William smiled enigmatically. "So you want to become the mistress of your own home."

Mary, completely flustered, retreated and took refuge behind the chair.

"Do you remember our wedding night?" he demanded harshly.

She blushed, but was unable to speak.

"I told you then that you would not have to pursue me again. I said I would come to you." He paused and looked at her intently. "Come here."

Mary was afraid she would burst into tears, and made an effort to calm herself before obeying.

But William was too impatient to wait. Reaching out, he caught hold of her arm and wrenched her toward him.

Mary lost her balance and fell heavily against him. Before she quite realized what was happening, William's arms encircled her and he was kissing her passionately. . . .

Other titles in the Ace Hall of Fame series:

THE SCIMITAR
THE EMPEROR'S LADIES
DAUGHTER OF EVE
THE HIGHWAYMAN
THE RIVER DEVILS
DRAGON COVE
SAVAGE GENTLEMAN

A HALL OF FAME *Historical Novel*™

The Queen's Husband

SAMUEL
EDWARDS

ace books
A Division of Charter Communications Inc.
A GROSSET & DUNLAP COMPANY
360 Park Avenue South
New York, New York 10010

THE QUEEN'S HUSBAND

While based on historical characters and events, creative liberties have been taken by the author in this work of fiction.

An ACE Book

First ACE printing: June 1979

Produced by Lyle Engel

Published by arrangement with
Hall of Fame Romantic-Historical Novels, Inc.

2 4 6 8 0 9 7 5 3 1

Manufactured in the United States of America

for Paul R. Reynolds

Ah, but a man's reach should exceed his grasp,
Or what's a heaven for?

—Robert Browning

Chapter 1

PRINCE WILLIAM OF ORANGE had been taught by his tutors, by his professors at the University of Leyden, and by the ministers assigned to guide his spiritual growth that hatred was a vile, base emotion, and that civilized men had learned to overcome it since the Renaissance and the Reformation had spread their light over Europe. Nevertheless he had to face facts: Granting that it was the year 1669, and that at the age of nineteen he should know better, he despised John de Witt, the Grand Pensionary of the United Dutch Provinces.

His reasons for loathing de Witt were as logical as they were numerous. He himself was a prince in title only, and neither reigned nor ruled; de Witt had seized control of the country and had been its sole master since the death of William's father, who had succumbed to a sudden illness shortly before the birth of his son and presumed heir. It was true, of course, that the Dutch people had prospered during de Witt's stewardship, but the price they had been forced to pay for their material prosperity had been high. Abjectly, fearfully, the Grand Pensionary had signed treaty after treaty with King Louis XIV of France, who was determined to make his nation the greatest and most powerful on earth, and as a consequence, even though the United Provinces had been spared occupation by French troops, Dutch citizens were forced to obey edicts signed in Paris, and the government bowed meekly to the whims of Louis's ministers.

Some men, particularly the merchants and shipowners who had been allowed to trade without too much interference, preferred to blind themselves to the situation, but William could not forget his country's plight or his own, because he was, literally, Louis's prisoner. At the insistence of the French, de Witt forced him to live in complete obscurity in one small wing of the old royal palace in Amsterdam. He was granted an allowance no larger than the income of a peasant, he was forbidden to make any public appearances, and he was refused even the right to take part in ceremonies of state. Humiliated and ignored, he had been deprived of his heritage, and the world had forgotten him.

But now, today, he had forcibly called himself to de Witt's attention. Determined to live in isolated penury no longer, he had broken the Grand Pensionary's strict rule prohibiting him from leaving Amsterdam, and had come to The Hague, the capital, in a public coach. It was difficult for the young man to realize that he was actually sitting in de Witt's living room at this moment, but he was enjoying the unusual experience in spite of his bitterness, and he could not resist gazing scornfully at the middle-aged man who sat opposite him. Meeting de Witt's eyes was not easy, however, so after a moment William glanced around the room. It was the first time he had ever been here and he was forced to admit to himself, grudgingly, that the Grand Pensionary's "palace" was no more ornate than the home of any reasonably prosperous Dutch burgher. In fact, it was disappointing to discover that de Witt did not surround himself with luxuries. William had expected him to imitate the gaudy style of living that Louis XIV had made fashionable, and had been prepared to hate him all the more for it, so it was disturbing to think of his jailer as a sensible, moderate person.

"You aren't listening to me!" de Witt said quietly.

Prince William deliberately continued to study the room. There was a long silence. Finally he turned to look again at the Grand Pensionary, sitting calmly in his chair of heavy oak. De Witt was watching him with alert, intelligent eyes, and William knew he was behaving childishly, but thought fiercely that there was no reason to feel abashed.

"All young people engage in daydreams," de Witt said. "It's one of the prerogatives of youth, and it's part of the process of growing up. But you go to such absurd lengths that you forget the meaning of reality." His manner was stern, but there was a hint of compassion in his voice. "Times have changed since the age of William the Silent. He was a great hero who performed rousing deeds. The whole country worships his memory and you remember constantly that he was your ancestor. What you forget is that Louis XIV was not the ruler of France one hundred years ago, and his armies were not threatening all of Europe. So stop pretending to yourself that you're going to be another William the Silent. Be proud of your descent from him, be grateful that your country is intact, and accept the world as it is, boy."

William flushed, certain that de Witt was deliberately patronizing him by calling him "boy."

"Suppose," the Grand Pensionary continued logically, "we examine your maternal descent."

"I have no wish to discuss my mother with you," the young Prince said stiffly.

"You came to The Hague to complain to me. You like to think you're mistreated. I am doing my best to prove otherwise. Therefore we will indeed discuss your mother." De Witt still spoke quietly, but his eyes became hard. "Unfortunately for you, she was an English Stuart who lived at the wrong time. I certainly do not need to tell you that Lord Cromwell hated your mother's family above all others on earth, and that his attitude made it difficult for poor old Charles II of Spain to take up your cause. He's been ill for years, and even if he were in good health, his nature is vacillating."

William sighed petulantly; his tutors had lectured him for years on the reasons his relatives had been unable to help him, and he needed no fresh reminders of their indifference to him.

"As for Charles II of England, he's been taking bribes from Louis for the past nine years, ever since the Restoration, to keep him quiet. So who is there to stand up for you? Do you think our half-trained militiamen could beat the finest army on earth if Louis became annoyed with you and sent his regiments against us? You're comfortable enough in Amsterdam, you have no worries and no responsibilities, so go back there, and don't come to The Hague again unless I send for you, which is improbable." De Witt smiled sympathetically, but he was unyielding.

The young man tore at the weakest spot in the Grand Pensionary's argument. "Do you call my corner of the crumbling, dusty palace in Amsterdam comfortable?" he demanded resentfully.

"I assure you that you would be granted fewer privileges in a French prison." De Witt was annoyed but managed to control himself. He rarely lost his temper. "If I provided you with luxuries and gave you a court," he explained patiently, "Louis would believe we were trying to organize a coalition against him, and our fate would be that of certain other small countries. We still have our national existence, we're at peace, and our trade is making our people wealthy. Our religion is our own, and there isn't one French soldier on Dutch soil."

Pausing for breath, he looked at the Prince and felt sorry for him. There was bleak despair in the young man's blue eyes, but he was unconsciously demonstrating the effects of the rigorous training he had received, and only by running a hand through his thick, dark blond hair did he hint at the inner turmoil he was suffering. "Be sensible, boy," the Grand Pensionary said. "Isn't it better that our people—and you—enjoy relative freedom? Or would you rather rot in one of those fortresses that Louis reserves for royal upstarts who forget that he's their master?"

"He isn't my master, and it's my right to sit on my father's throne," William retorted angrily.

Sighing, de Witt shook his head. "There is no such thing as 'right' in our world. Think in terms of power, and leave questions of ethics to the ministers and the philosophers." He laughed, harshly but a trifle sadly. "If I hadn't taken charge of the government the moment your father died, either France or Spain would have absorbed us overnight. So accept facts and stop wishing for something unattainable."

The young Prince stood and hooked his thumbs in his worn leather belt. "It's easy for you to preach!" he shouted defiantly. "You've made yourself the only power in the United Provinces!"

"Sit down," de Witt said sharply, and waited silently until his guest reluctantly obeyed. "If it weren't for the love and respect I felt for your father and mother, I'd cane you, even though you are almost of age. If you had a fraction of the wits that have distinguished the House of Orange for the past one hundred years, you'd realize I have no alternative. Whether you believe me or not, I don't enjoy my position, and if I could, I'd retire to a little house I own in the province of Zeeland. Power, as such, means nothing to me. But I have responsibilities, and I discharge them because there's no one who can take my place."

It was painful for William to admit to himself that the Grand Pensionary was being frank. But a show of candor did not prevent him from hating the man who forced him to live in obscurity. "I was wrong when I called you powerful. You bend your back whenever the French envoy calls on you, and when Louis snaps his fingers, you jump."

The very young were cruel, de Witt reflected, because they were too inexperienced to know better. "I'm forced to pay a heavy tribute to France," he conceded, "and I'm forbidden to make alliances with other nations. As you say, the French ambassador gives me orders, and I obey them. But our people are alive and healthy, our merchant ships sail everywhere, even to the New World, and our farmers' storehouses are filled. The Alsatians tried to fight Louis, and thousands of them were killed. Their towns are occupied, they no longer have the right to worship as they please, and their profits are carried off to Paris. The Brabant resisted, too, so French troops march up and down the streets of Brussels, and the Belgians are starving."

"I'd rather resist than be a slave."

"A very pretty sentiment, but you've never seen death or famine or deliberate cruelty. A dwarf doesn't thumb his nose at a giant, particularly when the giant is a despot."

William felt foolish, but he glared at de Witt stubbornly.

"You like to picture yourself leading a victorious army against the French. Childish, romantic nonsense! This should be unnecessary, but apparently I must remind you that the Prince of Orange has an obligation to the Dutch people. Some of your ancestors were warriors, some were statesmen, but unfortunately for you, we live in an age dominated by one man. As you read about the deeds of your forefathers, you forget that we're about to enter the last third of the seventeenth century—that we no longer live in an era when brave men perform valiant acts." Leaning back in his chair wearily, de Witt closed his eyes for a moment. "There is only one way you can serve the United Dutch Provinces. Remain as inconspicuous as possible."

The advice was sound, but a sense of impotent rage made William reckless. "Suppose I refuse?"

"If you do anything rash," de Witt replied coldly, suddenly sitting erect, "it will be my unpleasant duty to restrain you. If I must, I shall place you under arrest."

"In other words, I'm your prisoner."

"Not if you behave yourself, not if you think and act like an intelligent man who keeps the welfare of the Dutch people always in mind." Rising, the Grand Pensionary put a hand on the youth's shoulder in an awkward gesture of affection. "I doubt if you'll believe this, but I know how you feel. I understand your ambitions and I sympathize with your frustrations. But there's nothing I can do for you, just as there's no way you can change the world to suit yourself. You don't enjoy being treated like my lackey. I don't enjoy being a French lackey. But I'd rather pay tribute to Louis than see our cities reduced to rubble by his artillery and watch our citizens being bayonetted by his infantry. Wouldn't you?"

The question was rhetorical, and William, averting his face, bit his lip. He had forgotten that on the infrequent occasions when de Witt had come to Amsterdam and they had clashed in one of these stormy sessions, he invariably felt ashamed of himself later.

"A prince," the Grand Pensionary said gently, "doesn't have to march at the head of an army or issue sweeping decrees to become a great man. There's another way, a far more difficult way." He paused, and his grip on William's shoulder tightened. "He can learn patience, and for the sake of his subjects, he can teach himself humility. Hate me, if it will help, and hate King Louis, if that will give you pleasure, but do nothing that will harm our nation. The welfare of the Dutch people is infinitely more important than your personal happiness."

By August, 1672, three years after his significant meeting with John de Witt, William of Orange was convinced that the world was decaying and that his own situation was hopeless. The armies of France continued to expand the borders of Louis XIV's realm, the Dutch people still paid tribute to the great monarch who ruled most of Europe from Paris, and William's own existence remained dreary and boring. What he failed to realize was that he had matured during the past three years, that, as de Witt had suggested, he had learned patience and taught himself humility. Even more significant, he had developed the fine art of practicing constant self-discipline. Though his feelings toward de Witt were still bitter, and he hated Louis of France with a consuming passion, he now refused to lose his temper. He tried to think of the future in practical rather than romantic terms, and he passed his time by studying incessantly, reading history books, propaganda tracts, and philosophical treatises.

He still lacked the worldly experience that gave a man true wisdom, but his attitude of thoughtful calm, his deliberately cultivated manner of weighing his words and speaking quietly, and even the new firmness of his mouth were signs that he was becoming more adult. Certainly he was at ease as he sat in the audience chamber of the old palace in Amsterdam, where he was receiving an unexpected visitor, the elderly Count von Langbein, a special envoy from the Elector of Brandenburg, the most powerful of the German states. Not long before, William would have been uncomfortable in the presence of a noble guest because the greater part of the palace was closed off, and he would have been embarrassed by the shabby furniture and threadbare rugs, but now he realized there was no need to make apologies.

On the contrary, the Count had made the journey to Amsterdam to propose a marital alliance between the houses of Brandenburg and Orange, and the notion was so unsound that William was amused. The envoy had come to the United Provinces on a fool's errand, and William felt obliged to deal with the situation realistically. He smiled faintly, and when he spoke his voice was sardonic; without knowing it, he had evolved the technique of using irony to shield himself from the world.

"Perhaps it would be helpful if I tell you something about the way I live," he said. "When my desire for a woman becomes overpowering, I hire a prostitute for an evening. The really attractive ones command higher prices than I can afford to pay, and the fastidious find this old palace drafty and damp. They're right, too. It's a depressing place. No ladies have been entertained here since most of the rooms were boarded up after my mother died nearly eleven years ago, and as only Amsterdam's more questionable whores come here willingly, I enjoy very little feminine companionship."

He laughed quietly, and as he raised his head his gaze fell on the portrait of the illustrious William the Silent. "You should also know," he continued, a trace of acid in his voice, "that I'm the last member of a dying line, a useless appendage in the brilliant and glittering world of the fabulous Sun King of France. There's no place for me in Louis's realm, you see, but as I seem harmless and docile, he graciously consents to let me live. Perhaps that isn't his real reason, though. There may be a few patriotic Dutchmen still loyal to my family, and rather than anger them unnecessarily, the inferior grade of beef I'm served hasn't been sprinkled with poison. Not yet."

Count von Langbein smoothed his white hair with his hand, stared at his host, and shifted uncomfortably in his chair. After a life spent in his country's diplomatic service, he was unaccustomed to such blunt talk. "Your Highness," he said feebly, "has a remarkable sense of humor."

There was no rancor in William's smile. "You're very observing, Count. Most people think I lack a sense of humor, but I assure you I would have gone mad long ago without one. However," he added emphatically, "I don't mean to give you the impression that I'm wallowing in self-pity. I'm not."

The visitor coughed behind his hand and glanced uneasily around the chamber.

"You're wondering," William said candidly, "whether John de Witt has learned that you're here. In all probability he hasn't yet, but eventually he will. He and Cornelius, his brother, know everything that happens in the United Provinces. Oh, the three servants and the gentleman in waiting I'm permitted to have as members of my staff are loyal to me, but de Witt's spies are everywhere." He grinned at the expression of alarm on the old man's face. "Let me set your mind at rest. I have no intention of revealing to him that the purpose of your visit was to explore the possibility of a marriage between one of the Elector's nieces and me."

"The Elector will appreciate your tact."

"Of course he will, particularly when you report back to

him that I have no future—that the only reason I'm alive at all is because the French believe I'm a spineless creature."

Color rose in the envoy's face.

"I'll have an unpleasant interview with de Witt, of course, but it won't be the first or the last." William imperturbably smoothed a crease in his inexpensive, worn wool breeches and idly swung a foot. "However, luckily for me, he's a busy man these days." His voice became cynical again. "The French are massing an army on our frontiers."

The nobleman from Brandenburg sat erect. "Louis is going to invade Holland?"

"Certainly not. Why should he bother?" William seemed tranquil, and only a hard light in his eyes betrayed his real feelings. "How strange that you aren't familiar with the scheme. I thought that every diplomat in Europe understood it. Every two or three years Louis sends an army to the Dutch frontier. De Witt then levies a special defense tax on the people, as heavy a tax as he dares inflict. But not one guilder is spent equipping an army or building a navy. A few regiments of volunteer militiamen are allowed to parade for the sake of show, and then de Witt and Louis quietly share the profit. The French army marches off again, and de Witt's paid followers hail him as the savior of peace."

Veins stood out prominently at Count von Langbein's temples, and he tugged nervously at his white beard. "How many Protestant rulers will Louis pull into his net?" he murmured. "It's no secret that he subsidizes Charles of England, but I hadn't realized that de Witt was so completely under his control. Are the Protestant nations doomed?" he asked querulously. "Is Louis going to swallow us one at a time?'

William smiled faintly. "Perhaps the Elector of Brandenburg would have displayed less interest in me if he had known that at the same time I started writing to him, I also opened a correspondence with the Pope."

"Is Your Highness turning papist?" the old man demanded, aghast.

William's smile broadened, and he shook his head. "Persecution, I've discovered, makes a man tolerant. What concerns me is whether a man is good or bad. I care nothing about his religious views, provided he believes in God. I've learned to respect Pope Innocent, and I'm proud to say that his letters indicate he has a high regard for me, too. My dear Count, you look confused. I have more time to study and think than most men, and I've come to the conclusion that civilization has reached a point in its progress where religious wars are absurd. Louis of France is a menace to the world because he's a tyrant, not because he uses the title 'His Christian Majesty.' We Protestants are inclined to forget that his worst enemy is Spain, the most Catholic of all countries. You may be surprised to learn, although I was not, that Pope Innocent dislikes Louis intensely. The French try to dictate to him, as they do to everyone else, and continually threaten to occupy some of the Papal States."

The envoy tried to regain his composure. "May I ask the purpose of Your Highness' unusually voluminous correspondence?"

"I have one aim in life." William continued to speak softly, but gradually he grew tense. "The power of Louis must be destroyed or contained. People everywhere, not only in the United Dutch Provinces, have the right to live without fear of a French invasion. That's why I've been spending most of my small allowance hiring messengers who elude the secret police and carry letters for me. Someday England and the Emperor Leopold and the Swedes and Brandenburg will unite with the Dutch in an alliance against Louis. What's more, the Pope and Spain will join us. As for me, John de Witt won't live forever, and one day our provinces will have the right to elect me stadholder and captain general."

Count von Langbein began to realize that this shabbily dressed young Prince understood the limitations of his present position, but was looking far into the future. Perhaps, the visitor reflected, he kept his sanity by making long-range plans.

"Don't be sorry for me, please, and don't worry about me.

Even if Louis has heard of my efforts to weld a league against him, he knows I'm helpless and can't hurt him. I'm in somewhat the same position as that of one of his nobles who offended him. I've been told the poor wretch was caged, naked, for the edification and amusement of the French court."

The visitor was speechless.

"At present," William continued briskly, "there's no danger either to my correspondents or to me. Louis has known for a long time just what we think of him. However, I must apologize to you and to the Elector, for causing you to make a long journey because you believed me to be what I am not. I beg you to remind the Elector that not one of our seven provinces has elected me its stadholder, so I am not, technically speaking, an eligible partner for a princess." His face became a mask and he betrayed no feeling as he added dryly, "Personally, I'm inclined to believe I'm the worst match in Europe, but I'm flattered that the Elector thought of me."

"I'll convey your message to him." The Count stood and bowed suavely.

William wanted to laugh, but remained grave. "Will you stay for dinner? As I've been given fillet of herring for the past two nights, I imagine there may be meat on the table."

"Thank you, Your Highness, but as you'll understand, the longer I remain here, the more curious the Grand Pensionary will become. Relations between Brandenburg and the United Dutch Provinces may not be cordial, but at least they're correct, and having learned the true nature of de Witt's relationship with the French, I know you'll sympathize with my anxiety to—"

"I wish you a pleasant journey home," William interrupted, rising and terminating the interview.

He escorted his visitor to the door, then returned to his chair and gazed listlessly out of the open window. Rarely had he felt so chastened, so discouraged, and he knew he had no one to blame but himself. He had corresponded with Leopold I, the Holy Roman Emperor, and with the Pope, with Sweden and

Brandenburg, because he had been restless and bored, but he had accomplished nothing. Condemning himself bitterly, he reflected that the leaders opposed to the French would know now that his firm, confident correspondence, which had been sufficiently impressive to bring Count von Langbein on a long journey from Berlin to Amsterdam, was only a sham. The story of the envoy's humiliating experience would spread, and soon every monarch in Europe would know that the Prince of Orange was a weak, vain peacock who deserved to be treated with contempt.

William examined a hole in his left stocking, plucked at the coarse wool unthinkingly, and told himself it was no wonder that so many Dutchmen were migrating to the New World. Whenever he looked at the dust-coated furniture and grimy drapes in what had once been a magnificent throne room and was now one of the six chambers that had been left open for his use, he wanted to flee to America, too. There, in colonies established by both Dutch and English, men were free to believe what they pleased, free to make what they could of their lives. The very concept of liberty made him restless, and going to the open window, he tried to concentrate on some of the landmarks of his beloved Amsterdam.

The sight of them usually soothed him, but today, as the warm summer breeze blew across his face, he found no comfort in the solid, Gothic mass of the Nieuwe Kerk, sometimes called Saint Catherine's, on the far side of the Gracht, or canal. Often in the past he had taken pride in the knowledge that great Protestant churches could stand side by side with such structures as Saint Nicholas' Catholic Church and the synagogue erected by Jewish refugees from Portugal, but his interview with Count von Langbein had stripped away his flimsy illusions. He had been playing an adolescent game, and the religious liberties of the Dutch, which he had neither created nor protected, would soon be lost, just as all other freedoms had disappeared from the United Provinces.

Someday the French, ever more greedy, would march on

Amsterdam, and the lovely canals would be choked with the bodies of citizens who would resist the invaders in vain. William knew how his people felt, for he shared their frustration, but his plight was even more miserable than that of a cobbler or swineherd; they were doing the best they could, living their lives to the full. Meanwhile he was stagnating, passing time by writing to great men who respected the name of Orange because of deeds his ancestors had performed, but who would now know, as the envoy of the Elector of Brandenburg had learned, that he was totally wanting in authority. Although it was painful to admit the truth to himself, he realized he was so insignificant that his jailers had not even bothered to erect a pasteboard throne for him. Other rulers in other lands had been shorn of power throughout history, but many of them had been permitted to pretend they were kings. Louis of France was denying him even that shred of dignity.

He would live and die in anonymity, William concluded, and it was likely that the only Dutchman who would be remembered in the era of the French Sun King were two natives of Amsterdam, Rembrandt van Rijn, an artist whose work was attracting attention everywhere, and Baruch Spinoza, a lens grinder whose philosophical tracts were creating a stir in the major universities of every nation. Shame burning his face, William vowed that never again would he play at wooden soldiers.

It was easy enough to justify his stupidity, of course; his life had been so monotonous that he had turned to letter-writing, to feeble scheming against his archenemy, as an outlet for his feelings. Certainly every day was the same. After a breakfast of grilled herring and watered wine, he and his gentleman in waiting, William Bentinck, spent the morning fencing. They devoted their afternoons to a continuation of the studies in which they had been engaged when they had been fellow students at the University of Leyden, and William invariably enjoyed this part of the day. The fiasco of the correspondence had been a direct result of the fact that their evenings were idle, William could see now. Bentinck, who was only a year his senior, was bored, too. Fiercely loyal to the House of Orange, as his ancestors had been before him, Bentinck had encouraged his Prince.

Bentinck's devotion and his interest in the affairs of the world had made them both look like fools, William realized as he reached irritably for the bell rope behind his chair. Bentinck had gone to have a rip in the sleeve of his one good coat mended by a tailor, but he should have returned long ago. William, his annoyance increasing, reasoned that his friend had learned the reason for Count von Langbein's visit and had prudently decided to spend the rest of the afternoon elsewhere. Even if he was in the palace he was taking his time answering the summons, and William tugged at the rope again. After a long wait an elderly serving woman came to the door.

"Where is my Lord Bentinck of Diepenheim, Anna?" William asked.

The old woman grinned at his sarcastic tone and pulled the heavy black shawl that she wore in all seasons more tightly around her shoulders. "Out," she said.

"Out where?" William rarely addressed his servants so sharply, for he understood and appreciated their motives in staying with him. Their wages were inadequate, far smaller than they would receive from other employers, and they were frequently subjected to close questioning by de Witt's representatives, yet they stubbornly refused to abandon him. Anna, who was a grandmother, could have retired long ago and gone to live with one of her children, but she had served William's parents, and he felt sure she would stay with him until the day she died. Suddenly contrite, he reached out a hand to her. "I'm sorry."

Her toothless grin broadened. It was plain she had taken no offense. "Never mind. All I know is that he's out, and whether you're angry or not won't put knowledge into my head."

"He's probably found a new girl." Bentinck had a disconcerting habit of imagining himself in love with young courtesans who, unaware that he was penniless, were dazzled by the attentions of a member of one of the oldest and most aristocratic families in the province of Gelderland.

"Probably," Anna agreed cheerfully.

"In that case, I'll go to my room and read." William could always find some measure of relief from his plight in books. "If you see him when he comes in, tell him I want a word with him."

"Understood. Shall I bring you ale and a cut of cheese?"

"No, thank you."

"Gertrude will be disappointed." The cook was Anna's closest friend. "She bought it this morning at a bargain price from a farmer who knew she worked for you. It's a good, sharp cheese, William."

"Maybe I'll have a small slice with my dinner. I'm not hungry."

"You're never hungry," she said severely. "Take a glass of Spanish wine, then. There are still a few jars in the cellar that haven't turned sour."

"I'm not thirsty, either."

The old woman shook her head in exasperation. "You're too thin, that's your trouble!"

"What difference does it make if I'm thin or fat?" he asked petulantly, and unaware that there were tears of concern in her eyes, he walked to his bedroom. It was a room as simply furnished as his student's chamber at Leyden had been. A bed occupied one corner. Opposite it was a chest of drawers, and a few shelves were piled high with books, most of them economic or political treatises. Two chairs stood on the far side of the room, and between them was a table.

Aware for the first time that it was growing dark, William took a flint and tinderbox from the top drawer of the chest and lit the candle that stood on the table in a holder. It immediately began to smoke. Smiling to himself, William reflected that even if he could afford the new French tapers that did not smoke, he would not buy them. In small ways, at least, he could remind himself constantly that it was possible to escape from the influence of Louis XIV. Taking a book at random from the nearest shelf, he sat down with it and saw that it was in English; putting it aside, he stared with unseeing eyes at the flickering candle. In spite of his efforts to refrain from reverting to the subject that was foremost in his mind, he could not help thinking that no coalition against the French would be effective without the active support of England. He had realized it for the first time several years ago, when John de Witt had found it expedient to let him visit England, and since that time the conviction had grown in him that the British Isles comprised a natural fortress, that with the assistance of her king and people the French could be contained, but that without such help, an alliance was probably doomed to fail.

There, he thought, was the weak link in his schemes, for although he had made many friends among the English during his sojourn at Hampton Court, he had felt only disgust for Charles II. William's own experiences had taught him that the would belonged to the strong, but Charles was as capricious, vacillating, and venal in his capacity as the head of his state as he was depraved and abandoned in his personal life. A man who lacked moral character was not a fit ruler, and Charles, who bought jewels and silks for his many mistresses with the secret funds that Louis supplied him, would surely never raise a hand against the monarch on whom his pleasure depended. His brother James, Duke of York, the heir to the English throne, was an even worse specimen than Charles, for he was equally dissolute, but maintained a sanctimonious façade. At least the English king was no hypocrite. William had felt sorry for the Duchess of York, an intelligent and spirited woman whom he had admired, and perhaps because of her he continued to nourish the hope that someday England might join the forces opposed to France.

The bedroom door burst open unceremoniously, and William looked up to see his gentleman in waiting on the threshold. William Bentinck, Lord of Diepenheim, was a short, dark young man, inclined to overweight, who engaged in physical exercise only at the insistence of his prince. Apparently he had heard that he had been expected long ago and had dashed up the stairs, for he was breathing heavily, and for the moment could not speak.

William smiled at him frostily. "You left me alone with Count von Langbein almost all afternoon. He made me feel like a twelve-year-old schoolboy who deserved a whipping. You weren't there to share my misery, even though you're as much to blame as I am for the incident. You knew why he was here, and you deliberately avoided seeing him."

Bentinck, gasping, shook his head vehemently.

"I suppose I'll have to hear about your newest sweetheart before you'll be willing to discuss more sensible matters." William sat back in his chair. "Does this new one remind you of Beatrice or Venus or Juliet? Is she blond, or is she another of those black-haired slatterns you find in the shadows of the canals? Tell me about her, and then we can talk about more important matters."

Bentinck had caught his breath at last. "I've spent the past four hours down at the market place trying to confirm a rumor. And it's true, William, it's true!"

Hurrying to the window, Bentinck drew aside the faded drapes and pointed down into the square in front of the palace. "See the crowd gathering out there? They've heard the news, too."

For an instant William suspected that his friend might be drunk, for there was a wild, unnatural gleam in Bentinck's eyes. But after looking out the window and unexpectedly seeing a crowd of torch-bearing burghers, he changed his mind. Something out of the ordinary was indeed taking place, and he looked at his friend questioningly.

Bentinck made a supreme effort to steady himself, but his voice throbbed. "An announcement was made in The Hague this morning. People there were told they would have to pay a new tax because the French are threatening to invade the country. The citizens of the town have had to live with the de Witts for years. They doubted the threat. A mob formed and began to demonstrate. Cornelius de Witt came out of his palace and ordered the citizens to disperse." Bentinck sucked in his breath, and his excitement mounted. "I don't have many details, but they dragged him off to prison."

William was too stunned to display emotion. "Surely the Grand Pensionary stepped in and set his brother free? He pays his company of honor guards excellent wages."

"John de Witt marched to the prison with his company." Bentinck's voice cracked. He swallowed and went on: "Then his own men turned on him. They threw him into the same cell with Cornelius. You can imagine the effect that had on the mob."

A hint of a smile appeared at the corners of William's mouth. He was reacting unthinkingly.

"The people broke into the prison and tore both of the de Witt's apart, William."

"Do you know—that they are dead?" There was a trace of huskiness in William's tone.

"There's no longer any doubt about it. The courier who arrived at the market confirmed the story. From what he says, they suffered a horrible death."

"Spare me the details," William said sharply, glancing down at the crowd of burghers. He had always hated John de Witt, and as a child he had amused himself by imagining the tortures he would inflict on the Grand Pensionary if their positions were suddenly, miraculously, reversed. Because of de Witt, he had told himself, he had been unable to take his right place on the throne of his ancestors and in the world, but now, without warning, his bonds had been removed. He had believed that when this time came he would rejoice. Instead he was bewildered, frightened, and—to his surprise—sad.

De Witt, living, had been a symbol of oppression, but now that he was gone, a faint understanding of the meaning of responsibility stirred in William. He could no longer correspond with the rulers of other nations safely, knowing that de Witt and Louis would ignore his letter-writing as long as he did not interfere with their tidy arrangements. It was difficult to admit the truth, but William forced himself to face facts: The Grand Pensionary had been a wise man, and he himself had been an arrogant, stubborn child. But he could take refuge in his dream world no longer, and he knew he faced an immediate decision. Bentinck was eager to talk, of course, but William had to make his own choice.

If he wished, he could flee to a friendly court, and he felt reasonably certain there would be a polite welcome awaiting him in Sweden or Brandenburg. The alternative was to risk the wrath of Louis, and by remaining in the United Dutch Provinces to place his people in jeopardy and endanger his own life. De Witt had called him reckless and impatient, and he realized that the Grand Pensionary had known him better than he knew himself. Turning abruptly, he faced his friend.

"Open the doors of the palace and admit those who want to enter. Conduct them to the audience chamber. We will join you there presently." It was the first time in his life that William had ever used the prerogative of ruling monarchs—the plural personal pronoun—when referring to himself.

Bentinck straightened and stood at attention. "Yes, Your Highness!" He had called his friend by his Christian name ever since their student days at Leyden.

The door closed. William continued to stand immobile for a moment, then he bowed his head. "In Thee, O Lord, do I put my trust," he murmured. "Let me never be ashamed: deliver me in Thy righteousness. Bow down Thine ear to me; deliver me speedily; be Thou my strong rock, for an house of defense to save me. For Thou art my rock and my fortress; therefore for Thy name's sake lead me, and guide me."

Walking quickly to the chest of drawers, he took out his plumed hat and cloak lined in red silk, both of them items of apparel that John de Witt had allowed him to buy before he had made his trip to England. Then, kicking off his shoes, he pulled on a pair of stout, calf-high boots. Next, he opened the bottom drawer of the chest. Pausing, he gazed at the one object that he had been permitted to inherit from his father, a sword of Spanish steel with a carved gold hilt. His mother had given it to him shortly before her death, and he had sworn to her that he would never wear it until he could defend his country with it at the head of his army.

Buckling the sword on his broad belt, he gripped the hilt for a moment, thinking fleetingly of the past. Then, remembering that the palace corridors were always dark, he took up the candle from the table and started out of the room.

As he approached the staircase that led to the audience chamber below he heard the excited babble of the crowd. The sound sobered him. He had succumbed for an instant to a sense of exhilaration, but the presence of the burghers reminded him of his duty to them. Louis of France and Charles of England might believe they reigned by divine right and that they were above the laws of their countries, but the privations William had suffered had convinced him that rulers were as mortal as the lowliest of their subjects, and that they were obligated, in return for the power they held, to lead their people wisely and justly, curbing the strong and helping the weak. It was ironic to realize that the dead de Witt had been a temperate and able master.

William found that he could not think clearly. Perspiring heavily, he struggled against the wave of hysteria that rose up in him. Then the problems of the immediate future crowded everything else from his mind, and his face was grave as he stood in the open door of the audience chamber. Someone, in a shocking disregard for expense, had lighted all the dusty candles that were in the wall sconces, so he blew out his own candle and turned and handed it to Anna, who was waiting at the foot of the stairs. The old woman curtsied to the floor; a lump formed in William's throat, and he helped her to her feet before he moved into the chamber.

There was so much noise that the walls seemed to shake. People stood aside to let him proceed to the far end of the hall, where his father's throne had once stood. That part of the room was bare now, as even the dais had been removed, but Bentinck came to his Prince's aid and handed him a chair. William climbed onto it and held up his hand for silence.

The burghers became quiet, but one voice made itself heard. "Amsterdam wants you to be its stadholder, William!"

The Prince of Orange shook his head. "It is our devout hope that each of the United Provinces will soon have the right to elect a stadholder. That privilege is sacred to the Dutch people, and they have been denied it too long. But we cannot allow ourselves the luxury of holding free elections yet."

"John de Witt is dead!" a man at the rear of the chamber protested.

"Yes," William replied, "but an enemy far more powerful and infinitely more evil will crush us if he can. The French army poised at our borders was stationed there for the purpose of exacting tribute from us, but as soon as word reaches Paris that de Witt has died, Louis will need no further excuse. He will invade us, kill our men, make concubines of our wives and slaves of our children, put our cities to the torch, and devastate our land. Dutchmen, we must defend ourselves!" William knew his words were theatrical, but they were effective. At such a moment as this, effectiveness was important.

A burly young man wearing a tunic with fur-trimmed collar and cuffs elbowed his way to the front of the throng. He was carrying a sword, the mark of a gentleman, and drawing it, he saluted and dropped to one knee. "Your Highness, I am Nicholas Dykvelt, captain of a company of militia. I offer you the services of my company and myself."

A murmur of approval swept through the crowd, and William felt greatly relieved. He had been afraid that responsible men might laugh at his dramatic appeal. Everyone in the United Provinces had heard of Lord Nicholas Dykvelt, who had disrupted the scheme of the French and John de Witt two years ago by refusing to withdraw his troops from the field. His company, which had never numbered more than one hundred and twenty men, had outmaneuvered two regiments of French infantry and had captured seventeen cannon. Finally cornered by Condé, the greatest of the French generals, Dykvelt had calmly bartered for peace, and had obtained freedom for himself and his men by handing over more than four hundred prisoners to the enemy. This exceptionally able soldier had proved that French military invincibility was a myth. And now William had found a commander whose experience and advice would be extremely valuable.

"We accept your offer, Lord Nicholas, and we authorize you to augment your company with as many men as you see fit to add. However," William continued loudly, "we will accept only trained militiamen at present." He preferred to go into battle with a small army of seasoned troops rather than rely on patriotic amateurs who might become panic-stricken rabble after a taste of combat with Louis's disciplined veterans.

Dykvelt smiled in quiet appreciation. He had taken a risk in pledging allegiance to the House of Orange, since William was largely an unknown quantity, but now he seemed to recognize a sharp intelligence. "Are there any further orders, sir?"

"Yes," William replied, seemingly plucking the thought from his mind. "Enroll only those men who possess firearms and ammunition. Unfortunately, the late Grand Pensionary transformed the arsenals built by our father and grandfather into warehouses for the merchandise of the East India Company, so we have no weapons to distribute to those who would defend our soil."

Dykvelt's smile grew broader. "When do we march, sir?"

"At midnight."

Even Bentinck was surprised at the decision to move so swiftly, but before he could protest, another stranger came forward. Painfully thin, homely, and standing six feet, six inches tall, he made a grotesque appearance, but there was sincerity in his hearty voice as he boomed, "I like your methods. Damned if I've ever seen better. I'll join you, Your Highness."

William scrutinized him carefully. "Who are you?"

The tall man bowed stiffly. "George Frederick, Count of Waldeck."

Dykvelt stared at the count. Waldeck was a German mercenary colonel who had achieved fame in several wars. The Prince of Orange frowned regretfully. "We have no funds to pay a man of your abilities, my lord."

"Pay? Did I say anything about pay?" Waldeck demanded angrily. "I like your spirit and I hate the French!"

The burghers laughed as William and Waldeck shook hands. "Is this your chancellor?" the Count asked, glancing at Bentinck.

"He is," William replied promptly, although he had not previously considered the idea.

The tall German took Bentinck's arm. "You and I have work to do while Lord Nicholas is recruiting his troops. We must organize a supply train, find food and tents and wagons and mules. Come along. We've got to hurry if we're to obey Prince William's command and be ready by midnight."

As they started off, Dykvelt cupped his hands. "All men with military experience who own muskets will meet me on the palace steps," he called. "My sergeants will enroll you there." Saluting William smartly, he dashed away.

The crowd drifted out, and in a short time William found himself alone in the audience chamber. Except for the scores of lighted candles, the mud deposited on the floor by hundreds of boots, and the unending waves of sound from the throng outside, he might have dreamed the whole thing. Perhaps, he reflected, he was deluding himself in a more dangerous way. Waldeck and Dykvelt were brave men, but neither had ever commanded a unit larger than a regiment and both were still in their twenties. He himself had no practical experience in either government or war, and Bentinck, his mint-new chancellor, was neither a statesman nor a soldier.

It was ridiculous to think that four young men could lead an army of volunteers against the most formidable fighting machine that Europe had ever seen. Louis's divisions had never suffered defeat, his strategists were brilliant, his tacticians were resourceful and courageous, and he had unlimited supplies, weapons, ammunition, and money at his disposal. The Spaniards were afraid to fight the French, the King of England prostituted himself in order to keep the peace, and even the Pope dared not oppose Louis openly. Yet the United Dutch Provinces, one of the smallest states on the Continent, was preparing to defend itself against the most powerful monarch on earth.

William saw that Anna was standing at the entrance to the chamber. "If Gertrude can spare that cheese, I hope she'll pack it for me. I'll need some dried meat and bread, too." He saw tears in Anna's eyes; he tried to speak jovially. "I'm told that marching makes a man thirsty, so I'll have a use for those jars of Spanish wine, after all. The ones that haven't turned sour."

The old servant bobbed in a curtsy and went off to the kitchen.

William, alone again, looked slowly around the familiar room, and noticed the portrait of William the Silent. He walked to it, feeling frightened, lonely, and a trifle foolish. Standing stiffly before the painting, he drew his father's sword and raised it in salute.

Chapter 2

A FRENCH CORPS launched an assault against the impudent band of Dutchmen in September, 1672, and to the astonishment of Europe the invaders' attempt to capture the citadel of Ardenburg failed. The defenders' strategy was planned by Waldeck, Dykvelt commanded the infantry, and William, stubbornly rejecting the advice of his subordinates, foolishly risked his life by appearing on the field and personally leading a cavalry charge. His reckless valor heartened the three hundred horsemen who had rallied to his banner, and the troop knifed repeatedly through the lines of the stunned French cavalry, causing it to retire in confusion.

Humiliated, Louis XIV formally declared war against the United Dutch Provinces, and at his request Charles of England issued a similar proclamation. However, the English sympathized with the small nation that was fighting for its life, and the Duke of Buckingham's attempt to raise an army met a lethargic response. The French prepared to go into winter quarters, and the high command in Paris began planning a grand offensive for the spring. William, refusing to abide by the military conventions that had been accepted by generations of fighting men, remained in the field. His enemies believed he was mad, but he was taking a calculated gamble, hoping that disease would not decimate his little army: His people were enjoying true freedom for the first time in more than twenty years, and he wanted to organize and train his forces while the enthusiasm for his cause was rising.

Farmers and artisans, merchants and gentlemen enlisted by hundreds, then by thousands, and through the cold, wet days of the final months of the year Waldeck and Dykvelt worked to transform these civilians into professional soldiers. Meantime Bentinck traveled tirelessly from one end of the land to the other, talking to nobles and members of the States-General, the parliament that John de Witt had emasculated. The sincerity of William's beliefs and Bentinck's rapidly developing skill as a negotiator brought results early in January of 1673, when five of the seven provinces elected the Prince of Orange as their stadholder. The others did the same the following month, and in mid-February the States-General met at The Hague; the parliament's first act was to restore to William his traditional military rank, that of captain general of the army. He was also made grand admiral of the navy, but for the present that title was meaningless, the Dutch possessing no fighting fleet.

William promptly made Count Waldeck his lieutenant general, appointed Lord Nicholas Dykvelt a major general and sent both names to the States-General for confirmation, a gesture that the whole country appreciated. New taxes were levied for the prosecution of the war, measures were passed to encourage the growth of the merchant marine—for the nation's prosperity depended on its foreign trade—and William Bentinck, dazed by his sudden elevation to a place of prominence, initiated a vigorous correspondence with the foreign ministers of other countries in an effort to obtain allies.

The French professed to be amused at the spectacle of young, inexperienced men defying the strongest power on earth, but by the latter part of February it had become evident that the Dutch were growing strong enough to demand respectful treatment. Statesmen everywhere began to realize that the Prince of Orange was not a boy playing at being a ruler, and when Pope Innocent sent William a public message congratulating him on his accession to the throne of his ancestors, the Sun King decided to crush the upstart immediately, rather than wait until the weather became warm.

In the first week of March Waldeck learned that a French army, forty thousand strong, was approaching through the territories of German states friendly to Louis. The Dutch had erected breastworks on their western and southern frontiers. An attack from the east was completely unexpected. In a sense, it was a sign that the French strategists respected their foes.

William gathered his forces quickly and marched north and east to meet the threat. He set up temporary headquarters in the city of Groningen. Then, afraid the ancient university there would be destroyed and the citizens made to suffer if the French laid siege to the place, he moved to the open countryside and established his bivouac in the fields near the village of Finsterwolde, less than a mile from the sea. The troops were immediately put to work erecting earthworks, and William summoned Waldeck and Dykvelt to a council of war.

William's tent was like those of his senior officers, and was distinguished only by the flag of Orange that flew above it. The people of the province of Holland had offered him a silk pavilion as a gift, but he had declined with thanks, explaining that stout canvas was more practical and that he would be grateful if they used the money to buy blankets for the troops instead. His Spartan way of living was no pose, for his tent contained only his cot, two stools, and a table made of wood taken from crates that had contained supplies. He himself found one of the stools comfortable enough, but Waldeck preferred to prop himself on an elbow at the foot of the cot, and Dykvelt stood, his hands clasped behind him.

All three were silent for a time, but there was no sense of strain; they had come to know and understand each other during the several months they had fought and worked together, and each was lost in his own thoughts.

Waldeck was the first to speak. "My spies report that the enemy crossed the Ems River this morning." He blew on his fingers. "I wish you'd put a stove in here, William. You can afford a stove, you know."

The suggestion was ignored. "They know where to find us, George?"

"Oh, yes. I've seen to that. I contrived to let several documents fall into their hands shortly after they completed their crossing of the Ems."

Dykvelt chuckled and tugged at his small, pointed beard. "Then they should find us by noon tomorrow."

"It will be later than that, I think," Waldeck replied. "They're carrying sixty cannon, and it slows their rate of march."

"Sixty, eh?" William was unimpressed. "Enough to batter down the strongest wall in a siege, but useless here in the open, provided we don't concentrate our regiments too closely."

"I'm hungry," Dykvelt announced suddenly.

"You're always hungry, Nicholas. It's still daylight." William looked at him accusingly.

"Exactly. We won't eat supper for another three or four hours." The generals exchanged amused glances. "If you won't give me some bread and cheese from your larder, I'll send for some of my own."

William knew they were enjoying themselves at his expense, but he accepted their jesting good-naturedly. "If you insist, Nicholas, I'll find something for you." He picked up a small brass bell from the table and rang for his orderly. "You're going to be a fat old man, you know."

"If I live that long. How many cavalry troops is Louis sending against us, George?"

"Twenty."

Dykvelt whistled. "Four thousand horsemen. They want to smash us." He began to pace up and down, scowling, but he brightened when the orderly appeared. "His Highness wants some bread and cheese. And a jar of wine," he added as an afterthought.

Waldeck relaxed, and a grin creased his long face. "Be sure you bring us some good white bread, too."

The soldier looked bewildered. "His Highness eats only the black bread that's issued to the men, sir."

"They know it, Hanselmann," William said. "Black bread will do nicely. And if I remember correctly, there was some cheese left last night, so there's no need to cut a new one."

Dykvelt resumed his pacing. "I don't like this situation, gentlemen. The French obviously don't intend to take any chances."

"Neither do I," William replied. "We've spent the whole winter training and equipping ten thousand men, and I'm not going to lose them."

"If we should lose," Waldeck declared, rubbing the side of his nose reflectively with a bony finger, "it's a question whether the French will hang us if they capture us or whether the Dutch burghers will tear us apart if we escape."

"It's more likely, George, that we'll be killed in the battle," Dykvelt said. "Looking at our position objectively, I see that we're outnumbered four to one. The French cavalry can cut us off if we retreat, and their artillery can pound us to dust if we try to make a concerted attack."

William carefully folded the map that had been spread out on the table, placed it in the pocket of his plain, heavy wool tunic, and stood. "Our situation could be worse," he said casually.

Count Waldeck stood angrily, and the top of his head brushed the ceiling of the tent. "I took a deliberate risk when I joined you nearly seven months ago, William, and I'm not deserting you now," he said tartly.

"I'm concerned over your fear of the enemy, George, not your loyalty." William, stating a fact, spoke briskly, almost impersonally.

"I'd be stupid and incompetent if I weren't afraid," Waldeck retorted. "For the past two days I've been trying to work out a strategy that will hold down our casualties and prevent the French from marching as they please through the United Provinces. So far I've thought of nothing."

"That's because you've been seeking ways to prevent defeat instead of concentrating on achieving a victory," William said. "I'm frightened, too, but I'm trying not to let my fear numb my mind."

They were interrupted by the reappearance of the orderly, who brought them a loaf of coarse, dark bread, a thick chunk of yellow cheese, and a jar of wine.

A gleam of amusement appeared in William's eyes. "If Nicholas doesn't mind postponing his feast, perhaps you'll take a walk with me, and I can demonstrate my idea to you. It's hardly original, but it's the best I've been able to devise under the circumstances."

Dykvelt groaned as he reached for his burnished steel helmet. "I might have known you'd find a way to starve me." Taking a poniard from his belt, he cut a piece of cheese and popped it into his mouth.

All three men looked appropriately stern as they emerged from the tent and returned the salute of the sentries. The Dutch army knew that its fate and that of the nation depended on the trio, and this was certainly not a moment to appear before the troops in a frivolous mood. William started off in the direction of the sea wall, a mile away, and his generals fell in beside him. The raw March wind bit through their cloaks and tore at the plumes of their helmets; the soldiers digging breastworks were cursing the weather as William passed, but he told himself philosophically that their labor kept them warm.

"What is the meaning of that?" Dykvelt asked, observing a straggling line of men, women, and children heading south. All carried bundles, some seemed to have piled most of their earthly goods on carts drawn by mules or donkeys, and without exception the group, numbering about two hundred people in all, looked cold and miserable.

"I ordered Finsterwolde evacuated," William replied. "The French are sure to occupy the village, and I saw no need for innocent civilians to be hurt. They'll find refuge in Groningen, and with any luck their cottages will still be standing when they return." He saw no reason to reveal that he had ordered an aide to pay each family a liberal compensation out of the personal funds he received from each of the United Provinces in his capacity as stadholder.

He worried that the villagers might embarrass him by thanking him for his generosity, but was relieved when none of them recognized him as he approached. A few of the men and virtually all of the younger women stared at the three warriors curiously but blankly, and William was thankful that the new coins bearing his likeness were not yet in circulation. He breathed more freely after he had moved past the column of peasants.

When they arrived at the dike, William climbed onto it and stood staring at the churning gray waters of the North Sea inlet known as the Dollart. Off in the distance, hidden in the mists, were the Frisian Islands, and had the day been clear and bright, it would have been possible to see the soil of Germany. The scene was desolate and bleak, and Waldeck, shivering, drew his cloak more closely around him. "Well?" he demanded irritably.

Louis of France would have sent a subordinate into exile for using such a disrespectful tone, but William knew he deserved the rebuke. Though he had enjoyed his air of mystery, he now felt ashamed of his adolescent posturing, particularly as the plan he had conceived was far from startling. "Note the shape of the wall," hc said, getting down to business. "It curves like a huge horseshoe in this area. If it were to be broken at any point within this curve, the sea would pour in and inundate the whole area inside the horseshoe."

Waldeck sighed and shook his head. "We Dutch have been using this strategy for generations. It is precisely what the enemy will expect."

"Perhaps. But if we can think of nothing better, we'll have no choice, will we?" William made an effort to remain calm; he realized his idea would not make military history, but all the same something decisive was called for. "We can hope that the French will not look for us to rely on such an old trick."

Dykvelt stared at his companions. "Would one of you mind telling me what you're talking about?" he asked plaintively. "All I know is that our army is going to be beaten and scattered if we don't meet the enemy on high ground."

"Not necessarily," William replied, and continued quickly before Dykvelt could argue the point. "I have made a study of our dikes. You were annoyed with me yesterday, Nicholas, because I paid a visit to the university and delayed our march from Groningen. What I was doing was verifying my memory. I remembered that this area is particularly vulnerable. A break in the wall anywhere in this vicinity would let the sea pour in for approximately one mile."

"We'd be taking a terrible chance," Waldeck protested.

"Can you think of a better idea?" William retorted.

"It's good only if it succeeds," the second-in-command declared stubbornly.

Misgivings gnawed at William, but he had no alternative. "And we can't succeed if we don't try."

Dykvelt stamped his heavy boots and slapped himself to keep warm. "You two sound like a pair of quibbling schoolboys. Rather than listen to you, I would prefer to spend what may be my last night on earth sitting in front of a stove."

"It's very simple, Nicholas," William said loftily.

"Too simple. The French have thirty thousand infantrymen, twenty troops of cavalry, and sixty cannon, yet you stand here talking about what will happen to good farmland if the sea wall breaks."

"Not *if* it breaks. *When* it breaks. I'm picturing what will happen to those magnificent troops when the sea rushes in." The wind grew sharper and William's face felt numb.

"You mean you're going to open the dike deliberately." Dykvelt made no attempt to hide his contempt.

"Can you suggest another scheme?"

There was a long silence, followed by a surly, "No, damn me."

"Then we'll do what we must. Nicholas, your principal task tomorrow will be to entice the French into this sector, between us and the wall."

"I suppose one way of dying is about the same as another," was the gloomy response.

William made an attempt to sound briskly cheerful, but failed. "We'll station several men who know how to handle explosives on the dike, and at the right moment we'll send them a signal. George and I will hold the main line where we're now digging in."

Waldeck shrugged philosophically. "I've seen stupidity in battle more than once. Let's hope the French commander isn't bright and that his staff is incompetent."

Dykvelt studied the terrain carefully, and finally a resigned smile appeared on his wind-reddened face. "I may have to swim in order to join you."

"Thank you, Nicholas." William extended his hand. "I don't like the plan any more than you do. This land will be useless for years to come. But I understand there's an expert in The Hague who has been experimenting with methods of reclaiming soil. If we win I'll send for him."

He stood brooding, and the generals turned away; neither was interested in the peacetime future of Finsterwolde. Waldeck began to hunt for places on top of the dike where the vegetation was sufficiently thick to hide bags of gunpowder. The plan was less than brilliant, but having committed himself to it, he became the conscientious engineer. Meanwhile Dykvelt roamed up and down the wall, muttering to himself and pausing occasionally to evaluate the scheme he was developing to lure the French into the trap.

William, increasingly uneasy, waited for his subordinates to finish. They were loyally following orders, working out the details of the plan he had conceived, and knowing their military experience was greater than his, he made no attempt to interfere. Nevertheless he was depressed by the knowledge that the ultimate burden of responsibility was his alone. Thanks to his stubborn insistence on defying Louis, Dutch citizens would die tomorrow, and Dutch land would be ruined for generations. He himself had little to gain: If the battle was lost, he would be mocked all over Europe for using such hoary tactics; even if he won, Louis would mass an even bigger and stronger army to send against him. Perhaps, he thought wistfully, John de Witt had been right after all. Freedom was relative, not absolute, and he was calling on his subjects to pay a frightful price in the hope that he would achieve goals that were still far distant and might prove completely illusory.

But he reminded himself that this was no time to share his doubts with anyone, and when the generals rejoined him, shivering, he forced himself to speak heartily. "Gentlemen, I believe we've earned that wine and cheese. If you insist, I'll even see if I can find a loaf of white bread for you somewhere in camp."

The Prince of Orange and his immediate subordinates worked far into the night, debating and refining their strategy, but they were awake at dawn, and an hour later William reviewed his army. It was traditional for a commander to deliver an inspirational speech to his troops before a battle, but William decided this was an occasion when oratory was unnecessary. His ten thousand volunteers knew what was at stake, and he preferred to walk slowly up and down the lines, pausing to chat quietly for a moment here and there with a soldier.

Luck played a part in the day's developments, for the French were marching more slowly than the Dutch had anticipated, and it was two o'clock in the afternoon before a young cavalry ensign rode into the bivouac area to report that his patrol had sighted the enemy. The alert was sounded, and Nicholas Dykvelt immediately assembled his nine hundred horsemen, then reported to the Prince of Orange for final instructions.

"Delay them as long as you can," William told him. "The later in the day we make our move, the more effective it will be. I'd like to wait until sundown before we open the dike."

Dykvelt, his spirits improving now that action was imminent, grinned as he adjusted the chin strap of his helmet and drew on his steel-mesh gloves. "This will be a case where the little fish, caught and hauled ashore, proceeds to swallow the fisherman."

"We'll move out and support you if it becomes necessary," Waldeck assured him. "But remember, under no circumstances let yourself be forced into fighting a pitched battle. You've got to be moving away from the dike when we open it."

"I wouldn't be ashamed of death from an enemy bullet," Dykvelt replied lightly, "but I have no intention of drowning." Drawing his sword, he saluted, shouted an order, and then cantered off at the head of his troops.

William watched the departing horsemen regretfully. "I should like to be riding with them," he murmured.

The young officers who served as his personal aides exchanged glances, and Waldeck caught hold of his arm. "I forbid you to expose yourself!"

The knowledge that his second-in-command was right irritated William. "Do you presume to tell the captain general of the Dutch armies what to do?"

"Yes. Let someone else play the role of a hero!" The tall,

ungainly nobleman stared down at the Prince defiantly. "Without you, our cause would be lost, so I trust you will give me your word you won't do anything rash today. Otherwise you'll force me to instruct the staff to keep you from harm even if they have to resort to physical violence."

Were their situations reversed, William knew, he would be equally concerned over the safety of the man who had become the symbol of the nation's resistance to Louis XIV. He pondered for a time, and at last he said grudgingly, "I'll try to behave."

Waldeck had to be satisfied with his reply. The atmosphere became increasingly tense as he and William waited for an indication that Dykvelt had established contact with the enemy. The quiet of the Dutch countryside was undisturbed, and after a time the infantry regiments became restless. The cavalry had vanished, and some of the younger foot soldiers recalled hearing that the French possessed supernatural powers. Everyone strained to hear the sound of small-arms fire, but there was no sign that a mighty army was in the vicinity, or that it was being goaded by a band of courageous horsemen. Gray and white gulls, attracted by the Dutch troops' garbage, circled overhead in the dull gray sky.

An hour passed. William was tempted to send a patrol out for information, and knew Waldeck felt the same way, but neither gave in to the desire. The outcome of the forthcoming battle would depend as much on the spirit the badly outnumbered army would display as on the plan to flood the fields, and if the generals showed any symptoms of uneasiness, the men might become panicky at a critical moment. William therefore maintained an outward air of calm and continued to wait. Though he always found it difficult to indulge in small talk, he forced himself to chat at length with his aides.

Shortly after three o'clock there was a distant rumble, like that of thunder. Count Waldeck brightened. "The French artillery has come to life," he said, and turned to a stolid adjutant who had been standing behind him. "Be good enough to tell all regimental commanders to move into battle position," he directed politely.

Whistles blew, trumpets sounded, and the infantry moved into line behind the breastworks that had been prepared the previous day. Senior officers rode up and down inspecting their troops, supply sergeants moved spare bags of gunpowder into place, and the men, who had cleaned and loaded their muskets early in the day, checked them for the hundredth time to make certain they were ready for immediate use. Except for the group gathered in front of the tent flying the banner of the House of Orange, the entire army was busy.

"Would Your Highness care to observe our cannon before they go into action?" Waldeck inquired.

William concealed a smile. He had only eight fourteen-pounder guns and a few mortars. Since their combined strength was negligible, he had decided to scatter them, giving each of his major infantry units one cannon. The support they could give the foot soldiers in military terms was virtually meaningless, but he had reasoned that the roar of a big gun would encourage men who might otherwise become fainthearted when confronted by a solid mass of approaching French veterans. What Waldeck was actually proposing, then, was that they make a tour of their positions.

"By all means," William agreed. He leaped into the saddle as soon as his stallion was led forward, and he started off toward the left flank so quickly that the rest of the party was forced to hurry in order to catch up with him. He moved out into the open, and the troops called to him as he passed their breastworks. Looking at their eager faces as he raised his hand in salute, it suddenly occurred to William that these men were not fighting solely for their own freedom: They had formed a personal attachment to him, and were risking their lives so that he would triumph over his foes.

William knew that he had yet done nothing to deserve such loyalty. He swore to himself that if he could repel the invader, he would devote himself exclusively to his people. He was not qualified for real leadership, he reflected, for he lacked the brilliance and far-sighted wisdom of William the Silent, as well as the incredible courage his own father had shown when surrounded by enemies, but he would do his best to preserve Dutch liberties and to be worthy of his subjects' trust. Bowing his head, he prayed silently for guidance and strength.

Waldeck, who was riding directly behind him, suddenly cried, "Look at Dykvelt!"

Peering off into the distance, William could see his nine hundred horsemen near the sea wall. The units were still in formation, so he knew at once that Dykvelt had not lost control of the situation. Then he saw the French slowly pursuing his cavalry. The dazzling white and gold uniforms of the enemy were plainly visible, even at a distance, and he was amused to see that the foe's discipline was so strict that the French divisions marched as though on parade. Their cavalry rode in the van, and the straight lines of infantry followed, with the artillery bringing up the rear. Now and again the horse-drawn cannon would halt, and some of the guns would fire a salvo. No damage was done by these intermittent bombardments, and the only practical effect was to make the horses on both sides increasingly nervous.

Dykvelt was doing precisely as he had been told: retreating slowly before a superior force, he was leading the enemy straight toward the sea wall's great horseshoe formation. The French were advancing cautiously, however, and seemed to suspect a trick. William, powerless to halt what he had started, could only hope that the enemy high command would not foresee the obvious danger. It seemed impossible that the French would not soon realize that the Dutch intended to defend themselves as they had done for centuries. Any competent general should guess that the enemy was trying to draw him into a trap.

"Our Pied Piper is performing magnificently," Waldeck shouted above the roar of French artillery.

William, who was watching closely, saw the main body of

the French army draw to a halt, and after hesitating briefly, start inland toward his prepared earthworks. "They've seen us," he replied. "Nicholas has brought them to us, and now they're going to attack."

Waldeck glanced up at the sky. "It won't grow dark for another two or three hours. We'll have to hold them off."

The Prince thought of the expressions he had seen on the faces of his volunteers. "No," he said curtly. "The confusion in the French ranks would be greater if we waited and opened the sea wall at twilight, but I will not sacrifice one life unnecessarily. Open the dike now."

Count Waldeck hesitated.

"Fire your flares!" William said, speaking more sharply.

It had been arranged that Waldeck himself would give the signal to the demolition men hiding in the underbrush on top of the dike. He drew two massive pistols, held them high, and fired them into the air. There was a flash of green overhead, followed by a burst of orange-red, and the gulls, alarmed, headed toward the sea. The interval that followed seemed interminable, though William knew that the men stationed on the wall had probably lighted their fuses and were now scrambling away from the places where the breaks in the dike would occur. Even while fleeing, these soldiers would be doing their best to hide from the enemy, and William could not help thinking of the possible accidents and errors that might disrupt his scheme. Fuses were unreliable, the gunpowder might not explode, and there was always a chance that the men chosen to perform the delicate operation, even thought personally selected by Waldeck for calmness and reliability, might lose courage at the last moment. The worst danger was that the French might discover what was going on and stamp out the fuses or pour water on the gunpowder. In that event the Dutch army would be at the mercy of its enemy.

It was impossible, from the breastworks, to see all that was happening, and William knew only that Dykvelt had recognized the signal, for he was leading his horsemen away from the area near the wall at a gallop. The French cavalry did not bother to pursue him, however, for Louis's generals had now found the main body of the Dutch troops and were preparing to destroy it. The Prince of Orange and all his men watched in awed silence as the great French army spread out across the farmland and arranged itself in assault formation. The cavalry troops were placed in the lead, with lancers in the front ranks and swordsmen directly behind. Then, in long, solid rows, the infantrymen advanced, while the artillery, in the rear, took up positions in the shadow of the sea wall.

These moves were accomplished so deftly and quickly that even Count Waldeck was deeply impressed. White pennants bearing the gold fleur-de-lis emblems of the Sun King were unfurled to whip in the breeze, then three trumpets blared a single, sustained note, and the mighty French army started forward. The cavalry moved at a sedate walk. William knew that in a few moments the horses would begin to increase their speed. By the time they reached the Dutch line they would be cantering. The best armies in Europe had been unable to halt these horsemen, and it was too much to hope that recruits with only a few months' training would stand their ground.

There was a muffled roar in the distance, and William's temples throbbed. He looked at Waldeck, but as the enemy cavalry continued to move forward there seemed to be no need to ask whether the bags of powder had blown up. Obviously the sound had been made by the French artillery, which usually laid down a barrage ahead of its advancing van. The horses were trotting now, but gradually, almost imperceptibly at first, the ranks wavered, and William, standing in his saddle, could see that the infantrymen were milling around aimlessly. Some continued to move in the direction of the Dutch, but others halted, turned, and scattered.

"The dike has broken!" Waldeck cried.

A huge wave surged across the flat farmland, and William discovered that he was shouting wildly. The water, quickly growing deep, rendered the great French cannon useless, swirled around the foot soldiers, and finally caught up with the cavalry. The horses were terror-stricken, and scores of them stampeded, throwing their riders. For a few moments the confusion was so great that it was difficult to make out what was happening; all that was plain was that the sea continued to roll in across the plain. Its forward edge soon crept close to the earthworks the Dutch had erected. The French forgot their pride and their discipline, and as infantry and cavalry made desperate efforts to escape from the water that continued to rise higher, an army was transformed into a mob.

Louis's veteran generals and colonels were as helpless as their rawest infantrymen. Hundreds of Frenchmen were overtaken by the churning water and drowned. The units on the left flank stood on dry ground and had they advanced vigorously, it still might have been possible to defeat the Dutch, but the contagion of fear spread to them, and they bolted. Men and horses floundered into the sea swamp, and as the screams of the dying grew louder William turned away from the spectacle. His fierce joy was gone now, and a terrible sense of depression came over him as the French tried to escape from the trap he had set for them. His aides and Waldeck were fascinated by the sight, however, and when they began to cheer again William forced himself to look up. Nicholas Dykvelt, his uniform water-spattered, his horse bedraggled, was leading the Dutch cavalry toward the breastworks after making a wide detour of the inundated area.

Dykvelt called out something in hoarse triumph, but his words were lost, for the French, infuriated by the sight of the horsemen who had lured them near the dike, rallied sufficiently to form a ragged line and start forward once more. Their ranks were thinned, but their officers, beating at them with the flats of sabers, forced them to wade through knee-high water, and they fired their muskets as they advanced. Several of Dykvelt's cavalrymen fell, and Waldeck immediately ordered the exhausted troops to take refuge behind the breastworks.

William had hoped that the French survivors would be too discouraged to fight, but the case was otherwise. "Hold your fire until they come closer!" He drew his sword and flourished it as his regimental commanders repeated his order up and down the line.

"Come behind the earthworks!" Waldeck called urgently. "You're a perfect target out here!"

William pretended not to hear the advice. All through the long years of his lonely boyhood and adolescence he had dreamed that someday he would fight gloriously on the field of battle, like the heroes of Dutch history whose stories he had read so avidly. The desire to be remembered by his people as a great warrior was as overwhelming as it was unreasonable, and he deliberately moved forward a few paces toward the enemy. A bullet nicked the crown of his hat, another passed close to his ear, whining angrily, and suddenly he was more frightened than ever before in his life. A wave of nausea made him afraid he would disgrace himself in the presence of both armies.

It was so easy, when sitting alone in his tent, to think of French troops as the brutal instruments of the despot who had tried to keep his people in bondage and deny him his heritage. His opinion of the enemy now that he faced it in actual combat, was far different. Only a few moments ago he had taken pity on the dying French. Now he felt sorry for himself, for the furious men in soggy white uniforms and muddy boots were going to kill him if they could. His impulsive display of courage, he knew, was not bravery at all, but merely a desire to satisfy his vanity. It was humiliating to realize that such courage served no useful purpose.

While he debated with himself what to do next, a French bullet lodged in his stallion's head. He barely managed to kick his feet out of the stirrups and leap into the clear as the horse fell. Stunned, William stood for what seemed a long time and watched the enemy line drawing closer. He wanted to turn and run, but pride and fear paralyzed him, and he continued to watch the French advance until two staff officers, a lieutenant colonel and a captain, crawled up to him from behind the breastworks, dragged him to the ground, and hauled him unceremoniously to safety.

Waldeck came up to him, and for an instant William thought his second-in-command would strike him. "You damned, bloody fool," Waldeck shouted, "you deserve to be killed!"

William muttered an apology. The two staff officers, still holding his arms, tried to lead him further to the rear. Flushing, William refused to move. With the officers at his sides, he stood behind the parapet and watched the battle reach its climax. In vain he looked for individual heroes on either side. He saw instead that some men died shrieking and others fell quietly—that attackers and defenders alike were afraid.

After a quarter of an hour of close fighting, the French attack collapsed. Waldeck ordered his regiments to redouble their fire. The enemy troops, standing with their backs to the sea that had poured through the wall, tried to stand firm, but their cavalry had scattered, and when the Dutch refused to move out of their prepared positions, the French bugles sounded a retreat. King Louis's shattered army started off in the direction of the Ems River, and Waldeck, his mouth set in a straight, thin line, joined the Prince.

This was a moment of victory, but William was unable to enjoy it. "I'm very sorry I behaved as I did and caused you so much concern." It was the most difficult apology he had ever made.

"I've seen men do worse," Waldeck replied brusquely. "Even veterans who should have known better."

William was silent for a few moments as he watched the enemy move off. Then, rousing himself, he put his personal problems out of his mind. "If we could attack them now, they would never be able to reorganize."

Waldeck clenched and opened his bony fingers. "I know. It isn't often that a victor has an opportunity like this, but there's nothing we can do."

"Dykvelt's cavalry—"

"They're exhausted."

"And we have no horsemen in reserve." William made a mental note to build a large cavalry corps, no matter what the cost. The lesson was a bitter one, and he promised himself that he would never forget it: a few hundred men and a few hundred mounts, fresh and ready for action, could have destroyed what was left of a great and powerful French army. But a lack of reserves meant that another battle would someday be fought against this same foe.

Waldeck sensed his disappointment and gripped his shoulder. "You needn't feel so badly. We've done well today."

"We could have done better."

"True, but I have no complaints." The Count grinned, and for the first time in many hours he seemed relaxed. "You demand perfection, William. Luckily for my peace of mind, I do not."

As William started off toward the rear, he realized that his friend's comment was accurate. It had been intended as a compliment, but he took it as a criticism, and he knew that although there was ample cause for rejoicing, he felt bitter because so many of the enemy had escaped. The war, he reflected, glancing up at the gray sky, would be a long one, and again he wistfully remembered John de Witt.

The Dutch army was too tired to regret its inability to follow up its advantage. After a halfhearted attempt had been made to break into the French rear, which was protected by a strong guard that had regained its sense of discipline, an impromptu celebration began in the camp of the victors. Eleven of the seventeen men who had set off the charges that opened the dike had survived their experience, and each of them received a purse from William and a promotion in rank from Waldeck. Regimental commanders set up sentry outposts and then retired to their tents to toast one another. The men also began celebrating. For the first time since Louis XIV had started his campaign to make himself the supreme master of the Western world one of his armies had suffered a decisive defeat, and the Dutch casualties had been negligible, so there was ample cause for rejoicing.

William, who had been busy rewarding the demolition men, became aware of the revelry only after it was well begun. Still wearing his helmet and battle gloves, he stalked out of his tent. He was immediately surrounded by aides, and someone ran to tell Count Waldeck, who was supervising the opening of a jar of wine in his own tent, that the Prince of Orange seemed to be very angry. None of the lesser officers dared to ask what had displeased William, and the group fell silent as Waldeck, holding his wine jar under his arm, sauntered out into the open and approached his Captain General.

"There will be no celebration yet," William said.

"The men deserve it, and so do we," Waldeck replied, a hint of censure in his tone.

"Not while the dike remains open." William looked up at the sky. "There's still an hour of daylight. We owe a debt to the farmers of Finsterwolde, and the repayment will begin at once."

Waldeck frowned as he listened to orders for men to be put to work on the repair of the dike and the pumping of the flooded land. Knowing William as he did after half a year's service with him, he might have foreseen such orders.

Victims of French oppression in Alsace and the Brabant, and in the conquered German and Italian states, were heartened by the news of the unexpected Dutch victory, and Louis's enemies, realizing he could be beaten, drew up tentative plans to strengthen their alliances. William of Orange was acclaimed by every nation that cherished freedom, but his own army, laboring incessantly to drain the fields of Finsterwolde, came to regard him as something less than a hero. Until rain washed the sea's salt from the sodden earth, it would lie fallow, but when the dike was at last rebuilt William had the satisfaction of knowing that he had done everything possible for the peasants whose unexpected sacrifice had enabled him to defeat the legions of the Sun King.

The army forgave William when he gave the order to break camp, and the march across the United Provinces to The Hague became a triumphal procession. Citizens of Groningen, Meppel, and Hasselt pelted the conquerors with the spring flowers that were just beginning to bloom, William and his generals were guests of honor at ceremonies held in Kampen, Elburg, and Harderwijk, and people came from every part of the country to gaze at their deliverers, to cheer them and thank them. The problem of supplying the army vanished: farmers and townsfolk alike opened their larders and insisted on making gifts of hams, cheese, and onions, bread, potatoes, and turnips. The men quickly discovered they could obtain inexhaustible quantities of ale and wine, too, and William, trying to show leniency and moderation toward the army, gave orders that only those who became obnoxiously drunk or engaged in looting were to be placed under arrest.

Camp followers by the hundreds appeared and joined the march: yellow-haired Dutch wenches and dark-eyed women who slipped across the French border from the Brabant. By the time the town of Nijkerk, southeast of Amsterdam in the province of Gelderland, was reached, the army had discarded virtually all restraints, and William, sensitive to the reactions of respectable citizens, refused to allow any members of his command inside the gates of the staid community and insisted on pitching camp in the open fields.

He had grown so accustomed to snatches of bawdy song and high-pitched feminine laughter that the noises no longer interfered with his reflections as he sat alone in his tent, poring over a map by candlelight. Clergymen might condemn him for treating his troops so indulgently, but he knew what men of the cloth did not, that Louis would demand revenge, and that the victory at Finsterwolde had marked the start, not the end, of a war. Many of the young soldiers drinking and wenching tonight would be dead before the end of summer, and he, realizing the dangers in store for them, refused to deny them their fleeting pleasures.

His victory had solved many problems, of course: He would now have no difficulty in doubling the size of his army or persuading the States-General to levy new taxes so that the augmented regiments could be armed and equipped. What bothered him was the nagging question of where the enemy would strike next. As he studied his map he tried to put himself in the place of the French high command. Certainly there were weaknesses in the Dutch defenses; William was disturbed that he did not immediately recognize them. Tomorrow, he decided, he would summon his generals and regimental commanders to a council of war and learn their views. It might also be helpful, he thought, if he hired a few spies and sent them to learn the enemy's secrets.

The tent flap opened, and Count Waldeck, accompanied by two young women, entered unbidden. The tall lieutenant general, his breath heavily brandied, put a stone jar of liquor on the table and announced, "Your Highness has done enough work for one night. It isn't good for a man to spend all of his time alone."

One of the girls, a blonde, slipped her arm through William's and giggled. The other, a slender brunette with violet eyes, looked at William boldly, her hands on her hips, but said nothing. He was so startled by the intrusion of the trio that it was a moment before he could focus his attention on the silent brunette, but when he did return her insolent gaze he was pleasantly surprised. She was undoubtedly a whore, but she was plainly of a different caliber than the ordinary camp follower: her carefully brushed black hair was arranged in neat curls that hung over her bare shoulders, she wore long earrings and a necklace of amethysts that glittered in the light of the tapers, her gown was silk, and the tightly laced girdle that showed off her tiny waist and high breasts to such good advantage was made of velvet.

William had not enjoyed a woman in a long time.

"Here he is, ladies—the hero of Finsterwolde," Waldeck roared in a parade-ground voice. "What do you make of him?"

The blonde smiled vapidly and clung more closely, but the dark-haired girl dropped to the ground in a graceful curtsy. "This is a great honor, Your Highness," she said boldly, still staring intently at the young man in black.

The thought crossed William's mind that a night with a woman would cost him considerably more now than it had in the days when the whole country had known that John de Witt had paid him only a few guilders every month. Mildly amused at himself, he moved forward and helped the girl to arise. Her hand was warm, her skin smooth.

Waldeck broke the seal on the jar of brandy, thrust it at the blonde, and then took a deep swallow himself. "Tonight," he said, "we're going to have our own celebration."

"I approve," William told him, "provided you and your companion go off to your own tent." He took the jar of brandy from the Count and pushed him and the blonde good-naturedly toward the tent flap.

Alone with the brunette, William said, "I can't vouch for the quality of this brandy, but as George and his friend seem to have survived, I suppose we might try it."

"There's nothing I'd like more than to drink Your Highness' health."

As he took two silver mugs, which had been given to him by the grateful citizens of the province of Friesland, from the leather traveling box at the foot of his bed, it occurred to him that he had never encountered such a gracefully glib prostitute. He wondered why someone who might easily pose as a lady should choose her profession. But it was a passing thought. He stopped speculating about her as she edged close to him. Her proximity, as he poured brandy into two cups—the tantalizing scent she wore and her provocative, challenging air—aroused him. As they drank, William's tensions eased for the first time in many weeks. He smiled, the girl splashed more brandy into his cup, and when he sat on the bed she slipped deftly onto his lap. As she submitted to his caresses she sighed.

"You're the most handsome prince in Europe."

Her words momentarily dimmed William's ardor. Perhaps his imagination was playing tricks on him, but he thought he detected a trace of a foreign accent in her speech. French, it seemed to be. Well, there was a pleasant way to find out. He pulled her head down to his, kissed her passionately, then gradually forced her back onto the bed. He saw that she was responding to his love-making, and although he was anything but immune to her charms, his mind was functioning clearly. He cupped one of her breasts in his hand, and when she began to breathe more quickly he addressed her, deliberately, in French.

"You're the loveliest girl I've ever known," he said. "I'd like to make a permanent place for you in my suite."

The prospect of living under the protection of a prince pleased her even more than his advances, and flattered by the offer, she replied in the same language, "That would be wonderful."

William was not surprised to hear that her French was faultless. He knew now why someone with her beauty and obvious good breeding had come to his tent like a common prostitute. In short, she was a spy in Louis's pay. Common sense told him to denounce her. He knew that he ought to get rid of her immediately if he was to salvage his pride. But in spite of what he had learned about her, he still wanted her, and it was difficult to think highly of himself when he knew he had tricked her into revealing her true identity. A man who considered himself the leader of his people, a man who had received the benefits of the best education his country had been able to give him, was scarcely in a position to congratulate himself because he had fooled an ignorant young woman whose only weapon was her beauty. His father, William thought, would have refused to admit her to his tent in the first place, and William the Silent, although he might have been tempted, would have had her deported as soon as he had discovered that she was an enemy agent.

He, however, was continuing to make excuses to himself, and in spite of feeling ashamed of his weakness, he began to unlace her velvet girdle with his free hand. It was so easy to convince himself that she could do him no harm now that he was forewarned, and he could even pretend that he was outsmarting the French, but he knew he was evading the issue. He, who refused to deal with Louis's emissaries, who had forbidden the bookshops of the United Provinces to sell books or pamphlets published in Paris, and who would not allow the members of his household to use smokeless French tapers, was deliberately abandoning his principles. Not only was the girl French, but she had come here with the express intent of harming him and his cause; nevertheless his desire for her was stronger than his scruples, more powerful than his reason.

Someday, perhaps, he would be the force that would destroy French power, but for the present he had to admit that he was human, and therefore fallible. Unable to delude himself any longer, he gave in to the demands of the flesh and quickly stripped the girl's clothes from her body.

Some hours later, at dawn, a sentry came hesitantly into the tent to inform the Prince that William Bentinck had just arrived from The Hague after riding all night, and wanted an immediate audience. The soldier backed out hastily without waiting for a reply, and William made an effort to regain his composure. The girl, her dark hair tousled, was sleeping peacefully at his side, and his sense of shame and remorse became so intense that he hurriedly climbed out of bed, savagely donned his dressing gown, and began to pace up and down the tent. He did not want to see the French whore again, much less speak to her, and his self-contempt became transformed into a blind anger at her.

Striding to the bed, he caught hold of her bare shoulder and shook her roughly. She awakened slowly and smiled up at him, but grew alert and sober when she saw the expression in his eyes. "Get out," he said harshly, hating himself because of his inability to behave like a gentleman.

She stared at him silently.

"I know who you are and why you came here," he told her bluntly.

Shrugging, she sat up, reached for her shift, and drew it over her head.

To William's dismay the sight of her nude body revived the stirring of passion in him. His inability to control his lust infuriated him, and he knew that if he failed to handle the situation with dignity, the story of his behavior would soon be gossip in every court on the Continent. No nation would be likely to sign an alliance with a flighty and irresponsible ruler. William made a supreme attempt to master his emotions.

The girl, wise in the ways of men, understood his inner struggle. Gloating because she could still exercise power over him, she laughed triumphantly. There was no need for her to maintain the pose of a lady any longer, and the sound was so coarse and raucous that William turned away from her, afraid he would strike her.

Realizing she would tell the French everything he said and did, he forced himself to remain in one spot and gaze steadily at a small patch in the tent wall. He was trembling slightly. He hoped the girl did not notice this.

"When did you find out about me?" she asked, her voice heavy with sarcasm and amusement.

William made no reply. He felt nothing but disgust now, despising both the woman and himself. Although he knew there must be some pressing reason that Bentinck had traveled all night, he refused to give the girl the satisfaction of being told to hurry.

Again she laughed. She dressed with ostentatious care, apparently sensing that he had urgent reasons for wanting to be rid of her as soon as possible. At last she was ready to leave the tent. William would not allow himself to show his relief. Crossing the tent to his purse, he shook out three gold guilders, a considerable sum of money and several times the amount he had ever paid any woman.

"Here," he said, thrusting the coins into the girl's hand. "You can tell your masters I've paid you in full. I accept no favors from France."

The girl took the money, deliberately spat in his face, and swaggered out of the tent.

For a long moment William made no move. He had earned the contempt of a whore, and she had treated him as he deserved. However, the world had not come to an end because he had finally recognized the gross side of his nature. Wiping the spittle from his face, he roused himself. "Officer of the guard!"

A young ensign pushed open the tent flap, entered, and saluted.

"You saw the girl who was here just now?"

Embarrassed, the officer stared down at the tops of his polished boots.

"You saw her!" William insisted sharply.

"Yes, sir, I saw her," the ensign assured him hastily.

"Place her under arrest." William tried to speak without emotion.

The officer gaped.

"Anyone who harms or molests her will be personally answerable to me." To this extent, at least, William told himself, he could be a gentleman. "I want Captain Vanderhoort of my guard to form a detachment and take her to the border. There he will raise a flag of truce and deliver her to the commander of the French forces." He smiled ruefully. "With my compliments."

"Yes, Your Highness." The ensign departed quickly.

William paced up and down again briefly, composing himself, then asked that his chancellor be admitted. Obviously Bentinck had been waiting nearby, for he entered at once, brushing the dust of the road from his cloak. "I seem to have come at an inopportune time," he commented.

William remained unsmiling as he shook hands. "We'll wait until we're sure she's gone before we talk. She's in the employ of the French, so I'm having her escorted out of camp." Ignoring his friend's startled expression, William changed the subject abruptly. "Life as a diplomat agrees with you. I think you've gained ten pounds since the last time I saw you."

"Seven pounds," Bentinck replied defensively. "You'll want your generals to hear my news."

The Prince grinned wryly as he thought of Waldeck and his blonde. "I'll call them."

An aide came to the entrance when he heard William shout, then hurried off to get the generals. After a brief delay Waldeck and Dykvelt came in, both of them unshaven, bleary-eyed, and inclined to be surly. William ordered a breakfast of sausages and beer for his guests, and decided not to tell his lieutenant general immediately that the black-haired girl was a French spy. Waldeck was sitting on a stool, holding his head in his hands, and it was obvious that in his present physical condition the lesson would be lost on him. Later in the day, after he had recovered, would be a better time to caution him about his selection of bed companions.

An orderly arrived with the food, and both Dykvelt and Waldeck reached eagerly for their beer. Bentinck, choosing the largest chunk of sausage, bit into it with relish. "You're all wondering," he said cheerfully, "why I've arrived here at this unusual hour."

The generals glowered at him, but William knew his chancellor sufficiently well to realize that he was highly excited and was restraining himself with difficulty. "You didn't come here from The Hague because you enjoy riding in the night. Let's hear your news."

Bentinck put his sausage on a wooden tray and reached inside his cloak. "Last night as I was finishing my dinner—and an excellent meal it was, too—I was interrupted by the arrival of a private envoy from the man who is sometimes called the real King of England."

William displayed no emotion. "The Duke of Buckingham?"

"George Villiers himself, chief minister of the Crown, Master of the Horse, general-in-chief of the English army, lord admiral of the navy, and the holder of a few other titles that I can't recall." Bentinck handed his Prince a folded, sealed sheet of parchment.

William took it and glanced at the seal. "You're very pleased with yourself, so apparently you know the contents."

"The envoy gave me an idea of what his Grace has written to you, yes. But as I heard none of the details, I suggest that you read it."

Cracking the seal with his thumbnail, William unfolded the letter and read it rapidly, then went over it a second time more slowly. "This is a personal communication. Buckingham stresses the fact that it is not official. He's leaving himself a graceful escape if I reject his terms. Gentlemen, he offers us peace with England—and with France."

Dykvelt forgot his headache and Waldeck his blonde. Bentinck calmly went on eating sausage. "The envoy told me it was a peace offer," he said proudly.

William's expression did not change. "I gather from your attitude that he neglected to inform you of Buckingham's terms."

"Terms? What terms?"

"England and France will sign a peace treaty with us provided the United Dutch Provinces will place themselves under the benign protection of Louis and Charles."

Waldeck drained his mug of beer. "We've been fighting because they'd choke us to death with their benevolence," he said derisively. "They must think we're fools."

Bentinck looked crushed, and Dykvelt, clenching his fists, cursed under his breath.

Only William remained seemingly unruffled, but when he spoke his tone brought the others to their feet. "Milord Bentinck!"

This was no longer an informal discussion between close friends. "Yes, Your Highness?"

"We choose to reply publicly to His Grace of Buckingham's private communication. You will prepare such a reply for our signature."

"Yes, sir. I presume you'll want a copy sent to Paris?"

"Your presumption is correct." William stood, and although still attired in his shabby wool dressing gown, he had never shown greater dignity. "You may tell the kings of France and England that Prince William of Orange will never betray the trust of the country his ancestors have defended for so many years."

Dykvelt started to speak. William silenced him with a gesture. "You will also warn the Duke of Buckingham that if his country persists in following its present course, a proud nation will become no more than a French colony."

His courage inspired his subordinates, but his boldness alarmed Waldeck. "Do we dare shake our fist under the nose of a nation as powerful as England?"

"Why not? How does England prove her greatness these days?" William turned to Bentinck. "Tell Buckingham that we sympathize with the dilemma of his king and his people. Urge the English to follow the example of the Dutch, for there is only one choice in the world that France wants to dominate. Men will either fight for their liberty or let themselves be enslaved."

Bentinck nodded thoughtfully. "You won't persuade Charles to give up his alliance, you know. Brave words are no substitute for the pension that Louis pays him."

"Our reply has a double purpose," William said. "The English people love freedom, and will be reluctant to enter the fight against us, regardless of the attempts Buckingham will be forced to make to recruit an army and a navy after he receives our letter. And we want to prepare our own subjects for a long war. So you may conclude the message by informing the enemy that no matter what happens, we will defend our country, and, if necessary, die to the last man."

Chapter 3

THE DUTCH continued to amaze their friends and confound their enemies by winning one victory after another during the spring and summer of 1673. William and Waldeck laid siege to the town of Woerden, and although forced to retreat, inflicted enormous losses on the French. They captured the fortresses of Tongres and Walcheren, and after going into quarters for a brief rest, capped their previous triumphs by taking the city of Bonn. Spain, which had resisted Bentinck's repeated blandishments, now eagerly signed a treaty of alliance, and Louis became so alarmed that he withdrew the French fleet from the North Sea, where it had been blockading Dutch ports, and sent it to the Mediterranean. Sweden openly allied herself with the United

Dutch Provinces, and so did some of the independent German princes, the foremost of whom was the Elector of Brandenburg.

There were riots in Paris and Lyons. A unit of marines stationed at Brest mutinied. Even the sycophants at the court of the Sun King began to wonder whether a brazen young Dutch upstart was going to bring the most glorious era in French history to a premature close. Louis realized that he had to act decisively. In the spring of 1674 he assembled an army of more than one hundred thousand men under his best general, the Prince of Condé. William was not surprised, however; he had learned his lesson well from the French spy who had made her way to his bed following the battle of Finsterwolde, and his agents in France kept him informed of all developments. Accordingly, he and his allies were prepared and they marched out confidently to meet the enemy. The two forces met near the village of Seneff, in Hainault, and William distinguished himself in action, but in spite of his bravery and Waldeck's shrewdness, Condé was too strong and clever to be beaten, and the battle ended indecisively. Both sides withdrew after suffering heavy losses. Louis claimed that his army had won a great victory. The French, who had been waiting two years for such news, believed him, but the rest of Europe knew better. Emperor Leopold, the timid man who ruled over Austria, Hungary, and Bohemia, and was granting increasing self-rule to the German princes who nominally owed allegiance to him, finally agreed to become the ally of the Dutch. Charles of England rarely paid any heed to public opinion, but when London's street singers composed ballads extolling William of Orange, and when his chief officers announced that under no circumstances would they fight the Dutch, he decided to withdraw even his token support from Louis.

So, for all practical purposes, the Dutch had won their freedom by the summer of 1674. A state of war still existed, but Bentinck received unofficial hints that the enemy would be willing to begin discussions that might lead to a peace treaty. It was urgently necessary for Louis to continue winning victories, of course, if he hoped to maintain the myth that he was invincible, but he looked for less vigorous opponents, and soon became embroiled again in arguments with Pope Innocent, the Duke of Savoy, and the King of Naples.

William was at last in a position to devote himself to peacetime pursuits, and, turning the army over to Count Waldeck, he spent most of his time encouraging the building of a merchant fleet, providing assistance to farmers, and giving advice and grants of money to the rapidly expanding Dutch East India Company. His people now enjoyed complete personal and religious freedom, and in two years the United Dutch Provinces achieved a level of prosperity the nation had never before known. The States-General made several attempts to increase William's allowance, but he refused the offers, patiently explaining that he had no need for a larger income.

He maintained a small house at The Hague, and lived there during the months that the States-General was in session, but Amsterdam was still his home, and feeling as loyal to the city as its burghers were to him, he continued to make his headquarters there. The audience chamber of the palace was refurnished, and part of the ground floor was opened to accommodate secretaries and aides, but William still slept in the small room that had been his bedchamber when he had been John de Witt's prisoner. He refused to increase his personal staff, and told the nobles who felt that the Prince of Orange should live in a manner befitting his station, that Anna, Gertrude, and his groom made him comfortable enough. Most of the rooms of the palace remained closed until late in 1676, but William hated waste, and when he learned that the mayor of Amsterdam and his staff were occupying cramped quarters they had outgrown, he invited the city administrators to move into the building.

He spent most of his days in a small office adjoining the audience chamber, and there he worked, conferred with his ministers, and received visitors. The oak-lined walls were bare except for small portraits of his father and William the Silent. A table and a dozen chairs, which were used for meetings, stood at one end of the room, and William sat at a desk beneath the single window that looked out on the city. His lack of ostentation occasionally shocked foreign envoys, but his own associates grew accustomed to his bleak surroundings, and Bentinck, who had stopped trying to persuade the Prince to accept the trappings of his rank, deliberately closed his eyes to the atmosphere.

One afternoon in January, 1677, the chancellor, now growing stout, arrived at the palace from his own ornate office to find William signing documents. Amused, Bentinck stood and gazed at him for a moment: The ruler of the United Dutch Provinces was dressed in a suit of heavy, unadorned gray wool, there were no buckles on his shoes, and his only jewelry was a ring on the index finger of his left hand bearing the crest of the House of Orange, which he used to seal state papers. A stranger might have taken him for an unassuming clerk in the employ of a merchant, but his face reflected the burdens of responsibility he had assumed. His eyes were piercing now, rather than lively with a questioning intelligence, there were lines on his forehead, and although he wasn't yet twenty-seven, his hair was already sprinkled with gray. Sighing inaudibly and shaking his head, Bentinck removed his silk cloak, threw it over a chair, and moved to the hearth to warm himself.

"Is there any progress in your peace negotiations with the French?" William asked, not looking up.

"None. Every report from our envoys at Nimeguen is the same. Louis wants peace, but he will not agree to reasonable terms until we find some way to back him into a corner."

"It's as I thought." The scratching of William's quill pen was the only sound in the room for a moment. "I wanted to ask you about the state of affairs at Nimeguen at last night's reception, but your escort didn't leave your side all evening."

Bentinck grinned as he crossed the room and lowered his bulk into a chair beside the desk. "You sound as though you don't approve of the lady."

"Lady?" William raised an eyebrow as he reached for the next document on the pile before him. "You should have heard the comments of the Lord Treasurer and Lady Hausmann on the subject."

Bentinck laughed. "As I've seen Lady Hausmann, I can imagine. He was envious and she was jealous." He smoothed a crease in his green velvet breeches. "You've given me as good an opening as any, William. The reason I've come out in this foul weather is to discuss the ladies with you."

The Prince threw his quill pen onto the desk. "Again?"

"What alternative do you give me?" Unperturbed, Bentinck studied a ruby on the little finger of his left hand. It picked up the glow of the firelight and seemed to absorb his complete attention.

"You might leave me in peace for a while. Every time I've seen you lately you've been urging me to marry. If you approve so highly of matrimony, why don't you find yourself a wife and stop creating scandals?"

"Fortunately for me," Bentinck replied calmly, "I'm not the Prince of Orange. When I choose to marry it will be a strictly personal matter and not a state alliance."

William usually concealed his feelings, but saw no reason to hide his irritation from his oldest friend. "All right. Who is your candidate this time?"

"Count von Langbein of Brandenburg arrived in Amsterdam today. We've just spent a most interesting hour together. I told him that five years ago you weren't a fit consort for the Elector's niece, but that now the shoe is on the other foot."

"Was he offended?"

"No. He's a realist, and he didn't come here expecting the impossible. He told me in confidence that the Elector has persuaded Leopold to crown him King of Prussia. This will increase his niece's value."

William stared into the fire before replying. "If I'm to sacrifice my personal freedom, it must be for a good cause. Regardless of the Elector's title, his interests are inevitably opposed to those of the French, so he'll remain Louis's enemy whether I marry his niece or not. I'll take a wife only when you persuade me that such an act will help draw a ring around France."

"You said much the same when you were offered the Swedish princess two months ago. Not that I blame you, of course. I saw her miniature, too." Bentinck shuddered.

William smiled and picked up a paper from the desk. "As that disposes of the matter for the present, I'd like you to read this report from the province of Holland and give me your opinion of it. Some of the proposals for expanding trade are ingenious, and might help develop our New World colonies more rapidly."

"We haven't exhausted the subject of marriage." Bentinck airily waved aside the paper and settled more comfortably in his chair. "I've been devoting considerable thought to the problem, always keeping in mind, of course," he added hastily, "that your principal aim is to keep Louis of France contained and render him harmless."

The chancellor's tone was light, but William knew he was speaking seriously; Bentinck had proved that he was more devoted to the House of Orange than any other man in the United Provinces. "To the best of my knowledge you've dangled every eligible princess in Europe under my nose."

"Not all of them." Bentinck tried to appear casual and unconcerned. "I've been daydreaming lately. Do you realize that we would forge the most powerful alliance on earth if we could establish ties across the Channel? We would force Louis to sign that peace treaty quickly, I can tell you."

The subject was not a new one to William. "Charles of England has no legitimate children."

"Quite right. The heir to the throne is his brother James, who has two daughters. I've been informed on good authority that Princess Mary is an exceptionally pretty girl. Some of my English friends have admitted that Anne, the younger, is very plain, and as it's unlikely that she'll inherit the throne in any case, we can eliminate her from our considerations."

William made it obvious that he had weighed the possibilities of marrying one of his distant relatives. "As Mary is only fifteen years old we can forget her, too."

His argument failed to discourage Bentinck. "If the plague doesn't kill her, she'll grow older every year."

"In that event there will be a score of English noblemen who will want to marry her, and so will every bachelor prince on the Continent."

"Ah, then you're aware of the probability that she'll succeed to the throne of England someday, and that her husband will rule the country through her."

"The thought hadn't crossed my mind," William retorted a trifle too quickly.

Bentinck nodded, rose to his feet, sauntered to the conference table, and poured himself a small glass of wine. "I wish you'd keep a stock of Spanish sack. You can afford it."

"I prefer to encourage our domestic vintners."

Sipping experimentally, Bentinck made a wry face. "I might have known you'd actually use the consignment that the citizens of Utrecht gave you for Christmas." Shrugging, he drained the glass. "You refuse to contemplate the idea of marrying the English girl."

"I prefer to concentrate my thoughts and energies on practical possibilities."

The chancellor approached the desk and said solemnly, "You have a unique opportunity at present—if you care to exploit it."

"I'm listening."

"There's a rumor, unverified but persistent, that King Charles has become a convert to Catholicism." Bentinck had the satisfaction of seeing William start. "The Duke of York is said to be a convert, too," he went on. "He's been asked outright whether he's become a Catholic, but he refuses to discuss the matter, which is practically an admission that he's become a papist."

England was the strongest Protestant nation on earth, and although William firmly believed that every man had the right to worship as he pleased, he realized that the conversion of Charles and James, if true, could lead only to a stronger alliance with Louis of France. "Is the House of Commons conducting an investigation?"

"Charles refuses to call a meeting of the Parliament."

William sank back in his chair, toying with his quill pen. "If these stories are true, the French will invade us within a year."

"The English dukes and earls are is disturbed as you are." Bentinck's manner changed, and he spoke briskly. "They've insisted that both of James's daughters be raised as Protestants, and they keep constant watch over both girls. I'm further informed," he continued, raising his voice, "that Charles is terrified by the storm his alleged conversion has raised. The ghost of Cromwell has arisen, and the King remembers his years in exile. In fact, he recalls them so vividly he'll do anything to avoid being deposed."

"Anything?" William's mind was racing.

"It is no secret in England that you are not fond of Louis XIV. The Privy Council is aware of your views, and believes the King's popularity would be restored overnight if he married his niece to the man who has become the symbol of opposition to France. Naturally, the fact that you're a Protestant will dispel the fears of the English people, too, so the match would benefit everyone."

William drummed on the desk with his finger tips before replying. "You've been conducting secret negotiations with the English government."

"Not exactly. But," Bentinck admitted, "I have found it convenient to correspond with the Duke of Buckingham. He may be an extravagant libertine, as we've both heard, but he's no fool. And we understand each other."

The possibility that England might be brought into the coalition against France was so exhilarating that William did not allow himself to dwell on it. "Many years may pass before Charles and James die."

"That's one of the risks we'll be taking."

"There's an even greater one." Although the room was drafty,

William felt warm and loosened his stock. "There's always the chance that James's new wife may give birth to a son."

Bentinck smiled triumphantly. "I've made it my business to look into the English law on that subject. As the new Duchess of York was born a Catholic princess and practices her religion, any children she may bear James will be excluded from the succession. Only death or another revolution will prevent Mary from becoming Queen of England. And if you marry her there will be no revolt."

It was quiet in the room, and the logs burning on the hearth crackled and hissed. William realized that through the English Princess he might achieve his greatest ambition; with England and the United Dutch Provinces as the base of a firm alliance, the Sun King would never again menace civilization. Nevertheless he hesitated, for in spite of his many conversations with his chancellor on the subject, he had never seriously considered marriage as a means of forging his coalition against the French. Warfare and economic pressure were legitimate weapons, but he felt he would lose his honor if he used a girl who was scarcely more than a child in order to attain his goal. On the other hand, he could not let himself forget the Dutch soldiers who had died at Seneff, the men and women of the neighboring Brabant who were forced to endure Louis's harsh rule, the people of the Italian and German states who had been conquered by force of arms and paid reluctant tribute to the Sun King.

Sentiment, William decided, had to be discarded, and the only code of ethics that mattered was that imposed by a victorious army. If he failed in his efforts to hold Louis at bay, a French army even more powerful than that commanded by the Prince of Condé would someday cross his borders, and thousands of brave Dutchmen would die trying to preserve their liberties. He was reluctant to give up his quiet, ordered bachelor existence, but neither his personal happiness nor that of the young English princess was significant when he thought of all that was at stake.

"How soon can you sail to London?" he asked gruffly.

Bentinck was fully prepared for the question. "If I write Buckingham today he'll receive my letter in ample time for the Privy Council to extend me a formal invitation at its next meeting, which will take place a week from Thursday. We'll have to exchange the usual amenities, and then I'll have to apply to Charles for permission to visit his country. He'll reply as soon as he hears from me, as he's afraid there may be street riots in London when the weather grows warmer, so I dare say I'll be able to leave in about six weeks."

"You didn't mention his fear of riots. That strengthens our position. Wait until April, and you'll be better able to drive a bargain. With a threat of domestic violence hanging over his head, Charles will be more inclined to sign a firm treaty of alliance and settle a generous dowry on his niece."

Bentinck liked to think of himself as the leading statesman of Europe, but he had to concede that his talent for diplomacy was inferior to that of his Prince. "The dowry," he said with a chuckle, "will undoubtedly be paid in French gold."

"Don't expect much," William warned him. "Louis will stop paying Charles a subsidy when he hears that Princess Mary is going to become my wife." It was impossible for him to think in impersonal terms of the change that would take place in his life, and he stared moodily at the ceiling as Bentinck, still laughing, drew on his cloak.

"We're going to change the balance of power!" the chancellor declared exuberantly.

William had no desire to discuss the obvious and continued to look up at the ceiling with unseeing eyes. "As you remarked," he murmured, "she won't always be fifteen. Do you think your informants were telling the truth or were they exaggerating when they said she'll become an unusually handsome woman?"

Life at Hampton Court was always quiet and usually dull, but Mary Stuart was content to dwell in tranquil obscurity at Henry VIII's rambling old palace in the country, vastly preferring her bucolic existence there to the frenzied, dissolute atmosphere of her uncle's court in London. She and her sister Anne spent their mornings studying. After lunch they exercised their horses and played games of hide-and-seek in the elaborate garden mazes. When they could, they passed their evenings singing and reading with their governesses and tutors. In recent months grave-faced gentlemen from the Commons and the House of Lords had disturbed the quiet of Hampton Court at least two or three nights a week, but Mary no longer resented their invasion of her privacy, and patiently answered their questions about her education, her religious beliefs, and her opinions of papists.

Even these annoying intrusions were far less cause for concern than a journey into London, and as Mary sat erect in the carriage beside Lady Pamela Burghley, who had been sent to fetch her, she hoped she would be able to return to Hampton Court by evening. She had last stayed overnight at Whitehall during the Christmas holidays, and events during that visit had disgusted her. One afternoon she had entered the chamber that had been assigned to her, to find one of her stepmother's ladies in waiting and a young army officer making love on her bed. Unabashed at being caught, they had sauntered off without offering even a token apology for their outrageous conduct.

Far worse was the humiliation Mary herself had been forced to endure. On Christmas Eve she had worn her first real court gown, made of peach-colored silk with a square, low-cut neckline. She had been horrified during the course of the evening when Lord Arlington, one of the first peers of the land and a member of the Privy Council, had hauled her onto his lap and slipped his hand inside her dress. She had tried desperately to break away from him, but his strength had been too great for her, and she had finally managed to escape only when she had bitten his wrist hard enough to draw blood.

Instinct had told her that King Charles would have thought the incident amusing, so she had tried to find her father instead. Eventually she had described the incident to her stepmother. The Duchess of York had displayed a callous lack of sympathy for the sobbing girl, and had turned her away with the curt observation that, having reached the age of fifteen, it was time she stopped behaving like a prude. Since that night Mary had actively hated her stepmother, and, as she had confided to her sister, Anne, she had been unable to feel even a semblance of respect for the King or their father.

Lady Pamela Burghley was typical of the depraved young women of Charles's court, and Mary, stealing a glance at her in the carriage, vowed that if she ever became Queen she would forbid highborn ladies to appear before her looking like common prostitutes. Lady Pamela's gown was cut so low that only her nipples were concealed, and she drew additional attention to her breasts by wearing a beauty patch a fraction of an inch from her cleavage. Another patch was pasted on her powdered cheekbone, black salve was heavy on her lashes and lids, her lips and face were smeared with rouge, and an ornate wig hid her hair. In Mary's opinion she resembled a member of a traveling company of actors far more than she did a lady in waiting at His Majesty's court.

Unaware of the gesture, Mary raised her hand to touch her own hair; it was blond, with red highlights in it, and she was so proud of it that it had never been cut. Lady Pamela, who had been conscious of the girl's scrutiny, saw the move and smiled. "If you wish, ma'am," she said slyly, "I'll gladly loan you one of my wigs when we reach Whitehall."

"No, thank you," Mary replied primly, and looked out of her window at the rolling fields, which were turning green under a bland April sun.

"Oh? As you please, ma'am." Lady Pamela reached out and patted the girl's arm patronizingly. "But surely you'll borrow one of my gowns. We're approximately the same size, and I trust you don't intend to appear in a dress that doesn't have lace cuffs or a single ribbon at the hem."

Mary turned to face her companion, and her blue-green eyes were cold. "I'd freeze in one of your gowns."

The heavily perfumed young woman chose to regard the remark as humorous, and laughed heartily. Then she took hold of Mary's chin and studied her face carefully. "With a touch of rouge on your lips and a bit of salve on your eyelashes you'd be quite attractive, you know."

The Princess shrank from the tapering fingers. "I've never heard it said that my appearance is offensive," she murmured.

"No disrespect meant, ma'am, but you look more like one of Cromwell's psalm-singing Roundhead women than you do a Stuart."

Mary knew that Lady Pamela was one of her uncle's current mistresses and therefore had a measure of influence at court. It was never wise to make enemies, but the girl's dignity had been her greatest protection since her mother had died, and she refused to tolerate insults, even from someone who was enjoying the King's favor. "As I am a Stuart," she said distinctly, "I have no need to prove it. And if I'm satisfied with what I see in my mirror, who is to tell me I must change?"

Lady Pamela bit back an angry retort, recalling just in time that her outspoken companion was the heiress presumptive to the throne. Nevertheless it was disconcerting to be put in one's place so sharply yet deftly by a mere child, and the lady in waiting seethed. Courtiers might joke about the "little Puritan Princess," but it was less than pleasant to be rebuked by her. Under no circumstances, Lady Pamela decided, would she repeat the details of their conversation to her intimates.

Mary saw that she had scored and, realizing that the brazen woman would not again try to embarrass her, she relaxed. "Why am I being summoned to court?"

"I don't know, ma'am." Lady Pamela stared sullenly at the floor.

"My father didn't tell you why he wants to see me?"

"His Grace of York didn't call you, ma'am. It's Charles himself who sent me for you."

Ordinarily Mary would have been quick to resent the informal reference to the King, for her tutors had instilled the belief in her that protocol should be observed at all times. But the knowledge that it was the King who wanted to see her drove everything else from her mind. She could claim only a vague acquaintance with her uncle, and although she was required to appear before him at several state functions every year, she could recall having had no more than two private audiences with him. On one of these occasions he had been in an expansive mood and had made her a gift of a castle in Norfolk; then, last year, he had given her a diamond and emerald bracelet, and his generosity had stunned her until she had learned that he had planned to give the bracelet to his principal favorite, Louise de Kerouaille, the Duchess of Portsmouth, but had bestowed it on her instead in order to humiliate his mistress after quarreling with her.

In any event, a summons from the King probably meant that something exciting and pleasant was going to happen, and the prospect of visiting Whitehall again became less dismaying. Mary hummed a tune under her breath and, removing her right hand from her fur muff, studied her wrist. Had she known that she was going to see her uncle, she would have worn his bracelet as a sign of grateful respect, but she consoled herself with the thought that if he questioned her about it, she would tell him frankly that the lady in waiting who had escorted her to the city had been remiss in her duties. According to the gossip-loving servants at Hampton Court, Charles appreciated truth, and never punished a courtier for speaking plainly. With all his faults, she thought, there was much good in him, and she wished, as she so often had in the past, that he, not James, had been her father.

It was wicked not to love or honor her father, Mary knew, and she had struggled with her conscience for years. Sometimes she managed to convince herself that he wasn't as weak and degenerate as he seemed, but whenever she saw him the small store of good will toward him that she had accumulated promptly vanished. She could never forgive him for paying court to the Princess of Modena so soon after her mother's death, and she was still shocked whenever he brought one of his loose women to Hampton Court for a secret stay. The King conducted his affairs openly, and if his moral standards left something to be desired, at least he was honest. But James pretended to the world that he was faithful to his Duchess, and only his daughters knew better. Once or twice a month he would come to Hampton Court in a carriage with closed blinds, and Mary no longer bothered to spy on the painted, underdressed women who accompanied her father to a private wing of the palace and remained there with him for as long as four or five days.

Anne was still too young to know what was happening, but soon, in spite of Mary's efforts to protect her, she would learn, too, that James of York ostensibly went to the country to visit his children, but rarely saw them for more than a few moments. Mary had felt sorry for her stepmother until the incident on Christmas Eve, but she had hardened herself deliberately during the past few months, and had become convinced that she cared about no one on earth except Anne and herself. Her favorite pastime was to dream of the day when she would become Queen, and she was fascinated by the idea that it would be within her power to emulate the life and career of Elizabeth the Great. Many suitors would ask for her hand, but she would marry no one and would devote all of her energies to the people of England. Once, when she had confided in one of her governesses, she had been told she was a lonely, romantic girl with a headful of foolish notions. Since then she had kept her secret to herself, but she certainly had not abandoned it; she had gleaned from some of her tutors that the Stuarts were a stubborn breed, and she was determined to make her dream come true.

The carriage pulled to a halt, and Mary blinked in surprise when she saw she had arrived at the main entrance to Whitehall. An equerry opened the coach door, bowing low, and the sentries on duty at the gate stood stiffly at attention. These soldiers were typical of the loyal, decent citizens whom she admired, and she smiled broadly at them. Then, remembering that a stocky, blond corporal had been an expectant father when she had last seen him at Christmas, she paused to ask after his family. He extolled the virtues of his twin sons, and she listened raptly, even though aware that the other men were grinning at her. Anne, who was a very jealous child, frequently complained that Mary was the most popular member of the royal family and although it was a sure sign of vanity to admit that her sister had spoken the truth, Mary could not deny that wherever she went her uncle's subjects invariably greeted her warmly.

Lady Pamela touched her arm, but Mary stood her ground and refused to enter the palace until the corporal had finished telling her about his sons. Then, after congratulating him, she went inside and walked slowly through anterooms crowded with gentlemen who removed their plumed hats and ladies who curtsied to the floor when they saw her. Their exaggerated obsequiousness never failed to amuse her, but she controlled a desire to giggle and demurely followed a major-domo to the suite where the King transacted his business. She was kept waiting only a few moments, which surprised her, and then was admitted to the royal study. When she had been smaller she had played in the room one afternoon with two of her illegitimate cousins, and although she had not seen the inside of the chamber in at least eight years, she remembered it well.

Heavy drapes of pure white silk hung from the windows, a thick rug imported from the Ottoman Empire covered the floor, and the walls were covered with portraits of English monarchs, the largest and most prominently placed being a picture of the present King. A huge desk of carved oak stood beneath leaded windowpanes, and behind it was an enormous armchair with the letter C embroidered in the tapestried back. The King was perched on one edge of the desk, idly swinging a boot trimmed with ermine tails, and Mary thought he looked exceptionally healthy. There were the usual shadows beneath his eyes, of course, and tiny creases wrinkled his forehead, but his manner was animated, and when she curtsied before him he jumped to the floor, took her hand, and helped her to her feet.

"Welcome to Whitehall, niece," he said heartily.

"Your Majesty," Mary murmured, and then noticed that her father was scowling in a wing chair on the far side of the room. She hurried to him and kissed him dutifully, but he made it clear immediately that he was less than overjoyed to see her.

Muttering unintelligibly, he reached for a goblet of spiced wine that sat on a table beside him and drank deeply.

King Charles, however, compensated for his brother's surliness by exercising the charm for which he was famous. "We demand the privilege of looking at you," he said, and spun Mary around.

She hated herself for blushing, but could not prevent her cheeks from burning.

"The stories we've heard are true. You've become a young woman." He blithely ignored the fact that he had seen her every day for a week less than four months past. "Don't you agree, James?"

"She's a child," the Duke of York replied curtly.

Mary reacted as though her father had struck her with a whip. She knew she did not think like a child, and she certainly did not resemble one any more; in fact, one of the gardeners at Hampton Court had told her in the strictest confidence that the last young woman James had brought there had been less than two years her senior.

"Pay no attention to him," Charles said rudely, and granted Mary the honor of waving her to a chair while he remained standing. "Niece, you've been much on our mind lately. We've been thinking of your welfare."

Something in his expression that she could not quite define made her a trifle uneasy, but etiquette permitted only one reply. "Thank you, Your Majesty."

"Of all our many burdens, we can think of none more enjoyable than settling the future of such an extremely lovely young woman. Niece, please accept our felicitations. We completed arrangements today for your marriage to the stadholder of the United Dutch Provinces, Prince William of Orange."

"She's too young," James said angrily.

Mary hastily revised her opinion of herself, and for the first time in her life she agreed with her father. "Indeed, Your Majesty, I'm still a child."

"Nonsense," Charles replied briskly. "Didn't you hear us say that arrangements have been completed?"

Too crushed and horrified to speak, she nodded dumbly.

"We could not have done better for you if you were our own daughter," the King said fondly. "Prince William is a distinguished young man."

"Young?" Mary's voice sounded strange and distant.

"He's only eleven years older than you, we believe. And in recent years he's acquired a magnificent reputation as a soldier, as a statesman, and as a ruler."

James dug his lacquered heels into the rich pile of the rug. "He also happens to be the leader of a cabal against France."

"Your father," Charles told Mary imperturbably, "has developed a genuine liking for the French. We appreciate Louis's money, but we're realistic enough to know that the people of England insist that their Protestant Princess marry a Protestant. We'll miss Louis's gold, but we prefer going without it to losing our throne. We have a strong desire to keep our head attached to our body," he added sardonically, raising his voice for the first time, "and that, we fear, is a most unusual trait in our family."

James drained his drink and crashed the goblet on the inlaid mother-of-pearl table top. "I've done what I could for you, my child, but he won't listen to reason."

King Charles raised an eyebrow. "For her, did you say?" he demanded mockingly. "You've had your heart set on marrying her to the Dauphin, so you could rule France through her after Louis is dead. James, we tremble for the future of England. When will you learn to follow our example and let practical considerations guide your judgment? Oh, we indulge our personal tastes, but we take care never to offend our subjects or act contrary to the principles in which they believe. Remember that, if you can, when you succeed us."

Mary's tutors had taught her very little about political affairs, and she neither understood nor cared about the differences of opinion that were causing her uncle and her father to quarrel. All she knew was that her cherished dream of following in the footsteps of Elizabeth the Great was ended, and that she was being forced to marry a total stranger. The captain of the guards at Hampton Court was twenty-six, and she and Anne thought of him as an old man. The realization that the foreigner who was to become her husband might be fat and have gray hair at his temples was too much for her. Unable to control herself, she burst into tears.

Charles patted her shoulder, and when he spoke his voice was surprisingly compassionate. "We know how you feel, niece, and we sympathize with you. But this marriage is necessary for the stability of England and the continuity of the Stuart reign. The ceremony won't be held until the autumn, as we don't want to give the French an opportunity to mount an offensive against us this summer. However, you'll become the Princess of Orange in November, and neither your father's bad temper nor your tears will alter the situation. So dry your eyes and make up your mind that you'll do what you must—for the family, and for your country."

Chapter 4

WILLIAM WAS UNABLE to remember a birthday anniversary that he had enjoyed, although he recalled dimly that when he was very small his mother had always given a party in his honor. During the years John de Witt had ruled the United Provinces, the fourth of November had been the same as any other day, and it had been difficult, after William had become his own master and his country's, to change the habits of a lifetime. Therefore he had continued to observe his birthday quietly, but today, as he sat on the right of the King of England at a long banquet table, he wondered what absurd impulse had led him to choose the twenty-seventh anniversary of his birth as his wedding day. The other men at the table, thirty in all, were eating heartily, drinking heavily, and obviously enjoying themselves, but William had never felt lonelier or more miserable in his life.

The English weather was partly responsible, of course. Everyone had been telling him since he had landed at Dover the previous day that there had never been such a raw, damp November. The opulence and licentiousness of Whitehall depressed him, too, and his quarrel with his future father-in-law shortly after his arrival had not improved his disposition. He had assumed that he and Princess Mary would be married in Westminster Abbey, and had been disconcerted, then angered, when James of York had insisted that the ceremony take place in a private chapel at the palace. Bentinck, who was now conversing with the Duke of Buckingham and Lord Danby further down the table, had ferreted out the truth: the King and his brother had been afraid that Louis of France would become annoyed if the wedding were made a public ceremony.

To an extent, William reflected, gazing over the Duke of York's shoulder at hickory logs blazing on a hearth at the far side of the dining hall, King Charles's fears were justified. It had been heartening to receive such a cordial welcome from members of the nobility and to realize that the committee from the House of Commons that had called on him had been sincere in its declaration of friendship. And this morning, when he had wanted to escape from the palace for a walk, it had been flattering to hear from Lord Edward Russell, the young English admiral who had been assigned as his aide during his stay, that he was so popular with the people that he would risk being mobbed if he left Whitehall. So, after all, he could hardly blame the King for staging the wedding so discreetly; had he been in Charles's place, he would not have wanted to give his subjects the chance to demonstrate in favor of his benefactor's most implacable enemy.

Charles, who had been conversing in an undertone with his brother, turned to William. "You look unhappy, Nephew," he said. "Is there anything we can do to relieve you?"

"Perhaps you can satisfy our curiosity, Uncle." William knew that a number of the gentlemen were listening, but he recklessly decided to meet the issue squarely. "We were wondering whether Louis of France will continue to pay your subsidy after our marriage tonight."

The guests grew silent and James of York became red-faced, but Charles seemed to find the question amusing. "We hope he will."

"In that case, Your Majesty's caution is understandable."

Charles's smile broadened. "The wedding itself is sufficient cause for Your Highness' boldness." Though he had drunk too much, his eyes were hard as he regarded the young Dutchman. "It is customary, we believe, for a bridegroom to display nervousness."

"True enough," William agreed, then added quietly, "particularly when he has neither met nor seen his bride."

Some of the Englishmen in the party looked abashed, and Charles, unaccustomed to such bluntness, seemed uncertain what to reply. But the Duke of York, who had been drinking steadily since mid-afternoon, made no attempt to hide his anger. "My daughter," he said, his words slurring, "is too young to take part in the festivities that usually precede a wedding."

William knew it was senseless to quarrel openly with the man who was about to become his father-in-law, but he could not control his temper. Everyone he had met, including young Russell, whom he felt inclined to trust, had assured him that Mary was an attractive girl, but for all he knew they were lying and she might be the ugliest creature in England. "Your daughter is not too young, sir, to be married," he said distinctly, and glared at the heir to the throne.

The English and Dutch guests exchanged startled glances, and for a moment it seemed as though either William or James would stand and draw his sword. But King Charles, who was at his best in the role of a pacifier, had no intention of allowing the Prince of Orange to leave England without his bride. If that should happen, the people would certainly riot and possibly revolt. Charles did not like the plain-spoken, somberly dressed

Dutchman, but he proved himself capable of handling the delicate situation. Laughing heartily, he clapped William on the shoulder.

"You have already learned why you have not met her, Nephew. It would have embarrassed all of us had it been necessary to hold a formal levee. We should have been compelled to invite the French ambassador, and in that case you would not have attended." The King shook his head, then laughed again, ingratiatingly. "You may take our word for it that our niece is the prettiest girl in England."

"Then she must be very lovely, Uncle." William felt far from reassured, but reflected that if there was any substance to Charles's claim, the Princess, in spite of her extreme youth, must be a real beauty. Some of the ladies who had been presented to him a few hours since had been very attractive. He remembered one in particular, Lady Pamela Burghley, who had appealed to him enormously.

Perhaps he was guilty of disloyalty to his future wife to be thinking of another woman immediately prior to his wedding, but his marriage was an affair of state, no more and no less, and as his bride was only a young girl, there seemed to be no reason he should not let his mind linger on Lady Pamela. He wondered, not for the first time, whether she herself had conceived the idea which she had presented to him without much subtlety—that she would like to join his entourage as one of Princess Mary's ladies in waiting. If she was a spy who would report back to Whitehall, he wanted nothing to do with her, but it was possible that she was merely bored with England and wanted to sample court life in another country. Bentinck was too busy just now to investigate her background for him, and William, glancing down the table, caught the eye of one of the more able and discreet of his courtiers, Arnold von Keppel.

He decided to take Arnold aside for a moment on their way to the chapel and give him the assignment. If Lady Pamela proved trustworthy, she could certainly add zest to his court, and would help to compensate for the presence of an adolescent female member of the House of Stuart. Looking obliquely at James of York across the table, William thought that even if Mary were pretty, she had probably inherited her father's morose disposition. His feeling of depression increased. He had to remind himself sternly that he was making a personal sacrifice for the good of his country and the future of Europe, and that regardless of his wife's personality, England would eventually become his firm ally in the coalition against France.

William roused himself sufficiently to join gracefully in drinking a toast to the King, managed to preserve a dignified front when the company drank to him, and remembered in time to offer a toast to Princess Mary. Then the King announced that the hour had come to go to the chapel, and the party broke up, Charles and James hurrying off to join their waiting wives. Arnold von Keppel came to William at once, and showed no surprise over the unusual instructions he was given. He seemed to accept the explanation that Princess Mary would want compatriots as ladies in waiting, and if he thought it strange that his Prince was interested in a woman other than the one he was about to marry, the young nobleman managed to hide his views.

The palace chapel in which the ceremony was to be held was so small that it would accommodate only a few guests, and as William had no near relatives, he had chosen his closest associates to accompany him. William Bentinck and Nicholas Dykvelt fell in behind him, and Count Waldeck, who had himself been married the previous year, went quickly to his own suite to fetch his wife. Lord Edward Russell took William's arm and led him through the maze of palace corridors, and the Earl of Devonshire, an intense, homely young man who had said little during the dinner, quietly joined them.

"Our prayers have been answered through you, Your Highness." Devonshire spoke so softly that William had to strain to hear him.

"Oh?" Startled, William was instantly on his guard.

"We have been afraid of what would happen in this nest

of papists." The Earl exchanged a grim smile with Russell. "James of York has been trying for the past year to arrange a marriage between his daughter and the French Dauphin, and if that had happened, we should have sent the whole family into exile again."

"We are loyal to the Crown," Russell added, speaking in the same low, cautious tone, "but we insist that the Crown must be loyal to us, too."

"Thank you for taking me into your confidence, gentlemen," William replied carefully.

Edward Russell had gone to sea at age eleven, and he was still more sailor than diplomat. "We know we can rely on you in a crisis, Your Highness," he said bluntly.

William appreciated plain talk, and decided not to mince words either. "Is Princess Mary dependable?"

There was a silence broken only by the sound of leather heels clicking on the stone floor of the corridor. Then the Earl of Devonshire looked straight at William. "England suffered frightful losses when a Stuart was deposed," he said. "We do not want another Cromwell. Charles is too clever to make an open alliance with France, but there is no telling what James may do when he becomes King." His voice hardened. "If it should become necessary to get rid of him, we prefer to see him succeeded by the legitimate heir to the throne. You ask us if Princess Mary is dependable, sir. All I can reply is that at some future time we may put the same question to you. A man is responsible for his wife, and we beg you not to forget that the woman you are marrying may become Queen of England."

They had arrived at the chapel, and the Englishmen stood aside. William paused for a moment to give Countess Waldeck, a big-boned woman with dark hair and a pleasant countenance, a chance to primp. Then, his head high and his shoulders squared, as though he were leading his troops on parade, he walked into the chapel. The Archbishop of Canterbury was standing at the altar. Chandles were burning in wall sockets, and William noted idly that they were French candles. Then he caught the scent of burning incense, and felt sure the odor also annoyed his companions—Dutch churches scrupulously eliminated such refinements from their services. He bowed to the Queen, plump and ungainly in a high, elaborate wig, heavily powdered, then inclined his head a second time to the Duchess of York, whose face looked sallow in the candlelight. William approached the altar with Bentinck at his side, and the Archbishop, whom he had met that morning, smiled pleasantly at him. No one spoke, a clock in another room chimed eleven times, and King Charles, always bored by inactivity, stirred in his velvet-covered pew and coughed.

The doors opened again, and William heard footsteps approach; holding himself rigid, he tried not to turn, but could not resist a surreptitious glance. Princess Mary Stuart, supported by the arm of her father, was walking slowly toward the altar. To William's intense disappointment he could see only that she was tall and slender. Her gown of white satin was nipped in at the waist, indicating that she had no need to be ashamed of her figure, but her face and head were completely covered by a voluminous white veil, and it was impossible for William to make out her features beneath it. He guessed that she was not wearing a wig, which relieved him. It was absurd to realize that he was marrying a total stranger. Then, as she joined him before the altar, it occurred to him that she was trembling, and he felt sorry for her. For the first time the thought crossed his mind that the situation was probably no more pleasant for her than it was for him; at least he had agreed to this alliance of his own free will, but she had been given no choice in the matter.

Mary, peering at the man beside her through the thick web of her veil, found it hard to believe that he was about to become her husband. She had studied his likeness on several Dutch coins, but now she saw that he was stockier than she had imagined, and she certainly could not call him handsome. His face was too strong, there were too many lines at the corners of his eyes, and the set of his jaw was too stubborn. It was good to see that he did not wear a wig, for she considered false hair unsanitary, but she was shocked to see gray at his temples. Of course Anne, who had crept out of her room the night before to steal a glimpse of the Dutch prince, had warned her that he was old, but Mary had not believed her sister. She hoped that Anne was not gloating now, and had to control a desire to turn and glare at the younger girl, comfortably watching from a pew.

What bewildered Mary was that the man standing beside her seemed tense. She had been assured repeatedly by her governesses and tutors that he was a great warrior, and fearless champion of Protestantism, and a firm opponent of the French, yet now he was obviously ill at ease. She saw a trickle of perspiration run down the side of his face, even though it was chilly in the chapel, and she was fascinated by the twitching of a muscle in his jaw. What bothered her most, she decided, was that he dressed more like a servant than a prince. She had often criticized her father and Uncle Charles for their gaudy silks, and she supposed she should appreciate being married to a man who did not try to outdo a peacock, but if he was such a famous soldier he certainly could have worn a dashing uniform instead of this suit of somber black.

The Archbishop began to speak, and the bride and groom forced themselves to listen to him. William made his responses in a firm voice, and the girl at his side was pleasantly surprised to hear that he spoke perfect English, without the gutteral accent of so many Dutchmen. Of course, she reminded herself, his mother had been a member of her own family, and thus he was not a complete foreigner.

When Mary was called on to reply to the Archbishop, she whispered the words of the ancient formula, and William, scarcely able to hear her, thought she was probably very shy. If that was true, it would be a welcome change from the brashness of her uncle and her father. He would have brooded over her Stuart heritage, but Bentinck handed him the ring, a heavy band of plain gold, and when he slipped it onto Mary's finger he discovered that her hand was so cold as to seem lifeless. Then, suddenly, the ceremony was ended, and the Archbishop gently reminded William of his duty to kiss his bride. Slowly, almost reluctantly, he reached out and lifted Mary's veil.

His first reaction was one of happiness, caused in part by her beauty, which had not been exaggerated, but he was moved even more by the firm, sober intelligence he saw in her eyes. But his pleasure was short-lived, for he perceived that she was even more of a child than he had feared. There were girls in Amsterdam and The Hague who, at fifteen, were rapidly approaching maturity, but Mary was still a little girl and it was difficult to acknowledge the fact that this callow, inexperienced creature had become his bride. She was staring at him wide-eyed, so William bent quickly and bestowed a light, token kiss on her lips, sternly telling himself that it was stupid to feel cheated. He had known for months that he was going to marry a girl of fifteen. Sound reasons of state were responsible for the match and it would avail him nothing to wish that it might have been possible for him and his bride to create a romantic attachment. A diplomatic bargain had been made, and he would keep his end of it.

Turning stiffly, William offered his arm to Mary, and her touch on his sleeve was so light that he was scarcely aware of it as they walked together to the chapel entrance. After pausing to accept the congratulations of the English royal family and the Dutch entourage, the newlyweds, along with the rest of the party, proceeded to a brilliantly lighted salon. The Queen and the Duchess of York both disappeared, William noted, but no one seemed to mind their absence, and Charles, entering the salon, immediately occupied himself with a flamboyant redheaded girl in a flimsy gown who, someone said, had been forced to earn her living in her youth by selling oranges in a theater. James went off to a far corner with a pair of black-haired girls who looked like twins, and all three, ignoring the rest of the company, began to drink heavily.

William was impressed by Mary's poise and regal bearing

as she smiled at the ladies and gentlemen who offered her their good wishes. Perhaps she was frightened, as William had suspected in the chapel, but she gave no sign of it now, and her self-assurance was that of a mature woman. At least, he reflected, she would not disgrace him in public when they returned to the United Provinces. He had no idea why her proximity made him uncomfortable, and he relaxed only when her sister approached and made her obeisances. A gawky, homely child, Anne regarded William with such awe that he could not help feeling flattered, and he spent a quarter of an hour completely at his ease, exchanging pleasant nonsense with her.

Liveried servants hurried in and out of the chamber, serving a variety of wines, and William saw that most of the guests, including the members of his own party, were drinking freely. Bentinck, of course, remained sober as he took advantage of the occasion to converse seriously with various English leaders, and William noted with approval that Arnold von Keppel was not drinking either. Eventually von Keppel caught his eye, and William, excusing himself rather abruptly, left his bride and crossed the room.

"I've made the inquiries you requested, Your Highness," von Keppel said, speaking softly for fear of eavesdroppers. "The person about whom you asked has no attachments, either personal or political." His face devoid of expression, von Keppel was making it clear that he had attributes necessary for the diplomatic career to which he aspired. "For a brief period she enjoyed the King's favor, but he is notoriously fickle. She's at something of a disadvantage at present. She has no protector, and members of the court are a bit timid about striking up friendships with her. His Majesty has been known to turn back to a lady again, and his gentlemen do not want to incur his displeasure. The Burghley family, by the way, strongly dislike the French."

On the far side of the room Mary covertly watched her husband talking to his short, youthful aide for a few moments, and she was dismayed to see William look around the hall carefully, until he discovered the whereabouts of Lady Pamela Burghley. Mary had never beheld a streetwalker, but she felt certain that not even the most conspicuous member of the dubious profession would call attention to herself more vulgarly or ostentatiously than Lady Pamela, whose gown left very little to the imagination and whose face was heavily daubed with cosmetics. It was humiliating now to watch her laughing and flirting with William, and Mary felt close to tears. Then a hand touched her arm. Turning, she looked into the calm eyes of Countess Waldeck.

"A wise woman knows," the Countess said in heavily accented English, "that she who controls her husband best never pulls the reins too tight. Soon Your Highness will become a woman."

Too embarrassed to reply, Mary stood indecisively for a moment, then accepted a glass of wine from a passing tray and quickly finished it. She told herself repeatedly that the man she had married could not possibly enjoy the company of such an obvious whore as Lady Pamela, and her relief was infinite when, as she stood drinking another glass of wine, William reappeared at her side.

He glanced at her glass, frowned, and looked at the guests with distaste. They were becoming boisterous, and Mary wondered if he disapproved of their drinking. She had no way of knowing that he did not care what they did, but considered the atmosphere too abandoned for a girl of tender years. "Your sister is gone?" he asked.

"Yes, she left with Mistress Trumbull." It was strange and intoxicating for Mary to realize that she herself would never again be forced to submit to the dictates of a governess.

"Good. We suggest, madam, that we also retire." Bowing formally, William offered his arm.

Although Mary had practiced using the royal "we," she could not bring herself to use it. "I—I—of course," she stammered.

The gentlemen and ladies who had not drunk too much

bowed and curtsied as the Prince and Princess of Orange left the hall. A lackey, waiting in the corridor with a brace of lighted candles, led the way to the suite overlooking the gardens that William had been given on his arrival. His sitting room and bedchamber occupied one wing, and he knew that several other rooms had been made ready for his bride, but had paid no attention to the actual preparations other than to note that servants had been carrying clothing boxes into her quarters earlier in the day.

Neither he nor Mary spoke as they made their way down the long, drafty corridors, but William's spirits improved when they arrived at the suite and he found that someone had thoughtfully lighted a large fire on the sitting-room hearth. "This is better," he said, moving to the fire to warm his hands. "This English climate freezes the marrow."

"Is it warmer in Holland?" The question was stilted, as she well knew, but she could think of nothing else to say.

"Holland," he replied, correcting her gently, his manner like that of one of her tutors, "is only one of the United Dutch Provinces."

"I am sorry," Mary replied, abashed. "I knew that. I've been studying your country."

"Our country, if you please, madam." It was absurd, William thought, to call a child madam.

"Our country, then."

He took pity on her and smiled. "You'll find that our patriots praise our climate, but in my own view it is as nasty there as it is here." A sudden thought struck him. "I trust you have enough warm clothes in your trousseau?"

She wanted to retort that, if his conduct at the reception was any criterion, he seemed to prefer women who hardly covered their bodies. "My wardrobe is ample," she said, and managed to sound demure and prim.

"Well, whether it is or not, a surprise awaits you in Amsterdam." It was disconcerting to see her look like a woman one moment and an eager child the next.

"I love surprises!" In her enthusiasm she forgot her dignity.

William chuckled indulgently, feeling more like an uncle than a husband. "There's no doubt you'll like this one. It's a fur cape, a wedding gift from Czar Theodore of Russia. Actually, as he's an invalid, his sister probably selected it." He refrained from adding that had the Archduchess Sophia of Russia been a Protestant, she might have become his wife.

"What kind of fur?" Mary clasped her hands.

"White ermine."

"I've never owned ermine."

"You'll probably want to wear it when the States-General crowns you." William hoped he could persuade his government leaders to postpone that solemn occasion for at least a year or two, and preferably until his bride was eighteen, when she would come of age under Dutch law. He hated to admit to himself that the fate of John de Witt was always in his mind, but he could not deny the fact that the respect in which his people held him was due to his own efforts. He could hardly afford to appear ridiculous before subjects who, like the English, gloried in their ability to think for themselves, and he knew the coronation would be a travesty if the members of the States-General were forced to kneel before a wide-eyed adolescent. "Of course," he added hastily, "it will be some time before the ceremony is held."

Mary tried to hide her disappointment. "May I wear the cape before then?"

"Whenever you wish. It will belong to you." Irritated, he told himself he sounded like a nursemaid.

"Thank you."

She was so unexpectedly humble, so grateful, that his annoyance turned to shame. "That reminds me of something. Excuse me for a moment." William hurried to his bedchamber and returned with a small metal case. With a smile, he handed it to his child-bride.

Opening the case with care, Mary stared in speechless delight at the contents. A necklace of matched diamonds picked up the light of the fire on the hearth and dazzled her. "I've never seen anything so beautiful."

For an instant William thought she was going to fling her arms around his neck and kiss him, but to his relief she was overcome by shyness, and after a breathless pause silently held out the gems to him, indicating with a gesture that she wanted him to fasten them around her throat. He complied, fumbling with the catch, and was sufficiently aware of her intense joy that he refrained from expressing the opinion that she was too young to wear the jewels. "This necklace," he said carefully, "is officially your property under the law of the United Provinces. Should you have a son, you'll have to give it to his wife when he succeeds me as stadholder."

Mary blushed, and it was a moment before he understood the reason.

"You'll wear it only on state occasions," he said gruffly. "My grandmother and my mother were very careful about observing the tradition."

"Will there be any important functions before we leave for Hol—for the United Provinces?"

"There will not," he replied dryly. "Your illustrious uncle sees the shadow of the Sun King everywhere."

She had never heard anyone speak of Charles with such open contempt, and was shocked. "I—" Her thought turned swiftly to another matter. "Would it be all right if I show the necklace to my sister? She probably will not believe I own it if I just tell her about it."

"Of course." William smiled indulgently. "Send for her now, if you like."

Again Mary blushed. "Not tonight! I mean, I was told we are not sailing for two more days, so I shall have plenty of time tomorrow."

A distinct sense of uneasiness was growing in William; it was clear that the child persisted in thinking that this was to be a real wedding night, and he was afraid that no one had bothered to disabuse her of the notion. "As you wish," he said curtly.

The abrupt change in his mood bewildered Mary, and she wondered if she had said or done something that displeased her husband. She had never seen such a cold, remote expression in anyone's eyes, and his mouth had tightened into a thin, hard line. The realization struck her anew that she was no longer a sheltered member of the Stuart family living quietly at Hampton Court, but a woman, the wife of a foreign ruler who was a total stranger.

William saw that she was frightened, and although he could not imagine what he had done to upset her, he tried to make amends. "You haven't looked at yourself in the necklace to see how pretty it is," he said heartily. "There's a glass somewhere in this suite, I believe."

"Yes, one has been installed in my bedchamber. May I take my leave for a short time, sir?" she asked gravely, curtsying to the floor.

Her solemnity amused William. He bowed deeply to hide his smile. "By all means, madam." He could become quite fond of the child, he thought, and there was no doubt that she would grow up to become an exceptionally beautiful woman.

By the time he straightened, Mary was gone and he was alone in the sitting room—alone for the first time in many hours. It occurred to him that he had been forced to endure company ever since he had landed in England, a vexing state of affairs for a man who was accustomed to periods of solitude and enjoyed them. As he stood before the fire he glanced at the ancient tapestries that covered the walls. It was typical of Charles, he thought, to show ostentation in the public rooms of Whitehall but to ignore the comfort of guests in their private quarters. The tapestries were not keeping out the wind, and the chamber was chilly. He looked for a decanter of spirits, but saw none. Grimacing, he reflected that the King displayed little of the hospitality for which the English were renowned.

Opening the outer door of the suite, he found two sentries on duty in the corridor. A lieutenant in the scarlet and white dress uniform of the King's First Troop of Household Guards approached, drew his sword, and saluted.

The sarcasm in William's voice was heavier than he knew. "A glass of brandy might make it possible for a man to endure the chill here, provided such spirits are available."

"I'll see what I can find, sir."

The draft that blew in from the corridor was damp and disagreeable, so William hastily closed the door and retreated to the fire, where he remained until he heard a polite tap. "Come in."

The lieutenant entered, followed by a servant carrying a small silver tray bearing a decanter and two glasses. The lackey, accustomed to the licentious behavior of those he served at Whitehall, was wooden-faced, but the officer was grinning slyly, and it occurred to William that the lieutenant undoubtedly thought he wanted the spirits for a nuptial celebration. He dismissed the pair with a curt nod, and told himself that not even the French court could be more depraved than this Stuart household. The very idea of taking a fifteen-year-old girl to bed repelled him, and he wondered if anyone in the palace except his own countrymen felt as he did.

There would be ample opportunity to consummate the marriage when Mary grew up, he reflected grimly, and if she had any other thoughts on the subject, as he feared she did, he would disabuse her of them quickly. Charles and James, living under the influence of their mentor, Louis, might lead abandoned lives, but he was convinced that the English people, like his own subjects, would be shocked if a grown man made advances to an adolescent. As nearly as he could judge, the Dutch and English were remarkably similar, and he felt positive both nations would approve when word leaked out, as it inevitably would, that he had refused to violate a child.

It was vital that he retain the good will of the English, and if he made a single false step, his present popularity would vanish. The recent earnest words of the Earl of Devonshire and

Lord Edward Russell had made a deep impression on him, and he was determined to court the people of England through the years. An influential group of nobles shared his hatred of Louis, the common man thought of the French as their traditional enemies, and if he showed sufficient patience, the day would come when he could finally forge the grand alliance about which he had dreamed since he had been a boy.

In the meantime, of course, he was under no compunction to lead a celibate life. Pouring himself a glass of brandy and sipping it, William told himself that he would offend neither English nor Dutch public opinion if he failed to remain faithful to a bride who was still a little girl. A man was entitled to take his pleasure where he found it, and William had to admit to himself that Lady Pamela Burghley excited him. He saw her for precisely what she was, of course—a hard-headed, opportunistic courtesan—but that knowledge made her no less desirable. She took pains to advertise her charms in the most unmistakable manner possible, but that was no reason for him to turn away from her. She had made it clear that she would be delighted to accept his protection, and the more he thought about the idea, the better he liked it.

As a married man he could no longer bring women into the palace at Amsterdam or into his house at The Hague whenever he pleased; too many citizens, and particularly their wives, would consider such conduct reprehensible. But if Lady Pamela were established in his household as a lady in waiting to Princess Mary, no one would protest if he enjoyed an affair with her, always provided, of course, that he behaved with a measure of discretion. Charles, recklessly imitating King Louis, made a spectacle of himself by parading his mistresses before his subjects, and this was certainly one reason he had lost their respect. William had no intention of making the same mistake.

A door opened quietly behind him, and he turned. Then he gaped at the girl who stood before him. He had almost forgotten Mary, but she was reminding him of her presence in the most obvious and embarrassing way possible. She had daubed rouge on her lips, black salve covered her eyelids, and a beauty patch was prominent on her left cheekbone. Her blond-red hair now hung down her back in loose waves, and one lock fell forward, over her shoulder, curling daintily. What shocked him even more than her use of cosmetics, however, was her attire: she had changed from her wedding gown of stiff white satin into a negligee of sheer silk, and it was all too evident that she wore nothing beneath it. William was horrified when he perceived that she had rouged the nipples of her half-developed breasts. As he stared at her she struck what she obviously assumed to be a seductive pose, spoiling the effect by blushing furiously.

Mary had seen women at her uncle's court smile langorously and stand with one hip thrust forward, but it was impossible for her in her innocence to create the same provocative effect. Her smile wavered as she moved awkwardly toward her husband. Taking a deep breath, she said, "I see you've ordered some spirits. May I have a drink?"

William was too stunned to move or reply.

She hesitated for an instant, then poured herself a glass and raised it to her lips.

A sense of rage welled up in William. Had he stopped to think about it, he would have realized it was directed not so much at Mary herself as at the lascivious English courtiers whose standards were so lax that a child who had been married for reasons of state thought she had to deck herself out like a whore on her wedding night. But his mind was not functioning rationally and before he could stop himself, he knocked the glass out of her hand. It shattered on the hearthstone, the brandy caught fire and flared for a moment, and the tension in the room became greater.

Mary gasped, blinking back her tears.

William glared at her. "Wash your face!" he commanded.

She was too terrified to move.

Still wildly angry, he caught hold of her shoulders and shoved her into her bedchamber. A porcelain basin sat on a dressing table, he saw, and beside it was a pitcher of water. Dragging the frightened girl across the room, he poured a quantity of water into the basin, spilling a considerable quantity onto the floor in his haste, and still unable to control himself, shouted at her again as he pointed at the bowl. "Wash your face or I'll wash it for you!"

Mary began to sob.

"If you cry, that black grease will get into your eyes and they'll be red for a week!" The Prince of Orange, he told himself, had been reduced to playing the role of royal nursemaid.

Too alarmed to reply, Mary scrubbed her face with a rough cloth; she was weeping copiously now, and the black salve did sting her eyes, but she did not care. She was uncertain whether the man she had married was mad or a monster, but she was humiliated by the knowledge that he did not desire her. It had not occurred to her, even when she had been changing her clothes, that he might find her unattractive, and she was so crushed that she felt numb.

When she stood erect again, her face dripping, her water-soaked negligee clung to her; wet and miserable, she shivered before William. As he handed her a linen towel, he realized for the first time that she was still wearing the gems he had given her. "Take off the necklace!"

She tried to obey, but her fingers were trembling, and she could not unfasten the catch.

Cursing under his breath in Dutch, he spun her around, opened the necklace, and threw it on the dressing table. "Now," he said, "get into bed before you freeze."

The huge four-poster bed that dominated the room was a haven, and Mary fled to it. Pulling the silken coverlet over her head, she buried her face in the pillow and cried hysterically.

Feminine tears were alien to William and made him uncomfortable. As he stood helplessly beside the bed, shifting from one foot to the other, his anger subsided, and it occurred to him that he had wounded the girl's pride and damaged her spirit. It was not her fault that she had behaved in such an abandoned manner, and in all fairness he should not hold her responsible. In any event, she was now the Princess of Orange, and therefore had to regain her dignity. William was tempted to call for her women, particularly her governesses, but knew he would become the laughing stock of the palace if the story of tonight's farce leaked out. After standing indecisively for a time, he hurried into the sitting room, refilled his own glass with brandy, and brought it into the bedchamber.

Mary was still huddled beneath the covers. He leaned down to tap her on the shoulder. "I have something for you," he said, trying to speak calmly and soothingly.

"Go away!" she sobbed.

He had no intention of spending the night in this drafty room, coaxing a child to act like an adult. "Sit up!" he shouted.

Terrified, she obeyed.

"Drink this!"

She was afraid to refuse, and after a few moments the burning brandy spread through her body and she stopped sobbing.

William hooked his thumbs into his belt and made an effort to speak dispassionately. "Someday," he said, "you'll be a woman. When you are, I'll come to you. There will be no need for you to entice me into your bed. I'll come to it myself, of my own free will. Do you understand?"

Mary nodded miserably.

"Until then, you have much to learn. Have you been taught Dutch history?"

"A little." Her voice was barely audible.

"You'll have a special tutor in Dutch history," he informed her sternly. "Do you know English law? No? Then what have you been taught?"

It was difficult for her to catch her breath. "Languages. Music and dancing and—"

Exclaiming impatiently, he cut her off. "I'll get tutors from some of our best universities to teach you about your own country. No, better yet, I'll arrange for some Oxford professors to take leaves of absence from their posts. You should learn about your own nation from Englishmen, not foreigners."

It was bad enough that her husband had rejected her, but Mary was dismayed even more to learn that her education was not yet ended, as she had so confidently expected it was. "Why must I continue to study?" she demanded sullenly.

"Because," William replied, "you have become the Princess of Orange. That would be sufficient cause. But even more important, you may become Queen of England. Good night, madam." Turning, he stalked from the bedchamber. As a rule he used spirits moderately, but tonight he knew he would drink a large quantity of brandy.

After he had gone, the girl in the bed stared pensively at the closed door. Her mind whirling, she revised her estimates of William. He had indicated that her youth was the reason he had spurned her. Remembering her disgust over her father's affairs with young girls, she grudgingly admitted that she admired her husband's principles. She did not look forward to the prospect of resuming her studies, but she was not to have a choice in the matter. William had told her what would happen, and she expected there would be no second thoughts about his decision. Sighing, Mary Stuart, Princess of Orange, decided that William was the most forceful, dominating man she had ever met, and at that moment she fell in love with her husband.

Chapter 5

THE PRINCESS OF ORANGE became eighteen years old on April 30, 1680, and the following day her coronation took place. As she had already lived in the United Dutch Province for three years, her husband and his advisers decided that the ceremony should be simple and quiet, but when the royal couple rode out of their small palace in the Binnenhof, or inner court of government buildings, and started for the Nieuwe Kerk, where the actual crowning would take place, they were surprised to see the roads lined with people. Only a single squadron of household cavalry preceded their carriage, and William was mildly annoyed with himself. He hated to misjudge the mood of the public, and had he guessed that so many people would appear to catch a glimpse of their rulers, he would have planned a more elaborate parade.

Mary seemed to be delighted with the arrangements. Smiling broadly, she waved to the enthusiastic men and women and laughed in obvious pleasure when parents held their children in the air. Glancing at her covertly as he mechanically raised a hand, William reflected that she had certainly matured in the past three years. Her face was fuller now, her features showed more character, and her figure, although still exceptionally slender, was that of a young woman, not a child. Her long, blond hair, which still had red highlights in it, was gathered into a neat bun at the nape of her neck so that her coronet could be placed on her head without difficulty, and William admired her gown of white silk, trimmed with silver, which she displayed beneath a thin cloak she had thrown open.

A small amount of rouge had been applied to her lips and to the best of his ability to judge, there was a film of rice powder on her face, but she wore no other cosmetics, and her only jewelry other than her wedding ring was the diamond necklace William had given her in England. It showed up clearly against the soft, smooth skin of her throat, and the Prince of Orange stirred uncomfortably in his seat. It occurred to him, as it had with increasing frequency of late, that he and his wife were still almost complete strangers. He had been busy, of course, concluding the peace treaty with France and working hard since that time to make the United Dutch Provinces strong and wealthy. Mary had not been idle, either, and the reports he had received from her tutors certainly indicated that she was a serious student who now probably knew as much about history and economics, law and politics, as any woman in Europe.

What disturbed William was the knowledge that so many barriers separated him from this attractive girl, and that he had no one to blame but himself. They dined together only on state occasions or when they received foreign envoys, and William had to admit to himself that he knew virtually nothing about her temperament or the way she spent her time away from her studies. He had heard that she was an avid gardener, and although flowers meant nothing to him, even a desultory conversation was preferable to silence.

"Your tulips and roses will be blooming soon, I imagine."

Mary, surprised, did not turn from the window, but bestowed a particularly gracious smile on a man in laborer's clothes and his large brood of children, who were crowding into the road. "The tulips won't be out for another two or three weeks," she said, "and I don't expect to see roses until next month. But if the weather stays warm, they may blossom sooner."

That seemed to exhaust the topic. "I suppose the reason you didn't wear your Russian cloak today is because it's so warm."

This time she could not help looking at him. She laughed. It was difficult to pretend she was lighthearted in the presence of this man who had meant so much to her for so long, but who had seemed consistently unaware of her existence. However, she had learned to control her emotions and dissemble when nccessary, so, although she was amazed that William had actually made a personal comment, she was grateful for it. "This is not the season for ermine," she said lightly. "Our people are modest, and would think I was being ostentatious."

He was pleased that she thought of herself as Dutch, and encouraged, he leaned toward her. "You are very wise."

"Thank you." Mary shrank back into her corner, and took refuge by waving with more vigor than dignity to a large group gathered outside the gate of the Gavangen Poort, an old prison that William had closed after the murder of the de Witt brothers.

For a moment he thought she was deliberately avoiding him. Then he reminded himself that she was still young and shy. "This is a special occasion for you," he said, speaking a shade too heartily, "so we'll have to commemorate it. Is there something you want in honor of the day?"

Mary's mouth tightened as she thought of a matter that had been preying on her mind; however, she had promised herself that she would handle it in her own way, so she forced herself to relax, and when she turned to William her blue-green eyes were clear and seemingly untroubled. "Your're very kind, but I can think of nothing. I'll have my coronet, and that will be more than enough to satisfy me. Lord von Keppel showed it to me yesterday, and it's lovely."

"The coronet," he replied testily, "is state property, in a sense. I was thinking of something personal." He recalled dimly that the wife of a visiting Spanish grandee had complimented her on her dinner service at a recent state banquet. "You collect china, I believe?"

She thought with amusement of King Charles's solid silver plates and cups, and of the gold service, instituted by Henry VII, that was kept in the vaults at Hampton Court and was used only on rare occasions. "I suppose you might say I'm interested. In a modest way."

"Good!" William said vehemently. "We'll mark your coronation by furnishing you with a fine set of dishes. Order whatever you please, provided you avoid the French."

"I know." Like everyone else in the country, she was aware of his stubborn refusal to buy French products, and it was useless to tell him that the chinaware made in the Brabant, which was still under Louis's domination, was the best available. "You're very generous," she added belatedly, unable to resist wishing that he had selected a single plate himself rather than merely give her permission to make her own purchase.

He seemed to guess her feelings. "Unfortunately, I know nothing of such things," he said apologetically, "so I believe you'll be better satisfied with the ware you choose yourself." A sudden thought struck him, and he added hastily, "I'll tell the household treasurer to check on the state of my accounts and notify you of the maximum amount you may spend." Chinaware, he knew, could be very expensive.

"I'll be careful, never fear."

He glanced at her sharply, searching for some sign of malice, but her face was as guileless as her tone. Still, he could not forget that she was a Stuart, and was accustomed to lavish living.

Mary knew precisely what was going through his mind. "I feel as you do about expenditures," she said firmly. "And now that I'm going to be in charge of my own home, I think you'll be surprised at how much I can save."

William was startled by her calm announcement that she was planning to supervise the operation of their household.

"I've come of age," she declared, showing that she, too, could be stubborn, "and it's something I've wanted to do for a long time."

He was uncertain whether such activity was beneath the dignity of a reigning princess. "We have stewards who do that work."

"Yes, and they're wasteful. I've spent hours in the kitchens, I've gone over the lists of servants and watched them at work, and I know."

William had to admit that her attitude was sensible, and he remembered with pleasure how satisfied he had been with the modest standard he had maintained as a bachelor.

His silence encouraged Mary, and she became bolder. "I know it's considered fashionable for people in our position to keep half a dozen palaces and castles open, but I really don't see the advantage."

This was the first time William had ever discussed domestic matters with her, and he was struck by her intelligence. "Quite true," he murmured. "As a matter of fact, I've often thought that Louis of France is responsible for the royal custom of maintaining so many homes. It's sheer extravagance."

Mary turned away, ostensibly to smile and wave again, but actually to bolster her courage. "We spend most of our time at the palace in Amsterdam, and we come to the house here when the States-General is in session. I wonder if you realize that we've spent only three days at the castle at Maastricht since you recovered the town from France in the peace treaty."

"That's so, isn't it?" He sat silent for a moment, musing. "George Waldeck would love to get hold of that castle. I'll turn it over to the army. Thank you for the suggestion."

She took a deep breath. "That leaves the House in the Wood. It's a formidable expense keeping a staff there, and I feel we ought to close it, too."

William stiffened, but said nothing. The House in the Wood was a villa located in the forests near The Hague, and only last month he had gone there quietly with Lady Pamela for a week's holiday.

She had been afraid he would make a scene, but when he continued to stare into space, she wondered if it might be possible to bring their greatest problem into the open. "I don't like the place, and I certainly prefer not to go there."

It occurred to him that she had visited the House in the Wood only once, during her first spring in the United Provinces, and that since then he had used the villa exclusively as a private retreat when he and Pamela had wanted to escape from court life for a short time.

"So," Mary went on, her voice rising, "I'd like to transfer or dismiss the staff and close the House."

"I'll think about it." William stared gloomily out of the window and told himself he had been incredibly shortsighted. He had allowed himself to fall into a routine of living, devoting most of his time to affairs of state, taking his pleasure occasionally with Pamela, and assuming, foolishly, that Mary would remain a complacent, docile child. But the lovely, regal young woman sitting beside him had become an adult, and although he resented her interference, he had to admit that her attitude was justified. Even though they had lived apart, she was still his wife, and she was certainly old enough now to feel angry and hurt over his relationship with Pamela.

On the other hand, he reflected, it was a common practice for sovereigns, who married for reasons of diplomacy rather than love, to take mistresses when they pleased. Every other ruler did it, including Mary's notorious uncle, and her hint of censure outraged him. A man of thirty who had achieved renown throughout the civilized world because of his unwavering opposition to tyranny would lose his pride if he allowed an inexperienced girl of eighteen to dictate to him. "The villa costs very little," he said curtly. "After all, it's only a simple country house. I believe I'll keep it open."

Mary clenched her fists, but hid her hands in the folds of her skirt. For three arduous years she had obeyed her husband's instructions meekly, working hard so she could become a fit consort, and pretending to be unaware of his affair with King Charles's former mistress. She had been constantly sustained by the hope that when she became eighteen he would discard Lady Pamela and turn to her, but he was making it emphatically clear that he had no intention of altering his present arrangements. Perhaps he had forgotten his blunt statement on their wedding night that someday he would come to her himself, of his own free will. She had never forgotten his saying that, and now she was tired of waiting. A Stuart would shame herself if she became a supplicant for a man's love, and in any case Mary felt no reverence for the House of Orange. Her heritage was older than William's, and doubtless a good deal more distinguished.

Mary had not devoted all of her time to her studies since her marriage. A good deal of it had been spent in listening to the gossip of women, and although Mary had not acquired any firsthand experience with men, she had learned a great deal about them. The time had come to stop procrastinating with William, she thought. Countess Waldeck, who had become her confidante, would undoubtedly tell her she was recklessly jeopardizing her whole future, but Mary reminded herself that Bertha Waldeck was not a princess, and therefore could not really understand how she felt.

Her decision made, she surprised William by smiling at him sweetly. He had been prepared for a distasteful argument about the House in the Wood, and was therefore startled by her quick surrender. Relieved that they were not to squabble, he felt at the same time distinctly irritated with himself because he could not get rid of the notion that he was in the wrong. No matter how often he assured himself that his marriage was only a political alliance, he could certainly see that Mary was a charming and sensitive person, and he knew that his callousness must be hurting her. He was bothered, too, by the realization that Pamela was grasping, cold-blooded, and calculating, and that he continued to act as her protector because she satisfied his physical appetite, and for no other reason. It was extremely difficult for someone who longed for immortality to reconcile that desire with the recognition of his lust and his indifference to a girl who had done him no harm.

He was still disturbed when the carriage drew to a halt before the Nieuwe Kerk, and he responded unthinkingly to the salute of the troops drawn up before the church. Mary was smiling radiantly as he helped her to the ground, and she was exceptionally gracious as she held out her hand to Lord Bentinck to kiss. The occupants of three other carriages grouped themselves behind the Prince and Princess, and William became apprehensive when he saw that Pamela, acting contrary to the instructions issued to all ladies in waiting, had deliberately arranged the neckline of her pale gray bodice so that her breasts were half-exposed.

Mary was conscious of William's concern, and a single glance at his mistress was sufficient to enrage her. However, her smile did not waver as members of the States-General from each of the seven provinces approached and bowed low before her. Reminding herself that this was her day and that she would allow nothing to spoil it, she made a supreme effort to put Pamela out of her mind, and when Count Waldeck, who was acting as grand marshal came up to her, she greeted him warmly.

The representatives of the States-General entered the church, followed by members of the nobility and the diplomatic corps, led by the Earl of Somerset. The young Earl had arrived in The Hague only recently, but had been accorded the honor because he was the Princess' countryman. The generals of the

Dutch army and the admirals of the newly created Dutch navy filed solemnly down the center aisle of the unadorned church, accompanied by their wives, and one hundred children in the choir loft began to sing a hymn. Bentinck, whose scarlet cloak and brilliantly plumed hat made him the most conspicuous person present, took the heavy silver mace, the symbol of the House of Orange's authority, from an aide and moved slowly through the church to a pew in the first row on the left side.

William, removing his helmet, followed close behind his chancellor.

Mary placed her hand on the sleeve of Count Waldeck's uniform, and he looked down at her from his towering height. "How do you feel?" he asked.

"I'm frightened," she confessed.

His smile broadened. "I'm always afraid before a battle, too," he said, his words barely audible above the soaring voices of the children's choir.

Mary wondered how many of her confidences his wife had repeated to him, but there was no chance to speculate on the matter, for he started down the aisle, carefully trying to adjust his stride to her shorter step. She knew that everyone was looking at her, and for an instant she was reminded of her wedding. The church, her white gown, and the sight of William's broad back beneath the pulpit made her feel like a bride again, but she told herself angrily that the notion was as absurd as it was romantic, and again she forced herself to concentrate on the ceremony. When she reached the front pew her escort halted, moved back to join his Countess in the second row, and Mary was alone.

She stood motionless, as she had done during a rehearsal the preceding day, and then, when the children struck and held a high note, she made a slow half-turn and faced her husband. Bentinck knelt before the Prince, accomplishing the feat with difficulty because of his increasing girth, and extended the mace before him. William took it, and Bentinck, grunting slightly as he rose, also moved to a seat in the second pew.

Grasping the heavy ornamental weapon tightly, William turned and looked at his wife, and she thought she detected a fleeting expression of admiration in his eyes.

Then it was gone, the singing stopped abruptly, and there was no sound in the church but the faint rustling of the ladies' silk skirts. Mary had practiced her brief speech, and conquering a momentary feeling of panic, she spoke in a loud, clear voice. "We, Mary of Orange and of Stuart, do solemnly pledge our loyalty to our husband, our nation, and to all the people of the United Dutch Provinces, so help us God, whose guidance we implore." She sank to the cold stone floor in a full curtsy, and lowered her head.

"We accept your pledge," William replied in a deep voice. "Rise, Mary of Orange."

He held out his hand to her, and as he lifted her to her feet she realized it was the first time they had touched each other since their wedding night. Arnold von Keppel had taken William's place during the rehearsal. She realized now that she should have known that William would take her hand. She was angry at herself because she was trembling, but she managed to recover her poise almost immediately, and when she was standing again her smile was proud, her bearing erect and regal. William handed her the mace, which she held cradled in her arms, and with William at her side, she slowly mounted a short flight of steps to the pulpit, where three clergymen were waiting.

She stood before the ministers with bowed head while one recited the Lord's Prayer and a second read the Ninety-first Psalm. The mace seemed to grow heavier in her arms, and she remembered that Arnold, who was always thoughtful and considerate, had warned her that under no circumstances should she shift it to a more comfortable position. A young page, a distant cousin of William's, moved slowly down the center aisle, carrying Mary's coronet on a velvet cushion, and the diamonds in it were so clear and brilliant that it looked as though it had caught fire as it picked up the light of the candles that illuminated the church.

Mary, her arms aching, saw something gleam near her, and glancing surreptitiously at her husband, realized that he was wearing his coronet, too. She could not recall having seen him don it, and tried to occupy her mind with the puzzle, hoping it would help her forget the weight of the mace. She was convinced the page was dawdling purposely, but at last he climbed to the pulpit and knelt, holding the cushion before him. The most difficult moment of the ceremony had arrived for Mary, as she was expected to kneel, too, and her arms were so tired she was afraid she would fall.

But William apparently was conscious of her dilemma, for he ignored tradition, and catching hold of her shoulders, as he had done the night he had mortified her by forcing her to wash her face, he steadied her as she lowered herself to the stone floor.

She smiled at him gratefully, but he was looking not at her but at the third clergyman, who offered a prayer for Mary, blessed her and the coronet, and then drew back. There was a long pause during which Mary dared not look up. Then she had a glimpse of William moving forward, and knowing he was taking hold of the coronet, she braced herself. He placed it on her head, and she hoped, fervently, that he was making certain it would not slip when she stood. There was another brief prayer. Then, as William helped her to her feet, one of the clergymen said, "God bless Princess Mary."

"God bless Princess Mary," the congregation repeated, and the choir began to sing a triumphal hymn.

William took the mace from Mary, and holding it easily in the crook of his left arm despite its weight, he offered her his right. She was so grateful to be relieved of her burden as she placed her hand on the sleeve of his black doublet that it was a moment before she realized that everyone in the church had stood to pay homage to her. A feeling of fierce joy swept through her, and she promised herself that as long as she lived she would do everything in her power to keep the pledge she had just made. Even a glimpse of Lady Pamela's disgracefully low-cut gown could not spoil her elation, and as she walked beside William to their pew, she thought that this was undoubtedly the proudest moment of her life.

After the Prince and Princess had seated themselves the choir concluded its hymn, the rest of the congregation sat, and each of the clergymen delivered a short sermon. One spoke on the theme of Humility, a second discussed Duty, and a third talked about Devotion. Mary tried to listen, but was too excited to concentrate, and at last the service came to an end. Everyone rose and remained in place while the Prince and Princess of Orange left the church. The cavalrymen on escort duty drew their swords, and on the far side of the city, at the army barracks, cannon began to boom a twenty-one-gun salute.

William handed Mary into their carriage, and she had a chance to relax while the other members of the royal party went to their coaches. William took advantage of the delay to discuss some legislation pending in the States-General with the leader of the delegation from Utrecht, and when he rejoined her, the procession started off at once. The return to the palace was even slower than the ride to the Nieuwe Kerk had been, for even more citizens lined the roads and made it difficult for the cavalry detachment to clear the way. Mary's feeling of intoxication seemed to communicate itself to the people, and their response to her was so enthusiastic that she was kept busy smiling and waving.

Suddenly William broke the silence in the carriage. "You're beautiful," he said.

The compliment was so unexpected that it caught her off guard, but as she looked at him in amazement she saw that he was speaking sincerely and soberly. She could feel color rising in her face, but was incapable of accepting the gesture of admiration calmly. "Thank you very much," she replied, and hoped she did not sound close to tears.

There was another long silence, and she could feel him studying her. "I can recall my mother wearing the coronet on only two occasions. It's strange," he continued, "but you look very much the way I remember her."

Mary touched the circlet of diamonds lightly with the tips of her gloved fingers. "Perhaps it isn't so strange," she said. "After all, she was a Stuart, too."

He nodded thoughtfully, still scrutinizing her.

She wished that he would stop looking at her and pay more attention to his subjects; her embarrassment increased, and she laughed to hide it. "You couldn't have been more clever putting the coronet on my head. I don't mind admitting to you that I was terrified. Last night I even dreamed that it slid off during the ceremony."

William chuckled. "It's a good thing dreams don't come true. I had one, too, and when I woke up it seemed so real that I could have sworn it actually happened."

"Would you—care to tell me about it?" she asked hesitantly.

"Of course. I dreamed that you dropped the mace, and that it clattered down the steps from the pulpit. The noise it made was deafening!"

They laughed together, and all at once Mary understood why he had been so attentive during the ceremony. "That was why you helped me!"

William confirmed her guess with a nod. "The French would have talked about us for months. And Louis probably would have paid some of those cheap Parisian pamphleteers he hires to write dire prophecies predicting the fall of the House of Orange."

Mary should have known he had been thinking in terms of the political effect of an accident during the coronation, but the realization depressed her for no more than a moment. In less than an hour the nobles of the United Dutch Provinces and scores of visiting dignitaries would come to the palace to pay their respects to her, and she was not going to let anything or anyone mar the day for her. Anything or anyone, she repeated to herself, and when she smiled serenely, William thought she was appreciating his humor.

The carriage drew up before the entrance to the little palace, followed by a number of others, including those of the members of the Prince's intimate circle who had been granted the privilege of repairing their toilet here rather than being forced to drive to their own homes and wait there for the reception to begin. The ladies drifted off immediately to rooms that had been set aside for their convenience, but Mary lingered deliberately and exchanged a few private words with Count Waldeck, then called Lord von Keppel aside and spoke to him briefly. Then she climbed the stairs to her own suite on the second floor. Before she reached the top she heard someone following her, and when she entered her own small, private sitting room she was not surprised when Countess Waldeck, breathless and red-faced, came in almost at her heels.

Mary's smile faded. Bertha Waldeck had become her closest friend, but clearly this was not an occasion on which she was seeking advice.

"George told me just now!" the older woman gasped. "You can't do it. You mustn't!"

"George," Mary replied with a trace of annoyance, "should have learned years ago that certain state matters are not to be discussed with anyone, not even his wife."

Bertha paid no attention to the rebuke, and, her voluminous skirts swaying, she marched purposefully across the room and caught hold of the girl's arm. "I don't blame you for feeling as you do, Mary. Everyone sympathizes with you, but—"

"I don't want sympathy. I want to correct an impossible situation."

"You're taking enormous risks, my dear." The Countess' dark eyes were grave.

"Could the situation be worse than it is now?"

"Yes, infinitely worse. You have no idea how William may react. I believe I know George as few women know their husbands, but at times even he is unpredictable. Why, he's actually pleased at what you're planning. Apparently he doesn't see, any more than you do, that William may become actively antagonistic to you."

"That," Mary replied calmly, "is a chance I shall have to take." Walking past a heavy, old-fashioned table and chair whose new coats of ivory paint did not hide their ugliness, she pulled a bell rope. When a serving maid answered her summons, she said with unnecessary firmness, "Be good enough to inform Lady Pamela Burghley that we require her to attend us immediately."

When the door closed, Countess Waldeck sighed and shook her head dolefully. Then she kissed Mary on the forehead. "Whatever may happen," she said, "you know you can count on your friends to do everything in their power to make your burden easier to bear."

"Thank you, Bertha."

A moment later Mary was alone. Hurrying to her bedchamber, she glanced at herself in her dressing-table mirror, applied a fresh coat of rouge to her lips, dusted her nose and forehead with rice powder, and then recklessly dabbed herself with a strong scent that King Charles had sent her for her birthday. Her father, she thought, had either forgotten the occasion or had chosen to ignore it, but this was not the time to dwell on her relationship with him. Looking at her reflection again, she adjusted her glittering coronet precisely, then moved back into the sitting room just as she heard a tap at the door.

"You may enter," she called, wishing her heart would stop pounding so hard.

Lady Pamela, who had found the opportunity to glue a beauty patch above the neckline of her gown, walked slowly into the room. It was the first time she had visited the suite in many months, for she and Mary had long ago found it convenient to stop pretending that she had duties to fulfill as a lady in waiting. They stared hard at each other for an instant, then William's mistress dropped a token curtsy and said, "You wanted to see me."

"We require," Mary replied in a high, clipped voice, "that all who address us recognize our rank and conduct themselves accordingly."

Lady Pamela glared at her insolently, but could not match the Princess' steady gaze. "Yes, ma'am," she muttered at last, and this time she sank all the way to the floor.

Mary's legs were trembling, but her full skirt hid this weakness, and she moved slowly, deliberately, to a high-backed armchair. She had been planning this interview for many months, and it was not accidental that she had chosen a chair that had the coat of arms of the House of Orange woven into its tapestried back. Seating herself, she smoothed and arranged her skirts with care, rested her hands on the arms of the chair, and hoped she was successfully imitating the remote, impersonal attitude that Uncle Charles adopted when he issued edicts from the throne. "You have been on our mind recently," she said severely.

Lady Pamela's air of bravado returned. Striking a pose that she apparently thought enhanced her charms, she replied in a tone that was arrogant, almost flippant. "I'm flattered, ma'am."

There was no change in Mary's expression. "We have decided that the welfare of our realm makes it necessary for you to absent yourself from the United Dutch Provinces permanently and immediately." She had practiced and refined the statement so many times that she found herself making it flatly, without emotion.

A harsh, incredulous laugh was the only response.

"You will not attend the reception being held in honor of our coronation," Mary continued mechanically, "but you will prepare for an immediate departure. If you heed our advice, which we give you freely, you'll waste no time packing, since you will be leaving very soon."

There was a silence, and Lady Pamela's eyes blazed. She stood with her feet apart and her hands on her hips, and neither her expensive gown nor careful toilet could hide her resemblance to the blowsy shrews from Southwark, the slum district across the Thames from London, who sold fish and meats in the streets of the English capital. "You aren't serious!" she said in a rasping voice. "You couldn't be!"

"We have never been more in earnest," Mary assured her solemnly.

"You can't do it!"

"Do you question our authority to exile any person whose presence endangers the safety or well-being of the state?"

Lady Pamela lost her temper. "You may be wearing diamonds on your head, but William is the ruler of this country."

"His Highness is constantly in our thoughts, and as you heard today at the Nieuwe Kerk—if you were listening—we pledged him our full support." The interview was becoming easier to handle, and Mary, starting to enjoy herself, wondered what Lady Pamela's hair really looked like under her powdered wig. Several ladies who had seen it claimed it was a thin, lusterless blond, but it was possible they had been exaggerating, telling their Princess what she wanted to hear. "What's more," Mary continued crisply, "we will not tolerate your overbearing manner."

"Sorry, ma'am," Lady Pamela replied through clenched teeth. She made an attempt to control her rage, but failed. "You can't tell me what to do. I'm not Dutch!"

"You are a visitor in the United Provinces, and you have the privileges of a guest, but no rights," Mary said sweetly. She paused, then added casually, "We do not need to be reminded that you are English."

Lady Pamela smirked unpleasantly.

"It would appear, however, that you require instruction regarding our dual status. You know us as the Princess of Orange, but it seems to have slipped your mind that we are also the heiress presumptive to the throne of our uncle." Mary paused, and her grip on the arms of the chair grew tighter. "We hope you'll be sensible. It would grieve us, should we become Queen of England, if you forced us to sign an order banishing you from that realm, too."

Lady Pamela became pale beneath her thick coat of creams, rouge, and powder, and for the first time fear showed in her eyes. "What do you think William is going to say about all this? Do you imagine he's going to like you any better? You may think that because you've been crowned you can be a real wife to him now, but I know him far better than you, and if you send me away, he'll turn to someone else."

The woman was striking at Mary's weakest spot. With difficulty Mary managed to maintain her composure.

"I can guess how you feel, but there's no need to be so drastic." Lady Pamela changed her tactics, and her tone was wheedling now. "After all, ma'am, it isn't as though you loved him or he loved you. Your pride has been hurt, and you want to hit at him through me. Well, there's no need for that. I can make myself inconspicuous. I'll be happy to spend most of my time at the House in the Wood or some such place, and I'll be out of your way. It would be the best arrangement for all of us, ma'am."

Mary was infuriated by the bland observation that she and her husband cared nothing for each other, but she refused to give the painted whore the satisfaction of seeing that she had been hurt. "Arrangements for your departure have already been made. When you leave this suite, an escort will be waiting to take you to your room and he will gladly help you pack your personal belongings. Some of General Count Waldeck's most dependable cavalrymen will accompany you to Rotterdam to make certain you suffer no unpleasant incidents on the road. And as Lord von Keppel is arranging through the foreign ministry for a private packet ship to transport you to England, we feel sure your quarters on the vessel will be prepared for you by the time you arrive."

There seemed to be no escape, but Lady Pamela struggled desperately. "I can't go to Rotterdam today!" she wailed.

Mary could afford to smile now. "A comfortable carriage is being prepared for your convenience, and as you'll ride only fifteen miles, we feel confident you'll arrive in ample time to dine on board your ship."

Weeping but belligerent, the woman made a final stand. "I insist on seeing William first!"

"That, we fear, will not be possible." Mary's voice sounded

like that of her uncle in her own ears, and she was surprised. "Some of our guests have already arrived, and it would be harmful to the future of the United Dutch Provinces if he were not on hand to receive them."

Tears of frustration and indignation cut deep furrows in Lady Pamela's lavish cosmetic base and made her look old and ravaged. "Are you afraid to let me see William? Are you afraid he'll want me to stay and tell you to go?"

On this one point, at least, Mary knew she was on firm ground. "You say you know him. If that claim is even partly true, then you can't help but realize that he's the most ambitious man in Europe. As you've slept with a king and a reigning prince, we presume you hold a rather high opinion of yourself. But not even you could be so vain as to believe that His Highness of Orange would be willing to sacrifice his chance to become the consort of the Queen of England and make an alliance with the one country that can help him defeat France. You may have good cause for vanity, my dear, but no woman is that charming."

"You do love him," Lady Pamela said in astonishment.

"The interview is ended," Mary replied, irritated because she felt her face coloring. "You have our leave to withdraw."

For an instant it appeared as though William's mistress would throw herself at the Princess, but she recovered her sanity in time to remember that even in the United Provinces, the most enlightened of nations, an attack on the person of a crowned head of state was a crime punishable by hanging. She wanted to curse, but could not speak, so she lifted her skirts and stormed out of the room. Before she slammed the door, Mary caught a glimpse of two stolid cavalry officers waiting for her in the corridor. George Waldeck, always dependable, had promised to help and was keeping his word, although he certainly realized that William might not forgive him for the part he was playing in the conspiracy.

It was unnaturally silent in the sitting room. Wondering whether to laugh or cry, Mary continued to sit, her long, slender fingers curled around the carved ends of the chair arms. For an instant she felt elated, then she shuddered and wanted to go to sleep. A feeling of disgust stole over her, and she murmured aloud that a man who could make as obvious and promiscuous a tart as Lady Pamela his mistress was not worth the effort she had expended. She knew at once that she was telling herself lies, however: William's love was worth any price, and regardless of whether he achieved the greatness to which he aspired, regardless of whether he was faithful to her, she knew she could never care for anyone else. As she had done on countless previous occasions, she reminded herself that she had no right to blame him for his cheap affair. National policy, dictated by his own high principles and the good of the United Provinces, had compelled him to marry a child. He had treated her honorably, and no sensible girl could have expected him to remain celibate all these years.

Nevertheless, Mary reflected, William's taste had been deplorable. Rousing herself, she stood, walked to the window, and looked down at her gardens. The flat leaves of the budding tulips were a dark, shining green beneath the midday sun; the rosebushes, less well developed, were a more delicate shade. She smiled wistfully. She was tempted to seek the peace of the garden, to spend the rest of the afternoon there, but she could not shirk her duty. A rising hum indicated that guests were arriving, and she would be considered inexcusably rude if she tarried here.

She went again to her dressing-table mirror, seeking reassurance, and was surprised to see faint but distinct smudges under her eyes. It was the first time they had ever been there, but she could do nothing to erase them except dab at her face with rice powder. She smiled at her reflection experimentally, did not like the effect, and angrily told herself to stop wasting time. Drawing on her gloves, she decided to wear the bracelet King Charles had given her. As a final gesture she put on the diamond earrings that the King of Spain had sent her as a coronation gift.

Then, her head high, she left the suite and started slowly down the stairs. A major-domo, who had been watching anxiously for her, struck the tile floor three times with his staff, and called in a loud voice, "Her Royal Highness!"

The ladies and gentlemen gathered in the audience chamber fell silent; the men bowed, the ladies curtsied, and William, who stood alone on a dais at the far end of the chamber, looked relieved when he saw her. Guests jostled each other in an attempt to clear a path for her, but there was almost no sound save for the clicking of her own high-heeled white satin shoes as she crossed the room to join her husband. She noticed that he was wearing a sash of white watered silk across the front of his black suit, and that several decorations were pinned to it. He rarely displayed these symbols of his honors, and she was grateful to him. Smiling at him, she extended her hand, and he helped her to the top of the dais.

As soon as they turned, the guests started to surge forward to pay their respects, and William muttered in an undertone, "Where have you been?"

He had not yet learned about Lady Pamela's departure, she realized. "I was detained."

The explanation was inadequate, but he accepted it without question. "Whatever the reason," he declared, "you look even lovelier now than you did earlier today."

Either he had not bothered to look at her closely or the shadows concealed the dark patches under her eyes, but she was so pleased he thought her beautiful that her smile was radiant. They had no chance for further private conversation: the guests were mounting the dais, two by two, to make their obeisances and back off again. For the next half-hour Mary was content to exchange pleasantries with her subjects and the foreign envoys, and it was heartening to realize that so many of the Dutch guests, both nobles and commoners, were her friends, people who genuinely liked her.

Her heart beat faster when Arnold von Keppel winked surreptitiously as he bent over her hand; she knew he was telling her that there had been no unexpected complications, and she could scarcely curb an exuberant urge to hug him. However, she reminded herself that the real test was yet to come. She had won a skirmish, but the battle had not yet begun, and she had to face the possibility that William, when he learned the truth, might decide to recall Lady Pamela. Glancing at her husband, she wondered if she would ever understand him. He was a strange man, one who had voluntarily increased the power of the States-General, so that he governed his nation with the advice and consent of his people, yet a man who refused to allow anyone to interfere with his private life and, to the best of her knowledge, confided in no one, not even William Bentinck and George Waldeck.

After all of the guests had presented themselves, an orchestra of four violins and two bass viols struck up a lively air in an anteroom and servants appeared with trays of chilled fruit punch, spiced with wine, and a variety of foods. The French court would have sneered at the fare, but Mary, who had planned the menu herself, knew the Dutch appetite and realized, too, that many of those present would have eaten nothing since breakfast. She was pleased to see the guests reaching eagerly for slices of ham and cold beef, dried fillets of herring, and eggs stuffed with minced meat. Two lackeys brought in large quantities of jerked beef from the New World, which a few of the more adventurous sampled. Mary took care to explain that this delicacy had been sent to her by residents of New York, who had written to her that they were expressing their loyalty to their Dutch ancestry, and also to her person, as their colony, now English, had been renamed for her father, in his capacity as Duke of York. A variety of Dutch cheeses proved to be far more popular than the novelty from America, and although Mary was too excited to eat more than a few bites of food herself, she came to the conclusion, as she strolled around the chamber with her hand on her husband's arm, that her party was an unqualified success.

Then, an aide-de-camp pushed through the throng to whisper a few words in William's ear, and Mary watched a familiar, remote expression appear on William's face. His eyes were cold, his smile was forced as he politely excused himself and slipped away. Mary was terrified, but continued to act the role of the charming royal hostess, and only Bertha Waldeck, who was watching her with mounting concern, realized that she was worried, and with good cause. A few moments later Arnold von Keppel was called from the chamber, and then the aide returned for General Count Waldeck. Mary became so animated that some of the guests wondered if she had drunk too much wine, but the more discerning finally sensed that she was under some sort of tension, for she fell abruptly silent when her husband returned, accompanied by the two noblemen whom he had summoned.

Waldeck smiled at Mary, but she saw only William's hard eyes, and when he rejoined her but neither spoke to her nor indicated an awareness of her presence, and she knew he was furious. However, she could feel no regret for what she had done, and she told herself that no matter how much of a scene he might make, she would not hesitate to send Lady Pamela away again, if William brought her back to the court. Perhaps she should have consulted her husband before getting rid of his mistress, and it occurred to her, belatedly, that it might have been wiser to let him save his pride by dismissing the woman himself, but she refused to admit that she had done anything wrong.

Conscious of William's exceptional restraint, she became gay again, subtly defying him. She was relieved that circumstances made it impossible for him to talk to her privately, and when he continued to ignore her she chatted animatedly with the ladies and gentlemen who clustered around her. She laughed a shade too heartily at their witty remarks, her own voice was a trifle too loud, and, as her apprehension increased, she became reckless and accepted a glass of wine whenever one was offered to her. A member of the English delegation, whom she had known casually as a child, told her that anyone would know she was the niece of Charles II, and although she ordinarily would have resented the comparison, she thanked him for the compliment. She could see that some of the Dutch nobles and legislators, who had been bragging to the foreigners that their young Princess was sensible and dignified, were disturbed by her conduct, but this was one occasion when she cared not at all what they thought of her.

The reception had been scheduled to end in mid-afternoon, but evening came and lackeys were lighting the candles in the wall brackets when William touched Mary on the arm. "No one can leave," he said to her in an undertone, "until you withdraw."

She controlled a desire to giggle; perhaps she was being a coward, but she wanted to postpone the inevitable unpleasantness with him as long as she could. "I know," she replied, nodding brightly.

"I'm happy to hear you're not too intoxicated to understand," he said brutally, then raised his voice. "Ladies and gentlemen, Her Highness thanks you for your good wishes, which we also appreciate."

He offered Mary his arm, and with the whole company watching, she had no choice but to take it and walk slowly out of the chamber, trying to recapture her sense of decorum. When they reached the corridor outside, she let her hand fall to her side and would have moved off alone, but William caught hold of her elbow and firmly piloted her up the stairs. His mouth was set in a grim line, and Mary sobered instantly. William led her to her own sitting room, and when he closed the door behind them, it occurred to her that this was the first time he had ever come to her suite.

"Well?" he demanded belligerently. "What do you have to say for yourself?"

She wanted to hide, to pretend she did not know what he meant, but she reminded herself that he, not she, was at fault. "A great deal," she declared, and her voice was sharp and clear.

He had expected tears and excuses, and was so surprised that he could only blink at her.

"If you expect me to apologize for sending Lady Pamela away, I refuse." Mary's memories of the years of humiliation she had suffered gave her courage. "And I warn you, if you bring her back here, I shall leave at once."

William had been so angry he had found it necessary to caution himself not to strike her, but he had certainly not expected such a vigorous counterattack. "Since when," he asked coldly, "has it been a wife's prerogative to give orders to her husband?"

"I'm giving no orders." She began to tremble, and gripped the back of a chair for support, but her voice didn't falter. "You're free to do what you wish."

"Thank you." His tone was coldly sarcastic.

It was impossible for Mary to curb her own temper. "If you want to sleep with women you find on the streets, you have the right. But I refuse to let them contaminate my home."

"Your home, madam?" He could not deny that he had been guilty of infidelity, of course, but the problem had never really seemed difficult until now. It had been so easy to tell himself that he was married to a child, and therefore could do as he pleased. Now he was discovering that it was a disconcerting experience to stand facing a young woman as lovely as she was angry.

"You placed this coronet on my head yourself. I am the crowned Princess of Orange, and this is my home." Afraid he might think she was cowering behind the chair, she released her hold and stepped in front of it. "My position gives me certain rights. If you deny them, then I prefer to separate from you immediately."

Her impudence outraged him. "Oh? And just where to you imagine you would go?"

"If it becomes necessary, I shall return to England."

If she carried out her threat, William realized his years of careful planning would be disrupted; it was even possible that his precarious alliance with England would be destroyed, and that Charles would use the dissolution of his niece's marriage as an excuse to sign a new, open treaty of friendship with France. It was inconceivable that a girl who knew nothing about world affairs could alter the course of history because her vanity had been wounded, but this was precisely what Mary was proposing to do. "I forbid you to leave!" William shouted.

His rage frightened her, but she knew instinctively that she must not let him see she was afraid. So she smiled and said coolly, "And I forbid you to entertain women like Pamela Burghley under my roof."

William was reminded of the days when he had been forced to obey John de Witt, and color rose in his face. "You forbid, madam?"

Perhaps she was going too far, she thought, and looking at him, she knew he was capable of becoming violent, but it was too late to rereat now. "I've heard you criticize Louis's court as a brothel, and you've been contemptuous of my uncle, too. Are you any better than either of them?"

She had tripped him, and he recognized the validity of her argument. Either someone had coached her or she was unusually quick-witted. He suspected that her argument was her own. Certainly George Waldeck, whom he trusted completely, had sworn that she had concocted the whole scheme to get rid of Pamela, and von Keppel, whose loyalty was beyond question, had sworn that she alone had been responsible for the act. So, in spite of his anger at her high handed manner, William looked at his wife with grudging respect. "What is it you want?" he asked at last.

She was aware of a change in his mood, and even though her experience was limited, she realized that she could win a permanent victory only if she altered her own tactics. Now was the moment to show gentleness rather than indignation. "You've been very considerate these past three years, and I'm grateful to you for your kindness. I'll do the best I can to be a consort of whom you and the people of the United Provinces can be proud, and all I want in return is that you allow me to be the mistress of my own home." She wanted to be fair, and forced herself to add, "Have your affairs elsewhere, so that I'm not embarrassed by public scandals."

Her absolute honesty jolted William, and he stared at her in silence. Her behavior today had been insulting, but he had to concede that he had given her cause to act unreasonably, and that really only his pride had been wounded. It was actually a relief to realize that Pamela was gone, that she had bored him for a long time, and that her insatiable greed had always irritated him. What he could not quite grasp now was the fact that the girl who stood opposite him had become an adult; he had become increasingly aware of the change in her ever since they had driven to the Nieuwe Kerk this morning, but he had not really looked at her until this moment. He had stubbornly continued to think of her as a child, which was absurd, and he had no one to blame but himself for his blindness. He was probably the only man in the United Provinces who had remained unconscious of the fact that the Princess of Orange had become a supremely beautiful woman.

William's quiet, searching appraisal made Mary uneasy. During the past year, with increasing frequency, other men had looked at her as William was gazing at her now, but she had avoided possible complications by pretending to be unaware of such scrutiny. The situation that confronted her at this moment, however, was unprecedented: above all else she had yearned for William's approval, and she knew that his close inspection was a great compliment, but at the same time she was alarmed. She wanted him to make love to her, yet she was terrified by mysteries of which she knew nothing. She wanted time to compose herself, to prepare for her initiation, but she realized that she was caught in the trap she herself had set. She had exercised the rights of a wife when she had sent William's mistress away, and although she had hoped that he would turn to her, it had not crossed her mind that she would become utterly helpless if he called on her to fulfill her obligations to him.

He smiled enigmatically. "So you want to become the mistress of your own home." He repeated her words slowly, and took a single step toward her.

Mary, completely flustered, retreated and took refuge behind the chair again.

Had William been thinking clearly, he would have realized

that her withdrawal was merely a virgin's expression of timidity, but he interpreted the move as a sign of distaste. "Do you remember our wedding night?" he demanded harshly.

She blushed, but was unable to speak.

"I told you then that you would not have to pursue me again. I said I would come to you." William regretted that he sounded so accusing, and made an effort to become more gentle. "Well, I'm here."

Her dream was being realized, but she had been startled by the sudden change in his mood, and she was too numb to respond.

Their eyes met, and he halted. He, too, recalled every detail of her ludicrous adolescent performance at Whitehall, and his anger over the incident, long dormant, flared up again. She had thrown herself at him then, but he thought she was so disgusted by his affair with Pamela that she wanted nothing to do with him now. He had paid for every woman he had ever taken, and unable to recognize Mary's love, he misunderstood her rigid silence. Too disturbed to realize that she was confused and frightened, he felt certain she held him in contempt; his frustration and his unexpected desire for her overwhelmed him.

"You've told me your conditions," he said roughly, "but you haven't inquired about mine. It so happens I have some, too." He paused and looked at her intently. "Come here."

Mary was afraid she would burst into tears, and made an effort to calm herself before obeying.

But William was too impatient to wait. "You're my wife, not my ward," he said, his rage becoming greater. "I told you to come here." Reaching out, he caught hold of her arm and wrenched her toward him.

Mary lost her balance and fell heavily against him. Before she quite realized what was happening, William's arms encircled her and he was kissing her.

His desire for her mounted, yet simultaneously her passivity convinced him that she was rejecting him. Had he planned to make love to her, common sense would have told him to approach her carefully, but his ardor destroyed the last shreds of his objectivity, and crushing her to him, he kissed her again, savagely. Mary's gasp of pleasure sounded like dismay to him, and scarcely aware of what he was doing, he tore the rich fabric of her coronation gown, ripped the dress from her body, and began to caress her.

The only light in the room came through the open door of Mary's bedchamber, where a serving maid had placed a candelabrum on a table near the entrance, leaving hastily when she had heard her mistress and the Prince arrive. In the shadows of the sitting room, William was unable to see the strange mixture of ecstasy and fright on Mary's face. He only knew that, in spite of what he believed to be her resistance, she was finally responding to him, at least physically, and picking her up, he carried her to a divan at the far side of the room, where the shadows were the deepest.

Neither was able to recall later how they divested themselves of the rest of their clothes, nor could they remember the details of William's love-making. It was enough to know that he took her, and that afterwards they lay side by side on the divan, silent and spent.

After a considerable time, William recovered his reason. Mary's eyes were closed, and overcome by tenderness, a feeling that he could not remember having ever experienced, he reached out to stroke her face. Her cheeks were wet, and he drew back his hand instantly, unaware that in her exhaustion she was weeping tears of joy.

He had given her good cause to hate him, he reflected bitterly. Rising without a word, he dressed quickly and left the suite, filled with self-loathing. Mary, half asleep, did not realize he was gone until she heard the door shut. She then wept fresh tears, for she felt certain he did not love her, and she knew her pride would not allow her to reveal that she loved him.

Chapter 6

WILLIAM AND MARY gradually established a pattern of living that satisfied neither, but that, if it did nothing better, at least gave them some measure of relief from their burden of frustration. The House in the Wood was closed and the royal couple divided their time more or less equally between the palace in Amsterdam and the smaller establishment at The Hague. Several evenings each week William came to his wife's suite, made love to her, and then left her again, usually to return to his office. Some of the more observant members of the court noted that on these occasions he invariably worked far later into the night than was his custom, but the household was a dignified one, gossip was not encouraged, and the Prince's habits were rarely discussed openly.

But it was impossible for the ladies in waiting and the younger officers of the guard to refrain from whispering to each other occasionally that William and his Princess rarely spent any time alone with each other except on these evenings. They ate breakfast separately, in their suites, the Prince usually had a light meal in his office at noon, and although the royal couple dined together, official guests, friends, and visitors of state usually sat down at the table with them. If no one else was present, Mary insisted that her ladies accompany her to dinner, and William extended invitations to the officers or to someone on the staff of his foreign minister, Lord von Keppel.

Foreign visitors, less discreet than the Dutch guests, admitted that they were confused by the relationship between the Prince and Princess, for William and Mary addressed only polite, commonplace remarks to each other at dinner, and promptly went their separate ways when they left the table. But not even the French, who hired agents for the purpose, could uncover a trace of a scandal in the House of Orange. To the surprise of a great many people, including members of the Dutch nobility who thought they understood their Prince, William refrained from taking a new mistress after Lady Pamela Burghley returned to England. If he was less than content with a life that consisted of his work and brief visits to his wife's apartment, he voiced his complaints to no one. And everyone agreed that the conduct of the Princess was exemplary.

Mary acted as her own housekeeper, which won her the respect of her practical subjects, she devoted considerable time to her gardening, and she opened her doors for two hours every day to any woman in the United Provinces who wanted to see her, a custom that made her enormously popular with people of every class. No one guessed that she was unhappy, for she looked lovelier every year, and although the whole country was disappointed because she did not give birth to an heir, the Dutch kept hoping, as did the English across the Channel, that eventually she would have a son. No one wanted a baby Prince more than William, unless it was Mary herself, but on this subject, as on others, they were silent, both with outsiders and with each other.

They had made and sealed a bargain on the night of Mary's coronation as Princess of Orange, and neither complained. William was scrupulously faithful to his wife, and she, in return, made herself available to him whenever he wanted her. However, no couple could live under the same roof indefinitely in an atmosphere of coolness and tension, and in 1685, several months after Charles of England died and Mary's father was crowned as James II, the domestic tensions suddenly and unexpectedly became greater.

The States-General had adjourned for the summer, so the Prince and Princess were spending July and August in Amsterdam, as the high-ceilinged rooms of the palace were cooler than the more cramped quarters of the house in The Hague.

One sultry evening in late July promised to be similar to countless others—uneventful and dull. William went to his office after dinner for a meeting with a group of Dutch and English shipowners, who, with his encouragement, were trying to merge their interests for their common good. Mary retired to her sitting room with several of her ladies, and while she sat sewing, one of her attendants read aloud a new poem by John Dryden, the London dramatist, called *Absalom and Achitophel.* William had urged her to hear it, and as she listened she began to understand his reasons. The poem was a thinly veiled satiric attack on her father, and criticized him at length for his fear of his nephew, the Duke of Monmouth, the eldest of the late King Charles's illegitimate sons. Mary had known her cousin only casually, and had always thought of him as an older man; it was something of a shock to realize that he was approximately her husband's age.

She had never held a high opinion of Monmouth, and although she knew he aspired to the throne, she had never been able to take his pretensions seriously. Dryden, she discovered, shared her view, and was almost as uncomplimentary to Monmouth as he was to King James. The caustic wit of the poem amused her, but she averted her face whenever she smiled; it was possible that some of her ladies understood the allusions, too, and she had no intention of providing them with a juicy morsel of gossip. Uncomplimentary news always traveled quickly, and she knew that if she laughed, word would soon reach England that she had enjoyed the assault on her father and her cousin.

Politically minded people—and everyone in England seemed to be concerned with the succession these days—would be sure to interpret her reaction as a sign that she was anxious to secure the crown for herself, but nothing was further from the truth, and she did not wish to have London talking about her. Officially, of course, she was still the heiress to the throne, but she nourished the secret hope that if she remained quietly in the background she would be forgotten. She had no ambitions: as far as she was concerned, Monmouth could succeed James, and she would be content to remain in the United Provinces. She knew a great deal about political affairs, as Arnold von Keppel, acting on her husband's instructions, visited her twice every week and brought her up to date on the state of the world, but power meant nothing to her.

It was difficult, even degrading, to admit to herself that all she wanted in life was William's love, but she forced herself to face the truth squarely. She had been living with him for five years, but she still felt more like his mistress than his wife, and although there were times when she was convinced that he would never learn to care for her, she could not allow herself to give up hope. He still visited her twice each week, and she clung to the thought that he would not come to her if he did not find her attractive. But at the same time she was unable to rid herself of the fear that his own political ambitions were responsible for the attentions he paid her; his desire for a permanent, indissoluble alliance with England was undiminished, and he had made it plain to her, both through his own occasional crisp comments and via Arnold von Keppel, that she was the vital link in the chain he still wanted to forge around France.

Aware that her mind was wandering, she made an attempt to

listen to *Absalom and Achitophel,* but it was not easy to concentrate. She was willing to grant that James and Monmouth were fools, but her own happiness was at stake, and after paying close attention to the poem for some minutes, she discovered that she was unable to appreciate more than occasional bits of Dryden's humor. She wanted to halt the reading, but her sense of duty was too strong; if William asked her opinion of the work, she wanted to be able to discuss it intelligently with him. But she was relieved when the sitting room door opened, and told herself that any legitimate interruption would be welcome. Then, as her ladies rose hastily and curtsied, she looked in surprise at William himself. She certainly had not expected to see him this evening, for he had made love to her only the preceding night, and he had not come to her two days in succession since the first months they had been intimate.

Mary smoothed her hair and wished she was wearing her new pale green gown instead of the yellow dress that was more than a year old and that she had worn tonight because they had entertained no guests of importance at dinner. But it was too late now for regrets, as William seemed impatient as he said, "Good evening, madam."

"Good evening, sir." She turned to the ladies, who were awaiting her permission to leave. "We will have no further need of your services tonight."

The women backed out of the room, and William remained standing until they had gone. He was frowning, and when the door closed, he began to pace up and down. Occasionally he was in this sort of hurry, and Mary, trying to choke down a sense of shame, knew what was expected of her. "Shall we go into the other room?" she asked, rising and reaching for a hook at the shoulder of her short-sleeved gown.

"Sit down, please," William replied abruptly. "I want to talk to you."

The request was unusual, and as she resumed her seat she realized he was upset. She felt flattered that he had come to her when he was disturbed, but she concealed her pleasure, thinking it wiser to let him tell her what he wished, in his own way. "Would you care for something to drink?"

"No, I— On second thought, I will, provided it's mild."

She stood and went to a table on which a large silver bowl stood. "This is a plain fruit punch," she told him as she poured two cups. "There's no wine in it." She thought, as she had so frequently in the past, that their tastes were remarkably similar.

"Thank you." William took the offered cup. Watching her as she crossed the room again, he reflected bitterly that it was his own fault that she was so cool and reserved whenever they were together. He had to admit to himself that she had seemingly learned to enjoy his love-making, but the barrier that separated them whenever they tried to converse appeared to be impenetrable. He thought, as he had so often, that she considered him a boor, and in the past he had frequently wished he could summon the courage to apologize to her. But it was too late now; they had established their relationship, such as it was, and there were too many immediate, pressing problems to face. All the same, he told himself, it would be far easier on him if she were not so lovely.

Mary sipped her punch and glanced at her husband over the rim of her glass. William was drumming on the arm of his chair, a sure sign that he was under tension, and she longed to go to him, to clasp his head against her and stroke his hair. But he was too austere, too remote and dignified, so she told herself sternly to stop daydreaming.

"You may recall," he said suddenly, "that I had hoped you and I could pay a visit to the Vatican this October."

"I remember." He had mentioned the idea on one occasion, briefly, and Arnold von Keppel had later explained to her that William had hoped to prove to Pope Innocent that his enemy was France, not Catholicism. She had approved the plan heartily, and had said as much at the time, but apparently William had forgotten. "Aren't we going?"

"No." He did not mean to sound curt, but was trying to find the right words to express himself.

Mary felt a stab of disappointment. They had never made a journey outside the United Provinces together, and she had built up a false picture in her mind. The trip, she had told herself repeatedly, would bring them closer together, but now she had to abandon her hopes.

He gulped down his punch and placed his cup on the table beside him with unnecessary force. "Your father," he said, trying to conceal his hatred for James, "is responsible, I'm afraid."

She folded her hands in her lap and waited for him to continue. She had small reason to love her father, but it was painful to hear anyone else criticize him.

William saw the expression in her eyes and became defensive. "I said nothing when he became King and failed to send you an appropriate gift. I could have become very angry the day you received that little portrait of him—and nothing else. But I held my tongue."

Mary nodded, not trusting herself to speak. The incident had taken place only five months ago, and she still felt bruised when she thought of it. When a man became King of England, it was the custom for him to bestow expensive gifts on the members of his immediate family, but James had treated both of his daughters shamefully. Anne had written that she had wept every night for a week, but Mary had told no one about her own grief, and she certainly did not intend to say anything now to someone as coldly unsympathetic as William.

Unable to sit quietly, he jumped to his feet and roamed around the room. "Religious wars," he declared, finding it easier to talk in general terms than to discuss the specific issue that had brought him here, "have hampered the progress of Europe since the time of the Crusades. When people of one faith are made to suffer because of their beliefs, all religions suffer." He halted and stared at Mary. "Did you know this is the only nation on earth where complete freedom of religion is permitted?"

The question, she thought, was an insult to her intelligence—a deliberate attempt to ignore the interest she had shown in the Dutch people and their traditions. "You forget," she retorted icily, "that I've lived in the United Provinces for eight years."

Wlliam was lost in thought and did not hear her reply. "I had hoped that our visit to the Pope would show up Louis's revocation of the Edict of Nantes as the hypocritical gesture it is. He really doesn't care how the French worship. It just happens that there aren't many Protestants in France, so it's easy to persecute them. It's a convenient way to rally his country behind him while he occupies Alsace. His secret police are making so much noise arresting Huguenots that most countries still don't realize he sent three divisions into Strasbourg without a shot being fired."

"So you told me last week." Mary was sorry she sounded irritable, but she was unable to understand the connection between the French persecution of Protestants and the cancellation of William's plans to visit Rome, much less his anger at her father.

"When the Earl of Shrewsbury visited us early this month, he was obviously disappointed when I told him I wanted no part in a holy war. Spain and the Papal States are friendly to our country. Shrewsbury thought he would shock me by revealing that your father goes to Mass openly now, but he was a Catholic long before you and I were married."

Increasingly annoyed, Mary saw no reason why James's iniquities had to be paraded before her. It was almost as though William was accusing her of perfidy. And there was certainly no need to remind her of the Earl's embarrassing visit. "As I told you after that first unpleasant evening with Shrewsbury, he is a very impetuous young man. He was hot-headed even when we played together as children, and I don't think he's capable of understanding that you're trying to keep both your Catholic allies and your Protestant friends. He was hoping to goad you into making a statement he could repeat, and when you wouldn't say anything, he kept trying to press you harder. He just can't understand the delicacy of your position." Still in the dark regarding her husband's reasons for coming to her tonight, Mary refrained from adding that he himself was apparently insensitive to the nuances of her situation.

William listened to her attentively, nodding as he absently

sniffed some roses from her garden that floated in a bowl of water. Her observations were sound, and he reflected that although she was usually reluctant to comment on the state of the world outside her own home, she always made sense when she did. He wanted to compliment her on her shrewdness, but she had given him the perfect opportunity to explain why he had come to her apartment. At best his mission was extraordinarily difficult, and although Bentinck and von Keppel had volunteered to see her, he had not allowed himself to delegate the task to someone else.

"My position is so delicate," he said, taking a deep breath, "that events in England make it impossible for us to visit Rome this year. The Emperor wouldn't understand, nor would the Swedes."

He looked old and gray in the candlelight, and Mary, aware that he was going through some sort of inner struggle, felt such compassion for him that she hid her own alarm. Obviously there had been a crisis in England involving her father.

"How well did you know your cousin?" he demanded suddenly, his voice harsh.

"Which one?" she countered. Charles's various mistresses had given birth to so many children that there were some she had never met.

"Monmouth."

"He was always pleasant to me. And to Anne, too. He visited us at Hampton Court two or three times after he was made a general in the army. I always felt rather sorry for him, I think. He must have led an uncomfortable life in the years before his father granted him official recognition."

William planted his feet apart and hooked his thumbs in his black leather belt. "His Royal Highness, the Duke of Monmouth," he said grimly, "was a damned fool. He decided to make himself King, and led a rebellion against the Crown."

Mary gasped. Her hand over her mouth, she rose slowly to her feet.

"He persuaded more than one thousand men, nearly all of

them amateur soldiers, to follow him. There was a battle—if it can be called that—and the army shattered his band."

"Was he killed?" Mary asked in a hoarse whisper.

"No, captured."

"Then my father will send him into exile," Mary said, relieved. All at once she thought she understood the reason for William's unexpected call and his roundabout way of telling her the news. "If he asks for asylum in the United Provinces, please don't refuse his request because of me. Though I am James's daughter, I will not turn away my own cousin!"

"Monmouth won't be asking for asylum," William replied tonelessly, unable to meet her gaze. "According to the story that reached us this evening, two priests—King James's closest advisers—visited him in his cell last night. How much responsibility they bear for what happened, I honestly don't know, but there will be repercussions in every country in Europe. Monmouth was a member of the Church of England."

"Was?" Mary's lips formed the word silently.

"He was executed at dawn this morning for high treason. The death warrant was signed personally by King James."

Mary stood unmoving for a long moment, unable to believe that her father had actually put to death a nephew, even one who had conspired against him. Monmouth had been Charles's favorite son, and although he had made a vain and foolish blunder, it was horrifying to think of the price her father had forced him to pay. Suddenly, she began to weep helplessly, neither averting her face nor raising her hands to her eyes.

William stepped forward and took her into his arms awkwardly. This was not the moment to tell her that her father had made a mistake, that all of Protestant England would turn against him now. Nor was this the time to point out to her that she would benefit because Monmouth was dead and she was now the only claimant to the throne, either legal or illegitimate.

Sobbing, Mary buried her head in William's doublet and dug her nails into his arms.

He patted her clumsily, wishing desperately that he could

think of something to say that might comfort her. Her grief, he knew, was caused by her feeling—which the facts substantiated—that her father was a brutal, hypocritical despot, rather than by her sadness over the death of her cousin. It would be tactless to say that he had always been afraid James would upset the peace before Louis's allies were strong enough to unite against him. Nor could he, when her last illusions had just been destroyed, confide that he had always felt a deep contempt for the new King of England. So he remained silent and uncomfortable, not realizing that he, who had never been shown sympathy or tenderness, could not express his sentiments although he was acutely conscious of his wife's need.

Instinct rather than reason finally caused him to lead her, still sobbing, to her bedchamber. When she sank onto the bed he searched for a jug of brandy, but was so unfamiliar with her suite that he could find no spirits. Finally he had to summon a servant. He wanted no one else to see his wife in her present state, so he took the brandy from the lackey at the entrance to the sitting room, then hurried back to the bedchamber with it and stood over her, frowning.

"Drink this!" he commanded.

Mary obeyed unthinkingly. Then she smiled and made an attempt to wipe away her tears. William handed her a square of linen, which he carried in his sleeve. At that moment he began to laugh, overcome by a sudden surge of affection for Mary. Her nearness somehow gave him relief from the tensions he had been facing. Startled at first, Mary began to laugh too. Soon William, holding his sides, was sitting on the side of the bed. Members of the palace staff, unaccustomed to hilarity when William visited his wife's apartment, were astonished by the sounds they overheard.

Mary was the first to stop. Lying back against her pillows, exhausted, she closed her eyes, but opened them again when she felt William draw near. For an instant she was afraid he would make love to her. She wanted to push him away, but he surprised her by kissing her, very gently, on the forehead and cheeks. Then she surprised herself: she wanted William more than ever before, and shamelessly held out her arms to him. His impulsive gesture of kindness dissolved some of the barriers that separated them, and as he embraced her he recognized dimly that his need was as great as Mary's.

That night, for the first time in the eight years of their marriage, the Prince and Princess of Orange slept together until morning.

Even the most loyal monarchists in England were forced to admit by 1688 that James II was one of the most arrogant, inept, and misguided rulers who had ever sat on the throne. Openly declaring his desire to emulate his cousin, Louis of France, he proclaimed that the law is what the King wills, and set about proving it. Using dubious means, he secured the election of his sycophants to the House of Commons, offended the landed gentry by removing them from their hereditary offices and giving the positions to members of his small and increasingly powerful clique, and worst of all, made religion an issue in a nation that had learned a harsh lesson during the years of Cromwell's protectorate and yearned for universal tolerance. Refusing to realize that fear of France was at the root of English apprehension over growing Catholic power, James deliberately surrounded himself with Catholic advisers and, deaf to the rising murmurs of alarm, expelled the majority of the faculty of Magdalen College, Oxford, and gave their posts to Jesuits.

Pope Innocent sent a private message to London, warning the King that he was going too far, but Louis, increasingly convinced that he would soon be able to add the rich jewel of England to his growing collection of gems, endorsed every move that James made. Encouraged by the approval of the man he admired above all others and listening only to the counsel of the few extremists who believed as he did, James inflicted heavy taxes on the poor without the consent of Parliament, and when the courts refused to enforce his edicts, he summarily removed judges from office. The nation was edging closer to a revolution with each passing month, but James remained ignorant of the popular feeling, and when a few courageous men tried to tell him that the country was in peril, he haughtily quoted the famous statement of Louis XIV, "I am the State."

Across the Channel, William of Orange quietly watched the grim farce, biding his time. He gradually increased the strength of his army, built his navy more rapidly when he learned that James, piqued with his admirals, was cutting off their appropriations, and continued to cultivate the friendship of every ruler opposed to France. However, he rarely discussed James's folly with Mary, for he had discovered that she became disturbed whenever her father was mentioned, and William wanted no termination of the warmer, more relaxed relationship they had enjoyed since the night he had told her that James had murdered the Duke of Monmouth. Cautious in all of his dealings, William saw no reason to risk upsetting the truce that he and Mary had established.

William liked to tell himself that he was prepared for anything that might happen in England, but the totally unexpected upset his calculations. The States-General adjourned for the summer on the last day of June, 1688, and as both William and Mary were anxious to leave The Hague for Amsterdam early the following day, they ate a light, informal supper, attended only by Lord Bentinck and a few of the Princess' ladies, who chatted with her about the clothes and furniture they were to take with them from one palace to the other. The Prince, in a relaxed mood, paid little attention to their talk, discussing with his chancellor the legislation just passed by the States-General.

Bentinck, now considerably overweight, was the only person present who could eat heartily on such a warm night, but his appetite did not interfere with his political judgment, nor did it prevent him from covertly studying one of the newer ladies in waiting, an exceptionally pretty young noblewoman from Zeeland, with enormous eyes and a pouting, sensual mouth. According to Mary, the girl was seeking a husband, and William, aware of his old friend's interest in her, decided to tease Bentinck after the ladies left the table. The chancellor was still a bachelor, and insisted that he would remain one.

William was about to make a cryptic remark to Bentinck in an undertone when the major-domo came into the dining hall and hovered behind the Prince's chair. "Forgive the intrusion, Your Highness, but a visitor demands to see you."

Shaking his head, William took a sip of watered wine and looked with distaste at the platter of cold meats before him. "We have held our last audience in The Hague for the season. And we certainly do not grant interviews during a meal. Tell the fellow to see our chamberlain after we go to Amsterdam."

"I've already told him all that, Your Highness, but he claims his business with you is urgent." The man's tone was apologetic.

"Who is he?" William demanded.

"An English sailor, Your Highness."

Mary and her ladies were listening now, and William blinked in astonishment.

"He refused to give me his name, Your Highness, but his manner is not that of a common sailor, nor is his speech."

Bentinck sighed, wiped his mouth, and stood. "With your permission, William, I'll look into this matter. Don't let them take my plate away. I haven't finished my cold roast goose."

The interruption was odd, but William saw no cause for concern. He smiled politely at his wife, who sat at the opposite end of the table. "Are you taking your new set of chinaware to Amsterdam?"

"No, it would need special packing, and even then one or two pieces might break," she replied seriously.

He made himself a private wager that she would place an order for an identical set of dishes soon after they reached Amsterdam. Her one extravagance was collecting china, but he never protested, since the hobby was harmless and relatively inexpensive. Before he could comment, Bentinck reappeared. A glance at the chancellor's grave face brought William to his feet. "We'll return as soon as possible," he said hastily. "Please do not interrupt your meal."

Several servants and a pair of sentries stood in the corridor outside the dining hall, so Bentinck confined himself to a brief, cryptic remark. "I've taken him to your office."

They walked quickly and silently to the far side of the house, and when they entered the office, William saw a man in the rough wool breeches and short jacket of the English navy staring out of the window into the gardens. His hair was cut short, like that of any ordinary seaman, but he turned as he heard the door open, and his deep, accomplished bow was that of a nobleman familiar with court etiquette. William took a single step forward, stared at the visitor in the candlelight for a moment, then suddenly recognized Lord Edward Russell. He held out his hand.

"Welcome to the United Provinces, milord, and forgive me for being confused. According to the word I received a year or two ago, you were promoted to the rank of admiral-in-chief of the English navy, so I assume you're wearing a disguise and haven't been demoted."

His heavy-handed jocularity had no effect on Russell, who gazed at him solemnly. "If it hadn't been for my disguise and the cooperation of several patriotic gentlemen who risked their lives to help me, it would have been impossible for me to escape from England, Your Highness. The King has posted troops loyal to him at every port, and no one is being allowed to leave the country."

William sat down abruptly, waved his visitor to a chair, and saw that Bentinck, too excited to remember his manners, was perched on the edge of the desk. "You've had a falling out with the King?"

"Not I alone, sir. The whole country. The Queen has given birth to a son."

There was a silence, broken only by the sputtering of the candles. "Under your law," William said at last, speaking slowly, "only a Protestant may succeed to the throne of England. But in the past three years James has demonstrated to the whole world what he thinks of the law."

"Precisely." The admiral passed a hand wearily over his face.

"His record, I'm sorry to say, speaks for itself. We cannot trust him. And, Your Highness, it is not his Catholicism as such that we fear."

"I've been observing his tutor for a long time," William said quietly. "Louis has deprived the French people of all their rights under the guise of Catholicism, and James would like to do the same to the English."

"If he could." Russell paused while Bentinck, who had gone to a cupboard, blew dust from a mug, filled it with sack, and handed it to him. "That's why I'm here, sir." He glanced at the chancellor and hesitated.

"Milord Bentinck advises me in all matters," William assured him.

The admiral raised the mug to his lips, drank thirstily and leaned forward in his chair. "Then I'll come straight to the point. Your Highness, we want your help."

William's heart was pounding. He dared not look at Bentinck for fear he would reveal his feeling of triumph. It was possible that his goal, the formation of a solid alliance against France, was at last in sight, but the situation was complicated, and there was much he wanted to know. "You say 'we,' milord. To whom do you refer? And what is the nature of the help you want from me?"

A smile creased the admiral's tired face. "You're careful, Your Highness. I have a letter signed by six colleagues and myself that should answer most of your questions." He untied the thongs at the neck of his heavy shirt, reached inside, and drew out a pouch of oiled cloth, which he unfolded. "With your permission," he said belatedly, and removing a single sheet of somewhat crumpled parchment, handed it to the Prince.

William looked first at the signature, and his feeling of elation was mingled with that of relief. Russell was not the spokesman for a group of immature hotheads, so it seemed unlikely that the Duke of Monmouth's tragic fiasco would be repeated. The Earls of Devonshire and Shrewsbury were young but powerful nobles, Lord Danby had been a member of James's inner circle of advisers until his ouster a year ago, and Bishop Compton of London was, after the Archbishop of Canterbury, the most respected cleric in the Church of England.

The message itself was succinct. It asked William to come to England with as many troops as he wished to bring with him, and the signatories promised they would provide him with an army of trained men infinitely larger than the King's forces. The communication said the request was being made because the people of England were deeply concerned about their liberty, their religion, and their property. But, William was quick to note, the letter made no reference to the future, and the conspirators neither stated nor hinted whether they intended to depose James or allow him to remain on the throne provided he met their demands for safeguards.

Handing the letter to Bentinck, William stood and began to pace up and down the office, his hands clasped behind his back. The English admiral watched him anxiously, but said nothing, and it was Bentinck who broke the silence after he had studied the letter. "A very flattering invitation," he said in a noncommital tone.

William glanced at him over the top of Russell's head, and decided to leave the bargaining to his chancellor; he could not improve on Bentinck's approach. "Very," he agreed dryly.

Taking his time, the portly Dutch nobleman settled himself comfortably in a chair, folded his hands over his stomach, and looked politely at the haggard guest. "You must be tired and hungry after your journey, milord Admiral. Would you like something to eat?"

Russell curbed his impatience and managed to answer civilly, "Not at the moment, milord Chancellor."

Only an Englishman, William thought, could display such courtesy at a critical moment.

"I prefer," the admiral continued, "to discuss the matter that brought me here before I let myself relax." He addressed himself to Bentinck, as the Prince continued to move back and forth in the shadows on the far side of the room. "I'll grant you that the birth of James's son makes it necessary for my colleagues and me to act, but I'll admit to you that we've been searching for a valid reason for the past year. We do not believe in taking undue risks, and the venture we propose has an excellent chance to succeed in the next few months."

William found it difficult to keep out of the discussion, but Bentinck saved him the trouble. "You suggest an invasion," the chancellor said briskly. "That means the French will intervene."

"Forgive me for contradicting you, but they won't," Russell replied vehemently. "As you undoubtedly know, the bulk of the French fleet has been ordered to the Mediterranean."

That was true, William reflected. Charles of Spain, often reported on his deathbed, was ill again, and Louis, hoping to take advantage of the situation and win the throne of Castile and Aragon for his grandson, was sending virtually his entire naval force, the most powerful on earth, to hover off the Spanish coasts.

"As you maintain an excellent intelligence service," the Englishman continued, "I'm sure you also know that King Louis's dispute with the Pope has become very bitter, and every French division that can be spared from occupation duty is being mobilized on the borders of the Papal States. Therefore Louis has neither troops nor ships in the north to prevent you from crossing the Channel."

"I realize," Bentinck said thoughtfully, "that our navy would be useful to you. However, although I don't believe there are troops anywhere that are superior to Count Waldeck's, regiment for regiment, England can certainly raise a much bigger army than the United Provinces can muster. So, if you don't mind my asking, why have you extended this invitation to His Highness?"

William concealed a smile; Bentinck was handling the conversation magnificently. "The answers are obvious. He's the symbol of opposition to France, so our people regard him as a hero, naturally. What's more, he's the consort of Her Royal Highness, who must and will inherit the throne."

This could have been the moment for William to announce that he would never be satisfied with the role of a prince consort; however, since there was no need for him to express himself so early in the game, he remained silent.

Bentinck was in a position to press the guest more closely, and did so without hesitation. "His Highness would be taking an enormous risk."

Russell refused to be bullied. "I think not. And in any case, the prize would be worth it." He looked into the shadows, but could not see William's face. "Your Highness, it's no secret that you want England as an ally. Help us, and I guarantee you that we'll join you in any action you care to take against France."

It would be useless to inform the earnest admiral that the only way to insure England's cooperation would be for William to become King in his own right. Russell and the others who had signed the plea obviously had not yet gone that far in their thinking.

But Bentinck had no intention of losing the chance to clarify the issues at stake. "What are your plans for James? Are you going to execute him or send him into exile?" he demanded bluntly.

"His Majesty will decide his own future," the admiral said carefully. "If he's sensible, he'll agree to our terms." He finished his mug of sack and smiled. "There's a precedent, you know. King John acted wisely when the nobles gave him the choice of accepting the Magna Charta or being put to death."

William decided it was time for him to intervene, and stepped forward into the light. "I would be very reluctant," he said, "to be held responsible for the death of my father-in-law. The world has become sensitive to such unpleasantnesses, you know. If you'll look back a few years, you'll agree that James's troubles began when he executed his nephew, Monmouth. I would be severely criticized if I had to meet him in battle, and I have a strong suspicion I'd lose most of those troops you've offered me. If James should decide to make a stand, they'd rally to the King at the last minute."

Russell stood and wiped a film of perspiration from his brow. "We've considered that possibility, Your Highness, and you're right—as far as you've gone. James's subjects have no respect for him, but he represents established authority, and they'd join him if he put up a fight. What we're counting on, although this is plainly something I can't promise you, is that he'll flee when he realizes that virtually the whole country is opposed to him. Nearly everyone, including most of the Catholics who support him, hate him." He paused, then added contemptuously, "My colleagues and I have come to know His Majesty well, and I say—for the first time without regret—that in our unanimous opinion he is a coward."

Perhaps there was some truth to the charge, but William felt certain that the admiral, desperately seeking a leader who would make the revolt legitimate and respectable, was exaggerating. He could not blame the Englishman, of course; if their positions were reversed, he would do everything in his power to persuade the husband of the legally recognized heiress to the throne of England and Scotland to take at least nominal command of the forces that were going to challenge a tyrant. Bentinck cleared his throat and was about to speak, but William silenced him with a frown. Under most circumstances the opinion of the chancellor was valuable, but in the present situation the advice of an outsider, even a trusted associate, meant nothing. William was being called on to make the most important decision of his life, and only he could make it.

Lacing his fingers behind his back again, he started to pace once more, slowly and deliberately, as he weighed both sides of the question. If the scheme should succeed, he knew, his lifelong dream of containing France could be realized, and he was tempted by the thought that perhaps he could win the crown of England for himself, too. He had frequently told visitors that he had no desire to hold any post other than that of Prince of Orange, but he could not fool himself. The prospect of becoming King of England and persuading an intelligent, advanced nation to accept his concept of government fired his ambition. It was now possible for him to achieve far more than he had imagined when he had been the prisoner of Louis and John de Witt in his youth, and he considered it probable, if he could take James's place, that he could win a permanent place for himself in the annals of history.

However, ignominy and oblivion awaited him if he failed. The French would turn on him, James would send troops and ships to help Louis, and the United Provinces would be crushed. There was no way of guessing whether he would pay for his error with his life, but he could foresee a possibility that the admiral had not mentioned. If the conspiracy did not succeed, Mary would be disgraced for the rest of her life. It would be simple, should the plan be exposed, for James to brand her as a traitor, disinherit her, and name his infant son Prince of Wales. She would be known for the rest of her life as a woman who had plotted against her father, and if William should be killed in battle or executed, few countries would want to give her refuge. Examining the problem squarely, William had to admit to himself that Russell had not come to him solely because he had acquired a reputation as the foe of France. As Mary's husband, indebted to her for his present opportunity, he had to think of her future, too.

He struggled with the dilemma in silence, while the admiral and Bentinck watched him, and it finally occurred to him that he might be able to protect his wife if he kept her in ignorance of the whole scheme. Secrecy would be essential if he hoped to prepare his army and navy for an invasion before France could intervene, and he could think of no better way to shield Mary than to tell her nothing of the plan. He halted before the Englishman at last, his face set, and his voice was so soft that he sounded almost diffident. "I accept your invitation, milord Admiral, on one condition."

Russell rose to his feet and looked at his host anxiously.

"The Princess of Orange must know nothing of this discussion or of our preparations. I charge you to make it clear to your colleagues that she is not a participant in our venture."

The admiral thought for a moment before he replied. "Are you suggesting, sir, that Her Highness might not agree with us and might proclaim her loyalty to her father?"

That possibility had crossed William's mind, but he was unwilling to put Mary to the test. He knew she had no great love for her father, but had no idea what she really thought of her husband. If forced to express an opinion, he would have said that she was a sensible woman, and that consequently she was making the best of an arrangement that had been thrust upon her in her youth. Nevertheless it was a contract in which her own wishes had not been consulted, and he did not relish the prospect of asking her to choose between him and her father. This was not a moment for complete frankness, though; if he admitted that he felt insecure, he would be abandoning his stature as a ruler, his dignity as a husband, and his pride as a man.

"I take full responsibility for Her Highness," he said stiffly. "Do you accept my terms?"

"I do, sir. But surely it will not be easy to prevent the Princess from learning something about the preparations?"

"I trust my associates," William replied, and managed to smile at Bentinck, who would be responsible for keeping the secret from Mary.

The discussion continued for another quarter of an hour, and William promised to be ready to move as soon as he could assemble his forces. However, he refused to commit himself to a specific date until he conferred with his generals and admirals, and Russell had to be satisfied. A fishing boat was waiting at Rotterdam to take the Englishman back to Dover, and since he wanted to sail before dawn to avoid attracting attention, Bentinck agreed to send him word on the Dutch plans when they were formulated. It seemed advisable to work out a code so the conspirators could communicate freely, and William, bored by details of this sort, left the others in his office after first summoning a servant to bring the guest a platter of food.

Bidding the admiral good-by, he went back to the dining hall, only to find it empty. He made his way to the living quarters upstairs. The corridors were filled with a jumble of clothing boxes and packages, and aides, ladies in waiting, and serving maids were hurrying from one room to another, making last-minute preparations for the journey to Amsterdam. William resisted the temptation to go straight to his own suite and avoid seeing his wife until morning. There was really nothing to be gained by such a maneuver; they would be riding together in the morning, and as she would be sure to learn within the next day or two that her stepmother had given birth to a son, she might remember that his visitor tonight had come from England. If she pieced the bits together, she would think it strange that he had not brought her the news himself, so he told himself angrily not to be a coward. Waldeck and the admirals would need several weeks, at the very least, to prepare for the invasion, so he would have to practice countless deceptions in his relations with Mary. He might as well begin at once.

Forcing himself to head toward her apartment, he halted in the entrance when he saw half a dozen women energetically moving piles of clothing from one case to another, carrying hats and shoes and capes, and bickering loudly while they worked. Mary, completely engrossed, stood in the center of the room, directing the operation, but when she felt William's presence and glanced at his face, she came to him at once. He made an effort to sound jovial. "When I see this sort of confusion, I think it might be better if we stayed in one place."

"Oh, we aren't as inefficient as you seem to believe," she replied in the same bantering tone, but her eyes were serious.

"Where can we talk privately?"

"I can dismiss my ladies—"

"No, then we'll be delayed at least an extra hour in the morning."

"My dressing room?"

Nodding, he followed her as she threaded her way across the sitting room. When they reached the small chamber beyond it, a serving maid, who was placing toilet articles, jars of lotion, and bottles of scent in a satin-lined wicker basket, curtsied and backed out hastily. William closed the door, braced himself, and faced his wife. "I've just had word of an event that will be of interest to you," he said.

She had learned that his overly casual tone usually indicated concern, and felt herself grow tense.

"Her Britannic Majesty has given birth to a child. Your father's desire for a son has finally been realized." This was not the moment, William reminded himself, to resent the fact that he and Mary were still without an heir.

She studied the intricate pattern in the rug, which had been given to her by the envoy from the Ottoman Empire. "What have they named him?" she asked at last.

"I have not been told," William replied testily.

"You've heard from my father, I presume." It was unlikely that James had dispatched a letter, but Mary could not help hoping that on an occasion of this sort he had been sufficiently considerate to think of his elder daughter.

"I have not." William knew she was hurt and was sorry he sounded so brusque, but could think of no diplomatic way to cushion the blow.

Mary rallied quickly. "Then Anne and her husband have written to us," she said, a shade too brightly. Her sister had recently married Prince George of Denmark, and the couple had taken up residence in England after visiting the United Provinces on their honeymoon.

"There has been no letter from them as yet," William said carefully, "although I feel certain Anne will write to you about the event. Perhaps she's already done so, but there hasn't been time for the post to reach you. I don't believe the baby is more than twenty-four hours old."

"I see." Mary wished she could conquer the envy of her stepmother that threatened to overwhelm her. She had become convinced during the past three years that she and William could establish an ideal rapport if she could only produce a child, and her failure to fulfill her primary function as a woman constantly oppressed her. It was not enough that her husband had learned to relax in her presence and accept their marriage gracefully; if she had a baby, she felt certain, the last of his antagonism toward her would melt and he would give her the love she wanted so desperately. It was galling to realize that her dissolute father, who was incapable of caring about anyone except himself, and her indolent, self-centered stepmother had been granted the boon that would make such a difference in her own life. Depressed, she sat down heavily on the small bench before her dressing table and began to pluck aimlessly at a small lace handkerchief.

William hesitated for an instant, then patted her awkwardly on the shoulder. "Your rights to the succession will not be altered. I give you my word."

It had not crossed her mind that her political position might be threatened. She looked up at William, but remained silent, knowing from experience that he would become annoyed if she declared that the crown of England meant nothing to her.

"No matter how many children your father and his wife may have, you are going to become Queen of England," he continued firmly.

She nodded indifferently and, her mind wandering, thought to ask how he had learned of the birth. "Did the sailor who interrupted us at dinner bring you the news?"

The conversation was taking a dangerous turn. "Yes," he replied, deciding it was wiser not to elaborate.

He was so curt that Mary was afraid he had guessed the reason for her unhappiness. Accordingly, she forced herself to make conversation in order to hide her discomfort and embarrassment. "How strange to hear of an intimate family matter through an outsider, and an ordinary seaman at that."

Perhaps, William reflected, he had been too abrupt; she might become suspicious if he failed to offer some plausible explanation. "In this instance it isn't strange at all." He made a supreme effort to speak lightly. "I've known the man for many years."

Mary realized he was concealing something from her, and was shocked, but could not imagine what it could be or why he should feel it necessary to dissemble. "You've known a common sailor sufficiently well for him to—"

"I've already answered your question," he retorted, growing angry in spite of his attempt to control his temper. If she learned the seaman's real identity, he warned himself, it would not be long before she pieced together the plan to invade England. He forced himself to smile. "Besides, what's important is the message, not the messenger."

She knew beyond all doubt now that he was being evasive.

Her scrutiny made William uncomfortable. "As we're going to start early in the morning, I won't detain you longer." He bent down to kiss her. "Good night."

After he had gone, Mary remained in the dressing room, staring at the door. She could not recall an occasion when William had kissed her except as a prelude to love-making, and her uneasiness, combined with her jealousy of her father and stepmother, made her want to weep.

Chapter 7

ALL THROUGH the hot summer of 1688 the Dutch generals and admirals prepared for the invasion of England, and although they worked hard and conscientiously, the need for secrecy impeded them and made it impossible for them to sail while the weather remained warm. The French army was still maneuvering in Italy, Louis's powerful navy remained concentrated in the Mediterranean, and Paris was relying on its espionage service to observe developments in the north, so William and his subordinates had to proceed with great caution. Several French spies were captured and quietly executed, but as Count Waldeck said, there were undoubtedly twenty agents still at large for each one caught, and it would be catastrophic to take chances. Therefore only a very few high-ranking officers were entrusted with the secret, and the high command spent as much time creating ruses and diversions to fool the French as it did in preparing for the actual operation.

Veteran troops were stationed at half a dozen assembly points scattered along the seacoast, and the facilities of five ports were utilized to make the ships of the line, frigates, and smaller vessels of the navy ready for war. The duplication of effort in so many places was expensive, and the cost made William unhappy, but the precautions were essential to prevent French intervention, and he himself suggested that munitions and food supplies be gathered in arsenals and warehouses far removed from the military garrisons. Bentinck wrote in code to the impatient English conspirators that the fleet would sail in September, but a routine check of gunpowder supplies by an inspector who knew nothing of the scheme revealed that tons of the explosive were defective, and there was a maddening delay while Count Waldeck's agents scoured Sweden, Denmark, and the German states for replacements. At last they were secured, and word was sent to England that the Dutch were at last ready to move.

Louis of France inadvertently speeded the final phase of the invasion planning by sending an army into the German Palatinate, issuing a blistering manifesto attacking Pope Innocent, and making public a letter he had sent to the Holy Roman Emperor that was as insulting a communication as one sovereign had ever dispatched to another. Unfortunately, it was now mid-October, and heavy storms in the North Sea forced the Dutch warships to remain in port for two weeks. By the end of the month the weather cleared, however, and Waldeck ordered his troops to board ship. According to the schedule he had worked out, the vessels would sail separately and meet at a rendezvous at sea, where they would be joined by the Prince of Orange. A frigate had been prepared for his use and was waiting for him at Rotterdam.

William spent virtually the whole of his last day in the United

Provinces in his office in The Hague, where couriers brought him a stream of sealed reports telling him of the successful embarkation of one regiment after another. He had already written and carefully polished a statement to his subjects and another to the States-General, so he had little, really, to occupy him, and he spent hours sitting at his desk, staring gloomily into space while he tried to summon the courage to tell Mary the truth at last. Their relations had deteriorated in recent months, and he was aware that she knew he was hiding something from her, for she had hinted several times that she believed he had taken a new mistress.

She would be relieved, he reflected in ironic amusement, to learn he had been faithful to her, but he had no idea how she would react when she discovered that he was leading an armada to England. He could take satisfaction in the knowledge that he had succeeded in protecting her, and that even if the venture failed she could prove she had not been a party to the conspiracy. However, he could not deny to himself that he had treated her shabbily, and that one of his principal reasons for keeping her in the dark had been his fear that she would oppose the scheme. What troubled him now was what had disturbed him through the long weeks of preparation for the expedition: the knowledge that her status as the heiress to the throne of England gave the plot an aura of legitimacy that otherwise would have been lacking.

At dusk William knew he could procrastinate no longer, and his sense of shame became greater when he looked out at the darkening sky and told himself that he had fooled Mary so completely that even if she protested against the scheme, too many ships had already put to sea to halt the operation. Sighing, he pulled a bell rope. He frowned when an aide in breastplates and field boots answered his summons. "Send one of the servants to Her Highness. I'll be obliged if she'll join me here."

"Shall I go to her myself, sir?" the young officer inquired politely.

"No." William offered no explanation. After the officer had gone, he lit several candles and returned to his desk. Finding it impossible to sit quietly, he stood and began pacing. Mary surprised him by appearing almost immediately. When he saw her standing in the doorway, looking particularly attractive in a gown of subtle dark blue with a deep collar and cuffs of white lace, his throat turned dry.

She smiled uncertainly, but tried to appear poised. "I haven't been in this room in a long time. I had no idea you'd hung my portrait here." She glanced at a painting on the wall opposite the desk.

"It's been there for more than a year," he replied gruffly. Closing the door, he squared his shoulders as he turned to face her. "Thank you for coming here. I did not come to you simply because I am a coward."

Mary was too startled to reply.

"I thought I would feel safer and stronger talking to you in the place where I issue most of my orders, but I was mistaken." He forced himself to meet her questioning gaze. "I'm going away tonight on a rather long journey."

"So I gathered," she replied quietly.

It was William's turn to be astonished. "Oh?"

"I've seen your valet polishing your armor and your helmet, and I happened to be in the corridor when two huge leather clothing boxes were moved into your apartment. It didn't take much imagination to guess that you're going off to war."

"I see." He hesitated for an instant. "What else do you know of my activities?"

"Nothing." Mary could not conceal her bitterness.

"For the past four months I've told you a great many lies and half-truths. On two or three occasions you have almost openly accused me of taking a mistress."

She averted her face so she could blink away the tears that came to her eyes.

"However, when you hear what I have done, you may think I'm even more contemptible than if I'd been having an affair."

Mary was so relieved that she laughed aloud.

William's face remained grim. "I'm sure you remember the night I received word that your stepmother had given birth to a son. The man who brought me the news was not a common seaman. He was Admiral Lord Russell."

"Edward Russell?"

"He was wearing a disguise because the letter he brought me would have meant imprisonment in the Tower, had the King's men found it on his person." He walked to the desk, picked up a sheet of parchment, and handed it to her. "Read it for yourself."

Mary held the letter close to one of the tapers and studied it for a long time without comment, her face expressionless.

William waited for a reaction, and when there was none he had to use all of his will power to prevent himself from speaking first.

"So you're going to England," Mary said at last, in a flat tone.

"My fleet is even now transporting thirty thousand men across the Channel," he replied, a trifle defiantly. "All of them except my personal escort are already at sea. Devonshire and Shrewsbury will meet us with an army of one hundred thousand when we land."

She held out the letter to him, and he noted with amazement that her hand was steady.

"It was necessary," he continued, "to maintain absolute secrecy to prevent the French from attacking us before we could sail."

There was a hint of amusement in Mary's blue-green eyes. "Did you think I might send word to Louis of your plans?"

William flushed and raised his voice. "I agreed to lead this expedition on the condition that you knew nothing about it."

"Why?"

"I refuse to hide behind a woman's skirts."

For a moment her hopes had soared. Now she realized that

he had shielded her because of his pride in himself, not because he loved her.

"If we fail—and there are so many unknown factors that we may—no one can hold you responsible. I cannot guarantee that your position as heiress to the throne would have been as strong as it is now, but your father would find it extremely difficult to find legal grounds to disinherit you."

Mary searched his face, and wondered if she had jumped to a false conclusion. She felt faintly giddy, but reminded herself that this was not a moment to give in to sentiment. "Are you going to fight my father?"

This was the question William had dreaded. "I hope not. If James makes a sensible decision, no blood will be shed. The sole object of the expedition is to help the people of England. If the King permits a free Parliament to assemble and agrees to abide by the law, instead of putting himself above it, we'll sail home again. It's possible that I'll be back in The Hague within a week."

"You don't really believe that."

It was impossible to reply diplomatically to such a blunt statement.

"I don't believe it," Mary said, "and I know my father."

William had no idea whether she might insist on traveling to England herself and announcing that she supported James without qualification. He had refused to admit, even to himself, that such a possibility existed, but it did, nevertheless. After eleven years of marriage he still did not know his wife sufficiently well to be able to predict whether, in this hour of crisis, she would stand with him or with her father. He would be ruined if she chose James, but he refused to let himself dwell on the prospect. "I've prepared a declaration of intent that will be read in the States-General, and another for general public consumption. In both of them I've said substantially what I've told you." He did not realize that he was sounding more and more like a warrior. "If James behaves intelligently, there will be no battle."

"But you're prepared for battle, if he's arrogant."

William shrugged and took a deep breath. "My thirty thousand men are carrying enough arms, equipment, and ammunition for a long campaign."

They stared at each other. Finally, Mary nodded. "That's sensible."

The wild notion had crossed his mind that, if necessary, he could place her in protective custody until the invasion had taken place. Now he was ashamed of the thought. Yet at the same time he could not allow himself to believe that she realized she would be placing her whole future in jeopardy if she took any position other than a neutral one. "Be careful what you say, even to your ladies. If I'm defeated, I'm afraid your father will make every effort to prove that you've been a party to a conspiracy against him."

Mary felt as lonely as she had eleven years before, when she had stood at William's side in the chapel at Whitehall. "I'll always be sorry," she replied clearly, "that you did not take me into your confidence from the start. When you land, please convey a message from me to milords Russell, Shrewsbury, Devonshire and the others. Tell them that I intend to join my husband at the first opportunity, as soon as he deems it safe for me to travel to England."

"I'll tell them. Thank you." His voice was unexpectedly hoarse as he added, "I'm afraid we won't be able to celebrate our anniversary together." It would be indelicate to announce that he hoped he would be able to present her with the most valuable gift he had ever given her, the preservation of her inheritance. In any case it was difficult for him to think clearly; after so many weeks of uncertainty, he was dazed to discover that Mary seemed to be supporting him without reservation. Of course, he reflected, her attitude was not unselfish, for she obviously realized that drastic steps were necessary if her infant half-brother was to be prevented from usurping her rights.

"We won't be together for your birthday, either," she said, interrupting William's thoughts.

He had forgotten that he would be thirty-eight years old within a few days, but was not surprised that Mary had remembered. She had discovered that he had finally come to enjoy observing his birthdays, and although he had never admitted his feeling to her, she had given either a dinner or a reception for him every year. Looking at Mary, he told himself he was fortunate: Most royal marriages were completely unsuccessful, but he and Mary had achieved a pleasant, well-balanced relationship, even though they had no children.

She returned his smile, then sobered. "You'll be in no danger, will you?"

"Not if George Waldeck can help it," he assured her. "He always takes special precautions before a battle to make certain I'm not exposed unnecessarily to either infantry or artillery fire."

Long ago, before she had married William, Mary had heard how he had faced a French army alone. She had thought at the time that he had shown extraordinary courage, but then she had been a romantic child. Now, as a woman, she was aware of his tendency to give in to reckless impulses. "Please do not endanger yourself," she said earnestly.

Something in her expression stirred him, and he felt a strong desire to kiss her. He took a step forward, then halted abruptly as the thought crossed his mind that she might think he was offering her payment for her loyalty.

Mary knew only that he had moved closer to her, and rose to her feet, trembling slightly.

Her proximity aroused William even more, and he was startled by the realization that she could influence his emotions so strongly. Confused, he stared at her for a moment. "I've mentioned you in my declaration to the States-General," he said, trying unsuccessfully to rid himself of the feeling that he sounded inane. "I've charged them with the responsibility for your safety and welfare during my absence."

"Thank you, but what harm could come to me?" she asked, grateful but amused.

Her innocence irritated him. "Not all kings are ethical men, you know. If you were murdered or even abducted, my attempt to liberate England would collapse."

Mary's eyes widened. "Do you think Louis is so evil that he would make war on a woman?"

William shrugged, refraining from saying that he had been thinking of her father, not the King of France. In the past year hundreds of women in England had either been executed or sold into bondage and shipped off to plantations in the West Indies because of their inability to pay James's outrageous taxes. There were documents on William's desk proving beyond all doubt that his father-in-law pocketed the bulk of the profits from this illegal slave trade; he had been prepared to show Mary the papers had it been necessary to win her over to his cause, but there was no reason now to make her unhappy. It occurred to him for the first time that it must not be easy to be the daughter of James II.

"Nothing will happen to me," Mary said solemnly. "You're the one who will need to be careful." She took a deep breath and closed her eyes. "I shall pray to God to watch over you."

Unable to control himself any longer, he swept her into his arms. After he kissed her, without a word they started for her apartment. They were mounting the stairs when a clock chimed. William broke the silence. "I don't have to leave," he said huskily, "for another four hours."

On the first of November the Dutch ships met at sea as planned. Lords Bath and Dartmouth, English naval commanders who were believed to be loyal to James, were known to maintain a scouting force in the Channel and the North Sea, so it was likely that the invaders would be seen and an alarm sent to Whitehall. The Dutch high command had studied the dangers in this possibility, and an elaborate ruse had been prepared: The fleet, commanded by Count Waldeck, sailed northwest so that Dartmouth's scouts would assume that the landing would take place on the Yorkshire coast. But late that night signals were sent by lantern to all the ships' captains, and the fleet tacked and sailed south toward the Channel.

Heavy weather damaged some of the sloops, but not one vessel was lost, and at noon on the third of November the Dutch passed the Straits of Dover and made for Torbay, where Russell and Devonshire were assembling their forces. Capricious winds and a thick fog caused the pilot to miss his mark, however, and William, who had hoped to land on his birthday, was forced to spend the fourth of November impotently pacing the quarter-deck of his flagship. Finally, much to the relief of the admirals and the warship's captain, he retired to his cabin and spent the afternoon and evening reading. No one knew how much his exercise in self-discipline cost him, but when he came on deck the next morning, haggard after a sleepless night, his patience was rewarded.

The harbor at Torbay was directly ahead, and a pale November sun lighted the calm sea.

The landing itself was anticlimactic. Waldeck insisted on sending a party of marines ashore first, then disembarked three regiments of infantry before he considered it safe for the Prince of Orange to leave his ship. Russell and Devonshire were on hand, but when William raised his standard and went with the English nobles to inspect their troops, he was shocked to discover that they had mustered no more than a few hundred men. However, he could not turn back, and when Waldeck, always practical, pointed out to him that the gentry and common people of Torbay were greeting the invaders enthusiastically, William decided to maintain his original schedule.

Dutch seamen worked through the night and most of the following day to land cannon and supplies, and the army bivouacked in the open, outside Torbay. On the seventh William and his generals, preceded by a strong advance guard, rode at the head of a long column to Exeter, and even though Russell and Devonshire took pains to point out that the people who appeared at the roadside to watch the army march past were friendly, William was severely disappointed. When he reached

Exeter he set up his headquarters in a manor house owned by the Earl of Shrewsbury that had been made ready for him, and here, provided with many luxuries that his mounting anxiety would not permit him to enjoy, he waited for the English reinforcements that had been promised him.

His dilemma became greater as the days passed uneventfully, and at the end of his first week in England he and Waldeck sat down privately to decide whether they should return to the United Provinces. The outlook they faced was bleak: Their thirty thousand men, augmented by less than one thousand English irregulars, could not conquer a kingdom, and there was no sign of the reinforcements that Devonshire and Russell continued to insist would soon appear. Meanwhile, reports from London indicated that although there had been some riots in the city when the news of William's landing has been received, King James remained quietly at Whitehall, and there were rumors that the English army was refusing to break its oath of loyalty to the Crown.

After studying the situation, William and his lieutenant general finally concluded that they should neither advance nor retreat. Their prospects did not appear bright, but on the other hand, since James had not sent his forces to expel them from the country, they were in no immediate danger. The only course open to them, they realized, was to maintain a bold front as long as they could—it was humiliating and frustrating to have come to England to deliver the people from the oppression of an evil tyrant and to be received with seeming apathy by those whom they had come to save. William, realizing that even his loyal Dutch subjects would laugh at him if he was forced to return to the United Provinces without so much as issuing a manifesto demanding that James change his ways, became increasingly despondent.

That night Russell and Devonshire argued at dinner that surprise, not indifference, was responsible for the failure of the nation to join William. Many of the leaders whom they had visited during the summer had flatly refused to believe that the Prince of Orange would jeopardize his position in the United Provinces by leading an invasion force, but Russell swore that scores of influential men who had legitimate grievances against the King would soon appear in Exeter. William listened in polite, gloomy silence, and when the meal ended he retired to his bedchamber, a large room on the second floor of the Earl of Shrewsbury's house, and stood at the leaded windows for a long time, looking down at the Dutch sentries who stamped their feet to keep warm as they marched up and down. It was not an easy matter to conclude that perhaps he had miscalculated the temper of the English people; even more painful was the prospect that he might have to sail meekly back to Rotterdam and become a ridiculous figure in the eyes of the whole world.

Strangely, though he cared little what most people thought of him, he dreaded returning empty-handed to Mary. She had been so concerned, so filled with admiration when they had parted, that he was afraid he lacked the courage to face her with the news that his mission had been a dismal failure. It was odd, he reflected, that her good opinion should matter so much to him, but he was too tired and discouraged to try to understand why he felt as he did. He could not recall a time, even during his youth, when he had felt lonelier, but he had no desire to join his generals, who were chatting and drinking in the great hall of the manor. Instead, he went to bed. And that night, for the first time in years, he dreamed that he was nineteen or twenty again, and the prisoner of John de Witt and King Louis.

The next day began as uneventfully as those that had preceded it, and although it had long been William's custom to rise early, he remained in bed because there was nothing better to do. Finally, he sent his valet for a pitcher of hot water, but insisted on shaving himself. Then, still in his shabby dressing gown, he sat down to a breakfast of grilled fish and cold beef. He had no appetite, and sat staring at the food, wondering whether to send it away, when there was a loud knock at the door and Count Waldeck entered without waiting for an invitation. A single glance at his lieutenant general's face was enough to bring William to his feet.

"You'd better put on your uniform," Waldeck said unceremoniously. "You have visitors."

"Who are they?"

"Lord Colchester arrived an hour ago with a brigade of fifteen hundred horsemen. I've already accepted the services of his troops, but you'll want to see his lordship yourself."

"I certainly will." William removed his robe and laughed as he reached for his breeches. "Who is Colchester?"

"He was a close friend of the Duke of Monmouth, but no charges could be proved against him when Monmouth was executed."

William's sense of depression began to lift, and after slipping his shirt over his head, he hastily buckled on his armor. "I haven't believed a word that Russell and Devonshire have said to me, but it's barely possible that they've been right all along. Who is the other visitor?"

"Lord Abingdon."

William stared at his friend in astonishment. Abingdon, a Roman Catholic, was a member of the Privy Council and one of the King's closest advisors. "Has he come with word from James? Speak, George! Which is it—an offer or an ultimatum?"

"Neither," Waldeck replied quietly. "Milord Abingdon has come to join your cause and place himself at your disposal."

William's hands trembled so violently that he had difficulty in pulling on his boots. He regained his self-control quickly, and he was smiling confidently as he preceded Waldeck down the stairs to the great hall. For the first time since he had landed at Torbay, he thought, there was reason to hope the venture might succeed, and although he cautiously refused to allow himself to become optimistic, there was certainly cause to believe that the tide had turned.

By late afternoon there was no longer any doubt that England had at last awakened from her state of shock, for Lord Cornbury, eldest son and heir of the Earl of Clarendon, arrived in Exeter at the head of the three regiments he commanded, and when William came out of the manor house to greet him, the nobleman removed his right glove, threw it onto the ground at the Prince's feet, and then dropped to one knee in a dramatic gesture that made his position clear to everyone who witnessed the meeting.

The news that William was winning supporters spread rapidly, and during the next two days many influential men who had been waiting carefully on the sidelines found it convenient to slip out of London and ride to Exeter. A division of troops stationed at Nottingham made a forced march to William's headquarters, and embarrassed him by renouncing its allegiance to James. The Earl of Devonshire, who had been given the command of the growing body of English troops, received a report that there was an open insurrection in York, and that violent fighting was taking place between the rebels and regiments loyal to the King. There were stories, too, that riots had taken place in a number of other cities and towns, and that evening the high-ranking Dutch and English nobles gathered in the great hall of the manor house to celebrate.

William, however, retired alone to his room to give extended thought to his situation. It was far from favorable. The momentum of events was forcing England into fighting a civil war that might prove unnecessary. William decided that the time had come to send James the letter demanding justice that he had prepared before leaving The Hague. Dating it, he went down to the hall and read it to the group assembled there. It was short, and carefully worded, and William neither threatened his father-in-law nor showed him any lack of respect. The people of England, he said, had cause to fear that their ancient liberties, civil and religious, were in danger, and wanted firm assurances from the King that their rights would be respected. Acting as the spokesman for his wife, the future Queen, and for members of both the House of Lords and the Commons, William declared that he was willing to meet James anywhere, at any time, to obtain these guarantees.

The nobles accepted the letter without discussion, but several demanded the right to carry it to London, and William had to settle the dispute. Since the King had not yet made his position known, and might imprison any Englishman who brought him the communication, the messenger had better be Dutch, and an officer of sufficient rank to insure his personal safety. James, William said, would be reluctant to arrest a foreign general who had come to him under a flag of truce. The man who was obviously the best suited to carry out the mission was Nicholas Dykvelt, and he set out immediately, accompanied by an escort of forty cavalrymen. They carried their sabers but left their firearms in Exeter.

William hoped there would be peace, but during the next two days the generals continued to prepare for war, and troops from every part of England continued to swell his forces. Admiral Lord Russell estimated that there were at least eighty thousand of his compatriots in bivouac outside Exeter now, but it was impossible to obtain an accurate figure, for newcomers drifted into the camp throughout the whole of the next day; two more divisions marched down the road from London, their bands playing shrilly, and individual soldiers who had deserted from regiments still swearing allegiance to the King crept out of the woods, reported to the first officers they saw, and asked to be assigned to units.

The atmosphere at Shrewsbury's manor house became increasingly tense, and there was little conversation when William and his principal supporters sat down together for dinner two nights after Dykvelt's departure. However, as even the optimists considered it unlikely that the Dutch cavalry commander could return before noon the following day, the officers became more relaxed after jugs of wine and pitchers of bitter English beer had passed up and down the long tables several times. Gradually the talk became livelier, and several English peers tried to win William's favor by regaling him with stories of his wife's childhood. He admired their cleverness, as each of the speakers represented himself as having been one of Mary's closest friends, but the future was so uncertain that William could not afford to show partiality to any individual or faction. He smiled politely, declined the wine that was offered him, and maintained a dignified though uncomfortable reserve.

A short distance down the table Waldeck and Abingdon were engaged in a serious conversation, and William was interested in what the English peer was saying, but could hear only an occasional word. Leaning forward, he risked hurting the feelings of the young nobles who had bribed the steward for the privilege of sitting near him. "Milord," he called, "for our benefit, would you mind repeating what you've just said?"

"Certainly, Your Highness." Abingdon's dry, precise manner of speech reminded William of an elderly philosophy instructor whom he and Bentinck had disliked when they had been students. "I was telling milord Waldeck that the King's problem is to find an able commander. English soldiers think for themselves, and if they have confidence in a general, they'll follow him."

Small talk at the Prince's table died away, and William, who had spent endless hours speculating on this subject with Waldeck, exchanged a glance with his friend. "We have assumed that if James decides to fight, he'll give the command to Lord Bath."

Abingdon smiled wryly. "That would be his inclination, I'm sure. Unfortunately, although Bath is completely loyal to the Crown, he's a nincompoop, and the army knows it. Dartmouth is little better. He fancies himself as a soldier, though he's actually a sailor."

Admiral Lord Russell expressed his opinion of Dartmouth's seamanship with a derisive snort.

"That leaves Churchill," James's former aide continued.

"Our attention was caught when you mentioned his name,"

William admitted. Baron Churchill, the most competent of England's generals, had retired to his country estate in protest against the King's policies during the second year of James's reign, but Devonshire and Russell had assured William repeatedly that if a struggle developed he would remain neutral.

"Every regiment in the army would gladly follow Jack Churchill." Abingdon spoke as though he were addressing a class from a lecture platform. "Our people have confidence in him, and with good cause."

An ironic smile crossed Count Waldeck's face. "There's no need to tell us his qualifications, milord."

There was an embarrassed silence, as everyone present knew that, more than a decade ago, Churchill had led the English expeditionary force that had joined the French in their last campaign against the Dutch. His strategy and tactics had been so brilliant that he had disrupted Waldeck's plans repeatedly, although his corps had been only a small fraction of the size of his powerful French allies.

"We have been informed," William said, looking at Russell for confirmation, "that Lord Churchill dislikes many of the King's practices and no longer takes an active part in the affairs of the nation."

Russell nodded and was about speak, but Abingdon cut him off. "You may be right, Your Highness. For the sake of all of us, I hope so. But the Baron is a man who places his duty to his country above every other consideration, and I hesitate to predict what he might do if he believes that England is threatened."

"If he decides to oppose us," William said briskly, hoping he sounded more confident than he felt, "we shall have to beat him. No man is invincible, you know." He carefully refrained from adding that if Churchill joined the King, a long and bloody civil war would inevitably follow, and that it would be virtually impossible to prevent the French from intervening.

The Earl of Devonshire tactfully changed the subject by

telling an involved, amusing story of a hunting trip he had made into the highlands of Scotland, and by the time the roast was finished and a pudding was served, the company was in good spirits again. The junior staff officers and aides, sitting at the tables farthest removed from the Prince, had discovered that wine helped to minimize the language barrier, and no one minded when some of the Dutch and English failed to understand one another. Some illustrated their remarks with graphic gestures while others tried to make themselves understood by speaking more loudly, and their voices filled the hall.

Good food and amiable companionship made the higher-ranking nobles more convivial, too, and only William, who still felt the weight of the responsibilities he had assumed, remained aloof. Bored by the gossip of those around him, he paid little attention to the conversation, and therefore was the first to see Lord Nicholas Dykvelt stride into the room, his boots muddy, his long cloak travel-stained. William jumped to his feet, but Dykvelt reached his side before he could cross the room. Most of the officers had not realized that the message-bearer had returned, and continued to laugh and talk for a few moments, but one by one they fell silent.

Dykvelt's spurs clashed as he saluted. "Major general of cavalry at report, sir," he said, his voice hoarse with fatigue.

William dared not let himself show emotion. "You accomplished your mission, General?"

"I did, Your Highness."

They knew each other so well that William knew from the expression in his old comrade's eyes that the news was bad. "I delivered your letter to Whitehall, where it was taken from me by a man who did not identify himself." Dykvelt glanced at the English peers. "He had a long nose and bad teeth."

"That was Godolphin, James's chamberlain," Abingdon murmured.

"He left me waiting in an anteroom," Dykvelt continued, removing a gauntlet and wiping a smudge of caked dirt from his face. "My heels were already cool and I could have used a glass of brandy to warm me, but I was offered no refreshments of any kind. I stayed in that room so long that I began to wonder if I was a prisoner. Anyway, I knew what to expect. He took a deep breath and raised his voice angrily. "When the nobleman who took Your Highness' letter finally returned, he said the King refused to see me."

It was deathly quiet in the dining hall.

"His Majesty condescended to send me a verbal message. It was that he refused to grant audiences to brigands and cutpurses."

William made an effort to control his temper. If he gave in to his natural impulses and cursed his father-in-law, he would lose stature in the eyes of both his own subordinates and his English allies, so he forced himself to remain silent and unmoving.

"I was then dismissed," Dykvelt said. "However, as I was leaving the palace, either by chance or on the King's orders—and I suspect it was the latter—a gentleman who identified himself as Lord Halifax approached me."

"Halifax," Abingdon interrupted, "is closer to His Majesty than anyone these days. You may be sure he said nothing without the King's full knowledge and consent."

"He told me," Dykvelt declared, "that James is publishing a decree naming his baby son Prince of Wales."

William clenched his fists and the color drained from his face. Mary was being disinherited.

"He also told me that forces loyal to the Crown are being assembled to drive the Dutch from the country and hang all traitors. He said that the next time he saw me it would be on the battlefield."

William laughed, and was surprised that he could appear so nonchalant. "Is Halifax going to command James's army?"

Dykvelt looked at him solemnly. "No, sir. The post of lieutenant general has been accepted by Baron John Churchill."

Chapter 8

ESTIMATES on the size of the army being mustered in the King's cause varied, but the facts that emerged from the rumors and reports William received each day were not encouraging. Lord Churchill established his headquaters in the town of Salisbury and, precisely as Abingdon had predicted, regiments and brigades that had responded lethargically to James's orders now joined his lieutenant general. The opposing forces set up strong outposts, there were minor clashes when cavalry patrols met, and William, abandoning the hope that his wife's rights and those of the English people could be guaranteed by peaceful means, ordered his commanders to prepare with all possible haste for battle.

The Dutch troops, which held the most exposed positions in the open countryside facing Salisbury, were prepared to fight immediately, but many of the English units that had abandoned James had left their cannon behind them and needed ammunition, too, so Devonshire sent out parties to obtain munitions from arsenals that were not in Loyalist hands. Progress was maddeningly slow, thanks in large part to the Earl's lack of practical military experience, and Waldeck made strenuous but tactful efforts to speed the operation; however, the English nobles, who were jealous of their prerogatives, would have resented the appointment of the Dutch general as their commander, so Devonshire remained in charge and continued to direct his countrymen's efforts.

Each day a few more guns rolled into the encampment, and each day wagonloads of gunpowder and small arms arrived, but Waldeck insisted that the supplies were still insufficient for a major battle, and the basic situation remained unchanged for the next two weeks. The first day of December was bitterly cold and William, afraid that his English troops would desert him if they were forced to remain idle much longer, decided to visit each of the units and explain the reasons for the delay. Waldeck accompanied him, and two aides followed at a discreet distance, out of earshot, as the Prince and his general rode through the camp. The first two regiments that William visited listened to him politely but without enthusiasm, and as he and Waldeck started toward the next bivouac area, they shivered and drew their cloaks more closely around them.

"If I were in charge," Waldeck said bitterly, "we'd have all the cannon and powder we need within forty-eight hours. Devonshire doesn't know what he's doing."

"True, but I can't put you over him, George. I'm afraid that half the men who have come to us would disappear overnight. And what's more, I don't have the authority."

The Count twisted in his saddle so suddenly that his horse almost bolted. "Authority?" he demanded bitterly. "All you need to do is issue a proclamation saying that William and

Mary are King and Queen of England. That would give you all the authority you need!"

The idea had occurred to William, but he had been forced to reject it. "It wouldn't do, George. The English are trying to get rid of a tyrant." Any mention that hinted at his own secret ambitions to acquire the crown made him uncomfortable, so he changed the subject quickly. "Besides, it's to our advantage to force James to attack."

"Is it?" Waldeck asked with heavy irony. "If they strike us before we have enough artillery, they can cut us to ribbons."

"I was speaking politically."

"Well, I'm just a soldier, not a politician."

They realized they would soon be quarreling if they continued their conversation, so they said nothing more until they reached the crest of a hill on which two mounted sentries were stationed. The soldiers drew their sabers and saluted, and William, looking down at the tents at the base of the slope, called out to the nearer of the men. "What unit is this?"

"Colchester's cavalry brigade, sir."

William's spirits rose as he started down the hill; Colchester had arrived in Exeter when he had been on the verge of giving up and returning to the United Provinces, and the reckless peer held a special place in his affections.

Waldeck suddenly called out, "What's going on down there?"

They halted and stared in bewilderment at a strange scene taking place below. A party of approximately fifty horsemen wearing the uniforms of a number of English regiments had just ridden into the area from the opposite direction, and were surrounded by Colchester's troops, who milled around in seeming excitement, gesticulating. A babble of voices drifted up the hillside, but William was unable to make out what was being said, and Waldeck, puzzled and frowning, instinctively loosened his sword in its sheath.

"We'll wait here for a moment or two," he said, his sharp tone of command reminding William that he considered himself responsible for the Prince's safety.

A junior officer saw them and pointed up the hill, a soldier shouted something unintelligible, and then Lord Colchester began to walk up the slope, accompanied by a tall, heavy-set man with penetrating blue eyes, a round face, and a firm jaw. The stranger carried himself with the air of one accustomed to exercising authority, and William recognized him vaguely, but could not identify him. "Who is he?"

"I don't know, but he's wearing a general's epaulets," Waldeck muttered.

Colchester and his companion halted a few paces from the horses and raised their hands to the visors of their helmets. William returned the salute and studied the stranger covertly, trying to place him. Then Colchester, smiling broadly, said, "Your Highness, I have the privilege of presenting Baron Churchill. Milord, Count Waldeck."

"We met, so to speak, at Maastricht a number of years ago," Waldeck replied, recovering from his surprise.

William dismounted, removed his right glove, and held out his hand. James's lieutenant general grasped it, and Colchester, although obviously reluctant to leave, started slowly down the hill again. Waldeck, however, had every right to participate in the conversation, and leaping to the ground, hurried to his Prince's side.

"Welcome, milord General," William said stiffly. "Had we known of your visit, we would have sent an escort for you." He paused for an instant, then asked delicately, "We presume you have come at His Majesty's bidding to negotiate with us?"

"Sir," Churchill replied in the deep, resonant voice that would one day issue commands near a Bavarian village called Blenheim and win him immortality as the Duke of Marlborough, "I am here on my own initiative."

Waldeck was delighted, but William remained impassive. It was possible that Churchill had come to him conditionally, and he wanted to hear what James's commander had in mind before he allowed himself the luxury of feeling elated.

"I have spent the better part of the past two weeks trying to convince His Majesty that the letter you wrote him was reasonable and just. I've tried to persuade him to accept your suggestions and call the Parliament into session." Churchill sighed and shook his head. "He can be very difficult when he chooses. One day he promised to accept my advice, and the next he swore he would drive you into the Channel. I made it clear to him that under no circumstances would I fight against fellow Englishmen who believe as I do, or against the husband of our future Queen who has come to help us at great personal risk. Apparently he thought there was something to gain by temporizing, but I still don't know what it could be."

"Do we understand correctly that you have left James's service?" William asked quietly.

"I resigned my commission this morning, Your Highness."

William noted for the first time that Churchill's scabbard was empty.

"I became James Stuart's page when I was fifteen years old, Your Highness, and I've struggled with myself for a long time before taking this step. I spent more than a year in seclusion because I couldn't approve of what he's done, but I felt I owed it to him—and to England—to accept the command he offered me. I thought I could change his views, but I was mistaken." Churchill looked steadily at William. "Am I correct in assuming that you meant what you said in your letter, Your Highness?"

"You are correct, milord."

"Then, sir, I place myself at your disposal, and hope you can find employment for me. James, I'm sorry to say, is determined to fight a war."

"As it happens, milord, there is a position that no one has been able to fill." Relaxing at last, William smiled broadly. "Will you accept the post of lieutenant general of our English legions?"

Churchill's prompt, firm reply indicated that he had expected to be offered the appointment. "I am honored, Your Highness." He glanced obliquely at the Dutch lieutenant general standing beside the Prince. "I understand, of course, that I shall be operating under the command of milord Count."

Waldeck, who had always been jealous of his prerogatives and had long expounded the doctrine that no army could function successfully under more than one commander, surprised William by waving a bony hand in a self-deprecatory gesture. "That's unnecessary, Your Highness," he said, and turned to the Englishman. "You know as much about the business of making war as I do."

"I take that as a great compliment," Churchill replied warmly.

They seemed to understand each other, and Waldeck clapped him on the shoulder. "I suggest that we operate as equals, in consultation with each other. I'm sure we'll have no serious problems. And," he added politely, "if there are any minor differences between us that we cannot settle ourselves, we can always take our disputes to His Highness."

William wanted to laugh at them, but refrained; they were arranging a method of sharing command without even going through the formality of seeking his approval, but he had no cause for complaint. Not even the most celebrated of Louis's field marshals were better soldiers than these two giants, and the acquisition of Churchill's services was the greatest victory he had won since leaving the United Provinces. A gust of wind tore at his cloak and numbed his face. "Gentlemen," he said, "members of your profession are reputed to enjoy hardships, but do you suppose it might be possible to continue this discussion over a hot drink in front of a fire?"

The news of Churchill's defection created a sensation throughout England, and two regiments of infantry, a brigade of cavalry, and three companies of sappers followed him to Exeter, but there was no indication that King James intended to give up his plan to take the field against his rebellious subjects and their impudent Dutch allies. The Earl of Devonshire, delighted to be relieved of difficult responsibilities, happily turned over the command of his forces to the more experienced general, and within a few days ample cannon, gunpowder, and supplies had been acquired, firm discipline had been established, and every English officer and soldier in the camp outside Exeter knew what was expected of him.

Waldeck and Churchill began to urge William to take the initiative and strike first, and their pleas were echoed by the lesser generals. But the Prince, although anxious to settle the issue, was reluctant to lose the good reputation he had acquired in Europe, and knowing that the French would paint him as an unscrupulous scoundrel if he attacked his father-in-law without provocation, he hesitated. He missed Bentinck and Arnold von Keppel, and wished he had brought them with him from the United Provinces. Consulting with Lord Abingdon and the Earl of Shrewsbury, the latter possessing a talent for diplomacy in spite of his limited experience, William found both agreed that for the sake of world opinion James should be forced to make the first belligerent move, and although Waldeck and Churchill stormed and sulked, raged and pouted, William did nothing.

Time, he had concluded, was working in his favor now, and he could afford to wait. It was too late in the season for the French to send an army north from the Palatine or the borders of the Papal States and attack the United Provinces, and the longer James was paralyzed, unable to function as the head of a state, the more likely it was that he would capitulate, destroy the order granting the title of Prince of Wales to his infant son, and accept the demands of his subjects for justice. William had sent a few brief notes to Mary, but one afternoon, missing her far more than he was willing to admit to himself, he sat down in the drawing room of his suite in the manor house and wrote her a long letter. Even though he had rarely discussed his plans and thinking with her, he now felt compelled to explain the entire situation, and he filled so many sheets of paper that his fingers ached.

He was still writing when an aide interrupted him. Annoyed, William looked up with a frown.

"Beg your pardon, Your Highness, but your family has arrived."

William had been thinking so intently of Mary that he was

startled, and even though it was difficult to believe that she had come to England without his knowledge, a sense of excitement welled up in him. He nodded, and the aide backed out.

A moment later Princess Anne rushed into the room, followed by her husband. William embraced his sister-in-law, thinking it odd that Anne, who was considerably younger than Mary, should look so much older. And it was strange, too, that one sister should be so attractive and the other so homely, but after he had kissed Anne on the cheek, he was disturbed to discover that her eyes were remarkably similar to Mary's. Prince George of Denmark, tall and slender, was far more attractive than his wife, and looked dashing in the uniform of a cavalry general; he had never fought in a battle, studied military strategy and tactics, or even engaged in field exercises with troops, yet he managed to carry himself with an air that conveyed the impression he was a veteran soldier.

William conquered his initial feeling of disappointment, and as he began to realize the implications of this visit, he became expansive. "There's no one I'd rather see than you!" he declared.

Anne accepted the compliment with a smile, but when she saw the papers on the desk, it faded and she glanced at her brother-in-law uncertainly. "We've come at a bad hour, William. You're working."

"No, I'm just finishing a letter to Mary."

"Oh." Insatiably curious, Anne drifted toward the desk.

William reached it first, and shielded the letter with his body. "You must be hungry after your journey. Or thirsty."

Prince George sank indolently into the only cushioned chair in the room. "It so happens we're both. There are more pleasant experiences than traveling through the English countryside these days, I don't mind telling you." He sighed lugubriously.

William rang for a servant, and after ordering some cold beef, bread, and a bottle of wine for his royal relatives, turned back to Anne, who had moved to the hearth and was rubbing her plump hands together before it. "You came from London?"

"Yes," she replied. "We left yesterday, but it was so late by the time we drove away from Whitehall that we had to spend the night at an inn on the road." She shuddered, then pursed her small mouth angrily. "It was all Papa's fault, of course. He delayed us for hours. At first, when I told him we were coming here, I actually thought he was going to send us to the Tower. Imagine!"

It was difficult for William to understand why James had not imprisoned these two. Had he been in the King's place, he would certainly have arrested them.

"Our father-in-law, William," George said, his English marked by a flat Scandinavian drawl, "is not a reasonable man."

William agreed heartily, but silently; he and Mary had been irritated, when Anne and George had visited the United Provinces, to find that no couple could possibly take longer to say anything significant. They spoke as they apparently thought, vaguely and circuitously, and when interrupted, they had a distressing tendency to wander into irrelevant digressions. However, it was important to learn something of the King's activities. "I thought," William said tentatively, "that James was at Salisbury with his army."

"Nobody knows where he's going to be from one day to the next," Anne replied testily. She removed a huge emerald from the index finger of her right hand and rubbed her knuckle vigorously. "The way he races back and forth between Salisbury and London, I'm sure he hasn't the vaguest idea himself."

The servant arrived with the food, and for the next quarter of an hour William had to curb his impatience while his guests ate voraciously and said little.

When Anne was satisfied, she poured herself a second glass of wine, sat back in her chair, and relaxed. Suddenly she giggled. "You should have heard Papa yesterday!"

William waited for her to continue.

"Uncle Charles made a mistake when he reopened the theaters after the Restoration. Papa has seen too many of Shakespeare's plays."

It was impossible, William reflected dismally, to make sense out of what she was saying.

"George and I," James's younger daughter continued rapidly, "have wanted to join you ever since you landed. But we were afraid that if we left without my jewels, Papa would confiscate them and give them to his wife. He's kept them locked up ever since he heard you had arrived at Torbay."

"What we should have done," George interrupted, "was to have gone to you and Mary in Amsterdam last summer. Did we write you that after the birth of that insufferable infant, James cut off our allowance? We had been living at Kensington Palace, you know, but we had to close it because we didn't have the funds to pay for its upkeep, and we've been living on royal charity ever since."

"It's a wonder we have any pride left." Anne gave William no chance to speak. "But Papa isn't as shrewd as he likes to think." She smiled in malicious triumph. "Even his closest advisers don't know whether to stay with him or pledge their loyalty to you and Mary, so after he went off to Salisbury again the other day, I went to Lord Godolphin and made a frightful scene. The poor man was cowering."

"I feel very sorry for Godolphin," her husband said to no one in particular.

"Not I!" Anne was righteously indignant. "He's a vicious little weakling. But by the time I was through with him, he was meek enough. He brought me all of my jewels from Papa's strongbox, every last one of them, and he kept looking over his shoulder as though a whole regiment of Dutch cavalry was chasing him. He was trembling when I dismissed him, and he tried to make some sort of an apology, but I really didn't hear him. I was too busy counting the stones in my necklaces. I'm glad I always keep an inventory of my belongings."

"What," William asked weakly, "does all this have to do with your father seeing too many of Shakespeare's plays?"

Anne's glance indicated that she doubted whether her brother-in-law's reputation as one of Europe's leading statesmen was deserved. "When I told him that George and I were leaving," she said, "he decided he was King Lear. Well, he sounded like a madman, I must say, raving about the ingratitude of his daughters and cursing us for deserting him. What cause has he ever given us to be grateful to him, I'd like to know? He never did anything for either of us. Uncle Charles arranged Mary's marriage to you, and that's the best thing that ever happened to her."

The compliment was unexpected. William acknowledged it with a smile.

"And I decided myself that I wanted to marry George. I knew it the first evening we met, when he came to London on some sort of state visit."

Her husband was moved to protest mildly. "You seem to forget that I proposed to you, Anne."

"Of course, dear," she replied absently, still devoting her full attention to William. "If I hadn't refused again and again, Papa would have married me to a French prince. As I told him yesterday, he's never given me any cause to thank him. Just the opposite. When he made that spoiled, howling baby Prince of Wales, he didn't just disinherit Mary. I lost my chance to become Queen someday."

William stiffened, but made no reply.

Anne noted his reaction, and was quick to correct her slip. "Of course, if you and Mary have children, I'll move down in the line of succession. But that doesn't matter in the least. All I actually care about is seeing Mary on the throne. That will be wonderful."

She was taking far too much for granted, William thought, but he did not want to offend her. The news that James's younger daughter had joined the forces demanding justice could be put to good use. Yet he had to make his position clear, for she talked too much, and to anyone who would listen to her. "Your father," he said carefully, "is still King. I'm not a seer and I can't predict the future."

Anne's sense of insecurity always became evident when she was rebuked, and for a moment she looked flustered, but she recovered by changing the subject. "I hope," she said aggressively, "that George and I aren't inconveniencing you by coming here so unexpectedly. We saw officers coming in and out of nearly every house that we passed on our way through the town, so if you can't give us suitable quarters, please be frank with us."

The simplest solution, William knew, would be to order some of his staff officers to move in with others and give their rooms to the royal couple. But he shrank from the prospect of sharing his roof with Anne for an indefinite period, eating at least two meals a day with her, and being forced to listen to her unending stream of talk. Exeter was indeed crowded and his aides would have a difficult time arranging accommodations for a woman who was ever conscious of her exalted rank, but this would have to be done. "I'll see to it myself," he promised recklessly, "that you have a fine house of your own."

Events took a sudden, dramatic turn on the eleventh of December, when an excited messenger brought word to William's headquarters that James, with his wife and his son, accompanied by a small retinue, had left London secretly and in disguise. The party was making its way to a coastal port, and in one of his final statements to his subjects, the King had said he intended to take refuge with his cousin and good friend, Louis of France, because his life and that of the infant Prince of Wales were being threatened by a "foreign usurper." He ordered all regiments still loyal to him to disband, and as a last, irresponsible gesture, he granted pardons to many prisoners, the majority of them hardened criminals.

The time to take action had come at last, and William, who was able to congratulate himself because his policy of cautious waiting had resulted in a complete victory without the loss of a single man, ordered Waldeck and Churchill to break camp. Two hours later a long column began the march to the capital; William rode with the vanguard, composed of an honor battalion of Dykvelt's cavalry and another of Colchester's, and was flanked by his lieutenant generals. Anne was given the largest and most elegant carriage that the harried aides could find, and she spent the better part of the journey complaining bitterly to her husband that she had been given insufficient time to make herself ready.

The march started at a late hour, and William decided to call a halt at Windsor for the night, preferring to enter London in daylight. He arrived there the following morning, raised his flag above the turrets of the ancient castle that had been the principal residence of English sovereigns since the time of William the Conqueror, who had acquired it from the Church in exchange for Westminster Abbey. Anne and George, completely at home, retired immediately to the suite they had always occupied on their visits to the place, but William resisted the temptation to sleep in the apartment that traditionally had belonged to every monarch since Edward III.

He felt certain now that Mary would be asked by both Houses of Parliament to become Queen, but his own position was equivocal, and he told himself that he had to proceed with infinite care if he was to realize his own ambition. If he had to remain in the background as the Prince Consort, without holding power in his own right, it would be cumbersome and difficult to institute reforms and win the full support of an enthusiastic, united England in the war that Louis of France was sure to declare. However, he had confided in no one, and knowing that both the English and Dutch leaders were watching him closely, hoping to glean his intentions from small clues, he decided to keep his cohorts guessing, but to offend no one. He therefore chose to spend the night in the suite that had been built for the Black Prince and that Henry VIII had occupied when he had been Prince of Wales. The rooms were unusually small, but hickory fires blazed on the hearths, thick tapestries covered the stone walls, and William was comfortable.

He decided to eat alone in the small dining room of the apartment, and although the generals were disappointed, they understood his desire for privacy. While he waited for his meal to be prepared and served he dictated brief letters to Bentinck and von Keppel, requesting them to come to England immediately, then he wrote a letter to Mary in his own hand, asking her to prepare to join him. He said he would send his frigate for her, but refrained from mentioning that his own position would be stronger if she traveled in a Dutch rather than an English ship. For a few moments he stared at the heavy oak ceiling beams and smiled pensively; the English peers would not fail to take note of her ship, and would be reminded, subtly and distinctly, that she was, above all else, the wife of the Prince of Orange.

Windsor Castle's cooks, who knew nothing of the nuances of statecraft, instinctively believed they were preparing a meal for a new master. William was accustomed to plain fare, however, and found the chicken stuffed with olives, the beef simmered in wine, butter, and garlic, and the spiced mutton that had been oiled, baked, and sprinkled with chopped oysters and roast nasturtium seeds all too rich for him. He tried to show his appreciation of the cooks' labors, but the arrival of Lord Churchill gave him a perfect excuse to leave the meal unfinished, and he pushed the plates away in relief. The English general was more subtle and devious than most of the military men William had known, but he was still a soldier rather than a diplomat, and his forced smile, his casual air as he accepted the invitation to sit made it plain that something was bothering him. Like his Dutch colleagues, he wasted no time on frivolous amenities.

"We have been having trouble in London, Your Highness. There were riots when the people learned that King James had gone, and the city has been in a panic most of the day." Churchill tugged at his left ear lobe; he did this frequently when disturbed. "For a time the criminals released from Newgate Prison roamed the streets and robbed citizens at will. A few homes were looted, but some of the nobles still in London formed a provisional government of sorts, and fortunately the second regiment of House Guards did not disband. The troops were issued extra rations of ammunition, and they've been patrolling the city since sometime this afternoon. According to the reports that have come in, they had to send a company of troops across the Thames into Southwark and hang a few men who were caught with stolen goods."

"The city is quiet now?" William asked.

"Temporarily. Lord Feversham, the regimental colonel, is a disciplinarian, luckily, but one thousand men can't maintain order indefinitely in a community as large as London." The peer hesitated, shifted his position, and looked uncomfortable. "Count Waldeck and I were together when the messengers arrived, Your Highness, but both of us felt that since this is strictly an English problem, it would be appropriate for me to come to you alone."

William revised his opinion of the English commander's tact. Churchill could not have hinted more clearly that he felt it unwise to employ Dutch troops in keeping the city pacified. "How many men will you need to keep the peace, milord? Naturally," William added as a seeming afterthought, "you will use only your own units, since Waldeck's officers are unfamiliar with London."

A smile spread slowly across Churchill's face. He had been prepared to argue that the appearance of foreign troops might increase tensions in the city, but he had not known how to present his case diplomatically. It was difficult to relax in the presence of this austere Dutch Prince who was obviously lonely, yet kept even his highest-ranking subordinates at a distance. "One division of infantry will be sufficient, sir. And I'd like to give the general in command a troop of cavalry to use as messengers."

"Very well." William decided to be frank, too. "Send a general you can trust, and take no chances with a division that might become sentimental about James. It would be embarrassing if we had to fight our way into the city."

Churchill could hardly blame William for feeling apprehensive. No man could claim he had conquered England until he occupied London. "When I pledged my fealty to you, Your Highness, I did so without reservation. Let me state my position simply. I'm ambitious, and so is my wife. I'm aware of the significance of my shift in allegiance, and I'm confident that when Princess Mary becomes our Queen, she'll recognize the worth of my contribution to her cause."

William had made no specific commitments to anyone, and he would not begin now. If he offered to raise one man to higher rank in the peerage, every nobleman of consequence, every influential commoner in the country would besiege him with requests for favors, and in the scramble for honors and power he might not attain his own goal. "You're very sensible, milord," he replied quietly. "As you say, the Stuarts have excellent memories, and if James should ever return to the throne there's certainly no doubt that he would put your head on the block at the Tower." It could do no harm to remind a man who had a strong desire to better himself that he had voluntarily chosen the path he had followed, and that it was too late for him to turn back.

The shrewdness of the Prince's statement was plain to Churchill, but he took no offense. He had complete confidence in his own abilities. He was about to reply when an aide appeared in the entrance to the small dining room. "Your Highness, Lord Russell asks for an immediate audience."

"We shall see him in the living room." William pushed back his chair and glanced at his English lieutenant general.

Churchill shrugged indifferently; he neither knew nor cared about naval problems. "I'll send those troops off to London," he said, and started to leave the suite.

But he stopped short, as did William, when Lord Russell, Waldeck, and several other members of the high command came crowding in. William saw that Waldeck was the only member of the group who looked unhappy. The others appeared jubilant. Lord Russell stopped forward.

"Your Highness," he announced triumphantly, "I have the honor to inform you that a unit under my command has captured James Stuart, his wife, and his son."

William was too stunned to reply. Glancing about, he noted that Churchill seemed disconcerted and that Waldeck looked increasingly glum.

"Men of the squadron stationed on the Isle of Sheppey caught them as they were about to embark for France," Russell continued. "They're being held in a fortress on the coast, and I've given orders to have them brought to London as prisoners tomorrow."

For the first time in many years William completely lost his temper. He cursed fluently and at length, first in Dutch, then in English, and when he had exhausted his vocabulary of expletives in both tongues he switched to German. Russell and most of the others looked at him in blank bewilderment, unable to understand the reason for his rage. But Lord Churchill was biting his lower lip, and Waldeck came forward to put a restraining hand on the Prince's arm. His touch enabled William to regain a sense of balance.

The first person he addressed was Churchill. "You'd better send two divisions to the city, not one. London will explode like a bag of gunpowder that's been exposed to the sun too long when the people hear he's returning."

"Yes, sir." The lieutenant general quickly made his way out of the room.

"Count Waldeck!" William had difficulty catching his breath. "Dispatch the cavalry of both the Dutch and English armies to guard every road that leads to London. General Dykvelt will be in over-all command." The crisis was too grave to allow the two nationalities to retain their separate entities. "And tell General Dykvelt," William added grimly, "that if he allows James to enter the city, he'll be publicly stripped of his commission."

Russell, white-faced, was still confused. "Your Highness, what have I done wrong?"

William turned to him in a cold fury. "Perhaps you failed to realize," he said scathingly, "that James left no declaration of abdication among the many papers he distributed before he disappeared. What shall we do with him if you bring him back? Sit him on his throne again, while we spend the winter freezing in the countryside? Shall we remain idle for months while he procrastinates? Or shall we send him to the Tower, execute him, make a martyr of him, and plunge England into a new civil war?"

The admiral turned ashen as he finally realized the enormity of his error.

"James II is King of England until such time as he abandons the country, and the Parliament decides, by due process of law, that he has vacated the throne. If and when that should happen, the Commons and Lords will, in their wisdom, take up the question of the succession." William gazed at the solemn, stricken faces of the military leaders, and suddenly he recovered his sense of humor. "Milord Admiral, send a message to the King's jailers by the fastest post you can arrange."

"Yes, sir." Russell drew himself stiffly erect.

"Thank the men of the squadron on our behalf for their devotion to duty. Tell them we're proud of them." He paused significantly. "And inform them they'll win our undying gratitude if they not only permit His Majesty to escape, but see that he reaches his ship safely."

Even the abashed Russell joined in the general laughter.

The immediate problem was now solved, William reflected, but there remained one further point: He must not allow Lord Russell, one of the originators of the movement against James, to leave the suite feeling he had been belittled. There were too few competent admirals to risk losing him, and William was thinking in terms of the future. "While your gallant squadron is about it, Edward," he said familiarly, slapping Russell on the back, "you might instruct the men to put in a supply of milk for James's baby on the voyage. With our compliments."

Chapter 9

WILLIAM and the citizens of London succeeded in surprising one another thoroughly as they became acquainted. The Prince of Orange had grown accustomed to the curious stares and quiet gestures of friendship of people in the smaller towns, and was therefore unprepared for the vigor of the capital's reception. Thousands of Londoners lined the street to watch him enter the city at the head of his troops, faces peered from every window, and even the roof tops were crowded. William had always believed that the English, like his own subjects, were undemonstrative, consequently he was astonished when he heard men shout his name repeatedly, taking obvious pleasure in the noise they were making, and saw women weeping joyfully, without shame.

As for the Londoners, ever since the Restoration they had expected a show of ostentation from royalty, and it was difficult for them to believe that the stern-faced man in plain black was the sovereign of the United Provinces and the husband of Princess Mary.

His armor was made of steel rather than silver, there were no jewels in the hilt of his sword, and when he removed his right glove to wave to the people, they saw that he wore no rings. His helmet was an ordinary battle headgear, similar to that worn by every officer, and all that distinguished it from the helmets of the lowest ensigns and lieutenants was a small white plume. It was taken for granted that he would go to Whitehall, so the suite that James had vacated was made ready for him, and the nobles who had remained in London gathered there to await his arrival and assure him they secretly supported his cause from the first. But, in a move that surprised even his own staff, William decided to make his headquarters at St. James Palace, a comparatively small establishment in which various of the mistresses of Charles II had lived.

His choice of a residence surprised even the generals who were closest to him, and only a few shrewd observers guessed the truth —that he was proceeding with infinite care in order not to offend any political faction or give his enemies the opportunity to claim that he sought the crown for himself. His first act was to issue a proclamation assuring the people of England that their lives and property were safe and that their rights would be respected. He ordered the courts to observe the ancient common law, and sent word to the sheriff of every county that no man was to be arrested because of his religious beliefs. England had been expecting bloody reprisals against the Catholics, and men of moderation were relieved to know that the excesses of Cromwell's time would not be repeated.

William's principal concern was military rather than civil, for he felt certain that Louis of France would not meekly accept an Anglo-Dutch alliance. Accordingly, the regiments that James had disbanded were called back into service, and recruiting sergeants were sent into every part of the country, from the highlands of Scotland to the farthest reaches of Wales, to urge young men to join the colors. Messages from Ireland indicated that James's flight had caused great unrest there, and that troops stationed in Dublin were unable to prevent disorders in that city. However, Churchill and Waldeck advised the Prince to put his own house in order before sending a punitive expedition across the Irish Sea. William agreed that their conclusion was sound.

Bentinck arrived in London two days before Christmas, and with the aid of English nobles who had proved their loyalty to William's cause, quickly and energetically reorganized the bureaus and departments of the demoralized government, dismissing those men who were known to have accepted bribes during the reigns of Charles and James, and curbing the authority of petty officeholders who would have used their positions to obtain vengeance in private feuds. William and Bentinck spent the better part of Christmas Day conferring behind a closed door, and within the next forty-eight hours the results of their talk became apparent.

A call was sent out to members of both Houses of Parliament, urging the Commons and Lords to convene as soon as possible and take whatever steps the legislators deemed necessary and desirable. In the meantime Bentinck issued an order sharply reducing taxes on wool, bread, and agricultural produce; he also lowered tariffs, and in the general rejoicing most people failed to note that although they could import goods from the United Provinces, Spain, and the German states at lower costs, all trade with France was strictly prohibited.

Mary sent word to her husband that she was ready to sail for England, but William, after summoning Bentinck to another hasty meeting, decided that her appearance would have a greater impact if she delayed her arrival until the Parliament was in session. Afraid that a written communication might fall into the hands of the French, who would understand his ulterior motives and exploit them, William sent an aide to her with a verbal message, in the fastest sloop that Admiral Lord Russell could provide. He asked Mary to wait until arrangements could be made to receive her in style, but he had to curb his desire to instruct the aide to beg her to trust him. A man in his position could not afford to lower his dignity by sending such an entreaty through a subordinate, and he could only hope that Mary would be sufficiently perceptive to understand that he was consolidating his own position before the Commons and the Lords took charge of the nation's affairs.

He had been looking forward to seeing her in the immediate future, but knew his chances of realizing his own ambitions would be enhanced if she remained absent long enough for him to demonstrate to the people of England and their leaders that he should be made King in his own right. It was difficult to admit, even to himself, that he was selfishly depriving himself of Mary's company and that he missed her badly, but before the aide left, William impulsively handed him a rose from a vase standing on a table in the former sitting room of the voluptuous Duchess of Cleveland, which room he was using as an office. The flower was one of a large number that had been grown in a hothouse somewhere in Kent by a nobleman who hoped to curry favor by presenting them to him. Ordinarily William would have either thrown the roses out or given them to some member of his staff who admired flowers, but he had kept them because they reminded him of Mary. As he handed the largest blossom to the aide, he did not stop to think how his wife might react when she received it.

In general, people obeyed William's decrees without question, but when Shrewsbury reported that citizens were beginning to wonder why Princess Mary had not arrived, William promptly issued a statement saying that she would join him as soon as she could land without fear of being molested or killed by bands of fanatics who were faithful to her father. Luckily, a notorious highwayman captured near York at this time proved to be loyal to James, so he was brought to London and executed by hanging on Tyburn Hill. Thousands of people came to see the spectacle, and the majority of citizens accepted the continued absence of the Princess without the need for further explanation.

However, there were repercussions. A prolific writer of pamphlets and stories, whose name was sometimes written Defoe or De Foe, and sometimes Dafoe, published a scurrilous attack on the Prince of Orange in which he referred to him scathingly as "William the Conqueror." The Earl of Devonshire, incensed, issued a warrant for the author's arrest, but William heard of the incident and immediately countermanded the order. He then summoned all of the English nobles and prelates who were responsible for his presence in England, and told them blandly that the charges made by Defoe were all too true. The edicts he had issued certainly had no legal foundation, and were being enforced by armed men. Free Englishmen, precisely as the pamphleteer charged, were faced with the choice of obeying Dutch soldiers or being placed under arrest, and the English troops William commanded were being paid with funds collected by taxation, money which the Prince of Orange had no real right to use. It was unfortunate that Defoe's tone had been abusive, William said, but he himself did not consider his person sacred, and since the facts presented in the piece were indisputably accurate, there was no just reason for imprisoning the man who publicized them.

No one was more astonished by the lenient gesture than Defoe himself, but those who knew William and Bentinck were not surprised when another broadside appeared the following day. In it, the Prince was described as "William the Deliverer," and the anonymous author praised him at great length for unselfishly coming to the aid of the people of England and driving out a tyrant who had tried to deprive them of their liberties. Copies of this paper were carried to every part of the land by military courier, and were posted in all government buildings, inns, taverns, and other public meeting places. Devonshire complained nervously that William was making a mistake, that Daniel Defoe was a Dissenter, a trouble maker who thrived on argument, and that he would take advantage of his freedom by writing another embarrassing publication. However, he remained silent, for, as Bentinck confidently foretold, the treatment he had received was proof to the whole nation that the Prince was not a despot.

Members of the Parliament began to arrive in London on the

first day of January, 1689, and it seemed probable that both Houses would meet within a week. William, satisfied with the stability and progress of English affairs, turned to the routine problems of the United Provinces, and spent the afternoon reading diplomatic reports and studying the legislation passed by the States-General. Occasionally he sent for Bentinck or Arnold von Keppel to explain the intricacies of an unfamiliar bill. So much of this sort of work had accumulated during his absence from The Hague that he spent the whole dinner hour discussing Dutch affairs with his chancellor and foreign minister. Afterward he retired to the sitting room to continue his work alone. A frivolous, kidney-shaped desk of pale gray, decorated with an intricate design in gold—Charles had imported it from France—was piled high with papers, and William read them conscientiously, unaware of the passage of time.

He failed to hear the door open, or to note that someone had come into the room. Then he heard a familiar feminine voice. "I always imagined that the interior of St. James Palace must look like a brothel, and I was right." Mary, clad in a fur-lined cloak and hood, stood inside the door, looking with amusement at the red plush drapes, at the tapestried chairs with carved legs, the ornamental tables, and the fringes and tassels that decorated every piece of furniture. "I remember visiting the Louvre when I was a child, and I almost feel as though I was there right now."

William stood abruptly, knocking a sheaf of papers to the floor in his agitation. "Your presence here," he said, "is highly irregular."

Mary smiled at him mischievously, and he saw that she was carrying the rose he had sent her. It had withered, and most of its petals had fallen off, but he felt certain it was the same flower.

He crossed the room quickly, and as he took her in his arms he forgot, for the moment, that her premature arrival would upset all of his carefully laid plans. They kissed, and then Mary, a trifle breathless, opened her hood, sighed happily, and curled her arms around her husband's neck again.

It was difficult for William to think clearly when his face was buried in her hair. "You have no right to disobey me." He tried to sound stern, but knew she was conscious of his pleasure at seeing her.

Mary's face was pressed against his chest. As she murmured something unintelligible, William suspected that she was giggling.

"Obviously you received my message," he said. "You have the rose I sent you."

She leaned back in his arms and looked up at him. "That," she replied distinctly, "is why I came at once. My clothes were packed weeks ago. When your aide gave me this flower, I—well, I scarcely gave the captain of the sloop time to take on fresh provisions for the return voyage. I left in such a rush that I'm sure there are dozens of little things I've forgotten."

Unable to concentrate on anything when he breathed the fragrance of the light scent she wore, he released her. "You landed tonight?"

"The sloop cast anchor no more than half an hour ago in the Thames. The captain's gig brought me ashore, and I hired a commercial carriage." Again she laughed, delighted with her adventure. "I would have gone to Whitehall out of sheer habit, if I hadn't known you had taken over St. James." She glanced around the ornate room and shook her head. "This really is a dreadful place."

William's mind was functioning again. "Now that you're here, we'll have to move to Whitehall, and the sooner the better."

"Not tonight, I hope. I've already had all my clothing boxes brought here, and my ladies in waiting are unpacking them."

William glanced at an enameled clock on the mantel, and was surprised to discover that it was midnight. His enemies would invent all sorts of reasons to explain why Mary had arrived unheralded, so late at night, and every story would be detrimental. Even his friends and subordinates would speculate. William became increasingly nettled as he thought of these things. "We'll wait until morning," he said.

Mary looked up at him guilelessly. "I haven't been able to understand why you didn't take a suite there when you first occupied London. Anne and George have moved into their old apartment. You may recall I asked you about it in one of my letters. You ignored my question."

He spoke more sharply than he intended. "Anne is a Stuart and has the right to live at Whitehall if she chooses. I'm only the husband of a Stuart."

His anger revealed more than his words, and Mary's eyes widened, but she said nothing. During the long weeks she had spent alone in the United Provinces she had guessed what William wanted in England. However, she understood him too well to tell him that she knew he hoped to become King. She would have to wait patiently for him to reveal his desires to her, and if the Parliament failed to offer him the crown for some reason, she was prepared to remain silent for the rest of her life in order to save his pride.

"You think I've been reckless," she said, deliberately changing the subject, "but I haven't taken any chances. Two of my ladies came in the carriage with me, and the agreeable young aide borrowed a horse from an officer of a cavalry platoon that was on duty at the river front and rode beside me all the way here."

"Do you call that proper protection?" William was genuinely alarmed. "I'll have the aide court-martialed, and the commander of that cavalry detachment, too!"

"Please don't!" She was privately relieved that he had found an outlet for his annoyance. "It wasn't their fault. They wanted to give me an escort, but I refused."

"Why?" He knew he was shouting, but didn't care.

"You asked me to stay in the United Provinces until you sent for me," Mary replied meekly, "and I disobeyed you. I had no explanation from you, so I assumed that you either had reasons of state or were worried about my safety. So I thought I'd join you privately, without letting anyone know I had come."

William wondered whether to laugh or give her a shaking. "Are you naïve enough to imagine that every sailor on that sloop isn't now spreading the word of your arrival? Do you suppose for one instant that the members of that detachment of cavalry won't talk to their comrades as soon as they go back to their barracks? And do you think that the servants here aren't whispering? By dawn the whole city will know that Princess Mary, who will probably become Queen of England before the week ends, has reached her capital." He stared at her moodily, his mind racing. "We'll have to do what we can to make amends to the people. Baron Churchill can muster all of his troops in the morning, and they can accompany you on a triumphal procession through the streets. It will be expected."

She took a deep breath and hoped her voice would not tremble. "I didn't come here necessarily to become Queen of England." She tried to continue but faltered. She looked down at the rose, which she had placed on a table.

William stared at the dried petals, too, and made an attempt to summon enough courage to express his thanks. He hardly knew how to begin. No one had ever thought of him as a person; he had always been an abstraction—the Prince of Orange, a prisoner of those who held power or a ruler who was in a position to grant favors to others. Just now it was difficult for him to believe that Mary had joined him because she missed him. He gazed at her intently. Although she seemed to be telling the truth, he could not help wondering if a desire to sit on the throne in Westminster Abbey had not impelled her to cross the Channel prematurely.

His silence disturbed Mary. She had hoped he would reassure her, but when she stole a glance at him and saw the suspicion and uneasiness in his expression, her own lack of confidence increased. Her pride was injured, and she drew herself erect. "Perhaps," she said, thrusting aside the knowledge of his motives that she had gleaned, "you have some private reason for wanting me to be elsewhere."

Her tone made William bristle. "Be good enough to say what you mean."

"I think my meaning should be plain enough." She had not intended to reveal the fear that had gnawed at her ever since he had sailed to join the invasion fleet, but now she could not stop herself. "You've been known to be attracted to a certain type of Englishwoman in the past."

William stared at her incredulously. He realized she was intimating that he had resumed relations with Lady Pamela Burghley, and his first reaction was one of righteous anger. Then suddenly, inexplicably, he laughed. In all the weeks he had been in England he had not once thought of Pamela. It occurred to him that Mary had been suffering in silence, and he went to her. Removing her cloak, he placed his hands on her shoulders, vaguely aware that she was wearing a gown of soft yellow silk. Since such attire was inappropriate for a sea journey, he realized she had wanted to make a good impression on him and had probably changed her clothing before coming ashore.

"You've trusted me with your kingdom," he said, "so you need have no fear that I've abused your faith in lesser matters."

Mary was so startled that tears came to her eyes. Never before had he expressed his sentiments so clearly. Although he had not told her he loved her, she hoped this was what he meant. "Thank you," she replied, struggling for control.

"I want no thanks. I've done my duty, that's all."

"I've been prepared to do mine. If you had failed, I was ready to follow you into exile."

They looked at one another for a long moment, each sensing the candor and devotion of the other. There was no need for further words. William took his wife into his arms and pressed her close.

The following morning Londoners appeared on the streets early to see their Princess, but it was early afternoon before she emerged from St. James's Palace and rode with Lord Churchill's troops in a triumphal procession.

Members of the Parliament continued to arrive in the city all week, and almost without exception they visited Whitehall, where William and Mary had immediately moved and were now living in a suite. It soon became evident that the Commons, which had been rendered impotent and inarticulate since the Restoration, was determined to take the lead in fashioning the new government. William took care not to interfere, and devoted most of his time to Dutch affairs, but made himself available to Richard Hampden, who was elected Speaker, and to Gilbert Dolben, son of a late Archbishop of York, both of whom freely expressed their admiration for the help he had given England. He learned that Sir Robert Howard, one of the organizers of the new Whig party, was openly insisting that the crown should be offered jointly to the Prince and Princess of Orange, but that another group, calling themselves Tories, believed that only Mary should mount the throne.

Careful to avoid giving offense to those who might oppose him, William gently refused to grant a private interview to Sir Robert, and let it be known to Shrewsbury, Devonshire, and his other friends in the House of Lords that they would be doing him a service if they refrained from visiting him until matters were settled. Both Whigs and Tories agreed that the throne was vacant, but they quibbled for two weeks on whether James's flight constituted a legal abdication. Finally the Whigs demanded a vote, and were joined by enough moderate members of the other party to pass a resolution declaring that James had lost all rights, legal and personal.

The Parliament was now ready to get down to business, and its first act was to send a letter to William, thanking him for his great care in administering the affairs of the kingdom and asking him to continue to discharge his commission until such time as a permanent head of state was chosen. Bentinck and von Keppel helped him compose his reply, in which he said he was glad that he had pleased the legislators. Having disposed of the amenities, he pointed out in moderate but firm language that the safety of Europe depended on the stability of England, and urged the Parliament not to waste time filling the vacant throne.

He showed the document to Mary before he dispatched it. She praised it, but made no other comment, and William was content to let the subject drop. He and Mary had achieved a rapport that was new to both of them, but he was afraid that their relationship might become strained to the breaking point if the Parliament offered to make her Queen but withheld the prize from him. He was convinced that if the worst happened, she would be unable to refuse, and he made every effort to prepare himself for the blow. He told himself he would then sign a treaty with her and return to the United Provinces while she remained in England. This would be the most sensible action if the English rejected him, for the alliance against France had to be firm. Still, he wondered whether he was capable of paying such a high price. He realized that he depended on Mary, that her companionship meant more to him every day. Although he hated himself for feeling what he believed to be a weakness, he dreaded the thought of being separated from her.

A violent debate raged in the Commons and spread to the Lords, and it appeared as though William's worst fear would be realized. The legislators competed with each other in expressing their respect, gratitude and admiration for the Prince of Orange, but many members of both the Whig and Tory parties were clearly reluctant to offer the crown to a foreigner. William kept his own counsel, and Mary, apprehensive over the hurt he would suffer if the Parliament repudiated him, also said nothing.

The atmosphere at Whitehall became tense. Although the royal couple made it a practice to eat their meals privately in Mary's sitting room, the strain became almost unbearable when the debate dragged on into February. One day Mary decided to create a diversion by inviting her sister and brother-in-law to lunch. She was fond of Anne, and even though she knew that William might become irritated, she felt that the presence of such guests might distract him from the problem that was becoming more vexing each day.

The meal began badly. George of Denmark, greedily drinking his mushroom and claret soup, remarked cheerfully to William, "I felt certain I'd be calling you 'Your Majesty' by now, but apparently you and I must learn that we'll always be outsiders in this country. Strange, isn't it? You and I both come from small nations, but our people don't have the vanity of the English."

Mary interrupted hastily to compliment her sister on her gown, and began to discuss it in detail, but Anne ignored her.

"It's pride, George, not vanity," she said emphatically.

Mary, her heart sinking, glanced surreptitiously at her husband. His face blank, he sat toying absently with a spoon.

The young Dane carefully wiped his soup plate with a chunk of bread. "Pride?" he demanded scornfully. "Not all Englishmen are proud. Your father disgraced all of us by running away."

William tried to shut out the sound of their voices; their arrogant stupidity annoyed him.

"I wonder what's become of Papa," Anne said, sufficiently bemused to stop quarreling with her husband. "It seems as if the earth has swallowed him up."

"In a sense it has." William gave up all pretense of appetite and placed his spoon carefully on the table. "As we sit here, he's the guest of Louis at Versailles."

Mary signaled to a lackey, who began to clear away the soup dishes. The others were not yet finished, but she had planned an unusually large meal in the hope that one of the courses would appeal to William.

"At *where?*" Anne asked blankly.

"It's a small town outside Paris," William explained, trying to conceal his exasperation. "Louis has built a new palace there."

"Trust Papa to find a comfortable place to live," Anne said bitterly.

"Try the fish and cheese soufflé," Mary implored her husband. "It's a new recipe that Bertha Waldeck sent me from Amsterdam."

William waved away the servant who offered him a plate. "James will not remain at Versailles," he said grimly. "Louis will provide him with a headquarters of his own so he can create as much mischief as possible."

He was interrupted by a young Dutch cavalry officer, who saluted smartly as he entered the room. "A delegation from the English Parliament seeks an immediate audience with Their Highnesses of Orange," he declared.

William and Mary looked quickly at one another. Then they stood. Anne and George started to rise, too, but Mary spoke to them firmly. "We'll rejoin you as soon as we can. The chef has prepared some of your favorite dishes, and you will not want to miss them."

Anne, realizing she had been put in her place, subsided in her chair and began to sulk.

"Tell the gentlemen," William said, "that we shall meet them in the Privy Council chamber. Neither our sitting room nor this one is large enough for the purpose."

The moment for which William had been waiting so long had come at last, but he felt numb as he walked to the door, turned, and waited for Mary. She smiled at him and placed her hand on his arm, but neither spoke as they walked slowly down the long, cold corridors of Whitehall. Dutch troops stood on sentry duty outside their own quarters, for William had insisted on maintaining his identity as a foreign sovereign, but English soldiers guarded the rest of the palace, and two officers of Churchill's infantry were stationed outside the entrance to the Privy Council chamber. William stiffened as he returned their salute, and Mary, touching her hair and smoothing her lace collar, could not help wishing she was wearing a more elegant gown.

Thirty men were gathered in the chamber, talking in low voices, but conversation stopped abruptly as the Prince and Princess entered, and the delegation from the Parliament bowed. There was a brief, awkward silence, then William was surprised at the pleasantly calm sound of his own voice as he said, "Good day, gentlemen. We were told you sought an audience with us." He was acquainted with most members of the party, and a knot of uneasiness tightened inside him when he saw that his friends looked unusually solemn.

Lord Danby, who was a leader of the most conservative wing of the Tory party, took a single step forward; apparently he was the spokesman for the group, and conscious of the importance of the occasion, he cleared his throat and took a deep breath. "Madam, sir—we are grateful to you for receiving us."

There was no need for long, pompous speeches, and William shifted his weight restlessly from one foot to the other, but the pressure of Mary's hand on his arm soothed him. "The purpose of your visit is no secret, milord, either to us or to the whole civilized world," he said, "so be good enough to come to the point."

Danby's round face reddened, and he tugged at the gold tassel attached to the hilt of his dress sword. He was unaccustomed to plain speaking, and as this was a great hour in his life, one of the few occasions when he had ever been the center of attention, he was reluctant to obey. He had hoped to deliver a stirring address that would create a permanent niche for him in history, but it was exceptionally difficult for him to indulge in flowery rhetoric when the Dutch Prince was staring at him in cold disapproval. "Sir, madam," he stammered, "as you have no doubt been advised, the Parliament has been sitting in a joint session of both Houses since yesterday."

William nodded, and promised himself that he would never make Danby a member of the Privy Council. Apparently the man was incapable of expressing himself concisely.

"Madam, as you are the legitimate heiress to the throne that has recently become empty, it is the earnest wish of all England, Scotland, and Wales that you reign over our people as Queen."

Mary made no reply, but glanced at her husband, then raised her eyebrows as she turned to Danby, and her silence said much more than she could have put into words.

Lord Danby became increasingly flustered. "Your Highness," he said to William, "this nation can never repay its debt to you. Therefore we beg you to become the leader of our state."

"In what capacity, milord?" William spoke quietly, and only Mary, whose hand was still on his arm, knew that he was trembling.

"It is the hope of the Parliament, sir, that you will rule over us as Regent."

William gazed at the faces of the men who stood behind Danby, and when he saw his friends avert their eyes he knew he had to risk his entire future on a single, bold move. "We are unfamiliar with the title," he said icily.

Danby looked around for support, but no one else came forward, so he had to carry the burden unaided. "It was the thought of the Parliament, sir, that when Queen Mary sits on the throne, you would reign by her courtesy, so to speak."

Mary's fingers tightened on William's arm, and he smiled at her slowly, then patted her hand. Everyone was watching him closely, and he took his time replying. A veteran member of the Dutch States-General had once told him that a pause was the most potent weapon on earth, and he remembered the old politician's advice. When he started to speak his voice was so soft that the delegates at the rear of the chamber had to strain to hear him, and even the Tories who had opposed him the most vehemently had to admit that there was no rancor in his voice.

"No man," he said, "can esteem a woman more than I do the Princess." Again he paused, and those who had been crowding closer to him halted abruptly. "However, my nature is such that I cannot think of holding anything by apron strings, nor can I work effectively when my vision is blotted by someone else's shadow. You will observe, gentlemen," he added as a seeming afterthought, "that I have abandoned the royal form of address in speaking to you. I use the first person singular because I stand before you as your friend, nothing more. And I am compelled to be blunt and tell you that in my honest opinion it would be unreasonable for me to have any share in your government unless it be put in my own person, and for the term of my life."

Shrewsbury and Devonshire, he noted, were smiling, and Lord Edward Russell held a handkerchief to his face. Sir Robert Howard made no secret of his pleasure, and when he laughed aloud, Gilbert Dolben joined him.

Their reaction encouraged William. He was relying on the probability that his supporters, who had come to know him sufficiently well to realize that he would never consent to reign through a woman, had prepared another proposal to present to him when he rejected Danby's unflattering offer. He pretended not to hear their laughter, however. "I certainly have no intention of imposing my will on you, milord. If you do not want me to rule in my own name, I will not oppose you." He saw several of the Tories whispering to one another; they were obviously very much agitated, so he was taking the right approach. "Rather than meddle in your affairs, I'll go back to the United Provinces."

Lord Danby's thick fingers plucked nervously at a silver button on his doublet. England needed the Prince of Orange, and the country would certainly become embroiled in factional feuds that would develop into a civil war if he refused to guide the nation in this time of crisis. "Your Highness, I beg you to reconsider," he said hoarsely.

"Every man wants his own home," William replied. "You've been generous in extending your hospitality to me, but I'm growing weary of playing the role of a guest. So," he added, "are my troops. They'll be needed in the United Provinces, as Louis will undoubtedly want to pay me back for my audacity. Therefore I'll order them to embark at once."

A Tory member of the Commons stepped forward, his eyes desperate, but he was given no chance to speak.

"Naturally," William continued, "I'll release Lord Churchill's men from their oath of loyalty to me. I'd hate to see unpleasantness here, so I'll speak personally to the units that pledged their lives to me. I'm thinking in particular of Lord Colchester's cavalry."

Danby shuddered, and every man in the room shared his fear that as soon as William departed, the great lords would begin to maneuver for power, using armed men to help them gain their ends.

William had not allowed himself to look at his wife for fear his resolve would falter. He doubted that she realized he was gambling, that he was deliberately frightening the delegates in the hopes that they would change their minds and ask him to become King. She had known from childhood that someday she would become Queen, and the only time her future had been in jeopardy had been since the birth of her half-brother. Therefore, in William's opinion, she was a bystander in his duel with the delegates, and he was surprised when she suddenly began to speak.

"Milords and gentlemen," she said in a loud, clear voice, "like my husband, I prefer to address you in the first person singular."

Recovering from his initial astonishment, William saw that her eyes were bright and scornful.

"Many of you have known me since the time of the Restoration. I recognize some of you as members of the committee that visited me frequently at Hampton Court to make certain I was being raised as a Protestant. Therefore I feel free to talk to you as friends, not as my subjects." Her tone became sharper. "Do not think of me as a member of the house of Stuart or as someone you've asked to become your Queen. Remember, if you will, that I am a woman." She paused and looked up at William. "A married woman."

He had an inkling of what she intended to say, and his head started to throb.

"All of you have taken it for granted that the day would come when I would succeed my father. I am grateful for your loyalty to me, but my pleasure is somewhat tempered by the knowledge that if you do not offer the crown to me, it will eventually be placed on the head of the child my father has chosen to call the Prince of Wales."

Some of the men, unable to meet her angry gaze, looked down at the floor.

"Every one of you has assumed that I have no choice in this matter. You've believed that I'd bow to your will the moment you notified me that you wished me to become your Queen."

William reflected that he was as guilty as the others, and found it difficult to restrain an impulse to put an arm around her.

"What you haven't taken into consideration, milords and gentlemen," Mary declared, her voice rising, "is that I have never in my life sworn to accept the responsibility you want to thrust on me. I have taken a sacred vow, however, and you may recall the occasion. It was in the chapel of this very palace. I took an oath eleven years ago, and I intend to keep it until the day I die. I am the wife of William of Orange!"

There was a silence. William, overwhelmed, could no longer control himself. He put his left arm around her waist.

"Would you separate a wife from her husband?" Mary continued. "Would you have me break faith with the Dutch people? Perhaps, in your concern over your own affairs, you do not know that I already wear a crown, that of the Princess of Orange. Nothing will induce me to give up that position!"

Two or three men tried to interrupt, but Mary silenced them with an imperious gesture.

"If my husband returns to the United Provinces, I'll go with him! Good day, gentlemen."

William nodded stiffly, and together they started toward the door. There had been no opportunity for him to analyze the possible effects of her outburst, and at the moment he only knew that he felt curiously lighthearted. Eventually he would be forced to pay for her defiance and his own fierce pride, for the French would attack the United Provinces. Louis would muster his full strength in an attempt to crush a stubborn enemy who had caused so much trouble for him, and England, torn by conflicts, would be a useless ally. However, he and Mary would be together, William realized. His spirits soared. Although his gamble had failed, for the present it was enough to know that Mary thought more highly of him than of the kingdom that had been offered to her. No other husband on earth could claim such devotion, no other wife had sacrificed so much.

"Your Highness!" Richard Hampden, a short, swarthy man with bristling eyebrows, caught up with William and Mary in the corridor. "Forgive my impertinence, but I hope you won't plan to sail before tomorrow." There was an amused light in his eyes, and suddenly he grinned. "If I do say so, you've given the Tories the worst scare they've ever suffered, and if you'll be patient for just a few hours, I think I can promise that the Commons will pass a bill this afternoon offering the throne to you jointly, and that the Lords will ratify it before sundown." His smile faded, and removing his broad-brimmed black hat, he swept the floor with it as he bowed. "God save King William and Queen Mary," he said, and his voice was choked.

Chapter 10

LUXURY-LOVING COURTIERS who had enjoyed the dazzling state functions and spectacular entertainments provided by Charles and James were disappointed at the lack of pomp that marked the ceremony in which William and Mary formally became King and Queen in mid-February. The large audience chamber was crowded with officers in full uniform, civilians in fur-trimmed hats and cloaks, and ladies who were dressed in their finest satins and most glittering gems, yet Mary appeared before them in a simple gown of white silk, and William was attired in his usual black, relieved by a collar and cuffs of white lawn. Although several members of the Commons and the Lords had composed speeches praising the sovereigns, royal aides discreetly passed the word that as Mary's father was still alive and had been forced to abdicate under unusual circumstances, flattery would be inappropriate.

Lord Danby read a short resolution passed by the Parliament, requesting the Prince and Princess of Orange to become King and Queen, and when he had finished, William led his wife up to a dais on which two chairs draped with purple velvet had been placed. Mary sat in one, smiling graciously and calmly, but William preferred to stand. He thanked the nation for its confidence, and without further ado declared that he wished to issue a statement of principles. England, he said, had been torn by religious dissension for too many years, and from this time forward no man would be persecuted or denied the right to hold office because of his faith. Protestants, Catholics, and Jews would enjoy equal rights in the realm. Some of James's foes who had opposed him because he was a papist stared at each other in dismay, but William, his voice firm, announced that he and the Queen would exercise their royal prerogative of exiling anyone found guilty of religious intolerance.

He informed his quiet listeners, many of whom had been unprepared for such sobriety on this occasion, that censorship of the press and the theater was abhorrent to him, and that, as such control had been established by royal decrees, he was revoking them. He warned his audience, however, that England, together with the United Provinces, faced a difficult testing time; France would not watch idly while a great coalition of powers was being formed, and there was only one way to meet the threat. Smiling at Lord Churchill, who stood near the front of the hall, William said that the army would be placed on a regular footing immediately. From this time forward all troops would serve the Crown rather than the nobles who enlisted them, and all would be paid by the royal treasury. Churchill and the other professional soldiers were delighted, and William paused to give them a chance to digest what he had said before proceeding.

Asking members of the Parliament to pay particular attention to his views, he declared that it was his intention to utilize the system of government that had proved so successful in the United Provinces. He conceived of the elevation of the Queen and himself to the throne as a contractual arrangement rather than a God-given right, and both the Crown and the Parliament had obligations to the nation. He noted that there were two political parties of prominence and said that, having conferred with leaders of both, he was convinced that the affairs of state should be administered by one or the other, depending on which could muster the greater number of votes. However, he added, for the present he would ask both parties to help him.

Some of the Tories, who had been wondering whether to flee and join James in exile, were astonished to hear William appoint Lord Danby as president of the Privy Council, and the Whigs were amazed when he named Lord Halifax, a Catholic, as Lord Privy Seal. There were no other surprises, however, and the other positions were given to men who had supported the new King from the first.

The Earl of Shrewsbury was made Secretary of State, the post of president of the Treasury Board was given to Admiral Herbert, a friend of the Earl of Devonshire, who wanted no public office for himself, and Lords Churchill and Russell were confirmed in their ranks as commanders of the army and navy. William discreetly refrained from announcing that he had prepared his first honors list, and that he had made his two closest Dutch advisers, William Bentinck and Arnold von Keppel, English peers; they would be known as the Earl of Portland and the Earl of Albemarle, respectively, and regardless of the official ministries held by others, he planned to rely heavily on their counsel.

He closed his address by granting amnesty to all who had supported James, but he made it plain that anyone who committed treason in the future would be punished. Justice, he said, applied to all, and everyone in the audience chamber realized that a new era had begun when he stated solemnly that no one, not even the King or Queen, might stand above the law.

Members of the diplomatic corps came forward to extend their congratulations to the new sovereigns, and the guests were served mulled punch and sweet biscuits. But there was no banquet, no entertainment, no recitation of an ode by a poet laureate. William was too busy to bother with such frivolous refinements, and as soon as the last of the envoys had bowed before the dais, he called a meeting of members of the Privy Council, leaders of both political parties, and his new Earls, Portland and Albemarle. Such energetic efficiency had been unknown since the time of Cromwell, but the dumfounded courtiers quickly recovered and crowded around Mary.

However, she disappointed them, too. After listening absently to a few obvious compliments she showed distinct signs of restlessness, and before a quarter of an hour had passed she asked her sister and brother-in-law to act in her stead. She left the guests to finish their punch, and calling for the chamberlain, steward, and housekeeper, she made a systematic tour of the palace. She had always hated Whitehall, and had waited for years to get rid of the overly rich drapes and rugs, the ostentatiously vulgar furnishings. The palaces in Amsterdam and The Hague reflected her conviction that the homes of a nation's rulers should be dignified, and as she walked from room to room she startled the household staff by ordering virtually everything in sight removed.

Tables of solid oak and massive chairs would replace the delicately carved, expensively cushioned furniture; the canopies of sheer silk and fragile lace that adorned four-poster beds were to be removed, and sensible, substantial cloth of English make would be put up instead. The chamberlain and the steward made notes, and the housekeeper was near tears by the time the Queen was finished. As the woman had known Mary since childhood, she ventured to say what the men had been too timid to mention, that the redecoration of the place would cost a small fortune. There were insufficient funds available for the purpose, she complained, because the Queen had already cut the household budget to a fraction of what King Charles and King James had been accustomed to spend.

Mary surprised the trio by laughing mischievously and asking what they thought she intended to do with the items that were to be removed. The steward knew from experience that unwanted furniture was usually sent to one of the lesser palaces, and suggested that the royal homes at Greenwich and Kensington, which were in a state of disrepair, might be suitable storage places. Mary listened to him patiently, and he thought he had made an impression until Mary explained that she and King William hoped to use Greenwich as their principal country home and had no desire to fill it with gaudy reminders of her father and uncle. The staff members glanced at one another. It was easy for Mary to read their minds. It was evident they believed another imperious, capricious Stuart had mounted the throne, in spite of all the gossip in recent days to the effect that the new reign would be unique in English history.

Regretting the impulse that had led her to tease them, Mary quickly corrected their impressions. All of the contents of Whitehall that were being removed, she said, would be sold at auction, and although the proceeds might not be as great as the original investment, she was confident that the sale would enable her to refurnish the palace as she pleased and to show a handsome profit besides. The staff was stunned, as no member of the royal family had ever allowed personal property to be auctioned; the practice was usually considered a last, desperate move by nobles who were trying to avoid debtor's prison. The new Queen was setting a precedent that would cause all of London to whisper, but she seemed not to care, and her attitude was so sensible that the members of her staff looked at her with new respect.

In the weeks that followed, everyone at Whitehall came to know the ways of Queen Mary, and it was difficult for courtiers and servants alike to believe that she was the daughter of the dissolute James and the niece of the profligate Charles. She supervised the operations of the kitchens, ruthlessly dismissing chefs whose private arrangements with butchers and greengrocers were making them wealthy at the Crown's expense. She discovered that there were far too many lackeys and chambermaids on the staff; no one worked very hard. She changed that situation within a remarkably short time. The lazy, incompetent, and the arrogant were discharged summarily, but she quietly found new positions in the homes of peers for those who had ability but were not needed at Whitehall.

Three afternoons each week the Queen held receptions. The ladies who attended soon learned that they would be greeted coldly if their necklines were too low, if they applied cosmetics with a heavy hand, or if they were corseted too tightly. The gentlemen found Her Majesty unresponsive to boisterous humor, and after she turned her back on Lord Nottingham when he told a bawdy story, all her guests took great pains not to offend her again. Only a few courtiers complained, however, that history was repeating itself and that the whole country would soon become as joyless as it had been in the time of Cromwell. Most of the nobles, members of the Commons and their wives, and the merchants who were invited to Whitehall were pleased to find that Mary was charming and unaffected, that her modesty was genuine and her sense of humor lively.

As the days passed Mary made it her business to visit every part of London. Shocked by the squalor of the slum districts, she contributed a large parcel of land she owned to the people of the city, and gave the sum of ten thousand guineas, half of her annual allowance, for the building of a hospital to take care of young mothers and their children. She appeared unannounced at military and naval installations, and within three months even Daniel Defoe was moved to write a pamphlet describing her as the most popular sovereign since Elizabeth the Great.

King William, however, remained an enigma to most of his subjects, and only the members of the Privy Council, a few leaders of the Parliament, and his private advisers had any dealings with him. He was paying a great price for his ambition, rarely left Whitehall, never attended social functions, and spent sixteen to eighteen hours each day in the Council chamber or in the office that, for the sake of convenience, he had established in an adjoining room. The problems he faced were grave, and became increasingly complicated in spite of his strenuous efforts to solve them. England was suffering from years of misrule and overtaxation, so new laws had to be passed, and old, neglected ones enforced. The Commons, which had rarely been summoned by Charles or James, was making up for the years of humiliation it had been forced to endure, and was showing off its strength by behaving in an unruly manner. The members gloried in their new independence, the Whigs and Tories fought each other fiercely for the sheer pleasure of engaging in debate, and William's patience was strained to the breaking point as he alternately cajoled and threatened in an attempt to secure legislation that would enable the nation to become prosperous again.

William did not allow himself to forget his duties to his Dutch subjects, and when he finished his work as King of England each day, he became the Prince of Orange again and spent long hours reading reports from The Hague, dictating letters, and listening to the advice of Bentinck and von Keppel. William lost weight, could not rid himself of a head cold and cough that he attributed to the draftiness of Whitehall's corridors, and read so many documents that he began to wear spectacles when he sat at his desk.

His principal worry, the reaction of the French to his consolidation of power, was a matter of concern to both England and the United Provinces, of course, and he kept a sharp watch on the activities of Louis, employing scores of spies for the purpose. It was no great surprise when the French king gave James a palace of his own near the naval base at Brest. William and his generals and his admirals expected that the former monarch would presently be given an army and a navy by his mentor and sent on an expedition to regain his throne. Louis made no hostile moves against either the English or the Dutch in his own name, in part because he was having new troubles with rebellious subjects in some of the principalities he had conquered. As Bentinck pointed out, there was still another reason for his abstinence: He could pose as a man of peace, and use James as his tool. This theory was substantiated by the pamphlets, identical in content but printed in many languages, that appeared everywhere in Europe, describing James as an honorable leader who had been deceived by a treacherous son-in-law and faithless daughter.

There were signs that Louis intended to utilize Ireland as his puppet's base of operations, for disturbances continued to upset the peace in Dublin, and when Lord Churchill sent two fresh divisions there to enforce William's authority, the troops and their officers soon discovered it was dangerous to wander through the countryside at night, or, for that matter, to appear on the streets of the city alone or in small groups after dark. Shrewsbury, whose ministry was responsible for the administration of Irish affairs, personally questioned several agents who had been caught committing acts of sabotage, and although three of the men admitted that their wages had been paid in French gold, they carried no documents that would definitely establish that Louis was planning to make Ireland the first stepping stone in his cousin's return to the English throne.

The military men advised William to strike first, but he refused flatly. It he attacked, he said, he would be branded as the aggressor, and some of his German allies might refuse to join him; under such circumstances, he declared, he would be unable to count on the support or even sympathy of Spain. An even more pressing reason, which Bentinck and the English Treasury officials emphasized in every discussion, was that King William was not yet ready to move. He had not yet had time to put his own houses in order, and some months of grace would be needed before the new, equitable system of taxation would begin to bring in enough money to wage a major war. Some of the wealthier peers, whose taxes had been raised, praised the King loudly, but were curiously reluctant to pay the government what they owed.

The civilian contingent near the throne, headed by Bentinck, Shrewsbury, and Devonshire, had William's confidence, and a coolness developed between this faction and the military leaders, who had to be content with William's promise that they would be allowed to take the field as soon as he was sufficiently strong. In the meantime, as the result of an emphatically worded message he sent to the Parliament, fifty per cent of the total English budget, an unprecedented sum, was earmarked for arms and warships.

On April 11, William had to interrupt more pressing activities for his solemn coronation at Westminster Abbey. The oath that he and Mary took had been drawn up by members of the Commons, in consultation with the King, and it, more than anything else that had happened to date, indicated that England had reached a turning point in her history. The King and Queen swore they would rule by the statutes of the Parliament; the monarchy was hereditary, of course, but the Crown was no longer the sole lawgiver. Only a few of those gathered in the Abbey understood the significance of the oath, but William, relaxing in spite of the pomp, was satisfied.

When the royal party returned to Whitehall William announced a new honors list, in which he granted dukedoms to Shrewsbury and Devonshire, and then, leaving his wife to cope with the guests who crowded into the audience chamber, he returned to his office and the stacks of papers that had grown alarmingly in the hours he had been absent. Preoccupied, he forgot to change from his robes of state into more comfortable clothing, and it was almost midnight when, haggard and pale, he went to the Queen's apartment. Mary had arrived there only a short time previously, as the coronation guests had remained in the palace for hours, and she was chatting with several of her ladies in waiting before retiring. When William appeared she dismissed the women, and tried to hide her dismay when she saw that he looked exhausted. His shoulders sagged, and as he sat in one of the new chairs of heavy oak his appearance was that of a man approaching his fiftieth birthday rather than his fortieth.

"The celebration lasted very late," he said absently, rubbing a spot where his ermine collar chafed his neck.

"This was one time I could not leave." Mary tried to sound bright and cheerful. "Anne and George would have loved it, of course. Actually, I think they were rather disappointed because I stayed until the end."

William yawned, and when he raised his hand to his mouth, Mary saw there was an ink stain on his index finger. "I'm sorry you had to carry the burden alone," he told her, and removing his spectacles, closed his eyes for a moment.

"It was no burden, and the very least I could do," she replied quietly, and studied him intently. "Have you eaten anything tonight?"

He frowned in concentration as he tried to remember. "I believe an equerry brought me something at about six o'clock."

Mary saw no point in revealing that she had spoken to the officer afterward, and had been informed that His Majesty had scarcely tasted his food. "That was hours ago," she said briskly, "and the kitchen shelves are piled high with things from the reception."

William grimaced and shook his head. "The sauces are too rich."

"I'll order you something without sauces." She moved to a bell rope.

"I'm not hungry."

It had never occurred to Mary that at times he sounded like a small, petulant boy. She could even smile to herself as she recalled the period when she had felt more like his daughter than his wife because of the difference in their ages. But she put the past firmly in its place; her maternal instincts were aroused, and she intended to tolerate no nonsense. "I'm not going to let you starve yourself."

He glared at her, his dignity injured.

"I ordered some sausage from Rotterdam for you," Mary continued, giving him no chance to interrupt. "It came yesterday, and one of the Dutch chefs has been simmering it for hours in a pot of split-pea soup." She was rewarded by seeing a sudden spark of interest in his eyes.

"Well, as you've gone to so much bother, I suppose I could eat a small bowl," William conceded grudgingly.

The Queen sent her steward, who answered the summons, to the kitchens, and when he returned with a large tureen of soup and sliced sausage, she sat in companionable, discreet silence while William consumed the entire dish. Mary made no mention of the coarse black bread from Amsterdam that completed his meal; she had written specific instructions to the baker, telling him to wrap it in oiled cloth before sending it across the Channel, and apparently it was still fresh, for William ate every crumb of the loaf. Then, sighing happily, he leaned back in his chair and chuckled.

"You think you're very clever, I imagine," he said.

Mary raised an eyebrow and hoped she looked innocent.

"You think my mind is so filled with legislative bills and reports and financial figures that I don't realize how much planning and work was necessary to feed me this simple supper."

She shrugged and made an attempt to change the subject. "Lord Danby hinted very strongly tonight that he believes it's his due as president of the Privy Council to be made a marquis."

"In good time." William refused to be diverted. "How do I express my appreciation to you? I can't, any more than I can thank you for making me King of England." He had tried several times to tell her of his gratitude for her efforts on the day that she alone had been offered the throne, but embarrassment had overcome both of them on each occasion.

"I was a dutiful wife, nothing more. England would be lost without you, and the whole country knows it."

William thought she might be exaggerating, but had no desire to quibble and nodded complacently.

They were silent for a moment, then Mary spoke without

thinking. "I'm glad you came here tonight. I was afraid you'd work even later and go straight to your own suite." Suddenly realizing that he might interpret her remark as an invitation to love-making, she flushed.

William saw the color rise in her face and looked away. He had been so tired lately that the last few times they had been intimate he had disappointed her, and a sense of shame engulfed him. "This is a special occasion," he replied gruffly. "We aren't crowned every day."

His observation was as stupidly tactless as it was mundane, for it reminded both of them of Mary's coronation as Princess of Orange. Their memories of the aftermath of that event were refreshed, and the atmosphere became strained. Mary wanted to tell him she understood his problem, that she knew he was working under a great strain, and that she did not blame him for his recent failures as a lover, but the topic was so delicate she could not approach it openly. "We owe it to ourselves to celebrate," she said lightly. "Perhaps we can go to Greenwich soon for a holiday."

"I suggest that you go there and start putting the palace in order. I believe this is the right time of year to start planting your flower gardens, too."

She had been thinking of the Greenwich gardens, but there was something far more important on her mind. "And leave you here to neglect your health?" she demanded indignantly. "I'll do no such thing!"

William polished his spectacles with a square of linen before replying. "As it happens, I will not be here. The Parliament is going to adjourn in two weeks, and when it does, I intend to make a trip to the United Provinces."

"I shall come with you," Mary said promptly.

"It would be wiser if you stay in England for the present. I don't believe the French are going to attack us this year, but if both of us leave the country, your father might be irresistibly tempted to venture across the Channel."

She knew he was right. "I see," she said, attempting to hide her hurt.

William adjusted the arms of his spectacles behind his ears and pretended to be unaware of her reaction. "We've got to be sensible. And I can't neglect the Dutch."

Glancing at him covertly, Mary saw that he was anxious, and was assailed by guilt; he had so much on his mind, and she was adding to his burdens by letting him see that she was childishly piqued. "You're right, of course," she assured him, and forced herself to smile.

William's relief made it evident that he had expected opposition. "Bentinck and von Keppel are sailing tomorrow to co-ordinate preparations, so I should return in two months—three at the most."

She was shocked, and told herself that had she known he would be gone for so long she would have insisted on accompanying him. However, she realized it would be unfair to the Dutch people to ask him to shorten his stay in the United Provinces, and she controlled her voice carefully as she asked, "You'll live in the house at The Hague?"

"Yes, it will be more convenient, although I'd prefer to go to Amsterdam."

"I'll write to the housekeeper tomorrow."

A clock in an anteroom chimed once, and William raised his head. "I didn't know it was so late," he said, struggling to his feet. "I've called the leaders of both parties to a meeting at eight tomorrow morning—or, I should say, this morning. They've got to learn to resolve their differences." He stood lost in thought, brooding over the political quarrels that appeared to be inevitable when men were learning to govern themselves under a new system.

Mary hesitated, then took a deep breath. "Why don't you sleep here tonight?"

He forced himself to look at her. "I'm—very tired," he said bluntly.

"Yes, I know," Mary replied in the same tone, and not waiting for him to speak again, took his arm and led him toward her bedchamber.

She disrobed quickly, but William fumbled with the tassels and buttons and ties of his ceremonial garb, and it seemed a long time before he climbed wearily into the huge canopied bed where Mary was waiting for him.

Fatigue blurred his vision and his mind was numb, so he reacted instinctively, unthinkingly, when he saw that she was extending her arms to him. Neither spoke, and William moved to her; Mary embraced him, and he sighed as he closed his eyes. He was at peace, and in a few moments he was asleep, but Mary remained awake until dawn, his head on her breast.

The Queen spent the spring and summer at Greenwich, refurbishing the old palace there, working in her gardens, and holding informal receptions for the many peers who had followed her from London to the country. There was a brief flurry of excitement in July, when Princess Anne gave birth to a son, but the infant died the following day, which surprised no one, as she had lost three other babies previously. Unexpected complications in the administration of the affairs of state forced the King to remain in The Hague all summer, but he kept in close touch with developments in England, and after the death of his sister-in-law's newborn son, he wrote a memorandum to the Privy Council suggesting that the Parliament consider a bill settling the succession on the son of Princess Sophia of Hanover, who could claim descent from three royal English lines.

The proposal caused considerable comment in England, and virtually everyone in the country except Queen Mary expressed strong views on the subject. She said nothing, and after debating with herself whether to cancel her levees, finally decided that too many people would guess how she felt if she went into seclusion. Accordingly, she continued to appear in public each day, and no one guessed that she felt a deep sense of shame. William, by his memorandum, had tacitly admitted to the world that he believed her incapable of childbearing, and she knew that her failure to her husband and the nation was a burden she would carry as long as she lived.

Anne, whose own position as heiress to the throne was not being questioned, nevertheless took umbrage at the proposal, and announced to anyone who would listen that her brother-in-law had insulted her. Someday, she insisted, she would give birth to a future King, and although few people took her claims seriously, she was encouraged to take a positive stand by Prince George and the wife of Lord Churchill, with whom she had become friendly. She demanded her own palace, and Mary, secretly pleased to be rid of her, promptly granted the request. No sooner were Anne and George settled in their own home than she created a sensation by sending an insolent letter to the King demanding that her annual allowance be increased from thirty thousand to fifty thousand pounds. In order to obtain the widest possible hearing, she sent copies of her impudent communication to leaders of the Commons and the Lords, and for some days she became a focal point of gossip.

William, who was making a strenuous effort to force the Dutch and English East India Companies to cooperate rather than compete with each other, and who was working incessantly to increase the size of the navies of both countries in order to match the frantic shipbuilding activities of the French, was too harried to take care of the matter himself. He wrote to Mary, asking her to persuade her sister to stop acting like a lunatic, and the Queen immediately summoned Anne to Whitehall. As the whole controversy would not have arisen had Mary produced children, she was so dispirited that she used poor judgment: She tactlessly read aloud an excerpt from William's letter. In it he said forcefully that Anne was behaving stupidly, and that French agents, always quick to seize on any incident that would discredit the daughters of James II, were already making the most of the affair.

The sisters quarreled bitterly, and Anne left Greenwich in

a fury, declaring loudly that she herself had terminated the interview without waiting to be dismissed. Mary would have preferred to say nothing about the matter, but her sister's claim threatened the dignity of the throne, and having no alternative, she issued a brief formal statement to the effect that royal etiquette had been preserved throughout the unpleasant conversation and that the interview had been terminated by the Queen. Anne retaliated by taking her exorbitant demand direct to the members of the Commons' committee that drew up appropriations.

In general, people of every class sympathized with the King and Queen, and the argument would have been forgotten if Lady Churchill had not entered the dispute by openly siding with Princess Anne. Responsible men were worried, for Lord Churchill was immensely popular; he was unquestionably the most competent military leader in the country, and every sign indicated that at some time during the winter or early spring there would be a new war with France. William, who was still in The Hague, was kept informed of all developments, and it was he who solved the dilemma. He wrote a hurried letter of instructions to Mary, and the day she received it she announced a new honors list. The more perspicacious observers, glancing through the names of those who had been promoted, saw that Churchill had been made the Earl of Marlborough, and were relieved.

The distinguished warrior's wife, Sarah, now a Countess, was placed in an untenable position. If she continued to act as the champion and spokeswoman for her friend, Anne, she would be severely criticized by the whole nation, so she subsided into silence. And the new Earl, who had made strenuous efforts to avoid becoming embroiled in the dispute, buckled on his armor and went off to participate in troop maneuvers in Cornwall. It was unusual for an army to engage in mock battles so late in the season, but Churchill was making it clear that he was a professional soldier who did not wish to become involved in women's quarrels. The crisis lost its meaning, the military high command breathed more easily, and only Anne, who seemed to have inherited some of her father's less attractive qualities, kept the controversy alive by announcing unnecessarily that regardless of whether she received the increase in her income, she considered her estrangement from her sister and brother-in-law final.

She was not missed at Greenwich, however, for the Queen had more important matters on her mind. William, who had planned to return to England early in September, sent word that he would be delayed for another month, but would come straight to London during the first week in October, in time to confer with party leaders before the Parliament reconvened. Mary, who had been counting the days until she saw him again, concealed her disappointment, and decided to remain in the country. By mid-September she realized she had made a mistake.

The unpleasantness with Anne was a constant reminder of her inability to bear children. She could not rid herself of a sense of depression, and she sent for the royal physician. He examined her, then called in several colleagues, and after a long consultation they informed her that she was suffering from a malady that made it impossible for her to fulfill her ultimate function as a woman. Her blood was too thin, they said, and explained that her sister was a victim of the same disease; Anne's case was milder, which was why she could give birth to children, but her infants were too weak to survive. Mary paid the physicians liberally, ordered them to keep their findings secret so her father would not be able to use them to destroy her popularity, and for three days she remained alone in her apartment. She canceled her audiences, refused to see her ladies in waiting and allowed only one serving woman to wait on her.

The weather contributed to her gloom, too, and a cold, driving rain made life in the palace so uncomfortable that most members of the court, already bored by the austerity of their daily routines at Greenwich, wished they were in London. The

Thames, which could be seen from the upper floors of the palace, turned a sullen gray, and the trees in the royal hunting preserve of Henry VIII, which Mary had converted into a park, began to shed their leaves. The gardeners muttered to each other that this was an omen, as the forest usually remained green until mid-October, and several of the more influential peers prepared excuses that would enable them to escape back to the city.

Mary, however, gave them no opportunity to hand her their carefully worded petitions, for the sentries posted at the entrance to her suite admitted no one to her presence. She spent hours standing at the windows of her bedchamber, looking out at the dark sky and watching the rain fall onto her soaked gardens. She had long suspected, of course, that she could never found a dynasty, but she had always rationalized her fears and had continued to hope that someday she would become the mother of the future King of England and Prince of Orange. But the physicians had expressed their opinions so firmly that she knew she had to abandon her dreams, and her grief was so intense that it was a relief when a lethargic stupor robbed her of the ability to think clearly.

At night she dreamed wildly, and even though her windows were closed to keep out the raw air, she frequently awoke shivering. At last she forced herself to face her predicament without flinching: She was afraid that when William learned the truth, he would want no more to do with her and would take a mistress. For all she knew, it was possible that he was already sharing his bed with some other woman, and that personal pleasure rather than duty was keeping him in the United Provinces. His suggestion that the Parliament settle the line of succession on the royal family of Hanover was ominous, and she felt certain that even without hearing the reports of the doctors, he had given up hope that she would produce an heir.

She tried to be fair and had to admit that he had taken great care not to offend her by wishing aloud for a son, nor had he ever accused her of failure. But she had learned enough of human nature to realize that all men wanted immortality, and she could imagine William's disappointment when he learned, definitely and finally, that when he died, Anne would mount the throne of England, to be followed by a German princeling, and that a distant cousin who was almost a stranger to him would become stadholder of the United Provinces. Unable to weep, Mary thought miserably that it was unjust to deprive a man of his natural incentive; no monarch was more conscientious than William, and yet his wife was unable to give him children who could enjoy the rewards of his incessant labor.

Gradually, as the days passed, Mary found the strength to live with the inevitable. She began to understand that nothing had really changed, except that her own sense of loss had become a permanent part of her being. She shrank from the prospect of telling William what the physicians had said, and although she knew it was her duty to break the news to him, she was actually relieved that he continued to stay in the United Provinces. Perhaps, she reflected, she was taking refuge in cowardly silence by not writing to him, but she promised herself that she would find an appropriate occasion to discuss the situation with him, and her sense of dread and despair began to dissipate.

On the fourth day after the doctors had examined her, the sun appeared, the cold west winds died down, and Mary felt as though she was recovering from a long, severe illness. She caught a glimpse of herself in her dressing room mirror and was shocked by her appearance: her skin was pale, her eyes were dull, and her hair hung in lifeless strands down her back. Rousing herself, she tugged at the bell rope, and soon her serving maids were busier than they had been in many days. Ladies in waiting hurried in and out of the suite and the mistress of the royal wardrobe became increasingly flustered as the Queen, usually so easy to please, rejected one gown after another, insisting that she wanted to wear something livelier and more colorful.

For the first time since she had been a child Mary felt reckless, and giving in completely to her mood, she sent for the chamberlain and steward. She received the astonished officials in her dressing gown; one of her maids was applying lacquer to her fingernails, another was brushing her hair vigorously, and the wardrobe mistress, who was near tears, was standing in front of the Queen, holding up one dress after another, which she snatched from the arms of an assistant. Mary directed the chamberlain to inform all members of the court that she requested their presence at a reception that would begin late in the afternoon, and she ordered the steward to prepare a meal that would be served in the gardens adjoining the pavilion that Charles I had built. She wanted lanterns strung from tree branches, she said, and the music master, who had been enjoying something of a holiday at Greenwich, was to prepare a program that would continue into the evening.

The steward spent the busiest day of his career supervising the work of the chefs, conferring with the music master, and having the pavilion, which had been neglected all summer, freshly painted. The ladies and gentlemen of the court were surprised when they learned of the Queen's plans to hold a fete, and the more thoughtful were concerned. They had been worried for several days, as there had been rumors that Mary was ill; it was obvious now that these reports had been false, but she had lived so quietly all summer that the peers were startled by the hectic preparations for the festivities. One of the ladies in waiting who had attended Mary during the years she had lived in the United Provinces said that she could not remember an occasion when Mary had given a party during William's absence.

Shortly after noon the Earl of Marlborough arrived at the palace, accompanied by members of his staff, a large number of peers who were senior officers, and several younger men who also held commissions in the army. It was immediately assumed that the reception was being given in their honor, but Sarah Churchill, the Countess of Marlborough, who joined her husband an hour or two later, declared flatly that this could not be true, since the officers had come straight to the royal residence after their troop maneuvers in Cornwall had ended, and she told anyone who would listen to her that her husband had not sent advance word to Her Majesty that he was coming to Greenwich.

The lanterns were hung by mid-afternoon, perspiring lackeys set up long tables in the garden, and the painters who were gilding the pavilion finished their work by four o'clock. The orchestra of sixteen violins was supposed to play from the summerhouse, but as the paint was still wet, the musicians were forced to take up their places beside it. Pipes of wine and jugs of summer punch, consisting of three kinds of white wine laced with brandy, had been lowered into the waters of the Thames in nets to cool them, and the steward awaited the appearance of the Queen to send for the chilled containers. Shortly before five o'clock the nobles and their ladies began to gather on the lawn, and the military men, who were unprepared for a social event, were still wearing their uniforms, which had been hurriedly sponged.

The musicians began to play at the stroke of five, word was passed that the Queen had left her apartment, and the steward sent three men to bring several pipes of wine and as many jugs of punch as they could carry from the river. Mary entered the garden slowly, followed by her ladies, who were clustered behind her, and although the nobles tried to conceal their astonishment, they could not help gaping.

Mary wore her hair piled high on her head in an intricate arrangement, her combs glittered with gems, and she bore little resemblance to the sedate Queen the courtiers knew. Her lips were rouged, she wore delicate traces of salve on her eyelids, and for the first time in the memory of those who had known her all of her life, there was a black satin beauty patch on her right cheekbone. Her gown was not unusual according to the standards of those who had lived at the court of Charles II, but no one could remember when she had worn such a daring dress. Made of orange gauzelike silk that brought out the red highlights of her hair, it was cut low, revealing the cleavage between her breasts, and was tightly belted with a sash of yellow silk that emphasized her slender waist.

Although she gave no indication that she was conscious of the sensation she was creating, she secretly enjoyed the excitement. People were staring at her because she was an exceptionally attractive woman, not because she was their Queen, and she felt a measure of compensation for the frustration that had nagged at her since the physicians had examined her. Smiling animatedly, her eyes shining, she quickly established an air of informality by strolling around the garden rather than mounting the throne that had been placed near the pavilion for her. She made a point of extending a warm welcome to Churchill and the other officers, and then, her duty done, she announced that she wished to relax and hoped that everyone would have a pleasant time.

A few eyebrows were raised when she took a cup of punch instead of a glass of the milder wine, and several of the more conservative guests exchanged glances when she replied to the Duke of Shrewsbury's toast by draining her drink and calling for another. The lanterns were lighted shortly before sunset, and servants brought huge trays of food out to the tables, but Mary waved away the delicacies that were offered to her. The punch had made her giddy. She did not realize that her laugh was too loud or that she was looking at some of the men too boldly, when they, encouraged by her air of abandon, admired her openly.

Sarah Churchill remarked to a chosen few of her friends that she had always thought Mary's modesty was merely a pose. The Duchess of Devonshire, whose position at court was insecure in spite of her husband's influence, because she had reputedly been one of King Charles's mistresses, was even more pointed in her comments. Stuart blood, she said, could be disguised for a time, but the Queen's true nature was emerging at last. Members of the Privy Council wondered whether Mary was quarreling with King William, and several of the older peeresses, confused and upset, retired to their own quarters for the night as soon as they had eaten.

The army officers, who had been deprived of feminine company while they had been on maneuvers, made the most of their unexpected opportunity. The steward's messengers were kept busy bringing jugs of punch and pipes of wine to the garden from the river. The musicians entered into the spirit of the occasion by playing livelier tunes. As the evening progressed, couples strolled off into the gardens with a pretense of casualness that fooled no one. The reception was becoming increasingly reminiscent of daily court life during the reign of King Charles, and as the Queen was setting the example, cautious men like Churchill and Danby and Shrewsbury allowed themselves the luxury of drinking too much.

Mary seemed to be enjoying the party, but she could not rid herself of the feeling that her attitude of reckless gaiety was only a pose, and that if she gave in to her real feelings she would weep. She could not recall an occasion when she had drunk so much punch, and once or twice she wondered what William would have said of her conduct, had he been there to observe it. But as the evening progressed she forgot William—forgot everything except her pleasure. She chatted brightly with anyone who approached her, and even though she realized dimly that some of her more nonsensical statements would be repeated the following day, she did not care.

She had enough sense to know when to refuse still another cup of punch, however, and shook her head when Lord Colchester, his silver breastplates gleaming in the light of the lanterns, offered her one. "No more, thank you," she said, and smiled.

The cavalry officer held a cup in each hand, and looked first at one, then at the other in mock dismay. "What shall I do with these, ma'am?"

His tone was so solemn that Mary giggled. "Drink them yourself, milord."

"I obey Your Majesty's command," he replied promptly, and

the contents of the cups disappeared. The brandy gave him courage, and he looked her up and down slowly, speculatively. "Would you care to take a stroll, ma'am?"

Two or three other people had been talking to Mary, too, but they seemed to fade into the background, and she was aware only of Colchester's impudent stare. She realized she should put him in his place, but she could not help remembering that he had been the close friend of her cousin, the Duke of Monmouth, whom her father had murdered. He had been the first English military leader to join William's cause, too, and although she could not think clearly, she decided that a rebuke would be shabby repayment for his loyalty.

"I've been told," he persisted when she said nothing, "that you've made the gardens here into something that isn't to be seen anywhere else in the country. I'd be very proud if you'd consent to show me your handiwork."

No man except William had ever looked at her with such frank desire in his eyes, and Mary, anxious to blot everything but the immediate present from her consciousness, felt her heart beating more rapidly. "Your interest in flowers and landscaping is flattering, milord," she said, and even though she knew she was making a mistake, she started forward at his side. Surprised to discover that she was a trifle unsteady on her feet, she put her hand on his arm as they moved slowly out of the pool of lantern light.

The thought crossed Mary's mind that she had never touched such a strong, muscular arm, and she wondered if she were becoming wicked and depraved.

Colchester was watching her closely. "You're very silent, ma'am."

Mary could not prevent the color from rising in her face.

"May I know what you're thinking?"

"You may not, milord!" She spoiled the effect of her retort by stumbling over a tree branch that had fallen during the rainstorm, and Colchester immediately put his arm around her waist. She halted to regain her balance, and finally he withdrew his hand, slowly and reluctantly.

"Are you being discreet because you're a Queen, or are you simply exercising your right as a woman?"

She thought she detected an undertone of raillery in his voice, but replied seriously. "Even a Queen is a woman, milord."

Colchester chuckled, then murmured under his breath, "So I'm beginning to discover."

It was a moment or two before Mary understood the full meaning of his remark, and when she did, she became uneasy. She made an effort to concentrate, saw that they walked past the far end of the pavilion, and her misgivings increased. But instinct warned her that she would become more vulnerable if she showed fear. Halting, she gazed innocently at the summer-house. "I wonder," she said, "if the paint is dry." Too late it occurred to her that she had made still another error by speaking in the first person singular instead of using the royal plural.

Under the circumstances it was inevitable that the burly officer should interpret her informality as an invitation. He hurried to the pavilion, touched the wooden latticework, and returned to her, smiling slyly. "Your painters deserve a commendation, ma'am. It's dry—and empty." He held out his hand to her.

Mary hesitated, wondering how to retreat gracefully. She knew that her own carelessness was responsible for placing her in a compromising and embarrassing position, and her anger was as great as her alarm. Danger was sharpening her wits, and she no longer felt the brandy punch she had drunk.

Colchester was completely ignorant of her reaction, and having been given reason to believe she would permit him to take liberties, he interpreted her silence as coyness. Seizing her hand, he led her toward the pavilion. "I'll go first," he said, laughing, "and I'll prove to you that it's safe in here. It won't be the first time I've acted as an advance guard."

The reminder of his military service made Mary's position

more difficult. Just as she was not an ordinary woman who could commit an act of adultery lightly, so Lord Colchester, who now held the rank of major general and commanded all of England's cavalry, was not some nondescript, importuning lover who could be dismissed casually and forgotten. If she hurt his feelings or offended his dignity, it was possible that he would join her father, and that someday he might use his professional talents to kill men fighting under her banner.

The odor of fresh paint was strong in the dark pavilion, but Colchester was unaware of anything except the presence of the lovely young woman whose hand he still gripped. "No one can see us here," he said, speaking close to her ear to make himself heard above the violin players outside, "and no one would even think of looking for us!"

Before the terrified Mary knew what to say, he took her in his arms and kissed her savagely. Completely sober now, she struggled to free herself. Believing she was putting up a token resistance in order to appear more flirtatious, he held her tightly, his ardor mounting.

His strength was so great that he was able to hold her with one hand while, still kissing her, he began to caress her with the other, and she realized that no matter how hard she fought, she would not be able to break away from him. She could scream, of course, and the sound would carry to the guests in the garden above the music of the violins; she considered the possibility for an instant, but rejected it almost immediately.

If she cried out for help, Colchester would lose stature in the eyes of the whole court, and the disgrace would virtually force him to leave the country and offer his sword to James. Equally important, her own conduct would be open to question. People would wonder, and with good cause, how and why she had allowed herself to go off alone with a man other than her husband. The court would gossip interminably about the incident, Anne would relish the opportunity to tell the world that her sister pretended to be virtuous but was actually the most depraved woman in England, and it was impossible to predict how William would react when he heard the story, as he inevitably would.

It would be far better, Mary decided, to submit in silence, to hope the seduction would be mercifully brief. She stopped struggling, and stood quietly while Colchester, still holding her in a firm grip, deftly slid his free hand inside her gown and began to fondle her breasts. Her unresponsiveness puzzled him, and when he leaned toward her again to kiss her, he discovered that her cheeks were wet. Drawing back, he touched her face with his fingertips, and as he blinked at her in the darkness, she herself realized for the first time that she was weeping.

Colchester was confused, and seeing her standing unmoving and proudly erect, he reminded himself that she was no ordinary woman, but the Queen to whom he had sworn his allegiance. He still wanted her, but caution dampened his desire. "Have I offended you?" he asked in bewilderment.

Mary's shame overwhelmed her, but she could not remain silent. "No, it's I who have offended you by leading you to believe that you could take that which I'm unable to give you willingly."

There was a long silence, and at last it occurred to him that in spite of her dazzling appearance and provocative air, she was probably chaste. It was a waste of time to speculate on whether she had ever been unfaithful to her husband; Colchester knew that he did not want to take unnecessary risks. His own future would be in jeopardy if he made William a cuckold, and then had to flee the country and accept the dubious protection of James, whom he despised. There were too many women in the world, he told himself, to lose his place in the peerage and his rank in the army because of this one, however desirable. Had he been younger he would have been willing to tarry here with Mary and let the future shape itself, but it was senseless to make love to a reluctant Queen whose enmity could ruin him.

"You're very gracious, ma'am, but it was I who forgot myself," he said carefully.

Mary knew he was accepting the full blame deliberately, and smiled at him gratefully as she rearranged the front of her dress and dabbed delicately at her cheeks with a tiny lace handkerchief to smooth the rice powder that coated her face. "I'll always remember your kindness. I ask only one more favor of you. Forget the past quarter of an hour, and return to the reception without me."

Colchester reflected philosophically that his life would have been very complicated had the Queen become his mistress. She was far more valuable to him as a friend. "If I may make a suggestion, ma'am," he replied, "there will be far less talk if we return to the party together. People will suspect the worst if they see me wander back alone, but if we're together and make it obvious that there's nothing personal between us, the gossip-lovers won't be able to say a word."

She took the arm he offered her, and a few moments later, when the guests saw their seemingly serene Queen, no one guessed that she had almost made it impossible to live with William or with herself.

Chapter 11

MARY WAS RELIEVED beyond measure when the court settled back into its sedate routine following her unusual reception. Apparently no one attached any significance to her brief disappearance with Lord Colchester, for no scurrilous pamphlets dealing with her character were hawked in London's streets. The courtiers did not gossip about the episode, and neither Princess Anne nor the French agents in England said a word. But even though she had escaped so lightly, Mary could not forget the incident, and every shameful detail remained clear in her mind. She felt certain that William had been informed that she had acted as the hostess at a fete reminiscent of the reign of Charles II, but he made no mention of the party in his letters to her, and when he finally returned to England in October, he gave no sign that he had heard any unfavorable news of her.

Unable to rid herself of an ever-present sense of guilt, Mary still could not bring herself to confess the truth to him, and the longer she waited the more difficult it became for her to tell William that a group of the nation's most distinguished physicians had pronounced her incapable of childbearing. On three or four occasions during his first week in London she made an effort to blurt out the news, but each time something intervened, and she finally conceded to herself that she was seeking any excuse to avoid coming to an understanding with him. She knew he would become angry if she told him about her flirtation with Colchester and her near-seduction, and it was convenient to rationalize—to tell herself that she could not make a confession about the unfortunate evening without explaining the reason she had been depressed for so many days prior to the event.

William was still driving himself unmercifully, and as he landed in England only two weeks before the Parliament reconvened, he spent most of his time conferring with leaders of the Commons and Lords. The Tory and Whig parties had not been idle during the months that the Parliament had been in adjournment, and both were organized for the new session, ready for battle. The two groups were so bitterly opposed to each other now that William was afraid their disputes would paralyze the government, and consequently he wasted no opportunity to plead and argue that the welfare of the nation was more important than either party. Mary, who understood little and cared less about political matters, held herself aloof, and as far as she was concerned, her husband's incessant activity meant only that they spent virtually no private time together.

They entertained guests at Whitehall at dinner every evening, and on the few occasions when William joined her for lunch he was invariably accompanied by members of the Privy Council or by party leaders whose views he was trying to reconcile.

He spent long hours with the Earl of Marlborough and Admiral Lord Russell, too, and he devoted considerable time to studying the reports of army and navy quartermasters on the armed forces' state of preparedness. Protocol made it necessary for every foreign envoy stationed in London to call on the King and Queen after William's absence from the country, and although he tried to reduce such functions to a minimum, he could not eliminate them completely, and each week he had to waste a few hours at a diplomatic levee, sitting beside Mary on their twin thrones and exchanging pleasantries with the ambassadors.

Two or three evenings each week, after William finished his work, he came to Mary's apartment, and his need for her was so obvious that she did not then have the heart to tell him that she could never give him an heir. So she remained silent, enjoyed his love-making, and then, when he drifted off to sleep, stayed awake, trying to summon the courage to tell him the physicians' diagnosis when he awakened in the morning. But this form of procrastination was an evasion, too, as she knew they would have no opportunity to exchange intimate confidences at the beginning of the day. William began dictating letters while his valet shaved him; then, when Mary joined him at the table, his meal was repeatedly interrupted by aides and secretaries, and she was kept busy by the housekeeper and steward, who came to her during the meal to receive their orders for the day. All through the autumn and early winter Mary continued to temporize, hating herself for her weakness.

Then, shortly before Christmas, England's relations with France became worse. William was forced to devote all of his attention to the crisis, and Mary, pleased that there was a valid reason to pamper her cowardice, postponed her plans to speak to him. The English Parliament and the Dutch States-General were alarmed when it was revealed that King Louis had established the headquarters of a new army in Brussels and was mustering the largest force he had ever placed under a single command. Although naval operations were rarely conducted during this season, his fleet was gathering at Le Havre and several smaller Channel ports, and word was received from Madrid that the French Mediterranean fleet was sailing north, too.

It seemed likely that war would be declared at any moment, but William, who had spent the better part of his adult life preparing for this emergency, remained calm. He ordered Count Waldeck to mobilize the Dutch army, sent the Earl of Marlborough to Holland with his English regulars, and alerted both of his fleets. As the English and Dutch admirals cordially detested each other, the King granted them permission to operate separately, but made it clear to both groups that he expected them to forget their jealousies and work together if they were attacked.

The espionage agents in William's employ submitted contradictory figures on the size of the French army in the Brabant, but they agreed that new regiments were arriving each week, and late in January Waldeck and Marlborough, who were maneuvering cautiously on the Dutch side of the border, waiting for the enemy to strike first, signed a joint request to William, asking for reinforcements. The Parliament granted the King the right to send those battalions that had been enlisted for home defense to join their compatriots abroad, and he sent a plea for assistance to his allies. Brandenburg, which had now officially changed its name to Prussia, responded promptly with twenty-five thousand trained men who placed themselves at Waldeck's disposal, but the Holy Roman Emperor, who was more concerned about the safety of his own realm than participating in a foreign venture, sent only ten thousand infantrymen. The Papal States and Spain were too weak to give William anything except their moral support, and the few troops they could raise were stationed on their own frontiers. And Sweden, which was reluctant to participate in the wars of the great powers, temporized politely, kept up a lively correspondence with William, and carefully remained neutral.

Rumors reached London daily all through February that hostilities had begun, and the tension mounted steadily, but

Marlborough and Waldeck continued to report to the King that not one gun had been fired. Early in March Chancellor Bentinck of the United Provinces came to London, and attending a meeting of the Privy Council in his capacity as Earl of Portland, he expressed the opinion that King Louis had no intention of attacking the Anglo-Dutch army. His colleagues laughed at him, and even William, who had better reason than the others to respect his shrewdness and foresight, was unable to accept his evaluation. Why, he asked, had Louis put such an enormous army into the field if he did not intend to attack? Bentinck replied honestly that he did not know, and for the present that ended the speculation.

But Louis proved that he was still the cleverest man in Europe. The English and Dutch armies were being kept in a state of alert on the Continent, William's warships watched every move made by the ships flying the fleur-de-lis pennant as they sailed majestically from one Channel port to another, and while the attention of the world was being diverted, James II, accompanied by a force of approximately fifty thousand veteran French troops, landed unopposed in Ireland on the fourteenth of March, 1689. There was consternation in the House of Lords, a riot broke out in the Commons, and William, tight-lipped and silent, was helpless. The three southern provinces of Ireland declared themselves in favor of James, thousands of young men joined his army, and he entered Dublin in triumph on the twenty-fourth of March, a scant ten days after his landing.

The Dutch ministers of state hurried to London and met in almost continuous session with the English Privy Council, but nothing was accomplished. Marlborough and Waldeck sent word that if they abandoned their breastworks on the frontier, the army that stood poised in the Brabant would sweep through the United Provinces, and William, managing to keep his head even though he had been caught in a trap, followed the advice of his generals and left them at their posts.

James, meeting no organized opposition with his jubilant followers, announced that he would conquer England before the end of the year, then marched out of Dublin to occupy northern Ireland. But, as usual, the former king was his own worst enemy, and as he had permitted his enthusiastic aides to confiscate the property of Protestants in the southern provinces, he found the Ulstermen determined to oppose him. Londonderry, the Church of England citadel in the north, closed its gates to him, and when he tried to force his way in, the militia and the citizens put up such a spirited defense that he lost his appetite for battle and retreated to Dublin. Hoping to make amends to the Irish irregulars who had joined him, he stripped all but Catholics of their property rights and issued a long list of Protestants who, he said, were to be placed under arrest and executed when apprehended.

Protestants and Catholics alike in England were horrified, and William, who was aware of the evils of fighting a religious war, realized that his father-in-law was giving him no choice. If he hoped to accomplish his life's work and keep his thrones, he would now have to fight fire with fire, prejudice with prejudice, and after conferring at length with the Privy Council and the Dutch ministers, he finally decided on a course of action. But, realizing that his wife was Queen in her own right and that the enemy was her father, he thought it only fair to tell her his plans while his secretaries drew up the orders that required his signature.

It was late afternoon when he went to her suite, and he was annoyed to learn that she was in the small garden that she was cultivating in one of Whitehall's inner courts. There was not time to wait until an aide summoned her, as he wanted his proclamations read in the Commons before the day ended, so he made his way to the garden himself, growing increasingly irritable as he hurried through the endless corridors of the palace. Mary, an apron over her gown, was kneeling before some rosebushes, loosening the earth with a trowel, and when William saw her, she seemed so absorbed in what she was doing that he lost his temper. She was so calm, so unconcerned that she seemed unaware of the dangers that threatened the country and her own head.

"If you aren't too busy, madam, we'd like a word with you," William said angrily.

The Queen's ladies in waiting, who had been helping her half-heartedly, hastily withdrew, and Mary looked up in surprise. Her husband's tone had startled her, and when she saw his expression she was afraid that he had learned her secret or that Lord Colchester had boasted to another officer about her indiscretion in the pavilion at Greenwich and that William had heard of the incident. "What is wrong?" she asked, rising and removing a pair of heavy gloves.

"You may have heard that your father has proscribed two hundred and twenty Protestant nobles in Ireland, and that fourteen have already been murdered."

She nodded, relieved because he was still ignorant of her personal shame, yet depressed because of her father's outrageous behavior.

William stood in silence for a moment as she untied her apron and folded it neatly; she looked so contrite that he told himself it was wrong to use her as the outlet for his feelings. They were alone now in the little garden, and he lowered his voice. "I've waited for weeks, hoping we wouldn't have to fight a holy war. But James is giving me no choice. I thought you'd want to hear my plans before they're made public."

Mary shivered and wished she had worn a shawl. London could become unexpectedly cool in late April when the sun went down. "Shall we go inside?"

"There isn't time." He led her to a small bench that had not yet received its spring coat of whitewash; when he saw how grimy it was, he spread a linen handkerchief for Mary to sit on.

Her appreciation of his gesture was greater than the courtesy itself. She smiled up at him gratefully as he sat beside her.

"There are thousands of French Huguenots in England," he said. "I'm issuing a proclamation tonight, asking every able-bodied refugee to join me in a crusade."

Mary looked at him in dismay, knowing how deeply he felt about the right of all men to worship as they wished. "You're offering the Huguenots vengeance by appealing to them on religious grounds." It was an accusation, not a question.

"Your father and Louis have given me no alternative." He shrugged, but hesitated for a moment. "I'm calling for English volunteers, too, in your name and mine. The Privy Council thinks we should be able to raise a corps of fifteen thousand Dissenters, Calvinists, and sons of Cromwell's Roundheads. I can't afford to take chances on the possibility that there will be disturbances at home, so I'm issuing private instructions to the constabulary. Anyone who attacks Catholics in England or Scotland, anyone who either destroys Catholic property or desecrates a Catholic church, is to be placed under arrest. Quietly, that is, and without calling attention to the incident."

Mary continued to stare at him. "You've always said that hate breeds hate, but you're using the very methods you've always condemned in the French."

William smiled wryly. "I'm forced to admit the situation has its ironic elements. I intend to write to the Pope, explaining my position to him, but I'm afraid that won't make life any more comfortable for English Catholics in coming months. In a fight for survival, we've got to use every weapon that will help us, even the methods of tyranny. I'm telling you all this," he added, "because I'm willing to take sole responsibility for what I'm doing."

"I understand."

"I've always been careful to sign all state papers with both of our names. But if you wish, I'll omit your name, as I've already done in a letter to Denmark. Copenhagen will send us a full division of infantry and four batteries of artillery, provided there are only Protestants in the army. I've assured them I'll accept their conditions."

It was very quiet in the garden, and Mary gazed absently at the gray stone walls of the palace, then at the freshly turned earth of her flower beds. "You could have signed the letter with my name, too," she said softly.

"Thank you." No matter how long he was married to her, he

thought, he would always feel inadequate when he tried to express his gratitude for her gestures of loyalty. He made an attempt to hide his embarrassment by laughing. "Let's look on the bright side. This is one time when our relationship with George and Anne is a blessing. If we were on speaking terms with them, George would have the right to ask for the command of the Danish troops."

Mary smiled, but sobered quickly. "Who will you send to Ireland as your commander-in-chief?"

William had forgotten he had told her that the generals stationed in the United Provinces did not want to be transferred. "I thought of going myself."

"No!" she interrupted, alarmed for his safety.

Her response was so emphatic that he was hurt. "Apparently neither you nor the Privy Council has a good memory. Allow me to remind you that I've spent more time on active military service than any other ruler on earth. However, I've agreed that for the present, at least, it will be necessary for me to remain in London."

Rather than explain her reaction, Mary hid her relief.

"I'm giving the command to Marshal Schomberg."

She could not hide her astonishment. "But he's seventy-five years old!"

He volunteered for the post, and he's the best man available," William replied stubbornly, concealing his own misgivings by speaking loudly and belligerently. It was true that Field Marshal Friedrich Hermann Schomberg was an old man, but he was the most renowned general of the century. He had begun his military career in the United Provinces under William's grandfather, had served his own country, Brandenburg, and had gained fame as a mercenary by commanding Swedish troops and those of three other German states. Louis of France had awarded him his marshal's baton, and for a time he had even commanded the army of Charles II, who had given him an English dukedom. Subsequently he had returned to France and retired, but had fled to England as a refugee when Louis had begun to persecute

Huguenots, although his own fame was so great that neither he nor his family had been in personal danger.

"I don't mean to criticize," Mary said apologetically.

"Schomberg is a symbol of Protestant resistance to Louis," William declared. He added in an undertone, "I'm sending his son Charles with him. "It's the best I can do." He rose abruptly. "The documents must be ready for signature now."

Mary knew he was disturbed, but his inability to look straight at her made her realize that he was uneasy, too. Her knowledge of military affairs was severely limited, but even she could understand that he had good cause for concern. He was planning to send a force of amateur soldiers, Huguenot and English volunteers, together with a corps of Danes who had never fought a battle, against a large body of seasoned troops. And the general who would command the expedition was certainly a gallant old man, but even an ignorant woman knew he was no longer a warrior.

When William returned to the palace, Mary remained in the garden, and as dusk fell, her own sense of fear increased. Perhaps it was necessary, as William claimed, to abandon the principles of religious tolerance he had held all his life and make an appeal based on bigotry in order to raise a new army. Perhaps he was right, too, when he said that the competent young generals were indeed needed in the United Provinces to watch the huge French army massed in the Brabant. And it was even possible that inexperienced recruits could defeat trained, veteran divisions; Mary could vaguely recall a few such instances from the history she had been obliged to study as a child. But the only encouraging aspect of the situation was that the enemy was under the personal command, theoretically at least, of her father. For her father's abilities, she felt no respect. However, it was unlikely that James would have a chance to exercise his dubious talents, for Mary remembered that a recent dinner guest had remarked with brutal candor that if the French army in Ireland was threatened, its generals would promptly stop deferring to James. Louis demanded victories, and would not hesitate to reveal to the world that James was only a puppet if that was the price he had to pay to defeat William.

England celebrated and bonfires were lighted in every city and town when Marshal Schomberg landed unopposed at Carrickfergus, and the sixteen thousand men who had sailed with him took possession of the key Irish port. He remained in the town for the better part of a month, and was joined by more than twenty thousand more troops during that time. Speakers in the House of Commons competed with each other in heaping praise on the old marshal when word was received that he had left his base and marched to the town of Dundalk without losing a man. James and his French commander, General Lauzun, had set up headquarters at Dundalk, but at Schomberg's approach had retreated to the village of Ardee and taken up a position behind the Boyne River. England confidently awaited news that a major battle had been fought and won.

William and the Privy Council knew better, but remained silent. Censorship, the King declared, was necessary in time of war, and Schomberg's dispatches were carefully edited before they were made public. The people of England might become discouraged if they knew that the marshal's force of thirty-six thousand men had seen no living creature on the march from Carrickfergus to Dundalk; Irish irregulars had burned every hut to the ground, driven pigs and cows and chickens before them out of the area, and destroyed every scrap of food they had been unable to carry them. The English volunteers, French Huguenots, and Danes had to maintain long supply lines, and nightly raids on the wagons carrying food to the army from Carrickfergus were commonplace.

Schomberg dug breastworks on his side of the Boyne, James and Lauzun did the same on the opposite bank of the river, and the opposing forces spent the better part of the summer making menacing but meaningless gestures at one another. There was illness, principally dysentery, in both camps. Those men who remained healthy fell prey to boredom. Gradually the people at home became disillusioned. The temper of the Parliament changed, and Tories and Whigs alike made vigorous speeches demanding action. William wrote repeatedly to Schomberg, ordering an attack, but the old marshal calmly ignored the commands. He sent several private dispatches to the King, saying that he was afraid to trust his untried troops in a major attack, and rather than risk overwhelming defeat and the possible destruction of his entire force, he planned to let the enemy make the first move.

By August the impatience of the people and the nagging demands of the Parliament made it necessary for William to do something drastic. A huge army supported by English and Dutch taxpayers was idle in Holland, sailors of both navies were becoming so bored with their existence that captains were reluctant to cast anchor at Plymouth, Rotterdam or other major ports for fear their men would desert, and with the threat of a decisive French move still imminent, the volunteer force in Ireland sat behind its breastworks and listened to the taunts of the enemy.

From a strictly military point of view, Ireland was the least important sector, but James was a dangerous symbol; to some men, both in England and on the Continent, he was still the legitimate King, and the Privy Council agreed with Bentinck's cynical observation: If James conquered Ireland he would be regarded as a hero, and even those of his former subjects whom he had oppressed would be inclined to forget that he had made their lives miserable. William, listening and pondering, was forced to conclude that a ruler, if he hoped to keep his throne, had to succeed in all of his endeavors. His principles, his beliefs in tolerance and self-government, were secondary to success itself, and for the first time he felt he understood why the French blindly followed the despotic Louis.

Sentiment in favor of James was rising all over England, and even some members of the Parliament who had previously urged that he be executed if captured now referred to him cautiously, and emphasized in both their public and private statements that they respected him as a person. William, harried and sleepless, saw the distinct possibility that he and Mary would be driven into exile if he continued to play Louis's game. Confiding in no one except Bentinck and Shrewsbury, he made a private journey to Plymouth, and there he met secretly with the English and Dutch admirals. This was not the time for tact and diplomacy in dealing with men who were jealous of their prerogatives, and he ignored the feelings of both groups as he placed the combined fleets under the nominal command of Admiral Herbert, with Lord Edward Russell as his deputy in charge of sea operations.

The King's instructions were simple and direct: The two fleets were to act as one, and regardless of the cost in men, ships, or national pride, they were to lure the French armada into battle and destroy it. It was of no importance that English rear admirals would serve under Dutch vice-admirals, that Dutch captains would have to obey English rear admirals. Nothing mattered except the annihilation of Louis's fleet, and William swore grimly that any officer who failed in his duty would be dismissed in disgrace, regardless of his rank or experience.

Returning to London, where his field equipment was already packed and waiting for him, William visited his wife briefly, revealed to her that he was leaving for Ireland, and named her as his Regent during his absence. He told her to do nothing without the advice of the Privy Council and the Dutch Ministry. When she was in doubt, she was to write to him. Mary realized that she would be little more than a figurehead, but she had no desire to exercise power. Her only concern was William's safety, but he gave her no chance to express her feelings and left the city that same night after a brief, almost curt parting. It was small consolation for her to tell herself that it was too much to expect him to display tenderness when he faced the greatest crisis of his life. But she was sorry, all the same, that he hadn't lingered long enough to make love to her. If he had, she felt sure she would have found the strength to tell him of her inability to bear children.

Three days later William landed at Carrickfergus, and set out immediately for Belfast, where he formally took over the command of the army from Schomberg and, for the benefit of his loyal subjects in Ulster, reviewed token detachments of troops that had been withdrawn from the line for the purpose. He spent only one night in the city, and the following day, accompanied by the marshal, he started south. The army, which had grown lethargic, roused itself sufficiently to appear before him in clean uniforms when he inspected the positions facing the Boyne.

The enemy greeted him even more enthusiastically. General Lauzun set up two field pieces on a wooded hill, and both directed their fire at him. The first shot killed a man and two horses some distance from William, but the other gun was better aimed, and a heated iron ball struck the river bank and grazed the King's shoulder in its ricochet. The staff was alarmed, but William suffered no harm, and remarkingly dryly, "There's no need for any bullet to come nearer," he continued to move slowly up and down the line.

That evening he summoned a council of war, which was attended by the younger Schomberg, a competent officer of about William's own age, and Lord James Douglas, a Scotsman who commanded the cavalry. The meeting was held in Marshal Schomberg's tent rather than the King's, as maps of the area were already mounted on the canvas walls, and the old man, white-haired but still erect, sat in the folding leather chair he had carried with him on campaigns for more than fifty years as he smoked his pipe, sipped a dry white wine from a pewter mug, and waited to hear the King's views.

William wasted no words. "Gentlemen," he said crisply, "we will mount a full-scale attack at dawn tomorrow."

There was a silence, and the two juniors glanced uneasily at each other, then at the old marshal, who continued to suck calmly on his pipe. "Impossible, Your Majesty," he replied, his English accented by a mixture of German and French influences.

It was fortunate, William reflected, that he had been prepared for such obstinacy, or he might have become angry. "We hold no general in higher regard than we do Your Grace," he said. "But we have been forced to conclude that if we fail to defeat

James here, his strength in England will grow, and he can regain his throne by doing nothing other than sitting on the far side of that wretched river and defying us."

"I know nothing of political affairs, Your Majesty." Schomberg raised his mug to his lips, then slowly wiped his white mustaches. "I am a soldier, nothing more. And as a soldier I can tell you that in my opinion it would be catastrophic to send our men against the enemy. I'm not worried about the Irish. There are only six thousand of them, and I doubt if one in ten has ever had a day of real military training in his life. But Lauzun's veterans are of another caliber. Some of them served with me, some with Condé. You'll find no better troops anywhere."

His obvious pride in his former subordinates irritated William. "Apparently you forget, Your Grace, that we outnumber the enemy by at least five thousand, perhaps even ten thousand."

"I forget nothing," the marshal said gently. "All I can say is that we'd need a miracle to beat Lauzun if we attack, and as I'm a freethinker, I don't believe in miracles."

"I've never believed in them, either, but now I must," William retorted tartly, dropping the royal form of address. "I no longer have any choice. Regardless of the odds against us, we'll attack."

Lord Charles Schomberg, who was unaccustomed to hearing his father's word disputed, stared uncomfortably at his boots, and Douglas, a professional soldier who was in Ireland instead of the United Provinces only because he had been ill when the Earl of Marlborough had gone to the Continent with the bulk of the army, coughed behind his hand in obvious embarrassment.

But the marshal had spent more than half a century obeying the senseless whims of monarchs whose knowledge of military strategy was limited and whose ignorance of battle tactics was abysmal. "In that case," he declared, his light blue eyes still bright, "all of us must do our best. May I make a suggestion, Your Majesty?"

William was uncertain whether the old man's politeness was exaggerated. "Of course," he replied curtly.

"There's only one weakness I can find in the enemy position."

Schomberg pulled himself to his feet, walked to a map, and used the stem of his pipe as a pointer. "The hills behind Lauzun's lines are high, and the woods are thick. If he should be forced to retreat, there's only one pass open to him, and he'll try to send all of his troops through it."

Nodding thoughtfully as he stood beside the marshal, William concealed his chagrin. He had not thought as far as how to capitalize on the defeat of the enemy, and had to admit to himself that, as George Waldeck had frequently intimated, his renown as a soldier would never threaten the reputations of Caesar and Charlemagne.

"There is a bridge a few miles upstream," Schomberg continued. "Lauzun holds it, but he posts only a small guard there. I propose that we send part of our army across the bridge at midnight."

"For what purpose?"

The old man sighed patiently. "If our main attack is unsuccessful, the units that have crossed the river can create a diversion and give us a chance to draw back to our breastworks. On the other hand," he went on, his tone making it plain that he placed little faith in this possibility, "should we force Lauzun to retreat, we can reach the pass first and cut him off."

William concentrated on the map for some moments. "If we do not have enough experienced troops to execute an attack," he said at last, "I can't see how we dare risk losing part of our army by maneuvering behind the enemy's lines."

Schomberg was surprised by the validity of his argument and rewarded him with a sheepish smile. "You're right," he exclaimed, and taking advantage of his age and rank, slapped the King familiarly on the shoulder.

"Then your idea isn't feasible." William found it impossible to resent the impertinence; the marshal had attended this grandfather's councils of war and had fought at his father's side through three campaigns.

Schomberg returned to his chair, stretched his legs before him, and finished his wine. Then he smiled, and looked young and alert. "With any luck we might be able to achieve that miracle, after all. Milord Douglas!"

"Sir?" The Scotsman, who had been toying with the hilt of his sword, sat upright.

"Do you think your horsemen can play two roles? Are they capable of deploying as infantry to hold off the enemy if we're forced to draw back, or beat Lauzun to the pass in the hills if we cut through his lines?"

Douglas was anything but impetuous, and he weighed the question carefully. "We'll do all we can, Your Grace."

"That's all I ever ask of any general. Start moving upstream at midnight, and don't let Lauzun's sentries at the bridge sound an alarm. Charles, give me that list of troop units."

"Yes, sir." His son handed him a long sheet of paper.

The old man read it slowly, completely absorbed, and seemed to have forgotten that the King had superseded him as head of the army. But William was pleased to have him take charge, and now had no intention of making a show of his own authority.

"Charles, you'll take half the English troops and command the right wing. I'll take the center, with the Huguenots as my nucleus and the Danes to reinforce them. The rest of the English will deploy on the left." The marshal paused for an instant. "As Douglas will be across the river, I'll have to promote a brigadier to command the left flank. Does anyone have a suggestion?"

"I'd like to volunteer for the post," William replied.

Schomberg was startled. "This is very irregular."

"If you're afraid I won't obey orders, let me assure you that I have enough sense to follow the instructions of someone who was waging war before I was born. As to my experience—"

"I'm familiar with Your Majesty's military experience," the marshal interrupted, and his manner was so matter-of-fact that William did not find his rudeness offensive. "I think Your Majesty is an excellent choice for the position."

"I'm flattered, Your Grace."

"You needn't be." There was a gleam of amusement in the old man's watery blue eyes. "I don't need an expert tactician on the left. The river is straight and shallow there, and you'll either cross or be forced back. You'll be valuable because you'll be leading English recruits, and I hope the presence of the King in their midst will inspire them to hold steady when real soldiers begin to fire at them."

William managed to chuckle, but his laughter was hollow and fooled no one, including himself.

"Gentlemen," Schomberg said, "I shall send the final order of battle to your tents in an hour. Milord Douglas, I'll bid you good-by and wish you good luck. May all of us succeed tomorrow morning. And," he added a trifle belatedly after glancing at William, "God save the King."

Lord Douglas led his fourteen hundred horsemen out of the encampment at midnight, and at four o'clock in the morning, while William was shaving and preparing to dress in his armor, a messenger arrived with word that the bridge had been taken, that all James's guards there had either been captured or killed, and that the entire body of cavalry had crossed the Boyne safely. Breakfast consisted of three cold dishes, beef, fish, and potatoes, and as William ate by the light of a single candle that was shielded to prevent the enemy sentries on the far side of the river from seeing it, he felt so depressed that he had no appetite.

He missed Waldeck and Nicholas Dykvelt. He could not rid himself of a sense of uneasiness at the thought of leading recruits into battle, and he faced the truth that ambition forced him to walk a strange path. He, a Dutch Prince, was alone in the wild hills of Ireland; in less than an hour, obeying the commands of a German marshal, he would lead English troops against a French army that swore allegiance to his father-in-law. Rising abruptly from his table and buckling on his sword, William hoped that James would not take an active part in the battle. If he should be killed, the French would make a martyr of him and claim that his infant son had inherited the throne. Alive and bungling, James was far less of a menace than he would become if he died.

William strapped on his heavy battle helmet. As he left his

tent he wondered if he should take the precautionary step of ordering the army to spare James's life. Then he realized that such a command, given at the last moment, might create confusion in the ranks of men who were going into battle for the first time. And Schomberg, under whose authority he had promised to place himself, already had enough on his mind. He started toward the marshal's tent, which stood near his own, and saw that the old man was waiting for him. They exchanged salutes, then mounted their horses and made a rapid, token inspection of the army. The men were in position for the assault, and in theory at least, the sight of their King riding beside the most renowned soldier in Christendom raised their spirits, but they had been ordered to remain silent, so there were no cheers. Most of the faces William glimpsed looked pale and drawn in the predawn light.

When the tour was finished, William and Schomberg shook hands. "If you'll take your post, Your Majesty, I'll sound the order to attack in a quarter of an hour," the marshal said.

"Thank you for your devotion, Your Grace. The future of Europe depends on what we do today."

"The future of Europe has been at stake in so many battles I've fought," the old man commented. Then he turned and rode off.

Depressed by his cynicism, William watched him for a moment, then started toward the divisions drawn up on the left flank. His aides followed him, and he wished he had brought a few Dutch officers with him; in moments of great tension he had a tendency to speak in his native tongue, but today he would have to remember to use only English.

A brigade of light infantry was in the van of his force, with two divisions of heavy infantry behind it; a third division, together with two more brigades of light infantry, comprised the reserves. William halted directly behind the ranks of the brigade that would lead the assault, and tried to calm himself by taking stock of the situation. The first streaks of light had appeared in the sky. The stars were disappearing in a gray mist. The river was no more than one hundred and fifty yards ahead of him, and although he could not see it, he could picture it in his mind. There had been little rain all summer, so the light infantry, which wore no armor, would be able to wade across to the far bank without difficulty; even though the current was strong, the water would come no higher than the men's waists, and if the brigade remembered to hold its muskets high, there was every chance it could establish a foothold on the enemy side.

The crossing would not be easy for the heavy infantry divisions, however, and William realized that luck would play an important part in the day's developments. Each of the soldiers who made up the bulk of his striking force wore one hundred and fifty pounds of armor in the form of breastplates, leg guards, and helmets, and each carried a saber in addition to his musket. There might be stones on the muddy river bottom, and if a man slipped, he would wet his gunpowder and thus render himself helpless for anything except hand-to-hand fighting in which he could use his saber.

Sergeants moved up and down the lines to preserve silence, but it seemed to William that the enemy surely must know that a battle was imminent. A man dropped his musket and cursed. Somewhere in the distance the wheels of a cannon creaked as the gun was rolled into position. Near the river bank an officer's horse whinnied nervously. Trying to maintain an air of calm authority for the benefit of those who might be watching him, William drew his sword and gestured to his trumpeter to draw closer. A King, he thought, was the same as any other man: He wondered whether he would still be alive at sundown. He could not help speculating, too, on whether he and his father-in-law would meet face to face on the field. If he knew James, he reflected, the chances were slim.

Off to the right Marshal Schomberg's trumpeter sounded a single piercing blast, and William pointed his sword in the direction of the enemy. "Attack!" he called sharply.

Veterans would have started off at once, but the light infantry brigade was sluggish, and in spite of the exhortations of its officers and the threats of its cursing sergeants, the troops in the first rank did not wade into the Boyne until the last notes of the call played by the King's trumpeter died away. William spurred forward, but had to slow his pace and then halt impatiently as he waited for the infantrymen to ford the river. The lack of opposition from the French made up for the lethargy of his own men, however, and he was relieved, as he peered through the mist, to see neither cavalry nor foot soldiers waiting to repel his army.

French sentries began blowing long, warning blasts on shrill whistles, but for some moments there was no other sound. Then, off to the right, sporadic musket fire began, and William knew that either the center or the right wing had reached the French breastworks. He guided his horse purposefully across the river, and for an instant was elated as he emerged onto enemy territory. But his pleasure died quickly, for the brigade was milling about in disorganized fashion. He issued a sharp order to its commander, whom he instructed to take the enemy's earthworks. The brigade formed into three long lines, and these started up the rugged, hilly terrain toward the enemy position, some two hundred yards distant. William, remaining at the river edge for the moment, turned in his saddle to watch the first of his heavy infantry divisions struggle toward him. While it was difficult for him to believe that General Lauzun, one of the most experienced of French commanders, had been surprised by the attack, it certainly appeared as if the enemy had not anticipated the precise form it was taking. Day had broken now, the fog was lifting, and William, standing in his stirrups, could see thousands of soldiers in scarlet crossing the river.

Then, suddenly, the comparative quiet was broken by the roar of French artillery. It was impossible to guess whether Lauzun had actually been aware of the impending attack and had waited deliberately for the opportune moment to strike back, or whether he had indeed been caught off guard. The French gunners quickly proved that they deserved their reputations as the most accomplished artillerymen in Europe. They experimented with their first salvo, tested the range with their second, and then began to pour a steady rain of destructive fire on the men crossing the river.

Both of William's heavy infantry divisions were in the water now, and men hesitated as soldiers beside them screamed and flung their hands as they were struck or quietly disappeared beneath the surface of the Boyne. The river turned red, and officers, riding relentlessly back and forth, began to use the flats of their swords to drive their troops forward. Elsewhere down the line, William saw, other units were encountering similar difficulties, and only the Huguenots continued to advance grimly on their own initiative. Marshal Schomberg's doubts were being realized, and William stirred uneasily in his saddle.

Then, as he watched helplessly, the French infantry opened fire from behind its breastworks, and the advancing light infantrymen halted abruptly. Had they continued to advance they might have been able to overwhelm the enemy, for the line, judging by the spurts of flame, was thinly held. But the untried English troops became panicky when they saw some of their companions fall, and before their officers could rally them, they turned and streamed down the hills to the river. William, brandishing his sword and shouting in a vain effort to make himself heard above the artillery fire, tried to halt the fleeing brigade, and so did his aides, but the best they could achieve was to slow the wild rush to the Boyne.

In the meantime the heavy infantrymen, still being subjected to severe punishment from the enemy guns, saw their own comrades running toward them. Ignoring the threats and curses of their officers, they promptly made their way back to the safety of their own side of the river. William stubbornly remained on French territory, trying to encourage his men to form their lines anew and launch another assault, but he was so conspicuous and in such an exposed position that he finally listened to the aides, who pointed out to him that the French could come down the hill and capture him with ease, thus ending not only the battle but the campaign.

Reluctantly, his face burning with shame, he headed back across the Boyne, and it was little comfort to reflect that he was wiser and more cautious now than he had been in his youth, when George Waldeck had been compelled to remove him from a dangerous position by force. When he reached the English bank, several senior officers crowded around him trying to excuse the conduct of their men, but he waved them away and demanded a report on the progress of the battle in other sectors. Meanwhile, he said bitterly, the colonels could save their breath.

The demoralized divisions pulled back to reorganize, and the shattered light infantry brigade, recovering from its hysteria, discovered that the losses it had suffered had after all been slight. Men glanced at each other covertly, grinned sheepishly, and came to the conclusion that, having survived their baptism of fire, they were now veterans. William dispatched couriers to the other sectors, and while he awaited their return, a messenger arrived with word from the cavalry. Lord Douglas, the young officer said, had learned that James, afraid that his son-in-law and Marshal Schomberg might capture him, had fled from General Lauzun's headquarters the moment he had heard the English were attacking. Douglas' cavalry had tried to prevent his escape, but he had reached the pass in the hills five minutes before the English advance guard had arrived there, and by this time was presumably well on his way to Dublin.

William was secretly relieved, for now no one could accuse him of trying to murder his father-in-law, and when his couriers returned he gave them his complete attention. The attack on the right flank, led by Lord Charles Schomberg, had been repulsed, and only in the center, where the old marshal was supervising operations, had a secure foothold been established on the enemy bank. There the Huguenots had held firm, refusing to give ground in spite of a heavy artillery barrage and infantry counterattacks, and the Danes were now crossing the river to join them.

The couriers were followed by one of the marshal's aides, with a message of vital importance to the King. Lauzun's Irish allies were unsteady, and if William could advance again to protect the flank of the divisions in the center, Schomberg thought it might be possible to achieve a victory. A similar request, the aide said, was being delivered to Schomberg's son.

Determined not to be humiliated a second time, William ordered his troops to cross the Boyne again, and resisted the temptation to send his reserve light infantrymen in the van. The brigade that had been routed, he said, would have a chance to wipe out its disgrace, and as the troops moved forward, their uniforms water-soaked and stained, he rode up and down the lines, unsmiling. The French promptly resumed their artillery fire, and even though it was deadly, the English did not waver. William, trying to maintain an air of calm detachment, sat at the water's edge and pretended to ignore the heated iron balls that fell near him. Like his men, he was frightened, but he realized that he was under an obligation to them, just as they were being required to demonstrate their devotion to him. They were advancing because they were ashamed to show cowardice before their King; it was his duty, in return, to convince them that he, too, was courageous and was therefore worthy of their loyalty.

The mist had completely disappeared now, and the sun was shining down from a cloudless sky on the green hills. As the first line of the vanguard reached the enemy bank, William started off across the river, the heavy infantry directly behind him. The royal standard-bearer, Devonshire's nephew, pitched forward suddenly and toppled out of his saddle, and the King reached out and snatched his banner from the dying man's hand before it fell into the Boyne. Another aide rode up and took the flag from William, who pressed his mount forward doggedly. Neither Waldeck nor Marlborough would have permitted him to take such great risks, but he knew he had no choice, that if he wavered, his men would become panicky again and his whole cause would be lost.

After what seemed like a long time he reached the enemy bank, where he paused for a moment while his staff gathered around him. Three of his aides were missing and a fourth sat slumped in his saddle, a trickle of blood running down his right cheek. William ordered the officer to seek medical attention immediately, then watched the heavy infantry approach. Slowly the battalions and companies made their way across the stream, and when the first regiment had assembled on the French side, William rode up to the colonel in command and announced his intention of helping the unit storm the enemy breastworks. Giving no one an opportunity to argue with him, he started up the nearest hill, and the regiment hurriedly fell into line behind him.

Meanwhile the light infantry brigade was proving that it had truly learned its lesson. The first of its three lines had reached the French position, the second line was creeping forward, and the brigade was returning the foe's musket fire, ignoring its casualties and, although no one quite realized it at the time, helping to destroy the illusion still held by so many Englishmen that the army of Louis XIV was invincible. Men were firing at each other now from a distance of no more than fifty feet, and the ground was littered with dead and wounded, but William, screened by his aides, who refused to listen to his protests and rode in front of him, glanced back down the hillside over his shoulder and saw that his second heavy infantry division had successfully crossed the river.

Now, he thought, was the moment to summon his reserves, too. He was about to give the necessary order when he became aware of a strange quiet. Suddenly he realized that the enemy artillery had fallen silent, and at almost the same moment his light artillery brigade stormed the breastworks. French musket fire ceased abruptly, and William was puzzled as he spurred to the crest of the hill. One of his aides, a red-faced major, was waiting for him, his happiness plain to see.

"Your Majesty," he shouted, "the enemy is in retreat!"

Pushing forward, William saw that the breastworks had been abandoned. Then, off in the distance, he caught a glimpse of French infantry moving into a heavily wooded area. The enemy foot soldiers were being protected by a rearguard composed of a small cavalry detachment, and the horsemen were so efficient that the members of the English light infantry brigade who tried to give chase quickly lost their enthusiasm for the sport and halted.

"Our advance couldn't have been responsible for this," William murmured.

"It wasn't, Your Majesty," the aide replied. "General Lauzun ordered a retreat just as we stormed these positions."

It was difficult for William to realize that he had won. "Why?"

"Marshal Schomberg's Huguenots broke through his center, sir. So Lauzun has pulled in his flanks and drawn off." Only a few white French uniforms could still be seen in the distance as Lauzun's cavalry troops, converging, joined to beat off the scattered attacks of the English units that tried to follow them. "But the French are good, Your Majesty," the aide said in grudging admiration. "We'll probably have to beat them again before this campaign ends."

William realized that Schomberg would have ordered the army to follow the French and destroy them had the men been capable of executing such a move. Since no organized pursuit was being attempted, it was evident to William that his victory had been narrowly achieved. He planned to give the old marshal all the credit for a triumph that bordered on the miraculous.

Ordering his division and brigade commanders to take possession of the earthworks, to preserve any documents they captured, and to prevent battlefield looting, William started off toward the center to find the old man who had accomplished the impossible. It was difficult to ride up and down hills dotted with breastworks that English and Danish troops were now occupying, so William returned to the river bank and followed it until he saw the green plumes that distinguished the helmets of the Huguenots. A captain was directing the work of a burial party. Recognizing the King, he saluted as William rode up to him.

"Where will we find Marshal Schomberg?" There was a silence, and William, thinking that the refugee officer might not understand English, repeated the question in French.

The captain stared at him for a moment, then pointed in the direction of a grassy hollow between two hills.

As William approached the area he saw that the fighting here had been intense, for in this sector there were more dead of both sides than he had yet seen. At the far end of the little valley several officers had dismounted, and seeing the gold epaulets of two division commanders, William rode up to them. The senior officers and their aides stood aside as he drew near, and suddenly he realized why they had gathered at this particular spot. A score or more dead were sprawled on the ground. Some were Huguenots, but the majority were French, among them a brigadier and two colonels.

And in the center, staring with lifeless eyes at the bright sun, was Marshal Schomberg. The price of victory had been high.

Chapter 12

JAMES STUART, more convinced than ever that it was his destiny to suffer the fate of King Lear, fled from Ireland in such haste that he left most of his personal baggage in Dublin. He returned to France, where he found the palace placed at his disposal by Louis almost deserted; most members of the small band that had followed him into exile had discovered compelling reasons to take themselves elsewhere, and he was met only by his wife, his infant son, and a staff of French servants. For the present, at least, James's royal host had no use for him, but Louis apparently intended to let him stay in France. Someday, perhaps, it might be possible to seat him on his throne again, and although the prospects appeared dim at the moment, hope had not been completely extinguished.

The French commander in Ireland, General Lauzun, was disgusted by the craven behavior of the man whose cause he had defended, and he, too, found an immediate excuse to sail for home, leaving his army under the command of his hitherto undistinguished Irish deputy, Lord Sarsfield. The Irish irregulars, ashamed of their defeat, responded to Sarsfield's call for men, and together with the French professionals who remained in the country, they occupied Limerick, Cork, and Kinsale and waited for the opportunity to avenge their defeat at the Battle of the Boyne.

William, aware that his father-in-law had been discredited but that he still had to deal with the French, set up headquarters in the village of Finglas, near Dublin, and gave his troops a chance to rest after their victory. He himself took possession of a small castle abandoned by a minor member of the nobility, and tried to plan his next moves. It was difficult for him to concentrate, however, for he found he was depressed by the thought that so many hundreds had died fighting for his sake. When he went to bed at night in the chamber formerly occupied by the lord and lady of the castle, the staring, lifeless eyes of Marshal Schomberg appeared before him, obliterating all else from his mind, and he wondered, with weariness greater than he had ever felt, whether blood would continue to be shed as long as both he and Louis XIV lived. So many men had died either to win freedom from tyranny or in the name of French glory, and still there was no end in sight.

Two days after his arrival at Finglas, William received news that both relieved and saddened him: The combined English and Dutch fleets had fought a major battle against the French in the Channel off Beachy Head, and both sides had suffered tremendous losses. So many of Louis's warships had been sunk that his navy was no longer to be feared, but the Anglo-Dutch fleets had been badly crippled, too, and it would probably be years before they could be built back up to their full strength.

Staring listlessly at the maps of Ireland spread out before him, William reflected that this should be one of the crowning moments of his life. France was no longer the undisputed mistress of the seas, and even though he had suffered a severe blow, too, the naval triumph, together with his victory in the Battle of the Boyne, would greatly enhance his prestige. He would be hailed throughout the world as the only man who had ever defeated the French on both land and sea. Still, the future was not pleasant to contemplate. William was unable to convince himself that the victories in Ireland and off Beachy Head meant the end of Louis's dreams of controlling all Europe.

Only one dispatch from abroad was really cheering, and William perused it again. It was a brief letter from Count Waldeck saying that Louis had begun to withdraw his army from the Dutch border. This meant there would be a respite in one sector. Leaning back wearily in his chair, William reached for a decanter of brandy that the owner of the castle had left. Quickly drinking a glass, he closed his eyes and made an attempt to tell himself that he had achieved his life's ambition. The face of Marshal Schomberg materialized before him again. Jumping to his feet, for the decanter was now empty, William tugged at the bell rope beside the four-poster bed, then paced up and down the room savagely until a serving maid appeared.

"Brandy," he snapped. Realizing from the girl's bewildered expression that he had used the Dutch word, he repeated the order in English.

She smiled at him with the insolent sauciness of the Irish, curtsied, and twirled her skirt in such a way as she left the room that William caught a glimpse of her bare legs and thighs.

When she returned a few moments later with a dusty jar, he studied her more closely, and was ironically amused by the thought that she was the physical opposite of his wife. Tiny, with small bones, she had blue-black hair, bright blue eyes, and clear, pale skin; she moved with a deliberate awareness that men found her attractive, and William, recalling the women with whom he had slept in his youth, knew instantly that she was far from innocent.

Conscious of his scrutiny, she looked at him boldly. "Would you like me to open the jar, Your Majesty?"

"If you please," he replied gruffly, annoyed because he could feel his heart pounding. An old, half-forgotten sense of anticipation welled up in him as the girl slowly cut the wax from the top of the jar. It was no accident that her blouse fell from one shoulder, revealing an expanse of smooth, soft skin, and William knew that he was going to make love to her. The girl herself meant nothing to him: he was simply going to use her to forget, for a little while, that many men had been killed and maimed because of his principles, his ambition, and his stubborn pride, and that thousands more would die before he and Louis settled their account with one another.

"What's your name?" he demanded suddenly.

"Moira Cusack, Your Majesty."

"Well, Moira Cusack, pour a glass for yourself, too."

The girl did as she was bidden, then observed softly, "I've often wondered what it's like to be King. Now I know."

"Do you?" Her direct, challenging gaze made William uncomfortable.

"You're lonely, just like any other man."

He took the glass she held out to him, and raised it in salute, smiling sardonically. "To your wisdom. How old are you?"

"Twenty-two, Your Majesty."

"And you've already learned that all men are lonely?"

The girl laughed a trifle contemptuously. "I knew it years ago."

William emptied his glass, the brandy burned as it slid down his throat, and his temples throbbed.

"There are other things I know, too," she suggested boldly, refilling his glass.

This was the moment to end the interview, to send her back to the kitchen, but he lacked the strength, and his shame was almost as great as his desire for her.

"I know ways to make a man feel less lonely—for a time." She stood directly before him, her breasts outthrust, defying him to dismiss her.

"Lock the door," William said curtly, and was rewarded by a gleam of avarice in her eyes. It was probably true, as she had said, that she understood men, but he knew her type, too; the only thought in her mind was the size of the purse she would receive from the sovereign of England and the United Provinces.

She turned away, slid the bolt into place, and then moved toward him again, letting her blouse drop from her other shoulder. William seized her in a grip so strong, so demanding that she winced. But even as he pulled the girl to him the chilling realization struck him that no matter how frantically he made love to her, he could not forget the war.

Mary sat listlessly at the desk in her husband's study in Whitehall, signing the documents that the Privy Council had approved. From time to time she glanced out of the window at the mellow September sun. Each time she sighed and forced herself to continue her work. Soon it would be too late in the year to go to Greenwich, where her flower gardens were being neglected, but she could not allow herself to dwell on the pleasures she was missing. Duty required her to remain in London. Dipping her quill into the jar of ink before her, she wrote, "Mary II, Regina," on a bill passed by the Parliament, sanded the sheet of parchment, and picked up another. Someday, she thought, the numb sensation that enveloped her would pass, and she would begin to feel and think again. In the meantime she had no choice, and lived from one day to the next, doing what was expected of her.

There was a discreet tap at the door, and the chamberlain stood in the frame, nervously tugging at the gold chain of his office that hung from his neck. "Forgive the intrusion, ma'am," he said, "but you have a visitor whom I'm certain you'll want to receive despite your wish not to be disturbed."

Mary made no comment and waited for him to continue.

"Her Royal Highness would like the privilege of an audience, ma'am."

There was only one "Royal Highness" in England, and Mary could not conceal her surprise. "Our sister has come to Whitehall?"

"Yes, Your Majesty."

Anne had made herself conspicuous by her absence for more than a year. "We will receive her," Mary said, wondering what development could have caused Anne to change her attitude. Reaching for the next document on the pile before her, she pretended to study it while she waited, and as the door opened she signed it with a flourish.

"You look well, Your Majesty," Anne said, speaking so blandly that it was obvious she had rehearsed the greeting.

Mary carefully sanded the paper, then glanced up coolly. Her sister, she noted instantly, was overdressed as usual, in a gown of maroon velvet that clashed with the color of her skin, and it was too early in the season for the huge ermine muff that dangled from her left wrist. Mary regarded her impassively. At last Anne flushed, caught hold of her skirts, and curtsied. The chamberlain hovered at the door, and when the Queen nodded to him, he disappeared hastily, shutting the door silently behind him.

"We see no change in you," Mary said frigidly. She told herself she was lying. Anne was using cosmetics more heavily than she had in the past, but neither lip rouge nor plucked brows and salve could draw attention from the lines at the corners of her eyes and her tightened mouth, which looked smaller than Mary remembered it.

"Thank you, ma'am." Behind her bravado, Anne was distinctly ill at ease.

"Sit down!" Mary exclaimed, and refrained from adding that she refused to behave like a lunatic simply because her sister's conduct had left so much to be desired. "And as we're alone, there's no need for you to act as though this was a formal court levee. You may recall that we had the same mother and father."

"Oh, I've never forgotten it." Anne's expression became woebegone and her tone was self-righteous as she took a chair beside the desk and smoothed her skirt with nervous, ring-laden fingers. "I had hoped that you'd remember, too, when I petitioned for a larger allowance. But," she continued quickly, "I haven't come to reopen old wounds."

"I'm delighted to hear it," Mary replied vehemently.

Again color rose in Anne's face, but she controlled her temper. "I'd like to offer my congratulations and those of my husband on our victories in Ireland and at sea."

Mary inclined her head slightly. "I accept your felicitations on behalf of the King and myself."

"I could hardly believe the good news when I heard that the French army in the Brabant had gone into winter quarters."

"Rest assured," Mary said, with only a hint of sardonic humor in her voice, "that everything possible is being done to make the throne secure for you."

Anne refused to accept the challenge. She shook her head sadly and made a show of biting her lower lip, which smudged her rouge. "Poor Papa. Sometimes I feel so sorry for him."

Mary remembered how thoroughly Anne had always detested their father, and wanted to laugh. "Why?"

"He must be so lonely."

"You could always join him if you wished. That would cheer him, I'm sure." Since it had not occurred to Mary that Anne genuinely feared exile, she was surprised when she saw her sister's eyes widen. Suddenly she felt sorry for the bitter young woman who led such a frustrated life. Reaching out, she patted her hand. "Luckily for you, I'm not vindictive, and neither is the King," she said. "Your rights are protected in the Succession Law, and we'll do nothing to harm you."

"Thank you, Mary." Anne reached into her muff for a handkerchief and blew her nose vigorously. Able to relax at last, she leaned back in her chair and smiled. "I hear that William has sent for the Earl of Marlborough to take command of the forces in Ireland and finish the campaign for him there."

"You may tell your friend Sarah Churchill that she talks too much. As a matter of fact, I'll tell her myself," Mary declared angrily. "I'm astonished she hasn't the sense to realize we're making no advance announcement of the appointment. This was a deliberate move to protect her husband. The French would try to sink his ship if they learned that Marlborough is going to Ireland."

"Oh, Sarah hasn't said a word to anyone except me," Anne protested, then added smugly, "I can't blame her for bragging to me a bit, you know. It isn't every woman's husband who is called in to replace a King."

It was absurd to let herself feel increasingly irritated, Mary knew, but Anne must hear the reasons for the appointment. "Marlborough is a professional soldier. The King took command temporarily when Marshal Schomberg was unfortunately killed, but he's needed here far more than he is on the battlefield."

"I'm sure that's true," Anne said. She smiled. Her voice became soft. "I'm sure you'll be relieved when he leaves Ireland, too."

Mary knew now why her sister had come to Whitehall. She had hoped that William's disgraceful affair with an Irish serving maid, which at least half a dozen high-ranking peers had discreetly called to her attention, would be kept quiet. But she should have known that all of London would be gossiping about the incident.

"You and I haven't been on good terms, but I'm not one to shirk my duty," Anne said piously. "You won't love me for coming to you now, I'm sure, but you're my sister, after all, and when there's a crisis, blood is thicker than wine."

"Not necessarily," Mary said coldly. She wondered if she could silence Anne by reminding her that they had both played a role in forcing their father to abdicate. Probably not. Anne would surely return to her subject, no matter what the diversion might be.

"It pains me to tell you this, dear, but when you've had time to recover from the shock and reflect for a few days, you'll be glad it was your sister who came to you rather than some outsider." Anne paused and studied Mary closely. "William has pretended to be loyal to you ever since you got rid of that dreadful Burghley woman years ago. But I've been informed on excellent authority that he's been unfaithful to you again. And this time his mistress hasn't even been a noblewoman."

To Anne's astonishment, her sister smiled. Anne never knew how much the effort cost her.

"Your authority is correct. The woman is an ordinary slut." Mary was afraid her voice would tremble, and paused for breath. "The King spent one afternoon with her, and the following day she left for Dublin. I can't tell you the precise amount he paid her, but I can guess, judging from the wardrobe she bought for herself. She's now living in Dublin, by the way, and temporarily has become the mistress of Lord Waterford, one of the new Irish peers. Is there anything else you'd like to know, dear?"

For a long moment Anne was too astonished to reply, but finally she recovered sufficiently to say, with a touch of malice, "I'm too late. Someone else has come to you first." An exaggerated expression of sympathy appeared in her eyes. "I'm so sorry."

Mary was afraid she would lose her self-control if Anne made a gesture of affection, and knew she had to terminate the interview as quickly as possible. "Thank you for coming to me," she said crisply. "I won't forget your interest in the matter."

Anne knew she was being dismissed and recognized the implied threat, but having been assured that her own place in the hierarchy was secure, she made another attempt to continue the discussion. "What are you going to do about it?"

That, Mary thought bitterly, was the question that had kept her awake for the past three nights. No answer had yet offered itself. Making a supreme effort, Mary forced herself to smile enigmatically as she stood to indicate that the audience was at an end.

William handed the command of his army to the Earl of Marlborough, who spent less than a day checking supplies and ammunition, interviewing his principal subordinates, and inspecting the troops. Eighteen hours after he landed, the lieutenant general was on the march, and before the King sailed for England he captured Cork, took Kinsale, and laid siege to Limerick. William made a final gesture before he left: he issued a proclamation promising there would be no reprisals against the Irish who had rebelled. Three insurgent leaders promptly surrendered to Marlborough, and it seemed likely that the whole island would be in the Earl's hands before the end of the year.

Late on a rainy night William embarked for England, and a few hours later a violent storm blew his frigate off her course. The ship's officers and crew worked frantically to save their vessel, their monarch, and themselves. Finally, after two nights and two days at sea, the battered frigate dropped her anchor off Plymouth. William was rowed ashore past the hulks of what had been some of the finest ships in his navy, and their condition told him far more graphically than had any of the reports he had received that the battle near Beachy Head had been one of the most violent ever fought at sea.

He sat in the stern of his boat, huddled in a long cape, but made no attempt to protect his face from the cold rain that was still falling, and the men who comprised the gig's crew perceived for the first time that the King was after all as sensitive as the next man. They saw the sorrow and pain in his face as he gazed at the shattered warships, and they knew he was suffering, for they felt as he did.

The Lord Governor of Plymouth, who was waiting on shore, urged His Majesty to remain in the city until the weather cleared. The roads, he said, had been turned into rivers of mud, and the carriage that had been freshly gilded for the journey would bog down before it traveled more than a few miles. William was anxious to reach London as soon as possible, however, so he thanked the Lord Governor for his kindness, ordered horses for himself and his aides, and started for the capital at once, accompanied only by a half-troop of cavalry from the local garrison.

He set the pace himself, and after two days of hard riding, arrived in London shortly after sundown. It was still raining, though more lightly, and no one at Whitehall expected him in such weather. The sentries at the main entrance scarcely recognized the grimy figure who rode at the head of the company, and the officer in charge of the guard, deeply mortified, had no opportunity to assemble his men in time to give the King an appropriate welcome. The courtiers and servants who caught a glimpse of the bedraggled monarch were startled, too, but William wasted no time with them, and learning that the Queen was in his study, he went to her immediately.

He found Mary sitting at his desk, signing papers by the light of three candles set in a silver holder; the tapers flickered as the door opened, and she looked up in annoyance. Then she recognized her husband. She dropped her quill, spattering ink onto a bill granting a measure of tax alleviation to the sheep growers of Yorkshire, who had suffered a bad year.

William removed his soggy cape and threw it into a corner. "I'm home," he announced unnecessarily. He knew at once from his wife's expression that she was aware of his infidelity.

"So I see." She glanced at the spattered bill, then rose from her chair.

William removed his wet gloves with difficulty, then unfastened the chin strap of his helmet and dropped the heavy steel headgear onto a chair. "I should have sent word that I had landed, but I doubt if any messenger could have arrived here sooner than I."

She thought he looked haggard beneath his travel stains. He had certainly lost weight, and she noted irrelevantly that the strap of his helmet had left a mark on his face. "It doesn't matter." Mary made an effort to sound bright. "But I would have made preparations for you if I'd known."

They continued to stare at one another. "I don't deserve them," he said bluntly.

Mary's gaze faltered. "You've beaten the enemy in Ireland, you've destroyed his fleet, and you've forced him to abandon his plan to invade the United Provinces. I think you've accomplished marvels in these past weeks."

A wave of exhaustion made William feel ill. He closed his eyes for an instant, then opened them and looked straight at his wife. This was the worst crisis in their marriage, but he had to face it squarely; she probably wanted no more to do with him, but he would have to live with himself. "I've been unfaithful to you," he said hoarsely.

His bluntness was so startling that she was at a loss.

"I can see in your face that there's been gossip. I should have realized there would be talk, that a man in my position is under constant observation. If I'd had that much intelligence, I would have written to you. I don't know what you've been told, but I want you to hear the truth."

Mary shook her head. "Please—I'd rather you don't say anything about it."

"You have a right to know!"

"I—"

"I want you to know!" He had no idea he was shouting.

Mary gestured toward the door.

He realized that the sentries stationed in the corridor would overhear if he spoke loudly. He forced himself to lower his voice. "What I did in itself means nothing, if you can understand that. I committed an animal act with a whore. What is important is that I disgraced myself and humiliated you."

"Please, William—"

"I insist that you hear my reasons before you judge me. Something happened to me when Marshal Schomberg was killed. I spent all the rest of that day making certain that every man who died in the battle was given an honorable burial. Some of my officers thought I was mad, I suppose, and perhaps I was, but I refused to allow a common grave to be dug for the French dead. I insisted that they be given the same rights as the soldiers who had been killed fighting for me. Then, when I was making plans for the next battle, I received a report from Edward Russell. It wasn't very articulate, but the casualty figures spoke for themselves. I wondered if I had the right to order other men to fight—and die—for what I believe is a just cause. I even began to wonder if Louis is as sure of himself as he pretends to be. I had a strange feeling that with all his talk about the glory of France, there are moments when he realizes how much suffering he has caused. If that's true, then he wants to blot everything from his mind, as I did. That could be the reason he takes so many mistresses. He's been responsible for so much death, so much destruction. I've caused my share, too, and I couldn't let myself think about it. There was a woman available, so I took her. It was as simple as that. Or as complicated." He drew breath into his lungs, but couldn't seem to get enough of it.

Mary stood motionless before her husband. "I do understand," she said in a voice so low that it was difficult for him to hear her. "And I'm not judging you. I'm in no position to judge."

William blinked at her incredulously.

"Please, shall we sit down?"

"You sit, if you wish." He waved her toward his chair behind the desk. "I prefer to stand." Actually, his legs were aching, but he had no idea what Mary was going to reveal to him, and he preferred to take the blow with his feet planted far apart.

"You're stronger than I am, and more courageous." She was looking at a worn spot in the rug that she had never noticed before. With a great effort she raised her head. "There are some things I've been trying to tell you for the past year, but I've been too cowardly." She moved his helmet from the chair nearest her, sat abruptly, and held the headgear in her lap, unmindful of the drops of rain that fell from it and stained her gown of green silk.

William discovered that he was violently jealous, a feeling he had never before experienced, and his mood changed; no longer penitent, he became tense, suspicious, and possessive.

"I can imagine why you behaved as you did with that woman, because I had a somewhat similar experience." Mary saw the anger flare up in his eyes and became alarmed. "Technically," she added hastily, "I was faithful to you."

His sudden rage subsided, but he remained alert. Watching her, his eyes narrowed and his mouth compressed into a thin, hard line.

"Through no fault of my own, I wasn't seduced. I allowed myself to be placed in a very compromising situation. My escort could have done what he pleased, without censure, but he was a gentleman."

"I heard rumors about an evening at Greenwich, but I paid no attention to them at the time," he said thoughtfully.

Mary nodded, and wanted to cover her face with her hands. "That was the night."

He tried to recall the name of the courtier who had, as he remembered the story, disappeared with her for a half-hour or more, but he had refused to believe the gossip when it had been brought to his attention, and it occurred to him now that the identity of the man was as unimportant as that of the girl he had taken to bed in Ireland. Far more vital matters were at stake, he sensed, and he realized that the future of his marriage depended on how he conducted himself here and now.

"I ask only one favor," Mary whispered. "I encouraged him, but he treated me better than I deserved, and he did me no harm. So please don't punish him too severely. He has served you loyally for a long time."

William took a deep breath. "Does this man mean so much to you?"

Mary was able to look him in the eye at last. "He means nothing to me now, nor has he at any time in the past."

It was strange, William thought, that his knees should tremble and his legs feel so heavy. He decided to sit, after all. Without thinking, he moved to his own chair behind the desk, not bothering to glance at the tapestry-padded back in which he usually took so much pride. Neither the English lion nor the crest of Orange meant anything to him at this moment, and he did not see the gold-stitched inscription, WILLIAM III.

"In that case," he said in a strained voice, "I prefer not to hear his name."

"But—"

"The subject is closed."

Tears welled up in Mary's eyes, blurring her vision, and she brushed them away impatiently with the back of her hand.

"I've come to know you fairly well, and you certainly haven't inherited the Stuart leaning toward promiscuity, if my impressions are correct." William spoke briskly, biting off his words. "I've explained, to the best of my ability, why I made a fool of myself in Ireland. I assume you had a reason for abandoning your personal code of ethics, too."

"I did." Mary sobbed, and the room was very quiet as she fought for self-control. Somewhere in the distance an officer shouted commands and heavy boots thudded on cobblestones as the guard changed, but she was aware of no sound except the gentle splash of rain against the glass of the leaded windows. "I had been worried for a long time because I'd never conceived a baby." Her voice seemed remote and muffled, like that of a stranger. "I called in the best physicians in the country and submitted to their examination. They told me I'm not capable of bearing a child."

In spite of his weariness, William rose, went to her, and stood before her, his thumbs hooked in his belt. "Did it mean so much to you to have a child?"

His voice was so soft and gentle now that Mary wanted to look up at him, but she dared not. She tried to speak, then simply nodded.

"Why?" William asked in the same quiet tone.

She could produce only a strangled, inarticulate sound.

"Oh, I know the usual reasons," he said, "and I felt the same way. I hated the idea of seeing your sister become Queen after we're both gone, and I resented the thought of my cousin becoming stadholder of the United Provinces. But I've been corresponding with him since I first really came to know him last year, and he seems to be exceptionally intelligent. I've even thought of inviting him here so we can become better acquainted with him."

Mary raised her tear-stained face. She finally found her voice. "You've known, then, that I can't give you an heir?"

"It's been evident for some time. The physicians' findings simply confirm what I believed for years." He paused, and as he looked at her he found it was remarkably easy to admit the existence of an emotion he had long denied. "You still haven't told me why it meant so much to bear my child," he said.

Mary smiled at him tremulously.

The expression he read in her eyes, shy, yet at the same time positive and unequivocal, gave him an insight into his own problems and helped him to realize that his eighteen-year struggle against France had not been in vain. Understanding, he thought, had been waiting for recognition just below the surface of his mind, and at last he was able to see himself and his responsibilities in their true perspective.

"Will it help," he asked, "if I explain some things to you?"

She did not dare let herself hope that the dream she had cherished since she had been fifteen was going to materialize.

"The beliefs of men," William said, "are more important than anything else in this world. Socrates drank a cup of hemlock rather than sacrifice his principles, and Jesus was crucified. Their ideas, their concepts of right and wrong, of justice and truth, have survived for centuries." He hesitated, pondered, and continued more confidently. "Yes, and a girl in France was burned at the stake because she rebelled against tyranny and prejudice and terror."

Mary, still thinking about her inability to bear children, was puzzled.

William took her hand and held it. "Joan of Arc was a maiden, but all of us have inherited her ideas. Only the French, ironically, seem to have forgotten why she died. Did Socrates and Xanthippe have children? I think not, but it was he who first defined our concepts of freedom and dignity. And all of us are the sons and daughters of Jesus, or we wouldn't be striving to create a society based on brotherly love and forgiveness."

She began to see what he meant. Her tears dried and her eyes became bright.

"Our devotion to the cause of liberty hasn't been wasted, and the men who have died, the men who have been wounded, the women who have suffered have all played a part in the destruction of evil. I don't know how much longer we'll have to fight, but we and our allies will continue to grow stronger, and eventually the tyrant will be defeated. It doesn't matter whether you and I have children of our own. The principles that we hold dear will spread from England and the United Provinces to other lands, and if we're remembered, it will be because we've helped mankind to walk without fear. It will not matter that no son of ours was crowned in Westminster Abbey and the Nieuwe Kerk."

Mary gazed up at him silently, and only the tightening of her fingers in his grasp indicated that she was absorbing all that he said.

For a moment he became quiet, too, then he drew her up from her chair and put his arms about her. He knew that never again would he feel awkward in her presence. "Would it help," he asked, "if I tell you that without you I would not have the courage or strength to continue the fight? It's a little late for this, perhaps, but would it help if I tell you that I finally realize I've loved you for years, and will, as long as we live?"

Mary rested her head against his chest, sighed quietly, and was at peace. "Yes," she said. "It does more than help. It is all I want."

PREFACE

'It is perhaps, then, rather a duty than a piece of presumption for those who have had experience in word-judging to take any opportunity . . . of helping things on by irresponsible expressions of opinion.'

MEU: NEEDLESS VARIANTS

A Dictionary of Modern English Usage, by H. W. Fowler, was first published in 1926. Its author, ex-schoolmaster, classicist, and lexicographer, had started work on it, in collaboration with his brother, in 1911. The First World War intervened, and in 1918 Francis George Fowler died; H. W. Fowler completed the project alone. Today 'MEU' remains one of the most loved, and most provocative, reference books, as indispensable as a dictionary, in America as well as in England. Fowler not only teaches you how to write; he is a demon on your shoulder, teaching you how not to write, pointing out and exhibiting, with terrifying clarity, your most cherished foibles: Love of the Long Word, Elegant Variation, Genteelism, Pedantry, Battered Ornaments. To tamper with Fowler has taken both humility and courage—or perhaps foolhardiness—born of the quotation given above.

New words and idioms have come into the language since the publication of *Modern English Usage;* there are peculiarities of American speech and writing not recorded by Fowler; and many of us today, English and American, have neither the time nor the scholarship to follow through the fascinating but sometimes exasperating labyrinth of Greek and Latin parallels and Fowler's Socratic method of teaching by wrong examples. *American-English Usage* is an adaptation of MEU, not a replacement. AEU is a simplified MEU, with American variations, retaining as much of the original as space allowed. Many of the longer articles had to be shortened, many of the more academic ones and those less pertinent to usage today were omitted, to make room for new entries and illustrations. Fowler's own mannerisms and pedantries—and I am sure he would have been the last to deny them—have been left untouched. There was a temptation sometimes to soften the sting of 'illiterate,' 'journalese,' 'lady novelists,' 'uneducated writers'; perhaps Fowler himself would have tempered some of them had he revised his book, but only Fowler could decide that. They have been left as he wrote them.

It would be impossible to list the names of the many people whom I have consulted about the new material—specialists, friends, even casual acquaintances who have allowed me to interpose discussions of British and American usage at the most inappropriate times; I thank them for their help and their patience. I am deeply grateful to the Clarendon Press, England, and to Oxford University Press, New York, for allowing me to undertake this work in the first place, and to the staff of Oxford, New York, for its help and encouragement during the time the book was going through the press. I want to thank specifically Mr. R. W. Chapman, lately Secretary to the Delegates of the Clarendon Press, for his painstaking work in reading the first draft of the manuscript and for his many comments and suggestions, made with the wisdom and delicacy of wit that characterizes MEU. I also want to thank Mr. Henry Z. Walck of Oxford, New York, for his part in the conception of the project and for his continuing faith that brought it to a completion. Any errors and pitfalls that I have not avoided are my own.

A NOTE ON PRONUNCIATION: I have made no attempt to indicate general differences in English and American pronunciation—for example, the differences in pronouncing broad *a*, final *e*, short *o*, and the hard or slurred *r*—differences of this kind obtain within the United States itself, and also in different sections of the United Kingdom. Fowler says 'Pronounce as your neighbors do'; some of us on this side of the Atlantic could wish when we hear Englishmen and Americans speaking side by side—statesmen perhaps, or commentators or entertainers—that our neighbors would articulate a little more precisely, that *manufacture* were not pronounced as if it were spelled *mana-*, or that they recognized some difference in the value of the *a* in *cat, path,* and *laugh;* but that is not a matter for this book. The differences in English and American pronunciation that are given are not to express preference or censure, but to give the accepted pronunciation of each country.

If I could dedicate this book, and if it were not impertinent in the circumstances to think of doing so, I should dedicate it to the memory of Henry Watson Fowler, born 1858, died 1933. Since I must not, my hope is that AEU will be an instrument to lead some of the new generation who have not yet discovered it to the joys of *Modern English Usage.*

M. N.

Hillsdale, New York
29 *July* 1956

ABBREVIATIONS

ACD, *American College Dictionary*
Cent. Dict. & Cyclo., *Century Dictionary and Cyclopedia*
COD, *Concise Oxford Dictionary*
D.N.B., *Dictionary of National Biography*
Ency. Brit., *Encyclopedia Britannica*
Mencken, *The American Language*
MEU, *Modern English Usage* (Fowler)
Sat. Rev., *Saturday Review* (*of Literature*)
Webster, *Webster's New International Dictionary* (Abridged; Unabridged)

abbr., abbreviate, -ation
abs., absolute
adj., adjective, -ally
adv., adverb(ial)
Antiq., Antiquity
arch., archaic, -ism
Arch., Architecture
attrib., attributive(ly)
Bot., Botany
Brit., British (usage), Great Britain
c., century
c., circum
cap., capital(ize)
Chin., Chinese
colloq., colloquial(ly), -ism
conj., conjunction
constr., construe, -uction
d., died
derog., derogatory, -ially
dial., dialect(al)
dim., diminutive
Eccl., Ecclesiastical
ellip., elliptical
Eng., England, English
erron., erroneous(ly)
esp., especial(ly)
est., established (usage)
etym., etymology, -ically
exc., except
facet., facetious(ly)
F., Fr., French, France
fem., feminine, female
fig., figurative(ly)
fr., from
gen., general(ly)
Ger., German(y)
Gr., Greek
gram., grammar
Hist., History, -orical
Hort., Horticulture
indic., indicative
ind. obj., indirect object
inf., infinitive
It., Italy, -ian
L., Lat., Latin
lit., literal(ly); literature, -ary
Log., Logic
m., masculine
Med., Medicine
med. Lat., medieval Latin
Mil., Military
mod., modern
MS., MSS., manuscript(s)
Mus., Music
n., nn., noun(s)
Naut., Nautical
Nav., Naval
N.T., New Testament
obj., object(ive)
obs., obsolete
opp., opposite, opposed to
orig., origin(ally)
O.T., Old Testament
part., participle, -ipial
pers., person
pl., plural
Poet., Poetry, Poetics
poss., possessive
p.p., past participle
pref., prefer(ably), -red
prep., preposition
pron., pronounce(d); pronoun
prop., proper(ly)
R.C., Roman Catholic(s), -ism
rel., relative
Rhet., Rhetoric
sing., singular
Sp., Spain, Spanish
spec., specific(ally)
subj., subjunctive; subject
syn., synonym(ous)
trans., transitive
transf., transferred (senses)
unnec., unnecessary
v., vv., verb(s)
var., variant
vulg., vulgar(ly), -ism
&, and
&c., et cetera

Words in small capitals (e.g. GENTEELISM) refer to the article of that name (or e.g. WRONG to a usage not recommended).

KEY TO PRONUNCIATION

Pronunciation is given only for words that are unfamiliar or are often mispronounced. If only one syllable or the stress is in question, the other syllables may not be marked or may be omitted. For the pronunciation of FRENCH WORDS, see that article; of Latin words, see LATIN PRONUNCIATION. See also the article PRONUNCIATION, and the Note on pronunciation in the Preface.

VOWELS

a: māte, răck, stigm*a*, fäther, dȧnce, mâre, chåotic

e: mēte, rĕck, sil*e*nt, dêpend, makẽr

i: mīte, rĭck, cous*i*n

o: mōte, rŏck, *c*ontain, fôrbear, tôbacco

u: mūte, rŭck, s*u*bmit, ûrn, ûnited, ü (as Fr. *eu* in *coiffeur*)

ah: *bah;* aw: *law;* o͞o: *mo͞ot;* o͝o: *ro͝ok;* oi: *noise;* ow: *cow;* ou: *bough*

CONSONANTS USED IN RE-SPELLING

g (hard) as in *get*

h (aspirate) as in *hat*

j (soft *g*) as in *just, gest*

k (hard *c*) as in *kid, cat*

ng as in *singer*

ngg as in *finger*

y as in *yes*

s (sibilant, soft *c*) as in *said, city*

z (soft or voiced *s*) as in *fiz, music*

zh (g, *s, z*) as in *rouge, fusion, azure*

LIST OF GENERAL ARTICLES

N.B. *Webster's New International Dictionary* (Webster) and *The American College Dictionary* (ACD) have been cited in the text not because they are necessarily recommended as the best of the many available American dictionaries, but because they best reflect the contrast between traditional American spelling, pronunciation, and usage on the one hand and the modern, more liberal usage on the other.

A DICTIONARY OF AMERICAN-ENGLISH USAGE

A

a, an. 1. *A* is used before all consonants except silent *h* (*a history, an hour*). *An* was formerly the rule before an unaccented syllable beginning with *h* (*an habitual topic of conversation, an historical novel, an hotel*); the first two are still widely used in speech, less widely in writing. Since the *h* is now pronounced, *an* is usually nostalgic or pedantic.

2. The combinations of *a* with *few* & *many* are a matter of arbitrary but established usage: *a few, a great many, a good many* are idiomatic, but *a good few* is now facetious or colloq.; *a very few* is permissible but *an extremely few* is not; see FEW.

3. *A, an,* follow the adjectives *many, such,* & *what* (*many an artist, such a task, what an infernal bore!*); they also follow any adjective preceded by *as* or *how* (*I am as good a man as he; I knew how great a labor he had undertaken*), & usually any adjective preceded by *so* (*so resolute an attempt; a so resolute attempt* is also English, but suggests affectation); they often follow any adjective preceded by *too* (*too exact an,* or *a too exact, adherence to instructions*). The late position should not be adopted with other words than *as, how, so, too.* NOT: *which was quite sufficient an indication./Can anyone choose more glorious an exit?/Have before them more brilliant a future;* the normal order (*a quite* or *quite a sufficient, a more glorious, a far more brilliant*) is also the right one.

4. *A, an,* are sometimes ungrammatically inserted, especially after *no* (adj.), to do over again work that has already been done; NOT *No more signal* a *defeat was ever inflicted; no= not a,* & the *a* before *defeat* must be omitted; NOT *The defendant was no other* a *person than Mr. Disraeli,* but *no other person than . . .*

5. *A*+(noun)+*or two* takes a plural verb: *a year or two* are *needed for research;* but *a year or so* is *needed.*

abbreviate makes *abbreviable.*

abdomen. Traditionally pron. ăbdō′men; US dictionaries recognize ăb′dōmen also, but the former is here recommended.

abetter, -or. The *-or* ending always in legal contexts & more usual in others.

abide. Formerly, *abide, abode, abidden;* now usually *abided,* or (rarely US) *abode* for past & p.p. (*abidden* rare or poetic). *He abided* (or *has abided*) *by the terms of the contract.* In the sense 'tolerate,' 'put up with,' in use since the 16th c. but now heard only in the negative: *I can't* or *can scarcely abide it.*

abject. Pron. ab′-. For *my abject apologies,* see HACKNEYED PHRASES.

abjection, abjectness. There is little differentiation between the two, but the first is perhaps more usual for the condition, the second for the state of mind. *The women of Europe have never sunk to the* abjection *of the women of the East./He could look to God without* abjectness, *and on man without contempt.*

abjure, adjure. *Abjure* means to renounce an oath, forswear, repudiate: *abjure allegiance, abjure a former belief.* *Adjure* means to command solemnly, to appeal to or entreat (someone) earnestly, as if under oath: *I adjured him to stand on the truth.* *Adjure* is always followed by an infinitive or by a substantive clause.

-able, -ible, &c. The suffix *-able* is a living one & may be appended to any transitive verb to make an adjective. If the verb ends in a silent *e*, this is dropped except after a soft *c* or *g* (*usable, likable, pronounceable, manageable*).

Verbs ending in *-ate* that have established adjectives drop the *-ate* (*demonstrable, abominable,* &c.) & new adjs. should be similarly formed except when the verb is of two syllables (*accumulate* makes *accumulable, adulterate, adulterable,* but *dictate, dictatable, locate, locatable*). Nonce adjectives in *-able* may be formed even from those verbs whose established representatives are in *-ible* &c., especially when the established word has to some extent lost the verbal or contracted a special sense. Thus a mistake may be called *uncorrectable,* because *incorrigible* has become ethical in sense; *solvable* may be preferred because *soluble* has entered into an alliance with *dissolve;* & *destroyable by dynamite* may seem less pedantic than *destructible by.* The principle is that the normal form *-able* should be used when there is no objection to it. There is an objection when a word is itself well established with *-ible* &c. in general use, & therefore *digestable, perceivable,* are not to be substituted for *digestible* & *perceptible.* There is also an objection, though a less forcible one, when, though the word itself is not established in the *-ible* form, it is one of a set that includes an established word in *-ible.* Thus *incontrovertible* & *convertible* should decide the form *avertible, divertible, pervertible,* &c.; *digestible,* that of *suggestible;* in favor of *adducible, educible, producible,* &c., there is added to the influence of (*ir*)*reducible* & *deducible* a legitimate dislike to the ugly forms in *-eable.*

aboard. Originally on board, or into or onto a ship, & still sometimes so restricted in England; but generally it is now used also of trains & even busses and planes.

abolishment, abolition. There is no real difference in meaning & *abolishment* should not be used without careful consideration. If *abolition* is not wanted, *abolishing* (n.) will usually do.

A-bomb, atomic bomb, atom bomb. All three forms are used; the second is the original & is better in formal writing.

aborigines. The word being still pronounced with a consciousness that it is Latin (i.e. with ēz), the (etymologically unjustifiable) sing. *aborigine* (-nē), though gaining in popularity even among scholars, is still avoided or disliked by many; the adj. *aboriginal* used as a noun is the best singular.

about. In the sense *almost* (*he is about frozen*) still colloq. *It is about* (i.e. fig. *in the vicinity of*) 9:30 is established idiom. (But NOT *it is about* 9 or 10.)

above. Adv.: *The heavens above; the above-mentioned article;* prep.: *situated above the peaks; authority above that of civil law.* Although modern usage sanctions *above* as adj. & noun also, the (elliptical?) use (*the above argument; the above is my conviction*) is still avoided by careful writers. Recommended: *the foregoing argument*, or *the argument given above; the above-mentioned theory, the theory given above*, &c.

abridg(e)ment. The shorter form is preferred in the US & generally in Brit., although Oxford prefers the longer form. *Abridgeable* is given precedence in the US, whereas the OED lists *abridgable* first. A work is an *abridgment of* another, or *abridged from* another.

abrogate makes *-gable.*

absence. For *conspicuous by his absence* see HACKNEYED PHRASES.

absent, adj. & v. The accent of the adj. is on the first syllable, of the verb generally on the second. *Absent-minded, absent-mindedness,* so spelled.

absentee (n. & adj.) makes *absenteeism.*

absolute. (1) The use of *ab'solutely* for *very, absolute'ly* for *yes,* emphatic, are chiefly (US?) colloq. (2) For *In these pages they* absolutely *live,* see LITERALLY. (3) Grammar. An adj. or transitive verb is *absolute* when the adj. has no noun or the verb no object. *Fortune favors the brave; if looks could kill.*

absolute construction. Punctuation. *The king having read his speech, their majesties retired.* NOT *The king, having read* &c. The insertion of a comma between noun & participle in the absolute use is wrong. It arises from the writer's taking the noun, because it happens to stand first, for the subject of the main verb. Frequent use of the absolute construction gives a heaviness of style; it is best used sparingly.

ABSOLUTE POSSESSIVES. Under this term are included the words *hers, ours, theirs,* & *yours,* & (except in the archaic attributive-adjective use, as *thine eyes*) *mine* & *thine.* A mistake is often made when two or more possessives are to be referred to a single noun that follows the last of them. NOT *yours and ours and his efforts;* the correct forms are: *your & our & his efforts; either my or your informant must have lied* (NOT *mine*); *her & his mutual dislike* (NOT *hers*); *our without your help will not avail* (NOT *ours*). There is no doubt a natural temptation to substitute the wrong word; the simple possessive seems to pine at separation from its property. The true remedy is a change of order: *your efforts & ours & his; my informant or yours; our help without yours.* It is not always available, however; *her & his mutual dislike* must be left as it is.

absorbedly. Four syllables.

abstemious, abstinent. *Abstemious* (originally 'from wine') signifies habitual moderation in the gratification of appetite (particularly for wine & food). *Abstinent* (from *abstinence,* the refraining from gratification) may be of a single act or a general refraining from indulgence, *an abstinent enjoyment of life.*

abstract (adj.), **abstracted** (part. adj.). *Abstract* carries the significance of being withdrawn from material embodiment (as opposed to *concrete*); ideal, or abstruse, theoretical: *abstract reasoning, truth, speculations. Abstracted,* directly from the verb, 'withdrawn, removed,' now has the meaning withdrawn from contemplation of present objects, absent in mind: *He was in an abstracted mood; an abstracted gaze.*

absurd. The *s* pronunciation is preferred (NOT abzurd).

abysmal, abyssal. The first is the rhetorical word (*abysmal ignorance, degradation, bathos*); *abyssal,* formerly used in the same way, has now been appropriated as a technical term meaning 'of the bottom of the ocean,' or of a depth greater than 300 fathoms.

a cappella. In chapel style, i.e. unaccompanied (of vocal music). So spelled; ital.

accent(uate). In fig. senses (draw attention to, emphasize, make conspicuous, &c.) the long form is now much the commoner; in literal senses (sound or write with an accent), though either will pass, the short prevails; & the DIFFERENTIATION is worth encouraging.

acceptance, acceptation. The words, once used indifferently in several senses, are now fully differentiated. *Acceptation* means only the interpretation put on something (*the word in its proper acceptation means 'love'; the various acceptations of the doctrine of the Trinity*), while *acceptance* does the ordinary work of a verbal noun for *accept* (*find acceptance,* be well received; *beg* or *ask one's acceptance of,* ask him to accept; cf. *ask his acceptation of the terms*=ask how he understands; *endorses my acceptance of the terms,* agrees with me in accepting them; cf. *endorses my acceptation of them,* agrees with my view of their drift).

accepter, -or. The first form is now generally used for one who accepts. The second (earlier) form is the legal term, one who accepts, or undertakes the payment of, a bill of exchange.

accept of. This, formerly used almost as widely as the simple verb, is now restricted to the meaning consent to receive as a gift or benefit or possession. We can still *accept of a gift* or *favor, of a person's love* or *company,* & the like, though even these phrases tend to become archaic. But a theory, an emendation, advice, an apology, an invitation, we only accept.

access, accession. There are probably, in modern usage, no contexts in which one of these can be substituted for the other without the meaning's being modified. With regard to arriving, *accession* means arrival, *access* opportunity of arriving; accordingly *accession to the throne* means becoming sovereign, *access to the throne* opportunity of petitioning the sovereign; we can say *His access to fortune was barred,* or *His accession to fortune had not yet taken place,* but not the converse. The idea of increase, often present in *accession,* is foreign to *access; an access of fury, fever, joy, despair,* &c., is a fit or sudden attack of it, which may occur whatever the previous state of mind may have been, whereas *an accession of* any of them can only mean a heightened degree of the one that already existed; *our forces have had no accession,* have not been augmented in numbers, *have had no access,* have not been able to enter.

accessary, accessory. (Accent preferably -cess'ory.) Etymologically *accessary* is the noun, *accessory* the adj., but present US usage favors the latter for both.

accidentally. So spelled. *Accidently,* also an early form, is now obs.

acclimatize, acclimate, &c. *Acclimatize, acclimatization,* are the forms for which Brit. general usage seems to have decided; *acclimate, acclimation,* are more general in US. Pron. aklīm′atīz; both aklī′māt & ak′limāt are acceptable, but most US dictionaries give aklī′māt first.

accommodate, so spelled.

accompan(y)ist. The shorter form is now more prevalent in US, but either is permissible.

accord, account. The phrases are *of one's own accord, on one's own account;* NOT *of one's own account.* See CAST-IRON IDIOM.

according as means 'just as,' 'in a manner corresponding to the way in which.' Thus, *According as bodies become transparent they cease to be visible.* *According to* means 'in a manner agreeing with': *According to our ideas, this was the worst thing he could do.* *Accordingly as* means *according as,* but is obsolescent. There is a tendency to repeat the phrase *according as* (like BETWEEN), with a mistaken idea of making the construction clearer, in contexts where the repetition is not merely needless but wrong. NOT *The big production will be harmful or the reverse,* according as *it can command the Government to insure it a monopoly in all circumstances,* or according as it *works with the knowledge that, if it abuses its trust, the door is freely open to the competing products of other countries.* The second *according as it* should be omitted. *Or according as* is legitimate only when what is to be introduced is not the necessarily implied alternative or the other extreme of the same scale, but another scale or pair of alternatives. RIGHT: *Man attains happiness or not* according as *he deserves it or not.* (NOT *according as he deserves it* or according as he does *not deserve it*); but (RIGHT) *according as he deserves it* or according as he *can digest his food.*

accouchement &c. An established euphemism (*confinement,* also a euphemism, at least has the virtue of being English). Pron. ăkoosh′mĕnt or as Fr.

account. Unlike *regard,* & like *consider,* this verb does not in good modern usage admit of *as* before its complement; *I account it a piece of good fortune* (NOT *as a piece*); *you are accounted wise* or *a wise man.*

accouter, accoutre. Pron. ă kōō′ter. US usually *accouter, -tered, -tering;* Brit. *-re, -tred, -tring.* So *accouterment* (pron. -terment) *accoutrement* (pron. -trement).

accumulate makes *-lable.*

accumulative. The word, formerly common in various senses, has now given place to *cumulative* in most of them, retaining in ordinary use only the sense 'given to accumulating property, acquisitive.'

accursed, accurst. The *-ed* spelling is more prevalent in the US, except in poetic use. Whatever the spelling, the pronunciation is usually *this accursed* (ak ur′sed) *hour; of all men accurst* or *accursed* (akurst′).

accusal. An old but unnecessary form; *accusation* has the same meaning & is the more usual word.

accuse. *Accuse a person of* a thing; charge him *with* a thing.

achieve implies successful effort. Its use as a FORMAL WORD for getting or reaching should be avoided, e.g. *on achieving manhood.*

acid test. From testing for (the presence of) gold; transf. test of the value, genuineness, of something. Overused and often misused. See POPULARIZED TECHNICALITIES.

acknowledg(e)ment. Standard US & Brit. usage supports the shorter form (COD prefers the longer). *Acknowledgeable* retains the *e.*

acoustic. Pronunciation varies between -ow- & oo; in US oo is preferred. The noun *acoustics,* the science of sound, is both sing. & pl., but is usually treated as sing.

acquaintanceship is a NEEDLESS VARIANT for acquaintance. See RELATIONSHIP.

acreage. So spelled.

acronym. A word formed from initial letters of a phrase or title; WAC, loran, NATO, Unesco.

act, v. In the sense 'behave like,' the word, once used as freely as *play,* has contracted a slangy or colloquial tone, & is now more appropriate in such expressions as *act the giddy goat* than in *act the philosopher, lover, child,* or even *fool,* in all of which *play* is better.

act, action. The distinction between the two words is not always clear. The natural idea that *act* should mean the thing done, & *action* the doing of it, is not even historically quite true, but it has influence enough to prevent *act* from being commonly used in the more abstract senses. We can speak only of the action, not the act, of a machine, when we mean the way it acts; & *action* alone has the collective sense, as in *his action throughout* (i.e. his acts or actions as a whole) *was correct;* there are also other senses in which there is obviously no choice open. In contexts that do admit of doubt, it may be said generally that *action* tends to displace *act.* If we were making the phrases for the first time now, we should probably prefer *action* in *The Acts of the Apostles, By the act of God, Be great in act as you have been in thought, I deliver this as my act & deed.* This tendency, however, is by no means always effective; it is indifferent, for instance, whether we say we are *judged by our acts* or *by our actions;* there is no appreciable difference between *it was an act,* & *it was an action, that he was to regret bitterly.* And in certain contexts *act* more than holds its ground: (1) In the sense 'deed of the nature of': *it would be an act* (never *action*) *of folly, cruelty, mercy,* &c.; similarly in the sense 'deed characteristic of': *it was the act* (rarely *action*) *of a fool* (cf. *the actions of a fool cannot be foreseen,* where the sense is not characteristic deed, but simply deed). On the other hand, when for *of folly* or *of a fool* &c. *foolish* &c. is substituted, *action* is commoner than *act—a cruel, kind, foolish, noble, action* or *act.* (2) In the sense 'instant of doing': *caught in the act, was in the very act of jumping.* (3) In antithesis with *word, thought,* *plan*, &c., when these mean rather every word, every thought, a particular plan, than speech, thinking, planning: *faithful in word & act* (but *in speech & action*); *innocent in thought & act* (but *supreme in thought & action*); *the act was mine, the plan yours* (but *a strategy convincing in plan, but disappointing in action*).

actuate, activate. *Actuate* is now confined to the senses to move, impel, act upon the will: *actuated by the best motives. Activate* is the scientific and technical word, to make active (Chem.), set up or institute formally (Mil.); so *activate the muscles* (Med.). For *The Council* will be activated *with Mr. — in charge, to continue until further notice*, see POPULARIZED TECHNICALITIES.

acuity, acuteness. The longer form is the better & more general in both formal & literary usage. The shorter is largely confined to science & technical use.

acumen. Pron. ă kū′mĕn.

A.D., Anno Domini. Properly 'in the year of (our) Lord . . .' should be followed, not preceded, by the year in question, A.D. 1960, but the misuse (1960 A.D.) is so frequent as to be almost established. Also, it must be a specific year, NOT e.g. *the tenth century* A.D. B.C., however ('Before Christ'), follows the year or years, 25 B.C., & may follow a century or era.

adagio. Pl. *-os.*

ad captandum. (Rhet.): 'For catching [the common herd, *vulgus*].' Applied to unsound, specious arguments. *An* ad captandum *presentation of facts.*

addable, addible. Capable of being added. Both forms have existed since the 16th c.; *-able* is recommended.

addendum. Pl. *-a.*

addicted to. This should be followed by an ordinary noun or a verbal noun in *-ing* (*is addicted to whisky, is addicted to reading jokes aloud*) & never by an infinitive, as in *is addicted to read the jokes aloud.* The wrong construction, which occasionally occurs, is probably suggested by the commonest phrase, *addicted to drink,* in which *drink* is the noun.

addle, addled. The adjectival use of *addle* as in *an addle egg, his brain is addle,* is correct, & was formerly common; but to prefer it now to the usual *addled* is a DIDACTICISM. It still prevails, however, in compounds, as *addle-pate, addle-brained.*

address. Traditional usage places the stress on the second syllable for both noun & verb, but it is now often on the first syllable in US, esp. when the direction for delivery on a letter &c. is meant. See RECESSIVE ACCENT.

adducible, -eable. Use *-ible.*

adequate means equal to or sufficient (for some specific purpose) and should not be followed by *enough.* Constr. *to: A remedy not adequate to the disease.*

adherence, adhesion. The tendency is to confine *adherence* to the fig. use (mental or moral attachment), & *adhesion* to the literal (physical attachment). *Adherence to a fixed plan; adhesion of oysters to the rock.* The fig. sense of *adhesion* remains, however, in the established phrase *give in one's adhesion to a party,* &c., i.e. join as a supporter.

adieu. Now generally anglicized in pronunciation and the formation of the plural (*-s*): pron. ä dū′(z).

adjudge. To adjudicate upon, pronounce judicial sentence, award judicially, condemn (a person to a penalty, &c.). As a syn. for *judge, deem, hold,* it is obs.

adjudicate makes *-cable.*

administratrix. Pl. *-tratrices* (-trā′-).

admission, -ittance, -issible, -ittable. Of the nouns, *admission* is used in all senses (*No admittance* is perhaps the only phrase in which the substitution of *admission* would be noticed), while *admittance* is confined to the primary sense of letting in, & even in that sense tends to disappear. *You have to pay for admission* is now commoner than *for admittance,* & so with *What is needed is the admission of outside air; Admission* $2 is now the regular form; on the other hand *Such an* admittance (instead of *admission*) *would give away the case* is now impossible. The difference between the adjectives is that *admissible* is the established word, & *admittable,* though formerly current, is now regarded as merely made for the occasion, & used only when the connection with *admit* is to be clear; this is chiefly in the predicate, as *Defeat is admittable by anyone without dishonor.*

admit of. This combination, formerly used indifferently with *admit* in several senses, is now restricted to the sense 'present an opening' or 'leave room for,' & to impersonal nouns usually of an abstract kind as subject: *His veracity admits of no question* (but NOT *I can admit of no question*); *A hypothesis admits by its nature of being disputed* (but NOT *He admits of being argued with*).

admonishment, admonition. No real differentiation of meaning; *admonition* is the normal word in present usage.

adopted, adoptive. The incorrect use of *adopted* with *parents, father, mother,* &c., is to a certain extent excused by such allowed attributive uses as *the condemned cell;* that is the cell of the condemned, & the *adopted father* is the father of the adopted. But, while *condemned* saves a clumsy paraphrase, *adopted* saves only the trouble of remembering *adoptive.*

adult. The traditional pronunciation is *a*dult′, n. & adj. Ad′ult is heard increasingly often in US, esp. for the noun.

adulterate makes *-rable.*

adumbrate. Preferred pron. (US), ădŭm′- (ăd′ŭm- is also permissible & is preferred by COD).

adumbration: A representation in outline, a faint description, hence fig. a foreshadowing. A favorite of those who prefer not to say things simply (*Adumbrations of things to come in the field of mathematics are evident throughout the State Education Department*); see LOVE OF THE LONG WORD.

advance guard. Mil., a guard before or in front of the main troops (NOT *advanced guard*). *Avant-garde* (Fr.), in any art, the innovators & experimentalists. Pron. ävän(t)′ gärd.

advance(ment). Apart from a verbal noun use with *of* following, & from a technical sense in law, *advancement* has only the sense of preferment or promotion, never the more general one of progress. There are no contexts in which *advancement* can be substituted for *advance* without damage to or change in the sense; NOT *It will not be by the setting of class against class that* advancement *will be made* (use *advance*). It is true that both words can be used as verbal nouns of *to advance;* but *advance* represents its intransitive & *advancement* its transitive sense; *the advance of knowledge* is the way knowledge is advancing, whereas *the advancement of knowledge* is action taken to advance knowledge.

advantageous, adventitious. There is no reason for any confusion between the two words, but confusion does exist. *Advantageous* means favorable, useful, profitable; *adventitious* accidental, casual. *A decision advantageous to the Navy; an adventitious and external cause.* The occasional spelling *adventicious* is etymologically preferable but no longer customary.

adventurous, venturesome, adventuresome, venturous. Usage has decisively declared for the first two & against the last two. *Adventuresome* & *venturous,* when used, are due to either ignorance or avoidance of the normal.

ADVERBS. An adverb is a word (or phrase or clause) that modifies a verb, an adj., or another adv. The normal position of an adv. when used with a compound verb (e.g. *have seen*) is between the auxiliary (*have*) and the rest. *I have* never *seen her,* NOT *I* never *have seen her,* except for emphasis. The normal place for an adv. when used with a copulative verb (*is, are*) is between the verb & its complement: *It is* often *true; to be* fundamentally *wrong.* A transitive verb & its object should normally not be separated by the adv.: *Have they interpreted this situation* correctly?, NOT *Have they interpreted* correctly *this situation?* An infinitive should be split by the adv. only to clarify the meaning: *We must expect the committee* to at least neglect *our interests*—i.e. *not injure or oppose them.* For a complete discussion, see POSITION OF ADVERBS.

adverse. Unlike *averse,* this can be followed only by *to;* NOT *Politicians who had been very adverse* from *the Suez-Canal scheme.*

advertise. NOT *-ize. Advertisement,* accent traditionally on second syllable, though often on third in US.

adviser. Now properly so spelled. (Some US dictionaries include *advisor* as a variant.) Always *advisory.*

advocate. Unlike *recommend, propose, urge,* & other verbs, this is not idiomatically followed by a *that* clause, but only by an ordinary or a verbal noun. WRONG: *Dr. Felix Adler* advocates that *close attention be paid to any experiments;* RIGHT: *Dr. Adler urges that* &c. or *Dr. Adler* advocates the paying *of close attention to any experiments.*

Æ, Œ. These ligatures, of which the pronunciation is identical (ē), are also in some fonts of type so much alike that compositors often use one for the other & readers have their difficulties with spelling increased. It seems desirable that in the first place all words in common enough use to have begun to waver between the double letter & the simple *e*, as *phenomenon, pedagogy, medieval, ecumenical, penology* (a trend more general in US than in Brit.) should be written with the *e* alone; & secondly, in words that have not yet reached or can for special reasons never reach the stage in which the simple *e* is acceptable, *ae* and *oe* should be preferred to *æ* & *œ* (*Caesar, Oedipus;* the plurals and genitives of classical first-declension nouns, as *sequelae, Heraclidae, aqua vitae*). In French words like *chef-d'œuvre* the ligature *œ* must obviously be kept.

-AE, -AS, in plurals of nouns in *-a.* Most English nouns in *-a* are from Latin (or latinized Greek) nominative feminine singular nouns, which have in Latin the plural ending *-ae;* but not all; e.g. *sofa* is from Arabic; *stanza* & *vista* are from Italian; *subpoena* is not nominative; *drama* & *comma* are neuter; *stamina* & *prolegomena* are plural; & with all such words *-ae* is impossible. Of the majority, again, some retain the Latin *-ae* in English either as the only or as an alternative plural ending (*minutiae* only, *formulae* or *-las*), & some have always *-as* (*ideas, areas, villas*). The use of plurals in *-ae* therefore presents some difficulty to nonlatinists. For most words with which *-ae* is possible or desirable, the information is given in their dictionary places; for the principle of choice when both *-ae* & *-as* are current, see LATIN PLURALS.

aegis is preferred to *egis,* US & Brit.

aeon, æon, eon. The first is recommended.

aerate, aërate. The first is recommended. The form *ærated* is a mere blunder, but very common.

aerial, aërial. The first is recommended.

aeroplane. In US *airplane.*

aery, aerie, eyry, eyrie. The first two forms are preferable to the others, which are due to a theory of the derivation (from *egg; eyry=eggery*) that is known to be wrong.

aesthetic. More usual than *esthetic* (US & Brit.). The word means concerned with sensuous perception & was introduced into English to supply sense of beauty with an adjective. It is in place in such contexts as *aesthetic principles, from an aesthetic point of view, an aesthetic revival occurred.* It is less so in the meanings professing or gifted with this sense (*I am not aesthetic; aesthetic people*), dictated by or approved by or evidencing this sense (*a very aesthetic combination; aesthetically dressed; flowers on a table are not so aesthetic a decoration as a well-filled bookcase*); & still less so when it is little more than a pretentious substitute for *beautiful* (*that green is so aesthetic; a not very aesthetic little town*).

aestivate, aestivation. ('Summer-sleeping,' as opp. of *hibernate, hibernation.*) In US often *estivate, -tion.* Pron. ēs- or (US) often ĕs-.

aetat., aet. The words, being abbreviations of *aetatis suae* (of his, her, their, age) must be written with the period.

A.F. of L., A.F.L. (American Federation of Labor.) The latter is now more usual and is better printed without intervening space.

affect, effect. *Affect* (apart from other senses in which it is not liable to confusion with *effect*) means have an influence on, produce an effect on, concern, effect a change in; *effect* means bring about, cause, produce, result in, have as result. These verbs are not synonyms requiring differentiation, but words of totally different meaning, neither of which can ever be substituted for the other. *These measures chiefly* affect *the great landowners. It does not* affect *me. It may seriously* affect (i.e. injure) *his health. A single glass of brandy may* affect (alter for better or worse the prospects of) *his recovery. A single glass of brandy may* effect (bring about) *his recovery. This will not* affect (change) *his purpose. This will not* effect (secure) *his purpose. We hope to* effect *an improvement. I* effected *my escape.*

affiliate makes *-liable.*

affinity properly describes a reciprocal relation only. The prepositions normally used after this are, according to context, *between* & *with. The spiritual affinity* between *them; The sound of every instrument bears a perfect affinity* with *the rest.* When the sense is less relationship or likeness than attraction or liking, *to* or *for* are sometimes used instead of *with;* this should not be done. In places where *with* is felt to be inappropriate, the truth is that *affinity* has been used of a one-sided relation & should itself be replaced by another word. Cf. *sympathy with* & *for.*

affix. n. (Gram.): 'a thing fastened on.' A term including both prefixes and suffixes. *What is the stem when all affixes are removed?* Pron. affix′.

afflict, inflict. *I am* afflicted with *all the troubles in the world. He* inflicts *his troubles* on *me. His troubles* were inflicted on *me.*

à fond. Pron. äfawn′ or as Fr. It should be remembered that *à fond* & *au fond* mean different things, *à fond* to the bottom, i.e. thoroughly, & *au fond* at bottom, i.e. when one penetrates below the surface.

aforesaid. See PEDANTIC HUMOR.

a fortiori. (Logic): 'from yet firmer grounds.' Introducing a fact that, if one already mentioned is true, must also & still more obviously be true. *It could not have been finished in a week;* a fortiori *not in a day.*

afoul. Chiefly US: *Run afoul of the Internal Revenue Office.* (OED says 'prop. a phrase.') From *run foul of* (i.e. collide, become entangled with).

afraid. Constr. *lest, that,* inf., gerund. *We were afraid* lest we should *hurt them; afraid* that we might *hurt them; afraid* to hurt *them,* of hurting *them.*

after-effect, hyphen; *aftermath, afterthought,* single words.

afterward(s). *Afterward,* once the prevalent form, is now obs. in Brit. use, but survives in US.

again, against. US usually agĕn, Brit. agān. (The ĕ pronunciation is justified etymologically & historically.)

age. Often used interchangeably with *time, period* &c., *age* suggests a period identified by a dominant figure or marked characteristic: *The age of Pericles,* *the age of fishes in archeology, the Stone Age.* In mythology, Hesiod divides history into the Golden, Silver, Bronze, Heroic, and Iron ages. For synonymy, see TIME.

aged. Aged 54 or 54 years; NOT *aged* 54 *years old. An aged man* &c., ā′jed; *an aged horse,* ājd.

agenda. Although a plural (sing. *-um*) *agenda* is now often treated as a singular: *The* agenda *for the meeting* has *been distributed.* But *The most controversial* agendum *on the page; a correction is made in* agendum 6.

agent provocateur. 'Agent-provoker.' Agent employed to detect suspects by provoking them to overt action. Pl. *agents provocateurs.* A justifiable foreign importation since there is no exact English equivalent.

aggrandize(ment). The verb is preferably accented on the first syllable, the noun on the second.

aggravate, aggravation. *To aggravate* has properly only one meaning—to make (an evil) worse or more serious. Its use in the sense annoy, vex, is for the most part colloquial, but intrudes occasionally into the newspapers. RIGHT USE: *A premature initiative would be calculated rather to aggravate than to simplify the situation.* WRONG: *The reopening of the contest by fresh measures that would* aggravate their opponents *is the last thing that is desired.* It is in the participle (*and a very aggravating man he is*) that it is most frequently abused.

aggregate, v. *The load* aggregated *two tons.* This elliptical use in the sense 'amount in the aggregate of' is colloq. and should be avoided in writing.

agile. Pron. (US, & first in OED) ă′jĭl; (Brit.) ă′jīl.

aging. So spelled.

ago. If *ago* is used, & the event to be dated is given by a clause, it must be by one beginning with *that* & not *since.* RIGHT: *He died* 20 *years ago* (no clause); *It is* 20 *years since he died* (no *ago*); *It was* 20 *years ago* that *he died.* WRONG: *It is barely* 150 *years* ago since *it was introduced.* For similar mistakes, see HAZINESS.

agreeable. Constr. *to;* e.g. *conduct agreeable to our standard.* Its use followed by *with* is now obs.

agricultur(al)ist. Both forms are possible but the short one is recommended; the longer is in popular use in US (but not used by agriculturists themselves).

aid(e). In the sense 'helper, assistant' the English word (1596 on) was *aid; aide* was short for *aide-de-camp* (1670 to date in Brit. usage), an officer who assists the general (pl. *aides-de-camp*). The French spelling, however, is now firmly established in non-military use in US (*nurse's aide, aide to the chairman, aide of the Junior Senator*). *Assistant* and *helper* are both still good words.

aigrette, egret. The heron is usually *egret,* the ornamental plume or spray *aigrette.* Pron. ā′grĕt or -grĕt′.

aim. In Brit. the verb in the metaphorical sense of purpose or design or endeavor is idiomatically followed by *at* with the gerund. *Aim* followed by *to* with the infinitive is obs. in Brit. use, but survives in US. *He aimed* at *being* (US *he aimed* to be) *the power behind the throne* (the 'to be' constr.

is called in Brit. 'chiefly dial. or US'). *Aim for* is now chiefly colloq. (i.e. *We are aiming* for *complete enrollment*).

aîné. Elder (son) (cf. CADET). Used after proper names. Pron. ā'nā'.

ain't. *Ain't* used for *isn't* is illiterate; for its use for *am not*, see BE 7.

air-. In US *airplane* (Brit. *aeroplane*), *aircraft, airfield, airport, airtight*, single words; *air line, air raid, air mail* (Brit. *air post*), two words.

-AL NOUNS. There is a tendency to invent or revive unnecessary verbal nouns of this form. The many that have passed into common use (as *trial, arrival, refusal, acquittal, proposal*) have thereby established their right to exist. But when words of some age (as *revisal, refutal, appraisal* [q.v.], *accusal*) have failed to become really familiar & remained in the stage in which the average man cannot say with confidence offhand that they exist, the natural conclusion is that there is no work for them that cannot be adequately done by the more ordinary verbal nouns in *-ion* (*revision*), *-ation* (*refutation*), & *-ment* (*appraisement*). When there is need on an isolated occasion for a verbal noun that shall have a different shade of meaning from those that are current (e.g. *accusal* may suggest itself as fitter to be followed by an objective genitive than *accusation;* cf. *the accusal of a murderer, the accusation of murder*), or that shall serve when none already exists (there is e.g. no noun *beheadment*), it is better to make shift with the gerund (the *accusing*, the *beheading*) than to revive an unfamiliar *accusal* or invent *beheadal.* The use of rare or new *-al* nouns, however, is due only in part to a legitimate desire for the exactly appropriate form. To some writers the out-of-the-way word is dear for its own sake, or rather is welcome as giving an air of originality to a sentence that if ordinarily expressed would be detected as commonplace. They are capable of writing *bequeathal* for *bequest*, or *allowal* for *allowance.* Except for this dislike of the normal word, we should have had *account* instead of *recountal* in *Of more dramatic interest is the* recountal *of the mission imposed upon Sir James Lacaita. Surprisal, supposal, decrial* may be mentioned among the hundreds of needless *-al* words that have been actually used.

à la. The sex of the person whose name is introduced by this does not affect the form, *la* agreeing not with it but with an omitted *mode: à la reine; à la* (NOT *au*) *maître d'hôtel; a Home-rule Bill à la* (NOT *au*) *Gladstone. Au* with adjectives, as in *au naturel, au grand sérieux*, is not used in English except in phrases borrowed entire from French.

alamode has found its way into dictionaries, US & Brit., as est. spelling; *à la mode* nevertheless continues in good use.

alarm, alarum. *Alarum* is by origin merely a variant of *alarm*, & the two nouns were formerly used without distinction in all senses. In poetry *alarum* may still bear any of the senses except that of fear or apprehension; but in ordinary US usage, *alarm* is used in all senses. In Brit. use *alarum* is restricted to the senses of alarm signal, warning signal, or clock or other apparatus that gives these.

albeit. 'Even though.' (Pron. -bē'it.) To be used with care; see ARCHAISM.

albino. Pl. *-os;* pron. (US) ăl bīn'ō, (Brit.) ăl bē'no.

albumen, -in. *-en* the egg white; *-in* the proteins & in chemistry.

Algonquian, Algonkian (both pron. -kĭan), the (linguistic) family, made up of many tribes; *Algonquin* is an Indian tribe formerly north of Ottawa; *Algonkian* is also the geological name for pre-Cambrian rocks.

alibi (pl. *-is*) means 'elsewhere' (at the time under discussion). Hence, the plea of having been elsewhere. Used as *excuse* it is slang. RIGHT: *He established an alibi for Tuesday noon.* SLANG: *What's your alibi for not getting your work done?*

alien. The prepositions after the adj. are *from* & *to.* There is perhaps a slight preference for *from* where mere difference or separation is meant (*We are entangling ourselves in matter alien from our subject*), & for *to* when repugnance is suggested (*cruelty is alien to his nature*). But this distinction is usually difficult to apply, & the truth seems rather that *to* is getting the upper hand of *from* in all senses.

alienate makes *-nable.*

alight. The past & p.p. are *alighted* in ordinary use; but in poetry *alit* has been written by Byron, Shelley, & Poe.

align(ment), aline(ment). The first is now the established form.

alkali. The pronunciation in US is -lī, in Brit. usually -lĭ, but sometimes -lī. The plural should be & usually is *alkalis* (Webster prefers *-lies*).

all. RIGHT: *They had watched all‸his motions; all‸the people rose as he entered.* The insertion of *of* in this constr., except with pronouns (*all of us*) is 'recent' and more often heard in US than in Brit. It is usually unnecessary and, though permissible, undesirable.

Allegheny Mountains; pl. *-ies.*

allegory. (1) (Rhetoric): 'other wording.' A narrative of which the true meaning is to be got by translating its persons and events into others that they are understood to symbolize. *The Faerie Queen* & *The Pilgrim's Progress* are allegories. (2) *Allegory* & *parable* are almost synonymous but usage has given *allegory* the meaning of a longer story, its purpose less exclusively didactic, and the application less restricted; and *parable* the illustrative story designed to answer a single question or suggest a single principle. See SIMILE & METAPHOR.

allegro. Pl. *-os.*

alleluia. Now usually *hallelujah.*

alleviate makes *-iable.*

alliteration. (Rhet.): 'letter tagging.' The noticeable or effective use in a phrase or sentence of words beginning with or containing the same letter or word. *After life's fitful fever; In a summer season when soft was the sun.*

allowedly. Four syllables if used.

allow of. This is undergoing the same limitation as ADMIT OF, but the process has not gone so far; *Jortin is willing to* allow of *other miracles, A girl who* allows of *no impertinent flattery,* are hardly felt to be archaic, though *of* would now usually be omitted. The normal use & sense, however, are the same as those of *admit of*.

all right. The words should always be written separately; there are no such forms as *all-right, allright,* or *alright,* though even the last, if seldom allowed by the compositors to appear in print, is often seen (through confusion with *already* & *altogether*) in MS. This rule holds not only when the two words are completely independent, as in *The three answers, though different, are all right,* but also where they may be regarded as forming a more or less fixed phrase: *The scout's report was 'All right'* (i.e. all is right)./*Is he all right?*/*'Will you come for a walk?' 'All right.'*/*Oh, I know them apart, all right.* (Standard; est. idiom; colloq.; slang respectively.)

all-round. An all-round athlete. NOT *all-around* or *all-'round.*

all the time. The phrase is idiomatic English only when the time in question is a definite period fixed by the context as in: *I did not see you because I was looking at her all the time* (that you were present); *Well, I knew that all the time* (that you were supposing I did not); *He pretends friendship, & all the time* (that he pretends it) *he is plotting against one; I have been a free-trader all the time* (that others have been wavering). Used generally without such implied definition, in the sense all day & every day (*Actors act while they are on the stage, but he acts all the time; We hold that a Tariff Reformer must be a Tariff Reformer all the time, & not an opportunist*), it is slang.

allude, allusion. The words are much misused. *An allusion* is a covert or indirect reference; it is never an outright or explicit mention. *Allude to* has the same limitations. RIGHT: *We looked at each other wondering which of us he was alluding to; Though he never uses your name, the allusion to you is obvious; He is obscure only because he so often alludes* (or only owing to his frequent allusions) *to contemporary events now forgotten.* MISUSE: *When the speaker happened to* name Mr. Gladstone, the allusion *was received with loud cheers./The lecturer then* alluded at some length *to the question of strikes.* It may be added that *allude to* is often chosen, out of foolish verbosity, when the direct *mean* would do better; so *When you said 'some people cannot tell the truth,' were you* alluding to (did you mean) *me?;* but this is rather an abuse than a misuse.

ally, n. & v. Although the pronunciation alī′, aliz′, alīd′, is still preferred, in US the shift to the first syllable in the n. is becoming more prevalent and is given as the standard by some dictionaries & as a variant by others.

alma mater. See BATTERED ORNAMENTS, & SOBRIQUETS.

almanac. The only modern spelling. In old titles, however, the *k* spelling is usually right: *Poor Richard's Almanack, The Farmer's Almanack,* &c.

almighty. So spelled.

almost. (1) *Quite* means completely, wholely; *almost quite* is therefore an INCOMPATIBLE. (2) *Almost never* is slipshod for *hardly ever.*

alone. The adverbial use of *alone* with *not* in place of the usual *only* (*more might be done, & not alone by the authorities, but . . .*) is a SURVIVAL, & like other archaisms is to be avoided except in poetry or in prose of a really poetic type. In ordinary writing it is one of the thousand little mechanical devices by which 'distinction of style' is vainly sought. The following passage shows it in characteristic surroundings: *Recourse to porters savors more of operations in the West African bush than on the Indian frontier, so that* not alone *in the region passed through, but in its transport will our latest little war wear an interesting & unusual aspect.* This censure does not apply to the adjectival use (*It is* not *youth* alone *that needs . . .*), in which *not* & *alone* are usually separated.

along. Used as meaning 'some way on,' as *along toward the end of the year,* US colloq. The meanings 'in company' (*liberty along with order*) and 'with one' (*he carries a gun along*) are standard.

alongside. Adv. followed by *of: The losses* alongside of *the profits;* prep. (*of* omitted) *She kept* alongside *her companion. He brought the barge* alongside *the ship.*

aloof. Constr. *from* (NOT *to* or *of*): *He kept aloof from the struggle.*

aloud. *He cried aloud* (i.e. loudly); *he spoke aloud* (i.e. not to himself).

à l'outrance. ('To the utmost,' to death.) The French phrase is *à outrance* or *à toute outrance,* not *à l'outrance.* Those who use French phrases to suggest that they are at home with French should accordingly be careful to write *à outrance.* For those who use them merely as the handiest way of expressing themselves, the form that is commoner in English is as good as the other, & does not lay them open to the charge of pedantry.

already. The adv. is so spelled; this does not affect the use of the two separate words, as in *Tell me when you are all ready.*

alright. Spell ALL RIGHT.

also. The word is an adverb, & not a conjunction; nevertheless, it is often used in the latter capacity where *and* (*also*), *but also,* or *as well as* would be in place. In talk, where the informal stringing on of afterthoughts is legitimate, there is often no objection to this (*Remember your watch & money; also the tickets*); & the deliberate afterthought may appear similarly in print (*The chief products are hemp & cigars; also fevers*). But it is the writer's ordinary duty to settle up with his afterthoughts before he writes his sentence, & consequently the unassisted *also* that is proper to the afterthought gives a slovenly air to its sentence. WRONG: *Great attention has been paid to the history of legislation,*∧also *to that of religion./'Special' is a much overworked word, it being used to mean great in degree,*∧*also peculiar in kind.* Insert *and* in both.

alternative. 1. *Alternative*(*ly*) had formerly, besides their present senses, those now belonging only to *alternate*(*ly*). Now that the differentiation is complete, confusion between the two is inexcusable. WRONG:

Frenchmen have become accustomed to these changes in policy, singular methods which consist in blowing alternatively *hot & cold;* the needed word is *alternately.*

2. There are also difficulties about the correct use of the noun *alternative,* for dealing with which it is necessary to realize clearly its different senses. These are now distinguished with illustrations that may serve to show what is idiomatic & what is not:

a. Set, especially pair, of possibilities from which one only can be selected; this is often practically equivalent to *choice. The only alternative is success or* (NOT &) *death. We have no alternative in the matter.*

b. Either of such pair or any one of such set. *Either alternative is, any of the alternatives is, both alternatives are, all the alternatives are, intolerable. The alternatives, the only alternatives, are success &* (NOT or) *death.*

c. Second of such pair, the first being in mind. *We need not do it; but what is the alternative? We must do it; there is no* (NOT no other) *alternative. The* (NOT the other) *alternative is to die.*

d. Other of such a set, one at least being in mind. *If we decline, what are the alternatives? The only alternative is to die. You may say* lighted *or* lit *or* alight; *there is no other alternative. The only alternatives to it are gas &* (NOT or) *candles.*

although. No definite line can be drawn between *although* and *though* as complete conjunctions. The conditions in which *although* is likely to occur are (a) in a formal style of writing; (b) in a clause that precedes the main sentence: *Although he attained the highest office he was of mediocre ability;* (c) in stating an established fact rather than a mere hypothesis: *He wouldn't take an umbrella although it was already raining* (but *though it should rain cats and dogs*). *Although* cannot be used as an adverb; *though* can. *Although* cannot be placed last; *though* can. *Though* is alone possible in the *as though* idiom (see THOUGH).

altogether is right only in the senses 'entirely' or 'on the whole.' Confusion between this & *all together* is not uncommon. WRONG: *Until at last, gathered* altogether *again, they find their way down to the turf./A long pull, a strong pull, & a pull* altogether.

alto-relievo. Pl. *-os.* Preferable forms are the English *high relief* & the Italian *alto rilievo.*

aluminium. In US the usual word is *aluminum,* but the longer form is still used in some chemical texts. *Aluminium* is the standard Brit. form.

alumnus. Pl. *-ni* (pron. nī); feminine *-na,* pl. *-nae* (pron. -nē). Both words are more popular in US, where the older Latin pronunciation of the plurals (m. -nĭ; fem. -nī) is more usual.

a.m. Ante meridiem. Any time between midnight & noon. 10 a.m. (also written A.M.) NOT 10 *o'clock a.m.,* or 10 *a.m. in the morning.*

amateur. Pron. ă'matūr or -tûr; it is high time that vain attempts at giving the French *-eur* should cease, since the word is in everyday use.

amazedly. Four syllables.

ambidext(e)rous. Spell without the *-e-*.

ambiguity, ambiguousness. Although *ambiguity* in its objective sense means ambiguousness (*the ambiguity* or *ambiguousness of the word, of the language*), in the concrete sense of a word or phrase susceptible of more than one meaning, an equivocal expression, only *ambiguity* applies (*plausible ambiguities which so often occur in English law*); *ambiguousness* stresses the quality of being understood in various ways (*The ambiguousness of the term 'favorable exchange'*).

ambivalence, -ent. In psychology, simultaneous attraction & repulsion to the same object or person. Also the conflicting attractiveness & repulsion of that object or person. Pron. -bĭv′-.

ameliorate makes *-rable.*

amenable. Pron. -mēn′-.

amend, emend. Although both words come from the L. *emendare,* to free from fault, the first is now obs. in the sense of correcting a text or literary work (*emendate*); *amend a statement, a legal bill, your ways; emend a Greek text. Amends* is both sing. & pl. but is used as a collective singular with a sing. verb.

amenity. Pron. -mĕn′-; the restoration of -mēn- is pedantic.

America(n). The use of *America* for the United States & *American* for (citizen) of the US is open to as much & as little objection as that of *England* & *English*(*man*) for Great Britain, British, & Briton. It will continue to be protested by purists & patriots, & will doubtless survive the protests.

AMERICANISMS. Americans are often unhappy or resentful when they are told that a word, expression, idiom, pronunciation, or spelling is 'chiefly US' or an Americanism. So they should be, if a violation of grammar is involved, or if the Americanism is a vulgarism resulting from ignorance or carelessness. But there are many 'Americanisms' that were once in current usage in England and have survived here after becoming obsolete at home; others are good English words, current in both countries, but with different meanings or emphasis. Still others are of US coinage or were brought to us from our foreign population. To reject these words simply because they are 'chiefly US' is evidence of a sorry lack of faith in our own culture. So also with pronunciation and spelling. In this book 'chiefly US' or 'Americanism' is a statement of fact, not a recommendation or a condemnation. Occasionally what follows will give sufficient information so that the reader can decide whether it is an Americanism he wishes to preserve or one he will readily discard.

amiable, amicable. The first implies a lovable friendliness that causes one to be liked: *an amiable disposition;* the second a friendliness of intent, peaceableness, without force or quarreling: *amicable arrangement; an amicable manner.*

amid, amidst. 1. Both are LITERARY WORDS, subject to the limitations of their kind. In most contexts *in* & *among* serve more naturally.

2. As to the alternative forms, *amid* (esp. in Brit.) has dropped out of ordinary use still more completely than *amidst,* & is

therefore felt to be inappropriate in many contexts that can still bear *amidst*. When we find *amid* in a passage of no exalted or poetical kind (*A certain part of his work . . . must be done* amid *books*), our feeling is that *amidst* would have been less out of place, though *among* would have been still better.

amok. AMUCK is the usual form. See DIDACTICISM.

among, amongst. 1. There is no broad distinction either in meaning or in use between the two. *Among* is more usual in US, *amongst* now being chiefly literary. In Brit. both forms are used indifferently, though *amongst* is more usual before vowels.

2. *Among(st)* denotes a mingling with more than two objects: *An honest man among thieves* (*between* denotes two objects only).

amoral. Though originally a nonce word, *amoral* (pron. ā mor′al) is now accepted and in US has largely replaced *non-moral* in the sense 'not connected with morality.' *Immoral* ='wicked.'

amour-propre. *Vanity* usually gives the meaning as well, &, if as well, then better. See FRENCH WORDS.

amphibol(og)y. (Log.); 'aiming both ways.' A statement so expressed as to admit of two grammatical constructions, each yielding a different sense. *Stuff a cold & starve a fever* appears to be two sentences containing separate directions for two maladies, but may also be a conditional sentence meaning, 'If you are fool enough to stuff a cold you will produce & have to starve a fever.'

ample, used as an attributive adjective in the sense plenty of (*he has ample courage; there is ample time; ample opportunities were given*) is legitimate only with nouns denoting immaterial or abstract things. It is wrongly attached to nouns that, like *butter, oil, water, coal,* denote substances of indefinite quantity: NOT, e.g., *We have* ample water *for drinking.* Though *There is* ample coal *to carry us through the winter* is wrong, *The coal,* or *Our coal, is ample* is not wrong; the explanation is that *the coal, our coal,* denotes a quantity, & is an abstract phrase, though *coal* is a concrete word; this is only possible when *ample* is predicative & not attributive. Many words are sometimes abstract, sometimes concrete: *linen* may mean either the material (*ample* is then WRONG e.g. —*We have* ample linen *for half-a-dozen shirts*), or supply of linen articles (*ample* is then RIGHT —*They will start housekeeping with* ample linen, *plate, & crockery*). Other words with which in their concrete sense *ample* is wrong may in some figurative or abstract sense take it; a ship may have *ample water* (i.e. space) to turn in, though the crew cannot have *ample water* to drink; & *ample butter* may mean plenty of flattery though not plenty of butter.

amuck, the familiar spelling, due to popular etymology, but going back to the 17th c. & well established, should be maintained against the DIDACTICISM *amok.*

amusive serves no purpose not better served by *amusing,* & in spite of its actual age it always suggests either ignorance or NOVELTY-HUNTING.

an. See A, AN.

anachronic, anachronistic. The long form is better & more usual.

anagram. (Lit.): 'rewriting.' A shuffling of the letters of a word or phrase resulting in a significant combination. Bunyan tells his readers that John Bunyan anagram'd makes *nu hony in a B* (new honey in a bee). *Anagrammatize(d)* is the usual verb, but the now obs. *anagram'd* is less cumbersome.

analogous means similar in certain attributes, uses, or circumstances: *an analogous experience, but in the field of art. Similar* expresses a more complete likeness.

ANALOGY, 'accordance with proportion.' Inference or procedure based on the presumption that things whose likeness in certain respects is known will be found or should be treated as alike also in respects about which knowledge is limited to one of them. The conclusion that a State, because its development in some respects resembles that of a person, must by lapse of time grow feeble & die is analogical.

1. Analogy as a literary resource. The meaning of analogy in logic is given above; we are here little concerned with it; it is perhaps the basis of most human conclusions, its liability to error being compensated for by the frequency with which it is the only form of reasoning available; but its literary, not its logical, value is what we have now to do with. Its literary merits need not be pointed out to anyone who knows the Parables, or who has read the essays of Bacon or Montaigne, full of analogies that flash out for the length of a line or so & are gone: *Money is like muck, not good unless it be spread.* What does need pointing out is unfortunately its demerit—the deadly dullness of the elaborate artificial analogy favored by journalists who think it necessary to write down to their audience & make their point plain to the meanest capacity. Specimens fully bearing out this generalized description are too long to quote; but the following gives a fair idea of the essential stupidity of these fabricated analogies, against which no warning can be too strong: they are on a level with talking to a schoolboy about a *choo-choo.* Let it be read & compared with the money that is like muck: *The Government is playing the part of a man entrusted with the work of guarding a door beset by enemies. He refuses to let them in at once, but provides them with a large bag of gold, & at the same time hands them out a crowbar amply strong enough to break down the door. That is the Government's idea of preserving the Union.*

2. As an influence in word formation. In the making of words, & in the shape that they take, analogy is the chief agent. Wanting a word to express about some idea a relation that we know by experience to be expressible about other ideas, we apply to the root or stem associated with it what strikes us as the same treatment that has been applied to those others. That is, we make the new word on the analogy of the old; & in ninety-nine cases we make it right. Occasionally, however, we go WRONG: *The total poll*

midway in December was 16,-244 *so that upwards of half the electors were* abstentients. The writer wanted a single word for persons guilty of abstention, & one too that would not, like *abstainer,* make us think of alcohol; *dissension* came into his head as rhyming with *abstention.* If that yields, said he, *dissentients,* why should *abstention* not yield *abstentients*? Because the correspondence between *abstention* & *dissension* is not quite so close as he assumed; if he had remembered *dissentire* & *abstinere,* analogy would have led him to *abstinents* instead of to *abstentients.* That is a live instance of the fallibility of analogy, & dead specimens may be found in any etymological dictionary—dead in the sense that the unsoundness of their analogical basis excites no attention as we hear the words. Who thinks of *chaotic, operatic, dilation,* as malformations? Yet none of them has any right to exist except that the men who made them thought of *eros* as a pattern for *chaos, drama* for *opera, relate* for *dilate,* though each pattern differed in some essential point from the material to be dealt with. These malformations, it is true, have now all the rights of words regularly made; they have prospered, & none dare call them treason; but those who try their luck with *abstentients* & the like must be prepared to pass for ignoramuses. See also HYBRID derivatives, & (talking of ignoramuses, for which false analogy has been known to substitute *ignorami*) LATIN PLURALS.

3. As a corruptor of idiom. That is the capacity in which analogy chiefly requires notice in this book. Of the following extracts each exhibits an outrage upon idiom, & each is due to the assumption that some word or phrase may be treated in a way that would be legitimate if another of roughly the same meaning had been used instead; that other is given in parentheses, sometimes with alternative forms: (WRONG) *The double task was performed only at the* expenditure of *laborious days & nights* (cost)./*Those regulations about good husbandry so* unpopular to *farmers & landlords* (unpalatable.)/*Roumania indicated her* reluctance to *any step compromising her future good relations with Germany* (repugnance; or reluctance to take)./*Whether such a scheme would come under the category of 'public utility' is* ambiguous (doubtful).

analyse is the standard Brit. spelling, *analyze,* US; Americans may take comfort in the fact that the *-yze* ending was accepted by Johnson and according to OED is 'historically defensible.'

analytic, -al. The chief sense of the short form is that of pertaining to or in accordance with analysis: *an analytic science.* The longer form suggests the employment of the analytic method: *He had an analytical mind. A purely analytical process.*

anapaest. (Poet.): 'struck back.' A metrical foot, ◡ ◡ – (a reversed dactyl). And his Co′/horts were gleam′/ing with pur′/ple and gold′. Although *anapest* is given preference in some dictionaries, the *-ae-* is still standard in both Brit. & US.

anchoret, anchorite. Hermit. The two forms seem to be

equally common in Brit.; *-ite* is more usual in US.

anchovy. Traditionally anchō′vi; often (but not preferred) in US an′chovi.

ancien régime. Former political & social system, esp. that before the French Revolution.

and. 1. Bastard Enumeration. There is perhaps no blunder by which hasty writing is so commonly defaced as the one exemplified in (WRONG) *He plays good cricket, likes golf & a rubber of whist.* The writer thinks the items of his enumeration are three (as they would have been if he had said *& loves a rubber*), but they are in fact two.

The test of this slovenliness is fortunately very simple: in the form we all habitually use for enumerations of more than two items, there must be nothing common to two or more of the items without being common to all. In the *He plays* example the word *likes* is common to the golf & whist items, but has no relation to the cricket item. In the following examples, what is common to some but not all items is in roman type; corrections are added in parentheses; but it may be said in general that insertion of the missing *and,* from which ignorant writers shrink consciously or unconsciously, is usually attended with no more damage to euphony than that repetition of essential words by the fear of which ELEGANT VARIATION, in all its distressing manifestations, is produced. There is nothing to offend the ear in *He plays good cricket, & likes golf & a rubber of whist.* WRONG: *Hence* loss *of time, of money, & sore trial of patience* (time & money, &c.). It was *terse, pointed, & a tone of good humor made it enjoyable* (terse & pointed, &c.). *His workmen* are *better housed, better fed, & get a third more wages* (housed & fed, &c.).

Two bad enumerations are added for which carelessness rather than a wrong theory seems responsible. *The centuries during which the white man kidnapped, enslaved, ill-treated, & made of the black a beast of burden* (& made a beast of burden of; *or* & ill-treated the black and made him a)./*Many of these authoresses are rich, influential, &* are *surrounded by sycophants* (& surrounded).

2. *And* & commas in enumerations. *Every man, woman, and child was killed.* There is no agreement among writers and publishers about the punctuation in this kind of enumeration. This book advocates the comma before *and,* in the interests of clarity. In the sentence: *All of the most important documents, declarations & resolutions, as well as several minor state papers, are filed in the Library of Congress,* the reader cannot tell whether he has three separate items (documents, declarations, resolutions) or whether the second & third are the two items that make up the first. In *The smooth gray of the beech stem, the silky texture of the birch and the rugged pine & oak are the naturalist's delight* a comma before the *and* will keep the pine and oak from having silky texture.

3. *and which.* RIGHT: *The latest papers,* which *had just been delivered* and which *were already on his desk, contained the full account.* DOUBTFUL: *The Korean troops sent in as replacements,* and which *were woefully ill-equipped, faced one*

of the worst battles of the war. For full discussion of these and other difficulties, see WHICH WITH AND OR BUT.

4. *And* with infinitive. The use of *and* to connect two verbs, the latter of which would logically be in the infinitive with *to,* especially after *go, come, send,* & *try,* is established idiom: *Try and teach the erring soul; Come and see us.* After other verbs it is colloq. or dialect.

and/or. An ugly combination best confined to business and legal documents.

anemone. *An emine (nce),* not *an enemy,* gives the order of consonants. *Any money* is perhaps easier to remember (the US school-child variant), but is not a model for pronunciation.

anent, apart from its use in Scotch law courts, is archaic. See ARCHAISM.

angel. *Talk of an angel* is a GENTEELISM, for *Talk* (or *speak*) *of the devil* (*and he will appear*).

angle (v.) is current in US only in the fig. sense (when *fish* would often be better): *Angling for compliments; angler,* though still vital in Brit., is usually used by non-fishing Americans only with conscious recollection of *The Compleat Angler.*

Anglo-Indian. Traditionally, a person of English birth who has spent most of his life in India. Since 1911, in India, a person of mixed European & Indian parentage or descent; a Eurasian.

Anglophile (pron. -fil) (also *anglophil,* pron. -fil, but in US *-phile* is more usual). An admirer of England and things English. *Anglomania,* excessive admiration of English customs; *Anglophobia,* dislike or hatred of the English (hence *Anglophobe*). See also -PHIL(E).

annex(e). n. The shorter form is the rule in US & preferred in Brit.

annihilate makes *-lable.* The word means blot out of existence, destroy completely, and should not be used in combinations with *utterly, totally,* &c. See INCOMPATIBLES.

announce. A formal word, meaning to make public, declare, proclaim; as used as a synonym for *said,* see FORMAL WORDS.

annul, annulment. So spelled; but *-lled* &c.

annunciation (pron. -sia-)= announcement, but is restricted to the religious use.

another. (1) *Also, too,* are often used unnecessarily with *another*: NOT *There is* another *question* too *that we must discuss* (omit *too*). (2) Constr. *than,* NOT *from: Another house than mine.* (3) Poss. *one another's* (but *each other's* is more common) (see EACH 2). (4) NOT *some way (sort, kind) or another,* but *or other.* (5) *But that is another story,* see HACKNEYED PHRASES.

antagonize. As a synonym for *oppose, resist, neutralize, counteract,* the word is recognized in dictionaries; but it may safely be said that the occasions are rare when one of those words would not be preferable to it. The sense in which it does good service, & should certainly not be banned, is to rouse or incur the hostility of, to expose oneself by one's action to the enmity of. This sense probably comes from US, where it is commoner than in England. RIGHT: *But the President was* *afraid to* antagonize *Senator Aldrich & the other leaders of the Stand-pat Republicans./ Rather than* antagonize *the two New England Senators on whom the woolen manufacturers were leaning, he signed a re-enactment of the notorious Schedule K.*

ante-. Combining prefix meaning *before* (ANTI=against). Many US dictionaries omit the hyphen (*antemarital, antemundane*) except before proper nouns (*ante-Gothic, ante-Mormon*) and words beginning with an *e* (*ante-ecclesiastical, ante-eternity*). This book recommends keeping it in little-used words, and words of several syllables (*ante-dawn, ante-prohibition, ante-patriarchal*).

ante bellum ('before the war') as a noun, two words. Adj., *ante-bellum legislation,* hyphened.

antecedent. (Gram.). *A noun, clause, or sentence* to which a following pronoun (personal or relative) refers. (In the preceding definition, the italicized words are the antecedents of *which.*)

antenna. In zoology, biology, pl. *-nae;* in radio, mechanics, *-as.*

antepenult. (Gram.): 'before the nearly last.' Last syllable but two of a word. La bo ra-tor y (ra=antepenult).

Anthony traditionally is spelled with & pronounced without *h.* In US the *h* is often pronounced, especially in surnames (e.g. Susan B. Anthony).

anti-. Combining prefix meaning *against, opposite,* &c. In US often not hyphened except before proper nouns or words beginning with *i.* This book recommends the hyphen before words beginning with other vowels unless they are established & in common use (*anti-administration, anti-empirical, anti-optionist, anti-unionist*), and in NONCE words.

anticipate. 1. To forestall (*He anticipated the vengeance of heaven;* to accelerate (*Some jumped overboard as eager to anticipate their grave*); to take into consideration beforehand (*You shall not tempt me to anticipate the question*); to foresee (*My fears anticipate your words*); to look forward to (expect) an uncertain event (*They anticipated that all would be well*).

2. In the sense look forward to (expect), anticipate is followed by a simple object or by *that,* not an infinitive. RIGHT: *He anticipated an acquittal; he had anticipated that the sentence would be delivered by noon.* WRONG: *Exhibitions of feeling were, of course,* anticipated to take *place on Monday./A noteworthy act, which may be* anticipated to have *far-reaching effects.* The writers have thought their sentences with the homely *expect,* which would have served perfectly, & then written them with the FORMAL WORD *anticipate;* ANALOGY has duped them into supposing that since it vaguely resembles *expect* in sense it must be capable of the same construction.

anticlimax. (Rhet.): 'climax spoiling.' The annulment of the impressive effect of a climax by a final item of inferior importance. *In spite of our different backgrounds I liked her tremendously, I was impressed by her skill, and what's more, I was somewhat curious about her.*

anti-open-shop. So spelled, if necessary.

antipodes. Pron. antĭp′odēs. Though *antipode* (pron. -pōd) is said still to exist as a singular (*Selfishness is the very antipode of self-love*), the modern idiom is to use the plural form only, treating it as a singular when it means things diametrically opposite (*The antipodes of selfishness is self-love*).

ANTI-SAXONISM. There are, indeed, no anti-Saxonists, properly speaking; that is to say, anti-Saxonism is not, like its verbal counterpart SAXONISM, a creed; but, if it is not a creed, it is a propensity & a practice that goes far to account for the follies of Saxonism, & is here named on that ground. *Happenings* & *forewords* & *forebears* & *birdlore* & *wheelman* & *betterment* are almost justified as a revulsion from the turgid taste that finds satisfaction in *transpire* & *materialize* & *eventuate, optimism* & *mentality, idiosyncrasy* & *psychological moment, proposition* & *protagonist, in connection with* & *with reference to.* All of these are now in constant use, & often misuse. That the meaning of many of them is vague is a recommendation to one kind of writer as saving him the trouble of choosing between more precise synonyms, & to one kind of reader as a guarantee that clear thought is not going to be required of him; a further account of the attraction of such words will be found in LOVE OF THE LONG WORD. Others are chosen not because they are, like these, in constant use, but because they are not; to say *nomenclature* instead of *name, replica* for *copy, premier* for *first, major* for *greater, evince* for *show, malnutrition* for *underfeeding, prior to* for *before,* is AVOIDANCE OF THE OBVIOUS; & PEDANTIC HUMOR suggests *cacophonous, osculatory, sartorial,* & *cachinnation.*

Anti-Saxonism, then, is here used as a name for the frame of mind that turns away not so much from the etymologically English vocabulary as from the homely or the simple or the clear. It may perhaps have been observed that the word given above as preferable to *replica* was *copy,* which is no more Saxon than *replica;* it is more English, for all that, just as *ridiculous* is more English than *risible.* Readers who would like to study the effect of yielding to the practice will find quotations under nearly all the words that have been given as specimens, in their separate articles; & for others several are here collected, most of them containing rather a misuse than a mere use of the word concerned: *But he had the most tremendous* optimism *in the future triumph of his course./Neither France nor Great Britain could* indulge in such an eventuality *at the present* juncture./*The increase in the price of coal may not* materialize *after all.*

antithesis. (Rhet.): 'placing opposite' (-tith′). Such choice or arrangement of words as emphasizes a contrast. *Crafty men condemn studies; simple men admire them; & wise men use them.*

antitype. An antitype is one that corresponds as an impression to the die; it is what a type or symbol represents; what is foreshadowed in the type. The meaning *opposite* in the sense contrasting, although suggested in some US dictionaries, is not inherent in the word & leads to confusion. RIGHT: *The relation of the Old Testament to the New is that of type to antitype./ The type of mind that prompted this policy finds its modern antitype in the labor union.* WRONG: *This war figure is brought into dramatic contrast with his antitype.* (Should be opposite.) For complete discussion of *antitype, prototype,* &c., see TYPE.

anxious. (1) Constr.: anxious *for* their safety, *for* an issue desired; *about* a person or thing; *to* do, see, &c. (inf.) something, i.e. to effect some purpose. (2) The objections made to it in the sense 'eager' (*to hear, improve, go,* &c.) as a modernism, & in the sense 'calculated to cause anxiety' (*It is a very anxious business; You will find her an anxious charge*) as an archaism, are negligible. Both are natural developments, the first is almost universally current, & the second is still not infrequent.

any. 1. Compounds. *Anybody, anything, anyhow, anywhere,* are always single words (as is *anyone* in US, but not in Brit.), except when the individual element is meant to be stressed. *Anyone can see what I mean,* but *Any one of us could do it;* so also the adverb *anywise* (but *in any wise*); *any way* is two words (*I cannot manage it any way*) except when it means 'however that may be,' 'at any rate' (*Anyway, I can endure it no longer*); *at any rate,* NOT *at anyrate.*

2. *He is the most generous man of anyone I know.* This common idiom, which looks illogical (*of all I know* being the logical form), is no doubt defensible as a development or survival of the archaic type *Caesar, the greatest traveller, of a prince, that had ever been. Of* there means *in the way of,* & we should now write *for* instead of it. But that sense of *of* being preserved in this idiom alone, the idiom itself is not likely long to resist the modern dislike of the illogical. It therefore seems desirable to avoid such things as: *Edward Prince of Wales is the eighteenth who has borne that title, the most illustrious, perhaps, of any heir-apparent in the world* (more illustrious than that of any)./ *The Standard Oil Company is credited with having the largest Eastern trade of any American enterprise* (of all American enterprises; *or* a larger trade than any other).

3. *Any* used for *at all* is a (US) construction to be avoided: e.g. in *Even so it did not influence him any. Any place* for *anywhere* is US colloq.

anybody else makes *anybody else's.*

à outrance. See À L'OUTRANCE.

Apache. Indian tribe, US, pron. *a* păch'ē (pl. *-es,* or as sing.). The French word, pron. *a* päsh'.

apart from is the traditional idiom; *aside from* is US.

apex. Pl. *-es* is more general in both US & Brit., although *apices* is still used in some scientific and formal writing.

aplomb, from the French, *à plomb,* meaning 'perpendicularity,' 'plumb,' is now thoroughly anglicized in its fig. sense, self-possession, self-assurance. Pron. -plŏm' or as French.

apocrypha. Writings or statements of doubtful authorship or authority. Pl., but commonly used as a singular. (The sing. of the Greek form, formerly used in English, is *apocryphon.*) When a plural is needed, now *apocryphas,* formerly *apocryphy.*

apophthegm. Brit. usage prefers this spelling and the pron. ă′pofthĕm; US *apothegm* (which was more usual in Brit. until Johnson). The shorter form conceals the derivation, a Greek word meaning something clearly spoken, a terse saying. It is roughly synonymous with aphorism, maxim, but the word is not a popular one.

a posteriori. (Log.): 'from the hinder end.' Working back from effects to causes, i.e., inductively. *A posteriori* generalizations are those reached from facts or experience. *God's in his heaven—all's right with the world* is an *a posteriori* inference if it means the world is so clearly good that there must be a God in heaven (but it is an *a priori* inference if it means that since we know there is a God, the state of the world must be right).

apostle. In biblical reference, used interchangeably with *disciple.* The Apostles, the witnesses of the Resurrection 'sent forth' by Christ to teach his Gospel, to whom were added Barnabas and Paul; the Disciples, the personal 'followers' of Jesus Christ, often the Twelve, but also used of 'the 70 disciples' sent forth by him. In non-biblical use the words are not interchangeable. We may speak of an *Apostle of Temperance* but *a disciple of John Dewey.*

APOSTROPHE. (1) The apostrophe (') is used to indicate the omission of letters (*can't, ne'er*); the possessive use of nouns (*Jones's house, Mars' orbit, for conscience' sake;* see POSSESSIVE CASE); sometimes in forming the plural of letters, figures, &c. (*a's, 7's* or *as,* 7s; but *G.I.s, M.A.s;* see M.P.); & with the gerund (*John's going upset us all*). See POSSESSIVE PUZZLES, & -ED & 'D, for some points concerning its use. (2) (Rhet.): 'a turning away.' Words addressed to a present or absent person or thing, and breaking the thread of discourse.

apotheosis. Deification; hence, an ideal; *the apotheosis of virtue.* Pron. apŏthē ō′sis preferably.

appal(l). The double *l* is better.

Appalachian Mts. The preferred pronunciation is -ă′chian.

a(p)panage. (Orig. province or lucrative office given to younger children of kings; now perquisite; natural accompaniment.) Either form will do; *appa-* is preferred in US, and in Brit. is perhaps commoner in general use, & *apa-* in learned use.

apparatus. Pron. -ātus.

apparent(ly). (1) Commas before & after *apparently* give it more emphasis and should be used guardedly; compare *He had apparently forgotten it* with *He had, apparently, forgotten it.* See THEREFORE. (2) In the phrase *Heir apparent, apparent* has the sense, 'manifest, unquestionable.' *An heir apparent* is one whose title is indefeasible by any possible birth.

appeal. (1) n., in the sense 'power to attract or move the feelings,' although included in some US dictionaries, is usually considered commercial jargon or slang; e.g. *sex appeal, eye appeal; a young woman completely lacking in appeal.* (2) v., 'prove attractive,' as in *It doesn't really appeal to me,* it is often a GENTEELISM for *I don't like it.*

appearance. The idiom *to all appearance* has become in US *to all appearances. Keep up appearances, appearances are in your favor* are traditional uses of the plural.

appeared is liable to the same misuse as *seemed* with the PERFECT INFINITIVE. The right forms are: *He appears to enjoy opera. He appears not to have enjoyed the opera. He appeared to enjoy the opera until the last act. He appeared to have enjoyed the opera but was refusing to admit it.*

appendant, appendent. The first is preferred.

appendix. Pl. *-dices* (-sēz) or *-dixes.* The former is usually confined in US to scholarly and scientific writing (but *-dixes* in medical texts).

applicable. Pron. ăp′plĭk *a* b'l.

apposite. Appropriate (to), well put. *The truth most apposite to the whole argument; apposite illustrations.* Pron. ăp′*o* zĭt.

apposition. (Gram.): 'putting to.' The placing of a second description side by side with that by which something has first been denoted, the second being treated as grammatically parallel with the first. *Simon, son of Jonas, lovest thou me?*

appraisal. In the US, *appraisal* is the legal & commercial term, and more usual in all senses than *appraisement.* But *appraisement* is standard in Brit.; see -AL NOUNS.

appreciate makes *-ciable.* (1) Pron. -shĭ-, not -sĭ-. The pronunciation -sĭ- in *appreciation* (Brit. & sometimes US) is to avoid the ugly repetition, -shiashun. (See -CIATION.) (2) *Appreciate* has become a GENTEELISM, often incorrectly used, for *understand, realize, be grateful,* &c., esp. in business letters. It should always be followed by a noun, not a *that* clause. RIGHT: *I appreciate your kindness.* WRONG: *I appreciate that you have not had time to reply.*

apprehend, -ension, comprehend, -ension. So far as the words are liable to confusion, i.e. as synonyms of *understand(ing),* the *ap-* forms denote the getting hold or grasping, & the *com-* forms the having hold or full possession, of what is understood. *What is beyond my apprehension* I have no cognizance of; *what is beyond my comprehension* I am merely incapable of fully understanding. To apprehend a thing imperfectly is to have not reached a clear notion of it; to comprehend it imperfectly is almost a contradiction in terms. *I apprehend that A is B* advances an admittedly fallible view; *I comprehend that A is B* states a presumably indisputable fact.

apprise (not *-ize*), to notify, inform. In most contexts a stilted word for which *tell* or one of the words given above would be better. *Apprize* meaning *appraise* is obs. in Brit. except in Scottish law, but is still occasionally used in US.

approve=confirm, sanction (*He will not approve the treaties in their present form*); commend, pronounce to be good (with *of*) (*He has read all but approves of very few*).

approximately. Often used when *roughly, about, comparatively* would be better. (*Approximate* means very near, closely resembling, &c.)

apricot. The dictionaries all give long ā first.

a priori. (Log.): 'from the earlier part.' Working forward from known or assumed causes to effects, i.e. deductively. See A POSTERIORI above.

apropos is so clearly marked by its pronunciation as French, & the French construction is so familiar, that is is better always to use *of* rather than *to* after it. *Apropos of what we were saying* . . . The OED & Webster, however, both allow *to,* and it has been used by many well-regarded writers: *Is there not a passage in Spix apropos to this?* (Disraeli).

apt, liable. Followed by *to* with the infinitive in the senses 'having an unfortunate tendency' (*apt*), 'exposed to a risk' (*liable*), the words are so near in meaning that one of them (*liable*) is often wrongly used for the other. It may perhaps be laid down that *apt* is the right word except when the infinitive expresses not merely an evil, but an evil that is one to the subject. RIGHT: *We are* liable *to be overheard* (being overheard is an evil to us); *Matinee hat wearers are* liable *to be insulted; The goods are* liable *to suffer.* But: *Curses are* apt *to come home to roost* (the evil is not to the curses, but to the curser); *Damage is* apt *to be done; Matinee hats are* apt *to cause ill-temper; Difficulties are* apt *to occur; Lovers' vows are* apt *to be broken. Apt* is usually the right word in: *He is* apt *to promise more than he can perform* (but *liable,* if the evil suggested is the shame he feels); *Cast iron is* apt *to break* (but *liable,* if we are sorry for the iron & not for its owner). Since *liable* is apt to encroach, & *apt* is liable to suffer neglect, the best advice is never to use *liable* till *apt* has been considered & rejected.

aquarium. Pl. usually *-ums,* occasionally *-a.*

Arab, Arabian, Arabic. With exceptions for a phrase or two, such as *gum arabic,* the three adjectives are now differentiated, *Arab* meaning of the Arabs, *Arabian* of Arabia, & *Arabic* of the language or writing or literature of the Arabs. So we have an *Arab horse, child, chief; Arab courage, fanatics, traditions, philosophy; the Arabian gulf, desert, fauna & flora; Arabian gales; the Arabic numerals; an Arabic word; Arabic writing, literature. Arab* & *Arabian* can sometimes be used indifferently; thus an Arab village is one inhabited by Arabs; if it happens to be in Arabia it is also an Arabian village, & may be called by either name; the Arab war is one with Arabs; the Arabian war is one in Arabia; & the two may be one. Also *Arabian* may still be used instead of *Arab* of what belongs to or goes back to the past, as *Arabian records, monuments, philosophy, conquests.*

arbo(u)r. US *arbor;* Brit. *-our.*

arboretum. Pl. *-tums* is more usual in US, *-ta* in Brit. Pron. arborē′tum.

arc, v. (to form an electric arc) makes *arced* or *arcked, arcing* or *arcking;* the form without *k* is preferred in US.

arcanum. Pl. *arcana.*

arch-, arche-, archi-. Though the prefix *arch-* (=chief, &c.) is pronounced arch in all words except *archangel* & its derivatives, the longer forms are always pronounced arki: so *archbishop* (-ch-), but *archiepiscopal* (-k-); *archdeacon* (-ch-), but *archidiaconal* (-k-). The *ch* is hard (k) in *archetype, Archimedes, architectonic, architrave.*

archaeology. So spelled.

ARCHAISM. A certain number of words through the book are referred to this article, & such reference, where nothing more is said, is intended to give warning that the word is dangerous except in the hands of an experienced writer who can trust his sense of congruity. Archaic words thrust into a commonplace context to redeem its ordinariness are an abomination. More detailed remarks will be found in the general articles INCONGRUOUS VOCABULARY, REVIVALS, SUBJUNCTIVES, & WARDOUR STREET. Some words archaic in Brit. are in current usage in the US and will be so designated under the separate entries.

archipelago. Pl. *-os* best; see -O(E)S. Pron. arkĭpĕl′agō.

ardo(u)r. In US *-or,* Brit. *-our.*

area. In its fig. uses *area* has become a VOGUE WORD: *the* area *of foreign policy; more than two* areas *of the curriculum; we shall now deal with each subject-matter* area; *still another* area *of the Protestant Church's life in this period is the* area *of public worship.* For synonyms see FIELD.

are, is. When one of these is required between a subject & a complement that differ in number (*these things . . . a scandal*), the verb must follow the number of the subject (*are,* not *is, a scandal*). *The wages of sin is death* is an archaism; we do not now say *his wages is,* but *are, a dollar an hour;* & we do not say *a dollar are,* but *is, his wages.* When, as here, subject & complement can change places without alteration of sense, so that it may be doubted which is which, the verb must agree with what precedes, & not what follows. When, however, the undoubted subject happens to follow, as in a question, the verb agrees with it, as *But what proof are,* not *is, these facts of your theory?* In accordance with these rules, *are* & *is* should replace the romantype *is* & *are* in the following. WRONG: *Apparently what that school desires to see* are *pipeclayed & brass-buttoned companies of boys./But the moral inconsistencies of our contemporaries* is *no proof thereof./The only difficulty in Finnish* are *the changes undergone by the stem.*

Argentina. Also *the Argentine Republic* (hence, *the Argentine*); pron. usually -tēn, sometimes -tīn.

argot. (Pron. -gō.) The conventional slang of a group, esp. of thieves & vagabonds. For meaning & use, see JARGON.

arguing in a circle. (Log.): The basing of two conclusions each upon the other: *that the world is good follows from the known goodness of God; that God is good is known from the excellence of the world he has made.*

arise, in the literal senses of getting up & mounting, has given place except in poetic or archaic use to *rise.* In ordinary speech & writing it means merely to come into existence or notice or to originate from, & that usually (but cf. *new prophets arise from time to time*) of such abstract subjects as *question, difficulties, doubt, occasion, thoughts, result, effects.*

aristocrat. In US usually accented on the 2nd syllable (Brit. on the first).

arithmetical. In arithmetical progression the elements progress by a constant difference, e.g. 2, 5, 8, 11, 14, &c.; in geometric progression, by a constant factor, e.g. 2, 6, 18, 54, &c. For the use of the terms in non-scientific writing, see PROGRESSION.

armada. Brit. always armā′da; US often ar mä′da.

armadillo. Pl. *-os.*

armful. Pl. *armfuls.*

armo(u)r. US usually *-or;* Brit. *-our.*

arms (weapons). The singular is late, rare, & best avoided. Instead of describing a particular pattern of rifle or sword as 'a beautifully balanced arm,' it is worth while to take the trouble of remembering *weapon.* We do well to sacrifice the exhaustive brevity of *The report of a firearm was heard* & risk ambiguity with *gun,* inaccuracy with *rifle,* or extravagance with *pistol, rifle, or gun*—unless, of course, we have the luck to hit upon *shot.* The only sense in which the singular is idiomatic (*either arm*=cavalry or infantry; *each arm*=cavalry, infantry, & artillery) is made tolerable, perhaps, by suggesting the other arm & being interpreted as branch of the service (cf. *the secular arm*).

around is in Brit. use a disappearing variant of *round,* still the normal form in certain combinations only, as *around & about,* (the air) *around & above* (us), *all around* (are signs of decay); & it can be used without being noticeable in a few of the senses of *round,* as *seated around the table, diffuses cheerfulness around her, spread destruction around.* But in Brit. it is hardly possible to say *winter comes around, all the year around, win one around, send the hat around, a room hung around with pictures, travel around the world, show one around.* American usage is quite different: the following examples are normal US idiom (impossibilities for an Englishman): *He went through but I ran around; He turned around; The earth turns around on its axis; Go around to the post office; The church around the corner; Loaf around the city.* Used as 'here & there,' 'in the vicinity of' (*there must be some around somewhere*) or for about (*around 6 o'clock; around Christmas*), it is US colloq. See AMERICANISMS.

arouse. The relation of this to *rouse* is much like that of ARISE to *rise;* that is, *rouse* is almost always preferred to it in the literal sense & with a person or animal as object. *Arouse* is used chiefly with the senses 'call into existence,' 'occasion,' & with such abstracts as *suspicion, fears, cupidity, passions,* as object of the active or subject of the passive: *This at once aroused my suspicions; Cupidity is easily aroused.* NOT *I shook his arm, but failed to arouse him.* In the (WRONG) construction *All of us are aroused that our airmen have not been released,* 'by the fact' must be inserted before *that.*

arrière-pensée. 'A hidden or ulterior motive,' 'a mental reservation' are preferable in most contexts. (NOT *an afterthought,* as some writers seem to think.)

arrive. For the absolute sense 'reach success or recognition' (*a genius who had never arrived*), see GALLICISMS.

art. *Art* runs up through the meanings skill; human skill, as opposed to nature; skill displaying itself in perfection of workmanship; the skillful production of the beautiful in visible forms (painting, sculpture, engraving, architecture); and down from anything wherein skill may be displayed (the liberal arts); contrasted with science (*science teaches us to know, art to do*); hence craft, knack, artifice, wile, trick. Thus *artificial* often has a derogatory implication, & *artless* or *artlessness,* a favorable. For the broad distinction between art & science, see SCIENCE.

artefact, artifact. The second is preferred. There is no differentiation.

articulate, v., makes *-lable.*

artiste. 1. The word is applicable to either sex; *artists & artistes* as a phrase for male & female performers is a mere blunder.

2. In the sense professional singer, dancer, or other public performer, *artiste* serves a useful purpose. It is best restricted to this use, in which it conveys no judgment that the performance is in fact artistic; if it is desired to intimate that a cook, tailor, hairdresser, &c., or an artiste, makes his occupation into a fine art, *artist,* & not *artiste,* is the right word: *He is quite an artist; What an artist!*

as. This article is divided into 12 sections: 1. *Equally as.* 2. Causal *as* placed late. 3. *As to.* 4. *As if, as though.* 5. *As,* relative pronoun. 6. Omission of *as.* 7. *As*=in the capacity of. 8. Case after *as.* 9. *As a fact.* 10. *As well as.* 11. *As follow(s)* &c. 12. *As* for *that.*

1. *Equally as* (*good* &c.) is tautology; *as* is the comparative of equality. Use either *equally* or *as* by itself in *Unless retail prices are* (*equally* or *as*) *satisfactory.* For other examples see EQUALLY.

2. Causal *as,* meaning *since, because, seeing that, for,* &c. There is a tendency to overwork causal or explanatory *as* clauses. They are best used placed before the main clause (*As you are not ready, we must go without you*) or when the fact adduced is one necessarily known to the hearer or reader (*I need not translate, as you know, German*). Otherwise, placed after the main clause they are offensive to the ear and often ambiguous. NOT RECOMMENDED: *The Government has been induced to take this course* as *it is much impressed by the great value of the discoveries made./The sketch of Milton's life is inserted in this volume* as *it illustrates some points that occur in the Sonnets.* Either begin with the *as* clause or use one of the other conjunctions given above.

3. *As to.* This has a legitimate use—to bring into prominence at the beginning of a sentence something that without it would have to stand later (*As to Smith, it is impossible*

to guess what line he will take). It has, for instance, been wrongly omitted in:^*Whether the publishers will respond to Sir Charles Stanford's appeal or not it is too early to speak with any confidence.* A spurious imitation of legitimacy occurs when *as to* introduces what would even without it stand at the head of the sentence. In (WRONG): *As to how far such reinforcements are available this is quite another matter;* omit 'as to' & 'this,' & the order is unaffected; the writer has chosen to get out of the room by a fire escape when the door was open.

Apart from this, it is usually either a slovenly substitute for some simple preposition (*Proper notions* as to [of] *a woman's duty;/She has been sarcastic* as to [about] *his hunting*) or entirely otiose (*You ask the pertinent question* as to *how many of the doctors who signed the pledge were practicing./It appeared to be somewhat uncertain* as to *whether the bill would come up before this session or the next.* Omit *as to*).

As might be expected, those who put their trust in a phrase that is usually either vague or otiose are constantly betrayed by it into positive bad grammar. WRONG: *Unless it has some evidence* as to whom *the various ideas belong* (i.e. as to to whom). The popular favorites: *The question as to whether, The doubt as to whether,* may almost be included among the ungrammatical developments, since the doubt or question demands an indirect question in simple apposition; in such forms as *Doubts are expressed as to whether,* the 'as to' is not incorrect, but merely repulsive; An *interesting question therefore remains* as to how far *science will provide us with the power* may lawfully be written; The *interesting question* &c. may not.

4. *As if, as though.* These should invariably be followed by a past conditional, & not by a present form (*would,* not *will; could,* not *can; did,* not *does;* &c.). The full form of the INCORRECT *It is scanned curiously,* as if *mere scanning* will *resolve its nature* is *It is scanned curiously, as it* would be *scanned if mere scanning* would *resolve its nature;* & the omission of *it would be scanned* leaves *would resolve* unchanged. *As though,* about which the same demonstration is not possible, is precisely equivalent to *as if,* & is subject to the same rule; & the rule applies to the still more elliptical use of either form in exclamations (*As if,* or *As though, you didn't* [NOT don't] *know that!*) as well as to the use with an expressed main clause. The mistake of putting the verb in a present tense is especially common after *it looks* or *seems,* where there is the insufficient excuse that the clause gives a supposed actual fact; but it is spreading so fast that sometimes the supposition is admittedly false. WRONG: *But it looks for the moment* as if these will [should be *would*] *have to be abandoned./To the observer from without it seems* as if there has [*had*] been *some lack of stage-management.*

5. *As,* relative pronoun. The distinction between *as* the relative pronoun, capable of serving as subject or object of a verb, & *as* the relative adverb, not capable of so serving, must

be grasped if a well-marked type of blunder is to be avoided. WRONG: *The rate-payers have no direct voice in fixing the amount of the levy,* as is possessed *by the unions./Some nasty things were said about him,* as have been said *about others./There were not two dragon sentries keeping ward,* as in magic legend are *usually found on duty.* If these sentences, the faultiness of which will probably be admitted at sight, are examined, it will be seen that for each two cures are possible; one is to substitute for *as* an undoubted relative pronoun, *such as* or *which* (*such as is possessed; which has been said*); the other is to insert a missing subject or object (*as one is possessed; as such things have been said; as dragons are usually found*). Either method of correction suggests the same truth that *as* in these sentences is not a relative pronoun, & has been wrongly treated as one, though an adverb. The fact is that when *as* is used as a relative pronoun the antecedent is never a simple noun that has already been expressed (which must be represented by an ordinary relative–*such as, which, who, that*), but a verb or verbal notion, or a previously unexpressed noun, that has to be gathered from the main sentence. Thus we cannot say, *To affect poverty,* as *is now often* affected (i.e. which poverty is affected); but we can say, *To affect poverty,* as *is now often* done (i.e. which affecting is done).

On the other hand, failure to recognize that *as* is a relative pronoun sometimes produces mistakes of a different kind. WRONG: *Epeiros,* as it is *well known, was anciently inhabited by . . .* (*as*=which fact, & *it* is therefore impossible unless *as* is omitted)./*I do not think,* as apparently does *Mr. Thorne, that . . .* (*as*=which thinking, & the inversion is impossible; read *as Mr. Thorne apparently does*).

6. Omission of *as. As* is commonly but wrongly omitted after the verbs EXPRESS, REGARD, especially when complications arise with another *as.* WRONG: *But it is not so much as a picture of the time* as‸*a study of humanity that* Starvecrow Farm *claims attention* (*as as a study* has been too much for even a literary critic's virtue); cf. the omissions of *to* in the *as to* quotations (3 above). *As* is properly omitted after *account, consider.* RIGHT: *I account it a sin, I consider him wrong* (NOT *as a sin, as wrong*).

7. *As*=in the capacity of. When this is used, care must be taken to avoid the mistake corresponding to what is called the unattached participle. We can say He *gave this advice* as leader *of the oposition,* or *This advice was given by* him as leader, *he* & *him* supplying the point of attachment; but NOT *The* advice *which he tendered to the Peers* was given as leader *of the opposition.*

8. Case after *as.* It is a matter of no great practical importance, case being distinguishable only in a few pronouns, & these pronouns occurring so seldom after *as* that most of the examples given in illustration will have an artificial air; but some points may be noticed: (a) Sometimes a verb is to be supplied; the right case must then be used, or the

sense may be spoiled; *You hate her as much as I* implies *as I hate her; You hate her as much as me* implies *as you hate me.* (b) *As* is never to be regarded as a preposition; the objective case after it, when right, is due either to the filling up of an elliptic sentence as in (a) or to causes explained in (c) & (d). WRONG: *When such* as her *die, She is not so tall* as me. (c) The phrases *such . . . as he* &c., *so . . . as he* &c., may be treated as declinable compound adjectives (cf. German *was für ein*), which gives *Such men* as he *are intolerable,* but *I cannot tolerate such men* as him, *Never was so active a man* as he, but *I never knew so active a man* as him; to ban this construction & insist on writing *he* always, according to the (a) method, seems pedantic, though *he* is always admissible. (d) In many sentences the supplying of a verb supposed to have been omitted instead of repeated, as in (a), is impossible or difficult, & the case after *as* simply follows that of the corresponding noun before *as; as* is then equivalent to *as being.* RIGHT: *I recognized this* man as him *who had stared at me; You dressed up* as she, *You dressed* yourself *up* as her, *I dressed* you *up* as her, *You were dressed up* as she; *The entity known to me* as I, *The entity that I know* as me.

9. *As a fact;* the idiomatic expressions are 'in fact,' 'as a matter of fact.' For the use of 'as a fact,' see FACT.

10. *As well as* is a conj., not a prep. RIGHT: *I am going as well as* he (NOT *him*). See WELL.

11. For *as concern(s), regard(s), follow(s),* see CONCERN, FOLLOW.

12. After the verbs *say, know, think,* &c., the dependent clause should be introduced by *that,* not *as: I don't know* that *you'll like it* (NOT *as*).

ascendancy, ascendant. (Preferably so spelled, NOT *-ent,* US & Brit.) Both words mean domination or prevailing influence, & not upward tendency or rising prosperity or progress. *The ascendancy of, Have an* or *the ascendancy over, Be in the ascendant,* are the normal phrases; in the third, which is less detached than the others from its astrological origin, *ascendancy* is wrong: NOT *It is not recorded what* stars were in the ascendancy *when Winston Churchill was born* (must be *in the ascendant*).

ascertain. The only current use is to find out or learn for a certainty, by experiment, investigation, or examination; to make sure of, get to know. It is often wrongly used for a simple *discover* or *understand.* See ELEGANT VARIATION & WORKING & STYLISH WORDS.

ashen. In most contexts *ashy* is more usual, *ashen* being archaic (or pseudo-archaic), poetic, or ornamental. See -EN ADJECTIVES.

aside (adv.) means to or on one side (*He stood aside until the quarrel was over*). It does NOT mean on each side. WRONG: *We sat* five aside *in the suburban train; They were playing* three aside; *a side* must be written. As meaning *apart* (*Aside from what I have clearly told you . . . , jesting aside*) it is (chiefly) US.

askance has nothing to do with *ask,* but means obliquely, hence with indirect meaning, hence with disdain, suspicion, mistrust. (Pron. åskans′.)

aspirate. (Gram.): 'breathed.' Sound of the letter *h* as in *hot, greenhouse* (i.e. not fused as in *Philip* or *than, chin,* &c., or unaspirated as in *hour, heir*).

assay, essay, vv. A differentiation tends to prevail by which *assay* is confined to the sense 'test,' & *essay* to the sense 'attempt.' *Assay* is also used fig., to analyze or appraise critically. *Essay* itself has by this time the dignity attaching to incipient ARCHAISM.

assemblage, assembly. Both mean a meeting or gathering, but *assemblage* is less formal: *An assemblage of all ages & nations; assembly* usually connotes a gathering for some specific purpose: deliberative, political, religious. *Assemblage* is also applied to things (lit. & fig.)—a collection, cluster: *An assemblage of miscellaneous objects lay on the table.*

asset is a false form but through usage has been accepted in both US & Brit. Webster defines it 'any item of value owned; that which is a resource, i.e. *character is an asset.*' COD says '(loosely) any possession, (improp.) any useful quality' (e.g. *Trustworthiness is in itself a valuable asset*). Though it would be pedantic to try to outlaw it now, it should be used sparingly when *possession, gain, advantage, resource,* or some other synonym would be more effective. Most of those who use it are probably unaware that, though now treated as plural, *assets* is itself (cf. *riches*) a singular (from Fr. *assez,* enough). The right sense of the word is what suffices or should suffice to meet liabilities (see POPULARIZED TECHNICALITIES). The following quotations show how easily it may be avoided: *Hearne is playing splendidly and is* an *indispensable* asset *to the team* (omit *an . . . asset*)./His *experience in foreign affairs is* an *incalculable* asset *in the present international tension* (is invaluable).

assign. Derivatives & allied words are pronounced as follows: *assignable* (-īna-), *assignation* (-ĭg-), *assignat* (ă′sĭgnăt), *assignor* (ăsĭnor′), or *assigner* (ă sīn′er; so spelled in non-legal contexts only), *assignee* (ăsĭnē′).

assimilate makes *-lable.*

assist, in the sense 'be present' (at a performance &c.), is now a GALLICISM; in the sense 'help' (to potatoes &c.), it is a GENTEELISM. For *assist* & *help,* see WORKING & STYLISH WORDS.

associate. Pron. -shĭ-, not -sĭ-.

association. Pron. -sĭ ā′shn, not -shē-. See -CIATION.

assonance. The careless repetition of sound in words or syllables can ruin the effect of a sentence and should be guarded against, in both speech and writing: e.g. *to form an informal council.* For other examples see REPETITION.

assume, presume. Where the words are roughly synonymous, i.e. in the sense *suppose,* the object clause after *presume* expresses what the presumer really believes, till it is disproved, to be true; that after *assume,* what the assumer postulates, often as a confessed hypothesis. It may be owing to this distinction that the *that* of the object clause is usually expressed after *assume* & usually omitted after *presume* (I *presume you know; I assume that you know*). See PRESUME.

assure, assurance. 1. These words have never found general acceptance in the sense of paying premiums to secure contingent payments, though they are used by insurance offices & agents & so occasionally by their customers, especially when death is the event insured against (*life assurance; assure one's life*); apart from such technical use, *insure* & *insurance* hold the field.

2. *Assure* (make [a person] certain of a fact, or that it is true) for *ensure* (make certain the occurrence &c. of) is now rare. (RIGHT: *It will ensure your success, Let me assure you that you can't fail.*)

3. *Assure* cannot be used intransitively (i.e. it must have an object). NOT *After France* assured that *she would support the measure;* either insert the *committee* before *that* or change *assured* to *gave her assurance.*

ate, past of *eat,* pronounced āt in US, ĕt in Brit. (ĕt for *eaten* is illiterate in both countries).

athenaeum is still preferred to *atheneum* (US & Brit., though æ is optional).

atom, atomic. *Atom* is the noun, *atomic* an adj. If newspapers want to use *atom* in headlines (*atom bomb, atom conference*) to save space, it is their privilege, but the use should not creep into the article itself: *Although the actual construction of* an atom plane engine *was ruled out . . .* As short forms, both *A-bomb* & *atom bomb* are current; *atomic bomb* is best.

atom, particle, corpuscle, molecule. All these words have at one time or other stood for the smallest unit of matter—whence have been derived more general usages. (Cf. *He hasn't an atom* [or *particle*] *of sense.*) Democritus is believed to have been the first to call the units of matter *atoms—atomos* meaning indivisible. In the 20th c., physicists divided the 'indivisible' atom into a number of smaller particles, such as electrons, protons, neutrons, and so on. *Atom* continues to mean the smallest physical unit of matter of a specific kind—as an atom of hydrogen, oxygen, iron, uranium, &c. A molecule is the smallest chemical unit of a substance—the familiar matter with which everyone deals outside the physicists' laboratories (e.g. a molecule of hydrogen, the smallest unit that behaves like hydrogen in chemical reactions, has two atoms of hydrogen). While *atom* and *molecule* have acquired specific meanings, *particle* remains a general term, applied to the ultimate units of matter, such as electrons, and also, even in scientific usage, to any particular object—*dust particle, virus particle,* &c. *Corpuscle* is now an old-fashioned word seldom heard. A generation ago people still commonly talked of the red corpuscles of the blood, but now we speak of the red cells.

attempt. For *was attempted to be done* &c., an ugly and illiterate construction, see DOUBLE PASSIVES.

attorney. Pl. *-eys.* In US *attorney* (in the sense *solicitor* in Brit.) is restricted to a lawyer transacting legal business for his client. *Lawyer* is the general term, applying to anyone in the legal profession.

au with adjectives is not used in English except in phrases borrowed entire from French: *au naturel, au grand sérieux.* But *à la maître d'hôtel, à la Churchill.* See À LA.

audience. The battle of the purists to restrict the meaning to hearers is lost. It has been applied to spectators & reading public for over a century and insistence on the distinction is now pedantic.

au fond. At bottom; essentially. *À fond,* to the bottom, thoroughly. *It is* au fond *a matter of principle. Having investigated the subject* à fond, *he considers himself an expert.* But see FRENCH WORDS.

aught. *For aught I know* is the only phrase in which the word is still current in ordinary speech, & even there *all* is displacing it. The arithmetical cipher (zero) is a NAUGHT, not an *aught.*

autarchy, autarky. *Autarchy* is absolute sovereignty, autocratic rule, self-government. *Autarky* is national (economic) self-sufficiency. The distinction in spelling, though fairly recent and not universal, is worth preserving.

authentic, genuine. The distinction commonly drawn between the words is by no means universally observed, especially when either is used without special reference to the other; but, when it is present to the mind, *authentic* implies that the contents of a book, picture, account, or the like, correspond to facts & are not fictitious, & *genuine* implies that its reputed is its real author: *A genuine Hobbema; An authentic description; The Holbein Henry VIII is both authentic & genuine* (represents Henry as he was, or is really a portrait of him, & is by Holbein). The artificial character of the distinction, however, is illustrated by the fact that *authenticate* means to establish either as authentic or as genuine.

author. The verb *to author* was long seemingly obs., but has recently been (unnecessarily) revived: *authored ten bills in the last decade.*

authoress is a word regarded with dislike in literary circles—on the grounds, perhaps, that sex is irrelevant in art, & that the common unliterary public has no concern with its superiors' personality. The Brit. public thinks otherwise, & may be trusted to keep a useful word in existence, even though it has so far failed to bring into existence what it needs much more, a handy feminine for doctor. The American public is seemingly less enthusiastic about the word. See FEMININE DESIGNATIONS.

auxiliary verb. (Gram.): a 'helping' verb: *have, be, may, do, shall, can, must,* &c.—when combined with other verbs.

avail, v. The normal construction is *avail oneself of* (*I shall avail myself of your kind offer*). From this are wrongly evolved (esp. in US) such forms as *The offer was availed of. Emerson's Power must be availed of,* cited in the OED, should serve as a warning, not a model. The proper construction is *We must avail ourselves of the power.*

available. The modern senses are 'capable of being used'; 'at one's service'; 'within one's reach.' The editor who rejects a MS. by writing: 'We regret it is not available to us' would do better to say 'we regret we cannot use it.'

avenge, revenge, vengeance. *Avenge* & *vengeance* are one pair. The distinction between the two pairs is neither very clear nor consistently observed, but the general principle that personal feeling is the thing thought of when *revenge* is used, & the equalization of wrongs when *avenge* or *vengeance* is used, may assist choice. *Avenge* & *vengeance* suggest just retribution; *revenge,* vindictive retaliation. *Avenge your fallen brother. Take vengeance on them that do evil. He vowed to have his revenge.*

averse, aversion. To insist on *from* as the only right preposition after these, in spite of the more general use of *to* (*What cat's averse to fish?*—Gray. *He had been averse to extreme courses.*—Macaulay. *Nature has put into man an aversion to misery.*—Locke) is one of the pedantries that spring of little knowledge. Although many of the older writers used *from* (Donne, Walton, Locke), *to* has also been used since the 17th c. (Walton, Boyle). In modern usage *to* is much more prevalent.

avid. *The lion is avid for his prey.* Why not 'eager'? See AVOIDANCE OF THE OBVIOUS & WORKING WORDS & STYLISH WORDS.

avocation, originally a calling away, an interruption, a distraction, was for some time commonly used as a synonym for *vocation* or *calling,* with which it is properly in antithesis. In current usage it is used for an amateur or leisure-time interest as opposed to practical or professional work—colloquially, a 'hobby.' *Many scientists turn to music as an avocation.*

AVOIDANCE OF THE OBVIOUS is very well, provided that it is not itself obvious; but if it is, all is spoiled. Expel *eager* or *greedy* from your sentence in favor of *avid,* & your reader wants to know why you have done it. If he can find no better answer than that you are attitudinizing as an epicure of words for whom nothing but the rare is good enough, or, yet worse, that you are painfully endeavoring to impart some much needed unfamiliarity to a platitude, his feeling toward you will be something that is not admiration. The obvious is better than obvious avoidance of it. *Nobody could have written 'Clown' who had not been* (*as Mr. Disher is known to be*) an avid collector *of pantomine traditions & relics./Lord Lansdowne has done the Liberal Party a good turn by putting Tariff Reform to the front; about this there can be no* dubiety*./If John never 'finishes' anything else, he can at least claim by sheer labor to have completed over* five score *etchings.* There are some who would rather see *eager* & *doubt* & *a hundred* in those sentences than *avid, dubiety,* & *five score;* & there are some who would not; the examples are typical enough to sort tastes. *Avid* & *dubiety* are not yet hackneyed in the function of escapes from the obvious; they will be so one day if their qualifications in this kind are appreciated, & then their virtue will be gone.

Several words can be thought of that have been through this course. Starting as variants for the business word, they have been so seized upon by those who scorn to talk like other people as to become a badge by which we may know them; after which they pass into general use by the side of the words to which they were preferred, giving the language pairs of useless synonyms that have lost whatever distinction there may once have been between them. Such words are *cryptic, dual, facile,* & *Gallic,* as used without the justification of special meanings instead of *obscure, double, easy,* & *French.* On all of these except *cryptic* (a word whose sole function seems to be that which is our subject) comment will be found in their separate articles. A few examples of the uses deprecated are: '*A sensible young man, of rough but mild manners, & very seditious'; this description, excepting the first clause, is somewhat* cryptic./ *The World Conference has not proved to be so* facile *to arrange as it appeared.*/'*I blame the working of the Trade Board' said Mr. Newey,* forcefully, '*for keeping wages at an artificial figure.*'

avouch, avow, vouch. The living senses of the three words are distinct; but as a good deal of confusion has formerly prevailed between them, it is worth while to state roughly the modern usage. *Avouch,* which is no longer in common use, means guarantee, solemnly aver, prove by assertion, maintain the truth or existence of, vouch for (*A miracle avouched by the testimony of . . . ; Millions were ready to avouch the exact contrary; Offered to avouch his innocence with his sword*). *Avow* means own publicly to, make no secret of, not shrink from admitting, acknowledge one's responsibility for (*To think what one is ashamed to avow; Avowed himself my enemy; Avowed his determination to be revenged; Always avows,* & cf. in the contrary sense *disavows, his agents*). *Vouch* is now common only in the phrase *vouch for,* which has taken the place of *avouch* in ordinary use, & means pledge one's word for (*Will you vouch for the truth of it?; I can vouch for his respectability*).

await, wait. *Await* is always transitive, but *wait* is not always intransitive. NOT *I am* awaiting to hear *your decision.* But *I await,* & *I wait, your decision* are equally good.

awake, awaken, wake, waken. *Awake:* past *awoke* (rarely *awaked*); p.p. *awaked* (rarely *awoke*). *Wake:* past *woke* (rarely & then usually trans. *waked*); p.p. *waked* (rarely *woke* or *woken*). *Awaken* & *waken* have *-ed.*

Distinction between the forms is difficult, but with regard to modern usage certain points may be made. (1) *Wake* is the ordinary working verb (*You will wake the baby; Something woke me up; I should like to be waked at* 7:30; *Wake the echoes*), for which the others are substituted to add dignity or formality, or to suit meter, or as in (3) or (5) below. (2) *Wake* alone has (& that chiefly in *waking*) the sense 'be or remain awake' (*Sleeping or waking; In our waking hours*). (3) *Awake* & *awaken* are usually preferred to the others in figurative senses (*When they awoke,* or *were awakened, to their danger; This at once awakened suspicion; The national spirit awoke,* or *was awakened; A rude awakening*). (4) *Waken* & *awaken* tend to be restricted to the transitive sense; *when he wakens* is rarer for *when he wakes* than *that will waken him* for *that will wake him.* (5) In the passive, *awaken* & *waken* are often preferred to *awoke* & *wake*, perhaps owing to uncertainty about the p.p. forms of the latter pair; *it wakened me* is rare for *it woke* or *waked me,* but *I was wakened by it* is common for *I was waked* or *woke* or *woken by it;* see also the alternative forms in (3) above. (6) *Up* is very commonly appended to *wake*, rarely to *waken*, & hardly at all to *awake* & *awaken*.

aweigh. Of an anchor, just clear of the ground, so the ship can make headway. *Anchors* aweigh *and the ship is under* way (not *weigh.*)

awhile, adv., one word. *Let's rest awhile.* But *for a while* (i.e. *while,* **n.**).

awry. Pron. *a* rī′.

ax(e). The spelling *ax*, 'better on every ground of etymology, phonology, & analogy' (OED) is given first in most US dictionaries, but is 'unusual & pedantic' in Brit. *The New York Times* style book gives *axe.*

axis. Pl. *axes* (-ēz, not -ĭz).

ay, aye. The word meaning *yes* is pronounced ī, & the word meaning *ever* is pronounced ā; but which spelling corresponds to which pronunciation is disputed. The nautical *Ay, ay, sir* is usually written thus; & *aye* is probably the commoner spelling now for *ever.* On the other hand *the ayes have it* is usual, though *-es* may there be intended for the plural termination. *Ay* (ī) *yes* & *aye* (ā) *ever* seem likely to prevail.

B

Babbitt (from the Sinclair Lewis character), now est. usage as an exponent of middle-class business success and convention. So *Babbittry* (sometimes not cap.).

baby. *Baby carriage* is more usual in US than *perambulator* or *pram.* *Baby sitter,* no hyphen, but *baby-sit,* v., if used, so spelled. *Babied* but *babying, babyish, babyhood.*

baccalaureate. So spelled; the degree of bachelor (*Bachelor of Arts*=Baccalaureus Artium, B.A. or A.B.); often in US short for *baccalaureate sermon.*

bacchanal, bacchant(e). *Bacchanal* & *bacchant* are both used of males or females, or males & females, but with a tendency to be restricted to males; *bacchante* is used of females only. *Bacchant* is always pronounced bă′kant; *bacchante* bakănt′, bă′-kant, or bakan′ tĭ. *Bacchant* has *bacchants* or *bacchantes; bacchante* has *bacchantes* (-ts or -tĭs).

bacillus. Pl. *bacilli.*

BACK FORMATION. A dictionary definition of the term is: Making from a supposed derivative (as *lazy*) of the nonexistent word (*laze*) from which it might have come. It is natural to guess that the words *scavenger* & *gridiron* are formed from a verb *scavenge* & a noun *grid,* & consequently to use those if occasion arises. Those who first used them, however, were mistaken, & were themselves making the words out of what they wrongly took for their derivatives. Some back formations are not generally recognized as such, & have the full status of ordinary words, e.g. *diagnose* (from *diagnosis*), *drowse* (from *drowsy*), *sidle* (from *sideling=sidelong*), *grovel* (from *groveling*, an adv.). But more often they are felt to be irregular, & used only as slang or jocosely; so FRIVOL, ENTHUSE, LOCOMOTE, ORATE, REVOLUTE. Other articles that may be looked at are BRINDLE, FILTRATE, GRID, & SALVE.

back of as a preposition is an American, not a British, idiom. Much as it is deplored by many US scholars, it is seemingly established, at least colloquially, as in *Back of* (i.e. *behind*) *the house is a wide lawn bordered by flowers. In back of*, however, is less respectable, even in US.

background. The extended fig. use of *background* (the social, historical, or logical antecedents that explain something; the sum of person's training, education, experience) is comparatively recent and probably of US origin. Its popularity suggests that it has become an easy escape from precise thinking and expression: *The background of the present tension; He has no background for the job;* &c. See VOGUE WORDS.

backlog, orig. US (the large log placed in the hearth fire as a reserve), in its fig. use as *reserve, support,* is established in US commercial language, & is widely used elsewhere. Other est. Americanisms are *backtrack, backwoods,* &c.

backward(s). The adv. may be spelled either way with only rarely, and by the most careful writers, any difference in meaning. The OED suggests that *-wards* suggests manner as well as direction: *To back out is to move* backward *out of a place without turning; In backhand the hand is turned* backwards *in making the stroke.* Otherwise euphony is the guiding principle with some writers, who use the *-s* form before a vowel. Generally *-s* is more common in Brit., the shorter form in the US. The adj. is always *backward* (not *-s*): *a backward child, in a backward direction; backwards* as adj. now obs.

bacteria. Sing. *bacterium.*

badge (fig.), a distinguishing sign, emblem, token, or symbol. *The possession of land has become the badge of freedom.* For synonymy, see SIGN.

badly in the sense 'very much,' though still deplored by some, is rapidly becoming established (e.g. *The whole Act is badly in need of revision*). The colloq. idiom is *I feel* bad (-ill), NOT *badly.*

baggage, as applied to the belongings that a person travels with on land, one of its earliest uses, is now replaced in Brit. by *luggage.* Brit. *baggage* is used primarily for portable army equipment. US *baggage car, -master, -man,* &c.,=Brit. *luggage-car* &c.

bail is right, & *bale* wrong, in the sense throw water out; the derivation is from French *baille* =bucket. *Bail* is also the legal term; *bale* the commercial (i.e. bale of cotton, hay, &c.).

balance, in the sense *rest* or *remainder*, is, except where the difference between two amounts that have to be compared is present to the mind, a SLIPSHOD EXTENSION. We may fairly say 'you may keep the balance,' because the amount due & the amount that more than covers it suggest comparison; but in 'the balance of the day is given to amusement' such a comparison between amounts is, though not impossible, farfetched, & the plain word (*rest*, or *remainder*) is called for. (*Rest* & *remainder* are included as definitions in some US dictionaries but still usually considered colloq.)

balk, baulk. Pron. bawk. *Balk* is preferred, except in Brit. billiards. *A balky horse* (=Brit. *a balking horse*); *to be balked of one's prey* (i.e. to be frustrated, disappointed).

ballad. (Lit.): 'dancing song.' Originally a song as accompaniment to dancing; later any simple sentimental song, esp. of two or more verses each to the same melody, e.g. Jonson's *Drink to Me Only;* a separate modern use is as the name of simple narrative poems in short stanzas, such as *Chevy Chase. Ballade* (pron. balädʹ) is the technical term for the elaborate formal poem revived in France & England in the 19th c.

balm. For *balm in Gilead* see BATTERED ORNAMENTS & HACKNEYED PHRASES.

baloney. If the (US) slang word is used, the spelling is *baloney.* The sausage is *Bologna.*

bambino. Except in Italian contexts, the pl. is *-os;* in Italian, *-ni.*

bamboozle. First mentioned in the *Tatler* as current slang, *c.* 1700, along with *banter, sham, mob, bully,* &c. The OED defines it 'to trick, hoax, impose upon, mystify, & confound,' and uses it in defining other terms.

banal. Most dictionaries give bāʹnăl first, though the modified Fr. pronunciation, ba·nälʹ, is often heard; *banality,* pron. ba nălʹĭtĭ. But there are also *common, commonplace, trite, trivial, mean, vulgar, truism, platitude,* & other English words to choose among. See LITERARY CRITICS' WORDS.

banjo. Pl. *-os* is given first in most dictionaries.

bank. A river's right bank is that on the right of the river as a person looks downstream.

bank holidays. In England, Easter Monday, Whit Monday, the first Monday in August, and Boxing Day (26 December). If Boxing Day falls on Saturday or Sunday, the following Monday is observed.

bank on or *upon,* in the sense 'rely upon,' 'place your hopes on,' is still informal or colloq., but no longer considered slang.

bar. *Bar sinister,* used by novelists as a symbol of illegitimacy, is strictly incorrect, *bend* or *baton sinister* being the true term; it is, however, so familiar that to correct it, except where there is real need for technical accuracy, is pedantic; see DIDACTICISM.

barbarian, barbaric, barbarous. The difference in usage among the three adjectives is roughly, & setting aside special senses of the first, as follows: *Barbarian,* as an adjective, is now regarded as an attributive use of the noun *barbarian;* i.e. it is used only in such contexts as would be admissible for nouns like *soldier* or *German* (a soldier king; German ancestry), & means consisting of barbarians, being a barbarian, belonging to or usual with barbarians. So we have *barbarian tribes, hosts, frankness, courage; a barbarian* *king, home, empire; barbarian man* (the human race as barbarians); *the barbarian world.*

The other two words are ordinary adjectives, but differ in their implications. *Barbaric* is used with indulgence, indifference, or even admiration, & means of the simple, unsophisticated, uncultured, unchastened, tasteless, or excessive kind that prevails among barbarians. We speak of *barbaric taste, splendor, costume, gold, hospitality, simplicity.*

Barbarous, on the other hand, always implies at least contempt, & often moral condemnation; it means that is unfit for or unworthy of or revolts or disgraces or would disgrace the civilized: *barbarous ignorance, speech, customs, style, words, cruelty, treatment, tyranny.*

It should be observed that the same noun may be qualified by all three words according to the sense wanted: *barbarian gold* is money supplied by barbarians; *barbaric gold* is the metal used overlavishly in decoration; & *barbarous gold* is the material prosperity that blinds to higher things; a *barbarian king* is a king of barbarians; a *barbaric king* one throned in rude splendor; a *barbarous king* a cruel despot.

barbarism, barbarity, barbarousness. The three nouns all belong to the adj. *barbarous,* but the first two are now (putting aside intentional archaism & metaphor) clearly distinguished. *Barbarism* means uncivilized condition, grossly uncultivated taste, or an illiterate expression; *barbarity* means grossly cruel conduct or treatment, or a grossly cruel act; *barbarousness* may be substituted for either of the others where the sense quality or degree is to be given unmistakably: *They live in barbarism; The barbarism, or barbarousness, of his style; 'Thou asketh' is a barbarism; He treats prisoners with barbarity; The barbarity, or barbarousness, of the decree is irrelevant; Unheard-of barbarities.*

BARBARISMS is a hard word to fling about, apt to wound feelings, though it may break no bones; perhaps it would be better abstained from; but so too would the barbarisms themselves. What after all is a barbarism? It is for the most part some word that, like its name, is apt to wound feelings—'an offense against the purity of style or language,' spec. in the method of word formation.

There are unfortunately two separate difficulties, both serious. We may lack the information that would enable us to decide whether *bureaucrat* & *cablegram* & *electrocute* & *pleistocene* are or are not barbarisms. It is indeed obtainable for any particular word from a competent philologist; but life is not long enough to consult a philologist every time one of the hundreds of dubious words confronts us; and then, even if the philologist has been consulted, are we to talk geology or electricity & abstain from *pleistocene* & *impedance?* No; a barbarism is like a lie; it has got the start of us before we have found it out, & we cannot catch it; it is in possession, & our offers of other versions come too late.

That barbarisms should exist is a pity; to expend much energy on denouncing those that do exist is a waste; to create them is a grave misdemeanor;

& the greater the need of the word that is made, the greater its maker's guilt if he miscreates it. A man of science might be expected to do on his great occasion what the ordinary man cannot do every day, ask the philologist's help; that the famous *eocene-pleistocene* names were made by 'a good classical scholar' (see Lyell in D.N.B.) shows that word formation is a matter for the specialist.

It will have been gathered that in this book barbarisms have not been thought of the practical importance that would demand elaborate discussion. The object of this article is merely to suggest caution. When a word is referred to BARBARISMS without comment, it is to be understood that it is, in the author's opinion, improperly formed.

barely, hardly. The two are synonymous for working use; *barely* tends to emphasize the narrowness of the margin, *hardly* the effect of strain; *We could hardly survive the ordeal; We barely succeeded in making the train.*

baritone. The usual spelling in US; Brit. usually *barytone.*

bark, barque. In US, *bark* prevails in both senses, but in Brit. the two forms are now usually differentiated, *bark* being a poetic synonym for ship or boat, & *barque* the technical term for a ship of special rig.

baronage, barony, baronetage, baronetcy. The forms in *-age* are collectives, meaning all the barons (or peers), all the baronets, list or book of barons, &c. Those in *-y* are abstracts, meaning rank or position or title of a baron or baronet. See also LORD.

baroque. (Art): 'misshapen pearl.' Grotesque, whimsical stylistic tendencies of 17th- & 18th-c. art. Pron. ba rōk′. See also ROCOCO.

basal, basic. These un-English-looking adjectives, neither of which existed before the 19th c., were manufactured merely as adjuncts to certain technical uses of the noun *base* in botany, chemistry, & architecture, where *fundamental* would have been misleading. But they are now supplanting *fundamental,* with its 500-year tradition, in both general & fig. contexts. The native element of *basal* & *basic* is seen in: *The basal portion of the main petiole; Its capital resting on its basic plinth; Basic salts, phosphates, oxides.* On the other hand *fundamental* would be the natural word in: *Classification should rest on the most* basal *characteristics./This is our* basic *principle./The great* basic *industry is agriculture.* Ba̍sal *texts, reading, training.* A more basic *argument is an impossibility.*

basis. Pl. *bases.*

bas-relief, bass-relief, basso-relievo, basso-rilievo. The first form is French, the last Italian, & the other two are corruptions; the plural of the third is *basso-relievos,* & of the fourth *bassi-rilievi.* The first is recommended (pron. usually bä′rilēf, US; băs′rilēf, Brit.).

bassinet. This (NOT *bassinette*) is the right spelling; the wrong form is pseudo-French.

bath. In US the verb is usually *bathe.* As a transitive verb (chiefly Brit.) *bath* means to subject to washing in a bath: *to bath a baby* or *an invalid. Bathe* as a noun is chiefly Brit.

(=a swim).

bathetic, bathotic. These are made in imitation of *pathetic, chaotic;* but *pathetic* is not analogous, & *chaotic* is itself irregular. An adjective for *bathos* is, however, almost a necessity to the literary critic, & the OED states that *bathetic* is 'A favorite word with reviewers'; it is the better of the two.

batik. So spelled. Pron. bă'tik or (more usual in US) bătēk'.

baton should be written without the circumflex & pronounced (US) bătŏn'; (Brit.) bă'tn.

battalion has plural *battalions,* & not even in poetic style *battalia; battalia* is singular (It. *battaglia*) and means battle array; but being archaic, & often following *in* (*Friedrich draws out in battalia*—Carlyle), it is taken as meaning *battalions.*

batten. In modern usage usually fig.: thrive, prosper, glut oneself, grow fat (constr. *on* or *in*). *Skeptics who batten on the hideous facts of history.*

BATTERED ORNAMENTS. On this rubbish heap are thrown, usually by a bare cross reference, such synonyms of the ELEGANT-VARIATION kind as *alma mater, daughter of Eve,* & *sleep of the just;* such metonymies as *the buskin & the sock* for tragedy & comedy; such jocular archaisms as *consumedly* & *vastly;* such foreign scraps as *dolce far niente, gang agley,* & *cui bono?* such old phrases as *in durance vile* & *who was destined to be;* & such quotations customarily said with a wink or written instead of one as *Tell it not in Gath* or *balm in Gilead.* The title of the article, & their present company, are as much comment as is needed for most of them; but other articles from which the list may be enlarged are: FACETIOUS FORMATIONS; GALLICISMS; HACKNEYED PHRASES; INCONGRUOUS VOCABULARY; IRRELEVANT ALLUSION; MANNERISMS; MISQUOTATION; NOVELESE; POPULARIZED TECHNICALITIES; SOBRIQUETS; STOCK PATHOS; VOGUE WORDS; WARDOUR STREET; & WORN-OUT HUMOR.

battle royal. A free fight (of more than 2 people); fig. a general squabble.

baulk. See BALK.

bay, bow, window. A bay window, named as making a bay in the room, is one that projects outwards from the wall in a rectangular, polygonal, or semicircular form; bow window, though often loosely applied to any of these shapes, is properly restricted to the curved one.

bayou(s). Pron. bī'o͞o(z). The regular term in the lower Mississippi region for an arm or outlet of a lake or river, a minor river or tributary.

bazaar. So spelled.

B.C. Before Christ. 140 B.C. to A.D. 30 is 170 years. *The second century* B.C. Usually printed in small capitals.

be. 1. The number of the verb between a subject & a complement of different number agrees with the subject. *The only obstacle* is *the wide ditches.* See ARE, IS.

2. For abuse of *be* & *were* as subjunctives (WRONG: *If an injunction* be *obtained* & *he* defies *it; It* were *to be wished*), see SUBJUNCTIVES.

3. For mistaken fear of separating *be* from its particle &c. (AWKWARD: *If his counsel* still *is followed; The right wholly* to be *maintained*), see POSITION OF ADVERBS. The normal order is *is still followed; to be wholly maintained.*

4. *He is dead, & I alive* is permissible; but NOT *I shall dismiss him, as he ought to be;* the second must have *dismissed* after *to be.* For such forms see ELLIPSIS 1, 3.

5. Confusion of auxiliary & copulative uses. In *The visit was made* we have *was* auxiliary; in *The impression was favorable* we have *was* copulative. To make one *was* serve in both capacities is slovenly. WRONG: *The first visit* was *made & returned, & the first impression of the new neighbors on the Falconet family*^ *highly favorable; was* should be repeated after *family*—though, if *created* had stood instead of *highly favorable,* the repetition would have been unnecessary.

6. Case of the complement. The rule that the complement must be in the same case as the subject of the copula (*You believed that* it *was* he; *You believed* it *to be* him), is often broken in talk (*It wasn't me*), but should be observed in print, except when the solecism is preserved in dialogue as characteristic. The temptation in its simplest forms is rare, but may occur; Meredith, for instance, writes *I am she, she me, till death & beyond it,* where the ungrammatical *me* is not satirically intended; & this should not be imitated. Two special types of sentence, however, call for mention. One is that illustrated by (WRONG) *We feed children* whom *we think are hungry* (*who are hungry; we think* is parenthetical and does not affect the clause); for this see WHOM. The other is seen in *He has been, & not only passed for, our leader,* where it pains the grammarian to find that *leader* is subjective after *has been,* but objective after *for.* We might be tempted to disregard his pain as due merely to a pedantic familiarity with Latin, in which the cases are not so often indistinguishable in form; but if we pass *the leader* sentence as good enough for English, we are committed also to *This plan, which I have often tried & has never failed me;* & from that every well-regulated mind will shrink, if only because the step from *A man that hates me & I hate* to *Jones,* who *hates me & I hate* is so fatally easy. Whether resistance is desirable may be better judged from a genuine production of the ill-regulated mind: (WRONG) *It gave a cachet of extreme clericalism to the Irish Party* which *it does not deserve,* but^*must prejudice it not a little in the eyes of English Radicalism.*

7. Forms. Those that require notice are (a) *an't, ain't* (b) the singular subjunctives, & (c) *wast, wert.* (a) *Ain't* is unrecognized in modern English, & as used for *isn't* is an uneducated blunder and serves no useful purpose. But it is a pity that *a(i)n't* for *am not,* being a natural contraction & supplying a real want, should shock us as though tarred with the same brush. Though *I'm not* serves well enough in statements, there is no abbreviation but *a(i)n't I?* for *am I not?* or *am not I?;* & the shamefaced reluctance with which these full

forms are often brought out betrays the speaker's sneaking affection for the *ain't I* that he (or still more she) fears will convict him of low breeding (*Well, I'm doing it already, ain't I?; Yes, ain't I a lucky man?; I'm next, ain't I?*). *Aren't I*, used as an escape by some, is ungrammatical. (b) The present subjunctive has *be* throughout (*Be I fair or foul; If thou be true; Be it so*), the form *beest*, originally indicative but used for a time as second singular subjunctive, being obsolete. The singular of the past subjunctive is *were, wert, were* (*If I were you; Wert thou mine; It were wise*), *were* for the second person being obsolete. (c) *Wert*, originally indicative, was adopted like *beest* as a subjunctive form, & though it is still sometimes used alternatively with *wast* as indicative, the modern tendency is to differentiate the two & make *wert* subjunctive only (*when thou wast true; If thou wert true*)—a natural development that should be encouraged.

bear, v. As a substitute for *carry, bear* is a FORMAL WORD to be used sparingly. The past participle in all senses except that of 'birth' is *borne*. See BORN(E).

bear (market), bearish, with reference to the stock exchange, indicating a declining market, came into use in the 18th c.: *a bearskin jobber*, presumably suggested by the saying, 'to sell the bearskin before one has caught the bear.'

beat. The old p.p. *beat*, still the only form in *dead beat*, lingers colloquially also in the sense worsted, baffled (*I won't be beat; Has never been beat*), but now suggests ignorance rather than archaism. *To beat about* (US *around*) *the bush*, i.e. approach a subject in a roundabout manner, is not modern slang, but has a history back to the 16th c.

beau has pl. *beaux* (US sometimes *beaus*).

beau geste. A fine gesture; a display of magnanimity. But see FRENCH WORDS, & GESTURE.

beau-ideal. If the word is to be used it should be pronounced bō īdē′al, & written without accent. But neither in its only French sense of ideal beauty, nor in its current English sense of perfect type or highest possible embodiment of something, is there any occasion to use it, unless as a shoddy ornament. The English sense is based on the error of supposing *ideal* to be the noun (instead of the adj.) in the French phrase; & the English noun *ideal*, without *beau*, is accordingly the right word to use, unless *flower, perfection, very type, pattern*, or some other word is more suitable.

beau monde. People of fashion, 'the fashionable world.' But see FRENCH WORDS.

beauteous means beautiful; when not a poeticism it now usually suggests a sensuous, superficial beauty.

beautician. Chiefly US. See BARBARISMS.

beautiful. *But the* home beautiful *needs other growing greenery when the festive season arrives./The Bed Beautiful . . .* Such vulgarizing adaptations of Bunyan have upon readers the effect described in IRRELEVANT ALLUSION.

because. After such openings as *The reason is, The reason why . . . is,* the clause containing the reason should not begin with *because,* but with *that.* NOT: *The* reason was because *they had joined societies which become bankrupt./The chief* reason why *he welcomed this bill* was because *he regarded it as . . . Their joining & his belief* are the reasons; & these can be paraphrased into the noun clauses *that they had joined* &c., but not into the adverbial clauses *because they had joined* &c. For similar mistakes, see HAZINESS.

bedouin may serve as noun or as adj. As noun it is properly a plural but is used as both singular and plural in Brit. *Bedouins* is often used as the pl. in the US. On the use of the forms *bedawy* or *bedawee* (sing.) & *bedawin* or *bedaween* (pl.) as nearer to the Arabic, see DIDACTICISM.

beef. Pl. *beeves;* sometimes (US) *beef.*

been. In US usually pronounced *bĭn,* Brit. bēn (bĕn is dial. or illiterate).

beggar. So spelled.

begging the question. Founding a conclusion on a basis that needs to be proved as much as the conclusion itself: *Fox hunting is not cruel since the fox enjoys the fun.*

begin. (1) Past *began,* formerly also (& still rarely) *begun.* (2) For *It was begun to be built* &c., see DOUBLE PASSIVES.

behalf & behoof are often confused both in construction & in sense. *On* (or *in*) *his* &c. *behalf,* or *on behalf of all* &c. (*I can speak only on my own behalf; Application was made on behalf of the prosecutor*); *on* and *in* are the normal prepositions. The phrase means *on the part of, in the interest of;* it does NOT mean, except additionally & by chance, *for the advantage of;* it is still in common use. *For* or *to his* &c. *behoof,* or *for* or *to the behoof of all* &c., does mean *for* or *to the advantage of him, all,* &c. (*For the behoof of the unlearned; To the use & behoof of him & his heirs; Taking towns for his own behoof*); *for* & *to* are the prepositions; *the* is normally used; the meaning of *behoof* is simply *advantage;* the phrases are more or less archaic.

behavior. In US so spelled. Brit. *-iour.*

behemoth. (From Job, 'great or monstrous beast'; in modern usage a general symbol of largeness and strength. *Leviathan,* biblical sea monster.) Behē′mŏth is the correct pronunciation.

behest='command' is now poetic or archaic. The meaning vow, promise, is obs.

beholden, beholding. As p.p. of *behold, beholden* is now obs. except in poetry. In the sense 'bound by gratitude' (which it got when *behold* could still mean hold fast) it is still in use, though archaic by the side of *obliged; beholding* in that sense is an ancient error due to ignorance of how *beholden* got its meaning, & should be allowed to perish.

behoof. See BEHALF.

behoove, behove. Now usually impersonal: *it behooves me to follow his wishes;* i.e. is incumbent upon me. The first spelling, pronounced to rhyme with *prove,* is preferred in US, the second, now usually made to rhyme with *grove,* is Brit.

believable, credible. For emphasis *believable* is often used rather than *credible,* esp. in the negative: *It is simply not believable. Believableness* is an awkward substitute for *credibility.*

belittle, to make seem little, or less; to depreciate, minimize. An Americanism, formerly deplored by Brit. scholars, the word is now standard on both sides of the Atlantic.

belles-lettres. Now usually used of literature 'for its own sake,' not for information, narration, &c.; esp. of certain types of essays.

belly is a good word now almost done to death by GENTEELISM. It lingers in proverbs & phrases, but even they are being amended into up-to-date delicacy, & the road to the heart lies less often through the belly than through the stomach or the tummy. The slaying of the slayer now in course of performance by *tummy* (esp. Brit.) illustrates the vanity of genteel efforts; a perpetual succession of names, often ending in nursery ineptitudes (*smock, shift, chemise*), must be contrived. *Stomach* for *belly* is a specially bad case, because the meaning of *stomach* has to be changed before it can take the place of *belly* in many contexts. The tendency, however, is perhaps irresistible.

belong. The sense 'have its own proper place' (*The book is not where it belongs*) was originally, and is still chiefly, US.

beloved is, when used as a p.p. (*beloved by all; was much beloved*), disyllabic (-ŭvd); as a mere adjective (*dearly beloved brethren; the beloved wife of*), or as a noun (*my beloved*), it is trisyllabic (-ŭvĭd); the first of these rules is sometimes broken in ignorance of usage, & the second with a view to the emphasis attaching to what is unusual.

below, under. There is a fairly clear distinction between the prepositions, worth preserving at the cost of some trouble; but the present tendency is to obscure it by allowing *under* to encroach; & if this continues *below* will seem more & more stilted, till it is finally abandoned to the archaists. The distinction is that *below,* like its contrary *above,* is concerned with difference of level & suggests comparison of independent things, whereas *under,* like its contrary *over,* is concerned with superposition & subjection, & suggests some interrelation. *The classes below us* are merely those not up to our level; those *under us* are those that we rule. *Below the bridge* means with it higher up the stream; *under the bridge,* with it overhead. Contexts in which *below* is both right & usual are *below par, below the salt.* Contexts in which *under* is encroaching *are men below* 45, *below one's breath, no one below a bishop, incomes below* $5000. Contexts in which *under* is both right & usual are *under the sun, the sod, the table, the circumstances, the Stuarts, tyranny, protection, one's wing, one's thumb, a cloud.* Cf. also BENEATH.

beneath. The generally current sense is too mean(ly) or low for (*He married beneath him; It is beneath contempt; It would be beneath me to notice it*). Apart from this it is now usually a poetic, rhet., or emotional substitute for *under* or *below*.

Benedick, not *Benedict,* is the spelling in *Much Ado,* & should always be the spelling when the name is used generically for a confirmed or captured bachelor; but *Benedict* is often used (*Penalize the recalcitrant Benedicts by putting a heavy tax upon them*) either (& probably) in ignorance, or on the irrelevant ground that Shakespeare might have done well to use the more etymological form in *-ct.*

benefit makes *-fited, -fiting.*

Benelux (countries). BElgium, the NEtherlands, & LUXembourg, as a regional economic group.

Bengali, Bengalee. Pron. bĕng gaw′lĭ. The form in *-i* is now perhaps commoner in both US & Brit.

benign, benignant; malign, malignant. The distinction between the long & short forms is not very clear, nor is it consistently observed. But it may be said generally that *benign* & *malign* refer rather to effect, & *benignant* & *malignant* to intention or disposition: *Exercises a benign* or *malign influence; A benignant* or *malignant deity.* An unconscious possessor of the evil eye has a *malign* but not a *malignant* look; discipline is *benign* rather than *benignant,* indulgence *benignant* rather than *benign.* The difference is the same in kind, though less in degree, as that between *beneficent, maleficent,* & *benevolent, malevolent.* It is to be noticed, however, (1) that the impulse of personification often substitutes the *-ant* forms for the others, e.g. as epithets of destiny, chance, &c.; (2) that the distinction is less generally maintained between *benign* & *benignant* than between the other two (e.g. *of benign appearance* is common, where *benignant* would be better); (3) that nevertheless in medical use as epithets of diseases, morbid growths, &c., the forms are *benign* (as would be expected) & *malignant* (contrary to the rule); this use of *malignant* is perhaps a stereotyped example of the personifying tendency, which *benign* escaped because *benignant,* a recent formation, did not exist when the words were acquiring their medical sense. See also MALIGNANCY.

berate. Still in current usage in US (to scold, chide vehemently); obs. in Brit.

bereaved, bereft. The essential principle is perhaps that *bereaved* is resorted to in the more emotional contexts, *bereft* being regarded as the everyday form. The result in practice is that (1) *bereft* is used when the loss is specified by an *of* phrase, & *bereaved* when it is not, the latter naturally suggesting that it is the greatest possible (*Are you bereft of your senses?; The blow bereft him of consciousness; A bereaved mother; Weeping because she is bereaved*); but (2) *bereaved* is sometimes used even before *of* when the loss is that of a beloved person (*A mother bereft,* or *bereaved, of her children; Death bereft,* or *bereaved, her of him*).

Berkeley. Bishop Berkeley, pron. barkly; but Berkeley, Calif., pronounce burk-. *Berkeleian,* so spelled.

beseech. *Besought* is the established past & p.p., though *beseeched,* on which the OED comment is merely 'now regarded as incorrect,' still occurs, probably by inadvertence, & Milton has *beseecht.*

beside(s). The forms have been fully differentiated in ordinary modern use, though they are often confused again in poetry, & by those who prefer the abnormal or are unobservant of the normal. (1) *Besides* has all the adverbial uses; *besides* would have been normal in *And what is more, she may keep her lover beside. We talked of thee & none beside.* (2) *Beside* alone has the primary prepositional senses 'by the side of' (*Sat down beside her; She is an angel beside you*), 'out of contact with' (*beside the point, the mark, the purpose*). (3) *Besides* traditionally has the secondary prepositional senses 'in addition to,' 'except.' *Other men besides ourselves./I have no adviser besides you.*

besiege, so spelled.

bestir is now always used reflexively (*must bestir myself*), & never, idiomatically, as an ordinary transitive verb; *stirred* should have been used in (WRONG) *The example of the French in Morocco has* bestirred *Italy into activity in Africa.*

bet. Both *bet* & *betted* are in idiomatic use as past & p.p. *He bet me $5 I could not; They betted a good deal in those days; I have bet* $500 *against it; How much has been bet on him?* These examples, in which it will probably be admitted that the form used is better than the other, suggest that *bet* is preferred in the more usual connection, i.e. with reference to a definite transaction or specified sum, & *betted* when the sense is more general.

bête noire. 'Black beast'; bugbear, (pet) aversion. See FRENCH WORDS. Those who wish to use the phrase in writing must not suppose, like the male writer quoted below, that the gender can be varied. WRONG: *From the very first, & for some reason that has always been a mystery to me, I was his* bête noir.

bethink has constructions & meanings of its own, 'to stop to think' (*of, how,* or *that*); 'take it into one's head' (*to*); 'recall,' 'consider,' 'call to mind,' 'remind oneself' (*of, how, that*), always reflexive. It can never serve as a mere oramental substitute for *think;* NOT *They will* bethink themselves *the only unhappy on the earth.*

betide means *happen,* NOT *betoken* or *presage,* and is in modern usage only 3rd person sing. pres. subj.: *woe betide you.*

better. The idiomatic phrase *had better* requires care. CORRECT FORMS: *He had better be away, He had better have been away.* If the phrase *would find* (*have found*) *it wise to* is substituted for *had better,* it will be obvious that (WRONG) *He had better been away* is not English. *Better than* for *more than* (*I have better than a dozen answers already*) is colloq.

better, bettor. The first is the more usual for a person who places bets.

betterment has the specific use in law of improvement of real property which makes it better than mere repairing would do. For the use of the word in general contexts, see SAXONISM. WRONG: *The late Lady Victoria devoted her entire life to the* betterment *of the crofters & fishermen;* if the writer had been satisfied with the English for *betterment,* which is *improvement,* he would not have been blinded by the unusual word to the fact that he was writing nonsense; the lady's effort was not to better or improve the crofters, but their lot.

between is a sadly ill-treated word; the point on which care is most necessary is that numbered 5.

1. The illiterate *between you & I,* which is often said, perhaps results from a hazy remembrance of hearing *you & me* corrected in the subjective.

2. *Between* may be followed by a single plural (*between two perils*) as well as by two separate expressions with *and* (*between the devil & the deep sea*); but it must not be followed by a single expression in which a distributive such as *each* or *every* is supposed to represent a plural. NOT *A pitcher who tried to gain time by blowing his nose* between *every ball;* this must be corrected to *after every ball, between the balls,* or *between every ball & the next.* NOT *The absence of professional jealousy that must exist* between each member *of our profession;* read *between the members,* or if emphasis is indispensable, *between each member . . . & the rest.*

3. *Between . . . & between.* The temptation to repeat *between* with the second term, which comes in long sentences, must be resisted. *Between you & between me* is at once seen to be absurdly wrong; the following is as UNGRAMMATICAL: *The claim yesterday was for the difference* between *the old rate, which was a rate by agreement, &* between *the new, of which the Board simply sent round a notice.* See OVERZEAL.

4. *Between,* used after words like *difference,* seems to tempt people to put down for one of the terms the exact opposite of what they mean. WRONG: *My friend Mr. Bounderby would never see any* difference between leaving *the Coketown 'hands' exactly as they were* & requiring *them to be fed with turtle soup & venison out of gold spoons* (for *leaving* read *refusing to leave*)./*There is a very great* distinction between a craven truckling *to foreign nations* & adopting the attitude *of the proverbial Irishman at a fair, who goes about asking if anybody would like to tread on the tail of his coat* (read *avoiding* for *adopting*).

5. *Between . . . or* &c. In the commonest use of *between,* i.e. where two terms are separately specified, the one & only right connection between those terms is *and.* But writers indulge in all sorts of freaks. The more exceptional & absurd of these, in which *against, whereas, & to,* are experimented with, are illustrated in (WRONG): *It is the old contest* between *Justice & Charity,* between *the right to carry a weapon oneself* against *the power to shelter behind someone else's shield.* (Here ELEGANT VARIATION has been at work; to avoid repeating *be-*

tween . . . and is more desirable than to please the grammarian.)/*Societies with a membership* between *one thousand* to *five thousand.* These are freaks or accidents; the real temptation, strong under certain circumstances, is to use *or* for *and. They may pay in money* or *in kind* is wrongly but naturally converted into *The choice is* between *payment in money* or *in kind.* So (WRONG) *We have in that substance the link* between *organic* or *inorganic matter./Forced to choose* between *the sacrifice of important interests on the one hand* or *the expansion of the estimates on the other.* These again are simple, requiring no further correction than the change of *or* to *and.* Extenuating circumstances can be pleaded only when one or each of the terms is compound & has its parts connected by *and,* as in: *The question lies* between *a God & a creed,* or *a God in such an abstract sense that does not signify* (read *between a God & a creed on the one hand, & on the other a God in such* &c.).

betwixt. Now poetic, archaic, or dial. for *between.* See ARCHAISM.

bevel. Usually *beveled, -ing* (US); *-lled, -ling* (Brit.).

bevy. A company, 'properly of ladies, roes, quails, and larks' (COD).

beware is now used only where *be* would be the part required with *ware* regarded as = cautious, i.e. in the imperative (*Beware of the dog!*), infinitive (*He had better beware*), & pres. subjunctive (*Unless they beware*). *Bewaring, I beware* or *bewared, was bewared of,* &c., are obs.

bi-. Prefix usually meaning two or twice; not hyphened in est. words (*biennial, bilateral, bipartisan*) in US or Brit.; hyphened in Brit. in more recent combinations (*bi-weekly, bi-parietal*) but often not in US. *Bi-* prefixed to English words of time (*bihourly, biweekly, bimonthly,* &c.) gives words that have no merits & two faults: they are unsightly hybrids, & they are ambiguous. To judge from most dictionaries the first means only *two-hourly;* the second & third mean both *two-weekly, two-monthly,* & *half-weekly, half-monthly.* Under these desperate circumstances we can never know where we are. It is true that the present tendency (US) is to confine *bi-* to two-, *semi-* to half-, but the practice is far from universal (not followed by ACD, for example). Also the practice in US of writing them unhyphened makes them additionally objectionable: *biyearly, bihourly.* There is no reason why the *bi-* hybrids should not be allowed to perish, & the natural & unambiguous *two-hourly* & *half-hourly, fortnightly* & *half-weekly, two-monthly* & *half-monthly, two-yearly* & *half-yearly,* of which several are already common, be used regularly in place of them & the words (*biennial, bimestrial*) on which they were fashioned; these latter have now almost become ambiguous themselves from the ambiguity of their misshapen brood.

biannual, probably invented to stand to *biennial* as *half-yearly* to *two-yearly,* is sometimes confused with & sometimes distinguished from it.

Half-yearly is the better word; see BI-.

bias. *Biased, biasing* are better than *-ss-;* also in noun, pl. *biases* (cf. *atlases, crocuses*).

bicentenary, bicentennial. The former is more usual in Brit., the latter in the US; but both are used. The accent may fall on -tĕn′- (or -tēn′-) in both, but -cĕn′- is also possible for the first.

biceps, triceps. If plurals are wanted, it is best to say *-cepses,* the regular English formation; not *-cipites* (the true Latin), because it is too cumbrous, nor *-ceps,* which is a mere blunder.

bid. 1. In the auction sense the past & p.p. are both *bid* (*He bid up to* 10; *Nothing was bid*).

2. In other senses, the past is usually spelled *bade* & pronounced bad; the p.p. is *bidden,* but *bid* is preferred in some phrases, esp. *Do as you are bid.*

3. *Bid one go* &c. has been displaced in speech by *tell one to go* &c., but lingers in literary use.

4. In the sense command, the active is usually followed by infinitive without *to* (*I bade him go*), but the passive by *to* (*he was bidden to go*).

5. The noun *bid* has become a VOGUE WORD in modern journalism; *Russia's bid for peace; the bid for world power.*

bide. Apart from archaism & poetic use, the word is now idiomatic only in *bide one's time,* & its past in this phrase is *bided.*

biennial. Two-yearly. See BI-.

big, great, large. The differences in meaning & usage cannot be exhaustively set forth; but a few points may be made clear. Roughly, the notions of mere size & quantity have been transferred from *great* to *large* & *big; great* is now reserved for less simple meanings, as will be explained below; *large* & *big* differ, first, in that the latter is more familiar & colloquial, & secondly, in that each has additional senses—*large* its own Latin sense of generous, & *big* certain of the senses proper to *great,* in which it tends to be used sometimes as a colloquial & sometimes as a half-slang substitute. It will be best to classify the chief uses of *great* as the central work, with incidental comments on the other two.

1. With abstracts expressing things that vary in degree, *great* means 'a high degree of' (*great care, ignorance, happiness, tolerance, sorrow, learning, generosity*); *big* is not idiomatic with any of these; & though *large* is used with *tolerance* & *generosity,* it is in a special sense —broad-minded or prodigal. With words of this kind that happen themselves to mean size or quantity (*size, quantity, bulk, magnitude, amount, tonnage*) *large* & *big* are sometimes used, though neither is as idiomatic as *great,* & *big* is slangy.

2. With words denoting persons or things such that one specimen of the class deserves the name more fully than another (e.g. one fool is more a fool, but one boot is not more a boot, than another), *great* does not imply size, but indicates that the specimen has the essential quality in a high degree; so *a great opportunity, occasion, friend, landowner, majority, nui-*

sance, brute, haul, race (contest), *undertaking, linguist, age.* Here *large* could be substituted with *landowner, majority, haul,* & *undertaking,* but merely because a large quantity of land, votes, fish, or money is involved; *big* could stand with the same four on the same ground. *Big* is slangily used also with most of the others; this is bad; *a great fool* should mean a very foolish fool, & *a big fool* one whose stature belies his wit.

3. A *great* has the meaning 'eminent,' 'of distinction,' & *the great* the meaning 'chief,' 'principal,' 'especial' (*a great man; great houses; a great family; the great advantage,* or *thing, is*); & from these comes the use of *great* as a distinctive epithet (*Great Britain; Alexander the Great; the great toe*), with the idea of size either absent or quite subordinate. In these senses *large* cannot be used, though it would stand with many of the same words in a different sense (*a great family* has distinguished, but *a large family* numerous, members); *big* is here again slangily & ambiguously substituted for *great; a big man* should refer to the man's size, or be extended only (as in *the big men of the trade;* cf. *large* with landowner &c. in 2) to express the quantity of his stock or transactions. *The big toe,* however, & such examples as *the big gate,* show that *big* may serve as a distinctive epithet instead of *great* without slangy effect when difference of size is the salient point of distinction; & in such contexts it is now idiomatic.

4. Finally, *great* does sometimes mean of remarkable size—the sense that it has for the most part resigned to *large* & *big*—but it is so used only where size is to be represented as causing emotion; *large* & *big* give the cold fact; *great* gives the fact colored with feeling; e.g. *He hit me with a great stick* is better than *with a large* or *big stick* if I am angry about its size; but in *Perhaps a big* or *large stick might do* it would be impossible to substitute *great.* Similarly *Big dogs are better out of doors,* but *I am not going to have that great dog in here; His feet are large* or *big,* but *Take your great feet off the sofa. What a great head he has!* suggests admiration of the vast brain or fear of the formidable teeth it probably contains, whereas *What a large head he has!* suggests dispassionate observation.

bihourly. See BI-.

bill. As meaning paper money (*a dollar bill* &c), peculiar to US. So also *bill fold.*

billet-doux. Love letter (lit. 'a sweet note'), now jocular. Pron. bĭ'lĭ dōō. Pl. *billets-doux,* but pron. bĭ'lĭ dōōz.

billion, trillion, quadrillion, &c. It should be remembered that these words do not mean in American (which follows the French use) what they mean in British English. For the British they mean the 2nd, 3rd, 4th, &c., power of a million; i.e. a billion is a million millions (1,000,000,000,000), a trillion a million million millions, &c. For Americans they mean a thousand multiplied by itself twice, three times, four times, &c.; i.e. a billion is a thousand thousand thousands (1,000,000,000) or a thousand millions; a trillion is a thousand thousand thousand thousands or a million millions, &c.

bimonthly, biquarterly. See BI-.

bird's-eye, n. & adj., usually and best so spelled.

birth rate. In US two words; Brit., usually hyphened.

bishopric. The rank belonging to a bishop; also the province of a bishop, for which *diocese* is the more usual term.

bivalve. For *succulent bivalve* see PEDANTIC HUMOR.

bivouac. Pron. bĭv′wăk or bĭv′-ooak. Participles *-cked, -cking.*

biweekly, biyearly. See BI-.

black(en). The short form is used when the intentional laying on of coloring matter is meant, & otherwise the long; we *black boots* with blacking, *grates* with black lead, & *faces* with burnt cork; *we blacken a reputation, oak blackens* with age, & *the ceiling is blackened* with smoke; an exception is that *we black,* rather than *blacken, a person's eye* for him.

blackguard. Pron. blăg′ärd.

blamable. So spelled.

blame. A person is blamed or to blame *for* an offense; *blame on* & *blame it on* are slang or illiterate.

blank verse. (Poet.): strictly, any unrhymed verse. Spec. unrhymed iambic pentameter, as used by Shakespeare, Milton, &c.

blasé. Cloyed, surfeited. Pron. blä zā′ or blä′-. A circumlocution-saver for being so surfeited with pleasure &c. as to be unable to enjoy ordinary things.

blaspheme, -r, -y. Pron. blăs-fēm′, blăsfēm′er, blăs′fĕmĭ.

blended, blent. *Blended* is now the everyday form (*carefully blended teas; he successfully blended amusement with instruction*); but *blent* survives in poetic, rhetorical, & dignified contexts (*pity & anger blent*).

blessed, blest. The accent used below (blessėd) is for the purpose of the article only. The attributive adjective is regularly disyllabic (*blessėd innocence; what a blessėd thing is sleep!; the blessėd dead; every blessėd night; not a blessėd one*), & the plural noun with *the,* which is an absolute use of the adjective, is so also; but the monosyllabic pronunciation is sometimes used in verse, or to secure emphasis by the unusual, or in archaic phrases; the spelling is then *blest: our blest Redeemer; that blest abode; the Isles, the mansions, of the Blest.* The past tense, p.p., & predicative adjective are regularly monosyllabic; the spelling is usually *blessed* in the past tense, *blest* in clearly adjectival contexts, & variable in the p.p. (*He blessed himself; God has blessed me with riches; He is blessed,* or *blest, with good health, in his lot,* &c.; *Blessed,* or *blest, if I know; Those who win heaven, blest are they; It is twice blest*); in the beatitudes & similar contexts, however, *blessėd* is usual.

blessedness. For *single blessedness* see WORN-OUT HUMOR.

blithesome is a NEEDLESS VARIANT of *blithe.*

blond(e). The *-e* should be dropped; the practice now usual is to retain it when the word is used either as noun or as adjective of a woman & drop it otherwise (*the blonde girl; she is a blonde; she has a blond complexion; the blond races*); but this is by no means universal, & the doubt between *blond woman* & *blonde women* (with *blondes women* in the background) at once shows its absurdity.

bloom, blossom. Strictly, *bloom* n. & v. refers to the flower as itself the ultimate achievement of the plant, & *blossom* n. & v. to the flower as promising fruit; the distinction, as regards literal flowers, is perhaps rather horticultural than literary or general; at any rate it is often neglected; but *The roses are in bloom, The apple trees are in blossom,* & other uses, confirm it; & in figurative contexts, the blooming-time or bloom of a period of art is its moment of fullest development, when its blossoming-time or blossom is already long past.

blouse. Pron. -z, not -s.

board. Traditionally, you board a ship; to board a train is unjustifiable but (US?) established.

boatswain. The nautical pronunciation (bō′sn) has become so general that to avoid it is more affected than to use it.

bog(e)y, bogie. *Bogy* is the bugbear, & *bogie* in coach building; the golf word is usually *bogey*.

Bologna. The sausage, pron. bolō′nya or coloq. -nē. The slang word is spelled *baloney*.

Bolshevism. The doctrines, practices, &c., of the Bolshevik (i.e. 'larger,' 'major') party, renamed in 1919 the Communist party. See COMMUNISM.

bona fide(s). *Bona fide* is a Latin ablative, meaning in good faith; its original use is accordingly adverbial (*Was the contract made bona fide?*); but it is also & more commonly used attributively like an adjective (*Was it a bona fide,* or *bona-fide, contract?*); in this attributive use the hyphen is correct, but not usual; in the adverbial use it is wrong. *Bona fides* is the noun (*His bona fides was questioned*); the mistake is sometimes made by those who know no Latin of using *fide* instead of *fides.* Properly pronounced bō′nȧ fī dē (n. -dēs), but generally in US (& elsewhere) bō′na fīd.

bonhomie. Good nature, geniality. So spelled, not *-mm-*.

bon mot. 'Good word.' A witty remark, or adroit or happy expression. Pron. bôn mō; pl. (*bons mots*) -ōz (Eng.) or ō (Fr.). See FRENCH WORDS.

bon voyage. 'Good voyage'; farewell phrase, properly used when the trip is by water or by air (over water).

bookmaker. In US the professional bet-taker has appropriated this word so completely that the maker of books has virtually abandoned it. It is still used occasionally (derog.) of a mechanical compiler of books.

born(e). The p.p. of *bear* in all senses except that of birth is *borne* (*I have borne with you till now; Was borne along helpless*); *borne* is also used when the reference is to birth (a) in the active (*Has borne no children*), & (b) in the passive when *by* follows (*Of all the children borne by her one survives*). The p.p. in the sense of birth, when used passively without *by*, is *born* (*Was born blind; A born fool; Of all the children born to them; The melancholy born of solitude.*)

botanic(al). The *-ic* form is now almost superseded by *botanical,* except in names of some gardens & institutions. *The Royal Botanic Gardens* (Kew); *The Brooklyn, Elgin, California*

Botanic Gardens; but the *New York, Missouri, United States Botanical Gardens.*

both. 1. *Both . . . as well as. Both* must be followed by *and,* NOT by *as well as.* If *as well as* is used, *both* must be omitted. NOT *He has figured prominently* both *in the carters' strike, in which many of his members were involved,* as well as *in the more recent railway strike.* Correct to read *He has figured prominently* both *in the carters' strike . . .* and *in the more recent,* &c., or omit *both. The metrostyle will always be of exceeding interest,* both *to the composer* and (NOT *as well as*) *to the public.*

2. Redundant *both.* The addition of *both* to *equal(ly), alike, at once, between,* or any other word that makes it needless, is at least a fault of style, & at worst (e.g. with *between*) an illogicality. In the examples, *both* should be omitted, unless the omission of the other word(s) in roman type is preferable or possible. WRONG: *If any great advance is to be* at once both *intelligible & interesting./The currents shifted the mines, to the* equal *danger* both *of friend & foe./The International Society is not afraid to invite comparisons* between *masters* both *old & new.*

3. Common parts in *both . . . and* phrases. Words placed between the *both* & the *and* are thereby declared not to be common to both members; accordingly, *Both* in *India & Australia* is wrong; the right arrangements are (a) *Both* in *India &* in *Australia,* (b) *In* both *India & Australia;* of these (b) sounds formal, & is often shrunk from as a remedy worse than the disease; but there is no objection to (a), which should be used. Similarly, *Both* the *Indians &* the *Australians* is right & unobjectionable; *Both* the *Indians & Australians* is common but wrong.

4. Idiomatic usage. *We are both wrong. Both of us are wrong. They* (or *John & Jim*) *had both gone* (i.e. *both* follows the verb *be*—also, sometimes, *seem, become, appear,* &c.—and auxiliary verbs). *Both my friends saw it* (or *had seen it*) or for emphasis *My friends both saw it. Both arguments have some justification.* NOT IDIOMATIC: *We both, they both saw it* (for *both of us, of them*). *Both of the arguments* is colloq. for *both arguments.*

bottleneck. Fig. something that checks progress; in good standing, but overworked.

bottom. *The bottom of the list, the bottom of the page,* are good usage; insistence on *the foot of the page* &c. is a GENTEELISM or GALLICISM.

boughten for *bought,* p.p., is poetic or dial.

boulevard. Pron. (US) bo͞o′-lĕvärd (Brit., Fr., bo͞ol′vär); bo͞o′lĕvard (US var.) tends to deteriorate into bŭllyvard.

bound. The p.p. means obliged, compelled, destined (*a plan bound to succeed*); the meaning determined, resolved (*I am bound to go if I can possibly make it*), is US colloq.

bounden is still used, & *bound* is not, with *duty.* It is also used alternatively with *bound* as the p.p. of *bind* in the sense oblige (*I am much bounden,* or *bound, to you*); but the whole verb, including the p.p., is a mere ARCHAISM in this sense.

bounteous, -iful. The two

mean the same thing, but the first is literary or poetic, the second the usual word.

bouquet. Pron. bōō kā′.

Bourbon. The French family, pron. bŏŏr′bon; the whiskey, usually bûrbun.

bourgeois. Pron. bŏŏr zhwä′. Originally, one of the 'burghers' of the shopkeeping middle class; among socialists, anyone with private property interests. Often loosely & over-used. As the name of a printing type, in which sense the word is English, it is pronounced berjois.

bourn(e). There are two words, which were originally *burn* & *borne*, but are now not distinguished, consistently at any rate, either in spelling or in pronunciation. The first means a stream, but now in US occurs chiefly in poetry as an ornamental synonym for brook. The second means properly a boundary (from French *borne*) as in *The undiscovered country from whose borne No traveller returns*, but is used almost solely, with a distorted memory of that passage, in the sense of destination or goal. The OED prefers *bourn* stream, & *bourne* goal, & the differentiation would be useful.

bowdlerize. Expurgate; from the name of Thomas Bowdler, whose edition of Shakespeare (1818) omitted all 'offensive words & expressions.' Bow- rhymes with *cow*.

Bowery. A farm, plantation (fr. Dutch); the district & street in N.Y. so spelled, but *St. Mark's in The Bouwerie.*

bow window. A curved bay window. See BAY.

Boxing day. Brit. The first weekday after Christmas, on which Christmas boxes [tips] are given to servants &c. A legal holiday. Nothing to do with boxing matches.

boycott. To refrain by concerted action from communicating, purchasing, or using, &c. From the name of Captain Boycott, a land agent who was so treated in 1880 by the Irish Land League.

brace, n. (=two). Used esp. of dogs, game, and of things that are a pair, as *a brace of pistols.* When used after a numeral, usually in the singular form: *We shot* 20 *brace.* When used of people, usually facetious or contemptuous. See COLLECTIVES 3.

brachylogy. (Gram.): 'short speech.' Irregular shortening down of expression. *Less sugar, This is no use, & A is as good or better than B,* are brachylogies for *Less* of *sugar, This is* of *no use,* & *A is as good* as *or better than B.* The first is established as idiomatic, the others are still regarded by many as illegitimate.

brackets, parentheses, braces. Although all were formerly (& are still in Brit.) called brackets, the following differentiation is now general in US: brackets [ ]; parentheses ( ); braces {. In modern US typography the brackets (formerly 'square brackets') are used to indicate interpolated material or a second interpolation within parenthetical material. *'The report was given by* [*usually reliable*] *sources.'* (*Published in Volume I* [1950–55] *of the Western Encyclopedia.*) Braces are used to link together 2 lines of writing or printing: *The south* } *wind.*
east }

brain(s), in the sense of 'wits,' may often be either singular or plural, the latter being, perhaps, the familiar, & the former the dignified use. In *pick a person's brain(s)*, the number is indifferent; *Has no brains* is commoner than *Has no brain*, but either is English. Some phrases, however, admit only one number or the other, e.g. *cudgel one's brains, have a thing on the brain, have one's brain turned.*

brake, break, nn. The words meaning (1) bracken, (2) thicket, (3) lever, (4) crushing or kneading or peeling or harrowing instrument, (5) steadying-frame, though perhaps all of different origins, are spelled *brake* always. The word that means checking appliance is usually *brake*, but *break* sometimes occurs owing to a probably false derivation from *to break.* The word meaning horsebreaker's carriage frame, & applied also to a large wagonette, is usually, & probably should be, *break*, but *brake* is not uncommon. The word meaning fracture &c. is always *break.*

branch. Fig.='department,' 'subdivision': *branch of learning; branch of military service.* For synonymy see FIELD.

bran(d)-new. The spelling with *-d* is the right (fresh as from the furnace); but the *d* is seldom heard, & often not written.

brave in the sense fine or showy is an ARCHAISM, & in the sense worthy a GALLICISM; *make a brave show*, however, is fully current.

brazen. Current chiefly in secondary & metaphorical uses: *brazen impudence, brazen effrontery*, but *brass handles, a brass bowl.*

breeches &c. The singular noun & its derivatives (*breechloader, breeching*, &c.) have usually -ēch in pronunciation; *breeches* the garment has always -ĭch-, & the verb *breech* (put the child into breeches) usually follows this.

breve. (Printing): The symbol placed over a vowel to show it is short: căt, gĕt, lĕt, mŏp, cŭt.

brevet, n. & v. Pron. brĕ'vĭt; the past & p.p. are *breveted.*

brier, briar. (1) For the word meaning thorny bush, the spelling *brier* & the monosyllabic pronunciation brīr are nearer the original & preferable; *brere* is still nearer, but now a poetic archaism only. (2) The name of the pipe wood is an entirely different word, but also best spelled *brier.*

brilliance, -cy. The two words are for the most part synonymous; '*brilliancy*, however, is more distinctly a quality having degrees; as in the comparative brilliancy of two colours.' OED.

brindle(d), brinded. The original form *brinded* is archaic, & should be used only in poetry. *Brindled*, a variant of it, is now the ordinary adjective, & *brindle*, a BACK-FORMATION from this, & convenient as a name for the color (gray or tawny, marked with bars or streaks of darker colors) should be used only as a noun.

brio. Italian *liveliness.* For *An authentic picture of the old workaday West drawn with vigor, affection, and incontestable* brio, see LITERARY CRITICS' WORDS.

Britain, British, Briton. *Britain* is the proper name of the island which includes England,

Scotland, & Wales—now usually called Great Britain. It also is used for the British State or Empire as a whole. *British*, of Great Britain or its inhabitants, esp. in political or imperial connections: *the British army, colonies, ambassador, constitution. Briton* is used chiefly of the race found in England by the Romans; used for a native of Great Britain, it is now usually poetic or melodramatic. For the relation of these to *England, English(man)*, see ENGLAND. In this book the abbreviation *Brit.* is used both for Great Britain and for British (i.e. English) usage.

Briticism, the name for an idiom used in Great Britain & not in America, is a BARBARISM; COD prefers *Britishism,* and implies that *Briticism* is an Americanism.

Britisher is a word made in America, but now discountenanced in American dictionaries as 'in jocose use only' or as 'almost disused.' Fowler remarks that 'if the word is still current in America, Englishmen have both as little right to object to outsiders' applying it to them & as little occasion to use it themselves, as the Germans have to quarrel with us for calling them Germans & not Dutch or to change their name to please us.' Unfortunately the word still appears in US newspapers and book reviews: *Her most memorable characters are Americans and Britishers living in out-of-the-way places./Bogus Britisher Reported Touring U.S. Book Trade.*

broad, wide. Both words have general currency; their existence side by side is not accounted for by one's being more appropriate to any special style. What difference there is must be in meaning; yet how close they are in this respect is shown by their both having *narrow* as their opposite, & both standing in the same relation, if in any at all, to *long*. Nevertheless, though they may often be used indifferently (*a broad* or *a wide road; three feet wide,* or *broad*), there are (1) many words with which one may be used & not the other, (2) many with which one is more idiomatic than the other though the sense is the same, (3) many with which either can be used, but not with precisely the same sense as the other. These numbered points are illustrated below.

The explanation seems to be that *wide* refers to the distance that separates the limits, & *broad* to the amplitude of what connects them. When it does not matter which of these is in our minds, either word does equally well. If the hedges are far apart, we have a wide road; if there is an ample surface, we have a broad road; it is all one. But (1) *backs, shoulders, chests, bosoms,* are *broad,* not wide, whereas *eyes* & *mouths* are *wide,* not broad; *at wide intervals, give a wide berth, wide open,* in all of which *broad* is impossible, have the idea of separation strongly; & *wide trousers, wide sleeves, wide range, wide influence, wide distribution, the wide world,* where *broad* is again impossible, suggest the remoteness of the limit. Of the words that admit *broad* but refuse *wide* some are of the simple kind (*broad blades, leaves; the broad arrow*), but with many some secondary notion such as generosity or downrightness or neglect of the petty is the representative of the simple idea of amplitude (*broad daylight, broad jests, broad farce, broad hint, broad outline*).

(2) Some words with which one of the two is idiomatic, but the other not impossible, are: (preferring *broad*) *expanse, brow, forehead, lands, estates, acres, brim, mind, gauge;* (preferring *wide*) *opening, gap, gulf, culture.*

(3) Some illustrations of the difference in meaning between *broad* & *wide* with the same word; the first two may be thought fanciful, but hardly the others: *A wide door* is one that gives entrance to several abreast, *a broad door* is one of imposing dimensions; *a wide river* takes long to cross, *a broad river* shows a fine expanse of water; *a wide generalization* covers many particulars, *a broad generalization* disregards unimportant exceptions; *a wide distinction* or *difference* implies that the things are very far from identical, but *a broad distinction* or *difference* is merely one that requires no subtlety for its appreciation.

broadcast, v. In radio & television, *-ed* is permissible & perhaps preferable in the past tense, but unpopular and seldom used in US; p.p. always *broadcast.* Cf. FORECAST.

broadness is now usual instead of *breadth* only when the meaning is coarseness or indelicacy of expression.

Brobdingnag (NOT *-ignag*) is the spelling.

brochure, pamphlet. Pron. brôshōōr′.

brogue properly refers to the Irish speech, not the Scottish.

brooch. Best rhymes with *coach.*

brow. *In the sweat of thy brow;* properly *of thy face.* See MISQUOTATION.

Bruin (bear). See SOBRIQUETS.

bruit. Pron. brōōt. Archaic as a noun, but still used as a verb, esp. in the passive with *about, abroad*=rumored, noised.

brusque. In US usually pronounced brŭsk; Brit. brōōsk.

brutal, brute, brutish. *Brutal* differs from *brute* in its adjectival or attributive use, & from *brutish,* in having lost its simplest sense of the brutes as opposed to man & being never used without implying moral condemnation. Thus, while *brute force* is contrasted with skill, *brutal force* is contrasted with humanity. In torturing a mouse, a cat is *brutish* & a person *brutal.*

buck. The male of the reindeer, fallow deer, antelope, hare, rabbit, (US) goat, rat, colloq. sheep. But not properly applied to the male of the red deer (stag) or the elk or moose (bull).

buffalo. Pl. *-oes* or (usually) as sing. See COLLECTIVES 4.

buffet. In US, pron. bōō fā′. The OED pronounces this bŭ′fĭt in the sense sideboard or cupboard, & as French in the sense refreshment bar.

buncombe, bunkum. Although the COD prefers the shorter spelling, the first, from an American place name, is the original and is preferred in the US. The word was first used by Felix Walker in the 16th Congress: he was bound to make a speech for Buncombe (a county in his district in N.C.).

Hence the meaning, anything done for mere show; insincere publication, nonsense; the shorter form, *bunk,* is slang.

buoy is now pronounced bōō′ĭ (US) or boi (Brit.), & attempts to restore bwoi, the pronunciation 'recognized by all orthoepists British & American' (OED), are doomed to fail.

bur, burr. The word meaning prickly seed pod &c. is usually, & might conveniently be always, *bur;* the word describing pronunciation is always *burr;* in all the other senses, which are less common, *burr* is usual & might well be universal.

burden, burthen. The second form is, even with reference to a ship's carrying capacity, for which *burden* is now often used, a NEEDLESS VARIANT; & in other uses it is an ARCHAISM.

bureau. For a (bedroom) chest of drawers, chiefly US; for a desk or writing table with drawers, chiefly Brit. Both countries use it in its transf. sense, government department. The plural is regularly *-s* in US, often *-x* Brit.

bureaucrat &c. Pron. US bū′-rô krăt, bū rŏk′răsĭ (Brit. often -ŏ′kră-).

burgh, burgher. *Burgh,* still in English use, is pronounced like the English form *borough. Burgher,* an archaism, is pronounced ber′ger.

burglary. Originally (Law) breaking into and entering the dwelling of another, in the nighttime, with intent to commit felony. *Burgle* (chiefly Brit.), *burglarize* (chiefly US), are labeled 'humorous' or 'colloq.' in most dictionaries. A verb being undoubtedly wanted, & words on the pattern of *burglarize* being acceptable only when there is no other possibility, it is to be hoped that *burgle* may outgrow its present facetiousness & become generally current.

burlesque, caricature, parody, travesty. In wider applications the words are often interchangeable. Two distinctions, however, are worth notice: (1) burlesque, caricature, & parody have, besides their wider uses, each a special province; *action* or *acting* is *burlesqued, form & features* are *caricatured,* & *verbal expression* is *parodied;* (2) *travesty* differs from the others both in having no special province & in being more used than they (though all four may be used either way) when the imitation is intended to be or pass for an exact one but fails, & not to amuse by its mixture of likeness & unlikeness to the original.

burnt, burned. *Burnt* is the participial adj. (*a burnt offering*) and an alternative form of the past & p.p. (esp. in Brit.). *Burned* tends to prevail in the US for the simple past (often pron. burnt, though spelled *-ed*): *He burned his hands; he was badly burned* or *burnt.*

burr. See BUR.

burst, bust. In the slang expressions *bust up, go on a bust, bronco busting,* &c., the spelling *bust* is established, & should be used by those who use the phrases.

bus is sufficiently established to require no apostrophe; the plural is now usually *buses.*

business, busyness. The second form (pron. bĭ′zĭnis) is used as the simple abstract noun of *busy* (the state &c. of being busy) for distinction from the regular *business* with its special developments of meaning.

businessman, businesslike, are usually so spelled in US (& some Brit.) dictionaries, but many writers & publishers use the older *business man.* The advantage is seen in *a small businessman* vs. *a small* or *small- business man.*

buskin. For *the buskin* meaning the tragic stage &c. see BATTERED ORNAMENTS.

but. 1. Case after *but*=except. *No one knows but I. But* was originally a preposition meaning *outside,* but is now usually made a conjunctive, the subjective case being preferred after it when admissible. *Whence all but he* (NOT *him*) *had fled* exemplifies, in fact, the normal modern literary use. *All but him* is used (a) by those who either do not know or do not care whether it is right or not (& accordingly it is still good colloq.) & (b) by the few who, being aware that *but* was originally prepositional, are also proud of the knowledge and willing to air it (& accordingly it is still pedantic-literary). It is true that the conjunctional use has prevailed owing partly to the mistaken notion that *No one knows it but me* is the same blunder as *It is me;* but it has prevailed in literary use, & it is in itself legitimate. It would therefore be well for it to be universally accepted.

2. Redundant negative after *but. But* (now rare), *but that* (literary), & *but what* (colloq.), have often in negative & interrogative sentences the meaning *that . . . not.* But just as *I shouldn't wonder if he didn't fall in* is often heard in speech where *didn't fall* should be *fell,* so careless writers insert after *but* the negative already implied in it. Examples (all WRONG): *Who knows* but that *the whole history of the Conference might* not *have been changed?/Who knows* but what *agreeing to differ may* not *be a form of agreement rather than a form of difference?/How can he tell* but that *two years hence he may* not *be tired of official life?* (Omit *not* in all three.) For similar mistakes, see HAZINESS.

3. Illogical *but.* The right & wrong types in the simplest form are: (RIGHT) *It is not black, but white; It is not black; it is white; It is not black; but it is nearly black;* (WRONG) *It is not black, but* it is *white; It is not black, but it is nearly* white. A very common & exasperating use of *but* as the ordinary adversative conjunction is that illustrated in (WRONG): In vain *the horse kicked & reared,* but *he could not unseat his rider* (if the kicking was in vain, the failure to unseat involves no contrast; either *in vain* or *but* must be dropped)./*So far as Mr. Haldane's scheme tends towards the encouragement of local patriotism, it can do* nothing but good; but the only point *about the scheme which seems to me to be* doubtful *concerns the question of the divided responsibility.* (There being only one doubtful point is in harmony, not contrast, with the goodness admitted in the first clause. Omit *but,* or else write *But there is a doubtful point* &c.)/*It is in* no spirit of hostility *that these lines are written;* but it is a sincere appeal *to the men*

of courage & goodwill. (Either omit *but,* or convert the two clauses into one by writing *but in sincere appeal;* we then have the correct form *It is not black, but white* instead of the incorrect *It is not black, but it is white.*) Less excusable blunders than these, due to gross carelessness, occasionally occur (e.g. *It is* not an evergreen, *as is often represented;* but its leaves *fall in the autumn, & are renewed in the spring.* Omit *but.*)

4. Wheels within wheels. The following examples will show the disagreeable effect produced when inside one of the contrasted clauses connected by *but* an internal contrast, also indicated by *but,* is added: *I gazed upon him for some time, expecting that he might awake;* but *he did not,* but *kept on snoring./The reformers affirm the inward life,* but *they do not trust it,* but *use outward & vulgar means.*

5. *But . . . however* is perhaps always due to mere CARELESSNESS: *If any real remedy is to be found we must first diagnose the true nature of the disease;* but that, however, *is not hard.*/But *one thing,* however, *had not changed, & that was . . . /The enemy's cavalry withdrew with losses,* but *they returned,* however, *reinforced by . . .* (Omit *but* or *however.*)

6. *But which:* for the dangers, see WHICH WITH AND OR BUT.

buzz. So spelled, US & Brit.

by, prep., owing to the variety of its senses, is apt to be unintentionally used several times in the same sentence. When the uses are parallel & the repetition intentional (*We can now travel* by *land,* by *sea, or* by *air*), monotony is better than the ELEGANT VARIATION (by *land,* on *the sea,* or through *the air*) often affected; but such accidental recurrences of *by* as are here shown are slovenly (cf. OF): *The author's* feeble *attempt to round off the play* by *causing Maggie to conquer* by *making John laugh* by *her poor joke about Eve was not worthy of him./Palmerston wasted the strength derived* by *England* by *the great war* by *his brag.*

by, bye, by-. The spelling & usage in regard to separating the two parts, hyphening them, or writing them as one word, are variable. The following scheme might secure consistency without violating any usage that deserves respect.

1. The noun is *bye* (in sports, & in *by the bye*).

2. The adjective should be written *by-* (*by-product, by-election,* &c.). In US the hyphen is usually omitted in *bylaw, byword, byway;* and usage varies in *by-road, by-name, by-pass* (n.), *by-part, by-play;* the hyphen is therefore recommended.

3. The adverb should be spelled *by* & joined on without hyphen (*bygone, bystander,* &c.).

4. Some special words: *by & by* has the adverb or preposition twice, & should follow their spelling; *bye-bye* sleep, & *bye-bye* goodby, are unconnected with *by,* & have usually the *-e; by-law* is perhaps also unconnected, & is often spelled *bye-,* but may well be assimilated to words under rule 2.

A list is added for convenience: *by & by, by-blow, bye* (n.), *bye-bye, by-election, by-*

line, bygone, by-product, bystander.

Byzantine. The usual pronunciation is bĭzăn′tīn (or -ĭn); classical scholars, however, often accent the first syllable (cf. Flor′entine, Ap′ennine).

C

cab(b)alist(ic), cab(b)ala, &c. *Caba-*, the earlier spelling, is est. in US; *cabba-*, etymologically preferable, is est. in Brit.

cacao. Pron. kakā′ō, & see COCOA. Pl. *-os.*

cache. Pron. kăsh.

cachet (pron. kă shā′) is mainly a LITERARY CRITICS' WORD (*bears the cachet of genius* &c.), & should be expelled as an alien; *stamp, seal, sign,* are good enough for English readers. For synonymy, see SIGN.

cacodemon, cacodaemon. Pron. kă kō dē′mŏn. Evil spirit. The first spelling is better.

cacoethes scribendi. 'Itch for writing.' See BATTERED ORNAMENTS.

cacophony. Discord, dissonance ('ill-sound'). See ANTI-SAXONISM.

cactus. Pl. *-uses* or *-i.*

caddie, caddy. The golf attendant, *-ie;* the tea box, *-y.*

cadet. Younger son; student in a military or naval academy: pron. kă dĕt′. After the surname of a French younger brother (*Coquelin cadet*), pron. kȧ′dā′.

cadre should be anglicized in sound & pronounced kah′der, in pl. kah′derz; the French pronunciation is especially inconvenient in words much used in the plural. But in US military use, often kă′drê.

caduceus. Ancient herald's staff, esp. that of Hermes. The symbol of a physician and of the medical corps. Pl. *-cei.* Pron. kȧ dū′sĭŭs, -ēī.

caecum, Caesar, ca(e)sium, caesura, &c. *Cesium* is standard in US. The others so spelled.

caesura. (Poet.): 'cutting.' The point at which a verse line falls into two parts (in the middle of a foot or at the end). A rhythmic break, a sense pause in modern verse. *The stag at eve/had drunk its fill.*

café is naturalized in the sense coffee house or restaurant; in the sense coffee it is a French word (*café noir,* black coffee; *café au lait,* half milk, half coffee), and should be set in italics.

Caffre. See *Kaffir.*

caisson. (Ammunition chest, &c.) Pron. kā′sn.

calculate. (1) *Calculate* makes *calculable.* (2) The Americanism is an example of SLIPSHOD EXTENSION; the sense 'I consider-as-the-result-of-a-calculation' passes into the simple sense 'I consider.' *We shall win, I calculate, by a narrow majority* shows the normal use, the assumption at least being that the numbers have been reckoned & compared. *We shall be in time, I calculate* is (according to Brit. usage) correct if the time wanted & the time at disposal have been worked out in detail, but wrong if it is a mere general expression of sanguineness. *You don't know everything, I calcu-*

late is the full-fledged colloq. Americanism. So also *A story well-calculated to keep you in suspense.*

calculus. Pl. *-li.*

caldron is more usual in US, *cauldron* Brit.

Caledonian. Putting aside its special sense (inhabitant) of ancient Scotland, & its ornamental use in names of clubs, companies, &c., the word serves chiefly as material for POLYSYLLABIC HUMOR.

caliber, calibre. The first usual US, the second Brit.

caliph is the usual spelling, & kā′lĭf the pronunciation; the OED states, however, that 'orientalists now favour Khalif'; see DIDACTICISM.

calk, caulk. The first usual in US, the second Brit. Pron. kôk.

calligraphy &c. 'Beautiful handwriting.' NOT *calig-.*

cal(l)isthenics. Exercises to develop 'beautiful strength.' ('Chiefly a term of young ladies' boarding schools,' OED.) The *-ll-* is 'etymologically preferable' and is now standard Brit.; the single *-l-* is est. in US.

callus, n. Pl. *-uses.* Adj., *callous.*

calmative, being queer both in pronunciation (kăl′matĭv, not kah′matĭv) & in formation, should be left to the doctors, if even they have a use for it beside *sedative,* as a technical term.

calumny. Pron. kăl′ŭmnĭ.

camellia. Named by Linnæus for Kamel (latinized *Camellus*), the Jesuit botanist; properly pron. kam ĕl′ĭa, but the mispronunciation -mē- is now so prevalent as to be almost justified by usage.

camelopard does not contain the word *leopard,* & should be neither spelled nor pronounced as if it did. Pron. kamĕl′opard. (*Giraffe* is now the usual word.)

cameo. Stone carved in relief, esp. the sardonyx, giving a white figure on a red background. Pron. kăm′ĭō. Pl. *cameos* (earlier often *camei*). *Intaglio,* an incised figure depressed below the surface of the stone.

camera. A chamber; spec. a judge's chamber. *In camera,* in the judge's private room, not in open court; hence privately. The photographic instrument, orig. *camera obscura,* Lat. 'dark chamber,' i.e. dark box.

campanile. Bell tower. Pron. kămpănē′lė. Pl. *-les.*

campus. In Roman antiq., an open field for military exercises &c. Used for the grounds of a college or school, US.

can. (1) *Can* expresses power (physical or mental) to act; *may,* permission or sanction to act. The use of *can* for *may* is colloq. and permissible in spoken and informal (US) use. It is not justified in formal writing. (2) *Can't seem* is obviously absurd (not able to seem), as in *I can't seem to understand what you mean* (i.e. *I don't understand, I'm not able to* [*can't*] *understand*). Even though it is occasionally used by good writers, *can't help but* is colloq. (and awkward) as in *I can't help but despise a person like that* for *I can't help despising* &c. (3) *Cannot* is usually one word, except when special meaning or emphasis is needed.

Canaan(ite). The prevalent pronunciation in US is kā′nan(īt); Brit. kā′nyan(īt).

cancel. In US usually *-led, -ling;* Brit. *-lled, -lling.*

cancellation. Best so spelled.

candelabrum. The pl. *-bra* is still preferred to *-brums;* the false sing. *-bra* with pl. *-bras* should not be used.

cando(u)r. US *-or,* Brit. *-our.*

CANNIBALISM. That words should devour their own kind is a sad fact, but the guilt is perhaps less theirs than their employers'; at any rate the thing happens. WRONG: *The true facts should be made known in regard to*‸whom *is actually due the credit of first proving the existence of petroleum in this country.* (*To* has swallowed a *to.*) *It is more or less—& certainly*‸more *than less—a standardized product.* (*More* has swallowed a *more.*)/*The Council shall direct the Members as to*‸*which combatant is to be applied the Decree of Non-intercourse.* (*To* has swallowed a *to,* as its way is when employed by AS-*to* writers.)

cannon. Pl. *cannons* or collectively *cannon.*

cannot. See CAN.

canoe makes *canoeing, canoeist.*

cañon, canyon. The first is Spanish; the second now est. in English.

canorous. Pron. kanō'rus. *Melodious* is the usual word. See INCONGRUOUS VOCABULARY.

cant. The modern meaning is the insincere use of words implying piety or appealing to (religious, moral, political, &c.) principles that the speaker does not act upon or does not understand. For full discussion see JARGON.

cantaloup(e). The shorter form is Brit. (pron. -lo͞op); the longer, US (pron. -lōp).

cantatrice is usually pronounced as Italian (-ēchā), sometimes as French (-ēs); *singer* should be preferred when it is not misleading; other English substitutes, as *songstress, female singer,* are seldom tolerable; but see FEMININE DESIGNATIONS.

canto. Pl. *-os.*

canton(ment). The noun *canton* is usually kăn tŏn', sometimes kăn'ton. The verb is in civil and US military use kăntŏn', but in Brit. military use generally kăntoon'. The noun *cantonment,* which is military only, is generally kantŏn'ment US; kanto͞on'ment.

canvas(s). The material is best spelled *-as;* so also the verb meaning to line &c. with canvas; the plural of the noun is *-ses.* The verb meaning to discuss, ask votes, &c., has always *-ss;* so also the noun meaning the process &c. of canvassing in this sense.

capable. Constr. *of* (constr. with inf., e.g. *capable to do it,* now archaic). *Capable of giving happiness; capable of great things* (but *able to do great things*).

capitalist, properly a noun, is used attrib. rather than *capitalistic,* esp. in economics & Poli. Sci.: *The capitalist class; the theory of capitalist development.*

Capitol. The temple of Jupiter; US, the house of congressional meetings in Washington, D.C.; in many states, the state house. All other uses are *capital.*

caption, in the sense title or heading, is 'rare in Brit. use, &

might well be rarer,' but is firmly established in US.

carat, karat. The *c* is recommended; some US dictionaries give *k* for the measure of purity of gold (1/24; 14 karat gold is 14 parts gold, 10 parts alloy), *c* for the unit of weights of precious stones (*c.* 3½ grains), but the differentiation is not worth preserving.

caravanserai, -sera, -sary. The first spelling (pron. -rī) is the best etymologically; the last more usual in US.

carburetor, carburettor, carburetter. All three spellings are recognized; the first is more usual in US; the second in Brit.

carcass, -ase. The *-ss* form is better.

cardinal numbers. One, two, three, &c., as opposed to ordinal numbers, first, second, &c.

cardinal virtues. In scholastic philosophy the four natural virtues, justice, prudence, temperance, & fortitude, to which are added the 'theological' virtues, faith, hope, & charity.

careful. Constr. *of* (or *for*), inf., *that: Careful* of *the horses. More careful* for *his second child. Careful* to maintain *his obligations. Be careful* that *they are kept intact. Careful with* (*Do be careful with that knife*) is in general use colloq.

caret. A mark placed below the line or in the margin (‸) to indicate that something has been omitted.

cargo. Pl. *-oes.*

Caribbean. Pron. kar ĭ bē'an.

caricature. Grotesque or ludicrous representation by exaggeration or distortion. See BURLESQUE.

carillon. Pron. kăr'ĭ lŏn (US), kă'rĭlyon (Brit.), or as French.

carnelian. *Cornelian* is the original (and proper) spelling, standard in Brit. But *carnelian,* which came into use in the late 15th c. through false etymology, is standard US.

carnivore. (Pl. *carnivora.*) Any one of the flesh-eating mammalia.

carol. US usually *-ler, -ling,* &c.; Brit. *-ller, -lling,* &c.

carousal=drinking bout &c., so spelled. The Hist. cavalry tournament and the modern merry-go-round, *carrousel* (var. *carousel*); pron. -zĕl'.

carpet. For *on the carpet* ('under discussion') see GALLICISMS; a disadvantage peculiar to the phrase is that the sense required for carpet (*tablecloth*) is obs.

carte, quart(e), in fencing. The first spelling, still the commonest except in technical books following French authorities, should be preferred if only as keeping the pronunciation right.

carte blanche. 'White paper'; hence, full discretionary power.

cartel, in the old senses, is pronounced kar'tl; in the sense of manufacturers' combination it represents German *Kartell* & is often so spelled; it may therefore be expected to accent the last syllable for some time at least. The manufacturers' cartel is a contract between independent establishments regulating the amount of output for each, & in certain cases also the prices (Enc. Brit.); cf. TRUST.

carven for *carved* is a REVIVAL, not having been used between the 16th & 18th cc. *Carved* is usually better.

caryatid. (Female figure used

as a column.) Pron. kărĭă′tĭd Pl. *-ids* or *-ides*.

case. There is perhaps no single word so freely resorted to as a trouble saver, & consequently responsible for so much flabby writing. The following extract, in which the individual uses are comparatively justifiable, shows how the word now slips off the pen even of an educated writer: *In the majority of* cases *where reprisals have been the object, the blockade has been instituted by a single State, while in* cases *of intervention several powers have taken part; this is not, however, necessarily the* case.

To obviate the suspicion of an intolerant desire to banish it from the language, let it be admitted that *case* has plenty of legitimate uses, as in: *If I were in your* case; *A bad* case *of blackmailing; I am only stating a* case; *Circumstances alter* cases; *In* case *of fire, give the alarm; Take brandy with you in* case *of need; The plaintiff has no* case; *What succeeds in one* case *may fail in another; Never overstate your* case; *In no* case *are you to leave your post; It would be excusable for a starving man, but that was not your* case; *There are seven* cases *of cholera.*

Some of the bad uses are: *in any case* (meaning from any point of view), *in the case of* (meaning in this connection, or just superfluous), *in many cases* (often, many, usually), *in no case* (never, none, &c.), *as was formerly the case* (as it used to be), *that is not the case* (that is not so). It will be seen that *in the case of*, the worst offender, can often be simply struck out (parentheses are used to show this) & often avoided by the most trifling change, such as the omission of another word (also in parentheses). Many examples are given, in the hope that any writer who has inspected the misshapen brood may refuse to bring more of them into the world: *Older readers will, at least* (in the case of) *those who abhor all Jingoist tendencies, regret that the authors have* . . ./In no case *does the writer of any one of the four Gospels give his own name* (None of the four evangelists gives)./(In) *many* (cases the) *answers lacked care./He has large interests in various joint-stock enterprises, &*, in cases, *possesses a seat on the board* (& sits on the board of some of these)./*Even in the purely Celtic areas only in two or three* cases *do the first bishops bear Celtic names* (only two or three of the first bishops bear)./*That in all public examinations acting teachers* in every case *be associated with the universities* (teachers be always associated)./In this & other cases, *such as coal, the world is living on its capital.* (What, coal a case? we cry it mercy; we took it for fuel.)

The ELEGANT VARIATIONist is in clover with *case;* it is provided, in *instance*, with one of those doubles that he loves to juggle with, & *be the case* enables him to show his superiority to the common mortal who would tamely repeat a verb. We conclude with a few of his vagaries: *Although in eight* cases *the tenure of office of members had expired, in every* instance *the outgoing member had been re-elected* (Although the tenure of office of eight members . . . they were all re-elected)./*Thunderstorms have* in several cases *occurred, & in* most instances *they have oc-*

curred at night (There have been several thunderstorms, usually at night)./*We gather that he remained what his previous record had led us to anticipate* would be the case (to anticipate that he would remain).

casein. Pron. properly kā′-sĭĭn; kā′sēn, although used popularly in US, is not recognized by most dictionaries.

CASES. 1. General. The remaining case forms in English are the subjective (or nominative), objective (accusative), and possessive (or genitive). *I* (subject) gave *her* (indirect object) *my* (possessive) book (direct object). *Who* (subject) will choose *me* (object)? *Whom* (object) do *you* (subject) prefer? The sense of case is not very lively among English speakers because, very few words having retained distinguishable case forms, it is often needless to make up one's mind what case one is using. Mistakes occur chiefly, though not only, with (a) the few words having case forms, mostly personal pronouns, & (b) the relative pronouns. Accordingly, necessary warnings, with illustrations & discussion, are given in the articles I, ME, HE, SHE, WE, US, THEY, WHO 1, 2, THAT REL. PRON. 5, & WHAT 3; & to these may be added BE 6, LET, & THAN, which words are apt to deceive weak grammarians.

2. Specimens of case mistakes: A. *Three years of training are a preliminary* for he *who would defend his fellows* (should be *him*, object of *for*)./*Should not a Christian community* receive *with open arms* he *who comes out into the world with clean hands & a clean heart?* (should be *him*, object of *receive*)./*They came to fight in order to pick up the challenge* of he *who had said 'Our future lies on the water'* (should be *him*, object of *of*)./*But it is the whimsical perplexity of Americans contemplating the appearance of London that* provides he *who guides with most amusement* (*him*, object of *provides*).

B. *I saw a young girl gazing about, somewhat open-mouthed & confused,* whom *I guessed to be* she *whom I had come to meet* (should be *her*)./*It is not likely that other & inferior works were done at the same time* by an impostor *pretending to be* he (should be *him*). The temptation is to assume, perhaps from often hearing *It is me* corrected to *It is I*, that a subjective case cannot be wrong after the verb *to be*. But in these B examples it is not *to be* that decides the case of *he* & *she*; it is *whom* & *impostor*.

C. *One comes again to the problem* of Kant—he, *too, a cosmopolitan like Goethe* (should be *him* in apposition to *Kant*, object of *of*)./*It is sad to look in vain for a perambulator in Nursemaids' Walk & discover only one solitary* person, & he *a sentry* (should be *him*, in apposition to *person*, object of *discover*). It is hard not to sympathize with the victims of this trap. *Him, too, a cosmopolitan,* & *him a sentry,* do sound as if one was airing one's knowledge of the concords. Well, perhaps it is better to air one's knowledge than one's ignorance of them; but the escape from both is to be found in evading the pronoun (*another cosmopolitan,* or *also a cosmopolitan*) or sacrificing the apposition (*& he was a sentry*).

D. *Eye hath not* seen, *nor ear*

heard, *neither* have entered *into the heart of man,* the things which *God hath prepared for them that love him./Yet the coal is there in abundant quantities, & there is* nothing^*the world* wants *so much or*^can be dispensed *with such handsome profit to those who produce it.* The invisibility of case in nouns tempts us to try sometimes whether they may not be made to serve two masters. In the verse from Corinthians, *things* has to serve *seen-&-heard* as object, & *have entered* as subject. 1 Cor.ii.9 is the reference, & a glance at the R.V. shows, with its *which* in italics, that the Revisers did not regard its grammar as passable. The second example has the peculiarity that the word whose case is in question, viz. *that,* not only has no distinguishable cases, but is not on show at all; but the sentence is ungrammatical unless it is inserted twice—*nothing* that *the world wants so much, or* that *can be dispensed.*

E. *Let Gilbert's future wife be*^whom *she may.* In this difficulty write the sentence in full, *Let Gilbert's wife be* her who *she may be;* & the insertion of the omitted *her* having provided the first *be* with the objective complement that it requires, we find ourselves able to write *who* as the subjective complement required by the second *be; who* is in fact the grammatical English; cf. WHOEVER.

casket, a small chest or box, as for jewels. Its use for *coffin* is an Americanism, and so used in Brit. is a GENTEELISM.

cast, v., is a FORMAL WORD for *throw.* It is idiomatic in *cast off, cast out, cast eyes on,* &c.

cast(e). *Caste* is sometimes wrongly written for *cast* in certain senses less obviously connected with the verb *cast*—mold, type, tendency, hue, &c. The confusion is the more natural since *cast* was formerly the prevalent spelling for the hereditary class also; but the words are now differentiated & *cast* is the right form in such contexts as: *reflections of a moral* cast, *heroines of such a* cast, *a man of the* cast *of Hooker & Butler, my mind has a melancholy* cast, *his countenance was of the true Scottish* cast, *a strongly individual* cast *of character, their teeth have a yellowish* cast.

caster, -or. The word meaning pepper shaker &c., & swiveled chair-wheel, should be *caster,* meaning literally *thrower* & *veerer,* from the ordinary & an obs. sense of *cast;* this spelling is usual in US but *-or,* probably due to confusion with other *castors,* is now usual in Brit. *Castor oil,* so spelled.

cast iron used as a noun (*cast iron is more brittle*) should be written as two words; *cast-iron* is the attributive or adjectival form (*a cast-iron bracket*).

CAST-IRON IDIOM. Between Idiom & Analogy a secular conflict is waged. Idiom is conservative, standing in the ancient ways, insisting that its property is sacrosanct, permitting no jot or tittle of alteration in the shape of its phrases. Analogy is progressive, bent on extending liberty, demanding better reasons than use & wont for respecting the established, maintaining that the matter is what matters & the form can go hang. Analogy perpetually wins, is forever successful in recasting some piece of the cast iron; Idiom as perpetually renews the fight, & turns to defend some other object of assault. Idiom condemns 'We aim to prove it; This is claimed to be the best; They are oblivious to hardship; I doubt that it ever happened; In order that the work can proceed; He is regarded an honest man; A hardly won victory; With a view of establishing himself' as outrages on English; correct them, please, to: *We aim* at proving *it, They* claim that this is *the best, They are* insensible to *hardship, I doubt* whether *it ever happened, In order that the work* may (be able to) *proceed, He is regarded* as *an honest man,* A hard won *victory, With a view* to *establishing himself.* But why? retorts Analogy. Is not *to aim* the same as *to design?* is not *to claim* to *represent?* does not *oblivious* mean *insensible?* is not to *doubt* to *be unconvinced?* would not *so that* convey the same as *in order that?* is not *regarding considering?* is not *-ly* the adverbial ending, & is not *won* to be modified by an adverb? &, if *in view of* is English, why should *with a view of* be un-English? Away with such hair-splitting & pedantries! when one word is near enough to another to allow me to use either, I propose to neglect your small regulations for the appurtenances proper to each.

Not that Analogy, & those whom it influences, are offenders so deliberate & conscious as that account might seem to imply. They treat *regard* like *consider* not because they choose to flout the difference that Idiom observes, but because it comes natural to them to disregard distinctions that they have not noticed. In ANALOGY 2 it has been pointed out that it has very important functions to perform apart from waging its war upon Idiom; & therefore the admission that this book is wholly partisan in that war need not be interpreted as a condemnation of analogy always & everywhere; the Analogy that wars against Idiom is unsound or hasty or incomplete analogy.

The cast-iron nature of idiom may now be illustrated by a few phrases, shortened down to the utmost, in which some change that to the eye of reason seems of slight importance has converted English into something else. The idiomatic expression is supplied in parentheses: *He did it on his own* ACCORD (account); CONTENTED *himself* by (with) *saying; Spain* ('s prosperity) *was materially* ENHANCED; *We* ENTERTAINED *him* to (at) *dinner; Follow events* at close HAND (quarters); LEST *the last state* becomes (become, *or* should become) *worse than the first; Is* to (in) a great MEASURE *true; Had every* MOTIVE in (for) *doing it; A fact of which he took* every OPPORTUNITY (advantage); *Am not* PRIVILEGED (honored) with *his friendship; Has been* PROMOTED to captain (a captaincy); *The* RESENTMENT *I feel* to (at, *or* against) *this Bill; I cannot* STATE (insert *that*) *he was present; Stood me in* splendid (good) STEAD; *Guests came* by THE hundreds (hundred); *It was not* long UNTIL (before) *he called.* Discussion or actual quotations for these lapses will be found under the words in small capitals; & a few articles that have special bearing on the present subject are: AIM; CLAIM; DOUBT(FUL); FACT; FRI-

DAY; IN ORDER THAT; OBLIVIOUS; PLEASURE; PREFER 3; REGARD 2; RESORT; SUCH 1; THAT CONJ. 2; UNIDIOMATIC -LY; & VIEW.

castle. *Castle in the air* is English; *castle in Spain* is a GALLICISM.

castor. *Castor bean, castor oil,* but (US) CASTERS of a chair, a set of crystal *casters.*

catachresis (adj. *-estic*). (Gram.): 'misuse.' Wrong application of a term, use of words in senses that do not belong to them. The popular uses of *chronic*=severe, *asset*=advantage, *conservative*=low, & *mutual*=common, are examples.

catalogue. Although *catalog* will inevitably become the standard US spelling, most dictionaries still support those who prefer the traditional longer form.

catastrophe. A dénouement, sudden turn, conclusion; fig. a sudden disaster. Its use for ordinary misfortunes should be avoided.

catchup. Usual US spelling. Brit. usually KETCHUP.

catechize. So spelled.

category should be used by no one who is not prepared to state (1) that he does not mean *class,* & (2) that he knows the difference between the two; see WORKING & STYLISH WORDS, & POPULARIZED TECHNICALITIES. In logic it is a 'highest notion,' derived from logical analysis. It can therefore be applied to a class or division in any general scheme of classification, as the biological categories of species, genus, family. *Categorical* implies unqualified, absolute, direct, explicit. Kant's categorical imperative ('Act only on that maxim whereby thou canst at the same time will that it should become a universal law') is the absolute, unconditional command of the moral will—a law given by pure reason, & binding on every rational will. (OED.)

cathedra. From the Greek word for *chair,* esp. of a bishop, teacher, or professor. Hence *ex cathedrâ* (Lat.), from the seat of one with authority; i.e., officially uttered. (The circumflex is unnec. in English.) Pron. -ēd′ra or -ĕd′ra.

Catholic. *Catholic* means universal; in eccl. use, the Church universal, i.e. the whole body of Christians. Neither the desire for brevity (as in *the Catholic countries*) nor the instinct of courtesy (as in *I am not forgetting that you are a Catholic*) should induce anyone who is not Roman Catholic to omit the Roman.

catholic(al)ly. Both forms are rare, & consequently no differentiation has been established; *a catholicly* & *a catholically minded person* may mean either one of wide sympathies &c. or one inclined to (Roman) Catholicism.

cat's-paw. Best so spelled. (US sometimes *catspaw.*)

catsup. Either *catchup* (US) or *ketchup* (Brit.) is better.

caucus. Orig. US, probably of Algonquian orig.: a meeting of party or group leaders to decide on candidates, policies, &c. In Brit., a local political committee for fighting elections, defining policy, &c., generally used only of opponents' organizations.

ca(u)ldron. In US, usually *caldron,* Brit. *cauldron.*

caulk. In US usually *calk.*

cause. WRONG: *The main* cause *of the high price of meat is* due to the *exclusion of foreign cattle.* The main *cause* is the exclusion; the *price* is due to the exclusion; out of two rights is made a wrong. See HAZINESS for this type of blunder; with *reason* it is still commoner than with *cause.*

cause célèbre. Pron. kōz sā lĕbr′. 'A celebrated (legal) case'—a lawsuit, usually criminal, that excites much attraction. It does not mean 'a famous cause.'

causerie. Pron. kōz′*e* rē′. An informal newspaper article (or address) esp. on a literary subject, appearing as one of a series. Named after Sainte Beuve's *Causeries du Lundi* (Monday Talks).

cavalcade. A procession of persons on horseback. Transf. & fig., any procession, hence pageant. It has become a VOGUE WORD in (e.g.): *cavalcade of history, of fashion, of stars.*

caveat. Lat. 'let him beware.' Pron. kā′vĭăt. *Caveat emptor,* 'let the buyer beware' (he buys at his own risk).

cavil. US *caviled, -ing;* Brit. *-lled, -lling.* To raise captious frivolous objections; constr. *at, about: caviling* about *sects and schisms; cavil* at *the rule.*

-c-, -ck-. When a word ending in *c* has a suffix beginning with a vowel added to it, the hard *c* is preserved before the native suffixes *-ed, -er, -ing,* & *-y,* by the addition of a *k* (*mimicked, bivouacker, trafficking, panicky*), but not before the classical suffixes *-ian, -ism, -ist, -ity, -ize* (*musician, criticism, publicist, electricity, catholicize*).

cease is rapidly giving way to *stop,* as *cast* has given way to *throw.* It is no longer the word that presents itself first; we substitute it for *stop* when we want our language to be dignified. It is now poetic, rhetorical, formal, or old-fashioned, though not sufficiently so to have such labels attached to it in dictionaries. No effort should be made to keep words of this kind at work. The man who says he is *going to cease work* is, unless the statement has a rhetorical importance, merely pompous. *Cease fire,* the military command, remains. See FORMAL WORDS.

-ce, -cy. Among the hundreds of words corresponding to actual or possible adjectives or nouns in *-ant* or *-ent,* large numbers now present no choice of form: no one hesitates between *avoidance, forbearance, admittance, magnificence, coincidence,* or *intelligence,* & a form in *-cy;* nor between *buoyancy, constancy, vacancy, agency, decency,* or *cogency,* & a form in *-ce.* But about large numbers also it may easily happen that one has doubts which is the right form, or whether one form is as good as the other, or whether both exist but in different senses: *persistence* or *persistency? frequency* or *frequence? emergency* or *emergence?*

When there is doubt about a word not given in its place in this book, it is to be presumed that either *-ce* or *-cy* may be used, but three generalities may be added. First, that short words favor *-cy,* & longer ones *-ce;* it was not by design but by a significant accident that all the *-cy* words given above as having no *-ce* alternatives were metrical matches for *buoyancy*. Secondly, that many words tend to use the *-ce* form in the singular, but *-cies* rather than *-ces* in the plural, e.g. *irrelevance*, but *irrelevancies*. And thirdly, that euphony often decides, in a particular context, for one or the other ending. Of the first point a good illustration is provided by *frequency* & *innocence;* formerly both endings were common for each, but now from the shorter adjective *frequent -ce* is almost obsolete, & from the longer *innocent -cy* is an archaism preserved by Bible texts. On the second it may be added that words used concretely in the plural, meaning 'specimens of the quality' &c. (*truculencies*=truculent phrases, *irrelevancies*=irrelevant points, *inadvertencies*=acts of inadvertence), partly account for the peculiarity, since when there is differentiation it is *-cy*, not *-ce*, that tends to the concrete, as in *emergency*=event that emerges compared with *emergence*=the emerging. See also TRANSPARENCE.

cedilla. A mark placed under the letter *c* (ç), esp. in French and Spanish words, to show that it is pronounced 'soft,' as *s*. Though now omitted in many words in English, it is still generally used in *façade*.

celerity. Pron. se-. Swiftness, speed, now used chiefly with reference to living beings, as opposed to *velocity*, used for the rate of speed of objects.

cellar. Orig. a storeroom, either above or below ground; now usually an underground room or one at least partly underground, but not fitted for habitation. A *basement* is usually well lighted and used for some household purposes. *The cellar of a farmhouse; a basement apartment.*

'cello. Pl. *-os*. Being now much commoner than *violoncello*, it might well do without its apostrophe. Pron. chĕ′lō.

cellophane. So spelled.

Celt(ic), K-. The spelling *C-* & the pronunciation s- are the established ones, & no useful purpose seems to be served by the substitution of *k-*.

censer, censor. *-er*, the vessel in which incense is burned and the person who offers it; *-or*, the supervisor of public morals.

centenary, centennial, nn. meaning hundredth anniversary. *Centenary*, the usual Brit. form; *centennial*, chiefly used (as a noun) in US. Pron. sĕntĕn′ial, sĕn′tĕnary (US), or sĕntēn′arĭ (Brit.).

center, -re. US & Brit. spelling respectively (but *Centre Street*, N.Y.). Brit. *centreless, centremost, centring.*

centi-, hecto-. In the metric system *centi-* denotes division, & *hecto-* multiplication, by a hundred; cf. *deca-, deci-,* & *kilo-, milli-*.

centigrade. The centigrade 0°=Fahrenheit 32°; 100°C.= 212°F. Pron. sĕnt′-.

century. Each century as ordinarily named (the 5th, 16th, century) contains only one year beginning with the number that names it (500, 1600), & ninety-nine (401–499, 1501–1599) beginning with a number lower by one. Accordingly 763, 1111, 1900,

1901, belong to the 8th, 12th, 19th, & 20th, centuries.

cerebral, cerebrum. Preferred pronunciation, sĕr′ē-, but sĕrē′- is also common in US.

ceremonial, ceremonious, adjs. *Ceremonial* means connected with or constituting or consisting of or fit for a ceremony (i.e. a piece of ritual or formality): *the ceremonial law; a ceremonial occasion; for ceremonial reasons; ceremonial costume. Ceremonious* means full of or resulting from ceremony, i.e. attention to forms: *Why be so ceremonious?; ceremonious people; ceremonious politeness.* In these examples the termination not used could hardly be substituted, even with change of meaning. But with some words *-al* & *-ous* are both possible, though not indifferent: *a ceremonious court* is a sovereign's court in which ceremony is much observed; *a ceremonial court* would be a judicial court set up to regulate ceremonies; a visitor may make *a ceremonious entry* into a room, but an army *a ceremonial entry* into a town that has capitulated.

certitude is now restricted to the single sense of absolute conviction or feeling quite sure; *certainty* can, but often does not, mean this also, & the use of *certitude* may therefore obviate ambiguity. 'The Evangelist distinguishes between what we now call *certitude*—or the belief of the mind—and *certainty*, or the solid reality of the fact or truths believed in.' (E. White, quoted in OED.)

chagrin, pron. sh*a* grĭn′ (US) or sh*a* grēn′ (Brit.), makes *chagrined, -ining.* Orig. a species of rough leather (now usually spelled *shagreen*); fig. mortification arising from disappointment, frustration, or failure.

chairwoman. In US, *chairman* **is** used for either sex.

chaise longue. Pron. shāz lôɴg. The Fr. pl. takes a (silent) *s* on both words, but in US (esp. commercial) *chaise longues* is permitted (pron. longz).

chalet. A herdsman's wooden cottage in the Swiss mountains; a house or cottage of that style. Not just any house on a hillside, as many US house names would suggest. Pron. shă′lā′.

chamois (chamois leather) is best pronounced shă′mĭ; the goatlike antelope often shăm′-wah.

chance, n., makes *chancy.*

chance, v., as a synonym for *happen* (*it chanced that . . . ; I chanced to meet him*) stands in the same relation to it as *cease* to *stop.* See FORMAL WORDS.

chancellery, -ory, -erie. The first form (pron. chan′-) is that preferred.

change makes *changeable* &c.

chanty, sh-, sailors' hauling song. Spell *ch-*, but pronounce shă-; the anomaly is accounted for by the supposed derivation from French *chantez,* sing ye.

chaos. In its transf. & fig. sense, complete disorder & confusion. For *complete chaos* see INCOMPATIBLES.

chap, chop, jaw or cheek. In *lick one's chops, fat chops,* both spellings are common but *chops* is more usual.

chaparral, so spelled.

chaperon. The addition of a final *e* is wrong.

character is a valuable & important word with several well-marked senses. The worst thing that can happen to such a word is that it should be set to do inferior & common work, which, while it could be more suitably done by meaner words, has to be done so often that the nobler word is cheapened by familiarity. The average writer can perhaps not be expected to abstain from the word for the word's sake; but, if he realizes that at the same moment that he degrades the word he is making his sentence feeble & turgid, he will abstain from it for his own sake.

ABUSES: (a) *Character* is used with adjectives as a substitute for an abstract noun termination, *-ness, -ty,* &c.: *The very full* character *of the stage directions indicates . . .* (great fullness)./*On account of its light* Character, *Purity & Age Usher's whisky is a whisky that will agree with you* (lightness; but this is the kind of literature in which such idioms are most excusable)./*Unmoved by any consideration of the unique & ancient* character *of the fabric* (uniqueness & antiquity).

(b) A simple adjective *x* is watered into *of an x character;* the right water for such solutions, which are bad in themselves when not necessary, is *kind;* but the simple adjective is usually possible: *Employment of a* patriotic character (=*patriotic employment*)./*The attention which they receive is of* a greatly improved character./*His influence must have been* of a very strong character *to persuade her./The number of misprints is inconsiderable; we have noticed only one of* a disconcerting character (*kind;* or *one that need be disconcerting*)./*Payments* of the character *in question* (*of this kind;* or *such payments*).

(c) *Character* (colloq.) for an odd, strange, or eccentric person (*he's quite a character*) has a long history (Goldsmith used it in 1773), but its present renewed popularity has reduced it to slang.

character, characteristic, suggest likenesses that are distinctive to the type & distinguish it from every other member of its class or kind. *Superstition is not the* characteristic *of this age.* For synonymy see SIGN.

charade. Pron. US sh*a*rād′; Brit. sh*a*rahd′.

char(e), n. *Chore* has always been the usual word in the US; Brit. usually *char* or *chare. Charwoman,* however, is invariable.

charge. *In charge of* is used both actively & passively; a nurse is left *in charge of* the children; the children left *in charge of* a nurse. The archives are *in charge of* a clerk.

chargé d'affaires. Pron. shär′-zhā d*a* fâr′. Pl. *chargés d'affaires.*

charity. The widespread use of *charity* in the sense generosity to the poor has obscured for many its N.T. sense (Christian) love. Cf. Lincoln's Gettysburg address.

charivari. Pron. properly shar′ĭvar′ĭ, but throughout rural US shariv′arē or shĭvarēe′ (& so spelled), where it is still a local means of celebrating a wedding.

charlatan, &c. Pron. sh-.

Charles's wain. (The Big Dipper.) For *-s's* see POSSESSIVE PUZZLES 1.

charm suggests some quality of enchantment, secret means of attraction, fascination, allurement. For the noun in literary criticism see LITERARY CRITICS' WORDS.

chasse, chassé, chassis. *Chasse* (pron. shahs) is Fr. for the liqueur after coffee; *chassé* (pron. shăsā′, or colloq. US săshā′), the dance step; *chassis* (pron. shăs′ĭ), the framework (of car, plane, radio, &c.)—pl. also *chassis.*

chastise so spelled, not *z;* *chastisement,* pron. chăs′tĭzment.

château. Pl. *-s* or *-x* (pron. -z). The circumflex is often omitted in US, and should never be used with the *s* plural.

chauffeur. The stress (in US) is still usually on the second syllable, though the tendency toward shifting it to the first will probably be effective, as it has been in Brit.

chauvinism. The French parallel to *jingoism.*

cheap(ly). *Cheap* is an adv. as well as an adj. Thus Shakespeare's *sold cheap what is most dear* and Mill's *To sell cheaper* (NOT more cheaply) *in a foreign land.*

check (draft on bank). Brit. *cheque.*

checker is more common in US, CHEQUER in Brit.

(check)mate. *Mate* is the usual form in chess, & *checkmate* in fig. use.

cheerful, cheery. The latter has reference chiefly to externals—voice, appearance, manner, &c. Resignation may be *cheerful* without being *cheery;* & a person may have a *cheerful,* but hardly a *cheery,* spirit without his neighbors' discovering it. The *cheerful* feels & perhaps shows contentment, the *cheery* shows & probably feels it.

chef, chef-d'œuvre. *Chef* (head cook, male) is accepted as English. *Chef-d'œuvre* (pron. shĕ dû′vr′, pl. *chefs-d'œuvre*), though universally understood, has no particular superiority to *masterpiece.*

cheque, though merely a variant of *check,* is in Brit. usage differentiated from it with the sense of bank draft, *check* being chiefly American in this sense.

chequer, checker. The first spelling is very much commoner in Brit. for both the noun & the verb. The game, played on a chequer (chess) board, is called (Brit.) *draughts.* *Chequers* is the Prime Minister's official country house.

cherub, cherubic. (An order of angels ranking below the seraphim.) *Cherub* has pl. *cherubim* chiefly when the cherubim are spoken of as a celestial order; *cherubims* (an earlier form) is wrong; in fig. use *cherubs* is usual. *Cherubim* is the Hebrew pl., *cherubin* in the Vulgate. In English both have been treated as sing., pl., & collective. *Cherubic* is pronounced -oob-′.

chestnut. Spell with & pronounce without the first *t.*

chevy, chivy, n. A hunt or chase, usually spelled *chevy* & pronounced chĭvy. *Chivy* or *chivvy,* v., to torment or harass.

chiaroscuro. It., 'clear-dusk.' Pron. kyar′oskūr′ō. In art, the employment of light & shade, omitting the colors.

chic. (Fr. slang.) Artistic skill; hence style, stylish, 'smart.' Pron. shēk. But see FRENCH WORDS.

chicanery. Trickery, esp. in legal matters. Pron. shĭkān-′.

chide stands to *scold* as *cease* to *stop;* past *chid,* p.p. *chid(den).*

chief, adj. Orig. 'head,' by transf. at the head, or top, in importance; hence principal, foremost, greatest. *Chiefly,* above all, mainly but not exclusively. (As an adv. *chief* is now archaic.)

chiefest, formerly common, is now felt to be an unnatural form, & used only as an ornament.

childish, childlike. The distinction drawn is so familiar that *childish* is in some danger of being restricted to the depreciatory use that is only one of its functions; the rule that *childish* has a bad sense is too sweeping & misleads. *Childish,* as applied to a child, is not derogatory—*his sweet childish expression, his childish treble, bobbing her childish curls,* all natural to childhood. *Childish* used of adults or their qualities means 'that ought to have outgrown something or to have been outgrown,' & *childlike* 'that has fortunately not outgrown something or been outgrown'; *childish simplicity* in an adult is a fault; *childlike simplicity* is a merit; but *childish simplicity* may mean also simplicity *in* (& not *as of*) a child, & convey no blame; *childish enthusiasm* may be either a child's enthusiasm or a man's silly enthusiasm; *childlike enthusiasm* is only that of a man who has not let his heart grow hard.

chili, chilli. Spanish *chili* and so spelled in US; Mexican *chilli,* and so spelled in Brit. (The dried pod of the red pepper, capsicum. Pl. *-ies.*)

chill(y). The form *chill* (as adj.) is only a LITERARY WORD, *chilly* being that in general use.

chimera, -aera, -æra. Pron. kĭmēr′*a* or kīmē′*ra* (='she-goat'). The mythological monster; hence bogey; hence frightful or foolish fancy. The first (short) spelling is preferred.

chimpanzee. Accent last syllable (formerly often -pan′-).

Chinaman &c. The normal uses are: *A Chinaman* (rarely *Chinese*); *three Chinamen* (sometimes *Chinese*); 50,000 *Chinese* (sometimes *Chinamen*); *the Chinese* (rarely *Chinamen*); *she is Chinese.*

chipmunk. So spelled.

chisel makes *-led* &c., US; *-lled* &c., Brit. Its meaning 'to cheat, obtain by shrewd or unfair practices,' has been in slang use since 1808 (quoted in OED).

chivalry &c. The pronunciation sh-, instead of ch-, though based on a mistake, is now established. Of the adjs. *chivalrous* & *chivalric* (accent first syllable), the second should be either let die as a NEEDLESS VARIANT or restricted to the merely grammatical function of representing the phrase *of chivalry,* as in *the chivalric ages.*

choice, adj. In good standing historically, but overworked commercially (*choice fruits & vegetables, a choice selection,* &c.). *Hobson's choice,* the option of the thing offered or nothing.

choler(ic). *Choler,* except when used historically with reference to the four humors, is now a mere ARCHAISM; *choleric,* however, has survived it,

& is preferable in some contexts to irascible, quick-tempered, &c.; pron. kŏl′-.

chorale. Pron. korahl′. As to spelling, the *-e* is strictly incorrect, but both usual & convenient, obviating confusion with the adj. *choral;* cf. *locale* & *morale,* & see À L'OUTRANCE.

c(h)ord. There are two words *chord,* one of which, that used in Harmony, has no connection with *cord;* the other (*touch the right chord; the c(h)ord of an arc; the vocal c(h)ords; the spinal c(h)ord*) is the same as *cord,* but had its spelling corrected after the Greek original. It is well to remember that in the four phrases mentioned *chord* means simply string; but the spelling *cord,* which would have been legitimate & avoided confusion in any of them, is ruled out by custom in Brit. except in the last & possibly the last but one. For US usage, see CORD.

Christian name. The name given in baptism. *First name* and *given name* are equivalents.

chronic (continuing for a long time; confirmed) in the illiterate use for bad, intense, severe (*the weather has been chronic; that was a chronic fight last night*), is a SLIPSHOD EXTENSION. See POPULARIZED TECHNICALITIES. The adv. is *chronically.*

chronologic(al). The longer form is the more usual.

chrysalis has pl. *chrysalises, chrysalids,* or *chrysalides* (krĭsă′lĭdēz); the first should be made the only form.

chute, shoot. The fall of water, from a higher to lower level, is *chute* (from the equiv. Fr. word). The (artificial) water channel for conveyance (of logs &c.) is usually *chute* in US but may be *shoot.* The trough used for conveyance in mines, factories, &c., may be *chute* but is often *shoot* (always in Brit.). *Chute* is also short for parachute.

-ciation. Nouns in *-ation* from verbs in *-ciate* have, if they follow their verbs, the very unpleasant combination of two neighboring syllables with the *-sh-* sound (ĭmāshĭā′shn from *emaciate*). The alternative pronunciation -siashn, sometimes recognized by the OED (e.g. in *association*), avoids the bad sound, & is legitimate on the analogy of *denunciation, pronunciation, annunciation,* of which all might have had, & the last has in *annunciate,* a verb in *-ciate* as well as that in *-ounce.* Words in *-tiation* (as *initiation*) can perhaps hardly be treated in the same way, except those that, like *negotiation,* have alternative forms with *-c-* for *-t-;* nĭgōsĭā′shn seems possible, but not propĭsĭā′shn.

cicatrice, cicatrix. (Scar &c.) The first, pronounced sĭk′ atrĭs & in pl. sĭk′atrĭsĭz, is the English word. The second, pronounced sik′ atrĭks & in pl. sĭk′atrī′sēz, is the Latin, in surgical & other scientific use as well as in general use in US.

cider is a drink made from the juice of apples. *Apple cider* is tautological; *peach, raspberry,* &c., *cider,* from the meaning of the word, are impossible, but are used commercially.

cigarette. The short spelling, *cigaret,* though often seen, is not established. The accent is properly on the last syllable.

Cincinnatus. So spelled.

cinema, for motion picture (theater), has never been widely used in US but is standard Brit. (short for *cinematograph*). Pron sĭn-.

Cingalese. (Native of Ceylon.) In US *Singhalese.* COD gives *Cingalese* as the standard form; OED *Sinhalese.*

cinquecento. Pron. chĭngkwĭchĕn′tō. The 16th c., esp. in Italian art & literature.

cinq(ue)foil. Pron. sĭngk′foil. The longer form is preferred.

cion, scion. The detached shoot or portion of a plant. The OED lists the first as an obs. form of the second, but *cion* is used by most US horticulturists & nurserymen. Fig., *scion* is invariable: *the scion of a noble family.*

cipher. So spelled (NOT *cy-*). In cryptography, *cipher* is restricted to secret writing by means of disarranged letters or substitutions for letters (numbers, symbols, &c.), *code* to substitution of words, letter groups, &c., for words, phrases, or sentences.

circa. 'About,' with dates. Abbreviate *c.* (or *circ.*); *c.* 1850, but not *circa* (or *c.*) *the 17th century.*

Circe. Pron. ser′sĭ.

circumbendibus. Circumlocution. *Circum* + *bend* + Latin abl. pl. ending. (Examples in OED from 1681.) See FACETIOUS FORMATIONS.

circumcise, NOT *-ize.*

circumlocutional, -nary, -utory. Though an adj. is often wanted for *circumlocution,* none of these three has won any favor. It is better to make shift with *periphrastic.*

circumstance. The objection to *under the circumstances,* & insistence that *in the circumstances* is the only right form, because what is around us is not over us, is puerile. To point out that *around* applies as much to vertical as to horizontal relations, & that a threatening sky is a circumstance no less than a threatening bulldog (*Under the circumstances I decided not to venture*), might lay one open to the suspicion of answering fools according to their folly. A more polite reply is that 'the circumstances' means a state of affairs, & may naturally be conceived as exercising the pressure under which one acts. *Under the circumstances* is neither illogical nor of recent invention (1665 in OED), & is far more often heard than *in the circumstances.* The OED, far from hinting that either form is incorrect, assigns them different functions: 'Mere situation is expressed by "in the circumstances," action affected is performed "under the circumstances."'

cirrus (clouds &c.; curl, fringe) has pl. *cirri;* the adjs. are *cirrose* (for the curl), & *cirrous* (the clouds).

cither(n), cittern, gittern, zither(n). When the forms are distinguished *cither* is the general word including the ancient *cithara* & its more modern representatives, *zither(n)* is appropriated to the Tyrolese instrument, & *cithern, cittern, gittern,* all mean that common in the 16th & 17th cc.; *cittern* & *gittern* are perhaps NEEDLESS VARIANTS.

city. The City, in London, is the financial district; the City of Seven Hills, Rome. *City-born, city-bred, city-wide,* hyphened.

cityless. So spelled.

city-state. Keep the hyphen.

clad, past & p.p. of *clothe,* is now chiefly poetic or archaic. See CLOTHE.

claim. 1. A vulgarism that has made its way, probably through the advertisement column, into journalism, & is now of daily currency, is the use of *claim* in the senses of *assert, maintain,* or *represent,* with the infinitive construction admissible after them, but not after it (see ANALOGY). The only legitimate infinitive after *claim* occurs when *claim* is in the active (the subject is the one doing the claiming—*he claims to be the only survivor;* NOT *he* is claimed *to be the only survivor*) & also has the same subject as the infinitive (*he claims to have proved his case;* NOT *he claims* the book *to have proved his case*). Examples of the false idiom: *This new product, which Mr. Sandow* claims to be *absolutely pure* (asserts)./*An automatic self-starter, which* is claimed to be *very reliable* (represented)./*The gun* is claimed to be *the most serviceable weapon of its kind* (asserted).

2. The use of *claim* n. or v. followed by (or implying) a *that* clause, when *claim* means not *demand* but *assert(ion),* is also, though less grossly, contrary to British idiom; the old *Century Dictionary & Cyclopedia* said of it 'considered by many to be inelegant.' *I claim* (demand) *that it should be postponed* is English, but hardly *I claim* (assert) *that it is false.* WRONG: *The* claim *is made that there are a certain class of men out of work who . . .* (assertion). *Others* claim *there is little beyond the application of ice that the first aider can do* (maintain).

clamor. US so spelled. Brit. *clamour,* but *clamorous.*

clandestine. Pron. klăndĕs′tĭn.

clango(u)r, clangorous. US *-or,* Brit. *-our,* but both *clangorous.*

clapboard. Pron. (US) klăb′ẽrd. The Brit. equivalent is *weather-board.*

claque. Pron. klăk. Hired applauders.

clari(o)net. The two forms denote the same instrument, but the short form is now established.

classic(al). The adjectives are distinguished rather by suitability to different contexts than by difference of meaning. *Classical* is the usual word, & it would perhaps never be noticeably the wrong one, even where *classic* is more idiomatic (e.g. we can say, if we choose, *This is classical ground*); on the other hand, there are many combinations in which *classic* would sound ridiculous; *classic education, classic allusions,* are impossible. *Classic,* however, is often preferred (1) where the language is of an ornate kind (compare *steeped in classic lore* with *learned in classical mythology*); (2) where the speaker's emotion of admiration or respect is to be conveyed (compare *Do you prefer the classical or the romantic style?* with *A style classic in its perfect self-restraint; I did not ask for classical regularity of features* with *The classic regularity of his features; St. Andrews, the classic home of golf,* with *R.* v. *Hobbes was cited as the classical case*).

classified. In the sense (of material) 'forbidden to be disclosed except to specified people because of endangerment to national security'—modern US (*classified information*).

clause. (Gram.): A group of words having a subject & predicate but not standing as a complete sentence. The main or principal clause carries the main statement (*He left town*); a subordinate clause, a qualifying or modifying statement (*after I told him*); a co-ordinate clause is linked either to the main clause or to a subordinate clause by a co-ordinate conjunction (*and I haven't seen him since*).

claustrophobia. Pron. klôs trō-fō′bĭȧ (not klows-). Morbid fear of being enclosed. (*Agoraphobia,* morbid fear of open spaces.)

clayey. So spelled.

cleanly, adj. Pron. klĕn′lĭ. *Cleanly* applies to habit & tendency to cleanliness rather than to the actual state. 'A cleanly person may be for the actual moment dirty, but will as soon as possible make himself clean' (OED). Hence *cleanliness,* the quality of being cleanly; *cleanness,* the quality or state of being clean. Adv. *He hit the ball cleanly,* pron. klē-.

cleanse. In US used chiefly in fig. & transf. senses, as opposed to *clean,* the less elevated, literal word. *Cleanse your heart with tears.*

clear(ly). *Clear* is an adv. as well as adj. & n. & is so used idiomatically; *sing it loud & clear; clear cut; it vanished clear away; clear through; stand clear; ten dollars clear; it came out clear.* See UNIDIOMATIC -LY.

cleave, split, has past tense *clove* or *cleft* or *cleaved,* p.p. *cloven* or *cleft* or *cleaved.* A *cleft palate; a cleft stick* (i.e. a dilemma; a position in which neither advance nor retreat is possible). A *cloven hoof* or *foot.*

cleave, stick, has past tense *cleaved* or (arch.) *clave,* p.p. *cleaved.*

clench, clinch. The spellings are so far differentiated as to be generally applied thus: we *clench* a nail, a rivet, our hands, jaws, & teeth, an object held, a rope; we *clinch* an argument & a bargain, & the fact or statement that settles an argument is a *clincher.*

clerk. Pron. (US) -erk, (Brit.) -ark.

clever is much misused, and is constantly heard in the sense of learned, well read, bookish, or studious; a woman whose cleverness is apparent in all she does will tell you she wishes she was clever, that she cannot read clever books (meaning those of the graver kind), & that Mr. Jones must be a very clever man, for he has written a dictionary. But in fact ignorance & knowledge have no relation to cleverness, which implies ingenuity, adroitness, readiness, mental or manual quickness, wit, & other qualities incompatible with dullness, but not with ignorance or dislike of books.

clew, clue. The words are the same, but the more recent *clue* is now established in the usual sense of idea or fact that may lead to a discovery, while *clew* is retained in the nautical sense, & in the old-fashioned sense skein or ball of wool, from which the usual sense of *clue* has been developed.

cliché. 'Stereotype block.' A French word for such hackneyed phrases as, not being the simple or natural way of expressing what is to be expressed, have served when first used as real improvements on that in some particular context, but have acquired an unfortunate popularity & come into general use even where they are not more but less suitable to the context than plain speech. Such are *to be made the recipient of* for *to be given; make the supreme sacrifice* for *die in battle; stand to reason* for *be obvious;* & see for other examples HACKNEYED PHRASES.

clientele write without italics or accent, & pron. klĭĕntĕl′.

climacteric. The old pronunciation was klīmăktĕr′ĭk, which stands first in the OED; but klīmăk′tĕrĭk is now commoner & is likely to prevail.

climax (Rhet.): 'ladder.' An arrangement of a series of notions in such an order that each is more impressive than the preceding. (1) *Eye hath not seen,* (2) *nor ear heard,* (3) *neither have entered into the heart of man,/the things which God hath prepared;* three progressive stages of strangeness. *Climax,* v., means to arrange in a climax; popularly, but not properly, to bring to a culmination. LOOSE: *To climax a story; It was climaxed by a surprise ending.*

climb down, despite the purists' insistence on its absurdity, is in wide use & is accepted usage. *Descend* in many contexts would be formal or pedantic.

clime is distinguished from *climate* (1) in being more suited for poetic & rhetorical use; it occurs, however, in ordinary prose also, with the limitation that (2) it means always region (often with reference to its characteristic weather), & never, like *climate,* the weather conditions themselves; we say *strangers from every clime,* but never *the country has a delightful clime.*

clink (slang for *prison*); taken from the Southwark Clink, England, & found in English literature from 1515 on.

clique. Pron. klēk. Small exclusive set or coterie. (O.F. 'noise, clicking sound.') Usually derogatory. *Cliqu(e)y,* spell *-quy.*

clockwise. No hyphen. But *counter-clockwise.*

close. *Close the door, the window, your mouth,* used in the literal sense & in everyday speech instead of *shut,* expose the speaker to grave suspicion of GENTEELISM, though *The door is closed forever upon that possibility,* & similar figurative uses, are innocent. See also FORMAL WORDS.

close(ly). *Close,* adv., not *closely,* is idiomatic in some expressions. *The country was brought* close *to disaster. It was* close *upon noon. The* closer *they are examined, the more obvious they will be. Close-mouthed; close-hearted, close-drawn,* &c. See UNIDIOMATIC -LY.

closure. The name given to a provision by which debate in the House of Commons can be cut short in spite of the wish of a minority to continue it. In US Parl. Procedure, *cloture* is the traditional spelling (but in

New York Times always *closure*).

clothe has *clad* beside *clothed* both as past & p.p. While *clothed*, however, is suitable to all contexts (except where *dressed* is preferable as less formal), *clad* is (1) always slightly, & often intolerably, archaic in effect, & (2) never used absolutely, but always with some specification of the kind of clothing. Accordingly, *clad* cannot be substituted in *You were fed & clothed at my expense, He clothed himself hurriedly, When he was clothed he admitted us.* But *clothed* can be substituted in any of the following phrases, which are selected as favorable for the use of *clad*: *Lightly, well, insufficiently* clad; *He* clad *himself in shining armor;* Clad *with righteousness; Hills* clad *with olives;* Clad *in blue.*

clothes. The usual pronunciation is klōz, though this is often deliberately abstained from in the mistaken belief (confirmed by the OED) that it is 'vulgar or careless.' In Herrick's *The liquefaction of her clothes*, the rhyming word is *goes*.

clue. The usual spelling for the indication that leads to the solution. See CLEW.

co-. There are three ways of writing *cooperate* (*coop-, co-op-, coöp-*), & two of writing *copartner* (*cop-, co-p-*). The diaeresis should at once be rejected as possible only in some words (those in which *co-* is followed by a vowel), whereas the hyphen is possible in all. Next it should be recognized that hyphens in the middle of words are no ornament, & admittance should be refused to all that cannot prove their usefulness.

1. In some words the hyphen is never used: *coagulate, coerce,* &c.

2. Many are so common or so analyzable at a glance that the hyphen, though sometimes used, is entirely superfluous: *coefficient, coeducation.*

3. Some are used & seen only by the learned, who may be expected to know them at a glance without hyphens: *cosine, coaxial, cosecant.*

4. Some always have the hyphen apparently by way of a (*sic*), or announcement that the spelling is intentional: *co-respondent, co-religionist* (though Webster gives these unhyphened).

5. Some, if no hyphen is used, tend to fall at the first glance into wrong syllables & so perplex: *co-agent, co-worker.*

6. When a writer believes himself to be making a new word, he naturally uses the hyphen—*my co-secretary, their co-authorship,* &c. The tendency in US is to use the hyphen as little as possible, but US writers & the press do not always follow this rule. Webster gives all the *co-o-* words with a hyphen (*co-operate, co-ordinate,* &c.); some dictionaries use the diaeresis, but few of the more careful publishers do. Fowler preferred *cooperate, coordinate,* but the COD uses hyphens. The only recommendation possible is to think of the convenience of the reader. If the hyphen in *co-o-* words & in those of classes 4 & 5 saves a moment's hesitation in reading, it is worth while. *These ten coopted two more. He was co-opted a Senior Fellow.* Which?

coalesce makes *coalescing.*

cocaine. The pronunciation

kokān′, once stigmatized as vulgar, is now so general that attempts to maintain kō′kān are useless.

cockle. *The cockles of the heart* is of some age (quoted from 1671) but of disputed origin; such phrases are best not experimented with, but kept to their customary form & context (*rejoice, warm, the cockles of the heart*).

cock's-comb, cockscomb, coxcomb. The first for the comb of a cock, the second for the fool's cap & the plants, & the third for the fop.

cocksure (US one word, Brit. hyphen) has been in the language since 1520. The reference is presumably to the cock or tap of a spring, not to the bird.

coco(a). *Cacao* & *coco*, independent words, have corrupted each other till the resulting *cocoa* is used always for the drink & often for the coco(a)-nut palm. *Coconut, coco fiber*, &c., are still used, though the *-a* often appears; they should be kept in existence, if possible, & *cocoa* be restricted to the drink & the powder from which it is made; the uncrushed seeds & the plant are still usually spelled *cacao*.

codex has pl. *codices*.

codify. Pron. kŏ-, NOT kō-.

c(o)enobite &c. Pron. sēn-. In US, spell *cenobite*.

coercible. So spelled.

cog. The phrase *cogged dice* is due to a misunderstanding of the old *to cog dice*, which meant not to load them, but to cheat in throwing them; *loaded* should be used.

cogitate makes *-itable*.

cognate. (1) Of languages, descending from the same original language; of words, coming from the same root. (*Pater* & *father* are cognate, from the same Indo-European original; *paternal* is derivative, from Latin.) (2) *Cognate object* or *accusative*, an object of kindred sense or derivation, spec. one adverbially following an intransitive verb; *to die the death, to run a race*.

cognizance, cognizant, cognizable, cognize. *Cognize* alone has the *-g-* always sounded. Of the four, *cognizance* is the word from which the others have sprung, & it had for some time no *-g-* to be sounded; the introduction of the *-g-* has affected pronunciation, but kon- is still common in the first three, especially in legal use; *cognizable* should be either kŏn′ĭzabl′ or, if it is to be assimilated to *cognize*, kŏgnīz′abl′. In US the *-g-* in *cognizance* is usually sounded in popular use, but not in legal.

cognomen. Family name. The third of the three names of ancient Romans: *praenomen* (Caius), *nomen* (Julius), *cognomen* (Caesar).

coiffeur, coiffure. Pron. kwäfūr′ (fem. *-feuse*, pron. -fūz); kwȧ fūr′. The first is the person who dresses the hair, *coiffure* the result of the labor.

coin a phrase. See HACKNEYED PHRASES.

coincidence. *The long arm of coincidence*, see HACKNEYED PHRASES. Varying its form, endowing it with muscles, making it throw people about, & similar attempts at renovation, only make matters worse: *The author does not strain the muscles* of coincidence's arm *to bring them into relation./Nor does Mrs. Moberly shrink from a use of* 'the long arm' *quite unnecessarily.*

colander, cullender. Both are pronounced kŭl'ender; the first spelling, which is nearer the Latin stem (cf. *percolate*), is also more frequent.

coliseum. (A med. Lat. form of *Colosseum.*) The usual US spelling for any large structure for sporting events or other entertainment.

collaborator. 'Co-worker, esp. in lit., art, or science. The derogatory sense (of working with an occupying enemy government) arose in World War II.

collage. Pron. kô läzh'. Art: an assortment of fragments (cards, matchboxes, &c.) put together to make an artistic composition.

collation. The reporter who can be content with *repast* instead wins the moderate gratitude, & he who says *meal* the fervent admiration, of most of us; see WORKING & STYLISH WORDS.

collectible, -able. US *-ible;* Brit. *-able.*

COLLECTIVES. Applied primarily to (A) nouns denoting a whole made up of similar parts, such as *crew, flock, firm, Congress.* These are also called nouns of multitude (see NUMBER, 6). But other nouns, or uses of them, are often described by the term, & confusion may be saved by separating these. (B) Nouns whose plural is in form not distinguishable from the singular, as *sheep, deer, salmon, grouse, counsel* (=advocate). (C) Nouns whose singular is sometimes used instead of their plural, as *buffalo, duck, fish, shot, cannon.* (D) Nouns denoting either a thing or a material consisting of many of them, as *hair, straw.* (E) Nouns denoting either a material or a collection of things made of it, as *linen, silver, china.* (F) Nouns denoting either a thing or some or all of them, as *fruit, timber.* (G) Abstract singulars used instead of concrete plurals, as *accommodation* (=rooms), *kindling* (=pieces of wood), *royalty* (=royal persons), *pottery* (=pots); & even (H) nouns denoting substances of indefinite quantity, as *butter, water. Flock* (a number of sheep or parishioners) is a collective of one kind, & *flock* (woolen waste) is of another. *Flock* (1) may be treated as singular or plural (*His flock was attacked by wolves; His flock was without a pastor* or *were unanimous in disapproval*), & can itself be used in the plural with the ordinary difference in meaning from the singular (*shepherds tending their flocks*). *Flock* (2) can be used in the singular or in the plural, the meaning being the same, a material, & *flock* being treated always as singular & *flocks* as plural (*A flock mattress; A mattress of flock* or *flocks; the flock has, the flocks have, not been disinfected*). But the word *collective* is applied to both.

Reference of a word to this article means that it has the peculiarity indicated by the number of the following table that is given in the reference.

1. Words that have no separate plural form, but are the same in both numbers, e.g. *counsel, deer, grouse,* &c. (*Many counsel were briefed; The*

grouse were shy; We saw no deer.)

2. Words having a plural, but whose singular used in a collective sense, & treated as either singular or plural, is generally preferred to it, e.g. *shot, cannon.* (*The shot scatters too much; Three shot were extracted from his head.*)

3. Words of number or amount that when used after definite or indefinite numerals have often or usually the singular instead of the plural form, e.g. *brace, fathom, hundredweight.* (*We shot* 20 *brace; Six fathom deep; A few hundredweight of coal.*)

4. Names of an animal or vegetable that can have *a* & mean an individual or be used in the singular without *a* & mean the things as food or as objects of sport, e.g. *pig, potato, cabbage.* (*Went out sticking pig; Have some potato; Cabbage is a blood purifier.*)

5. Words having no plural, but able, being nouns of multitude, to take either a singular or a plural verb, e.g. *cattle* (*The cattle is sold; The cattle are in the hay*). For the many blunders occasioned by these words (*The Government* acknowledge *him as* its *official courier*) see PERSONIFICATION, & NUMBER 6.

colloquial. As used in this book=belonging to familiar speech, not used in formal or dignified speech or writing. *Colloquially, 'that's me' is permissible.*

collusion &c. The notion of fraud or underhandedness is essential to collusion, & the following is a MISUSE: *The two authors, both professors at Innsbruck, appear to be working in collusion;* the supposed arrangement is merely that their periods shall not overlap; *in collaboration* will therefore not do; if *in concert* will not, the thing must be given at length.

COLON. In modern writing the colon is used (a) after a formal introduction before an explanation, quotation, or example: *There are three possibilities: a colon in formal writing; a dash in less formal contexts; a comma in short simple sentences.* (b) After the salutation in a letter: *Dear John:* (c) In a compound sentence, especially when the two main clauses are in antithesis & not joined by a conjunction: *Man proposes: God disposes.* As long as the Prayer Book version of the Psalms continues to be read, the colon is not likely to pass quite out of use as a stop, chiefly as one preferred in impressive contexts to the semicolon; but the time when it was second member of the hierarchy, period, colon, semicolon, comma, is past. In general usage, it has acquired a special function (a), that of delivering the goods that have been invoiced in the preceding words; it is a substitute for such verbal harbingers as *viz., scil., that is to say, i.e.,* &c.

colonnade. So spelled.

colo(u)r. US *-or;* Brit. *-our. Color* makes *colorable, colorist,* (Brit. *-ourable, -ourist,* but *coloration, decolorize*). *Color-blind,* keep hyphen.

colorful is a fairly recent addition to the language & greatly overused by US writers as a synonym for *vivid, picturesque, striking,* &c.: *colorful writing, a colorful history; The manic is one of the most* colorful *of psychiatric types.*

colossal in the sense not of *enormous* (as in *colossal folly* &c.), but of indescribably entertaining or delightful or ridiculous, is a Germanism not deserving adoption; the similar use of IMMENSE, though we do not name it *honoris causa*, is at least of native development.

column. Pron. kŏl′ŭm (NOT kŏl′yūm). *Columnist*, pron. kŏl′ŭmnĭst (NOT kŏl′yūmnist or kŏl′ŭmĭst).

comatose. Pron. kŏm′ătōs, NOT kō- or -tōz.

combat makes *combating, -ed, -ant.*

combine. The verb is accented on the second syllable; the noun (US, a combination of persons for political or commercial advantage) on the first.

come. 1. For *come into one's life, come to grief, come home to roost*, &c., see HACKNEYED PHRASES.

2. *Come what may; I shall be 70 come Tuesday* are examples of the living subjunctive in modern speech & writing. See SUBJUNCTIVES.

come-at-able, get-at-able. Keep the hyphens. *Come-at-able* was made as long ago as the 17th c., but, except in *get-at-able*, the experiment has not been successfully repeated, & probably will not be (cf. US *stick-to-itiveness*).

comedian, tragedian, have, in the sense *actor*, the feminines *comedienne, tragedienne*, perhaps best pronounced komē′dĭĕn, trajē′dĭĕn, & written without accents. It is unfortunate that *tragedian* also means writer, which leads to ambiguity; but the introduction of *tragedist* for the writer is a remedy worse than the disease; we cannot begin now to talk of the Greek tragedists, for instance.

comedy, farce, burlesque. As species of drama, the three are distinguished in that *comedy* aims at entertaining by the fidelity with which it presents life as we all know it, *farce* at raising laughter by the outrageous absurdity of the situations or characters exhibited, & *burlesque* at tickling the fancy of the audience by caricaturing plays or actors with whose style it is familiar.

comely. Pron. kŭm′lĭ.

comestibles. The usual word is *food* or *eatables*. See WORKING & STYLISH WORDS.

comic(al). The broad distinction, sometimes obscured by being neglected, is that that is *comic* of which the aim or origin is comedy, & that is *comical* of which the effect, whether intended or not, is comedy. *A comic actor* is merely one who acts comedy; *a comical actor*, one who makes the audience laugh. *Comic hesitation* is that in which the hesitater is playing the comedian; *comical hesitation*, that in which observers find comedy, whether the hesitater meant them to or was unconscious of them. Accordingly, *comic* is the normal epithet (though *comical* may be used, in a different sense) with *actor, scene, relief, song, singer, paper; comical* is normal (subject to the converse reserve) with *face, effect, expression, deformity, earnestness, attempt, terror, fiasco*. There is some tendency (*The attempt was comic in the extreme; The disaster had its comic side*) to use *comic* where *comical* is the right word. This may possibly be a sign that *comical* is on the way to become archaic & obsolete; but, the difference of meaning being fairly definite & of real use, this would be regrettable.

comity, from Lat. *comis*=courteous, means *courtesy,* & *the comity of nations* is the obligation recognized by civilized nations to respect each other's laws & usages as far as their separate interests allow. It has nothing to do with Lat. *comes*= companion, & phrases based on this false derivation (*obtain admittance to the comity of states; entered into the comity of nations; a useful member of the civilized comity*), & implying the sense *company, association, federation,* &c., are wrong.

COMMA. 1. In ENUMERATIONS (see AND 2 & OR 3). This book recommends a comma before the *and* in enumerations, in the interests of clarity. Without the comma before *and* the following sentences would be ambiguous: *Since then he has been pulling out counterproposals for treaties, plebiscites, and special conferences, like rabbits from a hat./We shall find it necessary to deal drastically with the parental rights of drunken, criminal, & wastrel parents* . . . For complete clarity a comma is sometimes also necessary after the last element of the enumeration: *This new novel describes a love affair formed, precipitated, & rendered tragic, by the events of the Revolution./The resulting inquiry involves the consideration of the claims of consciousness, instinct, memory, habit, & desire, to be regarded as the determining factors of psychic life.*

2. In the absolute construction, a comma should not separate the noun and the participle. NOT *M. Maurice* Colin, having *called attention to the conditions of naval warfare, M. Pichon said* . . . (read *Colin having*)./*But these objections were overruled, & the* accused, having *pleaded not guilty, the hearing of evidence commenced* (read *&, the accused having*).

3. A comma should not separate inseparables, e.g. a verb from its subject or object or complement, a defining relative from its antecedent, or an essential modification from what cannot stand without it. NOT *The charm of Nelson's* history, is, the *unselfish greatness* . . . (read *history is the.* One comma parts verb from subject, the other complement from verb)./*He combines with Froissart's* picturesqueness, moral philosophy, *enthusiasm, & high principles* (*read picturesqueness moral.* The comma parts the object–*moral* . . . *principles*–from its verb *combines*)./*The right & wholesome atmosphere in this country, as in all* others, where *payment is the rule, is that it should be taken for granted as a normal incident* of *Parliamentary life* (read *others where.* The *where* clause starts a defining clause; see THAT, REL. PRON./*Situated,* as *we are, with our vast & varied overseas possessions, our gigantic foreign trade, & our unapproachable mercantile marine, we at any rate can gain nothing by war* (read *Situated as.* We should write not 'How, are we situated?,' but 'How are we situated?'; the *as* clause is exactly parallel to, & as essential as, *how*)./*We are assured that the Prime Minister will, in* no *circumstances & on no consid-*

eration whatever, consent *to . . .* (read *will in no circumstances . . . whatever consent.* The words that negative *will* must not be cut off from it).

4. In confluences, i.e. when alternatives &c. finish their course together, the necessary comma after the second is apt to be forgotten. NOT *As regards the form of the festival,* many, if not most of the customs *popularly associated with it may, perhaps, be traced to . . .* (read *most, of*)./*His craftsmanship, again, was superb*—more refined, more intellectual than *that of Frith* (read *intellectual, than*).

5. The comma is often forgotten in compound appendages to names. NOT *Mr. Haverfield has collected & edited a volume of 'Essays by Henry Francis Pelham, Late President of Trinity College,* Oxford & Camden *Professor of History'* (read *Oxford, &*).

6. In ambiguous appositions, insertion or omission of commas is seldom a sufficient remedy, & indeed is usually impossible. The thing is to remember that arrangements in which apposition commas & enumeration commas are mixed up are dangerous & should be avoided. AMBIGUOUS: *To the expanded 'Life of Shakespeare,' first published in* 1915, *& to be issued shortly in a third edition by* Mr. Murray, the author, Sir Sidney Lee, *besides bringing the text up to date, has contributed a new preface.* Which is the author?

7. The comma is often wrongly omitted between connected but independent clauses, or used instead of a semicolon between unconnected clauses. NOT *When the Motor Cars Act was before the House it was suggested that these authorities should be given the right to make recommendations to the central* authorities‸& that right *was conceded* (read *authorities, &*)./*'Will the mighty* Times *aid us in this historic struggle?' Dear to the heart of an editor must be such* an appeal, we wish *someone would seek for our aid in so flattering a formula* (read *appeal; we*).

commandant. Pron. kŏm'*an*dănt.

commander-in-chief. Pl. *commanders-in-chief.*

commando. Pl. *-os.*

commence(ment). The writers who prefer *ere* & *save* to *before* & *except* may be expected to prefer *commence(ment)* to *begin(ning)* in all contexts. *Begin* is the word always thought & usually said, but it is translated sometimes before it is said, & often before it is written, into *commence,* which is described by the OED as 'precisely equivalent to the native *begin.*' It is a good rule never to do this translation except when *begin* or *beginning* is felt to be definitely incongruous; see WORKING & STYLISH WORDS. In official announcements *commence* is appropriate; the program tells us when the performance will commence, though we ask each other when it begins. The grave historical style also justifies *commence,* & historians' phrases, such as *commence hostilities,* keep their form when transferred to other uses, though we *begin,* & do not commence, *a quarrel;* similarly we *commence operations,* but merely *begin dinner.* As against the precise equivalence mentioned above, it should be observed that *begin* has, owing to its greater commonness, more nearly passed into a mere auxiliary than *commence;* & from this it results (1) that *begin,* not *commence,* is even in formal style the right word before an infinitive; in *The landholders* commenced *to plunder indiscriminately,* anyone can perceive that *began* would be better; (2) that *commence* retains more than *begin* the positive sense of initiative or intention, & is especially out of place with an infinitive when this sense is absent, as in *Even his warmest supporters must be* commencing *to feel that he should give some slight consideration to . . .*

committee, in the original sense of person to whom something is committed, is pronounced kŏmītē′.

common. As applied to people & their qualities (=low-class, vulgar, unrefined), colloq.

commonplace, platitude, triviality, truism. The words are all often used as terms of reproach in describing the statements made by a speaker or writer; but none of them is identical in sense with any other, & if they are not to be misused a rough idea at least of the distinctions is necessary. It is something to remember that no one should welcome *platitude, triviality,* or *truism* in the strict sense, as a description of a statement of his own, whereas it may be a merit in a statement to be a commonplace or a truism in its loose sense.

A *commonplace* is a thing that, whether true or false, is so regularly said on certain occasions that the repeater of it can expect no credit for originality; but the commonplace may be useful.

A *platitude* is a thing the stating of which as though it were enlightening or needing to be stated convicts the speaker of dullness; a platitude is never valuable. The word is MISUSED in: *It is a* platitude *that the lack of cottages is one of the chief of the motive forces which drive the peasantry to the town.*

A *triviality* is a thing the saying of which as though it were adequate to the occasion convicts the speaker of silliness; a triviality is never to the purpose.

A *truism* in the strict sense (to which it might be well, but is perhaps now impossible, to confine it) is a statement in which the predicate gives no information about the subject that is not implicit in the definition of the subject itself. *What is right ought to be done;* since the *right* is definable as *that which ought to be done,* this means *What ought to be done ought to be done,* i.e. it is a disguised identical proposition, or a truism. *It is* not well *to act with* too great *haste; too great haste* being haste greater than it is well to act with, the sentence tells us no more, though it pretends to, than anyone who can define *too great haste* knew before the predicate *is not well* was added. But *What is right pays,* or in other words *Honesty is the best policy,* is not a truism in the strict sense (since it makes a real statement & not a sham one) or in the loose sense (since its truth is disputable); nor is *It is not well to act in haste* a truism of either kind. Both statements, however, are commonplaces, & often platitudes.

A *truism* in the loose sense is a thing that, whether in point or not, is so indisputably true that the speaker is under no obligation to prove it, & need not fear contradiction. This sense is a SLIPSHOD EXTENSION; the writer who describes his principle as a truism in order to justify his drawing conclusions from it would do better to call it an axiom; & the critic who depreciates someone else's statements as truisms, not in the strict sense, but meaning merely that they are too familiar to be of value, should call them platitudes or commonplaces.

common sense should be written as two separate words except when used attributively, & should then be hyphened: *The philosophy of common sense; The common-sense philosophy.*

communal. Pron. kŏm′ūnal.

communiqué. Pron. kŏmūnĭkā′. Some newspapers, or writers, print the word with no accent, presumably to be called kŏmūnēk′. This seems ill-advised, the literal sense 'communicated thing' & the difference from words like *critique* & *physique* being at present exhibited by the accent & surely worth preserving.

communism. In a general (philosophic) sense, any system of social organization in which all property belongs to the community, i.e. is held in common; thus Brook Farm was an experiment in communism. *Russian Communism* is a system of social organization based on revolutionary Marxism as developed by Lenin & the Bolshevik party in the USSR, in which all economic, social, & cultural activity is conducted by a single self-perpetuating party (i.e. a totalitarian state). It regards history as a class war eventually to result in a universal victory of the proletariat. See also SOCIALISM.

company, for guests or visitors, is often labeled 'colloq.,' but has seemingly been in good standing since 1579: 'one or more persons invited or entertained' (OED).

comparable. (Pron. cŏm′-.) Able to be compared *with;* worthy of comparison *to. There are many difficulties now not* comparable with *those existing in* 1590. Comparable *in its free use of idiom, though not in its dramatic impact,* to *the plays of Christopher Fry.*

comparative(ly). The idiom is *comparatively few* (NOT *a comparatively few*). For *a comparatively few, the comparative few,* &c., see FEW.

comparatives. For misuses, see -ER & -EST, MORE, & THAN.

compare, in the sense suggest or state a similarity, is regularly followed by *to,* not *with;* in the sense examine or set forth the details of a supposed similarity or estimate its degree, it is regularly followed by *with. He compared me* to *Demosthenes* means that he suggested that I was comparable to him or put me in the same class; *He compared me* with *Demosthenes* means that he instituted a detailed comparison or pointed out where & how far I resembled or failed to resemble him. Accordingly, the preposition in each of the following is the one required by idiom: *Witness compared the noise to thunder; The lecturer compared the British field gun with the*

French; The effect of a trumpet blast on the ear is comparable to that of scarlet on the eye; Shakespeare is hardly comparable with Milton; Compared with, or *to, him I am a bungler* (this is a common type in which either sense is applicable). After the intransitive verb (*Art cannot compare with Nature*), *with* alone is possible.

compass. *Within the compass of man's wit.* See also FIELD.

compendious means containing the substance in a concise form; comprehensive though brief (esp. of lit. works): *A compendious analysis of the chapters.*

compendium. Pl. *-ums* or *-a.*

compensate. (1) Formerly kompĕn'sāt, now kom'pensāt; but *compen'satory* &c. (2) *Compensate* makes *-sable.*

competence, -cy. Neither has any sense in which the other cannot be used; the first form is gaining on the second; & it would be well if *competency* could be abandoned as a NEEDLESS VARIANT.

complacence, -cy. There is no distinction that can be called established; the second form is the commoner, & is less liable to confusion with *complaisance* (see foll.); *complacence* might be dropped as a NEEDLESS VARIANT.

complacent, -ency; complaisant, -ance. 1. The two sets have clearly differentiated meanings but are often confused (see below); it would help to obviate this confusion if *complacency* were always preferred to *-acence* (see prec.).

2. He is *complacent* who is pleased with himself or his state, or with other persons or things as they affect him; the word is loosely synonymous with *contented.* He is *complaisant* who is anxious to please by compliance, service, indulgence, or flattery; the word is loosely synonymous with *obliging.* The choice made in each of these sentences is WRONG: *He owed such funds as he possessed to French* complacency./ *The display of the diamonds usually stopped the tears, & she would remain in a* complaisant *state until . . .*

complement (Gram.): 'filling up.' That which completes, or helps to complete, the verb, making with it the predicate. In the narrowest sense, and that most often used in US, *complement* is applied only to the noun or adjective predicated by means of a copulative verb (*be, become,* &c.) or of a factitive verb (*make, call, think,* &c.) of the subject (*He is* a fool; *He grew* wiser; *He was made* king) or of the object (*Call no man* happy); in such examples as the last, the complement is called an objective or an oblique complement. The case of the complement with *am, are, is,* &c., is the subjective or nominative. Meredith's *I am she, she* me, *till death and beyond it* is colloq. & perhaps poetically justified, but grammatically wrong; so also *whom* (for *who*) *would you rather be?* The number of a copulative verb agrees with the subject, not the complement: *His many achievements during this period* are (NOT *is*) adequate proof *of his ability.* See CASES, & NUMBER.

complete, v. In its simple meaning, 'to bring to an end' (an action, work, distance, period of time), *finish* is the normal word. But *complete* is a WORKING WORD in the meaning of 'bring to the full amount,' 'to make perfect,' 'to furnish or equip completely.' *After we had* finished *our tasks;* but *Let me* complete *your thought, if I can.* See FORMAL WORDS.

complex. (Psych.): A mental abnormality resulting from a repressed & unconscious system of desires & memories that in disguised form exerts a dominating influence on personality. Now loosely used as a VOGUE WORD. If a person is cautious about inflammables, he explains he has *a complex about fire.* If he prefers to travel by train rather than by air, he has *a height complex.* If he decides not to try to publish a story he has just written, he undoubtedly has *an inferiority complex.* In fact if he is afraid of anything, from mice to hydrogen bombs, he should immediately see his psychiatrist; he promptly admits, and his friends all agree, that he is suffering from a complex. See POPULARIZED TECHNICALITIES.

complex sentence. (Gram.) One having a principal clause & one or more subordinate clauses: *If I go down town, will you wait for me?* (The first is the subordinate, the second the principal clause.)

compost. Pron. US -ōst; Brit. ŏst.

compound, n. & v. The noun is accented on the first syllable, the verb on the second.

COMPOUND PREPOSITIONS, CONJUNCTIONS, &c. A selection of these is: *as to* (AS 3); *for the purpose of;* INASMUCH AS; in CONNECTION (2) *with; in favor of; in order that, to; in reference to; in relation to;* IN SO FAR *as, that; in so much that;* IN THAT; *in the absence of; in the* CASE *of; in the* INSTANCE *of; in the matter of; in the* NEIGHBORHOOD *of; in the region of; of the character of; of the order of; of the nature of; with a* VIEW *to; with reference to; with* REGARD *to; with relation to; with respect to.* Of such phrases some are much worse in their effects upon English style than others, *in order that* being perhaps at one end of the scale, & *in the case of* or *as to* at the other; but, taken as a whole, they are almost the worst element in modern English, stuffing up the newspaper columns with a compost of nouny abstractions. To young writers the discovery of these forms of speech, which are used very little in talk & very much in print, brings an expansive sense of increased power. They think they have acquired with far less trouble than they anticipated the trick of dressing up what they may have to say in the right costume for public exhibition. Later they know better, & realize that it is feebleness, instead of power, that they have been developing; but by that time the fatal ease that the compound-preposition style gives (to the writer, that is) has become too dear to be sacrificed. (See PERIPHRASIS & the words in small capitals in the list above.) Examples: *At least* 500,000 *houses are required, & the aggregate cost is* in the region of $4 million (why not *approximately, about,* or *nearly?*)./*Sir Robert Peel used to tell an amusing story of one of these banquets,* in the case of which *he & Canning were seated on oppo-*

site sides of Alderman Flower (at which?)./France is now going through a similar experience with regard to *Morocco to that which England had to undergo* with reference to *Egypt after the occupation* (a simple *with* in each case).

comprehend. '*To comprehend* is to know a thing as well as that thing can be known' (Donne). See APPREHEND.

comprise means include, embrace, NOT compose or constitute: WRONG: *The committee* is comprised of *one delegate from each major country* (should read *composed*).

comptroller, cont-. Both pronounced kŏntrōl′*er*. The first spelling is erroneous, being due to false association with *count* (Fr. *conter* from L. *computare*), but is retained in certain official titles.

conceal. The usual word is *hide.* See FORMAL WORDS.

concentrate. Pron. kŏn′-. See RECESSIVE ACCENT.

concept is a philosophical term, & should be left to the philosophers. The substituting of it for the ordinary word *conception* as below is due to NOVELTY-HUNTING: (a caricature has been described) *Now this point of view constantly expressed must have had its influence on popular* concepts. See POPULARIZED TECHNICALITIES.

concern. In (*so far*) *as concerns* or *regards,* the number of the verb (which is impersonal, or has for its unexpressed subject 'our inquiry' or some similar phrase) is invariable: *as concerns their demands, they must wait until later;* the change to plural, as in the quotation that follows, is due, like *as* FOLLOW, to misapprehension. WRONG: *Many of these stalks were failures, so far as* concern *the objective success.*

concernment has no senses that are not as well, & now more naturally & frequently, expressed by the noun *concern; concernment* should be dropped as a NEEDLESS VARIANT.

concerto. Pron. konchār′tō; pl. *-os* (It. pl. *-i*).

concession(n)aire. Omit the *-n-,* & pron. -sĕsh-.

concessive (Gram.): 'granting.' The name given to subordinate clauses beginning with *though* or *although,* to those or equivalent conjunctions, & to participles used with the corresponding effect, as in 'accepting your facts, I dispute your inference.'

conch. (Shell.) Pron. -k. Pl. *conchs.*

conciseness, concision. The first is the English word familiar to the ordinary man; *concision* is the LITERARY CRITIC'S WORD, more recent in English, used by writers under French influence, & often requiring the reader to stop & think whether he knows its meaning: *The writing of verse exacts* concision, *clear outline, & a damming of the waters at the well-spring.*

concomitance, -cy. The second is now a NEEDLESS VARIANT.

concord (Gram.): 'agreement.' The rules that an adjective is of the same number, case, & gender, as its noun, a verb of the same number & person as its subject, & a noun of the same case as that to which it is in apposition.

concretize. Orig. a NONCE word, unfortunately kept alive by social economists, among others.

concupiscence, -ent. Pron. -kū′-.

condign (pron. kŏndīn′) meant originally *deserved,* & could be used in many contexts, with *praise,* for instance, as well as with *punishment.* It is now used only with words equivalent to *punishment,* & means deservedly severe, the severity being the important point, & the desert merely a condition of the appropriateness of the word (*condign vengeance on the oppressor*); that it is an indispensable condition, however, is shown by the absurd effect of: *Count Zeppelin's* marvelous *voyage through the air ended in* condign *disaster.*

condolence. Pron. kondō′-lens.

conducive. Constr. *to* (conducive *of* now archaic).

conduit. Pron. kŏn′- or kun′-dit.

confederacy, -eration. In permanence & closeness of structure the order would seem to be *confederacy, confederation, federation* (*federation* the most closely united & permanent). See FEDERATION.

conferee. In the sense 'member of a conference,' chiefly US and not an adornment to the language. In the sense 'one on whom something is conferred,' *recipient* will usually do.

confer(r)able. The dictionaries give *confer′rable,* and so it is usually spelled & pronounced. But cf. *pref′erable* &c.

confessedly. Four syllables.

confidant, -ante, -ent, nn. *Con′fident* was in use as a noun meaning confidential friend or person to whom one entrusted secrets long before the other forms were introduced; but it is now an ARCHAISM, & to revive it is pedantry. *Confidant* is masculine & *confidante* feminine; they are indistinguishable in pronunciation, & accent the last syllable.

confines, n. Pron. con′-.

conform, conformable. Constr. *to* (rarely *with*).

confrère. *Fellow-member, colleague* are the usual English words. See FRENCH WORDS.

congé, congee. Dismissal (without ceremony; often jocular). The second, formerly est., is now obs. or archaic. Pron. kôn zhā′.

congeries. (sing. & pl.) A collection of things merely heaped together. *A curious* congeries *of towers, halls, churches, & chambers.* Pron. konjĕr′ĭēz.

conjunction. (Gram.): 'joining together.' A word whose function is to join like things together, i.e. a noun or its equivalent with another noun or its equivalent, an adjective &c. with another, adverb &c. with adverb &c., verb with verb, or sentence with sentence; cf. prepositions, which attach a noun to something different, esp. to verbs. The relation between the things joined is shown by the particular conjunction chosen (*but, and,* or *nor; if, although,* or *because; that* or *lest; since* or *until*). Some conjunctions, in joining two sentences, convert one into a dependency of the other, or clause in it, & are called *subordinating* or *strong* *conjunctions,* the others being *co-ordinating* or *weak* (strong—*I hate him* because *he is a Judas:* weak—*I hate him;* for *he is a Judas*). Many words are sometimes conjunctions & sometimes adverbs (*therefore, so, however, since,* &c.); & such words as *when* & *where,* though often in effect conjunctions, are more strictly described as relative adverbs with expressed or implied antecedent (*I remember the time* when (i.e. *at which*) *it happened; I will do it* when (i.e. *at the time at which*) *I see fit.*

conjunctive (*mood*) is a term that had much better be dropped. The forms denoted *conjunctive* & *subjunctive* are the same, & *subjunctive* is the much better name.

conjure, in the sense *beseech,* pron. konjo͞or′; in the other senses kŏn-′ or kun′jer.

conjurer, -or. The dictionaries give *-er* first.

connectable, -ible. The first is more usual in US, *-ible* Brit.

connection, -xion. (1) The first is US, the second Brit. (2) *In connection with* is a formula that everyone who prefers vigorous to flabby English will have as little to do with as he can; see PERIPHRASIS. It should clearly be admitted, however, that there is sometimes no objection to the words; this is when they are least of a formula & *connection* has a real meaning (*Buses run* in connection with *trains; The isolated phrase may sound offensive, but* taken in connection with *its context it was not so*). In the prevalent modern use, however, it is worn down into a mere compound preposition, with vagueness & pliability as its only merits. The worst writers use it, from sheer love of verbiage, in preference to a single word that would be more appropriate (*The three outstanding features* in connection with (i.e. *of*) *our 'Batchworth Tinted,' are as follows*). The average writer is not so degraded as to choose it for its own sake, but he has not realized that when *in connection with* presents itself to him it is a sign that laziness is mastering his style, or haziness his ideas. Of the examples that follow, the first two are characteristic specimens of compound-prepositional PERIPHRASIS: *The special difficulty in Professor Minocelsi's* case *arose* in connection with *the view he holds* relative to *the historical value of . . .* (Prof. M. was specially hampered by his views on)./*Regulations* with regard to *the provision of free places* in connection with *secondary education* (regulations for providing free places in secondary schools)./*Canvey Island, which is again coming into prominence* in connection with *the proposal to establish a great wharf there* (to which attention has been called by).

connoisseur. A critical judge, in the arts, in matters of taste, &c. Pron. kŏn*aser*′; the modern French spelling (*-nai-*) should not be used.

connote, denote. When *connote* & *denote* are in expressed or implied antithesis, *connote* means (of words) to imply in addition to the primary meaning; *denote* implies all that strictly belongs to the definition of the word. *Father* connotes male sex, prior existence, affection, guidance, &c.; it denotes one that has begotten.

conscience. Write *for conscience' sake* or *conscience sake;* see SAKE.

consensus means agreement, unanimity, or unanimous body (of opinion or testimony). *The consensus was that Mr. Hammarskjold's remarks had left the outlook on the airmen nebulous;* 'of opinion' is implied & need not be stated. The following, in which *consensus* is confused with census, is NONSENSE: *Who doubts that if a* consensus *were taken, in which the interrogated had the honesty to give a genuine reply, we should have an overwhelming majority?*

consequential is a word severely restricted in its application by modern idiom; it is now used only in the sense of 'self-important' or to indicate a secondary & incidental result. It is unidiomatic in several of the senses that it might have or has formerly borne.

1. Where doubt can arise between it & *consequent,* the latter should always be used when the sense is the simple & common one of *resulting.* Thus *In the* consequent *confusion he vanished,* but *The consequential amendments were passed.*

2. *Consequential* does NOT mean 'of consequence'; a consequential person may or may not be important; all we know is that he is self-important. RIGHT: *Mr. C. bustled about, the most* consequential *man in the town.*

3. *Consequential* does NOT now mean 'having great consequences.' For *so desperate & so* consequential *a war as this* there should be substituted *a war so desperate & so pregnant with consequences.*

4. A *consequential crime* &c. is an act that was not criminal in its own nature, but amounts to a crime in virtue of its consequences.

conservative. *Conservative* means 'preservative,' disposed to keeping existing institutions; hence by extension, of people, moderate, cautious ('similar to members of the Conservative party'). Perhaps the most ridiculous of SLIPSHOD EXTENSIONS is the rapidly spreading use of this word as an epithet, in the sense of *moderate, safe,* or *low,* with estimates, figures, &c.: *Seas that even the* conservative *ship's logs called 'mountainous.'/The figure is probably an overestimation, & a more* conservative *estimate is that of Kohler./The distributing side of the market takes* a more conservative *& certainly more hopeful view.*

conservatoire, conservatory. The French, German, & Italian musical institutions are best called by their native names—*conservatoire, conservatorium, conservatorio. Academy* or *School of Music* is better than *conservatory* for corresponding English and American institutions.

consider is not followed by *as* or *to be* when used in the sense regard, judge. RIGHT: *I consider him a rich man; He considers wealth of little importance.*

considerable, in the sense *a good deal of,* is applied in Brit. use only to immaterial things (*I have given it considerable attention; He went to considerable trouble*); applied to material things it is US colloq.: *Silk fabric containing* considerable gold or silver *thread./Certain pharmaceutical preparations* *similar to cerates, but containing* considerable tallow.

considerateness, consideration. *Consideration,* so far as it is comparable with *considerateness,* means thought for others, while *considerateness* means the characteristic of taking (or implying) such thought. It is therefore sometimes indifferent which is used (*He showed the greatest considerateness* or *consideration; Thanks for your considerateness* or *consideration*). But more often one is preferable: *His* considerateness *is beyond all praise; I was treated with* consideration; *He was struck by the* considerateness *of the offer.*

considering (=taking into account) is a prep. as well as a participle (i.e. it does not have to be attached to an agent noun). RIGHT: *It is scarcely possible to act otherwise,* considering *the frailty of human nature.*/Considering *his own circumstances, it was ironical that he should appear in such a cause.*

consist. *Consist of* introduces a material, & *consist in* a definition or a statement of identity; we must not say *the moon consists* in *green cheese* (no one would), nor *virtue consists* of *being good* (many do). ELEGANT VARIATION between the two is absurd: *The external world* consisted, *according to Berkeley,* in *ideas; according to Mr. Mill it* consists of *sensations & permanent possibilities of sensation.* WRONG: *The most exceptional feature of Dr. Ward's book undoubtedly* consists of *the reproduction of photographs.* Use *in.*

consistence, -cy. The *-cy* form is now invariable in the noun that means being consistent, i.e. not inconsistent (*consistency is an overrated virtue*). In the noun meaning degree of thickness in liquids usage varies; *A consistence something like that of treacle & Mud varying in consistency & temperature* are both from Huxley; it would be well if *consistence* could be made the only form in this sense, as *consistency* in the other.

consolatory. Pron. -sŏl′-.

consonant (adj., pron. kŏn′-) =agreeable *to,* consistent *with: consonant* to *our standards,* with *our aims.*

consort. Pron. the noun kŏn′-sort, the verb konsort′.

conspectus. General view of a subject; synopsis. Pl. *-uses.*

conspicuity, -ousness. The second is better.

conspicuous. For *conspicuous by absence* see HACKNEYED PHRASES (*Even in the examination for the M.D., literary quality & finish is often* conspicuous by its absence).

constitution(al)ist. Use the longer form. See -IST &c.

construct, construe, translate, with reference to language. *To translate* is to reproduce the meaning of (a passage &c.) in another language, or sometimes in another & usually more intelligible style. *To construe* is to exhibit the grammatical structure of (a passage &c.), either by translating closely (& so it is often tantamount to *translate*) or by analysis. A sense of *construe* formerly common, but now disappearing & better abandoned, is that in which *construct* is taking its place (*'Aim' should not be constructed,* or *construed, with an infinitive*). *Construe* retains, however, its sense of 'interpret':

The wording of the act has been variously construed.

consume means to devour, waste, destroy, spend, &c., completely. Hence it should not be accompanied by *totally, completely, utterly,* all of which it already implies. See INCOMPATIBLES.

consummate. The adj. (=perfect, complete) kŏnsum´ĭt, the verb (to accomplish, achieve) kŏn´sumāt.

consummation. For *a consummation devoutly to be wished* see HACKNEYED PHRASES.

contact. The use of *contact* as a verb except in technical language (*the two wires contacted to cause the spark*) is still avoided by many writers & speakers (e.g. *Please* contact *me at your earliest convenience*). Webster labels it 'slang.' Others defend it as useful, and it is rapidly becoming 'standard' in US, at least in business. *Contact* n.=(business) connection &c. is also chiefly US.

contemn. Pron. -eming, but -emner. Chiefly a literary word meaning to despise, scorn; not to be confused with *condemn* (to adjudge to be wrong, guilty).

contemplate &c. Pron. con´-; *contemplative,* pron. -tem´-.

co(n)temporary, -oraneous, &c. *Con-* is the only right spelling, & the *co-* form should be allowed to die.

contemptible, contemptuous. *Contemptible,* worthy of contempt, despicable; *contemptuous,* full of contempt, disdainful. WRONG: *Mr. Sherman, speaking in the Senate, called the President a demagogue who* contemptibly *disregarded the Government.* Mr. Sherman probably meant, & not improbably said, *contemptuously.* See PAIRS & SNARES.

content, v. *Content oneself with* (not *by*) is the right form of the phrase that means not go beyond some course; the following are WRONG: *We must* content ourselves *for the moment* by *observing that from the juridical standpoint the question is a doubtful one./The petition* contents itself by *begging that the isolation laws may be carried out.*

content(ment), nn. *Contentment* is now the usual word, *content* surviving chiefly in *to heart's content* & as a poetic or rhetorical variant.

contest. (1) Pron. the noun kŏn´tĕst, the verb kŏntĕst´. (2) The intransitive use of the verb (*Troops capable of* contesting *successfully* against *the forces of other nations;* cf. the normal *contesting the victory with*) is much rarer than it was, & is better left to *contend.*

continual, continuous. That is *continual* which either is always going on or recurs at short intervals & never comes (or is regarded as never coming) to an end. That is *continuous* in which no break occurs between the beginning & the (not necessarily or even presumably long-deferred) end. *His continual nagging; a continuous line.*

continuance, continuation, continuity. *Continuance* has reference to *continue* in its intransitive senses of last, go on; *continuation* to *continue* in its transitive senses of prolong, go on with, & (in the passive) be gone on with. Choice between the two is therefore open when the same sense can be got at from two directions. *We hope* *for a* continuance *of your favors* means that we hope they will continue; *We hope for a* continuation *of them* means that we hope you will continue them; & these amount to the same thing. But the addition that continues a tale or a house is its *continuation,* NOT its *continuance,* & the time for which the pyramids have lasted is their *continuance,* NOT their *continuation;* we can wait for a *continuation,* but NOT for a *continuance, of hostilities;* we like a thing for its *continuance,* but NOT for a *continuation;* &, generally speaking, the distinction has to be borne in mind. *Continuity,* though occasionally confused with *continuance,* is less liable to misuse, & it is enough to say that its reference is not to *continue,* but to *continuous.*

contract, n. & v. The accent is on the first syllable of the noun. In the verb it is in US often on the first syllable when the meaning is 'undertake by contract': *He* con'tracted *to have the work finished by spring.* Other senses of the verb are usually contract'.

contradictious, -tory. The meanings given to *contradicting* (captious, caviling, cantankerous, quarrelsome) do not belong to *contradictory.* If either word is to be used, it must be *contradictious;* but this, though not in fact a new word, is always used with an uneasy suspicion that it has been made as a temporary stopgap, & it is better to choose one of the many synonyms.

contralto. Pl. *-os.* (In English the Italian pl. *-ti* is usually felt to be an affectation.)

contrary. 1. The original accent (kontrar'i) lingers (1) with the uneducated in all ordinary uses of the adjective (not, perhaps, in *the contrary*); (2) with most speakers in the jocose or childish *contrary* for perverse or peevish, & in *contrariness, -ly,* used similarly; (3) with many speakers in *contrariwise,* especially when it either represents *on the contrary* rather than *in the contrary manner,* or is used playfully.

2. *On the contrary, on the other hand.* The idiomatic sense of *on the other hand* is quite clear; except by misuse (see below) it never means far from that, i.e. it never introduces something that conflicts with the truth of what has preceded, but always something reconcilable, though in contrast, with it. The following two examples should have *on the contrary* instead of *on the other hand:* (WRONG) *It cannot be pleaded that the detail is negligible; it is,* on the other hand, *of the greatest importance./The object is not to nourish* 10,000 *cats by public charity; it is,* on the other hand, *to put them to sleep in the lethal chamber.* RIGHT: *Food was abundant; water,* on the other hand (or, *on the other hand, water*), *was running short.*

The use of *on the contrary* is less simple. It may have either of the senses of which *on the other hand* has only one; i.e. it may mean either *on the other hand* or *far from that;* but if it stands first in its sentence it can only mean *far from that.* Thus *Food was abundant; water,* on the contrary, *was running short* is correct, though *on the other hand* is commoner &, with a view to future differentiation, preferable. If *on the contrary* is to stand first, it must be in such forms as *Food was not abundant;* on the contrary, *it was running short.*

contrary, converse, opposite. These are sometimes confused, & occasionally precision is important. If we take the statement *All men are mortal,* its contrary is *Not all men are mortal,* its converse is *All mortal beings are men,* & its opposite is *No men are mortal.* The contrary, however, does not exclude the opposite, but includes it as its most extreme form. Thus *This is white* has only one opposite, *This is black,* but many contraries, as *This is not white, This is colored, This is dirty, This is black;* & whether the last form is called the contrary, or more emphatically the opposite, is usually indifferent. But to apply *the opposite* to a mere contrary (e.g. to *I did not hit him* in relation to *I hit him,* which has no opposite), or to the converse (e.g. *He hit me* in relation to *I hit him,* to which it is neither contrary nor opposite), is a looseness that may easily result in misunderstanding. The temptation to go wrong is intelligible when it is remembered that with certain types of sentence (*A exceeds B*) the converse & the opposite are identical (*B exceeds A*).

contrast. (1) Pron. the noun kon′-, the verb -trast′. (2) The transitive use of the verb with one of the contrasted things as subject, in the sense *be a contrast to* or *set off by contrast,* was formerly common, but in modern writing is either an archaism or a blunder; *with* should always be inserted. The use meant is seen in: *Monks whose dark garments contrasted* ^*the snow.*

control makes *-lled, -llable,* &c.

contumac(it)y. (Defiance of authority.) The shorter form is more usual & is preferable. Pron. kon′-. See LONG VARIANTS.

contumely. (Insolent language or treatment; disgrace, insult.) Pron. kŏn′tû (or tū) mēlĭ (or mĭlĭ).

convenance, convenience. For *mariage de convenance* (a 'suitable' marriage; one arranged for reasons of position or money), & the *convenances* (conventional propriety; the conventionalities), see FRENCH WORDS, & MARRIAGE OF CONVENIENCE.

conversance, -cy. The words mean the same thing; *conversance* is more usual & therefore is recommended.

converse(ly). (1) Pron. the adj. kon′-, but the adv. ˌvers′-. (2) For the sense of *the converse,* see CONTRARY, CONVERSE.

cool makes *coolly.*

co-operate, co-opt, co-ordinate. The hyphen is recommended. But see CO-.

copulative, vv. & conjs. (Gram.): 'linking.' Copulative verbs are such as, like the chief of them, *to be,* join a complement to the subject (He *is* king; we *grow* wiser); among them are included the passives of factitive verbs (This *is considered* the best). Copulative conjunctions are those that make a combination (*and*), NOT a contrast or alternative (*but*).

copybook, copycat, and now (US) usually *copyreader,* each one word; *copy editor* still usually two (*copyedit, copyediting,* or with hyphens, US publishers' jargon).

copyright serves as n., adj., &

v. *I recently read a copyright article in the 'Times'* means that the article was on the subject of copyright; *I read a copyrighted article* means that the article had been copyrighted. In US the *Register* (NOT Registrar) *of Copyright.* See REGISTER.

coquet(te) &c. The noun is always *-ette,* & is applied to females only. The verb, formerly *coquet* only, is now usually *-ette;* the noun *coquetry* best pronounced kō′kĕtrĭ.

corbel gives *-led* (US), *-lled* (Brit.). The architectural supporting projection, not technically an ornament, but associated with the grotesque ornamentation by Sir Walter Scott. (Corbel=a raven.)

cord, chord. In US *cord* is invariable for rope or string, cloth, measure of wood, electricity; in physiology the usage varies between *spinal chord, vocal chord,* &c., & *spinal cord* &c.; but a *chord* in music. See CHORD.

cordon. Pron. kor′dn.

core. *Rotten at the core* is a MISQUOTATION for 'A goodly apple rotten at the heart' (*Merchant of Venice,* I.3).

co-respondent &c., in a divorce suit. The hyphen is often used to indicate the long *o* (kō′rē-spŏn dent) and to distinguish it from *correspondent,* but most US dictionaries list it without a hyphen.

cornelian. See CARNELIAN.

cornucopia. Pl. *-as,* NOT *-ae.*

corollary. (From *corollarium,* money paid for a chaplet or garland.) In geom. a proposition following immediately one that has been demonstrated, but without new proof. Hence transf., something that follows in natural course, a practical consequence. *The art of writing, of which printing is an inevitable corollary.* Pron. US kŏr′-, Brit. usually kŏrŏl′-.

corona. Pl. *-as* or *-ae.*

coronal. Pron. the noun (circlet) kŏr′onăl, the adj. (of the skull, of a corona) korō′-.

corporal, corporeal, adjs. *Corporal* means of the human body, & is common in *corporal punishment;* it is also rarely used with deformity, beauty, defects, & such words, instead of the usual *personal* or *bodily.* (The noun—non-commissioned officer—is not related.) *Corporeal* means of the nature of body, material, tangible; so *our corporeal habitation* (i.e. the body), *the corporeal presence of Christ in the Sacrament.*

corps. Pron. in sing. kōr, but in pl. (though the spelling is the same) kōrz. *Corpse,* which was originally the same word & so spelled and pronounced, is now completely differentiated; pl. *-ses.*

corpulence, -cy. There is no difference; *-cy* should be dropped as a NEEDLESS VARIANT.

corpus. Pl. *corpora.* Body; fig. the whole body of literature on any subject; a complete collection of writings; the main body, material substance; principal as opposed to interest or income. *Corpus delicti:* the basic facts necessary to the commission of a crime (not, as is sometimes supposed, the body of the victim).

corral. Pron. korăl′. (In some Western states commonly pronounced kor rĕl′); v., *corralled, corralling.*

correctitude, a recent formation (*correct+rectitude*), usually means merely *correctness* or *propriety.*

correlative, adj. & n. (Gram.): Having a mutual relation; regularly used together. Correlative conjunctions: *both . . . and; either . . . or; neither . . . nor; not only . . . but also; whether . . . or.*

corrigendum. Pl. (much commoner than the sing.) *-da.*

corroborate makes *-rable.*

Cortes. The national legislature (two chambers) of Spain & Portugal. Pron. kor′tĕs.

coryphaeus. The leader of the chorus (Greek drama). So spelled. Pl. *-aei.*

cosy, -zy. The former (for both adj. & teapot warmer) is est. in Brit.; the latter in US.

cot(e). The word for *bed* is or was Anglo-Indian, is unconnected with the other words, & is always *cot.* The poetic word *cottage* & the word for *shelter* (usually seen in compounds, as *sheepcote*), represent allied but separate Old English words; *cot* is now invariable in the sense *cottage,* & *cote* usual in the sense *shelter;* the latter, however, whether spelled *cote* or *cot,* is usually pronounced kŏt, especially in the commonest word *dovecote.*

cotemporary. Use CONTEMPORARY.

co-tenant. See CO-. Usually without a hyphen in US dictionaries, but hyphened in Brit. & often in US documents & by the press (long ō).

couchant. Lying down, esp. of an animal. Pron. kow′chant.

could, as a living subjunctive, is used to express an inclination (conditional): *I* could wish *he would be a little more considerate. I* couldn't think *of leaving you at such a time.*

council, -sel, -cil(l)or, -sel(l)or. (US usually *-cilor, -selor.*) A board or assembly, & the meeting of such a body, has always *-cil,* & a member of it is *-cil(l)or* (*the governor's council, the Town council*). The abstract senses consultation, advice, secret (*keep one's counsel*), belong to *-sel,* & one who gives advice is, as such, a *-sel(l)or,* though he may be a *-cil(l)or* also; *my council(l)ors* (i.e. my city's) are the members of my city council; *my counsel(l)ors,* those who advise me officially or otherwise. *Counsel,* however, has also the semi-concrete sense of the person or persons (never *counsels*) pleading for a party to a lawsuit (*The second of our three counsel was the best*).

counsel, v. intrans. (e.g. as in *I spent many happy hours* counseling with *the students*) is obs. & has no place in modern writing. Omit *with.*

counselee (one to whom counsel is given). An ugly word best eschewed.

countenance, face, physiognomy, visage. *Face* is the proper name for the part; *countenance* is the face with reference to its expression; *physiognomy,* to the cast or type of features; *visage* is now a LITERARY WORD, used ornamentally for *face* without special significance.

counter-. Combining prefix meaning opposite (*counterclaim*), complementary (*counterpart*), and their variations. In US the combinations are usually spelled as single words: *counteraccusation, counterrevolution, counterclockwise;* this book recommends retaining the hyphen in unusual & unusually long words that might not be recognized at first glance. *Counter-organization, counter-condemnation,* &c.

counterpart means thing, exactly similar to (NOT opposite to or contrasted with) another. WRONG: *All this is utterly false, the truth is its very* counterpart.

coup. Pron. kōō; pl. *coups,* pron. kōōz. *Coup* means a blow, a stroke, & in English now usually a successful one. *Coup d'état* (pron. dātä), a sudden & decisive stroke of state policy, spec. a violent or illegal change in government. *Coup de grâce* (pron. de gräs), a blow by which one mortally hurt or condemned is put out of his misery.

couple. When signifying a pair or brace, after a numeral, *couple* is often used as a plural. It is used loosely as a synonym for two &, colloq., for approximately two—a few. *Couple* is properly used only when there is some common function or relation. *A couple of people refused to sign* is loose but permissible; *I went out to mail a couple of letters* stretches this loose use too far.

couplet (Poet.): 'joining.' In verse two lines, especially when of equal meter, rhyming, & forming a whole:

'When simple kindness is misunderstood,
A little flagellation may do good.'

coupon. Pron. kōō'pŏn or -pon' (NOT kū).

course. *Of course,* as the herald of an out-of-the-way fact that one has just unearthed from a book of reference, is a sad temptation to writers: *From this marriage came Charles James Fox; his father was,* of course, *created Baron Holland in* 1763./*Milton* of course *had the idea of his line from Tacitus./He is,* of course, *a son of the famous E. A. Southern, of 'Lord Dundreary' fame.*

courtesan, -zan. Spell *-san,* & pron. kōr'tĭzăn.

courtier. Pron. kōr-'.

court-martial. Although the hyphen is not necessary for the noun, it is usual in the US. The verb always takes the hyphen. Pl. *courts-martial.*

Coventry. The dictionaries give preference to kŏv'-, but most people say kŭv-. *Send a person to Coventry* (an ancient town in Warwickshire)=refuse to associate with (him), exclude (him) from society because of objectionable conduct. There have been many conjectures about the origin of the phrase; the first use cited in the OED was by Clarendon in 1647.

covetous (pron. -tŭs) is often mispronounced -chus on the supposed analogy of *righteous* (& sometimes misspelled *-teous*).

coward(ly). The identification of *coward* & *bully* has gone so far in the popular consciousness that persons & acts in which no trace of fear is to be found are often called *coward(ly)* merely because advantage has been taken of superior strength or position; such action may be unchivalrous, unsportsmanlike, mean, tyrannical, & many other bad things, but not cowardly;

cf. the similar misuse of DASTARDLY.

coxswain. Pron. kŏk′sn.

coyote. Properly pron. koyō′tĭ. Webster gives the cowboy pronunciation, kī′ōt, first, a pronunciation popularized by 'Westerns' on radio & television.

cozy. So spelled (US). Brit. *cosy.*

crabbed (two syllables) for perverse, irritable, goes back to the 14th c.

cranium. Pl. *-ia, -ms.* The bones that enclose the brain; more widely, the skull. Joc. (or slang) 'head.'

crape, crepe. The first is the original English word, now retained only for the black crape of mourning.

crèche. The Christmas tableau usually pronounced (US) krĕsh. The (chiefly Brit.) day nursery, krāsh.

credence, credit. Apart from the isolated phrase *letter of credence* & the concrete ecclesiastical sense table or shelf, *credence* (pron. krē′-) has only one meaning—belief or trustful acceptance. WRONG: *Two results stand out clearly from this investigation . . . ; neither of these* gives any credence *to the assertions that Protectionist countries had fared better than Great Britain. Give credence to* means 'believe,' simply; *support* or *credibility* is the word wanted. *Credit,* on the other hand, is rich in meanings, & it is a pity that it should be allowed to deprive *credence* of its ewe-lamb; *credence* would be better in *Charges like these may seem to deserve some degree of* credit, & in *To give entire* credit *to whatever he shall state.* Even *give credit* (*to*) has senses of its own (*I give* him credit *for knowing better than that; No* credit given *on small orders*), which are all the better for not being confused with the only sense of *give credence to* (RIGHT: *One can* give no credence *to his word*).

credible, creditable. *Credible,* worthy of belief; *creditable,* worthy of praise. *Made* credible *by the sincerity of the speaker; a* creditable *use of his riches.*

crenel(le). Spell *crenel* & pron. krĕ′nl. *Crenal(l)ated* has *-l-* (US), *-ll-* (Brit.).

Creole. (1) A person of French or Spanish descent born & reared in a colonial region. (2) Spec. US, a white person descended from the French or Spanish settlers of Louisiana or the Gulf States (also a person of Negro & Creole blood who speaks the creole patois).

crepe. The usual US spelling (no circumflex, pron. crāp), except for mourning CRAPE.

crescendo. Pron. krĕsh-. Pl. *-os.*

cretin. Pron. krē′tĭn.

crisis. Pl. *crises* (krī′sēz). A stage or state of affairs, lit. or fig., at which a decisive change is imminent; a turning point. Loosely overused for any serious situation.

criteria is plural and must be followed by a plural verb. In (WRONG) *The basic* criteria *for clearance* was *so general that officials resolved any doubts in favor of dimissal,* the sing. *criterion* should have been used.

critique (pron. krĭ tēk′) is happily in less common use now than it was in the sense of review & criticism. It is still used (properly) for a treatise on a subject (e.g. *Kant's Critique of Pure Reason* &c.).

Croesus. Spell so. Pron. krē-.

crooked. (1) The figurative use of *crooked* (dishonest, perverted, &c.) is not colloq. but of long literary tradition (*A perverse & crooked generation,* Deut.). As applied to material things dishonestly come-by (*His whole output was crooked*) it is US colloq. (2) A stick that is not straight is a kro͝okĭd stick; one provided with a crook is a kro͝okt stick.

crosswise, crossways. The first is more generally used as adv. (but *dirty work at the crossways; Diana of the Crossway*).

croupier. Pron. kro͞o′pĭer.

crow. The past is now usually *crowed,* esp. in figurative use (*They crowed over us, The baby crowed loudly*). *Crew* is used always in *the cock crew* when there is reference to the N.T. passage, & alternatively with *crowed* when *cock* is the subject in other connections: *Three cocks crowed,* or *crew, at the same moment.*

crown. (1) *The Crown* is often used as a phrase for the king or queen regarded not as a person, but as a part of the constitution. It does not follow that pronouns appropriate to *king* or *queen* can be used after it, as in this absurdity: *The incontestable fact that the Crown nowadays acts, & can only act, on the advice of* her *Ministers.* (2) *Crown Colony* (preferably capitalized), one in which the legislation & administration are controlled by the home government (i.e. the Crown).

cruel. In US usually *-ler, -lest;* Brit. *-ller, -llest.*

cryptic. For this as compared with *mysterious, obscure, hidden,* & other synonyms, see WORKING & STYLISH WORDS.

crystalline. Pron. (US) krĭst′*a* lĭn; (Brit.) krĭ′st*a*lĭn (in poetic & rhet. use occas. krĭstă′lĭn).

crystallize. So spelled. In its figurative use (*crystallized public opinion; plans not yet crystallized*), a VOGUE WORD.

cubic(al). *Cubic* is the form in all senses except that of shaped like a cube. So *cubic measure, contents, foot, equation;* but *a cubical box* or *stone. Cubic,* however, is used of minerals crystallizing in cubes, as *cubic alum.*

cuckold. Pron. kŭ′kld.

cudgel makes (US) *-led, -ling;* (Brit.) *-lled, -lling.*

cue, queue. Both are pronounced kū. In billiards, & in the theatrical use (with the transf. applications, as in *take one's cue from*), *cue* is invariable. In the sense string of people &c. waiting their turn, *queue* is invariable. In the sense pigtail, *queue* is usual.

cui bono? As generally used, i.e. as a pretentious substitute for *To what end?* or *What is the good?*, the phrase is at once a BATTERED ORNAMENT & a blunder. The words mean *To whom was it for a good?* (i.e. *Who profited by it* or *had something to make out of it?*). Those who do not want it in this sense should leave it alone.

cuisine. Pron. kwē sēn′. Kitchen (department); also, the style of food prepared. But see FRENCH WORDS.

cul-de-sac. 'Bottom of the bag.' *Blind alley* is the English equivalent. Pron. as Eng. kōōl'de săk. See FRENCH WORDS.

culinary. Pron. kū'lĭnarĭ. The word is a favorite with the POLYSYLLABIC-HUMORIST, who often pronounces it kŭl-.

cullender. Use COLANDER.

culminate, v., to bring a thing to its highest point. *The mountains forming this cape* culminate *in a grand conical peak. A grand procession of dynasties of life, beginning from the lower forms &* culminating *in man.*

cult, as now used (=a group of admirers), dates only from the middle of the last century; its proper place is in books on archaeology, comparative religion, & the like; see ANTI-SAXONISM.

cultivate makes *-vable.*

cumulus. Pl. *-li.* The adj. is *-ous.*

cuneiform. The slovenly pronunciation kūn'ĭform, not uncommon, should be avoided, & to this end kūnē'ĭform is preferable to the more difficult kū'nĭĭform.

cunning means artful(ness), quaintly attractive (as a child), craft(y), dexterity (-ous), &c. Used for *pretty,* it is colloq. US.

cup. For 'cups that cheer' see HACKNEYED PHRASES.

cupola. Pron. kū'pola.

curaçao, -çoa. Spell -çoa (erron. but established); pron. kūr'asō.

curator. Pron. kūrā'tor (except in the Scotch law use in which it is kūr'ator).

curb, kerb. The first is usual in US for all senses. The second is a variant merely, but in Brit. is now much commoner than *curb* in the sense footpath edging, & seems likely to prevail in the closely allied senses fender, border, base, framework, mold. For the bit chain, & in the sense check n. or v., *curb* is invariable.

curé. Pron. kū rā'. (French) parish priest.

curio. Pl. *-os.* See CURTAILED WORDS.

curriculum. Pl. *-la* (*-ums* is permissible but seldom heard).

curse. For 'curses not loud but deep' see HACKNEYED PHRASES.

cursed, curst. The adjective *cursed* is disyllabic except sometimes in verse; the form *curst* is chiefly used either to show that the rare monosyllabic pronunciation is meant (esp. in verse), or to differentiate the archaic sense *ill-tempered.*

CURTAILED WORDS. Of these, some words establish themselves so fully as to take the place of their originals or to make them seem pedantic; others remain slangy or adapted only to particular audiences. A small proportion of them, including specimens of various dates & status, has here been collected as possibly useful to those who have, or wish to have, views on the legitimacy of curtailment: (air)*plane; bike* (bicycle); *brig*(antine); (omni)*bus; cab*(riolet); *cent*(um); *cons* (contras); (rac)*coon; curio*(sity); *cycle* (tricycle or bicycle); *dynamo* (-electric machine); (in)*flu*(enza); *gym*(nasium); *mob*(ile vulgus); *pants* (pantaloons); (tele)*phone; photo*(graph); *pro*(fessional); *props* (properties); *quotes* (quotation marks); *radio*(activity); *spats* (spatterdashes); *spec*(ulation); *Strad*(ivarius); *stylo*(graph); *super*(ior); *super*(numerary); *vet*(erinary); *Zoo*(logical gardens).

curtain raiser. A GALLICISM for which there is no short English equivalent. Also hyphened.

customs. Capitalized=the *US Bureau of Customs. Customs duties*–the payment levied upon imports from foreign countries (*excise*–duties charged on home goods before they can be sold).

cut. The idiom is *cut in half,* not *halves.*

cute. (From *acute.*) Colloq., clever, shrewd. US colloq., attractive, appealing, as a child.

cycle. (1) For the noun & verb as an abbreviation for 'bicycle or tricycle,' see CURTAILED WORDS. The verb is much more usual than *to bicycle.* (2) *Cycle* as a time-word is a succession of periods itself succeeded by a similar succession. See TIME.

cyclopedia, -ic. In US usually *-ped-,* Brit. *-paed-*. The longer forms *encyclo-* are in themselves better, & *encyclopedia,* being common in titles, is also the prevalent form; but *cyclopedic* is becoming the more usual form for the adjective.

cyclopaen, -pian. The first (sīklopē′*an*) is more usual than the second (sīklō′pĭan); but neither is wrong.

cyclop(s). The forms recommended are: for the singular *cyclops;* & for the plural the classical *cyclopes* (sīklō′pēz) except in jocular or familiar use, for which the English formation *cyclopses* is suitable.

Cymric. Pron. kĭ-.

cynic(al). As an adjective, *cynic* is used only in the sense of the ancient philosophers called *Cynics* (except in the technical terms *cynic year, cynic spasm*); the word that describes temperament &c. is *cynical.*

cypher. Use *cipher.*

Czar. Often so spelled, though *Tsar* is nearer the Russian.

Czech. Spell so, & pron. chĕk.

D

dachshund. Pron. däks′ho͝ont.

dactyl. (Poet.): 'finger.' The metrical foot –◡◡, as in pŏttĕrў or Jūlĭă.

dadaism. (Pron. dä′*da* ĭzm.) A movement in art, literature, &c., that flourished *c.*1920, esp. in Paris.

dado. Pl. *-oes.* Part of a pedestal between the base and the cornice; lower part of interior wall when finished differently from the upper part. Pron. dādō.

daemon, dæ-. Write *dae-*. Pron. dē-. This spelling, instead of *demon,* is to distinguish the Greek mythology senses of supernatural being, indwelling spirit, &c., from the modern sense of devil.

daguerreotype. So spelled. Pron. -gĕrō-.

dahlia. Pronounced dāl′ya in Brit. and by many US garden-club members. Standard US is dä- or dă-.

dais. In US usually dā′ĭs; Brit. dās.

damage makes *damageable.*

damning, in the sense cursing, is pronounced without the *n;* in the sense fatally conclusive, it usually has the *n* sounded: e.g. *dam'ning evidence.*

dampen is now chiefly US, having given place in Brit. to *damp.* Brit.: *Sorrow damped his zeal.* US: *Adversity dampened their ardor.*

damsel. Now poetic, archaic, or facetious. See ARCHAISM.

danger. (1) *In danger of his life* is still living idiomatic English, but *life* is the only word possible in this construction; with other words *in danger of* is followed by the evil (*in danger of losing his honor; of being thrown from the bridge*) not, as in the *life* idiom, of the thing exposed to the peril. (2) NOT *By refusing to cooperate he ran a* danger of *appearing mean.* One runs a risk, not a danger.

DANGLING PARTICIPLE. WRONG: *Having just returned from a long cruise,* the city *seemed unbearably crowded to us both.* But the city had not been on the cruise. Participles must be 'attached' to the noun responsible for the action. *Having just returned . . .* we *found the city unbearably crowded.* See UNATTACHED PARTICIPLES.

dare, v. 1. *Dare* as 3rd pers. sing. pres. indic. is the idiomatic form instead of *dares* when the infinitive depending on it either has no *to* or is understood; this occurs chiefly, but not only, in interrogative & negative sentences. Thus *dares,* though sometimes used in mistaken striving after correctness, would be contrary to idiom in *Dare he do it?; He dare not!* But *If he dares to say one word, he'll regret it. No one dares to* (or *dare*) *oppose him.*

2. *Durst,* which is a past indic. & past subj. beside *dared,* is obsolescent & nowhere now required, like *dare* above, by idiom. The contexts in which it is still sometimes preferred to *dared* are negative sentences & conditional clauses where there is an infinitive either understood or having no *to* (*But none durst,* or *dared to,* or *dared, answer him; I would do it if I durst,* or *dared*).

3. *Dare say* as a specialized phrase with the weakened sense 'incline to think,' 'not deny,' 'admit as likely' (cf. the unweakened sense in *I dare say what I think, Who dare say it? He dared to say he,* or *that he, would not do it*), has certain peculiarities: (a) even when not parenthetic (*You, I dare say, think otherwise*), it is never followed by the conjunction *that* (*I dare say it is a mere lie,* NOT *that it*); (b) it is never *dare to say* in direct speech, & the *to* is rare & better avoided in indirect speech also (*He dared say the difficulty would disappear; I told him I dared say he would change his mind; He dares say it does not matter*); (c) to avoid ambiguity, it is sometimes written as one word (*I dare say she is innocent,* I am sure of it; *I daresay she is innocent,* I can believe it); but this device is useless as long as it is not universally accepted. It is simpler to avoid *I dare say* in the unspecialized sense wherever it can be ambiguous.

dare, n., a challenge, is colloq. Brit. but accepted US: e.g. *To take a dare* &c.

dark(e)y. Spell *darky*, if used; pl. *darkies.* (Colloq., often offensive.)

darkly. In the biblical quotation (*We see through a glass, darkly*) the meaning is *dimly*, with obscure vision. In *He frowned darkly*, the meaning is *gloomily*, or ominously. WRONG: *The Democrats took the same view of the situation, but* darkly; the writer has confused the two meanings and added possibly his own meaning of *pessimistically.*

DASH. Conventional uses: 1. Instead of a colon, before an explanation: *There were* 12 *applications*–8 *from local posts,* 4 *from foreign.*

2. Before *all*, preceded by a complicated subject: *Careless driving, faulty mechanism, narrow or badly kept roads–all play their part in causing accidents.*

3. Instead of parentheses: *The truth is–and I say this advisedly–that the cause is lost no matter what we do.*

4. To indicate an unfinished thought: *But even if I dare*–. In formal writing three dots (. . .) are preferable to indicate missing material. See ELLIPSES.

dastard(ly). The essential & original meaning of the words is the same as that of *coward(ly)*, so far at least that both pairs properly connote want of courage; but so strong is the false belief that every bully must be a coward that acts requiring great courage are constantly described as cowardly or dastardly if they are so carried out as not to give the victim a sporting chance; the throwing of a bomb at a king's carriage is much less dastardly than shooting a partridge, because the thrower takes a very real risk; but even when he recklessly exposes himself to being torn to pieces, the absurd headline 'Dastardly Outrage' is inevitable. The true meaning is seen in 'A laggard in love & a dastard in war.' The words should at least be reserved for those who do avoid all personal risk.

data is plural only (*The data are,* NOT *is, insufficient./What* are *the data?*); the singular, comparatively rare, is *datum; one of the data* is commoner than *a datum;* but *datum line,* line taken as a basis, is common. WRONG: *My Intelligence Department has furnished me with so* much *valuable data*–a mistake of taking the plural for a singular; *much* should be *many. The* data *compiled from fall enrollments* is *noted below,* printed in a university report, proves that the error is made not only by the uninformed. Pron. dāta or däta.

dat(e)able. Spell *-ta-.*

-d-, -dd-. Monosyllables ending in *d* (*cad, dead*) double it before suffixes beginning with vowels if the sound preceding it is a single vowel but not if it is a diphthong or a doubled vowel or a vowel & *r: caddish, redden, bidding,* but *deaden, breeder, goodish.* Words of more than one syllable follow the rule for monosyllables if their last syllable is accented or is itself a word in combination (*forbidding, bedridden*), but otherwise do not double the *d* (*nomadic, nakedest, rigidity, periodical*).

dead letter, apart from its theological & post-office uses, is a phrase for a law that has still a nominal existence, but is no longer observed or enforced (e.g. the blue laws). The application of it to what was never a regulation but has gone or is going out of use, as quill pens, horse traction, &c., or to a regulation that loses its force only by actual abolition (*the one-sex franchise will soon be a dead letter*), is a SLIPSHOD EXTENSION.

dead line. Best spelled as two words. Orig. a line drawn around a (military) prison, beyond which a prisoner is liable to be shot. In printing, the time at which the forms of a newspaper are locked, after which no news can be added. Fig. (by extension) the final time for finishing anything. Other uses by extension are colloq. or slipshod.

deadly, deathly. *Deadly* is the usual word in most contexts except when the meaning is literally pertaining to death: e.g. *a deathly silence,* lit.; *a deadly silence,* fig.

deal, n. 1. The use of *a deal* instead *of a great* or *good deal,* though as old as Richardson & Johnson (the Shakespearian *what a deal!* can hardly be adduced), has still only the status of a colloquialism, & should be avoided in writing even when the phrase stands as a noun (*saved him* a deal *of trouble*), & still more when it is adverbial (*this was* a deal *better*).

2. A *deal* in the sense of a piece of bargaining or give-&-take is still slang or colloq. (US).

dear(ly) advs. With the verb *love, dearly* is now the regular form & *dear* merely poetic; but with *buy, sell, pay, cost,* &c., *dear* is still idiomatic (*He paid* dear *for his error*), & the tendency born of mistaken grammatical zeal to attach an UNIDIOMATIC -LY should be resisted.

dearth. *I think it of interest to point out* what a singular dearth of information exists *on several important points;* for this favorite journalistic device see PERIPHRASIS; read *how little we know.*

debacle. The accents are no longer necessary, but complete disregard of its French origin in pronunciation (dā băk′el), though admitted by one US dictionary, is not usual. Pron. dê bäk′l′. The literal meaning is a breaking up of ice in a river; a sudden deluge that breaks down all barriers, carrying stone and other debris before it. Transf. & fig. it is any violent disruption or sudden breakdown.

debar, disbar. There has been complete differentiation, *debar* having retained all senses of exclude, prohibit, prevent (usually with from—*debarred from holding office* &c.), & *disbar* now being used exclusively for (Law) expel from the bar.

debark(ation) are NEEDLESS VARIANTS for the est. *disembark(ation).*

debauchee. (An extreme sensualist, a libertine.) Pron. dĕbôsh ē′. *Debauch* and *debauchery,* however, are pronounced -bôch′-.

debonair. So spelled. Genial, gay, affable. Archaic in Brit. but still current in US.

debris, dé-. Write without accent, & pron. dĕ brē′ or dĕ′-brē.

debut, debutante. (1) *Debut*

can only be pronounced as French, & should not be used by anyone who shrinks from the necessary effort (in US it is usually dā bū or dā bo͞o). There is no reason why *debutante* should not be written without accent, & pronounced dĕ′būtänt. The masculine (*debutant*) is seldom used. (2) *Debut* is a noun, not a verb. The reviewer who wrote '*Sylvia* debuted *in the chorus at the age of* 19' would be hard put to read his own sentence aloud.

deca-, deci-. In the metric system, *deca-* means multiplied, & *deci-* divided, by ten; *decameter*, 10 m., *decimeter*, 1/10 m.; so with *gram, liter*, &c.

decadence. Most US dictionaries give dekā′dens first, but dĕ′cadens is often heard & is standard Brit.

decease, *the deceased,* should be reserved for legal and technical use. In other contexts they are still euphemisms for *die, dead.* So also *decedent* (pron. -sē′-) (US Law term).

decided, decisive. *Decisive* is often used loosely where *decided* is the right word. *A decided victory* or *superiority* is one the reality of which is unquestionable; *a decisive* one is one that decides or goes far toward deciding some issue; *a decided person* is one who knows his own mind, & *a decided manner* that which comes of such knowledge; *a decisive person,* so far as the phrase is correctly possible at all, is one who has a way of getting his policy or purpose carried through. The two meanings are quite separate; but, as the decided tends to be decisive also, it gets called so even when decisiveness is irrelevant. WRONG: *The sergeant,* a decisive man, *ordered . . ./A* decisive *leaning toward what is most simple./It was not an age of* decisive *thought./Poe is* decisively *the first of American poets.* The following suggests a further confusion with *incisive: The Neue Freie Presse makes some very* decisive *remarks about the Italian operations at Preveza.*

decimate meant originally to kill every tenth man as a punishment for cowardice or mutiny. Its application is naturally extended to the destruction in any way of a rather large proportion of anything reckoned by number, e.g. a population is decimated by the plague. Anything that is directly inconsistent with the proper sense (*A single frosty night* decimated *the currants by as much as* 80%) must be avoided. See SLIPSHOD EXTENSION.

declare implies explicitness, and usually formality. It should not be used when the sense is merely *express* or *say.*

déclassé (fallen or sunk in the social scale) is usually either a GENTEELISM or a euphemism. See FRENCH WORDS.

decline as a verb can be used as a polite or genteel equivalent of *refuse.* As a noun it cannot be used in the sense of *refusal.* (WRONG: *Our* decline *of this particular book is outside the option.*)

décolleté(e) is an adj. The noun is *décolletage. Her dress was excessively décolleté./Her décolletage was startling.* See FRENCH WORDS.

decorous. Pron. US dĕk′orus, Brit. usu. dĕkōr′us.

dedicate makes *-cable.*

deductible, NOT *-able.*

deduction (Log.): 'down-drawing.' Reasoning from the general to the particular; basing the truth of a statement upon its being a case of a wider statement known or admitted to be true. If I argue that I shall die because I have been credibly informed that all men do so, & I am a man, I am performing deduction. Cf. INDUCTION.

deed, v. An Americanism. 'To deed . . . We sometimes hear this word used colloquially but rarely except by illiterate people.' (1816 Pickering *Vocabulary,* quoted in OED.) Less than 100 years later (*Cent. Dict. & Cyclopedia*), it was the standard US word for convey by deed.

deem. The usual words are *think, suppose, judge.* See WORKING & STYLISH WORDS.

deep(ly). *Deep* is an adv. as well as a n. & adj., and in certain combinations *deeply* is unidiomatic. RIGHT: *Still waters run deep./Deep-rooted prejudice./Deep-seated emotion./They worked deep into the night./His hands were stuck deep in his pockets.*

deer is both sing. & pl. See COLLECTIVES 1.

defalcate. US (as also OED) prefers -făl′-; COD gives dē′- only.

defamatory. Pron. -făm′-.

defect. For *the defects of his qualities* see HACKNEYED PHRASES.

defective, deficient. The differentiation tends to become complete, *defective* being associated more & more exclusively with *defect,* & *deficient* with *deficit.* That is deficient of which there is either not enough or none, that is defective which has something faulty about it; so *deficient quantity, revenue, warmth, means; defective quality, condition, sight, pronunciation; a defective chimney, valve, manuscript, hat.* With some words quantity & quality come to the same thing; for instance, *much* or *great insight* is the same as *deep* or *penetrating insight;* consequently a person's insight may be described indifferently as *defective* or *deficient.* Again, deficiency in or of a part constitutes a defect in the whole, & consequently a person may be called either *deficient* or *defective in courage* or *knowledge* or *sympathy,* & milk may be *defective* (though *deficient* is commoner) *in fatty matter;* compare *The dialogue is not defective* (or *deficient*) *in ease & grace* with *Ease & grace are not deficient* (NEVER *defective*) *in the dialogue.* WRONG: *I wish you had a Fortunatus hat; it is the only thing* defective *in your outfit;* here *deficient* is required, though there would have been no objection to *It is the only thing in which your outfit is defective.* A verb or noun of which some part is deficient or wanting is called *defective,* where *deficient* would also be possible if the combination had not been stereotyped. Lastly, either word may sometimes be used, but with a difference of meaning from the other. *Deficient water* or *light* is too little water or light; but *defective water* is impure &c.; & *defective light* is uncertain &c.; similarly, *a defective* differs from *a deficient supply* in being irregular or unreliable rather than insufficient in the aggregate.

defence, -se. Brit. *-ce;* US *-se;* but both *-sible.*

deferrable. So spelled.

definite, definitive. Confusion between the two, & especially the use of *definitive* for *definite,* is very common. Many writers seem to think the words mean the same, but the longer & less usual will be more imposing; & mistakes are made easy by the fact that many nouns can be qualified by either, though with different effects. Putting aside exceptional senses that have nothing to do with the confusion (as when *definitive* means 'of the defining kind'), *definite* means defined, clear, precise, unmistakable, &c., & *definitive* means having the character of finality; or, to distinguish them by their opposites, that is *definite* which is not dubious, vague, loose, inexact, uncertain, undefined, or questionable; & that is *definitive* which is not temporary, provisional, debatable, or alterable. *A definite offer* is one of which the terms are clear; *a definitive offer* is one that must be taken or left without chaffering; *definite jurisdiction* is that of which the application or the powers are precisely laid down, & *definitive jurisdiction* is that from which there is no appeal. Either word can be applied, with similar distinctions, to *answer, terms, treaty, renunciation, result,* &c. But with many words to which *definite* is rightly & commonly applied (*a definite pain, accusation, structure, outline, forecast*) *definitive* either is not used except by mistake for *definite,* or gives a meaning rarely required (e.g. *a definitive forecast* means, if anything, one that its maker announces his intention of abiding by). WRONG: *We should be glad to see more* definitive *teaching./The Bill has not yet been drawn up, & the Government is not responsible for 'forecasts,' however* definitively *they may be written./The* definitive *qualities of jurisprudence have not often found so agreeable an exponent as the author of these essays.*

deflection, -xion. US *-ct-;* Brit. usually *-x-.*

defrayal. *Defraying* is better, or *defrayment.* See -AL NOUNS.

degree. The phrase *to a degree,* however illogical it seems as a substitute for *to the last degree,* is at least as old as *The Rivals* (*Your father, sir, is wrath to a degree*), & objection to it is futile.

deign. To deem worthy; to think it fit for oneself (to do something): *The very dog will hardly deign to bark at you;* to condescend (now usually with *answer, reply,* & in the negative): *She would not deign to reply.*

deism, theism. Though the original meaning is the same, the words have been so far differentiated that *deism* is understood to exclude, & *theism* (though less decidedly) to include, belief in supernatural revelation, in providence, & in the maintenance of a personal relation between Creator & creature.

delectable. Affording delight. In ordinary use the word is now ironical only; i.e. it is to be taken always, as *precious* is sometimes, to mean the opposite of what it says. In poetry, sometimes in fanciful prose, & in *the delectable mountains,* it retains its original sense; e.g. *Of all the fleeting visions which I have stored up in my mind I shall always remember the view across the plain as one of the most delectable.* Otherwise it is archaic.

deliberative. The word means pertaining to or characterized by deliberation: *Government by deliberative bodies./His more deliberative moments.* The sense 'not hasty in decision or inference,' which was formerly among those belonging to the word, has been assigned to *deliberate* by modern differentiation; the use of *deliberative* in that sense now (WRONG: *All three volumes are marked by a cautious &* deliberative *tone that commends them to thoughtful men*) instead of *deliberate* is to be classed with the confusions between ALTERNATIVE, DEFINITIVE, & alternate, definite.

delineate makes *-neable.*

delusion, illusion. It cannot be said that the words are never interchangeable; it is significant of their nearness in meaning that *illusion* has no verb corresponding to *delude* (*illude* having died out), & *delusion* has none corresponding to *disillusion* (*undeceive* & *disillusion* being used according as the delusion has been due to others' machinations or to the victim's own error). Nevertheless, in any given context one is usually better than the other; two distinctions are here offered:

1. A *delusion* is a belief that, though false, has been surrendered to & accepted by the whole mind as the truth, & may be expected to influence action; *delusion* is being possessed by *a delusion.* An *illusion* is an impression that, though false, is entertained provisionally on the recommendation of the senses or the imagination, but awaits full acceptance & may be expected not to influence action; *illusion* is the entertaining of *an illusion. We labor under delusions,* but *indulge in illusions. The delusions of lunacy, the illusions of childhood* or *of enthusiasm. A dangerous delusion, a pleasant illusion. Delusive hopes* result in misguided action, *illusive hopes* merely in disappointment. That the sun moves round the earth was once a *delusion,* & is still an *illusion.* The theater spectator, the looker at a picture or a mirror, experience *illusion;* if they lose consciousness of actual facts entirely, the illusion is complete; if the spectator throws his stick at the villain, or the dog flies at his image, illusion has passed into *delusion.*

2. The existing thing that deludes is a *delusion;* the thing falsely supposed to exist, or the sum of the qualities with which an existing thing is falsely invested, is an *illusion.* Optimism (if unjustified) is a *delusion;* Heaven is (if nonexistent) an *illusion.* If a bachelor dreams that he is married, his marriage is an *illusion;* if he marries in the belief that marriage must bring happiness, he may find that marriage is a *delusion.* A mirage, or the taking of it for a lake, is a *delusion;* the lake is an *illusion.* What a conjuror actually does—his real action—is a *delusion;* what he seems to do is an *illusion;* the belief that he does what he seems to do is a *delusion.* The world as I conceive it may for all I know be an *illusion;* &, if so, the world as it exists is a *delusion.*

demagogic &c. Although most US dictionaries give the soft *g* first (-jĭk), the hard g (-gĭk), is gaining popularity, especially in US academic circles. So *demagogy* may eventually replace the unfortunate US *demagoguery*.

demarcation. So spelled.

demean. There are two verbs. One, which is always reflexive, means to conduct oneself or behave, & is connected with *demeanor* & derived from old French *demener* (*He demeans himself like a king*). The other, which is usually but not always reflexive (*I would not* demean myself *to speak to him*), means to lower or debase. This seems to be the product of a confusion between the first verb & the adjective *mean*, &, though it is occasionally found as a normal word in good authors, it is commonest on the lips of the uneducated or in imitations of them, & is best avoided except in such contexts.

demesne. **1.** 'The prevailing pronunciation in the dictionaries & in the modern poets is dĭmēn′, but dĭmān′ is also in good legal & general use, & is historically preferable' (OED). Dĭmān′ is the more usual pronunciation in the US.

2. *Demesne, domain.* The two words are by origin the same, but in technical use there are several distinctions between them that cannot be set forth here. In the wide general sense of sphere, region, province, the established form is *domain;* also in Law, *eminent domain. Demesne* in legal terms is the possession (of land) as one's own: *land held in demesne.* The use of *demesne* in other contexts is usually due to NOVELTY-HUNTING.

demi-, used as a prefix to form temporary words (=half, or imperfect), now usually gives place to *semi-*. It survives in *demigod, demijohn, demimonde.*

demimonde. ('The half-world.') The class or world of doubtful reputation. *Demimondaine,* one of the women of that world.

demise, not *-ize.* Pron. -īz. Often a GENTEELISM for *death.*

democrat(ic). Democrat is a noun, *democratic* an adj. *The Democrat* (for *Democratic*) *party,* used presumably to indicate that the party has no exclusive claim to democracy, is a recent variation.

demonetize. Pron. -mŏn′-.

demoniac(al). The adjectives are not clearly differentiated; but there is a tendency to regard *-acal* as the adj. of *demon,* so that it is the form chosen when wickedness is implied, & *-ac* as the adj. of the noun *demoniac,* so that it is chosen to convey the notion of the intensity of action produced by possession (*demoniacal cruelty, demoniac energy*). Pron. -ō′nĭăk, -ī′akl'.

demoralize. So spelled. The most frequent modern use suggests *morale* rather than *moral;* to destroy the discipline, courage, cohesion or endurance, originally of troops; now transf., to reduce (a person &c.) to a state of weakness or disorder.

demote, the opposite of *promote* (*He has recently been demoted*), is heard and seen in news reports (US), but is so recent as to be in few dictionaries.

Denmark. For 'something rotten in the state of Denmark' see IRRELEVANT ALLUSION & HACKNEYED PHRASES.

denote. What a word *denotes*

is its actual meaning, by definition; what it *connotes* is what it suggests or implies. See CONNOTE.

dénouement. Pron. dā nōō-män′. (Lit.): 'untying.' The clearing up, at the end of a play or tale, of the complications of the plot. A term often preferred to the English *catastrophe* because that has lost in popular use its neutral sense. By transf., the final solution or issue of a complex situation, difficulty, or mystery.

dent. A variant of *dint* (influenced by *indent*), an impression in a surface such as is made by a blow with an edged or sharp instrument. In fig. use, *dint* is still sometimes used. *Dents in the wall, a dint in her character.*

dentifrice is a shop word, occasionally heard also as a GENTEELISM. *Tooth powder, tooth paste,* are what we say to ourselves.

denunciation. Pron. -sĭa-, & see -CIATION.

departed. For *the departed, the dear departed,* &c., see STOCK PATHOS.

department. In the sense of sphere, province, *department* is often used colloq. when one of its synonyms is idiomatically required. In *Religion is outside my department,* 'province' or 'field' is probably meant. But *Every department of human activity.* For synonymy see FIELD.

depend. Constr. *on, upon.* The slovenly construction illustrated below, in which *it depends* is followed by an indirect question without *upon,* is growing common, but is indefensible. WRONG: *It all* depends who *is going to read the criticism, & what he expects to learn from it.*

dependant, -ent. In US *-ent* is more usual for both noun & adj. In Brit. the noun has *-ant,* rarely *-ent;* the adj. *-ent,* rarely *-ant.*

dependence, -ency. The first is now usual, though not invariable, in all the abstract senses (*a life of dependence; no dependence can be put upon his word; the dependence of the harvest on weather; the gospel is our dependence*), & *dependency* is almost confined to the concrete sense of a thing that depends upon or is subordinate to another, esp. a dependent territory (*the cotton trade & its dependencies; India was a British dependency.*

depicture, though in fact an old verb, has never established itself in general currency, & perhaps always sets a reader wondering whether it is a blunder due to hesitation between *depict* & *picture;* it might well be abandoned as a NEEDLESS VARIANT.

depositary, -tory, are properly applied, *-tary* to the person or authority to whom something is entrusted, & *-tory* to the place or receptacle in which something is stored; & the distinction is worth preserving, though in some contexts (*a diary* as *the depositary of one's secrets; the Church* as *the depository of moral principles*) either may be used indifferently.

depot. (1) A place where military stores are deposited; (2) where troops are assembled and trained; (3) where goods are stored (a storehouse); (4) in US, a railroad station. Write without accents or italics, & pron. (1–3) dĕ′pō; (4) dē′pō.

deprecate (to express earnest

disapproval of, or an earnest wish against) & its derivatives *-cation, -catory,* often appear in print, whether by the writer's or the compositor's blunder, in place of *depreciate* (do the reverse of praise) & its derivatives *-ciation, -ciatory.* WRONG: *Mr. Birrell's amusing* deprecation *of the capacity of Mr. Ginnell to produce a social revolution./The* self-deprecatory *mood in which the English find themselves.* PROPERLY USED: *I cannot help* deprecating *their conduct./Its use is* deprecated.

depreciate. Intrans., to fall in value, become of less worth; trans., to lessen the value of, underrate, disparage. *The property has depreciated./He extolled his own actions and depreciated those of his father.*

deprival. *Deprivation* is the usual word and means the same thing.

deprivation. Pron. either dĕprī- or dēprī-, NOT dĕprī- or dēprī-.

Derby(shire). Brit. pron. där-. But the Kentucky Derby, US, dĕr-.

de règle. Customary, proper; *de rigueur,* required (by etiquette). See FRENCH WORDS.

derisory, derisive. Most dictionary definitions make no distinction, being almost in the same words for both (conveying derision, deriding); *derisory* only, however, has the sense ridiculously futile, not to be taken seriously, as in *a derisory offer* &c.; in other senses *derisive* is much commoner.

derring-do. This curious word, now established as an archaic noun meaning desperate courage, is traced to a misinterpreted passage of Chaucer, in which Troilus is described as second to none 'in dorryng don that longeth to a knyght,' i.e. 'in daring (to) do what belongs to a knight.' Spenser, a lover of old phrases, apparently taking it for a noun, as if the line meant 'in bold achievement, which is a knightly duty,' made *derring doe* in this sense a part of his regular vocabulary. The derivation is a surprise; but if Spenser did make a mistake, it does not follow that modern poetical writers should abstain from saying 'deeds of derring-do'; the phrase is part & parcel of an English that is suited to some occasions.

descendant, -ent. The noun (issue, offspring) is now always *-ant,* as is usually the related adj. The adj. meaning *descending,* i.e. coming or going down, is rare but when used is *-ent.*

description. The less this is used as a mere substitute for *kind* or *sort* (*no food of any description; crimes of this description*) the better; see WORKING & STYLISH WORDS.

desecrate makes *-crable.*

desert, nn., **desert,** v., **dessert,** n. The confusion is in the spelling. There are two nouns spelled *desert.* One is accented on the first syllable (the arid region &c.), the other on the second (*his condign deserts*). The verb (accent second syllable) means to abandon &c. *Dessert* (accent second syllable) is any sweet, fruit, &c., served at the close of a meal.

deserve. Although etymologically suggesting reward, deserts for virtue, *deserve* now may be used as worthy of good or evil (e.g. *he deserved his punishment,* or *the acclaim.*

déshabillé. Use *dishabille* (pron. dĭs ă bēl′), the anglicized form.

desiccate. So spelled.

desiderate (to desire with a sense of want, or regret) is a word that we should be better without. Most readers do not know the meaning of it, taking it for the scholar's pedantic or facetious form of *desire.* Writers are often in the same case (see the sentence quoted below; we do not 'desiderate' what we cannot be prevented from preserving), &, if they are not, are ill-advised in using the word unless they are writing for readers as learned as themselves. WRONG: *In this she acts prudently, probably feeling that there is nothing in the Bill that could prevent her, & those like-minded, acting as benevolently towards their servants as before, & so preserving the 'sense of family unity' she so much* desiderates.

desideratum. Pl. *-ta.* Pron. dĭsĭderā′t'm. Something desired; something lacking or required. *The great* desiderata *are taste and common sense* (Coleridge).

desire is not a synonym for *like.* It is stronger, & expresses a definite wish or longing. Used for *want* or *like* it is a GENTEELISM: *He doesn't* desire *it to be too successful./What do you* desire, *Madam?*

desist(ance). Pron. -zĭ- not -sĭ-.

desolated, as polite exaggeration for *very sorry* &c., is a GALLICISM. But an island can be desolated by a storm; a country by a war; a person by the death of a loved one.

despatch. Use DISPATCH.

desperado. Pron. -ādō. Pl. *-oes.*

desperation never now means, as formerly, mere despair or abandonment or loss of hope, but always the reckless readiness to take the first course that presents itself because every course seems hopeless.

despicable. Pron. dĕs′pĭk*a*b'l.

destine. (*Who was*) *destined to be* &c., when it means no more than who has since become or afterwards became, is a BATTERED ORNAMENT.

destructive. Constr. *to, of. Destructive of health; destructive to the morals of youth.*

detail. The verb is accented on the second syllable, the noun on either the first or second.

determinately, determinedly. Although *determinately* can be (and sometimes is) used in the sense with determination, its true meaning is precisely, in a definite manner, &c. (from *determinate,* limited, fixed, definable). The objection to *determinedly,* which is very general, is perhaps based on reluctance to give it the five syllables that are nevertheless felt to be its due. The recommendation is to use a substitute: resolutely, firmly, with determination, &c. An example or two will illustrate the ugliness of the word: *In causes in which he was heart & soul convinced no one has fought* more determinedly *& courageously* (with greater determination & courage)*./However, I* determinedly *smothered all premonitions* (firmly).

detour. In US, dē′- is heard more often and is given first in most dictionaries. The traditional Brit. pronunciation is dĕtōōr′. Write without accent or italics.

de trop. (Not wanted, in the

way.) Pron. dê trō′. But see FRENCH WORDS.

devil, n. *Devil's advocate* is very dangerous to those who like a picturesque phrase but dislike the trouble of ascertaining its sense. The real devil's advocate is one who, when the right of a person to canonization as a saint is being examined, puts the devil's claim to the ownership of him by collecting & presenting all the sins that he has ever committed; far from being the whitewasher of the wicked, the devil's advocate is the blackener of the good. In the following example the not unnatural blunder is made of supposing that it means a whitewasher, or one who pleads for a person who either is or is supposed to be wicked. WRONG: *Because the* devil's advocate *always starts with the advantage of possessing a bad case, Talleyrand's defender calls forth all our chivalrous sympathy.* And in this other the writer referred to is perhaps devil's advocate in 'the rest of his book,' & something quite different ('God's advocate,' say) in 'an early chapter': *He tries in an early chapter to act as* 'devil's advocate' *for the Soviet Government, and succeeds in putting up a plausible case for the present regime. But the rest of his book is devoted to showing that this Bolshevist case is based on hypocrisy, inaccuracy, and downright lying.*

devil, v., makes (US) *-led, -ling;* (Brit.) *-lled, -lling.*

devil(t)ry. The *-try* form is a mere corruption. It is so much commoner in US, however, that ACD gives it as the dominant form.

deviser, -sor. *Devisor* is the person who devises property, & is in legal use only; *-er* is the agent-noun of *devise* in other sense (cf. ADVISER).

devolute, though an old verb in fact, has been dormant for three centuries; it is unnecessary by the side of *devolve.*

devolve. Fig. to pass to or fall upon (a person); to delegate; to come upon (a person) as a charge. Constr. *to, upon. The stock devolved* to *them from ancient times./The duties of the government devolved* upon *the people.*

devotee. Pron. dĕ vô tē (equal stress).

dexter in heraldry means *right,* sinister *left,* i.e. of the person bearing the shield, not of the observer.

dext(e)rous. US dictionaries give the longer form first, Brit. the shorter.

diabetes. Pron. -ēz. Colloq. -ĭs. *Diabetic,* pref. pron. -ĕt′-.

diabolic(al). Roughly *-ic* means of, & *-ical* as of, the devil: *Horns, tail, & other diabolic attributes; He behaved with diabolical cruelty.*

DIAERESIS. (1) Spell -ae-, not æ. Pl. *-reses* (-sēz). Pron. dī ĕr′- or -ēr′-. (2) (Gram.): 'taking asunder.' The pronouncing of two successive vowels as separate sounds & not as a single vowel or diphthong; or the mark (¨) over the second, sometimes used to indicate such separation, as in Chloë. The mark, when used, should be placed over the second of the vowels that are to be kept unmixed (aërated). It should not not be regarded, however, as a permanent part of any word's spelling, but kept in reserve for occasions on which special need of it is felt. In combinations such as *co-operate, coöperate* (if not spelled without an indication of the prefix), the hyphen is better. See co-.

diagnosis. Pl. *-oses* (ōsēz).

diagram makes *diagrammatic.*

dialect. A local or provincial form of language. For *dialect, patois, vernacular,* &c., see JARGON.

dialectal, -ic, -ical. The natural adjective for *dialect* would be *-ic* or *-ical,* & both forms were formerly used as such, besides serving as adjectives to the noun *dialectic;* but to avoid confusion *dialectal* has recently been formed & found acceptance, so that we now speak of *dialectic(al) skill,* but *dialectal words* or *forms.*

dialectic(s). Log. (usually pl.), art of testing truth by discussion; logical disputation. Mod. Philos. (sing.), criticism dealing with metaphysical contradictions &c. (Kant, Hegel).

dialogue (Lit.): 'cross-talking.' Conversation as opposed to monologue, to preaching, lecturing, speeches, narrative, or description; neither confined to nor excluding talk between two persons; see DUOLOGUE.

diamond. Properly three syllables; popularly (US) two.

diapason. Pron. dīăpā'zn. In its fig. use (from music), = range, scope, entire compass. *The whole diapason of joy & sorrow.*

diarchy, dy-. Spell *di-.* Government by two rulers. *Diarchy* is to *monarchy* as *dioxide* & *disyllable* are to *monoxide, monosyllable,* & the other *mono-* words. *Monologue* & *dialogue* are not a relevant pair, *dialogue* having nothing to do with Gk. *di-,* two-. For the government in the Indian provinces from 1919 to 1937, Webster gives *dyarchy* ('of less etym. authority' —OED).

diastole. Pron. dīăs'tolĭ.

dice, see DIE.

dictator. Traditionally pronounced -tā'-; but dĭk'- now more often heard in US.

dictionary, encyclopedia, lexicon. A dictionary, properly so called, is concerned merely with words regarded as materials for speech; an encyclopedia is concerned with the things for which the words are names. But since some information about the thing is necessary to enable the words to be used rightly, & opinions differ upon the how much of this, most dictionaries contain some matter that is strictly of the cyclopedic kind. *Lexicon* means the same as *dictionary,* but is usually kept to the restricted sense, & is moreover rarely used except of Greek, Hebrew, Syriac, or Arabic dictionaries. By extension, *dictionary* is now also applied to reference books arranged in alphabetical order on various subjects: *Dictionary of Quotations, of Proverbs,* &c.

dictum. (A saying or utterance.) Pl. *-ta.* (1) An authoritative or formal statement. (2) A judge's pronouncement (Law). (3) A current saying. *This dictum must be our guide./The dicta of the judge concerning the privileges of Parliament./The dictum that truth always triumphs.*

didactic, orig. to instruct (*didactic poetry*), having the manner of a teacher, has now taken on, in popular use, a pejorative force, 'inclined to lecture others too much': *A didactic old lady.* See also DIDACTICISM.

DIDACTICISM. 'No mortal but is narrow enough to delight in educating others into counterparts of himself.' The statement is from *Wilhelm Meister.* Men, especially, are as much possessed by the didactic impulse as women by the maternal instinct. Some of them work it off *ex officio* upon their children or pupils or parishioners or legislative colleagues, if they are blessed with any of these. Others are reduced to seizing casual opportunities, & practice upon their associates in speech or upon the world in print. The orientalist whom histories have made familiar with *the Khalif* is determined to cure us of the delusion, implanted in our childish minds by hours with some bowdlerized *Arabian Nights,* that there was ever such a being as our old friend *the Caliph.* Literary critics saddened by our hazy notions of French do their best to lead us by example from *nom de plume* & *morale* to *nom de guerre* & *moral.* Dictionary devotees whose devotion extends to the etymologies think it bad for the rest of us to be connecting *amuck* with *muck,* & come to our rescue with *amok.* These & many more, in each of their teachings, teach us one truth that we could do as well without, & two falsehoods that are of some importance. The one truth is, for instance, that *Khalif* has a greater resemblance to Arabic than *Caliph.* Is that of use to anyone who does not know it already? The two falsehoods are, the first that English is not entitled to give what form it chooses to foreign words that it has occasion to use; & the second, that it is better to have two or more forms coexistent than to talk of one thing by one name that all can understand. If the first is not false, why do we say *Germany* & *Athens* & *Lyons* & *Constantinople* instead of *Deutschland* & the rest? or allow the French to insult us with *Londres* & *États Unis?* That the second is false not even our teachers would deny; they would explain instead that their aim is to drive out the old wrong form with the new right one. That they are most unlikely to accomplish, while they are quite sure to produce confusion temporary or permanent.

Seriously, our learned persons & possessors of special information should not, when they are writing for the general public, presume to improve the accepted vocabulary. When they are addressing audiences of their likes, they may naturally use, to their hearts' content, the forms that are most familiar to writer & readers alike; but otherwise they should be at the pains to translate technical terms into English. And, what is of far greater importance, when they do forget this duty, we others who are unlearned, & naturally speak not in technical terms but in English, should refuse to be either cowed by the fear of seeming ignorant, or tempted by the hope of passing for specialists, into following their bad example without their real though insufficient excuse.

die, n. (1) The plural of the cubes used in the game is *dice. The cast of a die* (or *of dice*) *is impossible of prediction./As straight as a die./The die is cast. /She hacked her toast into dice.*

(2) The plural of the cubical block (in Arch.), the engraved stamp used for impressing a design or figure on some softer material (metal, paper, &c.), and the various mechanical appliances, is *dies. Marble cut in small square dies./The variety of dies used in coining money./Before the use of dies, soles were rounded out by hand.*

dietitian. (Orig. US.) Modeled after *physician,* the spelling should be *dietician,* but the *-itian* form is established.

differ, in the sense be different, exhibit a difference, is followed only by *from,* not by *with.* In the sense have a difference of opinion, express dissent, dispute, it is followed usually by *with,* but sometimes by *from. Men* differ from *each other in appearance./Though I* differ with *him on minor points, I agree on all essentials./She may* differ from (*or* with) *me in opinion.*

difference. *There is all the* difference *in the world* between deceiving *the public by secret diplomacy* & carrying on *the day-to-day business of negotiation from the housetops.* Why, certainly; but was it worth while to tell us so obvious a fact? If the writer had put in a *not* before either *deceiving* or *carrying,* he would have told us both something of value & what he meant. See ILLOGICALITIES. *Difference* so often tempts to this particular illogicality as to deserve special mention.

different. 1. That *different* can only be followed by *from* & not by *to* is a SUPERSTITION. Not only is *to* 'found in writers of all ages' (OED); the principle on which it is rejected (you do not say *differ to;* therefore you cannot say *different to*) involves a hasty & ill-defined generalization. We cannot say *differing to;* but that leaves *different* out in the cold. The fact is that the objections to *different to,* like those to *averse to, sympathy for,* & *compare to,* are mere pedantries. (Fielding: 'It's a different thing within to what it is without.') This does not imply that *different from* is wrong; on the contrary, it is 'now usual' (OED); but it is only so owing to the dead set made against *different to* by mistaken critics.

2. *Different than* is now used chiefly when a preposition is inconvenient: . . . *in a different way than ever before.* It also has been used by many good writers, but is not recommended.

3. *Different* as an adv. is obs. and now is only in uneducated use: *He acts* different (should be *-ly*) *every time I see him.*

differentia. Pl. *-iae.* Fig., distinguishing mark or characteristic: *To be inconsistent . . . is the very differentia of myths.* For synonymy see SIGN.

differentiation. Pron. -shē ā′-shun.

DIFFERENTIATION. In dealing with words, the term is applied to the process by which two words that can be used indifferently in two meanings become appropriated one to one of the meanings & one to the other. Among the OED's 18th-c. quotations for *spiritual* & *spirituous* are these two: *It may not here be improper to take notice of a* wise & spiritual saying *of this young prince./The Greeks, who are* a spirituous & wise *people.* The association of each with *wise* assures us rather startlingly that a change has taken place in the meaning of *spirituous*. It & *spiritual* have now been appropriated to different senses, & it would be difficult to invent a sentence in which one would mean the same as the other; that is, differentiation is complete. In a living language such differentiation is perpetually acting upon thousands of words; to take a modern example, *airship*, when first used, meant any locomotive aircraft, whether lighter or heavier than air; now, by differentiation from *airplane*, it has been confined to the former kind. Most differentiations are, when fully established, savers of confusion & aids to brevity & lucidity, though in the incomplete state there is a danger of their actually misleading readers who have not become aware of them when writers are already assuming their acceptance. Differentiations become complete not by authoritative pronouncements or dictionary fiats, but by being gradually adopted in speaking & writing. It is the business of all who care for the language to do their part toward helping serviceable ones through the dangerous incomplete stage to that in which they are of real value. The matter is simple in principle, the difficulty being in the details; & all that need be done is to collect here, with some classification, a few differentiated words, those about which information is given in their places being printed in small capitals.

A. Words completely & securely differentiated: *adulteration* & *adultery; cloths* & *clothes; coffer* & *coffin; conduct* & *conduit; convey* & *convoy; costume* & *custom; dam* & *dame;* PRONOUNCEMENT & *pronunciation.*

B. Words fully differentiated, but sometimes confounded by ignorant or too learned writers: ACCEPTANCE & *acceptation; alternate* & ALTERNATIVE; CONTINUANCE & *continuation;* DEFINITE & *definitive;* ESPECIAL(LY) & *special(ly);* EXCEEDING(LY) & *excessive(ly); historic* & HISTORICAL: *intense* & INTENSIVE: *loose* & *loosen* (-EN VERBS); LUXURIANT & *luxurious;* MASTERFUL & *masterly;* OLYMPIAN & *olympic: proposal* & PROPOSITION: *slack* & SLACKEN: *transcendent* & TRANSCENDENTAL: TRIUMPHAL & *triumphant.*

C. Words in which an incipient or neglected differentiation should be encouraged; ASSAY & *essay* (vv.); COMPLACÉNT & *complaisant;* DEFECTIVE & *deficient;* FALSEHOOD, *falseness,* & *falsity;* FEVERISH & *feverous;* OBLIQUENESS & *obliquity;* OPACITY & *opaqueness.*

D. Words in which a desirable but little recognized differentiation is here advocated: APT & *liable;* CONSISTENCE & *consistency;* INCLUDE & *comprise;* INFANTILE & *infantine;* THAT & *which.*

E. Words vainly asking for differentiation: SPECIALITY & *specialty.*

F. Differentiated forms needlessly made: SPIRITISM for *spiritualism; stye* for STY; *tyre* for TIRE.

dig. *Digged* is archaic; *dug* should be used except when reference is intended to some biblical or other known passage.

digit has technical uses in mathematics, and in anatomy &c.; as a substitute for *finger*, it ranks with PEDANTIC HUMOR.

dike, dyke. The first is the right form.

dilemma. The use of *dilemma* as a mere finer word for *diffi-*

culty when the question of alternatives does not definitely arise is a SLIPSHOD EXTENSION. It should be used only when there is a pair, or at least a definite number, of lines that might be taken in argument or action, & each is unsatisfactory. See POPULARIZED TECHNICALITIES.

dilettante. Pl. *-ti* (pron. -tē). The final *e* in the sing. is pronounced ĕ or ĭ.

dilettant(e)ism. The shorter form is preferred.

dimeter. A verse of two measures (i.e. either two feet or four feet). *Iambic dimeter,* a line of eight syllables.

diminishment is a NEEDLESS VARIANT beside *diminution.* It was dormant for two centuries, but is now occasionally used (*Ireland is perhaps the only other European country that has shown a* diminishment *in its inhabitants*), perhaps inadvertently.

diminuendo. Pl. *-os.*

diminutive has a valuable technical sense in grammar; in general use (*a diminutive child, pony, apple, nose*) it is preferred to the ordinary words *tiny, small, stunted,* &c., chiefly by the POLYSYLLABIC HUMORist.

dint (archaic, stroke, blow) remains current in *by dint of.* See also DENT.

diocese, -cess. The right spelling is *-ese,* but the pronunciation is usually weakened to -ēs or -ĭs. For *diocese, bishopric,* & *see,* see SEE.

diphth-. *Diphtheria, diphthong,* & their derivatives are sometimes misspelled, & very often mispronounced, the first *-h-* being neglected; dĭfth- is the right sound.

diploma. The pl. is always *-mas* in the ordinary senses (certificate of degree &c.), though *-mata* lingers in unusual senses (State papers &c.) as an alternative.

diplomat(ist). The shorter form is standard in US, though the longer is often used by extension for 'one who is artful or tactful in meeting situations.' The longer form is standard Brit.

diptych. Pron. -ĭk.

direct(ly). 1. The right adverb in some contexts (e.g. *You should go* direct *to Paris, to the fountainhead*) is *direct,* NOT *directly;* see UNIDIOMATIC -LY.

2. The conjunctional use of *directly* (*I came directly I knew*) is quite defensible, but is chiefly colloq.

directress, -trix. See FEMININE DESIGNATIONS. As fem. of *director, -tress* is better, but *-trix* has a use in geometry (pl. *-trices,* see -TRIX).

direful is a NEEDLESS VARIANT for *dire* in sense, & in formation is based on a false analogy (*dreadful*).

disaffected. Disloyal, unfriendly, now almost always to the government or constituted authority.

disappoint. Constr.: usually *in, with. Disappointed* in *her, disappointed* with *its appearance;* rare, *disappointed* of *our hopes.*

disassociate, dissociate. The longer form is a NEEDLESS VARIANT.

disbeliever, unbeliever. A *disbeliever* is one who refuses to believe: *He attacks disbelievers but has little to say to mere unbelievers.* So *disbelief,* the rejection of an idea as untrue; positive or active unbelief.

disc. This is the standard spelling for the anatomical term (but not the botanical) and some dictionaries give it first for the phonograph record. But see DISK.

discharge. The verb is always accented on the second syllable, as is the noun traditionally, though there is a tendency now to accent the first.

disciplinary. The pronunciation dĭs′ĭplĭnarĭ is recommended in preference to dĭsĭplĭ′narĭ.

discomfit has nothing to do with *discomfort;* it means overwhelm or utterly defeat. There is a tendency to use it in too weak or indefinite a sense (WRONG: *Bell, conscious of past backslidings, seemed* rather discomfited). *Discomfiture* means rout, defeat, frustration.

disconnection, -xion. Spell *-ction* (US); *-xion* (Brit.)

discontent. For 'the winter of our discontent,' see IRRELEVANT ALLUSION.

discrete (separate, abstract, &c.) is accented on the second syllable in the US (and in OED). COD gives dĭ′skret, 'both natural in English accentuation (cf. the opposed adj. *concrete*), & useful as distinguishing the word from the familiar *discreet*' (Fowler).

discriminate, v., makes *-nable.*

disenthrall makes *disenthrallment* US or *-alment* (Brit.)

disfranchise, NOT -ize; NOT *disenfranchise* (a NEEDLESS VARIANT).

disgust. Constr. *at, with, by. I am disgusted* with *her;* at *her disobedience;* by *her habit of lying.*

disgustful was formerly common in the sense *disgusting,* but has now been so far displaced by that word as to be a NEEDLESS VARIANT in that sense.

dishabille. Pron. dĭsabēl′.

disinterested. The stress is strongly on *-in-*, not on *-est-*. The meaning is 'unbiased by personal interest,' as opposed to *uninterested* (=without concern, indifferent). A fair judge is *disinterested* in his cases; never *uninterested* (if he can help it). WRONG: *She exhibits a general nonchalance and* disinterest *in nursing* (should be *indifference to*).

disjunctive (Grammar): 'unjoining.' Conjunctions implying not combination but an alternative or a contrast (as *or, but*) are so called, the others (as *and*) being copulative. The distinction is of some importance in determining the number of verbs after compound subjects; disjunctive conjunctions are followed by a singular verb if both subjects are singular. *Not John* but *Mary* was *right.*/(Either) *John* or *Mary* is *equal to the occasion.* See NUMBER 2, 3.

disk, disc. 'The earlier & better spelling is disk' (OED). DISC, however, is established as the anatomical word.

dislike. Constr. *to, for, of. I have taken a dislike* to *him.*/*A strong dislike* for *crowds.*/*A dislike* of *crowded places.*

dislodg(e)ment. The shorter form is est. in US.

dispatch, des-, v. *Dis-* is preferred. In usual contexts the normal word is *send* (*off*). See FORMAL WORDS.

dispel means to drive away in different directions, & must have for object a word to which that sense is applicable (*darkness, fear, cloud, suspicions*), & not, as in the following sentence, a single indivisible thing. WRONG: *Carrington effectually* dispelled *yesterday* the suggestion *that he resigned the presidency because he feared . . .* He might dispel the suspicion, or repel the suggestion, *suspicion* being comparable to a cloud, but *suggestion* to a missile.

dispense with, apart from its legal and ecclesiastical uses, means do away with, render unnecessary, forego, do without. It does not mean *dispose of*.

disport is rapidly becoming archaic, remaining only in the reflexive, usually (would-be) humorous or poetic, third person: *disporting himself in the flowery paths of fancy.*

disposal, disposition. In some contexts there is no choice (*His disposition is merciful; The disposal of the empty bottles is a difficulty*); in some either word may be used indifferently (*The money is at your disposal* or *disposition*); & in some the choice depends upon the sense required (*The disposition of the troops* is the way they are stationed for action &c., & is general's work; *The disposal of the troops* is the way they are lodged &c. when not being used, & is quartermaster's work). When doubt arises, it is worth while to remember that *disposition* corresponds to *dispose*, & *disposal* to *dispose of*. *The testamentary disposition of property*, i.e. the way it is disposed or arranged by will, & *The testamentary disposal of property*, i.e. the way it is disposed of or transferred by will, describing the same act from different points of view, are naturally used without much discrimination. The same is true of *at one's disposal* or *disposition;* but in this formula *disposal* is now much commoner, just as *You may dispose of the money as you please* is now commoner than *You may dispose it.*

disproved, -en. The first is recommended. See PROVE.

disputable. Preferably accent first syllable.

disrobe is a GENTEELISM for *undress.*

dissemble, dissimulate. There is no clear line of distinction between the two. *Dissemble* is the word in ordinary use, & the other might have perished as a NEEDLESS VARIANT, but has perhaps been kept in being because it is, unlike *dissemble*, provided with a noun (*dissimulation*), & a contrasted verb (*simulate*), & is more convenient for use in connection with these.

dissociation is better than *disassociation* (there is no differentiation). Pron. -sĭ ā'shun. (But *dissociate,* dĭssō'shĭ āt.) See -CIATION.

dissoluble, dissolvable. *Dissoluble* may be used in all senses; but *dissolvable* often represents *dissolve* when it means make a solution of in liquid (*sugar is dissolvable* or *dissoluble in water*), & sometimes in other senses (*a Chamber dissoluble* or *dissolvable at the Minister's will*).

dis(s)yllable. Usually so spelled in US; but see DISYLLABLE.

distaff. For *the distaff side* see HACKNEYED PHRASES and WORN-OUT HUMOR.

distant. For *the not too distant future* see HACKNEYED PHRASES.

distendable, -dible, -sible. The last is established, US & Brit.

distention, -sion. The first is preferred US, the second Brit.

distich. A pair of verse lines, a couplet. Pron. -ĭk.

distil(l). The modern form in Brit. is *-il; -ill* is still standard US, but the shorter form is here recommended.

distinction, as a LITERARY CRITICS' WORD, is, like *charm*, one of those on which they fall back when they wish to convey that a style is meritorious, but have not time to make up their minds upon the precise nature of its merit. They might perhaps defend it as an elusive thing; but it is rather an ambiguous name for any of several things, & it is often doubtful whether it is the noun representing *distinctive* (markedly individual), *distinguished* (nobly impressive), *distingué* (noticeably well-bred), or even *distinct* (concisely lucid). A few quotations follow: (AMBIGUOUS) *His character & that of his wife are sketched with a certain* distinction./*The book is written with a* distinction (*save in the matter of split infinitives*) *unusual in such works./Despite its length, an inclination to excessive generalization, & an occasional lack of stylistic* distinction *verging upon obscurity, this book is a remarkable piece of literary criticism.*

distinctive means serving or used to discriminate, characteristic, so called by way of distinction, but it is often misused for *distinct*. WRONG: *The refugees at length ceased to exist as a* distinctive *people./*Distinctively *able & valuable.* On the other hand *distinctively* would have been the appropriate word in *The Swiss name of Edelweiss will be given to the village, the houses having the high-pitched roofs & other features of* distinctly *Swiss architecture.* In *During a long public life he served the interests of his class well in many* distinctive *positions* the right word would have been *distinguished.*

distinctly, in the sense 'really quite,' is the badge of the superior person indulgently recognizing unexpected merit in something that we are to understand is not quite worthy of his notice: *Quite apart from its instructive endeavors, the volume is* distinctly *absorbing in its dealing with the romance of banking.*

distingué. As used in English, *distingué* is not the equivalent of *distinguished,* but refers to an elegance of appearance and manner: A distingué person *with a genius for looking like a gentleman.* Pron. dĭs tăng gā', but see FRENCH WORDS.

distrait, -te. Absent-minded, inattentive. Pron. dē strā (t). Use *-ait* of males (-ā), *-aite* of females (-āt); of things (*expression, air, mood, answer,* &c.), *-ait* always. See FRENCH WORDS.

distraught, as opposed to *distrait,* means distracted to the extent of mental confusion, beset with mental conflict. Still current in US but listed as archaic in COD.

distributive (Gram.): 'allotting.' Those adjectives & pronouns are so called which expressly convey that what is said of a class is applicable to its individual members, not merely to it as a whole. *Either* (cf. *both*), *every* (cf. *all*), *each* (cf. *both* & *all*), *neither* (cf. *no*, *none*).

disyllable, diss-. The first is etymol. better; in English the prefix is *di-*, not *dis-*. But *dis-* is now in general use except among scholars (Fr. *dissyllabe*). Fowler consistently spelled with one *s*.

diurnal should not now be used in the sense of *daily*, i.e. recurring every day, though that was formerly one of its possible meanings. In modern use, (1) when opposed to *nocturnal* it means by day (*diurnal birds*), (2) when opposed to *annual* &c. it means occupying a day (*a planet's diurnal rotation*).

dive makes *dived* (sometimes US & colloq., *dove*), *dived*.

divers(e). The two words are the same, but differentiated in spelling, pronunciation, & sense, *divers* (dī'verz) implying number, & *diverse* (dĭvers') difference; cf. *several* & *various*, each of which has both senses without differentiation. In US, *divers* is now (usually) archaic or facetious.

divorce, v. The constr. is properly *from*, NOT *by*. Strictly a *divorced woman* is one whose husband has divorced her, not one who has divorced her husband; but (in US) the term is loosely used of both.

divorcé. In Fr. *divorcé* is masc., *-ée*, fem. The anglicized *divorcee* (pron. -sē) is masc. or fem.

do. 1. For *did* as in *Did I believe it, it would kill me* see SUBJUNCTIVES.

2. *Do have.* Protests are common against the use of *do* as an auxiliary to *have*. It is, however, often legitimate, as in *Did the Roman women have votes? Do you have coffee for breakfast? We did not have to pay. I did not have my hair cut.* In most of these the simple *had* or *have* is disagreeably formal, & in the *coffee* example *Have you coffee?* could only mean, *Is there any to make the drink with?* The objection should be limited to sentences in which the reference is to a single occasion or instance & also the sense of *have* is possess or something near it. This rule allows the examples given above & condemns the following: (WRONG) *Although I* do not have *any statistics, thousands of foreigners are settled there./ Counsel said the appellant took steps to have herself arrested, therefore she* did not have *any malicious intent./They* didn't even have *the grace to cover their refusal with an excuse.*

3. *Do* as substitute. The use of *do*, whether by itself or in conjunction with *as, so, it, which*, &c., instead of a verb of which some part has occurred previously, is a convenient & established idiom, but it has often bad results. WRONG: *They do not wish to see the Act of* 1903 *break down, as break down it is bound* to do; (omit *break down* or *do*)./*It ought to have been satisfying to the young man, & so, in a manner of speaking, it* did (should be *was*). *Do* &c. must not be substituted for a copulative *be* & its complement./ *The title of 'Don' is now applied promiscuously throughout Spain very much as we* do *the meaningless designation of 'Esquire'* (should read *apply* for *do*)./*It may justly be said, as*

Mr. Paul does, *that . . .* (*as Mr. Paul does say*)./*The Speaker said it ought to be withdrawn, & Mr. King* did so (i.e. *withdrew it*) *at once.* Unless the subject & the voice of *do* will be the same as those of the previous verb, it should not be used; but transgression of this rule results sometimes in flagrant blunders, & sometimes merely in what, though it offends against idiom, is (since *do so* means strictly *act thus*) grammatically defensible./*The ambassador gave them all the assistance which the nature of his office made it obligatory upon him to* do (*should* read *give*)./*To inflict upon themselves a disability which one day they will find the mistake & folly of* doing (*which one day they will discover to be a mistake & folly*). In these examples *do* is in grammatical relation to a noun (*assistance, disability*) that is only a subordinate part of the implied whole (the giving of assistance, the inflicting of a disability) to which alone it is in logical relation. The sentences, however, in which *do* is a transitive verb meaning *perform* are not properly examples of the substitute *do;* but the mistakes in them are due to the influence of that idiom.

do (the musical note). Pl. *dos.*

docile. Pron. (US) dŏ′sĭl, Brit. also dō′sīl.

doctor. In US, Dr. is used as a title for physicians, surgeons, dentists, and all holding similar medical and surgical degrees. It is used according to personal taste by those holding doctorates in other fields (science, theology, the liberal arts, &c.). As a v., *doctor* is colloq. or slang.

doctrinaire, n. A pedantic theorist; one who applies principle without regard to practical considerations. Adj., characteristic of a doctrinaire.

doctrinal. In US dŏk′trĭnal; Brit. also dŏktrī′nal.

document. (Orig. lesson, written evidence, proof.) It is sometimes forgotten that the word includes more than the parchments or separate papers to which it is usually applied; a coin, picture, monument, passage in a book, &c., that serves as evidence may be a document, & the following remark on 'Documents illustrative of the Continental Reformation' is absurd: *It is a collection not only* (*as the title implies*) *of* documents, but also *of passages from books & letters.* The phrase *human document* is more than a mere metaphor.

dodo. Pl. *-oes.*

doe. The female of most species of deer, antelope, hare, or other animals of which the male is called *buck.* Not applied to the female of the elk or moose (female, *cow*) or red deer (female, *hind*).

do(e)st. In modern, though not in older, use the auxiliary has DOST only, & the independent verb *doèst* only.

dog days. Associated with the 'pernicious influence' of the Dog-star (Sirius, the greater, or Procyon, the lesser), not with the fact that dogs go mad in hot weather. A period of from 4 to 6 weeks between early July and early September. Popularly the sultry, humid part of summer.

dogg(e)rel. The longer form is preferred.

dogma. Pl. *-mas,* formerly *-mata.*

dolce far niente. 'Delightful idleness.' See BATTERED ORNAMENTS.

Domesday, dooms-. *Domesday Book* is so spelled but pronounced doomz-; elsewhere the spelling is *doomsday.* Never *the* Domesday Book; RIGHT: *It is as indelible as Domesday Book.* (The record of the Great Inquisition, made by order of William the Conqueror in 1086.)

domestic, n., though it survives in legal & other formal use, in PEDANTIC HUMOR, & as a GENTEELISM, has been superseded for ordinary purposes by *servant* taken in a limited sense. Such losses of differentiation may be regretted, but usage is irresistible. The adj. in this sense survives in *domestic help, domestic employment.*

domicile, n. US (& OED) dŏm′ĭsĭl; Brit. also dō′mĭsĭl. Law: place of fixed or permanent residence. As a synonym for house, dwelling, in ordinary parlance, now only PEDANTIC HUMOR.

dominie. Orig. (chiefly Scot.) a schoolmaster. In rural US a pastor of the Reformed Dutch Church, or (colloq.) any minister.

domino. Pl. *-oes.*

don, v. A FORMAL WORD for *put on.*

donate is 'chiefly US' (OED). It is a BACK-FORMATION from *donation. Bestow, present,* or simply *give* would be the Brit. choice.

donor, formerly a formal or legal word, has come into current usage in *blood donor.*

dossier. Pron. US dōs yā, Brit. dŏ′syer. 'A bundle of papers,' set of documents, esp. a record of a person or matter.

dost. In late use *dost* is the auxiliary form: *Dost thou love me? doest,* the independent: *But that thou doest, do quickly.*

Douay Bible or Version. An English transl. (published, N.T. 1582 at Reims; O.T. 1609-10 at Douai, Fr.) from the Latin Vulgate, for R.C.

double. The common quotation (*Macbeth,* IV.i.83) is 'make assurance double sure' (not *doubly*). See MISQUOTATIONS.

DOUBLE CASE. WRONG: *An ex-pupil of Verrall's . . . cannot but recall the successive states of mind* that he possessed*—or, more truly,* possessed him*—in attending Verrall's lectures.* Here *that* is first objective & then (understood) subjective; it must therefore be repeated before the second *possessed.* See CASES 3 & 4, THAT REL. PRON., & WHICH.

DOUBLE CONSTRUCTION. WRONG: *They are also* entitled to prevent *the smuggling of alcohol into the States,* & to reasonable assistance *from other countries to that end.* 'Entitled to prevent (infin.) . . . & to assistance (noun)' is a change of a kind discussed in SWAPPING HORSES.

double entendre ('a double understanding,' a word or expression admitting of two interpretations, one usually indelicate) is the est. English form, & has been in common use from the 17th c.; the modern attempt to correct it into *double entente* suggests ignorance of English rather than knowledge of French. See DIDACTICISM.

DOUBLE PASSIVES. *The point is sought to be evaded:* monstrosities of this kind, which are as repulsive to the grammarian as to the stylist, perhaps spring by false analogy from the superficially similar type seen in *The man was ordered to be shot.* But the simple forms from which they are developed are dissimilar: *They ordered the man to be shot,* but *They seek to evade the point;* whereas *man* is one member of the double-barreled object of *ordered, point* is the object not of *seek* at all, but of *evade;* therefore, whereas *man* can be made subject of the passive *was ordered* while its fellow-member is deferred, *point* cannot be made subject of the passive *is sought,* never having been in any sense the object of *seek.*

To use this clumsy & incorrect construction in print amounts to telling the reader that he is not worth writing readable English for; a speaker may find himself compelled to resort to it because he must not stop to recast the sentence he has started on; but writers have no such excuse. Some of the verbs most maltreated in this way are *attempt, begin, desire, endeavor, hope, intend, propose, purpose, seek,* & *threaten.* A few examples follow: *Now that* the whole is attempted to be *systematized./The mystery* was *assiduously, though vainly,* endeavored to be *discovered./ No greater thrill can* be hoped to be *enjoyed.*

doubt(ful). It is contrary to idiom to begin the clause that depends on these with *that* instead of the usual *whether,* except when the sentence is negative (*I do not doubt . . . ; there is no doubt . . . ; It was never doubtful . . .*) or interrogative (*Do you doubt . . . ?; Is there any doubt . . . ?; Can it be doubtful . . . ?*). Even in such sentences *whether* is sometimes better (*I do not doubt* whether *I have a head on my shoulders*), but rules on that point are needless. The mistake against which warning is required is the use of *that* in affirmative statements. It is especially common (probably from failure to decide in time between *doubt* & *deny* or *disbelieve, doubtful* & *false*), but equally wrong, when the clause is placed before *doubt(ful)* instead of in the normal order. *Whether* should have been used in (WRONG): *It was generally* doubted that *France would permit the use of her port./So afraid of men's motives as* to doubt that *anyone can be honest.*/That *I have been so misled is extremely* doubtful./*It is very doubtful whether* (RIGHT) *it was ever at Dunstaffnage, & still more* doubtful that (WRONG) *it came from Ireland.*/That *his army, if it retreats, will carry with it all its guns we are inclined* to doubt.

doubtless, no doubt, undoubtedly, &c. *Doubtless* & *no doubt* have been weakened in sense till they no longer convey certainty, but either probability (*You have doubtless* or *no doubt heard the news*) or concession (*No doubt he meant well enough; It is doubtless very unpleasant*). When real conviction or actual knowledge on the speaker's part is to be expressed it must be by *undoubtedly,* *without* (*a*) *doubt,* or *beyond a doubt* (*He was undoubtedly guilty*).

dour rhymes with *moor,* NOT with *hour.*

dove. As past tense of *dive,* US (colloq.?). OED says 'occasional.'

dower, dowry. The two words, originally the same, are differentiated in ordinary literal use, *dower* being the widow's life share of her husband's property, & *dowry* the portion brought by a bride to her husband; but in poetic or other ornamental use *dower* has often the sense of *dowry;* & either is applied figuratively to talents &c.

dozen. Pl. *dozen* and *-s. Dozens of people,* but (after a number) *I bought six dozen.*

drachm, drachma, dram. *Drachm* was the prevalent form in all senses; but now the coin is almost always *drachma,* the indefinite small quantity is always *dram,* & *dram* is not uncommon even where *drachm* is still usual, in apothecaries' & avoirdupois weight. Pron. *drachm* drăm, *drachma* drăk'ma.

draft, draught, &c. *Draft* is merely a phonetic spelling of *draught,* but some differentiation has taken place. In US, *draft* is the usual spelling, *draught* being retained for the fishing term, the drinking term, and sometimes the air current. *A draught of fish; ale on draught; without a damper the draught* (or *draft*) *in the stove is faulty.* In Brit., *draft* has ousted *draught* in banking, & to a great extent in the military sense detach(ment); it is also usual in the sense (make) rough copy or plan (*a good draftsman* is one who drafts Bills well; *a good draughtsman* one who draws well). In all the other common senses (game of draughts, air current, ship's displacement, beer on draught, draught horse), *draught* is still the only recognized British form.

dragoman. The pl. is correctly *-mans,* but often *-men;* for insistence on the former, see DIDACTICISM.

dramatic irony. See IRONY, 2.

drapes, n. Properly *drape* is a verb; the noun is *drapery* (*-ies*).

draw is often a FORMAL WORD for *pull* as in *He drew his belt tighter; drew his hat over his face.*

dream. The ordinary past & p.p. is *dreamed* (US), *dreamt* (-ĕmt) (Brit.); *dreamed* (-ēmd) is preferred in poetry & in impressive contexts. Many people who write *dreamed* say drĕmt, in US as well as Brit.

drink has past tense *drank,* p.p. *drunk;* the reverse uses (*they drunk, have drank*) were formerly not unusual, but are now blunders or conspicuous archaisms.

droll. (Unintentionally) amusing, queer, quaint, strange. For synonymy see JOCOSE.

drunk(en). The difference, as now established, is complex. *Drunk* is in predicative use only, or at least is unidiomatic as an attribute; *Drunk as a lord,* but NOT *A drunk lord is a disgrace. Drunken* is the attributive word, whether the meaning is *now in drink* or *given to drink* or *symptomatic* &c. *of drunkenness* (*I saw a drunken man; A lazy drunken lying ne'er-do-weel; His drunken habits*); it may be used predicatively also, but only in the sense *given to drink* (he was *drunken and dissolute* means habitually so; *He was drunk & incapable* suggests his being so at a specific time); *He was drunken yesterday* is contrary to modern idiom.

dry, &c. The spelling in some derivatives of *dry* & other adjectives & verbs of similar form (monosyllables with *y* as the only vowel) is disputable. The prevalent forms for *dry* are, from the adjective, *drier, driest, dryly* (usually, US) or *drily* (usually, Brit.), *dryness, dryish,* & from the verb, *dryer.* The noun is *drier,* one who dries; a substance to make paint &c. dry more quickly; and *dryer,* an automatic device for drying clothes &c.

dual(istic). Both words are of the learned kind, & better avoided when such ordinary words as *two, twofold, twin, double, connected, divided, half-&-half, ambiguous,* will do the work. AVOID: Dual (double) *ownership./The* dual (connected) *questions of 'abnormal places' & a minimum wage would bring about a deadlock./ The Government is pleased with the agitation for electoral reasons, but does not desire to be too successful; the reason for this* dualistic (half-&-half) attitude *is that . . .* See POPULARIZED TECHNICALITIES.

dubiety. Pron. dūbī′ĭtĭ. The usual word would be *doubt, doubtfulness,* or *dubiousness.* See WORKING & STYLISH WORDS.

ducat. Pron. dŭk′*at.*

duck. The female is called *duck,* the male *drake.* Pl. *ducks, duck* (food). *A flock of ducks; enough duck to serve ten people.*

dudgeon (ill humor, anger, resentment) is obs. except in *high dudgeon.*

due. Under the influence of ANALOGY, *due to* is often used as though it had passed, like *owing to,* into a mere compound preposition. (See Webster's comment below.) *Due* must, like ordinary participles & adjectives, be attached to a noun & not to a notion extracted from a sentence: *His success was due to his diligence* is right, as is *The delay was due to the fact that the bridge had collapsed.* In all the examples below *owing* would stand, but *due* is impossible; it is not *the horse, the rooks, he,* or *the articles,* that are *due,* but the failure of the movement, the distrust of the rooks, & so on. WRONG: *The old trade union movement is* a dead horse, *largely* due *to the incompetency of the leaders./* Rooks, *probably* due *to the fact that they are so often shot at, have a profound distrust of man.* /Due *largely to his costume,* he *suggested a respectable organist.* /*Some* articles *have increased in price,* due *to the increasing demand.* (Webster says 'prepositional *due to,* meaning *because of . . .* is in common and reputable use.')

duel makes *duelist* or (chiefly Brit.) *duellist.*

dugout. (Orig. US) (hyphen, Brit.). Its earlier uses were for the canoe and for the colonists' (pioneers') dwelling dug out of a hillside.

dul(l)ness, ful(l)ness. Use *-ll-.*

dum(b)found. In US usually *dumfound.* Fowler says, 'Write dumbfound; it is probably *dumb* plus *confound.*'

duologue. A dialogue between two persons; now esp. a dramatic piece confined to two actors.

durance, duress. *Durance* now means only the state of being in confinement, is a purely decorative word, & is rare except in the phrases *in durance, in durance vile*—the latter a BATTERED ORNAMENT. *Duress* means the application of constraint, which may or may not take the form of confinement, to a person; it is chiefly in legal use, with reference to acts done under illegal compulsion, & is commonest in the phrase *under duress.* Pron. -dū rĕs′ (recommended), or dū′-.

durst. See DARE.

Dutch as referring to the Germans is now obsolete (or US local or slang) except in *Pennsylvania Dutch,* the language and descendants of the German (and Swiss) immigrants to Pennsylvania in the 17th and 18th cc.

duteous, dutiful. The second is the ordinary word; *duteous* (a rare formation,* exactly paralleled only in *beauteous*) is kept in being beside it by its metrical convenience (6 of the 7 OED quotations are from verse), & when used in prose has consequently the air of a poeticism; see also PLENTEOUS.

dwarf. Pl. usually *dwarfs,* rarely *dwarves.*

dwarfen. The verb is *to dwarf,* NOT *to dwarfen.*

dwell, in the sense have one's abode, has been ousted in ordinary use by *live,* but survives in poetic, rhetorical, & dignified use; see WORKING & STYLISH WORDS.

dyarchy. Used only of the government that obtained in the provinces of India, 1919–37 (Webster). Otherwise spell *diarchy.*

dye makes *dyeing* as a precaution against confusion with *dying* from *die.*

dynamic(al). Both words date from the 19th c. only, & *-ic* tends to become more & *-ical* less common; the only use in which *-ical* seems preferable is as the adj. of *dynamics* (*dynamical principles; an abstract dynamical proposition*).

dynamo (pl. *-os*) is a CURTAILED WORD (dynamo-electric machine).

dynast. Pron. dī′- (US); Brit. also dĭn′-.

E

each. 1. Number. *Each* as subject is invariably singular, even when followed by *of them* &c.: *Each of the wheels* has 12 *spokes* (NOT *have*). When *each* is not the subject, but in apposition with a plural noun or pronoun as subject, the verb (& complement) is invariably plural: *The wheels* have 12 *spokes each; the wheels* each have 12 *spokes* (this latter order is better avoided); *the wheels* are each 12-*spokers.* But the number of a later noun or pronoun & the corresponding choice of a possessive adjective depend upon whether *each* stands before or after the verb, & this again depends on the distributive emphasis required. If the distribution is not to be formally emphasized, *each* stands before the verb (or its complement, or some part of the phrase composing it), & the plural number & corresponding possessive are used: *We* each have our *own nostrums* (NOT *his own nostrum,* nor *our own nostrum*); *They are* each of them *masters in* their *own homes.* If the distribution is to be formally insisted on, *each* stands after the verb (& complement) & is followed by singular nouns & the corresponding possessives: *We are responsible* each *for* his *own vote.* The following forms are incorrect in various degrees (WRONG): *Brown, Jones, & Robinson* each has *a different plan./You will* go each your *own way./They have* each *something to say for* himself./Each *of these verses* have *five feet./They* each *of them* contain *a complete story.* A correspondent informs me that in the hymn lines 'Soon will you & I be lying Each within our narrow bed' *our* has been substituted for the original *his;* the corrector has been offended by *his* of the common gender, & failed to observe that he has restricted the application to married couples.

2. *Each other* is now treated as a compound word, the verb or preposition that governs *other* standing before *each,* instead of in its normal place, & *they hate each other, they sent presents to each other,* being usually preferred to *each hates the other*(*s*), *they sent presents each to the other*(*s*); but the phrase is so far true to its origin that its possessive is *each other's* (NOT *others'*), & that it cannot be used when the case of *other* would be subjective: *a lot of old cats ready to tear out* each other's (NOT *others'*) *eyes; we know* each *what* the other *wants* (NOT *what each other wants*). *Each other* is by some writers used only when no more than two things are referred to, *one another* being similarly appropriated to larger numbers, but the differentiation is neither of present utility nor based on historical usage.

3. *Between each.* For such incorrect expressions as 'three minutes between each scene' see BETWEEN.

earnest. There are two nouns, unrelated etymologically, one meaning seriousness, serious intention, surviving only in *in earnest* (*Are you in earnest or only jesting? He went at it in good earnest*), the other meaning money paid as an installment, fig. a token or presage, now chiefly legal or poetic (*earnest money; accepted by way of earnest; an earnest of his intention; an earnest of what is to come*). The adj. (*one earnest word; Life is real, Life is earnest; an earnest worker*) comes of course from the first.

earthen, earthly, earthy. *Earthen* is still in ordinary use (see -EN ADJECTIVES) in the sole sense made of earth (either soil or potting clay). *Earthly* has two senses only: (1) belonging to this transitory world as opposed to heaven or the future life, & (2, in negative context) practically existent or discoverable by mortal man. *Earthy* means of the nature, or having an admixture, of earth (soil, dross, gross materialism). *An earthen mound, rampart, pot. Earthly joys; the earthly paradise; their earthly pilgrimage; is there any earthly use, reason,* &c.?; *for no earthly consideration. An earthy precipitate formed in a few minutes; the ore is very earthy;* (fig.) *an upright man, but incurably earthy in his views & desires.*

easterly, northerly, southerly, westerly. Chiefly used of wind, & then meaning east &c. or thereabouts, rather from the eastern &c. half of the horizon; else only of words implying either motion, or position conceived as attained by previous motion: *an easterly wind; took a southerly course; the most easterly outposts of western civilization.* NOT *southerly* (but *south*) *aspect;* NOT *the easterly* (but *eastward*) *position;* NOT *the westerly* (but *west*) *end of the church;* NOT *westerly* (but *western*) *ways of thought.*

easy. As an adv. *easy* is illiterate except in some colloq. expressions: *easy come easy go; take it easy.* Also in the comparative & superlative: *All the easier led away* (or *more easily*); but *no easier said than done* is idiomatic.

eat. The past, spelled *ate* (archaic *eat*), is pronounced ĕt in Brit., āt US.

eatable, edible. The two words mean the same thing, but *eatable* implies a measure of palatability, whereas even tripe is *edible.*

eaves (the edge of the roof, overhanging the side) is really a singular, but in modern use is treated as a plural, with *eave* used as the singular. *Eavesdroppers* in English Law are 'such as stand under wals or windowes . . . to heare news' (1641, OED).

éclat. Now used in English chiefly in the sense of universal acclamation: *He was received with* éclat. Pron. ê klä′ & see FRENCH WORDS.

economic(al). Pref. pron. ē-, though ĕk- is also heard in US.) The nouns *economics* & *economy* having nearly parted company (though *Political Economy,* like the King's Proctor, impedes full divorce), it is convenient that each should have its own adjective. Accordingly, *-ic* is now associated only with *economics,* & *-ical* only with *economy; an economic rent* is one in the fixing of which the laws of supply & demand have had free play; *an economical rent* is one that is not extravagant; in practice the first generally means a rent not too low (for the landlord), & the second one not too high (for the tenant). NOT: *The question of* economical *help for Russia by sending her goods from this country.*

ecstasy. So spelled.

-ection, -xion. In US *connection, deflection, inflection, reflection,* are so spelled. In Brit. usually *-xion,* though *reflection* is also used.

eczema. Pron. ĕk′sĕ m*a*.

edgeways, -wise. No differentiation; both forms are in standard use.

edifice. Not a simple equivalent of *building,* but 'a large, stately structure, such as a temple, palace, or fortress.' See POMPOSITIES.

edify remains in current use only in the sense 'to improve or instruct,' esp. morally or spiritually, and is then used chiefly ironically or by those given to PEDANTIC HUMOR. It is related to *edifice,* not to *education.*

educate makes *educable,* 'capable of being educated,' & *educative,* 'tending to educate.'

educe makes *educible.*

eel-like. Keep the hyphen.

eerie, eery. The first is better.

effect, v. To bring about, accomplish, cause; *affect,* to move, touch, produce an effect on. See AFFECT. *He finally* effected *a reconciliation* (i.e. achieved one); *His action fatally* affected *any chance of a future reconciliation* (i.e. made one impossible).

effective, effectual, efficacious, efficient. The words all mean *having effect,* but with different applications & certain often-disregarded shades of meaning. *Efficacious* applies only to things (esp. now to medicines) used for a purpose, & means sure to have, or usually having, the desired effect. *Efficient* applies to agents or their action regarded as theirs or (with more or less of personification) to instruments &c., & means capable of producing the desired effect, not incompetent or unequal to a task. *Effectual* applies to action apart from the agent, & means not falling short of the complete effect aimed at. *Effective* applies to the thing done or to its doer as such, & means having a high degree of effect.

An efficacious remedy, efficacious (now rare) *cement; a drug of known efficacy.*

An efficient general, cook; efficient work, organization. Efficient cause is a special use preserving the original etymological sense 'doing the work.'

Effectual measures; an effectual stopper on conversation. Effectual demand in Political Economy is demand that actually causes the supply to be brought to market.

An effective speech, speaker, contrast, cross-fire; effective assistance, co-operation. An effective blockade, effective capital, effective membership, preserve the sense 'not merely nominal but carried into action.'

effectuate means 'to carry into effect, accomplish' (an intention or desire); 'to bring to pass' (an event). *Courts anxious to effectuate the intentions of the testators. To die without effectuating my purpose.* But often only a FORMAL WORD for *accomplish.*

effervescence, -cy. The *-ce* form means the act or process, or the product (bubbles &c.), of effervescing; the *-cy* form (now rare) means the tendency or capacity to effervesce (*has lost its effervescency*), though in this sense, too, *effervescence* is now more frequent.

e.g. is short for *exempli gratiâ,* & means only 'for instance.' WRONG: *Mr. . . . took as the theme of his address the existence of what he called a psychic attribute,* e.g. *a kind of memory, in plants;* i.e. should have been used. Italics, & a following comma, are unnecessary, but not wrong.

ego. (Brit. ĕgō, US often ēgō.) In Psych. *id*=the infantile or primitive element in personality, & *ego* the rational volitionary; *superego*='the conscious or unconscious conscience.'

ego(t)ism. The two words are modern formations of about the same date. Etymologically, there is no difference between them to affect the sense, but *egoism* is correctly & *egotism* incorrectly formed—a fact that is now, since both are established, of no importance. *Egotism* is restricted to the more popular senses—excessive use of *I* in speech or writing, & self-importance or self-centeredness in character. *Egoism* is used in metaphysics & ethics for the theory that a person has no proof that anything exists outside his own mind, & for the theory that self-interest is the foundation of morality.

egregious. The etymological sense is simply eminent or of exceptional degree (*e grege,* out of the flock). The use of the word has been narrowed in English till it is applied only to nouns expressing contempt, & especially to a few of these, as *ass, liar, folly, blunder, waste. The egregious Jones* &c. is occasionally used in the sense *that notorious ass Jones;* & with neutral words like *example egregious* is the natural antithesis to *shining—a shining example of fortitude, an egregious example of incapacity.* Reversion to the original sense, as in the following, is mere PEDANTRY: *There is indeed little forethought in most of our daily doing, whether gregarious or* egregious.

eighth. Spell thus, but pron. ātth, NOT āth.

eighties, 'ei-. *A man in his eighties;* the apostrophe would be wrong. *The architecture of the eighties* (or *'eighties*); the apostrophe is permissible to avoid ambiguity, but not required.

either. 1. In US usually pronounced ē-. The pronunciation ī-, though not more correct, is displacing ē- in Brit. educated speech, & will probably prevail in parts of the US.

2. The sense each of the two, as in *The room has a fireplace at either end,* is archaic, & should be avoided except in verse or in special contexts.

3. The sense any one of a number (above two), as in *either of the angles of a triangle,* is loose; *any* or *any one* should be preferred.

4. The use of a pl. verb after *either,* as in (WRONG) *If either of these methods are successful,* is a very common grammatical blunder.

5. *Either . . . or.* In this alternative formula *either* is frequently misplaced. The misplacement should be avoided in careful writing, but is often permissible colloquially. There are two correct substitutes for *You are either joking or have forgotten;* some writers refuse one of these, *You either are joking or have forgotten,* on the ground that it looks pedantic; but there is no such objection to the other, *Either you are joking or you have forgotten.* In conversation the incorrect form is defensible because a speaker who originally meant (*are*) *forgetting to answer* to answer to *are joking* cannot, when he discovers that he prefers *have forgotten,* go back without being detected (as a writer can) & put things in order; see UNEQUAL YOKEFELLOWS. Some examples follow of the slovenliness that should not be allowed to survive proof-correction. WRONG: *Their hair is usually worn* either plaited *in knots or* is festooned *with cocks' feathers* (omit the second *is*)./*It is not too much to say that* trade unions either *should not exist,* or that *all workers should join compulsorily* (*either* should follow the first *that,* omit second *that*).

Either . . . or is sometimes not disjunctive, but equivalent to *both . . . and* or *alike . . . and: The continuance of atrocities is* a fatal obstacle either to the granting *of an armistice* or to the discussion *of terms.* In such cases, *alike* (or *both*) . . . *and* should be preferred, or else proper care should be taken with *either;* 'an obstacle to either granting an armistice or discussing terms' would do it.

eke out. The meaning is to make something, by adding to it, go further or last longer or do more than it would without such addition. The proper object is accordingly a word expressing not the result attained, but the original supply. You can eke out your income or (whence the SLIPSHOD EXTENSION) a scanty subsistence with odd jobs or by fishing, but you cannot eke out a living or a miserable existence. You can eke out your facts, but not your article, with quotations. You can eke out ink with water or words with gestures, but not a rabbit hutch with or out of wire netting. RIGHT: *Mr. Weyman first took to writing in order* to eke out an insufficient income *at the Bar*. WRONG: *These disconsolate young widows would perforce relapse into conditions of life at once pitiful & sordid,* eking out *in dismal boarding-houses or humble lodgings* a life *which may have known comfort./A man the very thought of whom has ruined more men than any other influence in the nineteenth century, & who is trying* to eke out *at last a spoonful* of atonement *for it all.*

elaborateness, elaboration. *Elaborateness* means 'the quality of being elaborate': *Its beauty lay in the* elaborateness *of the design; Remarkable for the* elaborateness *of their structure. Elaboration* can mean elaborateness, but is better restricted to the process of working out in detail, perfecting, developing: *The first thought of Virgil was . . . the* elaboration *of his verse. He worked six months on the* elaboration *of the design* (or *plan*).

elapse. The noun corresponding to the verb *elapse* is *lapse.* The noun *elapse* is archaic. *Hearing nothing about it after* the elapse *of a month Mr. Cowen wrote to Mr. Redford* may be the words of a writer who knows that *elapse* was formerly a noun, but there is nothing in the context to call for ARCHAISM.

elder, -est. These forms are now almost confined to the indication of mere seniority among the members of a family. For this purpose the *old-* forms are not used except when the age has other than a comparative importance or when comparison is not the obvious point. Thus we say *I have an elder brother* in the simple sense a brother older than myself; but *I have an older brother* is possible in the sense a brother older than the one you know of; & *Is there no older son?* means 'Is there none more competent by age than this one?' *My elder (-est) cousin* would now be usually understood to mean the senior of a family of two (or more than two) who are my cousins; & *my older cousin* would be preferred in either of the senses 'my cousin who is older than I' or 'the senior of my two cousins of different families.' Outside this restricted use of family seniority, *elder* & *eldest* linger in a few contexts, but are giving place to *older* & *oldest.* Still idiomatic: *Who is the eldest man here? The elder men were less enthusiastic, An elder contemporary of mine, There was more character in the elder man, A tradition that has come down from elder times, Elder statesman.*

electric(al). The longer form,

once much the commoner (the OED quotes *electrical shock, battery, eel,* & *spark,* never now heard), survives only in the sense of or concerning electricity, & is not necessarily preferred even in that sense except where there is danger that *electric* might mislead; e.g. *had no electrical effect* might be resorted to as a warning that 'did not alter the state of the atmosphere as regards electricity' is meant, & not 'failed to startle'; on the other hand the difference between the 'electric book' that gives one shocks & the 'electrical book' that improves one's knowledge of science is obvious.

ELEGANT VARIATION. It is the second-rate writers, those intent rather on expressing themselves prettily than on conveying their meaning clearly, & still more those whose notions of style are based on a few misleading rules of thumb, that are chiefly open to the allurements of elegant variation. Thackeray may be seduced into an occasional lapse (*careering during the season from one great dinner of twenty covers to another of eighteen guests*—where however the variation in words may be defended as setting off the sameness of circumstance); but the real victims, first terrorized by a misunderstood taboo, next fascinated by a newly discovered ingenuity, & finally addicted to an incurable vice, are the minor novelists & the reporters. There are few literary faults so widely prevalent, & this book will not have been written in vain if the present article should heal any sufferer of his infirmity.

The fatal influence (see SUPERSTITIONS) is the advice given to young writers never to use the same word twice in a sentence —or within 20 lines or other limit. The advice has its uses; it reminds any who may be in danger of forgetting it that there are such things as pronouns, the substitution of which relieves monotony; the reporter would have done well to remember it who wrote: *Unfortunately Lord Dudley has never fully recovered from the malady which necessitated an operation in Dublin some four years since, during Lord Dudley's Lord-Lieutenancy.* It also gives a useful warning that a noticeable word used once should not be used again in the neighborhood with a different application. This point will be found fully illustrated in REPETITION, but it may be shortly set out here, a kind providence having sent a neatly contrasted pair of quotations: (a) *Dr. Labbe* seriously *maintains that in the near future opium smoking will be as* serious *as the absinthe scourge in France;* (b) *The return of the Nationalists to Parliament means that they are prepared to treat* seriously *any* serious *attempt to get Home Rule into working order.* Here (a) would be much improved by changing *serious* to *fatal,* & (b) would be as much weakened by changing *serious* to *real;* the reason is that the application of *seriously* & *serious* is in (a) different, the two being out of all relation to each other, & in (b) similar. *I am serious in calling it serious* suggests only a vapid play on words. *We will be serious if you are serious* is good sense. But the rule of thumb, as usual, omits all qualifications, & would forbid (b) as well as (a). Several examples are added of the kind of repetition against which warning is needed, to bring out the vast difference between the cases for which the rule is intended & those to which it is mistakenly applied: *Meetings at which they* passed *their time* passing *resolutions pledging them to resist./A debate which took wider ground than that* actually *covered by the* actual *amendment itself./Doyle drew the* original *of the outer sheet of Punch as we still know it; the* original *intention was that there should be a fresh illustrated cover every week.*

These, however, are mere pieces of gross carelessness, which would be disavowed by their authors. Diametrically opposed to them are sentences in which the writer, far from carelessly repeating a word in a different application, has carefully not repeated it in a similar application. The effect is to set readers wondering what the significance of the change is, only to conclude disappointedly that it has none: (1) *The Bohemian Diet will be the second Parliament to elect* women *deputies, for Sweden already has several* lady *deputies./*(2) *There are a not inconsiderable number of* employers *who appear to hold the same opinion, but certain* owners *hold a contrary view to this./*(3) *Mr. Redmond has just now a path* to tread *even more thorny than that which Mr. Asquith has* to walk. What has Bohemia done that its females should be mere women? Are owners subject to influences that do not affect employers? Of course they might be, & that is just the reason why, as no such suggestion is meant, the word should not be changed. And can Mr. Asquith really have taught himself to walk without treading? All this is not to say that *women* & *employers* & *tread* should necessarily be repeated—only that satisfactory variation is not to be so cheaply secured as by the mechanical replacing of a word by a synonym. The true corrections are here simple: (1) *several* alone instead of *several women* (or *lady*) *deputies;* (2) *some* alone instead of *certain employers* (or *owners*); (3) *Mr. Asquith's* instead of *that which Mr. Asquith has to tread* (or *walk*). But the writers are confirmed variationists—nail-biters, say, who no longer have the power to abstain from the unseemly trick.

Let us give special warning against two temptations. The first occurs when there are successive phrases each containing one constant & one variable. The variationist fails to see that the varying of the variable is enough, & the varying of the constant also is a great deal too much; he may contrive to omit his constant if he likes, but he must not vary it: *There are* 466 cases; *they consist of* 366 *matrimonial* suits, 56 *Admiralty* actions, & 44 *Probate* cases (strike out *suits* & *actions;* but even to write *cases* every time is better than the variation)./*At a higher* rate *or lower* figure, *according to the special circumstances of the district* (omit *rate*)./*It was Tower's third* victory, *& Buxton's second* win (drop either *victory* or *win*).

The second temptation is to regard *that* & *which* as two words that are simply equivalent & (the variationist would say *& which*) exist only to relieve each other when either is tired. This equivalence is a delusion, but one that need not be discussed here, & the point to be observed in the following quotations is that, even if the words meant exactly the same, it would be better to keep the first selected on duty than to change guard: *He provides a philosophy* which *disparages the intellect & that forms a handy background for all kinds of irrational beliefs* (omit *that*)./*A scheme for unification* that *is definite &* which *will serve as a firm basis for future reform* (omit *which*)./*A pride* that *at times seemed like a petty punctilio, a self-discipline* which *seemed at times almost inhuman in its severity* (repeat *that*).

elegy (Lit.): 'lamentation.' In the strict sense, a song or poem of mourning, & properly applied in English to such pieces as *Lycidas, Adonais,* & *Thyrsis.*

elemental, elementary. The two words are now pretty clearly differentiated, the reference of *elemental* being to 'the elements' either in the old sense of earth, water, air, & fire, or as representing the great forces of nature conceived as their manifestations (or metaphorically the human instincts comparable in power to those forces); & that of *elementary* being to elements in the more general sense of simplest component parts or rudiments. *Elemental fire, strife, spirits, passion, power; elementary substances, constituents, facts, books, knowledge, schools.* The *-al* form is often wrongly chosen by those who have not observed the differentiation, & think that an occasional out-of-the-way word lends distinction to their style. WRONG: *The evergrowing power of the State, the constant extension of its activities, threaten the most* elemental *liberties of the individual./Responsible government in Canada was still in its most* elemental *stage.*

elevator is standard US, *lift* Brit.

elf makes *elves, elfin, elvish* or *elfish.* Of the last two, *elvish* is the older, but *elfish* is more usual now and has been in the language since the 16th c.

eligible. So spelled. Fit or proper to be chosen; legally or morally suitable. *No person except a natural born citizen . . . shall be* eligible *to the office of president. A member of Parliament cannot be* eligible *for any other place.* Now loosely, available & qualified; *eligible for election; My daughter's most* eligible *admirer.*

élite. The choice part or flower (of society, or any body of persons). *The élite of comparatively civilized generations. One of the élite.* Pron. ā lēt′.

elixir. Pron. ē lĭk′ser. Orig. (in alchemy) the preparation (powder, stone) to turn metals into gold; a drug to prolong life indefinitely (*elixir of life;* fig. the quintessence or soul of a thing: *The elixir of [love's] nature is found . . . in the spirit that suffers for another's sake*).

ELLIPSIS. When a passage would, if fully set out, contain two compound members corresponding to each other, how far may the whole be shortened by omitting in one of these members ('understanding,' in grammatical phrase) a part that is either expressed in the other or easily inferable from what is there expressed? Possible varieties are so many that it will be better not to hazard a general rule, but to say that the expressed can generally, & the inferable can in specially favorable circumstances, be 'understood,' & then proceed to some types in which mistakes are common. 1. *Be* & *have*. 2. Second part of comp. verb. 3. With change of voice. 4. *That* (conj.). 5. After *than*. 6. With inversion. 7. *That* (rel. pron.).

1. Ellipsis of parts of *be* & *have*. Not only the expressed part can be understood, but also the corresponding part with change of number or person: *He is dead, & I‸alive; The years* have *passed & the appointed time‸come.* These are permissible; not all that is lawful, however, is expedient, & the license is not to be recommended outside sentences of this simple pattern. In the following quotation it is clearly ILL-ADVISED: *A number of stumbling-blocks* have been *removed, & the road along which the measure will have to travel‸straightened out.* It is the distance of *straightened* from *have been,* & not the change of number in the verbs, that demands the insertion of *has been.*

2. Ellipsis of second part of compound verb. Only the expressed part can be understood: *No State* can *or* will *adopt* would be regular, but (WRONG) *No State* has *or* can *adopt* is (however common) an elementary blunder. Equally common & equally wrong is the understanding of an infinitive with *to* out of one without *to.* WRONG: *A standard of public opinion which ought‸& we believe will strengthen the sense of parental responsibility.* Insert after *ought* either *to strengthen* or *to.*

3. Ellipsis with change of voice. Even if the form required is identical with that elsewhere expressed, it cannot be understood if the voice is different. WRONG: *We do not believe that the House would have really* revised *the Bill, as no doubt it could be‸with advantage;* to omit *revised* is out of the question. Still less can the passive *managed* be supplied from the active *manage* in (WRONG): *Mr. Dennett foresees a bright future for Benin if our officials will* manage *matters conformably with its 'customs,' as they ought to have been‸.* And with these may be classed expecting us to get *to be* from the preceding *to* in (WRONG): *If the two lines* are to *cross, the rate of loss‸reduced to zero, & a definite increase in the world's shipping to be brought about . . .*

4. Omission of *that* (conj.). Though this is strictly speaking not an ellipsis, but rather an exercise of the ancient right to abstain from subordinating a substantival clause (*And I seyde‸ his opinioun was good*—Chaucer), it may conveniently be mentioned here. Three examples will suffice to show the unpleasantness of ill-advised omission: *I am abashed to see‸in my notice of Mr. Bradley Birt's '"Sylhet" Thackeray' I have credited the elder W. M. Thackeray with sixteen children./Mr. Balfour blurted out* that *his own view was‸the House of Lords was not strong enough./I assert‸the feeling in Canada today is such against annexation that . . .* The first illustrates the principle that if there is the least room for doubt where the *that* would

come, it should be expressed & not understood. The second leads us to the rule that when the contents of a clause are attached by part of *be* to such words as *opinion, decision, view,* or *declaration* (a very common type), *that* must be inserted. It at the same time illustrates the motive that most frequently causes wrong omissions—the sensible reluctance to make one *that* clause depend on another; but this is always avoidable by other, though often less simple, means. The third involves a matter of idiom, & reminds us that while some verbs of *saying* & *thinking* can take or drop *that* indifferently, many have a strong preference for one or the other use (see THAT CONJ.); *assert* is among those that habitually take *that.*

5. Ellipsis after *than* is extremely common, & so various in detail as to make the laying down of any general rule impossible. The comparative claims of brevity on the one hand, & on the other of the comfort that springs from feeling that all is shipshape, must in each case be weighed with judgment. It will be best to put together two examples in which doubts whether all is right with the sentence obtrude themselves. *The evil consequences of excess of these beverages is much greater than*^*alcohol;* i.e. *than the evil consequences of excess of alcohol are great;* shall we (a) omit *are great?* yes, everyone does it; (b) omit *the evil consequences of excess of?* no, no one could do it but one who could also write, like this author, *consequences is;* (c) retain all this? no—waste of words; (d) shorten to *those of excess of?* yes, unless the knot is cut by writing *than with alcohol./This was due to the feeling that the Bill went further than*^*public opinion warranted or*^*was justified;* i.e. *than what public opinion warranted or what was justified;* either *what* could be omitted if its clause stood alone; but since the two *whats* are in different cases, one being subject & the other object, there is felt to be a grammatical blunder lurking under cover of *than.*

6. Ellipsis complicated by inversion. In questions, & in sentences beginning with *nor* & certain other words, inversion is normal, the subject standing after the verb or its auxiliary instead of before it (*Never heard I* or *Never did I hear;* NOT *Never I heard*). When a sentence or clause thus inverted has to be enlarged by a parallel member of the kind in which ellipsis would naturally be resorted to, difficulties arise. WRONG: *Why* is a man *in civil life perpetually slandering & backbiting his fellow men, &*^ is unable *to see good even in his friends?* The repetition of *is* without that of *why* & the subject is impossible; in this particular sentence the removal of the second *is* solves the problem as well as the reinsertion of (at the least) *why is such a man;* but often full repetition is the only course possible./*Not only* may such a love have deepened *& exalted,* &^may^ still deepen *& exalt, the life of any man of any age, but . . .* The inversion has to be carried on; that is, *not only,* & the subject placed after *may,* must be repeated if *may* is repeated; &, *may* being here indispensable, nothing less will do than *not*

only (with *and* omitted) *may it still deepen.*

7. For ellipsis of *that* (rel. pron.), & of prepositions governing *that* (rel. pron.), see THAT REL. PRON.

elliptic(al). The short form is more usual for the adj. of *ellipse;* the *-al* for that of *ellipsis. The* elliptic *motions of the planets; Style so* elliptical *as to be dry & obscure.*

else. The adverb *else* has come so near to being compounded with certain indefinite pronouns & words of similar character (*anybody, everyone, little, all,* &c.) that separation is habitually avoided, & e.g. *Nobody is ignorant of it else* is unidiomatic; correspondingly, the usual possessive form is not *everyone's* &c. *else,* which is felt to be pedantic though correct, but *everyone else's.* With interrogative pronouns the process has not gone so far; though *What else did he say?* is the normal form, *What did he say else?* (with which compare the very unusual *Nothing was said else*) is unobjectionable; correspondingly, *who else's* may be used colloquially, but *whose else* (cf. *anybody's else*) has maintained its ground; & of the forms *Who else's should it be?, Whose else should it be?, Whose should it be else?,* the last is perhaps the best, but is unlikely in US.

elusive, elusory. That is *elusive* which we fail, in spite of efforts, to grasp physically or mentally; *the elusive ball, halfback, submarine; elusive rhythm, perfume, fame; an elusive image, echo, pleasure.* That is *elusory* which turns out when attained to be unsatisfying, or which is designed to pass as of more solid or permanent value than it is; *elusory fulfilment, success, victory, possession, promises.* The *elusive* mocks its pursuer, the *elusory* its possessor; *elusive* is synonymous with *evasive, elusory* with *illusive.*

elvish. See ELF.

Elysium. Pl. *-ms.*

emaciation. Pron. -āsĭ-; but *emaciate,* pron. ē mā′shĭ āt; see -CIATION.

embargo. Pl. *-os* (in US also sometimes *-oes*).

embarkation. So spelled.

embarrassedly. A bad form. *Embarrassment,* so spelled.

embed, im-. Use *em-.* Past, *embedded.*

emblematic(al). The shorter form is recommended.

embrasure. Pron. ĕmbrā′zhyer; Nav. & Mil., also ĕmbrȧzhōōr′.

embryo. Pl. *-os.*

emend(ation). The words are now confined strictly to the conjectural correction of errors in MS. or printed matter, or to changes deliberately compared to this by metaphor. They are not used, like *amend(ment),* of improvement or correction in general.

Emerald Isle. See SOBRIQUETS.

emergence, emergency. The two are now completely differentiated, *emergence* meaning emerging or coming into notice, & *emergency* meaning a juncture that has arisen, esp. one that calls for prompt measures, & also (more recently) the presence of such a juncture (*in case of emergency*).

emigrant, émigré are the English and French forms of the same word—one who leaves his country to settle elsewhere. Because *émigrés* was used specifically for the royalists who fled at the time of the French Revolution, there is now a tendency to use it and not *emigrants* for political refugees, *emigrants* being reserved for people who change their countries under less pressure.

emolument. Usually a FORMAL WORD for *pay, profit,* or *salary.*

emotive, by the side of *emotional,* which means of the emotions as well as given to emotion, might well be left to the psychiatrists &c. In modern usage it is restricted to calling forth, or tending to incite, emotions.

empanel, impanel. *Impanel,* standard US (*impaneled* &c.); *em-,* Brit. (*-lled* &c.)

EMPHASIS. Double emphasis, the attempt to pack too much meaning in a single sentence, usually weakens the effect. *No government ever plunged* more rapidly *into a* deeper *quagmire. Deeper* weakens the sentence and changes the meaning: i.e. other governments may have plunged more rapidly into as deep quagmires—or as rapidly into deeper ones. See also FALSE EMPHASIS.

Empire City. See SOBRIQUETS.

empiric, -al, adjs. The longer form is more usual, esp. for philosophical empiricism; there is no real differentiation; *-ic* is becoming a NEEDLESS VARIANT.

employee, employé. The case for the English form (*ee*) is stronger than with most such pairs. One of them is needed, not for literary but for purely business purposes; & a good plain word with no questions of spelling & pronunciation & accents & italics & genders about it is therefore best.

emulate makes *-lable.* The word means to try to equal or excel; to imitate zealously; to rival. It should not be used for *copy* without this qualification.

-EN ADJECTIVES. The only adjectives of this type still in ordinary natural use with the sense made of so-&-so are *earthen, flaxen, hempen, wooden,* & *wool(l)en.* We actually prefer *earthen vessels, flaxen thread,* & *woolen cloth,* to *earth vessels, flax thread,* & *wool cloth.* Several others (*brazen, golden, leaden, leathern, oaken, oaten, silken, waxen*) can still be used in the original sense (made of brass &c.) with a touch of archaism or for poetic effect, but not in everyday contexts: *the brazen hinges of Hell-gate,* but *brass hinges do not rust; a golden crown* in hymns & fairy stories, but *a gold crown* in an inventory of regalia; *a lead pipe,* but *leaden limbs; a leathern jerkin,* but *a leather jacket; silken hose,* but *silk pajamas; an oaken staff,* but *an oak umbrella stand;* an *oaten pipe,* but *oat bread; the comb's waxen trellis,* but *wax candles.* Their chief use, however, is in secondary & metaphorical senses —*brazen impudence, golden prospects, leathern lungs, silken ease, waxen skin,* & the like. When well-meaning persons, thinking to do the language a service by restoring good old words to their rights, thrust them upon us in their literal sense where they are out of keeping, such patrons merely draw attention to their clients' apparent decrepitude—apparent only, for the words are hale & hearty, & will last long enough if only they are allowed to confine themselves to the jobs that they have chosen.

There are other words of the same formation (*ashen, bricken, cedarn, silvern,* &c.) that are solely archaic (or pseudo-archaic) & ornamental. The exceptional *olden* will be found in its place.

enamo(u)r. Usually *-or,* US; *-our,* Brit. Constr. now usually *of* (formerly also *with, on, upon*).

encase, incase. *Incase* is standard US; *en-* Brit.

enclose, inclose. In US *enclose* is standard except for legal use in respect to land. *I enclose my check; inclosed farm land.*

encomium. A 'formal or high-flown' expression of praise; a panegyric. Pl. now usually *-ums;* formerly, now rarely, *-a.*

encrust, incrustation. US both *in-;* Brit. *en-, in-* respectively.

endeavo(u)r. (In most contexts the WORKING WORD is *try.*) Usually *-or* US; *-our* Brit. NOT: *A somewhat ponderous jibe* has been endeavoured to be *levelled at the First Lord of the Admiralty because he . . .* For this use of *endeavor,* with which *somewhat* is in perfect harmony, see DOUBLE PASSIVES.

endemic, epidemic. An *endemic* disease is one habitually prevalent in a particular place; an *epidemic* disease is one that breaks out in a place & lasts for a time only.

endorse, indorse. Use *en-.* The use of *endorse* in advertisements (—— *cigarettes; endorsed by women of distinction*) is an example of unsustained metaphor (METAPHOR 2 A) worth mention because advertisements play a considerable part in forming the language of those who read little else. You can endorse, literally, a check or other paper, &, metaphorically, a claim or argument; but to talk of endorsing material things other than papers is a solecism.

endue, indue. Usually *en-.* Now chiefly fig., *endued with courage, endued with love for man and God.*

endways, -wise. Both forms are used, *-ways* probably being more usual in US.

enfold, infold. In US *in-* is standard; in Brit. *en-.*

enforce. WRONG: *They were prepared to take action with a view to* enforcing *this country into a premature & vanquished peace.* This use of *enforce* for *force* or *compel* or *drive,* with a person or agent as object, though common two or three centuries ago, is obs.; today we *force a person into peace,* or *enforce peace.* See NOVELTY-HUNTING, OBJECT-SHUFFLING.

enforceable. So spelled.

enfranchise, not *-ize.*

England, English(man). The incorrect use of these words as equivalents of *Great Britain, United Kingdom, British Empire, British, Briton,* is often resented by the Scotch, Irish, & Welsh; their susceptibilities are natural, but are not necessarily always to be deferred to. It must be remembered that no Englishman, & perhaps no Scot even, calls himself a Briton without a sneaking sense of the ludicrous. How should an Englishman utter the words *Great Britain* with the glow of emotion that for him goes with

England? He talks *the English language;* he has been taught *English history* as one tale from Alfred to Elizabeth II; he has heard of *the word of an Englishman* & of *English fair play,* scorns certain things as *un-English,* & aspires to be an *English gentleman;* & he knows that England expects every man to do his duty. In the word *England,* not in *Britain,* all these things are implicit. The case is not so strong against *British,* since we can speak of *the British Empire, the British army* or *navy* or *constitution,* & *British trade,* without feeling the word inadequate; yet even it is unfit for many contexts. Who speaks of *a British gentleman, British home life,* or *British tailoring?* On the other hand *the British matron, the British parent,* & *the British public* have an unenviable notoriety. The attempts to forbid people the use of the only names that for them are in tune with patriotic emotion, or to compel them to stop & think whether they mean their country in a narrower or a wider sense each time they name it, are doomed to failure. The most that can be expected is that the provocative words should be abstained from on the more provocative occasions, & that when Scots & others are likely to be within earshot *Britain* & *British* should be inserted as tokens, but no more, of what is really meant. See also BRITISHER & AMERICA(N).

engraft, in-. Use *en-*.

enhance. To heighten, intensify (qualities, powers, &c.: *Delights enhanced by the memory of passed hardships*); exaggerate; raise, increase (price, value, &c.: *Its value was enhanced by the almost indecipherable autograph*). But NOT *Spain felt that the war could not touch her, but that, on the contrary, while the rest of Europe was engaged in mutual destruction, she would be materially* enhanced. A dangerous word for the unwary. Her material prosperity may be enhanced, but *she* cannot be enhanced even in material prosperity, though a book may be enhanced in value as well as have its value enhanced. *Enhance* (& *be enhanced*) with a personal object (or subject) has long been obs. See CAST-IRON IDIOM.

enjoin. The ordinary modern use is *enjoin caution* &c. *upon* one, not *enjoin one to do* or *be.* The construction with a personal object & an infinitive (*The advocates of compulsory service* enjoin us to *add a great army for home defense to . . .*) is not recommended.

en masse. Pron. ĕn măs′ or as French. In a mass; *all together* will usually serve in English. See FRENCH WORDS.

ennui. Mental weariness and dissatisfaction; boredom, tedium. Pron. ŏnwē′. Do not italicize; the word is fully naturalized.

enormous(ness), enormity. The two words have drifted so far apart that the use of either in connection with the limited sense of the other is unadvisable. *Enormity* is confined to deviation from moral or legal rectitude; *enormous(ness)* to size, magnitude, intensity. *Enormous sin* & *The impression of enormity produced by the building* are both etymologically possible expressions; but to use the first lays one open to suspicion of pedantry, & to use the second to suspicion of ignorance.

enough & sufficient(ly). 1. In the noun use (= adequate amount), the preference of *sufficient* to *enough* (*have you had sufficient?*, *sufficient remains to fill another*) may almost be dismissed as a GENTEELISM. Besides being shorter, *enough* has the grammatical advantage of being a real noun. 2. In the adj. use (*is there enough*, or *sufficient butter?*) *sufficient* has the advantage of being a true adjective, while *enough* is only a quasi-adjective; *enough* evidence* is an abbreviation (as with *a hundred men, much difficulty*, &c.) for *enough of evidence;* the consequence is that *a sufficient supply* is possible, & *an enough supply* is not. In spite of the fact, however, that *sufficient* is always & *enough* only sometimes available, *enough* is to be preferred as the more natural & vigorous word wherever mere amount can be regarded as the only question: *is there enough butter*, or *butter enough, for the week?; he has courage enough for anything*. But where considerations of quality or kind are essential, *sufficient* is better; compare *for want of sufficient investigation* with *there has been investigation enough;* the first implies that it has not been thorough or skillful, the second that the time given to it has been excessive.
3. In the adv. use, neither word suffers from a grammatical handicap, *enough* being as true an adverb as *sufficiently*. Choice is dictated (often without the chooser's knowledge) in part by the feeling that a plain homely word, or a formal polysyllable, is appropriate (*he does not idle enough; he does not indulge sufficiently in recreation*), & in part by the limitation of *enough* pointed out above to mere amount or degree (*the meat is not boiled enough; he does not sufficiently realize the consequences*). Often, however, *enough* is so undeniably more vigorous that it is worth while to help it out with *clearly, fully, far, deeply*, &c., rather than accept the single word *sufficiently;* compare *he he has proved his point clearly enough* with *he has sufficiently proved his point.*

en passant. In chess, to take (a pawn) *en passant;* elsewhere *in passing* or *by the way* will usually serve. Pron. äɴ päsäɴ. See FRENCH WORDS.

enquire, enquiry, in-. *Inquire, -ry* are the preferred forms.

enrol(l). Enroll, -llment are preferred in US; the shorter forms Brit. For those who have the courage to defy editors & printers, *enrolment* is recommended; it is not a new form, but goes back to the 16th c.

ensign. In mil. & nav. use, the flag, banner, officer, usually pron. ĕn′sĭn; other uses sometimes ĕn′sīn.

ensure, insure, assure. Ensure *his recovery*, insure *his life*, assure *him that he will recover.* See ASSURE.

entail. In spite of the increasing tendency to differentiate (see NOUN & VERB ACCENT) the noun remains entail′.

entente. (Friendly) understanding, agreement; also the parties involved. Pron. äntänt′.

enterprise, not *-ize.*

enthral(l). Spell *enthrall.*

enthuse. Colloq. and undesirable. See BACK FORMATIONS.

entire. (1) The accent is on the second syllable. (2) *There is not a single county in the* entire *of Ireland in which . . .* This, which sounds like a foolish modern use comparable to that of VARIOUS, is in fact an old one, become 'somewhat rare' (OED). It may as well become rarer, for all that.

entirety. Three syllables (NOT four).

entitle. 1. To give a book a title. Hence, *A book entitled 'Storm over Europe' has recently been published.* See TITLE.

2. *Entitled* means having a right (to do something) or a just claim (to some advantage); it does not mean bound (to do) or liable (to a penalty); but it is often badly misused. WRONG: *Germany has suffered bitterly, & Germany is* entitled to suffer *for what she has done./If these people choose to come here (into court) & will not learn our heathen language, but prefer their gibberish or jargon, I consider they are* entitled to pay *for it.*

entity. The word is one of those regarded by plain people, whether readers or writer, with some alarm & distrust as smacking of philosophy. Its meaning, however, is neither more nor less recondite than that of the corresponding native word, which no one shies at; *entity* is *being, & an entity* is *a being.* The first or abstract sense is comparatively rare; *entity is better than nonentity* means the same as *it is better to be than not to be.* In the second or concrete sense, an *entity* differs only so far from a *being* that the latter as used by others than philosophers has come to exclude, while *entity* includes, any nonsentient or impersonal but actually existing thing. A plant or a stone or a State may be called an *entity,* but is not, outside of philosophy, called a *being. Each species is a distinct entity. Entity* therefore has a right to its place even in the popular vocabulary.

entrench, in-. *En-* is preferred.

entre nous. 'Between us'; *in confidence* will usually do. Pron. äɴtr' nōō, but see FRENCH WORDS.

entrust. Modern idiom allows only two constructions: *to entrust* (a task, a charge, a secret) *to* someone; *to entrust* (someone) *with* a task &c. The verb no longer means to put trust in simply (that is to *trust,* not *entrust*), nor to commission or employ or charge to do (for which those verbs, or again *trust,* will serve). The obs. use is seen in: *By victory the fighting men have achieved what their country has* entrusted *them to do.* See CAST-IRON IDIOM.

ENUMERATION FORMS. One of the first requisites for the writing of good clean sentences is to have acquired the art of enumeration, that is, of stringing together three or four words or phrases of identical grammatical value without going wrong. This cannot be done by blind observance of the rule of thumb that *and* & *or* should be used only once in a list. It will suffice here to illustrate very shortly the commonest type of error. WRONG: *The introductory paragraph* is sure, firm, & arouses *expectancy at once./If he* raises fruit, vegetables, or keeps *a large number of fowls./A matter in which the hopes & fears of so many are keenly concerned, & which, unless handled* with foresight, judgment, & in the spirit *of mutual concession, threatens to . . .* An *and* must be inserted after *sure,* after *fruit,* and before *judgment.* The matter will be found fully discussed under AND 2; *or* is liable to corresponding ill treatment; & a particular form of bad enumeration is set forth in the article WALLED-UP OBJECT.

enunciate (pron. -shĭ-) makes *-ciable, enunciation* (sĭ ā shun).

enure. Use *inure.*

envelope, n., **envelop,** v. (1) The French spelling (*-ppe*) has long gone, & the French pronunciation should no longer be allowed to embarrass us, but give way to ĕn′velōp. (2) The obs. spellings *envelope, envelopes,* in the verb, are now to be regarded as mere mistakes.

-EN VERBS FROM ADJECTIVES. It being no part of most people's business to inquire into such matters, the average writer would probably say, if asked for an offhand opinion, that from any adjective of one syllable an *-en* verb could be formed meaning to make or become so-&-so. A very slight examination shows it to be remote from the facts; *-en* cannot be called a living suffix. There are on the one hand some 50 verbs whose currency is beyond question; on the other hand as many adjectives may be found that, though they look as fit for turning into verbs by addition of *-en* as the 50, no one would dream of treating in that way. The despotism of usage is clear when it is noticed that we can say *moisten* but not *wetten, quicken* but not *slowen, thicken* & *fatten* but not *thinnen* or *leanen, deafen* but not *blinden, sweeten* but not *souren, sharpen* but not *blunten, cheapen* but not *dearen, greaten* but not *largen, freshen* but not *stalen, coarsen* but not *finen.* Between the two sets of adjectives whose mind is made up, some taking & some refusing *-en,* there are a few about which questions may arise. With some the right of the *-en* verb to exist is disputable, & with others the undoubted existence of two verbs (e.g. *loose* & *loosen*), one having *-en,* & one identical with the adj., raises the question of differentiated senses; discussion of these & the debatable words is given in the alphabetic listing of each.

envisage. In the 19th-c. sense an undesirable GALLICISM: *face, confront, contemplate, recognize, realize, view,* & *regard* seem equal between them to most requirements. There remains the current meaning, 'obtain a mental view,' 'set before the mind's eye': *Whatever way we envisage the moral attributes of God.* See WORKING & STYLISH WORDS.

epic, adj. An increasingly popular use is *epic laughter, combat, contest, struggle, siege,* &c. If the meaning is mainly 'such as we read of in Homer,' the word HOMERIC is perhaps better; in other contexts (*of epic proportions*), *heroic* or *imposing.*

epicene. Having no real function in English grammar, the word is kept alive chiefly as a more contemptuous synonym for *effeminate,* implying physical as well as moral sexlessness; for this purpose it is better suited than *common* or *neuter* owing to their familiarity in other senses.

epidermis. For its use instead of *skin,* see POLYSYLLABIC HUMOR.

epigram. (Lit.): 'on-writing.' Four distinct meanings naturally enough developed. First, now obs., an inscription on a building, tomb, coin, &c. Secondly (inscriptions being often in verse, & brief), a short poem, & especially one with a sting in the tail. Thirdly, any pungent saying. Fourthly, a style full of such sayings.

epigrammatic. So spelled.

epigraphy. (Lit.): 'study of inscriptions.' Inscriptions & the science of interpreting them &c. Cf. the original sense of EPIGRAM above.

episcopal ('of bishops') is an adj. only. *The Episcopal Church.* The noun, *an Episcopalian.*

epistle. Silent *t.* As a syn. for *letter* in ordinary contexts, see PEDANTIC HUMOR.

epoch, epoch-making. If an epoch were made every time we are told that a discovery or other event is epoch-making, our bewildered state of ceaseless transition from the thousands of eras we were in yesterday to the different thousands we are in today would be pitiful indeed. But luckily the word is a blank cartridge, meant only to startle, & not to carry even so imponderable a bullet as conviction. Cf. UNIQUE, & UNTHINKABLE.

equable. The quality indicated is complex—not merely freedom from great changes, but that as well as remoteness from either extreme, a compound of uniformity & moderation. A continuously cold climate or a consistently violent temper is not equable; nor on the other hand is a moderate but changeable climate or a pulse that varies frequently though within narrow limits.

equal. (1) The verb makes, US, *equaling* &c., Brit., *equalling* &c. (2) WRONG: *The navy is not* equal *in numbers or in strength* to perform *the task it will be called upon to undertake; perform* should be *performing;* see GERUND, & ANALOGY. (*Equal to* the task, *equal to performing* the task are idiomatic.) (3) WRONG: *This work is* the equal, if not better than *anything its author has yet done; equal* lends itself particularly to this blunder; see UNEQUAL YOKEFELLOWS, & read *is equal to, if not better than, anything . . .*

equally as. (1) The use of *as* instead of *with* in correlation with *equally* (*Hermes is patron of poets* equally as *Apollo*) is a relic of the time when *equally with* had not been established & writers were free (as with many other correlative pairs) to invent their own formulas. (2) The use of *equally as* instead of either *equally* or *as* by itself is a tautology, but one of which it is necessary to demonstrate the frequency, & therefore the danger, by quotation. WRONG: *'Stokehold' is* equally as *correct as 'stockehole.'/The Opposition are* equally as *guilty as the Government./The round seeded sort is* equally as *hardy & much pleasanter to handle.* Omit *equally.*

equanimity. Preferably pron. ē-.

equation. For the misuse of *personal equation* (=the allowance for individual slowness in noting phenomena) see PERSONAL.

equivalence, -cy. There appears to be no sort of differentiation; the first is now much commoner, & the second might well be let die.

equivocal. Ambiguous, doubtful, questionable; hence suspicious. *Equivocal & misleading language; an equivocal mode of life.*

equivocation. (Log.): 'calling alike.' A fallacy consisting in the use of a word in different senses at different stages of the reasoning. If we conclude from Jones's having a thick head (i.e. being a dullard) that he is proof against concussion, we take *thick head* to mean first *dull brain* & afterwards *solid skull,* which is an equivocation.

eradicate makes *-cable.*

-ER & -EST, MORE & MOST. Neglect or violation of established usage with comparatives & superlatives sometimes betrays ignorance, but more often reveals the repellent assumption that the writer is superior to conventions binding on the common herd. The remarks that follow, however, are not offered as precise rules, but as advice that, though generally sound, may on occasion be set aside.

1. The adjectives regularly compared with *-er* & *-est* in preference to *more* & *most* are (a) all monosyllables (*hard, sage, shy,* &c.); (b) disyllables in *-y* (*holy, lazy, likely,* &c.), in *-le* (*noble, subtle,* &c.), in *-er* (*tender, clever,* &c.), in *-ow* (*narrow, sallow,* &c.); (c) many disyllables with accent on the last (*polite, profound,* &c.; but cf. *antique, bizarre, burlesque,* & the predicative adjectives *afraid, alive, alone, aware*); (d) trisyllabic negative forms of (b) & (c) words (*unholy, ignoble, insecure,* &c.).

2. Some other disyllables in everyday use not classifiable under terminations, as *common, cruel, pleasant,* & *quiet* (cf. *constant, sudden,* &c.), prefer *-er* & *-est;* most of these are registered in their dictionary places. And many others, e.g. *awkward, brazen, crooked, equal,* can take *-er* & *-est* without disagreeably challenging attention.

3. Adverbs not formed with *-ly* from adjectives, but identical in form with them, use *-er* & *-est* naturally (*runs faster, sleeps sounder, hits hardest, hold it tighter*); some independent adverbs, as *soon, often, seldom,* do the same; *-ly* adverbs, though comparatives in *-lier* are possible in archaic & poetic style (*wiselier said, softlier nurtured*), now prefer *more wisely* &c.; but there is some freedom in the way of treating the comparative adjective, even where the positive is not so used, as an adverb (*easier said than done; he writes cleverer than he talks*); this, however, is chiefly colloquial.

4. Many adjectives besides those described in (1) & (2) are capable in ordinary use, i.e. without the stylistic taint illustrated in (5) & (6), of forming a superlative in *-est,* used with *the* & serving as an emphatic form simply, while no one would think of making a comparative in *-er* from them: *in the brutalest, civilest, timidest, cheerfullest, damnablest, manner.* The terminations that most invite this treatment are *-ful, -ing, -able, -ed,* & *-id.* On the other hand the very common adjective terminations *-ive, -ic,* & *-ous,* reject it altogether (*curiouser & curiouser* is a product of Wonder-

land). Though it is hard to draw a clear line between this use & the next, the intent is different; the words are felt to be little less normal, & yet appreciably more forcible, than the forms with *most;* they are superlatives only, & emphasis is their object.

5. As a stylistic device, based on NOVELTY-HUNTING, & developing into disagreeable MANNERISM, the use of *-er* & *-est* is extended to many adjectives normally taking *more* & *most,* & the reader gets pulled up at intervals by *delicater, ancientest, diligentest, delectablest, dolefuller, devotedest,* & the like. The trick served Carlyle's purpose, & has grown tiresome in his imitators. The extreme form of it is that which next follows.

6. The emotional *-est* without *the.* WRONG: *Mlle Nau, an actress of considerable technical skill & a valuable power of exhibiting* deepest *emotion.* This sentence is so obviously critical & unemotional that it shows fully the VULGARIZATION of a use that is appropriate only to high-poetic contexts. In so analytic a mood the critic should have been content with *deep emotion.* If he had been talking descriptively, he might have gone as far as 'she exhibited *the* deepest emotion.' Not unless he had been apostrophizing her in verse as 'deepest emotion's Queen,' or by whatever lyric phrase emotion (& not analysis) might have inspired, should he have dared to cut out his *the* & degrade the idiom sacred to the poets.

7. Certain illogicalities to which the comparative lends itself may be touched upon. WRONG: *Don't do it* more *than you can help,* meaning not what it says but the opposite (*than you cannot help*), is worth changing into *than you need* or *must* or *are obliged to,* unless it is to rank as a STURDY INDEFENSIBLE. *Better known than popular* is cured by resolving *better* into *more well. It is* more or less—& certainly‸more than less—*a standardized product* is a case of CANNIBALISM, one of the necessary two *mores* having swallowed the other. Unwise striving after double emphasis accounts for *He excelled as a lecturer* more than *as a preacher, because he felt* freer *to bring* more *of his personality into play,* & for *Were ever* finer *lines perverted to a* meaner *use?* In the first (a mixture of *freer to bring his* & *free to bring more of his*) the writer has done nothing worse than give himself away as a waster of words; but in the second (a confusion of *were ever fine lines more spoiled?* & *were ever finer lines spoiled?*—the former alone being the sense meant) we have the force actually diminished, if a reader chooses to work it out, by the addition designed to strengthen it.

8. In superlatives, *the fairest of her daughters Eve* is still with us: *Sir E. Cassel's Christmas gift to the hospitals of* £50,000 *is only* the latest of many acts *of splendid munificence by which he has benefited his fellows* before *now;* this gift is no more one (latest or not) of those 'before now' than Eve is her own daughter.

And here is a well contrasted pair of mistakes; the first is of a notorious type (for examples see ONE), & the second looks almost as if it was due to avoidance of the misunderstood danger. WRONG: *In which case one of the greatest & most serious* strikes *which* has *occurred in modern times will take place* (read *have*)./*Houdini was a wonderful conjuror, & is often reckoned* the greatest *of his craft who* have *ever lived* (read *has*).

-er & -or. The agent termination *-er* can be added to any existing English verb; but with many verbs the regular agent noun ends in *-or* & that in *-er* is an occasional one only, & with others both forms are established with or without differentiation of sense; see also -OUR & -OR.

ere. See INCONGRUOUS VOCABULARY, & VULGARIZATION. *Before* should in all ordinary prose be preferred; the following quotations show the fish out of water at its unhappiest: *The iniquitous anomaly of the plural voter will be swept away* ere *we are much older./There is reason to suppose that he will have arrived at the South Pole long* ere *this & at the season best fitted for accurate observation./In the opinion of high officials it is only a matter of time* ere *the city is cleared of the objectionable smoke pollution evil.*

ergo (Lat. for *therefore*) is archaic or obs. in serious use, but still serves the purpose of drawing attention facetiously to the illogical nature of a conclusion: *He says it is too hot for anything;* ergo, *a bottle of Bass.* See PEDANTIC HUMOR.

Erin. See SOBRIQUETS.

err. Rhymes with *her,* NOT *hair.*

errand. Unconnected with *err* & *errant;* probably from OE ár, *messenger.* See TRUE & FALSE ETYMOLOGY.

erratum. Pl. *-ta.* If only one error is corrected, *-um* should be used.

erst, erstwhile. *Erst* is an adj. and adv. (first, earlier); both are archaic or obs. in all senses. *Erstwhile* is properly an adv., archaic, meaning *formerly,* not an adj. meaning *former.* See PEDANTIC HUMOR, & VULGARIZATION. WRONG: *Incidentally, it may be mentioned that among Smithfield men 'boneless bag meat' has completely ousted the sausage from its* erstwhile *monopoly of jest & gibe.*

erudite. Pron. -ū- (sometimes -ū-). Except when sarcasm is intended or the use is facetious, *learned* will usually serve.

eschatology. Theology: the science of 'the four last things, death, judgment, heaven, and hell.' Pron. ĕsk*a*-.

eschew. Pron. ĕstchoo′. *Abstain from, avoid,* or *shun* would be the WORKING WORD in the usual context.

Eskimo(s), Esquimaux. The former is now the est. spelling; the pronunciation is the same either way.

esoteric. 'For the inner circle, the initiated'; hence words, theories, &c. for the experts only; NOT synonymous with *weird, strange,* or *profound.*

especial(ly). 1. The characteristic sense of *especial*(*ly*) is *preeminence* or the particular as opposed to the ordinary, that of *special*(*ly*) being *limitation* or the particular as opposed to the general. There is, however, a marked tendency in the adj. for *especial* to disappear & for *special* to take its place. It may be said that *special* is now possible in all senses, though *especial* is still also possible or preferable in the senses (a) exceptional in degree, as *My* especial *friend is Jones, He handles the matter with* especial *dexterity, architecture receives* especial *attention;* (b) of, for, a particular person or thing specified by a possessive adjective or case, as *For my* or *Smith's* especial *benefit, For the* especial *benefit* of *wounded soldiers.* In the adv. the encroachments of the shorter form are more limited; a writer may sometimes fall into saying *The reinforcements arrived at* a specially *critical moment,* where *an especially* would be better; but it is as little allowable to say (WRONG) *The candidates,* especially *those from Scotland, showed ability* as (WRONG) *Candidates must be* especially *prepared* or *An arbitrator was* especially appointed. Two examples follow of *especially* used where *specially* is clearly meant; in both the sense is not to *an exceptional degree,* but *for one purpose & no other.* WRONG: *Only Mohammedans were permitted to work within the sacred zones, & Turkish engineers were* especially *trained for this purpose./Agreeable features of the book will be the illustrations, including a number of reproductions of prints* especially *lent by Mr. Harcourt.*

2. *Especially* with inversion. The word is a favorite with victims of this craze (see INVERSION): *Springs of mineralized water, famous from Roman times onwards;* especially did they come *into renown during the nineteenth century./Mr. Campbell does not recognize a change of opinion, but frankly admits a change of emphasis;* especially is he anxious *at the present time to advance the cause of Evangelism.*

3. *Especially as.* It is worth notice that of the causal *as* clauses discussed in AS 2 some types intolerable in themselves are made possible by the insertion of *especially* before *as: I shall have to ask for heavy damages,*^as *my client's circumstances are not such as to allow of quixotic magnanimity; as* by itself is, as usual, insufficient to give the remainder of the sentence the fresh push-off that, introducing an unforeseen consideration, it requires; but *especially* inserted before *as,* by bespeaking attention, prevents the tailing off into insignificance that would otherwise ruin the balance.

espionage. Pron. ĕs′pyonij or (US usually) -ahzh′.

esquire. (1) The accent is on the second syllable, despite the popular pronunciation of the US magazine. (2) Orig. 'shield bearer.' In mod. Brit. used as a courtesy title for all who are regarded as 'gentlemen,' esp. in the addresses of letters (Esq.) after the surname (with no prefixed title as *Mr., Dr.,* &c.). *Esq.* used in the US on a letter to an American is an affectation.

essay. (1) *Essay,* to attempt; *assay,* to test. See ASSAY. (2) Pron. the verb essay′; the noun, in its now commonest sense of a kind of literary piece, es′say. But in the wider & now less usual sense of 'an attempt' the old accent is still often heard; *my second* essay′ *at authorship.*

essence & substance, essential(ly) & substantial(ly). It is natural that *essence* & *substance, essential(ly)* & *substantial(ly),* should on the one hand be sometimes interchangeable, & on the other hand develop, like most synonyms, on diverging lines with differentiations gradually becoming fixed. It may be said roughly that *substance* has moved in the direction of material & quantity, *essence* in that of spirit & quality. The strictly philosophical or metaphysical uses are beyond the scope of this book; but some examples of the words in popular contexts may serve to show how they agree & disagree.

1. Examples in which either is possible, sometimes with & sometimes without change of sense, or with degrees of idiomatic appropriateness: *God is an* essence (or less often a *substance*), i.e. a self-existent being./*I can give you the* substance *of what he said* (or less often the *essence,* implying the cutting out of all superfluous details)./*But he took care to retain the* substance *of power* (or less usually the *essence,* or archaically the *substantials,* or quite well the *essentials*)./*The* essence *of morality is right intention, the* substance *of it is right action* (the words could not be exchanged in this antithesis, but in either part by itself either word would do; the *essence* is that without which morality would not be what it is, the *substance* is that of which it is made up)./*Distinguish between the mere words of Revelation & its* substance (or *essence,* indifferently)./*They give* in substance *the same account* (or *in essence* rarely, or *substantially* or *essentially*)./*The treaty underwent* substantial *modifications* (or *essential,* but *substantial* means merely that they amounted to a good deal, *essential* that they changed the whole effect)./*Desire of praise is an* essential *part of human nature* (or *substantial;* if *essential,* human nature without it is *inconceivable;* if *substantial,* human nature is appreciably actuated by it)./*There is an* essential *difference* (or *substantial;* the latter much less emphatic)./*All parties receive* substantial *justice* (or rarely *essential,* which implies much less, if any, ground for dissatisfaction).

2. Examples admitting of *essence* only: *The* essence *of a triangle is three straight lines meeting at three angles./What is the* essence *of snobbery?/Time is of* the essence *of the contract./'Kubla Khan' may be called* essential *poetry./The qualities* essential *to success./An* essentially *vulgar person.*

3. Examples admitting of *substance* only: *Butter is a* substance./*Parting with the* substance *for the shadow./There is no* substance *in his argument./A man* of substance./*His failure to bring any* substantial *evidence./A* substantial *meal./A* substantially *built house.*

essential, necessary, requisite. The words so far agree in the sense in which they are all commonest, i.e. *needed,* that in perhaps most sentences containing one of them either of the others could be substituted without serious change of meaning. It often matters nothing whether we say *the essential,* or *the necessary,* or *the requisite, qualities are courage & intelligence only.* They have reached the meeting point, however, from different directions, bringing each its native equipment, of varying suitability for various tasks. For instance, in *We can hardly say that capital is as* requisite *to production as land & labor* the least suitable of the three has been chosen, the word wanted to class the relation of land &

labor to production being the strongest of all, whereas *requisite* is the weakest.

If we call something *essential* we have in mind a whole that would not be what it is to be or is or was if the part in question were wanting; *the essential thing* is such that the other thing is inconceivable without it. *Essential* is the strongest word of the three.

When we call something *necessary,* we have in mind the irresistible action of causality or logic; *the necessary thing* is such that the other cannot but owe its existence to it or result in it. *Necessary* doubles the parts of *indispensable* & *inevitable.*

When we call something *requisite,* we have in mind merely an end for which means are to be found; *the requisite thing* is that demanded by the conditions, but need not be the only thing that could satisfy their demands, though it is usually understood in that sense. The fact that *requisite* has no negative form corresponding to *unessential* & *unnecessary* is significant of its less exclusive meaning.

For a trivial illustration or two: In the taking of an oath, religious belief is *essential,* but neither *necessary* nor *requisite;* the unbeliever's oath is no oath, but the want of belief need not prevent him from swearing, nor will belief help him to swear. The alphabetical arrangement is *unessential,* but not unnecessary, & very requisite, in this book; the dictionary without it would be a dictionary all the same, but the laws of causality make the publishers demand & the writer supply alphabetical order, & without it the purpose would be very badly served.

essential. Constr. usually *to,* occasionally *for. Public recognition is* essential to *his happiness./Propositions . . . I consider* essential for *a right understanding of history.* Either would serve, but *to* is more idiomatic.

-est in superlatives. See -ER & -EST.

estate. *The three estates,* i.e. the Lords Spiritual, the Lords Temporal, & the Commons, is often wrongly applied to Sovereign, Lords, & Commons. The use of the phrase being now purely decorative, & the reader being often uncertain about what the user of it may mean, it is perhaps better left alone. *The third estate* is a phrase often used for the French bourgeoisie before the Revolution. *The fourth estate* is a jocular description of the newspaper press as one of the powers that have to be reckoned with in politics.

esthete, esthetic. *Aes-* preferred, US & Brit, though *es-* is sometimes used in US.

estimate, v. If an adj. is needed, use *estimatable. Estimable,* in the sense capable of being estimated, is obs.; it now means only worthy of esteem or regard.

estimate, estimation. (1) The sense judgment formed by calculation or consideration belongs to *estimate* & not to *estimation,* which means not the judgment itself, but the forming of it. The tendency described in LONG VARIANTS often leads writers astray. WRONG: *Norwegians can only wish that the optimistic* estimation *of Mr. Ponting will come true.* (2) The use of *in my* &c. *estimation* as a mere substitute for *in my* &c. *opinion* where there is no question of calculating for amounts or degrees is sloppy. WRONG: *The thing is absurd* in my estimation.

estivate, in US usually so spelled. Brit. *aestivate.*

estop is a useful word so long as it is restricted to the special sense that has secured its revival; but to revive its wider sense convicts one of pedantry. The special legal sense is (in the passive) 'to be precluded by one's own previous act on declaration from alleging or doing something.' Two quotations will show the right & the wrong use. RIGHT: *No one defended more joyously the silencing of Mr. Asquith last July, & Mr. Maxse is* estopped *from complaining, now that his own method has been applied to himself.* WRONG: *The road winds along the side of a barren mountain till it appears to be* estopped *by a high cliff.*

etc. To resort to *etc.* in sentences of a literary character (*His faults of temper* etc. *are indeed easily accounted for*) is amateurish, slovenly, & incongruous; e.g. *A timely compliment of this kind is calculated to increase their enthusiasm, courage,* etc., *to do their utmost.* On the other hand, in the contexts to which it is appropriate, it is needless PURISM to restrict its sense to what the words could mean in Latin, i.e. (a) *& the rest* as opposed to *& other things,* (b) *and the like* as opposed to *or the like,* (c) *& other things* as opposed to *persons.* The first restriction would exclude *His pockets contained an apple, a piece of string,* etc.; the second would exclude *'Good,' 'fair,' 'excellent,'* etc., *is appended to each name;* the third would exclude *The Duke of A, Lord B, Mr. C,* etc., *are patrons.* The reasonable punctuation with *etc.* is to put a comma before it when more than one term has preceded, but not when one term only has preceded: *toads, frogs, etc.; but toads etc.* (In this book the sign &c is used for economy of space & is not recommended for literary works.)

eternal. For *the Eternal City* (Rome) see SOBRIQUETS.

ethic(al), ethics. 1. *ethic, ethical. Ethic* has now been almost displaced as an adj. by *-al;* it is occasionally still used, but is noticeably archaic.

2. *ethic, ethics.* Of the two nouns the second is the one for ordinary use. It means the science of morals or study of the principles defining man's duty to his neighbors, a treatise on this, or a prevailing code of morality (*Ethics is,* or *are, not to be treated as an exact science; That is surely from 'The Ethics,'* i.e. Aristotle's; *Our modern ethics are not outraged by this type of mendacity*). *Ethic* in any of these senses has a pedantic air. It is chiefly in technical philosophic use, & its special meaning is a scheme of moral science (*The attempt to construct an ethic apart from theology*).

3. The grammatical number of *ethics,* as of most other *-ics* nouns, depends on the sentence. The science, or a treatise on the science (spec. Aristotle's), is always sing. RIGHT: *The 'Ethics' is our source for this statement. Ethics* is *the science of morals.* But *The Ethics of Paganism* were *part of a philosophy. Such ethics* are *abominable.*

4. *ethics, morals.* The two words, once fully synonymous, have so far divided functions

that neither is superfluous. They are not rivals for one job, but holders of complementary jobs; *ethics* is the science of morals, & *morals* are the practice of ethics: *His ethics may be sound, but his morals are abandoned.* That is the broad distinction. The points where confusion arises are three: (a) sometimes those who are talking about morals choose to call them *ethics* because the less familiar word strikes them as more imposing; (b) there is an unfounded impression that *ethics* is somehow more definitely than morals disconnected from religion; (c) the distinction is rather fine between the sense of *ethics* last given, & illustrated in (2), i.e. prevailing code of morals, & morals themselves; but, though fine, it is clear enough.

5. *ethical, moral.* It is in the nature of things that the dividing line between the adjectives should be less clear than with the nouns. For, if ethics is the science of morals, whatever concerns morals evidently concerns ethics too, & is as much ethical as moral; & vice versa. Nevertheless, we talk of *a moral,* but NOT *an ethical, man,* when practice is in question, &, in the region of theory, we perhaps tend more & more to talk of *the ethical* rather than the moral *basis of society, education,* & so forth. Cf. *unethical.*

ethos. Pron. ē′thŏs. It means the characteristic spirit informing a nation, an age, a literature, an institution, or any similar unit. In reference to a nation or State, it is the sum of the intellectual & moral tendencies of which what the Germans call the nation's *Kultur* is the manifestation. Like *Kultur* it is not in itself a word of praise or blame, any more than *quality.*

etymology. The origin or derivation of a word; the branch of philology concerned with etymologies.

euphemism, -mistic, -mize. The noun (cf. EUPHUISM) means (the use of a) mild or vague or periphrastic expression as a substitute for blunt precision or disagreeable truth: Euphemism *is more demoralizing than coarseness./'Mistress' is a* euphemism *for concubine./Protectionists have* euphemized *themselves into tariff reformers.*

euphuism. The word is often ignorantly used for *euphemism,* with which it is entirely unconnected. It is named from Lyly's *Euphues* (i.e. The Man of Parts), fashionable in & after the 16th c. as a literary model, & means affected artificiality of style, indulgence in antithesis & simile & conceits, subtly refined choice of words, preciosity. It is, unlike *euphemism,* a word with which no one but the literary critic has any concern. A single example of the common misuse will suffice. WRONG: *A financial* euphuism *christened railway construction a 'transformation of capital,' & not an expenditure.* See POPULARIZED TECHNICALITIES.

Eurasian. Of mixed European and Asiatic descent; formerly, esp. in Brit., it was used spec. for those of mixed English and Indian parentage. See MULATTO; ANGLO-INDIAN.

evacuate makes *-cuable.*

evacuee (from Fr. *evacué,* m.; *-ée,* f.) is now naturalized & applied to either sex. Pron. evăkūē′.

evaluate makes *-uable.*

evaluation in the sense of the action of appraising or valuing goods, or of a statement or calculation of value, is now displaced by *valuation. Evaluation* now is restricted to the action of evaluating or determining the value of (a mathematical expression &c.) or estimating the force of (probabilities, evidence, &c.) *The authors'* evaluation *of some of the terms . . .* but *The usual* valuation *of different articles of produce.*

evanish. Pron. ˈevan′ish. To vanish completely, die away. The word is effective in poetry & poetic contexts; for its use in such phrases as *The rapidly* evanishing *phantom of a home-rule majority,* see VULGARIZATION.

evasion, evasiveness. The latter is a quality only; in places where quality, & not practice or action, is the clear meaning, *evasion* should not be used instead of it. RIGHT: *His* evasion *of the issue is obvious; He is guilty of perpetual* evasion; but *The* evasiveness (NOT *evasion*) *of his answers is enough to condemn him.*

eve. RIGHT: *On Christmas Eve, on the Eve of St. Agnes, on the eve of the battle, on the eve of departure, on the eve of great developments.* The strict sense of *eve* being the evening or day before, the first two phrases are literal, the last is metaphorical, & the two others may be either, i.e. they may mean *before,* either with an interval of days or weeks, or with a night intervening, or actually on the same day. Nevertheless, in spite even of the chance of ambiguity, they are all legitimate. What is not legitimate is to use the word in its metaphorical sense & yet remind the reader of the literal sense by some turn of words that involves it. WRONG: *The most irreconcilable of landlords are beginning to recognize that we are on the* eve *of the* dawn *of a* new day. See METAPHOR.

Eve. For *daughter of Eve* see BATTERED ORNAMENTS, ELEGANT VARIATION, HACKNEYED PHRASES, PERIPHRASIS.

even. 1. Placing of *even.* It will be seen in POSITION OF ADVERBS that their placing is a matter partly of idiom & partly of sense; *even* is one of those whose placing is important to the sense. WRONG: *The time to see them is just after breakfast, when they emerge from every other door, Pugs, Poodles, Pekinese, Dachshunds, Dandies, & ever so many more whose names I do not* even know, *all chattering at the top of their voices as they walk, run, trot, waddle or pitter-patter along according to their kind.* The effect of putting *even* there is to contrast *know* with some other verb; what other verb? If it had run *I cannot* even *guess,* it would have been obvious to supply *much less know;* but *know* leaves no room for a *much less. Even* properly belongs before *names—I do not know even their names*—but since the *whose* construction makes this impossible the only solution is to recast the sentence.

2. *Even so.* This is a phrase that has its uses. It often serves as a conveniently short reminder to the reader that the contention before him is not the strongest that could be advanced, that deductions have been made, that the total is net

& not gross. But some writers become so attached to this convenience that they resort to it (a) when it is a convenience to them & an inconvenience to their readers, i.e. when it takes a reader some time to discover what exactly the writer meant by it, & (b) when nothing, or one of the everyday conjunctions, would do as well. The following passages are none of them indefensible, but all exemplify the ill-judged *even so,* used (when it conveys too much) to save the writer trouble, or (when it conveys too little) to gratify his fondness for the phrase: *I hope it won't come to this; but,* even so, *bridge players will continue to take their finesses & call it just their luck when they go down* (if it does)./*It is natural that France should be anxious not to lose on the swings what she gains on the roundabouts, & she has some reason for nervousness as to the interaction of commerce & politics.* Even so, *she will do well not to be over-nervous* (But)./*If the absent are always wrong, statesmen who have passed away are always gentlemen. But,* even so, *we were not prepared for this tribute to those statesmen who fought for Home Rule in* 1886 (omit 'even so').

evenness. So spelled.

event. OFFICIALESE: *In the event* (*of his death*)=if (he dies); *await the event*=await the result. For *blessed event* see WORN-OUT HUMOR.

eventuality, eventuate. ('Chiefly US'—COD.) In most contexts the working words would be *outcome, contingency; result, come about, happen.* See ANTI-SAXONISM. The words are chiefly used in flabby OFFICIALESE; some characteristic specimens are: *We shall of course be told before long that the Force is on the eve of a complete breakdown . . . ; that is very far from the case, however dear such an* eventuality *might be to our enemies./The bogeys that were raised about the ruin* did not eventuate, *yet employers still want the assistants to work for long hours.*

ever is often used colloq. as an emphasizer of *who, what, when,* & other interrogative words, corresponding to such phrases as *who in the world, what on earth, where* (can he) *possibly* (be?). When such talk is reproduced in print, *ever* should be a separate word—*what ever* &c., NOT *whatever* &c. *Seldom or ever* should be *seldom if ever* or *seldom or never.*

ever, adj. *Ever-blooming roses, our ever-esteemed friend, ever-increasing taxes,* &c., usually hyphened. But *everlasting,* one word.

ever so (*though it were ever so bad* &c.). This is the modern idiom; *never so,* the original form, is now archaic except in poetry. See NEVER SO.

everybody, everybody else. Always sing., always take a sing. verb and pronoun. NOT *Everybody else I know* do and say *what* they *please,* but *does, says,* and *he pleases.* Poss. *everybody else's.*

everyday. One word when an adj.: *My everyday clothes.* But *I see him every day.*

every one. *Every one* (2 words) should be used when the meaning stresses each individual: *Almost every one of them deserves a medal./What* *we every one of us can swear.* It is one word when used as a pronoun=everybody. *Everyone knows he is right.* (But *Every one of the twelve jurors knew he was right.*) *Everyone* is sing. Although the OED condones the use of pl. pronoun (and verb) because of the lack of a sing. pronoun of common gender: *Everyone had made up* their *minds that I was wrong,* this is not recommended. See ONE 6.

everywhere is an adv. meaning 'in or to every place.' NOT *everyplace.*

evidence. *To evidence* something is to be the proof, or serve as evidence, of its existence or truth or occurrence. *You* do not evidence care, i.e. that you are careful, but *your state of instruction* may evidence care, i.e. that either you or your instructors have been careful, & *you* may, by being obviously well instructed, evidence your instructors' care. It will be seen that *show* or *exhibit* could take the place of *evidence* in the places that have been said to allow of it, but also that they would stand where it has been said that *evidence* could not. Writers with a preference for the less common or the more technical-looking word are sometimes trapped by the partial equivalence into thinking that they may indulge their preference by using *evidence* instead of *show.* A right & a wrong sentence will make the limitation of meaning clearer, & another wrong sentence will illustrate the importance of the exact words used in the definition given above of the meaning. It must be borne in mind, however, that that definition does not pretend to cover all senses of *evidence,* but only those in which it is in danger of misuse. RIGHT: *This work of Mr. Phillipps, while it bears all the marks of scholarship, bears also the far rarer impress of original thought, &* evidences *the power of considering with an unusual detachment a subject which . . .* WRONG: *Mr. Thayer* evidences *a remarkable grasp of his material, & a real gift for the writing of history.* NEGATIVE: *We regret that his work should be so unambitious in scope, for it fails to include many of the popular superstitions of today & does not* evidence *any great care or research.* If *to evidence* means *to be the proof of,* or *to serve as the evidence of,* it is clear that it is one of those words that are in place only in affirmative sentences, & not in negative or neutral ones. Just as we say *This brandy is excellent,* but not *Bring me some excellent brandy* or *The brandy is not excellent* (*good* is the word), so we say that *work evidences care,* but not that *it does not evidence care* (*suggest* or *show* is the word). See POSITIVE WORDS.

evidently. The accent is on the first syllable, not the third. The word means obviously, manifestly, as may be clearly inferred. Its use as *seemingly* ('Is he suitable for the post? Evidently.') is colloq.

evince has lost most of its meanings by lapse of time, & only two remain. An example of each may be useful: *The contrivances of nature decidedly* evince *intention*—(i.e. are an evidence of); *The knees & upper part of the leg* evincing *muscular strength*—(i.e. giving tokens of possessing, or revealing the presence of).

But it may almost be said that its ANTI-SAXONISM is the word's only claim to be used any longer. Those who like a full-dress word better than a plain one continue to use & sometimes to misuse it. The writer of one of the quotations below, in putting it next door to *evident,* surely evinces a fondness for it that borders on foolishness; & the other must have been unaware that, though either a person or an attitude can evince an emotion, neither a person nor an emotion can evince an attitude; an attitude is nothing if not visible, & what is evinced is inferable but not visible. WRONG: *Both Parties* evinced *an evident anxiety to stir up trouble on the labor unrest in the railway world./The Opposition welcomed the Bill on first reading, & have, on the whole, only* evinced *a legitimately critical attitude in Committee.*

evolution. Pron. US ĕv-; Brit. ē-.

ex- meaning formerly but not now should be attached to single words only, not compound words. *Ex-president,* but not *ex-democratic nominee. Former* is usually the best solution in compound titles &c. For such patent yet prevalent absurdities as *ex-Lord Mayor, ex-Vice President,* see HYPHENS; & for alternatives, LATE.

exactly, just. Exactly *what has happened or what is about to happen is not yet clear;* Just *how the words are to be divided.* This now familiar idiom, in which *exactly* or *just* is prefixed to an indirect question, is a modern development. The *exactly* or *just* sometimes adds point, but is more often otiose, & the use of it becomes with many writers a disagreeable MANNERISM.

exaggerate. So spelled.

exceeding(ly) & excessive(ly). The difference is the same as that between *very great* or *very much* & *too great* or *too much.* It is not inherent in the words, nor very old, *excessive*(*ly*) having formerly had both meanings. But it is now recognized by most of those who use words carefully, & is a useful DIFFERENTIATION. It follows that *I am* excessively *obliged to you* is not now standard English, & that *I was* excessively *annoyed* should be said in repentant & not, as it usually is, in self-satisfied tones. A passage in which a good modern writer allows himself to disregard the now usual distinction may be worth giving. WRONG: *I have said that in early life Henry James was not 'impressive'; as time went on his appearance became, on the contrary,* excessively *noticeable & arresting. He removed the beard which had long disguised his face, & so revealed the* strong lines *of mouth & chin, which responded to the* majesty *of the skull.* 'Strong lines' & 'majesty' do not suggest excessive qualities.

excellence, -cy. *Excellence* is now the usual noun for the quality or virtue, *-cy* being reserved for the title.

excellent is one of the words used to express the speaker's strong opinion. After reading it, you may say a book is *excellent.* You ask for a *good* book. There is seldom justification for using *more* or *most excellent. I have never read a* *better book,* NOT *a more excellent book.* See POSITIVE WORDS.

except, as a conj. governing a clause, i.e. as a substitute for the *unless* or *if . . . not* of ordinary educated speech, is either an ARCHAISM resorted to for one or other of the usual reasons, or else an illustration of the fact that old constructions often survive in uneducated talk when otherwise obs. In the quotation, archaism for one of the less defensible reasons is the explanation: *But,* except *the matter is argued as a mere matter of amour propre, how is it possible to use such high-flown language about a mere 'change of method'?*

excepting as a prep. has one normal use. When a possible exception is to be mentioned as not made, the form used is, instead of *not except,* either *not excepting* before the noun or *not excepted* after it: *All men are fallible* except *the Pope; All men are fallible,* not excepting *the Pope* or *the Pope not excepted.* Other prepositional uses of *excepting* are unidiomatic, but the word as a true participle or a gerund does not fall under this condemnation. RIGHT: *He would treble the tax on brandy excepting only,* or *without excepting, that destined for medicine.* WRONG: *The cost of living throughout the world,* excepting in *countries where special causes operate, shows a tendency to keep level.* Use *except.*

exception proves the rule, & phrases implying it, are so constantly introduced in argument, & so much more often with obscuring than with illuminating effect, that it is necessary to set out its different possible meanings: (1) the original simple legal sense, (2) the secondary, rather complicated, scientific sense, (3) the loose rhetorical sense, (4) the jocular nonsense, (5) the serious nonsense. The last of these is the only one that need be objected to directly, though (3) & (4) must bear the blame of bringing (5) into existence by popularizing an easily misunderstood phrase. See POPULARIZED TECHNICALITIES.

1. 'Special leave is given for men to be out of barracks tonight till 11 p.m.'; 'The exception proves the rule' means that this special leave implies a rule requiring men, except when an exception is made, to be in earlier. The value of this in interpreting statutes is plain.

2. We have concluded by induction that Jones the critic, who never writes a kindly notice, lacks the faculty of appreciation. One day a warm eulogy of an anonymous novel appears over his signature, & we see that this exception destroys our induction. Later it comes out that the anonymous novelist is Jones himself; our conviction that he lacks the faculty of appreciation is all the stronger for the apparent exception when once we have found out that, being self-appreciation, it is outside the scope of the rule—which, however, we now modify to exclude it, saying that he lacks the faculty of appreciating others. Or again, it turns out that the writer of the notice is another Jones; then our opinion of Jones-the-first is only strengthened by having been momentarily shaken. These kinds of exception are of great value in scientific inquiry,

but they prove the rule not when they are seen to be exceptions, but when they have been shown to be either outside of or reconcilable with the principle they seem to contradict.

3. We may legitimately take satisfaction in the fact that since the discovery of antibiotics we need no longer fear fatality from certain virus diseases, the few people allergic to antibiotics being the exception that goes to prove the rule. On the contrary, it goes to disprove it; but no more is meant than that it calls our attention to & heightens by contrast what might otherwise pass unnoticed, the remarkable effectiveness of antibiotics in these diseases.

4. 'If there is one virtue I can claim, it is punctuality.' 'Were you in time for breakfast this morning?' 'Well, well, the exception that proves the rule.' It is by the joint effect of this use & the 3rd that the proverb comes to oscillate between the two senses: Exceptions can always be neglected, & A truth is all the truer if it is sometimes false.

5. It rained on St. Swithin's day (15 July), it will rain for forty days. July 31 is fine & dry, but our certainty of a wet August is not shaken, since today is an exception that (instead of at one blow destroying) proves the rule. This frame of mind is encouraged whenever a writer, aware or unaware himself of the limitations, appeals to the 2nd use without clearly showing that his exception is of the right kind. WRONG: *The general principle of Disestablishing & Disendowing the Church in Wales will be supported by the full strength of Liberalism, with the small* exceptions that may be taken as proving the rule.

exceptionable, exceptional, unex-. The *-able* & *-al* forms, especially the negatives, are often confused. *Exceptional* has to do with the ordinary sense of *exception,* & means 'out of the common'; *exceptionable* involves the sense of *exception* rarely seen except in *take exception to* & *open to exception;* it means the same as the latter phrase, & its negative form means offering no handle to criticism. WRONG: *The picture is in* unexceptional *condition, & shows this master's qualities to a marked degree.* Read *unexceptionable.*

excerpt. Accent first syllable of noun, second of verb.

excess. The accent is normally on the second syllable, except when the word is used attributively, *excess luggage, excess fare. Excess* as a true adj. is obs., *excessive* having taken its place. *In excess of* is usually a highfalutin way of saying *more than.*

excessive(ly). See EXCEEDING(LY).

excise, not *-ize. Excise taxes* = internal revenue taxes.

excitation. *Excitement* is the word used in usual non-technical language, *excitation* now being reserved chiefly for science.

EXCLAMATION MARK. Not to use a mark of exclamation is sometimes wrong: *How they laughed,* instead of *How they laughed!,* is not English. Excessive use of exclamation marks is, like that of ITALICS, one of the things that betray the uneducated or unpracticed writer: *You surprise me, How dare you? Don't tell such lies* are mere statement, question, & command, not converted into exclamations by the fact that those who say them are excited, & not to be decorated into *You surprise me! How dare you! Don't tell such lies!* Exclamations in grammar are (1) interjections, as *oh!*; (2) words or phrases used as interjections, as *Heavens! by Jove! my God! great Scott!*; (3) sentences containing the exclamatory *what* or *how*, as *What a difference it makes! What I suffered! How pretty she is!*; (4) wishes proper, as *Confound you! May we live to see it!*; (5) ellipses & inversions due to emotion, as *Not another word! If only I could! That it should have come to this! A fine friend you have been!*; (6) apostrophes, as *You miserable coward! You little dear!* Though a sentence is not to be exclamation-marked to show that it has the excited tone that its contents imply, it may & sometimes must be so marked to convey that the tone is not merely what would be natural to the words themselves, but is suitable to scornful quotation, to the unexpected, the amusing, the disgusting, or something that needs the comment of special intonation to secure that the words shall be taken as they are meant; so: *You thought it didn't matter! He learned at last that the enemy was—himself! Each is as bad as the other, only more so! He puts his knife in his mouth!* But NOT: *That is a lie! My heart was in my mouth! I wish you would be quiet! Beggars must not be choosers!* In all these the words themselves suffice to show the tone, & the exclamation mark shows only that the writer does not know his business.

excommunicate makes *-cable.*

exculpate. Free from blame, clear of guilt: exculpated *on both charges; he* exculpated *himself from the accusation; evidence that tends to* exculpate *the accused.* Pron. ĕks′kŭl pāt.

execrate makes *-crable* (abominable, detestable, deserving to be cursed). Used hyperbolically, *The versification was, to say no worse of it, execrable.*

executor. In the special sense (testator's posthumous agent) pron. ĕksĕk′ūtor, in other senses ĕk′zĭkūtor. The fem. is *executrix* (ĕkzĕk′-), pl. *-trices.*

exhalation, exhale. The *h* is pronounced in the verb, but usually not in the noun.

exhilarate. So spelled. The *h* is not pronounced.

exigence, -cy. Urgent need; requirement, emergency. *Exigency* is now the commoner form; *exigence* has no senses in which *exigency* would be unsuitable, while *exigence* sounds archaic in some; it would be well to make *exigency* universal.

-ex, -ix. Naturalized Latin nouns in *-ex* & *-ix* vary in the form of the plural. The Latin plural is *-ices* (-ĭsēz or -īsēz), the English *-exes* (-ĕksĭz). Some words use only one of these, & some both. See LATIN PLURALS.

1. Words in purely scientific or technical use (*codex, cortex, murex,* &c.) are best allowed their latinity; to talk of *cortexes, codexes,* & *murexes* is to take indecent liberties with physiology, palaeography, & ichthyology, the real professors of which, moreover, usually prefer *-ices.*

2. Latin words borrowed as trade names (*simplex, Bendix, duplex,* &c.) are for the period of their lives English; if in talk of apartments you say you find *duplices* better than one-floor penthouses, you are scarcely intelligible.

3. Words that have become the est. English for an object (*ilex*) use *-exes; under the shade of the ilices* shows ignorance of English more conspicuously than knowledge of Latin.

4. There are some words, however, whose use is partly scientific & partly popular, e.g. *apex, appendix, index, matrix, vertex, vortex;* of these both plurals are used, with some tendency, but no more, to keep *-xes* for popular or colloq. & *-ices* for scientific or formal contexts. *Six patients had their* appendixes *removed, & I hate books with* appendixes; but *The evidence is digested in five* appendices. *A dial like a clock face with two* indexes, but *Integral, fractional, & negative* indices. *A heap of old stereotype* matrixes, but *Some of the species of whinstone are the common* matrices *of agate & chalcedony. Arrange the trestles with their* vertexes *alternately high & low,* but *In the* vertices *of curves where they cut the abscissa at right angles. Whirlpools or* vortexes *or eddies,* but *The* vortices *of modern atomists.* There is thus considerable liberty of choice; but with most words of this class the scientific use, & consequently the Latin plural, is much commoner than the other.

ex officio. (By virtue or because of an office.) When used as an adj., the words should be hyphened: *I was there* ex officio, but *The* ex-officio members *of the committee.* Pron. -shĭo. In US now usually not italicized.

exorbitant. So spelled.

exordium. The introductory part (esp. of a discourse, treatise, &c.). Pl. *-ms* or *-ia.*

exoteric & exotic, of the same ultimate derivation, have entirely diverse applications. That is *exoteric* which is communicable to the outer circle of disciples (opp. *esoteric*); that is *exotic* which comes from outside the country (opp. *indigenous*); *exoteric doctrines; exotic plants. Exotic* has become a VOGUE WORD in US for 'unusual in appearance,' 'bizarre.'

ex parte (on or in the interest of), when used as an adj., should be hyphened: *speaking ex parte,* but *an ex-parte statement.*

expatiation. Pron. -shĭ ā′shn.

expect. Exception is often taken to the sense suppose, be inclined to think, consider probable. This extension of meaning is, however, so natural that it seems needless PURISM to resist it. *Expect* by itself is used as short for *expect to find that, expect that it will turn out that.* IDIOMATIC: *I* expect *he will be in time; I* expect *he is there by this time; I* expect *you have heard all this before.*

expectorate, -ation are (chiefly US) GENTEELISMS for *spit.*

expediency, -ce. The first is now commoner in all surviving senses; there is no differentiation.

expedient, expeditious, both come from the same root, but *expedient* in its modern sense means conducive to advantage, suitable, useful or politic as opposed to 'right' or 'just.' *The* *expedient, in the sense in which it is opposed to Right, generally means that which is expedient for the particular interest of the agent himself* (Mill). *Expeditious* means quickly given, ready, speedy; speedily performed: *Capable of making an expeditious passage./The German commission had been as expeditious as the Spanish had been dilatory.*

expedite. Usually a FORMAL WORD for *hasten.* See OFFICIALESE.

expendable. Formerly a rare word, *expendable* (that may be expended) has come into common language through its military use during the Second World War: 'normally consumed in service,' hence suitable to be sacrified according to plan, esp. in a delaying action.

expenditure. In the transf. sense, applied to time, energy, labor, &c., there is usually the implication of waste: *An unnecessary* expenditure *of energy.* For *He decided he should have to submit without* further expenditure of time *on it,* see LOVE OF THE LONG WORD.

expert. Pron. the noun ex′-, the adj. usually -pert′.

expiate makes *expiable, expiator.*

expiry. Pron. -ī′rĭ.

expletive. Pron., US, ex′-; Brit. also ĕxplē′-.

explicit & express. With a certain class of nouns (e.g. declaration, testimony, promise, contract, understanding, incitement, prohibition), either adj. can be used in the general sense of *definite* as opposed to *virtual* or *tacit* or *vague* or *general* or *inferable* or *implied* or *constructive.* One may nevertheless be more appropriate than the other. That is *explicit* which is set forth in sufficient detail; that is *express* which is worded with intention. What is meant by calling a promise *explicit* is first that it has been put into words & secondly that its import is plain; what is meant by calling it *express* is first, as before, that it has been put into words, & secondly that the maker meant it to bind him in the case contemplated. See also EXPRESS.

export. The verb is normally accented on the second syllable, but when contrasted with *import* often on the first.

exposition in the sense public show of goods &c. is a GALLICISM (or Americanism) for *exhibition.*

ex post facto. 'After the fact.' *Ex post facto legislation* is the making of an act illegal after it has been committed; but what is referred to in *facto* is not the 'doing' of the action but the 'enacting' of the law. (Properly *ex postfacto,* but the writing as three words is now est.)

express, adj., **expressed,** ppl. adj. Both mean 'made known in words,' but the former carries the additional sense of definite, unmistakable in import, not merely implied, *His* express *testimony; the* expressed *wishes of the deceased.* See EXPLICIT.

express, v. Idiomatic constr. is with *as.* WRONG: *Mr. Justice Sankey* expressed himself‸much troubled *by the views expressed in Lord Wrenbury's letter./Both men afterwards* expressed themselves‸perfectly satisfied. There is no authority for *to express oneself satisfied* &c.; at any rate the OED has no acquaintance with it; & it certainly requires the support of authority, whereas no such support is needed for the use with *as* (*He expressed himself* as *interested in the problem*). The fact is that ANALOGY is being allowed to confuse *express* with *declare* just as *regard* is wrongly given the construction of *consider*.

expressive. For *to use an expressive colloquialism,* see SUPERIORITY.

extant had formerly the same sense as *existent* or *existing,* & was as widely applicable. Its sense & its application have been narrowed till it means only 'still in existence or not having perished at the present or the given past or future time,' & is applied almost exclusively to documents, buildings or monuments, & customs. Now such phrases as *extant memory, the extant generation, the extant crisis, extant States,* are unlikely or impossible, & *the extant laws* would be understood only of such as were on record but not in operation, of laws as documents & not as forces.

extend. (1) The standard forms are *extendible, extensible.* (2) *Extend* for *give* or *accord, proffer* or *bestow,* is (Fowler) 'a regrettable Americanism'—*to extend sympathy, a call to a pastorate, a hearty reception,* and the like. The condemnation does not touch such sentences as *You should extend to me the same indulgence,* where the meaning is 'widen it so as to include me as well as someone else.' It is not maintained that *extend* has never had the sense of *give* or *accord* in native English—it had in the 16th–18th cc. —but only that the modernism in Brit. does not descend direct from the native use, but was reimported after export to America.

extent. In the phrase *to . . . extent, extent* should not be qualified by adjectives introducing any idea beyond that of quantity; *to what, to any, to some, to a great* or *vast* or *enormous* or *unknown* or *surprising, extent,* but NOT *Some of the girls even go* to the manlike extent *of holding meetings in the Park to discuss their grievances.*

extenuate. (1) *Extenuate* makes *-uable.* (2) The root meaning being 'to thin down or whittle away,' the proper object of the verb in its sense of 'make excuses for' is a word expressing something bad in itself, as *guilt, cowardice, cruelty,* & not a neutral word such as *conduct* or *behavior.* But since these latter, though neutral in themselves, are often converted by context into unmistakable words of blame, & are then legitimate objects of *extenuate,* the misapprehension arises that it can always govern them, & consequently that the meaning of *excuse* belongs to the verb, instead of to the combination between the verb & an object expressing something blamable. From this comes the further error of supposing that you can extenuate, i.e. make excuses for, a person. (Webster gives 'to excuse' as one definition.) In such cases etymology is of value.

exterior, external, extraneous, extrinsic. Etymologically the four differ only in the formative suffixes used, & there is no reason why any of them might not have acquired the senses of all; *outside* is the fundamental meaning. It will be best to take them in pairs.

1. *exterior* & *external.* That is

exterior which encloses or is outermost, the enclosed or innermost being *interior*. These opposites are chiefly applied to things of which there is a pair, & with conscious reference, when one is spoken of, to the other: *the exterior court* is one within which is an interior court; *the exterior door* has another inside it; *exterior & interior lines* in strategy are concentric curves one enclosing the other.

That is *external* which is without & apart or whose relations are with what is without & apart, that which is within being *internal*. *The external world, external things, external evidence,* illustrate the first part of the definition; *external appearances, worship,* & *action* (those that affect other persons or things somehow) illustrate the second part; *external relations* are those a country has to or with other countries.

In many phrases either *exterior* or *external* may be used, but usually with some difference of underlying meaning; e.g. the *exterior ear* is thought of as the porch of the interior ear, but the *external ear* is the ear as seen by the outsider. Again, *a building's exterior features* & *external features* are different things, the former being those of its outside only, & the latter all, whether of outside or inside, that are visible as opposed to the structure that can only be guessed at. Similarly, with the nouns, *exterior* has the definite narrow material meaning of the outside, as opposed to the inside of a building or the inner nature of a person, while *externals* includes all about a person that reveals him to us, his acts & habits & manner of speech as well as his features & clothes.

2. *extraneous* & *extrinsic*. That is *extraneous* which is brought in, or comes, or has come in, from without. A fly in amber, a bullet in one's chest, are *extraneous bodies; extraneous aid, interference, sounds; extraneous points* are questions imported into a discussion from which they do not naturally arise.

That is *extrinsic* which is not an essential & inherent part of something but is attached to it as a separable belonging, essential properties being *intrinsic*. A florin's *intrinsic value* is what the metal in it would have fetched before it was coined; its *extrinsic value* is what is added by the stamp. A person's *extrinsic advantages* are such things as wealth & family interest, while his courage & talent are *intrinsic advantages*.

It is worth notice that *extrinsic* is now rare, being little used except when a formal contrary is wanted for the still common *intrinsic*. *Extraneous* on the other hand exists on its own account; it has no formal contrary, 'intraneous' being for practical purposes nonexistent, & must make shift with *internal, intrinsic, indigenous, domestic, native,* or whatever else suits the particular context.

exterminate makes *-nable.*

exterritorial. Use EXTRATERRITORIAL.

extinguish. In ordinary contexts, *extinguish* is a pompous word for put out (lights, fire, &c.), e.g. in the US wartime directive, *Extinguish the illumination.* See OFFICIALESE.

extract, n. & v. Pron. noun ex′-, verb -tract′.

extraneous. See EXTERIOR.

extraordinary. Pron. as five syllables (-tror′-), NOT six (-traor-).

ex(tra)territorial(ity). The forms seem to be used quite indifferently. It would certainly be better to have one spelling, & *extra-* is recommended.

extricate makes *-cable.*

extrinsic. See EXTERIOR.

-EY & -Y IN ADJECTIVES. The adjectival suffix is *-y,* not *-ey.* Weak spellers are often in doubt whether, when *-y* is appended to nouns in MUTE E (as *grime*), the *e* is to be dropped or kept. With very few exceptions, it should be dropped (*grimy,* NOT *grimey*). A selection of a few of the commonest *-y* adjectives from nouns in mute *-e* will suffice to show the normal formation, & another list follows this, containing words of the kind in which the bad speller goes wrong. He often does so because he conceives himself to be making a new, or at least hitherto unprinted, word, & is afraid of obscuring its connection with the noun if he drops the *e*—a needless fear. The safe *-y* adjectives are: *briny, fluky, greasy, mazy, miry, oozy, prosy, scaly, shaky, slimy, snaky, spiky, spongy, wiry.* The shaky *-y* adjectives are: *chancy, gamy, horsy, mousy, nervy, nosy, stagy, wavy.*

Some of the exceptions are:

1. When an adjective in *-y* is made from a noun in *-y, e* is inserted to part *y* from *-y: clayey* & *skyey,* NOT *clayy* or *skyy.*

2. *Hole* makes *holey,* to prevent confusion with *holy*=hallowed.

3. Adjectives from nouns in *-ue* (o͞o) retain the *e: gluey* & *bluey,* NOT *gluy* or *bluy.*

eye, v., makes *eying.*

-EY, -IE, -Y, IN DIMINUTIVES. The most established type of all (*baby, daddy, granny*) has *-y.* Most proper names (*Tommy, Polly*) have *-y.* It would be a simplification if *-y* could be made universal; but *-ie* & *-ey* are the only forms in some proper names (*Charlie* or *Charley,* NEVER *Charly; Minnie; Sukey*); *-ie* is preferred in Scotland, the native land of some diminutives (*laddie, lassie, caddie*). The retention of mute *-e,* giving *-ey* (*dovey, lovey, nosey,* &c.), is more defensible than in the adjectives made with *-y;* & generally variety seems unavoidable. Many words about which there is doubt are given in their dictionary places.

eyot. Small island (Brit.). Pron. āt; the OED calls it 'a more usual variant of ait,' & 'an artificial spelling.'

eyrie. Spell US, *aerie;* Brit., *aery.*

F

fable. As distinguished from other short tales, a fable is one, usually with a moral, in which the speakers or actors are animals or inanimate objects. A *fabliau* (pl. *-aux*) is a metrical tale of early French poetry (12th & 13th cc.), usually characterized by broad humor & cynicism.

façade. The cedilla (ç) is usually kept.

facet. One 'face' of a many-sided body, esp. of a cut gem. *Facet* has become a VOGUE WORD in US. Subjects & problems no longer have many phases or aspects, but always *facets.* When tempted to use the word, the writer should remember not only the two alternatives mentioned, but also *sides, views,* and *angles.*

facetious. Witty, jocose, now often deliberately or inappropriately so. For synonymy see JOCOSE.

FACETIOUS FORMATIONS. A few specimens may be collected in groups illustrating more or less distinct types.

Pun or parody: *anecdotage* (anecdote, dotage); *correctitude* (correct, rectitude).

Mock mistakes: *mischevious, splendiferous.*

Portmanteau words: *galumph* (gallop, triumph); *chortle* (snort, chuckle).

Incongruity of Latin trimmings to common English words: *circumbendibus; omnium gatherum; disgruntled; contraption.*

Irreverent familiarity: *blimy* (God blind me); *crickey* (Christ).

Onomatopoeia, obvious or obscure: *ramshackle; pernickety; rumbustious.*

Long & ludicrous: *cantankerous; skedaddle; spiflicate.*

facile. Its value as a synonym for *easy* or *fluent* or *dextrous* lies chiefly in its depreciatory implication. *A facile speaker* or *writer* is one who needs to expend little pains (& whose product is of correspondingly little import); *a facile triumph* or *victory* is easily won (& comes to little). Unless the implication in parentheses is intended, the use of *facile* instead of its commoner synonyms (*a more economical & facile mode; with a* facile *turn of the wrist*) is ill-judged & usually due to AVOIDANCE OF THE OBVIOUS. *Facility* does not have the same derogatory implication.

facilitate. To make easier, help forward, an action or process. *We facilitate an operation,* NOT *the operator.* SLIPSHOD EXTENSION: *The officer was* facilitated *in his search by the occupants.*

fact. (1) *Fact* is well equipped with idiomatic phrases. There are unquestionably established *in fact, in point of fact, as a matter of fact, the fact is,* & *the fact of the matter is,* of which *in fact* is the shortest & usually the best. It is a pity that *as a fact* should be thrust upon us in addition to all these. It will be seen that in each of the quotations one or other of the familiar forms would have been more at home: *He says that a 'considerable part' of the 25 millions is spent on new officials like locusts devouring the land;* as a fact, *barely one-thirtieth of that figure is due to new officials* (as a matter of fact)./*It is quite arguable that the time given might have been better allocated, but* as a fact *nearly all the important points raised have been discussed* (in point of fact)./*The Pan-Germans & Nationalists can afford to be more independent than the Conservatives; &* as a fact *they are so* (in fact). (2) *Before the fact, after the fact,* are legal phrases in which *fact* retains its otherwise obs. meaning, *evil deed, crime.*

fact-finding, as *a fact-finding committee,* is recognized usage; *to fact-find* (*This mission was to* fact-find *on problems of speeding disarmament*) is colloq.

factious, factitious, fictitious. (Given to or pertaining to faction; not natural, artificial; imaginary, invented.) Though the words are not synonyms even of the looser kind, there is a certain danger of confusion between them because there are nouns with which two or all of them can be used, with meanings sometimes more & sometimes less wide apart. Thus *factious rancor* is the rancor that lets party spirit prevail over patriotism; *factitious rancor* is a rancor that is not of natural growth, but has been deliberately created to serve someone's ends; & *fictitious rancor* is a rancor represented as existing but imaginary. A party slogan has *a factious value;* a silver coin, *a factitious value* (cf. extrinsic); & a bogus company's shares, *a fictitious value.*

factotum. Pl. *-ms.*

faerie, faery. Pron. fā′erĭ. 'A variant of *fairy.* In present usage, it is practically a distinct word, adopted either to express Spenser's peculiar modification of the sense, or to exclude various unpoetical or undignified associations connected with the current form *fairy*' (OED). The distinction should be respected by all who care for the interests of the language & not only for their own momentary requirements.

fag(g)ot. US, usually *-g-;* Brit. *-gg-.*

fail. 1. *Failing*='in default of' is a participle developed through the absolute construction into a preposition; *if* or *since so-&-so fails* means the same as *in case of* or *on the failure of so-&-so.* Either the absolute or the prepositional use is accordingly legitimate, but not a mixture of the two. The form *whom failing,* familiar in companies' proxy notices, is such a mixture; it should be either 'failing whom' (preposition & objective) or 'who failing' (absolute & subjective).

2. *Fail* is one of the words apt to cause the sort of lapse noticed in NEGATIVES gone wrong: *New Year's Day is a milestone which the least observant of us* can hardly fail *to pass unnoticed.* Omit *fail to.*

fair(ly). (1) For the idioms *bid fair, fight* or *hit* or *play fair, fair between the eyes,* &c., *speak one fair,* see UNIDIOMATIC -LY. (2) For the avoidance of ambiguity it should be remembered that *fairly* has the two oddly different senses of *utterly* (*I was* fairly *beside myself*) & *moderately* (*a* fairly *good translation*), & that context does not always make it clear which is meant.

fairy. (1) For *fairyland* & *faerie,* see FAERIE. (2) *Fairy* & *fay.* The difference is not in meaning, but merely in appropriateness to different contexts; *fairy* being now the everyday form, *fay* should be reserved for occasions demanding the unusual.

fait accompli. 'Thing accomplished,' done, presumably irrevocable & no longer worth arguing about. Pron. fĕ tȧ kôɴ plē. But see FRENCH WORDS.

faithfully. (1) In *promise faithfully, faithfully* is an ultra-colloquial substitute for *definitely, explicitly, expressly, emphatically,* or *solemnly.* (2) *Deal faithfully with* is a phrase of biblical sound & doubtless of puritan origin, now used for the most part jocularly in the sense not treat with tenderness, punish or rebuke–one of the idioms that should not be spoiled by over-frequent use.

fakir, fakeer, faquir. For the religious mendicant &c., the first is the est. form. Pron. fāk′ẽr. The swindler is *faker.*

falcon. In US usually pron. fôl′kŭn, Brit. usually fawkn.

fall. The noun *fall* as a synonym for *autumn,* now chiefly US, was current in England as early as the 16th c. Americans should have the courage to keep it alive.

fallacious. Embodying a fallacy, hence misleading, as *fallacious reasoning;* disappointing, delusive, as *fallacious hopes, a fallacious peace.*

fallacy (Log.): 'deception.' A fallacy in logic is 'an argument which violates the laws of correct demonstration. An argument may be fallacious in matter (i.e. misstatements of facts), in wording (i.e. wrong use of words), or in the process of inference. Fallacies have therefore been classified as: (1) Material, (2) Verbal, (3) Logical or Formal' (Encycl. Brit.). Some types of fallacy are of frequent enough occurrence to have earned names that have passed into ordinary speech, & serve as a short way of announcing to a false reasoner that his conscious or unconscious sophistry is detected. Such are *arguing in a circle, equivocation, begging the question, ignoratio elenchi, argumentum ad hominem,* &c., *petitio principii, non sequitur, post hoc ergo propter hoc, false analogy, undistributed middle,* all of which will be found alphabetically placed.

false analogy (Log.): 'erroneous correspondence.' The unfounded assumption that a thing that has certain attributes in common with another will resemble it also in some attribute in which it is not known to do so; e.g. that of a pair of hawks the larger is the male, on the ground that other male animals are larger than female; or that *idiosyncracy* is the right spelling because words ending in the sound -krasi are spelled with *-cy.*

FALSE EMPHASIS. 1. *That being so, we say that it would be shameful if domestic servants were* the only class *of employed persons left outside the scheme of State Insurance.* What the writer means is 'It would be shameful for servants to be left out when all other employees are included.' What he says means 'It would be shameful for nobody except servants to be excluded'—which is plainly neither true nor his contention. The disaster is due to his giving too emphatic a place to a subordinate, though important, point; what is shameful is the servants' exclusion, not the inclusion of anyone or everyone else. Care must be taken that, an two men ride of a horse, the groom & not the master rides behind.

2. An especially common form of false emphasis is the use of the emphatic word *both* (which means one as well as the other, or in one case as well as in the other) in places where that full sense is either unnecessary or impossible, instead of *the two, they,* or nothing at all. The point is clear if the two sentences (a) *Both fought well* & (b) *To settle the matter both fought* are compared. In (a) emphasis is wanted; not only one fought well, the other did too; but in (b) of course one did not fight without the other's fighting, since it takes two to make a fight; the needless *both* makes the reader wonder whom else they both fought. Obvious as the mistake is, it is surprising how often it occurs in sentences little more abstruse than (b). WRONG: Both *men had something in common* (with whom?

with each other; then why not *the two*, or *the men*, or *the two men*, or simply *they*?)./*At present there is a complete divergence in the proposals of* both *Governments* (the two, *or* the). An instance at once more excusable & more fatal, both for the same reason, that hard thinking is necessary to get the thing disentangled, is: *This company has found that the men they employ in America can be depended on to produce a minimum of 40% more output than the men they employ abroad, & yet these men* both in America & elsewhere *may be of the same race & nationality at birth.* The point is not that in America, & just as much in (say) Italy, these men may be (say) Czechs, but that of any two men or any two sets of which one is employed in America & the other in Italy both may be (say) Italians; it is not that America & Italy are in some matter alike, but that the difference between the employee in one & the employee in the other is constant; *both,* inserted where it is, hopelessly disguises this; read *these men of whom one is employed in America & one elsewhere.*

falsehood, falseness, falsity. Differentiation has been busy with the three, but has perhaps not yet done with them. At present *a falsehood* is a lie; *falsehood* is lying regarded as an action, but it is also a statement or statements contrary to fact or the truth. *Falseness* is contrariness to fact regarded as a quality of statement, but it is also lying & deception regarded as an element in character. *Falsity* is interchangeable with *falseness* in its first but not in its second sense. In the following examples the word used is, except where an alternative is shown, the only one of the three consistent with modern usage: *You told a* falsehood; *He was convicted of a* falsehood; *Truth would be suppressed together with* falsehood; *Truth exaggerated may become* falsehood; *The* falseness (or falsity) *of this conclusion is obvious;* A falseness *that even his plausibility could not quite conceal.*

falsetto. Pl. *-os.*

famed. In the sense of famous, renowned, now obs. except when used as predicate (constr. *for*): *A man* famed for *his scientific discoveries;* famed for *humor;* or with a prefixed adj.: *far-famed, ever-famed.*

fanatic. The word tends to lose its fully adjectival use. We say *I call a man fanatical* (or *a fanatic,* but not simply *fanatic*) *who . . .*

fantasia. US usually făn tā′-zhȧ; Brit. fahntahzē′ah, fantah′-zĭa. The second (-zē′-) is the Italian pronunciation, advisable at least for the technical musical term.

fantasy, phantasy. In modern use the predominant sense of the former is 'caprice, whim, fanciful invention,' while that of the latter is 'imagination, visionary notion.'

far. 1. (*So*) *far from. So far from 'running' the Conciliation Bill, the Suffragettes only reluctantly consented to it.* This idiom is a curious, but established, mixture of *Far from running it they consented to it reluctantly* & *They were so far from running it that they consented to it reluctantly.* It is always open, however, to those who dislike illogically to drop the *so* in the short form—*Far from running it they consented* *to it reluctantly.* But it is waste labor to tilt against STURDY INDEFENSIBLES.

2. *Far-flung. The far-flung battle line, our far-flung empire,* &c. The emotional value of this as a VOGUE WORD is reckoned so high as often to outweigh such trifling matters as appropriateness: *Set against all its* [the war's] *burden of sorrow & suffering & waste that millions of men from* far-flung lands *have been taught to know each other better.* The lands are distant; they are not far-flung; but what matter? *far-flung* is a signal that our blood is to be stirred; & so it is, if we do not stop to think.

3. *As & so far as. As* or *so far as x* cannot be used short for *as far as x goes* or *so far as concerns x;* in the following examples *concerns, regards, is concerned, goes,* &c., should have been inserted where omission is indicated. WRONG: *As far as getting the money he asked for*^, *Mr. Churchill had little difficulty./The result was that the men practically met with a defeat so far as*^*obtaining a definite pledge in regard to their demands.*

As or *so far as,* regarded as a compound preposition, is followed primarily by a word of place (*went as far as New York*); secondarily it may have a noun (which may be an infinitive or gerund) that expresses a limit of advance or progress (*He knows algebra* as far as *quadratics; I have gone* so far as *to collect*—or *so far as collecting—statistics*). But when the purpose is to say not how far an action proceeds, but within what limits a statement is to be applied, as in the examples at the beginning of this section, *as* & *so far as* are not prepositions, but conjunctions requiring a verb. The genesis of the misuse may be guessed at thus: *I have gone so far as collecting statistics* (RIGHT). *As far as collecting statistics you have my leave to proceed* (CORRECT, but unnatural order). *As far as collecting statistics he is competent enough* (cf. knows algebra as far as quadratics; DEFENSIBLE, but better insert *goes;* the Churchill sentence quoted is just below this level). *As far as collecting statistics, only industry is necessary* (IMPOSSIBLE; *is concerned* or its equivalent must be inserted).

4. *So far as, so far that. His efforts were so far successful* (a) *as they reduced,* or (b) *as to reduce,* or (c) *that they reduced, the percentage of deaths.* The (b) & (c) forms mean the same, & their interpretation is not in doubt: he reduced the percentage, & had that success. The meaning of (a) is different: if you want to know whether & how far he succeeded, find out whether & how far he reduced the percentage; perhaps he did not reduce it, & therefore failed. But the (a) form is not infrequently used wrongly instead of (b) or (c): (WRONG) *The previous appeal made by M. Delcassé was* so far *successful* as *the Tsar himself sent orders to comply* (read *that* for *as;* the sending of orders clearly took place, & such sending is not a variable by the degree of which success could be measured).

5. *In so far* (*as*), by analogy with *inasmuch,* is often in US printed as one word and is a favorite with some writers. But see IN SO FAR.

6. *Far to seek* remains a cur-

rent idiom; *far to find* is archaic.

faraway, adj. US one word, Brit. usually hyphened.

farce (Lit.): 'stuffing.' ('That species of drama whose sole aim is to excite laughter.') The connection with the etymological sense lies in the meaning 'interpolation,' the farce having originated in interludes of buffoonery in religious dramas.

far-fetched, -flung, -reaching, -seeing, all hyphened.

farther, further. 'In standard English the form *farther* is usually preferred where the word is intended to be the comparative of *far,* while *further* is used where the notion of *far* is altogether absent; there is a large intermediate class of instances in which the choice between the two forms is arbitrary' (OED), with which most US dictionaries concur.

This seems to be too strong a statement, or a statement of what might be a useful differentiation rather than of one actually developed or even developing. The fact is surely that hardly anyone uses the two words for different occasions; most people prefer one to the other for all purposes, & the preference of the majority is for *further;* the most that should be said is perhaps that *farther* is not common except where distance is in question. The three pairs of quotations following are selected for comparison from the OED stores.

1. Comparative of *far: If you can bear your load no* farther, *say so.*—H. Martineau. *It was not thought safe for the ships to proceed* further *in the darkness.*—Macaulay.

2. No notion of *far: Down he sat without* farther *bidding.*—Dickens. *I now proceed to some* further *instances.*—De Morgan.

3. Intermediate: *Punishment cannot act any* farther *than in as far as the idea of it is present in the mind.*—Bentham. *Men who pretend to believe no* further *than they can see.*—Berkeley.

On the whole, though differentiations are good in themselves, it is less likely that one will be established for *farther* & *further* than that the latter will become universal. In the verb, *further* is very much more common.

fascist &c. The Italian words —*fascista,* pl. *-ti, fascismo*—are pronounced (roughly) fahshē'stah, -tē, -ē'smo. In English they should be fashĭ'sta, -tē, -iz'mo, or else anglicized to *fascist,* pl. *-s, -ism* (pron. făsh'ĭst &c.).

fastidious means over-nice, difficult to please in matters of taste or propriety, easily disgusted, squeamish. It does not mean merely sensitive or 'particular.'

fatalism, determinism. The philosophical distinction between the words cannot here be more than roughly suggested, & is itself more or less arbitrary. *Fatalism* says: Every event is preordained; you cannot act as you will, but only in the preordained way. *Determinism* says: You can act (barring obstacles) as you will; but then you cannot will as you will; will is determined by a complex of antecedents the interaction of which makes you unable to choose any but the one course. That is, *fatalism* assumes an external power decreeing irresistibly every event from the greatest to the least, while *determinism* assumes the dependence of all things, including the wills of living beings, upon sequences of cause & effect that would be ascertainable if we were omniscient. The difference between the two views as practical guides to life is not great; one assures us that what is to be will be, the other that whatever is cannot but be; & either assurance relieves us of responsibility; but those are *determinists* who decline to make assumptions (involving the ancient notion of Fate) about an external directing will.

Such, very roughly, is the difference between the two theories; but the popular distinction today is not between the names of two contrasted theories, but between the name of an abstract philosophy & that of a practical rule of life. *Determinism* is the merely intellectual opinion that the determinist or fatalist account of all that happens is true; *fatalism* is the frame of mind that disposes one at once to abandon the hope of influencing events & to repudiate responsibility for one's actions; *determinism* is regarded as a philosophy, & *fatalism* as a faith.

fateful. NOVELTY-HUNTING, the desire to avoid so trite a word as *fatal*, is responsible for many *fatefuls*. There was a reason good enough for inventing *fateful*, in the restriction of the older *fatal* to a bad sense; *fateful* could mean big with happy fate as well as with unhappy. But to use *fateful*, as in the quotation below, where *fatal* would do as well is to renounce the advantage gained by its invention, & to sacrifice the interests of the language to one's own momentary desire for a gewgaw. WRONG: *Will the Irish question, which has been* fateful *to so many Governments, prove one of the explosive forces which will drive the Coalition asunder?* Correct to *fatal.* See PAIRS & SNARES.

father, v., in the sense fix the paternity of, is followed only by *on* or *upon* (the father or author). WRONG: *The idea, which the advocates of compulsory service have attempted* to father on to *him . . .* Impossible English; see CAST-IRON IDIOM.

fathom. (Orig. the length of the outstretched arms, now 6 feet, used esp. in taking soundings. So the verb, penetrate, see through, thoroughly understand.) *Six* &c. *fathom,* rather than *fathoms;* see COLLECTIVES 3.

faucet for *tap* is est. US (Brit. dial.). Pron. fô-.

fault. *I am at fault*=I am puzzled; *I am in fault=I am to blame.* These are the traditional idioms, but in US the differentiation has almost disappeared. Webster still lists *'at fault*=in fault, *colloq.*,' but other recent dictionaries have ceased to so label it.

One finds *fault in* a person or thing (i.e. discovers or perceives a fault). *The only fault I find in our present practice . . .* To find *fault with* means to criticize unfavorably, express dissatisfaction, censure: *No fault was found* with *my suggestions.*

faun, satyr, yahoo. The first two are the Latin & the Greek names for woodland creatures, half beast & half man in form, half beast & half god in nature.

Horse's tail & ears, goat's tail & horns, goat's ears & tail & legs, budding horns, are various symbols marking not the difference between the two, but that between either of them & man. The *faun* is now regarded rather as the type of unsophisticated & the *satyr* of unpurified man. The first is man still in intimate communion with Nature, the second is man still swayed by bestial passions. *Satyr* has probably had its implications fixed by association with *yahoo,* the type of man at his most despicable, for which see *Gulliver* Pt. IV; *faun* has not been affected by this.

fauna, flora, are singular nouns used as collectives, not plurals like *carnivora* &c. Their plurals, rarely needed, are *faunas* & *floras,* or *faunae* & *florae.* They are Latin goddess names made to stand for the realm of animals & of flowers, esp. as represented in any given district.

faux pas. ('False step'), fig. a slip, esp. one that is against convention or propriety. Sing. & pl., pron. fō pä (or pl. pron. in Eng. fō päz). See FRENCH WORDS.

favo(u)r. US *-or,* Brit. *-our.* The verb in the sense 'to resemble' (*He favors his father's side of the family*) is colloq.; in the sense of 'sparing, dealing gently with' (*He favors the left foreleg*) colloq. or dial.

fay. In usual contexts, use FAIRY.

feasible. With those who feel that the use of an ordinary word for an ordinary notion does not do justice to their vocabulary or sufficiently exhibit their cultivation (see WORKING & STYLISH WORDS), *feasible* is now a prime favorite. Its proper sense is 'capable of being done, accomplished, or carried out' (OED). That is, it means the same as *possible* in one of the latter's senses, & its true function is to be used instead of *possible* where that might be ambiguous. A thunderstorm is *possible* (but not *feasible*). Irrigation is *possible* (or, indifferently, *feasible*). A counter-revolution is *possible;* i.e. (a) one may for all we know happen, or (b) we can if we choose bring one about; but, if (b) is the meaning, *feasible* is better than *possible* because it cannot properly bear sense (a) & therefore obviates ambiguity.

The wrong use of *feasible* is that in which, by SLIPSHOD EXTENSION, it is allowed to have also the other sense of *possible,* & that of *probable, likely.* This is described by the OED as 'hardly a justifiable sense etymologically, & . . . recognized by no dictionary.' It is, however, becoming very common; in the quotations, it will be seen that the natural word would be either *probable* or *possible,* one of which should have been chosen. WRONG: *I think it is very* feasible *that the strike may be brought to an end this week . . ./Witness said it was quite* feasible *that if he had had night binoculars he would have seen the iceberg earlier./We ourselves believe that this is the most* feasible *explanation of the tradition.*

feature, v. To make a feature of, give special prominence to, as *A new star is* featured *in this picture,* is US colloq. & should be left to the entertainment world.

fecund. Fertile, prolific, fruitful (in offspring or vegetation), lit. & fig. The OED gives precedence to fĕ′-; US dictionaries to fē′-.

federation, confederation, confederacy. There is no rigid distinction between the words. Politically they all mean a union of states on a federal basis, i.e. in which each state retains local or internal powers. *Federation* implies a closer union than the other two (e.g. the United States). *Confederation* is usually restricted to a permanent union of sovereign states for common action in relation to externals (the proposed 'United States of Europe'?). *Confederacy* suggests a looser and usually temporary union, but is often used interchangeably with *confederation.*

feel, v. The idiom is *to feel bad,* not *badly. Feel like* (*I feel like being alone,* i.e. have an inclination for) is chiefly (US) colloq. *Feel of* (*Let me feel of the texture*) is now chiefly dial. *Feel,* n., *the feel of spring is in the air, soft to the feel, the feel of an insect's bite, a homely feel,* is standard usage.

felicitate. A FORMAL WORD for *wish* (*you*) *joy, congratulate.*

fellow & hyphens. All the combinations of *fellow* with a noun (except *fellow-feeling,* for which see below) are best written without hyphens & are usually so given in US dictionaries. (Brit. dictionaries give a hyphen in some—*fellow-countryman, fellow-citizen,* &c.). *Fellow-feeling,* which in US is usually two words, would be better written with the hyphen. Combinations in which *fellow* is the second element—*bedfellow, schoolfellow, playfellow*—are given as single words.

female, feminine, womanly, womanish. The fundamental difference between *female* & *feminine* is that the first is wider, referring things to the sex, human or not, while the other is limited to the human part of the sex. This would leave it indifferent in many contexts which word should be used; & yet we all know that, even in such contexts, nearly always one & not the other is idiomatic: *female ruler* & *cook,* but *feminine rule* & *cookery; female attire, children, organs,* but *feminine gender, curiosity, arguments;* & *female* & *feminine education* mean different things. It is clearly not true that *feminine* is always to be preferred when the reference is to human females only, since *female attire, female servant,* are better than *feminine attire* & *servant.*

A *female* is, shortly put, a *she,* or, put more at length, a *woman-or-girl-or-cow-or-hen-or-the-like.* The noun use is the original; but, like all nouns, the word can be used attributively, & through the attributive use this noun has passed into an adjective. The *female sex* is the sex of which all members are *shes;* that is the attributive use. Passing to, or rather toward, the full adjectival use, we say so-&-so is *female,* meaning that it is of or for the female sex. Beyond that point as an adjective *female* has not gone; *feminine,* on the other hand, is not a noun that has gone part way to complete adjectivehood; it has been an adjective all its life, & means not merely of or for women, but of the kind that characterizes or may be expected from or is associated with women. That is, there are two factors in choosing between *female* & *feminine,* (a) that of the difference between all sex & human sex, & (b) that of the difference between the noun-adjective & the true adjective.

The result is this: when the information wanted is the answer to the question *Of* (or *for*) *which sex?* use *female,* provided that the context sufficiently indicates the limitation to humankind; when the question is *Of what sort?*, use *feminine.* So we get *female companion, Paul Pry,* but *feminine companionship, curiosity; female children, servants, the female ward* of a prison; *female education* is the education provided for (of course, human) females, while *feminine education* is that which tends to cultivate the qualities characteristic of women. *Feminine* is the epithet for *beauty, features, arguments, pursuits, sympathy, weakness, spite,* & the like. *The feminine gender* is the one that includes nouns resembling women's names; a man may be called *feminine,* but not *female,* if he is like women. (For *female* or *feminine rhyme* &c., see MALE 2.)

Womanly is used only to describe qualities peculiar to (a) good women as opposed to men (*womanly compassion, sympathy, intuition,* &c.) or (b) developed women as opposed to girls (*womanly beauty, figure, experience*). *Womanish* is usually used of a man, meaning resembling or like a woman. It is often used when the meaning is less derogatory than *effeminate.*

female, woman. *Female* in its noun use is sometimes convenient as a word that includes girls as well as women, & sometimes as including non-human as well as human female creatures. Where such inclusion is not specially desired, to call a woman a female is exactly as impolite as to call a lady a woman, without any of the sentimental implications that often make *woman* preferable to *lady;* it is reasonably resented. It is not reasonable to extend this resentment to the adj. use of *female;* but it is the mistaken extension that probably accounts for the apparent avoidance of the natural phrase *female suffrage* & the use of the clumsy *woman suffrage* instead. As with *female education* (for which see the previous article), *female suffrage* is the short for the suffrage of (of course, human) female creatures, i.e. women. To turn *woman* into an adj. with *female* ready made is mere perversity.

FEMININE DESIGNATIONS. This article is intended as a counter-protest. The authoress, poetess, & paintress, & sometimes the patroness & the inspectress, take exception to the indication of sex in these designations. They regard the distinction as derogatory to them & as implying inequality between the sexes; an author is an author, that is all that concerns any reader, & it is impertinent curiosity to want to know whether the author is male or female.

These ladies neither are nor pretend to be making their objection in the interests of the language or of people in general; they object in their own interests only. But general convenience & the needs of English, if these are against them, must be reckoned of more importance than their sectional claims.

With the coming extension of women's vocations, feminines for vocation words are a special need of the future. Everyone knows the inconvenience of being uncertain whether a doctor is a man or a woman; hesitation in establishing the word *doctress* is amazing in a people regarded as nothing if not practical. Far from needing to reduce the number of our sex words, we should do well to indulge in real neologisms such as *teacheress, singeress,* & *danceress,* the want of which drives us to *cantatrice, danseuse,* & the like; *authoress* & *poetess* & *paintress* are not neologisms.

But are not the objectors, besides putting their own interests above those of the public, actually misjudging their own? Their view is that the female author is to raise herself to the level of the male author by asserting her right to his name; but if there is one profession in which more than in others the woman is the man's equal it is acting; & the actress is not known to resent the indication of her sex. The proof of real equality will be not the banishment of *authoress* as a degrading title, but its establishment on a level with *author.* Nor, after all, does an authoress, a doctoress, a lioness, a prophetess, cease to be an author, a doctor, a lion, or a prophet because she ends in *-ess.* She should call herself, & still more allow us without protest to call her, by the common or the feminine title according to the requirements of the occasion; *George Eliot the authoress* would then be as much more frequent than *George Eliot the author* as the *prophetess Deborah* than the *prophet Deborah.*

feminineness, feminism, &c. *Feminineness, femininity,* & *feminity* are competitors for the sense of woman's nature & qualities, none of them perceptibly differentiated in meaning. *Feminineness* is a word that does not depend on usage or dictionary-makers for its right to exist. *Femininity* & *feminity* are both as old as the 14th c. & have been in use ever since; of the two, *femininity* is the more correct form, & has become the standard word in both US & Brit., *feminity* being much less commonly used.

Femininism & *feminism* now have meanings different both from the above & from each other. *Femininism* means (a) an expression or idiom peculiar to women (*'Fascinating' is a femininism*); & *effeminacy* now is used for the tendency in a man to feminine habits. *Feminism* (with *feminist* attached) means faith in women, advocacy of the rights of women, the prevalence of female influence.

feral. (Untamed, wild, brutal.) Pron. fē'-.

ferret, v., makes *-eted* &c.

fer(r)ule. The cap or ring for a stick has two *rs*; the teacher's implement (now in allusive use only) has one *r,* & is also spelled *ferula.* The two words are of separate origin.

fertile. US dictionaries (& OED) give precedence to -ĭl; -il is now usual in Brit.

fervent, fervid. Both in fig. use mean intense, ardent, impassioned. *Fervid* is in modern usage more poetical and less usual, and often carries a 'feverish' connotation.

fervo(u)r. US usually *-or,* Brit. *-our.*

festal, festive. Both words point to *feast* or *festival,* but the reference in *festal* is more direct; a person is in *festal mood* if there is a festival & he is in tune with it, but he may be in a *festive mood* even if he is merely feeling as he might if it were a festival. *A festal day, in festal costume; a festive scene, the festive board.* The distinction is not regularly observed, but, such as it is, it accounts for the continued existence of the two words. There is something of the same difference between *festival* & *festivity* or *festivities.*

fête. In US usually *fete.*

fetid, foetid. Spell & pron. fĕ′tid ('etymologically preferable,' OED).

fetish, fetich(e). The modern *-ish* seems to have superseded the older *-iche.* US usually pronounced fēt- (Brit. usually fĕt-). Though it has the air of a mysterious barbarian word, it is in reality the same as *factitious,* & means (like an idol, the work of men's hands) 'a made thing.' Its fig. use covers anything irrationally reverenced or held sacrosanct.

FETISHES, or current literary rules misapplied or unduly revered. Among the more notable or harmful are: SPLIT INFINITIVES; avoidance of repetition (see ELEGANT VARIATIONS); the rule of thumb for AND WHICH; a craze for English words (see SAXONISM); pedantry on the foreign spelling of foreign words (see MORALE); the notion that RELIABLE, AVERSE TO, & DIFFERENT TO are marks of the uneducated; the rule of thumb for *and* & *or* in ENUMERATION FORMS; the dread of a PREPOSITION AT THE END; the idea that successive metaphors are mixed METAPHOR; the belief that common words lack dignity (see FORMAL WORDS).

fetus. In US generally so spelled. Brit. FOETUS.

feverish, feverous. The differentiation is incomplete. What can be done to help it is to abstain from *feverish* in the sense apt to cause fever (of places, conditions, &c.), & from *feverous* both in the literal sense suffering from fever, feeling or showing symptoms of fever, & in the metaphorical sense excited or eager or restless. This would be in conformity with the present tendency, which, though often disregarded, is plainly observable.

few. 1. *Comparatively few* should not be preceded by *a* or *the.* The idiom is *A few* (people) *were there. Very few were there. Comparatively few were there. A very few* is grammatically permissible also, but NOT *a comparatively few* (e.g. *In a very few years all will be changed.* In this case, *very* is an adj., not an adv.). It may be added that *Very few people were there* is better than *A very few people were there,* because *few* means *some & not many,* while *a few* means *some and not* NONE, so that *few* is better fitted than *a few* for combination with words expressing degree like *very.*

2. *Fewer number(s)* is a solecism, obvious as soon as one thinks, but becoming common, correct to *smaller* in (WRONG): *Fortunately the* number *of persons on board was* fewer *than usual./ The* fewer number *of*

days or hours we are . . . the better it will be./ The bird seems to have reached us in fewer numbers *this year.*

fez. Pl. *fezzes,* adj. *fezzed.*

fiancé, -ée. These are now standard words for a betrothed person (m. & f.) and in US are no longer italicized. See INTENDED.

fiasco. Pl. *-oes,* or *-os.* The Italian word means 'bottle' or 'flask,' and *far fiasco,* fig., to break down or fail in a dramatic performance. Hence in general sense, *fiasco* is any ignominious or ridiculous failure.

fiber, -bre. US usually *-er,* Brit. *-re.*

fictitious, fictional. *Fictitious:* feigned, imaginary, unreal; *fictional:* pertaining to or of the nature of fiction. *Fictitious claims; The facts in poetry, being avowedly fictitious, are not false. Fictional literature, a fictional character.* See also FACTIOUS &c.

fiddle. If the word is, as the OED says, 'now only in familiar or contemptuous use' (Webster, 'colloq.'), it is matter for regret, & those who defy this canon deserve well of the language. Violinists like to speak of their *fiddles* (but few of them like to be called *fiddlers*).

fidget, v., makes *-eting* &c.

fiducial, fiduciary. The second is the ordinary form, *fiducial* being used only in some technical terms.

fidus Achates. (Faithful Achates, companion of Aeneas; hence devoted follower, trusted henchman.) Pron. fī′dus akā′tēz.

-fied. The spelling of the jocular compounds in which a verb in *-fy* hardly exists is unsettled (*countrified* or *countryfied* &c.). It seems best to use *-i-* when the noun or adjective does not provide a convenient connecting syllable, but, when it does, not to alter it; in US the spellings recommended are *cockneyfied, countrified, dandified, Frenchified, ladyfied,* &c.

field, in the sense of space proper to something (*field of action, each in his own field,* &c.). The synonyms for this are remarkably numerous; the distinctions & points of agreement between these are fortunately obvious enough not to need elaborate setting forth; but a characteristic phrase or so for each word, may be useful.

A debate covering a wide area. *Unsurpassed in his own* branch. *Expenses beyond my* compass. *In every* department *of human activity. Belongs to the* domain *of philosophy. Distinguished in many* fields; *is beyond the* field *of vision. In the whole* gamut *of crime. Stick to your* last. *Unconscious of his* limits. *Casuistry is not in my* line. *A very unsuitable* locale. *Talking beside the* point. *It is not our* province *to inquire. Comes within the* purview *of the Act. Constantly straying from the* question. *Outside the* range *of practical politics. Operating within a narrow* radius. *In the whole* realm *of Medicine. Don't travel outside the* record. *Such evidence is precluded by our* reference. *In the* region *of metaphysics. Any note in the lower* register. *Whatever the* scale *of effort required. A* scene *of confusion. Find* scope *for one's powers; limit the* scope *of the inquiry. Useful in his own* sphere. *Wanders from the* subject. *Get to the end of one's* tether. *Has chosen an ill-defined* theme. With all these to choose from it should be easy to avoid overworking the current VOGUE WORDS *area* and *department*.

fiend, even in its general & fig. sense, suggests cruelty, wickedness. Its use for *addict* is colloq.

fiery. Two syllables (fīr′ĭ).

fifth(ly). Both the *-f-* & the *-th* should be, but are often not, clearly sounded.

fifth column. (Orig. in Spanish Civil War.) Secret supporters of the enemy within the defense line. (Gen. Mala was leading 4 columns of troops against Madrid. The '5th column' referred to those supporters already inside the city.)

FIGURATIVE USE OF WORDS (fig.). Metaphorical, not literal; e.g. *fall,* n., lit. means a dropping down from a height, by force of gravity. Fig. it means a descent from a high estate or from moral elevation. In *He was killed in a* fall *from the roof, fall* is lit.; *in the* fall *of the Roman Empire, fall* is fig. See METAPHOR.

figure, figurant, figurative, &c. All pronounced fĭg′ūr- in US. In Brit., 'while it is pedantic to pronounce *figure* otherwise than as fĭ′*ger,* it is slovenly to let the natural English laxity go to this extreme with the less familiar *figuration, figurative, figurant, figurine,* &c.' (fĭgūrā′shn &c.).

filibuster, v. & n. In US, (to) delay action (in assembly) by dilatory motions, speeches, & other artifices. The word is not an Americanism in other senses now obs. It comes from a Dutch word meaning 'freebooter' and is found in English as early as the 16th c. (spelled then *flibutor*).

fils. Fr. son, used (as Jr. in US) after names: *Dumas fils.* Pron. fēs.

filthy lucre. See HACKNEYED PHRASES, & IRRELEVANT ALLUSION.

finance. Preferably pron. fĭnăns′ (both n. & v.); fī′năns is a US alternate. *Financier,* US usually fĭnansēr′, Brit. fĭnăn′sĭer.

fin de siècle. Lit. 'close of the century'; spec. of the (French) 19th c.; hence characteristic of it; hence (often) decadent. Pron. făɴ dē syâkl'. But see FRENCH WORDS.

fine, adj. *Not to put* too fine *a point upon it* is an apology for a downright expression, & means 'to put it bluntly.'

fine, n. *In fine,* a phrase now seldom used except in writing of a rather formal kind, has entirely lost the sense, which it once had, of *at last.* It is still sometimes used for *finally* or *lastly,* i.e. to introduce the last of a series of parallel constructions; but in the interests of clearness it is better that it should be confined to its predominant modern use, = *in short* or *in fact* or *to sum up,* introducing a single general statement that wraps up in itself several preceding particular ones.

finical, finicking, finikin. All that can be said with certainty about the derivation of the words & their mutual relations seems to be that *-al* is recorded 70 years earlier than the others. As to choice between them, the English termination *-cking* is best calculated to express a hearty contempt for the tenuity naturally symbolized by the three short *is*; *-cal* is now chiefly in lit. & not colloq. use. *Finicky* is a US variant.

fiord, fjord. The dictionaries give precedence to *fi-*. The other spelling is apparently used in English only to help the ignorant to call it fyord; as instead of helping them it only puzzles them, it should be abandoned.

firearms. 'The singular is late & rare in use' (OED; which, however, quotes 'the report of a fire-arm' from Thackeray). Brit. *fire-arms.*

fir, pine. Most of us have wished vaguely & vainly at times that we knew a fir from a pine. Although it is plain that the matter concerns the botanist more than the man in the street, the following from the Encycl. Brit. may be useful: 'The firs are distinguished from the pines & larches by having their needle-like leaves placed singly on the shoots instead of growing in clusters from a sheath on a dwarf branch. Their cones are composed of thin, rounded, closely imbricated scales.' Pines differ 'from the firs in their hard woody cone-scales being thickened at the apex, & in their slender needle-shaped leaves growing from a membranous sheath either in pairs or from three to five together.'

first. (1) For *first* &c. *floor*, see FLOOR. (2) For *first* &c. *form*, see FORM. (3) *First thing* is equally idiomatic with *the first thing* (*shall do it first thing when I get there*). (4) *The first two* &c., *the two* &c. *first*. When the meaning is not the possible but uncommon one of 'the two of which each alike is first,' modern logic has decided that *the first two* is right & *the two first*, though the older idiom, wrong. Since many find themselves unable to remember which is logical without working it out, & disinclined to do that afresh every time, the simplest way is to suit the treatment of 2, 3, & 4 to that of larger numbers; no one would say *the* 23 *first* instead of *the first* 23, & neither should one say *the two first* instead of *the first two.*

first(ly). The preference for *first* over *firstly* in formal enumerations is one of the harmless pedantries in which those who like oddities because they are odd are free to indulge, provided that they abstain from censuring those who do not share the liking. It is true that *firstly* is not in Johnson; it is true that De Quincey labels it 'your ridiculous & most pedantic neologism of *firstly*'; the boot is on the other leg now; it is the pedant that begins his list with *first;* no one does so by the light of nature; it is an artificialism. Webster says: 'Many prefer the word *first* for this use.' Idioms grow old like other things, & the idiom book of a century hence will probably not even mention *first, secondly.*

fiscal. The fiscal year is that between one annual balancing of financial accounts and the next. (US government: ending 30 June; Brit. & Can.: 31 Mar.)

fish. In usual contexts *fish* (collective sing.) is used for the plural. *Fishes* is used to signify diversity in kind or species, or in a distributive sense.

fisher(man). *Fisher* (a person) is archaic; *fisherman* usually implies one whose occupation is to catch fish, but is sometimes used of the sportsman, for whom *angler* is also used.

fix. (1) *Fixedly.* Three syllables. (2) *Fixedness, fixity. Fixedness* is preferable in the sense intentness, perhaps from the connection with *fixedly;* in other senses the doubt about its pronunciation (it should have three syllables) has caused it to give place to *fixity;* compare *Looking at her with mild* fixedness with *The unbending* fixity *of a law of nature.* (3) *Fix up* (arrange or organize) and *fixings* (apparatus or trimmings) were both orig. colloq. Americanisms but are now naturalized in England.

fixation has been almost completely appropriated by the psychologists and chemists; in general usage its psychological significance is usually meant—a strong attachment or association. But see POPULARIZED TECHNICALITIES.

fiz(z). Use *-zz.*

flaccid. (Limp, flabby.) Pron. -ks-.

flageolet. (Small wood-wind instrument.) Pron. flăjolĕt′.

flail-like. Keep the hyphen.

flair means keen scent, capacity for getting on the scent of something desired, a good nose for something. The following quotations illustrate the risks taken (see FOREIGN DANGER) by writers who pick up their French at second hand. WRONG: *And I was eager to burst upon a civilian world with all the* flaire [sic] *of a newly discovered prima donna./Mrs. —— has homely accomplishments; a* flair *for cooking goes with her* flair *for writing.*

flamboyant is a word borrowed from writers on architecture, who apply it to the French style (contemporary with the English perpendicular) characterized by tracery whose wavy lines suggest the shape or motion of tongues of flame. It is now fashionable in transf. senses; but whereas it should be synonymous with *flowing* or *flexible* or *sinuous* or *free,* it is more often made to mean *florid* or *showy* or *vividly colored* or *courting publicity.* A word of which the true & the usual meanings are at odds is ambiguous & could well be spared. See POPULARIZED TECHNICALITIES.

flamingo. Pl. *-os.*

flammable means the same as *inflammable:* capable of being easily ignited. It is used chiefly by technical writers (*flammable* and *non-flammable substances*); in ordinary contexts the older *inflammable* is better.

flatulence, -cy. The prevailing form is *-ce; -cy* might well be disused, unless it were worth while to assign it the fig. sense of verbosity, & that sense is hardly common enough to need a special form.

flaunt, flout. *Flaunt,* to wave proudly, display boastfully, to show off, parade (oneself); *flout,* with which it is sometimes confused, means to mock, insult, scoff at.

flautist, flutist. It is a comfort to learn from the OED that *flutist* (1603) is a much older word than *flautist* (1860). With three centuries behind us we can face it out against PRIDE OF KNOWLEDGE.

flavo(u)r. US *-or, -orous.* Brit. *-our,* but *flavorous.*

fledg(e)ling. In US, no *-e-*. (The OED gives *-e-* preference, but of the eight quotations given, not one has the *-e-*.)

flee. The verb is now little used except in the form *fled, fly*

& *flying* having taken the place of *flee* & *fleeing*.

fleece makes *fleeceable* & *fleecy*.

fleshly, fleshy. The distinction is much the same as between *earthly* & *earthy*. *Fleshy* has the primary senses consisting of flesh (*fleshy tablets of the heart*), having a large proportion of flesh (*fleshy hands, fruit,* &c.), and like flesh (*fleshy softness, pink,* &c.); while *fleshly* has the secondary senses proper to the flesh or mortal body, sensual, unspiritual, worldly (*fleshly pleasures, perception, inclinations, affairs,* &c.).

fleur-de-lis. Pl. *fleurș-de-lis;* pronunciation, alike in sing. & pl., flerdelē′.

flier, flyer. Both are in good use; the first is recommended.

flippant. 'Displaying unbecoming levity in the consideration of serious subjects or in behaviour to persons entitled to respect' (OED). *A flippant amusement at heavy-handed definitions.* For synonomy see JOCOSE.

flock. Pl. *flocks* or *flock.* The word orig. meant company or assemblage of persons. Now applied chiefly to birds traveling &c. together, or domestic sheep, goats, & geese, and to people only in a transf. sense—a Christian congregation.

floor, stor(e)y. (1) In the US the ground floor is the first floor, and the two words are, in this sense, synonymous. In Brit. the numbering of floors & stories is peculiar, the second floor, e.g., being the third story. The ground floor & the ground story are the same, but the first floor & first story are different, *first story* being another name for *ground story*, but the first floor above it. (2) In US, esp. in large hotels & hospitals, the 13th floor is often numbered 14 (no. 13 being omitted completely) to avoid offending the superstitious.

flora, n. sing., plants or plant life, as distinguished from fauna. Pl. (rarely used), *floras* or *-rae* (pron. *-rē*).

floruit (flŏr′o͞oĭt) is a Latin verb meaning *he flourished* used with a date to give the period to which the person's activity may be assigned; abbrev. *fl.* (*Caedmon, fl.* A.D. 670); it is also used as a noun—*his floruit* &c., i.e. the date at which he was active.

flotage, flotation. So spelled in US; Brit. *floatage, -ation.* (The Fr. form is *flottage.*) Pron. flō-.

flotsam & jetsam. The distinction is between goods found afloat in the sea & goods found on land after being cast ashore. The original sense of jetsam was what had been jettisoned or thrown overboard.

flower-de-luce. An archaic English form of *fleur-de-lis.*

fluid, gas, liquid. *Fluid* is the wide term including the other two. It denotes a substance that on the slightest pressure changes shape by rearrangement of its particles; water, steam, oil, air, oxygen, electricity, ether, are all fluids. Liquids & gases differ in that the first are incompressible & the second elastic; water & oil are liquid & fluid but not gaseous; steam & air & oxygen are gases & fluids but not liquids.

flunk(e)y. In US usually *-ky,* pl. *-ies;* Brit., *-ey, -eys.*

fluorine. Pron. flo͞o′ôrēn; so also *fluorescent* (4 syl.).

flute. *Fluty* (NOT *flutey*), *flutist;* see also FLAUTIST.

fly. (1) The verb makes *is flown* as well as *has flown.* (2) *Fly-leaf* is a blank leaf, esp. one before the title page or half title of a book, or at the end of a circular or leaflet.

foal, colt, filly. *Foal* is of either sex, *colt* male, & *filly* female.

foam, froth. The natural definition of *foam* would be froth of the sea, & that of *froth* the foam of beer. That is to say, *foam* suggests the sea, *froth* suggests beer, & while one word is appropriate to the grand or the beautiful or the violent, the other is appropriate to the homely or the ordinary or the dirty. One demands of *foam* that it be white; *froth* may be of what color it pleases. *Froth* may be scum, but *foam,* though it may become scum, ceases to be foam in the process. It is perhaps true that *froth* is thought of mainly as part of a liquid that has sent it to the top, & the *foam* as a separate substance often detached in the act of making from its source. But the difference is much less in the meanings than in the suitable contexts.

focus. (1) The noun has pl. *-cuses* or *-ci* (pron. -sī or -sē); the verb makes *focused, -cusing* (occasionally, but irregularly, written *focussed, -ing*). (2) The verb is liable to loose application. NOT: *At one moment it seemed to be quite near, & at the next far away; for the ears, unaided by the eyes, can but imperfectly* focus *sound or measure its distance.* The focus of a sound being 'the point or space towards which the sound-waves converge' OED), ears cannot *focus* sound except by taking their owner to the right point; the eyes do measure distance by focusing, having an apparatus for the purpose; the ears do not.

foetid. Usually so spelled in Brit., but see FETID.

foetus, fetus. In US usually *fetus;* Brit. usually *foetus.* According to OED 'The etymologically preferable spelling with *e* in this word & its cognates is adopted as the standard form in some recent dictionaries, but in [Brit.] actual use is almost unknown.'

foil, n. Transf. sense, anything (or person) that serves by contrast to adorn or set off another thing to advantage. No relation to verb *foil,* to defeat, baffle, frustrate.

foist. To put or palm off (something) on or upon (someone else). WRONG: *The general public is much too easily* foisted off *with the old cry of the shopman that 'there's no demand for that kind of thing.'* The public can be *fobbed off* with something, or the something can be *fobbed off* on the public; but *foist* has only the second construction; see ANALOGY, & OBJECT-SHUFFLING.

-fold. *Twofold, tenfold, fivefold,* &c. No hyphen.

folio. Pl. *-os.* The following account from a dictionary may be useful: Leaf of paper &c. of a book or MS.; two opposite pages, or single page, of ledger used for the two sides of account; number of words (US, 100, Eng. 72 or 90) as unit of length of document; (Bookbinding) once-folded sheet of printing-paper giving two leaves or four pages (*in folio, made of folios,* also *folio volume* &c.), also the size or form of a folio book; the size of paper; the page number of a printed book (even number on the left side, odd on right); a case or folder for papers.

folk has passed out of the language of the ordinary educated person, so far as he talks unaffectedly. It is still in use in such compounds as *folklore, folksong,* & *folk etymology,* &c. *Folk dance,* n., two words; adj., hyphened.

follow. The OED ruling is: 'The construction in *as follows* is impersonal, & the verb should always be used in the singular.' NOT *The main regulations of the new Order are* as follow: *First . . ./The principal items of reductions stand* as follow. *As follows* should be used in both.

font, fount. An assortment of type of one size & style. US usually *font,* Brit. *fount.*

fool's-cap, foolscap. The cap or hood often hyphened or two words. The name of the paper size (13x16 or 17 inches) is usually written *foolscap.*

foot, n. The combined forms, *foothill, footloose, footsore,* &c., single words, no hyphen. For *at the foot of the letter* see GALLICISMS.

footing. (Status, condition, relative position.) MISUSE: *We have not the smallest doubt that this is what will actually happen, & . . . we may discuss the situation* on the footing that *the respective fates of these two bills will be predicted.* To give *footing* the sense of *assumption* or *hypothesis* is a SLIPSHOD EXTENSION; the writer, in fact, on however intimate a footing he may be with lobby prophets, is on a slippery footing with the English vocabulary.

for, conj. 1. As a conj. *for* introduces the ground or reason for something previously said (=*seeing that, since*). As a conj. introducing a cause for a statement that precedes or follows (*because*), it is obs. RIGHT: *This oil must contain phosphorus* for *we find phosphoric acid in the residue.* OBS.: *I choose this one* for *it resembles my mother.*

2. Punctuation with *for: For* is a co-ordinating conj., i.e. one that connects two independent sentences; it is neither, like *therefore* & *nevertheless,* strictly speaking an adverb serving the purpose of a connection; nor, like *since* & *because,* a subordinating conjunction that joins a mere clause to a sentence. In *Therefore A is equal to B,* & in *Nevertheless he did it,* it is a mere matter of rhetoric, depending on the emphasis desired, whether a comma shall or shall not follow *therefore* & *nevertheless;* with *for* it is a matter of grammatical correctness that there should be no comma. NOT *For, within it is a house of refinement & luxury.* Omit comma. This naturally does not apply to places where a comma is needed for independent reasons, as in *For, other things being equal, success is a fair test.*

for-, fore-. The prefix of the words *forbear* (v.), *forbid, forfend, forgather* (assemble), *forget, forgive, forgo* (relinquish), *forlorn, forsake,* & *forswear,* is unconnected with the English words *for* & *fore,* & means *away, out, completely,* &c. All these should be spelled with *for-,* not *fore-.* On the other hand the noun *for(e)bears,* & *foregoing* & *foregone* in *the foregoing list, a foregone conclusion,* contain the ordinary *fore,* & should be spelled with the *e*. *Foreclose* & *forfeit* contain another prefix again (Lat. *foris,* outside), though *foreclose* has had its spelling affected by natural confusion with English *fore.* All the words, whether established or made for the occasion, compounded with *fore,* as *forebode, forewarn, foreman, fore-ordained,* are spelled with the *e.*

forasmuch as (=inasmuch as, seeing that). Write thus. Now somewhat formal & archaic.

forbears, n. In US, spell FOREBEARS, which see.

forbid. (1) *forbad(e).* The pronunciation is always -ăd, not -ād. The spelling *forbade* is perhaps more usual in US, but both forms are established. (2) NOT *To forbid one* from *doing* (e.g. *You may forbid him, if you like,* from *toiling ten hours a day*). An unidiomatic construction on the ANALOGY of *prohibit* or *prevent.* The idiom is, *forbid him to toil, forbid his toiling.*

forceful, forcible. The main distinction in sense is that, while *forcible* conveys that force rather than something else is present, *forceful* conveys that much as opposed to little force is used or shown; compare *forcible ejection* with *a forceful personality.* This leaves it often indifferent, so far as sense goes, which word is used; *a forcible style* is a style with force in it, *a forceful style* is one of great force. The sense distinction, however, is the less important part of the matter. In Brit., *forcible* is the ordinary word, & *forceful* the word reserved for poetical or other abnormal use, where its special value depends partly on its infrequency & partly on the more picturesque suggestions of its suffix.

force majeure does not mean *a 'major' force,* but *a 'superior' force,* irresistible compulsion, an act of God excusing the fulfilment of a contract. Pron. fôrs mäzhûr. See FRENCH WORDS.

forceps. Sing. Pl. the same or rarely *forcepses, -cipes.*

fordo. Obs. or archaic except possibly in the p.p: *By the end of the evening he was completely* fordone (i.e. exhausted, overcome).

fore. *To the fore* appears to mean 'properly' (OED) at hand, available, surviving, extant. In being borrowed by English from Scotch & Irish writers as a picturesque phrase, it has suffered a change of meaning & is now est. journalese for *conspicuous.* But in US the older meaning is almost unknown & it should not be used in that sense if there is any danger of ambiguity.

forearm. So spelled.

for(e)bears. (1) As to the form, the prevalent but not sole modern Brit. spelling is without the *e* (the newspaper extracts below are exact); but the *e,* preferred in US, seems better both as separating the noun from the verb *forbear* & as not disguising the derivation (*forebeers,* those who have been before). (2) As to the use of the word, its only recommendation is that being Scotch & not English, it appeals to the usually misguided instinct of NOVELTY-HUNTING. *Ancestors, forefathers,* & *progenitors,* supplemented when the tie is not of blood by *forerunners* & *predecessors,* are the English words. WRONG: *By his* forebears *Lord Tankerville is connected with the ancien régime of France. His great grandfather, the Duc de Grammont . . .* (read *an-*

cestors)./*Birmingham is now being afforded an opportunity for offering some kind of posthumous reparation for the great wrong its* forbears *inflicted, close upon* 120 *years ago, on the illustrious Dr. Priestly* (for *its forbears* read *it*. Birmingham's forebears would be not an earlier generation of Birmingham people, but any villages that may have stood where Birmingham now stands. If the writer had been content with an English word, he would hardly have fallen into that trap).

forecast. Whether we are to say *forecast* or *forecasted* in the past & p.p. depends on whether we regard the verb or the noun as the original from which the other is formed. If the verb is original (=to guess beforehand) the past & p.p. will of course be *-cast;* if the verb is derived (=to make a forecast) they will as certainly be *forecasted.* The verb is in fact recorded 150 years earlier than the noun, & we may therefore thankfully rid ourselves of the ugly *forecasted;* it may be hoped that we should do so even if history were against us, but this time it is kind.

forecastle. Usually pron. fō′ksl.

forego. *Forego*=to precede in time or place (*forgo,* to abstain from, relinquish). *Foregoing* is properly a part. adj.: *The foregoing material* &c. It is sometimes used absolutely & elliptically as a noun (*The foregoing must not be confounded with purely communistic theories*) but this use is not recommended.

forehead. Pron. fŏ′rĕd.

FOREIGN DANGER. Those who use words or phrases belonging to languages with which they have little or no acquaintance do so at their peril. Even in *e.g., i.e.,* & *et cetera,* there lurk unsuspected possibilities of exhibiting ignorance; with *bête noire, cui bono?, bona fide, qua,* & *pacè,* the risk is greater; & such words as *protagonist* & *phantasmagoria,* which one hesitates to call English or foreign, require equal caution. See all or any of the words & phrases mentioned, & *flair.* Two or three specimens follow, for those who do not like cross references: (WRONG) *I suggest that a compulsory loan be made* pro ratio *upon all capital* (pro rata)./*Ricasoli, another of his* bêtes noirs (noires)./*A man who claimed to be a delegate, but whose* bona fides were *disputed, rose to propose the motion* (was).

forenoon. See WORKING & STYLISH WORDS. *The Church Congress sat in two sessions this* forenoon. . . . *The afternoon program was divided into three sections.* Even in contexts that, by the occurrence as here of *afternoon* in contrast, most suggest the use of *forenoon,* the natural English is *morning. Forenoon,* having fallen out of use as the name for the first half of daylight, is now used by writers who dislike saying a plain thing in the plain way. See also FORMAL WORDS.

forever. In US one word. Brit. now usually two, but in earlier writers often one.

foreword, preface. *Foreword* is a word invented in the 19th c. as a Saxonism by anti-latinists, & caught up as a VOGUE WORD by the people who love a new name for an old thing. *Preface* has a 500-year history behind it in English, &, far from being antiquated, is still the name for the thing. A decent retirement might be found for *foreword* if it were confined to the particular kind of preface that is supplied by some distinguished person for a book written by someone else who feels the need of a sponsor.

But how one vogue word drives out another! Here is a book on whose title page is mentioned neither *preface* nor *foreword;* instead, it is *With a Prefatory Gesture by . . .* Poor old *foreword!* your vogue is past, your freshness faded; you are antiquated, *vieux jeu, passé, démodé;* your nose is out of joint. And, when *gesture* shall have followed you to limbo, we may hope to get back to *preface.*

forgather. Best so spelled.

forge makes *-geable.*

forget makes *-ttable.*

forgiveness. Pron. three syllables.

forgo. So spelled. The only sense not obs. or archaic is *abstain from, relinquish,* &c.

forgot, as a p.p. for the current *forgotten,* is now, except in uneducated speech, a deliberate ARCHAISM.

forlorn hope is not an abstract phrase transferred by metaphor to a storming party, but has the concrete sense in its own right, & only gets the abstract sense of 'desperate chance' &c. by misunderstanding. *Hope* is not the English word, but is a misspelling of the Dutch *hoop*=English *heap; the forlorn hope* is the devoted or lost band, those who sacrifice themselves in leading the attack. The spelling of *hope* once fixed, the mistake was inevitable; but it is well to keep the original meaning in mind; see TRUE & FALSE ETYMOLOGY.

form. School 'forms' are usually numbered from the *first* or lowest to the *sixth* or highest.

formalism, formality. It is only from the more abstract sense of *formality,* from *formality* as the name of a quality & not of an action, that *formalism* requires to be distinguished; & there, while *formality* means the observance of forms, *formalism* is the disposition to use them & belief in their importance; *formality* is the outward sign of formalism. RIGHT: *The cant and* formalism *of a degenerate faith. Dogmatic* formalism. BUT *Legal* formalities, *A mere* formality.

FORMAL WORDS. There are large numbers of words differing from each other in almost all respects, but having this point in common, that they are not the plain English for what is meant, not the form that the mind uses in its private debates to convey to itself what it is talking about, but translations of these into language that is held more suitable for public exhibition. We tell our thoughts, like our children, to put on their hats & coats before they go out; we want the window *shut,* but we ask if our fellow passenger would mind its being *closed;* we think of a room as being *well lighted,* but write of *adequate illumination.* These outdoor costumes are often needed; not only may decency be outraged sometimes by over-plain speech; dignity may be compromised if the person who thinks in slang also writes in slang. To the airman it comes natural to think & talk of his *bus,* but he does well to call it in print by another name. What is intended in this article is not to protest against all change of the indoor into the outdoor word, but to point out that the less of such change there is the better. A short haphazard selection of what are to be taken as formal words will put the reader in possession of the point; a full list would run into thousands. It must be observed that no general attack is being made on these words as words; it is only on the prevalent notion that the commoner synonyms given after each in parentheses ought to be translated into these: *accommodation* (room); *bear* (carry); *cast* (throw); *cease* (stop); *close* (shut); *commence* (begin); *complete* (finish); *conceal* (hide); *dispatch* (send off); *don* (put on); *donation* (gift); *draw* (pull); *emoluments* (pay); *endeavor* (try); *evince* (show); *expedite* (hasten); *extend* (give); *felicitate* (wish joy); *forenoon* (morning); *imbibe* (drink); *inquire* (ask); *luncheon* (lunch); *obtain* (get); *peruse* (read); *proceed* (go); *purchase* (buy); *remark* (say); *remove* (take away); *seek* (try, look for); *summon* (send for); *sustain* (suffer); *valiant* (brave); *veritable* (real or positive).

There are very few of our notions that cannot be called by different names; but among these names there is usually one that may be regarded as the thing's proper name, its *kurion onoma* or dominant name as the Greeks called it, for which another may be substituted to add precision or for many other reasons, but which is present to the mind even behind the substitute. A *destroyer* is a *ship*, &, though we never forget its shiphood, the reader is often helped if we call it a *destroyer.* A vessel also is a *ship,* but the reader is not helped by our calling it a *vessel,* for the most part; &, though *to evince* is *to show,* it does not help him to call *showing evincing.* What happens is first the translation of *show* into *evince* by the writer, & then the retranslation of *evince* into *show* by the reader; mind communicates with mind through a veil, & the result is at best dullness, & at worst misunderstanding. The proper name for a notion should not be rejected for another unless the rejector can give some better account to himself of his preference for the other than that he thinks it will look better in print. If his mental name for a thing is not the proper name, or if, being the proper name, it is also improper, or essentially undignified, let him translate it; but there is nothing to be ashamed of in *buy* or *say* that they should need translating into *purchase* & *remark;* where they give the sense equally well, they are fit for any company & need not be shut up at home. Few things contribute more to vigor of style than a practical realization that the *kuria onomata,* the sovereign or dominant or proper or vernacular or current names, are better than the formal words.

format. A French word, orig. (& still sometimes in Brit.) pronounced forˊmah, bŭt now naturalized in book & printing circles: the shape, size, and general make-up of a publication.

former. When *the former* is a pronoun its antecedent must be a noun, not another pronoun. See LATTER. When the reference is to one of three or more individuals, *the first*, not *the former*, should be used. WRONG: *Among the three representatives of neutral States, Dr. Castberg & Dr. Nansen stand for Norway & M. Heringa for Holland;* the former *is so convinced of . . .* who?

formidable. Stress first syllable.

formula. The plurals *-lae*, *-las*, are equally common.

fornicate. *Fornication*, as distinguished from *adultery*, implies that the woman is not a wife; it is sometimes but not always understood to imply further that neither party is married. Agent-noun, *fornicator*.

forte, person's strong point. The spelling should have been (but is NOT) *fort*. Pron. fort, not fortā (as the mus. term is pronounced).

forte (mus.). **Loud(ly), powerful(ly).**

forth. 1. *And so forth* is (cf. & THE LIKE) a convenience to the writer who does not wish to rehearse his list at length, but shrinks from the suggestion, now so firmly attached to *etc.* as to disqualify it for literary use, that he breaks off because it is too much trouble to proceed; the slightly antique turn of the phrase acquits him of unceremoniousness; *& so on* is in this respect midway between *& so forth* & etc.

2. *So far forth* has occasionally the advantage over *so far* of limiting the sense to extent & excluding the literal idea of distance; more often its only claim to preference is what is always the only claim of *so far forth* as against *so far as*—its superior pomposity.

forties, 'for-. See EIGHTIES.

fortitude means moral strength or courage in pain or adversity, not merely strength or endurance.

fortnight (pron. nīt) is more at home in England than US and often sounds self-conscious in American speech.

fortuitous means accidental, undesigned, &c. It is sometimes confused with *fortunate*, perhaps through mere sound, perhaps by the help of *lucky*. WRONG: *Reviewing my own experiences, I must say I should not have expected so* fortuitous *a termination of a somewhat daring experiment./When first produced, its popularity was limited. Nevertheless it may now sail into a more* fortuitous *harbor on the strength of its author's later reputation.* For such mistakes see MALAPROPS.

forward(s), adv. The OED says: 'The present distinction in usage between *forward* & *forwards* is that the latter expresses a definite direction viewed in contrast with other directions. In some contexts either form may be used without perceptible difference of meaning; the following are examples in which only one of them can now be used: "The ratchet-wheel can move only forwards"; "the right side of the paper has the maker's name reading forwards"; "if you move at all it must be forwards"; "my companion has gone forward"; "to bring a matter forward"; "from this time forward."' Since the publication of the OED, however, there has been a tendency, not yet exhausted, for *forward* to displace *forwards*, & in the US the shorter form is widely used in all contexts. The reader will notice that, while he can heartily accept the banishment of *forwards* from the last three examples, it is quite doubtful whether *forward* is not possible in some or all of the first three.

fossil. Pron. fŏ′sl.

foul. (1) The adv. is current only in certain idiomatic expressions meaning unfairly, contrary to the rules, and in comb. forms: *To play a person foul; foul-smelling, foul-spoken*, &c. (2) *Foul*, adj., as used in US publishing &c., means illegible, defaced by corrections: *foul copy, foul MS.; foul galleys* (or *proof*). (3) *Foul*, v., the navy slang expression, *all fouled up*, can be traced to the nautical use of the verb: to become entangled (as ropes, or two boats in collision).

foully. Pron. both *ls*.

four freedoms. (From F. D. Roosevelt's speech of 6 Jan. 1941.) Freedom of speech & expression, of worship, from want, from fear.

fourth estate. The public press, newspapers. See ESTATE.

fowl. The collective use of the sing. (*all the fish & fowl in the world*) still exists, but is not common.

fox. Fem. *vixen, bitch-fox, she-fox.*

foyer. The French word for a lobby, esp. in a theater. Most dictionaries give a modified French pronunciation first, foiā, but in US foi′ĕr is now commoner.

fracas. Uproar, brawl. US pron. frā′kas (pl. *fracases*); Brit. pron. fră′kah; pl. *fracas*, pron. fră′kahz.

fraction. (1) As a substitute for *portion, a little* (*he spent only* a fraction *of his time on politics*), loose or colloq. (2) For writing of fractions, see HALF.

fragile. (1) Only -ĭl is recognized by the OED and in US dictionaries; COD gives -īl. (2) *fragile, frail. Frail* is wider both in application & in sense. Whatever is fragile is also frail, but a woman may be frail (i.e. weaker than others in moral strength) who cannot be called fragile (i.e. weaker in physical strength). Where, as in most cases, either word is applicable, there is a certain difference of sense between (*fragile*) liable to snap or break or be broken & so perish & (*frail*) not to be reckoned on to resist breakage or pressure or to last long; that is to say, the root idea of *break* is more consciously present in *fragile* owing to its unobscured connection with *fragment* & *fracture.*

Frankenstein. From Mrs. Shelley's romance; now used generally for one destroyed by his own works. A sentence written by the creatrix of the creator of the creature may save some of those whose acquaintance with all three is indirect from betraying the fact: 'Sometimes I endeavored to gain from Frankenstein the particulars of his creature's formation; but on this point he was impenetrable.' *Frankenstein* is the creator-victim; the creature-despot & fatal creation is *Frankenstein's monster.* The blunder is very common indeed—almost, but surely not quite, sanctioned by custom: *If they went on strengthening this power they would* create a Frankenstein *they could not resist./In his belief they were in the miserable position of having* created a Frankenstein *which they could* *not control.* (Most US dictionaries now give as a second meaning of *Frankenstein* the monster so created.)

frantic makes *frantically.* Synonyms are *frenzied, furious, mad, passionate, rabid, raging, raving, wild.* Of these: *frantic* & *frenzied* both mean beside oneself or driven into temporary madness by a cause specified or apparent from context (*frantic with pain, excitement,* &c.; *the frenzied populace refused him a hearing*); in mere exaggerations, e.g. when joy is the cause, *frantic* is the word. *Furious* implies no more than anger that has got out of hand—or, of inanimate things, a degree of force comparable to this. *Passionate* applies primarily to persons capable of strong emotions, especially if they are also incapable of controlling them, & secondarily to the sort of action that results. *Rabid* now usually implies the carrying to a great excess of some particular belief or doctrine, religious, political, social, medical, or the like (*a rabid dissenter, teetotaler, faddist, rabid virulence*). *Raging* chiefly describes the violence in inanimate things that seems to correspond to madness in man (cf. *furious; a raging storm, pestilence, toothache*). *Raving* is an intensifying epithet for *madness* or *a madman.* The uses of *mad* & *wild* hardly need setting forth.

fraternize. Associate, make friends, hold fellowship (with) as brothers. Its derogatory connotation (World Wars I–II)—'fraternizing with the enemy' (i.e. occupation forces)—is not given in earlier US or Brit. dictionaries.

Frau, Fräulein. (As titles, Mrs., Miss.) Pron. frow, froi′-līn.

free. 1. *Freeman, free man.* The single word has two senses, (a) person who has the 'freedom' of a city &c., & (b) person who is not a slave or serf, citizen of a free State; in other senses (*at last I am a free man,* i.e. have retired from business, lost my wife, &c.) the words should be separate.

2. *free will, free-will, freewill.* The hyphened form should be restricted to the attributive use as in *a free-will offering, the free-will theory.* In non-philosophical use *free will* should be written & most dictionaries prefer it even for the philosophical term; if a separate form for the philosophical term is required, it should be *freewill.*

3. *free verse=vers libre.* Rhythmical or cadenced verse as distinguished from metrical or rhymed verse.

French leave. To depart or act without asking permission or giving notice.

FRENCH WORDS. Display of superior knowledge is as great a vulgarity as display of superior wealth—greater, indeed, inasmuch as knowledge should tend more definitely than wealth toward discretion & good manners. That is the guiding principle alike in the using & in the pronouncing of French words in English writing & talk. To use French words that your reader or hearer does not know or does not fully understand, to pronounce them as if you were one of the select few to whom French is second nature when he is not of those few (& it is ten thousand to one that neither you nor he will be so), is inconsiderate & rude.

1. Use of French words. It would be a satisfaction to have a table divided into permissible words, forbidden words, & words needing caution; but anyone who starts sanguinely on the making of it is likely to come, after much shifting of words from class to class, to the same conclusion as the writer of this article—that of the thousand or so French words having some sort of currency in English none can be prohibited, & almost none can be given unconditional licenses; it is all a matter of the audience & the occasion. Only faddists will engage in alien-hunting & insist on finding native substitutes for *tête-à-tête, agent provocateur, esprit de corps, chaperon, débris, habitué, laissez-faire,* & a hundred other words that save circumlocution. Only fools will think it commends them to the English reader to decorate incongruously with such bower-birds' treasures as *au pied de la lettre, à merveille, bien entendu, les convenances, coûte que coûte, quand même, dernier ressort, impayable, par exemple, sans doute;* yet even these are in place as supplying local color or for other special reasons on perhaps 5 per cent of the occasions on which they actually appear. It would be easy to make a set of pigeonholes to contain the French words; let us say:

A. The standard word for the thing (*aide-de-camp, ballet, chauffeur*).

B. Words accepted as practically English, though not indispensable (*beau, billet-doux, char-à-bancs*).

C. Circumlocution-savers (*blasé, au revoir, fait accompli*).

D. Diplomacy & politics (*communiqué, bloc*).

E. Dress & cookery (*moire antique, entrée, hors-d'œuvre*).

F. Local color & travel (*concierge, trottoir, lycée*).

G. Sport & theater (*savate, couloir, entr' acte*).

H. Art (*atelier, genre*).

I. Literature (*causerie, cliché, jeu d'esprit*).

K. Euphemism (*abattoir, accouchement*).

L. Pretentious decoration (*agréments, coûte que coûte, frappant*).

M. Needless substitutes for English words (*cul-de-sac, en route*).

N. Puzzles for the plain man (*acharnement, flâneur, impayable*).

But to distribute into such pigeonholes when made is a less simple affair, owing to the disturbing effects of audience & occasion. Every writer, however, who suspects himself of the bower-bird instinct should make & use some such classification system & remember that acquisitiveness & indiscriminate display are pleasing to contemplate only in birds & savages & children.

2. Pronunciation. To say a French word in the middle of an English sentence exactly as it would be said by a Frenchman in a French sentence is a feat demanding an acrobatic mouth. The muscles have to be suddenly adjusted to the performance of a different nature, & after it as suddenly recalled to the normal state. It is a feat that should not be attempted; the greater its success as a *tour de force,* the greater its failure as a step in the conversational progress; for your collocutor, aware that he could not have done it himself, has his attention distracted whether he ad-

mires or is humiliated. All that is necessary is a polite acknowledgment of indebtedness to the French language indicated by some approach in some part of the word to the foreign sound, & even this only when the difference between the foreign & the corresponding natural English sound is too marked to escape a dull ear. For instance, in *tête-à-tête* no attempt need or should be made to distinguish French *e* from English *a*, but the calling it tā′tah tāt′ instead of the natural English tāt′-*a*tāt rightly stamps it as foreign; again, *tour de force* is better with no un-English sound at all; neither *r* need be trilled, & *tour* & *force* should both be exactly like the English words so spelled. On the other hand, there are some French sounds so obviously alien to the English mouth that words containing them (except such as are, like *coupon*, in daily use by all sorts & conditions of men) should either be eschewed by English speakers or have these sounds adumbrated. They are especially the nasalized vowels (*an, en, in, on, un, am,* &c.), the diphthong *eu*, the unaccented *e*, & *u;* to say bong for *bon* is as insulting to the French language as to pronounce *bulletin* in correct French is insulting to the man in the English street; & ko͞oldēsăk′ for *cul-de-sac* is nearly as bad. In consulting the pronunciations given in the text the reader will bear in mind that it is no business of this dictionary to tell him how French words are pronounced in French; it has only to advise him how to pronounce them in English if he would neither exhibit a conscious superiority of education nor be suspected of boorish ignorance. The pronunciation is intended then to mitigate the precision of those who know French at least as much as to enlighten those who do not.

frenetic. Usually *phrenetic.* (Insane, fanatic.)

frequence, -cy. *Frequency* is now more usual in all contexts, and is standard in physics & biology.

frequently, as compared with *often*, is a FORMAL WORD.

fresco. Pl. *-oes.* The art of painting on freshly spread plaster. (*Alfresco,* one word, to paint in fresco.)

fresh, adv., 'newly,' retained chiefly in comb. forms: *fresh-caught, fresh-coined.*

friar, monk. By the word *friar* is meant a member of one of the mendicant orders, i.e. those living entirely on alms, especially 'the four orders' of Franciscans, Dominicans, Carmelites, & Augustinian Hermits. *Monk* is used sometimes of all male members of religious orders including friars, but properly excludes the mendicants. In the latter case the general distinction is that while the monk belongs essentially to his particular monastery, & his object is to make a good man of himself, the friar's sphere of work is outside, & his object is to do good work among the people.

Friday &c., *on Friday* &c. Normal US idiom: *The Puritan way of eating fish is, to eat it* Saturday *instead of* Friday./ *Can you dine with us* Tuesday? Brit. usage requires *on Saturday, on Friday, on Tuesday.* The OED says: 'The adverbial use of the names of the days of the week is now chiefly U.S. except in the collocations like "next Saturday," "last Saturday." '

friend. Some idiomatic constructions: *A friend* of *mine; he has been a friend* to *me; make friends* with *him; a friend* at (or *in*) *court.*

frier, fryer. The *-yer* is standard.

frightened. *At* is the traditional construction. In 1858 the following statement appeared in the *Sat. Rev.* (Brit.): 'It is not usual for educated people to perpetrate such sentences as . . . "I was frightened *of* her."' The OED (1901?) listed *frightened of* as colloq. The COD (1951) gives *at* when an occasion, *of* to a habitual fear. Webster gives *at* and *of* without differentiation. ACD gives *of* only.

frivol. A BACK-FORMATION from frivolous. *He frivolled* (or *-oled*) *away his time.* Given in modern dictionaries, without comment. (But OED: 'Not in dignified use.')

froth. See FOAM.

froward. Refractory, perverse (NOT a variant of *forward*). Archaic.

fruition. Pron. frooĭ′shn. The word means 'attainment of a thing desired,' 'enjoyment' (from *frui,* enjoy). Because of the popular (erroneous) connection with *fruit,* modern US dictionaries include 'state of bearing fruit,' 'a coming into fruit.'

fryable, preferred in US for the thing (able) to be fried. But *friable* (able to be crumpled) *soil.*

fuchsia. So spelled. Pron. fūsh *a.* (The generic name, pron. fo͝ok′sĭa.)

fuel, v., makes *-led, -ling* (US) or (Brit.) *-lled* &c.

-ful. The right pl. for such nouns as *handful, spoonful, cupful, basketful* is *handfuls* &c., NOT *handsful* &c.

fulcrum. Pron. fŭl-, NOT fo͞ol-; pl. *-crums* or *-cra.*

fulfil(l), fulfilled. US still prefers *-ll,* even in *fulfillment;* Brit. usually *fulfil, -filment.* One *l* is recommended. See ENROLL.

full for *fully* in such phrases as *full twenty, full as good as,* where it means *quite,* & such as *full sweet, full early,* where it means *quite sufficiently* or *rather too,* is idiomatic but colloq. In the sense *very* as in *full fain, full many a, full weary,* where *fully* cannot be substituted, it is poetical.

ful(l)ness. Use *-ll-,* US & Brit.

function, n., means the special activity or operation proper to any person or thing. It has now become a VOGUE WORD, as have also *function,* v., and *functional. The U.N. has no* function *in internal politics./Once the committee begins* to function *officially . . ./Functional furniture, functional literature.* 'Social function' comes from an earlier use (a special religious ceremony of the R.C. Church); hence *A large function in her honor.* See POPULARIZED TECHNICALITIES. As not everyone can cope unaided with mathematical technicalities, the following may be useful: 'When one quality depends upon another or upon a system of others, so that it assumes a definite value when a system of definite values is given to the others, it is called a function of those others.'

fundamental is the est. word

in literary use for which writers with a taste for scientific-sounding terms substitute *basic* or *basal.*

funebrial, funeral (adj.), **funerary, funereal.** The continued existence of the first & third words, which no one uses if he can help it, is due to what has happened to the other two. *Funeral,* though originally an adjective, has so far passed into a noun that it can no longer be used as an adjective except in the attributive position, as in *funeral customs, the funeral procession; funereal* has become so tied to the meaning as *of a funeral, gloomy enough for a funeral,* that it can no longer mean simply *of* or *for a funeral.* In such a sentence as *The origin of the custom is* ——, it only remains to choose between *funebrial* & *funerary,* the first of which is perhaps more usual.

fungicide. Pron. fŭnj-.

fungous, adj., is being replaced (in US) by the attributive use of the noun. When not used attributively (and by scientific writers generally), the distinctive spellings of adj. & noun are retained.

fungus. Pl. *funguses* or *fungi* (pron. -jī).

funnel makes *-led* (US) or *-lled* (Brit.).

funny. For *too funny for words* see HACKNEYED PHRASES.

furore. Three syllables (fū-rōr′ĭ); but in US generally supplanted by *furor* (fū′).

further, adj. & adv. See FARTHER.

fuse. (1) The verb makes *fusible.* (2) It is worth while to remember that *a fuse* is not so called because it fuses, being named solely from its shape (L. *fusus,* spindle), while the verb is from the L. *fundo,* pour.

FUSED PARTICIPLE is a name given to the construction exemplified in its simplest form by 'I like *you* pleading poverty,' & in its higher development by 'The collision was owing to the *signaling instructions* laid down by the international regulations for use by ships at anchor in a fog *not having been properly followed.*' The name was invented (*The King's English,* 1906) for the purpose of labeling & so making recognizable & avoidable a usage considered by the inventor to be rapidly corrupting modern English style. A comparison of three sentences will show the meaning of the term.

1. *Women* having the vote *share political power with men.* (RIGHT; true participle.)

2. Women's having the vote *reduces men's political power.* (RIGHT; gerund.)

3. *Women* having the vote *reduces men's political power.* (WRONG; fused participle.)

In the first, the subject of the sentence is *women,* & *having* (the vote) is a true participle attached to women. In the second, the subject is the verbal noun or gerund *having* (the vote), & *women's* is a possessive case (i.e. an adjective) attached to that noun. In the third, the subject is neither *women* (since *reduces* is singular) nor *having* (for if so, women would be left in the air without grammatical construction), but a compound notion formed by fusion of the noun *women* with the participle *having.* Participles so constructed, then, are called fused participles, as opposed to the true participle of No. 1 & the gerund of No. 2.

We are given to ridiculing the cumbrousness of German style, & the particular element in this that attracts most attention is the device by which a long expression is placed between a noun & its article & so, as it were, bracketed & held together. Where we might allow ourselves to say *This never-to-be-forgotten occasion*, the German will not crane at *The since-1914-owing-to-the-world-war-befallen-destruction-of-capital;* only a German, we assure ourselves, could be guilty of such ponderousness. But the fused participle is having exactly the same effect on English as the article-&-noun sandwich on German, the only difference being that the German device is grammatically sound, while the English is indefensible. The examples that follow, in which the two members of each fused participle are in roman type, exhibit both the bracketing capacity that makes this construction fatally tempting to the lazy writer, & its repulsiveness to a reader who likes clean sentences. In the last may be observed a special fault often attending the fused participle—that the reader is trapped into supposing the construction complete when the noun is reached, & afterwards has to go back & get things straight. FUSED PARTICIPLES: *Mr. Hall asked the Secretary if, in order to avoid the necessity of* men *who desired to work & were wantonly attacked by strikers* being *compelled to arm themselves with firearms, he would . . ./ The machinery which enables one man to do the work of six results only in the* others *losing their job, & in* skill *men have spent a lifetime acquiring* becoming *suddenly useless./ A dangerous operation, in which everything depends upon the* Election, *which is an essential part of the operation,* being *won.*

It need hardly be said that writers with any sense of style do not, even if they allow themselves the fused participle, make so bad a use of the bad thing as is shown above to be possible. But the tendency of the construction is toward that sort of cumbrousness, & the rapidity with which it is gaining ground is portentous. Some years ago, it was reasonable, & possible without much fear of offending reputable writers, to describe as an 'ignorant vulgarism' the most elementary form of the fused participle, i.e. that in which the noun part is a single word, & that a pronoun or proper name; it was not very easy to collect instances of it. Today, no one who wishes to keep a whole skin will venture on so frank a description. Here are a few examples, culled without any difficulty whatever from the columns of a single newspaper, which would be very justly indignant if it were hinted that it had more vulgarisms than its contemporaries. Each, it will be seen, has a different pronoun or name, a sufficient proof in itself of abundant material. *We need fear nothing from* China developing *her resources* (China's)./ *It should result in* us securing *the best airplane for military purposes* (our)./ *It is no longer thought to be the proper scientific attitude to deny the possibility of* anything happening (anything's). See also GERUND.

fuselage. Of an airplane, so spelled; pron. -z-.

fusillade, of firearms &c., pron. fū *zi* lād′.

fustigate, fustigation, are PEDANTIC-HUMOR words.

futurism. A movement in art, literature, &c., originating about 1910, marked by violent departure from traditional methods & by the use of arbitrary symbols in the expression of emotion.

G

gabardine. The modern fabric in US so spelled. The medieval garment *gaberdine.*

Gaelic. Pron. gā-, not gă-. The two longer forms, *Gadhelic* & *Goidelic,* are used chiefly by writers on philology & ethnology & mean the same thing. When precision is not required, *Gaelic* is the word chiefly used in both the narrow & the wide senses.

gage. A pledge, a challenge; *to throw down the gage. Gauge,* measure, so spelled.

gaiety, gaily, so spelled. See GAY.

gainsay is a LITERARY WORD, & now little used except in negative contexts such as *There is no gainsaying it, Without fear of being gainsaid, That can scarcely be gainsaid.*

gala. Pron gā-.

galaxy. Pron. găl′aksĭ.

gallant. The ordinary pronunciation is gă′lant. Certain senses, politely attentive to women, amorous, amatory, are traditionally distinguished by the pronunciation gălănt′. (*Gallant′,* n., is still heard in southern US.)

galley. Pl. *-eys.*

Gallic, Gallican, Gaulish, French. *Gallican* is a purely ecclesiastical word, corresponding to *Anglican. Gaulish* means only 'of the (ancient) Gauls,' & is, even in that sense, less usual than *Gallic.* The normal meaning of *Gallic* is the same as that of *Gaulish,* but it is also much used as a synonym in some contexts for *French.* It means not simply 'French,' but 'characteristically,' 'delightfully,' 'distressingly,' or 'amusingly,' French. We do not, or should not, speak of *Gallic wines* or *trade* or *law* or *climate,* but we do of *Gallic wit, morals, politeness,* & *shrugs;* & the symbolic bird is invariably the *Gallic cock.* So far as *Gallic* is used for *French* without any implication of the kind suggested, it is merely a bad piece of ELEGANT VARIATION OR AVOIDANCE OF THE OBVIOUS. (Pron. gălĭk, gâlish.)

GALLICISMS. By 'Gallicisms' are here meant borrowings of various kinds from French in which the borrower stops short of using French words without disguise.

1. One form consists in taking a French word & giving it an English termination or dropping an accent or the like, as in *actuality, banality,* & *redaction.*

2. Another in giving to an existent English word a sense that belongs to it only in French or to its French form only, as in *intrigue* (v.t., = interest, perplex, &c.), *arrive* (= attain success &c.), *exposition* (= exhibition).

3. Another in giving vogue to a word that has had little currency in English but is common

in French, such as *veritable* & *envisage*.

4. Another in substituting a French form or word that happens to be English also, but in another sense, as when *brave* is used for *honest* or *worthy*, or *ascension* for *ascent*.

5. Another in translating a French word or phrase, as in *leap to the eye, to the foot of the letter, knight of industry, daughter of joy, gilded youth, living pictures* (= tableaux vivants), *the half-world*, & *success of esteem*.

To advise the abandonment of all Gallicisms indiscriminately would be absurd. There are thousands of English words & phrases that were once Gallicisms, but, having prospered, are no longer recognizable as such; & of the number now on trial some will doubtless prosper in like manner. What the wise man does is to recognize that the conversational usage of educated people in general, not his predilections or a literary fashion of the moment, is the naturalizing authority, & therefore to adopt a Gallicism only when he is of the opinion that it is a Gallicism no more. To use Gallicisms for the worst of all reasons—that they are Gallicisms—to affect them as giving one's writing a literary air, to enliven one's dull stuff with their accidental oddities, above all to choose Gallicisms that presuppose the reader's acquaintance with the French original, these are confessions of weakness or incompetence. If writers knew how 'leap to the eye' does leap to the eye of the reader who, in dread of meeting it, casts a precautionary glance down the column, or how furious is the thinking that 'give furiously to think' stirs in the average English-speaking person, they would leave such paltry borrowings alone forever.

gallivant. Perhaps a humorous perversion of *gallant* (v.). See FACETIOUS FORMATIONS.

gallon. Four quarts in US, from the old English wine gallon. In Brit., the imperial gallon (4 imperial quarts) equals approx. 4.8 US quarts.

gallop makes *-oped, -oping.*

gallows, though originally a plural form, is now sing. (*set up a gallows* &c.); the plural is usually avoided, but when unavoidable is *gallowses.* Pron. găl′ōz; the pronunciation găl′ŭs is dial. or affected.

galop, the dance, is so spelled; the verb makes *-oped, -oping.*

galosh, golosh. The first is better.

galumph. From Lewis Carroll (gallop triumphant?). See FACETIOUS FORMATIONS.

gambit. In chess, from which the term comes, a gambit is the opening play in which a piece, usually a pawn, is sacrificed for the advantage of position. Hence *gambit pawn,* the pawn so sacrificed. The word has long been used figuratively (*The Emperor's genius in the art of war had devised a brilliant* gambit . . .), but should not be so used by writers who do not understand its meaning.

game. The meaning 'plucky, spirited,' is standard usage, not slang or colloq. *One of the* gamest *fish that swim; to die* game; *the* game *spirit of the pioneer. Gamy,* so spelled.

gamut. Pron. găm′ŭt. Music, the whole series of recognized notes; the diatonic scale. Transf. & fig., the entire range or compass of a thing. *The* gamut *of crime; Stocks were running up & down the* gamut *from* $1 *to* $7 *a share.* For synonyms, see FIELD.

gang agley (go away) is a BATTERED ORNAMENT.

ganglion. (Fig., a center of force or energy.) Pl. *-lia.*

gangway. (A passage, bridge of planks, in a boat or ship.) In the House of Commons, the cross-passage, about halfway down the House. *Below the gangway,* as a parliamentary phrase, is applied to members whose customary seat does not imply close association with the official policy of the party on whose side of the House they sit.

gantlet, gauntlet. The former is usual in US for the military punishment & its fig. connotations, *to run the gantlet* (a corruption from *Gantlope*); *gauntlet* for the glove. In Brit. use, usually *gauntlet* for both.

gantry, gaun-. In the modern engineering sense the first is usual.

gaol, gaoler, jail, jailor, &c. In US the *j-* forms are standard. In Brit. official use the forms with g are still current; in literary & journalistic use the *g-* & the *j-* forms are used indifferently.

garage. In US, gă räzh′ & găr′äzh; Brit., găr′ĭj or as French.

garble. The original meaning is to sift, to sort into sizes with a view to using the best or rejecting the worst. The modern transf. sense is to subject a set of facts, evidence, a report, a speech, &c., to such a process of sifting as results in presenting all of it that supports the impression one wishes to give of it & deliberately omitting all that makes against or qualifies this. Garbling stops short of falsification & misquotation, but not of misrepresentation. *A garbled account* is partial in both senses.

garret, attic. The two words mean the same thing but *attic* is now more usual in most contexts. *Garret* is usually chosen to suggest poverty, squalor, &c., or, in the US, the Middle West & rural communities.

garrot(t)e. The Spanish method of execution by strangulation. Hence throttling, esp. for robbery. US prefers *garrote* (the original Spanish spelling); Brit. *garrotte.*

gas. For the distinction in gas, fluid, & liquid, see FLUID. In US *gas* used for GASOLINE is colloq.

gaseous. (1) Pref. pron. găʹ-sĭus. (2) *Gaseous, gassy.* The first prevails in scientific use; in the US the latter is usually fig. or informal.

gasoline. US so spelled; Brit. *gasolene* (Brit. word in general use, *petrol*). See KEROSENE.

gauche(rie). Pron. gōsh, gō′-shĕ rē′. 'Left-handed,' hence awkward(ness) esp. in social graces.

gauge. So spelled, NOT *guage.* The verb makes *gaugeable.*

Gaul means ancient Gaul or one of its inhabitants; the use of it for *France* or *Frenchman* is poetic or facetious. See SOBRIQUETS.

Gaulish. See GALLIC.

gauntlet, the glove. See GANTLET.

gauntry. See GANTRY.

gay makes *gayer, gayest, gaily, gaiety.* (*Gayly, gayety* are given as variants in some US dictionaries.)

gelatin(e). The form without the final -*e* is standard for all uses in US; in Brit. it is in scientific (or pseudo-scientific) use only.

gender, n., is a grammatical term only. To talk of persons or creatures of the masculine or feminine gender, meaning of the male or female sex, is either a jocularity (permissible or not according to context) or a blunder.

genera. Pron. jĕn′ĕrä. Pl. of GENUS. Scientific names of genera are usually printed in italics. In US medical texts, however, they are often in roman.

general, adj., implies the inclusion of all, or nearly all: *general practice.* But *common occurrence, universal belief. Generally always* is self-contradictory. The use of *generally* for *usually* is not incorrect but may be misleading.

generalissimo. (Chief commander of military & naval forces or of combined armies.) Pl. *-os.*

generate makes *-rable, -tor.*

GENERIC NAMES AND OTHER ALLUSIVE COMMONPLACES. When Shylock hailed Portia as *A Daniel come to judgment,* he was using a generic name in the sense here intended; the *History of Susanna* was in his mind. When we talk of *the Mecca of Free Trade,* of the *Huns, draconic severity,* or *tantalizing opportunities,* we are using allusive commonplaces. They are an immense addition to the resources of speech, but they ask to be employed with discretion; this article is not intended either to encourage or to deprecate their use; they are often in place, & often out of place; fitness is all.

It is perhaps worth while to call attention to a practical difference between the useful & the decorative allusions. When an allusive term is chosen because it best or most briefly conveys the meaning, triteness is no objection to it, intelligibility being the main point. The choice for decorative purposes is a much more delicate matter; you must still be intelligible, but you must not be trite, & the margin in any audience between what it has never heard of & what it is tired of hearing of is rather narrow; it is necessary to hit it between wind & water.

These few remarks may suffice on the unanswerable question whether allusive terms should be sought or avoided. The purpose of this article is not to answer it, but to point out that if they are used it is inexcusable & suicidal to use them incorrectly. The reader who detects his writer in a blunder instantly passes from the respect that beseems him to contempt for this fellow who after all knows no more than himself. It is obvious that the domain of allusion is full of traps, particularly for the decorative allusionist, who is apt to take the unknown for the fine, & to think that what has just impressed him because he knows little about it may be trusted to impress his readers. For an example or two see the articles BENEDICK, CUI BONO?, DEVIL'S ADVOCATE, FRANKENSTEIN, ILK.

genie. A spirit, esp. in Arabian lore; loosely, any spirit or sprite. Pron. jē′nĭ; pl. *genii,* pron. jē-nĭī. Another form is *jinnee* or *jinni,* pl. *jinn.*

genitive case. See POSSESSIVE CASE.

genius. (1) Pl. *-uses;* the form

genii is now used only as pl. of *genie* (or of *genius* in the sense of *genie,* i.e. attendant spirit &c.); *the intervention of his better* genius; *their evil* genii. (2) *Genius* implies supreme native endowment, creative & original; *talent,* aptitude or acquired ability. For amplification, see TALENT.

genre. Pron. zhäɴ'r. Kind, style: *works of this genre.* As applied to the fine arts, the style in which scenes & subjects of ordinary life are depicted. *Genre painting,* depicting idylls of the fireside, the roadside, the farm. Do not italicize.

genteel is now used, except by the ignorant, only in mockery.

GENTEELISM. By 'genteelism' is here to be understood the substituting for the ordinary natural word that first suggests itself to the mind, of a synonym that is thought to be less soiled by the lips of the common herd. The truly genteel invite one to *step,* not *come, this way; take in* not *lodgers,* but *paying guests;* never *help,* but *assist, each other to potatoes;* & have quite forgotten that they could ever have been guilty of *tooth-powder* & *napkins* & *underclothing,* of *before* & *except* & *about,* where nothing now will do for them but *dentifrice, serviette, lingerie, ere, save, anent.*

The reader need hardly be warned that the inclusion of any particular word in the small selection of genteelisms offered below does not imply that that word should never be used. All or most of these, & of the hundreds that might be classed with them, have their proper uses, in which they are not genteel, but natural. To illustrate a little more in detail, 'He went out without shutting the door' is plain English; with *closing* substituted for *shutting* it becomes genteel; nevertheless, *to close the door* is justified if more is implied than the mere not leaving it open: 'Before beginning his story, he crossed the room & closed the door,' i.e. placed it so as to obviate overhearing; 'Six people sleeping in a small room with closed windows,' i.e. excluding air.

The reader may now be left to the specimen list of genteelisms, which he will easily increase for himself. The point is that, when the word in the second column is the word of one's thought, one should not consent to displace it by the word in the first column unless an improvement in the meaning would result.

Genteelisms	*Normal words*
anent	about
assist	help
cease	stop
distingué	striking
domestic	servant
edifice	building
endeavor	try
ere	before
expectorate	spit
hither	here
illuminate	light
inquire	ask
lady-dog	bitch
odor	smell
perspire, -ration	sweat
peruse	read
place	put
prior to	before
proceed	go
recreation	amusement
save	except
step	come, go
stomach	belly
sufficient	enough

genteelly. So spelled.

Gentile. As used by the Jews, one of a non-Jewish race; by the

Christians, a Christian distinguished from the Jew; in India, a non-Moslem; by the Mormons, a non-Mormon—in each case, any one outside the community.

gentle. *The gentle art.* This phrase, long a favorite with the anglers as an affectionate description of their pursuit, was cleverly used by Whistler in his title *The Gentle Art of Making Enemies.* The oxymoron was what made it effective; but the journalist, aware that Whistler made a hit with *the gentle art,* & failing to see how he did it, has now, by rough handling on inappropriate occasions, reduced it to a BATTERED ORNAMENT (cf. IRRELEVANT ALLUSION).

gentleman used indiscriminately for *man* is a GENTEELISM.

gentlewoman, lady. The first has no sense that does not belong to the second also, but *lady* has half a dozen for which *gentlewoman* will not serve—the Virgin, pl. of madam, titled woman, wife, beloved, woman politely described. It follows that in the one sense common to both (fem. of *gentleman,* i.e. a woman of good birth & breeding, or woman of honorable instincts) *gentlewoman* is sometimes preferred as free of ambiguity or as more significant. It is, however, an old-fashioned word, & as such tends to be degraded by facetious use, & to have associated with it constant epithets, of which some are derisive (*ancient, decayed, innocent*) & others are resorted to as protests against such derision (*true, Nature's,* &c.). It is therefore to be used with caution.

genuine. (Pron. -ĭn.) Not spurious: *how to tell the genuine from the false;* true, not feigned: *a genuine expression of his regard;* properly so called: *the mark of a genuine idler.* Of people, free from affectation or hypocrisy: *a man of great & genuine nature.* Cf. AUTHENTIC.

genus. Pron. jē-; pl. *genera,* pron. jĕn-. The genus ranks next above the species & under the family or sub-family. The generic & specific names, usually in Latin (or supposed to be in Latin), together form the scientific proper name. The generic name stands first & is begun with a capital letter: *Quercus alba,* white oak. *Genus homo* is a FACETIOUS FORMATION.

geographic(al). The longer form is the more usual; but *geographic latitude, geographic determinism, geographic environment.*

geometric(al). (1) There is no differentiation in meaning. In US the short form prevails, esp. in scientific use; in Brit., the longer form. (2) *Geometric progression,* one whose terms or elements progress by a constant factor: 2, 6, 18, 54, &c. (in arithmetic progression, the elements progress by a constant difference: 1, 3, 5, 7, 9). For the misuse of this, see PROGRESSION.

German. *High German* is the language known ordinarily as *German; Low German* is a comprehensive name for English, Dutch, Frisian, Flemish, & some German dialects. The words *High* & *Low* are merely geographical, referring to the Southern or mountainous, & the Northern or low-lying, regions in which the two varieties developed.

gerrymander. (From *Gerry,* Gov. of Mass., & *salamander,*

1812.) To divide into districts in such a way as to give a political party unfair advantage or reach unwarranted conclusions. The *g* is properly hard, from Gerry's name, but jeri- is so generally spoken that the origin may well be forgotten.

GERUND. The gerund in English grammar is a verbal noun having the same form as the present participle (i.e. ending in *-ing*). The gerundive (Lat. adj. having the same suffix as the gerund) has no proper function in English grammar & need not be discussed here.

Loving is a gerund in *I can't help loving him* but a participle in *a loving husband.*

If a gerund is the subject of a sentence or clause, a noun preceding it should be in the possessive: *I cannot prevent* Mary's *loving him.* This tends to be disregarded in modern informal (& sometimes formal) usage (see FUSED PARTICIPLE), but is observed by careful writers. The observance is more general when the subject of the gerund is a pronoun: His *leaving town was a great surprise to us all;* 'him leaving' would sound illiterate even to those who ordinarily will have no truck with formal grammatical rules.

The agent of the gerund may be omitted unless ambiguity would result—that is, if the receiver of the action is different from the subject: I *was sure of being admitted* (NOT *of* my *being admitted*), but They *were sure of* my *being admitted.*

Some words are idiomatically followed by the gerund, some by the infinitive. Examples of the former are: *confess, equal, object, resistance* (all followed by *to* & gerund): *I confess* to leaving *myself open to censure* &c.; *habit, idea, notion, thought, plan* (all followed by *of* & gerund): *His habit* of rising *at dawn lasted until old age; hesitance* (*about* doing something); *reason* (*for* doing something); *success* (*in* achieving something). (Examples of words followed by the infinitive, not the gerund: *promise, profess, tendency, heed, manage, threaten, avail.*) To sum up:

GERUND: *I object to John's* leaving *the decision to me.*

INFINITIVE: *I object to John's refusing* to make *the decision.*

PARTICIPLE: Refusing *to make the decision, John awaited my objections.*

gesticulation, gesture. *With vehement* gesticulation; *a* gesture *of impatience; a* gesture *more eloquent than words.* The usual relation between the two is that of abstract to concrete: *gesticulation* is the using of gestures, & a *gesture* is an act of gesticulation. On the other hand, *gesture* also is sometimes used as an abstract, & then differs from *gesticulation* in implying less of the excited or emotional or theatrical or conspicuous. Similarly, if *a gesticulation* is preferred to *a gesture,* it is in order to imply those characteristics.

The use of *gesture* in political & diplomatic contexts (=advance, manifestation of willingness to treat or compromise or make concessions, exhibition of magnanimity or friendliness, &c.) dates from the First World War & is apparently a GALLICISM, having been substituted for the French *beau geste.* For *a gesture of good will, a mere gesture,* see HACKNEYED PHRASES & VOGUE WORDS.

get. 1. *Have got* for *possess* or *have* is good colloq. but not good literary English. The verb means to obtain, procure, acquire, or receive.

2. *Gotten* still holds its ground in American English (there is a popular superstition that *got* is less 'refined' than *gotten;* see GENTEELISM). In Brit. it is in verbal uses (i.e. in combination with *have, am,* &c.) 'archaic & affected'; but as a mere participle or adjective it occurs in poetical diction (*On gotten goods to live contented*) & in mining technicalities (*There is no current wage rate per ton gotten*). It is also retained in many compounds of *get: forgotten, begotten.*

3. *Get-at-able.* So spelled. It is not modern slang; Southey used it in 1799.

4. *Get-away, get-up,* n. If used, keep the hyphen.

geyser. In US usually gī′zer; Brit. usually gā′ser (but both gī- and gē- are also heard in Brit.).

-g-, -gg-. Words ending in *g* preceded by a single vowel double the *g* before the suffix beginning with a vowel: *waggery, priggish, froggy, sluggard, zigzagging, humbugged.*

ghetto. Pl. *-os* (the Italian pl., *ghetti,* is now usually pedantic).

ghoul. An evil spirit that preys on corpses; also transf. & fig.: *Ghouls feasting on the fresh corpse of reputation.* Pron. gōōl.

gibber, gibberish. The first is usually pronounced with soft *g,* & occasionally spelled *ji-.* The second is also usually so pronounced in US; in Brit. it is pronounced with hard *g,* & was sometimes spelled *gui-* or *ghi-* to mark the fact. It is doubtful whether one is derived from the other. For *gibberish, lingo,* &c., see JARGON.

gibbous. Convex, of the moon. Pron. jĭb′-.

gibe, jibe. The word meaning to scoff, sneer, taunt, is usually spelled *gibe* (but pron. j-). *Jibe* is the nautical word (sometimes *gybe* in Brit.), & the US colloq. one meaning to agree (*His words & his actions do not jibe*).

gild, n. See GUILD.

gild, v. *Gild the lily* is a MISQUOTATION (*Paint the lily*). But *gild the pill* (fig.) is historically correct.

gill (or *ghyll*) ravine, & gills of fish, pron. gĭl; *gill,* the measure, & *Gill,* lass, pron. jĭl. In Jack & Gill, *Gill* (for Gillian) is the traditional form, but is now usually *Jill* in US.

gillie has *g* hard; *gilly-flower* has *g* soft.

gingerly. The word, which is at least four centuries old, has probably no connection with *ginger;* it originally meant daintily, delicately; then mincingly, effeminately; then cautiously, warily. See TRUE & FALSE ETYMOLOGY.

Giotto, Giovanni. (*c.* 1266–1337.) Pron jŏ-.

gipsy, gy-. *Gy-* prevails in US (& has etymological justification); the former in Brit. See GYPSY.

gird, encircle, has past & p.p. *girded* or *girt.*

gist has soft *g.*

given name. The name given at baptism, the Christian name, the 'first name.' (Orig. US.)

glacé. The adj. (glä′sā′), iced, candied, glazed, is still usually italicized. Webster admits the verb, *glacé, glacéed, glacéing,* in cookery (not italics).

glacial, glacier, glacis. The pronunciations preferred in Brit. are glā'sĭal, glă'sĭer, glā'sĭs; in US glā'shăl, glā'shẽr, glā'sĭs.

gladiolus. The pronunciation recommended by COD is glădĭō'lŭs or gl*a*dī'*o*lŭs; pl. *-luses* or *-li.* The OED gives glădī'ōlŭs & glădĭō'lŭs, in that order; in US dictionaries the order is reversed, but most of them point out that the accent on the antepenult (gladī'-) is correct technically & should be used to distinguish the genus from the plant. Popular US usage remains for the most part glădĭō'lŭs; garden-club usage glădī'ōlŭs. The Am. Gladiolus Society uses the singular with collective force as the plural, as have botanists & others historically (Evelyn, Bartram, &c.).

glamour makes *glamorous;* the *-our* ending of the noun is given first in US dictionaries that for other words give first place to *-or.* This is not because *-our* is 'more glamorous,' as one writer suggested, but because of its comparatively recent introduction & its Scottish derivation. (See -OUR & -OR.) It has been cheapened in US by advertising, society editors, & journalists. See VULGARIZATION.

glassful. Pl. *glassfuls.*

glean. The literal meaning is to gather or pick up (grain &c.) after the reapers; fig. to gather, collect, scrape together, chiefly immaterial objects. *To glean information* or *experience.* The careless usage making it synonymous with *acquire, obtain,* is wrong.

glimpse. *Glance* & *glimpse* are synonyms only in a very loose sense; the glimpse is what is seen by the glance, & not the glance itself; you *take* or *give a glance* at something, but *get a glimpse* of it. A glance *at the map will convince you. I had only a* glimpse *of it before the door was closed.*

glissade. Pron. glĭsahd'.

global. OED gives only the meanings spherical, globular, & lists the word as rare. Since World War II it has become (in US) a VOGUE WORD for worldwide, international, universal: *global problems, global war, global policy.*

globe. In their primary sense, *sphere, globe, orb,* & *ball* do not differ, except with regard to the contexts they suit. And their particular applications (*a* sphere *of action, circumnavigate the* globe, *his sightless* orbs, *a* ball *of wool,* &c.) are too familiar to need setting forth.

gloss. The two nouns—(1) comment, interpretation, translation; also a false commentary, a deceiving explanation; (2) brightness or luster, hence a superficial quality, fair semblance—are of different origins, the first Greek, the other Teutonic. The derived verbs (1) to explain by notes, to comment, hence to interpret speciously; (2) to give luster to, hence to color, give a specious appearance to; & (3) *gloze,* from *gloss,* to smooth over, palliate, as well as the secondary meanings of the nouns, have been confused by ignorance of their etymology. See TRUE & FALSE ETYMOLOGY.

glossary, vocabulary. Both are partial dictionaries, & so far synonymous; but the *glossary* is a list to which a reader may go for explanation of unfamiliar terms (see GLOSS), while the *vocabulary* is a stock in which he may hope to find words to express his meaning. A *glossary* in a technical book or school book; a *vocabulary* in a language text. *Vocabulary* has also the meaning of the whole stock of words used by a nation, by any set of persons, or by an individual. For *lexicon* &c., see DICTIONARY.

gloze. The original sense of 'commenting' (see GLOSS) is obs.

gluey. So spelled.

glycerin(e). In US generally & in Brit. pharmacy, manuals of chemistry, &c., the original spelling, *-in,* is preferred. In Brit. everyday use *-ine* is commoner, & *-in* something of an affectation.

G-man. 'Government man.' A special agent of the Federal Bureau of Investigation (F.B.I.) —NOT of the Secret Service (a 'T-man,' i.e. Treasury agent).

gnaw has p.p. *gnawed* or *gnawn,* but the *-n* form may be regarded as an ARCHAISM.

gnomic (Lit., Gram.): 'sententious.' *Gnomic literature* is writing that consists of or is packed with maxims or general truths pithily expressed. *The gnomic aorist* in Greek is the aorist used, though it refers normally to the past, to state a fact that is true of all times, e.g. in proverbs.

go, v. 1. *Goes without saying* is a GALLICISM, but perhaps one of those that are nearing naturalization, ceasing to serve as meretricious ornaments, & tending to present themselves as first & not second thoughts. Still, the English stalwart has 'needless to say,' 'need hardly be said,' or 'stated,' 'of course,' & other varieties to choose from.

2. *Go phut, fut(t),* or *foot.* The first spelling seems best, as suggesting by its obvious want of connection with any English word that the point lies in the mere sound (that of a collapsing bladder).

3. Mencken cites many uses of *go* in combinations of American origin that he feels are contributions to the language though they are still usually labeled 'slang': *go-getter, go (it) one better, go through—, go ahead, go back on—, go in for—.* Several of these are given with quotations in the OED.

god-. The following god-combinations are not hyphened but single words: godchild, goddaughter, godfather, godforsaken, godhood, godless, godlike, godmother, godparent, godsend, godson, godspeed.

God's acre, as a name for churchyard or cemetery, though its beauty be admitted, has not succeeded in establishing itself in England. It is not a phrase of home growth, but a translation from German; & it is interesting that of four quotations for it in the OED only one shows it used simply without a reference to its alien nationality. It has had a greater popularity & endurance in US, especially in rural communities (because of the many Americans of German descent?). It occurs in Longfellow (*Hyperion*), & the *Century Dict. & Cyclopedia* also gives an example from *Harper's Magazine,* LXXVI.

gold, golden, adjs. The first is chiefly literal, the second poetic & fig.: *a gold crown* in an inventory of regalia, but *a golden crown* in hymns & fairy stories.

golf. The natural pronunciation (gŏlf) is the best. The OED remarks: 'The Scotch pronunciation is (gōf); the pronunciation (gŏf), somewhat fashionable in England [and US], is an attempt to imitate this.'

golosh. Use *galosh.*

gondola. Pron. gŏn′dola.

good-by, good-bye. Both forms are used but the former is more common in US, the latter in Brit. *Good morning, good evening, good day, good night* are usually not hyphened.

goodness knows has two curiously divergent senses. In *Goodness knows who it can have been* it means God only knows, & I do not; in *Goodness knows it wasn't I* it means God knows & could confirm my statement. Ambiguity is unlikely, but not impossible. *For goodness' sake,* so written.

goodwill, good will, good-will. Except in the attributive use, which happens to be rare (as *a good-will token,* i.e. as a token of good will), the choice should be between the unhyphened forms. *Good will* (*men of good will*) is required when the notion is virtuous intent &c., & *goodwill* (*the goodwill of a business firm*) is better when it is benevolence &c.

gormandize, gourmandise. The first is the English noun (rare) & verb, the second the French noun (pron. gōōr′mändēz′), still not at home in English & usually unnecessary (see FRENCH WORDS). *Gormandizing on all they had caught; To gormandize books is as wicked as to gormandize food.*

gossip makes *gossiped, gossiping, gossipy* (US & Brit.).

Gotham. First applied to the City of New York in Washington Irving's *Salmagundi;* see SOBRIQUETS.

gotten. See GET.

gouge. Pron. gowj.

gourd. The sound gōrd is preferred to gōōrd.

gourmand, gourmet. Pron. gōōr′mand, gōōr′mā′. The first ranges in sense from greedy feeder to lover & judge of good fare; the second from judge of wine to connoisseur of delicacies. The first usually implies some contempt, the other not.

governance has now the dignity of archaism, its work being done, except in rhetorical or solemn contexts, by *government & control.*

governor, -nour. The second is obs.

grace. NOT *Your Grace can do as* he *wishes.* The Eng. idiom is *as* you *wish.* For pronouns after *your grace* &c., see MAJESTY.

graduate. Uses of *graduate* now peculiar to US: (1) a pupil who has completed a school course & passed the final examination: *There were* 15 graduates *from the local high school;* (2) to admit to a university degree: *The class was* graduated *with* 6 *men.* Also *graduation,* the ceremony of conferring degrees (also Scottish).

Gr(a)ecism, gr(a)ecize, Gr(a)eco-, &c. The spelling *grec-* is recommended. Pron. grēs′ism, grēs′īze, grēkō-, &c.

graffito. ('A scratching'): Inscription or drawing scratched on ancient wall (as at Pompeii); decoration by scratches through plaster showing different-colored undersurface. Pron. grăfē′-tō; pl. *-ti,* pron. -tē.

GRAMMAR, SYNTAX, &c. 1. Grammar is the general term for the science of language. The following list gives the chief parts of it, in their logical (not actual) order of development:

Phonology (Phonetics)—How sounds are made & depicted. *Morphology*—How words are made. *Accidence*—How words are inflected. *Orthoepy*—How words are said. *Orthography*—How words are written. *Composition*—How words are fused into compounds. *Semantics*—How words are to be understood. *Syntax*—How words are arranged in sentences. *Etymology*—How words are tested by reference to their source.

Of these, *orthography, accidence,* & *syntax,* as the bare essentials for writing & reading, represent for most of us the whole of grammar; & *morphology, orthoepy,* & *phonology* are meaningless terms to the average person. SEMANTICS was popularized in US by the publication of several books on the subject in the mid-20th c.

2. Purists rightly assure us that usage that does not conform to grammatical rules is *ungrammatical,* not *bad grammar.* Nevertheless, *bad grammar* & *good grammar* have long been used (colloq.?) & will probably continue to be.

gram(me). There seems to be no possible objection to adopting the more convenient shorter form, now standard usage in US, except that the *-me* records the unimportant fact that the word came to us through French.

granary. Pron. grăn-, NOT -ā-.

grand- compounds. The common-noun compounds of kinship (*grandchild, granddaughter,* &c.) are usually written without hyphens.

grangerize. Pron. -ānj-. From James Granger, who in 1769 published a *Biographical History of England* with blank leaves on which the reader could mount illustrations. Hence to 'extra-illustrate' a book with prints &c., esp. such as have been cut out of other books. The resulting noun *grangerism* has no relation to the US word, *granger,* which comes from *grange,* i.e. a farm; an agricultural society.

granted, granting, are 'converted participles' (see UNATTACHED PARTICIPLES); they may be regarded as prepositions & need not be attached to a noun. Granted *his honesty,* he *may be mistaken.* Granted *that two beings are so independent of each other, then . . .*

grave, v. (carve &c.), p.p. *graved* or *graven,* the second much the commoner; but the whole verb is archaic except in particular phrases, esp. *graven image, graven on one's heart.*

gravel makes in US *-led, -ling,* but *-lly;* Brit. *-lled* &c.

gray. Usually so spelled in US; Brit. GREY.

great. For the differences between *great, big,* & *large,* see BIG. The chief uses of *great* are as follows:

1. a high degree of (*great care; great generosity*);

2. of persons & things, possessing the essential quality in a

high degree (*a great schoolmaster; a great fool*);
3. eminent, of distinction (*a great man; a great family*), from which comes the distinctive epithet (*the great auk; Great Britain; Alexander the Great*);
4. sometimes, remarkable in size, but only when emotion is indicated (*He hit me with a great stick! Take your great feet off the sofa! What a great head he has!*).

great commoner, *the great unwashed,* are HACKNEYED PHRASES. See also SOBRIQUETS.

Grecian, Greek. The first is now curiously restricted by idiom to architecture & facial outline: *the Grecian bend & knot,* & *Grecian slippers.* We seldom talk of *Grecian,* but usually of *Greek, history, fire, calends, lyrics, tyrants, Church, dialects, aspirations,* though *Grecian noses & brows, colonnades & pediments,* & *and a good Grecian he is!* may still be heard.

Grecism, grecize, Greco-, &c. So spelled. See GR(A)ECISM.

greenness. So spelled.

Greenwich time, Village. The Brit. pronunciation is grĭn′ĭj; the US grĕn′ĭj. Webster gives the pronunciation of the Village (New York City) as Grēn′wĭch, but it is not commonly so called there.

grey, gray. 'In Great Britain the form *grey* is the more frequent in use, notwithstanding the authority of Johnson & later English lexicographers, who have all given the preference to *gray*' (OED).

greyhound is known to be unconnected with *grey,* though the meaning of its first part is doubtful; there is no justification, however, for the occasional US *grayhound.* See TRUE & FALSE ETYMOLOGY.

gridiron. Grating (hist. used for torturing by fire) for broiling food over coals. *Grid,* a frame, grating, network of lines (as on a map & mod. football field, &c.), a shortening of *gridiron; griddle* (from the same source as *gridiron*), now a (plate or) heavy pan on which cakes & scones are baked.

griffin, griffon, gryphon. *Griffon* is the regular zoological form, i.e. as the name of a kind of vulture; it is also the French dog name. For the monster, *griffin* is the ordinary, & *gryphon* an ornamental spelling.

grill, grille. The first, n. & v., is used in cooking (*to cook on a grill, to grill chops*); the second for the (architectural) ornament or sidewalk grille.

grimy. So spelled.

grippe, grisaille, grisette. See FRENCH WORDS. *Grippe* (=influenza) is anglicized in pronunciation, often in spelling (*grip*). *Grisaille* (=decorative painting in gray monotone, esp. on glass), pron. grĭsāl′ or grēsāl′, also anglicized. *Grisette* (=a girl of the French working class, esp. a shop assistant or seamstress) pron. grĭzĕt′ (the connotation 'lively & free in manners' reflects the observation of the foreigner in Paris).

grisly, grizzly. The first means inspiring horror, uncanny; the second gray, grizzled. The bear could be either, but is *grizzly.*

grosbeak. Pron. grōs′-.

grouse, the bird, both sing. & pl. The verb (slang = to grumble) was used by Kipling some 60 years ago.

grovel makes US *-ling, -led;* Brit. *-lling* &c.

grow. The use of *grown* for *grown up* is chiefly US (e.g. *Her children were both grown*). *Grown-up,* n. & adj., usually hyphened.

gruel makes US *-ling* &c.; Brit. *-lling* &c.

gruesome, grewsome. The first spelling is correct.

gryphon. An ornamental spelling of GRIFFIN.

guarantee, guaranty. For the verb *-ee* is now preferred; for the noun it is never wrong where either is possible. The contexts in which *-y* may still be reasonably preferred are those in which the giving of the security is meant rather than the security given or its giver: e.g. *contracts of guaranty; be true to one's guaranty.*

guer(r)illa. In US *-rr-;* Brit. usually *-r-*. (From Sp. diminutive of *guerra,* war.)

guess. The American's colloq. use of *guess* for *think, suppose, believe* identifies his caricature in England as *Oh, I say* identifies the caricature of an Englishman to US. There is nothing wrong with the word when used with its true meanings—conjecture, solve by conjecture, estimate, form a random judgment. See also RECKON.

guide makes *guidable.*

guidon. Small distinguishing flag or streamer. Pron. gī′dn.

g(u)ild, n. Though the form *guild* dates back only to 1600, it became so vastly predominant in the 17th & 18th cc. that the REVIVAL *gild* usually puzzles the reader for a moment, & should be abandoned as an affectation. The verb is always *gild.*

guillemet. The French quotation mark « ».

guillotine. Pron. gĭl′ōtēn. (After J. I. Guillotin, the French physician, who proposed it in 1789.)

guimp. Use *gimp.*

gulden. (Dutch & German coin.) Pron. gōōl-.

gullible. So spelled.

gunwale, gunnel. The pronunciation is always, & the spelling not infrequently, that of the second.

gusset makes *gusseted* &c.

guttural. Of the throat. The sounds *k, g,* & *ch* as in *keep, get,* & *loch* (Scottish).

guy, v., makes *guyed, guying;* n., a person of grotesque appearance, from Guy Fawkes. In US slang use, a person, a fellow, but not necessarily disparaging, as it is in Brit. (e.g. US *a good guy*).

gybe. The nautical term is usually so spelled in Brit., *jibe* in US. See GIBE.

gymnasium. Pl. *-ums* or *-a;* as the name of a German place of education, pl. *Gymnasien.*

gymp. Use *gimp.*

gypsy, gipsy. The first preferred in US, the second Brit. In contrast with the words into which *y* has been introduced instead of the correct *i,* apparently from some notion that it has a decorative effect (*sylvan, syren, tyre, tyro,* &c.), there are a few from which it has been expelled for no better reason than that the display of two *ys* is thought an excessive indulgence in ornament. In *gypsy* & *pygmy* the first *y* is highly significant, reminding us that *gypsy* means *Egyptian,* & *pygmy* foot-high (Gk. *pugme,* elbow to knuckles). It is a pity that they should be thus cut away from their roots, & the maintenance of the *y* is desirable.

gyves. The old pronunciation was with the *g* hard, as indicated by a former spelling *gui-;* but the *g* is now soft.

H

habiliments. Dress suited to spec. office or occasion; 'applied also jocularly or grandiloquently' (OED) to ordinary clothes. See POLYSYLLABIC HUMOR.

habitude. In some of its obs. senses (relation to, intimacy or familiarity) the word was not exchangeable with *habit.* But in the senses that have survived it is difficult to find or frame a sentence in which *habit* would not do as well or better, the only difference being a slight flavor of archaism attaching to *habitude.* The sense 'constitution' or 'temperament' is so rare as to be negligible, & *habitude* may fairly be classed as a SUPERFLUOUS WORD.

habitué. A habitual visitor or resident. Pron. as Eng., ha-bĭt û ā′.

HACKNEYED PHRASES. When *Punch* set down a heading that might be, & very likely has been, the title of a whole book, 'Advice to those about to marry,' & boiled down the whole contents into a single word, & that a surprise, the thinker of the happy thought deserved congratulations for a week; he hardly deserved immortality, but he has—anonymously, indeed—got it; a large percentage of the great British people cannot think of the dissuasive 'don't' without remembering, &, alas! reminding others, of him. There are thousands to whose minds the cat cannot effect an entrance unaccompanied by 'harmless necessary'; nay, in the absence of the cat, 'harmless' still brings 'necessary' in its train; & all would be well if the thing stopped at the mind, but it issues by way of the tongue, which is bad, or of the pen, which is worse. King David must surely writhe as often as he hears it told in Sheol what is the latest insignificance that may not be told in Gath. And the witty gentleman who equipped coincidence with her long arm doubtless suffered even in this life at seeing that arm so mercilessly overworked.

The hackneyed phrases are counted by the hundred, & those registered below are a mere selection. Each of them comes to each of us at some moment in life with, for him, the freshness of novelty upon it; on that occasion it is a delight, & the wish to pass on that delight is amiable. But we forget that of any hundred persons for whom we attempt this good office, though there may be one to whom our phrase is new & bright, it is a stale offense to the ninety & nine.

The purpose with which these phrases are introduced is for the most part that of giving a fillip to a passage that might be humdrum without them. They do serve this purpose with some readers—the less discerning—though with the other kind they more effectually disserve it. But their true use when they come into the writer's mind is as danger signals; he should take warning that when they suggest themselves it is because what he is writing is bad stuff, or it would not need such help; let him see to the substance of his cake instead of decorating with sugarplums. In considering the following selection, the reader will bear in mind that he & all of us have our likes & our dislikes in this kind; he may find pet phrases of his own in the list, or miss his pet abominations; he should not on that account decline to accept a caution against the danger of the hackneyed phrase.

Suffer a sea change./Sleep the sleep of the just./The cups that cheer but not inebriate./Conspicuous by his absence./Innocent bystander./A consummation devoutly to be wished./Which would be laughable if it were not tragic./But that is another story./Had few equals & no superior./Come into one's life./Has the defects of his qualities./Leave severely alone./In her great sorrow./More sinned against than sinning./Throw out the baby with the bath./My prophetic soul!/The irony of fate./The psychological moment./More in sorrow than in anger./There's the rub./Filthy lucre./The inner man./Too funny for words./My better half./Eagle eye./Young hopeful./Seriously incline./The turn of the century./The logic of facts, events./At the parting of the ways./Not wisely, but too well.

had. 1. *had, had have.* There are two dangers—that of writing *had . . . have* where *had* is required, & that of writing *had* where *had . . . have* is required. The first has proved fatal in the (WRONG) *Had she have done it for the Catholic Church, she would doubtless have been canonized;* & in *Had I* have *been there on Monday, I should certainly have been present at the first performance.* This is not uncommon, but is no better than an illiterate blunder. *Had she, had I,* are the inverted equivalents of *if she had, if I had;* no one would defend *if she had have done,* nor *if I had have been,* & it follows that *Had she done, Had I been,* are the only correct inverted conditionals.

The other error is seen in (WRONG) *The country finds itself faced with arrears of legislation which for its peace & comfort* had far better been *spread over the previous years.* It ought to be *had far better* have *been spread;* but the demonstration is not here so simple. At the first blush one says: This *had* is the subjunctive equivalent of the modern *would have,* as in *If the bowl had been stronger My tale* had been *longer;* i.e. *had far better been spread* is equivalent to *would far better have been spread.* Unluckily, this would involve the consequence that *you had far better done what I told you* must be legitimate, whereas we all know that *You had far better* have *done* is necessary. The solution of the mystery lies in the peculiar nature of the phrase *had better.* RIGHT: *You had better do it; It had better be done; You had better have done it; It had better have been done.* It will be granted at once that these are correct, & that *have* cannot be omitted in the last two.

2. *Had* in parallel inverted clauses. WRONG: Had *we desired twenty-seven amendments,* got *seven accepted, &* were *in*

anticipation of favorable decisions in the other twenty cases, we should think . . . To write *Had we desired & were in anticipation* is wrong (see ELLIPSIS 6); to write *Had we desired & were we in anticipation,* though legitimate, is not only heavily formal, but also slightly misleading, because it suggests two separate conditions whereas there is only a single compound one. This common difficulty is best met by avoiding the inversion when there are parallel clauses; write here *If we had desired & were in anticipation.*

3. For other uses of *had* (past subj.) see SOON, RATHER, GOOD, WELL.

haem- hæm-, hem-. *Hæmato-,* combining form meaning *blood.* Pron. hēm-. In US *haem-* is preferred in zoological & botanical names and derivatives, *hem-* in most other senses. *Haematoxylin,* a tree of the senna family and the dye derived from it; but *hemoglobin,* the pigment in the red corpuscles &c. Brit. usually *haem-* in all words. See Æ, Œ.

haggard. Originally said of a falcon 'that preyed for her self long before she was taken' (OED). Of a person, wild-looking from privation, want of rest, anxiety, terror, or worry. The modern use, 'gaunt from loss of flesh with age,' was apparently influenced by *hag* (repulsive old woman).

hagiarchy, hagiolatry, &c., have hard *g.*

hair do (pl. -s) is apparently est. in US in place of the formal *coiffure. Hairdress* has never been popular (except in *hairdresser*); *headdress* is properly the ornamental covering worn on the head.

halcyon (days). (Pron. hăl'sĭun.) Orig. 14 days near the winter solstice, from the bird that in ancient fables bred in a floating nest and charmed the wind & the waves so the sea was calm during that period. Hence calm, peaceful. *The halcyon days of youth.* But see HACKNEYED PHRASES.

half. 1. *A foot & a half, one & a half feet.* In all such mixed statements of integers & fractions (7½ mill., 3¾ doz., 27½ lb., &c.), the older & better form of speech is the first—*a foot & a half, seven millions & a quarter,* &c. In writing & printing, the obvious convenience of the second form, with figures instead of words, & all figures naturally placed together, has made it almost universal. It is a pity that speech should have followed suit; the 1½ ft. of writing should be translated in reading aloud into *a foot & a half;* & when, as in literary contexts, words & not figures are to be used, the old-fashioned *seven millions & a quarter* should not be changed into *seven & a quarter millions.* But perhaps the cause is already lost; we certainly cannot say *a time & a half as large* instead of *one & a half times.* For sing. or pl. after *one & a half,* use pl. noun & sing. verb: *One and a half* days is *all I can spare.*

2. *Half as much again* is a phrase liable to misunderstanding or misuse. *The train fares were raised this year 25%, & have again been increased by half as much again.* That should mean by a further 37½%, making altogether 62½%; the reader is justified, though possibly mistaken, in

suspecting that 12½ (*half as much*, not *half as much again*) was meant, making all together 37½% instead of 62½. The phrase is better avoided in favor of explicit figures when such doubts can arise.

3. *Half-world* = demi-monde, see GALLICISMS.

4. *Better half* = wife, see HACKNEYED PHRASES.

5. *Half of it* is, *half of them* are, *rotten;* for discussion, see NUMBER.

6. *Half past two* is more usual in both US & Brit. than *half after two*.

7. *Half binding.* In book binding, the back (covering the spine) and corners of the material specified (e.g. *half-morocco*), the two sides (front & back covers) being cloth or paper.

8. *Half title:* the short title of a book printed on the first page of text, or the title of a subdivision printed on a separate page before the part it introduces.

9. Hyphens are usual in *half-breed, -caste, -holiday, -mast, -sister, -wit; halftone, halfway* (adj.), single words.

hallelujah, halleluiah, alleluia. 'Now more commonly written as in the A.V. of the O.T. *hallelujah*'—OED. Pron. -lo͞o'ya. The mispronunciation lo͞olya should be avoided.

halliard. Use *halyard.*

hallmark. The official mark stamped on gold & silver articles at Goldsmiths' Hall, London; fig., a distinctive token of genuineness, excellence, &c. *The hallmark of military genius.*

Halloween. The traditional (and Brit.) spelling is *-e'en,* but in US now usually *-een.*

halo. US pl. usually *halos;* Brit. *-oes.*

hamstringed, hamstrung. No doubt of the right form is possible; in *to hamstring, -string* is not the verb *string;* we do not string the ham, but do something to the tendon called the *hamstring;* the verb, that is, is made not from the two words *ham* & *string,* but from the noun *hamstring;* it must therefore make *hamstringed.* In use, however, *-stringed* is rare, and the dictionaries give *-strung* as a variant. Esp. in fig. use (*the government hamstrung by protective legislation*) insistence on *-stringed* is pedantic. See DIDACTICISM.

hand. 1. *Hand & glove, hand in glove.* Both forms are common; the OED describes the second as 'later,' & *hand & glove* gives best the original notion, as familiar as a man's hand & glove are, while *hand in glove* suggests, by confusion with *hand in hand* (which is perhaps responsible for the *in*), that the hand & the glove belong to different persons. *Hand & glove* is therefore perhaps better.

2. *At close hand.* WRONG: *Those who follow the intricacies of German internal policy* at close hand *are able to . . .* This phrase seems to be a mixture of *close at hand* & *at close quarters.*

3. *Get the better hand.* WRONG: *If the Imperial troops* got the better hand, *the foreigners would be in far greater danger* similarly mixes *get the better of* with *get the upper hand.*

4. *Handful,* pl. *-ls.*

5. *On hand* in the sense of *in attendance* (*please be on hand early*) is chiefly US. In the sense of in one's possession (*any*

books you have on hand) it is est. idiom.

6. *To hand* (= within reach), *Any weapon that comes to hand;* (= received), *your letter which came to hand this week,* commercialese.

7. *In hand* (= at one's disposal), *cash in hand;* (= in process, preparation), *the work in hand now;* (= under control), *He kept his emotions well in hand.*

handicap makes *-pped* &c.

handkerchief. Pron. hang′ker-chĭf.

hang. Past & p.p. *hanged* of the capital punishment & in the imprecation; otherwise *hung. Hanger-on,* n., colloq., pl. *hangers-on.*

hangar. The aircraft shed is so spelled, & pronounced *-ngg-.*

hanker. To have a longing or craving. Constr. *after,* infinitive, rarely *for.* RIGHT: *The tendency of human nature to* hanker after *all that is forbidden./To be told what you've been* hankering *to* know *so long./*Hankering for *a glimpse of home.*

haply. By chance; perhaps. Now archaic or poetic.

happen. Followed by *in* or *into* (*I* happened into *a book auction; Some friends* happened in), obs. except in US, for which Webster lists it as dial.; at best it is colloq. *I* happen to *think* (*you're wrong, it's true,* &c.) is usually apologetic circumlocution. The mock-modest use (*I* happen to *know a little Greek*) is equally offensive. See SUPERIORITY.

happening(s). There is nothing to be said against *happening*(*s*) on the score of correctness; but it is a child of art & not of nature. It comes to us not from living speech, but from books; the writers have invented it, how far in SAXONISM (*event* is the English for it), & how far in NOVELTY-HUNTING, is uncertain. We cannot help laughing to see that, while the plain person is content that events should happen, the Saxonist on one side requires that there should be *happenings,* & the anti-Saxonist on the other that things should *eventuate.* The purpose of the quotations appended is to suggest that the use of the word is an unworthy affectation: *There was, first of all, one little* happening *which I think began the new life./Mr. William Moore* (*who has up to now played singularly little part in recent* happenings) *said . . ./So clear & vivid are his descriptions that we can almost see the* happenings *as he relates them.*

hara-kiri. NOT *-kari* or *hari-kari.*

harass. So spelled. Pron. har′ass, har′assment.

harbo(u)r. In US *-or,* Brit. *-our.* In place names, e.g. *Pearl Harbor, Harbour Grace,* the local spelling must be retained.

hardly. 1. *Hardly, hard.* Except in the sense *scarcely,* the idiomatic adv. of *hard* is *hard,* not *hardly:* 'We worked hard, lodged hard, & fared hard'—DeFoe. It is true that in special cases *hardly* may or must be substituted, as in 'What is made is slowly, hardly, & honestly earned'—Macaulay; if Macaulay had not wanted a match for his two other adverbs in *-ly,* he would doubtless have written *hard;* but there is now a tendency, among those who are not conversant enough with grammar to know whether they may venture to print what they would certainly say, to amend *hard* into *hardly* & make the latter the normal word; see UNIDIOMATIC -LY. It is even more advisable with *hard* than with other such adverbs to avoid the *-ly* alternative, since, as the following quotations show, a misunderstood *hardly* will reverse the sense: (AMBIGUOUS) *It must be remembered that Switzerland is not a rich country, & that she is* hardly *hit by the war./The history, methods, &* hardly won *success of the anti-submarine campaign.*

2. *Hardly . . . than.* This & *scarcely . . . than* are among the corruptions for which ANALOGY is responsible. *Hardly . . . when* means the same as *no sooner . . . than;* & the *than* that fits *no sooner* ousts the *when* that fits *hardly.* The mistake is so obvious that it should not need pointing out; it is however, surprisingly common. WRONG: *The crocuses had* hardly *come into bloom in the city parks* than *they were swooped upon by the children./* Hardly *has midsummer passed* than *municipal voters all over the country have to face the task of choosing new mayors.*

3. *Without hardly* is dial. or illiterate for *almost without.*

4. Equally bad is *no . . . hardly,* as in (WRONG) *There is* no *industry* hardly *which cannot be regarded as a key industry. There is hardly any* is the English. *Hardly* (= not quite) has the effect of a negative and must not be combined with a superfluous negative (eg. *couldn't hardly*).

harem, -am, -eem, -im. The est. spelling & pronunciation are *harem,* hār′em; hâr′em is also often heard in US. *Haram, harràm,* are antiquated; *hareem* & *harim* (pron. harēm′) may still fairly be called DIDACTICISMS.

harmless. To insist that *harmless* will not admit of comparison (*more* or *most*), that a thing is either *harmful* or *harmless,* is PEDANTRY. ('One of the most harmless of human vanities'—Coleridge.) For *harmless, necessary cat,* see HACKNEYED PHRASES.

harmony, melody. When the words are used not in the general sense, which either can bear, of musical sound, but as the names of distinct elements in music, *harmony* means 'the combination of simultaneous notes so as to form chords' & *melody* 'a series of single notes arranged in musically expressive succession' (OED).

Harpers Ferry, W.Va. NOT *Harper's.*

harquebus, arquebus. The *h-* form is established.

hart, stag, buck, hind, doe. The following extracts from OED definitions will make the distinctions clear:

Hart—the male of the deer, esp. of the red deer; a stag; spec. a male deer after its fifth year.

Stag—The male of a deer, esp. of the red deer; spec. a hart or male deer of the fifth year.

Buck—The he-goat, obs. The male of the fallow deer. (In early use perh. the male of any kind of deer.) The male of certain other animals resembling deer or goats, as the reindeer, chamois. Also, the male of the hare & the rabbit.

Hind—The female of the deer,

esp. of the red deer; spec. a female deer in & after its third year.

Doe—The female of the fallow deer; applied also to the female of allied animals, as the reindeer. The female of the hare or rabbit.

hashish, -eesh. The first spelling is better; pron. hash′-.

haste, v., is now literary or dial., displaced in modern usage by *hasten.*

hautboy. Pron. hō′boi; *oboe* (pron. ōbō) is now the usual form.

hauteur. Pron. hō tûr′. Do not italicize. *Haughtiness* is the English equivalent but *hauteur* has been used as an English word since the 17th c. The distinction between the two, when there is one, seems to be that *hauteur* is used of haughtiness of manner, not necessarily of spirit. *He seemed to think* hauteur *an essential feature of the clerical office./His* haughtiness *and disdain alienated him from everyone who would be his friend.*

have. Some common pitfalls: 1. *No legislation ever has*‸*or ever* will affect *their conduct.* The p.p. (*affected*) cannot be understood from *affect,* and must be inserted after *has.* For this common mistake see ELLIPSIS 3.

2. *Some Liberals* would have *preferred* to have *wound up the Session before rising.* After past conditionals (*should have liked, would have preferred,* &c.) the present inf. is almost invariably the right form. Hence substitute *to wind up* for *to have wound up.* For this mistake see PERFECT INFINITIVE 2.

3. *For if the Turks* had reason *to believe that they were meditating the forcible seizure of Tripoli, it was not to be expected that facilities for extending Italian inflence* would readily have been *accorded. Would have been,* as often happens, is wrongly substituted for *would be.*

4. *What* would have *Beaconsfield thought?* We need only substitute *he* for *Beaconsfield* to see that the right place for the subject in this type of question is between *would* & *have.*

5. Although many people object to using the auxiliary *do* with *have,* it is idiomatic colloq. and often legitimate, esp. when the meaning is 'is it (your) custom to have' (*Do you* have *coffee for breakfast?*); it is wrong when *have* means *possess* (*He* doesn't have *a nickel to his name*—i.e. he hasn't . . .). For other examples see DO 2.

6. *Have got* is often used colloq. for *have: I've* got *more examples now than I can possibly use.* (But *Have you got the number yet?* is legitimate.)

havoc, v., makes *-cking, -cked.*

hay. *Look for a needle in a bottle of hay.* This is the correct form of the phrase, *bottle* being a different word from the familiar one, & meaning *truss;* but having become unintelligible it is usually changed into *bundle.* (*Look for a needle in a haystack* is heard more often in US.)

HAZINESS. What is meant by this is a writer's failure to make a clear line between different members of a sentence or clause, so that they run into one another; if he does not know the exact content of what he has set down or is about to set down, the word or words that he is now writing will naturally not fit without overlapping, or a gap will be left between them. This sounds so obvious that it may seem hardly worth while to devote an article to the matter & find a heading for it; but even the more flagrant transgressions of the principle are so numerous as to make it plain that a warning is called for. Those more flagrant transgressions are illustrated first.

WRONG: *The* effect *of the tax is not likely* to be productive of *much real damage* (overlapping; part of *be productive of* has been anticipated in *effect;* omit either *the effect of* or *productive of*)./*It is a pity that* an account *of American activities in aircraft production cannot yet* be described (overlapping; *account* is contained in *described;* omit *an account of,* or change *described* to *given*)./ *The* need *of some effort, a joint effort if possible, is an urgent* necessity *for all the interests concerned* (*need* & *necessity* overlap)./A taste *for arboriculture has always* attracted *a wealthy & cultured class* (*taste* & *attracted* overlap).

Certain words seem to lend themselves especially to this sort of haziness, as AGO (*It is five years* ago since *I saw him*); REASON with BECAUSE (*The only* reason *his wages have not been higher is* because [i.e. that] *the profits of the industry have been miserably low*), or with DUE (*The* reasons *of his success were* due *not only to . . .*); the illogical TOO (*We need not attach* too much *importance to . . .*); PREFERABLE with *more* (*The former alternative being, in our view, on every ground the* more preferable); BUT with superfluous negatives (*Who knows* but *what this memorial exhibition may* not *prove the starting point?*); REMAIN with *continue* (*And yet through it all I* continue to remain *cheerful*); SEEM with *appear* (*These conclusions, it* seems *to me,* appear *to be reached naturally*).

Additional examples will be found under the words printed in small capitals.

he. In spite of the frequency with which we all claim to know the grammar of *he* & *him,* an illegitimate *him* occasionally appears even in less colloq. placings than 'That's him.' WRONG: *It might have* been him *& not the President who said . . .* The tendency to use *he* where *him* is required is, however, much commoner in print. The mistake occurs when the pronoun is to stand in some out-of-the-way or emphatic position; it looks as if writers, pulled up for a moment by the unusual, hastily muttered to themselves 'Heedless of grammar, they all cried "That's him!"' & thanked God they had remembered to put 'he.' WRONG: *The bell will be always rung* by he *who has the longest purse & the strongest arm./The distinction* between the man *who gives with conviction* & he *who is simply buying a title.*

headquarters, n. pl. (but occasionally used as sing. when the sense is the source of control: *Headquarters* has *no report at this time*).

healthful, healthy. The purist insists that in modern usage *healthful* means conducive to health (lit. & fig.), *healthy* possessing health; but the latter is also used as conducive to health, esp. of material things and fig.: *a healthy climate, influence, place to live,* &c. To insist on *-ful* is a disregarding of idiomatic usage.

heap. *Heaps* takes a sing. verb unless followed by *of:* Heaps *of magazines* are *piled in the corners;* but *There* is heaps *more to say.* See NUMBER.

hearken, harken. The second form is etymologically better (from *hark*) but *hearken* is given first in both US & Brit. dictionaries.

heave. Past & p.p. *heaved* or *hove.* In US *heaved* is more usual, esp. in fig. senses.

heaven. *For heaven's sake,* NOT *heavens' sakes.*

Hebraism, Hebraist, Hebraize, are the usual forms, not *Hebrewism* &c.

Hebrew, Israelite, Israeli, Jew, Semite. *Hebrew* suggests the pastoral & patriarchal, or the possession of a language & a literature; *Israelite,* the Chosen People & the theocracy, & him in whom was no guile; *Israeli,* a citizen of modern Israel; *Semite,* the failure of most modern nations to assimilate their Jews. The fact remains that *Jew* is the current word, & that if we mean to substitute another for it, it is well to know why we do so.

hecatomb. Pron. -ŏm. A great public sacrifice (orig. 100 oxen); hence any great slaughter.

heckle, hector, vv. The words are often confused in modern usage. The first means to question with a view to discover the weak points of the person being heckled (orig. in Scotland, of parliamentary candidates); hence to catechize severely, to tease with questions; the second, to intimidate by blustering or threats, to bully. RIGHT: *We are not to be* hectored *into compliance./ The audience proceeded to* heckle *him in a way dear to the local constituencies.*

hectic. The blossoming of *hectic* into a VOGUE WORD, meaning excited, intense, impassioned, wild, uncontrolled, & the like, is very singular. The OED (1901) explains its one quotation of the kind ('vehement & hectic feeling') as an allusion to the hectic flush—no doubt rightly. Now a hectic flush is one that is accounted for not, like other flushes, by exceptional & temporary vigor or emotion, but by the last stage of consumption, characterized by sudden rise of temperature, perspiration, and heightened color. Although some dictionaries admit the meanings given above without comment (i.e. as standard English) Webster lists this use of the word as colloq., COD as slang.

hecto-. Combining form meaning multiplied by 100 (*hectometer, hectoliter*). *Centi-* means divided by 100.

hedonist, Cyrenaic, epicurean, utilitarian. *The hedonist* (literally, adherent of pleasure) is a general name for the follower of any philosophy, or any system of ethics, in which the end or the *summum bonum* or highest good is stated as (in whatever sense) pleasure.

The Cyrenaic (i.e. follower of Aristippus of Cyrene) is the hedonist in its natural acceptation—the pleasure-seeker who only differs from the ordinary voluptuary by being aware, as a philosopher, that the mental & moral pleasures are pleasanter than those of the body.

The epicurean (or follower of Epicurus), bad as his popular reputation is, rises above the Cyrenaic by identifying pleasure, which remains nominally his *summum bonum,* with the practice of virtue.

The utilitarian, by a still more surprising development, while he remains faithful to pleasure, understands by it not his own, but that of mankind—the greatest happiness of the greatest number.

It will be seen that the *hedonist* umbrella is a broad one, covering very different persons. Both the epicurean & the utilitarian have suffered some wrong in popular usage. It has been generally ignored that for Epicurus pleasure consisted in the practice of virtue, & the utilitarian is unjustly supposed (on the foolish ground that what is useful is not beautiful & that beauty is of no use) to rate the steamroller higher than *Paradise Lost.* It may be worth while to quote the OED's statement of 'the distinctive doctrines of Epicurus: (1) That the highest good is pleasure, which he identified with the practice of virtue. (2) That the gods do not concern themselves at all with men's affairs. (3) That the external world resulted from a fortuitous concourse of atoms.

hegemony. Leadership, esp. of one state in a confederation (*The smaller countries, fearing the* hegemony *of France* . . .). The pronunciation hējĕm'onĭ is recommended.

hegira. (Flight.) *Hejira* is nearer the Arabic, but the word came into English from French, and *hegira* is established. Pron. US (usually) hejīr'a; Brit. hĕ'jira; *hijrah* is sometimes in scholarly use but for most of us it is an evidence of DIDACTICISM.

height, highth. *Highth,* though still heard (dial. or colloq.), is an obs. variant of *height.* NEVER *heighth.*

heinous. Pron. hā-. Infamous, atrocious, of crime or criminal; transf., of the accusation. *A heinous offender; a heinous sin. A heinous charge.*

heir. 1. *Heir apparent, heir presumptive.* These phrases are often used, when there is no occasion for either & *heir* alone would suffice, merely because they sound imposing. And those who use them for such a reason sometimes give themselves away as either supposing them to be equivalent or not knowing which is which. WRONG: *By the tragedy of the death of the Crown Prince Rudolph in* 1889 *the Archduke Ferdinand became* the Heir Apparent *to the throne.* Rudolph, it is true, was heir apparent; but by his death no one could become heir apparent except his child or younger brother (whereas Ferdinand was his cousin), since the Emperor might yet conceivably have a son who would displace anyone else. An heir apparent is one whose title is indefeasible by any possible birth; an heir presumptive is one who will lose his position if an heir apparent is born. Mistakes are no doubt due to the double sense of the word *apparent.* Its old sense, retained in *heir apparent,* & still possible elsewhere in literary use, but avoided for fear of confusion with the other & prevailing sense, is *manifest* or *unquestionable.* But the current sense is almost the same as that of *seeming,* though with slightly less implication that the appearance & the reality are different; *apparent* in this sense means much the same as *presumptive,* but in the other something very different; hence the error.

2. *Heir* can be either masc. or fem. and in legal documents is usually so used: *Sarah Lewis, heir to the said Rebecca Warren. Heiress* is used esp. in connection with the inheritance of wealth: *His ambition was to marry a young & attractive heiress.*

heliotrope. Pron. hē-.

Hellene, Hellenic. The function of these words in English, beside *Greek,* is not easy to define. They were formerly scholars' words, little used except by historians, & by persons concerned not so much with Greeks in themselves as with the effects of Greek culture on the development of civilization in the world. With the modern spread of education, the words have been popularized in such connections; at the same time the national aspirations of Greek irredentists have called newspaper attention to *pan-Hellenism* & to the name by which the Greeks & their king call themselves; so that the proportion of people to whom *Greek* means something, & *Hellene & Hellenic* nothing, is smaller than it was. Nevertheless, *Greek* remains the English word, into whose place the Greek words should not be thrust without special justification.

help, v. *Than,* & *as, one can help. Don't sneeze more than you can help, Sneeze as little as you can help,* are perhaps to be classed as STURDY INDEFENSIBLES. Those who refrain from the indefensible however sturdy it may be have no difficulty in correcting: *Don't sneeze more than you must, Sneeze as little as you can* or *may.* Out of *Don't sneeze if you can help it* is illogically developed *Don't sneeze more than you can help,* which would be logical, though not attractive, if *cannot* were written for *can.* And out of *Don't sneeze more than you can help* by a further blunder comes *Sneeze as little as you can help;* a further blunder, because there is not a mere omission of a negative—'you cannot help' does not mend the matter —but a failure to see that *can* without *help* is exactly what is wanted: the full form would be *Sneeze as little as you can sneeze little,* not *as you either can, or cannot, keep from sneezing.* The OED, which stigmatizes the idiom as 'erroneous,' quotes Newman for it: *Your name shall occur again* as little as I can help *in the course of these pages* (where *as little as may be* would have done, or, more clumsily, if the *I* is wanted, *as little as I can let it*).

helpmate, helpmeet. The OED's remark on the latter is: A compound absurdly formed by taking the two words *help meet* in Gen. ii. 18, 20 ('an help meet for him,' i.e. a help suitable for him) as one word. *Helpmate* is now the est. form.

hem-. The usual (US) spelling of the combining form of Gr. *haima,* blood, in all but botanical & zoological scientific names & derivatives. See HAEM-.

hemi-. A prefix meaning *half* (*hemisphere, hemiplegia*).

hempen. In US poetic or archaic. See -EN ADJECTIVES.

hendiadys. (Rhet.): 'one by means of two.' The expressing of a compound notion by giving its two constituents as though they were independent & connecting them with a conjunction. Little used in English, but *nice and warm, try & do better* are true examples. *Courage & intrepidity* is almost a hendiadys for *intrepid courage.* Pron. hĕn dī'ă dĭs.

her. 1. Case. For questions of *her* & *she,* see SHE, & cf. HE.
2. For questions of *her* & *hers* (e.g. *Her & his tasks differ*), see ABSOLUTE POSSESSIVES.
3. For *her* & *she* in irresolute or illegitimate personifications (e.g. *The United States has given another proof of* its *determination to uphold* her *neutrality./Danish sympathy is writ large over all* her *newspapers*), see PERSONIFICATION.

herb. In US usually pronounced urb (*an herb garden*), but *a herbal.* Brit. usually pron. hurb (*a herb*).

Herculean. Pron. her kū'lian. The normal sound of words in *-ean* is with the *-e-* accented & long; so Periclē'an, Cytherē'an, Sophoclē'an, Medicē'an, & scores of others. Of words that vacillate between this sound & that given by shifting the accent back & making the *-e-* equivalent to *i,* most develop a second spelling to suit; so *Caesarean* or *Caesarian, cyclopean* or *-pian, Aristotelean* or *-lian. Herculean,* like *protean,* changes its sound without a change of spelling; & many people in consequence doubt how the word should be said. The sound herkū'lian (preferred by most dictionaries) is not a modern blunder to be avoided, but is established by long use.

heredity. The word is now used, by good writers, only in the biological sense, i.e. the tendency of like to beget like. The extract below, where it has been substituted for *descent* solely because *descendant* is to follow, illustrates well what happens when zeal for ELEGANT VARIATION is not tempered by discretion: *The Agha Khan . . . is unique because of his* heredity*—he is a lineal* descendant *of the Prophet Mohammed.*

herewith. *Enclosed herewith please find . . .* Typical business jargon, to be shunned.

heroic (of meters). (Lit., Poet.): *Heroic* poetry=epic. *Heroic verse* or *meter,* or *heroics,* the meter used in heroic poetry, i.e. hexameters in Greek & Latin, & the five-foot iambic in English, whether blank as in *Paradise Lost* or in rhymed couplets (*the heroic couplet*) as in Chaucer's *Prologue* & in Dryden & Pope.

herr. German equivalent to English *mister.* Pl. *herren.*

hers. RIGHT: *A friend of* hers. *His wish and* hers. Hers *was the fault. This applied to her and* hers. See also ABSOLUTE POSSESSIVES.

herself. Intensive & emphatic form of *she.* Idiomatic uses: *She did it* herself. *She hurt* herself. *She* herself *first discovered it. She is not* herself. *Ask the woman* herself. *She had the habit of talking to* herself. *In the excitement she forgot* herself *completely.*

hesitance, hesitancy, hesita-

tion. There is little differentiation in the dictionary definitions, and the last has almost driven out the others. *Hesitancy* or *hesitance* is occasionally convenient when what is to be expressed is not the act or fact of hesitating, but the tendency to do so; indecision. *She rejected it without* hesitation./*That perpetual* hesitancy *which belongs to people whose intelligence & temperament are at variance./ Without* hesitance *& without regret.*

hetero-. Combining prefix meaning *different, other,* as in *heterogeneous, heterography* (=inconsistent or irregular spelling).

hew. In US the p.p. is now usually *hewed* in literal contexts, *hewn* in fig.: *It had to be* hewed *before it could be sawed;* hewn *down by the enemy.* Brit. usually *hewn.*

hexameter. (Poet.): 'six-measure.'

Hibernian differs from *Irish(man)* as GALLIC from *French,* & is of the nature of POLYSYLLABIC HUMOR.

hiccup makes *-uping, -uped.* The spelling *-ough* is a perversion of popular etymology, & 'should be abandoned as a mere error' (OED).

hide, v., p.p. *hidden* or *hid,* the latter still not uncommon.

hie makes *hieing.* Now usually poetic or facetious.

hierarchic(al). The long form is the commoner.

highfalutin(g). Colloq. (orig. US), high-flown, bombastic. The shorter form is better. (*High-flown* in this sense has been in the language since the 17th c.)

highly. 1. It should be remembered that *high* is also an adv., & better than *highly* in many contexts: e.g. *It is best to pay your men* high; High-placed *officials;* see UNIDIOMATIC -LY.

2. Though *highly* in the sense 'to a high degree' is often unobjectionable (*a highly contentious question*), it has acquired, when used with adjectives of commendation, a patronizing taint (*a highly entertaining performance*) like *distinctly,* & is best avoided in such connections.

Highness. Pronouns after *Your Highness* &c. are *you, your,* (NOT *her* or *his*). See MAJESTY.

hight. As a variant of *height,* dial. As v.=to name, call oneself, archaic.

him. Used as subj. after *is, than,* colloq.: *that's him now; You're really worse than him.* NOT acceptable in written or formal English. See HE.

Himalaya(s). The traditional pronunciation is hĭmä'layȧ(z), but himalā'ya(z) is also heard, esp. in Brit.

himself. For idiomatic uses, see HERSELF.

hind. Female of the (red) deer. For synonyms see HART.

hindermost. Archaic for *hindmost.*

hinge, v., makes *hinging.*

Hippocratic oath. The oath of Hippocrates (Gr. physician, 460?-357 B.C.), embodying the code of medical ethics.

hippogriff, -gryph. Fabulous winged creature, half-horse, half-griffin. The first spelling is recommended; cf. GRIFFIN.

hippopotamus. Pl. *-muses* better than *-mi.*

hircine, hirsute. The first means goat-like; the second hairy.

his. PITFALLS: 1. *A graceful raising of* one's *hand to* his *hat.* *His* should be *one's.* Since the repetition is ugly, however, it could be avoided in this case by substituting *the* for the first *one's.* For the question between *his* & *one's* in such positions, see ONE.

2. *The member for Morpeth has long been held in the highest respect by all who value sterling character & whole-hearted service in the cause of* his *fellows. His* should be *one's* (i.e. a man's). For this type of mistake see PRONOUNS.

3. *His,* POSSESSIVE ABSOLUTE: For uses, see HERS.

historic. *The historic present* is the present indicative used instead of the past, to give vividness. Unless used with great care it can be confusing and tedious.

historic(al). The DIFFERENTIATION between the two forms has reached the stage at which it may fairly be said that the use of one in a sense now generally expressed by the other is a definite backsliding. The ordinary word is *historical; historic* means memorable, or assured of a place in history; *historical* should not be substituted for it in that sense. The only other function retained by *historic* is in the grammarians' technical terms *historic tenses, moods,* &c., in which it preserves the notion appropriate to narration of the past of which it has been in general use robbed by *historical.*

historicity. The earliest OED example of this ugly word is dated 1880; but, being effective in imparting a learned air to statements that are to impress the unlearned, it has had a rapid success, & is now common. It has, however, a real use as a single word for the phrase 'historical existence,' i.e. the having really existed or taken place in history as opposed to mere legend or literature. To this sense, in which it makes for brevity, it should be confined. *The historicity of St. Paul* should mean the fact that, or the question whether, St. Paul was a real person. The following quotation shows the word in a quite different sense; in that sense it would not have been worth inventing (why not *accuracy?*); & as soon as it has two or more senses liable to be confused, it has lost the only merit it ever had—that of expressing a definite compound notion unmistakably in a single word: *He is compelled to speak chiefly of what he considers to be exceptions to St. Paul's strict* historicity *& fairness; & he tells us that he is far from intending to imply that the Apostle is usually* unhistorical *or unfair.*

hitch, v., is not slang, as some people suppose, but an old est. word meaning move (things) with a jerk; fasten with a loop &c. In the sense of *harness* (*an animal to a vehicle*), it is an Americanism (also fig., as in Emerson's *Hitch your wagon to a star*).

hither, described by the OED as 'now only literary,' is even in literature, outside of verse, almost disused. It is still tolerable, perhaps, in one position, i.e. as the first word in an inverted sentence following a description of the place referred to—*Hither flocked all the . . .*

Elsewhere, it produces the effect of a FORMAL WORD, being used mainly by the unpracticed writers who bring out their best English. The same is true of *thither;* but, as often happens with stereotyped phrases, *hither & thither* retains the currency that its separate elements have lost.

hoarhound. Var. of HOREHOUND.

Hobson's choice. A 'choice' without an alternative; the thing offered or nothing: (Thomas Hobson, who rented horses, *c.*1600, at Cambridge, England, required each of his customers to take the horse nearest the door).

hodgepodge. In the fig. sense, a mixture (derogatory); usually so spelled in US. *A hodgepodge of tragedy and bathos.* But see HOTCHPOT(CH).

hoe, v., makes *hoeable, hoeing.*

hoi polloi. These Greek words for the majority, ordinary people, the man in the street, the common herd, &c., meaning literally 'the many,' are equally uncomfortable in English whether *the* (=*hoi*) is prefixed to them or not. Unless the allusion is to Gilbert & Sullivan, the best solution is to eschew the phrase altogether.

hoist. *Hoist with his own petard* (*Hamlet*), blown up by his own bomb. *Hoist* is p.p. of (obs.) *hoise,* raise aloft, usually with exertion. The later form, present *hoist,* has the past & p.p. *hoisted.*

hold. (1) In the sense consider, regard as (*I hold him guiltless*), no longer followed by *as* or inf. (i.e. NOT *I hold him* to be *innocent;* or *I hold him* as *blameless*). (2) *Hold up* (i.e. stop and rob: *two men* held up *the train*) is still listed by some dictionaries as US colloq., but it is generally accepted as US standard. *A hold-up,* however, is still slang.

holidays, vacation. In US usually *Home for the holidays* (Christmas, Easter, &c.) but *summer vacation.* Brit. usually *summer-holiday(s),* but *vacation* for the interval between university or legal terms.

holily. *Piously, sacredly,* &c. are more at home in most contexts.

holo-. Combining form meaning *whole, entire. Holograph,* a document written and signed by the person under whose name it appears. *Holocaust:* orig. a sacrifice in which the whole offering is consumed by fire; fig. a wholesale sacrifice or destruction (esp. by fire).

home, n. (1) A home is a dwelling place of a family or household. Its commercial use for HOUSE (*A row of stucco homes is now under construction*) is incorrect and offensive. (2) The adj. is usually *homey* in US; Brit. often *homy.*

homely. (1) The meanings are: simple, plain, unpretentious; of people, plain (US, also ugly, ill-favored); *homelike,* comfortable, familiar. (2) For *to use a homely phrase* see SUPERIORITY.

homeo-. Combining form meaning *like: homeopathy.*

Homeric. *Homeric laughter* is usually defined 'loud, hearty laughter,' 'irrepressible laughter' and is usually so used. Properly it is 'laughter like that of the gods as they watched lame Hephaestus hobbling' (COD). For a discussion of its usage, see LAUGHTER.

homo-. Combining form meaning *same; homogeneous* &c.

homonym, synonym. Broadly speaking *homonyms* are separate words that happen to be identical in form, & *synonyms* are separate words that happen to mean the same thing. *Pole,* a shaft or stake, is a native English word; *pole,* the terminal point of an axis, is borrowed from Greek; the words, then, are two & not one, but being identical in form are called *homonyms.* On the other hand *cat,* the animal, & *cat,* the flogging instrument, though they are identical in form & mean different things, are not separate words, but one word used in two senses; they are therefore not homonyms. True *synonyms* are words exactly equivalent in meaning and use, as *furze* & *gorse;* such synonyms are rare, & the word is applied more frequently to pairs or sets in which the equivalence is partial only; see SYNONYMS.

homophones. Words having the same sound but a different meaning, *wright, right, rite.* See also SYNONYMS.

Hon. In the use of this prefix (*Hon.* or *the Hon*), which requires the person's Christian name or initial, not his surname alone (*the Hon. James* or *J. Brown,* NOT *the Hon. Brown*), a common mistake is to suppose that the Christian name is unnecessary before a double-barreled surname, as in *The Court, composed of Mr. Justice A. T. Lawrence,* the Hon. Gathorne-Hardy, *&* . . . The same remarks apply to the prefixes *Rev.* & *Sir.* With *Hon.* & *Rev.*, if the Christian name or initial is unknown, *Mr.* should be inserted (*the Hon. R. Jones* or *the Hon. Mr. Jones,* NOT *the Hon. Jones,* nor *The Hon. Pryce-Jones*).

honeyed, honied. The first is best.

honor. (1) US usually *-or,* Brit. *-our;* see -OUR, -OR. (2) *A custom more honored in the breach than the observance.* Whoever will look up the passage (*Hamlet* I. iv. 16) will see that it means, beyond a doubt, a custom that one deserves more honor for breaking than for keeping; but it is often quoted in the wrong & very different sense of a dead letter or rule more often broken than kept. WRONG: *The Act forbids entirely the employment of boys . . . 'by way of trade or for the purpose of gain.' Therefore, unless the Act* be honored more in its breach than in its observance, *the cherubic choirboy . . . is likely . . . to be missing from his accustomed place.* For a similar mistake, see DEVIL'S advocate.

honorarium. A fee, usually voluntary, for professional services; an honorary payment or reward. In US the *h* is not pronounced (*an honorarium*); in Brit. it usually is.

hoof. Pl. *-fs,* sometimes *-ves.*

hooping-cough. US *whooping-* (pron. hoop-).

hope. In the OED examples illustrating the use of the verb, not a single one bears the slightest resemblance or gives any hint of support to any of the sentences here to be quoted.

First, two examples of the monstrosity sufficiently discussed in the article DOUBLE PASSIVES: *No greater thrill* can be hoped to be enjoyed *by the most persistent playgoer of today than . . ./What* is hoped to be gained *by the repetition of these tirades just now I cannot conceive.*

Secondly, ANALOGY has been at work &, as *hope* & *expect* are roughly similar in sense, the construction proper to one (*I expect them to succeed*) is transferred to the other (*I hope them to succeed,* whence *They are hoped to succeed*) with which it is far from proper. WRONG: *I need not say how wide the same law ranges, & how much* it can be hoped to *effect./In the form of a bonus intended to cover the rise,* hoped to be temporary, *in the cost of living.* But the notion that, because *hope* means *hopefully expect,* therefore it can have the construction that that phrase might have is utterly at variance with the facts of language.

Thirdly, writers have taken a fancy to playing tricks with *it is hoped,* & working it into the sentence as an essential part of its grammar instead of as a parenthesis; the impersonal *it* is omitted, & *is* (or *are*) *hoped* is forced into connection with the subject of the sentence, with deplorable results (see also IT). WRONG: *The actual crest of the hill was not reached,* as^was hoped *might be possible./The final arrangements for what*^is hoped *will prove a 'monster demonstration.'* Read *as it was hoped; what it is hoped . . .*

hopeful. For *young hopeful* see HACKNEYED PHRASES.

horehound, hoarhound. Though the analogical spelling is *hoar-* (i.e. the word is connected with *hoary*), this is much less usual than *hore-,* in both US & Brit.

horrendous. Frightful, horrible; rare at best, the word is kept alive chiefly by those seeking ELEGANT VARIATION.

horrible, horrid. The distinctions between the two are (1) that *horrid* is still capable in poetical & literary use of its original sense of 'bristling' or 'shaggy'; & (2) that while both are much used in the trivial sense of 'disagreeable,' *horrible* is still quite common in the graver sense 'inspiring horror,' which *horrid* tends to lose, being now 'especially frequent as a feminine form of strong aversion' (OED).

hors de combat, hors-d'œuvre. Pron. (1) ôr dẽ kônbȧ, (2) ôr dûvr. *Hors* means *outside:* (1) 'out of the fight,' disabled; (2) 'out of the work,' i.e. out of the meal—relishes &c. served before the meal (pl. in English usually *-œuvres*).

horse makes *horsy,* NOT *horsey.*

hose (=stockings) is archaic, or a shop name, or a GENTEELISM.

hospitable. The stress should be on hos-ʹ, NOT on -pit-.

hospital(l)er. In US usually *-aler,* Brit., *-aller;* pl. *Knights Hospitallers.*

hostile. Pron. (US) hostĭl, (Brit.) -īl.

hostler (orig. stableman at an inn; now anyone who takes care of horses) is the usual form in US; *ostler* Brit.

hotchpot, hotchpotch, hodgepodge, hotpot. The first is nearest to the original form (Fr. *hochepot*=shakepot); 2, 3, & perhaps 4, are successive corruptions dictated by desire for expressiveness or meaning when the real sense was forgotten. *Hotchpotch* is the prevailing form in Brit.; *hotchpot* is the technical legal term; *hodge-podge* is the prevailing (non-legal) form in US.

hotel. The old-fashioned pronunciation with the *h* silent (cf. *humble, humour, humorous*) is certainly doomed, & is not worth fighting for. *A hotel* usually; but still sometimes, esp. Brit., *an hotel.*

houri. (Nymph of Mohammedan paradise.) Pron. hoor'ĭ or howr'ĭ.

house, home. Traditionally, *house* is the structure, *home* connoting family ties, domestic comfort, &c. The modern (US) tendency to make the two interchangeable (*A beautiful new home in North Main Street*) is best avoided.

houseful. Pl. *-ls.*

housewife. The shortened pronunciation (hŭ'zĭf or hŭz'wĭf), which is almost invariable for the sewing case, is usually an affectation in US when used for the mistress or domestic manager; displacement of the traditional hŭ'zif or hŭzwif by hows'wīf was in part brought about in the 16th c., when *housewife* & *hussy* were still realized to be the same word, by the feeling that a distinction between the two was due to the reputable matron.

Houyhnhnms. The 'human' horses of *Gulliver's Travels.* So spelled. Pron. hwĭnĭms.

hover. Pron. hŭ'ver, NOT hō- or hŏ-.

howbeit is archaic in one of its senses (*nevertheless*) & obs. in the other (*although*). The archaic has its place in modern writing, the obs. has not; see ARCHAISM. Those who, without much knowledge of the kind of literature in which archaism is in place, are tempted to use this word should carefully note the distinction.

however. Several small points require mention. 1. *However, how ever, how . . . ever.* In everyday talk, *how ever* is common as an emphatic form of the interrogative *how* (How ever *can it have happened?*). It should not appear in print except when dialogue is to be reproduced, being purely colloq. This does not apply to cases where *ever* has its full separate sense of 'at any time or under any circumstances,' but it is then parted from *how* by some other word or words. NOT *We believe that before many years have passed employers & employed alike will wonder* however *they got on without it;* this should have been *how they ever got on;* the other order is an illiteracy in itself, & the offense is aggravated by the printing of *however* as one word. See EVER.

2. *But however, but . . . however.* REDUNDANT: But *it must be remembered,* however, *that the Government had no guarantee.*/But *these schemes,* however, *cannot be carried out without money.* For other examples of this disagreeable but common redundancy see BUT 5; either *but* or *however* suffices; one should be taken, & the other left; sitting on two stools is little better than falling between them. It is noteworthy that *But however* with nothing intervening, which would seem the most flagrant case, is on the contrary better than the form

illustrated above; the juxtaposition suggests that there is more in it than mere carelessness, & that *however* has the definite sense 'in spite of all'—is in fact a full adverb & not a conjunction, & therefore strictly defensible as not trespassing on *but*'s ground. The usage is colloq. only.

3. *However* TOO LATE: *These extravagant counterattacks in mass on the Cambrai front,* however, *materially helped the French operations in Champagne.* The excuse for such late placing of the conjunction—that *these . . . front* is in effect a single word—is sound only against a suggestion that it should be placed after *attacks;* it, or *Nevertheless,* or *All the same,* could have stood at the head of the sentence. The undue deferring of *however* usually comes from the same cause as here, i.e. the difficulty of slipping it in where it interrupts a phrase, & should be recognized as a danger to be avoided.

4. *However* TOO EARLY. It should be borne in mind that the placing of *however* second in the sentence has the effect, if the first word is one whose meaning is complete (e.g. *He* as compared with *When*), of throwing a strong emphasis on that word. Such emphasis may be intended, or short of that may be harmless; but again it may be misleading. Emphasis on *he* implies contrast with other people; if no others are in question, the reader is thrown out. WRONG: *The Action Commission wished to get permission for meetings & had telephonic communication with Walraff, who declared that he would not negotiate with the workmen.* He, however, *would receive the Socialist members of Parliament.* The only right place for *however* there is after *would,* the contrast being not between *him* & anyone else, but between *would not* & *would.* The mistake is made with other conjunctions usually cut off by commas, but is especially common with *however* & *therefore.*

hue. Orig. a synonym for *color, hue* is now so used chiefly poetically or rhet.; it is usually a vaguer word, including quality, shade, tint, and can be applied to a mixture of colors: an *autumnal hue.* For synonymy see TINT.

hue-outcry. Obs. exc. in *hue & cry.*

human makes *humanness.* The use of *human* as a noun for *human being* is still generally regarded as colloq. or facetious.

humanist. Meanings: A student of human affairs (*such a* humanist *as Shakespeare*); a student of the humanities, hence a classical scholar; one of the scholars of the Renaissance who participated in the Revival of Learning; one of the modern schools believing in the supremacy of human, rather than divine, ideals (faith in man, not God; e.g. Paul Elmer More). The word is apt to puzzle or mislead, first, because it is applied to different things & a doubt of which is in question is often possible, & secondly because in two of these senses its relation to its parent word *human* is clear only to those who are acquainted with a long-past chapter of history. See HUMANITY.

humanity. *The Humanities,* or *Litterae humaniores,* is an old-fashioned name for the study of classical literature. The original humanists were those who in the Dark Ages, when all learning was theology & all the learned were priests or monks, rediscovered pre-Christion literature, turned their attention to the merely human achievements of Greek & Roman poets & philosophers & historians & orators, & so were named *humanists* as opposed to the divines; hence the meaning classical scholar; the humanities, classical literature. Now often extended to all literary, historical, philosophical, &c. students, as opp. to those of natural science.

humor, wit, satire, sarcasm, invective, irony, cynicism, the sardonic. So much has been written upon the nature of some of these words, & upon the distinctions between pairs or trios among them (*wit & humor, sarcasm & irony & satire*), that it would be both presumptuous & unnecessary to attempt a further disquisition. But a sort of tabular statement may be of service against some popular misconceptions. The constant confusion between *sarcasm, satire, & irony,* as well as that now less common between *wit & humor,* seems to justify this mechanical device of parallel classification; but it will be of use only to those who wish for help in determining which is the word that they really want. (Mencken defined *humor* as the 'capacity to discover hidden & surprising relations between apparently disparate things.')

humo(u)r, n., US usually *-or,* Brit. *-our.* (Brit. *humourless* but *humorist.*) *Humor* is still often pronounced without the *h* sound; the derivatives now being rarely without it, *humor* itself will probably follow suit.

hundred. Hundreds *of people; several* hundred *people.* See COLLECTIVES 3.

hundredfold. One word.

hung. P.p. of HANG, except when used for capital punishment or suicide.

hurt, v., intrans., meaning 'suffer pain' (*my arm hurts*) is colloq. only.

hybrid. Half-breed, crossbreed. *Hybrid derivative:* fig., a word composed of incongruous elements; e.g. *bi-daily* in which a Latin prefix is combined with an English word, or *sendee* in which an English

	MOTIVE or AIM	PROVINCE	METHOD or MEANS	AUDIENCE
humor	Discovery	Human nature	Observation	The sympathetic
wit	Throwing light	Words & ideas	Surprise	The intelligent
satire	Amendment	Morals & manners	Accentuation	The self-satisfied
sarcasm	Inflicting pain	Faults & foibles	Inversion	Victim & bystander
invective	Discredit	Misconduct	Direct statement	The public
irony	Exclusiveness	Statement of facts	Mystification	An inner circle
cynicism	Self-justification	Morals	Exposure of nakedness	The respectable
The sardonic	Self-relief	Adversity	Pessimism	Self

word is given a French suffix.

hyena, -aena. The first is better.

hygiene, hygienic. Pron. hī'-jīĕn, hījīĕn'ĭk. As the form of *hygiene* often puzzles even those who know Greek, it is worth while to mention that it is the French transliteration of a Greek word meaning art of health.

hyper-. Combining form meaning *over* (in excess of, exaggerated); *hypercritical.* The opp. of HYPO-.

hyperbole. Pron. hīper'bolĭ. (Rhet.): 'over-shooting.' Use of exaggerated terms for the sake not of deception, but of emphasis, as when *infinite* is used for *great,* or 'a thousand apologies' for an apology.

hyphen, hyphenate, hyphenize, vv. There is no differentiation in meaning; *hyphen* is the oldest and simplest, and though the second is established in US, both it and *-ize* may be regarded as NEEDLESS VARIANTS. *Hyphenation* is better than *-ization; hyphening* is perhaps best.

HYPHENS. 1. A hyphen is a symbol conveying that two or more words are made into one. The union may be for the occasion only, or permanent (as in *half-breed, make-believe*); the commonest form of temporary union is that in which a phrase (say *open shop*) is to be used attributively, i.e. as an adjective to another noun; to this end it must be marked as one word by the hyphen (*an open-shop policy*).

2. The hyphen is not an ornament; it should never be placed between two words that do not require uniting & can do their work equally well separate; & on the other hand the conversion of a hyphened word into an unhyphened single one is desirable as soon as the novelty of the combination has worn off, if there are no obstacles in the way of awkward spelling, obscurity, or the like.

3. The proper functions of the hyphen may be thus classified:

A. To convert two or more separate words into a single one acting as one adjective or noun or other part of speech. Such unions of the temporary kind are *Housing-of-the-working-classes* as an epithet of *Bill,* & *strong-Navy* as epithet of *agitation;* permanent ones are *ne'er-do-well, stick-in-the-mud,* & *what's-his-name,* serving as noun, adjective, & pronoun.

B. To announce that a compound expression consisting of a noun qualified adjectivally by the other element means something different from what its elements left separate would or might mean. Compare *Thrushes are not black birds* with *Thrushes are not black-birds* or *blackbirds.* The expressions coming under this head are chiefly those of which the second element is a noun & the first is an adjective (as in *black-bird, red-coat*) or an attributive noun (as in *water-rat*).

C. To render such compound expressions as a verb & its object or other appurtenances, or a noun & its adjective, amenable to some treatment to which it could not otherwise be subjected. Thus *Court Martial,* if it is to have a possessive case (the *Court-martial's decision was . . .*), must be one word; *storms beat, rend hearts, come home, handle by means of men, proof against bombs, go by,* can be converted into handy adjectives, nouns, or verbs, fit to receive suffixes or to play the part that may be required of them in a sentence, by being combined with a hyphen (often afterwards dropped out) into single words; so we get, *stormbeaten, heartrending, homecoming, man-handle, bomb-proof,* & (the) *go-by.*

D. To show that two adjectives, each of which could be applied separately to a noun (*I saw a red hot face,* i.e. one both red & hot), are not to be so applied, but are to form one epithet conveying a compound idea (*holding a red-hot poker*); such are *worldly-wise, mock-heroic, bitter-sweet.*

E. To attach closely to an active or passive participle an adverb or preposition preceding or following it that would not require hyphening to the parent verb (*you put up,* not *put-up, a job,* but the result is *a put-up job*).

In US the tendency is to drop the hyphen as soon as possible. *A near-by house* becomes *a nearby house* and even more unhappily *a house nearby. Dining room* and *dining room furniture* are more usual than *dining-room;* and *bathroom* is so spelled. The thug makes a successful *getaway* by wearing a *getup* resembling a plumber's. (But theatrical *make-up* is still so spelled.) In US the foe of the established hyphen is usually the typographer or dictionary maker (hence the copy editor), not the writer himself. In the works of many writers we still have *dining-room furniture, a near-by house,* and *a house near by.* The hyphening of compounds in the text of this book does not always follow that of US dictionaries.

hypo-. Combining form meaning *under, below* (*hypothesis,* foundation, hence, basis of an argument, from 'below' & 'placing'; *hypotension,* low blood pressure). See HYPER-.

hypothecate. *Hypothecate* means only to mortgage or pledge. (*He had no power to* hypothecate *any part of the public revenue.*) In (WRONG) *the Nahua race, which, by tradition, served the Aztecs in much the same way as to origin as the* hypothecated *Aryans serve ourselves* it is used as a verb corresponding to *hypothesis;* if an allied verb is really necessary, *hypothesize* is the right form, though it is to be hoped that we may generally content ourselves with *assume.*

hypothesis. Pl. *-theses,* pron. -ēz.

hypothetic(al). The longer is much commoner; there seems to be no distinction of meaning or usage.

hysteric(al). The short form has almost gone out of use as adj., and should be allowed to die.

hysteron proteron. (Rhet.): 'later earlier.' Putting the cart before the horse in speech, as in Dogberry's 'Masters, it is proved already that you are little better than false knaves, & it will go near to be thought so shortly.'

I

I. *Between you & I* is a piece of false grammar not sanctioned, like the contrary lapse *It is* ME, even by colloq. usage. Similar lapses are seen in (WRONG) *It was a tragedy of this kind which* brought home to my partner & I *the necessity for . . . /This has* led *Mr.* —, *Mr.* —, & I *to rethink the question in the light of recent developments.*

-i. The plurals with this ending need care in three points. (1) As plural of Italian words in *-o* or *-e* (*confetti, dilettanti, conoscenti,* &c.) *-i* is always pronounced ē, but as plural of Latin & Greek words in *-us* or *-os* (*bacilli, Magi*) it is now usually pronounced ī; for those to whom Latin & Italian words are indistinguishable, safety lies in *-uses,* which is now permissible in nearly all words, & better in most. (2) Many classical words in *-us* are given impossible plurals in *-i* by those who know little or no Latin. Such are *hiatus, afflatus, octopus, corpus, virus,* & *callus,* the Latin plurals of which end variously or do not exist; safety for the non-latinist again lies in *-uses.* (3) *Ignoramus, mandamus,* & *mittimus,* though now English nouns, are in Latin not nouns at all, but verbs (= we do not know, we command, we send); having become nouns only in English they can have only the English plurals *ignoramuses, mandamuses, mittimuses.*

iamb(us). The short form (pl. *iambs*) is more usual in US, the long form (pl. *-buses* or *-bi*) in Brit.

iambus. (Poet.): 'incentive.' The foot ⏑–, named as employed in early Greek satires.

Iberian. Of or pertaining to Iberia, the Spanish Peninsula. (Not to be confused with *Hibernian,* Irish [*Hibernia,* L. Ireland].) Also an Asiatic people near the Caucasus in modern Georgia.

ibidem. Stress second syllable. 'In the same place.' Abbr. *ibid.* Italics not necessary. Used to avoid the repetition of a reference, the meaning is 'in the same' book, chapter, passage, &c.

-IC(AL). A great many adjectives appear with alternative forms in *-ic* & *-ical.* Often the choice between them on any particular occasion is indifferent, so far as the writer's immediate object is concerned. To those who can afford time to think also of the interests of the English language it may be suggested that there are two desirable tendencies to be assisted.

The first of these is DIFFERENTIATION. There are many pairs in *-ic* & *-ical,* each form well established & in constant use, but with a difference of meaning either complete or incipient. The final stage of differentiation is seen in *politic* & *political,* which are not even content, as usual, to share an adverb in *-ically,* but make *politicly* by the side of *politically.* Between *economic* & *economical* the distinction is nearly as clear, though the seal has not been set upon it by a double provision of adverbs; most writers are now aware that the two words mean different things, & have no difficulty in choosing the one required. This can hardly be said of *comic(al),* the short form of which is often made to do the other's work. And so differentiations tail off into mere incipiency. Every well-established differentiation adds to the precision & power of the language; every observance of an incipient one helps it on the way to establishment, & every disregard of it checks it severely. It is therefore clear that writers have a responsibility in the matter.

The second laudable tendency is that of clearing away the unnecessary. When two forms coexist, & there are not two senses for them to be assigned to, it is clear gain that one should be got rid of. The scrapping process goes on slowly by natural selection. Sometimes the determining cause is apparent, as when *hysteric, cynic,* & *fanatic,* give way to *hysterical, cynical,* & *fanatical,* because they have themselves acquired a new function as nouns. Sometimes the reasons are obscure, as when *electric* & *dynamic* supersede the longer forms while *hypothetic* & *identic* are themselves superseded. But that one or other should prevail is a gain; & it is further gain if the process can be quickened. With this end in view, it is stated in this dictionary, about many *-ic(al)* words, which appears to be the winning side, that writers may be encouraged to espouse it.

ice makes *iceable, iceberg, icebound, iceman;* but *ice water, ice cream.*

icon. Also spelled *ikon* & *eikon,* but the first is best, US & Brit.

-ICS. 1. *-ics, -ic.* Among the names of sciences, arts, or branches of study are a few words in *-ic* that rank as real English; the chief are *logic, magic, music,* & *rhetoric;* but the normal form is *-ics,* as in *acoustics, classics, dynamics, ethics, mathematics, physics, politics, tactics.* The substitution of *-ic* for *-ics* (*dialectic, ethic, gymnastic, linguistic, metaphysic,* &c.) in compliance with French & German usage has the effect, whether it is intended or not, of a display of exotic learning, & repels the possibly insular reader who thinks that 'English is good enough for him.' It should be added, however, that the *-ic* & *-ics* forms can sometimes be usefully kept for separate senses; thus, *dialectic* meaning the art of logical disputation, *dialectics* would mean rather a particular person's exhibition of skill in it; but it is not with many words that this need arises, & it is not usually with this end in view that the *-ic* words are made.

2. Grammatical number of *-ics.* This is not so simple a matter as it is sometimes thought. The natural tendency is to start with a fallacy: We say *Mathematics is* (& not *are*) *a science;* therefore *mathematics* is singular. But the number of *is* there is at least influenced, if not (whether legitimately or otherwise) determined, by that of *science.* The testing should be done with sentences in which there is not a noun complement to confuse the issue: *Classics are,* or *is, now taking a back seat; Tactics are,* or *is, subordinate to strategy.* The rules that seem to emerge are: (1) Singular for the name of a science strictly so used; *Metaphysics,* or *Acoustics,* deals *with abstractions,* or *sound.* (2) Plural for those same names more loosely used, e.g. for a manifestation of qualities; often recognizable by the presence of *his, the,* &c.: *His mathematics are weak; Such ethics are*

abominable: The acoustics of the hall are *faulty.* (3) Plural for names denoting courses of action or the like: *Heroics* are *out of place; Hysterics* leave *me cold.* (4) The presence of a singular noun complement often makes the verb singular: *Mathematics,* or even *Athletics,* is *his strong point.*

idea. WRONG: *Humperdinck had the happy* idea *one day* to write *a little fairy opera. Idea* in this sense takes the GERUND, not the infinitive: *the happy idea of writing.*

idée fixe. A 'fixed idea' (one that dominates the mind); monomania. Pron. ē dā fēks′, but see FRENCH WORDS.

idem. 'The same.' (In) the same book, chapter, passage, title as already mentioned.

identic(al). (1) The short form has been so far ousted by the long as to be now a mere archaism except in the language of diplomacy (*identic note, declaration, action,* &c.). (2) If A and B are identical, A is identical *with* B (NOT *to*).

ideology. The pronunciation with long *i* is recommended, but ĭd- is also acceptable, US & Brit. *Ideologist* &c., so spelled, not *ideal-*.

id est. 'That is (to say).' See I.E.

IDIOM. This dictionary being much concerned with idiom & the idiomatic, some slight explanation of the terms may perhaps be expected. (For some synonyms, see JARGON.) 'A manifestation of the peculiar' is the closest possible translation of the Greek word. In the realm of speech this may be applied to a whole language as peculiar to a people, to a dialect as peculiar to a district, to a technical vocabulary as peculiar to a profession, & so forth. In this book, 'an idiom' is any form of expression that, as compared with other forms in which the principles of abstract grammar, if there is such a thing, would have allowed the idea in question to be clothed, has established itself as the particular way preferred by those whose mother tongue is English & therefore presumably characteristic of them. 'Idiom' is the sum total of such forms of expression, & is consequently the same as natural or racy or unaffected English. To suppose that grammatical English is either all idiomatic or all unidiomatic would be as far from the truth as that idiomatic English is either all grammatical or all ungrammatical. Grammar & idiom are independent categories; being applicable to the same material, they sometimes agree & sometimes disagree about particular specimens of it. The most that can be said is that what is idiomatic is far more often grammatical than ungrammatical; but that is worth saying, because grammar & idiom are sometimes treated as incompatibles. The fact is that they are distinct, but usually in alliance. To give a few illustrations: *You would not* go for to *do it* is neither grammatical nor idiomatic English; *I doubt* that *they really mean it, The distinction* leaps *to the eyes,* & *A* hardly earned *income,* are all grammatical, but all for different reasons unidiomatic; *It was not* me, Who *do you take me for?, There* is *heaps of material,* are idiomatic but ungrammatical; *He was promoted* captain, *She* all but *capsized,* Were *it true,* are both grammatical & idiomatic. For examples of special idioms see CAST-IRON IDIOM.

idiosyncrasy, -cratic. The right spelling (*-sy*, NOT *-cy*) is of some importance, since the wrong distorts the meaning by suggesting a false connection with the many words in *-cracy*. Those words are from Greek *kratos*, power; this is from Greek *krasis*, mixture. Its meaning is 'peculiar mixture,' & the point of it is best shown in the words that describe Brutus: *His life was gentle, & the elements So mixed in him that Nature might stand up And say to all the world 'This was a man.'* One's idiosyncrasy is the way one's elements are mixed, & the nearest synonyms for it are *individuality* & *character;* both of these, however, having positive implications not present in *idiosyncrasy*, the continued existence of the latter in its proper sense is very desirable, & it should be kept to that sense. Thus it is reasonable to say that a person has no character or no individuality, but a person without an idiosyncrasy is inconceivable. (Webster's definition, 'eccentricity,' is misleading, as is the ACD's 'susceptibility esp. to food, drugs, etc.') Since *idiosyncrasy* means all the ingredients of which a unit is composed, & their proportions & reactions—a valuable compound notion that we may be thankful to find compressed into a single word—it is a pity that it is often used as a polysyllabic substitute for various things that have good simple names of their own. It is both pretentious & absurd to say that so-&-so is one of your *idiosyncrasies* when you mean one of your habits, ways, fads, whims, fancies, or peculiarities. See POPULARIZED TECHNICALITIES. In *The errors a person is liable to make owing to his* idiosyncrasy, the word is used correctly. In the quotations following, read 'characteristic,' 'peculiarities,' 'antipathy': *It is* an idiosyncrasy *of this grumbler that he reads his own thoughts into the mind of others./I do not find him, though he is very quick in observing outward* idiosyncrasies, *a truthful or an interesting student of the characters, the minds & hearts, the daily actions & reactions, of men & women./There are several kinds of food freaks; some people have an* idiosyncrasy *to all fish, particularly shellfish & lobsters.*

Idiosyncratic is the adjective of *idiosyncrasy*—unfortunately, because it encourages by an accident the confusion between *-crasy* & *-cracy*. If *idiosyncrasy* is a word that has a real value, but should be much less used than it is, *idiosyncratic*, its hanger-on, should be kept still more severely in its place. In the quotations below, what the reader feels is not that his author has used the word in a wrong sense—he has not—but that he would have done better to circumvent, somehow, the need of it: *What we cannot help learning of their maker, or discoverer—his philosophy, his* idiosyncratic *view of things—is there, not because he wittingly put it there, but because he could not keep it out* (personal)*./He never hesitates at any joke, however* idiosyncratic (however little amusing to anyone but himself?).

idola fori, *idols of the market* (place). This learned phrase, in Latin or English, is not seldom used by the unlearned, who guess at its meaning & guess wrong.

It is the third of Bacon's four divisions of fallacies, more often mentioned than the other three because its meaning seems, though it is not in fact, plainer. There are the idols (i.e. the fallacies) of the tribe, the cave, the market, & the theater, which are picturesque names for (1) the errors men are exposed to by the limitations of the human understanding (as members of the tribe of man); (2) those a person is liable to owing to his idiosyncrasy (as enclosed in the cave of self); (3) those due to the unstable relation between words & their meanings (which fluctuate as the words are bandied to & fro in the conversational exchange or word market); & (4) those due to false philosophical or logical systems (which hold the stage successively like plays). The *tribe* is the human mind, the *cave* is idiosyncrasy, the *market* is talk, & the *theater* is philosophy; who would guess all that unaided? Who, on the contrary, would not guess that *an idol of the market-place* was just any belief to which the man in the street yields a mistaken deference? The odd thing is that no better instance could be found of an idol of the market than the phrase itself, oscillating between its real meaning & the modern misuse, so that the very person who pours scorn on *idola fori* is often propagating one in the very act of ridiculing the rest. Well, 'tis sport to have the engineer hoist with his own petard.

idolize, idolatrize, in their transf. sense (venerate, adore, love or admire excessively) are nearly synonymous and the former has almost displaced the latter. If there is a differentiation, it is that *idolize* is more personal (adore, love excessively) and *idolatrize* more often fig. (venerate, admire): *He idolizes you; An age that idolatrizes the material.* (COD does not list *-atrize.*)

idyl(l). Both forms are accepted; in US the shorter is more general, in Brit. the longer. In US (and OED) pron. ī'dĭl; COD also ĭdĭl.

idyllic. Of the nature of an idyl; hence full of natural charm or picturesqueness. NOT just *poetic, romantic.*

ie, ei. In most cases, the old rule holds; *i* before *e* except after *c* or when sounded as *a;* so *siege, niece; neighbor, either* (earliest pron. ayther); *seize, seizure* are notable exceptions.

i.e., id est. 1. To write, or even to say, this in the full instead of in the abbreviated form is now so unusual as to convict one of affectation.

2, *i.e.* means 'that is to say,' & introduces another way (more comprehensible to the hearer, driving home the speaker's point better, or otherwise preferable) of putting what has been already said; it does not introduce an example, & when substituted for *e.g.* in that function, as in the following extract, is a BLUNDER: *Let your principal stops be the full stop & comma, with a judicious use of the semicolon & of the other stops where they are absolutely necessary* (i.e. *you could not dispense with the note of interrogation in asking questions*).

3. It is invariable in form; the changing of it to *ea sunt* &c.—(WRONG: *which deals with persons:* ea sunt, *all present & future members*)—is due to the same misconception (explained under FOLLOW) as the incorrect

as follow; cf. also INTER ALIA.

4. It is always preceded by a stop; whether a comma follows it or not is indifferent, or rather is decided by the punctuation pitch of the writer of the passage.

if & when. Any writer who uses this formula lays himself open to entirely reasonable suspicions on the part of his readers. There is the suspicion that he is a mere parrot, who cannot say part of what he has often heard without saying the rest also; there is the suspicion that he likes verbiage for its own sake; there is the suspicion that he is a timid swordsman who thinks he will be safer with a second sword in his left hand; there is the suspicion that he has merely been too lazy to make up his mind between *if* & *when.* Only when the reader is sure enough of his author to know that in his writing none of these probabilities can be true does he turn to the extreme improbability that here at last is a sentence in which *if & when* is really better than *if* or *when* by itself. This absurdity is so common that it seems worth while to quote examples, bracketing in each either 'if &' or '& when,' & asking whether the omission would in any way change the meaning or diminish the force of the sentence: *The Radicals do not know quite clearly what they will be at* (if &) when *the fight is renewed. But* if (& when) *the notices are tendered it will be so arranged that they all terminate on the same day./We were under an honorable obligation to help France,* if (& when) *the time came for her to assert her claims.*

It was admitted above that cases were conceivable in which the *if* & the *when* might be genuinely & separately significant. Such cases arise when one desires to say that the result will, or does, or did, not only follow, but follows without delay; they are not in fact rare, & if a really good writer allows himself an *if & when,* one such must have presented itself; but in practice he hardly ever does it even then, because any strong emphasis on the absence of delay is much better given by other means, by the insertion of *at once,* or some equivalent in the result clause. So true is this that, when the devotees of *if & when* have had the luck to strike a real opportunity for their favorite, they cannot refrain from inserting some adverb to do over again the work that was the only true function of their *& when.* In the quotations, these adverbs that make *& when* otiose are in roman type: *The electors knew perfectly well that* if & when *the Bill was placed on the statute book it would* immediately *be used./*If & when *the party wins an election we are to have* at once *a general tariff on foreign manufactured goods.*

When or if is not so purposeless as *if & when; or if* does serve to express that the writer, though he expects his condition to be realized, has his doubts: *An official pronouncement as to what particular items of legislation it is proposed to repeal,* when, or if, *the opportunity arrives.*

Unless & until is open to the same objections as *if & when,* but is much less common.

ignitable, -ible. Both forms are accepted.

ignoramus. Pron. -āmus. Pl. *-uses,* not *-i.*

ignoratio elenchi. In English, the fallacy of the irrelevant conclusion.

ikon. Use ICON.

ilk means *same;* it does NOT mean *family* or *kind* or *set* or *name.* (Webster gives these but says 'a use arising from a misunderstanding . . . and still regarded as improper by many authorities.') *Ilk* is a form constructed for the case in which proprietor & property have the same name; *the Knockwinnocks of that ilk* means *the Knockwinnocks of Knockwinnock.* See POPULARIZED TECHNICALITIES. The common maltreatments of the phrase, several of which are illustrated below, are partly unconscious & due to ignorance of the meaning of *ilk,* & partly facetious; indulgence in such WORN-OUT HUMOR is much less forgivable than ignorance of what a Scotch word means. *Robert Elsmere, the forerunner of so many books* 'of that ilk.'/ *This publication was undertaken by John Murray, the first* of that ilk./*'Mystified' & others* of his ilk *do not seem to understand that the money that farmers & other producers make is . . .*

illegible, unreadable. The *illegible* is not plain enough to be deciphered; the *unreadable* is not interesting enough to be perused.

ILLITERACIES. There is a kind of offense against the literary idiom that is not easily named. The usual dictionary label for some specimens of it at least is *vulg.;* but the word *vulgar* is now so imbued on the one hand with social prejudices & on the other with moral condemnation as to be unsuitable. The property common to these lapses seems to be that people accustomed to reading good literature do not commit them & are repelled by them, while those not so accustomed neither refrain from nor condemn them; they may perhaps be more accurately as well as politely called *illiteracies* than *vulgarisms.* A few familiar types may be here collected for comparison, with just enough in the way of illustration to enable each usage to be recognized. Actual quotations will be found under many of the words mentioned in their dictionary places:

Like as conj. (*if I could think* like *you do*).

However, whatever, whoever, &c., interrogative (However *did you* find *out?;* Whatever *can this mean?*).

Same, such, & *various,* as pronouns (*Will submit* same, *or* the same, *for approval: Have no dealings with* such; Various *have stated*).

Frequent use of split infinitives (*Am ready* to categorically *affirm*).

Re in unsuitable contexts (*The author's arguments* re *predestination*).

Write with personal object only (*Though she had promised to* write him *soon;* generally accepted in US colloq. but usually avoided by good writers).

Think to=remember to (*I did not* think to *tell them when I was there*).

Negative after *should not wonder* (*I* shouldn't wonder *if it* didn't *come true yet*).

Present &c. after *as if* & *as though* (*It looks* as if *we* are *winning* or shall *win*).

Me &c. for *my* &c. in gerund construction (*Instead of* me *being dismissed*).

Between . . . or for *between . . . &* (*The choice is* between *glorious death* or *shameful life*).

Almost quite, rather unique, more preferable.

Aggravating or *provoking* for *annoying.*

Individual for *person.*

Rev. Jones; the hon. Smith.

illiterate. *Il*=not, *literate*= learned, liberally educated. Though *illiterate* is used in census reports &c. as unable to read, its general use is that suggested by the discussion above: 'not accustomed to reading good literature.'

ILLOGICALITIES. The spread of education adds to the writer's burdens by multiplying that pestilent fellow the critical reader. No longer can we depend on an audience that will be satisfied with catching the general drift & obvious intention of a sentence & not trouble itself to pick holes in our wording. The words used must nowadays actually yield on scrutiny the desired sense; to plead that anyone could see what you meant, or so to write as to need that plea, is not now permissible; all our pet illogicalities will have to be cleared away by degrees.

Take the following comment on a quotation the commentator thinks unjustified: *Were ever* finer *lines perverted to a* meaner *use?* We know well enough what he is trying to do—to emphasize the meanness of the use—; it is in expressing the emphasis that he has gone wrong; it has escaped him that *Never were lines perverted to a meaner use* is made weaker, not stronger, if changed to *never were* fine *lines* &c., & that again is further weakened, not strengthened, by a change of *fine* to *finer;* everything that narrows the field of rivals for the distinction of meanest perversion, as *fine* & *finer* do progressively, has an effect contrary to what was intended; it may be worth while to insert *fine* in spite of that, since it adds a qualification of importance; but the change to *finer* weakens the force without adding to the accuracy.

Another common, & more conspicuous, illogicality is the unintended anticlimax. *It will, I think,* delight *the reader as if it were something told by Meadows Taylor;* indeed *the mysterious 'sadhu' who figures in it, & the account of the fight with the yellow leopard, are not* unworthy *of the suggested comparison* (not *unworthy,* quotha? but *indeed* led us to expect *more than worthy,* a climax instead of an anticlimax).

The abandonment of blind confidence in *much less* is another compliment that will have to be paid to the modern reader's logic. It is still usual to give no hearing to *much more* before deciding for its more popular rival; sometimes a loose but illogical excuse is to be found in the general effect of the context, sometimes even that is wanting; these two varieties appear in the quotations: *The machine must be crushed before any real reforms can be initiated,* much less *carried./It is a full day's work even to open,* much less *to acknowledge, all the presents.* See MUCH 2.

A stray variety or two may now bring this subject, which might be treated at much greater length, to an end: *The schedule we shall have to face will be* a much longer one *than it would have been if we had undertaken the work this year,* & longer still *than it would have been if we had been able to do the work last year.* We may deeply sympathize with a writer who has brought himself to the pass of having to choose between saying *still more longer* & being illogical, but we cannot let him off that *more./That would quite easily & fairly redress what he* admitted *to be the* only grievance *he could see in Establishment.* The *he* is a supporter of the Established Church; he would *maintain,* not *admit,* that it is the only grievance, & should have said 'what he admitted to be a grievance, though it was the only one he could see.'

Other examples or remarks will be found on BECAUSE, BUT 3, -ER & -EST 7, 8, HAZINESS, REASON, THOUGH, TOO, YET, & passim.

illusion. *An optical illusion; the illusion of the theater; the illusions of childhood.* (The *delusions* of lunacy; labor under a *delusion.*) See DELUSION for the differences between the two words.

illustrate. The pronunciation ĭl'ustrāt (as opp. to -lŭ'-) has been slowly arrived at, but is now general. For *illustrative* Brit. use accepts ĭlŭ'strativ only. US dictionaries list il'- second.

imaginary, imaginative. The meanings of the two are quite distinct and never interchangeable. That is *imaginary* which exists only in someone's imagination; he, or his power or products, is *imaginative* who is able or apt to form mental pictures. Any confusion between the two is due to the fact that there are things to which either can be applied, though in different senses, & with some such things the distinction is not always apparent. The difference between *an imaginary* & *an imaginative person* is clear enough, but that between *imaginary* & *imaginative distress* is elusive; the begging impostor exploits the former; the latter is created & experienced (*Such a price The Gods exact for song, To become what we sing*) by the tragic or lyric poet. *The place is described with such wealth of detail as to lead one to the conclusion that it must have existed; but, of course, on the other hand, it may have been purely* imaginative; justifiable, or not?

imbed, em-. *Em-* better.

imbibe makes *-bable.* As a synonym for *drink* (*in*), *absorb,* or *inhale,* see FORMAL WORDS.

imbroglio. A state of confusion or entanglement; a complicated (esp. political or dramatic) situation. Pron. -ō'lyō; pl. *-os.*

imbue makes *imbuable.* The word means permeate; inspire; constr. *with. Imbued* with *wisdom. Imbued* with *the spirit of his authors.* See also INFUSE.

imitate makes *imitable, imitator.*

immanent. The word is something of a stumbling block and it is thought by some that the divines & philosophers who chiefly affect it should be asked whether they would not gain in intelligibility what they might lose in precision by choosing according to context between *indwelling, pervading, pervasive, permeating, inherent,* & other words that do not mystify us. 'All which though I most powerfully & potently believe, yet I hold it not honesty to have it thus set down,' & shall not venture to label *immanent* & *immanence* SUPERFLUOUS WORDS.

The OED's note on the use of *immanent* may be useful to those who, not reading philosophic & religious books, find it an enigma when it makes one of its occasional appearances in the newspaper: 'In recent philosophy applied to the Deity regarded as permanently pervading & sustaining the universe, as distinguished from the notion of an external transcendent creator or ruler.' See POPULARIZED TECHNICALITIES. The word meaning *impending* is *imminent.*

immaterial. Not material; hence, loosely, unimportant, of no consequence. (*It's immaterial to me whether you do this or that;* now accepted usage in this sense, but *indifferent* is usually better.)

immediately, conj. (=as soon as, the moment that), is obsolescent & out of place in most writing (e.g. *I'll tell him* immediately *he arrives*); cf. *directly.*

immense. Both the common slang use in the senses *excellent amusing* & the odd freak illustrated in the extract below are instances of NOVELTY-HUNTING, though the first has lost its freshness & grown stale, as such perversions do, whereas the second has not yet got beyond the circles in which the detection of generally unappreciated infinities makes one a luminary: *These memories yield what is probably an* immensely *true account of Nelson's career.*

immesh. Use *en-.*

imminent. Impending. Almost always of evil or danger. See IMMANENT.

immortal, as a compliment to an author or one of his productions or personages, requires to be used with caution. Its real use is to make sure that a reader who may or may not be an ignoramus shall realize that the person or book referred to is well known in the literary world, & that without telling him the fact in too patronizing a manner. But, delicate as the device may originally have been, it is now too well known to escape notice; & whether the reader will be offended or not depends on the exact depth of his ignorance. There are few who will not be angry if they are reckoned to require 'the immortal Shakespeare,' or *'Don Quixote,'* or *'Pickwick Papers'*; those who can put up with 'the immortal Panurge,' or 'Dobbin,' or 'Mrs. Poyser,' will be rather more numerous; & so on in many gradations. The author of the following was probably ill inspired in immortalizing Cervantes; but not so ill as if he had done the same—& he might have—for *Don Quixote: Lovers of* Don Quixote *will remember that the* immortal Cervantes *fought with great courage in this battle.*

immovable, NOT *-veable.* Though the differentiation between *immov-* & *irremov-* is fully established, blunders sometimes occur. WRONG: *The President, save for successful impeachment, is* immovable *by Congress./By suspending conscription & restoring the* immovability *of the judges.*

impale, em-. *Im-* better.

impanel, em-. In US *im-* is standard; COD prefers *em-.* Past &c., *-led, -ling,* US; *-lled, -lling,* Brit.

impassable, impassible. The two are different in derivation, spelling, & meaning. The first is ultimately from Latin *pando,* stretch, the second from Latin *patior,* feel; the first means 'that cannot be passed,' the second 'that cannot feel.' *An* impassable *road; an* impassible *spirit.* See also IMPASSIVE.

impasse. 'A blind alley.' Fig. a predicament from which there is no escape. Pron. preferably ĭmpăs′ or as French (NEVER *impassé*). See FRENCH WORDS.

impassive, impassible. The words are from the same root and have or had several meanings in common. *Impassible* alone now has the theological sense, not subject to suffering: *Corinthus . . . taught . . . that Christ was* impassible. *Impassive* alone has the sense deficient in or incapable of feeling or emotion; not liable to be disturbed by passion: *Even the* impassive *Chesterfield cried in despair. . . .* It also has the connotation serene, not exhibiting emotion: *an impassive countenance.*

impawn, em-. *Im-* better.

impediment. Hindrance, obstruction; in speech, a stammer. The pl. *impedimenta* is used chiefly of (military) baggage supply trains and in legal contexts. Otherwise, pl. *impediments.*

impel makes *-lled, -llable,* &c.

impenitence, -cy. There is no perceptible difference of meaning; *-ce* is recommended.

imperil, NOT *em-;* past &c., US *-led, -iling;* Brit. *-lled* &c.

impersonate makes *-nable, -tor.*

impetus. Pl. *-tuses,* NOT *-ti.*

impinge makes *-ging.* In fig. sense, to encroach or infringe, constr. *on* or *upon. To impinge* upon *the province of reviewers.*

impious. Pron. ĭm′pĭus. Not pious; spec., irreverent, profane. *Impious heretics; an impious disregard of all that is sacred.*

implicate makes *-cable.*

implicit. The human mind likes a good clear black & white contrast. When two words so definitely promise one of these contrasts as *explicit* & *implicit,* & then dash our hopes by figuring in phrases where the contrast ceases to be visible—say in 'explicit support' & 'implicit obedience,' with *absolute* or *complete* or *full* as a substitute that might replace either or both—we ask with some indignation whether after all black is white, & perhaps decide that *implicit* is a shifty word with which we will have no further dealings. It is in fact noteworthy in more than one respect. First, it means for the most part the same as *implied* &, as it is certainly not so instantly intelligible as that to the average man, it might have been expected to be so good as to die. That it has nevertheless survived by the side of *implied* is perhaps due to two causes: one is that *explicit* & *implicit* make a neater antithesis than even *expressed* & *implied* (*all the conditions whether explicit or implicit;* but *all the implied conditions; implied* is much commoner than *implicit* when the antithesis is not given in full); & the other is that the adv., whether of *implicit* or of *implied,* is more often wanted than the adj., & that *impliedly* is felt to be a bad form; *implicitly,* preferred to *impliedly,* helps to keep *implicit* alive.

Secondly, there is the historical accident by which *implicit,* with *faith, obedience, confidence,* & such words, has come to mean 'absolute' or 'full,' whereas its original sense was 'undeveloped' or 'potential' or 'in the germ.' The starting point of this usage is the ecclesiastical phrase *implicit faith,* i.e. a person's acceptance of any article of belief, not on its own merits, but as a part of, as 'wrapped up in,' his general acceptance of the Church's authority; the steps from this sense to *unquestioning,* & thence to *complete* or *absolute* or *exact,* are easy; but not everyone who says that *implicit obedience is the first duty of the soldier* realizes that the obedience he is describing is not properly an exact one, but one that is based on acceptance of the soldier's status. See POPULARIZED TECHNICALITIES.

imply. His words *imply* his intention; I *infer* from them what he means. When *imply* is followed by a substantive clause as object the *that* is expressed: *The text* implies that *Sidon was the leading city.*

impolitic (not politic, not according to good policy, inexpedient) makes the unusual adverbial form *-icly,* NOT *-ically.*

importunate, importune (adjs.). There is little differentiation in meaning (urgent, pressing in solicitation) and the shorter form is becoming increasingly rare as an adj.

importune, v. In modern usage, the stress is usually on the last syllable.

impotence, -t, -cy. Accent first syllable.

impregnable. In US used both as 'unconquerable' and as 'capable of being impregnated.' For the second, Brit. uses *impregnatable,* and the differentiation seems desirable.

impresario. Properly pron. -zär'ĭō, but -sär'ĭō is now much more usual in US; pl. *-os.*

imprescriptible. An *imprescriptible* right is a right not subject to negative prescription, i.e. a right that is not invalidated by any lapse of time, that cannot be legally taken away (e.g. Paine: *the natural & imprescriptible rights of man*).

impress, n. Pron. im'-. A mark made by a seal or stamp; fig. characteristic mark. *The impress of genius.* For synonymy see SIGN.

imprimatur. Pron. -mā'-. 'Let it be printed.' Official sanction to print (publish), now usually by the R.C. Church; fig., any sanction.

impromptu, n. Pl. *-us* (*Two sets of pieces by Shubert, known as* Impromptus). It is also an adj. (*an impromptu speech*) and an adv. (*It was made almost impromptu.*)

improvisator. One who composes and recites or sings (short poems) extempore. An improviser. Pron. ĭm prŏv'ĭzātor. (Italian form *-vvisatore* pron. -ahtor'ĭ, fem. *-vvisatrice* pron. -ahtrē'chā, pl. *-ori* pron. -or'ē, *-ici* pron. -ē'chē.)

improvise, NOT *-ize.*

impuissant. Powerless, weak, impotent. Mod. pron. ĭmpū'ĭsant. (In Browning *impuissance* is stressed ĭmpūĭ'sans.)

in. The combinations *inasmuch as, in order that* or *to, in so far, in that,* & *in toto,* are taken separately in their alphabetical places.

in-. (1) A Lat. prep. & prefix meaning *in, into, within, on,* &c.: *indwelling, innate.* (2) A Lat. prefix expressing negation (=*un-*): *inanimate, inse-*

cure. See IN- & UN-

inacceptable. *Un-* is better.

inaccessible. So spelled.

inadequate. Though it is true that *adequate* & *inadequate* originally meant made & not made equal, & therefore might be & were followed by *to* with any suitable noun or infinitive, modern usage has restricted the words to the notion (un)equal to requirements, so effectually that it may now be regarded as unidiomatic to express the particular demand; vague additions like *to the need, to the occasion, to the task,* are still possible, though felt to be pleonastic; but specifications like *His revenues were found* inadequate to *his expenses* (Gibbon) or *Is language* adequate to *describe it?* (W. Collins) are abandonments of the differentiation that has taken place between *adequate* & *equal, inadequate* & *unequal. His resources were inadequate,* or *inadequate to the occasion,* but NOT *inadequate to those of his opponent,* nor *to take the town.*

inadvertence, -cy. No differentiation. The first is recommended.

inadvisable, un-. The first is now more usual in US; Brit. usually *un-*.

inalienable is now the est. form (but in the US Constitution, Goldsmith, Macaulay, & others, *unalienable*).

inalterable, un-. There seems to be a differentiation worth preserving: *inalterable well being; an unalterable law.*

IN- & UN-. There is often a teasing uncertainty—or incertitude—whether the negative form of a word should be made with *in-* (including *il-, im-, ir-*), or with *un-*. The general principle that *un-* is English & belongs to English words, & *in-* is Latin & belongs to Latin words, does not take us far. The second part of it, indeed, forbids *inwholesome* & thousands of similar offenses; but then no one is tempted to go astray in this direction. And the first part, which is asked to solve real problems—whether, for instance, *unsanitary* or *insanitary* is right—seldom gives a clear answer; it forbids *undubitable, uneffable, unevitable,* & other such words of which the positive form does not exist as an English word; but about *sanitary* & the rest it says you may consider them English words and use *un-*, or Latin words & use *in-*. Fortunately the number of words about which doubts exist is not large; for the great majority usage has by this time decided one way or the other. The modern tendency is to restrict *in-* to words obviously answering to Latin types, & to prefer *-un* in other cases, as in *unavailing, uncertain, undevout.* Some suggestive contrasts may serve to show the conflicting tendencies that are at work: *unjust* but *injustice, unable* but *inability, unquiet* but *inquietude, uncivil* but *incivility,* show the influence of markedly Latin as opposed to nondescript endings in producing *in-*. *Undigested* but *indigestible, unanimated* but *inanimate, undistinguished* but *indistinguishable, unlettered* but *illiterate, unlimited* but *illimitable, unredeemed* but *irredeemable, unreconciled* but *irreconcilable,* illustrate the aversion of *-ed* to *in-; unceasing* but *incessant, undiscriminating* but *indiscriminate,* do the same for

-*ing*. *Unapproachable* but *inaccessible, undestroyable* but *indestructible, undissolvable* but *indissoluble, unbelievable* but *inconceivable, unprovable* but *improbable,* bring out well the tendency for *in-* to be restricted to the forms that are closest to Latin even in the very open-minded *-ble* group; & *uncertainty* but *incertitude* does the same for nouns. Lastly, *unaccountable* but *insurmountable,* & *unmelodious* but *inharmonious,* are examples of apparent caprice fixed by usage.

The words about which doubt is most likely, with a statement of the prefix recommended, appear in their dictionary places.

inappeasable. Un- is better.

inapt, inept, unapt. In modern usage, though the three words still occasionally overlap, there is a tendency for each to control a separate field. *Inept* alone means absurd, wanting in judgment, silly, foolish: *This policy of meddle and muddle, this* inept *influence with local administration . . . Unapt* alone means not likely, not accustomed: *He is* unapt *to take offense. Inapt* seems to be the chosen word for unskillful, unfitted, without aptitude or capacity: *A well-meant but hopelessly* inapt *attempt.* The sense in which the three vie for position is 'not suitable, inappropriate, out of place': *An inept* (or *inapt*, rarely *unapt*) *allusion in this place.*

inartistic, un-. *In-*, lacking an artistic taste; *un-*, not conforming to art. *An* inartistic *person; a powerful but* unartistic *painting.*

inasmuch as (so spelled) has two meanings: one the original, now rarely met with, i.e. to the same extent as or to whatever degree or so far as (*God is only God* inasmuch as *he is the Moral Governor of the world*); & the other worn down, with the notion of a correspondence between two scales gone, & nothing left but a four-syllable substitute for *since* (*I am unable to reply that I am much the better for seeing you,* inasmuch as *I see nothing of you*). This is the ordinary modern use, & its only recommendation as compared with *since* is its pomposity. On the other hand the old sense has been supplanted by *so far as* & *in so far as* & is now unfamiliar enough to be misleading when a literary-minded person reverts to it. *At any rate, his proposals,* inasmuch as *they were intended to secure continued loyalty & union among the people, were considered altogether unnecessary.* Do we gather that the proposals were in fact rejected, & the reason for this was that their intention was so-&-so? or that, whether rejected or accepted on other grounds, that intention was not held to justify them? In other words, does *inasmuch as* mean *since,* or *so far as*? We cannot tell, without extraneous information. A word that in one sense is pompous, & in another obscure or ambiguous, & in both has satisfactory substitutes, is better left alone.

incarnation. 'Embodiment in (human) flesh.' WRONG: *This unfortunately is not the prisoner's first lapse from honesty, for when the Chief Constable of Peterborough said 'he was the very quintessence of cunning &* the incarnation *of a book-thief,' he was not speaking without knowledge.* Either the C.C.

has been misreported or he was playfully suggesting that a book thief is not a human being, but a fiend or possibly a Platonic Idea; for so eminent a person must be aware that the incarnation of what is incarnate already is as idle as painting the lily, & much more difficult. Some of us, however, do need to be reminded that while a person may be *an incarnation of folly*, or *Folly clothed in flesh*, it is meaningless to call him *the incarnation of a fool*, because all fools are flesh to start with & cannot be fitted with a new suit of it. See POPULARIZED TECHNICALITIES.

incase. *En-* better.

inchoate, adj. US usually ĭnkō′ĭt; Brit. ĭn′kōat.

incident, adj., **incidental.** Two tendencies may be discerned; one is for the shorter form with its less familiar termination to be displaced by the longer; thus we should more usually, though not more correctly, now write *incidental* in such contexts as: *All the powers* incident *to any government; The expedition & the* incident *aggressive steps taken; The* incident *mistakes which he has run into.* The other tendency, cutting across the first, is a differentiation of meaning, based on no real difference between the two forms, but not the less useful on that account; while *incidental* is applied to side occurrences with stress on their independence of the main action, *incident* implies that, though not essential to it, they not merely happen to arise in connection with it but may be expected to do so. A consequence of this distinction is that *incident* is mostly used in close combination with whatever word may represent the main action or subject, & especially with *to* as the link; *Youth & its* incident *perturbations*, or *The enthusiasms* incident *to youth.* It would be well if the swallowing up of *incident* by *incidental* could be checked, & a continued existence secured to it at least in the special uses indicated. *Half the money has gone in* incidental *expenses*, & *Our failure brought us an* incidental *advantage;* but *Office & the* incident *worries*, & *The dangers* incident to *hunting.*

incidentally is now very common as a writer's apology for an irrelevance or afterthought. Naturally, those who find it most useful are not the best writers.

incise, not *-ize.*

incline. *Inclined to think* means nothing more than *think* (e.g. *I am* inclined to think *you are right*). For 'seriously inclined,' see HACKNEYED PHRASES.

inclose. Generally *-en* except in specific US legal use.

include, comprise. As often used, these may be called a pair of WORKING & STYLISH WORDS. The one used in ordinary life is *include;* the inferior kind of writer therefore likes to impress his readers with *comprise.* The frequent confusion between *comprise* & *compose* is an indication that *include*, which writer & compositor alike know all about, would be in general a safer word. Given the two, however, it would be possible to turn our superfluity to much better purpose than as a chance for the stylish writer. The distinction in meaning between the two seems to be that *comprise* is appropriate when the content of the whole, & *include* when the admission or presence of an item, is in question. Good writers say *comprise* when looking at the matter from the point of view of the whole, *include* from that of the part. With *include,* there is no presumption (though it is often the fact) that all or even most of the components are mentioned; with *comprise,* the whole of them are understood to be in the list. In England the Guards, for instance, *include* the Coldstreams or the Life Guards, but *comprise* the Life Guards, Horse Guards, Dragoon Guards, & Foot Guards. *Comprise* is in fact, or would be if this partly recognized distinction were developed & maintained, whereas *include* is not, equivalent to *be composed of.* In the following extract *include* would be the right word: *The Commission points out that the ample crop of information it has gathered only* comprises *irrefragably established facts.*

including may be used as meaning *inclusive of,* or *if we include: Including the impressionists, there have been six artistic movements in as many decades. Inclusive* may be used as quasi-adv. (=inclusively): *From Monday to Friday, inclusive.*

incognito. Pron. incŏg′-. Of the personal noun, *incognito, incognita, incogniti,* are the masculine, feminine, & plural, =man, woman, people, of concealed identity. The abstract noun (=anonymity &c.) is *incognito* only, with possible plural *incognitos* (*never dropping their incognitos,* or usually *incognito*). The adv. or predicative adj. (*traveling incognito*) is usually *incognito* irrespective of gender & number.

incognizant &c. Pron. US usually ĭnkŏg′n*i*zant; Brit. -kŏn′-.

incommunicative, un-. Both forms have been in general use since the 17th c.; un- is perhaps better. See IN- & UN-.

INCOMPATIBLES. Under this heading are collected some phrases each consisting of ill-assorted elements. The object of this list is first to give the reader, when referred to it, a conspectus of mistakes similar to the one he was investigating, & secondly to give the mistakes themselves an extra advertisement. Typical incompatibles are *almost quite; without scarcely; scarcely . . . than; finally scotched; major portion; rather unique; somewhat amazing; quite all right; more preferable; undue alarm.* Each misuse is discussed in this book under one or the other of the terms composing the phrase.

incompetence, -cy. The form recommended is *-ce,* cf. competence; in legal use, however, often *-cy.*

incompleted. *Un-* is the right form. A thing is *incomplete* if it is *uncompleted.*

incondite. Pron. ĭnkŏn′dĭt. The word is of the learned kind, & should be avoided except in what is addressed to a definitely literary audience. *Artless, rude, rough, unpolished,* come near the sense.

INCONGRUOUS VOCABULARY. *Austria was no longer in a position,* an' she would, *to shake off the German yoke.* 'Be in a position to' is a phrase of the most pedestrian modernity; 'shake off the yoke,' though a metaphor, is one so well worn that no incongruity is felt between it & the pedestrianism; but what is *an' she would* doing here? Why not the obvious *even if she had the desire?* or, if *an' she would* is too dear to be let go, why not *Austria now could not, an' she would?* The goldfish *an'* cannot live in this sentence-bowl unless we put some water in with it, & gasps pathetically at us from the mere dry air of *be in a position.* Only a child would expect a goldfish to keep his beauty out of his right element; & only the writer who is either very inexperienced or singularly proof against experience will let the beauties of a word or phrase tempt him into displaying it where it is conspicuously out of place. Minor lapses from congruity are common enough, & a tendency to them marks the effect of what a man writes more fatally than occasional faults of a more palpable kind, such as grammatical blunders; but they do not lend themselves to exhibition in the short form here necessary. A few of the grosser & more recurrent incongruities, connected with particular words, must suffice by way of illustration. The words out of their element are printed in roman type, & under most of them, in their dictionary places, will be found further examples: *Christmas books are put in hand long* ere *the* season *comes round./It is really very difficult to imagine that the reply of the ballot can be* aught but *an answer in the affirmative./There are, it may be noted, fewer marquises than any other section of the peerage* save *dukes./The Civil Service with its old traditions & its hereditary hatred of interlopers,* be they *merchants, journalists, doctors, etc.* (*be they* is nothing if not stiff, *etc.* nothing if not slack).

inconsolable, un-. *In-* is better.

incontrollable. *Un-* is better.

incorporate makes *-rable.*

incredible means 'beyond belief.' For the use of the weakened sense, 'such as it is difficult to believe,' see POSITIVE WORDS.

incrust, en-. *Incrust,* the standard US form, has now been ousted in Brit. by *en-.* But *incrustation,* US & Brit.

incubus. Evil spirit supposed to descend on persons in their sleep; hence nightmare; a person or thing that oppresses or burdens. Pl. *-bi* or *-buses.*

inculcate. (US usually ĭncŭl′-; Brit. ĭn′-.) The word means to urge or impress (a fact, idea) persistently (*upon, on,* a person's mind). RIGHT: *The teachers* inculcated *the duties of order, obedience, and fidelity* on *the slaves.* A curious mistake often occurs, shown in the quotations following: (WRONG) *A passer-by saved him, formed a close friendship with him, &* inculcated him with *his own horrible ideas about murdering women./An admirable training place wherein to* inculcate the young mind with *the whys & wherefores of everything which concerns personal safety.* Whether the explanation is that *inculcate* is one of the words liable to the maltreatment called OBJECT-SHUFFLING (*inculcate one with a doctrine* being substituted for *inculcate a doctrine upon one*), or whether the compositor has each time found *inoculate* & printed *inculcate,* is impossible to determine; if the latter, writers should take warning that *inoculate* is a word to keep an eye on in proofs.

incur makes *-rred, -rring.*

indecorous. (Improper, in bad taste.) In US usually ĭndĕk′-, Brit. ĭndĭkōr′-.

indefeasible, indefectible. That is *indefeasible* which is not liable to defeat, i.e. to being impaired or annulled by attack from outside; the word is therefore applied to *rights, titles, possessions,* & the like. That is *indefectible* which is not liable to deficit, i.e. to failing for want of internal power; the word is therefore applied to qualities such as *holiness, grace, vigor, resolution, affection,* or *abundance;* the sense *faultless* suggesting the noun *defect* rather than *deficit,* seems to be a modern change of meaning, & one not to be encouraged. Neither word lends itself to the sort of everyday use seen in: *And yet Mr. Barnstaple had the most subtle* & indefeasible doubt *whether indeed Serpentine was speaking.*

indescribable. So spelled.

index. Plural, *-exes, -ices.* The latter is more common in scientific and scholarly use; *refractive indices;* but *the indexes of the several volumes.*

Indian. To distinguish between the natives of India and the original inhabitants of America and the West Indies, American and Continental usage adopted *Hindu* (properly an adherent of Hinduism as opposed to Mohammedanism). Brit. usage is *Indian,* & *American Indian* (or formerly & still sometimes *Red Indian*). With the formation of India and Pakistan, all subjects of the former are now *Indians,* whether Hindu, Moslem, or Christian; the Pakistan subjects are *Pakistani.*

Indian summer. A period of warm or mild weather with hazy atmosphere occurring in late fall or early winter. Of US origin, but also used in England, where when it falls in October it is also known as *St. Luke's summer* and in November as *St. Martin's summer.*

indicate. When *indicate* is followed by a *that* clause, *that* is better expressed, not left to be understood. WRONG: *He said nothing to* indicate‸the *un*belligerent attitude *would be changed.*

indict, -able, -ment. Pron. -īt′-. *Indict* means accuse, & *indite* compose or write.

indigested. *Un-* is the usual form; *in-* is retained in a transf. sense, not thought out, shapeless: *a huge mass of indigested facts.*

INDIRECT OBJECT. Some verbs (*give, send, write, pay,* &c.) take an indirect object as well as a direct (accusative) one: *Give* me *the book,* or *give the book* to me. The preposition may (and should) be omitted when the indirect object precedes the direct object; it should be used (though in US often is not) when the direct object follows the verb immediately. *I shall write* him *a letter,* but *I'll send a note* to *him.* Variations are (1) when no direct object is expressed, as *You told* me *yourself,* (2) when the direct object is a mere pronoun & is allowed to precede, as (now poetic or archaic) *I told it* you *before* (but NOT *I told the story* you *before*), (3) when the indirect object is after a passive verb, as *It was told* me *in confidence.*

INDIRECT QUESTION is the grammarian's name for a modification of what was originally a question, such that it does not stand by itself as a sentence, but is treated as a noun, serving for instance as subject or object to a verb outside of it. Thus: direct question, *Who are you?;* indirect question, *I asked who he was,* or *Tell me who you are,* or *Who you are is quite irrelevant.* Two points arise, one of grammar, & one of style.

1. It must be remembered that an indirect question is in grammar equivalent to one noun in the singular; the number of its internal subject has no influence on the number of the external verb; to disregard this fact, as when *rest* is written instead of *rests* in the following extract because *terms* happens to be plural, is an elementary blunder. WRONG: *What terms Bulgaria may be ultimately given* rest *with the Peace Conference.*

2. The point of style is of much greater interest. How far is it legitimate to substitute in an indirect question the order of words that properly belongs to direct questions? The lamentable craze for INVERSION among writers who are fain to make up for dullness of matter by verbal contortions is no doubt responsible for the prevailing disregard of the normal order in indirect questions; for inversion, i.e. the placing of the subject later than its verb, is a mark of the direct, but not of the indirect question.

Take these five types:

A. How old are you?

B. Tell me *how old you are* or Tell me *how old are you?*

C. He wondered *how old she was* or He wondered *how old was she?*

D. He doesn't know *how old I am* or He doesn't know *how old am I?*

E. *How old I am* is my affair or *How old am I* is my affair.

A is the direct question; in B, C, D, & E, the first form contains the normal, & the second the abnormal form of the indirect question. It will be seen that the abnormal form is progressively disagreeable as we recede from interrogative governing verbs, until in E it might fairly be thought impossible. To contortionists, however, all things are possible; readers possessed of the grammatical sense, or of literary taste, will find the following examples of the abnormal order repugnant in the same degree as the types to which the letters B, E, &c., assign them: *I have been asked by the Editor to explain* what are the duties *of the Army toward the civil power,* how is it *constituted,* to whom does it owe *allegiance,* by whom is it *paid, & what* is the source *of its authority* (B. The reason why the first & last clauses here are less distasteful than the others is explained later)./*It shows inferentially* how powerless is that body *to carry out any scheme of its own* (D. Normal order—*how powerless that body is*)./How bold is this attack *may be judged from the fact that* . . . (E. Normal order—*How bold this attack is*).

The further remarks on the first example are these: three of the five indirect-question clauses in that are clear cases of abnormal order—*how is it* instead of *how it is, to whom does it owe* instead of *to whom it owes*, & *by whom is it paid* instead of *by whom it is paid*—; but about the other two, which whether designedly or not act as advance-guard & rearguard covering those between & almost preventing us from discovering their character, it is not so easy to say whether they are abnormal or not. That is a characteristic of the special type of question consisting of subject, noun complement, & the verb *be;* in the answer to such questions, subject & complement are transposable. Question, *What are the duties?;* answer, indifferently, *These are the duties,* or *The duties are these;* to the first form corresponds in the indirect question *Explain what are the duties,* & to the second, *Explain what the duties are;* & it can therefore hardly be said that one is more normal than the other. But to questions made of other elements than subject + *be* + noun complement, e.g. *How is it constituted?*, the two answers (*It is constituted thus,* & *Thus is it constituted*) are far from indifferent; one is plainly normal & the other abnormal. This minor point has been discussed only because sentences like *Explain what are the duties* might be hastily supposed to justify all other uses of direct-question order in indirect-question constructions.

indiscreet, indiscrete. The first 'wanting in discretion' (*You may do much harm by* indiscreet *praise*); the second, 'not divided into distinct parts' (*An* indiscrete *mass of confused matter*). Traditionally & still generally in US the stress is on the last syllable in both. In modern Brit., the -dis′- is stressed in the second.

indiscriminating. *Un-* is perhaps better, but *indiscriminate,* adj.

indite. Compose or write. Usually formal, poetic, or facetious.

individual, n. The remarks to be made concern the noun only, not the adj. 'Individual, which almost made the fortune of many a Victorian novelist, is one of the modern editor's shibboleths for detecting the unfit'; so it has been said, but editors seem to relax their vigilance occasionally. The test for the right use of the word as opposed to the 'colloquial vulgarism' (OED) is the question whether the writer means or not to contrast the person he calls an *individual* with society, the family, or some body of persons; if he does, he may say *individual* with a clear conscience. A pair of examples will make the difference clear; in the first, the *individual* is directly contrasted with, though a member of, the House of Commons, & is therefore rightly so called; in the second it is true that there is a body of persons in question, but the *individual* is so far from being contrasted with this body that he is it; the right way to have written the sentence is added, & the efficiency with which *his* does all the work of *this long-suffering individual* reveals the writer's style as one not to be imitated. RIGHT: *The House of Commons settled down very quietly to business yesterday afternoon; all trace of the preceding sitting's violent protestation appeared to have been obliterated from the political mind;* the only individual *who attempted to revive the spirit* *of animosity was Mr. ——./* WRONG: *We are little inclined to consider the urgency of the case made out for the patient agriculturalist; it would seem at first sight as if the needs of* this long-suffering individual *were such as could be supplied by* . . . (as if his needs could).

indoctrinate. To instruct *in* a subject: *He indoctrinated them* in *systematic theology;* to imbue *with* a doctrine &c.: *Fully indoctrinated* with *a sense of the magnitude of their office;* to bring *into* a knowledge of something: *He indoctrinated them* into *the communist philosophy.* (The derogatory sense is comparatively recent.)

induce makes *-cible.*

induction, deduction. *Induction* is the drawing, from observed or known cases, of the conviction that something established of them is true either of all similar cases, or of any particular similar case, that may afterwards be met with. The child who, having observed that all the persons known to him have two legs, confidently expects two legs on the newborn brother he has not yet seen has made an induction. *Deduction* is the drawing from a general principle, however derived, of the conviction that a particular fact is true because if it were not, the general principle, which has been accepted as undeniable, would not be true. The child who, being told that if you take a seed & sow it you may expect thirtyfold or so of what you took it from to spring up, sows a caraway seed & awaits the thirty copies of the seedcake from which he saved it is acting on a deduction. Whether the conclusion reached by induction or deduction is true depends on many conditions, which it is the province of Logic to expound; but the broad difference between the two is that *induction* starts from known instances & arrives at a generalization, or at the power of applying to new instances what it has gathered from the old, while *deduction* starts from the general principle, whether established by induction or assumed, & arrives at some less general principle, or some individual fact, that may be regarded as being wrapped up in it & therefore as having the same claim to belief as the general principle itself.

indue. To invest with a power, quality, &c., often in the passive. The est. modern form in Brit. is *endue;* in US both *in-* and *en-* are used (reflecting the usage of the 18th- & 19th-c. quotations in OED). The word is often used interchangeably with *endow: indued with love for God & men.*

indulge. You may *indulge* your emotion, or *indulge in* emotion, or *indulge yourself in* emotion; further, you may *indulge in,* or *indulge yourself in,* a note of emotion; but you cannot *indulge a note,* whether of emotion or of anything else. WRONG: *But here & there flashes out a phrase or a sentence that strikes* the note of emotion & pride *in the achievements of our armies* which *the most reticent of men* may indulge. That passes the limit of what even this very elastic verb can be stretched to. The object of *indulge* as a transitive verb must be either a person or at least something that can be credited with a capacity for being pleased or gratified; a passion, a fancy, an emotion, may be gratified, but not a note. The mistake is less a misunderstanding of the meaning of *indulge* than an example of HAZINESS, *note of emotion* being confused with *emotion,* & the confusion escaping notice under cover of *which.*

inebriate. 'To be "drunk" is vulgar; but if a man be simply "intoxicated" or "inebriated" it is comparatively venial' (Rogers, quoted in OED); see GENTEELISM. For 'the cups that cheer but not inebriate,' see WORN-OUT HUMOR.

inedited, un-. *In-* is retained chiefly in the sense 'unpublished': *Letters still extant but inedited.*

ineffaceable, un-. The first is recommended.

ineffective, -fectual, -ficacious, -ficient. For distinctions see EFFECTIVE.

inept. See INAPT.

inescapable, inessential. These & the *un-* forms are both & have long been current. *Un-* is recommended. See IN- & UN-.

inevitable(ness), -bly. To those of us who read reviews of books & acting & music it has been apparent for some time that these words have been added to what may be called the *apparatus criticus,* making up, with *distinction, charm, meticulous, banal, sympathetic,* & a few other LITERARY CRITICS' WORDS, the reviewing outfit. *And even when a song is introduced, such as Ariel's 'Where the bee sucks there suck I,' its effect is so great because it seems* dramatically inevitable./ *The mere matters of arrangement, of line therein, show how great was his power, how true his perception; he has* the inevitableness *of the Japanese.*

Better examples than these might be desired for the purpose of extracting the words' sense; they are the ones that happen to be at hand, recorded possibly for the very reason that they were open to objection. What the literary critic means by *inevitable* is perhaps this: surveying a work of art, we feel sometimes that the whole & all the parts are sufficiently consistent & harmonious to produce on us the effect of truth; we then call it, for short, *convincing;* thus & thus, we mean, it surely may have been or may be; nothing in it inclines us to doubt. To be convincing is a step short of being inevitable; when the whole & the parts are so far in concatenation accordingly that instead of *Thus & thus it may have been* we find ourselves forced to *Thus & thus it must have been* or *was* or *is,* when the change of a jot or tittle would be plain desecration, when we know that we are looking at the Platonic idea itself & no mere copy, then the tale or picture or the music attains to *inevitableness.* This is an outsider's guess at the meaning; whether the guess is a good one or not, the meaning seems to be one deserving expression in a single word—but only on the condition that that word shall be strictly confined to the works or parts of works that are worthy of it. Now it is, in fact, so often met with that one is compelled to infer the existence of a great deal more inevitability in 20th-c. art of all kinds than one at all suspected; so many things seem *inevitable* to the reviewer in which the reader could contemplate extensive alterations without a pang. The question is whether *convincing* or *true to nature* would not be nearer the critic's private meaning than *inevitable,* & indeed whether he does not choose *inevitable* just because the reader would understand the other words too easily & miss being impressed by his command of mysterious terms.

inexplicable. Pron. ĭnĕx′-.

inexpressive, un-. The second is recommended, but both are established.

infantile, -ine. Pron. -īl, -īn. The dictionaries do not lay down any distinction, giving as the sole definition of *-ine* '=infantile.' But OED quotations for the two words do on the whole bear out one that might well (see DIFFERENTIATION) be encouraged, something like that between *childish* & *childlike,* though less established: *infantile* means of or in infancy, & *infantine* infantlike or as of an infant. If this is accepted, each of the following quotations from the OED would be the worse if *-ile* & *-ine* were to change places: *The interest which his story first impressed upon her* infantile *imagination./The countenance is so innocent &* infantine, *you would think this head belonged to a child of twelve.* It may be said roughly that *infantile* records a fact, & *infantine* an impression. *Infantile paralysis, infantile dresses; an infantine credulity.*

infer makes *-rred* &c., but *inferable.* The word means to draw an inference in conclusion, to deduce; to lead to (something) as a consequence, and in this sense, to imply; RIGHT: *Socrates argued that a statue inferred the existence of a sculptor.* To use it in the other sense of *imply,* hint, insinuate (*He* inferred *that it was none of my business*) is, as Webster points out, erroneous; many dictionaries include *imply* in the definition without comment.

inferno. Pl. *-os.*

infinite(ly). There are naughty people who will say *infinite(ly)* when they only mean *great* or *much* or *far.* After quoting an amusing exchange of letters on this sin, Fowler adds a comment by his brother, F. G. Fowler: 'Rot. *Infinite* is no more a vulgarism than any other deliberate exaggeration.'

INFINITIVE. (1) The infinitive is that form of the verb that expresses merely its meaning without any subject or object (in Latin, *amare*=to love; in French *aller*=to go). In modern English it is, except in certain circumstances, preceded by *to*—*to go, to see, to have seen* (perfect inf.). (The exception is the use of the inf. with auxiliary verbs *can, may,* &c., and some other verbs such as *dare, let.*) Since *to* is a part of the infinitive form, normally it should not be separated from the verb by intervening word(s), but see SPLIT INFINITIVE. (2) For unidiomatic infinitives after nouns that prefer the gerund, as in the extract, see GERUND. WRONG: *The* habit *of mapmakers* to place *lands & not seas in the forefront has obscured the oneness of the Pacific* (read *of placing*).

infinitude does not appear to be now entitled to any higher rank than that of a NEEDLESS VARIANT of *infinity.* It might well have been, but can hardly now be, differentiated with the sense quality of being infinite. Milton & Sterne, however, will keep it in being for poets to fly to & stylists to play with when *infinity* palls on them. An escape from *-ity* is sometimes welcome: *It is just this* infinitude *of possibilities that necessitates* unity & continuity *of command.*

infirmity. 'The last infirmity of noble minds' is a MISQUOTATION. (*Mind,* not *minds*). (From 'Lycidas'; subject, Fame.)

inflame. *Inflam(e)able,* formed from the English verb, & used in 16th & 17th cc., has been displaced by *inflammable,* adapted from French or Latin. *Inflammable* (easily set on fire; hence easily excited, irascible) & *inflammatory* (tending to inflame —with passions &c., usually in a bad sense: excite anger, sedition, tumult) must not be confused. See PAIRS & SNARES.

inflection, -xion. (1) The first is more usual in US; the second Brit. (2) (Gram.): 'making curved.' The general name, including declension, conjugation, & comparison, for changes made in the form of words to show their grammatical relations to their context or to modify their meaning in certain ways. *Cats, him, greater, sued,* are formed by inflection from *cat, he, great,* & *sue.*

inflict is, owing especially to confusion with *afflict,* peculiarly liable to the misuse explained in the article OBJECT-SHUFFLING. The right constructions are: *he inflicted plagues* on *them, he afflicted them* with *plagues, plagues were inflicted* on *them, they were afflicted* with *plagues.* Examples of the BLUNDER: *At least the worst evils of the wage system would never have* inflicted *this or any other present-day community./The misconception & discussion in respect of the portraits of Shakespeare with which the world is in such generous measure* inflicted *are largely due to . . .*

infold. *En-* is recommended.

inform has almost completely ousted *tell* in business correspondence, and is doing its best to crowd out *notify, instruct, advise.* It is also an instrument for adding extra and unnecessary words: *This is to inform you . . ./For your information . . ./Kindly inform your clients,* &c. So confident is it that it attempts to take on the construction of some of its victims. WRONG: *Kindly* inform *all department heads* to attend *a meeting at* 4 *p.m. sharp.* Ask them *to attend;* inform them *that they must attend.* See OFFICIALESE.

informer, -ant. In US usage, *-er* is one who informs against another, *-ant* one who gives any sort of information. Because crime fiction and reporting have made the former a term of opprobrium, law-enforcement officials are now adopting the latter.

infringe. (1) *Infringe* makes *infringeable* but *infringing.* (2) *Infringe, infringe upon.* Many of those who have occasion for the word must ask themselves before using it what its right construction is: do you *infringe* (or *infringe upon*) a rule? do you *infringe* (or *infringe upon*) a domain?

There is no question that *infringe* is properly transitive only; *infringe* means *break in*= damage or violate or weaken, NOT *break in*=intrude; but it has been identified in sense with *trespass* & *encroach* & assimilated to them in construction, this being further helped by confusion with *impinge upon.* Pretentious writers like to escape from *encroach* & *trespass,* familiar words, to *infringe,* which will better impress readers with their mastery of the unfamiliar, and they find justification in most dictionaries. For those who care about the real meaning of words, however, the advice tendered is (1) to conceive *infringe* as a synonym rather of *violate* & *transgress* than of *encroach* & *trespass;* (2) to abstain altogether from *infringe upon* as an erroneous phrase; (3) to use *infringe* boldly with *right, rule, privilege, patent, sovereignty, boundary,* or the like, as object; & (4) when the temptation to insert *on* or *upon* becomes overpowering, as it chiefly does before words like *domain* & *territory,* to be content with *trespass* or *encroach* rather than say *infringe upon.*

infuse. 1. *Infusable, infusible. Fusible* being the word for that can be fused, & *infusible* being therefore the word for that cannot be fused, it is convenient as well as allowable to make from the verb *infuse* not infusible but *infusable. Infusable,* then=that can be infused; *infusible*=that cannot be fused.

2. *Infuse, imbue. Infuse* is one of the verbs liable to the OBJECT-SHUFFLING mistake. You can *infuse* courage *into* a person, or *imbue* or *inspire* him *with* courage, but NOT *infuse* him *with* courage. WRONG: *One man, however, it has not affected; say, rather, it has* infused *him* with *its own rage against itself./He* infused *his pupils* with *a lively faith in the riches that were within.*

-ING. 1. WRONG: *I would also suggest that, while* admitting *the modernity,* the proofs *offered by him as to the recent date are not very convincing* (should be, *while I admit their modernity*). For liberties of this kind taken with the participle, see UNATTACHED.

2. For the difference between participles in *-ing* & the gerund, see GERUND.

3. WRONG: *On the Press Association's* representative informing *a leading liberal of . . . , he replied . . .* (should be *representative's*). For such mixtures of participle & gerund, see FUSED PARTICIPLE.

4. WRONG: *In all probability he suffers somewhat, like the proverbial dog, from* his *having received a bad name.* For needlessness of his & other possessives in such contexts, see GERUND.

5. Tender grammatical consciences are apt to vex themselves, sometimes with reason & sometimes without, over the comparative correctness of the *-ing* form of a verb & some other part, especially the infinitive without *to,* in certain constructions. It is well, on the one hand, not to fly in the face of grammar, but eschew what is manifestly indefensible; & on the other hand, not to give up what one feels is idiomatic in favor of an alternative that is more obviously defensible.

WRONG: *The wearing down, phase by phase, has been an integral part of the plan, & it has enabled the attack to be kept up* as well as insuring *against hitches.* We can all condemn this without a regret. *As well as* is not a preposition but a conjunction; it therefore cannot govern the gerund *insuring,* as *besides* would have done. If *as well as* is to be kept, *insuring* must become *insured* to match *enabled.*

UNIDIOMATIC: *We suspect that Italy is doing something more* than raising *a diplomatic question.* Everyone's first idea would be *raise; raising* is easily defensible but unidiomatic. A defense for *raise,* which is idiomatic, is more difficult, but can be constructed as follows: I will raise the question; I will do more-than-raise-the-question (i.e. the hyphened group is treated as a single word, as *court-martial* has the pl. *courts-martial*). Hence we suspect Italy of doing more-than-raise-the-question.

RIGHT: *Dying at their posts rather than* surrender. There are misguided persons who would actually write *surrendering* there; but they are few, the rest of us feeling that we must either find a justification for *surrender* or else write it without justification. This feeling is strengthened if we happen to remember that we should have no such repugnance to *rather than surrendering* after a participle if the relation to be expressed were a quite different one; compare *acquiring rather than surrendering* with *dying rather than surrendering;* one must have its *-ing,* & the other must not. Well, the justification is the same as with *raise: I will die rather than surrender;* it is true that the form of *surrender* there is decided by *will,* like that of *die,* so that, when *will die* is changed to *dying, surrender* is left depending on air; but meanwhile *die-rather-than-surrender* has become a single verb of which *die* is the conjugable part: *they died rather than surrender; dying rather than surrender.*

-ing prepositions. Certain *-ing* participles have taken on the function of the preposition; that is, they do not have to be attached to a noun as do other participles. Among these are REGARDING, CONSIDERING, OWING, CONCERNING, FAILING, SEEING, PROVIDING.

ingeminate. The phrase *ingeminate peace* means to say *Peace, peace!* again & again (Latin *geminus,* double). The following sentence looks as if *ingeminate* were in danger of confusion with *germinate* or *generate* or some such word. WRONG: *We have great hopes that the result* [of a discussion on a Commission's report] *will be to* ingeminate *peace and avoid the threatened recurrence of hostilities.*

ingenious, ingenuous. *Ingenious* of people, clever at contriving or making things, is often used in contrast with those having solid inventive skill; *ingenuous,* open, frank, candid, artless, innocent. *Ingenious contrivances; an ingenuous confession.* So *ingenuity, ingenuousness.* (*Ingeniousness* means nothing more than *ingenuity* & is more easily confused with *ingenuousness.*)

ingénue. A naïve girl (esp. on stage). The masc. is *ingénu,* but seldom used.

ingrain(ed), not *en-.*

ingratiate has one sense & one construction only in modern English; it is always reflexive & means only to bring (oneself) into favor (with): *His desire was to ingratiate himself with* (or rarely *to*) *his neighbors.*

inherit makes *-tor,* with fem. *inheritress* or (in technical use)

-trix.

initiate. (1) *Initiate* makes *initiable, -ator.* (2) *Initiate* is liable to the OBJECT-SHUFFLING mistake; you initiate persons or minds in knowledge, not knowledge into person or minds. WRONG: *The Review, a quarterly which is doing so much* to initiate into the minds *of the public what is requisite for them to know.* *Instill* is perhaps the word meant.

initiative. 1. After *take the initiative* the construction is *in.* NOT: *The Congress delegates to the various committees the* initiative of *taking necessary action.*

2. The sense of *initiative* has been narrowed down by modern usage. Taking 'the first step' as the simple-word equivalent, we might understand that of the first step as opposed to later ones, or of the lead as taken by one person & not another or others; the latter is the only current sense, & it appears in all the special uses: (a) the military, where the *initiative* is the power of forcing the enemy to conform to your first step, so deciding the lines of a campaign or operation; (b) the political, where the *initiative,* technically so called, is the right of some minimum number of citizens to demand a direct popular vote on any constitutional question; (c) the two phrases in which *initiative* is chiefly used, 'take the initiative,' i.e. act before someone else does so, & 'of (or on) one's own initiative,' i.e. without a lead from someone else.

inmesh. *En-* better.

innavigable, un-. The second is recommended.

inner. For *the inner man,* see HACKNEYED PHRASES.

innocence, -cy. The latter is an ARCHAISM, chiefly kept alive by Ps. xxvi. 6 (*I will wash mine hands in innocency*).

innocent of, in the sense *without* (*windows* innocent of *glass*) is a specimen of WORN-OUT HUMOR. 'She might profitably avoid such distortions as "windows innocent of glass" & trays "guiltless of any cloth" '—says a *Times* review.

innocuous, so spelled.

innuendo. Pl. usually *-oes.*

inobservance (used chiefly in respect to laws, treaties, &c.) but *unobservant;* see IN- & UN-.

inoculate. For danger of misprints, see INCULCATE.

in order that is regularly followed by *may* & *might: in order that nothing may,* or *might, be forgotten.* In archaic writing, the subjunctive without a modal verb may be used instead: *In order that nothing* be *forgotten.* In some contexts, but not in most, *shall* & *should* may pass instead of *may* & *might: in order that nothing* should be *forgotten;* but certainly the second, & perhaps the first also, of the *shall* examples below is unidiomatic. The other examples, containing *can,* are undoubtedly WRONG: *The effort must be organized & continuous* in order that Palestine shall *attract more & more of the race./To influence her in her new adolescence* in order that we shall *once more regain the respect & admiration we enjoyed under the old Russia./Farmers object to portions of their farms being taken* in order that small holdings can *be created./It will conclude before lunch time* in order that delegates can *attend a mass meeting in London.* These solecisms are all due to ANALOGY, *in order that* being followed by what could properly have followed *so that.*

in petto. 'in the heart,' secretly. Spec. as applied to the appointment of cardinals, not named in consistory. See FOREIGN DANGER.

inquire. Often a FORMAL WORD for *ask.*

inquire, -ry, en-. *In-* is better.

insanitary, un-. Both forms are used in US; but see UNSANITARY.

inside of, in reference to time (*I'll be there* inside of *a week*) is colloq. *Inside of* for prep. *inside, within* (*He went* inside of *the house*) is illiterate (chiefly US).

insignia is pl.,=distinguishing marks (of office &c.), badges. The sing. is *insigne,* badge, emblem, but seldom used.

in so far. (If used, better as 3 words.) He must have a long spoon that sups with the devil; & the safest way of dealing with *in so far* is to keep clear of it. The dangers range from mere feebleness or wordiness, through pleonasm or confusion of forms, & inaccuracy of meaning, to false grammar. The examples are in that order, & the offense charged against each is stated in a word or two, & left undiscussed for the reader to decide upon. If he is sufficiently interested to wish for fuller treatment, he should turn to FAR 4, 5, where different uses of *so far* are considered; the prefixing of *in* is for the most part not dictated by reasons either of grammar or of sense, so that much of what is there said applies to *in so far* also. WORDY: *He did not, with such views, do much to advance his object,* save in so far that *his gracious ways won esteem & affection.* (Read *though* for *save in so far that.*)/ *The question . . . is not in any way essentially British,* save in so far as *the position of Great Britain in Egypt makes her primarily responsible.* (Read *except that.*) PLEONASTIC: *Some of the defects are inevitable, at least* in so far as *that no one can suggest an improvement.* (Omit *in* & *as.*)/UNGRAMMATICAL: *It has the character of a classic* in so far as *the period it covers.* (*In so far as* is not a preposition, & cannot govern *period.*)

insoluble, insolvable, unsolvable. *Insoluble* means (1) incapable of being dissolved, (2) incapable of being solved (*unsolved if not insoluble problems*), as does also *insolvable. Unsolvable* can mean incapable of being solved. It is suggested that *insoluble* be restricted to the sense not dissolvable, *unsolvable* to not solvable, and *insolvable* be allowed to die as a NEEDLESS VARIANT.

insomuch, adv. In modern English, *in* (*that*), *so* (*as*), *so* (*that*) are usually less wordy and less liable to ambiguity. If used, written as one word.

instal(l)(ment). Two *l's* are preferred in US, but *instalment* in Brit. Cf. ENROL(L).

instance. The abuse of this word in lazy periphrasis has gone far, though not so far as that of *case.* Here are two examples: *The taxation of the unimproved values in any area, omitting altogether a tax on improvements, necessarily lightens the burden* in the instance of *improved properties./The stimulation to improve land is more clearly established whenever the* *outgo is direct & visible,* such as in the instance of *highly priced city lands.* In the first *in the instance of* should be simply *on;* & in the second *such as in the instance of* should be *as on.* There is some danger that, as writers become aware of the suspicions to which they lay themselves open by perpetually using *case,* they may take refuge with *instance,* not realizing that most instances in which *case* would have damned them are also cases in which *instance* will damn them. The crossing out of one & putting in of the other will not avail; they must rend their heart & not their garments, & learn to write directly instead of in periphrasis. *Instance* has been called *case's* understudy; in the articles CASE & ELEGANT VARIATION will be found examples of the substitution.

instil(l), US usually *-ill,* Brit. *-il,* but always *-lled, -lling.* The word is liable to the OBJECT-SHUFFLING confusion. WRONG: *His words will undoubtedly* instill the Christians of Macedonia with *hope.* You can *inspire* men *with* hope, or hope *in* men; but you can only *instill* it *into* them, not them with it.

instinct. 'Instinctive acts are performed without any previous experience & are characteristic for each type of animal.' (Instinct=inherited behavior.) For the contrast with *intuition,* see INTUITION.

institute, institution. The two nouns have run awkwardly into & out of one another. The neat arrangement would have been for *institution* to mean instituting, & *institute* a thing instituted; but *institution* has seized, as abstract words will, on so many concrete senses that neatness is past praying for. *Institution* is in fact the natural English word capable of general use, & *institute* a special title restricted to, & preferred for, certain institutions. An *institute* is deliberately founded; an *institution* may be so, or may have established itself or grown. A man leaves his fortune to institutions, but perhaps founds a local or a mechanics' institute, i.e. an institution designed to give instruction or amusement to a special class of people. Whether a particular institution founded for a definite purpose shall have *-ute* or *-ution* in its title is a matter of chance or fashion—*The Royal Institute of Painters in Water Colours,* but *The Institution of Civil Engineers; The Smithsonian Institution.* A child is to be got into some institution, & is placed in the *National Institute for the Blind* or the *Masonic Institution for Boys.* Baseball, the cocktail hour, a hospital, the National Gallery, marriage, capital punishment, the law courts, are all institutions & not institutes.

insubstantial. *Un-* is usually better. (*In-* is used sometimes as 'immaterial,' 'apparitional,' in contrast with *un-,* flimsy.')

insufficient is an adj. As a noun it is obs. It must be attached to *quantity, amount, quality,* or some other noun. WRONG: *But Austria also excludes altogether a food product like meat, of which she produces* insufficient. This noun use (=not enough or too little) is worse than the corresponding use of SUFFICIENT.

insupportable, un-. The first is recommended.

insure, en-. *In-,* against loss; *en-,* make certain. See ENSURE.

insusceptible, NOT *un-*.

intaglio. Pron. -ăl′yō. Pl. *-os*. *Intaglio* is opposed to *relief* as a name for the kind of carving in which the design, instead of projecting from the surface, is sunk below it (*carved in intaglio*); & to *cameo* as the name for gems of the same kind but carved in intaglio instead of in relief.

integrate makes *-grable, -tor*.

intelligent, intellectual. While an intelligent person is merely one who is not stupid or slow-witted, an intellectual person is one in whom the part played by the mind as distinguished from the emotions & perceptions is greater than in the average man. An intellectual person who was not intelligent would be, though not impossible, a rarity; but an intelligent person who is not intellectual we most of us flatter ourselves that we can find in the looking glass. *Intelligent* is often a patronizing epithet, while *intellectual* is a respectful one, but seldom untinged by suspicion or dislike.

intelligentsia, -tzia. The 'intellectuals,' the intellectual (real or self-styled) class. Both forms are current, *-sia* being more usual in US, *-zia* in Brit. (The *s* is closer to the Russian, the *z* to the Italian.)

intended, n. It is curious that betrothed people should find it so difficult to hit upon a comfortable word to describe each other by. 'My intended,' 'my fiancé(e),' 'my sweetheart,' 'my love(r)'—none of these is much to their taste, too emotional, or too French, or too vulgar, or too evasive. The last two objections are in fact one; evasion of plain words is vulgarity, & 'my intended' gives the impression that the poor things are shy of specifying the bond between them, an ill-bred shyness; & in *fiancé(e)* they resort to French instead of to vague English for their embarrassing though futile disguise. Is it too late to suggest that 'my betrothed,' which means just what it should, i.e. pledged to be married, & is not vulgarized but only out of fashion, & would be a dignified word for public use, should be given another chance?

intensive. Just as *definitive* & *alternative* are ignorantly confused with *definite* & *alternate,* & apparently liked the better for their mere length, so *intensive* is becoming a fashionable word where the meaning wanted is simply *intense.* It must be admitted that there was a time before differentiation had taken place when Burton, e.g., could write *A very intensive pleasure follows the passion;* it there means *intense,* but the OED labels the use 'obsolete.' *Intensive* perished as a mere variant of *intense,* but remained with a philosophic or scientific meaning, as an antithesis to *extensive;* where *extensive* means with regard to extent, *intensive* means with regard to force or degree: *The record of an* intensive *as well as extensive development./Its* intensive, *like its extensive, magnitude is small.* This is the kind of word that we ordinary mortals do well to leave alone; see POPULARIZED TECHNICALITIES. Unfortunately, a particular technical application of the philosophic use emerged into general notice, & was misinterpreted—*intensive method,* especially of cultivation. To increase the supply of wheat you may sow two acres instead of one—increase the extent—or you may use more fertilizers & care on your one acre—increase the intensity; the second plan is *intensive cultivation,* the essence of it being concentration on a limited area. Familiarized by the newspapers with *intensive cultivation,* which most of us took to be a fine name for very hard or intense work by the farmers, we all became eager to show off our new word, & took to saying *intensive* where *intense* used to be good enough for us. The war gave this a great fillip by finding the correspondents another peg to hang *intensive* on—*bombardment.* There is a kind of bombardment that may be accurately called *intensive;* it is what in earlier wars we called concentrated fire, a phrase that has the advantage of being open to no misunderstanding; the fire converges upon a much narrower front than that from which it is discharged; but as often as not the *intensive bombardment* of the newspapers was not concentrated, but was *intense,* as the context would sometimes prove; a bombardment may be intense without being intensive, or intensive without being intense, or it may be both.

intensive (Gram.): 'tightening up.' Said of words or word elements that add emphasis; in *vastly obliged, vastly* is an intensive.

intent, adj. *The case has its moral for librarians all over the country; all hoods make not monks, nor are all visitors to libraries* on serious studies intent. When *intent* in its inverted construction (*on mischief intent,* instead of *intent upon mischief*) is mixed up with words so pedestrian & far from archaic as *visitors to libraries,* a tepid half-hearted jocularity results; see INCONGRUOUS VOCABULARY.

intention. Ordinary use: *the* intention *of doing* something, intention *to do.* A defining phrase is so often appended to *intention* that the question between gerund & infinitive, treated generally under GERUND 3, is worth raising specially here. Choice between the two is freer for *intention* than for most such nouns, & it can hardly be said with confidence that either construction is ever impossible for it. It will perhaps be agreed, on the evidence of the illustrations below, offered as idiomatic, that when *intention* is used in the singular & without *the, his, an, any,* or other such word, *to do* is better, but otherwise *of doing:* Intention to kill *is the essential point./You never open your mouth but with* intention to give *pain./He denied* the intention of killing./Some intention of evading *it there may have been./I have* no intention of allowing *it.*

inter, v., makes *-rred, -rring.*

inter-, prefix (=*between, among,* interval or reciprocal, &c.), in est. words and usually even in nonce words, no hyphen (*intercontinental, interdependency*), but the hyphen is retained before a proper noun (*inter-American*). Not to be confused with INTRA=within.

inter alia is Latin for 'among others' when 'others' are things. If the others are persons, *alia* must be changed to *alios* or rarely *alias* (the OED quotes, from 1670, *The Lords produce* inter alios *John Duke of Lancaster*); but when persons are meant, it is much better nowadays to use English.

intercalary. Inserted in the calendar; hence, interpolated. Stress -ter′-.

interest, v., **interestedly, disinterested,** &c. Stress on in′-, NOT est-.

interior, internal, intrinsic. Opposites of *exterior, external,* and *extrinsic.* An *interior* wall, trade, ear. *Internal* evidence, peace, medicine. *Intrinsic* value, beauty, advantages. See EXTERIOR.

intermediary, n., is, even in its concrete sense of a go-between or middleman or mediator, a word that should be viewed with suspicion & resorted to only when it is clear that every more ordinary word comes short of the need. In its abstract sense of medium or agency or means (*The only European people who teach practical geometry through the recondite* intermediary *of Euclid's Elements*), it is worthy only of the POLYSYLLABIC HUMORist.

intermezzo. Pron. -dzo. Pl. *-os* or *-i.*

intermit makes *-tted, -tting, -ssible.*

intern. The word meaning a graduate medical student in a hospital &c. came into English from the Fr. *interne* through US and is now best spelled without the *e.* The word meaning an interned alien &c. is also chiefly US, the Brit. equivalent being *internee.*

internal. See INTERIOR.

internecine (deadly, destructive, characterized by great slaughter) has suffered an odd fate. Being mainly a literary or educated man's word, it is yet neither pronounced in the scholarly way nor allowed its Latin meaning. It should be called ĭnter′nĭsĭn, & is called ĭnternē′sĭn, or -sĭn (US). And the sense has had the Kilkenney-cat notion imported into it because *mutuality* is the idea conveyed by *inter-* in English; the Latin word meant merely of or to extermination, without implying that of both parties. Internecine war is properly war for the sake of slaughter, war to the death. The imported notion, however, is what gives the word its only value, since there are plenty of substitutes for it in its true sense—*destructive, slaughterous, sanguinary, mortal,* & so forth. The scholar may therefore use or abstain from the word as he chooses, but it will be vain for him to attempt correcting other people's conception of the meaning or their pronunciation. See POPULARIZED TECHNICALITIES.

interpellate, -ation. An *interpellation* is the action of interrupting the order of the day by demanding an explanation from a (French) minister or other executive. The two words are little used now except in the technical sense proper to parliamentary proceedings. They are felt to be half-French words, & so the unnatural pronunciation (ĭnterpĕl′āt, ĭnterpĕlā′shn) is perhaps accounted for. These renderings, whether really current or not, have the advantage of distinguishing the sound from that of *interpolate, -ation.*

interpretative, NOT *interpretive,* is the right form; although *interpretive* is widely used in US, the longer form is preferred.

interstice. Pron. ĭnter´stĭs. Pl. *-ces,* pron. -stĭsēz.

in that is a conj. that has gone a little out of fashion & does not slip from our tongues nowadays. It is still serviceable in writing of a formal cast, but like other obsolescent idioms, is liable to ill treatment at the hands of persons who choose it not because it is the natural thing for them to say, but because, being unfamiliar, it strikes them as ornamental. WRONG: *This influence was* so far *indirect* in that *it was greatly furthered by Le Sage./The legislative jury sat to try the indictment against Mr. Justice Grantham* in that *during the election petition he displayed political bias.* In the first, two ways of saying the thing are mixed (*was so far indirect that,* & *was indirect in that*); & in the second *in that* is used in a quite suitable context, but wrongly led up to; a man is guilty in that he has done so-&-so, but an indictment against him is not *in that* anything. After *the less, the more,* the clause that responds to *the* should not begin with *in that,* but with plain *that;* WRONG: *Nor are they any the less pleasing* in that *the colorings are of the rich not gaudy type.* Omit the *in* & see THE 5.

intimidate. (1) *Intimidate* makes *-dable, -tor.* (2) WRONG: *Similar threats were uttered in the endeavor to* intimidate Parliament from *disestablishing the Irish Episcopal Church. From* is idiomatic after *deter* & *discourage,* but not after *intimidate* or *terrify;* but the threats might have intimidated Parliament *into abandoning* its attempt to disestablish the Church.

into, in to. The two words should be written separately when their sense is separate. WRONG: *The doors of the great opera house let out the crowd; when we went* into *the opera, the streets had been swept, but when we came out the snow was inches deep again. Opera house* shows that *opera* means not the building, but the performance, & you do not go *into* that, but go *in to* it. Correct similarly: *Lord Rosebery took her* into *dinner.*

in toto means not on the whole, but wholly, utterly, entirely, absolutely, & that always or nearly always with verbs of negative sense—*condemn, decline, deny, reject, disagree, in toto.* The following is NONSENSE: *Nor do we produce as much* in toto *as we might if we organized.*

intra- means *within* (*inter-,* between.) So *intracollegiate,* within the college; *intra-urban,* within the city; *intrastate,* within the state; *intramural,* within the walls (of a city, or college, or village, &c.).

intransigence, -cy. There is no differentiation. The *-ce* form is perhaps more usual.

intrench. *En-* is better.

intrigue, v. intrans. To carry on an underhand plot; to employ secret influence (*with*); to have a liaison (*with*); as a journalistic GALLICISM, v.t., 'rouse the interest or curiosity of' (COD). To this Webster adds 'to trick, cheat, entangle, complicate; to puzzle, perplex; to arouse the interest, desire, or curiosity of, as by an engaging, beguiling, or baffling quality.' ACD contributes, 'to take the fancy of: *Her hat intrigued me.*' This is one of the GAL-

LICISMS that have no merit whatever & at the same time the great demerit of being identical with & therefore confusing the sense of a good English word. Besides *puzzle* & *perplex*, there are *fascinate, mystify, interest,* & *pique* to choose from. Will the reader decide for himself whether the Gallicism is called for in any of the following places? *A cabal which has* intrigued *the imagination of the romanticists./The problem, however, if it* intrigues *him at all, is hardly opened in the present work./Nor is this the only problem raised by this* intriguing *exhibition./But her personality did not greatly* intrigue *our interest.*

intrinsic. See INTERIOR.

intrust. *En-* better.

intuition & instinct. The word *intuition* being both in popular use & philosophically important, a slight statement of its meaning, adapted from the OED, may be welcome. In modern philosophy it is the immediate apprehension of an object by the mind without the intervention of any reasoning process: *What we feel & what we do, we may be said to know by intuition;* or again (with exclusion of one or other part of the mind) it is immediate apprehension by the intellect alone, as in *The intuition by which we know what is right & what is wrong,* or immediate apprehension by sense, as in *All our intuition takes place by means of the senses alone.* Finally, in general use it means direct or immediate insight: *Rashness if it fails is madness, & if it succeeds is the intuition of genius.*

How closely this last sense borders on *instinct* is plain if we compare *A miraculous* intuition *of what ought to be done just at the time for action* with *It was by a sort of* instinct *that he guided his open boat through the channels.* One of the OED's definitions of *instinct,* indeed, is: 'intuition; unconscious dexterity or skill'; & whether one word or the other will be used is often no more than a matter of chance. Three points of difference, however, suggest themselves as worth keeping in mind: (1) an *intuition* is a judgment issuing in conviction, & an *instinct* an impulse issuing in action; (2) an *intuition* is conceived as something primary & uncaused, but an *instinct* as a quintessence of things experienced in the past whether by the individual or the race; & (3) while both, as faculties, are contrasted with that of reason, *intuition* is the attribute by which gods & angels, saints & geniuses, are superior to the need of reasoning, & *instinct* is the gift by which animals are compensated for their inability to reason.

intwine, intwist. *En-* is better.

inundate. Pron. ĭn′-. (Literally, to overspread with a flood of water; also used fig.: *Inundated with letters.*)

inure, enure. Pron. -ūr′. Both the connection between the verb's different senses (*The poor,* inured *to drudgery & distress; The cessions of land* enured *to the benefit of Georgia*) & its derivation are so little obvious that many of us, at any rate when minded to use the less common sense, feel some apprehension that we may be on the point of blundering, & that, again, there is a tendency to spell *in-* & *en-* for the two meanings as if they were different words (1. accustom, habituate [to]; 2. come into operation, take effect). The origin is the obs. noun *ure* (*We will never enact, put* in ure, *promulge, or execute, any new canons*), which is from French *œuvre*, which is from Latin *opera*, work. *To inure a person* you set him at work or practice him; *a thing inures* that comes into practice, or operates, in such & such a direction. Variant spellings are therefore unnecessary, & *in-* is preferred.

inveigle. Pron. (preferably) -vē′gl (also often -vā′gl).

INVERSION. By this is meant the abandonment of the usual English sentence order & the placing of the subject after the verb as in *Said he,* or after the auxiliary of the verb as in *What did he say?* & *Never shall we see his like again.* Inversion is the regular & almost invariable way of showing that a sentence is a question, so that it has an essential place in the language; & there are other conditions under which it is usual, desirable, or permissible. But the abuse of it ranks with ELEGANT VARIATION as one of the most repellent vices of modern writing.

In questions & commands, as contrasted with the commoner form of sentence, the statement, inversion is the rule: *Doth Job fear God for nought?/Hear thou from heaven thy dwelling-place.* The subject being usually omitted in commands, these do not much concern us; but in questions the subject regularly follows the verb or its auxiliary except when, being itself the interrogative pronoun or adjective, it has to stand where that pronoun almost invariably stands: *Who did it? What caused it?* In the other exceptional sentence form, the exclamation, inversion is not indeed the rule as in questions, but is, & still more used to be, legitimate: *How dreadful is this place!/What a piece of work is a man!/Bitterly did he rue it.* To these forms of sentences must be added the hypothetical clause in which the work ordinarily done by *if* is done in its absence by inversion: *Were I Brutus./Had they known in time.*

Interrogative, Imperative, Exclamatory, & Hypothetical Inversions form a group in which inversion itself serves a purpose. With statements it is otherwise; inversion is there not performed for its own significance, but comes about owing to the writer's wish to place at the beginning either the predicate or some word or phrase that belongs to it. He may have various reasons for this. The usual reason for putting the whole of the predicate at the beginning is the feeling that it is too insignificant to be noticed at all after the more conspicuous subject, & that it must be given what chance the early position can give it; hence the *There is* idiom; not *No God is,* but *There is no God.* That is Balance Inversion in its shortest form, & at greater length it is seen in: *Through a gap came a single level bar of glowing red sunlight peopled with myriads of gnats that gave it a quivering solidity;* if *came through a gap* is experimentally returned to its place at the end of that, it becomes plain why the writer has put it out of its place at the beginning. Another familiar type is *Among the guests were A, B, C . . . Z.*

Often, however, the object is not to transfer the predicate bodily to the beginning, but to give some word or words of it first place. Such a word may be meant to give hearer or reader the connection with what precedes (Link Inversion), to put him early in possession of the theme (Signpost Inversion), or to warn him that the sentence is to be negative (Negative Inversion): *On this depends the whole course of the argument./By strategy is meant something wider./Never was a decision more abundantly justified. On this, by strategy, never,* are the causes of inversion here; each belongs to the predicate, not to the subject; & when it is placed first it tends to drag with it the verb or auxiliary, so that the subject has to wait; tends, but with different degrees of force, that exercised by a negative being the strongest. We can if we like, instead of inverting, write *On this the whole course of the argument depends,* or *By strategy something wider is meant,* but not *Never a decision was more abundantly justified;* & *Not a word he said* is a very out-of-the way version of *Not a word did he say.*

If we now add Metrical Inversion, our catalogue of the various kinds may perhaps suffice. Where the Bible gives us *As the hart panteth after the water brooks,* & the Prayer Book *Like as the hart desireth the water-brooks,* both without inversion, the hymn books have *As pants the hart for cooling streams.* That is *metri gratiâ,* & it must not be forgotten that inversion is far more often appropriate in verse than out of it for two reasons—one this of helping the versifier out of metrical difficulties, & the other that inversion off the beaten track is an archaic & therefore poetic habit. A very large class of bad inversions will be seen presently to be those in subordinate clauses beginning with *as;* they arise from failure to realize that inversion is archaic & poetic under such circumstances, & non-inversion normal; it is therefore worth while to stress this contrast between *As pants the hart* & both the prose versions of the same clause.

To summarize these results:

Interrogative Inversion: *Doth Job fear God for nought?*

Imperative Inversion: *Hear thou from heaven thy dwelling-place.*

Exclamatory Inversion: *How dreadful is this place!*

Hypothetical Inversion: *Were I Brutus, & Brutus Antony.*

Balance Inversion: *There is no God./Among the guests were* . . . (long list).

Link Inversion: *On this depends the whole argument./Next comes the question of pay.*

Signpost Inversion: *By strategy is meant something wider.*

Negative Inversion: *Never was a decision more abundantly justified.*

Metrical Inversion: *As pants the hart for cooling streams.*

Though bad inversion is extremely common, non-inversion also can be bad. It is so rare as to call for little attention, but here are two examples: *But in neither case* Mr. Galsworthy tells *very much of the intervening years./Least of all* it is *to their interest to have a new Sick Man of Europe.* In negative sentences there is the choice whether the negative shall be brought to the beginning or not, but when it is so placed inversion is necessary; read *does Mr. G.*, & *is it*.

We may now proceed to consider with the aid of grouped specimens some of the temptations to ill-advised inversion. It is hardly credible, after a look through the collection to follow, that the writers can have chosen these inversions either as the natural way of expressing themselves or as graceful decoration, so ungraceful are many of them. It follows that the motive must have been a severe sense of duty, a resolve to be correct, according to their lights, at any sacrifice. And from this it follows that no demonstration that the inversions are incorrect is called for; the task is only to show cause why non-inversion should be permitted, & these idolators will be free of the superstitions that cramped their native taste.

INVERSION AFTER RELATIVES & COMPARATIVES

1. *A frigate could administer roughly half the punishment that* could a 74. Compare some everyday sentence: *You earn twice the money that I do,* never *that do I.* The misconception is perhaps that the putting of the object first (here *that*) should draw the verb; but this is not true of relative clauses; *the people that I like,* not *that like I.*

2. *It costs less* than did *administration under the old companies.* A simple parallel is *I spend less than you do,* for which no one in talk would substitute *than do you.* Many, however, would write, if not say, *I spend less* than do *nine out of ten people in my position.* The difference must lie in the length of the subject, & the misconception must be that it is a case for balance inversion, i.e. for saving the verb from going unnoticed; but so little does that matter that if the verb is omitted no harm is done; *did* in the quotation should in fact either be omitted or put in either of its natural places, after *administration,* or after *companies.*

3. *He looked forward,* as do we all, *with great hope & confidence to Monday's debate. As,* in such sentences, is a relative adverb; it & the unexpressed *so* to which it answers are equivalent to (*in the way*) *in which,* & what was said above of relatives & inversion holds here also. *Try to pronounce it as I do,* not *as do I;* & when the subject is longer, e.g. *the native Frenchman,* though *as does the native Frenchman* becomes defensible, it does not become better than *as the native Frenchman does,* nor as good.

4. *Each has proven ably that the other's kind of protection would be quite as ruinous* as would be *Free Trade.* This differs from that of 3 in that its fellow *as* of the main sentence belongs to an adjective (*ruinous*). This allows the inversionist a different defense, which he needs, since balance inversion is clearly not available for *as would be Free Trade* with its short subject. He might appeal here to exclamatory inversion. When the compound sentence is reduced to its elements, they are either (a) *Free Trade would be ruinous; protection would be equally ruinous* (the first clause being a statement); or (b) *Ruinous would Free*

Trade be! Protection would be equally ruinous (the first clause being an exclamation). He chooses, how reasonably let the reader judge, the (b) form, & retains its order in the compound sentence. The truth is that in this sentence the verb should have been omitted.

5. *Bad* as has been our record *in the treatment of some of the military inventions of the past, it may be doubted whether the neglect of the obvious has ever been more conspicuously displayed than in . . .* The meaning of this *as* idiom is clear; it is *Though our record has been so bad,* or *However bad our record has been;* but how it reached its present shape is less apparent. Some light is thrown by the presence in earlier English of another *as,* now dropped; Swift writes *The world, as censorious as it is, hath been so kind . . . ;* this points to (*Be our record as*) *bad as our record has been* (*bad*) for the unabbreviated form. Omission of the bracketed words gives the uninverted order, which will only be changed if exclamatory inversion (*Bad has been our record!*) or balance inversion is needlessly applied.

6. *It is not all joy to be a War Lord in these days, & gloomy* though is the precedent, *the only thing left for a War Lord to do is to follow the example of Ahab at Ramoth Gilead. Gloomy is the precedent!* is a not impossible exclamatory inversion; &, if the words were kept together with the effect of a quotation by having *though* before instead of in the middle of them, the exclamatory order might be tolerable, though hardly desirable, even in the subordinated form; but not with *though* where it is. This may be tested by trying a familiar phrase like *Bad is the best. Though bad is the best,* yes; but not *Bad though is the best;* instead of that we must write *Bad though the best is.*

7. *The work stands still until* comes the convenient time *for arranging an amicable rupture of the old engagement & contracting of the new.* There is no doubt about the motive. It is a balance inversion, & one that would be justified by the great length of the subject if the only place for the uninverted *comes* were at the end of the whole sentence. But what is too often forgotten in such cases is that there is usually a choice of places for the verb; here *comes* would be quite comfortable immediately after *time.*

The conclusion suggested is that, so far as relative clauses, & especially those containing *as,* are concerned, the writer whose taste disposes him to use the natural uninverted order is at the very least free to indulge it.

INVERSIONS OF THE LITERARY PARAGRAPHIST

The gentlemen who provide newspapers with short accounts of newly published books have an inversion form all to themselves. The principle seems to be that the title of the book is to be got to a place where the reader shall be able to find it; at the same time the catalogue look is to be avoided that results if the title is printed at the head before the description; & a literary air is to be so given to the paragraph. The title is therefore worked to the end, by the use of odd inversions that

editors would do well to prohibit:
Most racily written, with an easy conversational style about it, is *Mr. Frank Rutter's* 'The Path to Paris.'/*Diplomatic & military* are the letters *that comprise the Correspondence of Lord Burghersh, edited by his daughter-in-law./Lively & interesting* are the pictures *of bygone society in town & country presented in the two volumes, 'The Letter-bag of Lady Elizabeth Spencer-Stanhope.'*

FALSE EXCLAMATORY INVERSION

It has already been pointed out that a statement may be turned into an exclamation by inversion; an adjective or adverb that conveys emotion is first put out of its place, & inversion follows. If Jacob had said *The days of the years of my life have been few & evil,* he would have been stating a bald fact; by beginning *Few & evil have been,* he converts the statement into a groan, & gives it poignancy. Writers who observe the poignancy sometimes given by such inversion, but fail to observe that 'sometimes' means 'when exclamation is appropriate,' adopt inversion as an infallible enlivener; they aim at freshness & attain frigidity. In the following examples there is no emotional need of exclamation, & yet exclamatory inversion is the only class to which they can be assigned: *Finely conceived* is this *poem, & not less admirable in execution./By diligent search in sunny & sheltered places* could *some short-stalked* primroses be *gathered* (this is perhaps, however, a negative inversion gone wrong by the omission of the necessary *only* at the beginning)./*Little by little* are these *poor people being hemmed in & ground down by their cruel masters* (*Little by little* is quite the wrong expression to start an exclamatory inversion with, since its effect is not to enhance, but to diminish, the emotional effect).

YET, ESPECIALLY, RATHER, &C.

A curious habit has grown up of allowing these & similar words to dictate a link inversion when the stressing of the link is so little necessary as to give a noticeable formality or pomposity to the passage. It is a matter not for argument, but for taste; will the reader compare the quoted forms with those suggested in parentheses? *Especially* & *rather* usually change their place when inversion is given up, but *yet* remains first. The last example, in which the unusual *in particular* with this construction is felt to be intolerable, is strong evidence that the order to which custom has reconciled us with certain words only is not good on the merits: *His works were burnt by the common hangman;* yet was the multitude *still true to him* (yet the multitude was)./*It is to be hoped that some supervision will be exercised in the reproductions;* especially will care be needed *in the painting process* (care will be needed especially in)./*His book is not a biography in the ordinary sense;* rather is it *a series of recollections culled from . . .* (it is rather)./*An undefeated Prussia is ultimately the end of England, &*, in particular, is it *the end of fortune & security for . . .* (& it is the end in particular).

INVERSION IN INDIRECT QUESTIONS

This point will be found fully discussed under INDIRECT QUESTION. Examples of the wrong use are: *How bold* is this attack *may be judged by . . ./Why* should we be *so penalized must ever remain a mystery.* (*How bold this attack is* & *Why we should be so penalized* would be the right order.)

SUBORDINATED INVERSIONS

It is often well, when a sentence that standing by itself would properly be in the inverted form is subordinated as a clause to another, to cancel the inversion as no longer needed. The special effect that inversion is intended to secure is an emphasis of some sort, & naturally emphasis is more often suitable to a simple independent sentence than to a dependent clause. Examples are grouped under A, B, & C, according to the kind of inversion that has been subordinated:

A. Negative Inversion. *To give to all the scholars that firm grounding* upon which alone can we hope *to build an educated nation./Now that not only* are public executions long extinct *in this country, but the Press not admitted to the majority of private ones, the hangman has lost his vogue./But it had only been established that on eighteen of those days* did he *vote.* In the first it will be admitted that, while *Upon this alone &c.* (the independent form) would require the inversion, *upon which alone &c.* (the subordinate form) is at least as good, if not better, without it. The second example (*executions*) will on the other hand be upheld by many who have no inordinate liking for inversion; *not only* is so little used except in main clauses, & therefore so associated with inversion, that *not only public executions are long extinct,* though legitimate, has an unfamiliar sound even after *Now that.* The subordinate inversion in the last example is not quite what it seems, being due to irresolution between an inverted & an uninverted form; the former would be, *But only on eighteen of those days had it been established that he voted;* & the latter, *But it had only been established that he voted on* 18 *of those days.*

B. Exclamatory Inversion. *Suffice it to say that in almost one half of the rural district areas* is there *an admitted dearth of homes./Though once, at any rate,* does that benign mistily golden irony *of his weave itself in./While for the first time, he believed,* did naval & military history *appear as a distinctive feature.* The subordination in two of these only makes more conspicuous the badly chosen pegs on which the inversion is hung. *In almost one half of the rural district areas,* & *once at any rate,* are not good exclamatory material; *Many a time have I seen him!* shows the sort of phrase that will do. Even if main clauses had been used with these beginnings, they should have been put as statements, i.e. without inversion, & still more when they depend on *Though* & *Suffice it to say that.* In the third example *for the first time* is not incapable of beginning an exclamation; it would pass in a sentence, but becomes frigid in a clause.

C. Link Inversion. *When,*

three years later, came the offer *of a nomination, it was doubtless a welcome solution./While equally necessary* is it *to press forward to that unity of thought without which . . .* About these there can hardly be a difference of opinion. If the *when* & *while* constructions were absent, it would have been very natural to draw *Three years later, Equally necessary,* to the beginning to connect the clauses with what preceded, & inversion might or might not result. But with the interposition of *when* & *while* they lose their linking effect, & the natural order should be kept—*When the offer came three years later, While it is equally necessary.*

INVERSION IN PARALLEL CLAUSES

As with combinations of a negative & a positive statement into one, so with inverted & uninverted members of a sentence care is very necessary. *Not only in equipment but in the personnel of the Air Battalion* are we suffering *from mal-administration* (*Not only in equipment* requires *are we suffering; in the personnel* requires *we are suffering.* To mix the two is slovenly; the right form would be *We are suffering not only in* &c.)./*Even* were this tract *of country level plain & the* roads lent themselves *to the maneuver, it would be so perilous to . . .* (*were this tract* is inverted; *the roads lent themselves* is not, & yet, since there is no *if*, it absolutely requires it. Begin *Even if this tract were;* for the only ways to invert the second clause are the fantastic *& lent themselves the roads* & the clumsy *& did the roads lend*).

INVERSION IN DIALOGUE MACHINERY

Novelists & others who have to use dialogue as an ingredient in narrative are some of them unduly worried by the machinery problem. Tired of writing down *he said* & *said he* & *she replied* as often as they must, they mistakenly suppose the good old forms to be as tiring to their readers as to themselves, & seek relief in whimsical variations. The fact is that readers care what is said, but the frame into which a remark or a speech is fitted is indifferent to them; or rather, the virtue of frames is not that they should be various, but that they should be inconspicuous. Among those that are not inconspicuous, & are therefore bad, are many developments of the blameless & inconspicuous *said he*, especially the substitution of verbs that are only by much stretching qualified for verbs of saying, & again the use of those parts of verbs of saying that include auxiliaries. A few examples will make these points clear: *'Yes,'* moodily consented John, *'I suppose we must.'*/*'Oh?'* questioned he./*'But then,'* puzzled John, *'what is it that people mean when they talk about death?'*/*'You misunderstand your instructions,'* murmured rapidly Mr. Travers./*'I won't plot anything extra against Tom,'* had said Isaac./*'I am the lover of a Queen,'* had often sung the steward *in his pantry below.*

The ordinary *said he* &c. (*Thou art right, Trim, in both cases,* said my uncle Toby) was described above as blameless & inconspicuous. Its place among inversions is in the 'signpost' class. But only such insignificant verbs as *said, replied, continued,* will submit to being dragged about like this; verbs that introduce a more complicated notion, or that are weighted with auxiliaries or adverbs (compare 'went on my uncle Toby' with 'continued my uncle Toby'), or that cannot rightly take a speech as object, stand on their dignity & insist on their proper place.

inverted commas. See QUOTATION MARKS. For the use as apology for slang (*Democratic adhesion is a necessity for members to 'get along'*), see SUPERIORITY.

involve has many legitimate meanings, lit., transf., & fig., all having some connection with *enwrapping, entwining, complicating, entangling.* A sense found only in US dictionaries—'to be highly or excessively interested in' 'to occupy oneself absorbingly'—seems to strain the figure too far (e.g. *She is also* involved *in Red Cross work*).

inwrap. *En-* better.

iodine. For this, as well as for the three parallel element names *bromine, chlorine,* & *fluorine,* US chemists prefer the sound -īn, with -ĭn allowed as alternative. Popular use is almost universally for -īn in iodine, but varies in the other three. OED prefers -ĭn in all.

-ION & -MENT. Many verbs have associated with them nouns of both forms, as *commit, commission* & *commitment; require, requisition* & *requirement; excite, excitement* & *excitation.* When both are well established, as in these cases, the two nouns usually co-exist because they have come by differentiation to divide the possible meanings between them & so tend to lucidity. How little the essential difference of meaning is may be seen by comparing *emendation* with *amendment* (where the first means rather correction made, & the second rather correcting) and *requisition* with *requirement* (where the first means rather requiring & the second rather thing required), & then noticing that the two comparisons give more or less contrary results. Further, when there is only one established form, it is not apparent to the layman why one form exists & the other does not—why e.g. we say *infliction* & not *inflictment,* but *punishment* & not *punition.* The conclusion is that usage should be respected, & words that have been rarely used or may easily be coined, such as *pollutement, incitation,* & *punition,* should not be lightly resorted to when *pollution, incitement,* & *punishment* are to hand. To illustrate what is meant by 'lightly': if a writer suddenly realizes or suspects that he cannot say 'by chastisement of actual & admonition of prospective offenders,' & changes to *admonishment* as fitter for the construction wanted, without taking the trouble to think either of *chastising* & *admonishing* or *chastisement* & *dissuasion,* he is treating the language with levity.

-ION & -NESS. The question between variants in *-ion* & *-ness* differs from that discussed in the previous article in several respects. First, *-ness* words can be made from any adjective or participle, whereas the formation of *-ment* words from verbs is by no means unrestricted; by the side of *persuasion* you can make *persuasiveness,* but not *persuadement.* Secondly, there is more possibility of a clear distinction in meaning; *-ion* & *-ment* are both attached to verbs, so that neither has any more claim than the other to represent the verbal idea of action; but between *-ion* & *-ness* that line does exist. Though *-ion* & *-ness* are often appended to exactly the same form, as in *abjectness* & *abjection,* one is made from the English adjective *abject,* & the other from the Latin verbal stem *abject-,* with the consequence that *abjectness* necessarily represents a state or quality, & *abjection* naturally at least a process or action. Thirdly, while both *-ion* & *-ment* pass easily from the idea of a process or action into that of the product—*abstraction* e.g. being equivalent either to abstracting or to abstract notion—to subject *-ness* to that treatment is to do it violence; we can call virtue an *abstraction,* but not an *abstractness;* in compensation for this disability, the *-ness* words should be secured as far as possible the exclusive right to the meaning of state or quality; e.g. we should avoid talking of the *abstraction* or the *concision* of a writer's style, or of the *consideration* that marks someone's dealings, when we mean *abstractness, conciseness,* & *considerateness. Concision* means the process of cutting down, & *conciseness* the cut-down state; the ordinary man, who when he means the latter says *conciseness,* shows more literary sense than the literary critic who says *concision* just because the French, who have not the advantage of possessing *-ness,* have to say it, & he likes gallicizing. It is not always easy to prove that writers do not mean the process rather than the quality, but appearances are often against them; in the following examples, if the epithet *short-winded,* & the parallel *pungency,* are taken into account, it is pretty clear that the quality of the style was meant, & *conciseness* would have been the right word: *It is better than Tennyson's* short-winded & artificial concision—*but there is such a thing as swift & spontaneous style./But then as a writer of letters, diaries, & memoranda, Mr. Gladstone did not shine by any habitual* concision or pungency *of style.* If it were not for this frequent uncertainty about what is really meant, it would be as bad to say *concision* for *conciseness* as to use *correction* (which also could be defended as a GALLICISM) for *correctness,* or *indirection* (for which *Hamlet* II. i. 66 might be pleaded) for *indirectness.*

Simple reference of any word in *-ion* to this article may be taken to mean that there is a tendency for it to usurp the functions of the noun in *-ness.*

irascible. The traditional long *i* (īrăs′-) is given first in the dictionaries.

iridescent. So spelled, NOT *irri-* (the origin is Greek *iris,* rainbow).

IRONY. For a tabular comparison of this & other words, see HUMOR. Irony is a form of utterance that postulates a double audience, consisting of one party that hearing shall hear & shall not understand, & another party that, when more is meant than meets the ear, is aware both of that more & of the outsider's incomprehension. (1) *Socratic irony* was a profession of ignorance. What Socrates represented as an ignorance & a weakness in himself was in fact a noncommittal attitude toward any dogma, however accepted or imposing, that had not been carried back to & shown to be based upon first principles. The two parties in his audience were, first, the dogmatists, moved by pity or contempt to enlighten this ignorance, &, secondly, those who knew their Socrates & set themselves to watch the familiar game in which learning should be turned inside out by simplicity. (2) The double audience is essential too to what is called *dramatic irony,* i.e. the irony of the Greek drama. The drama had the peculiarity of providing the double audience—one party in the secret & the other not—in a special manner. The facts of most Greek plays were not a matter for invention, but were part of every Athenian child's store of legend; all the spectators, that is, were in the secret beforehand of what would happen. But the characters, Pentheus & Oedipus & the rest, were in the dark; one of them might utter words that to him & his companions on the stage were of trifling import, but to those who hearing could understand were pregnant with the coming doom. (3) And the double audience for the *irony of Fate?* Nature persuades most of us that the course of events is within wide limits foreseeable, that things will follow their usual course, that violent outrage on our sense of the probable or reasonable need not be looked for; & these 'most of us' are the uncomprehending outsiders; the elect or inner circle with whom Fate shares her amusement at our consternation are the few to whom it is not an occasional maxim, but a living conviction, that what happens is the unexpected.

That is an attempt to link intelligibly together three special senses of the word *irony,* which in its more general sense may be defined as the use of words intended to convey one meaning to the uninitiated part of the audience & another to the initiated, the delight of it lying in the secret intimacy set up between the latter & the speaker; it should be added, however, that there are dealers in irony for whom the initiated circle is not of outside hearers, but is an *alter ego* dwelling in their own breasts.

For practical purposes a protest is needed against the application of 'the irony of Fate,' or of 'irony' as short for that, to every trivial oddity: *But the pleasant note changed to something almost bitter as he declared his fear that before them lay a 'fight for everything we hold dear'—a sentence that the groundlings* by a curious irony *were the loudest in cheering* (oddly enough)./'*The* irony of the thing,' *said the dairyman who now owns the business, 'lies in the fact that after I began to sell good wholesome butter in place of this adulterated mixture, my sales fell off 75 per cent.' The* irony (*of fate*) is, in fact, to be classed now as a HACKNEYED PHRASE.

irrefragable. Unanswerable, indisputable. *An irrefragable authority, argument.* Pron. ĭrrĕf′ragabl.

irrefutable. Stress -ref′-.

irregardless seldom gets into print, but is occasionally heard in speech from people who should know better.

irrelevance, -cy. The first is recommended.

irrelevant. It is stated in the OED, which does not often volunteer such remarks, & which is sure to have documentary evidence, that 'a frequent blunder is *irrevalent*'; that form, however, does not get into print once for a hundred times that it is said. The word is one of those that we all know the meaning of, but seldom trouble to connect with their derivations. It is worth remembering that *relevant* & *relieving* are the same word; that, presumably, is irrelevant which does not relieve or assist the problem in hand by throwing any light upon it.

IRRELEVANT ALLUSION. We all know the people—for they are the majority, & probably include our particular selves—who cannot carry on the ordinary business of everyday talk without the use of phrases containing a part that is appropriate & another that is pointless or worse; the two parts have associated themselves together in their minds as making up what somebody has said, & what others as well as they will find familiar, & they have the sort of pleasure in producing the combination that a child has in airing a newly acquired word. There is indeed a certain charm in the grown-up man's boyish ebullience, not to be restrained by thoughts of relevance from letting the exuberant phrase jet forth. And for that charm we put up with it when one draws our attention to the methodical by telling us there is *method in the madness*, though *method* & not *madness* is all there is to see; when another's every *winter* is the *winter of his discontent;* when for a third nothing can be *rotten* except *in the state of Denmark*. Other phrases of the kind will be found in the article HACKNEYED PHRASES. A slightly fuller examination of a single example may be useful. The phrase *to leave severely alone* has two reasonable uses—one in the original sense of to leave alone as a method of severe treatment, i.e. to send to Coventry or show contempt for; & the other in contexts where *severely* is to be interpreted by contraries—to leave alone by way not of punishing the object, but of avoiding consequences for the subject. The straightforward meaning, & the ironical, are both good; anything between them, in which the real meaning is merely to leave alone, & *severely* is no more than an echo, is pointless & vapid. Examples follow: (1, STRAIGHTFORWARD) *You must show him, by* leaving him severely alone, *by putting him into a moral Coventry, your detestation of the crime;* (2, IRONICAL) *Fish of prey do not appear to relish the sharp spines of the stickleback, & usually seem to* leave them severely alone; (3, POINTLESS) *Austria forbids children to smoke in public places; & in German schools & military colleges there are laws upon the subject; France, Spain, Greece, & Portugal,* leave the matter severely alone. It is obvious at once how horrible the faded jocularity of No. 3 is in print; &, though things like it come crowding upon one another in most conversation, they are not very easy to find in newspapers & books of any merit; two samples follow: *The* moral, as Alice would say, *appeared to be that, despite its difference in degree, an obvious essential in the right kind of education had been equally lacking to both these girls* (as Alice, or indeed as you or I, might say)./*Resignation* became a virtue of necessity *for Sweden* (If you do what you must with a good grace, you make a virtue of necessity; without *make,* 'a virtue of necessity' is meaningless.

irremediable. Pron. -mē′-.

irremovable. So spelled.

irreparable. Pron. -rĕp′-.

irrespective(ly), adv. When *of* does not follow, the adverb still takes *-ly: Mercy that places the marks of its favor absolutely &* irrespectively *upon whom it pleases.* When *of* follows, the modern tendency is to drop *-ly* in the adverb, as in *All were huddled together,* irrespective of *age & sex;* see UNIDIOMATIC -LY. But good writers perhaps retain the *-ly* in sentences where *irrespective* might be taken for an adjective agreeing with the subject & meaning *not taking account,* whereas what is desired is an adverb meaning *without account taken;* so *He values them,* irrespectively of *the practical conveniences which their triumph may obtain for him* (quoted from Matthew Arnold, who would doubtless have refused to drop the *-ly* here). This rather fine (if not imaginary) point of idiom does not practically affect the meaning of a passage, but does imply a view of the exact meaning & construction of the word *irrespective*—the view, namely, that it does not mean careless & does not agree with a person.

irresponsive, un-. The second is recommended.

irretentive, un-. The first is recommended.

irrevocable. Pron. -rĕv′-.

is. 1. *Is* & *are* between variant numbers. WRONG: *What* are *wanted* are *not small cottages, but larger houses with modern conveniences./The plausible suggestions to the contrary so frequently put forward* is *an endeavor to kill two birds with one stone.* In the first example both *ares* should be *is;* in the second, *is* should be *are;* for discussion see ARE, IS. Mistakes are especially common with the word *what: What* is *really at issue* are *not questions of . . ./What* is *needed* are *a few recognized British corporations.* For these wrong forms, see WHAT.

2. *Is* & *are* in the multiplication table. *Five times six* is, *or* are, *thirty?* The subject of the verb is not *times,* but *six,* the meaning of the subject being 'six reckoned five times.' Before we know whether *is* or *are* is required, then, we must decide whether *six* is a singular noun, the name of a quantity, or a plural adjective agreeing with a suppressed noun; does it mean 'the quantity six,' or does it mean 'six things'? That question each of us can answer, perhaps, for himself, but no one for other people. It is therefore equally correct to say *twice two is four* & *twice two are four.* Moreover, as the two are equally correct, so they appear to be about equally old; *four times six* was plural as long ago as 1380, & *ten times two* was singular in 1425.

3. Confusion between auxiliary & copulative uses. WRONG: *The risk of cards' being lost or mis-*

laid under such circumstances is considerable, & great inconvenience‸experienced by any workman to whom this accident occurs. This mistake of leaving the reader to supply an *is* of one kind out of a previous *is* of another kind is discussed under BE 5.

4. *Is* after compound subjects. WRONG: *The Allies are prepared to retire if & when proper* pledges & security is *given./ Their* lives, their liberties, & their religion is *in danger.* In both these *is* should be *are;* they seem to point to a mistaken theory that, when the parts of a compound subject differ in number, the verb follows the nearest; that might reasonably, though it hardly does in fact, hold for *or* groups (*whether* we or she is *right*); but it is entirely wrong for *and* groups, which always require a plural verb unless they are, like *bread & butter*, compound words rather than mere groups. See also NUMBER.

-ise, -ize. On the general question of the spelling of verbs ending in the sound -īz, see -IZE. If *-ize* is accepted as the normal form, there are still a number of verbs in which the question between the two spellings does not arise, but *-ise* is for various reasons necessary (*advertise, supervise,* &c.). Many of these are listed in their dictionary places.

-ISM & -ITY. Many adjectives have each ending appended & give two words of different meaning. Occasionally choice between the two is doubtful. Roughly, the word in *-ity* usually means the quality of being what the adjective describes, or concretely an instance of the quality, or collectively all the instances; & the word in *-ism* means the disposition to be what the adjective describes, or concretely an act resulting from that disposition, or collectively all those who feel it. A few of the more notable pairs follow, to enable the reader to judge how far this rough distinction will serve him in deciding where the difference is less established: BARBARITY & *barbarism;* FORMALITY & *formalism; humanity* & HUMANISM; *latinity* & LATINISM: *reality* & *realism; spirituality* & *spiritualism; universality* & *universalism.*

isolate. Best pron. īs-; ĭs- is a US variant.

Israeli. Of (the state of mod.) Israel. *Israeli troops, citizens, Ambassador, The Egyptian-Israeli Commission. An Israeli, three Israelis.*

-IST, -ALIST, -TIST, -YIST, &c. The use of the suffix *-ist* in English is so wide & various that any full discussion of it is not here possible. But there are some words whose exact form is still uncertain & should be fixed, & there are others that are both established & badly formed, so that there is danger of their being used as precedents for new formations.

agricultur(al)ist, constitution(al)ist, conversation(al)ist, education(al)ist, & others of the kind. Either form is legitimate; the shorter, besides being less cumbersome, usually corresponds more naturally to the sense; expert in agriculture (*-turist*), for instance, is simpler than expert in the agricultural (*-turalist*); but in *constitution(al)ist,* perhaps, knowledge of or devotion to what is constitutional, rather than of or to the constitution, is required. Unless there is a definite advantage of this kind in the *-al-* form, the other should be preferred: *agriculturist, constitutionalist, conversationist, educationist.*

accompan(y)ist. Neither form is satisfactory & it is a pity that *accompanier* was not taken; but of the two *-nyist* (cf. copyist) is better than *-nist: accompanyist* (but US usually *-ist*).

ego(t)ist. The *-t-* is abnormal; but both forms are established, & a useful differentiation is possible if both are retained; see EGO(T)ISM.

analyst, separatist, & *tobacconist* are open to objection, though they are all firmly established.

isthmus. Pron. ĭsth′- or ĭs′mus. Pl. *-uses.*

it. 1. First, there is a present tendency to omit in relative clauses the anticipatory *it*, i.e. the *it* that heralds a deferred subject as in *It is useless to complain.* An example of this omission is (WRONG): *The House is always ready to extend the indulgence which‸is a sort of precedent that the mover & seconder of the Address should ask for.* If we build up this sentence from its elements, the necessity of *it* will appear, & the reader can then apply the method to the other examples. *That the mover should ask for indulgence is a precedent;* that, rearranged idiomatically, becomes *It is a precedent that the mover should ask for indulgence;* observe that *it* there does not mean *indulgence*, but means *that the mover should ask for indulgence, it* being placed before the predicate (*is a precedent*) as a harbinger announcing that the real subject, which it temporarily represents, is coming along later. *It is a precedent that the mover should ask for indulgence; the House extends the indulgence;* there are the two elements; to combine them we substitute *which* for *indulgence* in the clause that is to be subordinate, & place this *which* at the beginning instead of at the end of that clause: *the House extends the indulgence which . . . ;* now, if *it* had meant *indulgence,* i.e. the same as *which* now means, it would have become superfluous; but, as has been mentioned, it means something quite different, & is just as much wanted in the compound sentence as in the simple one. A parallel will make the point clear: *A meeting was held, & it was my duty to attend this;* whether *which* or *& this* is placed at the beginning of the second member instead of the present arrangement, no one would dream of dropping *it* & writing *which was my duty to attend,* or *& this was my duty to attend.* After this rather labored exposition it will suffice to add to the more or less similar examples that follow mere hints of the essential construction. WRONG: *It has already cost the two millions which‸was originally estimated would be the whole cost.* The missing *it* means *that which would be the whole cost* (*that* the conjunction, not the pronoun)./*The great bulk of the work done in the world is work that‸is vital should be done.* Elements: (a) *That certain work should be done is vital,* or *It is vital that certain work should be done;* (b) *Most work done is that work.* The missing *it* means not *work,* as *that* does, but *that which work should be done./ What‸was realized might happen has happened.* Elements:

It was realized that a thing might happen; that thing has happened.

2. Secondly, certain points have to be remembered about the anticipatory *it* besides the fact that it may be wrongly omitted. WRONG: *In connection with this article,* it *may be worth recalling the naïve explanation given to Dickens by one of his contributors.* Anticipatory *it* heralds a deferred subject; *it* cannot be used when there is no subject to herald; where is the subject here? *explanation* is engaged as object of *recalling; recalling* is governed by *worth; worth* is complement to *may be; it* neither has any meaning of its own nor represents anything else. The way to correct it is to write *worth while* instead of *worth,* which releases *recalling* to serve as the true subject; see WORTH for other such mistakes./It *is such wild* statements *as that Mr. Sandlands has made* that does *harm to the cause.* By strict grammatical analysis *does* would be right; but idiom has decided that in the *it . . . that* construction, when *that* is the relative, it takes its number not from its actual antecedent *it,* but from the word represented by it—here *statements./It is impossible to enter on the political aspects of the book but*‸*must suffice to say that he suggests with great skill the warring interests.* The reader of that at once thinks something is wrong, & on reflection asks whether the anticipatory *it,* which means *to enter* &c., can be understood again before *must suffice* with the quite different meaning of *to say* &c. It cannot; but some more or less parallel types will show that doubts are natural.

Here are (A) two in which the understanding of *it,* though the subjects are different, is clearly permissible. RIGHT: *It is dangerous to guess, but humiliating to confess ignorance./It must please him to succeed & pain him to fail.* And here are (B) two that will not do. WRONG: *It is dishonest to keep silence, &*‸*may save us to speak./It cannot help us to guess, &*‸*is better to wait & see.* The distinction that emerges on examination is this: in the A examples *is* & *must* are common to both halves; in the B examples it is otherwise, *is* being answered to by *may,* & *cannot* by *is;* it appears that *it* may be understood, even if the real subject is changed, when the verb or auxiliary is common to both parts, but not otherwise.

3. Examples of *it* & *its* used when the reference of the pronoun is obscure or confused, or its use too previous or incorrect. These faults occur with *it* as with all pronouns, & are discussed generally under PRONOUNS. A few examples are here printed without comment. WRONG: *This* local option *in the amount of outdoor relief given under the law has always operated inequitably & been one of the greatest blots on the system. To extend* it *to the first great benefit under the Insurance Act will greatly lessen* its *usefulness./Again, unconsciousness in the person himself of what he is about, or of what others think of him, is also a great heightener of the sense of absurdity.* It *makes* it *come the fuller home to us from his insensibility to* it.*/Both these lines of criticism are taken simultaneously in a message which* its *special correspondent sends from Laggan*

to the Daily Mail *this morning.*

4. The possessive of *it*, like that of *who*, & the absolute forms in *-s* of *her, their, our,* & *your,* has no apostrophe: *its, hers, theirs, ours, yours,* NOT *it's* &c.

ITALICS. The practiced writer is aware that his business is to secure prominence for what he regards as the essence of his communication by so marshaling his sentences that they shall lead up to a climax, or group themselves around a center, or be worded with different degrees of impressiveness as the need of emphasis varies; he knows too that it is an insult to the reader's intelligence to admonish him periodically by a change of type, like a bad teacher imploring his boys to attend for a moment, that he cannot safely go to sleep just now. But to those who, however competent on their special subject, have not had enough experience of writing to have learned these rudiments it comes as natural to italicize every tenth sentence or so as it comes to the letter-writing school girl to underline whatever she enjoys recording.

The true uses of italics are definite enough to admit of classification. Some of them may be merely mentioned as needing no remark: a whole piece may be in italics because italics are decorative; text & notes may be distinguished by roman & italic type just as they may by different-sized types; quotations used as chapter headings, prefaces, dedications, & other material having a special status are entitled to italics. Apart from such decorative & distinctive functions, too obvious to need illustration, italics have definite work to do when a word or two are so printed in the body of a roman-type passage. They pull up the reader & tell him not to read heedlessly on, or he will miss some peculiarity in the italicized word. The particular point he is to notice is left to his own discernment; the italics may be saying to him:

a. 'This word, & not the whole phrase of which it forms part, contains the point': It is not only *little* learning that has been exposed to disparagement.

b. 'This word is in sharp contrast to the one you may be expecting': It would be an ultimate benefit to the cause of morality to prove that honesty was the *worst* policy.

c. 'These two words are in sharp contrast': But, if the child never *can* have a dull moment, the man never *need* have one.

d. 'If the sentence were being spoken there would be a stress on this word': The wrong man knows that if he loses there is no consolation prize of conscious virtue awaiting *him*.

e. 'This word wants thinking over to yield its full content': Child-envy is only a form of the eternal yearning for something better than *this* (i.e. the adult's position with all its disillusionments).

f. 'This word is not playing its ordinary part, but is a word as such': Here *will* is wrongly used instead of *shall*.

g. 'This is not an English word or phrase': The maxim that deludes us is the *progenies vitiosior* of one to which the Greeks allowed a safer credit.

h. 'This word is the title of a book or a newspaper, or the name of a fictitious character': The Vienna correspondent of *The Times* reports that . . .

i. 'This word is important & likely to be overlooked': Good Friday services at *10 a.m.* (because the usual hour is 11 a.m.).

Such are the true uses of italics. To italicize whole sentences or large parts of them as a guarantee that some portion of what one has written is really worth attending to is a miserable confession that the rest is negligible.

italicize makes *-zable.*

itemize, itemization, are 'chiefly US,' permissible and useful in business practice. They have no place, however, in literary speech or writing.

its, pronoun, NOT *it's; it's*=a contraction of *it is.*

-ize, -ise, in verbs. In the vast majority of the verbs that end in *-ize* or *-ise* & are pronounced -īz, the ultimate source of the ending is the Greek *-izo.* Many English printers follow the French practice of changing *-ize* to *-ise;* but the OED, *The Times,* and American usage, in all of which *-ize* is the accepted form, carry authority enough to outweigh superior numbers.

It must be noticed, however, that a small number of verbs, some of them in very frequent use, like *advertise, devise,* & *surprise,* do not get their *-ise* even remotely from the Greek *-izo,* & must be spelled with *-s-;* the more important of these are given in their dictionary places in this book.

J

jaguar. Pron. pref. jăg'wär (but in US the car popularly jag'ūar).

jail, jailer, standard US spelling, make *jail-like, jailkeeper, jailmate,* &c. Brit. usually GAOL, *gaoler,* &c.

jam, n., the act of squeezing or crushing; *jamb,* n., in architecture &c. The verb is *jam* (*crowds jam the room; the cable was jammed*).

James. *St. James's* so spelled, NOT *James'* or *James* (*Court of St. James's; St. James's Palace*). *The King James Version* of the Bible (the so-called *Authorized Version*), 1611.

Jap, Japanese, Nipponese. *Jap* is colloq. & understandably resented. The use of *Nippon(ese),* current after World War II, seems unlikely to become general. *Japanese* is the normal English word.

Jaques, in *As You Like It,* pron. jā kwēz or -kwĭz.

jargon is perhaps the most variously applied of a large number of words that are in different senses interchangeable, & under it the distinctions between them may be pointed out. The words are: *argot, cant, dialect, gibberish, idiom, jargon, lingo, parlance, patois, shop, slang, vernacular.*

argot is primarily the vocabulary of thieves & tramps serving to veil their meaning, & is applied secondarily to the special vocabulary of any set of persons. There is in these senses no justification for its use instead of whichever English word may be most appropriate, except in writing concerned with France.

cant in current English means the insincere or parrotlike appeal to principles, religious, moral, political, or scientific, that the speaker does not believe in or act upon, or does not understand. It is best to restrict it to this definite use; but its earlier sense—special vocabulary of the disreputable (thieves' jargon)—is still used by philologists & in etymological discussions; & it means sometimes what is now more often expressed by *jargon* or *slang*, the special vocabulary of an art, profession, &c.

dialect is essentially local; a dialect is the variety of a language that prevails in a district, with local peculiarities of vocabulary, pronunciation, & phrase.

gibberish is the name for unintelligible stuff; applied by exaggeration to a language unknown to the hearer (for which, as a familiar term, *lingo* is better), & to anything either too learnedly worded, or on the other hand too rudely expressed, for him to make out its meaning.

idiom is the method of expression characteristic of or peculiar to the native speakers of a language; i.e. it is racy or unaffected or natural English (or French &c.), especially so far as that happens not to coincide with the method of expression prevalent in other languages; & *an idiom* is a particular example of such speech. (An earlier sense, the same as that of *dialect*, still occurs sometimes.)

jargon is talk that is considered both ugly-sounding & hard to understand: applied especially to (1) the sectional vocabulary of a science, art, class, sect, trade, or profession, full of technical terms (cf. *cant, slang*); (2) hybrid speech of different languages; (3) the use of long words, circumlocution, & other clumsiness.

lingo is a contemptuous name for any foreign language. It is sometimes used instead of *jargon* (1) & (2).

parlance, which means manner of speaking, has the peculiarity of possessing no significance of its own & being never used by itself; you can say *That is dialect, That is slang,* &c., but not *That is parlance; parlance* is always accompanied by an adjective or defining word or phrase, & that adjective, not *parlance,* gives the point: *in golfing* or *nautical parlance, in the parlance of the literary critics,* &c.

patois, as used in English, means nothing different from *dialect,* & therefore, like *argot,* should not be used except about France.

shop describes business talk indulged in out of business hours, or any unseasonable technical phraseology, & is thus distinct, in the special-vocabulary sense, from *jargon, cant,* & *slang.*

slang is the diction that results from the favorite game among the young & lively of playing with words & renaming things & actions. Many slang words & phrases perish, a few establish themselves; in either case, during probation they are accounted unfit for literary use. *Slang* is also used in the sense of *jargon* (1), & with two distinctions: in general it expresses less dislike & imputation of ugliness than *jargon;* & it is naturally commoner about sporting vocabularies (*golf slang* &c.) than *jargon,* because many of the terms used in sports are slang in the main sense also.

vernacular describes the words that have been familiar to us as long as we can remember, the homely part of the language, in contrast with the terms that we have consciously acquired. *The vernacular* was formerly common, & is still occasional, for English as opposed to any foreign language; &, by an unessential limitation, it is often applied specially to rustic speech & confused with dialect.

Currently *goobledegook* & *officialese* are used to describe the circumlocutions & unnatural wordiness of business and official letters & circulars (*Herewith are enclosed the requisite documents Government employees are requested to submit subsequent to the termination of their period of probation*). See OFFICIALESE.

jasmine, jessamine. The first is now established.

jazz, from the Creole word meaning 'to speed up,' is standard for a type of syncopated music, or a quality (of literary style) suggested by that music. The verb *jazz* (*jazz up*) is slang.

jealous. The normal constr. is *of*: *jealous of his honor, jealous of a person,* though *for* and *over* also are possible; *jealous about* is colloq.

jeep, the US army vehicle, probably from GP, General Purpose, though one US dictionary suggests a comic-strip animal as the source. *Jeep* for an escort carrier is US Navy slang.

jejune. Orig. 'fasting' (now obs. in this sense), meager, scanty, unsatisfying to the mind; esp. of speech or writing, insipid, dull: *a jejune account of his travels.* Pron. jêjo͞on′.

jemmy, a crowbar used by burglars, usually *jimmy* in US, & so pronounced in Brit.

Jenghiz Khan. Use GENGHIS KHAN.

jeopardy. Pron. jĕp′-. The verb is *jeopardize.*

jetsam, jettison. *Jetsam* is the goods, cast overboard and found on land; *jettison* is, as a noun, the action. *Flotsam* is goods found afloat.

Jew. For *Jew, Israelite,* &c., see HEBREW.

jewel makes, US, *-led, -ling, -ler;* Brit., *-lled* &c.

jewel(le)ry. In US the shorter form is general for all uses. In Brit. the longer is the commercial & popular form, the shorter the rhetorical & poetic. The pronunciation is always jo͞o′ĕlrĭ.

jibe, gibe. In US the first is the preferred spelling for the nautical term, and also for the colloq. meaning of to agree. *His words and actions don't jibe. Gibe* is preferred for scoff, taunt, &c.

Jill. *Jack and Jill* commonly so spelled in US. Brit. GILL.

JINGLES, or the unintended repetition of the same word or similar sounds, are dealt with in the article REPETITION OF WORDS & SOUNDS. A few examples of the sort of carelessness that, in common courtesy to his readers, a writer should remove before printing may be given here:

The sport of the air is still far from free from *danger./The situation had* so far *developed* so little *that nothing useful can be* said *about it,* save *that* so far *the Commander-in-Chief was* satisfied./*He* served *his* apprenticeship *to* statesmanship./ *I* awaited *a* belated *train./The* earliest lists, still so sadly & probably irretrievably *imperfect* (for this commonest form of the jingle, see under -LY).

jingo. The noun (blatant patriot, Chauvinist) is replaced by *jingoist* in US.

jinn. Pl. of *jinni, jinnee.* See GENIE.

jiu-jitsu. US usually *jujitsu;* Brit. JU-JUTSU.

jockey, n. Pl. *-eys.*

jocose, jocular, &c. These & several other words—*arch, facetious, flippant, jesting, merry,* & *waggish*—are difficult to separate from each other. They are marked off from *funny, droll,* & others, by the fact that in the latter the effect, but in these the intent, is the main point; that is *funny* &c. which amuses, but that is *jocular* &c. which is meant (or, if a person, means) to amuse. In the following remarks no definition of the whole meaning of any word is attempted; attention is drawn merely to the points of difference between the one in question & some or all of the others. All of them are usable in contrast with *serious,* but for some an opposite may be found more appropriate than that for the present purpose, & that word is given in parentheses.

arch (opp. *serious*) implies the imputation of roguery of some sort; the imputation is ironical, or the offense is to be condoned; the meaning is conveyed chiefly by look, tone, or expression. *An arch look, girl, insinuation.*

facetious (opp. *glum*) implies a desire to be amusing; formerly a laudatory word, but now suggesting ill-timed levity or intrusiveness or the wish to shine. *A facetious remark, fellow, interruption.*

flippant (opp. *earnest*) implies mockery of what should be taken seriously, & want of consideration for others' feelings. *A flippant suggestion, young man; flippant treatment.*

jesting (opp. *serious*) differs from the rest in having perhaps no distinctive implication. *A jesting mood, parson, proposal.*

jocose (opp. *grave*) implies something ponderous, as of Adam & Eve's elephant wreathing his lithe proboscis to make them mirth. *A jocose manner, old boy, description.*

jocular (opp. *literal*) very commonly implies the evasion of an issue by a joke, or the flying of a kite to test the chances. *A jocular reply, writer, offer.*

merry (opp. *melancholy*) implies good spirits & the disposition to take things lightly. *A merry laugh, child, tale.*

waggish implies on the one hand willingness to make a fool of oneself & on the other fondness for making fools of others. *A waggish trick, schoolboy, disposition.*

jocund, chiefly a lit. word; pron. jŏk′und, rarely jō′-.

Johnsonese. In the literary style of Dr. Johnson, used derogatorily. Contrast *Johnsonian,* applied to style abounding in Latin derivatives, not necessarily derogatory.

join. Ally (oneself), constr. *with: join* with *men of good will;* take part, constr. *in: join* in *the common cause.*

jollily, jolly. As a (Brit.) slang substitute for *very* (*a jolly good hiding; you know jolly well*) the adv. is *jolly;* in other uses (*he smiled jollily enough*) it is *jollily.*

jostle has *t* silent.

journal. Objections are often made to the extension of this to other periodicals than the daily papers. But 'Our weekly journals o'er the land abound' (Crabbe, 1785); see PEDANTRY.

journalese. Style of writing characteristic of hasty or inferior newspaper writing. The word was first slang, then colloquial, and now is accepted as standard in most dictionaries.

journey, n. Pl. *-eys.* *Journey* is usually applied to land travel, *voyage* to sea. *Trip* applies to either.

joust, just. Though *just* (jŭ-) is 'the historical English spelling' (OED), *joust* (jo͞o-) was preferred by Johnson & used by Scott, & is consequently now more intelligible & to be preferred. Webster gives *joust* as the preferred spelling but the pronunciations jŭst, joust, jo͞ost in that order.

jubilate, n. Pron. -lah'tĭ or -lā'tē.

judg(e)ment. Modern US usage favors *judgment;* Brit. sometimes *judgement.*

judicial, judicious. Roughly, *judicial*=of a judge or law court, *judicious*=exhibiting judgment. *Judicial murder* is murder perpetrated by means of a legal trial; *judicious murder* is murder that is well calculated to serve the murderer's interests. The distinction is clear enough, except that *judicial* has one use that brings it near *judicious;* this use is *impartial* or such as might be expected of a judge or a law court, applied to such words as *view, conduct, care, investigation,* to which *judicious* is also applicable in the sense of *wise* or *sagacious* or *prudent.* In the following example, one may suspect, but cannot be sure, that the writer has meant one word & written the other: *The chapter on the relations between Holland & Belgium after the war in connection with a suggested revision of the treaty of* 1839 *is fairly written in a* judicious *spirit.* For other such pairs, see PAIRS & SNARES.

jugular. The older dictionaries all want us to say jo͞og-; more recent dictionaries give jŭg- first.

ju-jutsu, jujitsu. The first is preferred in Brit. and is closer to the orig. Japanese; the second is more usual in US.

Juliet. Accent first syllable.

jumbo. Pl. *-os.*

jump. *Jump to the eye(s)* is a bad GALLICISM (5); e.g. *The desperate discomfort of these places as living houses judged by our standards* jumps to the eyes.

junior. US usually abbr. *jr.;* Brit. *jun.*

Junker. Pron. yo͝on'gker.

Juno. Pl. *-os.*

junta, junto (council; political faction or clique). The first is the Spanish form, which is used in English also. *Junto,* pl. *-os,* is a corruption more used in English than *-ta-*. Pron. jŭn- or hŭn-.

juror, jurist. A *juror* is a member of a jury; *jurist,* one versed in law; *juryman* & *jurywoman*= *juror.*

just, v. & n. Use JOUST.

just, adv. 1. *Just exactly* is bad tautology. WRONG: *Mr. Gladsone's dearest friend in political life, who himself passed away* just exactly *half a century ago.*

2. *Just how many* & similar indirect-question forms are (colloq.) AMERICANISMS. Just what *makes the best lodgment for oyster spawn has been greatly discussed.*

3. Frequent repetition of *just* is a danger. *A running hand was* just *what the name says, handwriting at a run, written in a hurry, as so many people write today. The letters were at first, we might say,* just *like*

those capital letters.

4. Pron. jŭst; a warning against the vulgarism jĕst is not superfluous.

justiciable. Subject to jurisdiction. Pron. -tĭsh′-. The word not being very common, those who use it should take care it is not printed *justifiable.*

juvenile. Pron. -īl (Brit. always); US sometimes ĭl, esp. attributively (*juvenile court* &c.) but *His reasoning was juvenile* (īl).

K

Kaf(f)ir. *Kaffir* is more usual, although *Kafir* (pron. kah-) is more nearly correct. But see PEDANTRY.

kail, as in *kailyard* &c., is a variant of *kale. A kailyard novelist* is one who writes of Scottish life in the vernacular (e.g. J. M. Barrie).

kalendar, kalends. Use CALENDAR, *Calends.*

Kalif, see CALIPH & DIDACTICISM.

kangaroo. In US, *a kangaroo court* is an informal or unauthorized tribunal, such as one conducted by prisoners in a jail, or one in a frontier district. In Brit. parliamentary sense, in *a kangaroo closure,* the chairman of Committees selects the amendments to be debated, the unselected ones being voted on without debate.

Kant makes *Kantian, Kantianism.*

karat, carat. See CARAT.

Kapellmeister (choirmaster, orchestra conductor) is both sing. and pl.

katharsis. Spell *catharsis.*

keenness. So spelled.

kelpie, -py. Water sprite, usually in form of a horse, present at the drowning of travelers. The *-ie* is usual.

kelter, kilter (health, condition, as in *out of kilter*). The *-i-* form prevails in US, the *-e-* in Brit.

Kelt(ic). Use CELT(IC).

kempt (p.p. of *kemp,* 'comb,' v.) survives in *well-kempt, unkempt.*

ken, range of sight or vision, survives in *within her ken, not in my ken.* In these phrases the word is not the verb *ken*= to know.

kennel makes US *-led,* Brit. *-lled.*

Kenya. Pron. kē′-.

kerb. In US *curb* is used for all meanings. Brit. use is *kerb* for border, edging, &c., *curb* for check, n. & v.

kerosene, paraffin, petrol, gasoline, petroleum. The popular use of the words is all that is here in question. In the US, *kerosene* is what is popularly called 'coal oil,' used in old-fashioned lamps &c.; *paraffin* the waxy substance; *gasoline* the refined product used in cars. In Brit. *petroleum* is the crude mineral oil; *petrol,* or *petroleum spirit,* is refined petroleum as used in motors; *kerosene* & *paraffin* (oil) are oils got by distillation from petroleum or coal or shale (*kerosene* being the usual name in America, & *paraffin* in England).

ketchup is the est. spelling in Brit. Most US dictionaries give *catchup* first, but many commercial products have the *k*-spelling, & some *catsup.*

key, v., makes *keyed, keying.*

Key, n., has been converted into an adj. VOGUE WORD in US journals & political & economic jargon: *Legislators and other* key *figures; Korea is the* key *topic; The* key *industries of the country.* One dictionary defines it 'pivotal, fundamental.'

khaki (olive drab), pron. kä'kē.

kidnap makes US usually *-ped, -ping, -per;* Brit. (& sometimes US), *-pped, -pping.*

kiln. Properly pronounced without *n,* but in popular speech the *n* is often heard.

kilo-, milli-. In the metric system, *kilo-* means multiplied, & *milli-* divided by, 1000; *kilometer* 1000 meters, *millimeter* 1/1000 of a meter. Pron. kĭl'ometer; kilŏm'eter is a false analogy with *barometer.* Brit. *-metre.*

kilty, Highlander. So spelled.

kimono makes *kimonos, -ed.* NOT *kimona,* though often so pronounced.

kin. Kinsfolk, relatives, collectively, now the prevailing meaning (*next of kin*). Often confused with *kith,* friends, acquaintances.

kind, n. The correct idiomatic uses are *this kind of tree, all kinds of trees, What kind(s) of tree?* Colloq. but grammatically INCORRECT: *What* kind of trees *are those? It had a* kind of *sour taste.* The IRREGULAR USES—*Those* kind of *people,* kind of *startled,* a kind of *a shock*—are easy to avoid when they are worth avoiding, i.e. in print; & nearly as easy to forgive when they deserve forgiveness, i.e. in hasty talk. *A kind of a shock* is both the least criticized & the least excusable of the three (i.e. the *a* before *shock* is unnecessary & unjustifiable).

kindhearted, so spelled.

kindly. *Authors are* kindly *requested to note that Messrs. —— only accept MSS. on the understanding that . . . Messrs. ——* may be kind in making the request, but did they really mean to boast of it? This misplacement is very common; for the ludicrous effect, compare the confusion between *It is our* PLEASURE & *We have the pleasure.*

kindred. *He is a* kindred *soul;* but *His soul is* akin *to mine* (NOT *kindred to*).

kinema(tograph). See CINEMA.

king. (1) Under *King-of-Arms,* the OED says 'less correctly King-at-Arms'; but, as both phrases are shown by its quotations to have been in use at all periods, & as the *at* form is certainly the one familiar to people without special knowledge, insistence on the other seems pedantic. (2) For *The King of Beasts* (i.e. lion), see SOBRIQUETS.

kinsfolk is pl. without the addition of *-s; kinfolks* is dial.

kneel. Both *kneeled* & *knelt* are est., past & p.p.; the latter is perhaps more generally used.

knife makes *knives;* v., *knifed, -ing.*

knight. For *knight of industry,* see GALLICISMS; for *knight of the rueful countenance* (Don Quixote), SOBRIQUETS.

knight errant, pl. *knights errant.*

Knight Templar, biblical, makes pl. *Knights Templars;* the Masonic order, *Knights Templar.*

knit(ted). Both forms are still in use for the past & p.p., but the short form is now unusual in the special sense of making with knitting needles. *She knit(ted)*, or *had knit(ted), her brows*, but *She knitted* or *had knitted a pair of socks; a well-knit frame*, but *knitted goods* in ordinary use (though *knit goods* survives in the trade). *Knitten* is a pseudo-archaism.

knoll. Pron. nōl. The word being chiefly literary, so that most of us have to guess its sound from its spelling, & the sound of final *-oll* being variable (*doll, loll, Moll,* against *droll, roll, stroll,* among clear cases), it is regrettable that the rival spelling *knole* has not prevailed, but *-ll* seems now established.

knot means nautical *mile* (6080.20 feet) *per hour.* Hence *the ship's speed is* 6 *knots* (NOT 6 *knots an hour*).

know. *I don't know* that *you are right* (NOT *as*).

knowledge. Pron. nŏl-. The OED says that nŏl-, 'used by some, is merely a recent analytical pronunciation after *know*'; it is on the same level as *often* with the *t* sounded.

knowledgeable. So spelled.

Koran. The pronunciation kō-rahn′ is better than kor′an.

kotow, kowtow. The second is more usual. Properly pronounced kō′tow.

Ku-Klux Klan. The secret society formed after the Civil War, so spelled. But *Knights of the Ku Klux Klan, Inc.*, the organization founded in 1915.

Kyrie eleison. Of many competing pronunciations COD prefers kē′rĭĭĭlā′ĭsŏn, Webster kĭr′- &c. (7 syllables). But the pronunciation is accentual; it is the only Greek that has got into the Western liturgy. The Greek is *Kurie eleēson* and should best be pronounced kĭ′-.

L

label makes US usually *-led* &c., Brit. *-lled.* In fig. use, describe or designate: *We cannot label Voltaire either spiritualist or materialist;* set down in a category as: *labeled either as curable or incurable.*

labor, -our. US & Brit. respectively. But *Labor Day*, US, always; *Labour party*, Brit., always.

laboratory. The orthodox pronunciation is lă′boratorĭ, but the four successive unaccented syllables are usually reduced to labŏ′ratorĭ (Brit.) or lăb′ratorĭ (US).

labyrinthian, -ine. The second form is preferred for both the lit. and fig. uses.

laches is a sing. noun (pron. lă′chĭz) meaning negligence of certain kinds, rarely used with *a* but often with *the* & *no*, & not requiring italics (*A right forfeited by the laches of the tenant*). Its formation is similar to that of *riches* (formerly *lachesse, richesse*), but not having become a popular word it has escaped being taken for a plural.

lackadaisical, affectedly languid (orig. 'resembling someone given to saying "Lackaday"'); NOT merely listless, as it is often used.

lackey, lacquey. Pl. *-eys;* the *-key* form is recommended.

lacquer. So spelled.

lacrim-. The better spelling (*lacrima*, tur), but *lachrym-* is est.

lacuna. In a MS., inscription, or other writing, a hiatus, a missing portion. Pl. *-nae* (pron. -nē) or *-nas.*

lade, apart from the passive use of the p.p., is now almost restricted to the loading of ships. Even *laden,* though still in use, tends to be displaced by *loaded* & to sound archaic except in particular phrases & compound words: *heavy-laden buses,* but *loaded* rather than *laden buses; sin-laden, sorrow-laden;* but *loaded,* rather than *laden, with hay;* on the other hand *a soul laden with sin,* because the dignity attaching to slight archaism is in place.

lady. 1. *Lady Jones, Lady Mary Jones, Lady Henry Jones.* The first form is proper only for a peeress or a baronet's or knight's wife or widow; the second for one called *Lady* because she is the daughter of a peer (earl, marquis, or duke); the third for a courtesy lord's wife or widow. See also LORD.

2. *Lady* by itself in the vocative is a wrong substitute, now common among the uneducated, for *madam* (*You dropped your glove, lady*).

3. *Lady* prefixed to names indicating vocation as a mark of sex (*lady doctor, author, clerk,* &c.) is a cumbrous substitute for a FEMININE DESIGNATION, which should be preferred when it exists; in default of that, *woman* or *female* would be better than *lady,* not confusing the essential point with irrelevant suggestions of social position.

ladyfied. So spelled.

laid, lain. See LAY & LIE.

laissez aller. Pron. lĕ sā ȧlā. ('Let go.') Absence of constraint, abandon: *A magnificent . . .* laissez-aller *neglect.* If used, italize, but see FRENCH WORDS.

laissez faire. Pron. lĕ sā fâr. ('Let [people] do [as they will].') In Econ., (governmental) non-interference. The noun (also *laisser faire*) not hyphened or necessarily italicized; the adj. not italicized but usually hyphened. *A* laissez-faire *political economy; a policy of* laissez faire.

lam. Thrash &c.; also (US) escape, flee (*on the lam*); both uses now slang, but if used so spelled, NOT *lamb.*

lama, llama. *La-* for the priest; *lla-* for the animal.

lamentable. Pron. lam′-.

lamia. (Man-devouring monster; a vampire.) Pron. lā′mĭa; pl. *-ae* or *-as.*

lamina. Pl. *-ae.*

lampoon, libel, pasquinade, skit, squib. There is often occasion to select the most appropriate of these words, & the essential point of each may be briefly given. A *lampoon* is a bitter satirical published attack (in US, usually by ridicule, possibly from the *Harvard Lampoon*); a *libel* is a defamatory statement made publicly or privately (see also LIBEL); a *pasquinade* is a published attack of unknown or unacknowledged authorship; a *skit* is a making game of a person or his doings especially by parody; a *squib* is a casual published attack of no elaboration.

lamprey. Pl. *-eys.*

land, n. *Land of the leal* means heaven, not Scotland.

languor, languorous, languid, languish. Pron. -gger, -ggerus,

-gwid, -gwish. *Languor* means lassitude, inertia, fatigue, and (of a mood, feeling) softness, tenderness (i.e. the lassitude caused by sorrow, longing, or love). Hence *languorous music, eyes,* &c.

lank(y). The short form is almost only literary, the long chiefly slang.

lantern, -thorn. The second, now seldom seen, is a corruption due to the use of horn for the sides of old lanterns.

Laocoön. Pron. lā ŏk′ō ŏn.

lapis lazuli. Pron. lă′pĭs lă′-zūlī.

lapsus. (Lat., a slip, error.) Pl. *lapsus* (not *-si*), pron. *-ūs. Lapsus calami,* a slip of the pen; . . . *linguae,* . . . of *the* tongue.

larboard. 'The loading side,' as opposed to starboard. Now superseded by *port.*

large. For a comparison of this with *great* & *big,* see BIG. *Large* makes *largish. Large-sized,* if used, NOT *large-size. Large-scale map,* or, fig., *operations* (i.e. of great scope); used for 'very extensive' (e.g. *going in for languages on a large scale*), slang.

large(ly). After the verbs *bulk* & *loom,* the idiomatic word is *large,* not *largely;* cf. UNIDIOMATIC -LY. WRONG: *The Monroe Doctrine of late years has* loomed so largely *in all discussions upon . . . /A phase of the question which has* bulked largely *in the speeches of the leaders.*

largess(e). Pron. lar′jĭs, & omit the final *-e.* The word means 'a liberal bestowal of gifts, or the gifts so bestowed.' If it had remained in common use, it would doubtless have come to be spelled, as it often formerly was, *larges;* cf. *riches* & *laches.*

larva. Pl. *-vae.*

lassitude, weariness of body or mind. See also LANGUOR.

lasso is pronounced lăsōō′ by those who use one; Brit. lă′sō, & some US dictionaries give that first. Pl. *-oes* better than *-os.*

last. 1. *The last two* &c., *the two last* &c. Ordinarily *the last two.* But *Both poems are traditional. The* two last verses *are typical.* See also FIRST 4.

2. *Last, lastly.* In enumerations *lastly* is recommended on the same grounds as *firstly,* for which see FIRST 5. In most other contexts *lastly* is obs. or archaic.

3. *At (the) long last* is an idiom that has experienced a revival, due more perhaps to its odd sound than to any superior significance over *at last,* & is now often heard & seen; 'in the end, long as it has taken or may take to reach it' is the sense.

4. *Last, latest.* In this now favorite antithesis (*Dr. Marshall's latest, but we hope not his last, contribution*) we are reminded that *latest* means *last up to now only,* whereas *last* does not exclude the future. The distinction is a convenient one, & the use of *latest* for *last* is described by the OED as 'now archaic & poetical.' But no corresponding agreement has yet been reached for abstaining from *last* when *latest* would be the more precise word, & many idioms militate against it (*last Tuesday; last year; for the last fortnight; on the last occasion*).

late, erstwhile, ex-, former(ly), quondam, sometime, whilom. With all these words to choose from we are yet badly off: *erstwhile* & *whilom* smack of affected archaism; *ex-*, which tends to swallow up the rest, is ill fitted for use with compound words such as *Vice President* (see HYPHENS), which nevertheless constantly need the qualification; *late* is avoided because of the doubt whether it means that the person's life, or his tenure of office, is over; *quondam* & *sometime* have become, partly owing to the encroachments of *ex-*, unusual enough to sound pedantic except in special contexts (*my quondam friend; sometime rector of this parish*). The best advice is to refrain from *ex-* except with single words (*ex-President,* but NOT *ex-Vice-President,* & still less *ex-vice president*), & from *late* except either in the sense of no longer living & to give *former(ly)*, & perhaps *quondam* & *sometime,* more work to do.

latent means hidden, not visible. It cannot always be used as an equivalent of dormant, undeveloped, delayed, though in some cases these words also apply. *Latent powers and capacities. The latent force of character under her gentleness.*

lath (strip of wood &c.) rhymes with *bath* in the sing., in the pl. with *paths. Lathe* (the machine), rhymes with *bathe.*

latifundia is pl., 'large estate.' The sing. is *latifundium.*

Latin America. The 20 republics south of US whose official language is a romance derivitive (Spanish or Portuguese).

latine (=in Latin) is a Lat. adv.; pron. in English latī′nē; similar advs. are *anglice* (-sē), *celtice, gallice, graece, hibernice, scot(t)ice, teutonice.* All these are sometimes printed with *-è* to show that the *-e* is sounded.

latinism, latinity. The first is a disposition to adopt Latin ways, especially of speech, or a particular idiom that imitates a Latin one; the second is the quality of Latin (classical, debased, &c.) that characterizes a person's or a period's style. *Milton's latinism; The last remains we possess of classical latinity are the biographies of the late emperors.* (In US, both sometimes, but not necessarily, capitalized.)

LATIN PLURALS (or latinized-Greek). Of most words in fairly common use that have a Latin as well as or instead of an English plural the correct Latin form is given in the word's alphabetical place. A few general remarks may be made here.

1. No rule can be given for preferring or avoiding the Latin form. Some words invariably use it; nobody says *specieses, thesises,* or *basises,* instead of the Latin *species, theses,* & *bases* (bā′sēz). Others nearly always have the Latin form, but occasionally the English; *bacilluses, lacunas,* & *genuses* are used at least by anti-Latin fanatics instead of *bacilli, lacunae,* & *genera.* More often the Latin & English forms are on fairly equal terms, context or individual taste deciding for one or the other; *dogmas, formulas, indexes, hiatuses,* & *gladioluses* are fitter for popular writing, while scientific treatises tend to *dogmata, formulae, indices, hiatus* (hīā′tūs), & *gladioli.* Sometimes the two forms are utilized for real differentiation as when *genii* means spirits, & *geniuses* men. All that can safely be said is that there is a tendency to abandon the Latin plurals, & that when one is really in

doubt which to use the English form should be preferred.

2. Latin plurals in *-i* should be pronounced (Reformed pronunciation) distinctly -ī, & not -ĭ like the Italian *dilettanti, pococuranti,* &c.; Latin plurals of words in *-is* (*theses, metamorphoses, neuroses*) should be plainly pronounced -ēz, not -ĭz like English plurals.

3. In Latin plurals there are naturally some traps for non-latinists; the termination of the singular is no sure guide to that of the plural. Most Latin words in *-us* have plural in *-i,* but not all, & so zeal not according to knowledge issues in such oddities as (WRONG) *hiati, octopi,* & *ignorami.* Similarly most Latin nouns in *-a* have plural in *-ae,* but not all: *lacuna, -nae; dogma, -mata; Saturnalia,* not singular but plural. And though *-us* & *-a* are much the commonest Anglo-Latin endings, the same danger attends some others (*-ex, -er, -o,* &c.).

4. The treatment of a Latin noun as an English plural because it ends in *-s* is, when a modern introduction, surprising. The Latin plural of *forceps* is *forcipes,* & the English plural should be *forcepses; a forceps, a set of forcipes* or *forcepses;* & both these were formerly in use. But *shears* & *scissors* & *pincers* & *pliers* have so convinced us that no such word can have a singular that instead of *a forceps* we usually say *a pair of forceps,* & *forceps* has to serve for both singular & plural.

LATIN PRONUCIATION. There are two schools of pronouncing Latin, the Reformed and the Roman or Classical. The differences need not be outlined in this book; but it may be well to mention that although US dictionaries now generally give the Reformed pronunciation (which is almost invariable in England) many Americans still use the Classical. Some typical differences are that the vowels in Reformed Latin are for the most part pronounced as long vowels are in English; in Classical as broad (or Continental); so *veni, vidi, vici* is pronounced Reformed: vēnī, vīdī, vīsī; Classical: wānē, wēdē, wēkē; *-ae* in Reformed is ē; in Classical ī; *pater,* Reformed: pāter, Classical päter, &c. Those who have had no training in Latin will find the Reformed pronunciation easier and will also be following the present trend. Those who are accustomed to using the Classical will do better to ignore the dictionary pronunciations, and those given in this book.

latter survives almost solely in *the latter,* which provides with *the former* a pair of pronouns obviating disagreeable repetition of one or both of a pair of previously mentioned names or nouns. Such avoidance of repetition is often desirable; for the principles, see ELEGANT VARIATION & REPETITION. But *the latter* is liable to certain special misuses: (1) *The latter* should not be used when more than a pair are in question; WRONG: *The difficult problems involved in the early association of Thomas Girtin, Rooker, Dayes, & Turner are well illustrated by a set of drawings that . . . ; & what was undoubtedly the best period of* the latter artist *is splendidly demonstrated by . . .* (2) Neither should it be used when less than two are in question; the public & its shillings cannot be reasonably regarded as a pair of things on the same footing in (WRONG): *The mass of the picture-loving public, however, may be assured of good value for their shillings–whatever be the ultimate destination* of the latter. (3) The true elegant-variationist, who of course works *the latter* very hard, should observe that a mere pronoun will not do for the antecedent of *the latter,* even though there may be a name in the background. AMBIGUOUS: *Mr. Hake was a cousin of the late General Gordon, of whom he entertained a most affectionate remembrance. On one occasion, when the hero of Khartoum was dining with* him, the latter *invited his relative to take wine with him, but Gordon imperiously declined.* (4) The true use of it is not to mystify. If the reader has to look back to see who *the latter* means, the name or noun should be repeated.

latterly used where most of us would say *lately, recently,* or *of late* has little to recommend it except a quaint air of archaism (*For some time she had tried to close her mind to the things her brother said, but* latterly *it had become increasingly difficult*).

laudable means praiseworthy; the quotation shows it confused with *laudatory* (praise-giving); see PAIRS & SNARES. WRONG: *He speaks in the most* laudable *terms of the work carried out in the Anglo-Egyptian Soudan.*

laughable. For *would be laughable if it were not tragic* &c., see HACKNEYED PHRASES.

laughter. *Homeric laughter* is a phrase whose meaning must be vague to many readers. The shorter dictionaries give 'irrepressible laughter,' 'loud, hearty laughter,' 'laughter like that of the gods as they watched lame Hephaestus hobbling.' Obviously it is a dangerous phrase for the uninformed to use. See POPULARIZED TECHNICALITIES.

launch. The traditional pronunciation is law-, not lah-.

lavabo. Pron. *la* vā′bō. Pl. *-os.*

lay & lie. (1) Verbs. *To lay* is transitive only (= put to rest), & makes *laid; to lie* is intransitive only (= be at or come to rest), & makes *lay, lain,* NEVER *laid.* But confusion even between the words *lay* & *lie* themselves is very common in uneducated talk; & still commoner, sometimes making its way into print, is the use of *laid* (which belongs to the verb *to lay* only) for *lay* the past tense, & *lain* the p.p. of *lie* (e.g. WRONG: *we* laid [*lay*] *out on the grass, & could have* laid [*lain*] *there all day*). (2) Nouns. *Lie* & *lay* are both used in the senses configuration of ground, direction or position in which something lies (*the proper lie* or *lay of the land*); *lie* seems the more reasonable form, and is the only one given by COD; *lay* is more usual in US, but both are heard. (3) *Lay,* adj., means of the people as distinguished from the clergy (*lay helpers* in the church); in a transferred sense, nonprofessional, not expert, esp. in law and medicine (*lay opinions; the view of the layman*). (4) *Lay figure* has no connection with any of the English words *lay,* but is from Dutch *led* = joint, & means literally jointed figure.

leaded, & *double-leaded,* in printing, mean set with more than the ordinary space between the lines; the space is made by inserting strips of lead.

leaden is less disused in the literal sense than most of the words of its type; *lead roof* or *pipe* is commoner than *leaden*, but *a leaden pipe* is not as unidiomatic as *a golden watch.* See -EN ADJECTIVES.

leading question is often misused for a poser or a pointed question or one that goes to the heart of the matter (as though *leading* meant principal). Its real meaning is quite different; a leading question is not hostile, but friendly, & is so phrased as to guide or lead the person questioned to the answer that it is desirable for him to make, but that he might not think of making or be able to make without help: it is used especially of counsel examining one of his own witnesses & unfairly prompting him. To object, as people do when they are challenged to deny or confirm an imputation, 'That is a leading question' is meaningless. See POPULARIZED TECHNICALITIES.

(-) leafed, (-) leaved. *A broad-leafed* or *-leaved plant.* Both forms are used, but the second is recommended. See -VE(D).

lean. Of *leant* (pron. lĕnt) & *leaned, leaned* is more general (US); both forms are current in Brit.

leap. Of *leapt* & *leaped,* both are used; Americans usually write *leaped* but often say *leapt* (lĕpt). Of *leap to the eyes,* as wearisome a GALLICISM as exists, some examples must be given to suggest its staleness. *Bath, it may be admitted, does not* leap to the eyes *as an obvious or inevitable meeting-place for the Congress./I won't weary you with rehearsing all the possible consequences of the Bulgarian surrender;* they leap to the eye./*We have not the smallest doubt that there is a perfectly satisfactory explanation of these widely differing totals, but certainly it does* not leap to the eyes.

learn. Both *learnt* & *learned* are used; see LEAN & LEAP. The existence of the disyllabic *learnèd* as an adj. is a reason for preferring *-nt* in the verb.

least. The common confusion between *much less* & *much more* is mentioned & illustrated in the article ILLOGICALITIES; *least of all* & *most of all* get mixed up in the same way: *If that is the case, what* justification *exists for the sentences,* least of all *for the way in which they were carried out?* (read *most*).

leastwise, -ways. The OED labels the first 'somewhat rare,' the second 'dialectal & vulgar'; Webster calls the first colloq. & the second dial.

leather. In *leather or prunella* (usually misquoted *leather & prunella*) the meaning is not two worthless things, but the contrast between the rough leather apron of a cobbler & the fine gown of a parson. It is true, however, that this difference is slighted in comparison with that between worth & the want of it: 'the rest is merely a question of whether you wear rough or fine raiment.'

lecher &c. Pron lĕch-.

lectureship, -turership. The first is of irregular formation, but it is long established, & those who use the second instead perhaps make it in momentary forgetfulness that the irregular form exists.

leeward. (Opp. to *windward.*) Pron. lū′*ard*.

leeway in the sense of margin, extra (space, time, money, &c.), chiefly US colloq.

left. (1) The left bank of a river is that to its left if it is imagined as a person walking downstream, & may therefore be north, south, east, or west, of it; as this is often in conflict with the idea of left (= westward) acquired from maps, some care is needed. (2) *Left hand* has no hyphen except when used attributively (*the left-hand drawer*). (3) A *left-handed compliment* is one of doubtful sincerity or one that is ambiguous, but not necessarily a malicious one.

legalism, legality. The first is exaltation of the law, hence stressing of formula, red tape. The second is the normal word for lawfulness.

LEGERDEMAIN WITH TWO SENSES, or the using of a word twice (or of a word & the pronoun that represents it, or of a word that has a double job to do) without observing that the sense required the second time is different from that already in possession. A plain example or two will show the point: *The inhabitants of the independent lands greatly desire our direct* government, *which* government *has, however, for years refused to take any strong measures./ Mark had now got his first* taste *of print, & he liked it, & it was a* taste *that was to show many developments.* In the first of these, *government* means successively *governance,* & *governing body*—either of them a possible synonym for it, but not both to be represented by it in the same sentence. In the second whereas the *taste* he got was an experience, the *taste* that showed developments was an inclination. Such shiftings from one sense to another naturally occur sometimes in reasoning, whether used by the disingenuous for the purpose of deceiving others, or by the over-ingenuous with the result of deceiving themselves; but we are here concerned not with their material, but with their formal, aspect; apart from any bad practical effects, they are faults of style.

The examples that follow are less flagrant than the typical specimens above; what leads to them is a want of clear thinking on small points, & in this they resemble the contents of the article HAZINESS: other examples will be found under I & WE.

If the statements *made are true,* they *constitute a crime against civilization.* (Whereas the *statements* means the things alleged, *they* means the things done.)/*The vital* differences *of their respective elders make* none *to their bosom friendship.* (Whereas *the differences* are quarrels, *none* is [no] alteration.)/*Admission is by* ticket, which *can be obtained from Mr. . . .* (Whereas *ticket* means a system, *which* means a piece or pieces of paper.)

legible, readable. *Legible,* of handwriting or print=easy to read; *readable*=interestingly written.

legitimate, v., legitimatize, legitimize. The second & third are mere substitutes without difference of meaning for the first, which has a longer history by two or three centuries, & is neither obs. nor archaic. It may be guessed that they exist only because *-ize,* now so common, saves a moment's thought to those who want a word & forget that there is one ready to hand; they might well be placed among SUPERFLUOUS WORDS. The *-able* adj. should be *legitimable* (*-atizable, -izable*).

leisure. The OED puts the pronunciation lĕzh- (not lēzh-) first. US dictionaries reverse the preference, but both pronunciations are heard.

leisurely is both adj. and adv., but the adverbial use is chiefly literary in US. *He walked* leisurely *down the street* would usually be *in a leisurely manner.*

leit-motiv, -f. The right (German) spelling is with *-v.* Pron. lītmōtēf.

lemma. Pl. *-s* or *lemmata.*

lend (p. & p.p. *lent*) is now the est. verb in Brit.; *loan* is a noun. As a verb LOAN is now chiefly US.

lengthways, -wise. Both forms are used, without differentiation. In US *-wise* is perhaps more common.

lengthy. Orig. an Americanism (?). Used of discussions, arguments, speeches, or writing, in the sense of long to the point of tedium. When used of physical length, (US) colloq.

lenience, -cy. The second is recommended.

lens. Pl. *lenses.*

lèse-majesté. Pron. lĕz′mȧ-zhĕs tā′. The English *lese-majesty* is not now a legal term, *treason* having taken its place; the French form is often used of treason in foreign countries; both are applied jocularly (cf. PEDANTIC HUMOR) to anything that can be metaphorically considered treason.

less. 1. *Nothing less than* means *quite equal to* usually, but can be ambiguous. See NOTHING.

2. The illogical use of *much less* instead of *much more* is discussed under ILLOGICALITIES & MUCH. Here are two examples of *still less* for *still more,* interesting in different ways: (WRONG) *Of course social considerations,* still less *considerations of mere wealth, must not in any way be allowed to outweigh purely military efficiency.* Here, if *still . . . wealth* had been placed later than *must not,* it would have passed; coming before it, it is wrong; you can understand *must* out of a previous *must not,* but not out of a *must not* that is yet to come./ *Perhaps Charles's most fatal move was the attempted arrest of the five members, undertaken on the Queen's advice, & without the knowledge, &* still less *without the consent of his three new advisers.* The writer of this has curiously chosen, by needlessly inserting that second *without,* to deprive himself of the usual excuse for using *less* instead of *more,* i.e. the fact that the ellipsis of some word prevents the illogicality from being instantly visible & permits a writer to lose sight of what the full phrase would require while he attends to the broad effect.

3. *Less, lesser, smaller, lower, fewer,* &c. UNIDIOMATIC: *The letters & memoirs could have been published, we should imagine, at* a less price./*While Colonel Seely adheres to the determination to keep open the competition for the best aeroplane,* a lesser prize *will probably be offered which will be confined to British manufacturers.* These extracts suggest ignorance of, or indifference to,

modern idiomatic restrictions on the use of *less* & *lesser.* The grammar of both is correct; but, when the context—unemotional statement of everyday facts—is taken into account, *at a less price* ought to be *at a lower price,* & *a lesser prize* ought to be *a smaller prize.*

The modern tendency is so to restrict *less* that it means not *smaller,* but *a smaller amount of;* it is the comparative rather of *a little* than of *little;* & it is consequently applied only to things that are measured by amount & not by size or quality or number, nouns with which *much* & *little,* not *great* & *small,* nor *high* & *low,* nor *many* & *few,* are the appropriate contrasted epithets: *less butter, courage;* but *a smaller army, table; a lower price, degree; fewer opportunities, people.* Plurals, & singulars with *a* or *an,* will naturally not take *less; less tonnage,* but *fewer ships; less manpower,* but *fewer men; less opportunity,* but *a worse opportunity,* & *inferior opportunities;* though a few plurals like *clothes* & *troops,* really equivalent to singulars of indefinite amount, are exceptions: *could do with less troops* or *clothes.* Of *less*'s antipathy to *a,* examples are: *I want to pay* less *rent,* but *a* lower *rent is what I want.*/Less *noise, please,* but *a* slighter *noise would have waked me.*/Less *size means* less *weight,* but *I want a* smaller *size.* Such is the general tendency: to substitute *smaller, lower, fewer,* or other appropriate word, for *less* except where it means 'a smaller amount of,' & for *lesser,* & to regard the now slightly archaic *less* in other senses as an affectation. There are no doubt special phrases keeping it alive even in quite natural speech, e.g. *in* or *to a less degree,* where *lower* is hardly yet as common as *less;* but the general tendency is unmistakable, & is moreover, since it makes for precision, one that should be complied with.

-LESS. Bare reference of any word in *-less* to this article means that the use of it in ordinary prose is deprecated.

The original & normal use of this suffix is to append it to nouns, producing adjectives meaning 'without the thing,' e.g. *headless, tuneless;* to this use there are no limits whatever. Words made from verbs, with the sense 'not able to do' or 'not liable to suffer the action or process,' as *tireless, fadeless,* & *describeless,* are much fewer, are mostly of a poetical cast, & when new-minted strike the reader of prose at least as base metal. They have an undeniable advantage in their shortness; compare *resistless,* & *weariless,* with *irresistible,* & *unwearіable;* but this is outweighed for all except fully established ones by the uneasy feeling that there is something queer about them. Apart from a few so familiar that no thought of their elements & formation occurs to us, such as *dauntless, -less* words made from verbs are much better left to the poets. This does not apply to the many in which, as in *numberless,* formation from the noun gives the sense as well, if not as obviously, as formation from the verb (*without number?* or *not able to be numbered?*); *dauntless* itself may perhaps have been made from the noun *daunt,* which in the 15th & 16th cc. was current in the sense *discouragement.*

If the verb compounds become much more frequent, we shall

never know that *pitiless* & *harmless* may not mean 'that cannot be pitied' & 'secure against being harmed' as well as 'without the instinct of pity' & 'without harmfulness'; we ought to be able to reckon that, with a few well-known exceptions, *-less* words mean simply without what is signified by the noun they contain; & the way to keep that assumption valid is to abstain from reckless compounding of *-less* with verbs.

lesser. See LESS.

lest. The idiomatic construction after *lest* is *should,* or in exalted style the pure subjunctive (*lest we forget; lest he be angry, lest public opinion be alienated*). Instead of *should* good writers rarely use *shall, may,* & *might.* The variations in the quotations below are entirely against modern idiom. WRONG: *There must be loyal cooperation,* lest *the last state of the party* becomes *worse than the first./The German force now lost no time in retreat,* lest *they* might *be cut off & surrounded by General Mackenzie.* See also IN ORDER THAT.

let. Mistakes in case are very rare in English; forgetfulness of the construction, when *let* is used in exhortations, is responsible for a wrong pronoun now & then. WRONG: *And now, my dear,* let you & I *say a few words about this unfortunate affair./Our work is to inform & permeate the party, not to leave it; if anybody must leave it,* let *it not* be we. Read *me, us.*

let up, v. (*until the storm lets up*) & n. (*no let-up*), are US, colloq. and slang.

lethargy (=a condition of torpor, inertness, apathy). WRONG: *Mr. —, discussing the* lethargy *of the dental profession to the shocking condition of the teeth of the working classes, said . . .* *Lethargy to* is unidiomatic, made on the ANALOGY of *indifference to,* but not justified by it.

levee. (The embankment [US] & the reception.) Write without an accent, & pron. lĕ′vĭ.

level makes *-led, -ler,* US; Brit. *-lled* &c. *Do one's level best,* originally American, has lived long enough in England to be no longer slang. *Level*=well-balanced, steady (*a level head*), is colloq.

lever. Pron. lē-.

lewd. 'Of difficult etymology' (OED). Obs. meanings: *Lay, nonclerical, ignorant, good for nothing, worthless, base, unprincipled;* only surviving meaning, *unchaste, indecent.*

lexicon. Used chiefly of Greek, Hebrew, Syriac, or Arabic dictionaries. See DICTIONARY. Pl. *-ns, -ca.*

liable, possibly because it is a more or less isolated word lacking connections to keep it steady, constantly has its meaning shifted. For its proper use 'exposed to a risk' (of something undesirable), see APT, with which there is much excuse for confusing it. The first quotation illustrates that confusion. WRONG: *Political & religious bias are also* liable to operate./ *At every inn you have to fill out forms about the color of your wife's hair, & every policeman* is liable to demand *the production of a variety of tickets* (should be *may demand* or *is likely* or *not unlikely to demand*)./*Duncan has been for several years* liable to win *one of the big prizes of golf* (the sporting reporter should have stuck to his last & said *in the* *running for* instead of *liable to win*).

liaison. US usually lē ā zŏn′; Brit. often lĭā′zn.

libel makes US *-led, -lous;* Brit. *-lled* &c.

libel & some synonyms. The much-quoted saying, 'The greater the truth the greater' (or 'worse') 'the libel' makes us all occasionally curious about what a libel is. Its synonyms are *calumny, defamation,* & *slander.* The definitions that follow are taken verbatim from the OED and are similar to those in Webster; the presence or absence in the definitions of the words *false, malicious, published,* &c., should be carefully noticed.

Calumny: False & malicious misrepresentation of the words or actions of others, calculated to injure their reputation.

Defamation: The action of defaming, or attacking anyone's good fame.

Libel: (Law) any published statement damaging to the reputation of a person ('The judge answered . . . that it was clearly possible to publish a libel for the public good'). (Pop.) any false & defamatory statement in conversation or otherwise.

Slander: The utterance or dissemination of false statements or reports concerning a person, or malicious misrepresentation of his actions, in order to defame or injure him ('Falsehood & malice, express or implied, are of the essence of the action for slander').

liberal. (1) In *liberal education* (=academic *vs.* technical or vocational, &c.) the adj. retains a sense that is almost obs., & yet is near enough to some extant senses to make misunderstanding possible. A liberal education is the education designed for a gentleman (Lat. *liber,* a free man), & is opposed on the one hand to technical or professional or any special training, & on the other to education that stops short before manhood is reached. (2) In politics, *liberal*=favoring progress or reform (e.g. the Brit. Liberal party).

libido. US dictionaries give lĭ bī′dō first, second, -bē′-; COD gives -bī- only.

libretto. Pl. *-etti* (pron. -ē) or *-os.*

Libyan. So spelled, NOT *Lybian* (but *Lydian*).

licence, -se. US usually *-se* for n. & v. (also *licensee*). In Brit., the first is the n., the second the v.

lichen. Pron. lī′kn.

licorice. So spelled in US; Brit. *liquorice.*

lie, be prostrate. See LAY & LIE.

lief. Gladly, willingly, now used only in *had as lief, would as lief* (do something). Not *as leave,* with which the word has no connection but is often confused.

lien, n. Best pron. lē′ĕn but lēn is also accepted.

lieutenant. In US pron. lū-; in Brit. left- or lĕft- & in nautical & naval use, letĕ′nant. (The *f,* the OED concedes, is 'difficult to explain.')

life. For *come into one's life,* see HACKNEYED PHRASES (e.g. *We sense the tragedy of Anna Wolsky as she steps lightheartedly* into Sylvia Bayley's life).

lift, n. (Brit.)=(US) elevator.

ligature. In printing or writing, a character composed of two or more letters combined: æ, œ. But see Æ, Œ.

light, n. (1) For *dim religious light,* see IRRELEVANT ALLUSION. (2) *In light of* will not do for *in the light of,* as in (WRONG) *That it should have been so,* in light of all the facts, *will always be a nine-days wonder to the student of history;* see CAST-IRON IDIOM.

light, v. Both verbs (kindle, descend) make *lighted* or *lit* for past & p.p.; but *lighted* is commoner for the p.p., especially that of the first verb used attributively: *Is the fire lighted* or *lit?* but *Holding a lighted candle.*

lightning, n. So spelled, NOT *-tening.*

like, adj. *And the like*=& *similar things,* to avoid enumeration, is better in literary contexts than *&c.* See FORTH.

like in questionable constructions. 1. *Like* used for *as.* It will be best to dispose first of what is, if it is a misuse at all, the most flagrant & easily recognizable misuse of *like.* A sentence from Darwin quoted in the OED contains it in a short & unmistakable form: *Unfortunately few have observed* like *you have done.* The OED's judgment is as follows: 'Used as conjunction:="like as," as. Now generally condemned as vulgar or slovenly, though examples may be found in many recent writers of standing.' Besides the Darwin quoted above, the OED gives indisputable examples from Shakespeare, Southey, Newman, Morris, & other 'writers of standing.' The reader who has no instinctive objection to the construction can now decide for himself whether he shall consent to use it in talk, in print, in both, or in neither. He knows that he will be able to defend himself if he is condemned for it, but also that, until he has done so, he will be condemned. It remains to give a few newspaper examples so that there may be no mistake about what the 'vulgar or slovenly' use in its simplest form is: *Or can these tickets be kept* (like *the sugar cards were*) *by the retailer?/Sins that were degrading me,* like *they have many others./The idea that you can learn the technique of art* like *you can learn the multiplication table or the use of logarithms.*

2. The rest of this article is intended for those who decide against the conjunctional use that has been already discussed, & are prepared to avoid also some misuses of a less easily recognizable kind.

The first type is perhaps not really different from that discussed in (1). Examples are: *Or should he have a palace some distance away,* like *the Bishop of Winchester has at Farnham?/ The club doctor was the friend & adviser of its members, something* like *the country parson has to be to his parishioners in the present day.* The peculiarity of these is that in each there is a previous noun, *palace, something,* with which *like* may agree as an adjective, & an ellipsis of 'what' or 'the one that' may be supposed. Such a defense is neither plausible nor satisfactory, & the sentences are no better than others containing a verb.

Of sentences in which *like* is not followed by a verb, certain forms are unexceptionable, but are liable to extensions that are not so. The unquestioned forms are *He talks* like *an expert* & *You are treating me* like *a fool,* in which *like* is equivalent to a prepositional adverb=similarly to; & *You,* like *me, are disappointed,* in which *like* is equivalent either to an adverb as before, or perhaps rather to a prepositional adjective=resembling in this respect. The second, third, & fourth faulty types represent neglect of various limitations observed in the correct forms.

Second type: *The Committee was* today, like yesterday, *composed of the following gentlemen./It is certain that* now, unlike the closing years *of last century, quotation from his poetry is singularly rare.* The limitation here disregarded is that the word governed by *like* must be a noun, not an adverb or an adverbial phrase. *Yesterday* is not a noun, but an adverb: & *the closing years,* meaning *in the closing years,* has also only a deceitful appearance of being a noun.

Third type: *People get alarmed on each occasion* on which (like *the present case*) *dying children suddenly appear./And then came the war;* like *many another village, it filtered slowly, very slowly, through* to his. The limitation (suggested with diffidence) that has here been disregarded is that the preceding noun to which *like* is attached must be not one governed by a preposition, but subject or object of the main verb. The preceding nouns are *which* (i.e. *occasion*) & *his* (i.e. *village*), governed by *on* & *to;* instead of *like,* read *as in the present case* & *as to many another.*

Fourth type: Like his Roman predecessor, *his private life was profligate;* like Antony, *he was an insatiate gambler.* The limitation is that the word governed by *like* must be *in pari materia* with the one to which it is compared. The *predecessor* is not so related to *life;* but *Antony* is to *he,* & that clause will pass muster. This mistake, however, of comparing unlike things is not, like the others, peculiar to *like,* but is a slovenly parsimony of words that may occur in many other constructions.

-like. In established words, US dictionaries usually omit the hyphen. In nonce words, or words not generally current, the hyphen is ordinarily used. Nouns ending in *-l,* however, require the hyphen: *cowl-like, eel-like, owl-like, pearl-like, rebel-like, veil-like.*

like, v. (1) *Like* makes *likable.* (2) *I would like.* In US *I would* in all senses is now accepted usage by a great many people. But even on those who still use *should* & *would* traditionally under all ordinary temptations the verb *like* seems to exercise a corrupting influence; a couple of examples follow *pro formâ,* but anyone can find as many as he pleases with very little search: *We* would like *to ask one or two questions on our own account./There is one paragraph in it that I* would like *to refer to.* There is indeed no mystery about why people go wrong: it is because, if the thing had to be said without the use of the verb *like, would* & not *should* is the form to use: *We would ask, that I would refer to;* but that has nothing to do with what is right when the verb *like* is used. Putting aside one idiom that with this particular verb is negligible (*When the post came I* would like *to be* *allowed to carry it in*=I used to like), *I would like* is no better than any of the *wills* & *woulds* that are not English English. If the SHALL & WILL idiom is worth preserving at all *I would like* is wrong, & *I should like* right.

likely, adv. In Brit. educated speech & writing the adv. is never used without *very, most,* or *more,* except by way of poetic archaism or, as presumably in the extract, of stylistic NOVELTY-HUNTING: *Yet it was not easy to divine the thought behind that intentness of gaze:* likely *it was far from the actual scene apparently holding its attention.* (Webster's Collegiate and the ACD give no qualification to the definition 'in all probability; probably,' but the unabridged Webster's says 'usually with *most, quite, very,* etc.')

likely, adj. Of *likely, liable,* and APT, *likely* is the only one meaning *probable,* or *to be expected. Apt* means having a tendency to (usually unfortunate); *liable,* exposed to a risk. *It is* likely *to rain; he is* apt *to deceive us on the slightest provocation; We are* liable *to be deceived if we trust him.*

likewise. The use of *likewise* as conj. (WRONG: *Its tendency to wobble & its uniformity of tone color,* likewise *its restricted powers of execution*) is, like the similar use of ALSO, an ILLITERACY.

-LILY. Avoidance of the adverbs in *-lily,* i.e. adverbs made regularly from adjectives in *-ly,* is merely a matter of taste, but is very, & increasingly, general. Neither the difficulty of saying the words nor the sound of them when said is a serious objection so long as the three syllables are not passed; *holily* & *statelily* & *lovelily* are not hard to say or harsh to hear; but with *heavenlily* & *ruffianlily* hesitation is natural; & the result has been that adverbs in *-lily,* however short, are now with a few special exceptions seldom heard & seldomer seen. Methods of avoidance are various:

1. It is always possible to say *in a masterly manner, at a timely moment,* & the like, instead of *masterlily, timelily;* or again to be content with *decorously* &c. instead of *mannerlily;* the method of periphrasis or synonym.

2. A large number of adjectives in *-ly* are established as adverbs also. So *early,* (*most* or *very*) *likely,* & the adjectives of periodical recurrence like *daily* & *hourly.*

3. Before adjectives & adverbs the *-ly* adjective often stands instead of the *-lily* adverb, making a kind of informal compound. Though we should say *horribly pale* & not *horrible pale,* we allow ourselves *ghastly pale* rather than use *ghastily;* so *heavenly bright, beastly cold,* &c.—all without the hyphen that would mark regular compounds.

4. In sentences where it is just possible, though not natural, for a predicative adjective to stand instead of an adverb, that way is sometimes taken with an adjective in *-ly* though it would not be taken with another: *it happened timely enough,* though not *opportune enough; she nodded queenly,* though not *she nodded significant.*

5. Perhaps any adjective formed by appending *-ly* either to an adjective (*kind, kindly; dead, deadly*) or to a noun of the kind that is easily used in apposition like an adjectival epithet (*cowardly,* cf. *the cow-*

ard king; soldierly, cf. *a soldier colonist*) is sometimes, though always consciously & noticeably, allowed to pass as an adverb: *it was ruffianly done; a kindly thought, & kindly uttered.*

On the other hand, avoidance is not always called for; some *-lily* words are current, though not many. Those that naturally present themselves (*sillily complacent; live holily; dodged it wilily*) seem to be all from adjectives in which *-ly* is not the usual adjectival ending, but the *l* is part of the word stem; & though we are most of us not conscious of that fact nowadays, it may have had its effect in separating these from the others.

limb. (1) *Limb* used to avoid *leg* is a GENTEELISM rapidly (and fortunately) becoming antiquated. (2) When we first come across an eclipse in the newspapers & read of *the sun's lower limb,* we suspect the writer of making jokes or waxing poetical. It is a relief to learn that *limb* does mean edge without a metaphor; the *limb* in Astronomy &c. is from Lat. *lĭmbus,* hem, & the *limb* of ordinary speech is a separate & native word.

limbo. Pl. *-os.*

limit, n. *The limits of knowledge; unconscious of his limits.* For some synonyms in sense of *tether* &c., see FIELD.

limited. (1) *Limited company* (Ltd.) is an elliptical phrase for *limited-liability company,* & implies not that the number of members is limited, but that their liability for its debts is so. (2) *Limited income* is often a EUPHEMISM or GENTEELISM, since few people have incomes with no limits. Usually *a small income* is meant.

limpid. Pellucid, clear, 'usually of atmosphere, liquids, eyes, literary style.'

linage, number of lines. Spell thus and pron. līn-; the other spelling, *lineage,* is, owing to the existence of *lineage*=descent, still less desirable than other spellings with intrusive MUTE E.

line, n. For some synonyms in sense *department* &c., see FIELD. Johnson considered this use a colloq. barbarism, and *the banking line, the furniture line* still smack of commercialese. It survives with respectability, however, in *not in my line, out of my line.*

lin(e)age. *Lineage* (lĭnēĭj), descent, ancestry, *linage* (līnaj), number of lines (printing &c.). See LINAGE.

lingerie. Pron. läɴ zhẽ rē. Orig. linen goods, then linen underwear, now esp. a (shop) word for all kinds of women's underwear—a GENTEELISM.

lingo. Pl. usually *-oes.* Contemptuous for a foreign language or (specialized) strange speech: *The general public . . . does not know the critics' lingo.* See JARGON.

links, golf course. Sometimes used as sing. (*There is a good links here*).

Linnaeus. Latinized form of (Carl von) Linné, Swedish naturalist. Hence *Linnaean* or *Linnean* (the first is more usual).

lionize. In contemporary US, usually confined to the sense 'to make a social lion of a person'; other meanings, 'to see the sights of a place'; 'to show (them) to a visitor.'

liquefy. So spelled. So *liquefaction,* but *liquidity.*

liqueur. Pron. lēkûr′. A sweetened (& usually flavored) alcoholic liquor.

liquid. See FLUID for fluid, gas, &c.

liquidate. In recent fig. senses, 'kill off (secretly),' 'ruthlessly destroy'; hence, get rid of, dispose of, anyone or thing; overworked to the point of becoming slang. Still in good use, however, for political murder &c. in a police state.

liquorice, the est. form in Brit.; US *licorice.*

lira, Italian franc, has pl. *lire* (pron. lēr ā) or anglicized *liras.* WRONG: *A meal in a second-class restaurant costs from eight to ten* lira.

lissom(e). Lithe, supple. In US usually *-ome,* Brit. *-om.* Pron. lĭs′um. Now chiefly poetic.

list, please. The third sing. pres. is *list* or *listeth* (*let the wind blow as it list*), the past *list* or *listed.* The verb being in any form archaic, it is of no great importance whether the more obviously archaic impersonal construction (*as him list* &c.) or the now commoner personal one (*as he list* &c.) is used.

litany, liturgy. The two words have come so close to each other in use that it is a surprise when one first finds that the initial syllables are not the same in origin, or even connected. For those who know the Greek words, a *litany* is a series of prayers, a *liturgy* is a canon of public service; the latter in practice includes prayer, but does not say so.

literally. We have come to such a pass with this emphasizer that where the truth would require us to insert with a strong expression 'not literally, of course, but in a manner of speaking,' we do not hesitate to insert the very word that we ought to be at pains to repudiate (*Our eyes were* literally *pinned to the curtain*); cf. VERITABLE; such false coin makes honest traffic in words impossible. *The strong tête-de-pont fortifications were rushed by our troops, & a battalion crossed the bridge* literally *on the enemy's shoulders. Practically* or *virtually,* opposites of *literally,* would have stood.

LITERARY CRITICS' WORDS. The literary critics here meant are not the reputable writers of books or treatises or essays of which the substance is criticism; readers of that form of literature are a class apart, between which & its writers if a special lingo exists, the rest of us are not concerned to take exception to it. The better the critic, the fewer literary critics' words he uses. The good critic is aware that his public wants to understand, & he has no need to convince it that he knows what he is talking about by parading words that it does not understand. With the inferior critic the establishment of his status is the first consideration, & he effects it by so using, let us say, *actuality, inevitable,* & *subvent,* that the reader shall become aware of a mysterious difference between the sense attaching to the words in ordinary life & the sense now presented to him. He has taken *actuality* to mean *actualness* or *reality;* the critic perplexes him by giving it another sense, which it has a right to in French, where *actuel* means present, but not in English, i.e. up-to-dateness, or resemblance not to truth in general but to present-day conditions; & he does this without mentioning that he is gallicizing. And so with the other words; the reader is to have it borne in upon him that a more instructed person than himself is talking to him. One mark of the good literary critic is that he is both able to explain his meaning without resort to these lingo words, & under no necessity to use them as advertisements.

Specimens of literary critics' words, under some of which (printed in small capitals) further remarks will be found, are: *actuality,* BANAL(*ity*), charm, CONCISION, DISTINCTION, IMMENSE, INEVITABLE, INTRIGUE, METICULOUS, MOT JUSTE, *risibility,* SYMPATHETIC.

LITERARY WORDS. A literary word, when the description is used in this book, is one that cannot be called archaic, inasmuch as it is perfectly comprehensible still to all who hear it, but that has dropped out of use & had its place taken by some other word except in writing of a poetical or a definitely literary cast. To use literary words instead of the current substitutes in an unsuitable context challenges attention & gives the impression that the writer is a foreigner who has learned the language only from books. See also what is said of FORMAL WORDS. *Chill* for *chilly, eve* for *evening, gainsay* for *deny* &c., *loathly* for *loathsome, visage* for *face* &c., may be instanced; but literary words are reckoned by thousands.

literate, adj. Orig. 'acquainted with letters or literature,' hence, educated; it is now used chiefly in contrast with *illiterate,* able to read and write. The earlier meaning is obvious in 'No literate person would use the expression' (not necessarily no one able to pass the voter's literacy requirements).

literature for any printed material is colloq. or trade jargon (e.g. *He had two briefcases full of advertising* literature).

lithesome is, between *lithe* & *lissome,* a SUPERFLUOUS WORD.

litotes. (Rhet.): 'frugality.' A figure of speech in which the affirmative is expressed by its opposite with a negative: *not a few* for *many, a citizen of* no mean *city.* A variety of MEIOSIS. Pron. lī′to tēz.

litre, -ter. In US usually *-ter,* except in French contexts; Brit. *-re.*

litter (brood) may be used of the young (pl.) of any four-footed animal; *brood* refers usually to those brought forth from eggs. *Farrow* is exclusively used for a litter of pigs.

littérateur. A literary man. Usually used when *writer, scholar,* or *author* is what is meant. Or man of letters? See FRENCH WORDS.

little. Used as the opp. of *much* in expressions of quantity or amount (*much* or *little damage was done*); the opp. of *great* in distinctive names (*The Great & Little Bear*); the opp. of *big* (often colloq. for *large* & *small,* i.e. size—*big and little cars*). For full discussion see SMALL. Comparative *less*(*er*) (for limitations of sense see LESS 3), *least,* or more usually *smaller, -est.*

littoral, n., has a technical sense in which it is doubtless of value; marine life being distributed into abyssal, pelagic, & littoral, the littoral is the (zone or region of) shallow waters near the shore. For the land region bordering & including the shore, it may be important in treaties, but in ordinary contexts it should never be preferred to *coast.* See FORMAL WORDS.

liturgy. See LITANY.

livable. So spelled.

-lived. In *long-lived* &c. the right pronunciation is līvd, the words being from *life* & not from *live.*

liven. Colloq. for *enliven.*

livid means of a bluish leaden color; discolored (black & blue) as by a bruise; hence fig., of people, blue or ashy pale, from rage or other emotion. It is often used mistakenly for *flushed.*

llama, the beast; *lama,* the priest.

-LL-, -L-. Final *l* is treated differently in Brit., but not American, usage from most final consonants, the Brit. rule being to double it, if single, in inflection & in some derivatives irrespective of the position of the accent. In US it is not doubled if the accent falls on the first syllable. Hence (US) *traveler, equaling, labeled;* (Brit.) *-ller, -lling, -lled.* In other words Brit. spelling calls for a single *l,* US for two: Brit. *instil, enrol, fulfil, enrolment, instalment, skilful, wilful,* &c., all spelled with double *l* in US. (The extra *l* serves no purpose; the spelling with a single *l* is recommended to those US writers who have the courage to defend it.) Many words of which the spelling differs will be found in their alphabetical places.

Lloyd's, underwriters. So written, NOT *-ds* or *ds'.*

load, lode. In the compounds with *stone* & *star* it is usual to spell *loadstone,* but *lodestar.* The first element is the same, & is the ordinary *load,* of which the original sense was *way,* connected with the v. *lead.*

loan. The verb has been expelled from idiomatic southern English by *lend,* but was formerly current, & survives in US & locally in UK.

loath, adj., disinclined, reluctant. (Rhymes with *both.*) *Loth* is a variant spelling.

loathe. The verb always has the *a,* and the *th* is voiced as in *then;* so also *loathsome.*

lobby, v. (chiefly US), makes *lobbied, lobbying;* also *lobbyist.*

local(e), n. (1) The 'erroneous form' (OED) *locale* is recommended. (2) Pron. the noun lōkahl′, whichever way it is spelled. (3) The word's right to exist depends on the question whether the two indispensable words *locality* & *scene* give all the shades of meaning required, or whether something intermediate is useful. A *locality* is a place, with features of some sort, existing independently of anything that may happen there. If something happens in a locality, the locality becomes that something's *locale,* or place of happening. If the something that happens is seen or imagined or described in connection with its locale, the locale becomes its *scene* or *visible environment.*

locate. Chiefly US (and unnecessary) in the sense of 'establish in a place,' be situated (*The bank is* located *on the south corner*); US colloq. (and overworked) in the sense *find* (*Have* *you* located *the file yet?*); justifiable in 'to search and discover the position of' (Locate *the enemies' camp*), US colloq. in 'take up one's residence in' (*We've* located *in California*).

locus. Pl. *-ci* (-ō′sī). *Locos classicus,* the standard or most authoritative passage to explain a subject. Pl. *loci classici. The report of* [*his action*] *is now a* locus classicus *in the law of life insurance.*

locution is a potentially convenient word as equivalent to word or phrase; not more than potentially, because it so far smacks of pedantry that most people prefer to say *word or phrase* on the rare occasions when *expression* is not precise enough for the purpose, & *locution* gets left to the pedants. *His style is comparatively free from* locutions *calculated to baffle the English reader;* does anyone really like that better than *expressions?*

lode. (1) 'Strictly, a mineral deposit that fills a fissure in the native stone' (Webster). Generally, any vein of metal ore. (2) *Lodestar,* a guiding star (the pole star). But *loadstone* so spelled.

lodg(e)ment. US usually *lodgment.*

loggia. A roofed open gallery or arcade. Pron. lōjĭa or lōj*a;* pl. *loggias* (It. *loggie*) or *-as.*

logia. Maxims (of a religious teacher); principally used of sayings of Christ not recorded in the Bible. (The sing. is *logion* from *logos,* word.

logrolling. US. Originally, the action of rolling logs in the water by treading; a combining, esp. among politicians, to assist each other for political ends; (*literary*) *logrolling,* praising (a book &c.) in hope of being praised in return.

lone. Now poetic or rhet. except in *a lone hand, a lone game;* or humorous, *a lone female. Lonely* is the usual adj.; *lonesome* now has an overtone of quaintness.

long-lived. Pron. -līvd.

LONG VARIANTS. 'The better the writer, the shorter his words' would be a statement needing many exceptions for individual persons & particular subjects; but for all that it would, & especially about US & English writers, be broadly true. Those who run to long words are mainly the unskillful & tasteless. They confuse pomposity with dignity, flaccidity with ease, & bulk with force; see LOVE OF THE LONG WORD. When a word for the notion wanted exists, some people (1) forget or do not know that word, & make up another from the same stem with an extra suffix or two; or (2) are not satisfied with a mere current word, & resolve to decorate it, also with an extra suffix; or (3) have heard used a longer form that resembles it, & are not aware that this other form is appropriated to another sense. Cases of (1) & (2) are often indistinguishable; the motive differs, but the result is the same; & they will here be mixed together, those of (3) being kept apart.

1 & 2. Needless lengthenings of established words due to oversight or caprice: *administrate* (administer); *assertative* (assertive); *contumacity* (contumacy); *cultivatable* (cultivable); *dubiety* (doubt); *epistolatory* (epistolary); *experimentalize* (experi-

ment, v.); *filtrate* (filter, v.); *preventative* (preventive); *quieten* (quiet, v.).

3. Wrong use of longer forms due to confusion: *advancement* (advance); *alternative* (alternate); *creditable* (credible); *definitive* (definite); *distinctive* (distinct); *estimation* (estimate); *excepting* (except); *intensive* (intense); *partially* (partly); *reverential* (reverent).

The differences of meaning between the longer & shorter words in (1) & (2) are not here discussed, but will be found, unless too familiar to need mention, under the words in their dictionary place. Examples of (3) (WRONG): *It was only by* advancement *of money to the farmers that the calamity could be ended./When the army is not fully organized, when it is in process of* alternative *disintegration & rally, the problems are insoluble./It is* creditably *stated that the length of line dug & wired in the time is near a record./But warning & suggestion are more in evidence than* definitive *guidance./Trade relations of an ordinary kind are quite* distinctive *from those having annexation as their aim./The Allies were able to form a precise* estimation *of Germany's real intentions./The sojourn of belligerent ships in French waters has never been limited* excepting *by certain clearly defined rules./The covered flowers being less* intensively *colored than the others./The two feet, branching out into ten toes, are* partially *of iron &* partially *of clay./Their behavior in church was anything but* reverential.

longways, -wise. Both are used. No differentiation.

lookout, n., *look out,* v.

loom, v. To appear indistinctly; to come into view in a vague and magnified form (orig. of a ship). The idiom is *to loom large,* NOT *largely.*

loony, lunatic. So spelled.

loose, loosen, vv. Now usually differentiated: *loose,* undo or set free; *loosen,* make looser.

loquacity. Pron. lōkwăs'ĭtĭ.

lord. A baron, whether a peer or a peer's eldest son, is called by his title of peerage, either a surname or territorial name: *Lord Byron, Lord Tennyson.* If the Christian name is to be mentioned it comes first: *George Gordon (Byron) Lord Byron; Alfred, Lord Tennyson.* Younger sons of Dukes & Marquises are spoken of by the title of lord followed by Christian & family name, as *Lord Arthur Smith.* Omission of the Christian name is wrong; the permissible shortening is not *Lord Smith,* but *Lord Arthur.* For *lord* as an undress substitute for *marquis, earl, viscount,* see TITLES. *Lord Bacon* is a mixture; the possible correct styles are *Bacon, Francis Bacon, Sir Francis Bacon, Lord Verulam, Lord* or *Viscount St. Albans,* of which the first is usually the best.

Lord Justice. Pl. *Lords Justices.*

lose. (1) *Lose no time in* is a notoriously ambiguous phrase: *No time* should be lost *in exploring the question.* Should it be explored at once or not at all? (2) *Lose face,* i.e. suffer loss of prestige, orig. Chinese. *Save face* has become a popular opposite.

lot. *A lot of people* say *so, Lots of paper* is *wanted,* &c. (colloq.), are the idiomatic forms. See NUMBER, 12.

loth. Spell *loath.*

Lothario. From Rowe's *The Fair Penitent;* a libertine. Pl. *-os.*

lotus. Pl. *-uses.*

loud, loudly. The idioms are *Don't talk so loud, laughed loud and long; loud-spoken,* &c., but *insisted loudly on his rights, a loudly dressed person,* &c. See UNIDIOMATIC -LY & ALOUD.

Louis, Fr., pron. lo͞o ĭ. The kings: *Louis Treize* (trāz; XIII), *Quatorze* (kȧtôrz; XIV), *Quinze* (kăNZ; XV), and *Seize* (sâz; XVI). The coin *louis d'or* (lo͞oĭ dôr). St. Louis, Mo., should be pron. as English.

lour, lower. Pron. lour. The meaning is to frown. In US usually spelled *lower,* Brit. *lour.* The word is not connected with *low* & the other v. *lower* (lō′er). The confusion is due chiefly to the word's being often applied to clouds, but the meaning is 'threatening' clouds, not 'descending' clouds.

love. For *the scenes he loved so well* &c., see HACKNEYED PHRASES, & STOCK PATHOS.

LOVE OF THE LONG WORD. It need hardly be said that shortness is a merit in words; there are often reasons why shortness is not possible; much less often there are occasions when length, not shortness, is desirable; but it is a general truth that the short words are not only handier to use, but more powerful in effect; extra syllables reduce, not increase, vigor. This is particularly so in English, where the native words are short; & the long words are foreign. There are many good reasons, however, against any attempt to avoid, because it is a polysyllable, the word that will give our meaning best. What is here deprecated is the tendency among the ignorant to choose, because it is a polysyllable, the word that gives their meaning no better or even worse. Attention is here confined to certain words frequently used where unrelated shorter ones would be better. They are doubtless chosen primarily not for their length, but because they are in vogue; but their vogue is in turn due to the pompous effect conferred by length. They are: *mentality, meticulous,* PERCENTAGE, PROPORTION, PROPOSITION, PROTAGONIST; there are many similar words, under which bare references to this article may be made; but these will serve as types.

Mentality: No one has so wide a knowledge of Afghan politics & of the mentality *of the Pathan* (mind).

Meticulous: These meticulous *calculations of votes which have not yet been given rather disgust us* (exact)./*Owing to a* meticulous *regard for the spirit of the party truce, their views have not been adequately voiced by their leaders* (strict).

Percentage: Our tax revenue is now fully 160 *millions, & the Single Land Tax would not yield more than a* percentage *of this* (part).

Proportion: The greater proportion *of these old hands have by this time already dropped out* (part).

Proposition: The agriculturist asks that corn growing shall become a paying proposition (enterprise).

Protagonist: The great Western Powers who have acted as protagonists *in this war* (leaders).

A few lines of the long-word style we know so well are added: *Vigorous* condemnation *is passed on the foreign policy of the Prime Minister, whose* temperamental inaptitude for diplomacy & preoccupation *with domestic issues have* rendered his participation in external negotiations gravely detrimental *to the public welfare.* Vigorous indeed; a charging hippopotamus hardly more so.

lower, adj. (1) *Lower case, upper case,* are printers' names for small letters, capitals. (2) *Lower Empire* is a name for the Roman Empire from the time of Constantine (A.D, 323–37), when the seat of empire was shifted from Rome to Constantinople, & Christianity became the State religion. Also called *Later, Greek, Byzantine,* & *Eastern, Empire.* (3) *Lower House,* as a syn. for the House of Representatives (US), usually capitalized.

lower, lour, v. See LOUR.

lucrative. VOGUE WORD for *profitable.*

lucre means profit, pecuniary advantage, now always in an unfavorable sense.

luminary, fig. a person who is a source of light in his field. *The great luminaries of philosophy and science.*

lung(e)ing. Omit the *e.*

lupin, lupine. In US both the flower (pron. lū′pĭn) and the adj. 'wolflike' (pron. lūp′īn) are spelled with final *e.* (Brit. plant sometimes *lupin.*)

lurid has two different color senses, likely to be confusing: (1) yellow, wan, dismal, ghastly: *a lurid paleness of skin;* (2) shining with a red glow amid darkness: *the lurid reflection of immense fires.* Either or both could account for the fig. meanings, terrible, ominous, marked by violent passion or crime; hence sensational. *A lurid story and luridly told.*

luster, -tre. In US usually *-ter,* Brit. *-tre;* both *lustrous.*

lustrum. Pl. *-tra,* sometimes *-trums.*

luxe. Elegance (usually preceded by *de*), *articles de luxe.* Pron. dĕ lo͞oks, lŭks, or as French lüks, if it must be used. *De luxe editions, models,* &c., usually signifying more expensive, are in commercialese 'dē lŭx.' See FRENCH WORDS.

luxuriant, luxurious. *Luxurious* is the adj. that belongs in sense to *luxury* & conveys the ideas of comfort or delight or indulgence. *Luxuriant* has nothing to do with these, implying only rich growth, vigorous shooting forth, teeming; as *luxurious* to *luxury,* so *luxuriant* to *exuberance.* Luxurious *houses, habits, life, people, climate, idleness, times, food, cushions, dreams, abandonment, desires;* luxuriant *vegetation, crops, hair, imagination, invention, style.* The points at which they touch & become liable to confusion are, first, that abundance, essential to luxuriance or exuberance, also subserves luxury, though not essential to it; &, secondly, their common property in the v. *luxuriate,* which means both to enjoy luxury & to show luxuriance. *A luxurious fancy* is one that dwells on luxury; *a luxuriant fancy* one that runs riot on any subject, agreeable or other.

-LY. (1) For the tendency among writers & speakers who are more conscientious than literary to suppose that all adverbs must end in *-ly,* & therefore to use *hardly, largely, strongly,* &c., when idiom requires *hard, large,* & *strong,* see UNIDIOMATIC -LY. (2) The commonest form of ugly repetition is that of the *-ly* adverbs, see JINGLES. As many *-ly* adverbs as one chooses may be piled on each other if one condition of sense is fulfilled—that all these adverbs have the same relation to the same word or to parallel words. *We are* utterly, hopelessly, irretrievably, *ruined; It is* theoretically *certain, but* practically *doubtful; He may* probably *or* possibly *be in time.* Euphony has nothing to say against repetition of *-ly* if there is point in it, which there is if the adverbs are parallel; but, when parallelism is not there to comfort her, Euphony at once cries out in pain, though too often to deaf ears. ILL-ADVISED:

Russian industry is at present practically completely *crippled. Practically* is not marching alongside of *completely,* but riding on its back; read *almost./He found himself* sharply, & apparently completely, *checked. Sharply* & *completely,* by all means; but not *apparently completely;* read *as it seemed./The earliest lists, still so* sadly & probably irretrievably *imperfect.* Whereas *irretrievably* qualifies *imperfect, probably* qualifies *irretrievably;* read *perhaps,* or *it is to be feared.*

Lyceum. Pl. *-ms.* The garden of Athens in which Aristotle taught; hence his philosophy and followers. Transf., a teaching place, lecture hall, literary institution. In US used also of an association providing inspirational lectures, concerts, &c.

lynch (orig. US, from Lynch['s] law) means to inflict punishment, esp. death, without legal sanction, as by a mob. It is not restricted to illegal hanging.

lyric(al). *Lyric* is now the est. adj. for most uses; we speak of *lyric poets, poetry, verse, drama, muse, elements,* & NOT *lyrical. Lyrical* is in some sort a parasite upon *lyric,* meaning suggestive of lyric verse. *Lyric* classifies definitely, while *lyrical* describes vaguely. With some words either can be used, but with different effect; *a lyric rhapsody* is one actually composed in lyric verse; *a lyrical rhapsody* is talk full of expressions, or revealing a mood, fit for lyric poetry. *Lyrical emotion, praise, sorrow,* &c.; or again, a person may *grow lyrical.*

lyrics. (Lit.): 'of the lyre.' The OED definition (as regards modern usage) is: 'Short poems (whether or not intended to be sung), usually divided into stanzas or strophes, & directly expressing the poet's own thoughts & sentiments.' The short pieces between the narrative parts of Tennyson's *Princess* (Home they brought her warrior dead &c.) are typical examples. Wordsworth's 'Daffodils,' Shelley's 'Skylark,' Keats's 'Grecian Urn,' Milton's 'Penseroso,' Burns's 'Field Mouse,' Herrick's 'Rosebuds,' Lovelace's 'Lucasta,' Shakespeare's 'It was a lover,' may serve to illustrate; but attempts to distinguish lyric poetry clearly from other kinds (epic, dramatic, elegiac, didactic, &c.) have not been successful, the classes not being mutually exclusive.

M

Ma'am. Contraction of *madam,* colloq.: *A school ma'am* (often *-marm*). At the English court, used in addressing the Queen or Royal Princess (pron. măm).

macabre. Pron. mȧkah'ber or mȧ kä'br. Orig. a proper name. From the dance of Macabre (properly *Macabré*), the dance of death; hence 'gruesome,' used esp. of works of art, literature, &c.: *A representation of the ghastly, the grim, and the macabre.*

macaroni. Pl. of the 18th-c. dandy, *-nies;* pl. of the foodstuff, *-nis.*

machete. Pron. mä chā'tā or (Span.) mä chĕ'tĕ (Brit. *matchet,* pron. mătch'ĕt). Broad knife used for cutting cane, clearing paths, &c.

Machiavel(li)(an)ism. The formerly current shortening *Machiavel* is now less common than *Machiavelli; a very Machiavel,* once much used, has become rare. The adj. is accordingly now spelled *Machiavellian,* not *-elian.* For the *-ism* noun, *Machiavellianism,* in spite of greater length, is the better.

machination. Pron. măk'-. Now almost always used of contriving, scheme, intrigue in a bad sense.

Mackinac, mackinaw. Both pronounced -aw. The straits, spell *-ac;* the adj., blanket, boat, coat, and trout *-aw.*

mackintosh. So spelled.

macro-. Combining form meaning long, large; *macrocosm,* the great world, the universe (as opposed to *microcosm*).

macron. The horizontal mark placed over a vowel to show that it is long: fāce, bōne, sīte, mēte, cūbe.

mad, v. Formerly an active verb, esp. in its intrans. sense, to be or become mad, now obs. (COD, 'rare'); it was so used in Gray's *Elegy,* 'the madding crowd,' in which it is often mistakenly interpreted as 'distracting' (and misread *maddening*).

mad, adj. Insane, crazy; hence, rashly foolish, infatuated, &c. Its use for *angry, annoyed* is US slang.

madam(e). In the English word, whether as appellation (*I will inquire, Madam; Dear Madam; What does Madam think about it?*), as common noun (*the city madams*), or as prefix (*Madam Fortune, Madam Venus*), there should be no *-e.* As a prefix to a foreign lady's name instead of *Mrs., Madame* (*Mme*) is right, with pl. *Mesdames. Madam,* the appellation, suffers from having no pl., *Ladies* being the substitute, for which *Mesdames* is sometimes used (abbr. *Mmes*) in writing.

Madeira. So spelled.

mademoiselle. Pron. mȧd'-mwȧ zĕl'. Pl. *mesdemoiselles.* (Abbr. *Mlle, Mlles.*)

madness. For *method in madness,* see IRRELEVANT ALLUSION.

maelstrom. A whirlpool, spec. the famous one off the west coast of Norway. Also fig.: *a maelstrom of luxury and extravagance.* Pron. māl'strom.

maenad. A bacchante; transf., any frenzied or wildly excited woman. *Furious as a maenad.* Pron. mē'năd.

maestro. 'Master,' spec. in

music, a great teacher, composer, or conductor. Pron. maĕs'trō.

maffia, mafia. The Italian spelling is *-ff-*, in English often *-f-*. In Sicily the (spirit of) hostility to law; in other countries, an organization of Sicilians & Italians who show their hostility through crime.

magazine. The warehouse, munitions, &c., usually accented on the last syllable; the periodical, usually (in US) on the first.

Magdalen(e). 1. In the names of the Oxford (*-en*) & Cambridge (*-ene*) Colleges, pron. mau'dlĭn.

2. In the use as a noun meaning reformed harlot &c., use *magdalen* & so pronounce.

3. When used with *the* instead of the name *Mary M.*, *the Magdalene* (-ēn) & *the Magdalen* (ĕn) are equally correct.

4. In the full name *Mary Magdalene* the four-syllable pronunciation (măgdalē'nĭ) is the best, though if it were *Mary the Magdalene* -lēn would be right, as it is in *the Magdalene*, i.e. the famous person of Magdala. *Mary Magdalen*, however, is also possible. To summarize:

Magdalen (mau'dlĭn) *Coll., Oxford*
Magdalene (mau'dlĭn) *Coll., Cambridge*
A Home for magdalens (măg'dalĕnz)
The Magdalene (-ēn) or *the Magdalen* (-ĕn)
Mary Magdalene (măgdalē'nĭ) or *Magdalen*.

maggoty. So spelled.

magic(al), adjs. *Magic* tends to lose those adj. uses that cannot be viewed as mere attributive uses of the noun. That is, first, it is very seldom used predicatively; *the effect was magical* (NEVER *magic*); *The ring must be magical* (NOT *magic*, though *must be a magic one* is better than *a magical one*). And, secondly, the chief non-predicative use is in assigning a thing to the domain of magic (*a magic ring, carpet, spell, crystal; the magic art*), or in distinguishing it from others & so helping its identification (*magic lantern, square*), rather than in giving its characteristics descriptively (*with magical speed; what a magical transformation*); this second differentiation, however, is not yet strictly observed.

Magna C(h)arta. The Great Charter of English liberty obtained from King John, 15 June 1215. *The personal & political liberties secured by Magna Charta* (NOT the *Magna Charta*). Authority seems to be for spelling *charta* & pronouncing karta, which is hard on the plain man. But outside of histories & lecture rooms the spelling & pronunciation *charta* will take a great deal of killing yet.

magnum opus. Lat. 'great work'; esp. a great & important literary work; one's greatest work.

magus. Member of the ancient Persian priestly caste; a magician; *the Magi*, the three wise men of the N.T. Pl. *-gi*, pron. -jī.

Magyar. Pron. mŏ'dyar (or anglicized măg'yär).

maharaja(h). The Hindu spelling has no *h*, but the anglicized *-rajah* is more frequent; see DIDACTICISM.

Mahomet, Muhammad, &c. The est. spelling is now *Mohammed(an)*.

maieutic. Pron. mīū'tĭk or

(OED) māū′tĭk. The word means performing midwife's service (to thought or ideas); Socrates figured himself as a midwife (*maia*) bringing others' thoughts to birth with his questionings; *educative* contains the same notion, but much overlaid with different ones, & the literary critic & the pedagogue consequently find *maieutic* useful enough to pass in spite of its touch of pedantry.

Majesty, Highness, &c. When *your Majesty, her Grace,* &c., has been used, & need arises for a pronoun or possessive adjective to represent it, grammar would require *it, its;* but instead of these either the full title is repeated (*Your Majesty can do as your Majesty will with your Majesty's ships*), or *you, your, she, her,* &c., is ungrammatically substituted for *it* or *its* (*Her Grace summoned her chef*). Stevenson writes: *Your Highness interprets my meaning with his usual subtlety.* The English idiom requires either *your Highness's,* or *your, usual subtlety.*

major means *greater,* & those who like POMPOSITIES are within their rights, & remain intelligible, if they call the greater part *the major portion;* they can moreover plead that *major part* & *portion* have been used by good writers in the times when pomposity was less noticeable than it now is. Those who do not like pomposities will call it *the greater part* & deserve our gratitude, or at least escape our dislike. *I, who had described myself as 'sick of patriotism' . . . found myself unable to read anything but a volume* the major portion *of which consisted of patriotic verse.*

major (in Logic). See SYLLOGISMS.

major-domo. The chief official of a princely household; a head steward; jocularly, a butler or steward.

majority. 1. Distinctions of meaning. Three allied senses, one abstract & two concrete, need to be distinguished if illogicalities are to be avoided: (1) *majority* meaning a superiority in number, or, to revive an obs. unambiguous word, a plurity (. . . *was passed by a bare* majority; *The majority was scanty but sufficient*); (2) *majority* meaning the one of two or more sets that has a plurity, or the more numerous party (*The* majority *was,* or *were, determined to press its,* or *their, victory*); (3) *majority* meaning most of a set of persons, or the greater part numerically (*The* majority *were fatally wounded; A* majority *of my friends advise it*).

2. Number. After *majority* in sense (1) the verb will always be singular. After *majority* in sense (2), as after other nouns of multitude, either a sing. or a pl. verb is possible, according as the body is, or its members are, chiefly in the speaker's thoughts. After *majority* in sense (3) in which the thought is not of contrasted bodies at all, but merely of the numbers required to make up more than a half, the verb is almost necessarily plural, the sense being *more people than not,* out of those concerned.

3. *Great* &c. *majority.* With *majority* in sense (1) *great, greater, greatest,* &c., are freely used, & cause no difficulty. With *majority* in sense (2) they are not often used, & then to

give the special sense of party having a great, greater, plurity as compared with that enjoyed by some other (*This* great majority *is helpless; Having* the greatest majority *of modern times devoted to him*). With *majority* in sense (3) *great* is possible & common, *the great majority* meaning most by far, much more than half; but the use of *greater* & *greatest* with it, as if *majority* meant merely part or number, is, though frequent, an illiterate blunder. WRONG: *By far* the greatest majority *of voters have never even read the amendments in question./By far* the larger majority *of the entries are not words.*

majuscule. (Paleography): a large letter (in contrast to minuscule); pron. -jŭs′-.

make. (1) Idiomatic usage: *Make him repeat it* (very rarely *to repeat*); *He must be made to repeat it* (very rarely *made repeat*). (2) *Make over,* in the sense remake, refashion (*We shall do our best to* make them over *into good citizens*), is chiefly US.

make-believe is the n.; *make believe* (no hyphen), the v. (which has meant *to pretend* since the 14th c.).

MALAPROPS. When Mrs. Malaprop, in Sheridan's *Rivals,* is said to 'deck her dull chat with hard words which she don't understand,' she protests, 'Sure, if I reprehend anything in this world, it is the use of my oracular tongue, & a nice derangement of epitaphs'—having vague memories of *apprehend, vernacular, arrangement,* & *epithets.* She is now the matron saint of all those who go word-fowling with a blunderbuss. Achievements so heroic as her own do not here concern us; they pass the bounds of ordinary experience & of the credible. Her votaries are a feebler folk; with them malaprops come single spies, not in battalions, & not marked by her bold originality, but monotonously following well-beaten tracks. In the article PAIRS & SNARES a number of words is given with which other words of not very different sound are commonly confused, & under most of the separate words contained in that list illustrations will be found; *predict* & *predicate, reversal* & *reversion, masterful* & *masterly* will suffice here as examples. Another kind of malaprop, in which two words are confused rather in construction than in meaning, is dealt with in OBJECT-SHUFFLING; *substitute* & *replace, instill* & *inspire, afflict* & *inflict* are specimens. And a long list might be made of words commonly so used as to show misapprehension of their meaning; a few, under which quotations will be found, are: *asset, comity, e.g., eke out, glimpse, oblivious, polity, proportion, protagonist, prototype.* But it is perhaps hardly decent to leave the subject without a single concrete illustration. Here are one or two less staled by frequent occurrence than those mentioned above: *Mr. —— has circulated what* portends *to be a reply to a letter which I had previously addressed to you./His capacity for continuous work is* incredulous./ *It was a great* humility *to be kept waiting about, after having been asked to come.*

malapropos. Pron. mălăpropō′.

male. 1. *Male, masculine.*

The distinction drawn between *female* & *feminine* is equally true for *male* & *masculine;* the reader will perhaps be good enough to look through the article FEMALE, FEMININE, & make the necessary substitutions. The only modification needed is in the statement about the original part of speech of *female; male* was not, like that, a noun before it was an adj.; but this difference does not affect present usage.

2. *Male* &c. in prosody. *Male* & *masculine, female* & *feminine,* are used to distinguish rhymes & line endings having a final accented syllable (*male* or *masculine: Now is the winter of our discontent′*) from those in which an unaccented syllable follows the last accented one (*female* or *feminine: To be or not to be, that is the ques′tion*).

malefactor. Four syllables.

malign. Pron. malīn′. (1) *Malign* refers to effect (=injurious: *a malign influence*); *malignant* refers to intention or disposition (=intense ill-will; *destroyed by some malignant spirit.*) In medicine, however, *malignant* is usually used rather than *malign: a malignant tumor.* See also BENIGN. (2) *Malign,* v., means to speak evil of, to slander: *I do not want to malign the person who has befriended me.*

malignancy, -nity. These nouns almost reverse the relation between the adjectives to which they belong. It would be expected that *malignancy* would be the word for spitefulness, & *malignity* for harmfulness; but the medical use of *malignant* has so strongly affected *malignancy* that *malignity* has had to take over the sense of spite, & almost lost that of harm.

malinger. To pretend illness (orig., of soldiers, to escape duty, work); now also to pretend illness, inability, in order to obtain charity, drugs, &c.

Mall. Pron. măl; *the Mall* (măl), but *Pall Mall* (pĕlmĕl) (the US cigarette pronounced pĕlmĕl by its manufacturers, but often pălmăl or pälmäl by those who smoke it).

mammon. Riches, but personified in the N.T. & often mistaken for a proper name; hence =Wealth, an idol or evil influence.

man. For the *inner, outer, man,* see HACKNEYED PHRASES.

manageable. So spelled.

mandamus. Pl. *-uses.* Pron. măndā′mus.

mandatary, -tory. The *-ary* form is noun only=one to whom a mandate is given; the *-ory* form is primarily an adj.=of the nature of a mandate, & secondarily a noun=*mandatary.* A distinction in spelling between the personal noun & the adj. is obviously convenient, & the form *mandatary* is therefore recommended for the noun.

manes, spirit of dead person. Pron. mā′nēz; a pl. noun, with pl. construction though sing. in sense. (*We may hope* the manes *of the burnt-out philosophies* were *then finally appeased.* —Huxley)

maneuver. The spelling now given first in most US dictionaries; Brit. always (and still often in US) *manœuvre.*

mango. Pl. *-oes.*

mangy. So spelled.

maniacal. Pron. manī′-. The (Med.) adj. *manic* (*manic-*

depressive) is properly mā- but often pop. mă-.

Manichee. Believer in the doctrine of Manez, 216?–276? (that Satan is coeternal with God). Pron. măn′ĭ kē.

manifest, adj. (Orig.=palpable.) Clearly revealed to the eye, mind, or judgment; open to view or comprehension; obvious. (The Lat. roots are probably *manus*=hand, & *festus* =struck.)

manifesto. A public declaration making known past actions & explaining the motives for actions announced as forthcoming. *The Communist Manifesto* by Marx & Engels (1848). (US pl. *-oes;* Brit. usually *-os.*)

manifold. Pron. măn-, NOT mĕn-. The word is no longer felt to be a member of the series *twofold, threefold, a hundredfold,* & attempts to treat it as such result in unidiomatic English. It is better to coin *manyfold* for the occasion than to imitate the writers of the quotations below. Both the uses illustrated in them are obsolete & the revival of them after centuries of dormancy is perhaps accounted for by the adaptation of the word to a commercial use in *manifold writing,* & its consequent popularization. NOT *Such elimination would recoup that expense,* manifold, *by the saving which it would effect of food valuable to the nation./ This organization in capable hands should repay* in manifold *the actual funds raised on its behalf.* Use *many-fold* or *many times.*

manikin, mannequin. *Manikin*=‘little man’; an anatomical model. *Mannequin*=person who models costumes. The artist's lay figure is *mannequin* (US); *manikin* (Brit.).

manipulate has *-lable.*

manner. *To the manner born,* i.e. destined by birth to be subject to the (specified) custom (*Hamlet* I.iv.15). (NOT *manor,* though even the usually careful *N.Y. Times* can be guilty of the error: (WRONG) *Mr. Ritchard, as Captain Cook, was to the* manor *born.*)

MANNERISMS. Mannerism consists in the allowing of a form of speech that has now & again served us well to master us. Pater has a *so: Ubiquitous, tyrannous, irresistible, as it may seem, motion, with the whole* so *dazzling world it covers, is—nothing./Once for all, in harshest dualism, the only true yet* so *barren existence is opposed to the world of phenomena./In the midst of that aesthetically* so *brilliant world of Greater Greece.*

Macaulay has an antithesis: *In some points it* has been fashioned to suit our feelings; *in others, it* has gradually fashioned our feelings to suit *itself./ At first they were only* robbers; *they soon rose to the dignity of* conquerors./*To enjoin* honesty, *& to insist on having* what could not be honestly got, *was then the constant practice of the Company.*

Meredith has a circumvention system for ‘said so-&-so’: *‘Now that is too bad,’* she pouted./ *‘I must see Richard tomorrow morning,’ Mrs. Doria* ended the colloquy by saying./*‘She did all she could to persuade me to wait,’* emphasized Richard.

Kipling has ‘But that is another story.’

Wells has a *Came:* Came *a familiar sound.*/Came *the green flash again.*/Came *that sense again of unendurable tension.* And so on, & so on. Perhaps few of those who write much escape from the temptation to trade on tricks of which they have learned the effectiveness; & it is true that it is a delicate matter to discern where a peculiarity ceases to be an element in the individuality that readers associate pleasantly with the writer they like, & becomes a recurrent & looked-for & dreaded irritation. But at least it is well for every writer to realize that, for his as for other people's mannerisms, there is a point at which that transformation does take place.

mannikin. Var. of MANIKIN.

manœuvre. US, usually *maneuver. Manœuvre,* v. makes *-vred, -vring.*

man of war. Pl. *men of war.*

man power. In the sense 'the strength in terms of men available' for military service &c., Webster and the *N.Y. Times* style book, but few other US dictionaries, give as one word. Brit. *man-power* (hyphen).

manslaughter. Law: unlawful killing of a human being without malice aforethought, as contrasted with (willful) murder.

mantel (piece, -shelf). So spelled. The cloak is *mantle.*

manumit makes *-tted, -tting.*

manuscript. The abbrev. is MS. in sing., & MSS. in pl. To insist on restricting the meaning of *manuscript* to handwritten material, & using *typescript* for the typed copy, is pedantry. A word is nevertheless needed; *longhand,* sometimes so used in US, is absurd in any sense except opposed to *shorthand.*

many. WRONG: *While there have been* many a *good-humored smile about the Cody 'Cathedral,' we may yet shortly witness . . . Many a* requires a sing. verb.

Maori. Pron. mowr′ĭ; pl. *-is.*

maraschino. Pron. măr*a*skē′-nō; pl. *-os.*

mare, the female of the horse family, including the zebra, ass, &c., but esp. the domestic horse. *Mare's nest:* a wonderful discovery that turns out to be illusory. *Professor X's advice led us only to a mare's nest.* (Often misused for hornets' nest; i.e. a confused or turbulent situation.) *Shanks's* or *Shanks' mare,* one's own legs, as opp. to riding &c.

margarin(e). The pron. marj- instead of marg- is etymologically wrong (the derivation is through a Fr. word *margaron,* pearl; hard *g*) but is so firmly established in US that it is useless to insist on marg-. In Brit., however, the marg- pronunciation is still sometimes used. Last syllable, Brit. & US pron. -ēn.

marginalia (marginal notes) is pl.

mariage de convenance. A marriage for money & position (not *convenience* in the English sense).

marquis. In English pron. mar′kwĭs, Fr. mȧr kē′.

marquise (pron. -kēz′) is French for *marchioness,* NOT for *marquis.*

marriageable. So spelled.

Marseillaise. Pron. marsel*ā*z′ or mär sĕ yāz.

Marseilles. The seaport, pron. mär sālz′ or mär sā; the fabric always -sālz.

marshal, v., makes US *-led, -ling;* Brit. *-lled, -lling.*

marten, -in. The beast has *-en,* the bird *-in.*

martinet. A strict disciplinarian (usually military & usually derogatory). Pron. -ê′.

marvel, makes US *-led, -ling, -lous;* Brit., *-lled,* &c.

masculine. *Masculine* understanding, appearance, nature, companionship; *male* sex, servants, voice, choir; see FEMALE.

mask, masque. The first is preferred for all uses except the dramatic entertainment.

Mason and Dixon's Line. Also *the Mason-Dixon Line.* Roughly, southern boundary of Pennsylvania, as surveyed in the 1760's; later considered the line between free & slave states.

massacre makes *massacring.*

massage, -eur, -euse. Pron. masahzh′, măser′, măserz′.

masterful, masterly. Some centuries ago both were used indifferently in either of two very different senses: (1) imperious or commanding or strong-willed, & (2) skillful or expert or practiced. The DIFFERENTIATION is now complete, *-ful* having the (1) & *-ly* the (2) meanings; & disregard of it is so obviously inconvenient, since the senses, though distinct, are not so far apart but that it may sometimes be uncertain which is meant, that it can only be put down to ignorance. *Masterly* is not misused; but *masterful* often appears, especially in journalism, instead of *masterly.* In the following examples *masterly* should have been the word: *The influence of the engineering & mechanical triumphs of the staff has been dealt with by* masterful *writers./Yates played a truly* masterful *game in defeating Reti.*

mate, checkmate. The full form is now chiefly in metaphorical use, while the shortened one is usual in chess.

materfamilias. Pl. *matresfamilias* or *materfamiliases.*

material, adj. There are at least four current antitheses in aid of any of which *material* may be called in when an adjective is required: there is matter & form (*material & formal*); there is matter & spirit (*material* & *spiritual*); there is matériel & personnel (*material* & *personal,* see MATÉRIEL); & there is what matters & what does not matter (*material* & *trifling*). Before using *material,* therefore, with reference to any of these, the writer should make sure that there is no risk of confusion with another. In the following sentences, *material* is AMBIGUOUS: *Agriculture, though the most* material *of all our pursuits, is teaching us truths beyond its own direct province./The old bonds of relationship, & community of* material *interests./A comparison between the French peasant-proprietor & the English small-holder as he might conceivably become under a freehold system, a comparison, be it said, to the* material *advantage of the former.*

materialize. The word has uses enough of its own (*Those who would materialize spirit. A soul materialized by gluttony. Virgil having materialized a scheme of abstracted notions. Ghosts or promises of ghosts which fail to materialize*) without being forced to do the work of *happen* or *be fulfilled* or *form.* WRONG: *There would* *seem to be some ground for hope that the strike will not* materialize *after all./Year after year passed & these promises failed to* materialize.*/Out of the mist of notes & protocols a policy seems gradually to be* materializing. In these latter senses *materialize* is on the level of *transpire* (happen), *eventuate* (happen), *unique* (notable), *individual* (man), & such abominations. See OFFICIALESE.

matériel. In antitheses with *personnel,* expressed or implied, the French spelling & pronunciation (mȧ tē rĭĕl′) should be kept, & not replaced by those of the English *material.*

mathematics (pl. usually treated as sing.). *Mathematics* derives *its accuracy from Logic. Mathematics* is *his strong point.* BUT *His mathematics* are *weak.*

matrix. Pl. *-ixes* or *-ices.*

matter. WRONG: *The distribution shows that, as exceptional bravery is confined to no rank in the Army, so recognition is given to it* by no matter whom *it is displayed.* If elliptical phrases like *no matter who* are to be treated freely as units, care must be taken that the ellipsis can be filled in correctly; *by it is no matter whom it is displayed* is wrong, & *it is no matter by whom it is displayed* is right; accordingly the order should be *no matter by whom.* The real cause of the mistake here is the superstition against prepositions at the end; *no matter whom it is displayed by* would have been correct; but the writer was frightened at his final preposition, made a grab at it, & plumped it down in a wrong place; see SUPERSTITIONS, & OUT OF THE FRYING PAN. The offense is aggravated by the inevitable impulse to connect *by* with *is given.*

mature. Pron. -tūr.

matutinal. Of or occurring in the morning; hence early. Chiefly in POLYSYLLABIC HUMOR: *Here they were found by a* matutinal *gardener.* (Pron. US m*a*tū′tĭn*a*l; Brit. also -ī′n*a*l.)

maudlin. (Effusively sentimental; a tearful stage of drunkenness.) So spelled. The origin is the name MAGDALEN.

maximal. In most non-technical contexts *greatest* is better.

maximum. Pl. *-ma,* sometimes *-mums.*

maybe. (1) In present US usage *maybe* is confined almost exclusively to informal conversation, *perhaps* being the normal word in writing and in formal speech. *Maybe* has still, however, a real function—to replace *perhaps* in a context whose tone demands a touch of primitive dignity; so *Our Lord speaking quite simply to simple Syrian people, a child or two* maybe *at his knees.* (2) Care should be taken to write the two words separately when used as a verb form: *He is probably right but* may be *mistaken.*

mayonnaise. Pron. mā-.

mayoralty. Pron. mār′ăltĭ.

me is technically wrong in *It wasn't me* &c., but, the phrase being of its very nature colloq., such a lapse is of no importance; & this is perhaps the only temptation to use *me* instead of *I.* There is more danger of using *I* for *me,* especially when *& me* is required after another noun or pronoun that has taken responsibility for the grammar & has not a separate objective case; *between you & I, let you & I try,* are not uncommon but are illiterate even colloquially (see BETWEEN, LET). WRONG: *A rich friend of ours wrote & asked my husband & I to dine at the most expensive restaurant & go to the theatre on his birthday.*

meager, -re. US usually *-er;* Brit. *-re* (*meagreness, meagrely*).

mealy-mouthed has a long literary tradition, going back to the 16th c.; soft-spoken, afraid to speak out or speak one's mind. Sometimes spelled as one word, but the hyphen is recommended.

mean, adj., makes *meanness.* In the sense ill-tempered, pettily selfish or malicious, US colloq.

means, n. In the sense *income* &c., *means* always takes a pl. verb: *My means* were (NEVER was) *much reduced.* In the sense *way to an end* &c., *a means* takes a sing. verb; *means,* & *the means,* can be treated as either sing. or pl.; *all means* (pl.) & *every means* (sing.) are equally correct. (WRONG: Every means *of exit from the city—rail, bus, and air terminals*—were *being closely watched*). *The means* do not, *or* does not, *justify the end; the end is good, but the means* are, *or* is, *bad; such means* are (NOT is) *repugnant to me,* because *such* without *a* is necessarily pl.; cf. *such a means* is *not to be discovered;* & similarly with other adjs., as *secret means* were *found,* but *a secret means* was *found.*

meantime, meanwhile. Although both words are nouns & advs. & mean the same thing, modern usage tends to restrict the former to its function as a noun (*In the* meantime *both countries will hold conferences; This order will be effective for the* meantime), the latter to its function as an adv. (*Do what you can,* meanwhile, *to stop all controversy;* Meanwhile *I shall draw up my report*).

measure. The idioms are *in great measure* & *to a great extent.* In the following quotation they are confused: (WRONG) *Lord Curzon's policy has been overthrown by the present announcement, which* to a great measure *restores Bengal to her former greatness.* See CAST-IRON IDIOM.

measuredly. Three syllables.

media, n. pl., see MEDIUM.

medi(a)eval. The shorter spelling is recommended.

medicate makes *-cable.*

medicine. In US usually three syllables; in Brit. usually two (mĕ′dsn).

mediocre. Pron. mē′dĭoker.

Mediterranean. So spelled. As a common noun the word means of land, remote from coast; of water, landlocked.

medium. In the spiritualistic sense, the pl. is always *-ums.* In all other senses—(intervening or enveloping substance, element, liquid vehicle, means or agency) *-a* & *-ums* are both in use, & *-a* seems to be the commoner.

meerschaum. So spelled.

megrim. Pron. mē′-. The headache is usually *migraine* in US, *megrim* Brit. *Megrims,* low spirits, the 'blues.'

mein Herr. German for *Sir.* See also MYNHEER.

meiosis. (Pl. *-oses.*) Pron. mīō′sĭs. (Rhet.): 'lessening.' The use of understatement not to deceive, but to enhance the impression on the hearer. Often applied to the negative opposite illustrated under LITOTES, but taking many other forms, & contrasted with hyperbole. Very common in colloq. & slang English; the American *some* (*This is* some *war*), the schoolboy *decent* (=first rate &c.), & the strangely inverted hyperbole *didn't* half *swear* (=swore horribly), are familiar instances.

mélange. A mixture, a medley. Pron. mā länzh′.

melee. In US now so spelled, Brit. *mêlée.* If one accent is kept, the other must also be. Pron. mĕ lā.

melodic, melodious. The two are not synonymous, but are often so used. *Melodic* is contradistinguished from *harmonic: The melodic scale; a melodic minor.* A given musical composition may be both *melodic* & *melodious.* A voice, however, is *melodious.* To say a popular tune is *melodic* is a truism, in view of modern taste in music, but unhappily not all popular tunes are *melodious.* See MELODY.

melodrama is a term generally used with some contempt, because the appeal of such plays as are acknowledged to deserve the title is especially to the unsophisticated whose acquaintance with human nature is superficial, but whose admiration for goodness & detestation of wickedness is ready & powerful. The melodramatist's task is to get his characters labeled good & wicked in his audience's minds, & to provide striking situations that shall provoke & relieve anxieties on behalf of poetic justice. Whether a play is or is not to be called a melodrama is therefore often a doubtful question, upon which different critics will hold different opinions. The origin of the name is in a form of play intermediate between opera, in which all is sung, & drama, in which music has no essential part. The early melodrama was 'a form of dramatic musical composition in which music accompanied the spoken words & the action, but in which there was no singing . . . This is the source of romantic dramas depending on sensational incident with exaggerated appeals to conventional sentiment rather than on play of character, & in which *dramatis personae* follow conventional types—the villain, the hero wrongfully charged with crime, the persecuted heroine, the adventuress, &c. (Enc. Brit.) What the melodrama now so called inherits from the early form is the appeal to emotion; the emotional effect of musical accompaniment is obvious, & it is on emotional sympathy that melodrama still depends for success.

melody, harmony. Melody, as contradistinguished from harmony, means 'a series of single notes arranged in musically expressive succession.' Harmony, 'the combination of simultaneous notes so as to form chords.' (OED)

melt. *Molten* as in the verbal use (*will be molten* &c.) is now confined to poetry; as an adj. (*like molten glass* &c.) it can still be used without archaism, but only in literary contexts.

membership. The sense 'number of members' (of a club &c.) is, though not a very desirable one, more or less established (*The necessity of adding to the membership of the House;* A *large membership is necessary*). Much less desirable still is the extension from *number of members* to *members* (*The Committee being chosen from the* membership *of the two Houses./ The employers' proposals may be distasteful to a large section of our* membership). Needless substitution of the abstract for the concrete is one of the surest roads to flabby style.

memento. Pl. *-os* is recommended. (NOT *momento.*)

memorabilia, n., pl. (The sing. is rarely used.) Memorable things; things serving as record, or the record of such things.

memorandum. Pl. *-da* or *-dums.* Colloq. *memo* (pron. mĕm′ō, not mē′-).

ménage. The early meaning, members of a household, is now obs. In modern usage, household management, domestic establishment. Pron. me näzh, but see FRENCH WORDS.

mendacity, mendicity. The first is the conduct of a liar, the second that of a beggar.

-ment. For differences between this & *-ion,* see -ION & -MENT. The stems to which *-ment* is normally appended are those of verbs; freaks like *oddment* & *funniment* should not be made a precedent of; they are themselves due to misconception of *merriment,* which is not from the adj. but from an obs. verb *merry,* to rejoice.

mentality. *Mentality* is often thrust into the place of many old familiar words—*mind, idiosyncrasy, disposition, character, nerve, mood, intellect,* & a dozen others—for which it can possibly be made to do duty (e.g. *The* mentality *of the politician is a constant source of amazement to the engineer*). Other examples of it will be found in LOVE OF THE LONG WORD. Some like it because it is longer than *mind;* some because it is a VOGUE WORD; & some because it has a pseudo-scientific sound about it that may impress the reader; see POPULARIZED TECHNICALITIES. Its meaning while it had one of its own instead of many borrowed ones was purely intellectual power; or more often the preponderance of that over the other faculties (*An insect's very limited mentality./ Pope is too intellectual & has an excess of mentality*); in which senses *intellect*(*uality*) was far more common, so that *mentality* is a truly SUPERFLUOUS WORD.

menu. US usually mĕn′ū; Brit. mĕ′nōō.

Mephistopheles. The adj. is *Mephistophelean* (mĕfĭstŏfĭlē′-an) or *Mephistophelian* (mĕfĭstŏfē′lĭan): the second is more general & is recommended.

mercy. For *the tender mercies of,* see HACKNEYED PHRASES.

merit makes *-ited* &c. The adj. is *meritorious.* Although usually having the connotation of 'worth,' 'reward for excellence,' &c., the verb can also be used with punishment &c.: *He merited the censure he received.* (*Meretricious* is a completely unrelated word.)

mésalliance. The English form, *misalliance,* has been in good literary use for over 200 years. See FRENCH WORDS.

Messieurs. As the pl. for *Mr.,* pron. mĕs′erz. Abbrev. *Messrs.* (French, pron. mā′syû′.)

metamorphosis. Now usually accented on -mor′- but the more regular accent on -phō′- is still often heard. Pl. *-oses,* pron. (Eng.) -mor′fosēz, but Ovid's -fō′sēs.

METAPHOR. 1. Live & dead metaphor. In all discussion of metaphor it must be borne in mind that some metaphors are living, i.e. are offered & accepted with a consciousness of their nature as substitutes for their literal equivalents, while others are dead, i.e. have been so often used that speaker & hearer have ceased to be aware that the words used are not literal. Thus, in *The men were sifting meal* we have a literal use of *sift;* in *Satan hath desired to have you, that he may sift you as wheat, sift* is a live metaphor; in *the sifting of evidence,* the metaphor is so familiar that it is about equal chances whether *sifting* or *examination* will be used, & that a sieve is not present to the thought—unless indeed someone conjures it up by saying *All the evidence must first be sifted with acid tests,* or *with the microscope—;* under such a stimulus our metaphor turns out to have been not dead but dormant. The other word, *examine,* will do well enough as an example of the real stone-dead metaphor; the Latin *examino,* being from *examen,* the tongue of a balance, meant originally to weigh; but, though weighing is not done with acid tests or microscopes any more than sifting, *examine* gives no convulsive twitches, like *sift,* at finding itself in their company; *examine,* then, is dead metaphor, & *sift* only half dead, or three-quarters.

2. Some pitfalls: A. Unsustained metaphor: *He was still in the middle of* those 20 years *of neglect which only began* to lift *in* 1868. The plunge into metaphor at *lift,* which presupposes a mist, is too sudden after the literal 20 *years of neglect;* years, even gloomy years, do not lift./*The* means *of education* at the disposal *of the Protestants were* stunted & sterilized. The *means at the disposal of* names something too little vegetable or animal to consort with the metaphorical verbs. *Education* (personified) may be stunted, but *means* may not.

B. Overdone metaphor. The days are perhaps past when a figure was deliberately chosen that could be worked out with line upon line of relentless detail. The present fashion is rather to develop a metaphor only by way of burlesque. All that need be asked of those who tend to this form of satire is to remember that, while some metaphors do seem to deserve such treatment, the number of times that the same joke can safely be made, even with variations, is limited. The limit has surely been exceeded, for instance, with 'the long arm of coincidence'; *The author does not strain* the muscles of coincidence's arm *to bring them into relation./Then* the long arm of coincidence rolled up its sleeves & set to work *with a rapidity & vigor which defy description.*

Modern overdoing, apart from burlesque, is chiefly accidental, & results not from too much care, but from too little: *The most irreconcilable of landlords are beginning to recognize that we are* on the eve of the dawn of a new day.

C. Spoiled metaphor. The essential merit of real or live metaphor being to add vividness to what is to be conveyed, it need hardly be said that accuracy of detail is even more needed in metaphorical than in literal expressions; the habit of metaphor, however, & the habit of accuracy do not always go together: *Yet Jaures was the* Samson who upheld the pillars *of the Bloc./He was the very essence of cunning, & the* incarnation *of a book thief*. Samson's way with pillars was not to uphold them; & what is the incarnation of a thief? too, too solid flesh indeed!

D. Battles of dead metaphors. In *The Convenanters took up arms* there is no metaphor; in *The Covenanters flew to arms* there is one only—*flew to* for *quickly took up*—; in *She flew to arms in defense of her darling* there are two, the *arms* being now metaphorical as well as the *flying;* moreover, the two metaphors are separate ones; but, being dead ones, & also not inconsistent with each other, they lie together quietly enough. But dead metaphors will not lie quietly together if there was repugnance between them in life; e'en in their ashes live their wonted fires, & they get up & fight: *It is impossible to* crush *the Government's* aim *to restore the means of living & working freely. Crush* for *baffle, aim* for *purpose,* are both dead metaphors so long as they are kept apart; but the juxtaposition forces on us the thought that you cannot crush an aim./ *National military training is the* bedrock *on which alone we can hope* to carry through *the great struggles which the future may have in store for us. Bedrock & carry through* are both moribund or dormant, but not stone-dead./*They are* ciphers living under the shadow *of a great man.*

E. Mixed metaphors. For the example given in D, tasteless word selection is a fitter description than mixed metaphor, since each of the words that conflict with others is not intended as a metaphor at all. Mixed metaphor is more appropriate when one or both of the terms can only be consciously metaphorical. *This is not the time* to throw up the sponge, *when the enemy, already weakened & divided,* are on the run to a new defensive position. A mixture of prize ring and battlefield.

In the following extract from a speech it is difficult to be sure how many times metaphors are mixed; readers versed in the mysteries of oscillation may be able to decide: *No society, no community, can* place its house *in such a condition that it is* always on a rock, oscillating between *solvency & insolvency. What I have to do is to see that* our house is built upon a solid foundation, *never allowing the possibility of the Society's* life blood *being sapped. Just in proportion as you are careful in looking after* the condition *of your income, just in proportion as you* deal with them *carefully, will* the solidarity *of the Society's financial condition* remain intact. *Immediately you begin* to play fast & loose *with your income* the first blow *at your financial stability* will have been struck.

Writers who are on the defensive apologize for change & mixture of metaphors as though one was as bad as the other. The two things are in fact entirely different. A man may change his metaphors as often as he likes; it is for him to judge whether the result will or will not be unpleasantly florid; but he should not ask our leave to do it. If the result is bad, his apology will not mend matters, & if it is not bad no apology was called for. On the other hand, to mix metaphors, if the mixture is real, is an offense that should not have been apologized for, but avoided. Whichever the phrase, the motive is the same—mortal fear of being accused of mixed metaphor: *Time sifts the richest granary, & posterity is a dainty feeder. But Lyall's words, at any rate*—to mix the metaphor—*will escape the blue pencil even of such drastic editors as they.* Since all three metaphors are live ones, & *they* are the *sifter* & *the feeder*, the working of these into grammatical connection with *the blue pencil* does undoubtedly mix metaphors. But then our author gives us to understand that he knows he is doing it, & surely that is enough. Even so some liars reckon that a lie is no disgrace provided that they wink at a bystander as they tell it; even so those who are addicted to the phrase 'to use a vulgarism' expect to achieve the feat of being at once vulgar & superior to vulgarity. *Two of the* trump cards *played against the Bill are* (1) *that 'it makes every woman who pays a tax-collector in her own house,' &* (2) *that 'it will destroy happy domestic relations in hundreds of thousands of homes'; if we may at once* change our metaphor, *these are the* notes *which are most consistently* struck *in the* stream of letters, *now printed day by day for our edification in the Mail.* This writer need not have asked our leave to change from cards to music; he is within his rights, anyhow, & the odds are, indeed, that if he had not reminded us of the cards we should have forgotten them in the three intervening lines; but how did a person so sensitive to change of metaphor fail to reflect that it is ill playing the piano in the water? *a stream of letters*, it is true, is only a picturesque way of saying *many letters*, & ordinarily a dead metaphor; but once put your seemingly dead yet picturesque metaphor close to a piano that is being played, & its *notes* wake the dead—at any rate for readers who have just had the word *metaphor* called to their memories.

metaphysics & metaphysical are so often used as quasi-learned & vaguely depreciatory substitutes for various other terms, for *theory* & *theoretical, subtle(ty)*, (the) *supernatural, occult(ism)*, *obscure* & *obscurity, philosophy* & *philosophic, academic(s)*, & so forth, that it is pardonable to forget that they have a real meaning of their own. *Metaphysics* is the branch of philosophy that deals with the ultimate nature of things, or considers the questions, What is the world of things we know? &, How do we know it? 'Three kinds of definite answers are returned. *Metaphysical materialism* is the view that everything known is body or matter. *Metaphysical idealism* is the view that everything known is mind, or some mental state or other. *Metaphysical realism* is the intermediate view that everything known is either body or soul, neither of which alone exhausts the universe of being' (Prof. T. Case in Enc. Brit.). Such being the subject of Metaphysics, it is not wonderful, in view of the infinity of theories & subtlety of arguments evoked, that it should have come by some or all of the wrong acceptations mentioned above.

mete, n., boundary stone, limiting mark, remains alive chiefly in (legal & fig.) *metes & bounds.*

mete, v., to measure, is archaic or poetic; to allot, portion out (rewards, punishment), *to mete out justice,* is now chiefly literary.

metempsychosis (transmigration of souls). Pl. *-oses* (-ēz). Pron. mĕtĕmpsīkō′sĭs.

meter, metre. The instrument for measuring (*gas meter, water meter*) can be only *meter,* US or Brit. The word used of verse, music, or the metric system is usually US, *meter;* Brit., *metre.* (In the metric system the meter=39.37 inches.)

-meter. (Poet.): 'measure.' A little-used sense of the word *meter* is the unit (itself consisting sometimes of one foot, sometimes of two) that is repeated a certain number of times in a line of verse. But the compounds made from it—*monometer, dimeter, trimeter, tetrameter, pentameter, hexameter*—are in regular use as one part of the full technical names of meter (e.g. *iambic trimeter acatalectic*); the feet of which two & not one make a meter in this sense are the *iambus, trochee,* & *anapaest,* so that six iambi (or equivalents) make a trimeter, but six dactyls (or equivalents) make a hexameter.

methinks (methought), 'it seems to me'; see WORN-OUT HUMOR.

method. For *method in madness,* see IRRELEVANT ALLUSION.

methodic, -al. The usual adj. is the longer. There is a possible differentiation (*extensive & methodic inquiries; a methodical arrangement of detail*), but it is so slight that *methodic* might well be dropped as a NEEDLESS VARIANT.

meticulous. Originally meaning fearful, timid (now obs.), *meticulous* now means careful of minute details, overscrupulous (*labored mannerism & meticulous propriety*). In the collection of examples that follows, the first illustrates fairly the legitimate sense in which shrinking from any possible wrong element is the point; the last is ludicrous in that it excludes not merely the idea of fear, but even that of care; & the intermediate ones are arranged roughly in a descent from the less bad to the worse. RIGHT: *It will be good for the New Englanders to contemplate Mr. Joseph Southall's quiet* & meticulous craftsmanship. SUPERFLUOUS OR WRONG: *That on the French artillery, with its plea for* less meticulous care *& more simplicity in our own batteries, should be read & digested by . . ./Japanese writers have not yet acquired either the methods of our art criticism or* the meticulous attention *to detail which our habits* demand./*Mr. —, who has succumbed to the wounds inflicted upon him ten days previously by a pet lion, had his fate foretold with* meticulous accuracy *more than* 2000 *years ago by the greatest Greek dramatist.*

métier. One's trade, profession, or line; the field or occupation for which one is especially skilled or adapted. Pron.

mĕ′tyā. See FRENCH WORDS.

metonymy. (Rhet.): 'name-change.' Substitution of an attributive or other suggestive word for the name of the thing meant, as when the *Crown, Homer, wealth,* stand for the sovereign, Homer's poems, & rich people.

metre, -ter. See METER.

mettle. Orig. a variant of *metal,* now used exclusively in the fig. sense: quality of disposition, courage, spirit; *To put him on his mettle, try his mettle,* &c. Hence *mettlesome,* spirited.

mews, orig. a pl. (a mew was a cage for hawks while 'mewing,' i.e. molting; *the Mews,* the Royal stables, built on the site of the hawks' mew), now used freely as sing. with *a.* Modern usage, a row of stables, usually around an open yard; now also applied to a row of garages, studios, or houses built on the site of earlier mews.

mezzanine. A low story between two higher ones; usually between ground floor & second.

mezzo-rilievo (pl. *-os*) is the Italian spelling, & the corresponding pron. is mĕ′dzō rĭlyā′vō; if the spelling is, as often, corrupted to *rel-,* pron. mĕ′dzō rĭlē′vō.

mezzotint (engraving). Pron. *medz-.*

miaow, miaul. It is better to be content with *mew* & *caterwaul* than to multiply phonetic approximations.

Michelangelo (Michelagniolo Buonarroti, 1475–1564); in English pron. mī- (Italian, mē-). (Shaw always spelled *Michael Angelo,* as did many earlier writers.)

mickle & muckle are merely variants of the same word, & the not uncommon version *Many a mickle makes a muckle* is a blunder; the right forms are *Many a little* (or *Mony a pickle*) *makes a mickle* (or *muckle*), with other slight variations.

micro-, combining form meaning small; *microscope,* an instrument for magnifying minute objects. *Microcosm,* man (the small world) as the epitome of the universe. See MACRO-.

mid, prep., is literary or poetic for *amid;* better written *mid* than *'mid.*

middle. Middle class is hyphened as an adj. (*middle-class education*), but not as a noun (*belongs to the middle class*). *Middle age,* the period of middle life, makes *middle-aged,* adj. *The Middle Ages,* about 1000–1400, or in wider sense, 400 (or 600)–1500.

Middle West, Middle Western, are still preferred to *Midwest, Midwestern.* (But Sinclair Lewis uses *Middlewestern, -er.*)

middling(ly). The *-ly* is unusual & undesirable: *a middling good crop; did middling well; it went only middling.* See UNIDIOMATIC -LY.

midst, n. Now rare except following a prep., as *in the midst. In our* (*your, their*) *midst* (for *in the midst of us* &c.) is of fairly recent use and is still condemned by some, but is given without qualification by COD. Webster says 'its propriety has been much disputed.'

mien, air, bearing, manner, expressive of character or mood, is now a literary word: *a man of noble mien.* (As 'expression of the face, aspect,' it was erron. & is now obs.)

migraine is usual for the headache (US); MEGRIM Brit.

milage, mileage. There is no reason to keep the *e*, & COD gives *milage* only. OED & US dictionaries give *mileage* as the standard & *milage* as a variant.

milieu. Environment, (social) state of life. Pron. mē′lyû′.

militate. (Of facts, evidence, &c.): to have force, tell *against*, some conclusion or result (rarely *for*, or *in favor of*): *The whole history of science militates* against *such a conclusion./The same reasons that militated* in its favor *before, militate* for *it now.*

millenarian, of the, believer in the, millennium. So spelled, NOT *-nnarian.*

millennium. So spelled. Period of a thousand years, esp. that during which Christ is to reign in person on earth (Rev. xx: 1–5); hence any anticipated period of great happiness, goodness, &c.

milli-. A combining form meaning 1000; in the metric system, divided by 1000 (*kilo-*, multiplied by).

milliard means a thousand millions; it is chiefly a French term, though perhaps advancing in general currency. In France it is the equivalent in ordinary use for the mathematical French (which differs from the English) BILLION.

million. 1. *A million & a quarter, two million & a half,* better than *one & a quarter million(s)* & *two & a half millions;* see HALF.

2. *It is safe to say, therefore, that the total is considerably less than* 2½ millions *although it must be well over* 1½ million. This change from 2½ *millions* to 1½ *million* is wrong (see ONE) unless 1½ million is meant merely for the printed form that is to be said as 'a million & a half.' Otherwise, 1½ *millions.*

3. *Forty-five million people* rather than *forty-five millions of people* (on the analogy of *dozen, score, hundred, & thousand*); but, with *a few* & *many, millions of* is perhaps more usual.

4. *Among the eight* million *are a few* hundred *to whom this does not apply*—rather than *millions, hundreds;* but *He died worth three* millions rather than *million;* this because 'a million' is an established noun (as distinguished from a mere numeral) in the sense $1,000,000, but not in the sense a million people.

millionaire. So spelled (NOT *-nn-*).

milord. French word for an English lord or man of wealth & rank. Pron. mēlor′ (Brit.) or mĭ lord′ (US).

mimic, v., makes *-cked, -cking.*

minacious, minatory. Threatening, menacing. Both words smack of pedantry; but while the first is serviceable only for POLYSYLLABIC HUMOR, the second is not out of place in a formally rhetorical context. *A doctrine minatory to the armies of France.*

mince, v., makes *-ceable. Mincemeat* but *minced meat; mince pie.*

mine. *Your future & mine will both be affected;* but *my & your futures depend upon it;* see ABSOLUTE POSSESSIVES.

miniature. Picture in an illuminated MS.; small-scale portrait; reduced image; hence *in miniature,* on a small scale. The word has nothing to do with *minimus*, 'smaller,' but comes from an Italian word *miniature* from the Lat. root *miniare*, to color with minium. Its justifiable transf. & fig. use: *This stream contains many lovely miniature cascades;* but NOT *a miniature miss with dancing eyes.*

minimize. *Minimize* is both a rightly formed & a current word, but unfortunately current in more senses than it has any right to. It should be kept strictly to the limits imposed by its derivation from *minimus* (NOT less or little, but *least*), & therefore always mean either to reduce to the least possible amount (*We must minimize the friction*) or to put at the lowest possible estimate (*It is your interest to minimize his guilt*). The meanings given to *minimize* in the following quotations, i.e. reduce & underestimate, ignore the essential superlative element. WRONG: *The utility of our convoy would have been considerably* minimized *had it not included one of these./An open window or door would greatly* minimize *risk.*

minimum. Pl. usually *-ma.*

minion. A favorite: *minions of fortune;* opprobriously, a 'creature' of someone in power: *He helps himself from the treasury & allows his minion to do so too;* a servile dependent or an agent: *minions of the law.*

Minoan. Pron. mĭnō'-.

minor (in logic). See SYLLOGISM.

minority is like *majority*, only more so, in its meanings, with which odd tricks can be played. *Minority* means inferiority of number or fewerness or pauciority, (2) a party having a pauciority, & (3) less than half of any set of people. In a board of 51 a minority of one may be either 25 persons (1) or one person (2). The point need not be labored, but should be appreciated. There is a tacit convention, in the interests of lucidity, that adjs. naturally appropriate to magnitude shall not be used with *minority* (e.g. *vast, large*, &c.) to emphasize smallness of number, & another that *a minority of one* shall always mean one person. But the first is not always kept to: e.g. (WRONG) *With* a considerable minority *of the votes polled, the Party has obtained a clear & substantial majority over all other parties in the House.*

minotaur. Generally pron. mĭn'-.

minuscule. 'Somewhat smaller.' See UNCIAL.

minutia, n. sing. Pl. *-iae.* A precise detail; a small or trivial matter or doing. Pron. mĭnū'shĭa, -shĭē. The sing. is often wrongly used as a pl.: (WRONG) *All* those minutia *of daily living* (should be *minutiae*).

mirabile dictu, 'wonderful to relate.' Pron. mĭră'bĭlĭ dĭk'tŭ.

misalliance, though formed after the French *mésalliance*, is so natural an English word that it is free of the taint of gallicism, & should always be preferred to the French spelling.

misanthrope, a hater of mankind; *pessimist*, one who believes that reality (life) is essentially evil; *cynic*, one who believes that human conduct is motivated by self-interest.

miscellany. Pron. mĭ'sel*a*nĭ or

mĭsĕ′lanĭ; the OED & US dictionaries put the former first.

mise-en-scène. The scenery, properties, &c. of a play; hence, setting, milieu. Pron. mēzäɴ sâɴ′.

misogynist. A hater of women. Pron. usually -sŏj′- (sŏg- is academically better but seldom heard). *Misogamist,* a hater of marriage (always -sŏg′-, NOT sŏj-).

MISQUOTATION. The misquoting of phrases that have survived on their own merits out of little-read authors (e.g. of *Fine by degrees* &c. from Prior, usually changed to *Small* &c.) is a very venial offense; & indeed it is almost a pedantry to use the true form instead of so established a wrong one. It would be absurd to demand that no one should ever use a trite quotation without testing its verbal accuracy. But when a quotation comes from such a source as a well-known play of Shakespeare, or 'Lycidas,' or the Bible or Prayer Book, to give it wrongly at least requires excuse, & any great prevalence of such misquotation would prove us discreditably ignorant of our own literature. Nevertheless, such words as *A poor thing, but my own* are often so much more used than the true form that their accuracy is sure to be taken for granted unless occasional attempts are made to draw attention to them. A few of the more familiar misquotations are entered in their alphabetical places in the book.

Miss. *The Misses Smith* &c. is the old-fashioned pl., still used when formality is required, e.g. in printed lists of guests present &c.; elsewhere *the Miss Smiths* is now usual.

misshapen &c. The hyphen, formerly usual in compounds of *mis-* with words beginning with *s,* is disappearing in US, but still sometimes retained in Brit.

missive. An official letter; 'a somewhat high-flown equivalent of "letter"' (OED).

mistaken makes *-nness.*

mistral. Cold N.W. wind in Mediterranean provinces of France &c. Pron. mĭs′trăl or mĭsträl′.

miter, -re. Usually *-er* US; Brit. sometimes *-re.*

mitigate (to temper, to moderate) makes *-gable, -tor.*

mixed metaphor. See METAPHOR.

-M-, -MM-. Monosyllables ending in *m* double it before suffixes beginning with a vowel if it is preceded by a single vowel, but not if it is preceded by a diphthong or a doubled vowel or a vowel & *r: hammy, gemmed, dimmest, drummer;* but *claimant, gloomy, worming.* Words of more than one syllable follow the rule for monosyllables if their last syllable is a word in composition, as *bedimmed, overcramming,* but otherwise do not double the *m, diademed, emblematic; but* words ending in *-gram* double the *m;* compare *diagrammatic* with *systematic*).

mnemonic. Of, or designed to aid, the memory. Pron. nĕmŏn′ĭk.

moccasin. So spelled.

model makes *-led, -ling,* US; Brit. *-ll-.*

modern makes *-nness.*

modest. For *our modest home, a modest income, a modest but continuing sale,* see GENTEELISMS.

modicum. Small quantity. Pron. mŏd′-, NOT mōd-.

modus vivendi (lit. 'way of living') is any temporary compromise that enables parties to carry on pending settlement of a dispute that would otherwise paralyze their activities. Pron. mō′dus vĭvĕndī (or -dĭ).

Mogul. (Pron. -gŭl′.) *The Great Mogul,* emperor of Delhi. Hence, transf., any great personage, autocrat. For the spelling *Mughal* see DIDACTICISM.

Mohammed(an). So spelled.

Mohave or Mojave. Indians now *-have* (pron. mō hä′vē), but the *Mojave Desert.*

moiety (one of two equal parts; loosely 'about half'), apart from uses as a legal term & a FORMAL WORD, exists merely for the delight of the ELEGANT-VARIATIONIST in such triumphs as: *The candidate was returned by exactly* half *the number of votes polled, the other* moiety *being divided between a Labour & an Independent opponent.*

moire, moiré. *Moire,* or *moire antique,* is the name of the watered silk material; *moiré* is first an adj. meaning watered like *moire* (often of metal surfaces), & secondly a noun meaning watered surface or effect. *A moire dress; velvets & moire antiques; a moiré surface; the moiré has been improved by using the blowpipe.* Pron. mwahr, mwar′ā.

mold. The usual US spelling. See MOULD.

molecule, atom, electron, corpuscle. To the mere literary person without scientific knowledge, the relations of these words to each other are puzzling, & not easy to learn, even in an elementary way, from consulting each by itself in dictionaries. Here are the etymological meanings: *molecule,* small mass; *atom,* uncuttable (particle); *electron,* amber; *corpuscle,* small body. For modern differentiation, see ATOM.

mollusc, -k. US usually *mollusk,* Brit. *-llusc.*

molt, moult. The first usual US, the second Brit.

molten, adj. *Molten glass, a molten image, the molten material of his mind.* See MELT.

momentarily, momently. The first means for a moment (*he was momentarily abashed*), the second from moment to moment or every moment (*am momently expecting a wire from him*). The differentiation is well worth more faithful observance than it gets; & the substitution of either, which sometimes occurs, for *instantly* or *immediately* or *at once* is NOVELTY-HUNTING.

momentary, momentous. The first means lasting only for a moment, or transitory; the second means of moment, i.e. of great consequence.

momentum. Pl. usually *-ta.*

monachal, monastic, monkish. Each has its own abstract noun—*monachism, monasticism, monkery.* Of the three sets *monastic (ism)* is the one that suits all contexts; it is useful that *monkish* & *monkery* should also exist, as serving the purpose of those who wish to adopt a certain tone. *Monachal* & *monachism,* though they would have passed well enough if *monastic(ism)* did not exist & were not much better known, seem as it is to have no recommendation unless it is a good thing that scholars writing for scholars should have other names for things than those generally current, even though the meaning is the same. If that is, on the contrary, a bad thing, *monachal* & *monachism* should be allowed to die.

monadism, monism. Both terms owe their existence to the metaphysical problem of the relation between mind & matter. The view that regards mind & matter as two independent constituents of which the universe is composed is called *dualism.* In contrast with dualism, any view that makes the universe consist of mind with matter as a form of mind, or of matter with mind as a form of matter, or of a substance that in every part of it is neither mind nor matter but both, is called *monism* (see also METAPHYSICS). *Monadism* is the name given to a particular form of monism, corresponding to the molecular or atomic theory of matter, & holding that the universal substance (according to the third variety of monism described in the previous sentence) consists of units called *monads.*

monarchical, -chic, -chal, -chial. The first is the current form; *-chic* is occasionally used for antithetic purposes (*the monarchic, the aristocratic, & the democratic branches of the constitution*); *-chal* with a slight rhetorical difference, where *kingly* might serve (*the royal harangue has a certain monarchal tone*); *-ial* seems superfluous.

Monday. See FRIDAY.

moneyed, moneys, monied, monies. The first two are better. *Monies* is still occasionally used, however, for amounts of money: *Of the monies now due all but one or two will be collected on schedule.*

mongoose. Pl. *-ooses.*

mongrel. Pron. mŭng-.

monism. See MONADISM.

monk. Member of a male religious community living apart under vows of poverty, chastity, & obedience; monks are cloistered & carry on all their activities within the monastic establishment. For *monk* & *friar,* see FRIAR.

monogamous. Believing in but one marriage during life (now rare); in marriage to but one person at a time. Often mispronounced as if it were spelled *mona-.*

monologist. Webster gives mônŏl′ŏjĭst first, but both mŏn′ŏlŏgĭst (OED & many US dictionaries) & mŏnŏl′ōgĭst (COD) are more usual. The earlier spellings, *-guist* & *-gueist,* are now seldom seen in US or Brit.

monologue. (Lit.): 'sole speech.' This & *soliloquy* are precisely parallel terms of Greek & Latin origin; but usage tends to restrict *soliloquy* to talking to oneself or thinking aloud without consciousness of an audience whether one is in fact overheard or not, while *monologue,* though not conversely restricted to a single person's discourse that is meant to be heard, has that sense much more often than not, & is especially used of a talker who monopolizes conversation, or of a dramatic performance or recitation in which there is one actor only.

monotonic, -nous. The secondary sense of *monotonous* (same or tedious) has so nearly swallowed up its primary (of one pitch or tone) that it is well worth while to remember the existence of *monotonic,* which has the primary sense only.

Monroe Doctrine. Its status is that of a MANIFESTO, not that of a treaty or a piece of international law. Its name is taken from President Monroe, who in 1823 made a declaration to Congress to the effect that the American continents were no longer open to European political acquisition. The original policy, at least, had the official approval of Great Britain.

monseigneur, monsieur, monsignor, -ore. The first is a French title given esp. to princes & church & court dignitaries; pl. *messeigneurs* (pron. mŏn′sâ nyûr′, mĕsânyûrz′). *Monsieur* is the equivalent of *Mr., sir;* pl. *messieurs* (pron. mĕ syû′, mā syû′; abbr. *M., MM.* or *Messrs.*). *Monsignor* is a title given to prelates & officers of the Papal court (pron. mŏn sēn′yôr). *Monsignore,* the Italian form of *Monsignor* (pron. -ēnyor′ē, pl. *-ori,* pron. -yorē).

monsoon. Periodic wind in S. Asia, esp. in the Indian Ocean; also the seasons accompanying it. (Accent 2nd syl.)

mood. The grammar word (*indicative, subjunctive, imperative, mood*) has nothing to do with the native word meaning frame of mind &c., & is merely a variant of *mode.*

moral, adj. Morals are the practice of ethics; hence *moral ideas, a moral life.* For distinctions between *moral, ethical, morals,* & *ethics,* see ETHICAL 5. *Moral victory* is often applied to an event that is from another point of view a defeat; *moral certainty* is always applied to what is in fact an uncertainty. Though this peculiar sense of *practical* or *virtual* in combination with *certainty* is hard to account for, it is established as idiomatic.

moral(e), n. The addition of an *e* to the French word *moral* to distinguish it in meaning & pronunciation from the English *moral* is frowned upon by many purists. *Morale* is now established, however, & its usefulness is obvious.

morass. A marsh, bog. Pron. -ass′.

moratorium. A legal period during which payments may be postponed; also transf. & fig. Pl. *-ia,* sometimes *-ums.*

more. (1) *The more.* Idiomatic uses: *The more the merrier. A is more careful than B; of the two B is the more careful. As the hour approached I grew the more nervous.* But for limitations on the use of *the more,* see THE. (2) RIGHT: *It is impossible to do it under a year, much* more *in six months. Social considerations, still* more *considerations of mere wealth, must not be allowed to outweigh military efficiency.* But for the common confusion between *much more* & *much less,* see ILLOGICALITIES, LESS, & MUCH. (3) *More than one,* though its sense is necessarily pl., is treated as a sort of compound of *one,* following its construction, & agrees with a sing. noun & takes a sing. verb; *More than one workman* was *killed,* NOT *workmen* or *were.* (4) For *more in sorrow than in anger,* see HACKNEYED PHRASES. (5) WRONG: *The new dock scheme affects the whole of the northern bank of the Thames in* a more or less *degree.* This is wrong because, though *a less de-*

gree is English, *a more degree* is not. (6) *More like* for *nearer* is colloq. or slang (e.g. *What I finally collected was* more like *ten than a hundred*). (7) Some adjectives are by their very meaning absolute & therefore cannot be modified: *unique*=having no like or equal; hence, *A* more unique *person I never saw* is an INCOMPATIBLE. So also *outstanding, essential, perfect*, &c., each mentioned in its alphabetical place. This rule is often broken colloq. & in informal writing, occasionally in formal (*in order to form* a more perfect *union*), but if it is to be done it should be deliberate, for effectiveness, not through carelessness. (8) Most adjectives & adverbs of more than one syllable & all of more than two normally form their comparatives with *more* rather than *-er*. A few monosyllables (e.g. *right, just*) also form their comparatives in this way; some allow of either *more* or *-er:* e.g. *true, busy, often*. See -ER, -EST.

mores. (Lat.) n. pl. Customs, esp. established folkways that have ethical significance; conventions that have the force of law. Pron. mō′rēz. A word useful to sociologists but often used in general contexts where *customs* or *manners* would be as accurate & more readily understood. See POPULARIZED TECHNICALITIES.

Mormon. Member of the Church of Jesus Christ of Latter-day Saints, founded by Joseph Smith (in N.Y.) in 1830; *the Book of Mormon*, divine revelations translated by Smith.

Morpheus. Properly pron. Môr′fūs (popularly often mor′-fē ŭs); the god of dreams (NOT sleep). *In the arms of Morpheus*, see BATTERED ORNAMENTS.

mortal. For *all that was mortal of*, & *the mortal remains of*, see HACKNEYED PHRASES, & STOCK PATHOS.

mortician. An unfortunate (professional) US GENTEELISM for *undertaker* (see BARBARISMS).

mortgagee, -ger, -gor. *The mortgagee* is the person who lends money on the security of an estate, the *mortgager* or *-or* the person who pledges his property in order to get the loan. But, as the owner of a mortgaged estate is often himself described as 'mortgaged up to the eyes' &c., & as *-ee* suggests the passive & *-or* & *-er* the active party, those who are not familiar with the terms are apt to have the meanings reversed in their minds. The *-or* spelling is standard in US (& OED); *-er* is given first in COD.

Moslem, Muslim. The first is the ordinary English form. For correcting it to *Muslim*, see DIDACTICISM. *Moslem* can be used as adj. or as noun, & the pl. of the noun is preferably *-ms*, but sometimes the same as the sing.; the use of the pl. *Moslemin* or *Muslimin* is bad didacticism.

mosquito. Both *-oes* & *-os* are used as the pl.; *-os* is recommended.

most. For the use of *most* in forming the superlative of adjs. & advs., see MORE 8.

mostly. See UNIDIOMATIC -LY. The only idiomatic sense of *mostly* is for the most part. (*The goods are mostly sent abroad./Twenty-seven millions, mostly fools.*) But it is often wrongly used for *most;* WRONG: *The internecine conflict has* *largely killed sentiment for any of the factions, & the Powers* mostly concerned *have simply looked on with a determination to localize the fighting.*

mot. 'Word.' Pron. mō. The *mot juste* has the disadvantage that you can find examples of it, if you want to know more about it, neither in French dictionaries (at any rate, not in *Littré*) nor in English, & must be content to associate it vaguely with Flaubert. *Mot* in French means both *word* & a (pithy & witty) *saying. Mot juste,* a pithy saying, phrase (or word occasionally), expressing the most precise shade of the meaning intended; the 'perfect expression.' See FRENCH WORDS.

mother-of-pearl, -o'-pearl. The dictionaries favor the *of* form; but *o'* gives the usual pronunciation, & perhaps is what most people would print if the compositors would let them.

motif. Pron. mōtēf'. Salient feature, esp. theme, in literature & the fine arts (in music, however, most musicologists prefer *motive,* perhaps because of possible confusion with *leitmotiv*). *Motif* should not be used in other ordinary contexts in place of *motive.* See FRENCH WORDS.

motion picture(s) seems to be established as the preferred formal term in US (*cinema* is still used in Brit.); *moving picture(s)* is colloq.; *movies,* slang.

motive. (1) UNIDIOMATIC: *The victorious party has* every motive in claiming *that it is acting not against the Constitution, but in its defense.* An or *every interest* in *doing,* but *a* or *every motive* for *doing.* See ANALOGY, & CAST-IRON IDIOM. (2) For the use of *motivation* in contexts in which the simpler & older *motive* would be the normal word (*There was* no motivation *for such an attack*), see LOVE OF THE LONG WORD.

motto, in the sense of *maxim,* is one adopted as a rule of conduct. Pl. *-oes.*

mould. In US the older form, *mold,* is established. The three common words so spelled (shape, n. & v.; earth; fungous growth) are probably all unconnected; but the identity of form has no doubt caused the second to be tinged with the meaning of the third, & the original notion of powdery earth has had associated with it the extraneous one of rottenness.

moustache is the usual Brit. spelling, *mustache* US. The accent, traditionally on the second syllable, is now (US) often on the first.

mouth. Pron. the *-th* in the verb, & the pl. of the noun, as in *both;* that in *foul-mouthed* &c. as the *-th* in *then.*

mouthful. Pl. *-ls.*

move makes *-vable,* NOT *-veable.*

mow, v. The p.p., when used as an adj., should be *mown* (*the mown,* NOT *mowed, grass; new-mown* &c.); when it is verbal, both forms are current (*The lawn was mown,* or *mowed, yesterday*).

M.P. (also other initials used in place of nouns, G.I., U.N., &c.). Four forms are wanted: ordinary sing., ordinary pl., possessive sing., & possessive pl. Those recommended are: M.P. (*He is an M.P.*); M.P.s (*M.P.s now travel free*); M.P.'s (*What is your M.P.'s name?*); M.P.s' (*What about income tax & M.P.s' salaries?*).

MS. *Manuscript.* Pl. MSS. (NOT Ms.; NOT ital.)

much. 1. *Much* & *very*. RIGHT: *Attic taste is* much celebrated by *the poets,* but *He is* very celebrated; *The Government,* much worried, *withdrew the motion,* but A very worried *official; You seem* much annoyed, but *His tone was* very annoyed. For the use of *much* rather than *very* with participles (*much pleased* &c.), see VERY.

2. *Much more* & *much less*. The advs. *more* & *less* are used in combination with *much* or *still* to convey that a statement that is being or has been made about something already mentioned applies more forcibly yet to the thing now to be mentioned. RIGHT: *The abbreviating,* much more *the garbling, of documents does great harm./ Garbling was not permitted,* much less *encouraged.* The choice between *more* & *less* is under some circumstances a matter of difficulty. With sentences that are affirmative both in effect & in expression it is plain sailing; *much more* is invariable. With sentences that are negative in expression as well as in effect there is as little doubt; *much less* is invariable: *I did not even see him,* much less *shake hands with him.* It is when the effect is negative, but the expression affirmative, even if technically affirmative only, that doubts arise. The meaning of *technically,* & the distinction between effect & expression, must be made clear. *It will be a year* before *it is done;* the effect of that is negative, since it means that the thing will not be finished in less than twelve months; but its expression is affirmative, there being no negative word in it. *It is* not *possible to do it* under *a year;* the effect & the expression of that are obviously both negative. *It is* impossible *to do it under a year;* the effect of that is negative, but the expression is technically affirmative. Though the difference in meaning between the last two is undiscoverable, the difference of expression decides between *more* & *less*. RIGHT: *It is* not possible *to do it under a year,* much less *in six months; It is* impossible *to do it under a year,* much more *in six months.* What governs the decision is the right words required to fill up the ellipsis: *It is not possible to do it under a year, much less (is it possible to do it) in six months; It is impossible to do it under a year, much more (is it impossible) to do it in six months.* In the following quotations *more* should have been written instead of *less:* (WRONG) *It is a full day's work even to open,* much less *to acknowledge, all the presents which arrive on these occasions.* Expression fully affirmative./ *But of real invention & spontaneity,* much less *anything approaching what might be classed as inspiration, there is little enough.* Expression technically affirmative./*I confess myself altogether unable to formulate such a principle,* much less *to prove it.* Less *unable* to prove it?

muchly. Obs. except as slang or WORN-OUT HUMOR.

muck-rake. Orig. in Bunyan's *Pilgrim's Progress,* 'the Mare with a Muck-rake,' i.e. searching for worldly gain. Used as a verb by Theodore Roosevelt (1906)=to seek out habitual corruption in public men & corporations. Hence *muckraker* (usually derog.), one who seeks out & publicizes such corruption, often for sensational appeal or selfish interest.

mucous, -cus. The first is the adj., the second the noun; *mucous membrane.*

mugwump. (1) A chief (among the Algonkian Indians); hence a conceited or self-consequential person. (2) A bolter from the Republican party in 1884 (so called by the journalists because most of the bolters were influential Republicans 'suffering from superiority complexes,' according to Mencken); hence an independent voter.

mulatto. US, pl. usually *-oes,* Brit. *-os.* By definition, any person of a mixed race (from *mule*). As used in US, the first generation offspring of a pure Negro & a white person; loosely, any person of mixed Caucasian & Negro blood. Brit., the offspring of a European & a Negro.

mumps. Usually treated as sing.

Munchausen (Baron). Hero of a book of extravagantly improbable adventure travels by Rudolph Eric Raspe, 1785. Pron. -chaw′zn.

murk, mirk. Darkness, gloom. Now archaic, poet., or dial. *The murk & the rain; the land of murk & mist.* (*Murk* is preferred.) So *murky.*

Muses. The nine were daughters of Zeus & Mnemosyne (nĕmŏz′ĭnē), Memory. Their names & provinces are: *Clio,* history; *Melpomene* (-ŏ′mĭnĭ), tragedy; *Thalia* (-ī′ă), comedy; *Euterpe* (-pĭ), music; *Terpsichore* (-ĭ′korĭ), dance; *Erato* (ĕ′ra-), lyric; *Calliope* (-ī′opĭ), epic; *Urania,* astronomy; *Polyhymnia,* rhetoric.

museum. Pl. *-ms.* (Stress 2nd syl.)

musicale. Chiefly US & fortunately losing its popularity.

Muslim. Use MOSLEM.

mussel, bivalve. So spelled.

Mussulman. A Mohammedan. Pl. *-ans,* not *-en,* the last syllable not being the English word *man.* It is perhaps to impartial dislike of the incorrect *-men* & the queer *-mans* that the comparative disuse of *Mussulman* is due; the pl. is needed at least as often as the sing., & *Mohometan, Mohammedan,* & *Moslem,* being resorted to for the pl., get the preference in the sing. also.

must, need. The following questions with their positive & negative answers illustrate a point of idiom: *Must it be so? Yes, it must; No, it need not./ Need I do it? No, you need not; Yes, you must.* But *you must not infer . . . , you must never complain.*

mustache. So spelled in US.

mustachio. Pl. *-os. Mustachio* is now archaic for *mustache,* but the adj. derived from it is often preferred to the other; spell *mustachioed.*

muster. *Pass muster* is one of the many idioms that must be taken as they are or left alone. WRONG: *The general condition of these women* [the WAVES] *would pass* a very fair muster. *Muster* in this phrase means *inspection* & should not be modified.

MUTE E. Uncertainty prevails about the spelling of many inflexions & derivatives formed from words ending in mute *e.* Is this *-e* to be retained, or omitted? The only satisfactory rule, exceptions to which are very few, is this: When a suffix is added to a word ending in mute *e,* the mute *e* is dropped before a vowel but not before a consonant.

The chief exception is that *e* remains even before a vowel when the soft sound of *c* or *g* is to be made possible (as before *-able*) or to be insisted on (as in distinguishing the participles of *singe* & *sing*).

A second exception, less justifiable, is that of the power (most arbitrarily & inconsistently exercised at present) of indicating the sound of an earlier vowel by insertion or omission of the *e* (*mileage* for fear that *milage* may be pronounced mĭl-). There are no other general exceptions; *duly, truly,* & *wholly* are individual ones merely; *hieing* is specially so spelled to avoid consecutive *i*'s, much as *clayey* has an *e* actually inserted to separate two *y*'s; & *gluey, bluey,* are due to fear that *gluy, bluy,* may be pronounced after *buy* & *guy.* Words about which there is any question of retaining or dropping the *e* are entered in their dictionary places.

mutual is a well-known trap. The essence of its meaning is that it involves the relation, *x is or does to y as y to x* (*they are mutual well-wishers*); & NOT the relation, *x is or does to z as y to z* (*a country that is our mutual enemy,* i.e. an enemy of both the US & Britain); from which it follows that *our mutual friend Jones* (meaning Jones who is your friend as well as mine), & all similar phrases, are misuses of *mutual.* In such places *common* is the right word, & the use of *mutual* betrays ignorance of its meaning. It should be added, however, that *mutual* was formerly used much more loosely than it now is, & that the OED, giving examples of such looseness, goes no further in condemnation than 'Now regarded as incorrect . . . Commonly censured as incorrect, but still often used in the collocations *mutual friend, mutual acquaintance,* on account of the ambiguity of *common.*' Webster says, 'this use is now avoided by careful writers.' The Dickens title has no doubt much to do with the currency of *mutual friend.*

Another fault is of a different kind, betraying not ignorance but lack of the taste or care that should prevent one from saying twice over what it suffices to say once. This happens when *mutual* is combined with some part of *each other,* as in: *It is this fraternity of men serving a common cause,* mutually comprehending each other's *problems & difficulties, & respecting* each other's *rights & liberties, which is the foundation of the structure.* The sole function of *mutual*(*ly*) is to give the sense of some part of *each other* when it happens to be hard to get *each other* into one's sentence; if *each other* not only can be, but is, got in, *mutual* is superfluous; in the quotation it adds nothing whatever, & is the merest tautology.

A few bad specimens follow: *The ring was* mutually *chosen by* the Duke & Lady Elisabeth *last Wednesday./They have affinities beyond a* mutual admiration *for Mazzini.*/Mutual *exchange of prisoners.*

For the distinctions between *mutual* & *reciprocal,* see RECIPROCAL.

my. For *my* & *your work* &c. (NOT *mine*), see ABSOLUTE POSSESSIVES.

Mycenaean. The pre-Greek civilization in the Mediterranean area, *c.*1000–1100 B.C. Pron. mī sê nē′*an*.

mynheer, mein Herr, Herr. The first is Dutch & can mean *gentleman, sir,* or *Mr.;* the second is German for *sir;* the third is German for *gentleman* & *Mr.*

myopic. Near-sighted; also, fig. shortsighted. Pron. mīŏ′pĭc (but mīō′pĭă). Fig.: *The correspondent is typical of those who have mental myopia.*

myriad (n. & adj.) is generally used of a great but indefinite number; but it is well to remember that its original sense, still occasionally effective, is ten thousand. It is used in both sing. & pl.: *myriad of planets; the moon and the starry myriad that attend her; a myriad of infinitesimal bells; its myriad progeny.* (Chiefly poet. or rhet.)

myself. *I saw it myself* (i.e. I was an eyewitness). *I myself am doubtful* (I, for my part, . . .); *I am not myself* (not in my normal health, state of mind, &c.); idiomatic colloquially, *Enough to make a better man than myself run into madness;* WRONG: *one of the party & myself.*

mystic has been much slower than *mysterious* in becoming a popular word & thereby losing its definitely spiritual or occult or theological implications. Everything that puzzles one has long been called *mysterious* (who committed the latest murder, for instance), but not *mystic.* It is very desirable that *mystic* should be kept as long as possible from such extensions. Unfortunately the NOVELTY-HUNTERS, tired of *mysterious,* have now got hold of it: *But I don't want to be* mystic, *& you shall hear the facts & judge me afterwards.*

mystic, mystical. By definition, the two words are in many senses truly interchangeable, but there is a difference in feeling & overtone; spiritual, allegorical, or symbolical: *the* mystic *union of the soul with Christ; the* mystical *body of Christ;* occult, esoteric: *the* mystic *rites of initiation; a* mystical *cloud of smoke. Mystical,* not *mystic,* is now used in reference to theological mysticism: *The basis of whose life* [St. Paul's] *was profoundly* mystical.

mystifiedly. A bad form.

myth is a word introduced into English in the 19th c. as a name for a form of story characteristic of primitive peoples & thus defined by OED: 'A purely fictitious narrative usually involving supernatural persons, actions, or events, & embodying some popular idea concerning natural or historical phenomena.' By those who wish to mark their adherence to this original sense the word is still sometimes pronounced mīth. But the meaning popularly attached to the word is little more than a tale devoid of truth, or a nonexistent person or thing or event; always in these senses & usually even in the original one, the pronunciation is mĭth.

N

n. *To the nth.* As a mathematical symbol *n* means an unspecified number. It does not mean an infinite number, nor the greatest possible number, nor necessarily even a large number, but simply the particular number that we may find ourselves concerned with when we come to details; it is short for 'one or two or three or whatever the number may be.' It follows that the common use of *to the nth* for 'to the utmost possible extent' (*The Neapolitan is an Italian* to the nth *degree*) is wrong. It is true that sentences can be constructed in which the popular & the mathematical senses are reconciled (*Though the force were increased* to the nth, *it would not avail*), & here, no doubt, the origin of the misuse is to be sought. Those who talk in mathematical language without knowing mathematics go out of their way to exhibit ignorance. See POPULARIZED TECHNICALITIES.

nadir. The point of the heavens opposite to the zenith, i.e. directly under the observer. Hence, fig., lowest point, time of greatest depression: *the nadir of wickedness, of his career.* Pron. nā′dēr.

naiad. Nymph of river or spring; water nymph. Pron. nī′ad. Pl. *-ds* or *-des* (-dēz).

naïf, naïve. *Naïve* is now the prevalent spelling, & the use of *naïf* (either in all contexts or whenever the gender is not conspicuously feminine) is usually a conscious correction of other people's supposed errors.

naïve, naïveté, naive, naivety. The slowness with which the naturalization of the words has proceeded is curious & regrettable, for they deserve a warm welcome as supplying a shade of meaning not provided by the nearest single English words. The OED definition, for instance, 'Natural, unaffected, simple, artless,' and Webster's 'Ingenuous, unsophisticated' clearly omit elements—the actor's unconsciousness & the observer's amusement—that are essential to the ordinary man's idea of *naïveté.* Unconsciously & amusingly simple; *naïve* means not less than that, & is therefore a valuable word. Although most dictionaries give *naïve* first (pron. nä ēv′) many by this time write *naive* (& some call it nāv); but *naivety,* though it was used by Hume & other 18th-c. writers, has not yet made much headway against *naïveté* (pron. nä ev′tā′).

name. (1) The recent (US) use of *name* as an adj. (=recognized, front-rank), as in *name writers, a name brand,* is at best colloq. and reflects the success of publicity and the best-seller lists. (2) *By name* is an idiom going back to 900; *a man by the name of John* is now chiefly US (why not *a man named John?*). (3) *Given name* is normal US but rare in Brit.; *first name,* US & Sc. (4) The fig. use of *middle name* (*obstinacy is his middle name*) is slang but often effective. (5) The traditional idiom is *named after* (but US, *for*) *his grandfather.* (6) *Name* makes *namable.*

naphtha. So spelled. Pron. năf-, not năp-.

narcissus. Pl. *-ssuses* or *-ssi.* The noun, used chiefly in Psych., is *narcissism.*

narcosis. Pl. *-oses* (-ō′sēz).

nasal. (Gram.): 'of the nose.' Sounds requiring the nose passage to be open, as in English those of *m, n,* & *ng,* are so called. For *nasal organ* see PEDANTIC HUMOR.

nature. 1. Periphrasis: The

word is a favorite with the lazy writers who prefer glibness & length to conciseness & vigor. *The accident was caused* through the dangerous nature *of the spot.* The other way of putting this would be *The accident happened because the spot was dangerous./It must not be supposed that when we speak of Mr. —— as unwilling to snatch at office we are suggesting any feeling of* a converse nature *in Mr. ——.* 'Any feeling of a converse nature' means the converse (or rather, perhaps, the opposite) feeling. It is true that *nature* slips readily off the tongue or pen in such contexts, but the temptation should be resisted; see PERIPHRASIS.

2. *One touch of nature makes the whole world kin.* What Shakespeare meant was: There is a certain tendency natural to us all, viz. that specified in the following lines (of *Troilus & Cressida,* III. iii. 176–9), which is, so far as one word may express it, *fickleness.* What is meant by those who quote him is: A thing that appeals to simple emotions evokes a wonderfully wide response. This is both true & important; but to choose for the expression of it words by which Shakespeare meant nothing of the kind is unfair both to him & to it. That the first words of a cynicism appropriately put in the mouth of the Shakespearian Ulysses should be the stock quotation for the power of sympathy is an odd reversal.

naught, nought. COD makes no distinction between the two, & OED & Webster give *naught* for the cipher, all other uses *nought.* ACD gives *naught* for all uses, *nought* only a variant. It would seem that the choice must be up to the writer.

Navaho, Navajo. Indians, blanket, &c. Pron. nȧ′vahō. Although *-jo* is the earlier (Span.) spelling (*Apaches de Navajo*), *-ho* is given first in most recent dictionaries.

Nazi, Nazism. Pron. -ts- (in Brit. often -z-). *Naziism* is now less usual.

near is both adv. (followed by *to*) & prep. (no *to*); in the literal sense of *close to,* the prep. is perhaps more common: *Don't come near me; he stood near the door.* But *she is nearer* to *heaven; near and dear* to *us.*

near(ly). The use of *near* in the sense of *nearly* (*Not* near *so often;* near *dead with fright;* near *a century ago*) has been so far affected by the vague impression that adverbs must end in *ly* as to be obsolescent (see UNIDIOMATIC -LY). Those who still say *near* for *nearly* are suspected, if provincialism & ignorance are both out of the question, of pedantry; it is a matter in which it is wise to bow to the majority.

near by (also *near-by, nearby*) is an Americanism, & one becoming increasingly popular, for *close by, neighboring.* The spelling *nearby,* although given preference by Webster, ACD, &c., is not accepted by many US writers (or publishers). RECOMMENDED *A* near-by *farmhouse; a farmhouse* near by.

nebula. Pl. *-lae.*

necessarily. Stress first syllable (but *necessar′ily* is often heard for emphasis in US).

necessary. For *essential, necessary,* & *requisite,* see ESSENTIAL.

necessitarian. One who believes that all action is determined by a sequence of causes & who therefore denies free will; *determinism* is the more usual word in general philosophy. *Necessarian* should be regarded as a NEEDLESS VARIANT.

necro-. Combining form meaning *corpse,* hence *death: necrology,* death role, obituary notice(s); *necropolis,* cemetery. *Necromancy* (art of predicting by means of communicating with the dead) was early confused with the root *nigro,* black, & thus took on the meaning *black magic;* hence magic in general, conjuration.

nectar has kept the word makers busy in search of its adjective; *nectareal, nectarean, nectareous,* &c., have all been given a chance. Milton, with *nectared, nectarine,* & *nectarous,* keeps clear of the four-syllabled forms in which the accent is drawn away from the significant part; & we might do worse than let him decide for us.

née, fem., 'born.' *Mrs.* or *Jane Smith, née Gray* (NOT *née Jane Gray;* she was born with the family name only; the other was given later). The masc. form *né* is much less usual, but *Jane Austen's brother, Edward Knight, né Austen.*

need. The rules for the use of *need* instead of *needs* & *needed* are: It is used only in interrogative & negative sentences; in such sentences it is more idiomatic than the normal forms, which are, however, permissible. If *need* is preferred, it is followed by infinitive without *to,* but *needs* & *needed* require *to* before their infinitive. Idiomatic form, *They* need not be *counted;* normal form, *They* did not need to be *counted,* or *They* needed not to be *counted;* WRONG FORMS: *They* need not to *be counted; They* needed not (or *did not need*) be *counted.* The following extracts suffice to show the lapses in grammar or idiom that may occur with *need.* WRONG: *He seems to think that the bridgehead was abandoned earlier than* need *have been.* This looks like some confusion between the verb & the noun *need;* at least the two right ways of putting it would be (a) *earlier than it* (i.e. the bridgehead) *need have been* (sc. abandoned), where *need* is the verb, & (b) *earlier than need was* (sc. to abandon it), where *need* is the noun./*It was assumed that the reserves had been used up and* need no longer to be taken *into account as a uniform, effective body.* The writer has missed the point of idiom that, while *needs* & *needed* are ordinary verbs followed by infinitive with *to,* the abnormal *need* is treated as a mere auxiliary, like *must,* requiring no *to; the reserves needed no longer to be taken,* or *did not need any longer to be taken,* but *need no longer be taken, into account.*

needle. *A needle in a bottle of hay* is the right wording (Matt. XIX.24), *bottle* being an old word, now dial. only, for *bundle;* it is often mistaken for a mistake, & changed to *bundle of hay* (or *in a haystack*).

needless to say. Since this always prefaces something that the speaker or writer has determined to say anyway, it often suggests either arrogance or foolhardiness.

NEEDLESS VARIANTS. Though it savors of presumption for any individual to label words *needless*, it is certain that words deserving the label exist; the question is which they are, & who is the censor that shall disfranchise them. Natural selection does operate, in the worlds of talk & literature; but the dictionaries inevitably lag behind. It is perhaps, then, rather a duty than a piece of presumption for those who have had experience in word-judging to take any opportunity of helping things on by irresponsible expressions of opinion. In this book, therefore, reference is made regarding many words that either are or ought to be dead, but have not yet been buried, to the present article or to that called SUPERFLUOUS WORDS. Those only belong here which can be considered by-forms differing merely in suffix or in some such minor point from other words of the same stem & meaning. Sometimes the mere reference has been thought sufficient; more often short remarks are added qualifying or explaining the particular condemnation. Here the general principle may profitably be laid down that it is a source not of strength, but of weakness, that there should be two names for the same thing, because the reasonable assumption is that two words mean two things, & confusion results when they do not. On the other hand, it may be much too hastily assumed that two words do mean the same thing; they may, for instance, denote the same object without meaning the same thing if they imply that the aspect from which it is regarded is different, or are appropriate in different mouths, or differ in rhythmic value or in some other matter that may escape a cursory examination. To take an example or two: it is hard to see why *necessarian* & *necessitarian*, or *hydrocephalic* & *hydrocephalous*, should coexist & puzzle us to no purpose by coexisting; but it would be rash to decide that *dissimulate* was a needless variant for *dissemble* on the grounds that it means the same & is less used & less clearly English, without thinking long enough over it to remember that *simulate* & *dissimulation* have a right to be heard on the question.

Some of the words under which reference to this article is made (not always concerning the title word itself): *acquaintanceship, blithesome, burden, chivalry, competence, complacence, concomitance, corpulence, debark, depicture, diminishment, direful, dissemble, infinitude, quieten.*

negative. 'The answer is in the negative' is Parliament language, but deserves much severer condemnation (as a pompous PERIPHRASIS for *No, sir*) than most of the expressions described as unparliamentary language.

NEGATIVE & AFFIRMATIVE IN PARALLEL CLAUSES. Of actual blunders, as distinguished from lapses of taste & style, perhaps the commonest, & those that afflict their author when he is detected with the least sense of proper shame, are various mishandlings of negatives. Writers who appear educated enough to know whether a sentence is right or wrong will put down the opposite of what they mean, or something different from what they mean, or what means nothing at all, apparently quite satisfied so long as the reader can be trusted to make a shrewd guess at what they ought to have said instead of taking them at their word. It is parallel clauses that especially provide opportunities for going wrong, the problem being to secure that if both are negative the negative force shall not be dammed up in one alone, & conversely that if one only is to be negative the negative force shall not be free to spill over into the other. Some classified specimens of failure to secure these essentials may put writers on their guard. The corrections appended are designed rather as proofs of the error than as satisfactory, or at any rate as the best, emendations.

1. If you start with a negative subject you may forget on reaching the second clause to indicate that the subject is not negative there also. WRONG: No lots *will therefore be put on one side for another attempt to reach a better price, but*‸must *be sold on the day appointed* (but *all* must be sold). *Very few people* even got out *of bed*, &‸went *through their ordeal by fire as an inescapable fate* (& *the majority* went). Neither editor nor contributors *are paid*, but‸are *moved to give their services by an appreciation of the good work* (but *all* are).

2. You may use negative inversion in the first clause, & forget that the second clause will then require to be given a subject of its own because the inversion has imprisoned the original subject. WRONG: *Not only* was Lord Curzon's Partition detested *by the people concerned*, but‸was *administratively bad* (*it* was)./*In neither case* is this due *to the Labour Party*, but to *local Socialist aspirations* (This is due in neither case).

3. Intending two negative clauses, you may enclose your negative between an auxiliary & its verb in the first & forget that it cannot then act outside its enclosure in the second. WRONG: *There is scarcely a big hotel which* has not sunk *a well deep into the chalk* & is drawing *its own supply of water from the vast store* (& succeeded in drawing; if *has* continues, *not* does so with it)./*No scheme run by civil servants sitting in an office is likely to succeed if these gentlemen* have not *themselves lived on the land*, & *by experience* are able *to appreciate actual conditions of agriculture* (& learned to appreciate).

4. Conversely, intending a negative & an affirmative clause, you may so fuse your negative with a construction common to both clauses that it carries on to the second clause when not wanted. WRONG: *These statements* do not seem *well weighed* & to savor *of the catchword* (*& savor* —cutting the connection with *do not seem*).

5. You may negative in your first clause a word that when supplied without the negative in the second fails to do the work you expect of it. WRONG: *To raise the standard of life of the many it is* not sufficient *to divide the riches of the few* but also to produce in *greater quantities the goods required by all* (it is also necessary to produce).

6. You may so misplace the negative that it applies to what is common to both clauses instead of, as was intended, to what is peculiar to one. WRONG: *It is* not expected *that*

tomorrow's speech will deal with peace, but will be confined *to a general survey of . . .* (It is expected . . . will not deal).

7. You may treat a double negative expression as though it were formally as well as virtually a positive one. WRONG: *It would* not be difficult *to quarrel with Mr. Rowley's views about art,* but not with *Charles Rowley himself* (It would be easy). Such blunders require only care for their avoidance, to be conscious of the danger is enough to induce that care, & those who would realize the danger may easily do so. Abundant illustrations of it will be found in the articles on NEITHER, NO, NOR, NOT, & NOTHING LESS THAN.

neglect (n.), **negligence.** Though in some contexts the two words are interchangeable, *neglect* is more often used in the sense of disregarding, slighting, paying no attention to a specific person or thing, at a specific time; *negligence* a habitual inattention to what ought to be done. *A child suffering from* neglect; *punished for* neglect *of duty. Criminal* negligence; negligence *in handling his affairs; contributory negligence.*

neglect, v., may be followed by either the infinitive or the gerund: *He neglected* to follow *instructions; Don't neglect* taking care *of that cold.* The *to* const. is seemingly more usual.

negligee. Usually so spelled in US; *néglígé,* Brit. (& Fr.).

negligible, -geable. The first is recommended.

negotiate makes *-tiable, -tor, -tion.* (Pron. -shĭ-.) The use of the verb in its improper sense of tackle successfully (Webster: 'colloq.') is comparable in faded jocularity with the similar use of *individual,* & stamps a writer as literarily a barbarian (*Dark Star* negotiated *the distance without effort*). See POLYSYLLABIC HUMOR.

Negro. Pl. *Negroes.* In US always capitalized.

neighbor, -our, US & Brit. spelling respectively.

neighborhood. *In the neighborhood of* for *about* is a repulsive combination of POLYSYLLABIC HUMOR & PERIPHRASIS.

neither. 1. The more usual pronunciation in US is nē-, in Brit. nī-. (The earliest pron. was nā-.)

2. The proper sense of the pronoun (or adjective) is 'not the one nor the other of the two.' Like *either,* it sometimes refers loosely to numbers greater than two (*Heat, light, electricity, magnetism, are all correlatives;* neither *can be said to be the essential cause of the other*); but *none* or *no* should be preferred. This restriction to two does not hold for the adv. (conj.). (*Neither fish nor flesh nor fowl*).

3. The number of the adjective & pronoun is properly singular & disregard of this fact is a recognized grammatical mistake, though, with the pronoun at least, very common. WRONG: *The conception is faulty for two reasons,* neither of which are *noticed by Plato./ What at present I believe* neither of us know. (Grammar requires *is noticed,* & *knows.*) The same mistake with the adjective is so obviously wrong as to be almost impossible: not quite, however: *Both Sir Harry Verney & Mr. Gladstone were very brief,* neither speeches

exceeding fifteen minutes. An almost equally incredible freak with the pronoun is: *Lord Hothfield & Lord Reay were born the one in Paris & the other at The Hague,* neither being British subjects *at the time of his birth* (as indeed neither could be unless he were twins).

4. Number & person after *neither . . . nor.* If both subjects are singular & in the third person, the only need is to remember that the verb must be singular & not plural. This is often forgotten; the OED quotes from Johnson, *Neither search nor labour* are *necessary,* &, from *Ruskin, Neither painting nor fighting* feed *men,* where *is* & *feeds* are undoubtedly required. Complications occur when, owing to a difference in number or person between the subject of the *neither* member & that of the *nor* member, the same verb form or pronoun or possessive adjective does not fit both: *Neither you nor I* (was?, were?) *chosen; Neither you nor I* (is?, am?, are?) *the right person; Neither eyes nor nose* (does its?, do their?) *work; Neither employer nor hands will say what* (they want?, he wants?). The wise man, in writing, evades these problems by rejecting all the alternatives—any of which may set up friction between him & his reader—& putting the thing in some other shape; in speaking, which does not allow time for paraphrase, he takes risks with equanimity & says what instinct dictates. The COD gives *Neither you nor I* know; *neither I nor he* knows—i.e. the verb agrees with the second member, the one nearest it. But, as instinct is directed largely by habit, it is well to eschew habitually the clearly wrong forms (such as *Neither chapter nor verse* are *given*) & the clearly provocative ones (such as *Neither husband nor wife is competent to act without* his *consort*). About the following, which are actual newspaper extracts, neither grammarians nor laymen will be unanimous in approving or disapproving the preference of *is* to *are* or of *has* to *have;* but there will be a good majority for the opinion that both writers are grammatically more valorous than discreet: *Neither apprenticeship* systems nor *technical* education is *likely to influence these occupations* (why not have omitted *systems?*)./*Neither* Captain C. nor I has *ever thought it necessary to . . .* (Neither to Captain C. nor to me has it ever seemed . . .).

5. Position of *neither . . . nor.* WRONG: *Which* neither suits *one purpose nor the other. Suits* being common to both members should not be inserted in the middle of the *neither* member. Read *which suits neither . . .* Such displacement has been discussed & illustrated under EITHER 5, & need only be mentioned here as a mistake to be avoided.

6. *Neither . . . or.* When a negative has preceded, a question often arises between *nor* & *or* as the right continuation, & the answer to the question sometimes requires care; see NOR, OR. But when the preceding negative is *neither* (adv.), the matter is simple, *or* being always wrong. WRONG: *Diderot presented a bouquet which was* neither *well* or *ill received./Like the Persian noble of old, I ask 'that I may* neither *command* or *obey.'* Here again, to say that

Morley & Emerson have sinned before us is a plea not worth entering.

7. *Neither* alone as conjunction. This use, in which *neither* means 'nor yet,' or '& moreover . . . not,' & connects sentences instead of the ordinary & *not* or *nor* (*I have not asked for help, neither do I desire it; Defendant had agreed not to interfere, neither did he*) is much less common than it was, & is best reserved for contexts of formal tone.

8. *Neither* with the negative force pleonastic, as in *I don't know that neither* (instead of *either*), was formerly idiomatic though colloq., but is now ignorant or archaic or affected.

neo-, combining form of *new,* is usually hyphened before proper nouns (*neo-Catholic, neo-Darwinism*), but sometimes makes one word with those that have been long established (*neoplatonism* or *neo-Platonism*). Before common nouns, esp. those more often & longer in use, usually one word without hyphen (*neoclassical, neopaganism, neoplasticism; neoromantic* or *neo-; neoimpressionism* or *neo-*).

nepenthe(s). A drug to cause forgetfulness of pain or sorrow; hence anything causing oblivion. Three syllables, whether with or without the *-s.* The *-s* is part of the Greek word, but it has very commonly been dropped (except in Botany, where the classical word is naturally used).

nephew. In US usually pron. nĕf′ū, Brit. nĕv′ū (the *v* sound comes from the early spellings, *neveue, nevue,* &c.).

nepotism. Now usually bestowal of patronage because of relationship rather than merit. (Orig. favoritism to 'nephews,' i.e. illegitimate sons.)

Nereid. Pron. nē′rēĭd. A sea nymph (daughter of Nereus, pron. nē′ro͞os).

-ness. For the distinction between *conciseness* & *concision,* & similar pairs, see -ION & -NESS.

net. In the commercial sense (free from deduction &c.) the spelling should, as elsewhere, be *net,* not *nett.*

nether. For *nether garments, nether man,* &c., see PEDANTIC HUMOR.

neurasthenia. Pron. -thē-, NOT -thĕ-.

neurosis. Pl. *-oses.*

never so, ever so, in conditional clauses (*refuseth to hear the voice of the charmer, charm he never so wisely*). The original phrases, going back to Old English, are *never so,* & *never such. Ever so,* however, is the normal modern form, not *never so,* & it is in vain that attempts are occasionally made to put the clock back & restore *never* in ordinary speech. In poetry, & under circumstances that justify archaism, *never so* is unimpeachable; but in everyday style the purism that insists on it is futile.

new (adv.), **newly.** *New-mown hay, new-made bread,* the *new-crowned Queen;* but *the hay had been* newly *mown, the bread* newly *made,* &c.

newfangled. Not recent colloq. but long established. Novel, new-fashioned, in a derogatory sense. *The newfangled notions.*

news. The number varied (*the news* is *bad, are bad*) for more than two centuries, but has now settled down permanently as singular.

Newfoundland, the province, pron. nū′fun(d)lănd′ or nū′-fŭn(d)land (Webster says 'locally'). The dog, usually nū-fownd′lănd.

New Style (of reckoning dates) refers to the Gregorian Calendar. Abbr. N.S. See STYLE.

New Year's, short for *New Year's Day* &c., should have the apostrophe.

next. 1. RIGHT: *The* next three *weeks will be my busiest./ First three boys, then two boys and a girl, and the* three next *were all girls.* For the question between *the next three* &c. & *the three* &c. *next,* see FIRST 4.

2. *Next June, next Friday,* &c., can be used as advs. without a preposition (*Shall begin it next June*); but, if *next* is put after the noun, Brit. idiom requires a preposition (*may be expected* in *June next,* on *Monday next*). See FRIDAY.

3. *Next best* = second best. Hence, colloq. with other words: *My next oldest brother, my next worst enemy.* That idiom requires a superlative, & such words as *oldest, worst, narrowest, weightiest,* suit it well; but it is ugly with adjs. having no superlative but that with *most,* & there is a temptation to try whether, for instance, *next important* will not pass for *next most important.* WRONG: *The party had the rank & file at their back because they fought to the last ditch to save the grandest institution in the country; do they expect support now in wrecking the two* next important *institutions?* The natural sense of the *two next important institutions* is 'the two next institutions that are of importance,' which need by no means be the two that are next in importance.

nexus. Connection, tie, link (*the nexus of cause & effect*). The English pl. *nexuses* is intolerably sibilant, & the Latin, *nexus* (-ōōs), sounds pedantic; the plural is consequently very rare.

nice. (1) *Nice* makes *nicish.* (2) *Nice &* as a sort of adverb= satisfactorily (*I hope it will be* nice & *fine; Aren't we going* nice & *fast?*) is an established colloq., but should be confined, in print, to dialogue. (3) Meaning. *Nice* has been spoiled, like CLEVER, by its *bonnes fortunes;* it has been too great a favorite with the ladies, who have charmed out of it all its individuality & converted it into a mere diffuser of vague & mild agreeableness. Everyone who uses it in its more proper senses, which fill most of the space given to it in any dictionary, & avoids the modern one that tends to oust them all, does a real if small service to the language.

Nicene. The name of the place from which the creed is so called is *Nicaea* or *Nicea,* NOT *Nicoea.*

nick-nack. Use KNICKKNACK.

Nietzscheism, so spelled. Pron. nē′chē ĭz′m. The philosophy of Friedrich Wilhelm Nietzsche, Ger. philosopher, 1844–1900.

Nigger is sometimes used familiarly between two Negroes with affection. Used by a non-Negro it is offensive.

nihilism, -ist. Pron. nī′ĭ-, with the *h* silent.

nimbus (halo). Pl. *-bi* (-ī).

nimrod, for hunter, see SOBRIQUETS.

nine makes *ninety, ninefold, ninth,* the *nineties* or *'nineties* (see EIGHTIES).

Nipponese is preferred by the Japanese. *Japanese* remains the normal English word.

niter, -re. The first is more usual in US, *-re* in Brit.

-N-, -NN-. Monosyllables ending in *n* double it before suffixes beginning with vowels if the sound preceding it is a single vowel, but not if it is a diphthong or a double vowel or a vowel & *r: mannish,* but *darning; winning,* but *reined; conned,* but *coined; runner,* but *turned.* Words of more than one syllable follow the rule for monosyllables if their last syllable is accented, but otherwise do not double the *n: Japanned* & *beginner,* but *dragooned, womanish, turbaned, musliny.*

no. 1. Part of speech. *No* is (A) an adj. meaning in the sing. *not a* (or *not any*), & in the pl. *not any;* it is a shortened form of *none,* which is still used as its pronoun form: *No German applied; No Germans applied; None of the applicants was* (or now often *were*) *German. No* is (B) an adv. meaning *by no amount* & used only with comparatives: *I am glad it is no worse. No* is (C) an adv. meaning *not* & used only after *or,* & chiefly in the phrase *whether or no: Pleasant or no, it is true; He must do it whether he will or no. No* is (D) a particle representing a negative sentence of which the contents are clear from a preceding question or from the context: *Is he there?—No* (i.e. he is not there). *No, it is too bad* (i.e. I shall not submit; it is too bad). *No* is (E) a noun meaning the word *no,* a denial or refusal, a negative vote or voter: *Don't say no; She will not take a no; The Noes have it.*

2. Confusion of adj. & adv. If the tabulation in (1) is correct, it is clear how the worse than superfluous *a, the,* & *her,* made their way into the following extracts. The writer of each thought his *no* was a B or a C adv., against which the absence of the invariable accompaniments should have warned him, & did not see that it was the adj., (A) which contains *a* in itself & is therefore incompatible with another *a, the,* or *her.* WRONG: *We can hardly give the book higher praise than to say of it that it is* a no *unworthy companion of Moberly's 'Atonement'* (omit *a,* or write *not* for *no*)./*The value of gas taken from the ground there & sold amounted to* the no *insignificant value of* $54 *million* (the not)./ *Paintings by Maud Earl, who owes* her no small reputation *as an artist to the successes which* . . . (her reputation, no small one).

3. *No* in negative confusions. *No,* used in the first of two parallel clauses, ensnares many a brave unwary writer; the modifications necessary for the second clause are forgotten, & bad grammar or bad sense results. See NEGATIVE & AFFIRMATIVE IN PARALLEL CLAUSES. WRONG: *He sees in England* no attempt to mould *history according to academic plans,* but to direct *it from case to case according to necessity* (it is rather directed)./ *Although* no party has *been able to carry its own scheme out,* it has been *strong enough to prevent any other scheme being carried* (each has been).

4. Negative parentheses. The rule here to be insisted on con-

cerns negative expressions in general, & is stated under *no* only because that word happens to be present in violations of it oftener perhaps than any other. The rule is that adverbial qualifications containing a negative must not, like qualifications that, not being negative, do not so vitally affect the sense, be set off by commas from the words they belong to as though they were mere parentheses. The rule only needs stating to be accepted; but the habit of providing adverbial phrases with commas often gets the better of common sense. It is clear, however, that there is the same essential absurdity in writing *He will, under no circumstances, consent* as in writing *He will, never, consent,* or *He will, not, consent.* It is worth while to add, for the reader's consideration while he glances at the examples, that it would often be better in these negative adverbial phrases to resolve *no* into *not . . . any* &c. WRONG: *We are assured that the Prime Minister will,* in no circumstances & on no consideration whatever, *consent* (will not in any . . . or on any . . . Or omit the commas, at the least)./*And Paley & Butler,* no more than Voltaire, *could give Bagehot one thousandth part of the confidence that he drew from* . . . (could not, any more than . . . Or could no more than Voltaire give.

5. *No one* (or *nobody*) *else's,* see ELSE.

6. *No place, any place;* the traditional adverbial forms are *nowhere, anywhere.*

Nobel prizes. Pron. nōbĕl′. Annual awards for achievement in the sciences, promotion of peace, or other fields in the interest of humanity, provided by the will of Alfred B. Nobel, 1833–96, the inventor of dynamite.

nobody, no one. As a pronoun the latter is now more literary and formal.

noblesse oblige. Pron. nôblĕs′ ôblēzh′. 'Nobility obligates,' i.e. privilege entails responsibility.

nom de guerre, nom de plume, pen name, pseudonym. *Nom de guerre* is current French, but, owing to the English currency of *nom de plume,* is far from universally intelligible to English-speaking people, most of whom assume that, whatever else it may mean, it can surely not mean *nom de plume. Nom de plume* is open to the criticism that it is ridiculous for English writers to use a French phrase that does not come from France; not perhaps as ridiculous as the critics think (see MORALE), but fear of them will at any rate deter some of us. Nobody perhaps uses *pen name* without feeling either 'What a good boy am I to abstain from showing off my French & translate *nom de plume* into honest English!' or else 'I am not as those publicans who suppose there is such a phrase as *nom de plume.*' For everyone is instinctively aware that *pen name,* however native or naturalized its elements, is no English-bred word, but a translation of *nom de plume. Pseudonym,* lastly, is a queer out-of-the-way term for an everyday thing. But it is perhaps the best of the bunch except for those who take the common-sense view of *nom de plume*—that it is the established word for the thing, & its antecedents do not concern us.

nomenclature. 'A system of

naming or of names.' It does NOT mean *name;* see LOVE OF THE LONG WORD. WRONG: *The forerunner of the present luxurious establishment was the well-known Gloucester Coffee House,* the nomenclature *of which was derived from that Duke of Gloucester who . . ./ A small committee of city men had just launched a society, under the* nomenclature *of the 'League of Interpreters,' with the object of . . .*

nominative. 1. The grammatical word is always pronounced nŏm'ĭnatĭv; the adj. connected in sense with *nominate* & *nomination* (e.g. in *partly elective & partly nominative*) is often, & perhaps more conveniently, nŏm'ĭnātĭv.

2. *Nominative case.* (Gram.): the case used as or in agreement with the subject of a verb, in English discernible chiefly in pronouns. In the following sentences, the words in roman type are in the nominative: He *gave me the book.* It *is* she who *is mistaken. The three* victors, John, Alfred *and* I, *will meet the next contestants.*

3. *Nominative absolute,* an English construction like the Latin ablative absolute (Fowler says in *The King's English,* 'not much to be recommended'): *John was my worst threat but,* he having been defeated, *I had a chance.* The current use least offensive is *that being so . . .*

non-. As a prefix, pron. nŏn, rarely nŭn. In US *non-* joins with proper nouns usually by a hyphen: *non-Aryan, non-Christian,* but otherwise usually forms one word. In Brit. usage the hyphen is often retained except in some of the older and most used words: *nonconformist,* but *non-resistance, non-intervention* (all single words in US).

nonce. 'Time being,' 'present occasion,' chiefly in *for the nonce* (i.e. temporarily); *nonce words,* words coined for one occasion and not of general usage.

nonchalant, -ance. Pron. nŏn'-sh*a*lant, -*a*ns (i.e. as English words, but with the sound -sh- rather than -ch-).

none. (1) It is a mistake to insist that the pronoun is singular only & must at all costs be followed by sing. verbs &c.; the pl. construction is now common (e.g. *None* are *more fortunate than those who . . .*). (2) The forms *none so, none too,* are idiomatic (*It is* none so *pleasant to learn that you have only six months to live; The look he gave me was* none too *amiable*), but are perhaps seldom used without a certain sense of archaism or condescending to the vernacular as an aid to heartiness of manner or emphasis; & condescension is always repellent.

nonentity, in the now rare abstract sense of nonexistence, should have the *non-* pronounced clearly nŏn, & perhaps be written with a hyphen (*non-entity*). In the current concrete sense of a person or thing of no account, it is written *nonentity* & said with the *o* obscured (n*o*nĕn'tĭtĭ).

nonesuch, nonsuch. The first is the original form and still standard US; the second the now usual Brit. one. (Pron. nŭn-.)

nonpareil. Unrivaled, without peer. Pron. nŏnp*a*rĕl'.

nonplus (baffle, confound) makes US *-sed, -sing.;* Brit.

-ssed, -ssing. (Pron. nŏn-.)

non sequitur. (Log.): 'does not follow.' The fallacy of assuming an unproved cause. Thus: It will be a hard winter, for holly berries (which are meant as provision for birds in hard weather) are abundant. The reasoning called *post hoc, ergo propter hoc* is a form of non sequitur.

no one. So spelled in US and often in Brit.; but *no-one* is also used in Brit.

nor. 1. The negative forms of *He moves & speaks, He both moves & speaks,* are *He moves not nor speaks, He neither moves nor speaks;* or, with the verb resolved as usual in modern negative sentences, *He does not move or speak, He does not either move or speak.*

2. *Nor* is a word that should come into our minds as we repeat the General Confession. Most of us in our time have left undone those things which we ought to have done (i.e. failed to put in *nor* when it was wanted) & done those things which we ought not to have done (i.e. thrust it in when there was no room for it). The tendency to go wrong is probably due to confusion between the simple verbs (*moves* &c.) & the resolved ones (*does move* &c.). If the verb is resolved, there is often an auxiliary that serves both clauses, &, as the negative is attached to the auxiliary, its force is carried on together with that of the auxiliary & no fresh negative is wanted. Two cautions are necessary on this carrying on of the negative force & consequent preference of *or* to *nor.* The first is that it will not do to repeat the auxiliary & yet use *or* under the impression that the previous negative suffices. WRONG: *Sir Guy Granet was naturally & properly at pains to prove that his company had* not acted *negligently or carelessly* or had been *unduly influenced by reasons of economy.* There was a choice here between *or been* & *had not been; or had been* makes nonsense.

The other caution, much more often required, is that if the negative is attached not to an auxiliary (or other word common to two clauses) that will carry it forward, but to some other part of the first clause, the negative force is cut off & has to be started afresh by *nor.* RIGHT: No treaty could *override the power of an individual state* nor could one *take effect unless it were implemented by legislation.* The following examples illustrate the danger; in each *or* must be corrected into *nor* if the rest of the sentence is to remain as it is, though some slight change of arrangement such as is indicated would make *or* possible. WRONG: *In its six months of power it has* offered not one *constructive measure* or done *a single thing to relieve suffering* (it has not offered one)./*It is with* no unfriendly intention *to Germany* or with any desire *to question her right or her need to possess a powerful Navy* (it is not with any).

These are the ordinary types of mistake with *nor.* Others that should hardly require mention are *either . . . nor,* & the poetical omission of the first negative. *Either . . . nor* is as bad as *Neither . . . or;* WRONG: *There was* not, either *in* 1796 *in Italy* nor *on the Mediterranean coast of Spain in* 1808, *any force at work which . . .*

3. *Do nor undo* is legitimate in poetry, but not in prose of so ordinary a kind as: *For her fingers had been so numbed that she could* do nor undo *anything.*

normalcy (=normality) is a HYBRID derivative of the 'spurious hybrid' class, & seems to have nothing to recommend it. Popularized by President Harding (*back to normalcy*), it was accepted in US but is now losing its vogue use.

north-. Compounds *northeast* &c. are single words in US, hyphened in Brit.

northerly. *A northerly wind, course; the most northerly outpost.* But *the north end of the church, northern ways of thought.* See EASTERLY.

nostrum. A medicine prepared by the person recommending it; a quick remedy. Hence a pet scheme, favorite device. Pron. nŏs-.

not. 1. *Not all, all . . . not. All is not gold that glisters; Every land does not produce everything.* Precisians would rewrite these sentences as *Not all is gold that glisters* (or *Not all that glisters is gold*) & *Not every land produces everything.* The negative belongs logically to *all* & *every,* not to the verbs, & the strict sense of the first proverb would be that glistering proves a substance to be not gold. The precisians have logic on their side, logic has time on its side, & probably the only thing needed for their gratification is that they should live long enough. The older a language grows, & the more consciously expert its users become, the shorter shrift it & they may be expected to grant to illogicalities & ambiguities. *All . . . not* for *Not all,* like *the two first* for *the first two,* is already denounced by those who have time to spend on niceties; but it is still, like many other inaccuracies, the natural & idiomatic English. It will pass away in time, for *magna est veritas et praevalebit.* In the meantime it is worth anyone's while to get on speaking terms with the new exactitudes (i.e. to write *Not all* himself), but worth nobody's while to fall foul of those who do not choose to abandon the comfortable old slovenries.

2. *Not inconsiderable* &c. 'We say well & elegantly, *not ungrateful,* for *very grateful*'—OED quotation dated 1671. It is by this time a faded or jaded elegance, this replacing of a term by the negation of its opposite; jaded by general overuse; faded by the blight of WORN-OUT HUMOR with its *not a hundred miles from, not unconnected with,* & other once-fresh young phrases. But the very popularity of the idiom in English is proof enough that there is something in it congenial to the English temperament, & it is pleasant to believe that it owes its success to a stubborn national dislike of putting things too strongly. (US, it is true, cannot claim this as a national characteristic, but many Americans cherish the idiom, and revel in its 'elegance.') It is clear too that there are contexts to which e.g. *not inconsiderable* is more suitable than *considerable.* By using it we seem to anticipate & put aside, instead of not foreseeing or ignoring, the possible suggestion that so-&-so is inconsiderable. The right principle is to acknowledge that the idiom is al-

lowable, & then to avoid it except when it is more than allowable. Examples in which their authors would hardly claim that elegance or point was gained by the double negative, & would admit that they used it only because they saw no reason why they should not, are: *The style of argument suitable for the election contest is, no doubt,* not infrequently *different from the style of argument suitable for use at Westminster* (often)./*One may imagine that Mr. —— will* not be altogether unrelieved *when his brother actor returns tomorrow* (will be much relieved).

3. *Not* in exclamations. WRONG: *But if you look at the story of that quadrilateral of land, what a complex of change & diversity do you* not *discover!* A jumble of question & exclamation. The right exclamation would be: *What a complex you discover!* The possible question would be: *What complexity do you not discover? What a complex* & the exclamation point are essentially exclamatory: *not* is essentially interrogative; *do* is characteristically interrogative, but not impossible in exclamations. The forms in a simpler sentence are (RIGHT): Exclamation: *What I have suffered!* Question: *What have I not suffered?* Exclamation with inversion: *What have I suffered!* Confusion: *What have I not suffered!*

4. *Not* pleonastic. We all know people who habitually say *I shouldn't wonder if it didn't turn to snow soon* when they mean *if it turned.* The same mistake in print is almost as common and as inexcusable as it is absurd. WRONG: *Nobody can predict with confidence how much time may* not *be employed on the concluding stages of the Bill./Who knows but what agreeing to differ may* not *be a form of agreement rather than a form of difference?*

5. *Not . . . but.* WRONG: *Mrs. Fraser's book, however, is* not confined *to filling up the gaps in Livingstone's life in England,* but it deals *most interestingly with her father's own early adventures in Africa.* See BUT 3 for more flagrant mishandlings of *not* followed by *but.* The difference between right & wrong often depends on the writer's seeing that the subject, for instance, of the *not* clause must not be repeated (or taken up by a pronoun) in the *but* clause, but allowed to carry on silently. The compound sentence above, which is not idiomatic English as it stands, is at once cured by the omission of *it.* The relation between one form & the other is exactly that between *It is not black, but it is white* (which is impossible except in special conditions) & *It is not black, but white.*

6. *Not only* out of its place is like a thumbtack loose on the floor; it might have been most serviceable somewhere else, & is capable of giving acute & undeserved pain where it is. All of the following extracts required only a preference for order over chaos to have tidied them up. WRONG: *Ireland, unlike the other Western nations,* preserved not only *its pre-Christian literature,* but *when Christianity came,* that literature received *a fresh impulse from the new faith* (Not only did Ireland . . . preserve)./Not only had *she now a right to speak,* but to speak *with authority*

(She had now a right not only to speak)./Not only does *the proportion of suicides vary with the season of the year,* but with *different races* (The proportion of suicides varies not only with).

nota bene, 'note (mark) well'; observe what follows. Abbr. N.B. (NOT *N.b.*).

notch in US, esp. in place names, a narrow opening or pass in the mountain; *Crawford Notch* &c.

note, v. *It is interesting to note* . . . see HACKNEYED PHRASES.

nothing less than. The OED remarks: 'The combination *nothing less than* has two quite contrary senses,' & gives as the first, 'quite equal to,' 'the same thing as,' with, for illustration, *But yet methinks my father's execution* Was nothing less than *bloody tyranny;* & as the second, 'far from being, anything rather than,' with, for illustration, *Who trusting to the laws, expected* nothing less than *an attack.* To the second sense it adds the description, 'Now rare.' As a matter of grammar, either sense is legitimate, *less* being different parts of speech in the two, as appears in the light of paraphrases: my father's death was no smaller thing than tyranny (i.e. *less* is an adj.); they expected nothing in a lower degree than they expected an attack (i.e. *less* is an adv.). Grammar, then, leaves the matter open. But the risks of ambiguity are very great. If the sense of *they expected nothing less than an attack* did not happen to be fixed by *trusting to the laws,* who would dare decide whether they expected it very much or very little? The sense called by the OED 'now rare' should, in the interests of plain speaking, be made rarer by total abandonment. It is unfortunately less rare than the label would lead one to suppose. Passages like the following are not uncommon, & are to many readers very puzzling: *Now we are introduced to inspired 'crowd-men' or heroes who have a passion for making order out of the human chaos & finding expression for the real soul of the people; these heroes or crowd-men resemble* nothing less than *the demagogue as popularly conceived.*

nought. See NAUGHT.

noumenon. In Kant, opp. of *phenomenon:* a non-empirical concept (US usually no͞o'mē-nŏn; Brit. now'mĭnŏn); pl. *-ena.*

NOUN & ADJECTIVE ACCENT. When a word of more than one syllable is in use both as a noun & as an adj., there is a certain tendency, though much less marked than the corresponding one with nouns & verbs (see next article), to differentiate the sound by accenting the last syllable in the adj. but not in the noun; thus *He is an expert' golfer,* but *He is an ex'pert in handwriting.* So *compact'* adj., com'pact n.; minute' adj., min'ute n.; content' adj., con'tent(s) n. (sometimes).

NOUN & VERB ACCENT, PRONUNCIATION, & SPELLING. When there is both noun & verb work to be done by a word, & the plan of forming a noun from the verb, or a verb from the noun, by adding a formative suffix (as in *stealth* from *steal*) is not followed, but the one word doubles the parts, there is a strong tendency to differentiate by pronunciation, as in *use* (n. ūs, v. ūz). Such a distinction is sometimes, as in *use,* unrecorded in spelling, but sometimes recorded as in *calf* & *calve.* The impulse is still active, & as a consequence the pronunciation of many words is for a time uncertain.

1. The largest class is that of words whose accent is shifted; these, not being monosyllables, are mostly of foreign origin. (A) Words in which the differentiation is established, for example: *commune′* v., *com′mune* n.; *compress′* v., *com′press* n.; *decrease′* v., *de′crease* n.; *escort′* v., *es′cort* n.; *import′* v., *im′port* n.; *produce′* v., *prod′uce* n.; *subject′* v.; *sub′ject* n. (B) Words in which accent-shifting is tentative only; for example: *construe′* v., *con′strue* n.; *detail′* v., *de′tail* n.; &c.

2. Other words, especially but not only monosyllables, are differentiated not by accent but by a modification in noun or verb of the consonantal sound at the end, which is hard in the noun & soft in the verb. This difference is often for the ear only & does not affect spelling; so *abuse, excuse, grease, house, misuse, mouth.* In this class are words about which usage varies & material for comparison is therefore useful. More often the change of sound is recorded in the spelling; about such words no doubts arise; but examples are worth giving to confirm the fact that the distinguishing of the parts of speech by change of sound is very common, & that its extension to words whose spelling fails to show it is natural: *advice* & *advise, belief* & *believe, cloth* & *clothe, device* & *devise, life* & *live, proof* & *prove, relief* & *relieve, sheath* & *sheathe, teeth* & *teethe, wreath* & *wreathe.* Many words about which usage varies are listed in their alphabetical places.

nous. (Greek Phil., the mind, intellect.) In US usually pron. nōōs; Brit. nows.

nouveau riche. 'Newly rich' (usually disparaging); pl. *-veaux riches.* Pron. nōō vō rēsh.

NOVELESE. This heading is not to be taken as a suggestion that writers of novels are all alike in yielding to certain professional weaknesses. A single warning only is intended, & that on a point so elementary that it concerns only the beginner. What is here meant by *novelese* is the set phrases that the young writer remembers to have had his emotions stirred by in the days when he was reading novels instead of writing them, & relies upon to affect his own readers in turn. The phrases have had some wear & tear since he was first struck by them, & the emotional value of such things depreciates quickly. Influences that 'have come into' somebody's 'life,' fallen ones 'more sinned against than sinning,' unfortunates 'hoping against hope,' *strong silent men, living deaths, that supreme moment, devilish ingenuity, magnetic personalities* & *sinister machinations, utter abandon* & *pathetic indifference* & *innocent guile,* all these & hundreds of the like phrases, which thrilled our own youth, will not thrill but bore those on whom we sanguinely try the same experiment. The emotions may be sempiternal; the stimuli to which they will react lose their power with use, & must be varied.

novella. A short story or tale (of the type in Boccaccio's *De-*

cameron). Pl. *novelle* (pron. -lā).

NOVELTY-HUNTING, or the casting about for words of which one can feel not that they give one's meaning more intelligibly or exactly than those the man in the street would have used in expressing the same thing, but that they are not the ones that would have occurred to him, is a confession of weakness. Anyone can say *improvement* & *complexity* & *conception* & *ancestors;* I will say BETTERMENT & COMPLICACY & CONCEPT & FOREBEARS. Why? Obviously because, there being nothing new in what I have to say, I must make up for its staleness by something new in the way I say it. And if that were all, if each novelty-hunter struck out a line for himself, we could be content to register novelty-hunting as a useful outward sign of inward dullness, & leave such writers carefully alone. Unluckily they hunt in packs, & when one of them has such a find as ASSET or HAPPENINGS or FORCEFUL or MENTALITY they are all in full cry after it, till it becomes a VOGUE WORD, to the great detriment of the language. Further notes on the point will be found under most of the words already mentioned. Other specimens are FEASIBLE for possible, MOMENTLY for instantly, LIKELY for probably, adverbs like embarrassedly (see -EDLY).

noviciate, -itiate. Usually US *-iti-*, Brit. *-ici-*.

nth. For *to the nth,* see N.

nuance. A shade of difference, a subtle variation (of meaning, opinion, color, tone, &c.). Pron. nū äns′.

nucleus. Pl. *-lei* (lĭī), or sometimes *-uses* in non-scientific use.

nude, adj., is often a GENTEELISM for *naked.*

nuisance. Pron. nū′sans (not 3 syllables).

NUMBER. Several kinds of mistake are common & various doubts arise involving the question of number. The following sections are arranged with the purely grammatical points coming first. 1. Subject & complements of different numbers. 2. Subject of mixed numbers. 3. *Or.* 4. Red herrings. 5. Harking back with relatives. 6. Nouns of multitude. 7. Singular verb preceding plural subject, & vice versa. 8. *As follow(s)* &c. 9. *Other(s).* 10. *What.* 11. Pronouns & possessives after *everyone* &c. 12. Quantity words. 13. Nonsense.

1. If subject & complement are of different numbers, how is the number of the verb to be decided? That is, shall we use *are* in *Clouds are vaporized water,* & *was* in *The last crop was potatoes,* because the subject *clouds* is plural & the subject *crop* singular, or shall we prefer *is* & *were* to suit the number of the complements *water* & *potatoes?* The natural man, faced with these examples, has no doubt: 'Of course, *Clouds are, The crop was,* whatever may be going to follow.' The sophisticated man, who thinks of *The wages of sin is death,* hesitates, but probably admits that that is an exception accounted for by the really singular sense of *wages* (=guerdon). It may in fact be fairly assumed that when the subject is a straightforward singular, or a straightforward plural or separate items (as in *he & she*), the

verb follows the number of the subject, whatever that of the complement may be. That it is not as needless as it might seem to set this down will be plain from the following violations of the rule. WRONG: *Our only* guide were *the stars./For Germany's great* need are *colonies./ The plausible* suggestions *to the contrary so frequently put forward* is *an endeavor to kill two birds with one stone.* The only comment necessary on these is that when it makes no difference to the meaning which of two words (*stars* or *guide, need* or *colonies*) is made the subject & which the complement, the one that is placed first must (except in questions) be regarded as subject & have the verb suited to its number: *Our only* guide was *the stars,* or *The* stars were *our only guide.*

When the words *which* or *what* take the place of the subject, mistakes are more intelligible, but still mistakes. WRONG: *The* grass plots *intersected with graveled* drives which is *the ordinary achievement of the English gardener in India. What puzzles us most* are *the references to . . . ,* &c. The traps laid by WHAT are so many & various that it is better to refer the reader to that word.

2. Subject of mixed numbers. In *Mother & children were killed* we have a compound subject; in *Mother or children are to die* we have not one compound subject, but two alternative subjects; the rules for the number of the verb differ in the two types. The compound subject is necessarily plural, whether its components are both plural, or different numbers, or both singular. To make the verb singular, as has been done in the extracts below, is accordingly WRONG: *Those who have been encouraging these people to believe that* their lives, their liberties, & their religion is *in danger have assumed a great responsibility./They are prepared to cease operations if & when proper* pledges & security is *given.*

If the verb in sentences of this type precedes the compound subject (*There* were a table & some chairs *in there*), it becomes legitimate to use a singular verb under some circumstances (see 7 below).

3. *Or.* When both alternatives are singular in grammar & in sense the verb can only be singular. So *Mother or child* is (NOT are) *to die.* But when the alternatives differ in number, as in *Mother or children are to die, Is the child or the parents to be blamed?*, the methods in order of merit are: (a) Evade by finding a verb of common number: *Mother or children must die, Shall the child or the parents be blamed?* (b) Invoke ellipsis by changing the order: *The mother is to die, or the children, Is the child to be blamed, or the parents?* (c) Give the verb the number of the alternative nearest it: *Mother or children are to die, Is the child or the parents to be blamed?* What should NOT be said is *Mother or children is to die, Are the child or the parents to be blamed?*

4. Red herrings. Some writers are as easily drawn off the scent as young hounds. They start with a singular subject; before they reach the verb, a plural noun attached to an *of* or the like happens to cross, & off they go in the plural; or vice versa. This is a matter of carelessness

or inexperience only, & needs no discussion; but it is so common as to call for a few illustrations. WRONG: *The* results *of the recognition of this truth* is . . ./*The* foundation *of politics* are *in the letter only./An immense* amount *of confusion & indifference* prevail.

5. Harking back with relatives. *Who, which,* & *that* can in themselves be singular or plural, & there is a particular form of sentence in which this produces constant blunders. RIGHT: *He is one of the best* men *that* have *ever lived* (with which compare *He is* one *that* has *lived honestly*). In the first sentence there are two words capable of serving as antecedent to *that,* viz. *one* & *men.* A moment's thought shows that *men* is the antecedent necessary to the sense: *Of the best men that have ever lived* (or *of the best past & present men*) *he is one.* But with *one* & *men* (or their equivalents) to attach the relative to, writers will hark back to *one* in spite of the nonsense it gives, & make their verbs singular. WRONG: *They have gone through one of those complete* changes *of occupation which* does *everybody good./One of the many well-known* actresses *who* wears *Sandow's corset.*

An example or two offering peculiarities may be added. WRONG: *Mr. Edwin Pugh is one of those intriguing* people who are *able to write well in any style &* does; but who *constantly* leaves *us with the impression that he is not quite serious;* this writer wants to have it both ways; *who* is to be plural with *are,* but singular with *does* & *leaves;* read *& he does, but./Describing him as one of those busy* men who *in some remarkable way* find *time for adding to* his *work;* to have got safely as far as *find,* & then break away with *his,* is an odd freak.

6. Nouns of multitude. Such words as *army, fleet, government, company, crowd, number, majority* may stand either for a single entity or for the individuals who compose it, & are called nouns of multitude. They are treated as singular or plural at discretion—& sometimes, naturally, without discretion. *The Cabinet* is *divided* is better, because in order of thought a whole must precede division; & *The Cabinet* are *agreed* is better, because it takes two or more to agree. That is a delicate distinction, & few will be at the pains to make it. Broader ones that few will fail to know are that between (RIGHT) *The army* is *on a voluntary basis* & *The army* are *above the average civilian height,* & that between (RIGHT) *The party lost* their *hats* & *The party lost* its *way.* In general it may be said that while there is always a better & a worse in the matter, there is seldom a right & a wrong, & any attempt to elaborate rules would be waste labor. A single example will illustrate sufficiently: *More money will be wanted if the* number *of teachers* are *to be adequate.* No one will misinterpret that; yet everyone will admit that the singular would have been what the plural is not, foolproof; the writer meant *if there are to be enough teachers;* he did not mean what his words ought to mean—*if the numerous teachers are to be skillful enough.*

But if the decision whether a noun of multitude is to be treated as a singular or as a plural is often a difficult business, & when ill made results at worst in a venial blemish, failure to abide by the choice when made, & plunging about between *it* & *they, have* & *has, his* & *their,* & the like, can only be called insults to the reader. A waiter might as well serve one on a dirty plate as a writer offer one such untidy stuff as (WRONG): *The* University Press hopes *to have ready the following additions to* their *series of . . ./The latter* Government has *now attempted to link up with the Czechs & have* have *published a program./The* village is *at work now & ready to do* their *bit.*

7. Singular verb preceding plural subject & vice versa. The excuse for this in speaking—often a sufficient one—is that one has started one's sentence before fixing the precise form of the subject, though its meaning may have been realized clearly enough. But the writer both can & ought to do what the speaker cannot, correct his first words before the wrong version has reached his audience. If he does not, he too, like the waiter with the dirty plate, is indecently & insultingly careless. WRONG: *For the first time* there is *introduced into the Shipyard Agreement* clauses *which hold the balance equally./A book entitled 'America's Day,' in which* is *discussed the pressing* problems *of home & foreign policy that . . ./On these questions there* is *likely to be acute* differences *among the political groups & parties.*

The converse mistake is seldom made; in the following, the influence of *these* no doubt accounts for *are* (WRONG): *The Thames has certain natural disadvantages as a shipbuilding center; to these* are *added* an *artificial disadvantage.*

When the verb precedes a subject compounded of singular & plural, some questions of more interest than importance may arise. *There* were *a table & some chairs in there; were* is better because the compound subject is compact. *There* were *a plain deal table in there & some wicker armchairs which Jorgenson had produced from somewhere in the depths of the ship.* The alteration of *were* to *was* would now be an improvement; but why, if *were* was best in the bare framework given first? First & least, the author has made *table & chairs* less homogenous, less the equivalent of 'some articles of furniture,' by describing one as *plain deal* & the others as *wicker;* secondly, he has attached to *chairs* & not to *table* a long relative clause; third & most important, he has had, in order to cut off the relative clause from *table,* to shift *in there* to an earlier place. But it results that the verbal clause (*there were . . . in there*) is so arranged that it encloses one item of the compound subject (*table*) & leaves the other (*chairs*) out in the cold. The author would have done better to write *was* & let the second part be elliptical with *there were in there* to be understood out of *there was in there.*

8. *As follow(s), concern(s), regard(s),* &c. WRONG: *For higher incomes the new rates will be* as follow. *As follow* is not English; *as follows* is; for discussion of the point see FOLLOW.

9. *Other(s).* WRONG: *The wrecking policy is, like* other *of their adventures in recent times, a dangerous gamble.*

Other should be *others;* for discussion see OTHER.

10. *What.* WRONG: *What provoke men's curiosity are mysteries.* See WHAT for the reason it cannot be plural.

11. Pronouns & possessives after *each, every, anyone, no one, one,* &c. *Each* & the rest are all singular; that is undisputed; in a perfect language there would exist pronouns & possessives that were of as doubtful gender as *they,* & yet were, like them, singular; i.e. it would have words meaning *him-or-her, himself-or-herself, his-or-her.* But, just as French lacks our power of distinguishing (without additional words) between *his, her,* & *its,* so we lack the French power of saying in one word 'his-or-her.' *But, as* anybody *can see for* themselves, *it is wrong.* There are three makeshifts: (A) *as anybody can see for* himself or herself; (B) *as anybody can see for* themselves; & (C) *as anybody can see for* himself. No one who can help it chooses (A); it is correct, & is sometimes necessary, but it is so clumsy as to be ridiculous except when explicitness is urgent, & it usually sounds like a bit of pedantic humor. (B) is the popular solution; it sets the literary man's teeth on edge, & he exerts himself to give the same meaning in some entirely different way if he is not prepared, as he usually is, to risk (C); but it should be recorded that the OED, which quotes examples of (B) under *every, they,* & *themselves,* refrains from any word of condemnation. (C) is here recommended. It involves the convention that where the matter of sex is not conspicuous or important *he* & *his* shall be allowed to represent *a person* instead of *a man,* or say *a man* (*homo*) instead of *a man* (*vir*). Whether that, with (A) in the background for especial exactitudes, & paraphrase always possible in dubious cases, is an arrogant demand on the part of the male, everyone must decide for himself (or for himself or herself, or for themselves). Have the patrons of (B) made up their mind yet between *Everyone* was *blowing their nose* & *Everyone* were *blowing their noses?*

12. Quantity words. WRONG: *There* are heaps *more to say, but I must not tax your space further.* The plurals *heaps* & *lots* used colloq. for *a great amount* now always take a singular verb unless a plural noun with *of* is added: *There* is heaps *of ammunition,* but *There* are heaps *of cups; There* is lots *to do,* but Lots *of people* think *so.* Compare the use of *half* in *Half of it* is *rotten,* but *Half of them* are *rotten.*

13. NONSENSE. *He comes for the first time into the Navy at an age when naval officers—unless* they are *so meritorious or so fortunate as to be* one *of the three Admirals of the Fleet—are compelled by law to leave it.* Naval officers cannot be one admiral; & what is wrong with *unless they are Admirals of the Fleet?*

numerous. (1) The repeated use of *numerous* in every combination requiring *many, some, various,* &c. (*on numerous occasions, numerous attempts, numerous examples,* &c.) is a characteristic of writers suffering from LOVE OF THE LONG WORD. (2) *Numerous* is not, as the following extract makes it, a pronoun. WRONG: *These men* *have introduced no fewer than* 107 *amendments, which they know perfectly well cannot pass, &* numerous of which *are not meant to pass.* See VARIOUS, which is much more often misused in the same way.

numskull, NOT *numb-*.

nuncio. Pron. -shĭō. Pl. *-os.*

O

O & oh. Usage has changed, *oh* having formerly been prevalent in many contexts now requiring *O,* & is still by no means fixed. The present tendency (stronger in Brit. than in US) is to restrict *oh* to places where it has a certain independence, & prefer *O* where it is proclitic or leans forward upon what follows: which means for practical purposes that as the sign of the vocative (*O God our help; O mighty-mouthed inventor of harmonies*) *O* is invariable, & as an exclamation the word is *O* when no punctuation immediately follows it, but before any punctuation *oh* (*Oh, what a lie! Oh! how do you know that? O for the wings of a dove!*).

oaf. Pl. *-fs,* rarely *-ves.*

oaken. Now usually replaced by *oak* except in poetic or slightly archaic contexts. *An oak chest* but *an oaken staff.*

oasis. Pron. ō ā′sĭs; pl. *-es* (ēz).

oath. Pl. rhymes with *clothes.*

obbligato. So spelled. Pl. *-os.*

obdurate, adj., 'hardened,' against tender feelings, against moral influence; stubborn. Pron. ŏb′- (in some poetry -dūr′-).

obeisance. Now usually in *to do, make,* or *pay obeisance,* i.e. a gesture of submission, respect, or deference. Pron. -bās′-.

obelus. A critical mark (— or ÷) in ancient MSS. to indicate a spurious word or passage; now also, in printing, the obelisk (dagger †) as a reference sign. Pl. *-li* (-ī). *Obelize,* to mark with the obelus or obelisk as spurious.

obfuscate. US (and OED) ŏbfŭs′kāt; COD ŏb′-; to darken, obscure, (fig.) the mind; hence bewilder, confuse. *Obfuscated by wine and brandy.*

obiter dictum. 'By the way saying' (pron. ob′-). An incidental opinion, by a judge, not binding; generally, any incidental remark or opinion. Pl. *dicta.*

object, v. The idiomatic constr. after *object* is *to* with the gerund: *I object* to using *it; I object* to your (or *John's*) using *it.* See GERUND.

object, n. (1) In the sense purpose, end, aim, &c., *object* has a long and legitimate history, but should be used with care. The commercial use (*money is no object*) should not be imitated. (2) In grammar, a noun or its substitute governed by a verb or its preposition: *I gave the* ball *to* Mary; *ball* is the direct object, *Mary* the indirect. *I wrote* her *a* letter; *her* is the indirect object, *letter* the direct.

objection. As with *object* v., the idiomatic constr. is the gerund. WRONG: *They have been blocked by the* objections *of farmers & landlords* to provide *suitable land;* read *to providing.*

objective. The use of *objective* for the more normal *aim, propose, object,* or *end* is usually an example of a writer's LOVE OF THE LONG WORD. (This sense came from *objective point,* in military use: the point to be reached as an aim or end of action. By ellipsis, *objective point* became *objective,* which has now become a VOGUE WORD.)

OBJECT-SHUFFLING. The conferring of a name on a type of mistake, making it recognizable and avoidable, is worth while if the mistake is common. *Object-shuffling* describes what unwary writers are apt to do with some of the many verbs that require, besides a direct object, another noun bearing to them a somewhat similar relation, but attached to them by a preposition. You can *inspire courage in* a person, or *inspire a person with courage;* the change of construction is object-shuffling, which with the verb *inspire* is legitimate & does not offend against idiom; but with *instill* the object-shuffling would be wrong; see INSTILL. Wherever reference is made under any word to this article, the meaning is that with that word object-shuffling is not permissible. Two or three specimens may be here given; the reader who wishes for more will find them under the words *prefix, infuse, enforce, ingratiate,* & others. WRONG: *The attempt to convict Mr. Masterman of an indiscreet utterance in a public speech & to affix the Government with responsibility therefor utterly failed* (& to affix responsibility to the Government)./*A quarterly which is doing so much to initiate into the minds of the public what is requisite for them to know* (to initiate the public in what is requisite)./*The ecclesiastical principle was* substituted by *the national* (The national principle was substituted for the ecclesiastical).

objet d'art. Pl. *objets d'art.*

obligated as a synonym for *obliged* (having received a favor &c.) is now a mere solecism; but in the full sense of bound by law or duty to do something it is still used, esp. in legal language. *You may feel* obligated *to vindicate yourself,* but NOT *deeply* obligated *for kindness.*

obligatory. Pron. (preferably) oblĭg′atorĭ.

oblige. The derivatives of *oblige* & *obligate* (see OBLIGATED above) are troublesome. There are two possible adjs. in *-able: obligable* from *obligate* (=that can be legally bound; pron. ŏb′lĭgabl) and *obligeable* (=that can have a favor conferred; pron. oblī′jabl). *Obligee* & *obligor* belong in sense to *obligate,* & have curious legal meanings: *obligor,* not one who confers an obligation, but one who binds or obligates himself to do something; *obligee,* not one who is obliged, but one to whom a service is due (toward whom a duty has been undertaken).

obliqueness, obliquity. There is some tendency to confine the latter to the secondary or fig. senses; *obliquity of mind* or *judgment* or *outlook,* but *obliqueness of the ground, a Chinaman's eyes,* or the *alignment.* It is perhaps well to fall in with such DIFFERENTIATION.

obliterate makes *-rable.*

oblivious. A word badly misused in two ways. (1) Its right sense (which has been disregarded so generally that even the dictionaries have given up the struggle to maintain the restriction) is *no longer aware* or *no longer mindful* (*Happily for him, he was soon* oblivious *of this*); it is not simply unaware or unconscious or insensible. The following examples offend against this principle: *A contempt to which the average man in his happy self-sufficiency is generally* oblivious./*He may have driven off quite* oblivious *of the fact that any harm had been done.*/*And they are ingenuously* oblivious *to the 'howlers' so constantly perpetrated.* (2) Even when the word might bear its true sense of *forgetful* (as opposed to *unaware*), it is often followed by the wrong preposition (*to*); this is an indirect result of the mistake explained in (1); it will be noticed that two of the quotations there given show *to* instead *of:* that is on the analogy of *insensible to.* But in the following examples *to* has been used even where the meaning might otherwise be the correct one of *forgetful: Each of them* oblivious to *the presence of anybody else, & intent on conversation.*/*A principle to which the romances of the eighteenth century were curiously* oblivious./*Mr. Humphreys is always* oblivious to *the fact that the minority in one part of the kingdom is represented by the majority in another part.*

The making of these mistakes is part of the price paid by those who reject the homely word, avoid the obvious, & look about for the imposing; *forgetful, unaware, unconscious, unmindful,* & *insensible,* while they usually give the meaning more precisely, lay no traps.

obnoxious has two very different senses, one of which (exposed or open or liable to attack or injury) requires notice because its currency is now so restricted that it is puzzling to the uninstructed. (*A similar case, and* obnoxious *to similar criticism.*) It is the word's rightful or *de-jure* meaning, & we may hope that scholarly writers will keep it alive, as they have hitherto succeeded in doing. Meanwhile the rest of us need not scruple to recognize the usurping or *de-facto* sense, offensive or objectionable; this has perhaps no right to exist ('apparently affected by association with *noxious,*' says the OED), but it does & will, &, unlike the other, it is comprehensible to everyone.

oboe makes *oboist.* Pron. ō'bō.

observance, observation. The useful differentiation in virtue of which neither word can be substituted for the other, & each is appropriated to certain senses of *observe,* should not be neglected. *Observance* is the attending to & carrying out of a duty or rule or custom (*a custom more honored in the breach than in the observance*); it has none of the senses of *observation* (watching, noticing, &c.), & *observation* in turn does not mean performing or complying. Though the distinction is modern, its prevalence in good writing may be judged from the OED's having only one 19th-c. & no 20th-c. example of *observance,* as against many of *observation,* in the sense consciously seeing or taking notice. Unfortunately, a perverted taste for out-of-the-way forms is undoing this useful achievement, & such uses as the following, almost unknown for two or three centuries, have again become common. WRONG: *That the Americans are & will remain interested in Europe, & that a close* observance *of European & Asiatic affairs is an essential & important part of the life of the citizen of the U.S./Emerson does not check his assumptions; he scorns* observance./*Mr. Abbott's verse, basing its claims to beauty on significant* observance, *is apt for that very reason to . . .* In all these the word should be *observation;* one quotation is added in which *observation* is wrongly used for *observance: The Government has failed to secure the* observation *of law & has lost the confidence of all classes.*

obsolescent, obsolete. Of words, *obsolescent*=going out of use, becoming obsolete (*durst* is obsolescent); *archaic*=no longer in use but retained for special purposes (*perchance* is archaic); *obsolete*=no longer in use (*simule* is obsolete).

obstacle. After *obstacle,* idiom requires *to,* NOT *of.* WRONG: *Their apathy, fatalism, & resentment of interference constituted, & still constitute, a formidable* obstacle of *progress* (to progress).

obtain. (1) Used in the sense *get, procure, acquire,* see FORMAL WORDS. (Customer—Can you get me some? Shopman—We can obtain it for you, madam.) (2) Be established, prevalent, or in vogue: *Morals that obtained in Rome;* right, but for learned contexts only—*prevailed* will usually do.

obverse. 'Front,' facing the observer, opp. of reverse; of a coin, the side bearing the head & (in US) the date; 'counterpart': *sin cannot be explained as the obverse of good.*

obviate. To meet & dispose of (a difficulty &c.): *The defect cannot be obviated by these measures.* To prevent, neutralize: *The risk has now been obviated.* WRONG: *Their action in emergencies* obviates *the thoroughness of their training;* 'makes obvious' or 'reflects' is meant.

occult. 'Hidden.' Hence, secret, mysterious; magic(al). Accent second syllable. So *occultism.*

occupancy, as compared to *occupation,* is reserved for the act of taking possession, the actual possession (of land &c.), the term during which one is an occupant.

occur makes *-rred, -rring, occurrence.*

ocher, ochre. The first is standard US, but the second (Brit.) is still the usual spelling in US art books &c.

ochlocracy. Mob rule. Pron. ŏklŏk′-.

octaroon. Use OCTOROON.

octavo. A book of sheets folded into 8 leaves (usually written 8 vo.). Hence a book size, usually about 6x9 inches. Pl. *-os.* Pron. ŏktā′vō.

octet(te). Spell *-et.*

octodecimo. (Size of) book or page given by folding sheets into 18 leaves (18 mo.); usually about 4x6½ inches. Pl. *-os.*

octopus. Pl. *-uses;* the Greek or Latin pl., rarely used, is *-podes* (-ēz), NOT *-pi.*

octoroon, -taroon. (A person of ⅛ Negro blood; offspring of a quadroon and a white.) Both are bad forms, but the second is worse than the first.

odd. (1) The sense eccentric, though often labeled 'colloq.,' has been accepted usage since the 16th c. (2) *Forty-odd people attended;* keep the hyphen to avoid ambiguity.

oddment. 'An odd thing,' remnant; an article belonging to an incomplete or broken set; in Printing, any portion of a book except the text—e.g. the index, table of contents, frontispiece. Though the word itself is established & useful, its formation is anomalous & should not be imitated.

Odysseus. Pron. -sūs.

odyssey. Pl. *-eys.*

Œ, Æ, E. In US, words beginning with *oe-* are usually spelled with *e-*, *ecology, ecumenical, edema* &c.; but *Oedipus, oestrum.* The pronunciation in all is traditionally (and properly) ē, though ĕ is often heard in US. See Æ, Œ.

-O(E)S. The writer has a legitimate grievance against the words ending in *-o.* No one who is not prepared to flout usage & say that for him every word in *-o* shall make *-oes* or shall make *-os* can possibly escape doubts. One kind of whole-hogger will have to write *heros* & *nos* & *potatos* & *gos* & *Negros,* while the other kind must face *embryoes, photoes, cameoes, duodecimoes,* & *generalissimoes.* In this book many words in *-o* have been entered with the plurals that seem advisable, & with a notation of differences in US & Brit. spelling. Here, one or two guiding principles may be indicated. Although there are several hundred nouns in *-o,* the ending is one that is generally felt to be exotic, & the plural in *-oes,* which is shown by its being indispensable with the most familiar words (*no, go, cargo, jingo, hero, Negro,* &c.) to be the normal form, is allowed only to a small minority, most words having *-os.* It must be understood that the following rules are not more than generally true, & that sometimes they come to blows with each other over a word.

1. Words used as freely in the plural as in the singular usually have *-oes,* though there are very few with which it is invariable; names of animals & plants fall naturally into this class. So *bravoes; cargoes; dominoes; heroes; potatoes.*

2. Monosyllables take *-oes;* so *goes, noes.*

3. Words of the kind whose plural is seldom wanted or is restricted to special uses have *-os;* so *dos* (the musical note); *bravados; calicos; crescendos; dittos; guanos; infernos.*

4. When a vowel precedes the *-o, -os* is usual, perhaps because of the bizarre look of *-ioes* &c.; so *arpeggios; cameos; embryos; folios.*

5. The curtailed words made by dropping the second element of a compound or the later syllables have always *-os;* so *chromos; dynamos; magnetos; photos.*

6. Alien-looking or otherwise queer words have *-os;* so *albinos; altorelievos; centos; commandos; ghettos.*

7. Long words tend to *-os;* so *archipelagos; armadillos; generalissimos.*

8. Proper names have *-os;* so *Gallios; Lotharios; Neros; Romeos.*

of shares with another word of the same length, *as,* the evil glory of being accessory to more crimes against grammar than any other. But, in contrast with the syntax of *as,* which is so difficult that blunders are very excusable, that of *of* is so simple that only gross carelessness can lead anyone astray with it. Fortunately, the commonest type of blunder with *of* is very definite & recognizable, so that the setting of it forth with illustration has a real chance of working some improvement. That type is treated in the first of the following sections, the list of which is: (1) Wrong patching. (2) Patching the unpatchable. (3) Side-slip. (4) Irresolution. (5) Needless repetition. (6) Misleading omission. (7) Freaks of idiom. (8) Archaisms &c.

1. Wrong patching. In the examples to be given, the same thing has happened every time. The writer composes a sentence in which some other preposition than *of* occurs once but governs two nouns, one close after it & the other at some distance. Looking over his sentence, he feels that the second noun is out in the cold, & that he would make things clearer by expressing the preposition for the second time instead of leaving it to be understood. So far, so good; care even when uncalled for is meritorious. But his stock of it runs short, & instead of ascertaining what the preposition really was he hurriedly assumes that it was the last in sight, which happens to be an *of* that he has had occasion to insert for some other purpose; that *of* he now substitutes for the other preposition whose insertion or omission was a matter of indifference, & so ruins the whole structure. In the examples, the three prepositions concerned are in roman type; the reader will notice that the later of the two *of*s can be either omitted or altered to the earlier preposition, & that one of these courses is necessary. WRONG: *An eloquent testimony* to *the limits* of *this kind of war, & of the efficiency of right defensive measures./Which clearly points the need* for *some measure* of *honesty & of at least an attempt at understanding of racial ambitions./He will be in the best possible position* for *getting the most out* of *the land & of using it to the best possible advantage.*

2. Patching the unpatchable. These resemble the previous set so far as the writers are concerned. They have done the same thing as before; but for the reader who wishes to correct them there is the difference that only one course is open; *of* must be simply omitted, & *between* or *without* cannot be substituted. We can say *for you & for me* instead of *for you & me* if we choose, but not *between you & between me* for *between you & me; with cries & with tears* means the same as *with cries & tears*, but *without cries or without tears* does not mean the same as *without cries or tears;* on this point, see OVERZEAL. WRONG: *It could be done* without *unduly raising the price* of *coal, or* of *jeopardizing new trade./He will distinguish* between *the American habit* of *concentrating upon the absolute essentials, of 'getting there' by the shortest path, &* of *elaboration in detail & the love of refinements in workmanship which mark the Latin mind.*

3. Side-slip. Besides the types given in the previous sections, so beautifully systematic in irregularity as almost to appear regular, there are more casual aberrations of which no more need be said than that the sentence is diverted from its track into an *of* construction by the

presence somewhere of an *of*. Analogous mistakes are illustrated in the article SIDE-SLIP. WRONG: *The primary object was not the destruction of the forts, or of the airplane shed, or of whatever military equipment was there, or even* of *killing or capturing its garrison./Its whole policy was, & is, simply to obstruct the improvement of the workingman's tavern, &* of *turning every house of refreshment & entertainment in the land into that sort of coffee tavern which . . .*

4. Irresolution. WRONG: *Here again we have illustrated her utter contempt for her pledged word &* of *her respect for nothing but brute force./His view would be more appropriate in reference to Hume's standpoint than* of *the best thought of our own day.* These are the results of having in mind two ways of putting a thing & deciding first for one & then for the other: *we have illustrated,* & *we have an illustration of; to Hume's standpoint* (*than* to *the thought*), & *to the standpoint of Hume* (*than* of *the thought*).

5. Needless repetition of *of: There is a classical tag about the pleasure of being on shore &* of *watching other folk in a big sea.* A matter not of grammar, but of style & lucidity; in style the second *of* is heavy, & in sense it obscures the fact that the pleasure lies not in two separate things but in their combination.

6. Misleading omission: *The prohibition of meetings &*‸*the printing & distribution of flysheets stopped the agitation.* Unless an *of* is inserted before *the printing,* the instinct of symmetry compels us to start by assuming that *the printing* &c. *of flysheets* is parallel to *the prohibition of meetings* instead of, as it must be, to *meetings* alone.

7. Some freaks of idiom: *You are the man* of all others *that I did not suspect. He is the worst liar* of any man *I know. That long nose* of his. The modern tendency is to rid speech of patent ILLOGICALITIES, & all of the illustrations above either are, or seem to persons ignorant of any justification that might be found in the history of the constructions, plainly illogical: *the man of all men; the worst liar of all liars; a friend of mine,* i.e. among my friends, but surely not *that nose of his,* i.e. among his noses: so the logic-chopper is fain to correct or damn; but even he is likely in unguarded moments to let the forbidden phrases slip out. They will perhaps be disused in time; meanwhile they are recognized idioms—STURDY INDEFENSIBLES, possibly.

8. Uses of *of* now archaic, dial., colloq., or illit.: *We sat on the porch reading* of *an evening. Feel* (or *smell*) of *it. He fell off* of *the roof. Your letter* of *this date* (chiefly US). *What do you want* of *him?* (i.e. with him). *In back* of *the house* (behind). *Outside* of *the house.*

off. *Off of* for *off* is now obs., dial., or colloq. US. *Off-color* is est. in the sense out of condition, below standard; for 'risqué' 'of doubtful propriety,' it is chiefly US colloq.

offense, -ce. US & Brit. spellings respectively.

OFFICIALESE. Almost simultaneously England & US became aware of a new kind of writing first used in Government publications and letters during World War II, which was eagerly adopted by business houses & other groups dealing with the public. England borrowed the GI name for it, 'gobbledegook.' US more staidly called it Officialese. The stylistic rules seem to be: Use as many and as long words as possible. Whenever possible make use of circumlocutions. Salt well with 'in the event of,' 'as to,' 'in case of,' 'in connection with,' & other such circuitous connectives. When the US Government at last brought out a style book for its civil servants, in counterattack, the *New York Times* epitomized the now condemned style in the headline *Government Will Finalize Inadvertency.* Examples of officialese are: You are correct in your assumption that no action has been taken on the application in question; therefore it would appear that due to an inadvertency, you were not informed that the application failed to meet the requirements for evidence in accordance with regulations promulgated./(A business specimen): No manuscript has yet been seen and this is therefore a competitive situation prior to the materialization of any copy./(Professional): In your own sphere, a number of independent confluences are quite certain to produce soon a full-scale emergence./(Public Notice): Before leaving, extinguish all illumination.

Characteristics of officialese are discussed in this book in the articles ANTI-SAXONISM, AVOIDANCE OF THE OBVIOUS, FORMAL WORDS, LONG VARIANTS, LOVE OF THE LONG WORD, PERIPHRASIS, POMPOSITIES, WORKING WORDS & STYLISH WORDS, and many others.

officious has a meaning in diplomacy so oddly different from its ordinary one that misunderstanding may arise from ignorance of it. A diplomatist means by an *officious communication* much what a lawyer means by one *without prejudice;* it is to bind no one, &, unless acted upon by common consent, is to be as if it had not been. The word is used as the antithesis of *official* & the notion of meddlesomeness attaching to it in ordinary use is entirely absent.

offspring=progeny, issue, can be sing. or pl. and can refer to one child or to an indefinite number of children. *He is the offspring of a genius and an idiot. Their offspring are all typical.*

often. Pron. aw′fn or ŏ′fn. The sounding of the *t*, which as the OED says is 'not recognized by the dictionaries,' is practiced by two oddly consorted classes—the academic speakers who affect a more precise enunciation than their neighbors' & insist on dĕ′vĭl & pĭk′tūr instead of dĕ′vl & pĭk′cher, & the uneasy half-literates who like to prove that they can spell by calling *hour* & *handkerchief* howr & handkerchēf instead of owr & hangkerchĭf. (The OED & Webster point out more charitably that ŏf′ten is not uncommon 'in the South of England' (OED), 'among the educated in some sections' (Webster), and 'is often used in singing' (both).

often times, ofttimes. Both now chiefly poetic or archaic.

ogre. So spelled; adj. *ogreish,* pron. ō′gerĭsh.

oh. See O.

O.K. All right; approved. Standard in US business usage (v. better *O.K.'d, O.K.'ing,* than *okayed* &c.). As a substitute for *yes,* I agree, &c., in speech, a US national disease.

old. (1) *Older, oldest* are the usual words except when seniority among members of a family is to be indicated (*The* oldest *man on the board; my* eldest *brother*). (2) Idiom allows *a boy ten years old, a boy ten years of age, a ten-year-old boy, a boy aged ten* (years). (3) For *the old lady of Threadneedle Street* (Bank of England) see SOBRIQUETS.

olden. The adj., which is of a strange formation & not to be reckoned among the numerous -EN ADJECTIVES, is also peculiar in use; *the olden time(s)* is common, but outside that phrase the word is usually as ridiculous as *Ye* substituted for *the* in sham-archaic advertisements. The combination of *olden* with *regime* in the following example is what one might expect the author to call very tasty; see INCONGRUOUS VOCABULARY: *They form part of the* olden railway regime, *when every mainline train was deliberately halted for ten minutes for refreshment.*

old-fashioned (adj.), so spelled and pronounced; NOT *old-fashion.*

old-fogyish. So spelled.

Old Glory. See SOBRIQUETS.

Old Style (abbr. *O.S.*) with dates refers to the system used before the adoption of the Gregorian Calendar. See STYLE.

olfactory. For *olfactory organ,* see POLYSYLLABIC HUMOR.

olive branches. See HACKNEYED PHRASES, & SOBRIQUETS.

Olympian, Olympic. The distinction, not as old as Shakespeare & Milton, but now usually observed, is useful. *Olympian* means of Olympus, of or as of the Greek gods whose abode was on it: *Olympian Zeus, splendor, indifference. Olympic* means of Olympia, of the athletic contests there held: *Olympic games, victors.*

ominous. Pron. ŏm′-.

omit makes *-tting* &c., *omissible.* Constr.: *He omitted* to *mention* or *mentioning* (both idiomatic).

omni-. Combining prefix meaning *all* (*omnipotent, omnivorous;* accent second syllable of each).

omnibus. Pl. *-uses.* The public vehicle is now usually *bus* (no apostrophe). *An omnibus volume,* one containing reprints of a number of works bound together (often by the same author or from a single source, i.e. the same magazine, publisher, &c.).

omnium gatherum. (Miscellaneous collection; a medley.) See FACETIOUS FORMATIONS.

omnivore. Pl. *-a.* Animal that eats both animal and vegetable food.

on. For *onto, on to,* & *on,* see ONTO.

-on. Of words derived from Greek & having in English the termination *-on:* (1) Some may, & often or always do, form the plural in *-a;* so *criterion, organon, phenomenon.* (2) Others seldom or never use that form, though it would not be incorrect, but prefer the ordinary English *-s;* so *electron, lexicon, skeleton.* (3) In others again, the substitution of *-a* for *-on* to form the plural would be a blunder, their Greek plurals being, if they are actual Greek words, of some quite different form, & *-s* is the only plural used; such are *canon, demon, mastodon, pylon, siphon, tenon.* Words about which mistakes are possible are listed in their dictionary places.

once. 1. The use as a conjunction (i.e.=if once or when once, as in *Once you consent you are trapped*) is sound English enough, but it is sometimes forgotten that it is not for all contexts. There is a vigorous abruptness about it that makes it suitable on the one hand for highly literary expression, in poetry for instance, & on the other for the short sentences of actual conversation or dramatic dialogue. Between these extremes it is better to be content with *if* or *when,* supplemented or not by the adverb *once.* In the first quotation *if,* & in the second *when once,* would be better: *It is to be explained perhaps by the fear that* once *foreign affairs become predominant, home affairs take a back place./But their aloofness might have quite the opposite result of that which they desire; for*^once *the crisis had arrived, home affairs would indeed be swamped.*

2. *Once & away; once in a way.* The two phrases seem properly to have distinct meanings, the first 'once & no more' (*It is not enough to harrow once & away*—1759 in OED), & the second 'not often'; but the present custom is to use both in the second sense, each person choosing the form that he considers fittest to convey that sense, & *in a way* being the favorite.

one. 1. Forms: *anyone* &c. 2. *One & a half years* &c. 3. *One of, if not the best book(s).* 4. *One of the men that does things.* 5. Kind of pronoun. 6. Poss. & other belongings. 7. Mixtures of one with we &c.

1. The compound forms recommended are *anyone, everyone, no one, someone. Anyone knows that answer* but *Does* any one of you *know the answer?* For discussion see EVERYONE.

2. *One & a half years; a year & a half.* The second is recommended, when words & not figures are used; for discussion, see MILLION 1, 2, & HALF 1. The wrong form is seen in *India has shown her loyalty by the fact that* one & a half millions *of her sons volunteered; a million & a half of her sons* is obviously preferable.

3. *One of the, if not the, best book(s).* Grammar is a poor, despised branch of learning; if it were less despised, we should not have such frequent occasion to weep or laugh at the pitiful wrigglings of those who feel themselves in the toils of this phrase. The nature of the problem is this: we have two expressions of the type 'one of the best books' & 'the best book'; but we have been taught to avoid repetition of words, & therefore desire that part of one of these nearly similar expressions should be understood instead of said or written. When, as always happens in this idiom, there is a change of number, the only thing is to see that the place from which the understood word is omitted is after, not before, the word from which it is to be supplied; for from a word that has already been expressed the taking of the other number is not forbidden. Accordingly, the right form is: *One of the best books yet written, if not the best; One of the most spacious, if not the most spacious, of salons; One of the greatest export articles*

of Norway, perhaps the greatest.

It may be thought that for the second example the best has not been done, & that *One of the, if not the, most spacious of salons* would have been less clumsy, & yet legitimate. But it is not legitimate, because *most spacious* has to be taken as at the same time singular & plural; English disguises that fact by its lack of inflexions, but does not annul it; &, though most people are not quite sure what is the matter, they can feel that there is something the matter.

4. WRONG: *One of the men who* does *things.* This blunder will be found discussed in NUMBER 5.

5. Kind of pronoun. *One* is a pronoun of some sort whenever it stands not in agreement with a noun, but as a substitute for a noun preceded by *a* or *one:* in 'I took one apple' *one* is not a pronoun, but an adjective; in 'I want an apple; may I take one?' *one* stands for *an apple* or *one apple,* & is a pronoun. But for the purpose of this article it is more important to notice that *one* is not always the same kind of pronoun; it is of three different kinds in these three examples: *One of them escaped; One is often forced to confess failure; One knew better than to swallow that.* In the first, *one* may be called a *numeral pronoun,* which description will cover also *I will take one, They saw one another, One is enough,* & so on. In the second, *one* has a special sense; it stands for *a person,* i.e. the average person, or the sort of person we happen to be concerned with, or anyone of the class that includes the speaker. It does not mean a particular person; it might be called an indefinite, or an impersonal, pronoun; for the sake of contrast with the third use, *impersonal pronoun* will here be the name. In the third, *one* is neither more nor less than a substitute for *I,* & the name that best describes it is the *false first-personal pronoun.* The distinction between the numeral & the impersonal, which is plain enough, is important because on it depend such differences as that between *One hates his enemies* & *One hates one's enemies;* those differences will be treated in section 6. The distinction between the impersonal & the false first-personal, a rather fine one in practice, is still more important because it separates an established & legitimate use from one that ought not to exist at all. Outside this section, it will be assumed that it does not exist except as a mere misuse of the impersonal *one.*

Let us take a fictitious example & pull it about, in order to make the point clear: *He asked me to save his life, & I did not refuse;* the true first-personal pronoun, twice. *He asked me to save his life; could* one *refuse?* true first-personal pronoun, followed by impersonal pronoun. *He asked me to save his life, &* one *did not refuse;* true first-personal pronoun, followed by false first-personal pronoun. The *one* of *could one refuse?* means I or anyone else of my kind or in my position, & is normal English; the *one* of *one did not refuse* cannot possibly mean anything different from *I* by itself, & is a fraud. But the self-conscious journalist has seen in this fraud a chance of eating his cake & having it; it will enable him to be impersonal &

personal at once; he has repined at abstention from *I*, or has blushed over not abstaining; here is what he has longed for, the cloak of generality that will make egotism respectable. The sad results of this discovery are shown in the following extracts; in none of them is there any real doubt that *one* & *one's* mean *I* & *my* simply; but in some more than in others the connection with the legitimate impersonal use is traceable. The journalist should make up his mind that he will, or that he will not, talk in the first person, & go on the sound assumption that *one* & *one's* do not mean *I* & *me* & *mine*.

THE FALSE FIRST-PERSONAL ONE: *But* one *must conclude* one's *survey* (*at the risk, I am afraid, of tedious reiteration*) *by insisting that . . ./I have known in the small circle of* one's *personal friends quite a number who . . ./This is not, I think, ecclesiastical prejudice, for* one *has tried to be perfectly fair.*

6. Possessive, & other belongings, of *one*. By other belongings are meant the reflexive, & the form to be used when the pronoun *one* has already been used & is wanted again either *in propria persona* or by deputy; as, when Caesar has been named, he can be afterwards called either *Caesar* or *he*, so, when *one* has been used, is it indifferent whether it is repeated itself or represented by *he* &c.?

In the first place, there is no doubt about the numeral pronoun *one;* its possessive, reflexive, & deputy pronoun are never *one's*, *oneself*, & *one*, but always the corresponding parts of *he, she*, or *it*. RIGHT: *I saw* one *drop* his *stick; Certainly, if* one *offers* herself *as candidate;* One *would not go off even when I hammered* it.

Secondly, the impersonal *one* always can, & now [Brit.] usually does, provide its own forms —*one's, oneself*, & *one;* thus One *does not like to have* one's *word doubted; If* one *fell*, one *would hurt* oneself *badly*. But, in US, in older English, & in a small minority of modern Brit. writers, the sentences above would run: One *does not like to have* his *word doubted; If* one *fell*, he *would hurt* himself *badly*. The prevailing Brit. fashion (*one's, oneself*, &c.) gives a useful differentiation between the numeral & the impersonal, which however is not reliable till it is universal; & it makes recourse to the horrible *their* &c. (One *does not like to have* their *word doubted*) needless.

The difference between *One hates* his *enemies* & *One hates* one's *enemies* is at once apparent if to each is added a natural continuation: *One hates* his *enemies & another forgives* them; *One hates* one's *enemies & loves* one's *friends*. The first *one* is numeral, the second impersonal, & to make *his* & *one's* exchange places, or to write either in both places, would be plain folly.

Let it be added, for anyone who may regard *one's* & *one(self)* in the use here concerned as fussy modernism, that they are after all not so modern. *I hope, cousin*, one *may speak to* one's *own relations*—Goldsmith.

7. Mixtures of *one* with *we, you, my*, &c. These are all bad, though the degrees of badness differ; for instance, it is merely slipshod to pass from *one* in an earlier sentence to *you* in the next, but more heinous to bring two varieties into syntactical relations in a single sentence.

WRONG: *As* one *goes through the rooms,* he *is struck by the youth of most of those who toil; the girls marry,* you *are told. He* belongs to section 6; *you* illustrates the more venial form of mixture./*As* one *who vainly warned* my *countrymen that Germany was preparing to attack her neighbors for many a long day before the declaration of war,* I *say that . . . My* should be *his, one* being the numeral pronoun; but this kind of attraction in relative clauses (*my* taking the person of *I* instead of that of *one* & *who*) is very common./*To listen to his strong likes & dislikes* one *sometimes thought that* you *were in the presence of a Quaker of the eighteenth century.* A bad case; *you were* should be *one was.*/ *No* one *likes to see a woman who has shared* one's *home in distress; no one* contains the numeral, not the impersonal, *one,* & *one's* should be *his.*

Oneida. The Indian tribe and the Lake. Pron. ō nī′da.

oneself. The usual reflexive and emphatic form, though *one's self* is also permissible.

one-sided makes *one-sidedness.*

only, adv.: its placing & misplacing. *I read the other day of a man who 'only died a week ago,' as if he could have done anything else more striking or final; what was meant by the writer was that he 'died only a week ago.'* There speaks one of those friends from whom the English language may well pray to be saved, one of the modern precisians who have more zeal than discretion, & wish to restrain liberty as such, regardless of whether it is harmfully or harmlessly exercised. It is pointed out in several parts of this book that illogicalities & inaccuracies of expression tend to be eliminated as a language grows older & its users attain to a more conscious mastery of their materials. But this tendency has its bad as well as its good effects. The pedants who try to forward it when the illogicality is only apparent or the inaccuracy of no importance are turning English into an exact science or an automatic machine. If they are not quite botanizing upon their mother's grave, they are at least clapping a strait jacket upon their mother tongue, when wiser physicians would refuse to certify the patient.

The design is to force us all, whenever we use the adverb *only,* to spend time in considering which is the precise part of the sentence strictly qualified by it, & then put it there—this whether there is any danger or none of the meaning's being false or ambiguous because *only* is so placed as to belong grammatically to a whole expression instead of to a part of it, or to be separated from the part it specially qualifies by another part.

It may at once be admitted that there is an orthodox placing for *only,* but it does not follow that there are not often good reasons for departing from orthodoxy. For *He only died a week ago* no better defense is perhaps possible than that it is the order that most people have always used & still use, & that the risk of misunderstanding being chimerical, it is not worth while to depart from the natural. Remember that in speech there is not even the possibility of misunderstanding, because the intonation of *died* is entirely different if it, & not *a week ago,* is qualified by *only;* & it is fair that a reader should be supposed capable of supplying the decisive intonation where there is no temptation to go wrong about it. But take next an example in which, ambiguity being practically possible, the case against heterodox placing is much stronger: *Mackenzie* only *seems to go wrong when he lets in yellow; & yellow seems to be still the standing difficulty of the color printer.* The orthodox place for *only* is immediately before *when,* & the antithesis between *seeming to go* & really *going,* which is apt to suggest itself though not intended, makes the displacement here ill advised. Its motive, however, is plain—to announce the limited nature of the wrong before the wrong itself, & so mitigate the censure: a quite sound rhetorical instinct, &, if *goes* had been used instead of *seems to go,* a sufficient defense of the heterodoxy. But there are many sentences in which, owing to greater length, it is much more urgent to get this announcement of purport made by an advanced *only;* e.g. the orthodox *It would be safe to prophesy success to this heroic enterprise* only *if reward & merit always corresponded* positively cries out to have its *only* put after *would,* & unless that is done the reader is led astray; yet the precisian is bound to insist on orthodoxy here as much as in *He died only a week ago.*

The advice offered is this: there is an orthodox position for the adverb, easily determined in case of need; to choose another position that may spoil or obscure the meaning is bad; but a change of position that has no such effect except technically is both justified by historical & colloquial usage & often demanded by rhetorical needs.

The OED remarks on the point should be given: *'Only* was formerly often placed away from the word or words which it limited; this is still frequent in speech, where the stress & pauses prevent ambiguity, but is now avoided by perspicuous writers.' Which implies the corollary that when perspicuity is not in danger it is needless to submit to an inconvenient restriction.

onomatopoeia. (Gram.): 'name-making.' (Pron. -pē'*ya.*) Formation of names or words from sounds that resemble those associated with the object or action to be named, or that seem suggestive of its qualities: *babble, cuckoo, croak, tintinnabulation,* are probable examples. (Rhet.): use of words whose sound suggests the sense: *a hurrying sound of wings that westward whirr.*

onomatopoeic, -poetic. The first form (pron. -pē'ĭk) is decidedly preferable, because the other inevitably suggests, at least to those who do not know Greek, irrelevant associations with *poet.*

onto, on to, on. Writers & printers should make up their minds whether there is such a preposition as *onto* or not. If there is not, they should omit the *to* in contexts that are good English without it; if there is & they like it better than the simple *on* or *to* (an odd taste, except under very rare conditions), they should make one word of it. Abstain from the preposition if you like; use it & own up if you like; but do not use it & pretend there is no such word; those should be the regulations. The use of *on to* as separate words is, however, correct when *on* is a full adverb; & very rarely doubts may arise whether this is so or not. Is *on* an adverb, or is *onto* a preposition, for instance, in *He played the ball* on to *his wicket?* As *He played on* could stand by itself, it is hard to deny *on* its independent status. Occasions for *on to: We must walk* on to *Keswick; Each passed it* on to *his neighbor; Struggling* on to *victory.* Occasions for *on* or *to* or *onto,* but on no account *on to: Climbed up* on(to) *the roof; Was invited* (on)to *the platform; It struggles* (on)to *its legs again; They fell* 300 *ft.* on(to) *a glacier. The logic of this electioneering leads straight to the abolition of the contributions & the placing of the whole burden* on(to) *the State./The Pan-Germans are strong enough to depose a Foreign Secretary & force their own man* on(to) *the Government in his place.*

onus. Burden, responsibility. No plural. Pron. ō′nŭs.

onward(s). The shorter form is much commoner in all senses, except possibly in phrases of the type *from the tenth century onwards.*

oö-. Comb. form meaning egg(s). In US the diaeresis is usually kept (*oölite, oölogy*); in Brit. *oo-*. *Oölite,* pron. ō′olīt.

opacity, opaqueness. The fig. senses are avoided with the second, but the literal senses are not confined to it, though there is perhaps a tendency to complete differentiation: *The* opacity *of his understanding; Owing to the* opaqueness (*or opacity*) *of the glass.*

open-. Webster gives *openmouthed, openhanded, openhearted,* as single words, but many other US dictionaries retain the hyphen, as does Brit. practice.

opera, Lat. n. pl., 'works,' rare in English; sing. *opus;* n. sing. 'music drama,' pl. *operas.* See OPUS.

operate makes *-rable.* The senses manage, work, conduct, chiefly US: *owned and* operated *by the Pennsylvania Railway; the cost of* operating *the cars; the lamps* operated *by the lighting companies.*

operative, n. Formerly a worker, esp. an artisan; now used (US?) for agents of government bureaus (Secret Service, F.B.I., &c.); also of detectives generally.

opere citato. 'In the work cited.' Abbr. *op. cit.* Italics not necessary.

opine. To think, suppose, express an opinion (*that*); now archaic or (usually) WORN-OUT HUMOR.

opinionated, -ative. Both have existed long enough in English to justify anyone in using either. But for those who do prefer a sound to a faulty formation it may be said that the first is unobjectionable, the second not.

opportunity. Constr. *of*+gerund; *to*+inf.; for+noun. *The opportunity* of meeting *you,* to meet *you,* for *a meeting.* WRONG: *A fact* of which *he took every* opportunity. You take *the opportunity,* or *an opportunity,* or *every opportunity, of doing* something. You take *advantage,* or *all possible advantage, of* a fact or event or state of affairs. The two sets of phrases must not be mixed; see

CAST-IRON IDIOM, & ANALOGY.

opposite. (1) Constr. *to* or *from*: *opposite to what I had expected*; *opposite from my beliefs*. It must not be followed by *than* (WRONG: *Opposite than I had hoped*). (2) *Opposite* tempts careless writers to the slovenly clipping seen in: *He can thwart him by applying it to the* opposite *purpose*ʌ*for which it was intended* (*he* is pupil, *him* teacher, & *it* the teaching). Insert *from* (or *to*) *that* after *purpose*. (3) For the distinction between *opposite*, *contrary*, &c., see CONTRARY, CONVERSE, OPPOSITE.

oppress makes *-ssible*, *-ssor*.

oppugn. Pron. ŏ pūn'. The only living senses are to controvert, to call in question.

optative. The natural pronunciation is op′tativ and it is so pronounced in US. In Brit. those who deal in grammar often call it ŏpta′tiv, and it is not worth while to attempt to reform them.

optic. For the noun=eye, see PEDANTIC HUMOR. 'Formerly the learned & elegant term' (OED).

optimism, -ist(ic). (Belief that this is the best of all possible worlds; that good must ultimately prevail over evil.) The first two quotations show the words in their proper sense, the last two in their modern popular triviality. RIGHT: *Besides optimism, which affirms the definitive ascendency of good, & pessimism, which affirms the definitive ascendency of evil, a third hypothesis is possible.*/ *The optimistic or sentimental hypothesis that wickedness always fares ill in the world.*/ LOOSE: *The company had suffered severe losses, but at the last meeting the chairman spoke with a fair amount of* optimism./ *He is* optimistic *if he really thinks that he, or whoever represents the Foreign Office, can leave Paris by October.* They have become VOGUE WORDS, and owe their vogue to the delight of the ignorant in catching up a word that has puzzled them when they first heard it, & exhibiting their acquaintance with it as often as possible; & they displace with what differs more or less from the idea intended the familiar words that would express it exactly. In the third & fourth quotations, *hope* & *sanguine* would have given the sense not less but more exactly than *optimism* & *optimistic*. See POPULARIZED TECHNICALITIES.

opus. Work, composition, esp. music, used in citing individual numbers (e.g. Beethoven, op. 15). Pl., seldom used, *opera*. *Opus magnum*, see MAGNUM OPUS.

opusculum. Minor musical or literary work. Pl. *-ula*.

or. 1. *Or, nor*. There are sentences in which it is indifferent, & affects neither meaning nor correctness, whether *or* or *nor* is used. Compare with *I can neither read nor write* (in which *nor* is requisite), & with *I cannot either read or write* (in which *or* is requisite), *I cannot read nor* (or indifferently *or*) *write*. The alternatives in the last are differently arrived at, but are practically equivalent: *I cannot read nor* (can I) *write*; *I cannot read*(-) *or*(-)*write*, where the supposed hyphens mean that *write* may be substituted for *read* if desired. The use of *nor* in such cases was formerly in fashion, & that of *or* is now in fashion; that is all. But the modern preference for *or* where it is equally legitimate with *nor* has led to its being preferred also where it is illegitimate. WRONG: *It is of great importance that they should face them* in no *academic spirit,* or *trust too much to conclusions drawn from maps.*/No *Government Department* or any *other Authority has assisted.* The test of legitimacy has been explained in NOR; & it suffices here to say that in the first extract it is the position of *no* (alter to *they should not face them in any*), & in the second the presence of *any* (precluding the carrying on of *no*), that forbid *or.*

2. Number, pronouns, &c., after *or.* When the subject is a set of alternatives each in the singular, however many the alternatives, & however long the sentence, the verb must be singular; for discussion see NUMBER, 3. WRONG: *Either the call of patriotism & the opportunity of seeing new lands, or conscription, or the fact that tramping was discouraged even by old patrons when the call for men became urgent,* account *for it.* (Read *accounts.*) If alternative members differ in number &c., the nearest prevails (Were *you or he,* was *he or you, there?; either he or you* were, *either you or he* was), but some forms (e.g. *Was I or you on duty?*) are avoided by inserting a second verb (*Was I, or were you . . . ?*). Forms in which difference of gender causes difficulty with pronouns (*A landlord or landlady expects* their, his or her, his, *rent*) are usually avoided, *their rent* or *the rent due to them* being ungrammatical, *his or her rent* or *the rent due to him or her* clumsy, & *his rent* or *the rent due to him* slovenly; some evasion, as *expects rent,* or *the rent,* is always possible.

3. *Or* in enumerations. WRONG: *I never heard a sermon that was simpler, sounder,* or *dealt with more practical matters.* In the very numerous sentences made on this bad pattern there is a confusion between two correct ways of saying the thing: (a) *that was simpler, sounder, or more practical,* (b) *that was simpler or sounder or dealt with more practical matters.* See ENUMERATION, & for full discussion AND 2.

4. Wrong repetition after *or.* A misguided determination to be very explicit & leave no opening for doubt results in a type of mistake illustrated in the article OVERZEAL. It is peculiarly common with *or,* & to put writers on their guard a number of examples follow. False analogy from *and* explains it; with *and,* it does not matter whether we say *without falsehood & deceit* or *without falsehood & without deceit,* except that the latter conveys a certain sledge-hammer emphasis; but with *or* there is much difference between *without falsehood or deceit* (which implies that neither is present) & *without falsehood or without deceit* (which implies only that one of the two is not present). WRONG: *No great economy* or no *high efficiency can be secure* (omit *no*)./ *There would be nothing very surprising* or nothing *necessarily fraudulent in an unconscious conspiracy to borrow from each other* (omit *nothing* or change *or* to *and*)./*To no conference*

of pacifist tendencies or to no *gatherings where representatives of the enemy people will be found, will American labor organizations send delegates* (omit *to no*)./*Every arrangement ends in a compromise, & no one* or no *party may be expected to carry its own views out in their entirety* (no person or party).

-or, see -OUR & -OR.

oral=spoken; *verbal*=of words, written or spoken. But the two are used interchangeably; a verbal agreement could be in writing, but it is generally understood to be oral.

orang-outang is the popular spelling (US & Brit.), but *orang-utan* 'more nearly correct.' See PEDANTRY.

orate. A BACK-FORMATION from *oration,* & marked by the slangy jocularity of its class.

orbit. Course, path; transf. & fig., scope of activity; not to be confused with *orb*=sphere, globe.

ordeal. All the verse quotations in the OED (Chaucer, Spenser, Cowley, Butler, Tennyson) show the accent on the first syllable; but modern dictionaries give ôr dēl′ or (better) ordē′*a*l first.

order. *In order that* is followed by *may* and *might,* NOT *can* and *could.* See IN ORDER THAT.

ordinal numbers, first, third, tenth, &c. (*Cardinal,* one, three, ten.)

ordinance, ordnance, ordonnance. The first, the decree, regulation (in US local or municipal law); *ordnance,* cannon, military supplies, &c.; *ordonnance* (rare), the arrangement of parts in an architectural, literary, or artistic composition; (also, in France=*ordinance*).

oread. A nymph of the mountains or hills. Pron. or′ĭad.

oreography &c. See ORO-.

organon. 'Instrument' of all reasoning; system or treatise on Logic. Pl. *-ana,* rarely *-ns.*

orient, orientate, vv. There is no differentiation. The shorter form is the older and more usual both in lit. and fig. senses. *Orientate* might well be abandoned as a NEEDLESS VARIANT.

orison. Usually pl. Archaic, a prayer. Pron. ŏ′rĭzn.

Orleans. The preferred pronunciation for New Orleans is or′lĭaNZ′ (not the older orlēnz′).

oro-. Combining form meaning mountain (e.g. *orogeny, orography*); also, that meaning mouth (*oropharynx*). The identical representation of Greek *oros,* mountain, & Latin *os,* mouth, by *oro-* is regrettable. The most convenient arrangement consistent with correctness would have been to make *ori-* the combining form meaning mouth & *oreo-* that of *oros,* mountain. *Ori-* does exist in *orinasal* & some other mouth-words, but it is too late to do anything about those that are est. with *oro-.*

orotund. The odd thing about the word is that its only currency, at least in its non-technical sense, is among those who should most abhor it, the people of sufficient education to realize its bad formation; it is at once a monstrosity in its form & a pedantry in its use. If the elocutionists & experts in voice production like it as a technical term, they are welcome to it. The rest of us should certainly leave it to them, & not regard it as a good substitute for *magniloquent, high-sounding, inflated, pompous, imposing,* & the like.

Orpheus. Pron. (properly) ôr′fūs (popularly often or′fēŭs).

oscillate makes *-llable, -tor.*

osculatory. A favorite POLYSYLLABIC HUMOR word: *The two ladies went through the* osculatory *ceremony./At the end of one letter were a number of dots which he (counsel) presumed were meant to represent an* osculatory *performance.*

ostler, var. of *hostler.* Stableman at an inn; groom. (*Hostler* is the est. word in US.) Pron. ŏs′ler; the form without *h-* is now the est. one in Brit. though etymologically wrong; *hospital, hostel, hotel* & *hostler* belong together.

ostracize makes *-zable.*

other. 1. *Each other* makes *each other's* (poss.), and can be used both when the reference is to two and when it is to be a larger number. For the syntax & for the distinction sometimes made between *each other* & *one another,* see EACH 2.

2. *On the other hand.* For the difference between this & *on the contrary,* see CONTRARY 2.

3. *Of all others. You are the man* of all others *I wanted to see.* A mixture of *You are the man of all men* &c. & *You are the man I wanted to see beyond all others.* A still popular ILLOGICALITY, perhaps to be counted among the STURDY INDEFENSIBLES that are likely to survive their critics.

4. *Other, others,* or *another.* The writers of the following sentences may be supposed to have hesitated between *other* & *others;* if they had decided for *others,* they would have been more in tune with modern usage: *We find here, as in* other *of his novels, that he has no genius for . . . /Mrs. — will, we hope, incite* other *of her countrymen to similar studies./ A Privy Councillorship, an honor which has but rarely been won by* other *than those who were British subjects from the moment of their birth.*

In two of these we have what the OED calls the absolute use of the adjective, the noun represented by *other* being present elsewhere in the sentence, but not expressed with *other* (*other novels of his novels*); in the third we have the full pronoun use, *other* meaning *other persons,* & *persons* not being expressed either with *other* or elsewhere. But alike of the absolute & the pronoun use the OED describes the plural *other* as archaic, & the plural *others* as the regular modern form. In older English, however, *other* was normal in such contexts, so that those who like the archaic can justify themselves; *others* is here recommended.

If it is now contrary to usage to prefer *other* to *others,* it is much worse to prefer it to *another,* which is the modern absolute & pronominal form in the singular just as *others* is in the plural; but that is what has been done in: *A number of writers on various subjects serve to give interest to the review on* other *than its political side*—unless indeed the meaning is *its other than political side,* which would stand or fall, as the equivalent of its non-political side, with the examples discussed at the end of 5; but, if so, the order of words has been dislocated.

5. Abuses of *other than.* The existence of an adverbial use of *other* is recognized by the OED, but supported by very few quotations, & those from no authors whose names carry weight; although recent dictionaries give '*other,* adv. = *otherwise*' without comment, its use should be avoided as both ungrammatical & needless: *So that no new invention could come in* other than *through a specific company* (except)./*Yet how many of the disputants would know where to look for them*—other than *by a tiresome search through the files of the daily press—if they desired to consult them?* (short of)./*Although the world at large & for long refused to treat it* other than *humorously* (otherwise).

But simple confusion between *other* & *otherwise* does not account for every bad *other than.* A notion seems to prevail that one exhibits refinement or verbal resource or some such accomplishment if one can contrive an *other-than* variant for what would naturally be expressed by some other negative form of speech: *with other than apprehension* is thought superior in literary tone to *without apprehension: Up to the very end no field company would look with* other than apprehension *to meeting the 25th on even terms./Mr. Collier has some faults to find, but no Englishman can be* other than *flattered by the picture which he paints of British activities.* *Other than* should be registered as a phrase to be avoided except where it is both the most natural way of putting the thing & grammatically defensible.

otherwise. Modern usage, US & Brit., tends to disregard the fact that *otherwise* is properly an adv., *other* an adj. For careful writers, who may wish to follow grammatical tradition in spite of the changing idiom, the examples of the deprecated uses are listed: *No further threats, economic or* otherwise, *have been made* (should be *no further economic or other threats*)./*Large tracts of land, agricultural &* otherwise (*some agricultural and some not*)./*The success or* otherwise *of the undertaking* (*the success or failure*). Often *or otherwise* is superfluous, even if grammatically justifiable: *I am not concerned with the accuracy* or otherwise *of the figures given./To discover the truth* or otherwise *of his statements.* What does *or otherwise* add?

Or otherwise in this construction is not quite always superfluous. It is not superfluous in *With the view of showing the applicability* (or otherwise) *to the practical affairs of government of the principles which . . .* That is due to the particular verb *showing,* which prevents *applicability* from including as usual its opposite. But, while such cases are rare, it is better even in these to give the sense in some other way, e.g. *to showing how far the principles which . . . are applicable.* Similarly, in *It has an area of under* 100 *square miles, & enjoys*—or otherwise—*a very heavy rainfall* 'or does not enjoy,' 'or endures,' &c., would be better in grammar, as good in sense, &, considering the dimness with which *or otherwise* now so often sparkles, not inferior in brilliance.

The reader may perhaps be

curious about the statement that such phrases as *applicability or otherwise* are grammatically not quite indefensible. In *He never conveyed to me any intimation that he disapproved, strongly* or otherwise, *of my conduct,* we have an unquestionably legitimate use, *otherwise* being parallel to *strongly,* another adverb. In *Yesterday he was our hero, but today he is* otherwise, *otherwise* is parallel not to an adverb, but to the noun *hero;* nevertheless grammar is not offended, because the complement of *to be* can be noun, adjective, or adverb, indifferently: *He is a hero, He is dead, He is abroad.* That is why *Governor Sulzer is the hero* or otherwise *of a quaint election story* is excusable; though not itself legitimate, it is a slight & natural extension of something that is legitimate. The type with *or otherwise* answering to abstract nouns like *applicability* or *truth,* is similarly accounted for. *Is it applicable or is it otherwise?* is sound enough English; when we want to turn these questions into a noun, *its applicability or otherwise* not unnaturally presents itself as a short form of *its being applicable or being otherwise;* it can claim a sort of second-hand soundness; like an addled egg, it has in an earlier phase been good.

To sum up, *or otherwise* is in grammar occasionally quite correct, often indefensible, but usually capable of a rather far-fetched justification; in meaning it is, except when strictly correct, nearly always superfluous, & always less exact than some equivalent; & in style (again except when correct) it has the disadvantage of suggesting, even when the user is innocent of any such intent, a sort of insipid jocosity.

otiose. Orig. 'at leisure.' The only sense in which it is likely to be used today is 'without any practical function, purposeless': *the word sometimes has point but is often otiose.* Pron. ō′shĭōs.

ottava rima (Poet.): 'octave verse.' (Pron. -tä-′, rē-′.) The stanza invented by Boccaccio and used by Byron in *Don Juan.* Eight five-foot iambic lines, rhyming abababcc.

ought, n., is a wrong form for NOUGHT.

ought, v., is peculiarly liable to be carelessly combined with auxiliary verbs that differ from it in taking the plain infinitive without *to. Can & ought to go* is right, but NOT *Ought & can go.* WRONG: *We should be sorry to see critics suggesting that they* ought or could have *acted otherwise;* insert *to* after *ought,* or write *that they could or ought to have acted.* See ELLIPSIS 2. *Had ought* (vulg. or illiterate) is still occasionally seen in print.

our. 1. *Our, ours.* WRONG: Ours *& the Italian troops are now across the Piave.* The right alternatives are: *The Italian troops & ours, The Italian & our troops, Our & the Italian troops;* see ABSOLUTE POSSESSIVES.

2. The editorial *our,* like *we* & *us* of that kind, should not be allowed to appear in the same sentence, or in close proximity, with any non-editorial use of *we* &c. In the following, *our* & the second *we* are editorial, while *us* & the first *we* are national: *For chaos it is now proposed to substitute law, law by which* we *must gain as neutrals,*

& which in our *view, inflicts no material sacrifice on* us *as belligerents.* We *do not propose to argue that question again from the beginning, but . . .*

3. *Our, his.* WRONG: *Which of us would wish to be ill in* our *kitchen, especially when it is also the family living room?* If a possessive adjective were necessary, *his* & not *our* would be the right one, or, at greater length, *his or her.* People of weak grammatical digestions, unable to stomach *his,* should find means of doing without the possessive; why not simply *the kitchen,* here? But many of them, who prefer even the repulsive THEIR to the right forms, are naturally delighted when *of us* gives them a chance of the less repulsive but at least slovenly *our.* It is undeniable that *which of us* is a phrase denoting a singular (=which one of us), & that the possessive required by it is one that refers to a singular.

-OUR & -OR. In US usually *-or* (except in *glamour* and *Saviour*). [Fowler's discussion follows verbatim.] The American abolition of *-our* in such words as *honour* & *favour* has probably retarded rather than quickened English progress in the same direction. Our first notification that the book we are reading is not English but American is often, nowadays, the sight of an *-or.* 'Yankee' we say, & congratulate ourselves on spelling like gentlemen; we wisely decline to regard it as a matter for argument; the English way cannot but be better than the American way; that is enough. Most of us, therefore, do not come to the question with an open mind. Those who are willing to put national prejudice aside & examine the fact quickly realize, first, that the British *-our* words are much fewer in proportion to the *-or* words than they supposed, &, secondly, that there seems to be no discoverable line between the two sets so based on principle as to serve any useful purpose. By the side of *favour* there is *horror,* beside *ardour pallor,* beside *odour tremor,* & so forth. Of agent-nouns *saviour* (with its echo *paviour*) is perhaps the only one that now retains *-our, governor* being the latest to shed its *-u-.* What is likely to happen is that either, when some general reform of spelling is consented to, reduction of *-our* to *-or* will be one of the least disputed items, or, failing general reform, we shall see word after word in *-our* go the way of *governour.* It is not worth while either to resist such a gradual change or to fly in the face of national sentiment by trying to hurry it; it would need a very open mind indeed in an Englishman to accept *armor* & *succor* with equanimity. Those who wish to satisfy themselves that the above denial of value to the *-our* spelling is borne out by facts should go to the article *-or* in the OED for fuller information than there is room for here.

-OUR- & -OR-. Even those nouns that in Brit. usage still end in *-our* (see -OUR & -OR), as opposed to the American *-or,* e.g. *clamour, clangour, humour, odour, rigour, valour, vapour, vigour,* have adjectives ending in *-orous,* not *-ourous: humorous, vaporous,* &c.

Derivatives in *-ist, -ite,* & *-able* are regarded as formed directly from the English words, & in Brit. use retain the *-u-;* so *colourist* & *humourist, labourite* (cf. *favourite,* of different formation), *colourable* & *honourable.* But derivatives in *-action* & *-ize* are best treated, like those in *-ous,* as formed first in Latin, & therefore spelled without the *-u-;* so *coloration, invigoration, vaporize,* & *deodorize.*

ours, our. See OUR 1.

ourself, ourselves. The former, 'denoting a single person in legal or editorial style,' is now usually facetious or pompous: *By the time* we ourself *reached the scene the excitement was over./ We cannot persuade* ourself *that the government is in earnest.*

outcome is one of the words specially liable to the slovenly use described in the article HAZINESS. WRONG: *The* outcome *of such nationalization would undoubtedly* lead *to the loss of incentive & initiative in that trade.* The outcome of nationalization would *be* loss; nationalization would *lead to* loss.

out-herod. In view of the phrase's great popularity & many adaptations, two cautions are perhaps called for. The noun after *out-herod* should be *Herod* & nothing else (the OED quotes 'out-heroding the French cavaliers in compliment'; cf. *Ecclesiastical functionaries who* outheroded *the Daughters of the Horse-leech*), &, after adaptions like *out-milton* & *out-nero, Milton* &c. should be repeated (*out-zola Zola,* NOT *out-zola the Realists*). Secondly, the name used should be one at least that passes universally as typifying something; to *out-kautsch Kautsch* (*The similar German compilation edited by Kautsch was good; but Charles easily* out-kautsches Kautsch) is very frigid.

out loud. Colloq. when the simple *aloud* is meant (e.g.: *He read it* out loud, *not to himself*).

OUT OF THE FRYING PAN. A very large proportion of the mistakes that are made in writing result neither from simple ignorance nor from carelessness, but from the attempt to avoid what are rightly or wrongly taken to be faults of grammar or style. The writer who produces an ungrammatical, an ugly, or even a noticeably awkward phrase, & lets us see that he has done it in trying to get rid of something else that he was afraid of, gives a worse impression of himself than if he had risked our catching him in his original misdemeanor; he is out of the frying pan into the fire. A few typical examples will be here collected, with references to other articles in which the tendency to mistaken correction is set forth more at large.

WRONG: *Recognition is given to it* by no matter whom *it is displayed.* The frying pan was 'no matter whom it is displayed by,' which the writer did not dare keep, with its preposition at end; but in his hurry he jumped into nonsense; see MATTER, & PREPOSITION AT END./*When the record of this campaign comes* dispassionately to be written, *& in just perspective, it will be found that . . .* The writer took 'to be dispassionately written' for a SPLIT INFINITIVE, & by his correction convinces us that he does not know a split infinitive when he sees it./*In the hymn & its setting there is something which,* to use a word of Coleridge, *'finds' men.* 'A word of Coleridge's' is an idiom whose genesis may be doubtful, but it has the advantage over the correction of being English; *a word of Coleridge* is no more English than *a friend of me.*/*The object is to bring before the public many ancient & modern aspects of the* theater's art *which have too long been disregarded.* 'The theater's art' is a phrase that, apart from surroundings, no one would prefer in prose to 'the art of the theater.' What the writer has shied at is the repetition of *of* in *of the art of the theater,* which is however much more tolerable than this 's INCONGRUOUS./*But the badly cut-up enemy troops were continually reinforced &* substituted *by fresh units.* The frying pan was REPLACE in the sense 'take the place of'; the fire is the revelation that the writer has no idea what the verb SUBSTITUTE means./*Sir Starr Jameson has had one of the most varied & picturesque careers of any Colonial* statesmen. 'Of *any* statesman,' idiomatic but apparently illogical, has been corrected to what is neither logical (*of all* would have been nearer to sense) nor English./*The claim yesterday was for the difference* between *the old rate, which was a rate by agreement,* & between *the new.* The writer feared, with some contempt for his readers' intelligence, that they would not be equal to carrying on the construction of *between;* he has not mended matters by turning sense into nonsense; see OVERZEAL./*The reception was held* at the bride's aunt. The reporter was right in disliking *bride's aunt's,* but should have found time to think of 'at the house of.'

The impression must not be left, however, that it is fatal to read over & correct what one has written. The moral is that correction requires as much care as the original writing, or more. The slapdash corrector, who should not be in such a hurry, & the uneducated corrector, who should not be writing at all, are apt to make things worse than they found them.

outré. Outside the bounds of propriety. Pron. ōō trā'. But see FRENCH WORDS.

outside. (1) RIGHT: *The outside* of *books; to ride on the outside* of *a bus.* But *Outside the bounds of propriety* (NOT *outside of*); *natural forces are outside morality.* (2) *Outside of*=beyond the number of, with the exception of (*outside of those who are personally interested, no one will agree with him*) is US colloq. and has little to recommend it.

outstanding, 'that stands out,' (fig.) prominent, conspicuous: *of outstanding importance; an outstanding exception.* VOGUE use: *one of the* outstanding *artists of our generation; one of the* most outstanding *historians I have read.*

over-all, adj.,=including everything, is best hyphened and best not overused (cf. *over-all policy, over-all estimate, over-all values,* &c.; *comprehensive, total, whole* are the older, more normal words). *Overalls,* n. pl., the garment, is one word.

overly=excessively, is chiefly US and Scotch. Often *over* itself is the normal word; *it pays not to be* overly *zealous*=*it pays not to be* overzealous.

overthrowal. WRONG: *The drama lies in the development of a soul toward the knowledge of itself & of the significance of life, & the tragedy lies in the* overthrowal *of that soul. Overthrow* itself is a noun, or *overthrowing* if a more active sense is wanted; *overthrowal* is unknown to dictionaries, US & Brit.

OVERZEAL. Readers should be credited with the ability to make their way from end to end of an ordinary sentence without being pulled & pushed & admonished into the right direction; but some of their guides are so determined to prevent straying that they plant great signposts in the middle of the road, often with the unfortunate result of making it no thoroughfare. In the examples the signpost word, always needless, often unsightly, & sometimes misleading, is enclosed in brackets: *But it does not at all follow* that *because Mr. Long is* 65 [that] *he will not be equal to . . .* See THAT, conj., for more./*We agree that the Second Chamber would be differently constituted* according as *we went forward to other schemes of devolution & federation,* [& according as we] *decided to make Home Rule for Ireland our one & only experiment.* Read *or decided;* see ACCORDING for more./*The working man has to keep his family on* what *would be considered a princely wage,* but [which] *in point of fact, is barely enough to keep body & soul together.* See WHAT for more./*But what* no *undergraduate or* [no] *professor in the art of writing verse could achieve is . . .* See OR 4 for more./*There are others who talk* of *moving & debating a hostile amendment, & then* [of] *withdrawing it. Moving, debating, & then withdrawing* make up a single suggested course; but the superfluous *of* implies that the talkers vacillate between two courses.

ovum. Pl. *ova.*

owing to is here inserted not because it is misused, but in the hope of calling attention to it as a phrase that should be more used. Its rights are now perpetually infringed by DUE TO (in US the infringement is so general that it is now accepted by many as standard usage). The difference is that while *owing to* can be either adjectival or adverbial (*The accident was not* owing to *carelessness;* owing to *my carelessness he broke his leg*), *due to* is grammatically only adjectival (*The accident was not* due to *carelessness*). In the following examples (& see DUE for others) those who prefer the traditional distinction would substitute *owing* for *due:* Due *to this omission* he *has unfortunately committed himself to views he finds it difficult to go back on./But,* due *largely to the fact that the hall was situated a long distance from the Congress building,* the visitors *did not attend in such large numbers as previously.* See QUASI-ADVERBS.

owl-like. Keep the hyphen.

ox. Pl. *oxen.*

Oxford Movement=Tractarianism. A movement toward revival of Roman Catholic doctrine & observance, set forth in *Tracts of our Times* (1833–41), ending with tract No. 90, by John Henry Newman. *Oxford Group Movement,* Buchmanism, founded 1921 by Frank Buchman; belief in a return to primitive Christianity and the confession of sins.

oxymoron. Pl. *-s* or *-ra.* (Rhet.): 'sharp-dull.' (Pron. -mō-ʹ.) The combining in one expression of two terms that are ordinarily contradictory, & whose exceptional coincidence is therefore arresting. (*A cheerful pessimist; Harmonious discord; His honor rooted in dishonor stood; And faith unfaithful kept him falsely true.*) The oxymoron was what made *The Gentle Art of Making Enemies* effective.

P

pace. Pron. pā sē̂. This latinism (*pace tua* 'by your leave,' or 'if you will allow me to say so'; *pace Veneris* 'if Venus will not be offended by my saying so') is one that we could well do without in English. Minor objections are that the construction is awkward in English (*pace Mr. Smith* is the best we can do for *pace Caesaris* in the genitive), & that the Latinless naturally extend the meaning or application as they do those of VIDE, RE, & E.G. WRONG: *But in the House of Lords there is no hilarity*—pace *Lord Salisbury's speech last night. Pace* does NOT mean *notwithstanding a fact or instance,* but *despite someone's opinion.*

padrone. (It. patron.) In US an Italian employment agent. Pron. pad rō′nĕ; pl. *-ni* (-ē).

paean. Hymn (orig. to Apollo) of joy, thanks, praise. Pron. pē′*an.*

pageant. Best pron. pă′jant.

pailful. Pl. *pailfuls.*

painedly. A bad form not listed in most dictionaries.

paint the lily is the right wording of the quotation from Shakespeare (*King John,* IV, ii. 11), not *gild.* See MISQUOTATIONS.

painterly, adj., adv., characteristic of a painter, artistic (ally), was listed as rare in the OED and is seldom included in more recent dictionaries. It has recently been revived in the sense 'worthy of a painter, befitting a painter' (*His composition and execution are always* painterly, *even in his most trivial watercolors*), but sounds odd & un-English to the average man. See REVIVALS.

pair, n. Formerly (and still occasionally) used as a pl. after a numeral: *six pair of horses; pairs* is now more usual, at least in US.

PAIRS & SNARES. Of the large number of words that are sometimes confused with others a small selection is here given. Those who have any doubts of their infallibility may find it worth while to go through the list & make sure that these pairs have no terrors for them. Under one of each pair in its dictionary place they will find remarks upon the difference & usually proofs that the confusion does occur. While vagueness about suffixes or prefixes is the most frequent cause of mistakes, it is not the only one. Often the two words might legitimately have been, or actually were in older usage, equivalents, & the ignorance is not of Latin elements but of English idiom & the changes that DIFFERENTIATION has brought about. And again there are pairs in which the connection between the two words is only a seeming one. To exemplify briefly, *contemptuous* & *con-*

temptible are a pair in which suffixes may be confused; *masterful* & *masterly* one in which differentiation may be wrongly ignored; & *deprecate* & *depreciate* one of the altogether false pairs. The list follows:

acceptance & acceptation
advance & advancement
affect & effect
alternate & alternative
antitype & prototype
ascendancy & ascendant
ceremonial & ceremonious
comity & company
complacent (-ency) & complaisant (-ance)
immovable & irremovable
inflammable & inflammatory
judicial & judicious
laudable & laudatory
legislation & legislature
luxuriant & luxurious
oblivious & unconscious
observance & observation
compose & comprise
consequent & consequential
contend & contest
continuance & continuation
definite & definitive
derisive & derisory
e.g. & i.e.
euphemism & euphuism
fatal & fateful
forceful & forcible
fortuitous & fortunate
hypothecate & hypothesize
perspicacity (-acious) & perspicuity (-uous)
policy & polity
precipitate & precipitous
predicate & predict
proportion & portion
purport & purpose
regretful & regrettable
resource, recourse, & resort
reversal & reversion
transcendent & transcendental
triumphal & triumphant
unexceptionable & unexceptional

pajamas. In US usually so spelled. Brit. *pyjamas.*

palaeo-, palæo-, paleo-. Combining form meaning *old, ancient.* In US the usual spelling is *paleo-,* Brit. *palaeo-.* (Usually pron. pā′lēō-.)

palaestra. (Wrestling school; gymnasium.) Pl. *-trae, -tras.*

pale, adj., makes *palely, palish. Pale,* n. (stake, picket; rarely, an enclosure) now usually fig., as in *beyond the pale.*

palindrome. A word, phrase, sentence, &c., that reads the same backwards as forwards: *lewd did I live & evil I did dwel.*

palladium. Statue of Pallas Athena (cap.); fig. a safeguard (not cap.): *a kind of* palladium *to save the city; the* palladium *of our civil rights.* Pl. *-ia.*

pall-mall. A game played with ball and mallet, pron. pĕl mĕl; the London street (where it used to be played), pron. păl măl or as the game. The US cigarettes, pron. pĕl mĕl or päl mäl. The Mall, măl.

palmetto. Pl. *-os.*

palpable. *Palpable* means literally touchable, or perceptible by touch; that meaning is freely extended to perceptible by any of the senses, & even to appreciable by the intelligence. But (WRONG) *The work that has yet to be done is* palpable *from the crowded paper of amendments with which the House is faced* is a good illustration of the need of caution in handling dead metaphors. The final extension is necessary here, & would pass but for the *from* phrase that is attached. *From the paper* &c. implies not sensuous perception, but intellectual inference; the dead metaphor in *palpable* is stimulated into angry life by the inconsistency; see METAPHOR. *Palpable* is one of the words that are liable to clumsy treatment of this sort because they have never become vernacular English, & yet are occasionally borrowed by those who have no scholarly knowledge of them.

pan-. Combining form meaning *all, every*. Thus, *panacea,* orig. an herb that cured all diseases, hence a universal remedy (not for only one disease or distress); *Pan-American,* of both N. & S. America; *Panhellenic,* of all Greece.

pandemonium. Pl. *-ums.* Abode of all demons (in Milton, the capital of Hell); hence a wild tumult, utter confusion.

pander, n. & v. (From Pandarus, who procured Cressida for Troilus, in Boccaccio, Chaucer, & Shakespeare.) Though *-ar* is the older & better form, it is useless to try to restore it.

panel. US usually *-led, -ling;* Brit. *-lled* &c.

panful. Pl. *-ls.*

panic makes *panicky, panicked.*

papier mâché. In US now naturalized in pronunciation; pāper măshā. Do not italicize.

papilla. Pl. *-ae.*

papyrus may be the sedge, the writing material, the scrolls, or the MS. written on them. Pl. *-ri.*

par. ('Equal, equality'; hence normal, average.) *On par, up to par, below par,* all accepted terms in commerce & economics, are little less than slang when used in literary contexts.

parable. A short allegorical narrative designed to answer a single question or suggest a single principle, & offering a definite moral. See SIMILE & METAPHOR.

paradise rivals NECTAR in the number of experiments that the desire for a satisfactory adjective has occasioned. But, whereas *nectar* is in the end well enough provided, no one uses any adjective from *paradise* without feeling that surely some other would have been less inadequate. Some of the variants are *paradisaic**(*al**), *paradisal, paradisiac*(*al*), *paradisian**, *paradisic*(*al*), of which the asterisked ones are badly formed. *Paradisal* is perhaps the least intolerable, & that perhaps because it retains the sound of the last syllable of *paradise;* but the wise man takes refuge with *heavenly, Edenlike,* or other substitute.

paraffin. In US, usually the wax used for sealing jellies &c.; Brit. paraffin oil=US kerosene. See KEROSENE.

Paraguay. The OED pronunciation is -gwā, which is also preferred in US; but -gwī, the Sp. pronunciation, is also often heard.

parakeet, paroquet. The first is est., US & Brit.

parallel. (1) In both US & Brit., the verb makes *paralleled* &c. (2) The noun, where *parallel* itself will not serve, is *parallelism,* NOT *parallelity;* the latter is not even recorded in the OED. WRONG: *We have already had occasion to comment on the remarkable* parallelity *between . . . & . . .* (3) Constr. *to, with* (*to* perhaps more frequent), *between* (two things).

PARALLEL-SENTENCE DANGERS. 1. Negative & affirmative. A single example may be given here to show the kind of difficulty that occurs.

WRONG: *There is not a single town in the crowded district which* is not *open to these attacks,* & must *be prepared for defense with guns, troops, & airplanes.* The *not* spoils the second clause. Correct by putting a semicolon after *attacks* and continuing *everyone must be prepared.* But, for discussion & illustration of this & many other varieties, see NEGATIVE & AFFIRMATIVE.

2. Inverted & uninverted. WRONG: *And* not merely *in schools & colleges,* but as *organizers of physical training,* are women *readily finding interesting & important employment.* The *not merely* part requires the inverted *are women finding;* the *but* part requires the uninverted *women are finding.* The right solution is to start the sentence with *And women are finding employment not merely* &c. In INVERSION the section headed *Inversion in parallel clauses* is devoted to this & similar types.

3. Dependent & independent. WRONG: *The municipality charged itself with the purchase of these articles in wholesale quantities, &* it was to the Town Hall that poor people applied for them, & were served *by municipal employees.* The parallel clauses in question were, in their simple form, (a) *The poor people applied for them to the Town Hall,* & (b) *The poor people were served by municipal employees.* The writer has decided, for the sake of emphasizing *Town Hall,* to rewrite (a) in the *it was . . . that* form; but he has forgotten that he cannot make (a) dependent & leave (b) independent unless he supplies the latter with a subject (*& they were served*). The correct possibilities are: (i, both independent) *The people applied to the Town Hall for them, & were served by municipal employees;* (ii, both dependent) *It was to the Town Hall that the people applied, & by municipal employees that they were served;* (iii, dependent & independent) *It was to the Town Hall that the people applied, & they were served by municipal employees.*

paralyse. Brit. (and etymolog.) so spelled; US usually *paralyze.*

paramount. 'Pre-eminent, supreme': a non-comparable absolute: *of paramount importance* (but NOT *of* most *paramount importance*); 'superior (*to*)': *their first duty is* paramount *to all subsequent engagements.*

paranoea, -noia. (Mental derangement, esp. when marked with delusions of grandeur &c.) The first would be the regular form, but the other, with unlatinized Greek spelling, is more used. Pron. -noiă (Brit. sometimes -nēa).

parcel. US usually *-led, -ling;* Brit. *-lled* &c.

parenthesis. Pl. *-theses* (-ēz). The marks ( ) in US (in Brit. called round BRACKETS).

PARENTHESIS. (Gram.) A word, phrase, clause, or sentence not grammatically essential to the passage in which it is inserted; usually set off by commas, parentheses, or dashes.

1. Relevance. A parenthesis may have or not have a grammatical relation to the sentence in which it is inserted. In *This is,* as far as I know, *the whole truth* there is such a relation, & in *This is,* I swear, *the whole truth* there is not; but one is as legitimate as the other. It is

not equally indifferent whether the parenthesis is relevant or not to its sentence; parentheses like the following cannot possibly be justified. WRONG: *In writing this straightforward & workmanlike biography of his grandfather* (the book was finished before the war, & delayed in publication) *Mr. Walter Jerrold has aimed at doing justice to Douglas Jerrold as dramatist, as social reformer, & as good-natured man.* The time of writing & the delay have no conceivable bearing on the straightforwardness, workmanlikeness, grandfatherliness, justice, drama, reform, or good nature, with which the sentence is concerned. If it had been called *a long-expected* instead of *a straightforward* biography, it would have been quite another matter; but, as it is, the parenthesis is as disconcerting as a pebble that jars one's teeth in a mouthful of plum pudding. The very worst way of introducing an additional fact is to thrust it as a parenthesis into the middle of a sentence with which it has nothing to do. WRONG: *Napoleon's conversations with Bertrand & Moncholon* (it is unfortunate that there are several misprints in the book) *are a skilful blending of record & pastiche.*

2. Identification. Still more fatal than readiness to resort to parenthesis where it is irrelevant is inability to tell a parenthesis from a main clause. WRONG: *A remarkable change had come over the Government,* he suggested, *since the Bill had left the Committee,* & expressed doubts *as to whether Mr. Masterman altogether approved of the new turn of affairs.* In this, *he suggested* is as much a parenthesis as if it had been enclosed in brackets; if it were not parenthetic, the sentence would run, *He suggested that a change had come.* But the writer, not knowing a parenthesis when he sees (or even when he makes) one, has treated it as parallel with *expressed,* & so fully parallel that its *he* may be expected to do duty with *expressed* as well as with *suggested.* Either the first part should be rewritten as above, with *suggested* for its governing verb, or the second part should be cut off from the first & begin *He expressed doubts,* or else another parenthesis should be resorted to—*It was doubtful,* he continued, *whether Mr. . . .*

parenthetic(al). In most uses the longer form is obsolescent; but it has still a special sense worth preserving, i.e. full of or addicted to parentheses (*a horribly parenthetical style*). The adv. is *parenthetically.*

par excellence. 'By (virtue of) special excellence'; preeminently; above all others that could be so called. Pron. pär′ ĕk sê länz′. But see FRENCH WORDS.

pariah. In India, a member of a low (or no) caste; fig., a social outcast. US dictionaries give pä rī′*a* first, but in Brit. usage the stress is always on the first syllable.

pari mutuel. (French, 'mutual stake.') A form of betting in which those who have bet on the winning horse share the total stakes. Now naturalized in pronunciation; do not italicize. (Sometimes hyphened)

parlance. Way of speaking. *In common parlance, legal parlance,* &c. See JARGON.

parliament. Pron. par'lament.

parlo(u)r. US usually *-or,* Brit. *-our.*

parlous is a word that wise men leave alone. It is the same by origin as *perilous* ('hazardous': *parlous roads, weather,* &c.; 'risky': *a parlous plea, a parlous bird to hit*); but it had centuries ago the same fate that has befallen *awful* & *chronic* within living memory; it became a VOGUE WORD applied to many things very remote from its proper sense. It consequently lost all significance, 'died of its own too much,' & was for a long time (for most of the 18th c.) hardly heard of. In the 19th c. it was exhumed by ARCHAISM & PEDANTIC HUMOR, & the adepts in those arts should be allowed exclusive property in it.

Parmesan. Pron. -z-.

parody. An imitation for comic effect or ridicule. See BURLESQUE for synonyms.

parricide, patricide. The first is the orthodox form. *Patricide* has no doubt been substituted by some deliberately, in order to narrow the meaning to murder(er) of a father, as *matricide* & *fratricide* are limited, & by others in ignorance of the right word. *Parricide* includes not only the murder of either parent or any near relative or anyone whose person is sacred, but also treason against one's country; & the making of *patricide* to correspond to *matricide* is therefore natural enough.

parson is properly applied only to a rector or incumbent of a parochial church. Loosely (or colloq.) applied to any clergyman.

partially is often used where *partly* would be better. This is, no doubt, because it is formed normally, by way of the adjective *partial,* while *partly* formed direct from the noun *part* is abnormal. There is between the two words much the same difference as between *wholly* (opp. *partly*) & *completely* (opp. *partially*). In other words, *partly* is better in the sense 'as regards a part & not the whole,' & *partially* in the sense 'to a limited degree': *It is* partly *wood; This was* partly *due to cowardice; A* partially *drunken sailor; His* partially *re-established health.* Often either will give the required sense equally well; *partly* is then recommended, since it is *partially* that tends to be overused; see LONG VARIANTS for other such pairs. The wrong choice has been made in: *Whether 'The Case is Altered' may be wholly or* partially *or not at all assignable to the hand of Jonson./Lightning had struck the* partially *completed skeleton of a barn he worked on.*

PARTICIPLES. 1. Unattached participles. Knowing *how much you need it,* the book *will be in your hand tomorrow.* But it is the writer, not the book, that knows. For this danger, as insidious as it is notorious, see UNATTACHED PARTICIPLE.

2. Absolute construction. WRONG: The Municipal Council, having refused the clerks' demand for a rise in salary, *those in the Food Supply offices today declared a strike.* This false stopping (there should be no comma after *Council*) is an example of what is perhaps both the worst & the commonest of all mistakes in punctuation. See ABSOLUTE CONSTRUCTION.

3. Fused participles. WRONG: *Jimmy Wilde's first fight in the United States resulted in* him being beaten *by Jack Sharkey./ They are so well chosen that there is little fear of the* reader *to whom the more familiar aspects of the subject have ceased to appeal* being wearied *by them.* 'Him being beaten,' 'the reader being wearied,' are examples of a construction regarded in this book as a corrupting influence in modern English, & fully discussed in the articles GERUND & FUSED PARTICIPLE.

4. Initial participle &c. If newspaper editors, in the interest of their readers, maintain any discipline over the gentlemen who provide inch-long paragraphs to stop gaps, they should take measures against a particular form that, by a survival of the unfittest, bids fair to swallow up all others. In these paragraphs, before we are allowed to enter, we are challenged by the sentry, being a participle or some equivalent posted in advance to secure that our interview with the C.O. (or subject of the sentence) shall not take place without due ceremony. The fussiness of this is probably entertaining while it is quite fresh; one cannot tell, because it is no longer fresh to anyone. Examples: Described *as 'disciples of Tolstoi,' two Frenchmen sentenced to two months' imprisonment for false statements to the registration officer are now to be recommended for deportation.*/Aged *seventy-nine, the Rev. F. T. Wethered, vicar of Hurley, near Marlow, whose death is announced, bathed daily in the Thames, winter & summer, till a few months ago.*

parti-colored, party-. *Parti-* is best. US hyphen, Brit. usually one word (a reversal of the usual custom).

particular used to intensify a demonstrative adj. (*this, that, these,* &c.) weakens the sense and the style: *This* particular *book was a present from my brother. This* does the work alone. *Particularly* for *very, more than usually* (*I'm not* particularly fond *of music*) is colloq. or slang.

parting. *The British Empire is at the parting of the ways.* Empires & men are now so familiar with that position that, when told they are there once more, they are not disquieted; their only impulse is to feel in their breeches pockets for the penny with which they may toss up. See HACKNEYED PHRASES.

partisan, -zan. The *-san* form is preferred for the weapon, the adherent of a party, & the soldier. US accents the first syllable whatever the meaning; COD prefers -san′ for the person.

PARTITIVE. (Gram.): 'of division.' Partitive words are such nouns & pronouns as by their nature imply the separating or distinguishing of a part of some whole from the rest, such as *part, portion, half, much,* superlatives, *some, any, each;* the partitive genitive is that of the word denoting the whole, which is made to depend on a partitive word by being put in the genitive in fully inflected languages, but in English attached to it by *of. But the* greatest of these *is charity; greatest* is the partitive word, & *of these* the partitive genitive.

partly. In respect to a part;

not wholly: *Written partly in prose, partly in verse.* See PARTIALLY.

party. *The* party *who called you could not wait* typifies the commercial or colloq. use of *party* for *person* (possibly justified here by the fact the person was a party to the attempted telephone message); *who was the old* party *you were with last night?* typifies the vulgar or jocular use. For *party* in the sense *person* without the qualification 'one participating in a contract, suit, legal action, &c.,' see POPULARIZED TECHNICALITIES.

parvenu. 'Arrived.' A person of obscure origin who has risen to wealth or position (derog.); an upstart. Pron. pär′vê nū or as French, but see FRENCH WORDS.

pasquinade. (Pasquino, a statue in Rome on which Latin verses were posted.) A squib posted in a public place, of unknown authorship. See LAMPOON.

pass makes *passed* for its past tense (*You passed me by*), & for its p.p. used verbally (*It has passed out of use*); but when the p.p. has become a mere adj. it is spelled *past* (*In past times*). The distinction between p.p. & adj. is rather fine in *Those times have passed away* (p.p.), *Those times are passed away* (intransitive p.p.), *Those times are past* (adj.).

passable, passible. The first word (pron., usually, pá-) is the adj. from the verb *pass* (esp., able to pass muster, i.e. fairly good; mediocre); the second (pron. păs-) is a separate word in learned & especially theological use, meaning capable of feeling. See also IMPASSABLE.

passe partout. In picture framing, a mat, or the type of framing held together by heavy strips of gummed paper. In French ('pass everywhere'), a master key. In US two words, COD hyphened. Pron. päs partoo′.

passer-by. Keep the hyphen. Pl. *passers-by.*

passim. Here and there. In every part. *Reference to it is found in the Ethics, Book II* passim. (Usually italicized.)

PASSIVE DISTURBANCES. The conversion of an active-verb sentence into a passive-verb one of the same meaning—e.g. of *You killed him* into *He was killed by you*—is a familiar process. But it sometimes leads to bad grammar, false idiom, or clumsiness.

1. The double passive. *People believed him to have been murdered* can be changed to *He was believed to have been murdered;* but *They attempted to carry out the order* cannot be changed to *The order was attempted to be carried out* without clumsiness or worse. For full discussion see DOUBLE PASSIVES.

2. Passive of *avail oneself of.* WRONG: *We understand that the credit* will be availed of *by three months' bills, renewable three times, drawn by the Belgian group on the British syndicate.* A passive is not possible for *avail oneself of;* see AVAIL.

3. Active of *do* after passive verb. WRONG: *Inferior defenses could then, as now, be tackled, as Vernon* did *at Porto Bello.* The active form would be *An admiral could then, as now, tackle inferior defenses;* if *defenses could be tackled* is substituted, the voice of *did*

must be changed too—*as was done*, or *as they were*, *by Vernon* &c. This lapse is a common one; see DO 3 c.

4. *As.* WRONG: *The great successes of the co-operators hitherto have been won* as *middlemen.* Active form, sound enough—*The co-operators have won their successes as middlemen.* Conversion to the passive has had the effect of so tying up *the co-operators* with *of* that it is not available, as in the active form, for *as middlemen* to be attached to. A common lapse.

past. See PASS. *Past master*, two words unhyphened. *A past master of a lodge* (=one who has filled the master chair); *a past master of electioneering tactics*, or *in verbal fluency* (=an adept, a 'master' in the field).

pastel. The plant (woad), pron. păs′tel. The pigment and the adj., in US păstĕl′, Brit. păs′tel. (The spelling *pastelle* is erron.)

pasteurism, -ize. Pron. pas′-tēr- (NOT -tūr-). From (Louis) Pasteur, chemist, 1822–95.

pastiche. (It. *pasticcio*, 'any manner of pastie or pye.') A (lit. or mus.) medley or 'hodgepodge'; a literary or artistic work in imitation of another style; an artistic composition made up of fragments. Pron. păs tēsh′.

pastor. One in charge of a flock. Hence a minister or priest in charge of a church or parish. In Brit., used only of foreign Protestant clergy.

pastorale. Music. Pron. -ahlĕ; pl. *-li* (*-ē*). (*Pastoral*, adj. & n., 'of shepherds,' country life, esp. of poetry, art, &c.)

pat, adv. & adj. Opportune(ly); pertinent(ly), apt(ly): *He had the whole story pat; a pat answer.* Colloq.=firmly: *to stand pat.*

patent. Pā-, or pă-? Pā- predominates in England, pă- in America. But even in England some retain pă- for the sense connected with *letters patent*, i.e. for the technical uses as opposed to the general or etymological senses 'open & plain.' And in US pā- is often used for the sense 'evident' (*a patent truth, patently absurd*) and the Bot. & Zool. senses (spreading, open).

paterfamilias. Head of a family. In Roman history, or references to it, the pl. should be *patresfamilias;* but as an adopted English word it makes *paterfamiliases.* Pron. usually pā-.

pathetic fallacy is a phrase made by Ruskin; the OED quotes from *Modern Painters: All violent feelings . . . produce . . . a falseness in . . . impressions of external things, which I would generally characterize as the 'Pathetic fallacy.'* In ordinary modern use *pathos* & *pathetic* are limited to the idea of painful emotion; but in this phrase, now common though little recognized in dictionaries, the original wider sense of emotion in general is reverted to, & *the pathetic fallacy* means the tendency to credit nature with human emotions. *Sphinxlike, siren-sweet, sly, benign, impassive, vindictive, callously indifferent the sea may seem to a consciousness addicted to* pathetic fallacies.

pathos. Pron. pā-.

patois. Dialect spoken by the common people of a particular district. Pron. pă′twä. For *patois, dialect*, &c., see JARGON.

patriot(ic). In US usually pā-. Brit., the adj. often pă-.

patrol makes *-lling, -lled, -llable.*

patron, -age, -ess, -ize. In US pā- prevails in all but possibly the second. The OED gives the sound of the *-a-* as pātron, pătronage, pātroness, & pătronize.

pea. Pl. formerly *pease,* now usually *peas.*

peaceable. So spelled. A *peaceable* country is one not disposed to war; a *peaceful* one, one not at war.

peaked. *A peaked hat* (pēkt), i.e. pointed; *she looks peaked* (pēk′ĕd), i.e. pinched, wasted. The verb *peak,* to waste away, survives chiefly in *peak & pine.*

pean, var. of PAEAN.

peccadillo. (Now so spelled.) A trifling offense (dim. of *pecado,* sin). In US pl. usually *-oes;* Brit. *-os.* Pron. pĕk-.

pedagogy, -gical. In US usually -gŏj-, though the hard -g- (-gŏg-), nearer the Greek, is also heard, esp. in academic circles.

PEDANTIC HUMOR. No essential distinction is intended between this & POLYSYLLABIC HUMOR. One or the other name is more appropriate to particular specimens, & the two headings are therefore useful for reference; but they are manifestations of the same impulse, & the few remarks needed may be made here for both. A warning is necessary, because we have all of us, except the abnormally stupid, been pedantic humorists in our time. We spend much of our childhood picking up a vocabulary; we like to air our latest finds; we discover that our elders are tickled when we come out with a new name that they thought beyond us; we devote some pains to tickling them further; & there we are, pedants & polysyllabists all. The impulse is healthy for children, & nearly universal—which is just why warning is necessary; for among so many there will always be some who fail to realize that the clever habit applauded at home will make them insufferable abroad. Most of those who are capable of writing well enough to find readers do learn with more or less of delay that playful use of long or learned words is a onesided game boring the reader more than it pleases the writer, that the impulse to it is a danger signal—for there must be something wrong with what they are saying if it need recommending by such puerilities—& that yielding to the impulse is a confession of failure. But now & then even an able writer will go on believing that the incongruity between simple things to be said & out-of-the-way words to say them in has a perennial charm. It has, for the reader who never outgrows hobbledehoyhood; but for the rest of us it is dreary indeed. It is possible that acquaintance with such labels as *pedantic & polysyllabic humor* may help to shorten the time that it takes to cure a weakness incident to youth.

An elementary example or two should be given. The words *sartorial* (of clothes), *interregnum* (gap), are familiar ones: *While we were motoring out to the station I took stock of his* sartorial *aspect, which had changed somewhat since we parted./In his vehement action his breeches fall down &*

his waistcoat runs up, so that there is a great interregnum.

These words are, like most that are much used in humor of either kind, both pedantic & polysyllabic. A few specimens that cannot be described as polysyllabic are added here, & for the larger class of long words the article POLYSYLLABIC HUMOR should be consulted: *ablution; aforesaid; bivalve* (the succulent); *digit; eke* (adv.); *ergo; erstwhile; nasal organ; nether garments; parlous.*

PEDANTRY may be defined, for the purpose of this book, as the saying of things in language so learned or so demonstratively accurate as to imply a slur upon the generality, who are not capable or not desirous of such displays. The term, then, is obviously a relative one; my pedantry is your scholarship, his reasonable accuracy, her irreducible minimum of education, & someone else's ignorance. It is therefore not very profitable to dogmatize here on the subject; an essay would establish not what pedantry is, but only the place in the scale occupied by the author; & that, so far as it is worth inquiring into, can be better ascertained from the treatment of details, to some of which accordingly, with a slight classification, reference is now made. The entries under each heading are the names of articles; & by referring to a few of these the reader who has views of his own will be able to place the book in the pedantry scale & judge what may be expected of it. There are certainly many accuracies that are not pedantries, as well as some that are; there are certainly some pedantries that are not accuracies, as well as many that are; & no book that attempts, as this one does, to give hundreds of decisions on the matter will find many readers who will accept them all.

Spelling niceties: See DIDACTICISM; *amuck; morale.*

Pronunciation: See *Christmas; diphtheria; margarine.*

Long or learned words: See *dual(istic)*; LOVE OF THE LONG WORD; *intermediary; meticulous.*

Synonyms: See *apt; authentic; broad; classic(al); exceedingly.*

Variants & differentiation: See *acceptance; act(ion); alternative; ascendancy; complacent; masterful.*

Symmetry: See *between; both; either; nor.*

Logic & pleonasm: See *ago; because; equally as;* HAZINESS.

Rules of style: See *and* 2; ELEGANT VARIATION; FUSED PARTICIPLE; *only;* PREPOSITION AT END; SPLIT INFINITIVE.

Reversion to etymological senses: See *dastardly; decimate; egregious; enormous; infinite; internecine.*

Objections to particular words or constructions: See *aggravate; case; conservative; different; doubt(ful); feasible; ilk;* INVERSION; *like; oblivious; quieten.*

peddler, -lar. The first is the usual US spelling; the second Brit.

pejorative. Depreciatory. (Of words, whose orig. sense is depreciated by a suffix, e.g. *poetaster.*) Preferred pronunciation, pē′-; sometimes pejor′-.

pellucid. A scientific & literary word, rare in speech. Literally, allowing the passage of light, *pellucid ice;* fig., showing the sense clearly, mentally clear; clear in style or expression; *pellucid writers, a pellucid mind.*

pen, v., to write (down), is now chiefly poetic or formal; in ordinary contexts it suggests archaism or affectation.

penalize. Pron. pē′-.

penates. Household gods (Rom. myth.). Pron. pĭnā′tēz.

penchant. A strong inclination, a liking (constr. now usually *for*): *A penchant for ancient music.* Pron. pĕn′chant or as French.

pendant, pendent, pennant, pennon. There is much confusion between these; the reasonable distribution of meanings to forms would be as follows: *pendent,* adj., hanging; *pendant,* n., a hanging ornament or appurtenance; *pennant,* n., in nautical use for certain pieces of rigging & certain flags; *pennon,* n., in heraldic & military use for a lance streamer or the like. See DIFFERENTIATION.

pendente lite. ('Pending the suit.') Pron. pĕndĕn′tĭ lī tĭ.

pendulum. Pl. *-ms.*

penetralia. Innermost recesses (esp. of a temple). A plural noun.

penetrate makes *-trable, -tor.*

penicillin. So spelled.

peninsula(r). Uses of the noun (*-la*) instead of the adj. (*-lar*), as the *Peninsula War,* or vice versa, as *the Spanish Peninsular,* are wrong, but not uncommon. The former is indeed defensible, on the ground that nouns can be used attributively, but at least ill advised.

penman should be used with reference to handwriting only, not to the writing of books or articles; in the sense *writer* or *author* it is an affectation—not indeed a new invention, but a REVIVAL.

pen name. An unnecessary translation of *nom de plume.* See NOM DE GUERRE.

pennant, pennon. See PENDANT.

Pennsylvania Dutch. Descendants of 17th- & 18th-c. immigrants to Pennsylvania from Germany and Switzerland; their dialect, still spoken in parts of Penn.; the adj., of their style of architecture, furniture, &c. The *Dutch* is from the German *Deutsch,* NOT 'of Holland.'

penny. Colloq. US, a cent. Brit., the coin worth 1/12 of a shilling, pl. usually *pence* (written d. = denarias, as 6d.); but *pennies* of the separate coins as such (*pennies only will work the machine*) or as objects (*buttons the size of pennies*).

pentameter ('five measure'). Specifically the short line of the classical elegiac couplet; loosely, *iambic pentameter,* the English blank-verse or heroic-couplet line.

penult. (Gram.): 'nearly last.' The last syllable but one of a word. In gladiolus, *-o-* is the penult. *Antepenult,* last but two: the third syllable from the end.

penurious. The earlier sense, poverty-stricken, is obs. The meaning is now usually merely stingy, penny-pinching.

people is both sing. & pl., and has the occasional pl. *peoples. The history of a people; the people are the masters; the English-speaking peoples.*

per. Prep.=through, by, by means of; so *per diem, mensem, annum* (day, month, year); *per se,* by or in itself, intrinsically. As an English preposition (*$3 per volume*) it is established in econ., business, &c., but has no place in literary writing.

peradventure is archaic as both n. and adv. and should not be used in ordinary contexts. See ARCHAISM.

per capita. *The entire production of opium in India is two grams* per capita *yearly.* This use is a modern blunder, encouraged in some recent dictionaries, and long a STURDY INDEFENSIBLE in US. '(So much) a head,' or 'per man' (which is the meaning here) would not be *per capita* (any more than it would be 'per men'), but *per caput. Per capita* describes the method of sharing property in which persons, & not families, are the units, & its opposite is *per stirpes.* RIGHT: *Patrimonial estates are divided* per capita; *purchased estates,* per stirpes; it is out of place, & something of a barbarism, however lately popular, except in such a context.

per cent. Dictionaries, Brit. & US, differ, giving *per cent, per cent., percent.* The first is recommended. The amount before *per cent* is usually written in numerals: 5 (NOT *five*) *per cent.* The sign (%) is convenient and appropriate in tables, statistics, &c., but has no place in a literary work.

percentage. (Rate per hundred.) See LOVE OF THE LONG WORD. The notion has gone abroad that *a percentage* is *a small part.* Far from that, while a part is always less than the whole, a percentage may be the whole or more than the whole. There is little comfort to be had in 1957 from reflecting that our cost of living can be expressed as a percentage of 1940's. There is a widespread belief that the public prefers a word that sounds scientific, even if it gives the sense less well, to another that it can understand; see POPULARIZED TECHNICALITIES. In all the following examples but the last, the word *percentage* has no meaning at all without the addition of *small* or of something else to define it; & in the last *the greater part* would be the English for *the largest percentage.* WRONG: *But in London there is no civic consciousness; the London-born provides only* a percentage *of its inhabitants./It is none the less true that the trade unions only represent a* percentage *of the whole body of workers./The largest* percentage *of heat generated is utilizable, but the rest escapes & is lost.* For an exact parallel, see PROPORTION. The final degradation is its current slang use (US): *There's no* percentage *in that.*

perchance is very much out of place in pedestrian prose, as, for instance, in *There is nothing,* perchance, *which so readily links the ages together as a small store of jewels & trinkets.* See ARCHAISM & INCONGRUOUS VOCABULARY.

père. 'Father.' Often used after a surname, to distinguish father from son: *Dumas père.* Pron. pār.

PERFECT INFINITIVE, e.g. *to have done* &c. These are forms that often push their way in where they are not wanted, & sometimes, but less often, are themselves displaced by wrong presents.

1. After past tenses of *hope, fear, expect,* & the like, the perfect infinitive is used, incorrectly indeed & unnecessarily, but so often & with so useful an im-

plication that it may well be counted idiomatic. That implication is that the thing hoped &c. did not in fact come to pass & the economy of conveying this without a separate sentence compensates for lack of logical precision. So: *Philosophy began to congratulate herself upon such a proselyte from the world of business, & hoped to have extended her power under the auspices of such a leader./It was the duty of that publisher* to have rebutted *a statement which he knew to be a calumny./I was going* to have asked, *when . . .*

2. After past conditionals such as *should have liked, would have been possible, would have been the first to,* the present infinitive is (almost invariably) the right form, but the perfect often intrudes, & this time without the compensation noted in (1), the implication of nonfulfilment being inherent in the governing verb itself. WRONG: *If my point had not been this, I should not have endeavored* to have shown *the connection* (to show)./*Jim Scudamore would have been the first man* to have acknowledged *the anomaly* (to acknowledge). Sometimes a writer, dimly aware that 'would have liked to have done' is usually wrong, is yet so fascinated by the perfect infinitive that he clings to that at all costs, & alters instead the part of his sentence that was right. WRONG: *On the point of church James was obdurate; he* would like to have insisted *on the other grudging items* (would have liked to insist).

3. With *seem, appear,* & the like, people get puzzled over the combinations of the present & past of *seem* &c. with the present & perfect of the infinitive. The possible combinations are: *He seems to know, He seems to have known, He seemed to know, He seemed to have known.* The first admits of no confusion, & may be left aside; the last is very rarely wanted in fact, but is constantly restorted to as an *en-tout-cas* by those who cannot decide whether the umbrella of *He seems to have known* or the parasol of *He seemed to know* is more likely to suit the weather. WRONG: *I warned him when he spoke to me that I could not speak to him at all if I was to be quoted as an authority; he* seemed to have taken this *as applying only to the first question he asked me* (seems to have)./*It was no infrequent occurrence for people going to the theater in the dark to fall into the marshes after crossing the bridge; people* seemed to have been *much more willing to run risks in those days* (seemed to be).

perfect. (1) Pron. verb perfect′. (2) The purist argues that since *perfect*=free from imperfection, faultless, it is not capable of comparison. The OED is more charitable and points out that it is used as a 'near approach' to perfection; hence *in order to form a more perfect union* need not embarrass Americans.

perfume. Noun, per′- (formerly and still occasionally, -fume′). Verb, -fūme′.

pericranium. The membrane encasing the skull; facetiously, the skull, brain, intellect. Chiefly in POLYSYLLABIC HUMOR.

peril makes US, *-ling* &c; Brit. *-lling* &c., but both *perilous.*

Imperil is now more usual as a verb.

period. 1. The period (Brit. 'full stop') is the point used to mark the end of a complete declarative sentence or of an abbreviated word. Contractions (*can't, Miss*) are not followed by a period, and the tendency in modern printing is to omit the periods in initials that have wide currency (*POW, CIO, NATO,* &c., but see UNITED STATES).

2. The spot plague. The style that has been so labeled, the essence of which is that the matter should be divided into as short lengths as possible, with few commas & no semicolons or conjunctions, is tiring to the reader, on whom it imposes the task of supplying the connection, & corrupting to the writer, whose craving for brevity persuades him that anything will pass for a sentence: *It was now clear. The light was that of late evening. The air hardly more than cool./They demand long years of accurate study—even when the student has the necessary aptitude for such things. Which three students out of every four have not.*

periodic(al). The *-ic* form is not used of publications (*periodical literature, periodicals*); the *-ical* form is not used of literary composition (*Johnson's periodic style*); otherwise the two words do not differ in meaning, but the longer tends to oust the shorter.

PERIPHRASIS (-rif'-) is 'putting' things in a roundabout way. *In Paris there reigns a complete absence of really reliable news* is a periphrasis for *There is no reliable news in Paris. Rarely does the 'Little Summer' linger until November, but at times its stay has been prolonged until quite late in the year's penultimate month* contains a periphrasis for *November,* & another for *lingers. The answer is in the negative* is a periphrasis for *No. Was made the recipient of* is a periphrasis for *was presented with.* The periphrastic style is hardly possible on any considerable scale without much use of abstract nouns such as *case, character, connection, dearth, nature, reference, regard;* the existence of abstract nouns is a proof that abstract thought has occurred; abstract thought is a mark of civilized man; & so it has come about that periphrasis & civilization are by many held to be inseparable. (See OFFICIALESE.) These good people feel that there is an almost indecent nakedness, a reversion to barbarism, in saying *No news is good news* instead of *The absence of intelligence is an indication of satisfactory developments.* Nevertheless, *The year's penultimate month* is not in truth a good way of saying *November.*

Strings of nouns depending on one another & the use of compound prepositions are the most conspicuous symptoms of the periphrastic malady, & writers should be on the watch for these in their own composition. An example or two may be illuminating: (A) nouns: *I merely desired to point out the principal reason which I believe exists for the great exaggeration which is occasionally to be observed in the estimate of the importance of the contradiction between current Religion & current Science put forward by thinkers of reputation.* (B) compound prepositions: *A resolution was moved & carried in favor of giving facilities to the public vaccination officers of the Metropolis to enter the schools of the Board for the purpose of examining the arms of the children with a view to advising the parents to allow their children to be vaccinated.* Other examples will be found under some of the words that lend themselves especially to periphrasis—*case, character, connection, eventuality, instance, nature, neighborhood, not* 2, *reference, regard.*

permanence, -cy. One of the pairs in which the distinction is neither broad & generally recognized, nor yet quite nonexistent or negligible. Writers whose feeling for the distinctions is delicate will prefer *-ce* for the fact of abiding, & *-cy* for the quality or an embodiment of it: *We look forward to its* permanence; *The* permanency *of the orthodox marriage bonds.*

permeate makes *-meable, -tor.*

permit makes *-tted* &c., *-ssible.* The noun is accented on the first syllable. *Permit of,* see ADMIT OF.

perorate (to sum up and conclude a speech) is not in fact one of the modern BACK-FORMATIONS like *revolute, enthuse,* & *burgle,* but it suffers from being taken for one, & few perhaps use it without some fear that they are indulging in a bold bad word.

perpetrate makes *-rable,* & *-tor.* The thing perpetrated is always associated with evil & crime, blunder, hoax.

persiflage. (Rhet.): 'whistle-talk.' Irresponsible talk, of which the hearer is to make what he can without the right to suppose that the speaker means what he seems to say; the treating of serious things as trifles & of trifles as serious. 'Talking with one's tongue in one's cheek' may serve as a parallel. Hannah More, quoted in the OED, describes French persiflage as 'the cold compound of irony, irreligion, selfishness, & sneer'; irony, paradox, & levity are perhaps rather the ingredients of the compound as now conceived. Pron. pûr′sĭ fläzh.

persistence, -cy. The distinction is the same as with *permanence, -cy,* but is more generally appreciated: *the* persistence *of poverty* or *of matter; courage &* persistency *are high gifts.*

PERSON. (Gram.) 1. When a compound subject consists of two or more alternative parts differing in person, there is sometimes a doubt about the right verb form to use (*Are you or I next?* &c.). As a general rule, the nearest noun governs the verb (*Are you or I . . . Am I or you*). The skillful writer avoids the problem by rewording: *Are you next or am I? Which of us is next?* See NEITHER 4, OR 2, for discussion.

2. Person of relative. Two questions arise, for which see WHO; these are exemplified in (a) *To me, who has* (or *have?*) *also a copy of it, it seems a somewhat trivial fragment,* & (b) *Most of us lost our* (or *their?*) *heads.* Relatives take the person & number of their antecedents: in (a), *who*=I; in (b) *most* of us=most people; hence read *have* and *their.*

persona. Pl. *-ae. Dramatis personae:* the people of the drama; *persona grata:* an acceptable person; - *non grata,* an unacceptable . . . Pron. persōn′a.

personal equation is a phrase of definite meaning; it is the correction, quantitatively expressed, that an individual's observation of astronomical or other phenomena is known by experiment to require; minutely accurate assessment is essential to the notion. The learned sound of *equation,* however, has commended it to those who want some expression or other with *personal* in it, & are all the better pleased if a commonplace word can be replaced by something more imposing. WRONG: *Let us hope that the improved* personal equation (between two state leaders) *will count for something./In general there is too much* personal equation *in American politics.* See POPULARIZED TECHNICALITIES.

personal(i)ty. Personal property in the legal sense is *-alty;* the other noun work of *personal* is done by *-ality;* cf. *real(i)ty.*

PERSONIFICATION, Nouns of Multitude, Metonymy. When a country is spoken of as *She,* we have personification; when we doubt whether to write *The Cabinet refuse* or *The Cabinet refuses,* we are pulled up by a noun of multitude; when we call Queen Elizabeth *the Crown,* we use metonymy. Some mistakes incident to these forms of speech run into one another, & are therefore grouped together here under the headings: (1) Ill-advised personification. (2) Vacillation. (3) Unattached possessives.

1. Ill-advised personification. To figure 'the world' as a female, a certain 'quarter' as sentient, or 'Irish womanhood' as a woman, is to be frigid—the epithet proper to those who make futile attempts at decoration. Such personifications are implied in *Just now the world wants all that America can give* her *in shipping* (read *it* for *her*), in *But on application to* the quarter *most likely to know I was assured that the paper in question was not written by Dickens* (*the quarter* is no doubt a person or persons, & capable of knowledge; but it will surely never do to let that secret out), & in *The womanhood of Ireland stands for individualism as against co-operation, & presents the practical domestic arguments in* her *support* (whether *her* implies the personification of womanhood or of individualism does not much matter; it must be one or the other, & neither is suited for the treatment). It is in places like these, where a writer hardly intends personification, but slips unconsciously or half-heartedly into implying it, that he reveals his want of literary instinct. Far the commonest form taken by the weakness is that of which many examples are given under 'S INCONGRUOUS. To write *famine's* or *Austria's* instead of *of famine, of Austria,* is virtually to personify them; & the modern writer is perpetually doing this in the most prosaic contexts. So: *A particular character of a monsoon season may reduce to* famine's verge *millions of industrious ryots* (the writer was afraid of *verge of famine* before *millions of ryots;* see OUT OF THE FRYING PAN)./*Crowded toward* the bed's edge *by Susan's warm body, Louise wondered about the campaign,* etc.

2. Vacillation. *The Government, the Times, the Party,* & the like, are nouns of multitude, which can be treated as units & therefore referred to by the

words *it, its,* & followed by singular verbs, or as bodies of people to which *they, them, their,* & plural verbs are appropriate. *America* & the like are words naturally admitting of personification, & can be referred to in their literal sense by *it* & *its,* or in their personified sense by *she* & *her.* So much everyone knows; what will perhaps surprise the reader is to find from the examples below how many writers are capable of absurdly mixing the two methods in a single phrase or staggering, in longer sentences, from one to the other & back again. The noun-of-multitude examples (for yet more of which see NUMBER 6) are placed first, the personification ones afterwards; & the words in which the vacillation is exhibited are in roman type. WRONG: *'The Times' also gives some interesting comments by* their *special correspondent./During* their *six years of office the Government* has *done great harm./That will gain ground or not in proportion as the public is secure in* their *minds about the Navy./The excuse of the Admiralty, which* were *responsible for these proceedings, is . . .* (which was, or who were)*./Japan* itself *now ceases to be an island Power, & for the first time accepts responsibilities on the continent which* it *cannot abandon;* her *frontier is no longer the sea./The United States has given another proof of* its *determination to uphold* her *neutrality.*

3. Unattached possessives. WRONG: *Danish sympathy with Finland is writ large over all* her *newspapers, literature, & public speeches. Her* means 'of (the personified) Denmark'; we can all see that; but we most of us also resent, nevertheless, a personification that is done not on the stage, but 'off'; a Denmark personified & not presented is a sort of shadow of a shade./*This is a timely tribute from a man who has spent a large part of his life in Friendly Society work, & who would be the last to sanction anything that imperiled* their *interests. Their* means 'of the Friendly Societies'; but where are they? The adj. *Friendly Society* is as unavailing here as *Danish* in the previous example./*The true doctrine is that every public act of the Crown is an act for which* her *advisers are responsible.* It is in some contexts indifferent whether one says *the Queen, Her Majesty,* or *the Crown;* but while *the Queen* has *her* advisers, *the Crown* can only have *its;* as to the possessive proper to *Her Majesty,* see MAJESTY.

personnel, NOT **-sonel.** Pron. personel'.

perspic-. *Perspicacious, -acity,* mean (having or showing) insight (*The greatest wits lack* perspicacity *in things that respect their own interests./Far too* perspicacious *to be imposed upon by any such false analogy*). *Perspicuous, -uity,* mean (the being) easy to get a clear idea of (*I am willing to be tedious in order to be sure I am* perspicuous./*There is nothing more desirable in composition than* perspicuity); see PAIRS & SNARES. *Shrewd* & *shrewdness, clear* & *clearness,* or other short words, are used in preference by those who are neither learned nor pretentious. The learned, however, can safely venture on the *perspic-* pairs; when the unlearned pretender claims acquaintance with them, they are apt to punish the familiarity by showing that he is in fact a stranger to them. The usual mistake is to write *-uity* for *-acity*. WRONG: *Sometimes, however, Dr. Bell's* perspicuity *was at fault./The high-class provincial tailors are displaying considerable* perspicuity *in buying checks.*

perspire, perspiration. See GENTEELISMS.

persuade makes *-dable* as well as *persuasible;* the former is recommended.

persuasion. Parodies of the phrase 'of the Roman, Protestant, &c., persuasion,' e.g. *Hats of the cartwheel persuasion,* are to be classed with WORN-OUT HUMOR; see also HACKNEYED PHRASES.

pertinacity is persistency, usually in a bad sense, carried to a fault; obstinacy.

pertinence, -cy. There is no useful distinction; the first will probably prevail.

peruse means to read carefully or thoroughly, but is generally used as a high-flown substitute for *read.* See FORMAL WORDS.

pessimism is the (Phil.) doctrine that this is the worst possible world and all things tend toward evil; hence it is the tendency to look at the worst aspect of things. See OPTIMISM for comments on the popular use, & POPULARIZED TECHNICALITIES.

pestle. Pron. without *-t-*.

petal usually makes *-led* (US); *-lled* (Brit.).

petit. Fr., little; fem., *petite.* Pron. pĕtē′, -ēt′. The obs. English *petit* (*petit jury, petit larceny*) is now replaced by *petty.*

petitio principii. (Logic): 'assumption of the basis.' The fallacy of founding a conclusion on a basis that as much needs to be proved as the conclusion itself. Arguing in a circle (q.v.) is a common variety of *petitio principii.* That foxhunting is not cruel, since the fox enjoys the fun, & that one must keep servants, since all respectable people do so, are other examples of begging the question or *petitio principii* in which the argument is not circular.

petrel. The sea bird, *stormy petrel.* Pron. pĕt-.

petrol(eum). *Petroleum,* the natural mineral oil; *petrol* (Brit.) =gasoline (US). See also KEROSENE.

phalanx. Ordinary pl. *-xes,* but in Anatomy *phalanges* (falăn′-jēz).

phallus. Pl. *-li.*

phantasm, phantom. The two are by origin merely spelling variants, differentiated, but so that the differences are elusive; the following tendencies are discernible, but sometimes conflict. (1) *Phantom* is the more popular form, *-asm* being chiefly in literary use. (2) Both meaning roughly an illusive apparition, *phantom* stresses the fact that the thing is illusive, & *-asm* the fact that it does appear, so that they give respectively the negative & the positive aspect. (3) A *phantom* presents itself to the eye, bodily or mental, a *phantasm* to any sense or to the intellect. (4) *Phantasm* has an adj. (*phantasmal*) of its own; *phantom* has not, but is used attributively (*phantom hopes* &c.) with much freedom, & where a true adj. is necessary borrows *phantasmal;* the two nouns are no doubt kept from diverging more definitely than they do by this common property in *phantasmal.*

phantasmagoria is sing., not pl. WRONG: *We shall then be able to reach some conclusion as to the meaning & effect of* these *bewildering* phantasmagoria. The word was invented for an exhibition of optical illusions produced by means of a magic lantern, in 1802. The inventor, says the OED, 'probably only wanted a mouth-filling & startling term . . .'

Pharaoh. So spelled. Pron. fā′rō.

Pharisee. One of an ancient Jewish sect distinguished by their strict observance of traditional and written law; in the N.T. deplored for their pretensions to superior sanctity. See also SCRIBE. The adj. *Pharisaic* is preferable to *Pharisaical.* The *-ism* noun is *Pharisaism,* not *-seeism.*

pharmaceutic(al). The long form is established. The shorter one as an adj. (*pharmaceutic company*) is rare and might well be dropped.

phenomenal means 'of the kind apprehended by (any of) the senses'; that is, everything that is reported to the mind by sight, hearing, taste, smell, or touch—& that whether the report answers to reality or not—is phenomenal. If the report is correct, the thing reported is also real; if not, it is 'merely phenomenal.' The question of real existence & its relation to perception & thought is the concern of Metaphysics, & *phenomenal* is a metaphysical word, contrasted variously with *real, absolute,* & *noumenal.* But the object here is not to expound the metaphysical meaning of these terms; it is only to point out that *phenomenal* is a metaphysical term with a use of its own. To divert it from this proper use to a job for which it is not needed, by making it do duty for *remarkable, extraordinary,* or *prodigious,* is a sin against the English language. It has gone through the phases, Philosophic term, POPULARIZED TECHNICALITY, & VOGUE WORD, & is now in the state of discredit that follows upon unreasonable vogue. That is the moment when believers in sound English may deliver their attack upon such usages with hope of success.

phenomen(al)ism. The longer form is recommended.

phenomenon. Pl. *-ena. Phenomenon* in the sense 'notable occurrence' or 'prodigy' is open essentially to the same objections as PHENOMENAL used correspondingly; but less practical inconvenience results, since there is little danger of misunderstanding.

philately, -ist. Pron. fĭlăt′ĕlĭ, -ĭst. It is a pity that for one of the most popular scientific pursuits one of the least popularly intelligible names should have been found. The best remedy now is to avoid the official titles whenever *stamp collecting* & *collector* will do.

-phil(e). Suffix='lover of.' The *-e* originally taken on from French is now often dropped in Brit., with the good result of bringing back the pronunciation from the queer -fīl to -fĭl. In US, however, the *-phile* forms are still usual, and pronounced usually fīl (*bibliophile*). There is no justification for -fēl.

philharmonic, philhellenic, &c. The *-h-* is better unsounded in these, but not in syllables on which the accent falls, as in *philhellenism, -ist.*

Philippine Islands. (*The Republic of the Philippines,* now the official name.) So spelled. The natives are *Filipinos.*

Philistine. The special modern meaning is thus given by the OED—A person deficient in liberal culture & enlightenment, whose interests are chiefly bounded by material & commonplace things. (But often applied contemptuously by connoisseurs of any particular art or department of learning to one who has no knowledge or appreciation of it; sometimes a mere term of dislike for those whom the speaker considers 'bourgeois'.) (Accent first syllable.)

philosophic(al). Except where *-cal* is stereotyped by forming part of a title (*Philosophical Transactions* &c.), the *-ic* form is now commoner in all the more specific senses; *-ical* still prevails in the very general sense 'resembling' or 'befitting a philosopher,' i.e. wise or unperturbed or well balanced; & this gives a basis for differentiation.

philtre, -ter. A love potion; *-ter* is more usual in US, but *-tre* is also used. Brit. always *-tre.*

phlegm &c. The *g* is silent in *phlegm,* & *phlegmy,* but sounded in *phlegmatic.*

-phobe, -phobia, are combining suffixes meaning (one who has) fear, dread, horror of the noun to which it is attached. By extension it has also come to include aversion to, dislike of (*Russophobe, Anglophobia, xenophobe—xeno*=strangers, i.e. foreigners).

Phoenician, phoenix. Best so written.

phone, for telephone is colloq. See CURTAILED WORDS.

phonetics. The science of speech sounds; the study of the phenomena of language. In US usually used as a sing. noun (*Phonetics* is *that department of linguistic science that treats of the sounds of speech*); Brit. often plural (*Provincial phonetics go still further*).

photo. Pl. *-os.* See CURTAILED WORDS.

phylo-, combining form meaning *race* (pron. usually fīl-): Hence *phylogeny* (the history of racial evolution of an animal or plant type, as opposed to *ontogeny*).

phylum. Pl. *-la.*

physic makes *-cked, -cking, -cky.*

physician, doctor, surgeon, in ordinary parlance. 'The physician' & 'the doctor' may be used to denote the same person, viz. one whose vocation is to heal physical troubles, physician being the FORMAL WORD, & no particular relation to *surgeon* being implied by either. A surgeon is always a doctor who undertakes to perform manual operations, but not necessarily one who confines himself to them. *Physician* is also used in contrast with *surgeon* to denote one who deals with medicines & treatment, not with surgical instruments.

physics, physiology. The two words had once the same wide meaning of natural science or natural philosophy. They have now been narrowed & differentiated, *physics* retaining only the properties of matter & energy in inorganic nature, & *physiology* only the normal functions & phenomena of living beings.

physiognomy. The *g* is now usually pronounced; even the

OED says, 'the pronunciation fĭzĭŏ′nōmĭ is somewhat old-fashioned.'

physiology. See PHYSICS. For the adj., *-ical* is so much the commoner that it should be accepted as the only form.

pi(e). Printing. A confused mass of type. The verb makes *pied, piing.* In Brit., always *pie;* US the noun is often *pi,* the verb *pie.*

pianist. The older & Brit. pronunciation is pē′*a*nĭst; in US also pĭăn′ĭst.

piano. The instrument is pĭăn′ō; pl. *-os.* The musical direction is pĭ ä′nō.

piazza. Pron. pĭă′z*a*; (in Italian pyah′tsa). A public square or market place. Only in US is a *piazza* a veranda or porch.

picaresque. The picaresque novel is defined in the Enc. Brit. as: 'The prose autobiography of a real or fictitious personage who describes his experiences as a social parasite, & who satirizes the society which he has exploited.' The type is Spanish, but the most widely known example is the French *Gil Blas. Picaro* is a Spanish word meaning vagabond.

picayune. US, a small coin; hence anything worthless or trifling; hence petty, mean (colloq.).

piccolo. Pl. *-os.*

pickax(e). US usually *pickax,* Brit. *-axe.* (See AXE.)

picket, v., makes *-eted, -eting,* &c.

picket, picquet, piquet. The second form serves no purpose at all; the third should be reserved for the card game, & *picket* be used for all other senses, including that of the military outpost often spelled with *-qu-* or *-cqu-.*

picnic makes *-cking, -cked,* &c.

picture. Pĭk′tūr is academic; pĭk′tyer is impossible except with a deliberate pause after the *t* (though many people think they say it who do not); pĭk′cher is the form used by ordinary mortals.

picturesque suggests the striking, effective, interesting qualities of a picture rather than sublimity or the highest beauty; so in *picturesque writing, language,* fact may be disregarded for effect.

pidgin, pigeon. 'Business-English' was the name given by the Chinese to the Anglo-Chinese *lingua franca;* but they pronounced *business* 'pidgin' & we have confused the meaningless *pidgin* with the significant *pigeon;* cf. AMUCK. *Pigeon,* however, is two centuries younger in print than *amuck,* so that there is not the same reason to protest against *pidgin* as against *amok.*

piebald, skewbald. *Piebald* is properly of white & black, *skewbald* of white & some color.

piece makes *-ceable.*

pièce de résistance. The most substantial dish of a meal, not necessarily the most elegant, difficult to make, &c., as is sometimes implied in its fig. use (perhaps from the mistaken notion that it is the piece 'not to be resisted'). Pron. pyĕs′ dẽ rā-sēs tänz′.

pierce makes *-ceable.*

pietà. The representation of Mary mourning over the body of Christ. Pron. pyā′tah.

pigeon English. See PIDGIN.

pigmy. Use PYGMY.

pilfer makes *-ered, -ering,* &c.

pill. *To gild the pill* is to soften or tone down something unpleasant (from the practice of gilding a bitter pill to make it easier to swallow).

pilot, v., makes *-ted, -oting,* &c.

pilure. A little pill. So spelled, not *-ll.*

pimento. Pl. *-os.*

pince-nez. Pron. (Eng.) păns nā.

pincers, n. pl. In US often (colloq.?) *pinchers.*

pinch hitter. In baseball a substitute batter sent in when a hit is particularly needed. Hence someone supposedly better (at batting) than the person whose place he takes. This fact is often ignored in the fig. use by non-baseball fans (also *pinch hit*).

Pindarics. (Poetry): 'of Pindar.' The form imitated in English verse in which a poem consists of several stanzas often of unequal length, with the rhymes within the stanza irregularly disposed of, & the number of feet in the lines arbitrarily varied.

piquant. Pron. pē'kant.

piqué, piquet. The first is the cotton fabric, the second the card game.

pis aller. 'To go worst.' The only course possible, a last resource. *As a* pis aller *one might put up with him.* Pron. pē zä lā. But see FRENCH WORDS.

pistachio. Pl. *-os.*

piteous, pitiable, pitiful. There are three broadly different senses for the words: (1) Feeling pity; (2) Exciting pity; (3) Exciting contempt. It would have been easy, then, if the problem had been posed beforehand, to assign a word to a sense, *piteous* to No. 1, *pitiable* to No. 2, & *pitiful* to No. 3. But language-making is no such simple affair as that, & spontaneous development has worked badly here; *piteous* has senses 1 & 2, *pitiable* senses 2 & 3, & *pitiful* senses 1, 2, & 3—a very wasteful confusion, but too inveterate to be got into order at present.

pity, n. *In the meantime, we can only muse* upon the pity of it. For *the pity of it,* & *pity 'tis 'tis true,* see STOCK PATHOS, & HACKNEYED PHRASES.

pixy, -ie. The first is better.

pizzicato. Pron. pĭtsĭkä'tō. Pl. *-os.*

placable. Best pron. plăk-. The negative form, *implacable,* is more in use.

placate. US usually plā'kāt; Brit. often plakāt'. The word is much more in American than in Brit. use, but is quoted from the 17th c. Beside the adj. *placable, placatable* can be made for the gerundive use.

place, v., makes *-ceable. Any place, some place,* &c., should not be used for *anywhere, somewhere.*

placebo. A 'medicine' given to satisfy the patient; hence fig. a soothing or ingratiating remark, act, &c. Pron. plasē'bō.

plague makes *-guable, -guing, -guy.*

plaice (fish). So spelled.

plaid. Pronounced plād in Scotland, but plăd in England and US.

plain makes *plainness. Plain sailing* is ('probably'—OED) a popular use of the nautical term *plane sailing,* which means navigation by a plane chart, 'a simple & easy method, approximately correct for short distances.' The corruption, if it is one, is so little misleading, since *plain sailing* is as intelligible in itself as *clear going* or any such phrase, that any attempt to correct it is needless as well as vain.

plait. US usually plāt or plēt; Brit. usually plăt; but all three are heard.

plane sailing. See PLAIN.

plangent. The sound of waves; loud, reverberant, thrilling, or plaintive (depending, seemingly, on the writer's idea of the sound of waves beating on the shore).

plantain. Pron. plăn'tĭn.

plateful. Pl. *-ls.*

plate glass. Two words, unhyphened.

plateau. Pl. now usually *-s,* sometimes *-x.*

platform. The political sense of 'party program' is still rather American than Brit., but in England too is now not uncommon.

platitude, -dinous. (A flat, dull remark; insipid.) The words are misused in the following extracts. WRONG: *He would probably have avoided the use of certain phrases & arguments which, though he clearly means them to be innocuous & even* platitudinous, *have none the less been the subject of vehement controversy./ The miners acknowledge the force of this principle or* platitude *as freely as the rest of us.* For the differences between *platitude, commonplace, & truism,* see COMMONPLACE.

Platonic love. For the origin of the expression, see Plato's *Symposium.* For its meaning, the definition & one or two quotations from the OED here follow: (Definition) Applied to love or affection for one of the opposite sex, of a purely spiritual character, & free from sensual desire. (Quotations): (Howell) 'It is a love that consists in contemplation & idaeas of the mind, not in any carnall fruition.' (Norris) 'Platonic Love is the Love of Beauty abstracted from all sensual Applications, & desire of Corporal Contact.' (Lewes) 'This is the celebrated Platonic Love, which, from having originally meant a communion of two souls, & that in a rigidly dialectical sense, has been degraded to the expression of maudlin sentiment between the sexes.'

platypus. Pl. *-puses,* not *-pi.*

plausible means (etym.=commendable) apparently believable, hence (only) superficially reasonable, hence (often) specious; of persons, usually derog. *Implausible* means not to be believed.

plead. The past and p.p. are *pleaded. Pled* is now colloq. or dial. (or Sc.). The legal phrase is *to plead* not *guilty. To plead guilty,* often heard, is technically wrong: one confesses guilt.

pleading. In law, *special pleading* alleges special or new matter in avoiding the allegations of the other side. Popularly, *special pleading* is used of an argument that presents only the favorable features of a question. For discussion see SPECIAL.

pleased. The battle against *very pleased* is apparently a losing one. In *The ABC of Plain Words* Sir Ernest Gowers writes, 'There can be no objection to "very pleased," which means no more than "very glad."' For Fowler's opinion see VERY.

pleasure. *I have the pleasure*

of doing so-&-so means I do it, & am glad to do it—a courteous announcement that one is conferring some favor. *It is my pleasure to do so-&-so,* or *that so-&-so should be done,* means I choose to, & therefore of course shall, do it or have it done—an imperious statement of intention. The second idiom is based on the definite special sense of *pleasure,* with possessives (*my, his, the king's,* &c.), viz. one's will, desire, choice. *It is a pleasure to do,* on the other hand, means the same as *I have the pleasure of doing.* But insensibility to idiom often causes *It is my* or *our* (NOT *a*) *pleasure* to be substituted for *I* or *We have the pleasure;* see CAST-IRON IDIOM. WRONG: *Once again* it is our pleasure *to notice the annual issue of 'The Home Messenger.'/In the experiment which* it was my pleasure *to witness, M. Bachelet used only two traction coils.*

plebeian makes *-nness* (abstract noun).

plebiscite. Pron. plĕ′bĭsĭt.

plectrum. Pl. *-tra.*

Pleiad. US usually plē′ad, Brit. plī′-. Pl. *-ds* or *-des* (-ēz). The use in the sing. for a group of brilliant people comes from the *Pléiade,* a group of seven poets of the French Renaissance. *The Pleiades,* the group of seven stars (named for the seven daughters of Atlas).

plenteous, -iful. As with other pairs in *-eous* & *-iful* (e.g. from *bounty, beauty, duty, pity*), the meaning of the two is the same, but the *-eous* word is the less common & therefore the better suited to the needs of poetry & exalted prose; for these it should be reserved.

plenty. *Excuses are plenty* (i.e. plentiful), *There is plenty wood* (i.e. plenty of), *That is plenty hot enough* (i.e. quite), are irregularities of which the first is established in literature, the second is still considered a solecism (though the omission of *of* is easily paralleled, as in *a little brandy, a dozen apples, more courage, enough food*), & the third is recognized colloq., but not literary, English.

PLEONASM is redundancy; the using of more words than are required to give the sense intended.

1. It is often resorted to deliberately for rhetorical effect (*Lest at any time they should* see *with their* eyes & hear *with their* ears). The writer who uses pleonasm in that way must be judged by whether he does produce his effect & whether the occasion is worthy of it.

2. There are many phrases originally put together for the sake of such emphasis, but repeated with less & less of impressiveness until they end by boring instead of striking the hearer. Such are the pairs of synonyms *if & when, unless & until, save & except, in any shape or form, of any sort or kind.* These & many others have long worn out their force, & what those who would write vigorously have to do with them is merely to unlearn them; see IF & WHEN, the apparently least pleonastic of these stock phrases, for fuller discussion. Those who use this form of pleonasm can hardly be unconscious that they are saying a thing twice over, the *and* or *or* being there as a reminder.

3. In other phrases, the offender is evidently unconscious, & expresses the same notion twice over in the belief that he is

saying it once. Such are EQUALLY AS 2, *more* PREFERABLE, & *continue to* REMAIN, which mean neither more nor less than *equally* (or *as*), *preferable*, & *remain* by themselves, but which can be defended, by those who care to defend them, as not worse than uselessly pleonastic. With these may be classed the queer use of *both*, repugnant to sense but not to grammar, where *they* or *the two* is replaced by it though the emphasis necessarily attaching to *both* is absurd. REDUNDANT: Both *men had something* in common. See BOTH 2 for more varieties of this very common ineptitude.

4. A further downward step brings us below the defensible level, & we come to the overlappings described in the article HAZINESS: *It is singular how* apparently *slow some minds* seem *to learn the elementary truth./We have been enabled to make large economies* while at the same time *increasing the efficiency of the fleet.* See also AGO & BECAUSE.

5. Lastly, there are the pleonasms in which by wrongly repeating a negative or a conjunction the writer produces a piece of manifest nonsense or impossible grammar. WRONG: *It should be a very great thing* that *before guns, shells, mountings, rangefinders, &c., are adopted,* that *the opinion of real & not of soi-disant experts shall be taken.*/I *should* not *wonder if I could* not *lick you into shape.*

plethora. Pron. plĕth′ŏră (the etym. preferable plĕthō′ra is now pedantic). Med., excess of red corpuscles; fig., any overabundance, unhealthy repletion: *a plethora of words.*

pleurisy. So spelled, NOT *plu-;* the derivation is from *pleura,* rib, not *plus, pluris.*

plexus. Pl. *-uses* or (rarely) *plexus;* NOT *-xi.*

pliable, pliant. There is little differentiation in either the lit. or fig. meanings; the following illustrations are from the OED: *Leather soaked in water to make it* pliable./*Shells* [*made*] *soft &* pliant *in warm water./Men* pliant *to good advice.*/Pliable *judges were previously chosen./A voice clear and* pliable./A pliant *voice.*/A pliant *style.*

plow, plough. The first usual US (and 18th-c. Eng.); the second modern Brit.

plumb- (=lead). The *b* is silent in *plumber, plumbery, plumbing,* & *plumbless,* but sounded in *plumbago, plumbeous, plumbic, plumbiferous,* & *plumbism.*

plumb. Ball of lead used on end of line to test perpendicularity &c. So *plumb line, out of plumb, the wall is plumb* (and US slang *plumb crazy*).

plume makes *plumy.*

plurality. With three-cornered contests as common as they now are, there are occasions for a convenient single word for what the English now call *an absolute majority,* i.e. a majority comprising more than half the votes cast. In US the word *majority* itself has that meaning, while a poll greater than that of any other candidate, but less than half the votes cast, is called a *plurality.*

pneumatic, pneumonia, &c. Pron. nū-. Formerly *pneumatology, pneumonometer* were pronounced pn- but nu- is now standard for them too.

pocketful. Pl. *-ls.*

podium. Arch., a continuous projecting base or pedestal. A raised platform around an arena or amphitheater; a continuous bench around a room. Its use for *dais,* as for an orchestra conductor, seems to be chiefly US. Pron. pō-; pl. *-ia.*

poetaster. A versifier, a petty or paltry poet. In US now usually pō′ĕtăster, Brit. pōĕtă′ster.

poetess. Long-established, though most women who write poetry prefer to be called *poets.* See FEMININE DESIGNATIONS.

poeticize, poetize. *Poetize* is the older word and the one more used in US. There seems to be little differentiation. *A* poeticized *account./He* poeticized *over the ruins./All have* poetized *about the sea./It is irrational to* poetize *the moon and ignore the sun.*

pogrom. US usually pō′grum; Brit. pogrŏm′.

poignant. In US now usually poin′yant; Brit. always poi′nant.

poinsettia. So spelled. Pron. -tĭa.

point. *Point of view* is the native phrase now being ousted by *standpoint.* What is killing *point of view* is no doubt the awkwardness of following it, as is constantly necessary, with another *of* (*from the point of view of history*); the process may be expected to continue, & there is no valid objection to *standpoint; point of view* will linger for a time where the *of* difficulty does not present itself (*from my,* or *Mill's, point of view*). *Viewpoint,* another (esp. US) solution to the dislike of the two *of*s, has the disadvantage of calling to mind what *standpoint* allows to be forgotten, that the idiomatic English is undoubtedly *point of view.* The perplexed stylist is at present inclined to cut loose & experiment with *angle.* What is here recommended is to use *point of view* as the normal expression, but not be afraid of *standpoint* on occasion. *Point of view* for *view* (*I can't agree with* your point of view) is nonsense.

poke makes *-kable* & *poky.*

Polack for *Pole* is archaic or contemptuous.

polemic(al). Controversy, controversial (esp. theol.). It would be convenient, & not be counter to any existing distinctions, if *-ic* were kept for the noun & *-ical* for the adj.

police, v., makes *-ceable.*

polite normally takes *more, most.* Mackenzie's *The French are the* politest *enemies in the world* should not serve as a guide. See -ER & -EST.

politic(al). An example of complete differentiation. *Politic* makes *politicly; -ical, politically.*

polity is a word that has emerged from its retirement in the writings of philosophic historians or political philosophers, become a newspaper word, & suffered the maltreatment usual in such cases. It has been seized upon as a less familiar & therefore more impressive spelling of *policy* (with which it is indeed identical in origin), & the differences that have long existed between the two have been very vaguely grasped or else neglected. A useful indication that the two words are of widely different meanings is that *policy* is as often as not without *a* or *the* in the singular, whereas *polity* in its right senses is very rarely so. *Polity* is not (like *policy* or *principle*) a line of action, nor (like *politics*) a branch of activity, nor (like *statesmanship*) an art or quality.

The true meanings of *polity* are: (1, now rare) a condition, viz. the being organized as a State or system of States; (2, & most frequent) some particular form of such organization, e.g. a republic, monarchy, empire, confederation, Concert of Europe, or United Nations; & (3, not uncommon) a people organized as a State. RIGHT (sense 2): *Dr. Hazeltine's lecture is an interesting account of the influence of English political & legal ideas upon the American* polity./*If the terms are accepted the future* polity *of Europe must be more than ever based on force./Mr. Keynes points out that the commercial & industrial system of Europe has grown up with the pre-war* polity *as its basis.*/(Gladstone, sense 1) *At a period antecedent to the formation of anything like* polity *in Greece.*/(Huxley, sense 3) *Those who should be kept, as certain to be serviceable members of the* polity.

But in the following extracts it will be seen that one of the senses of *policy* or *politics* is required, & that one of those words, or at any rate some other word, would be the right one instead of *polity*. WRONG: *This newspaper trust has during the last two years increasingly assumed the right & the power to upset ministries, to nominate new ministers & discharge others, & to dictate & veto public* polity./*The main obstacles to advancement have always been social superstitions, political oppressions, rash & misguided ambitions, & gross mistakes in* polity./*Habits of living from hand to mouth engendered by centuries of crude* polity *will not die out in a month.*

polloi. 'Many,' i.e. people, majority, rabble. *Hoi*=the. See HOI POLLOI.

poltergeist. 'Noise-ghost.' Mischievous spirit that makes itself known by knockings and other noises. Pron. pôl′tergīst.

polyandry, plurality of husbands; *polygamy,* plurality of wives or of husbands (i.e. plurality of marriage, but usually refers to a plurality of wives); *polygyny,* plurality of wives or concubines.

polyglot makes *-ttal, -ttic, -ttism.*

POLYSYLLABIC HUMOR. See PEDANTIC HUMOR for a slight account of the impulse that suggests long or abstruse words as a means of entertaining the hearer. Of the long as distinguished from the abstruse, *terminological inexactitude* for *lie* or *falsehood* is a favorable example, but much less amusing at the hundredth than at the first time of hearing. *Oblivious to their pristine nudity* (forgetting they were stark naked) is a less familiar specimen. Nothing need here be added to what was said in the other article beyond a short specimen list of long words or phrases that sensible people avoid. *Caledonian, Celestial,* & *Hibernian* for Scotch, Chinese, Irish. *Olfactory organ* for nose. *Osculatory, pachydermatous, matutinal, diminutive, culinary,* & *minacious,* for kissing, thick-skinned, morning, tiny, kitchen, & threatening. *Individual, equitation, intermediary,* & *epidermis,* for person, riding, means,

& skin. *Negotiate* & *peregrinate* for tackle & travel.

pommel, pu-. The first spelling is usual for the noun, the second for the verb, though the verb is merely a use of the noun, & not of different origin. Both are pronounced pum-, & both make *-led* (US), *-lled* (Brit.).

POMPOSITIES. Such words as *collation, comestibles, consort, edifice, ere, evince, exacerbate, munificent, save* (except), *spouse, vituperate,* have all 'a certain use in the world, no doubt'; but they are seen in print very much more often than occasions for those certain uses occur, & may serve as specimens of hundreds that are habitually substituted for others merely as pompous ornaments.

pontifex. (Member of Pontifical College; the Pope.) Pl. *-fices* (-ēz).

pontificate (v.), pontify. In the transf. sense, to speak as a pontiff, with an air of infallibility, both are used (*Victor Herbert* pontificating *in his own salon./Stevenson was always inclined to preach, to* pontify, *to be didactic*), seemingly without differentiation. The first is more usual & the second might well be spared as a NEEDLESS VARIANT.

poor. For *poorness* & *poverty* see the latter. For 'A poor thing but mine own' (i.e. 'A poor virgin . . . an ill-favored thing . . . but mine own') see MISQUOTATION.

POPULARIZED TECHNICALITIES. The term of this sort most in vogue [when the first edition of MEU was in preparation in 1920] was *acid test* (*The measure, as our correspondent says, provides* an acid test *for every Free Trader*), which became familiar through a conspicuous use of it during the war by President Wilson. In contrast with this acquisition may be set *intoxicated,* so long popular as to be not now recognizable for a medical term at all; it is just a ponderous GENTEELISM for *drunk.* A few examples of these popularized technicalities may be gathered together; they will be only as one in a score or a hundred of those that exist, but will serve as specimens. Upon most of them some remarks will be found in their dictionary places. Two general warnings will suffice: first, that the popular use more often than not misrepresents, & sometimes very badly, the original meaning; & second, that free indulgence in this sort of term results in a tawdry style. It does not follow that none of them should ever be used.

From Philosophy–*optimism* & *pessimism, category, concept, dualistic.*

From Mathematics–*progression, arithmetical* & *geometrical, to the nth degree, to be a function of* & *functional, percentage* & *proportion* (=part).

From Religion–*devil's advocate, immanent, implicit, incarnation.*

From Psychology–*personal equation, idiosyncrasy, psychological moment, inferiority* (&c.) *complex.*

From Law–*special pleading, leading question, party* (=person), *re, exception that proves the rule.*

From War–*decimate, internecine.*

From Logic–*dilemma, idols of the market.*

From Commerce–*asset, liquidate.*

From Agriculture–*intensive,*

hardy annual, common or garden variety.

From Astrology—*ascendant.*

From Politics—*conservative* (=small).

From Chemistry—*eliminate.*

From Literature—*protagonist, euphuism, pathetic fallacy.*

From Medicine—*chronic, expectorate, hectic.*

populate makes *-table.*

port, harbor, haven. The broad distinction is that *a haven* is thought of as a place where a ship may find shelter from a storm, *a harbor* as one offering accommodation (used or not) in which ships may remain in safety for any purpose, & *a port* as a town whose harbor is frequented by naval or merchant ships.

port, larboard. The two words mean the same, but *port* has been substituted for *larboard* (the earlier opposite of *starboard*) because of the confusion resulting when orders were shouted from the too great similarity between *larboard* & *starboard; larboard,* however, has not yet perished in US.

porte-cochère. 'Gate (for the) coach.' A large gateway & passage for vehicles to drive through the house into the courtyard. In US used (erron.) for the porch at the entrance of a building to protect people alighting from the vehicle. Pron. pōrt kô shâr′.

portfolio. Pl. *-os.*

portico. Pl. *-os.*

portion. *The Prime Minister, at the banquet on Saturday, devoted* the major portion *of his speech to Russia.* See FORMAL WORDS for *major portion* as compared with *greater part.* A favorite piece of buckram. See also MAJOR.

portmanteau. Pl. *-s* (or *-x*). For *portmanteau word* the OED quotes from *Through the Looking-glass:* 'Well, "slithy" means "lithe & slimy" . . . You see it's like a portmanteau—there are two meanings packed up into one word.'

pose makes *-sable.* The verb meaning *puzzle, nonplus* (with its noun *poser,* unanswerable question) is a different word from that meaning to lay down or place, being shortened from *appose.*

poseur. One who poses, an affected person. *Poser* is also used in this sense, but the French spelling survives to distinguish it from *poser,* puzzle. Pron. pôzûr′.

POSITION OF ADVERBS. The word *adverb* is here to be taken as including adverbial phrases (e.g. *for a time*) & adverbial clauses (e.g. *if [it is] possible*), adjectives used predicatively (e.g. *alone*), & adverbial conjunctions (e.g. *then*), as well as simple adverbs such as *soon* & *undoubtedly.* Many readers may justly feel that they do not require advice on so simple a matter as where their adverbs should go, &, to save them the trouble of reading this long article, each section will start with a sentence exhibiting the type of misplacement to be discussed. Those who perceive that the adverb is wrongly placed, & why, can safely neglect that section. The misplacements to be considered will be taken under the heads: (1) Split infinitive. (2) Fear of split infinitive. (3) Imaginary split infinitive passive. (4) Splitting of the compound verb. (5) Separation of copulative verb & complement. (6) Separation of transitive verb & object. (7)

Separation of preposition & gerund. (8) Heedless misplacings.

1. Split infinitive: *The people are now returning & trying to again get together a home.* The heinousness of this offense is estimated in the article SPLIT INFINITIVE. Here the general result of that estimate is merely assumed: (a) that *to get* is a definitely enough recognized verb form to make the clinging together of its parts the natural & normal thing; (b) that there is, however, no sacrosanctity about that arrangement; (c) that adverbs should be kept outside if there is neither anything gained by putting them inside nor any difficulty in finding them another place; but (d) that such gain or difficulty will often justify the confessedly abnormal splitting. (C) is illustrated in the example above. It is easy to write *to get a home together again,* &, as *again* does not belong to the single word *get,* but *to get a home together,* nothing is gained by its abnormal placing. An example illustrating (d) is: *With us outside the treaty, we must expect the Commission* to at least neglect *our interests.* Here, *at least* cannot be put before *to* because it would then go with *Commission* (=the Commission even if not other people), nor after *neglect* because it would then be doubtful whether it referred back to *neglect* or forward to *interests,* nor after *interests* because it would then belong either to *interests* or to *neglect our interests,* neither being what is meant. Where it stands, it secures our realizing that the writer has in mind some other verb such as *injure* or *oppose* with which the weaker *neglect* is to be contrasted.

In a split infinitive, however, we have not so much a misplacing of the adverb as a violence done to the verb. It is by repulsion, not by attraction, that the infinitive acts in effecting the many misplacings for which it is responsible.

2. Fear of split infinitive: *He came* to study personally *the situation.* The order of words in that example and in those following is bizarre enough to offend the least cultivated ear. The reason why the writers, whose ears were perhaps no worse than their neighbors', were not struck by it is that they were obsessed by fear of infinitive splitting. It will be seen that the natural (not necessarily the best) place for the adverb in each of the following sentences is where it would split an infinitive: *Such gentlemen are powerless to*‸*analyze* correctly *agricultural conditions./A body of employers which still has power to*‸*influence* greatly *opinion among those who work for them.* But the terrorism exercised by the split infinitive is most conspicuous where there is in fact (see next section) no danger.

3. Imaginary split infinitive passive: *He exercised an influence that is still potent & has yet* adequately *to be*‸*measured.* In this example it is again clear that the natural place for the adverb is not where it now stands, but after the words *to be.* To insert an adverb between *to* & *be* would be splitting an infinitive; to insert one between *to be* & *measured* is nothing of the kind, but is a particular case of the construction explained in (5). The position after *to be* is not only the natural one, but the best. The

mistake—& that it is a definite mistake there is no doubt whatever—is so common that other examples are called for. WRONG: *The awkward necessity for getting to work & working as hard as possible & with hearty goodwill* altogether *seems to be‸forgotten./Every citizen worth the name ought* vitally *to be‸concerned in today's election./We think the public will not fail* unfavorably *to be‸impressed by the shifting nature of the arguments./An Act has been passed enabling agricultural land* compulsorily *to be‸acquired at a fair market price.*

4. Splitting of the compound verb: *It deals with matters about which most persons* long ago *have‸made up their minds.* By compound verb is meant a verb made up of an auxiliary (or more than one) & an infinitive (without *to*) or participle (e.g. *have made*). When an adverb is to be used with such a verb, its normal place is between the auxiliary (or sometimes the first auxiliary if there are two or more) & the rest. Not only is there no such objection to thus splitting a compound verb as there is to splitting an infinitive, but any other position for the adverb requires special justification: *I have* never *seen her,* not *I* never *have seen her,* is the ordinary idiom, though the rejected order becomes the right if emphasis is to be put on *have* (*I may have had chances of seeing Bernhardt, but I* never *have seen her*). But it is plain from the example above & those now to come that a prejudice has grown up against dividing compound verbs. It is probably a supposed corollary of the accepted split-infinitive prohibition; at any rate, it is entirely unfounded. In each of the first three extracts there is one auxiliary, & after that instead of before it the adverb should have been put; the other three have two auxiliaries each, which raises a further question to be touched upon afterwards. WRONG (single auxiliary): *If his counsel* still *is‸followed, 'the conflict' is indeed inevitable./Its very brief span of insect-eating activity* hardly *can‸redeem its general evil habit as a grain-devourer./Politicians of all sorts in the United States* already *are‸girding up their loins for the next election.*/(Double auxiliary) *Oxford must* heartily *be‸congratulated on the victory./If the desired end is ever attained it* earnestly *may be ‸hoped that especial care will be taken with the translation./The importance which* quite rightly *has‸been given to reports of their meetings.* The minor point of whether the adverb is to follow the first auxiliary or the whole auxiliary depends on the answer to the question: Do the adverb & verb naturally suggest an adjective & noun? If so, let them stand next each other, & if not, not. *Heartily congratulated, earnestly hoped,* suggest *hearty congratulations,* & *earnest hope;* but *rightly given* does not suggest *right gift* or *right giving;* which means that the notion of giving is qualified by *rightly* not absolutely but under the particular limitations of the auxiliaries, & that the adverb is better placed between the auxiliaries than next to *given.* This, however, is a minor point, as was said above; the main object of this section is to stress the certain fact that there is no objection

whatever to dividing a compound verb by adverbs.

5. Separation of copulative verb & complement: *It would be a different thing if the scheme had been found* fundamentally *to be^faulty, but that is not the case.* This is on the same footing as the separation of the compound verb discussed in (4); that is, it is a delusion to suppose that the insertion of an adverb between the two parts is a solecism, or even, like the splitting of the infinitive, a practice to be regarded as abnormal. On the contrary, it is the natural arrangement, & in the following example *often* has been mistakenly shifted from its right place owing to a superstition: *The immense improvement which they have wrought in the condition of the people, & which* often *is^quite irrespective of the number of actual converts.*

6. Separation of transitive verb & its object: *The Ministry must either take action or^defend* effectively *their inactivity.* The mistakes discussed in sections 2 to 5 have this in common, that they spring from a desire, instinctive or inculcated, to keep the parts of a verb group together & allow no adverb to intrude into it. But there is one kind of group whose breaking up by adverbs that ought to have been placed not in the middle of it, but before or after the whole, is only too common. That is the group consisting of a transitive verb & its object: *I had to second* by all the means in my power *diplomatic action. To second diplomatic action* is the verb & object, separated by a seven-word adverb; it is a crying case; everyone will agree to deferring the adverb, & the writer had either no literary ear or some grammatical or stylistic fad. The longer the adverb in proportion to the object, the more marked is the offense of interpolating it. But the same mistake is seen, though less glaringly, in the following examples. The roman-type adverb in each should be removed, sometimes to a place before the verb, sometimes to one after the object. WRONG: *Are they quite sure that they have^interpreted* rightly *the situation?/I should counsel,* then, *the schoolboy^to take plenty of exercise in the open./A lull of the breeze kept* for a time *the small boat^in the neighborhood of the brig./Continuation with the university courses would most certainly^elevate* further *the people.*

There are conditions that justify the separation, the most obvious being when a lengthy object would keep an adverb that is not suitable for the early position too remote from the verb. *Failure of the Powers to enforce their will would expose* to ridicule *an authority, which, as it is, is not very imposing;* the shortness of 'to ridicule' compared with the length of the object makes that order the best & almost necessary one. But anyone who applies this principle must be careful not to reckon as part of the object words that either do not belong to it at all or are unessential to it; else he will offend the discerning reader's ear as cruelly as the authors now to be quoted: *They are now busy issuing blueprints & instructions, & otherwise helping* in all sorts of ways *our firms^to get an efficient grip of the business in a hurry.* The object is *our firms* alone, not that & the rest of the sentence; put it next to *helping./Who are risking* every day with intelligence & with shrewdness *fortunes‸on what they believe. Fortunes* alone is the object; put it after *risking./His make-up, which approached* too nearly *sheer caricature‸to be reckoned quite happy.* A very odd piece of tit for tat; *too nearly* divides *approached* from *caricature,* & in revenge *caricature* divides *to be reckoned* from *too nearly;* put *sheer caricature* next to *approached.*

7. Separation of preposition & gerund. *To decry the infantry for the sake* unduly *of*‸piling *up artillery & what not, is the notion of persons who . . .* This hardly needs serious treatment. It is an amusing example of somebody's terror of separating *of* & *piling* by an adverb—which is no more than an exaggeration of the superstitions dealt with in 3, 4, & 5.

8. Some heedless misplacings: *Dressings of cotton & linen are reserved* only *for‸the most serious cases‸./The terms upon which the governing classes have obtained their influence are those upon which‸*it alone *may be retained./Should,* too, *not our author be considered?* (*too* might go after *not,* or *author,* or *considered,* according to the meaning wanted; but no meaning can justify its present position).

POSITIVE WORDS IN NEUTRAL PLACES. There are words whose essential function is to express the speaker's strong opinion; specimens are *excellent, admirable, remarkable, incredible, disgraceful.* To use these in a negative, conditional, or interrogative sense is an offense against idiom too obvious to be common. You cannot stipulate that a thing shall be *excellent;* you can only pronounce it excellent on trial. To ask for a *most delicious peach,* a bottle of *admirable claret,* a *profoundly interesting novel,* is absurd (unless you are playfully quoting someone else's commendation; Martin Chuzzlewit, for instance, with his experience of remarkable men, could legitimately ask whether Mr. Choke was one of the most remarkable men in the country). Examples: *If they heard of the pecuniary trouble of* an excellent scholar or man of letters, *they should communicate the fact to their secretary./An American soldier who was serving on the special staff told him that exceptional care is now being taken to secure railway engines that are* in admirable condition*./The amphibious part of the operation, then, would be limited to what he could do in an* incredibly short *time./You should have written to your cousin the moment they had begun to treat you* disgracefully (*so* before *disgracefully,* implying 'as I consider they have treated you,' would have cured this)*./All Governments who get into power by a* most violent & unscrupulous *use of party tactics try to prolong their advantage by . . .* (omit *most*)*./When will Church leaders realize that unity in action is* so much more important *than unity of belief?* (omit *so*).

posse. From *posse comitatus,* 'the force of the county'—'the body of men above the age of 15 (exclusive of peers, clergymen, & infirm persons) whom the sheriff may summon to repress a riot &c.'; hence a force armed with legal authority.

Two syllables.

possession. *In possession of,* holding; *in* the *possession of,* held by: *Prisoner was found* in possession of *a revolver; The necklace was found* in the possession of *prisoner's wife.*

POSSESSIVE PUZZLES. 1. *Septimus's, Achilles'.* It was formerly customary, when a word ended in *-s,* to write its possessive with an apostrophe but no additional *s,* e.g. *Mars' hill, Venus' Bath, Achilles' thews.* In verse, & in poetic or reverential contexts, this custom is retained, & the number of syllables is the same as in the subjective case, e.g. *Achilles'* has three, not four; *Jesus'* has two. But elsewhere we now add the *s* & the syllable, *Charles's Wain, St. James's Palace, Jones's children, the Rev. Septimus's surplice, Pythagoras's doctrine.* For *goodness' sake, conscience' sake,* &c., see SAKE.

2. *Whose, of which.* See WHOSE for illustrations of the absurdity of prohibiting *whose* to be used as a possessive of the inanimate, and allowing it to be used only of persons; e.g. *My thought, Whose murder yet is but fantastical.*

3. (A) *Mr. Smith (now Lord London)'s intervention was decisive?* or (B) *Mr. Smith's (now Lord London) intervention?* or (C) *Mr. Smith's (now Lord London's) intervention?* or (D) *The intervention of Mr. Smith (now Lord London)?* (C) is clearly wrong because the intervention was not Lord London's; (B) is intolerable because we cannot be happy without the *'s* close before *intervention,* just as we cannot endure *someone's else umbrella* though we can with an effort allow the umbrella to be *someone's else;* (A) is the reasonable solution, but has no chance against the horror of fussy correctness; &, failing it, the only thing is to run away, i.e. to use (D).

4. *In 'The Times"s opinion.* This also has to be run away from. To write *in 'The Times's' opinion* is not running away but merely blundering; if the newspaper title is to be in quotation marks & the possessive is to be used, the form at the top with two independent apostrophes jostling each other is the only correct possibility. But there are two escapes; one is to write the title in italics instead of quotation marks, but the possessive *s* in roman type (*The Times*s), & the other is to fly to *of* (*in the opinion of 'The Times'*).

5. For the idiomatic use of *somebody else's* rather than *somebody's else* see ELSE.

possible. 1. *Do one's possible* is a GALLICISM; &, with *do what one can* in established existence, it is superfluous.

2. Construction. Unlike *able,* which ordinarily requires to be completed by an infinitive (*able to be done, to exist,* &c.), *possible* is complete in itself & means without addition *able to be done* or *occur.* WRONG: *But no such questions* are possible, *as it seems to me,* to arise *between your nation & ours./No breath of honest fresh air is suffered to enter, wherever it* is possible to be *excluded.* The English for *are possible to arise* & *is possible to be excluded* is *can arise, can be excluded.* The mistakes are perhaps due to the frequency of such forms as *It is possible to find an explanation,* in which *it* is not an ordi-

nary pronoun, but merely anticipatory; that is, the sentence in its simpler form would NOT be *An explanation is possible to find*, but *To find an explanation is possible.* When it is felt that *possible* does require to be amplified, it is done by *of* with a verbal noun—*Limits that are* possible of *exact ascertainment;* but *susceptible* or some other word is usually better.

3. *Possible, probable.* It would be too much to demand that *possible* should always be kept to its strict sense & never so far weakened that *impossible* (or *possible* in a negative context) means no more than *very unlikely;* but, when *probable* & *possible* are in explicit contrast, the demand may fairly be made. WRONG: *The Prohibition Amendment could only be revoked by the same methods as secured its adoption. I met no one in America who deemed this* probable, *few who thought it* even possible. As all sensible people knew it, whatever its improbability, to be possible, the picture of American intelligence is uncomplimentary; but this absurdity is common enough, & ranks with the abuse of LITERALLY.

post. (1) *Post* is used in Brit. for what in US is usually *mail,* both n. & v. (2) Technically, in US the card with an official government stamp printed on it is *a postal card;* in Brit. *a post card.* The unofficial card to which the user attaches a stamp is in US *postcard,* Brit. *postal card.* Popularly the two terms are used interchangeably in both countries.

poste restante is the equivalent of US General Delivery (i.e. held at the post office until called for).

post hoc, ergo propter hoc. (Log.): 'after it, therefore due to it.' The fallacy of confusing consequence with sequence. On Sunday we prayed for rain; on Monday it rained; therefore the prayers caused the rain.

posthumous. The *-h-* is silent, & also, though never omitted, etymologically incorrect (Lat. *postumus,* 'last'; *a posthumous child,* so called because it must be the dead father's last; but *posthumous books* &c., published after the author's death).

postil(l)ion. One *l* is better.

postpone. Silent *t.*

postprandial. 'After dinner.' Chiefly in PEDANTIC HUMOR.

postscript. For insistence on pronouncing the first *t,* see PRONUNCIATION.

potency, -nce. In general senses *-cy* is much commoner; &, as *-ce* has technical senses in engineering, watch making, &c., it would be better to confine *-ce* to these, & make *-cy* universal in the general senses.

potential has no longer the meaning of *potent,* which should have been the word in (WRONG): *The Labour Party . . . was exercising a most* potential *influence on some social problems.* See LONG VARIANTS.

potful. Pl. *-ls.*

pother is now, except in dialects, a LITERARY WORD. The more correct, but now less usual, pronunciation rhymes with *other.* There is no proof of connection with either *bother* or *powder,* though it is thought that *bother* may be an Irish corruption of *pother.* Between *pother* & *bother* there is the difference in meaning that *pother* denotes ado or bustle or confusion in itself, while *bother* emphasizes the annoyance or trouble caused.

pot-pourri. A mixture, of spiced flower petals in a jar; fig. a medley of music, literature. Pron. pō′po͞o′rē′.

potter, v. In US *putter* (dawdle, trifle) is more usual.

poverty, poorness. The dominant sense of *poor* is having little money or property. The noun corresponding to this dominant sense is *poverty,* & *poorness* is never so used in modern English. The further the dominant sense is departed from, the more does *poverty* give way to *poorness*—Poverty *is no excuse for theft; The* poverty (or *poorness*) *of the soil; The* poorness (or *poverty*) *of the harvest; The* poorness *of his performance.*

POW=prisoner of war (usually no periods).

practicable, practical. 1. The recommended negative forms are *impracticable*, but *unpractical* (*impractical* is listed in US dictionaries, however, without comment).

2. Meanings. Each word has senses in which there is no fear that the other will be substituted for it; but in other senses they come very near each other, & confusion is both natural & common. Safety lies in remembering that *practicable* means capable of being effected or accomplished, & *practical* adapted to actual conditions. It is true that the *practicable* is often *practical,* & that the *practical* is nearly always *practicable;* but a very *practical plan* may prove, owing to change of circumstances, impracticable, & a *practicable policy* may be thoroughly unpractical. In the extracts, each word is used where the other was wanted. WRONG: *In the case of a club, if rules are passed obnoxious to a large section of the members, the latter can resign; in our national relationships, secession is not* practical *nowadays.* The last clause is in clear antithesis to *the latter can resign,* & means *You cannot secede,* or in other words *Secession is not practicable./But to plunge into the military question without settling the Government question would not be good sense or* practicable *policy; & no wise man would expect to get serviceable recruits for the Army from Ireland in this way.* The policy was certainly practicable, for it was carried out; & the writer, though he had not the proof that we have of its practicability, probably did not mean to deny that, but only to say that it was not suited to the conditions, i.e. *practical./We live in a low-pressure belt where cyclone follows cyclone; but the prediction of their arrival is at present not* practical.

practice, -se. In US usually *-ce* for noun & verb. In Brit. n. *-ce,* v. *-se.*

praenomen. In Ancient Rome, the first of the three names. Pron. prēnō′men.

pragmatic(al). In the diplomatic, historical, & philosophical senses, the *-ic* form is usual. In the general sense of officious or opinionated, *-ical* is commoner. In the interest of differentiation these tendencies should be encouraged.

pragmatism. 'An American philosophical movement founded by C. S. Peirce and William James, & having as its characteristic doctrines that the meaning of conceptions is to be sought in their practical bearings, that the function of thought is as a guide to action, & that the truth is preeminently to be tested by the practical consequences of belief' (Webster).

pray. *Pray in aid*=pray or crave the assistance *of* (someone). One of the picturesque phrases that people catch up & use without understanding. WRONG: *We are disturbed to find that this principle of* praying in aid the domestic circumstances *of the woman appears to have been sanctioned officially by the Committee on production.* This writer, & most of those who use the words, suppose that *in aid* is an adv., & that *pray* is therefore free to take an object—here *circumstances.* The fact is that the object of *pray* is *aid,* & *in* is not a preposition but an adv., *to pray in aid* being word for word *to call in help;* if the helper or helping thing is to be specified, it must have an *of* before it, as in the following OED quotations (RIGHT): *A city or corporation, holding a fee-farm of the King, may* pray in Aid of him, *if anything be demanded of them relating thereto./An incumbent may* pray in aid of *the patron & ordinary.*

pre-. In compounds whose second part begins with *e* a hyphen is recommended (e.g. *pre-eminent*); Brit. usage hyphens also before *i,* US usually not. In others the hyphen is not necessary, and some US authorities frown upon its ever being retained. So the unwary reader comes upon *predata, a prechilled atmosphere.* The recommendation is that the hyphen should be freely used if the compound is one made for the occasion, or if any peculiarity in its form might prevent its elements from being instantly recognized, or if recurrence from the sense now developed to a more primitive one is to be marked by especial stress on the elements: *predetermine, prenatal, prearranged; pre-Coalition, pre-position* (in contrast with *preposition* the part of speech). *Pre-* with a hyphen is better than the un-English *prë-*.

precarious. Held during the pleasure of another: *precarious tenure;* taken for granted, unwarranted: *a precarious conclusion;* 'dependent on chance, uncertain': *makes a precarious living;* hazardous, perilous: *a precarious voyage.*

precession is the action of preceding in time, rank, or order. It has no relation to *procession* and is little used except in scientific or technical contexts (Astron., Physics, and Phonetics). Alone it usually stands for the precession of the equinoxes.

preciosity & preciousness illustrate well the differentiation that should be encouraged whenever there is an opening for it between the two terminations. The special sense of excessive fastidiousness in diction, pronunciation, & the like, is almost confined to *-ty,* & the more general senses are left to *-ness.* The opening here was provided by the fact that *preciosity* represents the French form & so calls up the *Precieuses Ridicules* of Molière.

precipitance, -ancy, -ation. The most economical way of dealing with the words would have been to let *precipitancy* perish, & make *precipitance* mean rashness of action or suddenness of occurrence or speed of motion, & *precipitation* the bringing or coming to pass with especial rashness or speed. But what is happening is that all three exist side by side, *-ance* & *-ancy* slowly giving way to *-ation* just as their parent *precipitant* has given way to *precipitate.*

precipitate. (1) The verb makes *-itable.* (2) Pron. v. -āt, adj. & n. *-at* or -ĭt.

precipitous means steep, like a precipice (*precipitous rocks, a precipitous ravine*). Formerly, it was freely used where we now always say *precipitate;* but that time has passed away. NOT *Are the workers justified in taking the* precipitous *action suggested in the resolution?/The step seems a trifle rash & precipitous when one remembers the number of banking & commercial failures that . . .* The writers either are ignorant of the established difference between *precipitous* & *precipitate,* or must not be surprised if they are taken to be so.

précis. 'Concise.' Noun, sing. & pl. A summary, abstract; a brief, clean-cut statement of essential facts. Pron. prā′sē′.

precisian, n. One who is rigidly precise in observing forms. See PURISM.

predaceous, -cious. Webster gives *-ceous* first; most other US dictionaries, as well as Brit., give *-cious.* The word means 'living by preying on other animals' and is applied to predatory animals. *Predacious attacks on the flock; the predacious habits of the weasel. Predatory* means 'plundering' and not only includes the qualities of predacious animals, but may be applied to predatory tribes, nations, &c. and to animals, birds, & insects that are destructive to crops, buildings, &c. as well as to animal life.

predecessor. US usually prĕ-, Brit. prē-.

predicate. (1) The verb makes *-cable.* (2) Pron. *predicate,* & its derivatives *predicable* & *predication,* with prĕd-, not prēd-. The verb is said with -āt, the noun with -ĭt. (3) *Predicate, predict.* The words are not interchangeable variants. *Predicate* is from Latin *praedicare,* to cry forth or proclaim, but *predict* from Latin *praedicere,* to say beforehand or foretell. *Predicate* makes *predicable* & *predication, predict* makes *predictable* & *prediction.* It is naturally *predicate* & its derivatives that are misused; Webster includes under *predicate,* 'To found; to base (upon) —not in good use'; and 'erroneously, to foretell.' Some other US dictionaries do not so qualify these definitions. WRONG: *The case for establishing compulsory & voluntary systems side by side in the same country is not only not proven, but involves a change in strategic theory that* predicates *nothing but disaster* (threatens? foreshadows? presages? just possibly *predicts;* certainly not *predicates*)./*A profound change in the balance of the Constitution,* predicable *by anyone who had searched the political heavens during the last four years & observed the eccentric behavior of certain bodies & their satellites, is now upon us* (predictable). (4) *Predicate* & its derivatives mean to assert, & especially to assert the existence of some quality as an attribute of the person or thing that is spoken of (*Goodness or badness cannot with any propriety be* predicated *of motives./To* predicate the *mortality of Socrates,* i.e. to state that Socrates is mortal). The words (apart from *predicate* n., the grammatical term) are mainly used in Logic, & are best left alone by those who have no acquaintance with either Logic or Latin. See PAIRS & SNARES. (5) Gram. In *time flies, time* is the subject, *flies* the predicate. In *time is flying, is flying* is the predicate (i.e. the predicate includes the verb & its copula). In the wider sense, the predicate includes the verb, its object, complement, &c. that express what is said of the subject.

preface. (1) The verb makes *-ceable.* (2) *Preface* and *foreword* can be used interchangeably. A distinction is made, however, by some US publishers: the *preface* is by the author; the *foreword* by some one not the author. Though arbitrary, the distinction is useful. *Introduction* is reserved for longer prefatory material that is more integral to the text.

prefect. Pron. prē-. The adj. is *prefectorial,* not *-toral.*

prefer(able). 1. *Prefer* makes *-rring, -rred,* but *preferable* (prĕf'erabl); the latter formation is anomalous but established.

2. *More preferable* is an inexcusable PLEONASM 3. WRONG: *The cure for that is clearly the alternative vote or the second ballot, the former alternative being, in our view, on every ground the* more preferable.

3. *To, rather than, than.* If the rejected alternative is to be expressed, the normal construction for it is *to: I* prefer *pears* to *apples, riding* to *walking.* The OED, defining the construction, gives nothing besides *to* except *before* & *above,* both of which it obelizes as archaic or disused. A difficulty arises, however, with *to:* the object of *prefer* is often an infinitive, but the sound of *I* prefer to *die* to to *pay blackmail,* or even of *I* prefer to *die* to *paying,* is intolerable. It is easy sometimes to make the change corresponding to that of *to die* to *death,* but by no means always. When the infinitive is unavoidable, the way out is to use *rather than* instead of *to: I* prefer to *die* rather than *pay blackmail.* To use simple *than* instead of *rather than* (*I* prefer to *die* than *pay*) is clean against established idiom, as bad as saying *superior than* or *prior than* instead of *superior* or *prior to.* Even the *rather than* mentioned above is not much to be recommended; but, if the writer is bent on using *prefer,* it will pass; a better plan is to change the verb *prefer* to *choose rather* or *would rather* (*He* chose to *die* rather than *pay; I* would rather *die* than *pay*). The main point is that *prefer . . . than* without *rather* is not English. WRONG: *We should greatly* prefer *to pay the doctors more* than *to limit the area of insurance* (We would much rather pay . . . than limit)./*The nine deportees would* prefer *to go home* than *to undergo sentence after trial by Court-martial* (would sooner go . . . than undergo)./*He is persuasive rather than dogmatic, & prefers to suggest* than *to conclude* (suggesting to concluding).

prefix. (1) (Gram.): 'attached in front.' An affix attached to the beginning of a word or stem to make a compound word, as *re-, ex-, be-, a-,* in *reform, ex-officer, belabor, arise.* (2) *Prefix, preface,* vv. *Prefix* is one of the verbs liable to the OBJECT-SHUFFLING abuse. You can *prefix* a title *to* your name, but not *prefix* your name *with* a title.

Several examples of the confusion follow; in each the construction must be turned inside out if *prefix* is to be kept, but in most of them the change of *prefix(ed)* to *preface(d)* would put things right. WRONG: *The speeches in the present volume are* prefixed *by a clear & connected account of the Administration./Every son is allowed to* prefix *his name with the title./ Every paragraph is* prefixed *with a kind of title to it.* The poor old word *preface,* with *foreword* assailing it on one front & *prefix* on another, is going through troubled times.

prejudg(e)ment. In US usually no *e.* Brit. usage varies.

prejudice, n, The prepositions after *prejudice* are *against* & *in favor of.* WRONG: *The Committee's Report adds that without doubt a marked* prejudice to *the eating of eels exists in Scotland.* In this *to* is transferred from *objection;* see ANALOGY. But *without prejudice to either side* is idiomatic.

preliminary, adv. RIGHT: *He was gathering up his books* preliminary *to leaving* (NOT *preliminarily*). See QUASI-ADVERBS.

prelude. Pron. prĕ-, not prē-.

premature. The pronunciation prĕ'matūr is recommended (prēma tūr' is perhaps more usual in US), but the sound of the *e* & the place of the accent are both variable; in any case, the last syllable is fully pronounced & not weakened to -chĕr.

première. Pron. prĕmyār'. (From Fr. *first.* The first performance of a play, in US often pronounced premēr'.)

premise(s),-ss(es). (1) The noun is prĕm'ĭs, the verb prĭmīz'. (2) The verb is spelled *premise,* not *-ize.* (3) The two noun spellings (*-ises* & *-isses* in the plural) may perhaps be thought useful; but ambiguity cannot often arise between the parts of a syllogism (*-isses*) & of a building or house (*-ises*); &, except practical utility, there is no reason for the variation. The two words are one, the parts of a syllogism being 'the previously stated,' & the grounds & appurtenances of a house &c. being 'the aforesaid' (facts, places, &c.). *Premiss* is the earlier & etym. spelling, but the modern uniform spelling *premise* (pl. *premises*) is recommended.

premium. Pl. *-ms* only.

preoccupiedly. A bad form.

preparatory. RIGHT: *They were weighing it* preparatory *to sending it to town* (NOT *preparatorily*); see QUASI-ADVERBS.

prepare makes *-rable* (pron. prepar'-, not as *reparable*).

PREPOSITION AT END. It is a cherished superstition that prepositions must, in spite of the incurable English instinct for putting them late ('They are the fittest timber to make great politics of,' said Bacon; & 'What are you hitting me for?' says the modern schoolboy), be kept true to their name & placed before the word they govern. 'A sentence ending in a preposition is an inelegant sentence' represents a very general belief. One of its chief supports is the fact that Dryden, an acknowledged master of English prose, went through all his prefaces contriving away the final prepositions that he had been guilty of in his first editions. It is interesting to find Ruskin almost reversing this procedure. In the text of the *Seven Lamps* there is a solitary final preposition to be found, &

no more; but in the later footnotes they are not avoided (*Any more wasted words . . . I never heard of./Men whose occupation for the next fifty years would be the knocking down every beautiful building they could lay their hands on*). Dryden's earlier practice shows him following the English instinct; his later shows him sophisticated with deliberate latinism. Gibbon improved upon the doctrine, &, observing that prepositions & adverbs are not always easily distinguished, kept on the safe side by not ending sentences with *on, over, under,* or the like, even when they would have been adverbs.

The fact is that the remarkable freedom enjoyed by English in putting its prepositions late & omitting its relatives is an important element in the flexibility of the language. The power of saying *A state of dejection such as they are absolute strangers to* (Cowper) instead of *A state of dejection of an intensity to which they are absolute strangers,* or *People worth talking to* instead of *People with whom it is worth while to talk,* is not one to be lightly surrendered. But the Dryden-Gibbon tradition has remained in being, & even now immense pains are daily expended in changing spontaneous into artificial English. *That depends on what they are cut with* is not improved by conversion into *That depends on with what they are cut;* & too often the lust of sophistication, once blooded, becomes uncontrollable, & ends with, *That depends on the answer to the question as to with what they are cut.* Those who lay down the universal principle that final prepositions are 'inelegant' are unconsciously trying to deprive the English language of a valuable idiomatic resource, which has been used freely by all our greatest writers except those whose instinct for English idiom has been overpowered by notions of correctness derived from Latin standards. The legitimacy of the prepositional ending in literary English must be uncompromisingly maintained. In respect of elegance or inelegance, every example must be judged not by any arbitrary rule, but on its own merits, according to the impression it makes on the feeling of educated readers.

In avoiding the forbidden order, unskillful handlers of words often fall into real blunders (see OUT OF THE FRYING PAN). A few examples of bad grammar obviously due to this cause may fairly be offered without any suggestion that a rule is responsible for all blunders made in attempting to keep it. The words in parentheses indicate the avoided form, which is not necessarily the best, but is at least better than that substituted for it. WRONG: *The day begins with a ride with the wife & as many others as want to ride &* for whom *there is horseflesh available* (& as there are horses for)./*It is like the art* of which *Huysmans dreamed but never executed* (the art that Huysmans dreamed of)./*Recognition is given to it* by no matter whom *it is displayed* (no matter whom it is displayed by)./*That promised land* for which *he was to prepare, but scarcely to enter* (that he was to prepare for).

It was said above that almost all our great writers have allowed themselves to end a sentence or a clause with a preposition. If it were not presumptuous, after that, to offer advice, the advice would be: Follow no arbitrary rule, but remember that there are often two or more possible arrangements between which a choice should be consciously made; if the abnormal, or at least unorthodox, final preposition that has naturally presented itself sounds comfortable, keep it; if it does not sound comfortable, still keep it if it has compensating vigor, or when among awkward possibilities it is the least awkward.

presage. The noun is prĕ′sĭj, the verb prĭsāj′. The verb makes *-geable.* Although sometimes used (and defined) as if it were neutral in tone, a synonym of *forecast,* for example, the word whether noun or verb, properly suggests the coming of something evil. Typical examples from OED: *presage of a storm; a presage that he had only a short time to live; omens presaging some dire calamity; presaging danger and disaster.*

prescience, -nt. The pronunciation prĕsh′- is given first by most dictionaries; OED gives it only; ACD gives prē′- first.

prescription. For the legal meaning, & its relation to IMPRESCRIPTIBLE, see that word.

present, adj. *The present writer* is a periphrasis for *I* & *me* that is not entirely avoidable under existing journalistic conditions, & is at any rate preferable to the false first-personal *one* see ONE 5) that is being tried as a substitute; but it is very irritating to the reader. Personality, however veiled, should be introduced into impersonal articles only when the necessity is quite indisputable. The worst absurdity occurs when a contributor or correspondent whose name appears above or below his article or letter assumes this coyness; but they often do it.

presentiment, presentment, presentient. Nine people out of ten, challenged to pronounce the first, will do it with z. On the other hand the OED gives only the pronunciation with s; that is undoubtedly the correct one, as in *sentiment;* but the sound has been assimilated to that of *present,* with which *presentment* is, but *presentiment* is not, connected; & with *presentient,* which is not in popular use, no one would make the same mistake. Mistake or not, however, even the OED's authority is hardly likely to cure *presentiment* of its z, & the pronunciations here recommended are prĭzĕn′tĭment, prĭzĕnt′ment, prēsĕn′shent.

presently=at once, now, has been obs. since the 17th c. (OED). Its only modern sense is soon, shortly.

presidency. Those who would have Americans say *candidate for the presidency, run for the presidency* (rather than *for President*) are undoubtedly right, but the battle is in vain.

prestidigitator, -tion. Now chiefly in POLYSYLLABIC HUMOR.

prestissimo, presto. (Mus., very quick; quick.) Pl. *-os.*

presume, assume. In the one sense in which the words overlap, 'take for granted,' *presume* is the stronger word, seemingly with more justifiable confidence in the thing tentatively accepted as true: *I* presume *that he will accept* (he has always accepted before, and seemed quite happy about it). *I* assume *that he will accept* so I am preparing an extra place. The technical uses suggest this. RIGHT: *If a man is missing for seven years* *he is* presumed *dead and his wife may remarry./If we assume that our hypothesis is right we can easily take the next step.* (*I am* assuming *it is right; I* presume, *from what you have told me, that it is.*)

presumptive. Giving grounds for presumption. So *presumptive evidence. Heir presumptive,* one whose title is liable to be defeated by the birth of a nearer heir.

pretence, -se. *Pretense* is the usual US spelling; *-ce* Brit. *Pretension* but *pretentious.*

preterite. In dealing with English grammar, it is better to say *past.*

pretermit makes *-tted, -tting;* the word (chiefly literary or formal) means omit, overlook (intentionally), neglect, interrupt. RIGHT: *Some points we advisedly* pretermit./*God* pretermits *many times errors in circumstances./For her the mastiff* pretermits *his incessant bark.* Pron. prētĕrmit′.

prevaricate makes *-tor.* It means be evasive, quibble, equivocate. It is not a syn. of *lie,* for which it is often loosely used.

prevent. Constr.: *Prevent him* from *going* or *prevent* his *going* (NOT *prevent* him *going*).

preventable, -ible. The first is recommended.

prevent(at)ive. The short form is better; see LONG VARIANTS.

previous. (1) For the construction in *will consult you previous to acting* (NOT *previously*), see QUASI-ADVERBS. (2) *Too previous,* originally amusing both because the sense of *previous* was a specially made one, & because *too* was with that sense deliberately redundant, has passed into the realm of WORN-OUT HUMOR. (3) *The previous question* is a phrase that does not explain itself. According to Webster, it is 'The question whether the main issue shall be voted on or not, at once, without further debate.' In England the object is to shelve the matter for the time being; in US it is to hasten action.

pre-war. 1. The hyphen is still widely used (Brit. always), though most US dictionaries spell as one word.

2. The only justification for saying *pre-war* instead of *before the war* is that *before the* war makes a very unhandy adjective, & we are now constantly in need of a handy one; *before-the-war conditions, politics, prices,* as phrases for everyday use, will never do, & the only justification is also sufficient. But it fails to cover the use of *pre-war* as an adverb. There is nothing unhandy in that use of *before the war,* which should be restored in all contexts of the kind here shown: *The suggestion is utterly untrue, as a comparison of present prices with those prevailing* pre-war *will show./The difference is made up, though not, of course, to the same extent as* pre-war, *by interest on our foreign investments./The season-ticket holder, too, is to pay more than he did* pre-war.

prick. Archaic, a goad for oxen. Now only in *Kick against the pricks* (from Acts IX.5), to hurt oneself by vain resistance.

pride. *Pride goeth before a fall* is a MISQUOTATION of Proverbs XVI.18: 'Pride goeth before destruction and an haughty spirit before a fall.' But see PRIDE OF KNOWLEDGE.

PRIDE OF KNOWLEDGE is a very unamiable characteristic, & the display of it should be sedulously avoided. Some of the ways in which it is displayed, often by people who do not realize how disagreeable they are making themselves, are illustrated in the following among many articles: *á l'outrance, amuck, averse, bedouin, course, different, double entendre, egregious, flautist, implement, ingeminate, moslem, naïf, nom-de-guerre, taboo.*

prie-dieu. 'Pray God.' A desk suitable for one kneeling at prayer. Pron. prē dyû.

prig is a word of variable & indefinite meaning; the following, from an anonymous volume of essays, may be useful: 'The best thing I can do, perhaps, is to give you the various descriptions that would come into my head at different times if I were asked for one suddenly. A prig is a believer in red tape; that is, he exalts the method above the work done. A prig, like the Pharisee, says: "God, I thank thee that I am not as other men are"—except that he often substitutes Self for God. A prig is one who works out his paltry accounts to the last farthing, while his millionaire neighbor lets accounts take care of themselves. A prig expects others to square themselves to his very inadequate measuring-rod, & condemns them with confidence if they do not. A prig is wise beyond his years in all the things that do not matter. A prig cracks nuts with a steam hammer: that is, calls in the first principles of morality to decide whether he may, or must, do something of as little importance as drinking a glass of beer. On the whole, one may, perhaps, say that all his different characteristics come from the combination, in varying proportions, of three things—the desire to do his duty, the belief that he knows better than other people, & blindness to the difference in value between different things.'

prima donna. Pron. prē-. Pl. (It.) *prime donne* (-ēmā -nā) but usually *prima donnas.*

prima facie. 'On first appearance.' *Prima facie evidence* is that sufficient to establish the fact in question unless it is proved wrong. Pron. prī'ma fā'shĭē.

primary colors. The fundamental or additive primary colors (lights, which when properly selected & mixed can produce any other colors) are red, green, and blue. In painting, red, yellow, and blue are the primaries.

primates, n. pl., the highest order of mammals including man, apes, monkeys, lemurs (and, in the Linnaean order, bats).

primer. The traditional pronunciation is prĭ'mer, & the word was very commonly spelled with *-mm-*. This pronunciation is standard US and still used in Brit. for the names of types; but in the names of modern school manuals prī'mer is now more usual in Brit.

primeval, -aeval. The first is recommended.

princess. As a prefix (*Princess Margaret, Princess Victoria, Princess Royal,* &c.) pron. prĭn'sĭs; as an independent noun, prĭn'sĕs (usual US), or prĭnsĕs'.

principal, principle. Misprints of one for the other are very frequent, & should be guarded against.

prior. For the adverbial use (*prior to*=before) see QUASI-ADVERBS. But the phrase is incongruous, & ranks merely with FORMAL WORDS, except in contexts involving a connection between the two events more essential than the simple time relation, as in *Candidates must deposit security* prior to *the ballot.* The use deprecated is seen in: *No manuscript has yet been received; this is a dubious situation* prior to *the materialization of any copy.* See OFFICIALESE.

prise. This spelling is sometimes used to differentiate the verb meaning to force up by leverage from the other verb or verbs spelled *prize;* it is also the old spelling of the nautical verb meaning to capture. But the pronunciation (always -z) is against the success of this distinction, & the ordinary form *prize* is recommended.

pristine. Belonging to the earliest period; primitive. Hence now often 'of its original condition'; uncorrupted. *Pristine purity, loveliness,* &c.

privacy. Pron. prīv-.

privative. (Gram.): 'taking away.' Prefixes that deny the presence of the quality denoted by the simple word are called privative or negative. The *a-* of *aseptic* & the *in-* of *innocent* are privative, whereas the *a-* of *arise* & the *in-* of *insist* are not.

privilege, v. WRONG: *He was generally believed to be an exceptionally taciturn man, but those who were* privileged with *his friendship say that this was a habit assumed against the inquisitive.* (On the ANALOGY of *honored with.*)

pro-. Prefix (Lat.) meaning forth, forward (*proceed*); substituted for (*pronoun*); in favor of (*proslavery, pro-British*). Prefix (Gr.) meaning before (*prologue*).

pro (=professional). Colloq. See CURTAILED WORDS. Pl. *pros.*

pro & con. Pl., as noun, *pros & cons.*

probable. Two temptations call for notice. The first is that of attaching an infinitive to *probable;* cf. POSSIBLE; a thing may be *likely to happen,* but NOT *probable to happen;* ANALOGY is the corrupter. WRONG: *Military co-operation against Russia is scarcely* probable to be *more than a dream.* The second temptation is the wrong use of the future after *probable. The result will probably be* is right; but *The probable result will be* is a mixture between that & *The probable result is.* WRONG: *It is believed that Said Pasha will be forced to resign, & that his most* probable *successor* will be *Kiamil Pasha* (is Kiamil Pasha).

probity. Moral excellence, uprightness, integrity. *A man of strict probity.* Prŏb'itĭ is traditional pronunciation, but prō- is now more often heard in US (ACD gives it first).

problematic(al). The longer form is slightly more common; there is no clear difference in usage.

proboscis. The pl. recommended is *-scises;* the Latin form is *-scides* (-ēz), & *probosces* is wrong. For *proboscis* =nose, see POLYSYLLABIC HUMOR.

proceed is often used as a FORMAL WORD. WRONG: *Mr. — expressed a particular hope* *that we might* proceed *to secure this important book* (that we might secure).

process. Prŏ'sĕs is more usual in US & is given first by OED; prō'- is more usual in Brit.

produce. Verb prodūs', noun prŏd'us. The verb makes *-cible.*

proem, proemial. Pron. prō'-ĕm, prōē'mi*a*l. But the words, not having made their way like *poem* & *poetic* into common use, remain puzzling to the unlearned & are better avoided in general writing. (*Proem*= preface, to a book or speech; prelude.)

professedly. Four syllables.

professorate, -riate. The differentiation that makes *-rate* the office of professor, & *-riate* the body of professors, deserves recognition.

proffer makes *-ering, -ered.* See FORMAL WORDS.

proficient. The usual construction is *in: Proficient* in *languages;* but *proficient* at *cards.*

profile. US (usually) prō'fīl; Brit. prō'fēl.

profoundly. A word that expresses the speaker's strong opinion. *I am profoundly interested,* but NOT *Have you* a profoundly interesting *problem for us to discuss?* See POSITIVE WORDS.

prognosis. Pl. *-oses* (-ēz).

prognosticate makes *-cable, -tor.*

program(me). In US usually *-am.* The OED's judgment is: 'The earlier *program* was retained by Scott, Carlyle, Hamilton, & others, & is preferable, as conforming to the usual English representation of Greek *gramma,* in *anagram, cryptogram, diagram, telegram,* &c.' *Programme* is now more usual in Brit.

progress. In US usually prŏ-', but the OED gives prō- as preferable. Noun prō'gr*e*s, verb progrĕs'.

progression. *Arithmetical progression* & *geometrical progression.* These are in constant demand to express a rapid rate of increase, which is not involved in either of them, & is not even suggested by *arithmetical progression.* Those who use the expressions should bear in mind (1) that you cannot determine the nature of the progression from two terms whose relative place in the series is unknown; (2) that every rate of increase that could be named is slower than some rates of arithmetical progression & of geometrical progression, & faster than some others; & consequently (3) that the phrases 'better than arithmetical progression, than geometrical progression,' 'almost in arithmetical progression, geometrical progression,' are wholly meaningless. The point of contrast between them is that one involves growth or decline at a constant pace, & the other at an increasing pace. Hence the famous sentence in Malthus about population & subsistence, the first increasing in a geometrical & the second in an arithmetical ratio, which perhaps started the phrases on their career as POPULARIZED TECHNICALITIES. Of the following extracts, the first is a copy of Malthus, the second a possibly legitimate use, according to what it is meant to convey, & the third the usual absurdity. RIGHT: *The healthy portion of the population is increasing by* arithmetical progression, *and the feeble-minded by* geometrical progression./AMBIGUOUS: *Scientific discovery is likely to proceed by* geometrical progression./WRONG: *As the crude prejudice against the soldier's uniform vanished, & as ex-regular officers joined the volunteers, & volunteers passed on to the Army, the idea that every man owes willing service to his country began to spread in an almost* geometrical ratio.

progressive, conservative. Except as names of established political parties, these are relative terms, and unless the position of the speaker is known, they are meaningless. A progressive to one man is a conservative to another. So also *liberal.*

prohibit. The modern construction, apart from that with an object noun as in an *Act prohibiting export,* is *from doing,* NOT *to do;* the OED marks the latter as archaic, but it is less archaism than ignorance of idiom & the analogy of *forbid* that accounts for it in modern contexts. WRONG: *He* prohibited *his troops* to take *quarter within the walls./The Government has decided to issue a decree* prohibiting *all Government officials* to strike.

prohibition. Pron. prōĭ-; the *h* is sounded, however, where the *i* following it bears the accent, as in *prohibit* itself.

prohibitive, -ory. There is no real differentiation. The first is recommended. See NEEDLESS VARIANTS.

prolegomena. Preliminary observations; prefatory remarks (to a book or speech). Pron. prōlĕg ŏm′ēna. A plural, of which the sing., rarely used, is *-menon.*

proletariat(e). Usually (US) no final *e.* In modern Polit. Econ., the wage-earning classes with no reserve capital; the laboring classes. *Dictatorship of the proletariat:* Communist ideal of domination by the laboring classes after the suppression of capitalism & the bourgeoisie.

prolific is in common use, but to make a satisfactory noun from it has passed the wit of man. *Prolificacy, prolificity,* & *prolificness,* have been tried & found wanting; substitutes such as *fertility, productiveness, fruitfulness,* are the best solution.

prologue, -logize, -loguize. The prevalent modern pronunciation is prō′lŏg, but the OED gives preference to prŏ′lŏg. For the verb Brit. usage prefers *-gize,* US *-guize.*

promenade. Pron. n. usually -ahd, v. usually -ād, but both are permissible for either.

promiscuous. Of heterogeneous & disorderly composition (*a promiscuous gathering*); indiscriminate (*a promiscuous massacre of women & children*); undiscriminating (*promiscuous social relations*); without control (e.g. *she was accused of being promiscuous*), now usually refers to sexual relations. The colloq. use for *random, chance, casual,* &c., springs from POLYSYLLABIC HUMOR.

promise. The noun *promisor* is confined to legal use, & *-er* is the ordinary word. *Promise,* v., is liable to the abuse discussed in DOUBLE PASSIVES: *If it had been taken down, even though* promised to be re-erected, *it might have shared the fate of Temple Bar.*

promissory. So spelled, NOT *-isory.*

promote. Constr.: You can

promote a person *to an archbishopric,* or promote him *to be archbishop,* or promote him *archbishop,* but not mix two of these & *promote him to archbishop.* The unidiomatic construction, however, is now commoner than it should be. WRONG: *The crowning glory of an executive naval officer's career is to be* promoted to *Admiral of the Fleet./Over* 1150 *cadets of the Military Academy were* promoted to *officers.*

promulgate makes *-atable, -tor.* Pron. prômul′- (or Brit. now usually prō′- or prŏm′-).

prone. (1) In the sense 'having a natural inclination or tendency' (disposed, liable) *prone* is used more often for something evil or undesirable than for something good: *Prone to quarrel.* (2) In regard to position, *prone* means lying face downward, as opp. to *supine.*

pronounce makes *-ceable. Pronouncedly* has four syllables. *Pronouncement* is kept in being by the side of *pronunciation* owing to complete DIFFERENTIATION; it means only declaration or decision, which the other never does.

PRONOUNS & pronominal adjectives are rather tricky than difficult. Those who go wrong over them do so from heedlessness, & will mostly plead guilty when they are charged. It is enough to state the dangers very shortly, & prove their existence by citations.

1. No pronoun without a principal (i.e. the thing to which it refers) expressed. WRONG: *The State Department press officer told the U.P. he knew nothing about the tanks but would look into* it. (*It* is the *matter* or *question;* but as neither word has been used we can only suppose the State Dept. officer to have agreed to look into the U.P.) / *The member for Morpeth has long been held in the highest respect by all who value sterling character & whole-hearted service in the cause of* his *fellows* (*his* means *a man's,* & not, as grammar requires since 'a man' has not been mentioned, the member for Morpeth)./*An American Navy League Branch has even been established in London, & is influentially supported by* their *countrymen in this city* (whose countrymen?).

2. The principal should not be very far off. We have to go further back than the beginning of the following extracts to learn who *he* & *she* are. SLOVENLY: *Yet, as we read the pages of the book, we feel that a work written when the story is only as yet half told amid the turmoil of the events which* he *is describing, can only be taken as a provisional impression./It is always a shock to find that there are still writers who regard the war from the standpoint of the sentimentalist. It is true that this story comes from America & bears the traces of its distance from the field of action. But even distance cannot wholly excuse such an exterior view as* she *permits herself.*

3. There should not be two parties justifying even a moment's doubt about which the pronoun represents. AMBIGUOUS: *Mr. Harcourt, who presided at a large public meeting, declared that* it *was* his *experience as Home Secretary which changed Sir William Harcourt's earlier views & convinced* him *that drastic legislation was nec-*

essary (Mr. H.'s experience, or Sir W.'s? See also 5)./*Professor Geddes's fine example of sociology applied to Civics, his plea for a comprehensive & exact survey of* his *own city as a branch of natural history required for the culture of* every instructed citizen (The professor's own city? Ah, no; here comes, perhaps better late than never, the true principal)./*As it is, the shortsighted obstinacy of the bureaucracy has given* its *overwhelming strength to the revolution* (not bureaucracy's, but revolution's, strength; see also 5).

4. One pronoun, one job. WRONG: *This opens up the bewildering question as to how far the Duma really represents the nation. The answer to this is far from solving the riddle, but without answering* it *it is idle even to discuss* it (*it* represents, first, the bewildering question, secondly, the discussion of that riddle, & last, the riddle itself—which is not the same as the question).

5. The pronoun should seldom precede its principal. WRONG: *For Plato, being then about twenty-eight years old, had listened to the 'Apology' of Socrates; had heard from* them *all that* others *had heard or seen of his last hours* (had heard from others all that they had heard &c.)./*The old idea of cutting expenditure down to the bone, so that* his *money might fructify in the pocket of the* taxpayer, *had given place to the idea of* . . . (the taxpayer's money might fructify in his pocket)./*Both these lines of criticism are taken simultaneously in a message which* its *special correspondent sends from Alberta to the* Daily Mail *this morning* (which the D.M. prints this morning from its correspondent &c.).

pronunciam(i)ento. The Spanish and usual US spelling is with the *i* (the OED gives the English word without it). Pl. *-os.*

PRONUNCIATION. The ambition to do better than our neighbor is in many departments of life a virtue; in pronunciation it is a vice; there the only right ambition is to do as our neighbors. It is true this at once raises the question who our neighbors are. To reply that some people's neighbors are the educated, others' the uneducated, & others' again a mixture, is not very helpful in itself, suggesting social shibboleths; but there is truth in it, for all that, which may serve us if we divide words also into classes: the words that everybody knows & uses, & the words that only the educated, or any other section of us, know & use. As regards the first of these classes, our neighbor is the average English-speaking person; as regards the second, our neighbor is our fellow member of the educated or any other section. The moral of which is that, while we are entitled to display a certain fastidious precision in our saying of words that only the educated use, we deserve not praise but censure if we decline to accept the popular pronunciation of popular words. To make six syllables of *extraordinary,* or end *level* & *picture* with a clear -ĕl & -tūr, or maintain the old accent on the middle syllable of *contemplate,* all everyday words—these feats establish one's culture at the cost of one's modesty, & perhaps of one's hearer's patience. But if, with some word that most of us pass their lives without uttering—*comminatory*, for instance, or *intercalary*—a scholar likes to exhibit his deftness in saying many successive syllables after a single accent where the vulgar would help themselves out with a second one (kŏʹmĭnatorĭ, kŏʹmĭnāʹtorĭ; ĭntĕrʹkalarĭ, inʹterkăʹlarĭ), why, no one need mind. The broad principles are: (1) Pronounce as your neighbors do, not better; (2) for words in general use, your neighbor is the general public. A few particular points may be touched upon:

Silent *t*. No effort should be made to sound the *t* in the large classes of words ending in *-sten* (*chasten, fasten, listen*) & *-stle* (*epistle, jostle, bustle*), nor in *often, waistcoat, postpone.* But some good people, afraid they may be suspected of not knowing how to spell, say the *t* in self-defense.

Silent *h*. In *Hunt has hurt his head,* it is nearly as bad to sound the *h* of *has* & *his* as not to sound that of *Hunt* & *hurt* & *head.* In many compounds whose second element begins with *h*, the *h* is silent unless the accent falls on the syllable that it begins; so *philhelʹlenism* sounds the *h*, but *philhellenic* does not; similarly *Philharmonic* has fĭʹlar-. In *nihilism* the *h* should be silent, though *nihil,* if there is occasion to say the word, sounds it.

Demonetize & *decolo*(*u*)*rize* raise the question whether the peculiar vowel sound of *money* & *color* (ŭ-) is to be extended to derivatives involving recurrence to the Latin nouns; -mŏn- is recommended, &, if *decolorize* is spelled as it should be, without *u*, then -cŏl-.

Clothes, forehead, fortune, fossil, knowledge are samples of the many words whose spelling & ordinary pronunciation do not correspond, but with which mistaken attempts are made to restore the supposed true sound. They should be called klōz, fŏʹrĭd, forʹchōōn, fŏʹsl, nŏʹlĭj, in accordance with the principles laid down above.

Obdurate & *recondite,* formerly accented on the middle syllable, but now more often on the first, represent many more whose accent has shifted or is shifting toward the beginning; see RECESSIVE ACCENT.

The variations ah & ă for *a,* aw & ŏ for *o,* lōō & lū for *lu,* are widely prevalent in large classes of words (*pass, telegraph, ask; gone, soft, loss; lucid, absolute, illumine*); it need only be said that the first two are roughly local distinctions while lōō is displacing lū, especially in certain positions, irrespective of locality. The difference between the British & the usual US pronunciation of the final *e* or *y* has also been disregarded in this book (Brit. ĭ, usual US ē, as in *opportunity*). (See also note on pronunciation in Preface.)

propaganda is sing., not pl.: *a propaganda, this propaganda,* &c.; & the plural, if required, is *-as* (*The difference between these* propagandas *is obvious enough*).

propel makes *-lled, -lling,* &c.

propellant, -ent. In US *-ant* is usual for the explosive or oxidizing agent for propelling projectiles, engines, &c., and *-ent* for the adj. & the fig. & non-technical uses of the noun. In Brit. *-ant* is not used, *-ent* serving all purposes.

propensity. Constr. *to do* or *for doing.* WRONG: *That propensity* of *lifting every problem from the plane of the understandable by means of some sort of mystic expression.* The ANALOGY of *practice, habit,* &c., is responsible.

property makes *propertied.*

prophecy, -sy. The noun *prophecy.* The verb *prophesy.*

prophetess. Est. usage. See FEMININE DESIGNATIONS.

prophetic. For *my prophetic soul* see HACKNEYED PHRASES.

prophetic(al). The *-al* form perhaps lingers only in such phrases as *the prophetical books,* in which the meaning is definitely 'of the Prophets.'

propitiate makes *-tiable, -tor.* Pron. -shĭ-.

propitiation. Pron. -shĭā'sh*u*n.

proportion. It has been recorded as a common misapprehension that *proportion* is a sonorous improvement upon *part.* What was meant will be plain from the following examples, in all of which the word has been wrongly used because the writers, or others whom they admire & imitate, cannot resist the imposing trisyllable; *the greater part, most,* &c., should be substituted; see POMPOSITIES for other such temptations. *A few years ago the largest* proportion *of the meat coming through Smithfield had its origin in the United States* (the greater part)./*The total number of all classes & all nationalities carried outward & inward on board foreign ships was* 6,053,-382, *of which* the great proportion *were carried in British ships* (the great majority)./The larger proportion *of the children received are those of unmarried mothers* (Most).

It is not merely that here are two words, each of which would give the sense equally well, & that the writer has unwisely allowed length to decide the choice for him; *proportion* does not give the sense so well as *part.* Where *proportion* does so far agree in sense with *part* that the question of an exchange between them is possible, i.e. where it means not a ratio but a quota or amount, there is nevertheless a clear difference between them. A proportion is indeed a part, but a part viewed in a special light, viz. as having a quantitative relation to its whole comparable with the same relation between some analogous whole & part. Thus a man who out of an income of $5000 spends $2000 upon house rent is rightly said to spend a large proportion of his income in rent, if it is known that most people's rent is about ⅕ of their income; *proportion* is there a more precise & better word than *part,* just because other ratios exist for comparison. But to say *A large* proportion (instead of *a large part*) *of these statements is unverified,* where there is no standard of what ratio the verified facts bear to the unverified in most stories, is to use a worse long word instead of a better short one. It is a clumsy blunder to use words like *greater* & *largest* with *proportion* when the comparison is between the parts of one whole & not between the ratios borne by parts of different wholes to their respective wholes. WRONG: *We passed the* greater proportion *of our candidates* (read *part*). RIGHT: *We hope to pass a* greater proportion *of our candidates* next year. For a parallel, see PERCENTAGE.

proportionable, -nal, -nate. All three adjectives have existed since the 14th c., & it is presumptuous to advise the superannuation of any of them. The statement may be ventured that the latest OED quotation for *-nable* is dated 1832, & that far from needing three words we can hardly provide two with separate functions; the *-al* word is better suited to the most general sense of all, 'concerned with proportion,' & the *-ate* word to the particular sense 'analogous in quantity to,' but *-al* & *-ate* are both so fully in possession of the most usual sense 'in proportion' or 'in due proportion' that it is useless to think of confining it to either.

proposal. See PROPOSITION.

propose. WRONG: *The Commissioners* proposed to be appointed *will give their whole time to the work of the Commission. Propose* is one of the verbs liable to be used in this ungainly construction, for which see DOUBLE PASSIVES.

proposition. The modern use as a VOGUE WORD is an Americanism. It runs riot in the newspapers, but is so slightly recognized in British dictionaries that probably few people realize its triumphant progress. (COD includes the meanings 'proposal,' 'thing proposed'; and, as 'US commerce, and slang, *task, job, problem, objective, trade, opponent, prospect,* &c.')

It may be granted that there is nothing unsound in principle about the development of sense. *Proposition* does or did mean *propounding,* &, like other *-tion* words, may naturally develop from that the sense of thing propounded, from which again is readily evolved the sense thing to deal with, & that sufficiently accounts for all or nearly all the uses to be quoted. And, on another line, there is no objection to *proposition*'s having the sense *proposal,* except one–that English idiomatic usage is clean against it, & that confusion between the two words has been, until the Americanism arose, very rare. It is much to be desired that *proposition* should be brought back to its former well-defined functions in Logic & Mathematics, & relieved of its new status as Jack-of-all-trades. Some of the uses deprecated are:

Used for *proposal:* 'Let us pull down everything' seems to be his proposition. (US, status dubious.)/He prefaced his speech by observing he intended to put Home Rule before them as a business proposition. (US, accepted usage.)

Used for *task, job, problem, objective:* Any Secretary of Agriculture is up against a tough proposition. (US, slang.)

Used for *undertaking, occupation, trade:* He has got a foothold mainly because the original manufacturer has been occupied with propositions that give a larger proportion of profit. (US, commercial.)/The agriculturist asks that 'corn-growing shall become a paying proposition.' (US, now also Brit., colloq.)/The future of the taxicab proposition in the Metropolis presents a very interesting problem. (US, slang.)

Used for *opponent:* The former is a very tough proposition as an opponent in singles. (US, slang.)

Used for *possibility, prospect:* Gas at 6½¢ or 7½¢ a gallon was hardly a commercial proposition. (US, commercial.)/The only way to increase the recruiting standard is to make the service a more attractive proposition to the man & the employer. (US, colloq.)

Used for *area, field:* The mining district, according to the best information obtainable, is a placer proposition, & placer mining ruins the land. (US, slang.)

Used for *method, experiment:* The territories will certainly require many novel propositions for their development. (US, slang.)

[Fowler had probably never heard the recent US slang, vulg. use of *proposition* as a verb.]

proprietary. So spelled (NOT *-tory*).

proprietress. Est. usage. See FEMININE DESIGNATIONS.

pro rata. Proportionately. Pron. prō rāt*a*, -rät*a*. *To prorate* is chiefly US.

prorogue makes *-gable, -gation.* In parliamentary practice =to discontinue meetings. Brit. Parliament is *prorogued* at the end of a session; *adjourns* for a recess; is *dissolved* at its end.

proscenium. Pl. *-ia.* Pron. -sēn′-.

proselyte makes *-tism, -tize.*

prosody. (Poetry): 'to song.' The science of versification, including (1) the rules of quantity & accent governing the pronunciation of words in a language, & (2) tables of the various meters showing the number & kind & arrangement of feet, lines, stanzas, &c., in each. The adj. recommended is *prosodic,* & the *-ist* noun *prosodist.*

prospect, n., in the sense of prospective customer, is chiefly US and should be confined to commercial use. *In prospect* is often chosen by those who like to use more elegant language than most of us, where we should say *expected,* e.g. *A modest but continuing sale is* in prospect.

prospectus. Pl. *-tuses,* not *-ti.*

prostrate=(strictly) prone, i.e. with face downward.

protagonist. Leading actor in a drama; hence one who takes the chief part in a play, novel, a story; but in recent use, also 'an active participant or leader' (Webster); 'leading person in contest, champion of cause' (COD). The word has no right whatever to any of these meanings (*champion* or *advocate* or *defender*), & almost certainly owes them to the mistaking of the first syllable (representing Greek *protos,* first) for *pro,* on behalf of—a mistake made easy by the accidental resemblance to *antagonist.* 'Accidental,' since the Greek *agonistes* has different meanings in the two words, in one *combatant,* but in the other *playactor.* The Greek *protagonistes* means the actor who takes the chief part in a play—a sense readily admitting of figurative application to the most conspicuous personage in any affair. But to talk of *several protagonists,* or of *a chief protagonist* or the like, is an absurdity as great, to any one who knows Greek, as to call a man *the protagonist of a cause* or *of a person,* instead of *the protagonist of a drama* or *of an affair.* In popular writing it is a rarity to meet *protagonist* in a legitimate sense; but two examples of it are put first in the following collection. All the others are recent corruptions of the meaning, because some of them distinguish between chief protagonists & others who are not chief, some state or imply that there are more protagonists than one in an affair, & the rest use *protagonist* as a mere synonym for *advocate.*

Traditional uses: *In* Jeppë *the subsidiary personages do little more than give* the protagonist *his cues./Marco Landi,* the protagonist *& narrator of a story which is skillfully contrived & excellently told, is a fairly familiar type of soldier of fortune.*

Pro- and *-ant:* Protagonists & antagonists *make a point of ignoring evils which militate against their ideals.* (Advocates and opponents?)

Use with *chief: It presents a spiritual conflict, centered about its* two chief protagonists *but shared in by all its characters.*

Absurd plural uses: *As on a stage where* all the protagonists *of a drama assemble at the end of the last act./*The protagonists *in the drama, which has the motion & structure of a Greek tragedy, are* . . . (Fie! fie! a Greek tragedy & *protagonists?*).

Confusions with *advocate* &c.: *Mr. —, an enthusiastic* protagonist *of militant Protestantism./ The* chief protagonist *on the company's side in the latest railway strike, Mr. —.*

Pro- in *protagonist* is NOT the opposite of *anti-; -agonist* is NOT the same as in *antagonist; advocate* & *champion* & *defender* & *combatant* are better words for the recent senses given to *protagonist,* & *protagonist* in its right sense of the (NOT *a*) chief actor in an affair has still work to do if it could only be allowed to mind its own business.

protean. Pron. prō′tĭan. Variable (in shape); versatile; like Proteus. (Do not confuse with *protein.*)

protégé. One under the protection (usually permanent) of another. Pron. prō tĕ zhā′. Fem. *-ée,* pl. *-ées.*

protestant, when used as adj. or noun without reference to the specialized sense in religion, is often pronounced protes′tant for distinction.

Proteus. Pron. prō′tūs.

prothalamium, -on. Spenser, who made the word, spelled it *-on.* Preliminary nuptial song.

protocol. The original draft or record (of a document, treaty, &c.); a preliminary memorandum; a formal statement of transaction; the rules of etiquette (deference to rank, correct procedure) in diplomatic and state ceremonies. The last syllable is -ŏl, not ōl.

prototype. 'First type.' The original pattern, from which any later specimen is copied. The following quotations show a complete misunderstanding of the meaning. WRONG: *William Hickey, gay young man about town . . . would be amazed if he could see his* prototype *of today drinking barley water at luncheon./It is perplexing to find the American Expeditionary Force described as 'the immortal* prototype *of Britain's gallant "First Seven Divisions,"' until you find that for Mr. — the word 'prototype' has exactly the opposite meaning of that which is given in the dictionary.* And by no means for Mr. — alone. See also TYPE.

prove. (1) *Proved,* NOT *proven,* is the regular p.p., the latter being properly from the verb *preve,* used in Scotland after it had given way to *prove* in England. Except in the phrase *not proven* as a quotation from Scotch law, *proven* is better left alone. (2) For *the exception proves the rule,* see EXCEPTION.

provenance, provenience. (Place of) origin, source. The word is, & will doubtless continue to be, in literary use only. It is therefore needless to take exception to the first much better-known form on the ground that it is French & try to convert the literary to the second, even if it is better in itself.

provided (that). Conj. On the condition, or understanding (that). The following examples show that care is needed in substituting this for *if*. WRONG: *Ganganelli would never have been poisoned* provided *he had had nephews about to take care of his life./The kicks & blows which my husband Launcelot was in the habit of giving me every night,* provided *I came home with less than five shillings.*

It will be agreed that *if* should have been written in both, & the object lesson is perhaps enough. Those who wish for an abstract statement in addition may find that the following test, applied to each of the examples, will compel their rejection: A clause introduced by *provided* must express a stipulation (i.e. a demand for the prior fulfilment of a condition) made by the person who in the main clause gives a conditional undertaking or vouches conditionally for a fact. RIGHT USE: *This nation agrees to sign,* provided that *at least two other members also will sign.*

providing (that), conj., =provided (that). Accepted usage, US & Brit.

proviso. Pl. *-os.*

provost. In the names of military-police officials, pron. prōvō′, elsewhere prŏ′vost.

prox(imo). 'Of next month.' Abbr. *prox. The 3rd prox.* See INSTANT.

prude. Strictly a prudish woman, but often used also of men.

prudent(ial). While *prudent* means having or showing prudence, *prudential* means pertaining to, or considered from the point of view of, or dictated by, prudence. To call an act *prudent* is normally to commend it; to call it *prudential* is more often than not to disparage it. A prisoner's refusal to go into the witness box is *prudential* but NOT *prudent* if he refuses for fear of giving himself away but actually creates prejudice against himself, *prudent* but NOT *prudential* if it deprives the prosecution of a necessary link in the evidence but is dictated merely by bravado, & both or neither in conditions as easy to invent. But the difference is sometimes neglected, & *prudential* preferred merely as a LONG VARIANT.

prunella. See LEATHER.

prurience, -cy. (Tendency toward impure or lascivious thoughts.) There is no differentiation; *-ence* is recommended.

pry makes *pryer* (US), or *prier* (Brit.).

pseud(o)-. Combining form meaning *false(ly)*. *Pseudepigrapha,* spurious writings (esp. those ascribed to O.T. prophets).

pseudo, adj. =sham, spurious,

is now chiefly US (colloq.?); in Brit. archaic (*the pseudo penitent*).

pseudonym. A fictitious name, esp. one assumed by an author. See NOM DE GUERRE.

psyche. Pron. sī′kē or psīkĭ.

psychic(al). Both forms have been & are in common use in all senses & differentiation has not yet started; the shorter form is more usual in US, but *-al* is frequent in antithesis to *physical.*

psychological moment. The original German phrase, misinterpreted by the French & imported together with its false sense into English, meant the psychic factor, the mental effect, the influence exerted by a state of mind, & not a point of time at all, *das Moment* in German corresponding to our *momentum,* not our *moment.* Mistake & all, however, it did for a time express a useful notion, that of the moment at which a person is in a favorable state of mind (such as a skilled psychologist could choose) for one's dealings with him to produce the effect one desires. But, like other POPULARIZED TECHNICALITIES, it has lost its special sense & been widened till it means nothing more definite than the nick of time, to which as an expression of the same notion it is plainly inferior. It should be avoided in the extended sense as a HACKNEYED PHRASE, & at least restricted to contexts in which *psychological* is appropriate; see also IRRELEVANT ALLUSION. Three examples follow, going from bad to worse: *It is difficult to believe that grievances which have been spread over many years have suddenly reached the breaking point at the precise* psychological moment *when the Franco-German settlement was reaching its conclusion./There is a feeling that the* psychological moment *has come to fight with some hope of success./Everything goes right, no sleeping calf or loud-crowing cock grouse is disturbed at the* psychological moment *the wind holds fair.*

psychopathic, psychotic, &c. The general public has become increasingly fond of using terms borrowed from Psychology (see POPULARIZED TECHNICALITIES). A number of these are used indiscriminately as synonyms; the following definitions taken from a medical dictionary indicate their differences: *Psychopathic,* anything relating to mental disease, derangement, disorder; abnormal sensitiveness to spiritual phenomena, extreme susceptibility to emotion, doubts, & fears. *Psychoneurotic,* a general term having to do with various functional disorders of the nervous system, with no ascertainable organic disease, & accompanied by a certain amount of mental impairment; an emotional state in which feelings of anxiety, obsessional thoughts, &c. dominate the personality. *Psychotic,* having a serious disorder of the mind that may amount to insanity, but without the legal implications of *insane. Neurotic,* a general term applied to any nervous disease, especially disorders of functions of parts of the nervous system, but not depending on discernible disease or injury. *Psychosomatic,* having physical manifestations in part due to emotional or mental factors.

pt-. In *ptarmigan* & in *Ptolemy* & its derivatives the *p* is always silent. In other words the OED favors its being sounded, but in US it is usually silent.

ptomaine. In US usually tō′mān, which the OED stigmatizes as an illiterate pronunciation; but, as with *cocaine,* it is impracticable to maintain the three-syllable (p)tō′maĭn.

puerile. ('Boyish.') Now in general contexts only derog.: childish, immature, trivial. Pron. pū′ẽrĭl or (always in Brit.) -īl.

puisne. (Law): younger or inferior in rank; *a puisne judge.* Pron. pū′nĭ (it is the orig. of English *puny*).

puissant. Mighty, potent. The disyllabic pwĭ′sant, the older pronunciation, is recommended, the word itself being archaic. But in US usually pū′ĭs sant.

Pulitzer prize. Annual prize in letters & journalism established by Joseph Pulitzer. Pron. pū′-.

pulley. Pl. *-eys.*

pulque. Fermented Mex. drink made from maguey (agave) sap. Pron. pōōl′kē.

pulse (heart beat). The OED says, 'Formerly sometimes construed erroneously as a plural.' The mistake is still made.

pummel, v. So spelled in US; see POMMEL.

pun. The assumption that puns are *per se* contemptible, betrayed by the habit of describing every pun not as a pun, but as a bad pun or a feeble pun, is a sign at once of sheepish docility & desire to seem superior. Puns are good, bad, & indifferent, & only those who lack the wit to make them are unaware of the fact.

punctilio. A nice point of behavior or ceremony; hence (often) a trifling formality. Pl. *-os.*

pundit. Hindu scholar; loosely (facet.?), learned teacher or critic. For the correction of this into *pandit,* see DIDACTICISM.

pupa. (Chrysalis.) Pl. *-ae.*

purchase. As a substitute for *buy* (goods for money), *purchase* is to be classed among FORMAL WORDS; but in fig. use (*purchase victory by sacrifice* &c.) it is not open to the same objection.

purée. Pron. pū̂ rā′ or pū′rā.

purely is rightly used for exclusively, merely, solely: *purely accidental; purely a formality.* In some contexts, however, it is unfortunate: *By* playing purely music *we may bring back that lost audience.*

PURISM. Now & then a person may be heard to 'confess,' in the pride that apes humility, to being 'a bit of a purist'; but *purist* & *purism* are for the most part missile words, which we all of us fling at anyone who insults us by finding not good enough for him some manner of speech that is good enough for us. It is in that disparaging sense that the words are used in this book; by *purism* is to be understood a needless & irritating insistence on purity or correctness of speech. Pure English, however, even apart from the great number of elements (vocabulary, grammar, idiom, pronunciation, &c.) that go to make it up, is so relative a term that almost every man is potentially a purist & a sloven at once to persons looking at him from a lower & a higher position in the scale than his own. The words have therefore not been very freely used. That they should be renounced altogether would be too much to expect considering the subject of the book.

But readers who find a usage stigmatized as *purism* have a right to know the stigmatizer's place in the purist scale, if his stigma is not to be valueless. Accordingly, under headings of various matters with which purism is concerned, a few articles are now mentioned illustrating the kind of view that may be expected in other articles of a similar nature:

New words: PROTAGONIST.

Old words: HOWBEIT.

Foreign words: GALLICISMS.

Foreign senses: INTRIGUE.

Distinction of sense: HAZINESS.

Popular misuses: POPULARIZED TECHNICALITIES.

Corrections: BAR SINISTER.

Bad constructions: DOUBLE PASSIVE.

Idiom: IDIOM.

Framework: POSITION OF ADVERBS.

Pronunciation: PRONUNCIATION.

Spelling: MUTE E.

Sound: JINGLES.

puritanic(al). The long form is commoner, & there is no perceptible difference in meaning. The existence of a third adj. *puritan,* which suffices for the mere labeling function (=of the puritans), makes the *-ic* form even less useful than it might otherwise be, & it will probably be squeezed out.

purport. The word is one that, whether as noun or as verb, requires cautious handling. The noun may be said to mean 'what appears to be the significance' (of a document, an action, &c.); its special value is that it is noncommittal, & abstains from either endorsing or denying, but lightly questions, the truth of the appearance. When such an implication is not useful, the word is out of place, & *tenor, substance, pith, gist,* or other synonym, should be preferred. But NOVELTY-HUNTING discovers *purport* sometimes in place of *scope* or *purview,* & even of *purpose.* NOT: *In 'A Note on Robert Fergusson' he touches a theme outside the general* purport *of the book.* Read *purview* or *scope.*

As to the verb, there are certain well-defined idiomatic limitations on its use, one of which, in an ugly development, is beginning to be neglected. This development is the use of the passive, as in: *Many extracts from speeches* purported to have been made *by Mr. Redmond are pure fabrications./He had no information of a Treaty between Japan & Germany* purported to have been made *during the war.* Though the verb is an old one, there is in the OED quotations only one passive use, & that dated 1894. The extracts above are doubtless due to the corrupting influence of the DOUBLE PASSIVE. That construction is especially gratuitous with *purport,* the sense of which fits it to serve, in the active, as a passive to *suppose, represent,* &c. In the extracts *supposed* would stand; pretentiousness has suggested *purport* as a less familiar & therefore more imposing verb, & ignorance has chosen the wrong part of it (*purported*) instead of the right (*purporting*).

The first idiomatic limitation, then, is that the verb, though not strictly intransitive only (*It purports,* i.e. it is to the effect, *that someone from Oxfordshire applied*), should never be used in the passive. The second is that the subject, which is seldom a person at all, should at any rate not be a person as such—only a person viewed as a phenomenon of which the nature is indicated by speech, action, &c., as the nature of a document is indicated by its wording. NORMAL SUBJECT: *The* story purports *to be an autobiography.* LEGITIMATE PERSONAL SUBJECT: *The Gibeonites sent* men *to Joshua* purporting *to be ambassadors from a far country.* ILLEGITIMATE PERSONAL SUBJECT: She purports *to find a close parallel between the Aeschylean Trilogy & The Ring.*/He is purported *to have said 'The F.A. are responsible for everything inside the Stadium.'*

purpose, n. WRONG: *It serves* very little purpose *to ask the Chancellor of the Exchequer to give a little more in this direction or in that.* There are three idioms: *Be to the, to (very) little, to no, purpose; Do something to some, to much, to no, to (very) little, purpose; Serve the, my* &c., *no, purpose.* These should not (see CAST-IRON IDIOM) be confused. *Serve very little purpose* is a mixture of the third with one of the others.

purposive ('an anomalous form'—OED). *Purposeful* in some contexts & *purposed* in others will meet most needs, & there are *deliberate, designed, adaptive, teleological* & many more synonyms. In the first of the following extracts *purposeful,* & in the second *adaptive,* would enable *purposive* to be dispensed with. NOT: *The tendency is all in the direction of what Mr. Masterman calls national self-consciousness; progress, steady* & purposive, *by the means of social science./The material origin of all* purposive *reactions would be adequately explained by the theory of natural selection.*

pur sang. (Of the full blood, genuine.) See FRENCH WORDS. WRONG: *The men who direct it are* pur-sang mandarins, *trained in all the traditions of a bureaucracy which lives not for, but on, the people.* If one is brave enough to use the French words, one should be brave enough to place them as such—*are mandarins pur sang.*

pursuant(ly). *Pursuant* is used adverbially in certain idiomatic phrases: *I have acted* pursuant *to our agreement* (i.e. according to). See QUASI-ADVERBS.

purulent. Pron. pūr′ōōlent.

purview. Scope, range. *Objects within the purview* of *his authority.* See FIELD.

pygmean, -aean. The first is recommended. Pron. pĭgmē′*an*.

pygmy, pi-. *Pygmy* is better; see GYPSY.

pyjamas. US *pa-*.

pyrites. Pron. pĭrī′tēz (also in US sometimes pī′rīts).

pyrrhic. *Pyrrhic victory,* one gained at too great cost, as that of Pyrrhus at Asculum.

Q

qua (='as,' in the capacity of) is sometimes misused like other Latin words; see E.G., I.E., RE, VIDE. The real occasion for the use of *qua* occurs when a person or thing spoken of can be regarded from more than one point of view or as the holder of various coexistent functions, & a statement about him (or it) is to be limited to him in one of these aspects. RIGHT: Qua lover *he must be condemned for doing what* qua citizen *he would be condemned for not doing.* The two nouns (or pronouns) must be present, one denoting the person or thing in all aspects (*he*), & the other singling out one of his or its aspects (*lover*, or *citizen*). In the extract below, *financier* &c. do not give aspects of the man to be distinguished from other coexistent aspects, but merely successive occupations; the fault is that the occasion does not justify the substitution of the very precise *qua* for the here quite sufficient *as*. WRONG: *The familiar gentleman burglar who, having played the wolf to his fellows* qua *financier, journalist, & barrister, undertakes to raise burglary from being a trade at least to the lupine level of those professions.*

quadrennium. Pl. *-ia.*

quadrille. Best pron. kw*a*-.

quadrillion. In US & Fr. a thousand trillions; in Brit. & Ger., a million trillions.

quadroon. Offspring of a mulatto and a white person (one-fourth Negro).

quaere, the original of *query*, is now little used, & nothing is gained by keeping it in being.

quagmire. A marsh, bog, lit. & fig. Pron. kwăg′mīr.

quaint means unusual, strange, but having some attractive or picturesque quality: *The quaint costumes of an earlier century.* Its use for peculiar or odd without the additional quality is condoned in US dictionaries but not in Brit.

Quakers. The Society of Friends, founded by George Fox *c.* 1650. But 'Quaker' is not used of themselves by members of the Society.

quality. For 'has the defects of his qualities' see HACKNEYED PHRASES.

qualm. Pron. kwahm.

quandary. In US now kwŏn′-d*a*rĭ. Brit. also kwŏndār′ĭ ('the original stressing'—OED).

quantit(at)ive. The long form is the right.

quantity. *A negligible quantity* is a POPULARIZED TECHNICALITY, often used where *negligible* by itself gives all that is wanted, in the way noted in IRRELEVANT ALLUSION.

quarantine. (Orig. a 40-day period of a ship's isolation.) So spelled.

quarrel makes US *-led* &c.; Brit. *-lled* &c.

quart (fencing). Use CARTE.

quarter, n. Const.: *For a quarter of the price; for quarter of the price; for a quarter the price; for quarter the price* are all blameless English. *After three & a quarter centuries,* or *three centuries & a quarter*—the second is better. See HALF.

quartet(te). Spell *-et.*

quarto. A sheet of paper folded twice to make 4 leaves (or 8 pages). The size of the page (or book so made); about 9½ by 12½ inches. Abbr. 4to or 4°.

quasi-. (Lat., 'as if.') *Seeming(ly)*, near(ly), almost, half —*A decided war instead of a* quasi-war; *public & quasi-*public *institutions.* Pron. kwā′-sī (or kwä′sĭ).

QUASI-ADVERBS. *He was rolling up his sleeves* preparatory *to punching my head.* From a narrowly grammatical point of view, the word should be *preparatorily;* but it never is, except in the mouths of those who know just enough grammar to be timid about it. Most of those who would correct, or be tempted to correct, *preparatory* to *preparatorily* feel no temptation to write *accordingly to his wishes* instead of *according to,* because the latter is so familiar as not to draw their attention. See also UNIDIOMATIC -LY, in which words of a slightly different kind are considered. It should be observed that it is only certain adjs. with which the use is idiomatic; for instance, *He did it* contrary *to my wishes,* but NOT *opposite to* nor *different from* them. A few of the adjs. concerned are: *according* & *pursuant; contrary; doubtless; preliminary, preparatory, previous* & *prior; irrespective* & *regardless.*

quatrain. A stanza of four lines. Pron. kwŏ′trān.

quatrefoil. Pron. kă′ter- or kă′tre- (OED gives only -ter- & Webster gives it first).

quattrocento. The 15th c., as a period in Italian art or literature. Pron. kwahtrōchĕn′tō.

quay. Pron. kē.

queer. The verb (*His opening address* queered *the whole conference*) is slang, as is the adj. in the sense spurious, counterfeit.

querulous. Pron. -rōō-, NOT -ū-.

question. (1) For *leading question* see LEADING. (2) For *previous question* see PREVIOUS. (3) For order of words in indirect questions (WRONG: *He asked* what was he *to do* &c., for *he was*), see INDIRECT QUESTION. (4) *To beg the question* is to take for granted the matter in dispute. ('He speaks with angels.' 'How do you know it?' 'He says so himself.' 'Perhaps he lies.' 'But how could a man who speaks with angels lie?'—Paraphrased from Enc. Brit.) (5) *The question as to . . .* This ugly & needless but now common formula is discussed & illustrated under AS 3; but it is worth while to repeat here that it is at its worst when *question* has *the,* as in: *When the nation repudiated Papal authority,* the question *naturally arose* as to *who were to have the endowments./From time to time there appears in the weekly revenue statement an item on the expenditure side of 'War Bonds,' & the question has cropped up as to its meaning.* The reason is that you do not say *the* instead of *a* question unless either it is already known what question is meant or you are about to supply that information at once. The function of the *as to* phrase is to fulfil the expectation of the latter procedure; that is, you explain in it what the question is, not what it concerns; & to do that you must use an interrogative clause in simple apposition with question (*the question who was to have*), or if a noun is to be used instead of such a clause, attach that noun to *question* by *of* (*the question of its meaning*). Another particularly offensive form is *the question as to whether.*

QUESTION MARK. The chief danger is that of forgetting that whether a set of words is a question or not is decided not by its practical effect or sense, but by its grammatical form & relations. Those who scorn grammar are apt to take *Ask him who said so* for a question, & *Will you please stand back* for a request, & to wrongly give the first the question mark they wrongly fail to give the second. But the first is in fact a command containing an INDIRECT QUESTION, & the question mark belongs to direct questions only, while the second is in fact a direct question, though it happens to be equivalent in sense to a request. When the natural confusion caused by the conveying, for instance, of what is in sense a statement in the grammatical form of a question is aggravated by the sentence's being of considerable length—e.g. when *Will it be believed that* is followed by several lines setting forth the incredible fact—the question mark at the end is often, but should never be, omitted. Still more fatal is a type of sentence that may be put either as an exclamation or as a question, but must have its punctuation adapted to the exclamatory or interrogative nature of the *what* or *how* whose double possibilities cause the difficulty. *How seldom does it happen!* can only be an exclamation, but *How often does it happen* may be either a question (answer, *Once a month* &c.) requiring *happen?*, or an exclamation (meaning, *Its frequency is surprising*) requiring *happen!* WRONG: *In that interval what had I not lost!* (either *lost!* should be changed to *lost?*, or *not* should be omitted)./*A streak of blue below the hanging alders is certainly a characteristic introduction to the kingfisher. How many people first see him so?* (read either *so!* or substitute *otherwise?* for *so?*). The archness of the question mark interpolated in parentheses infallibly betrays the amateur writer: *Sir, The following instance of the doubtful advantages* (?) *of the labor exchanges as media . . . seems to deserve some recognition.*

questionnaire. So spelled.

queue. The pigtail and the waiting line. Pron. kū.

quick, adv. Idiomatic uses (rather than *-ly*): *quick as lightning* &c. *As quick as thought* &c. *Quick, bring me my coat.* With (esp. present) participles: *quick-acting, quick-moving,* &c.

quid pro quo. 'Something for something.' Now usually compensation: *I must find him a* quid pro quo. Slang, the 'wherewithall': *I'll go if I can raise* the quid pro quo.

quiescence, -cy. The former is best. Pron. kwī ĕs′ens.

quiet, n., **quietness, quietude.** The first is much more used than the others. It is possible to distinguish roughly the senses to which each is more appropriate, but often there is a legitimate choice between two points of view. *Quiet* is a state of things or an atmosphere: *A period of quiet followed; Seeking quiet & rest. Quietness* is a quality exhibited by something: *The quietness of his manner, of rubber tires. Quietude* is a habit or practice: *Quietude is out of fashion in these days.* An example of each follows in which (if what has been said above is true) one of the others would have been preferable: *How becomingly that self-respecting* quiet *sat* *upon their high-bred figures* (quietude); *Enjoying the fruit of his victory, peace and* quietness (quiet); *The* quietude *of the meadows made them his favorite resorts* (quietness *or* quiet).

quieten (*'To quieten' the children is not English./They soon quietened down*) is a SUPERFLUOUS WORD. Webster calls it 'chiefly Brit.'; ACD, 'Brit. & US dial.'; COD, 'vulg.' At any rate, good writers seem to avoid it.

quietus. In modern usage usually 'extinction,' 'final riddance.' RIGHT: *This law gave the* quietus *to the theories of common origin./If an unlucky bullet should carry its* quietus *with it./That will give him his* quietus (i.e. kill him)./*The* quietus *of a rumor.* Pron. kwī ē′tus.

quintessence. Orig. the '5th essence' of ancient & medieval philosophy; fig. the essential feature, the purest or most perfect manifestation: *The* quintessence *of Pauline philosophy; the very* quintessence *of invective; You have escaped the very* quintessence *of bores.*

quintet(te). Spell *-et.*

quintillion. In US & Fr. a thousand quadrillions (1+18 zeros); Brit. & Ger., a million quadrillions (1+30 zeros).

quire. 24 (or rarely 25) sheets of paper of the same size & quality. *Quire* as a var. of *choir* is perhaps etym. preferable, but it is now obs.

quisling. A person co-operating (esp. as a leader) with an enemy who has conquered his country. (After Major Vidkum Quisling of the Norwegian Nazi party.)

quite. (1) Excessive use of *quite* often amounts to a MANNERISM, & many writers would do well to convict & cure themselves of it by looking over a few pages or columns of their work. (2) The favorite colloq. formula 'quite all right' is a foolish PLEONASM, *quite* & *all* being identical in sense; 'quite right' is all right, & 'all right' is quite right, but 'quite all right' is all quite wrong. (3) *Quite* (*so*). Many people are in the habit of conveying their assent to a statement that has just been made to them in talk by the single word *quite,* where the rest of us say *quite so.* Oddly enough, they are mostly of a class that should know better, the class that attaches some importance to the way things are said; *quite* sounds to them neater, conciser, than *quite so.* What they do not realize is that choice between the two is sometimes open to them, but by no means always. Used in wrong places, *quite* is an example of SLIPSHOD EXTENSION. Three specimen exchanges will make the matter clear: (a) He seems to be mad. *Quite.* (b) To demand that Englishmen should act on logic is absurd. *Quite* (*so*), but . . . (c) Well, anyhow, he did it. *Quite so,* but the question is . . . In (a), *quite so* would be out of place, because what is to be qualified by *quite* is simply the word *mad,* understood directly from what precedes. In (b), choice is open; *quite* will amount to *quite absurd,* as in (a); *quite so* will amount to *it is quite as you say;* & the general effect of each is the same. In (c) *quite* would be wrong, because the other speaker's words do not supply anything, as in (a) & (b), for *quite* to qualify; the sense is clearly not *he quite did* *it,* but, as in the second alternative of (b), *it is quite as you say=so.* The bad modern use, in actual life, is well shown in this scrap of law-court examination: *There was no power in anyone to bring the child back? Quite.*

qui vive. (From the sentinel's challenge, '[long] live who?' i.e. 'on whose side are you?'); *on the qui vive,* on the alert. Pron. kē vēv.

quiz, meaning (n.) an informal examination, (v.) to question closely, is US. The chief Brit. senses—'an eccentric person' (archaic), 'a hoax,' 'a burlesque'; 'to make sport of a person'—are reflected in *quizzical.*

quoin, quoit. Pron. koi-. (The second is also often kwoit in US.)

quondam. (Archaic.) Former, sometime. *My quondam friend* (the adj. equivalent of adv. *erstwhile,* which word is often misused for *quondam*). See also LATE.

quorum. The fixed number of members that must be present to make proceedings valid (not necessarily a majority).

QUOTATION. Didactic & polemical writers quote passages from others to support themselves by authority or to provide themselves with something to controvert; critics quote from the books they examine in illustration of their estimates. These are matters of business on which no general advice need be offered. But the literary or decorative quotation is another thing. A writer expresses himself in words that have been used before because they give his meaning better than he can give it himself, or because they are beautiful or witty, or because he expects them to touch a chord of association in his reader, or because he wishes to show that he is learned or well read. Quotations due to the last motive are invariably ill advised. The discerning reader detects it & is contemptuous; the undiscerning is perhaps impressed, but even then is at the same time repelled, pretentious quotations being the surest road to tedium. The less experienced a writer is, & therefore on the whole the less well read he is also, the more he is tempted to this error; the experienced knows he had better avoid it; & the well-read, aware that he could quote if he would, is not afraid that readers will think he cannot. Quoting for association's sake has more chance of success, or less certainty of failure; but it needs a homogeneous audience. If a jest's prosperity lies in the ear of him that hears it, so too does a quotation's; to each reader those quotations are agreeable that neither strike him as hackneyed nor rebuke his ignorance by their complete novelty, but rouse dormant memories. Quotation, then, should be adapted to the probable reader's degree of cultivation; which presents a very pretty problem to those who have a mixed audience to face. The less mixed the audience, the safer it is to quote for association. Lastly, the sayings wise or witty or beautiful with which it may occur to us to adorn our own inferior matter, not for business, not for benefit of clergy, not for charm of association, but as carvings on a cathedral façade, or pictures on the wall, or shells in a bower-bird's run, have we the skill to choose & place them? are we architects, or bric-a-brac dealers, or what? Enough has perhaps been said to indicate generally the dangers of quoting.

QUOTATION MARKS. ('Inverted commas.') There is no universally accepted distinction between the single form & the double. The more sensible practice is to regard the single as the normal, & to resort to the double only when, as fairly often happens, an interior quotation is necessary in the middle of a passage that is itself quoted. To reverse this is clearly less reasonable; but, as quotation within quotation is much less common than the simple kind, & conspicuousness is desired, the heavy double mark is the favorite. It may be hoped that *The man who says 'I shall write to "The Times" tonight'* will ultimately prevail over *The man who says "I shall write to 'The Times' tonight."* (Most US publishers prefer the double.)

In US the following rules are generally observed. Periods and commas are always placed inside the quotation marks: *'To Mary,' the first poem, he calls 'A Memorial.'* Exclamation marks, question marks, semicolons, and colons go inside if they are part of the quotation, outside if they belong to the main sentence: *He cried 'Stop!' Do you know 'The Nymphs'? They never call themselves 'Quakers': that term is only used by outsiders. 'Why not?' he asked. 'It seems to me the term "par excellence."'* In Brit. usage (as also older US usage) there is no difference in the treatment of the various kinds of punctuation; all are placed in accordance with their relation to the sentence–i.e. as are exclamation marks &c. in modern US usage.

quotes, n. pl., may be regarded as a CURTAILED WORD, & left to those whose occupation makes a shortening of 'quotations' & 'quotation marks' indispensable.

R

rabbet. The groove or slot &c. so spelled. The verb makes *rabbeted, rabbeting.*

rabbit. The rodent & *Welsh rabbit,* so spelled (NOT *rarebit*).

Rabelaisian, -aesian. The first is better.

raccoon, racoon. The first is given preference in US, *-c-* in Brit. (The word is of Algonquian origin & native to US.)

racialism, racism. Both comparatively new words meaning race prejudice (either favorable or unfavorable, but usually the latter); the assumption of the purity or superiority of some races and therefore discrimination against others. If there is differentiation, *racism* is more often applied to the doctrine, *racialism* to the practice of the doctrine.

rack & ruin. The OED, though it calls *rack* a variant of *wrack,* recognizes this spelling.

racket. In the sense of a fraudulent system of obtaining money, (orig. US) slang. *Racketeer,* however, is now the established word for the person who extorts money in such a way.

racket, raquet(te). In tennis &c., the first is better.

raconteur. Pron. ră kŏn tûr′,

or as French. A (skillful and amusing) teller of anecdotes. Fem. *-euse.*

radiance, -cy. The second is rare, but kept in being as metrically useful or rhetorically effective.

radiator. Pron. rā-.

radical. 'Of the roots'; hence fundamental, inherent, essential, primary. *A radical politician* is one who advocates fundamental and sweeping reforms, or destructive changes, according to the point of view of the speaker, in laws and government. See LIBERAL. *Radical* and *radically* are strong words & should not be used loosely: *a radical difference* of opinion is not just a considerable difference of opinion, but a fundamental one.

radio, v., makes *radioed, radioing.*

radius. Pl. *-ii* (-ĭī). Loosely, scope, reach (*destructive to everything within its radius*); see FIELD.

radix. Pl. *-ices* (-ĭsēz), or *radixes.*

Raffaelesque. From the Italian spelling *Raffaelo+esque.* But *Raphaelesque* is the usual spelling. See DIDACTICISM.

railroad. 'Now chiefly US, the usual term in Great Britain being railway'–OED. The fig. use of the verb, *to railroad a bill through Congress,* is US colloq.

rain or shine, as a phrase for 'whatever the weather,' has 'an American sound.' It is quoted, however, from Dryden–*Be it fair or foul, or rain or shine*– in the *Cent. Dict. & Cyclopedia.*

raise. (1) In the sense *rear* (a person), *raise* is chiefly US (in Brit. 'vulg.') (e.g. *born and raised in Indiana*). (2) Properly, a man receives a *rise* (NOT a *raise*) *in pay;* the US (colloq.) idiom, however, is *raise.* (3) The confusion between *raise* & *rise,* vy., is chiefly through ignorance and seldom seen in print.

raison d'être. 'Reason for being'; justification for existence. RIGHT: *After the Armistice the [service] society no longer had a* raison d'être *and therefore disbanded.* WRONG: *It has been proposed that it shall be sufficient for a candidate to affirm a belief in the Protestant Faith without pledging himself to be a member of the Church: the* raison d'être *is obvious.* Pron. rĕ zōn dâ'tr. But see FRENCH WORDS.

raja(h) & maharaja(h) have the *-h,* an English addition, much more often than not, & it is better to abstain from the DIDACTICISM of omitting it.

ramekin, -quin. The first is the English spelling, the second the French.

rampant. (From *ramp,* v., to climb, rear, bound, &c.) Of the lion, in heraldry: 'Standing on the sinister hindleg, with both forelegs elevated, the Dexter above the sinister & the head in profile.' Of things, unrestrained, having an unchecked course: *Vice was rampant; A rich soil makes [nasturtiums] too rampant . . .*

ranco(u)r. US usually *-or,* Brit. *-our,* but both *rancorous.*

range, v. (1) *Range* makes *-ging, -geable.* (2) WRONG: *Gratuities* ranging from 10 *lire for each of the singers in the Sistine Chapel choir* up to much larger sums *for higher officials.* If one has not provided oneself with figures for both extremes, one should not raise expectations by using *range from . . . to.* It is as bad as saying 'Among those present were A, B, & others.'

ransack (so spelled, NOT *ram-*) means both to search thoroughly, lit. & fig., and to search with intent of robbing, hence to pillage, plunder. *She ransacked her conscience . . . ; ransack a house,* or *country.*

ranunculus. Pl. *-luses* or *-li* (-ī).

rapine. Pillage, robbing. *All the bloodshed and* rapine *occasioned by their pride and injustice.* Pron. ră′pĭn.

Raphaelesque. See RAFFAELESQUE.

rapport, formerly common enough to be regarded & pronounced as English (rapor*t*′), may now perhaps be called again a FRENCH WORD, & will not be missed in English. It is used now chiefly in the phrase *en rapport,* in harmony (or in a harmonious relation). (Formerly, *in connection, in communication.*)

rapprochement. A coming together again; a re-establishment of harmonious relations, esp. of states. *A rapprochement between the French and Italian governments.* Pron. (usually) rȧ prôsh mäɴ (but often anglicized).

rapt, meaning originally carried off, raped, snatched away, but now usually absorbed or intensely concentrated, has perhaps been affected by the identical sound of *wrapped* or *wrapt,* though *ravish* is enough to show that such an explanation is not necessary. The best known passage (*Thy rapt soul sitting in thine eyes*) has doubtless helped. A concordance to Milton supplies also: *Wrapped in a pleasing fit of melancholy./Thus wrapped in midst of midnight./Rapt in a balmy cloud.*

rara avis (rare bird) is seldom an improvement on *rarity;* see IRRELEVANT ALLUSION.

rare in the sense *underdone* is now chiefly US.

rarebit is a mistaken spelling of RABBIT (i.e. *Welsh rabbit*).

rarefaction, NOT *-fication,* is the correct as well as the usual form (4 syllables).

rarefy. So spelled (in contrast with *rarity*), but pron. rārĭ-.

rarely. RIGHT: *Rarely ever, rarely if ever, rarely or never.* NOT *rarely or ever.*

rase (to level to the ground) is the older spelling, but *raze* now prevails.

raspberry. Pron. răz′-.

rather. 1. *Rather is it* &c. *Rather* often tempts the writer to inversion when it is not only unnecessary but results in a formality or pomposity. It is a matter not for argument, but for taste. The following examples should be rid of inversion as indicated: *Mr. Dooley seldom makes you laugh aloud;* rather does he *keep his readers continually in a state of the 'dry grins'* (rather he keeps, *or* he keeps his readers, rather,)./*I do not feel like one who after a day of storm & rain is glad to creep indoors, & crouch hopelessly over the fast-dying embers on the hearth;* rather do I feel *like one who . . .* (rather I feel). It should be remembered, however, with *rather,* that care is needed, in mending or avoiding the inversion, not to put *rather* where it might be interpreted as 'somewhat'; to write *I rather feel* or *it is rather felt* in the second example would be worse than the inversion itself.

2. *Rather superb* &c. *There is something* rather delicious *in the way in which some of these inventors ignore previous achievements./This was* rather *a revelation.* What is the use of fine warm words like *delicious* & *revelation* if the cold water of *rather* is to be thrown over them? 'Rather agreeable' if you will; 'rather surprising' by all means; 'rather enjoyed' certainly; but away with *rather delicious, rather a revelation,* & *rather loved!* Cf. SOMEWHAT.

3. *I had rather* is as idiomatic as *I would rather; had* is the old subjunctive (=*I should hold* or *find*) & is used with *rather* on the analogy of *I had liefer* (=I should hold it dearer). See HAD 1.

4. *Dying rather than surrender, He resigned rather than stifle his conscience,* &c. (NOT *surrendering, stifled*). The use of the infinitive after *rather than* in such contexts is discussed in -ING 5.

ratio. Pl. -os. Pron. rā'shĭō.

ratiocinate (to reason formally; go through logical processes) & its derivatives, as exclusively learned words, may fairly be pronounced rātĭ- rather than răshĭ-. The OED and Webster, however, give only răshi-.

ration. Either ră- or rā- is acceptable. But the army says ră-, & the military use is the prevalent one.

rationale (the fundamental reason, logical basis [*of*]) should be pronounced răshonā'-lĭ; but confusion with such French words as *morale* & *locale* (there is no Fr. *rationale*) naturally leads to its being pronounced similarly, & US dictionaries give răsh*u*năl' first.

raucous rhymes with *caucus.*

ravage makes *-geable.*

ravel. US, *-led, -ling;* Brit. *-lled* &c. The verb is curiously applied both to the tangling & the disentangling process. The verbs that can mean either 'to deprive of' or 'to provide with' what is expressed by the noun of the same spelling (compare *will but skin & film the ulcerous place* with *skin 'em alive*) are not parallel, because with them the noun is the starting-point. *The ravelled sleave of care* is the classic example of the Shakespearian use.

raze, rase. *Raze* now prevails.

re. 'In the matter of,' standard in legal and business use (used prepositionally, fór *in re*); 'vulg. as substitute for about, concerning, in ordinary use,' COD. For the use of this telltale little word see ILLITERACIES: *I am glad to see that you have taken a strong line* re *the railways situation./Why not agree to submit the decision of the Conference* re *the proposed readjustment to the people so that they alone can decide?*

re(-). In *re*(-) compounds, the hyphen is usual before *e* (*reentrant, re-examine,* &c.); permissible before other vowels (*rearmament* or *re-armament, re-urge* or *reurge*), although in the US the tendency is toward making these single words; common when the compound is used after the simple word (*make* & *re-make, discussion* & *re-discussion*); & necessary when a modern compound such as *re-cover*=put a new cover upon, *re-pair*=pair afresh, or *re-*

count=count again, is to be distinguished from a better known & differently pronounced old word. See HYPHENS.

reaction. *Reaction*, owing to its use in Chemistry and Psychology, has become a POPULARIZED TECHNICALITY liable like other such terms to be used by SLIPSHOD EXTENSION where it is not wanted, e.g. where nothing more is meant than response or effect or influence or the simple action. MISUSE: *Darwin's observations upon the breeds of pigeons have had a* reaction *on the structure of European society./Any apparent division in this country, even the threat of a vote of censure, might have had its* reaction *on public opinion in Italy.* This misuse is betrayed in the quotations by the word *on*, which suits *action* &c., but does not suit *reaction* except in senses in which it means more than any of those given below. The senses of *reaction* may be distinguished thus: (1) The process of reversing what has been done or going back to the *status quo ante: progress & reaction; the forces of reaction* (from this sense, *reactionary.*) (2) The recoil from unusual activity or inactivity, producing an equally unusual degree of the reverse: *extremes & reaction; the reaction from passion, despair,* or *a cold bath.* (3) The second half of interaction, B's retaliation upon the first agent A, making up with *action* the vicissitudes of a struggle &c.: *after all this action & reaction.* (4) The reflex effect upon A of his own actions: *the reaction of cruelty upon the cruel.* (5) The action called forth from B by A's treatment: *stimulus & reaction; the reaction of copper to sulphuric acid.* No. 5 is the sense that covers the chemical use, & the one also that is often interchangeable with *effect* &c.; but *on* or *upon* is out of place with it; NOT *the reaction of sulphuric acid* on *copper*, but either *the reaction of copper to sulphuric acid* or *the action of sulphuric acid on copper.* Similarly, NOT *the reaction*, but *the action* or *effect* or *influence, of Darwinism on Europe & of votes of censure on Italian public opinion.* The Englishman derides especially the Americanism *reactions* (=first impressions): *What are your* reactions *to New York?*

readable. The modern meaning of *readable* is 'easy to read because interestingly written' (legible=easy to read because of clearness of type, handwriting, &c.). The word is overworked by reviewers and book publishers: *Scientific but readable; This readable account of the conversion of St. Paul; abridged for readability.*

real. Another overworked adj. (also adv., *really*). It is properly used in contrast with *apparent, fictional, imaginary;* but often it is used unnecessarily as a means of emphasis, permissible in conversation but not in writing (e.g. *The real-life story of a great American statesman./This is really the best exposition presented so far*, implying that the writer has asserted that many others were the best, but has now changed his mind).

realize. *What*$_\wedge$*was realized might happen has happened.* The insertion of *it* between *what* & *was* is, however ugly, indispensable unless the sentence is to be recast. For discussion & parallels see IT 1.

realtor. Ugly as the word is, it was adopted in 1916 by the (US) National Assoc. of Real Estate Boards. The public, however, may continue to use the est. and unpretentious *real estate agent.* (Brit. equivalents: *land agent, house agent, estate agent.*)

-re & -er. Many words usually spelled (esp. in Brit.) *-re* are pronounced as if the spelling were *-er;* so *centre, fibre, acre, manœuvre.* In American usage the spelling of many of these is now *-er,* except when, as in *acre* & *lucre,* a preceding *c* would have its sound changed from k to s.

reason. 1. *Have reason*=be in the right, & *give one reason*= admit that he is in the right, are GALLICISMS.

2. *It stands to reason* is a formula that gives its user the unfair advantage of at once involving reason & refusing to listen to it; or rather, he expects it to do that for him, but is disappointed, few of us being ignorant nowadays that it is the prelude to an arbitrary judgment that we are not permitted to question.

3. *The reason is because* &c. WRONG: *The only* reason *his wages have not been higher* is because *the profits of the industry have been miserably low.* 'The reason is that . . .' is the English for this; for further examples see BECAUSE, & for analogous mistakes HAZINESS. Wrong forms nearly as common as this are *the reason is due to,* & *the reason is on account of,* as in (WRONG): *The* reason *of our success* is *largely* due to *unselfishness, power to combine, power to weather adversity, & superhuman bravery./The* reason why *I put such a poem as 'Marooned' so very high* is on account of *its tremendous imaginative power.* In itself, *reason why* is not a solecism. *Why* here is a relative (=for which, on account of which). *That is no* reason why *you should surrender.*

Réaumur. The thermometric scale, freezing point 0°, boiling point 80°, invented by R. A. F. Réaumur. Abrev. *R.* (55°R.). Pron. rā'ō mür. Still used to some extent in eastern Europe.

rebate (carpentry). Pron. ră'bĭt (usually spelled *rabbet*).

rebel, v., makes *-lled, -lling.*

rebuke makes *-kable.*

rebus. Pl. *-uses.* Representation of a word or name by pictures suggesting its syllables. A kind of riddle. Pron. rē'bus.

rebut makes *-tted* &c.

rebuttal. Contradiction, refutation: *He reserved the right to call in evidence in rebuttal.* In law the answer to the plaintiff's surrejoinder is the defendant's *rebutter.* See REJOINDER.

recalcitrant. Kicking against restraint; refractory. *The recalcitrant ministers; recalcitrant to the rules of his art.* Pron. -kăl'sĭ trant.

recapitulate makes *-lable, -tor.*

receipt, recipe. In the sense 'formula for the making of a food or medicine,' either word is as good as the other, except that *prescription* has almost displaced both as a name for a doctor's formula; *recipe* (pron. rĕ'sĭpĭ) is more usual for cooking directions.

recension. Revision of, or a revised, text, esp. a critical revision of (an ancient) text to establish a definitive version.

RECESSIVE ACCENT. The accentuation of English words is finally settled by the action of three forces on the material presented to them in each word. First, the habit of concentrating on one syllable, or in long words sometimes on two, & letting the others take care of themselves. This habit is responsible for that obscuring of the English vowel sounds which unnecessarily saddens some of our purists; but English words of three & four syllables are common in which there is only one clear vowel (*corruption, enlightenment,* &c.); it is a main characteristic of the language, to be recognized & not fought against or lamented over.

Secondly, recessive accent, or the drift of this usually single stress toward the beginning of the word. The most obvious illustration is what happens to the French words we borrow; *tableau, menu, charlatan, nonchalant,* & hundreds of others, come to us with their last syllables at least as clear & fully stressed as any but we soon turn them into tăb′lō & shar′l*a*t*a*n & the like. Again, other words that were long pronounced in English with stress on the middle syllable have it shifted to the first; recon′dite, obdur′ate, contrar′y, demon′strate, become rĕk′ondīt, ob′dūr*a*t, &c.

These first & second forces work well enough together, &, as they are always extending their influence & gradually assuming control of new words, account for a large proportion of the variant pronunciations so much more numerous in English than in most languages. In deciding which of two renderings should be preferred, it may be remembered that when recessive accent has once opened an attack it will probably effect the capture, & that it is well to be on the winning side.

But, thirdly, there comes into conflict with both these tendencies a repugnance to strings of obscure syllables. With the uneducated this is rather inability than mere dislike; their tongues cannot frame a rapid succession of light syllables hardly differing from each other; & the educated, who can manage it if they will, have the objection to fussy precision & often do not choose to, except where academic surroundings constrain them to academic elocution. *Laboratory* & *disciplinary* are not easy to say with a single first-syllable accent each, & the attempt is apt to result in omission of syllables —la′br*a*torĭ & dĭs′pl*i*nrĭ. Such dangers are shirked in Brit. by the use of two stresses (dis′-ĭplī′narĭ) or by shifting the stress forward again (lăbō′r*a*torĭ). *Hos′pitable, des′picable, ap′plicable,* are a few examples of the many quadrisyllables from whose orthodox accent many speakers seek relief. The unsatisfactory clipping of words like *voluntar*(*y*)*ism* & *accompan*(*y*)*ist* (see -IST) is perhaps due to this dislike of many syllables unrelieved by an accent. The word CONTUMELY, with its five pronunciations, is an interesting case, discussed separately.

recidivist. One who has a tendency to revert to (usually criminal or antisocial) habits.

recipe. Now usual in cookery. See RECEIPT.

recipient. *Wilfrid, who was seventy years of age yesterday, **was** the recipient of congratula-*

tions from . . ./Mr. Visetti, who has just been the recipient *of a pleasant presentation from his pupils.* Can any man say that sort of thing & retain a shred of self-respect?

reciprocal, mutual. To the difficulties presented by *mutual* itself must be added that of the difference between it & *reciprocal. Mutual* regards the relation from both sides at once: *the mutual hatred of A & B;* never from one side only (NOT *B's mutual hatred of A*). Where *mutual* is correct, *reciprocal* would be so too: *the reciprocal hatred of A & B;* but *mutual* is usually preferred when it is possible. *Reciprocal* can also be applied to the second party's share alone: *B's reciprocal hatred of A; reciprocal* is therefore often useful to supply the deficiencies of *mutual;* A, having served B, can say, 'Now may I ask for a *reciprocal* [but NOT for a *mutual*] service.' Two parties can take *mutual* or *reciprocal* action, & the meaning is the same; one party can take *reciprocal,* but NOT *mutual,* action. In the following passage, *mutual* could not be substituted for the correct *reciprocal: I trust your Government saw . . . the manifestation of friendly goodwill which the people of the United States hold for those of Britain. Believing in* the reciprocal friendship *of the British people it will be my aim in the future . . .* If the words had been not 'of the British people,' but 'of the two peoples,' *mutual* would have been as good as *reciprocal,* or indeed better; it must be added, however, that since it takes two to make a friendship which is essentially a mutual or reciprocal relation, to use either adjective is waste.

reciprocate has *-cable.*

recitative. Pron. rĕsĭtatēv′.

reckon makes *-oned* &c. Americans are sometimes needlessly cautious about using *reckon* because of its dial. parenthetical use (*There's no need to go, I reckon*). Besides its primary meaning of ascertaining by counting or calculation &c., it is also correctly used in the sense consider, think, or suppose that: *'I reckon,' said Socrates, 'that no one could accuse me of idle talking'* (Jowett, quoted in OED).

recluse, n. Best pron. rĕklo͞os′; now often (US) rĕk′lūs.

recognizance. Pron. US usually rĕkŏg′-. Law & Brit. often rĭkŏn′-. See COGNIZANCE.

re-collect, recollect, remember. To *re-collect* is to collect or rally what has been dissipated (*but he soon re-collected his courage* or *himself*); the distinction between this & the ordinary sense of *recollect* is usually though not always kept up in pronunciation, & should be marked by the hyphen. Between *recollect* & *remember* there is a distinction often obscured by the use of *recollect* as a FORMAL WORD for the dominant term, *remember. Recollect* follows *I can't* as naturally as *remember* follows *I don't;* i.e. *recollect* means not *remember,* but succeed in remembering, & implies a search in the memory. *Peter* remembered (NOT *recollected*) *the word of Jesus, which said unto him, Before the cock crow, thou shalt deny me thrice.*

recommend (in the sense of *advise, counsel*). Constr.: You can *recommend* a course of action *to* a person; you can *recom-*

mend that a person should take a course of action; you can *recommend that* the action be taken. WRONG: *After long deliberation I can only recommend*‸*the manuscript be declined.* Insert *that.*

reconcile makes *-lable.* Of the nouns *reconcilement* & *reconciliation,* the first is comparatively little used, but has the special function (perhaps as being more closely dependent on the verb) of representing the act of reconciling rather than the act or state of being reconciled, which means in practice that it is more fitly followed than *reconciliation* by an objective genitive, as in *The reconcilement of duty with pleasure is no easy problem.*

recondite. The traditional pronunciation rikŏn′dīt is maintained by some scholarly persons, but rĕk′ondīt is now usual; see RECESSIVE ACCENT.

reconnaissance. Pron. as English: rekŏn′ĭsans.

reconnoiter, -re. US usually *-er,* Brit. *-re* (US *-tering,* Brit. *-tring*).

recount, v. Narrate, tell in detail; *re-count,* count again. The noun *recount* or *re-count* (a new counting), accent first syllable. *Recountal* is an ugly and unnecessary substitute for *recounting, recital, narration.* (*When the very interesting stories of crime have been unfolded, we can follow the* recountal *of detection without any bewilderment.*)

recourse. See RESORT.

recover, re-cover, recreation, re-creation, &c. The hyphen is used when the meaning is cover again, created anew, the *re-* then being pronounced rē- and given equal stress.

recrudescence. RIGHT: *There is an alarming* recrudescence *of piracy in the West River.*/ WRONG: *A literary tour de force, a* recrudescence *two or three generations later, of the very respectable William Lamb (afterwards Lord Melbourne), his unhappy wife Lady Caroline Lamb, & Lord Byron. To recrudesce* is to become raw again or renew morbid activity, as a wound or ulcer may, or metaphorically a pestilence or vice or other noxious manifestation. That being so, the first example above is proper enough; but what has Lord Melbourne done that his reappearance should be a recrudescence? Nothing, except fall into the hands of a writer who likes POPULARIZED TECHNICALITIES & SLIPSHOD EXTENSION. This disgusting use is apparently of the 20th c. only; *recrudescence* is properly used with *abuses, calumny* & *malignity, paganism, epidemic,* a wound, & other regrettable occurrences.

recruital. An unnecessary variant. Use *recruitment.*

rectilinear, -neal. There is no objection to either in itself; but -ar is so much commoner that, as there is no difference of meaning, *-al* should be abandoned as a NEEDLESS VARIANT.

recto. Pl. *-os.* In books, the right-hand page (as opp. to *verso*); the front cover.

recuperate makes *-rable.* Best pron. -kū-, not -kōō-.

recurrent, -ing. In science, *recurrent nerves, sensibility; recurring curves, series.* In nonscientific contexts *recurring* is more usual in expressing the meaning of the verb: *the recurring seasons, festivities,* &c.

redact, -or, -ion. *Edit, revise, rearrange,* with their nouns, are the usual English words.

redintegrate (*re+integrate;* restore to wholeness, unity, or a perfect state) makes *-rable, -ation, -ative.*

redolent (fragrant) is now chiefly poetic or fig. (strongly suggestive of, reminiscent of); *redolent of past joys.*

redoubtable (formidable; worthy of respect) is still current (*a redoubtable opponent*); *redoubted* (=redoubtable, renowned) is now archaic.

reduce makes *-cible.* After *reduce to* & *be reduced to* the gerund, not the infinitive, is idiomatic; *He was reduced to retracting* (NOT *to retract*) *his statement.*

reductio ad absurdum. (Log.): 'reducing to absurdity.' The method of disproving a thesis by producing something that is both obviously deducible from it & obviously contrary to admitted truth, or of proving one by showing that its contrary involves a consequence similarly absurd. *A reductio ad absurdum* of the theory that the less one eats the healthier one is would be 'Consequently, to eat nothing at all gives one the best possible health.' The proof (as opp. to disproof) by *reductio ad absurdum* is the form often used by Euclid, e.g. where the contrary of the thing to be proved is assumed & shown to lead to an absurdity. An extreme case, such as the eating nothing of the instance above, is often called 'the reductio ad absurdum of' a plan.

redundancy, -ce. Superabundance, superfluity. In writing, PLEONASM, the use of more words than needed, e.g. *People who* profess to call *themselves Christians; But the* final climax *came when . . . ;* A false untruth. The *-cy* form is more usual.

reduplicate makes *-cable.*

re-enforce. Use *reinforce.*

reeve makes *rove* or *reeved* both in past & in p.p.

refection (meal). A FORMAL WORD.

refectory. Pronounced usually refĕk′- except in monastic use, in which the older rĕf′- still prevails.

refer makes *-rred, -rring,* but *referable* (pron. rĕf′erab'l).

reference. By SLIPSHOD EXTENSION, the word is now made to mean a person to whom reference is permitted as a witness to character (*Please give* three references *who know of your work*), & even a written testimonial (*Bring your* references *with you*). Most US dictionaries include both the person and the testimonial without comment; COD lists the person, but labels the testimonial 'loosely.'

referendum, properly meaning a question to be referred (to the people), has been appropriated as a name for the system of so referring questions & for any particular occasion of its exercise; the normal form would have been *reference,* but *referendum* has the advantage over that of not bearing several other senses. The plural *-da* is better avoided as too suggestive (cf. *memoranda, agenda,* &c.) of the correct sense—questions to be referred; use *-ms.*

reflection, reflexion. The spelling with *x* is the earliest, but *-ct-* is now usual in all senses (US &

Brit.). (*Reflexion* is sometimes, but not always, used in the anatomical & other scientific contexts.)

reflective, reflexive. *Reflexive* has now lost all its senses except the grammatical one & *reflective* has resigned that & kept the rest. But *reflective,* though it can at need have any of the adj. senses corresponding to *reflection,* is current chiefly as synonymous with *meditative,* & *reflecting* or *reflected* is substituted for it as often as possible in referring to the reflection of light &c.—*reflecting surface, reflected color,* rather than *reflective.*

reform, re-form. For 'shape again,' keep the hyphen.

refusal has been used in the sense of *option* (*gave him the refusal of . . .*) since the 16th c.

re-fuse. 'To fuse again,' keep the hyphen.

refutable. Pron. rĕf′-.

regalia. The word meaning royal emblems &c. is a plural.

regard. 1. *Regard* in periphrasis. *In regard to, with regard to, as regards.* The two examples that follow, in which *about* would have served for *with regard to,* & *in* for *in regard to,* are mere everyday specimens of a practice that is not strikingly bad on each occasion, but cumulatively spoils a writer's style & injures the language: *It is well said, in every sense, that a man's religion is the chief fact* with regard to *him.*/In regard to *three other seats there will be a divided Unionist vote.* See also COMPOUND PREPOSITIONS.

The verb is also much overused periphrastically in *as regards.* WRONG: *Any country the population of which is Christian* as regards *the majority of its inhabitants . . .* This should run —*any country* (a) *whose population is chiefly Christian,* or (b) *with a predominantly Christian population,* or (c) *in which the majority of the population is Christian,* or (d) *in which the majority are Christians,* or (e) *where Christians are in the majority.* See AS 3 for the disfigurements to which the very similar *as to* leads those who indulge in such phrases.

2. *Regard, consider. I consider it monstrous* or *a shame* is English; *I regard it monstrous* or *a shame* is not, but requires *as: I regard it* as *monstrous,* as *a shame. Regard* (*it*) *to be* (or *do*) is as unidiomatic as *regard it monstrous* &c., but far less common & therefore less in need of attention. A number of examples will be given, in the hope that when they are seen in the mass their badness will be glaring enough to repel.

A. *Regard to be* (or *do*), & *regard that.* WRONG: *Dr. Leonard* regards it to indicate *the looseness of popular opinion* (thinks or considers that it indicates)./*Some county associations* regard it to be *their first duty to accumulate large invested funds* (believe)./*Montenegro* regards *this treaty* to be *worthless because she was not previously informed of its existence* (considers, or *regards . . . as*).

B. Unprovoked omission of *as.* WRONG: *The present rulers will* regard *themselves*‸free *to pile up armaments./But the Generals present* regarded *the remedy*‸ worse *than the evil.* (Insert *as* in both, or use *consider* or *think.*)

C. Omission of *as* not excused, but perhaps caused, by proximity of another *as,* or by abnormal order of words. *Consider* is the remedy in all. WRONG: *We re-*

gard *no insult*‸so supreme *as the insult that we are intolerant./ Pufendorf went so far as to* regard *ratification*‸superfluous./ *Showing how fundamental they* regarded *the need of establishing the independence of the judiciary.*

regarding serves grammatically as a prep. meaning *respecting, about* (*I have no information* regarding *the subject*). But *about* is usually better.

regardless is used idiomatically as an adverb in such sentences as *He came* regardless *of my instructions.* See QUASI-ADVERBS. The colloq. uses (US, *I'll do it* regardless—i.e. of what you think, of what might happen; Brit., *got up* regardless—i.e. of expense) are but slightly removed from slang, but far better than the illiterate *irregardless.*

regime. The accent (*régime*) is now usually omitted, but the *g* is still pron. zh. But *ancien régime* (the government in France before the Revolution; hence, transf., any abolished or past system) keeps the accent & is best printed in italics.

register, v., makes *-trable;* the agent noun is now *registrar* but in the 17th & 18th cc. was often *register.* (In US, *The Register,* NOT *Registrar, of Copyright.*)

regress. The verb regrĕs′, the noun rē′grĕs.

regret makes *-tted, -ttable,* &c.

regretful means feeling or manifesting regret, not causing it; the latter sense belongs to *regrettable.* In the extracts below the wrong word has been chosen: see PAIRS & SNARES. WRONG: *The possession of those churches was unfortunately the reason of the* regretful *racial struggles in Macedonia./It was not surprising, however* regretful, *that Scotland had lagged behind.*

reindeer is sing. & pl. See COLLECTIVES 1.

reinforce, re-enforce. The ordinary form (*rein-*) has been so far divorced from the simple verb (formerly *inforce* or *enforce,* now always the latter) that it seldom or never means to enforce again, as when a lapsed regulation is revived. For that sense *re-enforce* should be used (*An attempt to* re-enforce *the Blue Laws*). Both make *-ceable.*

reiterant. WRONG: *But the booing &* reiterant *cries of 'No' grew louder, & at length he sat down.* This AVOIDANCE OF THE OBVIOUS, as often, has resulted in a blunder; *reiterant* means repeating, not repeated; but, at any rate, what are *booing & reiterant* doing in one sentence?

rejoin, re-join. The hyphened form should be restricted to actual reuniting (*The parts will* re-join *if laid close end to end,* or *should be re-joined with care*).

rejoinder. In Law, there is the plaintiff's declaration, the defendant's plea; the plaintiff's replication (reply), the defendant's rejoinder; the plaintiff's surrejoinder, the defendant's rebutter; and the plaintiff's surrebutter. In general use, therefore, *a rejoinder* is an answer to a reply and suggests *retort.* Used loosely for any answer or reply, it is usually a result of LOVE OF THE LONG WORD.

rejuvenate makes *-nable.*

relation, relationship, relative, as terms of kindred, have seen some changes. *Relative* started as an adj. meaning what we call *related,* but, being used as short for related person, became a noun denoting a person. *Relation* started as an abstract noun meaning our *relationship* (in its only right sense; see next article); but, being transferred from the abstract to the concrete, came also to denote a person. We have had to take to *related* & *relationship* because the others in their original senses have failed us, & now find ourselves with *relation* & *relative* as two names for the same thing, only so far different as *-ive* is something of a FORMAL WORD, & *-ion* the dominant term.

relation(ship). The word *relation* has many senses, most of which are abstract. It approaches the concrete in the rather rare sense 'a story or narrative,' & it is fully concrete in the very common sense 'a related person,' i.e. a son or mother or cousin or aunt or the like. Now, *sonship, cousinship,* &c., being words for which there is a use, it is entirely natural that *-ship* should be affixed also to the word that summarizes them; *sonship* the being a son, *relationship* the being a relation —with the extension (due to the generalizing sense of *relation*) into 'the being this, that, or the other relation,' or 'degree of relatedness.' To that use of *relationship,* then, there is no objection. But to affix *-ship* to *relation* in any of its other, or abstract, senses is against all analogy. The use of *-ship* is to provide concretes (*friend, horseman, lord*) with corresponding abstracts; but *relation,* except when it means related person, is already abstract, & one might as well make *connectionship, correspondenceship,* or *associationship,* as *relationship* from *relation* in abstract senses. Of the following extracts the first shows how *relationship,* when it is justifiable, may lend precision to the meaning; the second suggests, by the writer's shifting from one to the other, that *relationship* in the improper sense has no superiority whatever to *relation* or *relations;* & the rest show how needlessly the LONG VARIANT is often resorted to: (1) *The king was therefore not necessarily of royal blood, though usually he was the son of the previous Pharaoh; the* relation *of Tut-ankh-Amen to his predecessor is not known* (should be *relationship*). (2) *Why not leave the* relations *of landlord & farmers, as well as those of farmers & laborers, to the beneficial effects of the policy? Why is a tribunal necessary in the one case & not in the other if mutual frankness will adjust all* relationships? (all *relations*). (3) *A state of things may be created which is altogether inconsistent with the* relationship *which should properly exist between police & public* (relation). (4) *A step which must have great effect on the commercial* relationship *between America & Europe* (relations).

relative is a QUASI-ADVERB in idiomatic expressions such as *I wrote to him* relative *to renewing the lease; about* would be better.

relative pronouns. Pronouns that introduce a subordinate clause and refer to an expressed or implied element in the principal clause. See WHO, WHICH, WHAT, THAT, SUCH AS, AS.

relatively means 'in relation to something else.' RIGHT: *In view of the number that registered,* relatively *few actually attended.* It is meaningless unless the thing to which it is related may be assumed: *I worked* relatively *hard today*—in relation to how I usually work? to how other people worked? considering the kind of day it was? *Relatively* is often used when *quite, rather,* &c., is really meant.

relegate makes *-gable.* It comes from a word meaning 'sent back,' and now means consign or dismiss to some (usually inferior) position or sphere: You relegate certain material to footnotes; certain duties to your subordinates. WRONG: *The large terrace, usually a dining room, had also been* relegated *to the King's use, & was adorned with groups of Alpine plants.* Has the writer looked up *assign* in a synonym dictionary & decided that *relegate* is the least familiar of the list? familiar to him it does not seem to be; see NOVELTY-HUNTING.

relevance, -cy. *Relevance* is now more usual, US & Brit.

relict. Semi-legal or FORMAL WORD for *widow.* Pron. rĕl'ĭkt.

relievo. Pl. *-os.* But the form might well be dropped as a needless mixture between the Italian *rilievo* (rēlyā'vō) & the English *relief.*

religious, adj. For *dim religious light,* see IRRELEVANT ALLUSION. N. sing. & pl.=person(s) bound by monastic vows (=Fr. *religieux*).

remain. 1. WRONG: *There* remains *to be said* a few words *on the excellence of M. Radot's book.* The use of a singular verb before a plural subject is discussed in NUMBER 7. The present example is perhaps due to confusion between *It remains to say* & *There remain to be said.*

2. *Continue to remain. Remain* (in the sense that concerns us) means in itself 'continue to be'; *to continue to continue to be* is, except in some hardly imaginable context, a ridiculous tautology, & would not call for mention if it were not surprisingly common; see HAZINESS, PLEONASM. WRONG: *And yet through it all* I continue to remain *cheerful./It is expected that very soon order will be restored, although the people* continue to remain *restive.*

remark, v., has as one of its senses 'to say by way of comment' or 'say incidentally.' It would be absurd pedantry to insist that it should never be used for *say* except when 'by way of comment' is clearly justified, & often very difficult to decide whether it is justified or not. Nevertheless, it is well to remember the qualification, & be thereby saved from two bad uses of *remark,* (1) as a mere FORMAL WORD, & (2) as a word relied on to give by its incongruity a mildly facetious touch—one of the forms of WORN-OUT HUMOR: *You may drive out Nature with a pitchfork but she will always return, as Horace* remarked *in a language no longer quoted.*

remarkable is a POSITIVE WORD, expressing the user's personal feeling. *Very remarkable* is usually unnecessary, and adds nothing that the word itself does not say; but *one of the most remarkable* is idiomatic.

remedy. *Remediable* & *remedial* are pronounced remē'-.

remember is the usual opp. of *forget; recall* and *recollect* suggest an effort to remember. See RECOLLECT.

reminisce, a BACK-FORMATION of *reminiscent,* 'still somewhat colloquial or jocular' (OED). US dictionaries list it without comment in the senses 'indulge in reminiscences,' 'remember,' 'recall to memory,' but careful writers seldom use it seriously.

remise (Law, v.). Pron. rēmīz′.

remit makes *-tted, -tting,* &c.; but *remissible.* Of the nouns *remission* & *remittal,* the first is better in all senses but one, the act of referring a case from one court to another; *remittance* is restricted to transmittal of money, or the money remitted.

remonstrate. Pron. (in contrast with *demonstrate*) remon′strate, perhaps because the current noun is *remonstrance.* The other noun, *-ation,* is now rare & should not be used: *Although every attempt is made at this office to save people from being misled, our* remonstrations *have not hitherto met with success* (remonstrances).

remote is not one of the adjs. that can be used as QUASI-ADVERBS; it must have a noun with which it can be reasonably conceived to agree. WRONG: *Even somewhat* remote *from the main tourist routes* the knowledge *of English in ships is remarkable.* Read *Even some distance from . . .*

remove makes *-vable.* For *remove one's hat, the cloth,* &c. (i.e. take off), see FORMAL WORDS.

remunerate makes *-rable*: *Remunerate, -ation,* & *-ative* are, as compared with *pay(ing),* FORMAL WORDS, & should not be preferred without good reason.

renaissance is still the standard spelling for the French literary & artistic classical revival (pron. rĕn′ĕzäNS′ or rēnā′săns). It is also often used for similar periods of artistic & literary revivals. *Renascence,* the anglicized form, is usual when the meaning is simply (fig.) rebirth (pron. rēnăs′ĕns).

rend makes *rent, rending.* The noun (tear, cleft, &c.) is *rent.*

rendezvous. (Meeting place; a meeting by agreement; n. sing. & pl.) Pron. rŏn′devōō, -ōōz. The verb makes *-vouses* (pron. -vōōz), *-voused* (pron. vōōd), *-vousing* (pron. -vōōing).

rendition in the sense of performance (of music, a play, &c.) is chiefly US. See GENTEELISMS.

renege (Brit. *renegue*). Orig. (now archaic), to renounce, deny. Now in card playing, to fail to follow suit. US colloq., to go back on a promise. Pron. (traditionally) rēnēg′; popularly rēnĭg′.

renounce makes *-ceable.* Between *renouncement* & *renunciation* there is no differentiation & *renouncement* is accordingly passing out of use.

renunciation. Pron. -sĭ ā′shun. *Renunciative, renunciatory,* pron. Brit. -sh*a*tĭv, -sh*a*trĭ or, US, -shĭ ātĭv, -shĭ*a* tō rĭ).

repa(i)rable. *Reparable* (rep′*a*-) is used almost only of abstracts such as *loss, injury, mistake,* which are to be made up for or to have their effects neutralized; *repairable* sometimes in that way also, but chiefly of material things that need mending. The negatives are *irreparable,* but *unrepairable.*

repast. See GENTEELISMS.

repel makes *-lled* &c.

repellent, repulsive. That is *repellent* which keeps one at arm's length; that is *repulsive* from which one recoils; that is, the second is a much stronger word.

repertoire (pron. -twär) is still the usual word for the stock of parts, plays, music ready for performance. But *a repertory theater.*

REPETITION OF WORDS OR SOUNDS. The first thing to be said is that a dozen sentences are spoiled by ill-advised avoidance of repetition for every one that is spoiled by ill-advised repetition. Faulty repetition results from want of care; faulty avoidance results from incapacity to tell good from bad, or servile submission to a rule of thumb—far graver defects than carelessness. This article is accordingly of slight importance compared with that in which the other side of the matter is presented; see ELEGANT VARIATION, where the rule of thumb against repetition is shown to have the most disastrous consequences.

The fact remains, however, that repetition of certain kinds is bad; &, though the bad repetitions are almost always unintentional, & due to nothing worse than carelessness, & such as their authors would not for a moment defend, yet it is well that writers should realize how common this particular form of carelessness is. The moral of the examples that will be given is the extremely simple one—read what you have written before printing it. The examples are divided into batches under headings, & little comment need be added.

DEPENDENT SEQUENCES, i.e. several *of* phrases, or two or more *which* clauses or *that* clauses or *-ly* words, each of which is not parallel or opposed, but has a dependent relation, to the one before or after it. For this point of the distinction between dependent & parallel sequences, see -LY 3. *The founders* of *the study* of *the origin* of *human nature./The atmosphere of mutuality must be created* which *will make it possible to discuss proposals* which *would have seemed impracticable./I do not forget* that *some writers have held* that *a system is to be inferred./He lived* practically exclusively *on milk.*

TWO ACCIDENTALLY SIMILAR BUT NOT PARALLEL USES OF A WORD. Some other examples may be found in JINGLES. *The entire article would run to* several *columns, but there are* several *points which, if quoted, would give the impression that . . ./In these days American revolutionary upsets appear small* enough *beside the other afflictions of the world; yet the situation is interesting* enough. Doubtful specimens of this kind sometimes occur in which the repetition may have been intended, but the parallel or contrast is so little significant or so untidily expressed that it was probably accidental: *The Japanese are* affronted *at what they regard as an* affront *to their national dignity./They can, no doubt, do each other* enormous *injury, but the Bulgarians could only carry the trenches at* enormous *cost.*

HAPHAZARD REPETITION, IN A DIFFERENT SENSE, OF A WORD (or such use of one of its inflexions or derivatives or other belongings). *The cure for that is clearly the* alternative *vote of the second ballot, the former* alternative *being the more preferable./This may have been* due *to* undue *power placed in his hands by the Constitution.*

Here again it is sometimes possible to suspect a writer of what is worse than carelessness, a pointless but intended repetition that is to have the effect of a play on words or the mildest of puns: *The triple* bill *of* Bills *which are down for the autumn sitting: the Mines* Bill, *the Shops* Bill, *& the Insurance* Bill./ *Anonymity seems to be a peculiar delight to writers on naval* matters, *though perhaps necessity has something to do with the* matter.

ASSONANCE, RHYME, &C. *'Worser & worser' grows the plight of the Globe* over *the* overseas *trade figures./If no such council existed, the Secretary of State would have to* form *an* informal *one if not a* formal *one./The features which the* present *Government in this country* presents *in common with* representative *& responsible government are few & formal.*

repetitional, repetitionary, repetitious, repetitive. With all these on record, *repetition* would seem to have a good stock of adjectives at need; but few writers have the hardihood to use any of them. *Repetitious* is common in US use; *repetitive* is perhaps the least avoided in Brit. The first two are fortunately obsolescent.

replace makes *-ceable.* There is the literal sense of put (thing or person) back in the same place as before; & there are, broadly different from this, various uses in which substitution is the idea—return an equivalent for, fill or take the place of, find a substitute for, supersede, & so forth. All the dictionaries, or certainly most of them, give the *substitute* uses without comment, & they are established in the language; but some wise men of Gotham have lately discovered that, if one is perversely ingenious enough, one can so use *replace* that it shall not be clear whether literal putting back or substitution is meant. Here is an example in which a little thought is required: *We do not regard the situation as a simple one; a large proportion of the men on strike have been* replaced, *& as complete* reinstatement *is one of the demands of the union, there are obvious difficulties to be overcome.* To use *replace* there was foolish; 'have had their places filled' was the way to put it. But the wise men of Gotham are so proud of a discovery that ordinary people have made about hundreds of other words that they have issued a decree against using *replace* at all in the *substitute* senses. The consequences, in overuse & misuse of the verb SUBSTITUTE & the noun *substitution,* have been lamentable, but need not be set forth here; it is enough to state that the objections to the secondary senses of *replace* & *replacement* are idle, & that only the same kind of care is required that is taken not to use *trip* in the special sense *stumble,* or *mistress* in the special sense *female paramour,* where the context makes confusion likely with the unspecialized senses.

replenishment, repletion. The first is the process of filling something up or the amount of matter that effects the process; the second is the filled-up condition.

replete. WRONG: *No teacher's bookcase is* replete *without it.* Everyone at once rightly corrects to *complete;* but why not *replete?* you can say 'a bookcase replete with works of genius.' Because quite full (*replete*) is not the same as adequately filled (*complete*).

replica. 'Properly one made by the original artists,' says the OED, after defining *replica* as a copy or duplicate of a work of art. It is this proper sense that alone makes the foreign word *replica* worth maintaining in English by the side of the abundant English synonyms. ELEGANT VARIATION & NOVELTY-HUNTING account between them for much destruction of what is valuable in words.

repoussé. 'Thrust back.' Formed in relief, esp., of ornamental metal work. Pron. rē-pōō sā'.

repress makes *-ssible.*

reproduce makes *-cible.*

reptile. The prevailing pron. in US is -ĭl; Brit. -īl (but OED gives -ĭl first). *Reptilia* include snakes, lizards, crocodiles, alligators, turtles, & tortoises.

repudiate makes *-diable.*

repugn(ant). *Repugn,* formerly in common use, is now obs. in most senses, and rare in those still in use. It should be used with care. Pron. rĭpūn', but rĭpŭg'nant.

repulsive. Causing one to recoil; loathsome, disgusting. See REPELLENT.

request. WRONG: *The German Commission* requested *the Allied Commission* for *information as to whether an extension of the Armistice could be relied upon.* Request information *from* the Commission, request *to be* informed *by* the Commission, request *that* the Commission would inform; these will do, but the form in the text is unidiomatic, & due to the ANALOGY of *ask.*

requiem. The dictionaries give the pronunciation rē'- first.

requirement, requisite, nn. The two are so far synonyms that in some contexts either will do: *The requirements,* or *The requisites, are courage & callousness.* But *requirement* means properly a need, & *requisite* a needed thing; *That sum will meet my requirements,* never *my requisites;* but, just as the abstract *need* is often used for the concrete needed thing, so *requirement* may perhaps always be substituted for *requisite; Sponge, toothbrush, & other requirements* will pass, though *requisites* is better & more usual.

requisite, adj. Required by the circumstances; 'called for.' For *essential, necessary,* & *requisite,* see ESSENTIAL.

requite makes *-table.*

reredos. (Ornamental screen or partition wall behind altar.) Two syllables (rēr'dŏs).

rescind has *rescission.*

research. Pron. (preferably) reserch', but US often rē'-.

resentment. Constr. *of, at, against* (NEVER *to*). WRONG: *May I, as one in complete sympathy with the general policy of the Government, give expression to the strong* resentment *I feel* to *the proposed Bill?* *Repugnance* is probably what was meant; see ANALOGY, & CAST-IRON IDIOM.

reservedly. Four syllables.

reside, residence, -cy, have their proper uses (legal, official, diplomatic, fig.) but see FORMAL WORDS.

residue, -uum, -ual, -uary. There are two special uses, to each of which one noun & one adjective are appropriated—the legal sense concerned with what remains of an estate after payment of charges, debts, & bequests; & the mathematical, chemical, & physical sense of what remains after subtraction, combustion, evaporation, &c. The legal noun & adjective are *residue* & *residuary*, the chemical &c. are *residuum* & *residual*, though the differentiation is occasionally infringed in both directions. In more general use, *residuum* implies depreciation, differing from *residue* as *leavings* or *sweepings* differs from *remainder*. *Residuum* has plural *-dua*.

resign. *He resigned* from *office* (US)=*he resigned* his *office*, or *he resigned*.

resilience, -cy. Pron. with -zĭl′-. The very slight difference of sense—that *-ce* can & *-cy* cannot mean an act of rebounding—does not, since there is no chance of *-ce's* being confined to that special sense, make the existence of the two anything better than an inconvenience; it is therefore best to use *-ce* always.

resin, any of the natural organic substances; see ROSIN.

resist makes *-tible*. *Resistless* has no purpose with *irresistible* & *unresisting* both ready to choose from. See -LESS.

resoluble, resolvable. Both are in use without distinction of meaning, the first being more a literary, & the other more a colloq. word. The negatives should be *irresoluble*, but *unresolvable;* in *The number of* irresolvable *difficulties is relatively small,* correct either the prefix or the suffix.

resolution, motion. As names for a proposition that is passed or to be passed by the votes of an assembly, the two differ in that the passing of a motion results in action, & a motion is that something be done; while a resolution is not necessarily more than an expression of the opinion that something is true or desirable. Since, however, opinion often becomes operative, & since also resolutions as well as motions are moved, i.e. are at least in one sense motions, the distinction is elusive; it is nevertheless, if not too rigidly applied, of some value.

resorb, to absorb again, makes *resorption*.

resort, resource, recourse. Confusion between these three is very frequent, &, since in some senses each is really synonymous with each, the confusion is, if not excusable, at least natural. The usual mistake is to say *resource* when one of the others is required. WRONG: *Such ships as remain in the Southern Seas must now have* resource *to the many sparsely inhabited islands* (recourse)./ *She will not be able to do so, in Dr. Dillon's opinion, without* resource *to the sword* (recourse, resorting, resort)./. . . *binding all Powers to apply an economic boycott, or, in the last* resource, *international force, against any Power which . . .* (resort).

The words are chiefly used in certain established phrases, given below; when alternatives appear in parentheses, they are to be taken as less idiomatic. *To resort to; to have recourse* (resort) *to; without recourse* (resort, resorting) *to. Without resources; at the end of his resources; had no other resource left; the only resource* (resort); *as a last resource; in the last resort. His usual resource was lying; his usual recourse* (resort) *was to lying. A man of great* or *no resource; a man of many* or *no resources.*

Without resource in the sense 'irreparably,' though it has been used by good writers, is a GALLICISM, not an English idiom.

respect. The compound prepositions *with respect to, in respect of,* should be used not as often, but as seldom, as possible; see REGARD, & PERIPHRASIS.

respecting may function legitimately as a preposition (=relating to). RIGHT: *Respecting Canada, one or other of the two following will take place.* (This does not encourage the slipshod or commercial *Respecting yours of the eighth, the order was never received.*)

respective(ly). Delight in these words is a widespread but depraved taste. Like soldiers & policemen they have work to do, but, when the work is not there, the less we see of them the better. The evil is considerable enough to justify an examination at some length: examples may be sorted into six groups: (A) in which the words give information needed by sensible readers; (B) in which they give information that may be needed by fools; (C) in which they say again what is said elsewhere; (D) in which they say nothing intelligible; (E) in which they are used wrongly for some other word; & (F) in which they give a positively wrong sense.

A. RIGHT: *There are two other chapters in which Strauss & Debussy take* respectively *a higher & a lower place than popular opinion accords them.* But for *respectively,* the reader might suppose that both composers were rated higher on some points & lower in others./ *That training colleges for men & women* respectively *be provided on sites at Hammersmith & St. Pancras.* But for *respectively* we might take both colleges to be for both sexes./*This makes it quite possible for the apparently contradictory messages received from Sofia & Constantinople* respectively *to be equally true. Respectively* shows that the contradiction is not, e.g., between earlier & later news from the Near East, but between news from one & news from the other town.

B. FOOLPROOF: The particular fool for whose benefit each *respective* is inserted will be defined in parentheses. *Final statements were made by Mr. Bonar Law & M. Millerand in the House of Commons & the Chamber of Deputies* respectively (*respectively* takes care of the reader who does not know which gentleman or which Parliament was British, or who may imagine both gentlemen talking in both Parliaments)./ *The Socialist aim in facing a debate was to compel the different groups to define their* respective *attitudes* (the reader who may expect a group to define another group's attitude)./*It is very far from certain that any of the names now canvassed in Wall Street will secure the nomination at the* respective *Republican & Democratic Conventions* (the reader who may think Republicans & Democrats hold several united conventions).

C. TAUTOLOGICAL: After each is given in parentheses the expression of the fact that makes *respective* superfluous. *Having collected the total amount, the collector disburses to each proper authority its* respective *quota* (each . . . its)./*He wants the Secretary of War to tell the House in what countries they are at present stationed, & the numbers in each country* respectively (each)./*Madame Sarah Bernhardt & Mrs. Bernard Beere* respectively *made enormous hits in 'As in a Looking Glass'* (hits, plural).

D. UNINTELLIGIBLE: *The writing room, silence room, & recreation room have* respectively *blue & red armchairs./A certain estate is for sale; its grounds border three main roads, namely, Queen's, Belmont, & King's* respectively.

E. RESPECTIVELY FOR ANOTHER WORD: The writers of these mean no more than *both* (to be placed in the second after *Fellow*). *The two nurses' associations* respectively *organized in Scotland make no secret of their membership./He was a Fellow*^ *of Balliol College, Oxford, & of the University of London* respectively.

F. REVERSAL OF SENSE: *It is recognized that far too little is known by Englishmen & Americans about their* respective *countries; in this country there is only one lectureship on American history, & that is at King's College, Strand.* This can only mean that Englishmen know too little of England, & Americans know too little of America—which is no doubt true, but is not the truth that the writer wished to convey; 'about each other's countries' would have served both writer & reader.

The simple fact is that *respective*(*ly*) are words seldom needed, but that pretentious writers drag them in at every opportunity for the air of thoroughness & precision they are supposed to give to a sentence.

respite, n. & v., pron. rĕs′pĭt.

resplendence, -cy. The first is recommended.

responsible in the sense of answerable, morally accountable (for), is applicable to people, not things. Loose, chiefly US: *The three-day* holiday was responsible *for over two hundred traffic accidents.*

restaurateur. Restaurant keeper. So spelled, if used. See FRENCH WORDS.

restive (orig. *restiff;* of a horse, stubborn, balky, refractory) when applied to a person means intractable, resisting control. It is often confused with *restless.* The two effects are comparable, but the distinction should be kept in mind. A child will become *restless* if he is bored; he will become *restive* if he dislikes what he is being told to do and refuses to co-operate.

resurrect, a BACK-FORMATION from *resurrection,* is listed as colloq. in Brit. dictionaries, but is accepted usage in US.

resuscitate makes *-itable.* (Pron. -sŭs′ĭ tāt, -tab′l.)

retaliate makes *-iable.*

reticent means reserved in speech, taciturn, &c. It is not interchangeable with *shy.*

retina. Pl. *-as* or *-ae.*

retrace makes *-ceable.* In the literal sense to trace (a drawing) over again, the hyphen should be kept. *He retraced his steps* but *The map will have to be re-traced.*

retrieve. Of the nouns *retrieve* & *retrieval,* the first is used in particular phrases (*beyond, past, retrieve*), & the other elsewhere (*for the retrieval of his fortunes* &c.).

retro-. Combining form meaning 'back.' In most words the usual pronunciation in US is rĕtrō: *retrospect, retrograde, retrospective, retrospection, retrogression, retrogressive, retrogradation.* In physiological terms, however, it is often rētrō- (as it is in many general words in Brit.).

retrograd-, retrogress(-). There are two series: (1) adj. & v. *retrograde,* n. *retrogradation;* (2) v. *retrogress,* n. *retrogression,* adj. *retrogressive.* But, as most of us have a preference for *retrograde* as the adj. & *retrogression* as the noun, & no great liking for either verb, there is unfortunately little prospect that one series will oust the other.

revaluate, -ation mean the same things as, and are better than, *re-evaluate, -ation.*

reveille. In US service, usually pron. -rĕv′elĭ; Brit. rĕvĕl′ĭ.

revel makes (US) *-led, -ling, -ler;* (Brit.) *-lled* &c.

Revelation(s). Though the Bible title is *The Revelation of St. John the Divine,* the plural *Revelations* is quite established in ordinary speech, & to take exception to it is PEDANTRY; but *The Revelations* is a confusion of the correct *The Revelation* with the popular *Revelations.*

revenge. For *revenge* v. & *avenge, revenge* n. & *vengeance,* see AVENGE. *Revenge* makes *-geable. Revengeful* can usually be discarded in favor of *vindictive.*

reverberate makes *-rable, -tor.*

reverend, rev., reverent(ial). (1) *Reverend* means deserving reverence, & *reverent* feeling or showing it. (2) *Reverend* is now usually abbreviated *Rev. Rev. Smith,* instead of *Rev. J. Smith* or *the Rev. Mr.* or *Dr. Smith* is an illiteracy. Reporters giving lists of clergy have difficulties with the plural of the abbreviation; but, since *reverend* is an adjective (& not, like *parson* in the now disused 'Parson Jones & Smith,' a noun), there is neither occasion for nor correctness in such forms as *Revs.* & *Revds.; the Rev. J. Smith, W. H. Jones, P. Brown, & others* is the way to put it. If the initials, or some of them, are not known, it should run *The Rev. J. Smith, Messrs. Jones & Brown, Dr. Robinson, & other clergy.* (3) Between *reverent* & *reverential* the difference is much the same as that between PRUDENT & *prudential, reverential* being as applicable to what apes reverence as to what is truly instinct with it, while *reverent* has only the laudatory sense; but *reverential* is often wrongly chosen merely as a LONG VARIANT. When *reverent* would not be out of place, *reverential* is a substitute as much weaker as it is longer.

reverie, -y. The first is better.

reverse, n. Such phrases as 'remarks the reverse of complimentary,' meaning uncomplimentary remarks, are cumbrous specimens of WORN-OUT HUMOR.

reverse, v. For the adj. *-sible* is the usual form; negative *unreversable,* or *irreversible.*

reversion has various senses, chiefly legal or biological, to be found in any dictionary, & not needing to be set forth here. It suffices to say that they all correspond to the verb *revert,* & not to the verb *reverse,* whose noun is *reversal.* WRONG: *The* reversion *of our Free Trade policy would, we are convinced, be a great reverse for the working class.*

revieweal. Use *review*, n.

REVIVALS. It is by no means uncommon for very ordinary words to remain latent for long periods and then come back into use. The occasion may be one on which a name has to be found for a new thing, & a question arises between a foreign word & a disused English one that might well have served if the thing & the word had been alive together. To take only some notable cases in the letter *B*, the OED records such disappearances of *balsam* (600 years), *bloom* (the iron-foundry word; 600 years), *braze* (to make of brass; 550 years); but the reappearance of these was not so much a deliberate revival as a re-emergence out of the obscurity of talk into the light of literature. It is only with deliberate revivals, however, that it is worth while to concern ourselves here —words like *carven* (carved), *childly*, *dispiteous*, & *dole* (grief), or uses of words in obsolete senses such as *egregious* meaning excellent or *enormity* meaning hugeness. *Carven* seems to have been disused for 300 years, *childly* for 250; *dispiteous* (formerly *despite/ous* full of despite, now *dis/piteous* unpitying) for 200; *dole* for a long time in England at least. Revivals like these, & those of obsolete senses, not to fill gaps in a deficient vocabulary but to impart the charm of quaintness to matter that perhaps needs adornment, are of doubtful benefit either to the language or to those who experiment in them. Is it absurdly optimistic to suppose that what the stream of language leaves stranded as it flows along consists mainly of what can well be done without, & that going back to rake among the debris, except for very special needs, is unprofitable? At any rate, the simple referring of any word to this article is intended to dissuade the reader from using it.

revoke makes *revocable* (rĕv′-*okab'l*), *revocation*.

revue. (Lit.): 'review.' A loosely constructed play or series of scenes of spectacles, satirizing, exhibiting, or referring to current fashions & events.

Reynard (=fox), see SOBRIQUETS.

rhapsodic(al). The short form is now usually limited to the original sense 'of the Greek rhapsodes,' while *-ical* has usually & might well have only the secondary sense of ecstatically expressed or highflown.

rhetorical question. (Rhetoric.) A question is often put not to elicit information, but as a more striking substitute for a statement of contrary effect. The assumption is that only one answer is possible, & that if the hearer is compelled to make it mentally himself it will impress him more than the speaker's statement. So *Who does not know . . . ?* for *Everyone knows, Was ever such nonsense written?* for *Never was* &c.

Rh factor. The Rhesus factor, so called because it was found in the blood of the rhesus monkey. No period.

rhinoceros. Usually used as both sing. & pl., but pl. may be *-oses* (older forms of pl., *-otes* & *-i*).

rhombus. Pl. *-buses* or *-bi.*

RHYME, RIME. 1. (Poetry): 'rhythm.' As now understood in English verse, rhyme is identity of sound between words or lines extending back from the end to the last fully accented vowel & not farther; *greet* & *deceit, shepherd* & *leopard, quality* & *frivolity, stationery* & *probationary* are rhymes; *seat* & *deceit, station* & *crustacean, visible* & *invisible* are not. Words that, to judge from spelling, might have been rhymes, but have not in fact the required identity of sound, as *phase* & *race, love* & *move* & *cove,* are often treated as rhyming, but are called *imperfect rhymes.* One-syllable rhymes are called *male* or *masculine* or *single,* two-syllable *female* or *feminine* or *double,* three-syllable & four-syllable *triple* & *quadruple. Rhyme royal,* a meter in stanzas of seven five-foot iambic lines rhyming ababbcc. Chaucer's *Clerk's Tale* is a well-known example.

2. *rhyme, rime.* Nothing seems to be gained, except indeed a poor chance of the best of three reputes (learning, pedantry, & error), by changing the established spelling. The OED states that *rhyme* 'finally established itself as the standard form,' & that the revival of *rime* 'was to some extent due to the belief that the word was of native origin & represented OE *rim*' (=number). *Rhyme* is in fact the same word as *rhythm;* it is highly convenient to have for the thing meant a name differently spelled from *rhythm,* but that convenience *rhyme* gives us as fully as *rime,* while it has the other advantage of being familiar to everyone.

RHYTHM. 'Flow.' Rhythmless speech or writing is like the flow of liquid from a pipe or tap; it runs with smooth monotony from when it is turned on to when it is turned off, provided it is clear stuff; if it is turbid, the smooth flow is queerly & abruptly checked from time to time, & then resumed. Rhythmic speech or writing is like waves of the sea, moving onward with alternating rise & fall, connected yet separate, like but different, suggestive of some law, too complex for analysis or statement, controlling the relations between wave & wave, waves & sea, phrase & phrase, phrases & speech. In other words, live speech, said or written, is rhythmic, & rhythmless speech is at the best dead.

rhythmic(al). Both forms are too common to justify any expectation of either's disappearance; yet there is no marked differentiation. What there is perhaps amounts to this, that *-al* is the more ordinary pedestrian term, & therefore better suited for the merely classifying use (*& other rhythmical devices:* cf. *so rhythmic a style*).

riant (Fr. laughing, cheerfully gay), though it is completely naturalized, having been used as an English word since the 17th c., is still chiefly a literary and artistic word (*riant landscapes; wild and riant profusion*). Pron. rī'ant.

ribbon, riband. The second is now archaic in general senses but is still used occasionally for the decorative or honorary ribbon.

riches. *But the promoters will certainly not need to go back to ancient history for it; they will have* an embarrassment of riches *from the immediate past.* See GALLICISMS.

rickety, NOT *-tty.*

ricochet. The spelling, accent, & pronunciation recommended are: *ricochet* (rĭk'oshā); *ricocheted* (rĭk'oshād); *ricochet-*

ing (rĭkoshā'ing).

rid. There is no clear line between *rid* & *ridded* in past inflections, but the prevailing usage is: past tense, *ridded* (*When he ridded,* sometimes *rid, the world of his presence*); p.p. as active, *ridded* (*We have ridded,* or *rid, the land of robbers*); p.p. as passive, *rid* (*I thought myself well rid,* rarely *ridded, of him*).

rider (=corollary). A clause tacked on to a bill at a late stage with some addition or restriction or other alteration; a corollary naturally arising out of a more general principle; a problem soluble by means of some principle & used to test a learner's grasp of it.

right. (1) *Right away* in the sense 'at once,' 'without delay,' originated in US, & is still far from comfortable in England. (Webster lists it as US colloq.) Other colloq. uses: right *here & now,* right *across the way* (=exactly); *he's said so* right along (=continuously); *blows fell right & left* (=in every direction); *set things to rights* (=in order); *everything's* all right (=in order, satisfactory); right *you are,* all right, right oh! (=approval, acquiescence); right *smart* (=quite, dial.). But *Your opinions are all* right (=correct, true) is standard. See ALL RIGHT. (2) *Right, righten,* vv. *Right* is the established verb; *righten* was 'rare' when the OED was compiled; it is now archaic or dial. (3) *Right*(*ly*), advs. *Right* in the senses 'properly,' 'correctly,' is being squeezed out by the tendency to UNIDIOMATIC -LY. It is well, before using *rightly* in these senses, to consider whether *right* is not better, though usage is much less decided than with many alternative adverbs of the kind. In all the following types *rightly* is possible, but *right* is better: *He guessed or answered* right (cf. *He* rightly *guessed that it was safe* or *answered twenty-seven*); *You did* right *in apologizing* or *to apologize* (cf. *You rightly apologized*); *If I remember* right (cf. *I cannot* rightly *recollect*); *I hope we are going* right; *If it was tied* right, *it will hold; Teach him to hold his pen* right. (4) The right bank of a river is on the right-hand side of one looking down stream. The right side of a stage is to the left of the audience.

righteous. Pron. rī'chus.

rigmarole. So spelled.

rigo(u)r. In US (usually) *-or,* Brit. *-our.* But *rigorous* for both, and *rigor mortis.*

rilievo. (It.) Relief; *alto-rilievo,* high relief, &c.

rime. See RHYME 2.

ring, v. Both *rang* & *rung* are still used for the past, but *rang* is much commoner, & likely to become universal. The verb from the noun *ring* (=encircle &c.) makes *ringed,* past & p.p.

riot makes *rioted, -ting.*

riposte. The noun (in fencing, a quick return thrust) is fairly well at home in its transf. sense, a counterstroke, retort; the verb is less usual & an English equivalent is recommended. Pron. as Eng., rĭpōst'.

Rip Van Winkle. So spelled (NOT *van*) by Washington Irving.

rise. (1) The noun meaning increase in wages is properly *rise* but often *raise* (colloq.) in

US. (2) *Rise to the occasion* &c. WRONG: *It is hoped that the Joint Committee will* rise equal to *the occasion, & give India a constitution which . . .* Either *rise to* or *be equal to;* see CAST-IRON IDIOM.

risible. Pron. rĭz′ĭbl. The word has nearly perished except in the special sense 'of laughter' (*risible faculty, nerves, muscles,* &c.). To use it in the sense 'ridiculous,' 'ludicruous,' correct enough, but now unfamiliar, is a REVIVAL not to be recommended. See LITERARY CRITICS' WORDS.

risqué, verging on indecency, suggestive of impropriety. The fem. is *risquée,* but is seldom used.

rival, v. US usually *-led, -ling;* Brit. *-lled* &c.

rive. Past *rived;* p.p. *riven,* rarely *rived.* The word now occurs most often in the passive, *riven.*

rivet has *-eted, -eting, -eter.*

roast. (1) The use of the p.p. *roast* is very narrowly limited; *roast beef* or *lamb,* but *roasted coffee berries* or *cheeks; a roast joint,* but *a well-roasted joint; is better roasted than boiled; should certainly be roasted.* (2) For *rule the roast,* see RULE.

robot. An automaton. (From Karl Capek's play, *R.U.R.*) Pron. rō′bot.

robustious. One of the words whose continued existence depends upon a quotation (*Hamlet* III, ii. 10): *O! it offends me to the soul to see a robustious periwig-pated fellow tear a passion to tatters.*

rococo. (Art): 'rockwork.' This & *baroque* are epithets applied, sometimes indifferently, sometimes with the distinction noted below, to tendencies prevailing in the architecture & furniture of the late 17th & early 18th c. in France & imitated elsewhere, esp. in Germany & Italy. Departure from the normal or expected, incongruous combinations, bristling surface, profuse ornament, strange or broken curves or lines. The distinction referred to is that rococo is regarded as a form taken by baroque when it aimed no longer at astounding the spectator with the marvelous, but rather at amusing him with the ingenious.

rodeo. Rōdā′ō is the older (correct) pronunciation, but rō′dēō has now almost displaced it in US.

rodomontade, NOT *rho-.* Boastful, boasting, to boast. (From Rodomente, in *Orlando Furioso.*) Pron. -tād′.

role, rôle. Though the word is etymologically the same as *roll,* meaning the roll of MS. that contained an actor's part, the differentiation is too useful to be sacrificed by spelling always *roll.* Italics and accent no longer necessary.

roman numerals. I=1, V=5, X=10, L=50, D=500, M=1000. A bar over a letter multiplies it by 1000: $\overline{\text{M}}$=1 million. Roman IV=4, LV=55.

Rome makes *Romish.*

rondeau, rondel. (Poetry): 'round.' Poems of fixed form (named as ending where they began) with the common characteristics that the opening word, words, line, or two lines, recur at stated places, & that all rhymes are set by the first two different endings. In a *rondeau,* which is of 13 lines exclusive of refrain, the first half line or less recurs as refrain after the eighth & the last lines. In a *rondeau of Villon,* which is of 10 lines, the similar refrain is after the sixth & the last. In a *rondel,* which is of 14 or 13 lines according as it ends with a refrain of the first two or only the first, the first two lines recur after the sixth, & the first two or the first only at the end. The word *roundel* is, as ordinarily used, the English for *rondeau* or *rondel,* either or both. But it is also applied to a meter of Swinburne's, of 9 lines exclusive of refrain, with a refrain of the rondeau kind after the third & the last lines.

rondo. Pl. *-os.*

röntgen, roentgen. Of or pertaining to X rays. After Wilhelm Konrad Röntgen, Ger. physicist, 1845–1923, their discoverer. Pron. US rûnt′gen, Brit. rŭ′ntyen. Sometimes capitalized.

roomful. Pl. *-ls.*

Roosevelt. Pron. Rō′zevelt.

root (1) Pron. rōōt, NOT rŏŏt. (2) (Philol., Gram.) Roots are the ultimate elements of language not admitting of analysis. In the word *unhistorically, un-, -ly, -al, -ic, -tor,* can all be set aside as successive affixes modifying in recognized ways the meaning of what each was added to. There remains *HIS,* which would be called the root if *unhistorically* were an isolated word; investigation shows that the same element, with phonetic variations that are not arbitrary, is present in many other words, e.g. in English *wit,* in the Latin-derived *vision,* & in the Greek-derived *idea;* & that the Indo-European or Aryan root is *VID,* with the sense *sight* or *knowledge.* Cf. STEM.

root, rout (poke about). The second is an 'irregular variant of' the first.

rope makes *-pable, -py.*

rosary, -ery (rose garden). The first is the old word (from 15th c.), direct from Latin *rosarium.* The second is a 19th-c. formation made presumably, from *rose+-ery,* by someone not aware that *rosary* has this sense. *Rose garden* or *bed* is recommended for ordinary use, & *rosary* for verse.

Rosicrucians, or Brethren of the Rosy Cross, much talked of in the 17th c., paid homage by their name not to anything symbolized by *cross* or *rose,* but to an alleged 15th-c. founder named Rosenkreuz (=cross of roses). The Rosicrucians were 'moral & religious reformers, & utilized the technicalities of chemistry (alchemy), & the sciences generally, to make known their opinions, there being a flavor of mysticism or occultism promotive of inquiry & suggestive of hidden meanings discernible or discoverable only by adepts' (Enc. Brit.).

rosin is by origin merely a form of *resin* changed in sound & spelling; but the two are now so far differentiated that *resin* is usual for the liquid in or taken from the tree, & as the general chemical term for substances having certain qualities, while *rosin* denotes the distilled solid. *Rosin* makes *rosined, -iny.*

roster. Though US dictionaries are almost unanimous for rŏster, the army, which is the chief user of the word, says rōster; & Skeat remarks: 'The *o* is properly long: pron. roast-er.'

rostrum. Pron. rŏs′-. Pl., in the orignal sense (ship's beak), usually *-ra;* in the secondary sense (pulpit or platform), *-rums* or *-ra.*

rota(to)ry. There is no important difference in meaning either essential or customary, & therefore the short *rotary* should be preferred & *rotatory* avoided as a SUPERFLUOUS WORD.

rote is now used only in the phrase *by rote,* i.e. from memory, by heart (usually without any understanding).

rotten makes *-nness.* For *something rotten in the state of Denmark,* see IRRELEVANT ALLUSION.

rough(en), vv. (1) The intransitive verb (=become rough) is always *roughen,* except that the addition of *up* occasionally enables *rough* to serve (*the sea, his bristles, its scales, their tempers, began to rough up*). (2) In the simple transitive senses also (=make rough), *roughen* is usual, but if *up* is added *rough* is preferred, & *rough* by itself is the word for arming horseshoes against slipping (*rough the shoes* or *the horse*). (3) In the other transitive senses of to treat roughly or shape roughly (the latter usually with adverbs, *in, off, out*), the verb is *rough: rough a horse*=break it in; *rough a calf*=harden it by exposure; *rough a person*=abuse or maltreat him; *rough in the outlines; rough off timber; rough out a scheme; rough a lens=shape* without polishing it. (4) To *take things in the rough* is to *rough it.*

round, adv. & prep. (often *around* in US). Brit. usage: *Summer comes round; he turned short round; a room hung round with portraits; station them round the field,* &c. See AROUND.

roundel, roundelay. Not, like *rondeau* & *rondel,* precise terms. *Roundel* is sometimes used loosely for *rondeau-or-rondel; roundelay* is defined in the OED as 'A short simple song with a refrain.'

rouse is usually preferred in the literal use: *We were roused at daybreak by the whistle of a train. Aroused* is often preferred with abstracts: *This aroused my fears.* See AROUSE.

rout (=poke about), var. of ROOT.

route (usually pron. rōōt) is pronounced, in military phrases such as *route-march, column of route,* rowt.

routine makes *routinism, -ist* (rōō tēn′-).

-r, -rr-. Monosyllables ending in *-r* double it before suffixes beginning with vowels if the sound preceding it is a single vowel, but not if it is a diphthong or a double vowel: *barring* but *nearing, stirred* but *chaired, currish* but *boorish.* Words of more than one syllable follow the rule for monosyllables if their last syllable is accented (with the exception noted below), but otherwise do not double the *r; preferred* but *proffered, interring* but *entering, abhorrent* but *motoring.* Exception: *confer, infer, prefer, refer,* & *transfer,* though accented on the last, give adjs. in *-erable,* & shift the accent to the first syllable: *pref′erable* &c.

rub, n., in the sense hindrance, obstruction, of a non-material source, remains in living English only through Hamlet's 'To sleep, perchance to dream; Ay, there's the rub.'

Rubaiyat. Pron. rōō bī′yät′ (in US popularly rōō′bīyät′). The word in Arabic means *quatrain.*

Rubicon. A stream in Italy; *cross* or *pass the Rubicon,* to take an irrevocable, decisive step (as Caesar before the war with Pompey).

rubricate. To mark or distinguish with red, as the title of a book; to make rubrics (orig. written or pointed in red).

rucksack. Usually rŭk′săk in US; Ger. (& Brit.) rŏŏk′săk.

ruffed grouse (Bonasa umbellus) is called *partridge* in the north (US), *pheasant* in the south, and *birch partridge* in Canada.

ruination is not, like *flirtation, floatation,* & *botheration,* a hybrid derivative, being regularly formed from *ruinate;* but it now has the effect of a slangy emphatic lengthening of the noun *ruin.* This is only because *ruinate,* which was common in serious use 1550–1700, is no longer heard; but the result is that *ruination* is better avoided except in facetious contexts.

rule. (1) *Rule of three* & *rule of thumb* should not be hyphened except when used as compound adjs. (2) *Rule the roast* (*roost*). The OED gives no countenance to *roost,* & does not even recognize that the phrase ever takes that form; but most unliterary persons say *roost* & not *roast.* Writers should take warning, at any rate, that *rule the roast* is the orthodox spelling, & that when they have written it the compositor must be watched.

rumo(u)r. US usually *-or;* Brit. *-our.*

run. In the sense to manage (*run a hotel, the administration, a business,* &c.) orig. US but now often used also in Brit.

rune. (Lit): 'secret.' In the plural, the letters of the earliest Teutonic alphabet, used especially by Scandinavians & Anglo-Saxons, & developed perhaps in the 2nd or 3rd c. by modifying Roman or Greek letters to facilitate the carving of inscriptions. In the singular, a name given to certain Finnish (& sometimes incorrectly to old Scandinavian) poems or their cantos.

ruse. Stratagem, trick. Pron. rōōz.

S

's. 1. *For art's sake, for goodness' sake, for conscience' sake;* see SAKE.

2. *Achilles', Jones's, Jesus', St. James's,* &c.; see POSSESSIVE PUZZLES.

3. For *England's* &c. & *of England* &c., see 's INCONGRUOUS, & PERSONIFICATION 1.

4. *To use a word of Coleridge's* is the idiom, NOT *of Coleridge;* see OUT OF THE FRYING PAN.

Sabbatic(al). The short form is still a var. of the (Jewish) religious use; the longer one is established in the academic *sabbatical year* or *leave.*

saber, -bre. The first is usual in US, the second Brit.

saccharin(e). *Saccharin* is

more usual for the noun & *saccharine* for the adj.

sacerdotal. Pron. săs-.

sacrifice makes *-ceable*. For *the supreme* &c. *sacrifice*, see STOCK PATHOS. Pron. -ĭs, not -īs.

sacrilegious. So spelled. It is often misspelled from confusion with *religious*. *Sacrilege* orig. meant the crime of stealing sacred things (*sacer*, sacred; *legere*, to gather).

sacrosanct. Orig. 'most sacred.' Now 'inviolable,' often ironically.

sadism. A form of sexual perversion exhibiting a gratification from cruelty. Popularly & loosely used of any abnormal delight in cruelty. Properly pron. sä'dĭsm (from Fr. *sadisme*, after Count de Sade, 1740–1814); often, esp. US, să- or sā-.

saga. (Lit.): 'story.' 'Any of the narrative compositions in prose that were written in Iceland or Norway during the Middle Ages; in English use often applied spec. to those which embody the traditional history of Icelandic families or the kings of Norway' (OED). Also (incorrectly) used of historical or heroic legend as distinguished from authentic history and intentional fiction (e.g. Indian sagas &c.). Hence transf., an account of a series of adventures; a series of connected books giving the history of a family (*The Forsyte Saga*).

sagacious, sagacity, mean acuteness of mental discernment, shrewdness (no relation to *sage*=wise). *Sagacity in money matters; sage counsel. Sagacious* & *sage* may be applied to the same things, but the distinction should be borne in mind.

sage. For *the sage of Chelsea* (Carlyle), see SOBRIQUETS.

said. 1. (*The*) *said.* In legal documents, phrases like 'the said Robinson,' 'said dwelling-house,' are traditional. Jocose imitation of this use (*regaling themselves on half-pints at* the said *village hostelries*), no longer indulged in by writers not desperately anxious to relieve conscious dullness, is to be classed with WORN-OUT HUMOR.

2. *Said he, said N.* or *M.*, placed after the words spoken, is entirely unobjectionable; the ingenuity displayed by some writers (see 3) in avoiding what they needlessly fear will bore their readers is superfluous. But two points should be noticed: the sprightliness of *Said N.* or *M.* placed before instead of after the words said, & the ponderousness of *had said* &c. instead of plain *said*, are alike intolerable. (*Said a Minister: 'American interests are not large enough in Morocco to induce us to . . .'/'I won't plot anything extra against Tom,' had said Isaac.*)

3. Substitutes for *said he.* Many verbs, such as *whispered, cried, shouted, asked, answered, continued, groaned,* imply or suggest the use of words, & are naturally used after what is uttered, as equivalents of *said* with an adverb. With these (*asked Jones* &c.) to relieve the monotony of *said he,* no writer need be afraid of boring; he may safely abstain from the very tiresome MANNERISM initiated perhaps by Meredith (*'Ah,' fluted Fenellan*) & now staled by imitation: *'Hand on heart?' she doubted./'Need any help?'*

husked A./'They're our best revenue,' defended B./'I know his kind,' fondly remembered C. See also INVERSION.

sail. PLAIN *sailing* (NOT *plane*). By the side of *sailor,* the normal agent noun *sailer* exists for use in such contexts as *She (ship) is a slow* sailer.

Saint. In US usually abbr. *St.,* Pl. SS. *St. Agnes's Eve* (20 Jan.); *St. George's Cross* (the Greek cross): *St. James's Palace; St. Vitus's dance* (chorea) (OED *St. Vitus'*). Brit. often S. & *Sts.*

saith. Archaic 3rd person sing. of *say.* Pron. sĕth.

sake. *For God's sake, for mercy's sake, for Jones's sake, for Phyllis's sake;* but when the enclosed word is both a common noun & one whose possessive is a syllable longer than its subjective, the *s* of the possessive is not used; an apostrophe is often, but not always, written; *for conscience sake, for goodness' sake, for peace' sake.* (Modern usage in US prefers the apostrophe: *conscience' sake.*)

salable, salability. So spelled.

salad days (one's raw youth) is one of the phrases whose existence depends on single passages (*Ant. & Cleop.* I. v. 73: 'My salad days, when I was green in judgment, cold in blood'). Whether the point is that youth, like salad, is raw, or that salad is highly flavored & youth loves high flavors, or that innocent herbs are youth's food as milk is babes' & meat is men's, few of those who use the phrase could perhaps tell us; if so, it is fitter for parrots' than for human speech.

salamander, *gnome, sylph,* & *nymph* are spirits of fire, earth, air, & water, in Paracelsus's system.

Salic, Salique. In the most frequent use, i.e. in the name of the law excluding females from dynastic succession, 'still often spelt *Salique* & pronounced salēk' (OED).

saline. Pron. sā'līn.

salmon. The *l* is not pronounced.

Salome. Pron. (Eng.) salō'mē; the Fr. opera, sȧ'lō mā'.

salon. Reception hall of great (Fr.) house: a reception esp. for celebrities; a hall for the exhibition of art; (Cap.) the annual exhibition of living artists' work in Paris. *Saloon,* the Eng. equivalent, has most of its meanings; *saloon* in the sense 'drinking bar' is US only (Brit., 'pub').

Salonica. Pron. sălonī'ka or -ē'ka, NOT salŏ'nĭka.

salubrious, salutary. *Salubrious* (conducive to health) is used esp. of air, climates, places, lit. & fig.: *Religions, like winds, are not equally salubrious. Salutary* in non-technical use (conducive to well-being, beneficial) is often used as *wholesome: a salutary dread of guns.*

salve. The noun & verb meaning remedy are pronounced sahv. The verb meaning save or rescue is an entirely separate one, a BACK-FORMATION from *salvage,* pronounced sălv. Both verbs make *-vable.* The Latin word meaning *Hail!* is pronounced să lvē.

salvo. Pl. *-os.*

same. 1. *Same* or *the same,* in the sense the aforesaid thing(s) or person(s), as a substitute for a pronoun (*it, him, her, them, they*) is one of the usages whose effect is discussed in ILLITERACIES. It has the peculiarity that it occurs chiefly in writing, not often in speech, & yet is avoided by all who have any skill in writing. As the working man puts on his Sunday clothes to be photographed, so the unliterary adorns himself with '(the) same' when he is to appear in print; each seems bent on giving the worst possible impression of himself. In all the extracts below, the writers would have shown themselves much more at their ease if they had been content with *it, them,* or other pronoun. *Shops filled to the doors with all kinds of merchandise & people eager to acquire* the same./*Again, the doctors declaim against patients by contract, while they largely themselves set up the machinery for carrying on* the same (the system?)./*If not directly, at least through the official presence of their representatives, or by a chosen delegation of* the same.

2. Constr. with *that* or other relative pronoun or adv. clause. RIGHT: *He defends it on the* same *grounds* that *he would defend 'Lycidas.'* With ellipsis of rel., also permissible: *This is the* same *book*‸*my brother gave me last year.* Ellipsis of both rel. & copulative, in careless use only: *It is regarded with the* same *interest*‸*accorded in Europe to its relative* (supply *that is*). The adv. use of *same,* as in *You'll never think* the same *of me again,* is colloq.

Samson. So spelled in Judges, and as a generic name.

samurai. In Jap. feudal system, gentry or lesser nobility; member of military caste. Pron. să′mōōrī.

sanat-, sanit-. The chief words as they should be spelled are: *sanatorium,* a healing place; *sanatory,* curative; *sanitary,* conducive to wholesomeness; *sanitation,* securing of wholesomeness; *sanitarium* is an equivalent of *sanatorium* and is more usual in US. *Sanitorium, sanatarium,* & *sanitory* are wrong.

sanction, n. The popular sense (permission, authorization, countenance, consent) has so far prevailed over the more original senses still current especially in Law & Ethics that it is worth while to draw attention to these. The *sanction of a rule* or *a system* is the consideration that operates to enforce or induce compliance with it: *The death penalty is the* sanction *of the law against murder.* The OED quotes from T. Fowler: 'Physical sanctions are the pleasures & pains which follow naturally on the observance or violation of physical laws, the sanctions employed by society are praise & blame, the moral sanctions . . . are . . . the approval & disapproval of conscience; lastly, the religious sanctions are either the fear of future punishment, & the hope of future reward, or, to the higher religious sense, simply the love of God, & the dread of displeasing Him.' In this sense, penalty to enforce compliance, *the economic sanctions* applied by the League of Nations.

sand-blind. A defect of the eyes; purblind. Its modern existence depends on one passage (*M. of V.* II, ii. 35–80), & it can rank only as an ARCHAISM.

sang-froid. 'Cold blood.' Composure, coolness in disturbing circumstances. Pron. säɴ frwä′. But see FRENCH WORDS.

sanguine is in danger of being superseded by the very inferior OPTIMISTIC. Candor, however, compels the admission that *optimistic, optimism,* & *optimist* have the advantage in mechanical convenience over *sanguine, sanguineness,* & *sanguine person.*

Sanhedrim, -in. 'The incorrect form *sanhedrin* . . . has always been in England [from the 17th c.] the only form in popular use' (OED).

sans. (1) As an English word, pron. sănz. For *The poet whom he met* sans *hat & coat one four-o'clock-in-the-morning,* see WORN-OUT HUMOR. (2) *Sans serif,* printing type with no serifs (Brit., *sanserif*); pron. sănz. (3) *Sans-souci,* without worry, care free, and other Fr. phrases, pron. as French (säɴ).

Santa Claus. Orig. US; *Santa* is not fem. but comes from a Dutch dialect form of *Saint* (*Ni*)*cholas.* The use of *Santa* alone (or *Santy*) is US, not Brit.

sapid, unlike its negative *insipid,* is a merely LITERARY WORD.

sapient. Chiefly a LITERARY WORD, & usually ironical (of fancied sagacity). Pron. sā′.

Sapphic, Sappho. Pron. săf-.

sarcasm ('flesh-tearing') does not necessarily involve irony, & irony has often no touch of sarcasm. But irony, or the use of expressions conveying different things according as they are interpreted, is so often made the vehicle of sarcasm, or the utterance of things designed to hurt the feelings, that in popular use the two are much confused. The essence of sarcasm is the intention of giving pain by (ironical or other) bitter words. See also IRONY, & HUMOR.

sarcophagus. Pl. *-i,* or *-uses.*

sardine (stone; Rev. iv. 3). Pron. sȧr′dīn. ('Prob. erron.; RV gives sardius [sard]'; COD.)

sardonic. 'Bitter' is the essential element. See HUMOR for some rough distinction between this, *cynical, sarcastic,* &c. Novelese: *The hollow laugh or at least the* sardonic grin *that is a sine qua non of every self-respecting poisoner.* (*A sardonic smile,* yes—but *grin?*)

sartorial. See PEDANTIC HUMOR.

Satanic(al). The *-al* form is now rare.

satiate. Adj. (now rare). Pron. sā′shĭ ȧt; v. -āt. The verb makes *-tiable.*

satiety. Pron. satī′ĭtĭ.

satire. 'Poetic "medley" aimed at vices or follies' (Rom. Antiq.). For rough distinction from some synonyms, see HUMOR.

satiric(al). The senses *addicted to, intending, good at, marked by, satire* are peculiar to the long form (*a satirical rogue; you are pleased to be satirical; with satirical comments; a satirical glance*). In the merely classifying sense, of or belonging to satire (the — poems of Pope; the Latin — writers), either form may be used, but *-ic* is commoner. This differentiation might well be hastened by deliberate support; but the line of demarcation between the two groups is not always clear.

satiric, satyric. The two spellings represent two different & unconnected words; *satyric,* which is in learned or literary use only, means of satyrs, & especially, in *satyric drama* (a form of Greek play), having a satyr chorus.

satrap. Pron. sā′trăp.

saturate makes *-rable.*

Saturday. See FRIDAY.

Saturnalia. The word was originally plural, but, as being the name of a festival, is now construed, both in literal & metaphorical use, more often as sing. (*the* Saturnalia was, or *were, at hand; now follows* a saturnalia *of crime*). When a real plural is required (*the sack of Magdeburg, the French Revolution, & other such* saturnalia *of slaughter*), the form is *-ia,* NOT *-ias.*

satyr. Pron. să′ter. Woodland deity, half-beast, half-man in form. See FAUN for distinctions.

satyric. See SATIRIC.

Sault (*Ste. Marie*). Pron. sōō. (A 17th-c. colonial spelling of Fr. *saut*—pron. sō—a waterfall or rapid.)

savant. A man of learning or science. Pron. savăɴ′, or anglicized, săvănt′.

save (except). 1. *Save & except* is a stock PLEONASM that is fortunately losing its popularity. 2. Though nearly everyone uses *except* or *but,* not *save,* in speaking, & perhaps everyone in thinking, & though the natural or dominant word *except* is neither undignified nor inferior in clearness, mediocre writers have made up their minds that it is not good enough for print, & very mistakenly prefer to translate it, irrespective of context, into *save; save* is becoming a FORMAL WORD, like the reporter's invariable *proceed* for *go.* Does anyone not a writer—& does any good writer—think that the substitution of the formal *save* for the natural *except* or *but* in the following sentences has improved them? *The handful of ship's officers could do nothing* save *summon the aid of a detachment of the Civic Guard./One marked trait of Dr. Griffith John has been displayed in his refusal to leave China* save *at long intervals./There can be no question,* save *in the minds possibly of fanatics,* &c.

save, v. (1) *Save face* (avoid being humiliated or disgraced) originated in the English community in China, after the Chinese 'lose face.' So *face-saving.* (2) *Save the mark* (with variants *God save* &c.) is a stylistic toy, of which no one can be said to know, though different people make different guesses at, the original meaning. The OED's description of it, as it now survives, is: 'In modern literary use (after some of the examples in Shakespeare), an expression of indignant scorn appended to a quoted expression or to a statement of fact.'

Saviour. The *-our* is usually retained in US (always in Brit.) when the reference is to Christ. Otherwise US *savior.*

savory, the herb, so spelled US & Brit. The adj., Brit. *savoury.*

Savoyard. A native of Savoy —but more importantly in US & Brit., having to do with Gilbert & Sullivan, whose works were first produced at the Savoy Theatre, London.

saw. Proverb or maxim; now usually combined with *old* or *ancient;* often suggesting that the saying is sententious or pedantic.

saw, v., has p.p. *sawed,* & (US rarely) *sawn.*

SAXONISM is a name for the attempt to raise the proportion borne by the originally & etymologically English words in our speech to those that come from alien sources. The Saxonist forms new derivatives from English words to displace established words of similar meaning but Latin descent; revives obsolete or archaic English words for the same purpose; allows the genealogy of words to decide for him which is the better of two synonyms. Examples of the first kind are FOREWORD (earliest OED quotation, 1842) for *preface, bodeful* (1813) for *ominous;* of the second, BETTERMENT for *improvement,* HAPPENINGS for *events;* of the third, BELITTLE & *depreciate, love* & *charity* (1 Corinthians xiii, A.V. & R.V.). The wisdom of this nationalism in language—at least in so thoroughly composite a language as English—is very questionable. We may well doubt whether it benefits the language, & that it does not benefit the style of the individual, who may or may not be prepared to sacrifice himself for the public good, is pretty clear. The truth is perhaps that conscious deliberate Saxonism is folly, that the choice or rejection of particular words should depend not on their descent but on considerations of expressiveness, intelligibility, brevity, euphony, or ease of handling, & yet that any writer who becomes aware that the Saxon or native English element in what he writes is small will do well to take the fact as a danger signal. But the way to act on that signal is not to translate his Romance words into Saxon ones; it is to avoid abstract & roundabout & bookish phrasing whenever the nature of the thing to be said does not require it. We can almost see the writer of the following sentence striking out *improvement* (which did not clash with *better* a few words later) & inserting his Saxon *betterment* in its place: *Instead of breaking heads over a* betterment *of Anglo-German relations, it would be better to study British finance.* But *betterment* has no single advantage over *improvement* except its Saxonism.

say. (1) To *have a say* (i.e. voice) *in a matter* has been idiomatic English since 1614 (first quoted in OED). *To have* the *say* is US idiom but not Brit. (2) When modern writers indicate that a character is illiterate by putting in his dialogue 'he ses,' the reader only wonders how else *says* is now pronounced. (Formerly sometimes spelled *sais, sayes,* pron. *sāz,* but now only dial.) (3) For variations on *he said,* see SAID, INVERSION, & MANNERISMS.

saying. 'As the saying is,' or 'goes,' is often used by simple people, speaking or writing, who would fain assure us that the phrase they have allowed to proceed from their lips or pen is by no means typical of their taste in language; no; it only happens to be 'so expressive' that one may surely condescend to it for once. Well, *qui s'excuse s'accuse;* if the rest of their behavior does not secure them from insulting suspicions, certainly the apology will not. See SUPERIORITY.

scalawag. See SCALLYWAG.

scallop, sco-. The spelling is usually with *-a-*, but the pronunciation with -ŏ-. The verb makes *-oping, -oped.*

scallywag, -ala, -alla-. The first is preferred by the OED, but the word is of US origin & Webster gives *scalawag* first.

scan in its non-technical sense means to examine minutely, scrutinize; the sense to look over hastily (*scan the headlines*) is US ('colloq.' Webster).

scant, adj., is a LITERARY WORD, preferred in ordinary contexts to *scanty, small, few, short,* &c. (*The attendance was* so scant *as to suggest that many members must have anticipated the holiday*) only by those who have no sense of incongruity. It survives as a current word, however, in some isolated phrases, as *scant courtesy, scant of breath.*

scarce, adv., used instead of *scarcely,* is a LITERARY WORD.

scarcely. WRONG USES: (1) *Scarcely . . . than.* Scarcely *was the nice new drain finished* than *several of the children sickened with diphtheria.* For this construction, condemned in OED s.v. *than* as erroneous, see HARDLY 2. *Before* or *when* is what should be used instead of *than.* (2) *Not* &c. . . . *scarcely.* We most of us feel safe against even saying 'I don't scarcely know,' with *not* & *scarcely* in hand-to-hand conflict; but, if a little space intervenes, & the negative is disguised, the same absurdity is not very rare in print. *It has been* impossible *to tell the public* scarcely anything *about American naval co-operation with the British.*

scarf. Pl. *-fs* or *-ves.*

scavenge(r), vv. *To scavenge* is a BACK-FORMATION from the n. *scavenger,* the normal verb being *to scavenger. Scavenge,* however, is now much commoner.

scenic. Long *e* (sēnĭk) is better than sĕn-.

scepter, -tre. The first usual US, the second Brit. Pron. sĕp-.

sceptic &c. Brit. so spelled. US, *skeptic,* pron. sk-. *Skeptical* (or *sc-*) is the adj. except in the sense *the skeptic* (or *sc-*) *philosophy.*

schedule. Pron. US skĕd′ūl; Brit. shĕ′dūl.

schema. Plan, outline, diagram; Log., a syllogistic figure; Kantian Philos., general type, essential form. Pron. skē′ma. Pl. *-mata.*

scherzando, scherzo. Pron. skārtsăn′dō, skār′tsō (pl. *-os*).

schism(atic). Pron. sĭ-.

schizo-, combining form meaning cleavage or division. Pron. skĭzo-.

scholar. Though there is no apparent reason why *scholar* or *scholars* should not mean *pupil(s)* at a school, *schoolboy, schoolgirl, school children,* &c., it is not often now so used in US, and never in Brit. The usual modern meanings are 'one who holds a scholarship' (e.g. *Rhodes Scholar*); one engaged in advanced study (*one of the eminent scholars in the field*); one who learns (*an apt scholar*).

scholium. A marginal note, esp. by an ancient grammarian on a classical text. Pl. *-ia.* So *scholiast,* the annotator. Not to be confused with *scolium,* a form of Greek verse, and *sciolist,* a pretender to scholarship (pron. sī′ō lĭst).

school. *There are two schools of thought* (on how to open a can or other trivia) is WORN-OUT HUMOR.

school (of fish &c.), **shoal.** The two words are etymologically one, & equally unconnected with the ordinary word *school;* both are also current, & without difference of sense. The form *school* has the disadvantage of being liable to be taken for a figurative use of the other *school.*

schoolhouse, schoolboy, schoolbook, &c. In US all usually single words (except *school board*). In Brit., many are written as single words, but *school-teacher, school-book* hyphened.

sciagraphy &c., ski-. In Brit. usually *sci-* (pron. usually sī- sometimes skī), US *ski-* (pron. skī-).

science & art. Science knows, art does; a science is a body of connected facts, an art is a set of directions; the facts of science (errors not being such) are the same for all people, circumstances, & occasions; the directions of art vary with the artist & the task. But, as there is much traffic between science & art, &, especially, art is often based on science, the distinction is not always clear; *the art of self-defense,* & *the boxer's science*—are they the same or different? The OED, on *science* 'contradistinguished from *art,*' says: 'The distinction as commonly apprehended is that a science is concerned with theoretic truth, & an art with methods for effecting certain results. Sometimes, however, the term *science* is extended to denote a department of practical work which depends on the knowledge & conscious application of principles; an art, on the other hand, being understood to require merely knowledge of traditional rules & skill acquired by habit.'

scilicet, usually shortened to *scil.* or *sc.,* is Latin (*scire licet,* you may know) for 'to wit.' It is not so often misused as *e.g.* & *i.e.,* not having been popularized to the same extent. Its function is to introduce: (a) a more intelligible or definite substitute, sometimes the English, for an expression already used: *The policy of the I.W.W.* (sc. *Independent Workers of the World*); *The Holy Ghost as Paraclete* (scil. *advocate*); (b) a word &c. that was omitted in the original as unnecessary, but is thought to require specifying for the present audience: *Eye hath not seen, nor ear heard* (sc. *the intent of God*).

scintilla. Spark, a minute particle. Also fig. (*not a scintilla of evidence*). Pron. sĭntĭl′*a.* Pl. *-lae.*

scion. Hort., a graft, a shoot or slip for grafting. Transf., a descendant (*scion of a royal family*). US horticulturists and nurserymen use CION. Both pron. sī′*un.*

score, n. (=20). *Four score,* but *scores of people.*

score, v., makes *-rable.* The fig. use=censure, scold severely (*He scored the reporters for their rudeness*) is US.

scoria (dross, slag) is sing., pl. *-iae;* but, as the meaning of the singular & of the plural is much the same (cf. *ash* & *ashes*), it is no wonder that the singular is sometimes followed by a plural verb (WRONG: *The* scoria were *still hot* &c.), or that a false singular *scorium* is on record.

scot. *Scot-free,* orig. without being taxed; now usually *unharmed, unpunished.*

scotch. This verb owes its currency entirely to the sentence in *Macbeth*—'We have scotch'd the snake, not kill'd it.' The contrast is between *scotching* (or disabling) & *killing* & is understood to be implied even when it is not expressed. *Scotch,* then, can say in six letters & in one syllable 'put temporarily out of action but not destroy'—a treasure, surely, that will be jealously guarded by the custodians of the language, viz. those who write. Although US dictionaries include in their definition 'to crush, stamp out,' *finally* or *entirely* with *scotch* should be, in view of the history of the word, an impossibility; but it is now often met with. WRONG: *It is well that this legend should be* finally scotched./ *The idea is so preposterous that by the time this is in print it may be* definitely scotched./*We hope the proposal for a Government news service is* finally scotched *by the debate.*

Scotch, Scots, Scottish. (1) (as adjs.): The third represents most closely the original form, the first and second being the contractions of it usual in England & Scotland respectively. *Scottish* is still both good English (esp. in formal contexts) & good Scotch. Thus, *Scottish literature, a Scottish lawyer, Scottish emigrants* (but *Scotch tweed, a Scotch terrier, Scotch whiskey,* & *Scots law*). (2) (as nn.): For the name of the Scotch dialect, the noun *Scottish* is little used; *Scotch* is the English noun, & *Scots* the usual Scotch noun.

Scot, Scots(wo)man, Scotch(wo)man. In England and US the third forms are used by nature, the first sometimes for brevity or for poetical or rhetorical or jocular effect, & the second in compliment to a Scotch hearer, *Scots-* being the prevalent form now used by Scotch people. *The* Scotch *have always been good gardeners; a* Scot *by birth; he is a* Scotsman *or* Scotchman *or a* Scot.

Scotticism. Idiom peculiar to the Scottish people.

scream, screech, shriek. The first is the dominant word for a cry uttered, under emotion, at a higher pitch than that which is normal with the utterer. Those who wish to intensify the pitch & the emotion substitute *shriek;* those who wish either to add the notion of uncanny effect, or to make fun of the matter, substitute *screech.*

screw *your courage to the sticking place* (NOT *point*) (*Macbeth* I. vii. 60); see MISQUOTATION.

scrimmage, scru-. *Scrimmage* is used in US football; the form with *-u-* is preferred in Rugby (Brit.); that with *-i-* in more general uses.

scrupulous should have its claims considered before the gallicism METICULOUS is substituted for it.

scull, skull. The single-handed oar has *sc-,* the cranium *sk-.*

sculptress. An accepted FEMININE DESIGNATION since the 17th c.

sculpture is a verb as well as a noun (*sculp* is slang). *It was sculptured in marble.*

Scylla. Six-headed monster living on a rock, opposite *Charybdis,* the whirlpool, in the Straits of Messina (*Odyssey,* XII); hence one of two dangers, neither of which can be avoided without encountering the other. (Both personified as female monsters.)

sea. *Sea change. Suffer a sea change* is from Ariel's song in *The Tempest:* 'Of his bones are coral made . . ./Nothing of him that doth fade/But doth suffer a sea-change/In to something rich and strange.' It is one of the most importunate & intrusive of IRRELEVANT ALLUSIONS & HACKNEYED PHRASES. *We hope that the Prime Minister will on this occasion stick to his guns, & see that his policy does not for the third or fourth time* suffer a sea change *when its execution falls into the hands of his colleagues.*

Seabees. From *Construction Battalion* (C.B.) of US Navy, est. 1941 to build airfields, landing facilities, &c. in combat areas. So spelled.

seagreen incorruptible (Robespierre). See SOBRIQUETS.

seamstress, semps-. Use *seams-;* the second is a variant.

séance. Pron. sā′äns′. The accent is retained in US, often omitted in Brit.

sear, sere. OED gives *sear* for the nouns (part of gunlock, mark of burn), & for the verb (burn); *sere* for the adj. (withered). US prefers *sear* for all, with *sere* as a variant of the adj.

secede. So spelled.

second. 1. *Second chamber,* in a Parliament, the upper house, which does not initiate (important) legislation.

2. *Second class. I sent it second class. Second-class mail* (US).

3. *Second(-)hand.* The *second hand* of a watch is so written in US (Brit. *second-hand*). The adj., meaning not new or original, & the adv., meaning not for or in first use, are best written as one word (*dispenses secondhand clothing* or *information; always buys secondhand*); & the phrase (*heard only at second hand*) should be two words, unhyphened.

4. *Second-rate,* adj. Inferior, mediocre (usually vaguer and more depreciatory than *second-class*). *A second-rate performance.*

5. *Second sight.* Two words unhyphened.

secondary education is that which comes after the primary or elementary but before that of the universities.

secretive. The OED & ACD give only sĭkrē′tĭv; Webster gives that first but adds that sē′krĭtĭv is often heard when the meaning is 'fond of secrets.' COD gives sē′krĭtĭv first.

secure. *Secure* in the sense 'succeed in getting' implies that the object is something coveted, or competed for. *There is nothing she would not do to secure her end.* It is not a syn. for simple *get.*

seduce makes *-cible.*

see, bishopric, diocese. A *bishopric* is the rank belonging to a bishop; a *diocese* is the district administered by a bishop; a *see* is (the chair that symbolizes) a bishop's authority over a particular diocese. A *bishopric is conferred on,* a *diocese* is *committed to,* a *see* is *filled by,* such & such a man. *My predecessors in the see; All the clergy of the diocese; Scheming for a bishopric.*

seeing is a quasi-conj.=*considering, inasmuch as. Which isn't to be wondered at,* seeing *that he has just finished six weeks at . . . ;* Seeing *that there is no alternative . . .* (Cf. *excepting, providing, considering, supposing,* &c.)

seek is often used as FORMAL WORD for *try, look for.*

seem. 1. Pleonasms. *These*

conclusions, it seems *to me,* appear *to be reached naturally.* Such absurdities are not uncommon with *seem;* see PLEONASM 4, & HAZINESS.

2. The proper combinations are: *He seems to know what he means. He seems to have known what he meant (though I thought he didn't at the time). He seemed to know what he meant (though I suspect now he didn't).* For confusion between *seem(s) to have been* & *seemed to be,* very common, see PERFECT INFINITIVE 3. WRONG: *Lady Austen's fashionable friends occasioned no embarrassment; they* seemed to have preferred *some more fashionable place for summering in, for they* are *not again spoken of;* here *are* shows that *seemed* is wrong; read *seem.*

3. *To my* &c. *seeming* has been good English in its time; its modern representative is *to my* &c. *thinking,* & *to his seeming* will pass only in archaic writing. *From wherever he may start, he is sure to bring us out very presently into the road along which,* to his seeming, *our primitive ancestors must have traveled.* That the author of the extract is an archaizer is plain independently, from the phrase 'very presently'; but he has no business to be archaizing in a sentence made unsuitable for it by the essentially unarchaic 'primitive ancestors.'

4. *As seem(s) to be the case. As seem to be the case* is always impossible, because the relative pronoun *as,* for which see AS 5, never represents an expressed plural noun, but always a singular notion like *fact* or *state of affairs,* & that not expressed, but extracted out of other words. RIGHT: *Even if they acted in good faith and never anticipated the present impasse,* as seems to be the case, *they are now taking every advantage of it.* WRONG: *How can the Ministry acquire proper authority if it has powers so limited* as seem to be the case? *—seem* must be changed to *seems.*

seemly is both adj. & adv., but as an adv. it is rare. *Decorously* is better in most contexts.

seer has double pronunciation & meaning; sē-*er*, beholder, & sēr, prophet &c.

seisin, seizin. Properly *seizin* (pron. sē′-), though commonly *seisin.* (Law: possession of land by freehold.)

seismic, seismograph, &c. Pron. sīz′-.

seize (so spelled) makes *-zable.* The spelling *seise* is archaic except in legal use.

seldom. *Seldom if ever; seldom or never* (NOT *seldom if never*).

Seleucid. Pl. *-ids* or *-idae.*

self. WRONG: *As both* self & wife *were fond of seeing life, we decided that . . ./He ruined* himself & family *by his continued experiments.* Correct the first to *both I & my wife* (or better, *my wife and I*), & the second to *himself & his family.* Such uses of *self* are said by the OED to be 'jocular or colloquial' extensions of a 'commercial' idiom; & unless the jocular intent is unmistakable, they are best avoided.

self-. *Self-* compounds are sometimes used when the *self-* adds nothing to the meaning. For example, there is perhaps never any difference of meaning between *despondent* & *self-de-*

spondent. Self-evident, on the other hand, sometimes means evident without proof, or intuitively certain, which is a valuable sense, & sometimes no more than evident, not implying that proof is needless or has not been given, & therefore tending to confusion. Other words resembling *self-despondent* in being never preferable to the simple form without *self-* are *self-collected* (calm &c.), *self-opinionated.* And others resembling *self-evident* in having a real sense of their own but being often used when that sense is not in place are *self-assurance, self-complacent, self-confidence.* But these are samples only; there are scores that a writer should not use without first asking himself whether the *self-* is pulling its weight. It is not to be supposed that the otiose use of *self-* is a modern trick; on the contrary, the modern tendency is to abandon many such compounds formerly prevalent, & the object of this article is merely to help on that sensible tendency.

self-possessedly. A bad form.

selvage, -vedge. The first is more usual in both US & Brit.

SEMANTICS. ('Significant meaning.') The science of the meanings of words (as opposed to PHONETICS, the science of the sound of words): the reasons for their survival, decay, disappearance, & sometimes revival; the causes for the creation of new words; the historical and psychological examination & classification of changes in their meanings & forms as factors in the development of language. Especially significant are meliorative & pejorative tendencies, metaphor, adaptation, & multiple definition. In the terminology of semantics, the word is the *symbol;* the thing or abstraction to which it refers the *referent;* and the thought, feeling, or emotion for which it stands or which it evokes, the *reference.* Among other things, semantics enables a person to select that one of the various possible symbols of any given referent that seems best to meet his needs.

The word *semantics* seems to have come into English through the translation of Bréal's *Essai du semántique* by Mrs. H. Cust (London, 1900). As late as 1925 Fowler dismissed it as a 'meaningless term to the average person.' Largely through the works of I. A. Richards and C. K. Ogden, however, it was greatly popularized in the 1930's and now is an accepted branch of the science of language.

semi-. Prefix meaning *half, partly, incompletely.* In US hyphened before a proper noun (*semi-Christian, semi-Slavic*) and before words beginning with *i* (*semi-idleness, semi-independent*); all other combinations (except nonce words) are single words (*semiarid, semiofficial, semiurban*) according to most dictionaries. Many authors and publishers do not observe this rule, however, and use the hyphen (as the Brit. do generally) before a vowel except in well-established words, and before a consonant in long or little used combinations. In many combinations *half* is better (*a half-filled room,* NOT *semi-filled*).

SEMICOLON. After having been almost abandoned by all except the most self-confident writers, the semicolon is once more coming back into fashion.

Its most common use is to separate parallel elements after a colon. *There are roughly three kinds of approach to municipal reform: the political, or New Broom, or Throw-the-Rascals-Out; the legislative, or There-Ought-to-be-a-Law; and the technical administrative, or Somebody-Should-Watch-Those-Things.* It is also useful in the balanced sentence. *He says wise things gracefully; he is the master of an idiom at once exact and suggestive, distinguished yet familiar.* The use of semicolons to separate parallel expressions that would normally be separated by commas is not in itself illegitimate; but it must not be done when the expressions so separated form a group that is to be separated by nothing more than a comma, or even not separated at all, from another part of the sentence; to do it is to make the less include the greater, which is absurd. WRONG USE: *And therein lies a guarantee of peace & ultimate security, such, perhaps, as none of the States of South America; such as not even Mexico herself can boast* (read *America, such as not even Mexico herself, can*).

seminar, for group of (graduate) students engaged in research under a professor, is chiefly US (& German).

Semite. A member of any of the races supposed to be descended from Shem (Gen. x. 21ff.), now chiefly represented by the Jews and Arabs. The principal Semitic languages are Arabic, Aramean, Ancient Assyrian, Ethiopic, Hebrew, & Syriac. See also HEBREW.

sempiternal. Enduring constantly & continually (*semper,* always). Now chiefly a LITERARY WORD.

sempstress. *Seamstress* is the usual word now.

send-off, n., colloq., so spelled.

senile. Pron. sē′nīl.

sennight. So written; archaic, 'seven-night', i.e. a week.

señor, señora, señorita, Spanish titles. Pron. sĕnyor′, sĕnyor′*a,* sĕnyorē′t*a.*

sense, v. To perceive as by the senses, become aware of. Colloq. (US) to grasp, understand (e.g. *I cannot* sense *your meaning*). The use in the sense of feel something present, a fact, state of things, &c., not by direct perception but more or less vaguely or instinctively (*We* sense *the tragedy of Anna Wolsky as she steps lightheartedly into Sylvia Bailey's life*), has, no doubt, the advantage of brevity as compared with *become conscious of, get an inkling of,* & other possibilities; but whether that brevity is sufficient compensation for the irritation or suspicion of preciosity that most readers feel when confronted with it is not so certain.

sensibility. Just as *ingenuity* is not *ingenuousness,* but *ingeniousness,* so *sensibility* is not *sensibleness,* but *sensitiveness;* to the familiar contrasted pair *sense* & *sensibility* correspond the adjs. *sensible* & *sensitive* —an absurd arrangement, & doubtless puzzling to foreigners, but beyond mending.

sensible, sensitive, susceptible. In certain uses, in which the point is the effect produced or producible on the person &c. qualified, the three words are near, though not identical, in meaning. *I am* sensible *of your* *kindness,* sensitive *to ridicule,* susceptible *to beauty.* Formerly *sensible* could be used in all three types of sentence; but its popular meaning as the opposite of *foolish* has become so predominant that we are no longer intelligible if we say *a sensible person* as the equivalent of *a sensitive* or a *susceptible person,* & even *sensible of* is counted among LITERARY WORDS. The difference between *sensible of, sensitive to,* & *susceptible to* or *of,* is roughly that *sensible of* expresses emotional consciousness, *sensitive to* acute feeling, & *susceptible to* or *of* quick reaction to stimulus; *profoundly, gratefully, painfully, regretfully,* sensible of; *acutely, delicately, excessively, absurdly,* sensitive to; *readily, often, scarcely,* susceptible to *or* of.

sensitize is a word made for the needs of photography, & made badly. (It should have been *sensitivize;* one might as well omit the adj. ending of *immortal, human,* & *liberal,* & say *immortize, humize,* & *liberize,* as leave out the *-ive.*) The photographers, however, have made their bed, & must lie in it; the longer the rest of us can keep clear, the better.

sensuous is thought to have been expressly formed by Milton to convey what had originally been conveyed by the older *sensual* (connection with the senses as opposed to the intellect) but had become associated in that word with the notion of undue indulgence in the grosser pleasures of sense. At any rate Milton's own phrase, 'simple, sensuous, & passionate,' in describing great poetry as compared with logic & rhetoric, has had much to do with ensuring that *sensuous* shall remain free from the condemnation now inseparable from *sensual.*

SENTENCE, in grammar, means a set of words complete in itself, having either expressed or understood in it a subject & a predicate, & conveying a statement or question or command or exclamation. If it contains one or more dependent clauses in addition to the main clause it is a *complex sentence;* if it contains more than one independent clause it is a *compound sentence;* if it contains more than one independent clause and one or more dependent clauses, it is a *compound-complex sentence.* If its subject or predicate or verb (or more) is understood, it is an *elliptical sentence.*

SIMPLE SENTENCES: *I went.* (statement); *Where is he?* (question); *Hear thou from heaven.* (command); *How they run!* (exclamation).

COMPLEX SENTENCE: *Where he bowed, there he fell down dead.*

COMPOUND SENTENCE: *You commanded & I obeyed.*

COMPOUND-COMPLEX SENTENCE: *Although he thought it was hopeless, he continued to strive and finally he succeeded.*

ELLIPTICAL SENTENCES: *Listen. Well played. What?*

sententious, 'abounding in maxims,' now usually in a derogatory sense; affected or pompously formal. *Fond of uttering moral reflections in a style too sententious and oracular./A sententious pedant.*

sentinel, sentry. The first is the wider & literary word, & the fitter for metaphorical use; the second is the modern military term.

sepsis. Pl. (rare) *sepses* (-ēz).

septet(te). Spell *-et.*

septillion. See BILLION.

Septuagint. The Greek version of the O.T. (The name derives from the traditional story that the Pentateuch was translated by 72 Palestinian Jews in 72 days. The Church Fathers made it a round 70 and included the whole O.T.)

sepulchre, -cher. US dictionaries give *-er* first, but *-re* often is seen, esp. in religious writing. Brit. *-re.*

sequelae. Consequences. A plural word with the rare sing. *sequela.*

SEQUENCE OF TENSES. 1. The rule according to which the tense of verbs in a subordinate clause is changed to the past when the verb in the main clause is in the past tense, even though no notion of past time needs to be introduced into the dependent clause. *Two will do; I* think *that two* will *do; I* thought *that two* would *do; I* should think *that two* (normal sequence) would *do,* or (vivid sequence) will *do.* (In these examples, the usually omitted *that* has been inserted merely to make it clear that a real clause is meant, & not a quotation such as *I thought, 'two will do.'*) The point to be noticed is that the change to the past tense is normal sequence, & the keeping of the present (called vivid sequence above) is, though common & often preferable, abnormal. Some further examples are: *I wish* I knew *what 'relativity'* (normal) meant, *or* (vivid) means; Would *God it* (normal) might, *or* (vivid) may, *be so!* Abnormal (i.e. vivid) sequence was said to be often preferable; it is sometimes so much so as to be practically the only thing possible. Asking the time, I do not say *Could you tell me what the time* was?—which nevertheless is strictly correct—but *what the time* is.

2. Sequence out of place. *One* would *imagine that these prices* (normal) were, *or* (vivid) are, *beyond the reach of the poor; These prices, one* would *imagine,* are *beyond* &c. (NEVER *were*). The base is *These prices are;* if made dependent on *One would imagine, are* may be changed, or may not, to *were;* but if *one would imagine* is a parenthesis instead of being the main clause, the change is impossible; nevertheless it happens: (WRONG) *The shops have never had such a display of Christmas presents, but here again the prices, one would imagine,* were *beyond the reach of any but the richest person; one hundred francs* is asked *for a common rag doll.* The mistake, a common one, results from not knowing a parenthesis when one sees it; see PARENTHESIS 2.

seq., seqq., et seq(q)., are short for Latin *et sequentes* (*versus*) =& the subsequent lines, or *et sequientia*=& the words &c. following. Except in writing directed to scholars, it is kinder to the reader to use *f., ff.,* or *foll.,* of which he is sure to know the meaning.

seraglio. Harem. (Formerly, a walled palace, esp. of a Sultan.) Pron. sĭrahʹlyō. Pl. *-os* or *seragli* (-yē).

seraph. A BACK-FORMATION

from the pl. *-phim* or *-phin* (*-phin* is now archaic). *Seraphim* as a sing., sometimes used erron. with pl. *-ims* (see A.V. Is. VI. 2, 6), is now obs.

sere. In Brit., the adj. In US var. of SEAR, adj.

serif, ceriph, seriph. In printing the fine cross-stroke finishing off a letter. *Serif* is now the accepted spelling.

serjeant. Brit. var. of *sergeant.* (Hist.) lawyer of high rank: *Serjeant-at-Arms, Common Serjeant* (officer of City of London). But Mil., always *serg-*.

serum. Pl. *-rums, -ra.*

serviceable. So spelled.

serviette. A GENTEELISM for *napkin.*

servile. Pron sûr′vĭl, US. Brit. usually -īl.

sesqui-. Prefix meaning one and a half. *Sesquicentennial,* 150th anniversary.

sestet(te), sex-. The last six lines of a sonnet, usually *sestet;* other uses, SEXTET.

set-. The nouns *setback* (Brit. hyphen), *set-to, setup* so spelled.

set(t). The extra *t* is an arbitrary addition in various technical senses, from a lawn-tennis to a granite set, and is now generally abandoned.

seventies, 'seventies. See EIGHTIES.

sever makes *-ered* &c.

severely. *Leave severely alone* has two uses: (1) to leave alone as a method of showing contempt (*After his disgraceful behavior you should leave him severely alone*); (2) ironical, to leave alone to avoid consequence for the subject (*From now on I shall leave all such temptations severely alone*). Used when the meaning is simply 'leave alone,' the *severely* is pointless. See HACKNEYED PHRASES, & IRRELEVANT ALLUSION. There are degrees of badness; in the first of the following extracts, for instance, *severely* is less pointless than in the second: *That immortal classic which almost all other pianists are content* to leave severely *alone on the topmost shelf./If our imports & exports balance, exchanges will be normal, whatever the price, & I am glad that Mr. Mason agrees that exchanges should be left* severely alone.

sew, p.p. *sewed* or *sewn.* The first is both the older form & the commoner in modern English.

sew(er)age. It is best to use *sewage* for the refuse, & *sewerage* for the sewers or the sewer system.

sextet, 'an alteration of *sestet*' (OED), is now the normal word in music and (transf.) for any group of six. *Sestet* is still usual when speaking of the sonnet.

sforzando. Musical direction, 'accented.'

shade, n. Different *shades* (properly) of the same color, i.e. with respect to depth. *A deep shade of blue, almost a blue-black.* For color synonymy see TINT.

shade, shadow, nn.,=(1) comparative darkness; (2) a dark figure cast upon a surface by a body intercepting light; (3) protection from glare & heat. These apply to both nouns, the only significant point being that *shadow* is the normal word for (2), NOT *shade.* It is a sort of clue to remember that *shadow* is a piece of shade, related to it as, e.g., pool to water. So it is that *shade* is a state—viz. partial absence of light—& not thought of as having a shape, nor usually as an appendage of some opaque object, both which notions do attach themselves to *shadow*. So too we say *light & shade* but *lights & shadows, in the shade* but *under a shadow;* & so *too shady* means full of shade, but *shadowy* like a shadow.

shake makes *-kable.*

Shakers. Popular name for the religious sect (the Millennial Church) that originated in England, but shortly moved to the US (1774). Not to be confused with the QUAKERS.

shako. (Military hat.) Pron. shă'kō. Pl. *-os.*

Shakspere, Shakespear(e), -erian, -ean, &c. The forms adapted in the OED are *Shakspere* (from the signature in his copy of *Montaigne*) & *Shaksperian* ('*-ian* is alone correct'). But 'the commonest form is *Shakespeare*,' which is the usual spelling in US.

shaky, shaly. So spelled.

shall & will. The traditional use, which every English child and most American children are taught in school, is, simple future,

I shall go
You will go
He, they, will go.

If it is a matter of determination, obligation, or permission,

I will go
You shall go
He shall go.

In *The ABC of Plain Words* (1951) Sir Ernest Gowers says, 'But the idiom of the Celts is different. They have never recognized "I shall go." For them "I will go" is the plain future. American practice follows the Celtic, and in this matter, as in so many others, the English have taken to imitating the American. If we go by practice rather than by precept, we can no longer say dogmatically that "I will go" for the plain future is wrong . . .'

Nevertheless, the majority of Americans still use the traditional forms in formal & literary writing, and many do in speech. For a lucid exposition of traditional usage, see 'shall and will' in Fowler & Fowler, *The King's English,* & WILL.

shame, v., makes *-mable.*

shamefaced, -fast. It is true that the second is the original form, but those who would revert to *-fast* in ordinary use are rightly rewarded with the name of pedants; see PRIDE OF KNOWLEDGE. To use it as an acknowledged archaism in verse is another matter.

shamefacedly. Four syllables.

shanghai, v. Pron. -hī; for past & p.p. *-aied.*

Shangri-La. So spelled. A nonexistent idyllic land (in James Hilton's *Lost Horizon*); a secret base of operations, airfield, &c. used by US Army Forces.

shanty, sailors' song. Use CHANTY.

shape. *In any shape or form* is a stock phrase that weakens a writer's style and is now usually meaningless: *Mr. A— states that 'he is absolutely unconnected* in any shape or form *with the matter.'* See PLEONASM 2. The p.p. is *shaped* & *-en* is archaic.

shard. In the well-known phrase 'the shard-borne beetle,' the interpretation 'borne through the air on shards' (i.e. the wing cases), which has so far prevailed as to set up *shard* as an entomological term for wing case, appears to be an error. The real meaning was 'born in shard,' there being another word *shard,* now obs. except in dialects, meaning cow dung.

sharp, adv. In such phrases as *pull up sharp, turn sharp (a)round, at eight o'clock sharp, sharp* is preferable to *sharply;* see UNIDIOMATIC -LY.

Shavian, of or pertaining to G. B. Shaw.

Shays' Rebellion (in Mass., 1786–7), NOT *Shay's.*

she. 1. For *she* & *her* in bad personifications (e.g. *The world wants all that* America *can give* her), see PERSONIFICATION 1, 2.

2. Case. A few violations of ordinary grammar rules may be given; cf. HE. WRONG: *I want no angel, only* she (read *her*)./*When such as* her *die* (read *she*)./*She found everyone's attention directed to Mary, &* she *herself entirely overlooked* (omit *she*)./*But to behold her mother* —she *to whom she owed her being* (read *her*). *I saw a young girl whom I guessed to be* she *whom I had come to meet* (read *her*)./*Nothing must remain that will remind us of that hated siren, the visible world,* she *who by her allurements is always tempting the artist away* (read *her*).

sheaf. The noun has pl. *-ves.*

shear, v., has past *sheared* in ordinary current senses (*We* sheared *our sheep yesterday; A machine* sheared *the bar into foot-lengths, the nap quite short; This pressure* sheared *the rivets*), *shore* in archaic & poetical use (shore *through the cuirass, his plume away,* &c.). For the p.p., *shorn* remains commoner than *sheared* in fig. senses, less common in regard to sheep, and is not used in the technical sense of distorted by mechanical shear (i.e. strain), nor usually in that of divided with metal-cutting shears.

shear legs, sheer-. An apparatus for hoisting weights. The spelling *sheer* is due to & perpetuates a mistake. *Shear legs* is the usual spelling in US and is recommended. Also *shear-bulk.*

sheath(e). The noun (-th) rhymes with *wreath* in sing., but in the pl. with *wreaths. Sheathe* (v.) rhymes with *breathe.*

sheep. Pl. same; see COLLECTIVES 1.

sheer. The use of the adj. for fine, diaphonous, 'very thin' (*a sheer silk veil*) is now chiefly US & in Brit. only a commercial term. The senses undiluted, unqualified (*sheer nonsense; by sheer force*) are traditional.

sheik. So usually spelled (US) & pron. shēk. (OED prefers *sheikh* sometimes pron. -āk.)

shelf. There are two separate nouns, one meaning ledge, board, &c., & the other sand bank &c. Each has pl. *-ves,* verb *-ve,* adjs. *-ved, -fy,* & *-vy. Shelf-full* (of books &c.), n., is best written with hyphen; pl. *-ls* (unless the two words *shelves full* are suitable & preferred).

shellack, v., makes *-cked, -cking.*

shew, show. 'The spelling *shew,* prevalent in the 18th c. & not uncommon in the first half of the 19th c., is now obs. except in legal documents' (OED).

In *shewbread* the old spelling naturally persists.

shibboleth. For synonyms of the (transf.) sense (*Emancipation from the fetters of party shibboleths*), see SIGN.

shier, -est. See SHY.

shillelagh. The Irish cudgel made of blackthorn or oak. So spelled. Pron. -ā′la (often in US -ā′lē).

shine, v. In the sense 'to polish, make bright' (*to shine shoes, to shine the silver*—US colloq.), past & p.p. *shined.*

shingly, shiny. NOT *-ey.*

ship makes *shipyard, shipload, shipowner* (no hyphen).

shire. The Shires as the name of an English (hunting) country means Leics., Northants., & Rutland; it is also 'applied to other parts of England by the inhabitants of East Anglia, Kent, Sussex, Essex, & Surrey' (OED). As a suffix, pron. -shẽr, NOT shẽr or shīr. (In general use it can mean the counties whose names end in *-shire.*)

shockedly. A bad form.

shoe, v., makes *shoeing.*

shoot, chute. Between the English *shoot* & the French *chute* (lit. *fall*) there has been much confusion, & there seems to be no good reason against making *shoot* the only spelling & allowing it to retain such senses as it has annexed from *chute.* (US still prefers *chute* for the waterfall or rapid; the trough or channel for conveying things to a lower level; and the toboggan slope.)

shop makes *shoptalk* or (better) *shop-talk* (orig. from 'talk shop'); as compared with *cant, slang,* &c., see JARGON. US *bookstore, grocerystore*=Brit. *bookshop,* &c.

short circuit as a noun should not, & as a verb should, be hyphened.

shorthand. So written.

short-lived. Pron. -īvd.

shortly should not be used in the sense *briefly* when there is a possibility of ambiguity: e.g. *The President was heard* shortly *in reply* (*briefly* or *in a short time*?). *She answered* shortly (*briefly, in a short time,* or *curtly*?).

short shrift. 'Brief confession' (orig. of a criminal, before execution); hence a brief respite. To *give short shrift to*=to make short work of: *The House will give short shrift to the bill.*

short sight. No hyphen; but *short-sighted* or *shortsighted.* In US *nearsighted* is usually used in the lit. sense; *short-sighted* in the fig. (Most US dictionaries give as one word, but it is often hyphened in practice.)

shot, n. Pl. *shots* or *shot.* For the pellets used in shotguns, the latter is usually preferred: *About a dozen* shot *were extracted from his leg.* But *I distinctly heard three* shots.

should. *I should have liked to be there; I should like to have been there* (NOT *I should have liked to have been there*). *It is unlikely that he should have been there;* but *it is likely that he was* (or *may have been*) *there.* For *should* in inverted conditionals (*should it happen* for *if it should happen*), see SUBJUNCTIVE.

shoulder. *The cold shoulder* (no hyphen) but *to cold-shoulder* (OED gives quotations from Scott, Dickens, & Thackeray).

shovel. In US usually *shoveled, -ling;* Brit. *-lled* &c.

show. (1) v. The p.p. is usually *shown,* rarely *showed.* (2) n. In the sense 'theatrical performance,' colloq.

shred, v. In the p.p. *shredded* & *shred* are both old & both extant; the longer is recommended.

shriek. See SCREAM.

shrink has past *shrank* (archaic, *shrunk*), p.p. usually *shrunk* as verb or pred. adj., & *shrunken* as attrib. adj.: *has shrunk, is shrunk* or *shrunken, her shrunken* or *shrunk cheeks.*

shrivel makes, US, usually *-led, -ling,* &c., Brit. *-lled* &c.

shy. The adj. makes *shyer, shyest, shyly, shyness, shyish. Shier, shiest* (Webster's first) are alternative forms in US but not recommended.

sibilant. (Gram.): 'hissing.' A sound or letter of the nature of *s, z, sh,* &c. The careless inclusion of a number of words having several sibilants in close proximity should be guarded against.

sibyl(line). So spelled (NOT *sybi-*).

sic, Latin for 'so,' is inserted after a quoted word or phrase, usually in brackets, to confirm its accuracy as a quotation, or occasionally after the writer's own word to emphasize it as giving his deliberate meaning; it amounts to *Yes, he did say that,* or *Yes, I do mean that, in spite of your natural doubts.* It should be used only when doubt is natural. But reviewers & controversialists are tempted to pretend that it is, because (*sic*) provides them with a neat & compendious form of sneer. RIGHT: *The industrialist organ is inclined to regret that the league did not fix some definite date such as the year* 1910 (sic) *or the year* 1912–(*sic*), because the reader might naturally wonder whether 1910 was meant & not rather 1911. WRONG USE: *A circular with an appeal for funds to carry on the work of enlightening* (sic) *the people of this country.* What impudence! says (*sic*); but, as no one would doubt the authenticity of enlightening, the proper appeal to attention was not (*sic*), but quotation marks./'*A junior subaltern, with pronounced military & political views, with no false modesty in expressing them, & who* (sic) *possesses the ear of the public . . .*' The quoter means 'Observe, by the way, this fellow's ignorance of grammar; *& who* without a preceding *who*!'; as the sentence is one of those in which the *&-who* rule of thumb is a blind guide (see WHICH), & is in fact blameless, the (*sic*) recoils, as often, & convicts its user of error.

sick. Constr. *of, with, at. With* is now more usual in the literal sense: *Sick* with *a virus infection.* (But *Sick at* (NOT *to*) *the stomach.*) Fig. *of, with, for, at; Sick* of *flattery, sick* with *longing; sick* for *a sight of him; sick* at *heart. Sick* makes *lovesick, airsick, sick headache.* See also SICK, ILL.

sick. *The Sick Man of the East* or *of Europe* (the former Turkish Empire); see SOBRIQUETS.

sick, ill. (1) The original & more general sense of *sick* was 'suffering from any bodily disorder.' That sense remains to it in attributive use (*sick people, a sick child,* &c.), but is now uncommon in Brit. in predicative use (*be* or *feel sick*), in which it means vomiting or ready to vomit. In US & Scotch use the wider sense is still common. (2) Instead of either *iller* or *sicker, more ill* or *more sick, worse* is the comparative wherever it would not be ambiguous.

SIDE-SLIP. (The disturbing influence of what has been said on what is about to be said.) The grammatical accident to which a name is here given is most often brought about by the word *of,* & in the article OF its nature has been so fully explained that nothing more is now required than some examples of the same accident not caused by *of.* WRONG: *Their interest lies* in getting *through as quickly as possible in order* to put *in an extra journey, & consequently* to avoid *waiting for passengers* (read *in avoiding* for *to avoid*)./*In a plea* for *the setting aside* of this accord, *or at least* for *certain parts of the accord, by the Conference . . .* (read *of* for the second *for*)./*Today we can but be thankful* that *the nerve of Fisher proved cool at the crisis, &* that *to him we mainly owe it that we have not to record a disaster of almost historical importance in the history of the railway.* Who is Fisher, that we should prefer him as savior to other signalmen? The second *that* is there only because the first has sent the writer off at a tangent. To mend, omit the second *that,* or insert *feel* before it, or, omit 'to him we mainly owe it that.'/*If it can be done, &* only *if it can be done, shall* we be *in the position to re-establish civilization.* The intervention of the parenthesis with its *only* is allowed to upset the order of words, viz. *we shall be,* required by the start of the sentence; this variety of side-slip is further illustrated in INVERSION in parallel clauses./*Whether* the cessation of *rioting, looting, & burning which has been secured largely by the declaration of martial law & rigorous shooting of leaders of the rabble is merely temporary* or has been put an end to for good *remains to be seen.* If the *cessation* of rioting *has been put an end to for good,* a lively time is coming. To mend, read *is permanent* instead of the words just italicized; & for this variety see HAZINESS.

sidle makes *-dling.*

siege. So spelled.

sien(n)a, Sien(n)a, Sien(n)ese. In the color, the old-established *-nn-* is recommended; the two proper nouns are usually *-n-* in US, but may be either way in Brit.

sign (indication) & some synonyms. (*A visible* sign *of spiritual grace.*) The synonyms are so many that it seems worth while to collect some of them (in their dictionary places are sentences showing each of them in a context to which it is better suited than any, or than most, of the others). The selected words are: *badge, cachet, character, characteristic, cognizance, criterion, device, differentia, emblem, hallmark, impress, index, indication, mark, motto, note, omen, prognostic, seal, shibboleth, sign, slogan, stamp, symbol, symptom, test, token, touch, trace, trait, type, watchword.*

signal, v., makes US *-led* &c.; Brit. *-lled* &c.

signal, single, vv. CONFUSION: *But there is intense resentment that Japan should be* signaled *out for special legislation.* A specimen of a very common misprint or blunder; *singled* should be the word. Unfortunately, there is just nearness enough in meaning between the verb *single* on the one hand &, on the other, the adj. *signal* & the verb *signalize* to make it easy for the uncharitable to suspect writer rather than printer.

signatory, adj. & n., both now so spelled.

signify. In the intrans. use, 'to be of importance,' now usually only in the impersonal negative: *It does not signify.*

Signor(a), -rina, Italian titles. Pron. sēnyor′(*a*), sēnyorē′n*a.*

silhouette. So spelled.

silk(en). *Silken-winged, a silken touch,* but a *silk ribbon.*

sillily. One of the few current -LILY adverbs.

silvan, sylvan. There is no doubt that *si-* is the true spelling etymologically; there is as little doubt that *sy-* now preponderates, & OED & most US dictionaries do the word under that spelling, giving *silvan* as a variant. Fowler & COD prefer *sil-*.

silver-tongued. As used with *orator, oratory,* see HACKNEYED PHRASES.

similar, adj. 'Nearly corresponding; having a mutual resemblance (to).' *Similar* is apt to bring disaster to certain writers, those namely to whom it is a FORMAL WORD to be substituted in writing for *the like* or *the same* with which they have constructed a sentence in thought. WRONG: *It is claimed that the machine can be made to turn on its own centers,* similar to *the motorboats which the inventor demonstrated at Richmond* (*similarly to* or *like*)./ *Nevertheless, although adjoining New York all along its northern border & in its general industrial development swayed by* similar business considerations that *govern the Empire State, its people went as strongly for Roosevelt as their neighbors in New York went against him* (correct to *the same considerations* or *similar considerations to those that . . .*).

simile. A simile is always a comparison; but a comparison is by no means always, & still less often deserves to be called, a simile. To let this specialized & literary word thrust itself, as in the following quotation, into the place of the *comparison* or *parallel* that we all expect & understand is to betray that one has & uses a synonym dictionary, which is to some writers what the rhyming dictionary is to some poets. WRONG: *The advent of Kossovo Day cannot but suggest a* simile between *the conflict then raging & that in which we are engaged today.*

SIMILE & METAPHOR, ALLEGORY & PARABLE. *Allegory* (uttering things otherwise) & *parable* (putting side by side) are almost exchangeable terms. The object of each is, at least ostensibly, to enlighten the hearer by submitting to him a case in which he has apparently no direct concern, & upon which therefore a disinterested judgment may be elicited from him. Such judgment given, it is to be borne in upon him, whether or not a 'Thou art the man' is needed, that the conclusion to which the dry light of disinterestedness has helped him holds also for his own concerns. Every parable is an allegory, & every allegory a parable. Usage, however, has decided that *parable* is the fitter name for the illustrative story designed to answer a single question or suggest a single principle, & offering a definite moral, while *allegory* is to be preferred when the application is less restricted, the purpose less exclusively didactic, & the story of greater length. The object of a parable is to persuade or convince; that of an allegory is often rather to please. But the difference is not inherent in the words themselves; it is a result of their history, the most important factor being the use of *parable* to denote the allegorical stories told by Christ.

Between *simile* & *metaphor* the differences are (1) that a simile is a comparison proclaimed as such, whereas a metaphor is a tacit comparison made by the substitution of the compared notion for the one to be illustrated (*the ungodly flourishing like a green bay-tree* is a confessed comparison or simile; *if ye had not plowed with my heifer,* meaning *dealt with my wife,* is a tacit comparison or metaphor); (2) that the simile is usually worked out at some length & often includes many points of resemblance, whereas a metaphor is as often as not expressed in a single word; & (3) that in nine out of ten metaphors the purpose is the practical one of presenting the notion in the most intelligible or convincing or arresting way, but nine out of ten similes are to be classed not as means of explanation or persuasion, but as ends in themselves, things of real or supposed beauty for which a suitable place is to be found.

It cannot be said (as it was of *allegory* & *parable*) that every simile is a metaphor, & vice versa; it is rather that every metaphor presupposes a simile, & every simile is compressible or convertible into a metaphor. There is a formal line of demarcation, implied in (1) above; the simile is known by its *as* or *like* or other announcement of conscious comparison. There is no such line between *allegory* & *parable,* but in view of distinction (2) & (3) it may fairly be said that parable is extended metaphor & allegory extended simile. To which may be added this contrast: having read a tale & concluded that under its surface meaning another is discernible as the true intent, we say *This is an allegory;* having a lesson to teach, & finding direct exposition ineffective, we say *Let us try a parable;* to reverse the terms is possible, but not idiomatic.

simon-pure. Adj., genuine, authentic; also out-and-out. From the character in Mrs. Centlivre's *Bold Stroke for a Wife.* When used as a noun, two words capitalized.

simony. Traffic in Eccl. preferment. Preferably pron. sĭ′-m*o*nĭ, though sī-, a variant, is often heard.

simpleness, simplicity. *Simplicity* is the usual word in all senses, *simpleness* being fairly rare and usually now used in a derogatory sense (*the vapid simpleness of popular lyrics*).

simulacrum. Image; a semblance; a sham. Pron. sĭmūlā′-kr*u*m. Pl. *-cra.*

simulate makes *-lable, -tor.*

simultaneous. The older (and Brit.) pronunciation is sĭm-; sīm- is now more usual, however, in US.

sin. 'More sinned against than sinning' (*King Lear* III. ii. 60) has become a HACKNEYED PHRASE.

since. (1) RIGHT: *It is now five years* since *he died. He died five years* ago. *It was five years* ago that *he died.* For the very common mistake of using *since* after *ago,* see AGO. (2) *Since* conj.=seeing that, inasmuch as. (3) For 'P.S. Since writing this your issue of today has come to hand,' see UNATTACHED.

'S INCONGRUOUS (*drink's victims* &c.). Most careful writers still observe the rule that, with certain exceptions, possession is attributed only to animate objects and inanimate objects that are thought of as personified. It begins to seem likely, however, that *drink's victims* will before long be the natural & no longer the affected or rhetorical version of *the victims of drink;* but for the present generation, which has been instinctively aware of differences between *drink's victims* & *the victims of drink* & now finds them scornfully disregarded, there will be an unhappy interim.

It is the headline that is doing it. The fewer words to the headline, the larger can the type be, & *China's Integrity* is two words less than *The Integrity of China; Beatty & Haig's Reply* (i.e. *that of Beatty & Haig*), *Uganda's Possibilities, Navy & Army's Thanks* are others; but illustration is superfluous.

We could be content if only the modern possessive kept to its own territory, the modern headline; even *Ontario's Prime Minister* (so are we chastened!) we can bow down before while he is in capitals; but when he comes among us in the ordinary garb of lower-case text, we pluck up heart again & want to kick him: '*In no part of the world,*' says Ontario's Prime Minister, '*will . . .*'/*The object is to bring before the public many ancient & modern aspects of the* Theatre's Art *which have . . ./And the* narrative's charm, *which is that of . . . is due to . . .*

sinecure. Pron. sī'nĕkūr or sĭn'- (the latter is chiefly US & Scottish).

sine die. 'Without date,' i.e. without setting a day. Pron. sīnē dīē.

sine qua non. 'without which not'; indispensable. *A condition* sine qua non *of peace.* Pl. (seldom used) *sine quibus non.*

singeing. So spelled.

Singhalese (of or pertaining to Ceylon). The usual spelling in US. Brit. *Sinhalese.* (*Senegalese*=of Senegal, Fr. West Africa.)

SINGULAR -S (or sibilant ending). The feeling that the *z* sound at the end of a noun proves it plural has played many tricks in the past; *pea, caper* (the herb), & *Chinee,* have been docked under its influence of their endings, *riches* is usually treated as a plural, & many other examples might be collected, philologically interesting rather than of practical importance. On the other hand it may be worth while to notice that the *glasses* of spectacles are *lenses* & not *lens,* & that the plural of a *forceps* should certainly be, & probably will be again, what it unfortunately is not at present, *forcepses.*

sinister in heraldry means *left* (& dexter *right*), but with the contrary sense to what would naturally suggest itself, the left

(& right) being that of the person bearing, not of an observer facing, the shield. *Bar* (properly *baton* or *bend*) *sinister,* sign of bastardy. See BAR.

sink, v. (1) Past tense *sank* or *sunk,* the former now prevailing, esp. in intransitive senses. (2) *Sunk(en).* The longer form is no longer used as part of a compound passive verb: *the ship would have been, will be, was, sunk,* NOT *sunken.* But *sunken* has not a corresponding monopoly of the adj. uses: *sunken eyes; a sunken ship; a sunk* (or *sunken*) *fence; sunk carving; a sunk panel, shelf, story.* Roughly, *sunken* is used of what has sunk or is (without reference to the agency) in the position that results from sinking, i.e. it is an intransitive p.p.; & *sunk* is used of what has been sunk esp. by human agency.

Sino-. A combining form meaning *Chinese; Sinology,* the branch of knowledge that treats of China & the Chinese. *Sino-American, Sino-Japanese,* &c., hyphen. Pron. sīnō-.

sinus. Pl. *-uses* or *sinus.*

Sioux. Pron. sōō. Pl. (also *Sioux*) pron. sōō or sōōz. The adj. is *Siouan.*

sir (as prefix). 'The distinctive title of honor of a knight or a baronet, placed before the Christian name.' To say *Sir Jones* is as much a mistake as to say *Hon.* or *Rev. Jones.* But writers often (1) forget, as with *Hon.,* that a double-barreled surname will not do instead of Christian name & surname, & (2) play foolish games of elegant variation when a knight or baronet has two Christian names, ringing the changes between *Sir William Jones, Sir Henry Jones, Sir William Henry Jones, Sir William,* & *Sir Henry. Sir William Jones,* & *Sir William* or, less happily *Sir W. Jones,* are surely enough to provide relief. When a man chooses to be known by a name not his first he may be referred to as, e.g., *Sir (William) David Ross, Sir David, Sir David (Ross).*

siren, NOT *sy-.*

Sirius. The Dog Star. Pron. sĭr'*ĭŭs.*

sirloin. The knighting of the loin attributed to various kings seems to have been suggested by, & not to have suggested, the compound word; it has, however, so far affected the spelling (which should have shown French *sur*=upper) that *sir-* may now be taken as fixed.

sirocco, sci-. Both forms exist in Italian. The first is the standard English spelling.

sirup. The est. spelling in US; Brit. usually *syrup.*

sismograph. Spell *seismograph.*

sixteenmo. A book of sheets each folded into 16 leaves, approx. 4×6 inches (=*sextodecimo*).

sixties. See EIGHTIES.

sizable. So spelled.

skeptic(al), skepsis, &c. Pron. sk-, whatever the spelling. Fowler says, 'to spell *sc-* & pronounce sk- is to put a needless difficulty in the way of the unlearned. America spells *sk-;* we might pocket our pride & copy.' But Brit. spelling still *sceptic.*

skew, adj., though still current technically, e.g. in architecture, engineering, & carpentry, has so far gone out of general use as to seem, in other applications, either archaic or provincial.

Askew=oblique(ly) is still current. *Skewer,* the pin for holding meat together &c., is from a different source.

skewbald. Of horses, marked with white & some other color —not black. See PIEBALD.

ski, n. Pron. US skē, Brit. formerly & still occas. shē; pl. *ski* or *skis.*

ski, v. In US usually *skied, skiing;* Brit. usually *ski'd.* The agent noun is *skier.*

skiagraphy &c. (In Photography, Architecture, Astronomy, &c.) So spelled in US. Brit. usually *sciagraphy.* Both pron. skī-.

-skied. In combinations, *the blue-skied East, the leaden-skied midwinter;* chiefly poetical.

skilled. The skilled & the unskilled are sheep & goats, distinguished by having or not having had the requisite training or practice; the two words exist chiefly as each other's opposites, or terms of a dichotomy. The point of the limitation is best seen by comparison with *skillful: skilled* classifies, whereas *skillful* describes; you are *skilled* or not in virtue of your past history, but not *very* or *most* or *fairly skilled* (in idiomatic speech, at least); you are *skillful* according to your present capacity, & in various degrees.

skillful. US prefers *skillful,* but why insist on double *l,* when US usage drops extra letters whenever possible? *Skilful* (standard Brit.) is recommended to those US writers who have the courage to be unconventional & whose publishers allow them to be.

skin. With *the skin* of *my teeth,* NOT *by;* see MISQUOTATION.

sky blue. The name of the color is *sky blue;* the adj. *blue* qualified by *sky* becomes *sky-blue; sky blue will be best; a sky-blue tie; her eyes are sky-blue.*

skyey. So spelled. (Now chiefly poetical.)

slack(en), vv. The following distinctions are offered with the caution that they represent idiomatic usage only, & that quotations contravening them may be found in the OED & elsewhere. (1) *Slacken* is the ordinary word for to become slack, & for to make (or let become) slacker: *the tide, breeze, pace, demand, rope, one's energy,* slackens; *we* slacken *our efforts, grip, speed, opposition, the girth, the regulations.* (2) To *slack,* if it is to have such senses, is reinforced by *off, out, up,* &c.: *the train* slacked up; *had better* slack off; slack out *the rope.* (3) *Slack,* NOT *slacken,* trespasses on the territory of *slake:* slack *one's thirst, lime, the fire.* (4) *Slack,* NOT *slacken,* means to be slack or idle; *accused me of* slacking. (5) *Slack,* NOT *slacken,* means to come short of or neglect (one's duty &c.).

slake, slack, vv. Both are derived from the adj. *slack,* & *slake* had formerly such senses as *loosen* & *lessen,* which have now passed to the newer verb *slack* owing to their more obvious sense connection with it; *slake* tends more & more to be restricted to the senses *assuage, satisfy, moisten* (thirst, desire, vengeance, lips, lime). *Slake* is properly pronounced slāk, but slăk is often heard, esp. when the reference is to time.

slander. In Law, a false defamatory report, maliciously & orally uttered. For synonymy, see LIBEL.

slang. In the sense of words or phrases below the standard of cultivated language, slang differs from colloquialism in that the latter may be acceptable in conversation or informal writing. As time passes, some slang becomes accepted colloquially, some colloquialisms become standard English. For comparison with the many synonyms, see JARGON.

Slavic, Slavonic. The words are often used interchangeably, but usually *Slavic* applies to ethnic characteristics (*Slavic tribes, nations, civilization*), *Slavonic* to cultural (*Slavonic characters, dances, literature*).

slay makes *slew, slain.* But *slayed* is heard from people who should know better.

sleazy. Pron. slā'zĭ.

sleep. For *the sleep of the just* see HACKNEYED PHRASES.

sleeping partner. The (chiefly) Brit. equivalent of US *silent partner.*

sleight. Pron. slīt; it is related to *sly* as *height* to *high. Sleight of hand,* no hyphens.

slenderize, the unpleasant US GENTEELISM, is only a little more objectionable, because of its malformation, than the Brit. genteelism, *to slim* (v.), to reduce one's figure by dieting & exercise.

slice, v., makes *-ceable.*

sling, slink. Past & p.p. *slung, slunk,* NOT *slang, slank.*

SLIPSHOD EXTENSION. To this heading, which hardly requires explanation, reference has been made in the articles on many individual words. Slipshod extension is especially likely to occur when some accident gives popular currency to words of learned origin, & the more if they are isolated or have few relatives in the vernacular; examples are *protagonist, recrudescence, feasible, dilemma;* the last two of these offer good typical illustrations. The original meaning of *feasible* is simply *do-able* (L. *facere,* do); but to the unlearned it is a mere token, of which he has to infer the value from the contexts in which he hears it used. He arrives at its meaning by observing what is the word known to him with which it seems to be exchangeable; that is *possible;* & his next step is to show off his new acquisition by using it instead of *possible* as often as he can, without at all suspecting that the two are very imperfect synonyms; for examples see FEASIBLE.

The case of *dilemma* as a word liable to slipshod extension differs in some points from that of *feasible,* though *a dilemma* is confused with *a difficulty* just as *feasible* with *possible.* A person who has taken a taxi & finds on alighting that he has left his money at home is in a difficulty; he is not in a dilemma, but he will very likely say afterwards that he found himself in one. The differences are (1) that the ordinary person has still less chance than with *feasible* of inferring the true meaning from related words, it being an almost isolated importation from Greek; (2) that the user need hardly be suspected of pretension, since *dilemma* is in too familiar use for him to doubt that he knows what it means. Nevertheless, he is injuring the language, however unconsciously, both by helping to break down a serviceable distinction, & by giving currency to a mere token word in the place of one that is alive.

Slipshod extension, however, though naturally more common with words of learned antecedents, is not confined to them, & in the following list will be found several that would seem too thoroughly part of the vernacular to be in danger of misuse: *balance; calculate; chronic; commonplace* (or *truism*); *conservative; dead letter; decimate; eke out; evidence; forgather; liable; meticulous; mutual; optimism; possible* (3); *probable; precedent; reference; relegate; tribute; verbal.*

Of these words, all or most are habitually ill treated, & should be noted as needing care. A stray example may be added of a word with which such abuse is exceptional & apparently unaccountable, that slipshod extension may not be taken for the sort of blunder against which one is safe if one attends to a limited list of dangerous words. What is required is the habit of paying all words the compliment of respecting their peculiarities. WRONG: *An excellent arrangement, for there are thus none of those smells which so often* disfigure *the otherwise sweet* atmosphere *of an English home.* What has no figure or shape cannot be disfigured; not that the limitation need be closely pressed; not only a face or a landscape can be disfigured; so also can an action, a person's diction, or a man's career (to take things of which the OED quotes instances) be disfigured, because each of them can be conceived, with the aid of metaphor, as a shapely whole; but a *shapely atmosphere?*

sloe-eyed. The mystery and romance writers who describe their heroines thus seem to be thinking of the effects of sloe gin rather than the bluish-black plum, which gave the original meaning to the adj.

slogan. Originally a Highland war cry; in the 20th c., usually a motto, catchword: *Our slogan is Small Profits and Quick Returns.* For synonyms see SIGN.

slosh seems to be a more recent (19th c.) variant of *slush.* In US it is used chiefly as a verb (*sloshing about in mud*); in Brit. v. trans. *Don't slosh your tea over*); the noun is usually *slush;* hence *slushy* (adj.).

slough. The n. & v. meaning bog rhyme with *cow;* so *slough of Despond,* from Bunyan; in US the inlet from a river and the tideland creek are usually pronounced slōō and often spelled *slue* or *slew;* the n. meaning cast skin &c. & the v. meaning cast or drop off are pronounced -ŭf.

slovenly. Pron. slŭv-.

slow(ly), advs. In spite of the encroachments of *-ly* (see UNIDIOMATIC -LY), *slow* maintains itself as at least an idiomatic possibility under some conditions even in the positive (*how* slow *he climbs! please read very* slow; *my watch goes* slow), while in the comparative & superlative *slower* & *slowest* are usually preferable to *more* & *most slowly.* Of the 'conditions,' the chief is that the adv., & not the verb &c., should contain the real point; compare *We forged* slowly *ahead,* where the *slowness* is an unessential item, with *Sing as* slow *as you can,* where the slowness is all that matters. *Drive slow* is more effective for a road sign than *drive slowly.*

sludge. See SLUSH.

slue. See SLOUGH.

sluice makes *-ceable.* Pron. slōōs.

slumber. Apart from mere substitutions of *slumber* for *sleep* dictated by desire for poetic diction or dislike of the words that common mortals use, *slumber* is equivalent to the noun *sleep* with some adj., or the verb *sleep* with some adv. *Slumber* is easy or light or half or broken or daylight sleep, or again mental or stolen or virtual or lazy sleep. The implied epithet or adverb, that is, may be almost anything; but the choice of *slumber* instead of *sleep,* if not due to mere stylishness (e.g. the Brit. commercialism *slumberwear;* see WORKING & STYLISH WORDS), is meant to prevent the reader from passing lightly by without remembering that there is sleep & sleep.

slumb(e)rous. The shorter form is the older, but that with the *e* is now commoner, US & Brit.

slump, n. & v., are accepted usage, esp. in Econ. (*a slump in the price of wheat*).

slush, sludge, slosh. The differences are not very clear. There is the natural one, resulting from the stickier sound, that *sludge* is usually applied to something less liquid than *slush* or *slosh,* e.g. to slimy deposits or clinging mud; whereas thawing snow is typical *slush;* & of *slush* & *slosh* the latter is perhaps more often used to describe what is metaphorically watery stuff—twaddle or sentimentality. But see SLOSH.

slush fund. Orig. (Navy), fund for small luxuries, collected by sale of 'slush,' refuse, etc. Mod. US slang: any unallocated fund.

sly makes *slyer, slyest, slyly, slyness, slyish;* for comparison with other such words, see DRY.

small. Relations with *little* are complicated, & the task of disentangling them might excusably be shirked, if not as difficult, then as unprofitable; but examination of the differences between seeming equivalents does give an insight into the nature of idiom. Under BIG some attempt has been made at delimiting the territories of *great, large,* & *big; small* & *little* have to divide between them the opposition to those three as well as to *much,* & the distribution is by no means so simple & definite as the pedantic analyst might desire.

Of the possible pairs of opposites let some be called *patent pairs,* as being openly & comfortably used with both members expressed; & the rest *latent pairs.* The patent pairs start with three that are pretty clearly distinguishable in meaning. Contrasts of size or extent are given by *large* & *small,* those of quantity or amount by *much* & *little,* & those of importance or quality by *great* & *small:* 'large & small rooms,' 'of large or small size,' 'large or small writing,' 'large & small appetites,' 'large & small dealings, dealers'; 'much or little butter, faith, exercise, damage, hesitation, study'; 'the Great & the Small Powers,' 'great & small occasions,' 'a great or a small undertaking,' 'great & small authors.' To these, the main divisions, are to be added two minor patent pairs sometimes substituted for one or other of them—*great* & *little*, *big* & *little*. *Great* & *little* as a patent pair is preferred to *large* & *small* in distinctive names ('the Great & the Little Bear,' 'Great & Little Malvern,' 'the great & the little toe'); it is also common (see below) as a latent pair in two senses. *Big* & *little* is a patent pair often colloquially substituted for either *large* & *small* ('big & little wars, people').

The *patent pairs* are sets of opposites so far felt to correspond that one does not hesitate to put them together as in all the expressions given above; or again either member can be used when the other is not expressed but only implied; e.g. 'the Great Powers' is more often used alone, but 'the Great & the Small Powers' is also an ordinary expression; & 'the Little Entente,' 'the Big Four,' depend for their meaning on a 'Great Entente' & a 'Little Thirty (or so)' that are seldom mentioned. By *latent pairs* are meant sets of opposites in which one member has the meaning opposite to that of another with which nevertheless it could not be expressly contrasted without an evident violation of idiom. For instance, no one would put *large* & *little* together; 'large & little lakes' sounds absurd; but one speaks of 'a (or the) little lake' without hesitation, though 'large lakes' (not 'great lakes,' which ranks with the distinctive names above referred to) is the implied opposite. Another latent pair is *much* & *small;* though 'much or small hope' is impossible, & 'much or little hope' felt to be required instead, yet 'small hope,' 'small thanks,' 'small credit,' 'small wonder,' are all idiomatic when the irregular opposite *much* is not expressed. Similarly with *big* & *small;* we never contrast them openly, but in 'the big battalions,' 'big game,' 'a big grocer,' the opposite in reserve is *small*. *Great* & *little* was said above to rank both as a patent & as a latent pair. In the latter capacity it allows us to talk of 'great damage,' 'great doubt,' 'great hesitation,' & again of 'little damage' &c., but forbids us to put the pair together; it is 'much or little' (not 'great or little') 'doubt.' Again, when *great* is substituted for *large,* or *little* for *small,* with a view to charging either idea of size with contempt or indignation or affection, as in 'you great fool,' 'you little fool,' 'he hit me with a great stick,' 'a sweet little cottage,' the opposites naturally do not appear together, & we have another variety of latent pair. Tabulating now, we get:

Patent pairs

1. Large & small (of size or extent).
2. Much & little (of quantity or amount).
3. Great & small (of importance or quality).
4. Great & little (in distinctive names).
5. Big & little (colloq. for 1, 3, or 4).

Latent pairs

Large, little (for 1).
Much, small (for 2).
Big, small (for 1).
Great, little (for 2 or 1).

smash-up, n., though given as one word in some US dictionaries, is better with a hyphen.

smell, v. Past & p.p. in US

usually *smelled;* Brit. usually *smelt.* The intransitive sense to emit an odor of a specified kind is idiomatically completed by an adj., not an adv.; a thing smells sweet, sour, rank, foul, good, bad, &c., not sweetly, badly, &c. When the character of the smell is given by 'of so-&-so' instead of by a single word, an adv. is often added; compare *smells strong* or *delicious* (i.e. has a strong or delicious smell) with *smells strongly* or *suspiciously of whisky* or *deliciously of violets;* & when *to smell* is used, as it may be, for *to stink,* an adv. is the right addition—*this water smells outrageously; smells disgusting* & *smells disgustingly* are both idiomatic, but are arrived at in slightly different ways, the first meaning 'has a disgusting smell,' & the second 'stinks so as to disgust one.'

smell-less. Write so.

smite. *Smit* for *smote* is obs.; *smit* for *smitten* is archaic, but still in poetic use.

Smithsonian Institution, NOT *Institute.*

smog, though still labeled 'colloq.' in some US dictionaries, is now the accepted term.

smolder is the usual US spelling; *smoulder* Brit.

smooth(e(n). *Smooth* is now the standard spelling for both adj. and verb. *Smoothen* is a superfluous word with no difference in meaning.

snail-like. Keep the hyphen.

snake, serpent. *Snake* is the native & *serpent* the alien word; it is not a necessary consequence of this, but it is also true, that *snake* is the word ordinarily used, & *serpent* the exceptional one. The OED's remark on *serpent* is 'now, in ordinary use, applied chiefly to the larger & more venomous species; otherwise only rhetorical . . . or with reference to serpent-worship.' We perhaps conceive serpents as terrible & powerful & beautiful things, snakes as insidious & cold & contemptible.

so. This article is divided into 8 sections: 1. Phrases treated elsewhere. 2. *So long, & so to, do so.* 3. Appealing *so.* 4. Paterine *so.* 5. Repeated *so.* 6. *So* with p.p. 7. Explanatory *so.* 8. *So* with superlatives & absolutes.

1. For *so far from, so far as, so far that,* see FAR; for *so far forth (as)* see FORTH 2; for *& so on, & so forth,* see FORTH 1; for *quite (so)* see QUITE; for *so to speak* see SUPERIORITY: for *ever, never, so,* see NEVER.

2. *So long, & so to—, do so. So long* used colloq. for *good-by* or *au revoir.* Those who are inclined to avoid it as some sort of slang may be mollified by its naturalness as a short equivalent for *Good luck till we meet again. And so to a division, & so to dinner,* &c. The formula for winding up the account of a debate or incident, borrowed directly or indirectly from Pepys, is apt to take such a hold upon those who once begin upon it that, like confirmed cigarette smokers, they lose all count of their indulgences; it is wise to abstain from it altogether. *Do so.* WRONG: *It is a study of an elderly widower who, on approaching sixty, finds that he knows hardly anything of his three daughters, & sets out to* do so. For similar absurdities, which are too common, see DO 3.

3. The appealing *so.* The type is *Airlines are so uncertain.*

The speaker has a conviction borne in upon him, & in stating it appeals, with his *so*, to general experience to confirm him; it means as you, or as we all, know. A natural use, but more suitable for conversation, where the responsive nod of confirmation can be awaited, than for most kinds of writing. In print, outside dialogue, it has a certain air of silliness, even when the context is favorable, i.e. when the sentence is of the shortest & simplest kind, & the experience appealed to is really general. Readers will probably agree that in all the following extracts the context is not favorable; & the only object of exhibiting them is to give proof that the danger of yielding to this weakness ('feminine' it would have been called before the ladies had learned to write) is a real one. The principle underlying the restriction to short simple sentences is perhaps that this use of *so* is exclamatory. The examples are ranged from bad to worse: *Mr. Walsh is, like* so many *of the miners' leaders, a man who started life in the pit./But he does combine them ingeniously, though in instancing this very real power we feel that it might have been* so *much more satisfactorily expended./He was always kind, considerate, & courteous to his witnesses, this being* so *contrary to what we are led to expect from his successors.*

4. The Paterine *so*. This is a special form of the appealing *so: In the midst of that aesthetically* so *brilliant world of Greater Greece* is an example. The *so* is deliberately inserted before a descriptive adjective, & is a way of saying, at once urbanely & concisely, *Has it ever occurred to you how brilliant &c. it was?* It differs from the *sos* in 3, that is, in being not careless & natural, but didactic & highly artificial. Effective enough on occasion, it is among the idioms that should never be allowed to remind the reader, by being repeated, that he has already met them in the last hundred pages or so. See MANNERISMS for more examples from Pater himself; & here, from imitators, are others: *Here he has set himself to follow in outline its difficult but always* so *attractive development./And still no one came to open that huge, contemptuous door with its* so *menacing,* so *hostile air.*

5. *So* (& *such*) in repetition. From the artificial to the entirely artless. *So* is a much used word, but not indispensable enough to justify such repetitions of it as the following: *It would do away with any suggestion of State purchase of which the country is at the present time* so *nervous, as it would necessitate* such *large borrowing of money, which in the present financial condition of the country, is* so *inadvisable./The situation was well in hand, but it had* so far *developed* so little *that nothing useful can be said about it, save that* so far *the Commander-in-Chief was satisfied.*

6. *So* with p.p. The distinction usually recognized with VERY between a truly verbal & an adjectival p.p. is not applicable to *so;* but it is well worth while, before writing plain *so,* to decide between it & *so much, so well,* &c. *The batteries have been* so (much) *damaged that soldiers have been forced to retire into town./The Bill is not*

so (well) *suited to Ireland as to this country.*

7. The explanatory *so.* Type: *He could not move, he was* so *cold.* The second member is equivalent to a clause beginning with *for,* & the idiom is mainly, but not solely, colloq. What requires notice is that, when it is used in formal writing, it is spoiled if *for,* whose work is being done for it by *so,* is allowed to remain as a supernumerary. RIGHT: *The dangers of the situation seem to us very real & menacing; both sides, in maintaining a firm attitude, may* so *easily find themselves bluffing over the edge into the precipice.* WRONG: *It would seem particularly fitting that an American professor of literature should discuss the subject of Convention & Revolt,* for *in that country the two tendencies are at present* so *curiously & incongruously mingled.*

8. *So* with superlatives & absolutes. *So,* when it qualifies adjectives & adverbs, means *to such a degree* or *extent;* it is therefore not to be applied to a superlative, as in *The difficult & anxious negotiations in which he has taken* so foremost *a part.* Nor to words that are felt not to admit of degrees ('absolutes,' for convenience), including, besides essential positives like *unique,* such indefinites as *some, several.* Among the latter is *ofttimes,* though *often* is not, & 'so ofttimes' is as wrong, though not as unlikely, as 'so sometimes': *And now, as it* so ofttimes *happens, the pupil well may claim to have out-passed the master.*

sobriquet, sou-. The first is much longer established in English, besides being the only modern French form. Pron. sō′brĭkā.

SOBRIQUETS. Under this heading, for want of a better, are here collected a handful out of the thousands of secondary names that have become so specially attached to particular persons, places, or things, as to be intelligible when used instead of the primary names, each of which is thus provided with a deputy or a private pronoun. The deputy use is seen in 'It was carried to the ears of that famous hero & warrior, the Philosopher of Sans Souci,' i.e. Frederick the Great; & the private-pronoun use in 'He employed his creative faculty for about twenty years, which is as much, I suppose, as Shakespeare did; the Bard of Avon is another example . . . ,' where the 'Bard of Avon' means Shakespeare or *the latter.* Some names have a large retinue of sobriquets; Rome, e.g., may be the Eternal City, the City of the Seven Hills, the Papal City, the Scarlet Woman, the Scarlet Whore, the Empress of the Ancient World, the Western Babylon; & the list of sobriquets is only half told.

Now the sobriquet habit is not a thing to be acquired, but a thing to be avoided. The writers most of all addicted to it are the sports reporters; games & contests are exciting to take part in, interesting or even exciting also to watch, but essentially (i.e. as bare facts) dull to read about. The reporter, conscious that his matter requires enlivening, thinks that the needful fillip may be given if he calls fishing *the gentle craft,* a ball *the pigskin* or *the leather*, or a captain *the skipper*, & so makes his description a series of momentary puzzles that shall pleasantly titillate inactive minds.

It is by no means true, however, that the use of sobriquets is confined to this, or to any, class of writers; *the Philosopher of Sans Souci* & *the Bard of Avon* quoted above are from Thackeray & Conan Doyle, though they are unfavorable specimens of those authors' styles. And, moreover, the sobriquet deputy has its true uses; just as Bacon knows of 'things graceful in a friend's mouth, which are blushing in a man's own,' so the sobriquet may often in a particular context be more efficient than the proper name; though 'the Papal City' means Rome, its substitution may be a serviceable reminder, when that is appropriate, that Rome in one of its aspects only is intended. A famous example of effective use is in Gibbon: *The graver charges were suppressed; the* Vicar of Christ *was charged only with* (a list of appalling crimes). Again, many sobriquets have succeeded, like mayors of the palace, in usurping all or some of their principals' functions; *the Young Pretender* is actually more intelligible, & therefore rightly more used, than Charles Edward, & to insist on 'came over with William I' in preference to 'with the Conqueror' would be absurd.

No universal condemnation of sobriquets, therefore, is possible; but even the better sort of writer, seldom guilty of such excesses as the sports reporter, is much tempted to use them without considering whether they tend to illuminate or to obscure; 'the exile of Ferney,' he feels, at once exhibits his own easy familiarity with Voltaire the man (*Voltaire* the word, by the way, is itself one of the mayor-of-the-palace sobriquets) & gratifies such of his readers as know who is meant; as for those who may not know, it will be good for them to realize that there are others more cultured than they. The sobriquet style, developed on these lines, is very distasteful to all readers of discretion. Reference to this entry means that the sobriquet given is to be used with caution. Those who may become aware that these & similar substitutes are apt to occur frequently in their own writing should regard it as a very serious symptom of perverted taste for cheap ornament.

so-called, so called. In predicative use, properly without a hyphen: *The Mound Builders,* so called *because of the burial mounds they built on the Mississippi basin . . . ;* in attributive use, hyphened (often a juvenile way implying doubt): *The* so-called *Progressive party . . .*

sociable, social. There is a tendency to use *social* not where it is indefensible, but where the other would be more appropriate. Roughly, *social* means of or in or for or used to or shown in or affording society; & *sociable* seeking, or loving, or marked by the pleasures of, company. *Social* is rather a classifying, & *sociable* rather a descriptive adjective: man is a *social being,* Jones is a *sociable person;* people are invited to a *social evening,* & say afterwards (or do not say) that they had *a very sociable evening.* Obviously, overlapping is likely.

The OED, under a definition of *social* that includes 'sociable' as an equivalent, gives two quotations in which *sociable* should have been preferred (*His own friendly & social disposition*—Jane Austen/*He was very happy &* social—Miss Braddon), as well as one that is just on the right side of the border (*Charles came forth from that school with* social *habits, with polite & engaging manners*—Macaulay). For the noun use=a social gathering, *social* is better (*sociable* in this sense, US colloq.).

Socialism. A political & economic theory of social organization in which individual freedom is subordinated to the interests of the community, & the essential means & distribution of goods are vested in the State. Extreme Marxian Socialism tends toward Communism in the belief in the overthrow of Capitalism, & in Government (proletariat) control of land & capital as well as of the means of production. Mild or Liberal Socialism (cf. the Welfare State) is little more than democratic management of public utilities, public insurance against poverty & sickness, free education & feeding of children, & the abolition, through taxation, of inherited wealth. See also COMMUNISM.

socialite, US. colloq.; a society-page word.

sock. For *the sock*=comic stage (so called from the light shoe worn by comic actors in Ancient Greece & Rome) see BATTERED ORNAMENTS.

Socrates. Pron. sŏk-. *Socratic irony,* feigned ignorance to entice others into a display of their supposed knowledge; see IRONY. *Socratic method,* instruction by use of questions & answers; dialectic.

soddenness. So spelled.

Sodom (*& Gomorrah*). So spelled (see Genesis XVIII, XIX). Now used of any city or country notorious for vice and corruption.

soft. As an adv. now usually archaic or poetic except in the comparative: *play softer;* see UNIDIOMATIC -LY.

soi-disant. Pron. swä dēzäɴ, but see FRENCH WORDS. English is well provided, with *self-styled, ostensible, would-be, professed, professing, supposed,* & other words, for all needs.

sojourn. OED gives the pronunciations sŭ-, sŏ-, sō-, in that order. COD gives sŭ & sŏ. In US sō- is most often heard.

Sol=the sun. Pron. sŏl, NOT sōl. (But *sōlar, sōlarize.*) See SOBRIQUETS.

solace. Pron. sŏl-.

solder. Pron. sŏd*er*.

soldierly can serve as both adj. & adv. As the latter, it is preferable to *soldierlily* (*He marched* soldierly *toward his fate*), but is ill at ease in most contexts. See -LILY.

solecism. A violation of the rules of grammar; a blunder in speaking or writing; hence (transf. & fig.), a piece of ill-breeding, incorrect behavior.

solemnness, NOT *-mness.*

soliloquy. (Lit.): 'sole speech.' Talking to oneself or thinking aloud without consciousness of an audience; see MONOLOGUE.

solo. Pl. *-os,* or in technical use *soli* (-ē).

so long=goodby. See so 2.

soluble, solvable, make *insoluble, unsolvable.* Substances are *soluble* (or *dissolvable*), NOT *solvable;* problems are *soluble* or *solvable.*

sombre, -ber. US usually *-er;* Brit. *-re.*

some. 1, Meiosis. 'This is some war,' with strong emphasis on *some,* is modern colloq. for 'This is a vast war,' 'This is indeed a war, if ever there was one.' It is still felt as slang, & it originated in America; but it results from that love of meiosis which is shared by British and Americans alike. We say a place is *some distance off,* meaning a long way; we say 'It needs some faith to believe that,' meaning a hardly possible credulity. So far the effect is exactly parallel to the (Brit.) emphatic use of *rather* in answer to a question—'Do you like it?' 'Rather!' meaning not somewhat, but exceedingly. The irregular development comes in when *some,* meiosis & all, is transferred from its proper region of quantity or number to that of quality; *some faith* is a wonderful amount of faith; but *some war* is a wonderful kind or specimen of war, & *some pumpkins* (at least 70 years old, & said to be the original American phrase) were not a great number of pumpkins, but very superior pumpkins. It is this irregularity that makes the use both noticeable & popular; perhaps, when it has become so trite as no longer to sound humorous, it may perish. Compare with it the Brit. equivalent, which lacks the piquant irregularity only, 'something like a war.'

2. *Someone, some one.* In the sense *somebody, some person,* one word. But *Choose* some one person *to represent you:* see EVERYONE.

3. *Some time, sometime. I have been waiting* for some time (two words); *I must see him about it* sometime (i.e. at some time or other, US one word, Brit. *some time*); sometime *Rector of this Parish* (i.e. formerly) one word US & Brit.

4. *Somewhat* has for the inferior writer what he ought not, but would be likely, to describe as 'a somewhat amazing fascination.' WRONG: *The evidence furnished in* the somewhat extraordinary *report of the Federation . . ./His election experiences were* somewhat *unique./ The flocks of wild geese, to which the flamingo is* somewhat more or less *closely allied.* These are examples selected for their patent absurdity, & their authors are doubtless so addicted to the word that they are no longer conscious of using it. What moves people to experiment first in the *somewhat* style is partly timidity—they are frightened by the coming strong word & would fain take precautions against shock—& partly the notion that an air of studious understatement is superior & impressive; & so in our newspapers 'the intemperate orgy of moderation is renewed every morning.'

5. *Somewhen* should be regarded as the progeny of *somewhere* & *somehow,* & allowed to appear in public under the wing of either or both of its parents, but not by itself.

-some. The OED collects a number of adjectives in *-some,* grouping them according to their age. The most established words are here given in three sets for comparison.

A (older); *buxom, cumbersome, fulsome, gladsome, hand-*

some, lightsome, loathsome, noisome, wholesome, winsome.
B (medium); *awesome, darksome, gruesome, healthsome, quarrelsome, tiresome.*
C (younger): *blithesome, bothersome, cuddlesome, fearsome, lithesome, lonesome.*

Reading through the lists, one can hardly fail to notice that, while most words in the first are such as one feels to be independent wholes & is not tempted to resolve into root & suffix, the other lists are made up, with individual exceptions as for *quarrelsome* & *lonesome,* of artificial-looking & more or less fanciful formations. The inference is that *-some* has lost its efficiency as a suffix, & that it is wise to avoid such *-some* words, even including one or two of the older ones, as are not of quite unquestionable standing.

somersault, somerset, summerset. The first is recommended.

songstress. Now chiefly poetical. See FEMININE DESIGNATIONS.

sonnet. (Poet.): 'sound'; 'little song.' A kind of short poem of which there are in English three recognized varieties, the features common to all being (1) use of rhyme, (2) the line meter, of five iambi, (3) the number of lines, fourteen, & (4) division into an octave (first eight lines) & a sestet (last six). The three varieties are the Petrarchan, the Shakespearian, & the Miltonic.

The Petrarchan sonnet has a break in sense between octave & sestet, two rhymes only in the octave, arranged abbaabba, & two, or three, other rhymes in the sestet variously arranged, but never so that the last two lines form a rhymed couplet unless they also rhyme with the first line of the sestet. Wordsworth's 'The world is too much with us . . .' observes these rules.

In the Shakespearian sonnet, though the pause between octave & sestet is present, the structure consists less of those two parts than of three quatrains, each with two independent rhymes, followed by a couplet again independently rhymed—seven rhymes as compared with the Petrarchan four or five (e.g. 'Let me not to the marriage of true minds . . .').

Of the Miltonic sonnet, which follows the Petrarchan in the arrangement of the octave, the peculiarity is that the octave & the sestet are worked into one whole without the break of sense elsewhere observed ('When I consider how my light is spent').

sonorous. Pron. sonōr′-.

soot. Pron. -ŏŏ-, NOT sōōt.

sophist. Ancient Greek teacher of philosophy and rhetoric (often disparaged for teaching for payment, as opp. to philosopher); hence, now, a specious or fallacious reasoner. The adj. is *sophistic* or *-al. Sophistry,* the use of subtle arguments that are intentionally deceptive; dialectic as an art or exercise.

soprano. Pl. *-os.* or *-ni* (-ē).

sore, adv. Now archaic or poetic (*sore afflicted, sore oppressed,* &c.).

sorites (sorī′tēz). (Log.): 'heap.' Applied to two entirely different things. (1) A process by which a predicate is brought into the desired relation to a subject by a series of propositions in which the predicate of one becomes the subject of the next, & the conclusion has the first subject & the last predicate. Thus: Schoolmasters are teachers; Teachers are benefactors; Benefactors are praiseworthy; Therefore schoolmasters are praiseworthy. A sorites may be a short way of exhibiting truth, or, as in the example above, may conceal fallacies at each or any step. (2) A logical trick named from the difficulty of deciding how many grains of corn make a heap; is a man bald who has 1000, 1001, 1002, &c., hairs on his head? If the Almighty cannot undo the done, where is the line of almightiness to be drawn?

sorrow. For *more in sorrow than in anger,* & *in her* &c. *great sorrow,* see HACKNEYED PHRASES, & STOCK PATHOS.

sorry, sorrow. The two words do not, as it is natural to suppose, belong to each other, *sorry* being the adj. of the noun *sore. Sore* & *sorrow,* however, are so near in sense (especially in earlier & wider meanings of *sore*) that the mistake has perhaps no ill effects; still, the knowledge has its practical value; connection between *sore* & *sorry* helps to account for the use of *sorry*=(*scurvy*) *poor, inferior,* seen in *sorry rascal, meal, luck, excuse.*

sort. (1) *I* sort of *expected it; a lawyer of* sorts (or *of a sort*); *he's a good* sort; *he's out of* sorts; *these* sort *of things are out of my line*—all often heard, but varying in status, from colloq. to vulgarism. (2) *Any sort or kind* is needless repetition; see PLEONASM 2: *We can only repeat that there is no inconsistency* of any sort or kind *in our attitude.*

SOS (international signal of distress) is a code signal, not an abbreviation (no periods).

soubrette. In comedies, a maid servant, usually coquettish and pert; hence the actress who plays such a part.

soubriquet. See SOBRIQUET.

sough may rhyme with *rough, cow,* or (Sc.) hōōch. Fortunately it is chiefly a literary word & seldom need be pronounced.

soulless. So spelled.

sound, adv. *Sound asleep; sleep sound* (NOT *-ly*); see UNIDIOMATIC -LY.

soupçon. 'Suspicion'; a very small quantity; a dash, a touch. Pron. sōōp sôN. But see FRENCH WORDS.

southerly. Of wind, or motion; *a southerly gale, a southerly course.* For the special uses & meanings of this set of words, see EASTERLY.

soviet. ('Council.') Pron. sōvĭĕt′, sō′- (COD also sŏvĭĕt′). One of the governing bodies of the Union of Soviet Social Republics (abbrev. U.S.S.R.). See COMMUNISM.

sow, v. *Sowed* & *sown* are both current as p.p.

spa. Mineral spring (resort). Pron. spä.

spadeful. Pl. -ls.

SPAR. Women's Reserve of the US Coast Guard Reserve (from the motto, Semper Paratus —Always Ready). No periods.

special. 1. *Special*(*ly*), *especial*(*ly*). *Special* can be used in all senses, although there are some in which *especial* is preferable. *Especial* should not be used when the sense is not that of exceptional in degree or of or for a particular person or thing specified. RIGHT: *He is especially adept at figures; for his* especial *benefit.* A special *messenger; in* special *cases.* In the following quotations each is used where the other would have been better: *Ample supplies of food & clothing are now available, having been shipped from America* especially *for this purpose./The neighborhood is not* specially *well provided with places where soldiers can get amusement & refreshments.* See also ESPECIAL.

2. *Special pleading* is a POPULARIZED TECHNICALITY. In law, *special pleading* is the allegation of special or new matter as opposed to denial of allegations of the opposite side; but when we say that a person's argument is special pleading, we mean that he has tried to convince us by calling our attention to whatever makes for, & diverting it from whatever makes against, the conclusion he desires. But this is, not indeed the highest, but at any rate the almost universal argumentative procedure, & the word *special* adds nothing to the meaning; why then call it *special?*

specialty, -ity. In US the former has almost crowded the latter out. There is little real differentiation in meaning; *speciality* is commoner in most senses in Brit.

specie. Coin, as opposed to paper money (no pl.); *in specie,* in kind. Pron. spē′shĭ.

species. Pron. spē shēz. Pl. the same.

specific(ally). These words, like RESPECTIVE(LY), though their real value need not be questioned, are often resorted to by those who have no clear idea of their meaning for the air of educated precision that they are held to diffuse. A short table of the senses of *specific,* showing the relation of each to the central notion of *species,* follows; it is in the last rather loose sense that it is wise to avoid the word & choose one of the more generally understood synonyms.

1. Characterizing a kind or species. *Specific gravity* is that belonging to gold &c. as a kind or as such.

2. Constituting kind or species. *Specific difference* is that which entitles *courage, man,* &c., to be called by those names rather than by more general ones such as *fortitude, mammal.*

3. Indicating species in classification. In *Pinus sylvestris maritima* (Scotch Fir), the three words are the generic, specific, & subspecific (or varietal) names.

4. Applicable to a kind only. *Specific remedy* is one used for a particular disease or organ, not for ill health, or for the body, in general.

5. (LOOSE) Not universal but limited, not general but particular, not vague but definite. *Specific directions, accusation, cause,* &c.

specious (pron. spē′shus), orig. meaning fair, beautiful, fair-seeming, has deteriorated in non-technical use to outwardly attractive but not having the qualities it seems to possess; hence plausible, fallacious, sophistical: *a specious argument, appearance, story.*

specter, -re. The first is given as the dominant form in most US dictionaries, but many writers still use the second for the disembodied spirit; *-re* is standard Brit.

spectrum. Pl. *-tra, -ms.*

speculum. Pl. *-la, -lums.*

speed. Past & p.p. *sped;* but *speed up*=increase *the speed of,* as traffic, &c., makes *speeded* (*must be speeded up* &c.).

spell. (1) In US *spelled* is much more usual than *spelt* in writing, though many people use *spelt* in speech, esp. the p.p.: That's *spelt* wrong, but you *spelled* that wrong. (2) The sense amount to, mean, involve as inevitable result, seen in *Democracy spells corruption,* & esp. in *So-&-so spells ruin* ('common in recent use'—OED), had its merit, no doubt, when new, but now ranks with WORN-OUT HUMOR. (3) *Spell*=period of time, turn of work, &c. (*Let me drive for a spell*), is idiomatic; as applied to distance (*down the street a spell*) it is US colloq. or dial.

SPELLING POINTS. Spelling is a matter of usage as much as is the meaning of words. During a process of change no dictionary can say this is right, that is wrong (*by-pass, bypass; skillful, skilful; setup, set-up, set up*). There are also differences between US and Brit. usage in spelling (*center, -re; honor, -our; pajamas, pyj-*). In the spelling of words that are in flux, the writer has a choice; the important thing is to be consistent. But most words have a fixed spelling, and deviation occurs through ignorance or carelessness. Various points are discussed throughout the book, and many words whose spelling is disputed will be found in their alphabetical places. The following collection of rules may help the habitually bad speller.

Most words ending in a single consonant preceded by a single vowel (which excludes such combinations as *ee, ai, ea*), when they have added to them a suffix beginning with a vowel (e.g. *-ed, -er* of the agent or of comparison; *-able, -y* of adjs.), double the final consonant if they either are monosyllables or bear their accent on the last syllable; they keep it single if they have their last syllable unaccented; but in words ending with a final *l* & with a final *s* usage varies. Thus the addition of *-ed* to the verbs *pot, regret, limit, travel,* & *bias,* gives *potted* (monosyllable), *regretted* (accented final), *limited* (unaccented final), *traveled* or *travelled* (final *l*), & preferably *biased* (final *s*); the verbs *tar, demur, simper, level, focus,* give similarly *tarring, demurring, simpering, leveling* or *levelling,* & preferably *focusing;* the adjs. *thin, common, cruel,* give *thinnest, commonest,* & *cruellest;* the nouns *gas, Japan, gruel,* give *gassy, japanny,* & *gruelly.*

In forming advs. in *-ly* from adjs. in *-l* or *-ll,* neither a single nor a triple *l* is ever right; *full, purposeful,* & *dull,* have advs. *fully, purposefully,* & *dully*—no distinction being made between *fully* & *dully* though the two *l*s are sounded in *fully* as one letter & in *dully* as two. And in forming nouns in *-ness* from adjs. in *-n* both *n*s are retained—*commonness, rottenness, solemnness,* &c.

Words ending with a mute *e* retain the *e* before suffixes beginning with a consonant, drop it before suffixes beginning with a vowel. Exception: the *e* is retained after a soft *c* or *g.* Hence *milage, gaugeable, palish, wholly;* see MUTE E. *Judgment, acknowledgment* are usually so spelled in US; Brit. sometimes *-dgement.*

Words formerly written with a

ligature æ, œ are now usually written with the two letters separated: *Caesar, aesthetic, Oedipus.* There is a tendency in US to drop the *e* or *o*, esp. in common nouns *ecology, gynecology,* but since it is by no means universal & varies in different words, no rule can be given. See Æ, Œ.

Most verbs ending in *-ize* or *-ise* are spelled *-ize* in US (and by the OED). For a list of verbs in which *-ise* only is correct (*advertise, chastise,* &c.) see -ISE, -IZE.

The plural of *handful, spoonful,* &c., is *handfuls, spoonfuls.*

Words ending in either *-or* or *-our* are usually *-or* in US, *-our* in Brit.

The rule 'i before e except after c' is very useful; it applies only to syllables with the vowel sound ē; words in which that sound is not invariable, as *either, neither, inveigle,* do not come under it (& *seize* is an important exception) & it is useless with proper names (*Leigh, Monteith,* &c.). The *c* exception is in such common use (*receive, deceit, inconceivable;* cf. *relieve, belief, irretrievable*) that a simple rule of thumb is necessary.

The plural of all nouns in *-ey* should be in *-eys,* not *-ies—donkeys* (but *ponies*), *moneys* (but *bunnies*).

The writing of the very common *anti* (=against) instead of the rarer *ante* (=before) (*antedated,* NOT *antidated*) is to be carefully avoided.

Verbs in *-cede, -ceed,* are so many & so much used, & the causes of the differences are so far from obvious, that mistakes are frequent & a list will be helpful: *cede, accede, antecede, concede, intercede, precede, recede, retrocede, secede;* to which may be added *supersede;* but *exceed, proceed, succeed.*

Adjectives & nouns in *-ble, -cle, -tle,* &c., make their adverbs & adjectives not by adding *-ly* or *-y,* but by changing *-le* to *-ly: humbly, subtly, spangly.*

Adjectives in *-ale, -ile, -ole,* add *-ly* for their adverbs: *halely, vilely, docilely, solely;* but *whole* makes *wholly.*

Verbs in *-c* like *picnic* & *bivouac* add *k* before *-ed, -ing, -er,* &c.; *picnicker, bivouacking.*

Many words ending in *-bre, -tre,* &c., in Brit. are spelled *-er* in US: *center, meter, fiber* (exceptions: *acre, lucre*).

Of adjectives in -(*e*)*rous* some never use the *e,* as *disastrous, lustrous, monstrous, wondrous;* some have it always, as *boisterous, murderous, slanderous; dextrous* & *slumbrous* are perhaps better than *dexterous* & *slumberous* (but both are est. in US).

Spencerian, of Herbert Spencer, philosopher, d. 1903.

Spenserian, of Edmund Spenser, poet, d. 1599.

Spenserians. (Poet.). The meter of *The Faerie Queen,* often used by later poets, especially by Byron in *Childe Harold.*

sphere. *Extending principles that belong to building into* the sphere *of architecture proper.* For synonyms in the sense *province* &c., see FIELD.

sphinx, pl. *sphinxes; -ges* (pron. jēz) is now unusual & pedantic. *Sphinxlike.*

spice makes *spiceable.*

spill. In US the past & p.p. usually *spilled* (often pron. spilt); the adj. *spilt* (*spilt milk*). Brit. past & p.p. usually *spilt.*

spin. The past *span* is now archaic in US, but it is still current in Brit.

spiraea rather than *-ræa* or *-rea.*

spiritism & spiritistic mean the same as *spiritualism* in its most frequent & *spiritualistic* in its only acceptation. *Spiritism* is 'preferred by those specially interested in the subject, as being more distinctive than *spiritualism*' is the OED comment. To ordinary people the old noun with a new meaning comes much more natural than the recent invention, & it is to be hoped that they will not let themselves be dictated to by the specially interested with their craving for distinctiveness.

spiritual, -ous. The DIFFERENTIATION (*-al* of soul, *-ous* of liquor) is now complete, & neglect of it more often due to inadvertence than to ignorance.

spirituel(le). The meaning is not quite clear to everyone, & is therefore here given in the OED terms: 'Of a highly refined character or nature, esp. in conjunction with liveliness or quickness of mind.' And on the spelling the OED remarks: 'The distinction between the masc. & fem. forms has not been always observed in English.' That is undoubtedly so; the notion of masc. & fem. forms for adjectives is entirely alien to English, & if a French adjective is to make itself at home with us it must choose first whether it will go in male or female attire & discard its other garments. *Spirituel* is recommended (cf. *blond*).

spirt, spurt. The spelling is now very much a matter of personal fancy, & whether more than one word is concerned is doubtful. In US dictionaries *spirt* is listed as the variant; in Brit. *spurt.* There are, however, two distinguishable main senses —that of gush, jet, or flow (v. & n.), & that of sprint, burst, hustle (v. & n.); & for the second sense the form *spurt* is far the commoner. It would plainly be convenient if the DIFFERENTIATION thus indicated were made absolute; *a* spirt *of blood; works by* spurts; *oil* spirts *up; Jones* spurted *past.* See also SPRINT.

spit. (1) Past & p.p. *spat; spit* for past tenses is archaic in Brit., but it is still often heard in US. (2) The noun in transf. use has taken the sense 'counterpart': *The very spit of his father;* so (dial.?) *the spit and image* (NOT *spittin' image*). (3) For *expectorate,* see GENTEELISMS.

spite. *In spite of, despite, notwithstanding,* are often used interchangeably. *Despite,* shortened from *in despite of*, is more literary & formal than the other two. *I shall go* despite *my misgivings. In spite of* is stronger than *notwithstanding* and usually suggests active opposition or serious hindrances to be encountered. *He succeeded* in spite of *all their trickery and machinations. Notwithstanding,* although the least emphatic, suggests a hindrance. *They decided to continue the conference,* notwithstanding *the protests of the opposition.*

splendo(u)r. In US *-or,* Brit. *-our.*

splice makes *-ceable.*

SPLIT INFINITIVE: '*A book of which the purpose is thus—with a deafening split infinitive —stated by its author: Its main idea is* to historically, even while events are maturing, & divinely —from the Divine point of view —impeach *the European system of Church & State.*'

The English-speaking world may be divided into (1) those who neither know nor care what a split infinitive is; (2) those who do not know, but care very much; (3) those who know & condemn; (4) those who know & approve; & (5) those who know & distinguish.

1. Those who neither know nor care are the vast majority, & are a happy folk, to be envied by most of the minority classes; 'to really understand' comes readier to their lips & pens than 'really to understand,' they see no reason why they should not say it (small blame to them, seeing that reasons are not their critics' strong point), & they do say it, to the discomfort of some among us, but not to their own.

2. To the second class, those who do not know but do care, who would as soon be caught putting their knives in their mouths as splitting an infinitive but have hazy notions of what constitutes that deplorable breach of etiquette, this article is chiefly addressed. 'To really understand' is a split infinitive; 'to really be understood' is a split infinitive; but 'to be really understood' is not a split infinitive. The havoc that is played with much well-intentioned writing by failure to grasp that distinction is incredible. Those upon whom the fear of infinitive splitting sits heavy should remember that to give conclusive evidence, by distortions, of misconceiving the nature of the split infinitive is far more damaging to their literary pretensions than an actual lapse could be; for it exhibits them as deaf to the normal rhythm of English sentences. No sensitive ear can fail to be shocked, if the following examples are read aloud, by the strangeness of the indicated adverbs. Why on earth, the reader wonders, is that word out of its place? He will find, on looking through again, that each has been turned out of a similar position, between the word *be* & a passive participle. Reflection will assure him that the cause of dislocation is always the same. These writers have sacrificed the run of their sentences to the delusion that 'to be really understood' is a split infinitive. It is not; & the straitest non-splitter of us all can with a clear conscience restore each of the adverbs to its rightful place as indicated by the caret. FAILURE TO RECOGNIZE AN INFINITIVE: *He was proposed at the last moment as a candidate likely* generally *to be‸accepted./When the record of this campaign comes* dispassionately *to be‸written, it will be found that . . ./The leaders have given instructions that the lives & property of foreigners shall* scrupulously *be‸respected.*

3. The writers of class (2) are bogy-haunted creatures who for fear of splitting an infinitive abstain from doing something quite different, i.e. dividing *be* from its complement by an adverb; see further under POSITION OF ADVERBS. Those of class (3) who presumably do know what split infinitives are, & condemn them, are not so easily identified, since they include all who neither commit the sin nor flounder about in saving themselves from it, all who combine with acceptance of conventional rules a reasonable dexterity. But when the dexterity is lacking, disaster follows. It does not add to a writer's readableness if readers are pulled up now & again to wonder—Why this distortion?

Ah, to be sure, a non-split diehard! It is of no avail merely to fling oneself desperately out of temptation. One must so do it that no traces of the struggle remain; that is, sentences must be thoroughly remodeled instead of having a word lifted from its original place & dumped elsewhere. DISTORTIONS IN AVOIDING A SPLIT INFINITIVE: *What alternative can be found which the Pope has not condemned, & which will make possible* to organize legally *public worship* (to organize public worship legally?)./*If it is to do justice between the various parties & not* unduly to burden *the State, it will* . . . (burden the State unduly)./*Nobody expects that the executive of the Society is going* to assume publicly *sackcloth & ashes* (assume sackcloth & ashes publicly).

4. Just as those who know & condemn the split infinitive include many who are not recognizable, only the clumsier performers giving positive proof of resistance to temptation, so too those who know & approve are not distinguishable with certainty. When a man splits an infinitive, he may be doing it unconsciously as a member of our class (1), or he may be deliberately rejecting the trammels of convention & announcing that he means to do as he will with his own infinitives. It is perhaps fair to assume that each of the following specimens is a manifesto of independence. DELIBERATE BUT UNNECESSARY SPLIT INFINITIVES: *It will be found possible* to considerably improve *the present wages of the miners*‸ *without jeopardizing the interests of capital./But even so, he seems* to still be‸*allowed to speak at union demonstrations./The men in many of the largest districts are declared* to strongly favor *a strike*‸*if the minimum wage is not conceded.* It should be noticed that in these the separating adverb could have been placed outside the infinitive, as indicated by the caret, with little or in most cases no damage to the sentence rhythm (*considerably* after *miners, still* with clear gain after *be,* & *strongly* at some loss after *strike*), so that protest seems a safe diagnosis.

5. The attitude of those who know & distinguish is something like this: We admit that separation of *to* from its infinitive (*be, do, have, sit, doubt, kill,* or other verb inflectionally similar) is not in itself desirable, & we shall not gratuitously say either *to mortally wound* or *to mortally be wounded;* but we are not foolish enough to confuse the latter with *to be mortally wounded,* which is blameless English, nor *to just have heard* with *to have just heard,* which is also blameless. We maintain, however, that a real split infinitive, though not desirable in itself, is preferable to real ambiguity, & to patent artificiality. We will rather write *Our object is* to further cement *trade relations* than, by correcting into *Our object is* further *to cement* . . . , leave it doubtful whether an additional object or additional cementing is the point. And we take it that such reminders of a tyrannous convention as *in not combining to forbid flatly hostilities* are far more abnormal than the abnormality they evade. We will split infinitives sooner than be ambiguous or artificial. More than that, we will freely admit that sufficient recasting will get rid of any split infinitive without involving either of those faults, &

yet reserve to ourselves the right of deciding in each case whether recasting is worth while. Let us take an example: *The Commission has been feeling its way to modifications intended* to better equip *successful candidates for careers.* To better equip? We refuse 'better to equip' as a shouted reminder of the tyranny; we refuse 'to equip better' as ambiguous (*better* an adjective?); we regard 'to equip successful candidates better' as lacking compactness, as possibly tolerable from an anti-splitter, but not good enough for us. What then of recasting? *intended to make successful candidates fitter for* is the best we can do if the exact sense is to be kept; it takes some thought to arrive at the correction; was the game worth the candle?

After this inconclusive discussion, in which, however, the author's opinion has perhaps been allowed to appear with indecent plainness, readers may like to settle for themselves whether, in the following sentence, 'either to secure' followed by 'to resign,' or 'to either secure' followed by 'resign,' should have been preferred—an issue in which the meaning & the convention are pitted against each other: *He states that his agreement with Mr. Wyndham was never cancelled, & that Mr. Long was too weak* to either secure *the dismissal of Sir Antony or himself resign office.* For further discussion, see POSITION OF ADVERBS 1. (*Do you want to sit and read awhile? No, I want* to just sit.)

SPLIT VERBS. When an adverb is to be used with a compound verb, its normal place is between the auxiliary and the rest. If there are two auxiliaries the adverb stands next to the verb if adverb & verb suggest an adjective & noun. ABNORMAL: *There can be little doubt that the position of his troops all the way from Berat northward* will seriously be *imperiled.* The normal place for *seriously* is next to *imperiled.* See POSITION OF ADVERBS.

splutter, sputter. Without any clear or constant difference of meaning, it may be said that in *sputter* the notion of spitting is more insistent, & that it tends on that account to be avoided when that notion is not essential.

spoil. (1) *Spoiled* is more common in US in all senses, though *spoilt* is sometimes used as adj. (*a spoilt child*) & is often heard in speech. (OED uses in its definition *that can be spoiled, that which is spoilt.* (2) *Spoilation* is an error for *spoliation.*

spontaneity, -ousness. There is no differentiation; the first is more usual & to be preferred.

spoonerism. (Sometimes capitalized.) The accidental transposition of (initial) letters of two or more words: *a well-boiled icycle* for *a well-oiled bicycle.* From Rev. W. A. Spooner of Oxford, 'esteemed for Spoonerisms.' Of many apocrypha, *flattified & grattered.*

spoonful. Pl. *spoonfuls.*

spouse. For the use in ordinary writing in preference to *wife,* see FORMAL WORDS; but *spouse* is serviceable as short for husband-or-wife in some styles, e.g. in dictionaries or legal documents.

spring, v. The past *sprang* is more frequent than *sprung,* in all senses.

spring, n. The compounds are of interest to the hyphen-fancier. *Springboard, springtime, springtide* (the season) in US usually so written. *Spring tide* (the tidal term), *spring fever,* each two words. Brit., all *spring-* combinations usually hyphened.

springe (snare). Pron. -j.

sprint, spurt. The words are to a considerable extent interchangeable. *Sprint* is, at least apart from dialectal use, a 19th-c. word only, *spurt* going further back, but the newer word is displacing the older; a short race, or a run at high speed, is now a *sprint,* while for a quickening of pace, or a spasmodic effort bodily or mental, *spurt* is still the more usual term, but is tending to be displaced even in these senses; if that tendency could be checked, the DIFFERENTIATION would be useful. See also SPIRT.

spry makes (preferably) *spryer, spryest, spryly, spryness, spryish.* (OED says 'current in Eng. dialects but more familiar as an Americanism.')

spurt. See SPIRT & SPRINT.

Spuyten Duyvil. (Creek, N.Y.) So spelled. Pron. spīten dīval.

squalo(u)r, US usually *-or;* Brit. *-our.*

square makes *squarable* & *squarish.*

squib. Short satirical writing. For synonymy, see LAMPOON.

-s-, -ss-. So few monosyllables or words accented on the last syllable end in a single *-s* (cf. final *-l*) that rules need not be here stated. It will suffice to say that: (1) The plural of *bus* is usually *buses;* this irregularity is explained by the fact that *buses* is still regarded as an abbreviation of the regular *omnibuses;* when that is forgotten doubtless *buses* will become, as it should, *busses.* (2) *Biases* & *focuses,* nn., or vv., *biased* & *focusing,* are more regular than the *-ss-* forms (OED); similarly *canvas* (the fabric) gives *-ases* (pl. n.), *-ased,* & so too, *nimbuses, trellised, bonuses, atlases, cutlases,* &c. (3) *Nonplus* makes *nonplussed.*

St. Abbrev. for *Saint;* also S. (*S. Paul*), *Ste.* (*Ste. Agathe*). Pl. abbr. SS. See SAINT.

stable, adj., makes *stability; stabilize,* so spelled.

stadium. Pl. *-dia* for the Greek measure and racecourse; *-iums* for the modern athletic structures.

staff. (1) Pl. in music & in archaic senses, *staves;* in modern senses, *staffs.* (2) For *staff of life* (bread), see SOBRIQUETS.

stag. Male of the red deer.

stage makes *stageable, stagy;* of the chief compounds, *stage-struck* should be hyphened; *stagecoach, stagecraft, stagehand,* each one word & most others should be two words each —*stage direction, stage door, stage effect, stage fright, stage whisper. To stage-manage* (*He stage-managed the wedding*), hyphen.

stained glass. *A window made of* stained glass; *a* stained-glass *window.*

stalactite, stalagmite. Most dictionaries, US & Brit., give the stress on the second syllable first.

stale makes *stalish, stalely.*

stalemate. Chess, a draw resulting from the player's having no possible move; hence transf., a deadlock.

stalk, stem, trunk. *Stalk* is the stem of a plant less than tree or shrub; *trunk* is the stem of a large tree; *stem* is the general word applicable irrespective of size.

stamp, n. Characteristic mark, impress: *He bears the stamp of genius.* For synonymy, see SIGN.

stanch, staunch. Most US dictionaries give *staunch* as a variant. Brit. (& in US speech & many publications) the adj. is *staunch,* the verb *stanch: A* staunch *friend* or *ship;* stanch *his wounds, the flow of blood.*

stand. (1) For *it stands to reason* (the prelude to an arbitrary judgment we are not permitted to question) see REASON 2. (2) *Standpoint* is preferable to *viewpoint* or *point* alone; *point of view* is the idiomatic English expression; see POINT.

standard time. At 12 noon in Washington D.C. it is 11 a.m. in Chicago, 10 a.m. Denver, 9 a.m. San Francisco; 5 p.m. in London & Paris; 5 the next morning in Wellington, N.Z.

stanza. (Poet.): 'standing,' group of rhymed lines. Many poems consist of a succession of metrically similar line groups each of which has the same number & length of lines & the same rhyme scheme as the rest. This pattern unit is called, esp. when of more than two lines, a stanza. It may be of a generally accepted kind, as the alcaic or Spenserian or rhyme royal stanza, or one made for the occasion & observed throughout a single poem only.

starboard. (Naut., opp. to *port;* right side, looking forward.) Pron. star′bĕrd.

starlight, -lit, -litten. The first (in adj. use, e.g. *a starlight night*) may or may not be historically, but is certainly now to be regarded as, the noun used attributively. Attributive uses of nouns, like adverbial uses of apparent adjectives (see UNIDIOMATIC -LY), sometimes strike people whose zeal for grammar is greater than their knowledge of it as incorrect; & *starlit* is perhaps often substituted for *starlight* owing to this notion. No harm is done, *starlit* being a blameless word, & indeed better in some contexts. If 'a starlight night' & 'a starlit sea' have their epithets exchanged, both suffer to the extent at least of sounding unnatural. The further step to *starlitten* is not so innocent, *-litten* being not archaic but pseudo-archaic; the writer who uses *starlitten* is on a level with the tradesman who relies on such attractions as *Ye Olde Curyosytie Shoppe.*

Star-Spangled Banner. Keep the hyphen.

start. *Start in* (=begin) is US colloq. (e.g. *Let's* start in *now & see if we can finish by five. When do you* start in *working?*).

state, n. It is a convenient distinction to write *State* for the political unit, at any rate when the full noun use is required (not the attributive, as in *state trading,* but *Church and State*) & *state* in other senses. The following forms are recommended: *statecraft, stateroom, stateless, state's evidence, states' rights.*

state, v. *State* is one of the verbs that insist on proper ceremony & resent the omission of THAT, CONJ. WRONG: *He then stated, to our embarrassment,*^ *his family had long been mem-*

bers and . . . That must be inserted.

stationary, -ery. The adj. (not moving), *-ary;* the noun (paper &c.), *-ery.*

statist. In US the word meaning statistician, when used, is pronounced stătist. That meaning advocate of or advocating statism, stātist. Brit. both stātist, but the Brit. paper, *The Stătist.*

statistic(al), adj. The short form is almost obs.

status. The *status quo* is the position in which things (1) are now or (2) have been till now or (3) were when or (4) had been till then; in senses (2) & (4) *ante* (*the status quo ante*) is sometimes, but need not be, added. With *in* the phrase becomes *in statu quo* (*ante*), without *the,* & with *ante* similarly optional.

statutable, -tory. The two words are hardly distinguishable in meaning; *-table* is considerably older, & *-tory* perhaps now more usual; a natural DIFFERENTIATION would be that *-table* should take the sense permitted, & *-tory* the sense enjoined, by statute. *Statutable authority; statutory penalties.*

staunch, adj. In US also STANCH.

stave, v. The past & p.p. *stove* (instead of *staved*) is modern & (OED) 'chiefly Naut.'

staves. See STAFF.

stead, n. WRONG: *The atmosphere of the home life was favorable to the growth of qualities which were presently to stand him* in inestimable stead. *To stand one in good* or *better, much* or *more, little* or *less stead;* those are perhaps the limits within which the phrase can now, without affectation, be used; words like *inestimable* should not be substituted; see CAST-IRON IDIOM.

steadfast is now the established spelling, preferable as exhibiting the connection with *stead* & *steady; sted-* was formerly much the commoner, & is still seen.

steam. (1) In US the chief combinations beginning with *steam* are best written as follows (usage differs in Brit.): As one word: *steamboat, steamship, steampipe, steamcar, steamtight.* As two words: *steam brake, boiler, roller, whistle, engine, fitter, table, heat, shovel. Steam-roller* is hyphened as a verb or adj.: *He* steam-rollered *the bill through Congress; steam-roller tactics.* (3) *Steamship* is abbr. SS or S.S. *U.S.S.*=United States Steamer or Ship; *H.M.S.*=Her (or His) Majesty's Ship.

stele. Upright slab or pillar (gravestone); pron. stē'lē; pl. *-lae.* In Archery, the body of an arrow, pron. stēl; in Bot. stēlē or stēl.

stem. (1) (Gram.): A word's stem is the part from which its inflections may be supposed to have been formed by the addition of affixes; in the inflections it may be found unchanged, or may have been affected by phonetic tendencies. Thus the stem of *man* is *man,* giving *man's, men,* & *men's.* Cf. ROOT. Of the English verb *wit* the root is VID, but the stem, giving *wit, wot, wist, wottest,* &c., is *wit.* Different parts of a 'word' may be formed from different stems; there are e.g. several stems in what is called the verb *be.* (2) See STALK.

stemma. Pl. *-mata.*

stencil makes US *-lable, -led,* &c.; Brit. *-llable, -lled.*

step. For *step this way, step in,* &c., see FORMAL WORDS.

steppingstone. One word.

stereotype. Pron. four syllables.

sterile. The older spellings (*-il, -ill,* &c.) suggest that the pronunciation -īl is modern, & it is still probably less common than -ĭl (esp. in US). Noun *sterility.*

stern, adj. For *the sterner sex,* see BATTERED ORNAMENTS.

stet. 'Let it stand.' Printing direction to cancel a correction, accompanied by dots under the material to be stetted. *Glamo̶u̶r/stet* is printed *Glamour.*

sticking-place, -point. In the *Macbeth* passage, *-place* is the word (*But screw your courage to the sticking place, and we'll not fail.*) The reference is presumably to a peg in a musical instrument, screwed until it will stick; see MISQUOTATION.

stickler. One who contends or stands out for (something): *A stickler for official reticence.* The word is not modern slang but has been used since the 17th c.

stick-to-itiveness. US colloq. Seemingly so spelled.

stigma. Pl. *stigmata* in Eccl. & scientific senses; *stigmas* only in the fig. sense of imputation of disgrace, in which a plural is rare.

stigmatize. Things are not *stigmatized monstrous,* but *stigmatized as monstrous.* The mistake, fully dealt with under REGARD 2, occurs rarely with *stigmatize.* WRONG: *Bravely suffering forfeiture & imprisonment rather than accept what in this same connection Lord Morley* stigmatized‸*the 'bar sinister.'* Insert *as.*

stile, style. *Stile* is the spelling for the means of passage & for the carpentry term (*stiles & rails*); *style* for all other senses.

stiletto. Pl. *-os.*

stilly. Pron. the poetic adj. stĭ'lĭ, the adv. stĭl'lĭ.

stilted. (From 'artificially raised, as on stilts.') Fig., of language &c., affectedly lofty; pompous, artificially formal.

stimulus. Pl. *-li.*

sting. *Stung* is the past & p.p. (*stang* archaic).

stink. Past *stank* or *stunk,* both in current use.

stipend. A fixed periodical payment of any kind (e.g. a pension, or allowance); esp. a clergyman's official income. Often a FORMAL WORD or used facetiously for *wage* or *salary.* In Brit. *a stipendiary magistrate* is a 'paid police magistrate in large towns, paid by the Home Secretary.'

stirrup (properly pron. stĭr'up, pop. stûr'-) comes from a word meaning to climb, and has nothing to do with the verb to stir.

STOCK PATHOS. Some words & phrases have become so associated with melancholy occasions that it seems hardly decent to let such an occasion pass unattended by any of them. It is true that such trappings & suits of woe save much trouble. It is true that to mock at them lays one open to suspicion of hardheartedness. It is also true that the use of them suggests, if not quite insincerity, yet a factitious sort of emotion, & those are well advised who abstain from them. A small relection, which might be greatly enlarged, is: *In her great sorrow; The land he loved so well; The supreme sacrifice; The mortal remains of; The departed; One more unfortunate; More sinned against than sinning; A lump in one's throat; Tug at one's heartstrings; Stricken; Loved & lost; Hour of need.*

stoep. See STOOP.

stogie, stogy. The boot and the cigar. (From Con*estoga* wagon.) The dictionaries do not agree on the spelling, but the first is nearer the original and more often used.

stoic(al). Both forms are used as adjs., *-ic* being indeed the commoner; but points of difference are discernible. In the predicative use *stoic* is rare: *his acceptance of the news was* stoical, *he was* stoical *in temper,* rather than *stoic.* In the attributive use, *stoic* naturally preserves the original sense more definitely, while *stoical* forgets it. When we say *stoic indifference,* we mean such indifference as the Stoics taught or practiced; when we say *stoical indifference* we think of it merely as resolute or composed. The *stoic virtues* are those actually taught by the Stoics, *the stoical virtues* simply those of the sterner kind. Lastly, while either epithet is applicable to abstracts, *stoical* is the word for persons; *with stoic* or *stoical composure; stoic* or *stoical life* or *tone* or *temper* or *views; he is a stoical fellow; these stoical explorers; a stoical sufferer; my stoical young friend.*

stokehold, -hole. In US the first is used in the Naut. senses; in Brit. the second. In US *stokehole* is used only for the opening into a furnace.

stomach. For genteel use, see BELLY. The US expression of nausea is *sick at* (NOT *to*) *the stomach.*

stomacher, article of dress. The old pronunciation was with -cher, which should be kept to as long as the word is historical only, & not revived with the thing in modern use.

stone, n. *Rolling stone* should not be hyphened; *steppingstone* is one word. The measure of weight (of man, chiefly Brit. or US scientific)=14 pounds. (A man weighing 12 stone=182 lbs.)

stony. So spelled.

stool. 'To fall between two stools' is to fail through vacillating between two courses of action.

stoop. US, from Dutch *stoep* (pron. stōōp). Orig. a (covered) porch (with seats) at the entrance to a house, introduced into US in colonial N.Y.

stop, v. Those who use *stop* when others would use *stay* (*Where are you stopping?* &c.) are many, & are frequently rebuked. The OED deals very gently with them: 'Cf. *stay,* which is often preferred as more correct'; & it is not a case for denunciation, but rather for waiting to see which word will win. Meanwhile, careful speakers do prefer *stay;* & it is in its favor, & a sign of its being still in possession, that its noun, & not *stop,* is certainly the right one in the corresponding sense (*during our stay in New York,* NOT *our stop*). It may also be suggested that, if *stop* is a solecism, there are degrees of enormity in the offense: *Won't you* stop *to dinner?, I shall* stop in town *till I hear, We have been* stopping *at the Deanery,* of which the last is the worst, point to a limitation—that *stop* is tolerable only when postponement of departure rather than place of sojourn is in question.

stops &c. (Brit.)=(US) punctuation. *Full stop=period.* See PUNCTUATION; also *apostrophe, brackets, colon, comma, dashes, exclamation, hyphen, italics, period, semicolon, question & quotation marks.*

stor(e)y. Pl. *-eys* or *-ies,* adj. *-storeyed, -ied.* US usually *story.* The DIFFERENTIATION lacks the support of the OED; the 19th-c. quotations are found to show *-ry* & *-ries* four times as often as *-rey* & *-reys.* See also FLOOR.

story. For *But that is another story,* see HACKNEYED PHRASES. It is not mended by variations, such as: *He had read a story—but never mind that now.*

stouten. Now chiefly colloq. or dial.

stove. See STAVE.

Strad. Short for *Stradivarius,* violin made by Antonio Stradivari, of Cremona, Italy (1644–1737). See CURTAILED WORDS.

strafe. To bombard &c. (From 'Gott strafe England,' used by Germans in the First World War.) Pron. US strāf, Brit. & Ger. sträf.

straight(ly). *Straight* is an adv. as well as an adj. *Walk, stand,* &c. *straight.* UNIDIOMATIC: *Certain members of the Party have spoken very honestly &* straightly *about the growth of this idea./For once, he did not mince his words on a labor question; would that he had spoken as* straightly *on previous occasions!* These two examples, of which the first shows a perhaps defensible *straightly,* & the second a certainly indefensible one, throw some light on the regrettable but progressive extension of our old monosyllabic adverbs; it is the company of *honestly* that partly excuses the first *straightly;* see UNIDIOMATIC -LY.

straightforward, adj., one word; *straight-faced,* adj., hyphen.

strait(en). The chief phrases in which these, & not *straight(en),* must be used are: *the strait gate, the straitest sect, strait jacket, strait-laced, straitened circumstances.* (*Strait*= tight, narrow, &c.)

strata. Pl. of *stratum* (pron. strā- or strä-, NOT stră-). *He came from* the lowest strata *of society* is conceivably possible, if there are several strata all occupying that lowest place; *from one of the lowest strata* would be better even so. WRONG: *He came from* that strata *of society from which so many* &c.; use *stratum.*

stratagem. Artifice, trick, orig. of generalship, to outwit the enemy. Hence, deception.

strategy, tactics. *Strategy*= 'the art of a commander-in-chief; the art of projecting & directing the larger military movements & operations of a campaign. Usually distinguished from *tactics,* which is the art of handling forces in battle or in the immediate presence of the enemy' (OED).

stratum. Pl. STRATA.

stratus. Pl. *-ti.* Continuous horizontal formation of cloud, of comparatively low altitude.

streamline, adj., should be used only when the mechanical meaning is present or suggested —of a shape or body designed to meet the smallest amount of resistance when passing through air or water: *a streamline automobile* or *boat* or *aircraft*. In transf. and fig. use (still close to slang)=brought up to date, modernized, stripped of superfluities, *streamlined: a streamlined version of the classics.*

stress, strain, as technical terms in Physics. Any close examination of such matters is outside our scope, but the layman may be glad of a rough distinction. It is perhaps safe to say that *strain* is the result of stress; *stress* being mutual action exerted by bodies or parts, *strain* is the alteration of form or dimensions produced by it. *Stress,* v., fig., to lay stress or emphasize, was labeled 'chiefly US' in OED, but is now standard Brit.

strew, p.p. indifferently *-ed* & *-n.*

stria. Pl. *-iae.*

stricken. This archaic p.p. of *strike* survives chiefly in particular phrases, & especially in senses divorced from those now usual with the verb—*stricken in years, a stricken field, the stricken deer, for a stricken hour, poverty-stricken, panic-stricken.* The use of the word by itself as adj.=afflicted, in distress, is sometimes justified, but more often comes under the description of STOCK PATHOS.

stride, p.p. (rare) *stridden.*

stringed, strung. Accurately, a bow is *stringed* or *unstringed* according as it is provided with a string or not, & *strung* or *unstrung* according as it is bent to the string or not; cf. *stringed instruments* & *strung nerves;* so *a high-strung temperament* but *a gut-stringed racket. Overstrung piano,* which suggests a difficulty, is right because the notion is not that of providing it with overstrings as the racket is provided with gut strings (implying formation from the noun *string*), but that of stringing it transversely (from the verb *string* with the adverb *over*).

striped. Best pron. strīpt, not strīpĕd.

strive. Past *strove,* p.p. *striven;* but the OED adds that 'many examples of *strived*' for both 'occur in writers of every period from the 14th to 19th c.'

stroma. Pl. *-ata.*

strophe. Pron. strō′fĭ; pl. *-s* or *-phae.*

struma. Pl. *-mae.*

strung. See STRINGED.

stubbornness. So spelled.

studding-sail. Pron. stŭ′nsl.

student. A *University student, medical student, student of life, of manners; a good student, poor student;* but *a great scholar, a high-school pupil.*

studio. Pl. *-os.*

stuff. *Such stuff as dreams are made* on, NOT *of* (*Tempest* IV, i. 146). See MISQUOTATIONS.

stump. The senses to nonplus (slang: *the problem really* had me stumped) and to travel while electioneering (*During the campaign he* stumped *the Middle West*) were both orig. US (now also used in Brit.).

stupefy. So spelled.

stupor, NOT *stupour,* US or Brit.

STURDY INDEFENSIBLES. Many idioms are seen, if they are tested by grammar or logic, to express badly, even sometimes to express the reverse of, what they are nevertheless well understood to mean. Good people point out the sin, & bad people, who are more numerous, take little notice & go on committing it. Then the good people, if they are foolish, get excited & talk of ignorance & solecisms, & are laughed at as purists; or, if they are wise, say no more about it & wait. The indefensibles, sturdy as they may be, prove one after another to be not immortal. There was a time when no one was more ashamed to say 'You was there' than most of us now are to say 'It's me'; 'You was' is dead; 'it's me' has a long life before it yet; it too will die, & there are much more profitable ways of spending time than baiting it. It is well, however, to realize that there are such things as foolish idioms; that a language should abound in them can be no credit to it or its users; & the drawing of attention to them is a step toward making them obsolete. A few types follow, with references to articles in which each question is touched upon:

It's ME.

Don't be longer than you can HELP.

So far from hating him, I like him (FAR 2).

The man of all others for the job (OF 7).

The worst liar of any man I know (OF 7).

A child of ten years old (OF 7).

That long nose of his (OF 7).

It is no USE complaining.

Were ever finer lines perverted to a meaner use? (ILLOGICALITIES).

It is a day's work even to open, much less to acknowledge, all the letters (MUCH 2).

For two reasons, neither of which are noticed by Plato (NEITHER 3).

All men do not speak German. (NOT 1).

He ONLY died a week ago.

It should not be taken TOO literally.

I should not be SURPRISED if it didn't rain.

sty, nn. Pl. *sties.* The separate spelling *stye* (pl. *styes*), sometimes used for the pimple on the eyelid, has not the support of the OED, & the danger of confusion is too slight for artificial DIFFERENTIATION.

style. New Style, Old Style, in ref. to dates=according to the Gregorian and Julian calendars. The Gregorian calendar (introduced by Pope Gregory XIII in 1582 & adopted by Great Britain and the American colonies in 1752) added 10 days to dates from 1582 to 1700, 11 days from 1700–1800; 12 days from 1800–1900; and 13 days after 1900. Thus 5 October 1582 O.S.=15 October 1582 N.S.

stymie. So spelled in US; Brit. now *stimy* (but OED makes *stymie* the standard spelling). If used as a verb, usually *stymied,* but probably *stymying.*

suave. In US usually pron. swäv, Brit. swāv.

sub-. As a prefix, in US usually attached to words without hyphen: *subeditor, subgroup, subhuman;* Brit. *sub-editor, subheading, sub-title,* &c. *Sub rosa,* 'under the rose,' i.e. the symbol of secrecy; hence confidentially, in secret.

subdual. An old but ugly form; *subduing* will usually serve as the noun.

SUBJUNCTIVES. Subjunctives met with today, outside the few truly living uses, are either deliberate revivals by poets for legitimate enough archaic effect, or antiquated survivals as in pretentious journalism, infecting their context with dullness, or new arrivals possible only in an age to which the grammar of the subjunctive is not natural but artificial.

Alive: *If I were you . . .*

Revival: *When I ask her if she* love *me* (prose, *loves*).

Survival: *If this analysis* be *correct* (normal, *is*).

Arrival: *If this* were *so, it was in self-defense* (sense, *was*).

We may now proceed to illustrate the four classes—Alives, Revivals, Survivals, & Arrivals—& no concealment need be made of the purpose in hand, which is to discourage the last two classes.

ALIVES: Those uses are alive which it occurs to no one to suspect of pedantry or artificiality, & which come as natural in speech as other ways of saying the thing, or more so. The giving of a few specimens is all that will here be necessary.

Go away (& all 2nd-pers. imperatives).

Manners be hanged! (& such 3rd-pers. curses).

Come what may, Be that as it may, Far be it from me to . . . (& other such stereotyped formulae).

I shall be 70 come *Tuesday.*

If he were here now (& all *if . . . were* clauses expressing a hypothesis that is not a fact; *were* & not *be,* & not a fact, are essential).

I wish it were *over.*

Though all care be *exercised* (the difference is still a practical one between *Though . . . is*=In spite of the fact that, & *Though . . . be*=Even on the supposition that).

REVIVALS: *What care I how fair she* be?

Lose who may, *I still can say . . .*

If ladies be *but young & fair.*

But illustration is superfluous; there are no uses of the subjunctive to which poets, & poetic writers, may not resort if it suits them. The point to be made is merely that it is no defense for the ordinary writer who uses an antiquated subjunctive to plead that he can parallel it in a good poet.

SURVIVALS: In the examples that will be given there is nothing incorrect (the subjunctive with *if* & *though* was normal quite recently). The objection to the subjunctives in them is that they diffuse an atmosphere of dullness & formalism over the writing in which they occur. The motive underlying them & the effect they produce are the same that attend the choosing of FORMAL WORDS, a reference to which article may save some repetition. The normal form is given in parentheses.

If it have (has) *a flaw, that flaw takes the shape of a slight incoherence./It is quite obvious to what grave results such instances as the above may lead,* be they (if they are) *only sufficiently numerous./If these others* be (are) *all we can muster, it* were (would be) *better to leave the sculpture galleries empty.*

ARRIVALS: The best proof that the subjunctive is, except in isolated uses, no longer alive, & one good reason for abstaining from it even where, as in the Survival examples, it is grammatical, are provided by a collection, such as anyone can gather for himself from any newspaper, of subjunctives that are wrong. That two verbs whose relation to their surroundings is the same should be one subjunctive, & one indicative, is an absurdity that could not happen until the distinction had lost its reality; but it does happen every day. WRONG: *If that appeal* be *made & results in the return of the Government to power, then . . ./There are those who, if there* be *common security & they* are *all right, not only care nothing for, but would even oppose, the . . .* These *bes* are not themselves wrong; they are Survival subjunctives; but the fact that the verbs associated with them, which have subjunctives ready for use just as much as *to be*, are allowed to remain indicative shows that the use of *be* too is mechanical & meaningless.

Were in conditionals: The correct type, a common enough Survival, is *Were that true there* were *no more to say;* the first *were* is right only in combination with the other *were*, or with its modern equivalent, *would* (should) *be;* & neither of them is applicable to past time any more than *would be* itself. Their reference is to present or to undefined time, or more truly not to time at all (& especially not to a particular past time) but to utopia, the realm of non-fact. If it is hard to accept that *were* (sing.) in conditionals does not refer to past time, consider some other verb of past form in like case. Such a verb may belong to past time, or it may belong to utopia: (1) *If he* heard, *he* gave *no sign* (*heard* and *gave*, past time); (2) *If he* heard, *how angry he* would be! (*heard* & *would be*, not past time, but utopia, the realm of non-fact or the imaginary); in (1) *heard* is indicative, in (2) it is subjunctive, though the form happens to be the same. In the verb *be*, conveniently enough, there happens to be still a distinguishable form for the subjunctive, & what corresponds for the verb *be* to the two *heard* sentences is (1) *If it* was (NEVER *were*) *so, it did not appear;* (2) *If it* were (or nowadays alternatively *was*) *so how angry we* should be! *Were* (sing.) is, then, a recognizable subjunctive, & applicable not to past facts, but to present or future non-facts. It is entirely out of place in an *if*-clause concerned with past actualities & not answered by a *were* or *would be* in the following clause. WRONG (read *was*): *It is stated that, during the early part of the war, the Greeks massacred Mussulmans; if this* were *so, it was only in self defense./If rent* were *cheap, clothes were dearer than today./We must not look for any particulars as to that lost work, if it* were *ever written.*

Sequence: Perhaps from a hazy memory of the SEQUENCE OF TENSES and of moods in Latin grammar, some writers use a wrong or uncalled-for subjunctive in a clause following one containing an alive conditional or subjunctive. WRONG: *If I made a political pronouncement here I should feel that I* were *outraging the hospitality of the Movement* (use *was*). *Why should the front office enjoy a half-holiday while the staff behind the scenes, often working in overheated rooms and factory conditions,* be *denied this privilege* (use *is*).

Indirect question: Latin grammar is perhaps also responsible for the notion that indirect questions require the subjunctive. There is no such requirement in English; *Ask him who he is* (not *be*) is enough to show that. *Adams asked Sir Richard if he* were *aware that one of the miners' secretaries had been . . .* Read *was;* but again such subjunctives may be found in older writers.

Miscellaneous. WRONG: *He therefore came to the view that simple Bible teaching were better abolished altogether & that the open door for all religions* were *established in its place. Were better abolished* is a correct Survival; but dealing with the now unnatural has tempted the writer into an impossible continuation; read *should be./ He replied that if his department* were *to be successful, he must accommodate himself to the people who employed him.* His words were not 'If my department be to succeed,' but 'is to.' The sequence change of *is* should be to *was,* & *were* instead ruins the sense; 'were to be successful' means 'succeeded' or 'should succeed,' not 'was to have a chance.'

The conclusion is that writers who deal in Survival subjunctives run the risks, first, of making their matter dull, secondly, of being tempted into blunders themselves, thirdly, of injuring the language by encouraging others more ignorant than they to blunder habitually, & lastly, of having the proper dignity of style at which they aim mistaken by captious readers for pretentiousness.

subpoena. Best so written; p.p. *subpoenaed.* Pron. sŭbpēn'*a*, or sŭpēn'*a*.

subservience, -cy. The first is better.

subsidence. The OED and US dictionaries give preference to subsī'dence over (COD) sub'sĭdence. But *residence, confidence, providence,* & *coincidence,* all associated with verbs in *-ide,* are a very strong argument on the other side, against which perhaps no opposite instance of any weight can be brought. Sub'- is therefore recommended.

substantiate makes *-tiable, substantiation* (pron. -shĭā'-sh*u*n).

substitute, v., substitution. A change—according to the view here taken, a corruption—has been taking place in the meaning & use of these words; what the OED stigmatized in 1915 as 'Now regarded as incorrect' will soon, if nothing can be done to stop it, become normal usage & oust what is here held to be the words' only true sense. The meaning in question is (for the verb) 'To take the place of, replace,' & in 1925 an examination of other dictionaries (Century, Standard, Webster, Cassell's Encyclopaedic, & some small fry) proved that none of them recorded this sense at all, with the exception of the Standard, in which it is confined to Chemistry. They all agreed that the verb means something entirely different, viz. to put (a person or thing) in the place of another. By 1950 'replace by or with' may be found in most dictionaries and only the COD adds 'vulg.' It is clear, then, what the orthodox use of the verb is. The use of the noun follows it.

CORRECT: (A) *We had to* substitute *margarine* (*for butter*)./(B) *Aliens* are being substituted (*for Englishmen*)./(C)

Aliens are replacing *Englishmen.*/(D) *The* substitution *of margarine (for butter) is having bad effects.*/(E) *Let there be no more* substitution *of aliens (for Englishmen).*/(F) *Its* substitution (*for butter*) *is lamentable.* UNDESIRABLE: (A) *We had to* substitute *butter* (by *margarine*)./(B) *Englishmen are being* substituted (by *aliens*)./(C) *Aliens are* substituting *Englishmen.*/(D) *The* substitution *of butter* (by *margarine*) *is having bad effects.*/ (E) *Let there be no more* substitution *of Englishmen* (by *aliens*)./(F) *Its* substitution (by *margarine*) *is lamentable.*

It is high time that *replace* were reinstated & *substitute* reduced to its proper function.

subtle, subtil(e), &c. The modern forms are *subtle, subtler, subtlest, subtly,* but *subtilize; b* is silent in all. Spellings with the *i* retained (*subtile* &c.) are (except in *subtilize*) usually left to archaists of various kinds; &, as Milton was content with *suttle,* there seems little reason for going back beyond *subtle* to *subtile.*

subversal. *Subversion* is the standard form.

subversive is an adj., not a noun. *They are all subversives* may pass colloq., but not in serious writing.

succeed. Constr. *in* with the gerund, not *to* with infinitive. WRONG: *All the traditions in which she has been brought up have not* succeeded to keep *her back.* Read *in keeping,* & see GERUND.

success. For *success of esteem* (*succès d'estime,* a favorable reception from respect, not a popular or profitable success), see GALLICISMS 5.

succinct. Pron. -ks-.

succo(u)r. US *-or,* Brit. *-our.*

succuba, -bus. Pl. *-ae, -i;* the words mean the same, & are not respectively feminine & masculine.

such. This article is divided into 7 sections: 1. *Such which, who,* &c. 2. *Such that.* 3. *Such* exclamatory or appealing. 4. Illiterate *such.* 5. *Such*=so. 6. *Such as* for *as.* 7. *Suchlike.*

1. *Such which, who, that* (rel. pron.), *where* (rel. adv.). *Such* is a demonstrative adjective & demonstrative pronoun, to which it was formerly common to make other relatives besides *as* correspond, esp. *which, who, that,* & *where.* Modern idiom rejects all these, & confines itself to *as.* The OED's remark on the use of *such . . . which* &c. is 'Now rare & regarded as incorrect.' It is not in fact so very rare; but most modern examples of it are due either to writers' entire ignorance of idiom or to their finding themselves in a difficulty & not seeing how to get out of it. In the following extracts, when a mere change of *which* &c. to *as* is not possible, the way out, or a way, is indicated. WRONG: *The Government contends that it has only requisitioned* such things *of which there is abundance in the country* (*such things as are abundant,* or *as there is abundance of*)./*It is subject, of course, to* such *possible changes of plan* that (as) *any unexpected turn of events may bring about.*/*The first zone, where the regulations are not so onerous, covers* such *tracts* where *there are no real signs of war* (read *the* or *those* for *such;* or *as show* for *where there are*).

2. *Such that* rel., *such that*

conj. Now & then a *such that* for *such as* is perhaps due to the writer's hesitating between two ways of putting a thing, one with the relative *as* & the other with the conjunction *that,* & finally achieving neither, but stumbling into the relative *that.* WRONG: *They will never learn the truth from this system of inquiries, because they will only see the results if those are* such that *the Government would like them to see* (*such as the Government would like them to see?* or *such that the Government would like them to be seen?*)./*I cannot think that there is* such a different level *of intelligence among Englishmen & Germans* that *would prevent similar papers from being profitable property in Great Britain* (*such . . . as would prevent?* or *such . . . that it would prevent?*).

3. *Such* exclamatory or appealing. *A piece of constitutional antiquarianism of which Scott made* such *splendid use in 'Peveril of the Peak.'* *Such* is liable to the same overuse of this kind as *so;* reference to so 3 will make further illustration unnecessary here. Use & overuse of an idiom are different things, & there is no need to avoid this *such* altogether. In the quotation above it may be noticed that if the writer had said *the piece* of antiquarianism instead of *a piece* the *such* would have passed well enough.

4. The illiterate *such* (=that, those, it, them, &c.). The significance of the epithet will be found explained in ILLITERACIES, & a few examples with corrections will suffice. WRONG: *That there is a void in a millionaire's life is not disproved by anyone showing that a number of millionaires do not recognize* such *void* (recognize *it,* or *the* or *that void*)./*But when it comes to us following his life & example, all will, I think, agree that* such *is impossible* (that that is)./*An appeal to philanthropy is hardly necessary, the grounds for* such *being so self-evident* (for it being).

5. *Such*=so. Most people have no hesitation in saying *such a small matter, such big apples, with such little justice, such conflicting evidence;* others object that it should be *so small a matter, apples so big, with so little justice, evidence so conflicting.* It must first be admitted that the objectors are (with allowances for phrases of special meaning) entitled to claim the support of grammar. In 'such a small matter' it is usually *small,* not *matter* or *small matter,* that is to be modified by *such* or *so,* &, *small* being an adj., the adv. *so* is obviously the grammatical word to do the job. At the same time, *such a small matter,* though it usually means *so small a matter,* may also mean a small matter of the kind that has been described; but, speaking generally, the objectors have grammar on their side. Shall we then be meek & mend our ways at their bidding? Why, no, not wholesale. We will try to say *so* wherever idiom does not protest or stiffness ensue; for instance, we will give up 'with such little justice' without a murmur; but they cannot expect of us 'I never saw apples so big' instead of 'such big apples.' And they must please to remark that the *such* idiom has so established itself that the other is often impossible without a change of order that suggests formality or rhetoric; *so big ap-*

ples? so convincing evidence? no; the adjective has to be deferred (*apples so big*) in a clearly artificial way; but we grant that 'so small a matter' does strictly deserve preference over 'such a small matter,' &, if so partial a concession is worth their acceptance, let it be made.

6. *Such as* for *as.* WRONG: *Even the effects of unfavorable weather can be partially counteracted by artificial treatment* such as by *the use of phosphates.* The repetition of *by* results in a *such as* not introducing, as it should, a noun (*use*), but a preposition (*by*)—a plain but not uncommon blunder. Omit either *such* or *by./Some are able to help in one way,* such as *for instance* in speaking; *some in another, such as organization.* The second part is right; the first should be either *in one way such as for instance speaking,* or *in one way as for instance in speaking; such as* requires a noun (*speaking*), not an adverbial phrase (*in speaking*), as its completion.

7. *Suchlike.* That the word is a sort of pleonasm in itself, being ultimately=*solike-like,* is nothing to its discredit, such pleonasms being numerous (cf. *poulterer*=pullet+-er+-er); but, whether as adj. (*barley, oats, & suchlike cereals*) or as pronoun (*schoolmasters, plumbers, & suchlike*), it is now usually left to the uneducated, *such* being used as the adj. & *the like* as the pronoun. The OED, however, abstains from comment.

suddenness. So spelled.

sue makes *suable.*

suffer. (1) *She is suffering from a fit of depression,* NOT of. (2) *Sufferable* (that can be 'suffered,' endurable) is now rare except in the negative (*it simply isn't sufferable*), and then is usually *insufferable* except for emphasis. (3) For *Suffer a sea-change,* see SEA.

sufficiency. Usually archaic or WORN-OUT HUMOR (*an elegant sufficiency, a genteel sufficiency*).

sufficient(ly) & enough. *Sufficient* as a noun is a GENTEELISM or 'vulg.' (COD) for *enough.* The words are discussed under ENOUGH; for *sufficient* in the following extracts, see the first paragraph of that article. WRONG: *So far as the building trade is concerned, the complaint we have made to the Government is that* sufficient *has not been done to get materials organized./And there should be* sufficient of *a historic conscience left in the Capital to evoke a large subscription.*

suffix. (Gram.): 'attached below.' An affix (q.v.) at the end of a word or stem to make a derivative, as *-cy, -ship, -ful,* in *tenan(t)cy, lordship,* & *fearful.*

suffuse makes *-sable.*

suggest makes *suggestible.*

suggestio falsi. Pron. sujes'-tĭō făl'sī. (Rhet.): 'suggestion of the untrue.' The making of a statement from which, though it is not actually false, the natural & intended inference is a false one; e.g. if A, asked whether B is honest, replies, though he in fact knows no harm of B, that his principle is to live & let live & he is not going to give away his old friend, the questioner infers that A knows B to be dishonest. Cf. SUPPRESSIO VERI.

suicide, n., may properly be used of both the person & the act, but not as a verb. (*He is* *a suicide; he was driven to suicide* (n.) or *to commit suicide;* but NOT *I'm afraid he will suicide.*) WRONG: *At the end of the performance, after Brutus* had suicided, *another boy came forward to speak the epilogue.*

suit, suite, nn. (*Suite,* pron. swēt.) The two words are the same, & the differences of usage accidental & variable; but where, the sense being a set, either form would seem admissible, we do say at present *a suit of clothes, a suit of armor, a suit of sails, the four suits* at cards, *follow suit;* & on the other hand *a suite* (of attendants &c.), *a suite of rooms* or *apartments, a suite of furniture* or *chairs.*

sulfur, -phur. The *-fur* spelling is now more usual in US ('preferred by US chemists,' Webster) in the word and the *sulf-* derivatives. *Sulphur* is standard Brit.

sullenness. So spelled.

sumac, -ach. US usually *sumac* (pron. shōō- or sū-); Brit. usually *-ach.*

summarily. (Accent first syllable.) Meanings: (1) In a summary (i.e. compendious) manner, concisely, esp. of a statement: *It is my purpose summarily to sketch the broadest results.* (2) By summary legal procedure: *Restitution of the goods in the hands of the trustee may be claimed summarily.* (3) Without hesitation, unnecessary formality, or delay: *They summarily refused all suggestions.* When there can be any confusion, esp. between (1) & (3), another word should be chosen.

summer. *Summer time,* Brit.= US daylight saving time. *Summertime,* one word, is the summer season.

summersault, -set. Var. of SOMERSAULT.

summon(s). (1) For *summon & send for,* see FORMAL WORDS. (2) *Summons,* n., has pl. *summonses.* (3) *Summon* is the verb in ordinary use; *summons* should not be used as a verb except in the special sense to serve with a legal summons or issue a summons against, & even in that sense *summon* is equally good.

Sunday. See FRIDAY.

sunk(en). *A sunken garden, sunken eyes;* but *the ship would have sunk.* See SINK.

super. The use of this as an abbreviation for 'of a superior kind,' & in combinations such as *superman, super-dreadnought, super-critic,* & scores or hundreds of other words, is so evidently convenient that it is vain to protest when others indulge in it, & so evidently barbarous that it is worth while to circumvent it oneself when one can do so without becoming unintelligible.

superb. Of the most impressive or noble or exalted kind. As a mere emphatic (*the food was superb*), colloq. See POSITIVE WORDS for a caution on contexts to which the word is unsuitable.

supererogation. (Performance of more than is required.) For *a work of supererogation,* see HACKNEYED PHRASES.

SUPERFLUOUS WORDS. That there are such things in the language is likely to be admitted, & perhaps it might be safe even to hazard the generality that they ought to be put in a black list & cast out; but woe to the miscreant who dares post up the first list of proscriptions! Brevity & timidity will therefore be the marks of our specification; the victims will be mainly such as have no friends, with just one or two of other kinds slipped in to redeem the experiment from utterly negligible insignificance. Indeed, it is more necessary to account for the tameness of the list than to defend its boldness; & for this purpose it must be borne in mind that most of the words naturally thought of as conspicuously suitable for expulsion (say *meticulous, asset, protagonist, individual,* & the like), abominable as they are in their prevalent modern senses, are not superfluous, because each of them has somewhere in the background a sense or senses at least worth preserving, & often of importance; the use of them needs to be mended, but not ended, & they are dealt with elsewhere. The list follows; reasons for the condemnation should be looked for under the word concerned unless a special article is indicated: *emotive; épopée; faience; femineity* (FEMININENESS); *flamboyant; gentlemanlike; habitude; intrigue,* v.; *lithesome; minify; quieten; righten* (-EN VERBS); *rotatory; smoothen* (-EN VERBS); *un-come-at-able.*

superior. (1) For *has few equals & no superiors,* see HACKNEYED PHRASES. (2) The patronizing use (*a most superior woman*), in which one expects it to be understood always that the person one calls *superior* is nevertheless one's inferior, resembles the corresponding uses of *honest, worthy,* & *good,* in producing on the hearer an unfavorable impression of the speaker. (3) *Superior to,* NOT *superior than,* is required by idiom; but such is the power of ANALOGY that even people who obviously cannot be described as uneducated are sometimes capable of treating *superior* as we all treat *better* or *greater.* The quotations are purposely given at sufficient length to show that the writers are not mere blunderers. WRONG: *Mr. Ernle desired first to translate Homer, & in looking about for a meter decided on the hexameter as the most appropriate &* superior *for this style of the heroic* than *the blank or rhymed verse of the great English masters* (read *better . . . than,* or *superior . . . to*)./*Able & public-spirited men have refused to accept the dictation of the B.M.A., & are giving far* superior *attention to the insured persons* than *was possible under the cheap conditions of the old club practice* (read *greater . . . than,* or *superior . . . to what*).

SUPERIORITY. Surprise a person of the class that is supposed to keep servants cleaning his own boots & either he will go on with the job while he talks to you, as if it were the most natural thing in the world, or else he will explain that his servant is ill & give you to understand that he is, despite appearances, superior to boot-cleaning. If he takes the second course, you conclude that he is not superior to it; if the first, that perhaps he is. So it is with the various apologies (*to use an expressive colloquialism—if we may adopt the current slang—in the vernacular phrase—so to speak—in homely phrase—not to put too fine a point upon it*) to which recourse is had by writers who wish to safeguard their dignity & yet be vivacious, to combine comfort with elegance, to touch pitch & not be defiled. They should make up their minds whether their reputation or their style is such as to allow of their dismounting from the high horse now & again without compromising themselves; if they can do that at all, they can dispense with apologies; if the apology is needed, the thing apologized for would be better away. *A grievance once redressed ceases to be an electoral asset* (if we may use a piece of terminology which we confess we dislike)./*Turgenev had so quick an eye; he is the master of the vignette*—a tiresome word, but it still has to serve./*It is a play that hits you,* as the children say, *'bang in the eye.'*/*Palmerston is to all appearance* what would be vulgarly called *'out of the swim.'*/*May I take it that I can speak 'off the record,'* as our American friends say?

For another form of superiority, that of the famous 'of course,' as often exposed & as irrepressible as the three-card trick, see COURSE.

[Fowler adds a note that he found scribbled by his brother in his copy of *The King's English:* 'Some writers use a slang phrase because it suits them, & box the ears of people in general because it is slang; a refinement on the institution of whipping-boys, by which they not only have the boy, but do the whipping.']

SUPERLATIVES (the naked kind, stripped of *the* or *a*): *The problem is not one of Germany alone; many other States are in* worst *plight for food, so far as can be gathered./. . . addressed the Senate, declaring that* widest *diversity of opinion exists regarding the United Nations./Mr. Vanderlip is, therefore, in* closest *touch with the affairs of international finance.*

If the reader will be good enough to examine these one by one, he will certainly admit this much—that such superlatives are, for better or worse, departures from custom, & that in each sentence a change from 'worst,' 'widest,' 'closest,' to 'a worse,' 'the widest,' 'very close,' would be a return to normal English. If he will next try to judge what effect is produced by this artifice, it may be hoped, though less confidently, that he will agree with the following view. The writers have no sense of congruity (see INCONGRUOUS VOCABULARY), & are barbarically adorning contexts of straightforward businesslike matter with detached scraps of poetry or exalted feeling; the impression on sensitive readers is merely that of a queer simulated emotionalism.

supersede. So spelled.

SUPERSTITIONS. 'It is wrong to start a sentence with "But." I know Macaulay does it, but it is bad English. The word should either be dropped entirely or the sentence altered to contain the word "however."' That ungrammatical piece of nonsense was written by the editor of a scientific periodical to a contributor who had found his English polished up for him in proof, & protested; both parties being men of determination, the article got no further than proof. It is wrong to start a sentence with 'but'! It is wrong to end a sentence with a preposition! It is wrong to split an infinitive! See the article FETISHES for these & other such rules of thumb & for references to articles in which it is shown how misleading their sweet simplicity is. The best known of such prohibitions is that of the SPLIT INFINITIVE, & the hold of that upon the journalistic mind is well shown in the following, which may be matched almost daily. The writer is reporting a theater decree for hat-removal: '. . . the Management relies on the co-operation of the public to strictly enforce this rule.' *Even a split infinitive* [he comments] *may be forgiven in so well-intentioned a notice.* Theater managers are not stylists; the split this manager has perpetrated, is it not a little one? & to put him, irrelevantly, in the pillory for it betrays the journalist's obsession.

Well, beginners may sometimes find that it is as much as their jobs are worth to resist, like the champion of 'But,' their editors' edicts. On the other hand, to let oneself be so far possessed by conventions whose grounds one has not examined as to take a hand in enforcing them on other people is to lose the independence of judgment that, if not so smothered, would enable one to solve the numerous problems for which there are no rules of thumb.

supervise, NOT *-vize.*

supple. In US the standard spelling of the adv. is *supplely,* Brit. *supply.* The OED found more instances in print of *-plely* than of *-ply,* & therefore on its historical principles makes *supplely* the standard form. The pronunciation is undoubtedly sŭp′lĭ, NOT sŭ′pŭl-lĭ, & the long spelling has been due to the wish to distinguish to the eye from *supply* (sŭplī′), n. & v.

supposedly. Four syllables if used.

suppositious, supposititious. WRONG: *The* supposititious *elector who imagined that the Bill was a weapon for show & not for use is, we venture to say, a mythical being.* It is often assumed that the first form is no more than an ignorant & wrong variant of the other, like *pacifist* by the side of *pacificist.* Ignorant it often is, no doubt, the user not knowing how to spell or pronounce *supposititious;* but there is no reason to call it wrong. *Suppositious* & *supposititious* may as well coexist, if there is work for two words, as *factious* & *factitious;* &, if the support of analogy for the shorter form is demanded, there are *ambitious, expeditious, seditious, nutritious,* &c. to supply it. There are moreover two fairly distinct senses to be shared, viz. spurious, & hypothetical. *Supposititious* is directly from the Latin p.p. *suppositus*=substituted or put in another's place, & therefore has properly the meanings foisted, counterfeit, spurious, pretended, ostensible. *Suppositious* is from the English *supposition*=hypothesis (cf. *suspicious* similarly formed at an earlier stage, in Latin), & therefore may properly mean supposed, hypothetical, assumed, postulated, imaginary. It does not follow that *suppositious* is wanted; probably the work it might do is better done by the more familiar synonyms above given; it does follow that *supposititious* should not be given, as in the quotation at the head, senses proper to the synonyms of *suppositious,* but should be confined to those implying intent to deceive.

suppress makes *suppressible* & *suppressor.*

suppressio veri. (Rhetoric): 'suppression of the true.' Intentional withholding of a material fact with a view to affecting a decision &c.; cf. SUGGESTIO FALSI.

supra, adv., above; in book references, 'previously.'

supreme. (1) For *the supreme sacrifice,* see STOCK PATHOS. (2) Highest in authority or rank; greatest possible, uttermost; last and greatest or most important. See POSITIVE WORDS.

surcease, n. & v., is a good example of the archaic words that dull writers at uneasily conscious moments will revive in totally unsuitable contexts; see INCONGRUOUS VOCABULARY. The fact is that in ordinary English the word is dead, though the pun in *Macbeth* (*& catch, with his surcease, success*) is a tombstone that keeps its memory alive. There are contexts & styles in which the ghosts of dead words may be effectively evoked; but in pedestrian writing ghosts are as little in their element as in Wall Street at midday. The following quotations are borrowed from the OED: *It was carried on in all weathers . . . with no* surcease *of keenness./Private schools for boys give four days'* surcease *from lessons./There is no* surcease *in the torrent of Princes . . . who continue to pour into the capital./Intrigues & practices . . . would of necessity* surcease. These are all from 19th- or 20th-c. writers. It should be added that at least two of the verb examples in OED are American; but today the word is as archaic in US as in Brit.

sure, adv., is now archaic, or slang, except in such phrases as *sure as fate, as sure as death,* &c. Elsewhere, *surely.*

surety. Pron. shoor'tĭ; many verse examples show that the disyllabic sound is no innovation. (Most US dictionaries give -ĕtĭ second.)

surly. (Adv. *surlily.*) Orig. spelled *sirly* (from *sir*), it meant arrogant, haughty; now obviously ill-humored, uncivil.

surmise, NOT *-ize.*

surmisedly. Four syllables, if used.

surprisal. A NEEDLESS VARIANT.

surprise. (NOT *-ize.*) WRONG: '*I should* not *be surprised if the Chancellor does* not *agree with me.' Mr. Asquith added that . . .* If Mr. Asquith really said what the reporter attributes to him, which may be doubted, he meant 'agreed' or 'agrees,' not 'does not agree.' The mistake, for other examples of which see NEGATIVE 7 & NOT, is particularly common after *should not be surprised.*

surprisedly. Four syllables, if used.

surrealism. 'Twentieth-century movement in art & literature, influenced by Freudianism, seeking to express the subconscious mind by images without order or sequence.' Pron. sûr·rē'-alĭzm.

surveillance. Pron. servāl'ans.

suspense, suspension. In the verbal sense=suspending, the second is the right. *Suspense,* though it still retains that force in *suspense of judgment,* has become so identified with a state of mind that to revive its earlier use puzzles the hearer. In the following quotation it is clear that *suspense* compels one to read the sentence twice, whereas *suspension* or *suspending* would have been understood at first sight: *The state of war is inevitably the* suspense *of liberalism, & in all the nations at war there are some men who greatly hope that it may also be the death of liberalism.*

suspensible exists, but is perhaps not better than the normal *suspendable.*

suspicion. For *suspicion*=soupçon (*just a suspicion of garlic in it*) see GALLICISMS. *Suspicion,* v. (*I* suspicion *that he is not as honest as he pretends*), is US dial. or slang.

sustain. *Mr. —— has* sustained *a broken rib & other injuries through his horse falling.* The very common idiom here illustrated is described by the OED as 'in modern journalistic use'; but with such abstract objects as *injury, loss, leak, bruise,* &c., instead of broken rib it is as old as the 15th c., & the extension is not a violent one. Nevertheless, *sustain* as a synonym for *suffer* or *receive* or *get* belongs to the class of FORMAL WORDS, & is better avoided both for that reason & for a stronger one: if it is not made to do the work of those more suitable words, it calls up more clearly the other meaning in which it is valuable, viz. to bear up against or stand or endure without yielding or perishing, as in *capable of sustaining a siege.*

svelte is a society-column word. See FRENCH WORDS.

Swan of Avon (Shakespeare), see SOBRIQUETS.

swap, swop. The OED prefers *-a-*, which is standard in US; COD prefers *swop.*

SWAPPING HORSES while crossing the stream, a notoriously hazardous operation, is paralleled in speech by changing a word's sense in the middle of a sentence, by vacillating between two constructions either of which might follow a word legitimately enough, by starting off with a subject that fits one verb but must have something tacitly substituted for it to fit another, & by other such performances. These lapses are difficult to formulate & to exemplify, & any exposition of their nature naturally incurs the charge of PEDANTRY. Nevertheless, the air of slovenliness given by them is so fatal to effective writing that attention must be called to them whenever an opportunity can be made, as by this claptrap heading.

CHANGING OF WORD'S SENSE; *interest* is peculiarly liable to maltreatment: *His promised speech on reparations & inter-allied debts furnished all the* interest *naturally aroused. Interest* is here virtually, though not actually, used twice—the speech furnished interest, interest was aroused; but what was furnished was interesting matter, & what was aroused was eager curiosity; *interest* can bear either sense, but not both in one sentence. For similar treatment of other words than *interest,* see LEGERDEMAIN.

SHIFTING FROM ONE TO ANOTHER CONSTRUCTION: *But* supposing *nothing* changed & *this Pope* enjoys *a long life, we should look for a great decline in . . . Supposing* is followed first by an object (*nothing*) & adjectival complement (*changed*), & secondly, by a substantival clause (*this Pope enjoys*). Either is right by itself, but to swap one for the other means disaster.

TACIT MODIFICATION OF THE SUBJECT &c.: *This* barbarism could *be stopped in a very short time, if it were made a punishable offense to throw rubbish into the street,* & would have *the added value of reducing the number of scavengers.* It is not the barbarism, but the stoppage of it, that would have the added value./*Mr. A. C. Benson* recalls a *pleasant* fiction, supposed to have happened *to Matthew Arnold.* A *fiction* neither happens nor is supposed to happen to anyone; a fiction can be recalled, but before it can be supposed to have happened it must be tacitly developed into a fictitious experience; for it is itself a statement or narrative & not an event. See HAZINESS for other specimens of similar confusion.

swarm, swarthy, pron. sworm, sworthy.

sweat. Victim of GENTEELISM.

swell. *Swollen* is the usual form of the p.p., & that not less, but more, than formerly. The chief use of *swelled* as p.p. is now in *swelled head,* in which its supposed irregularity may have been a recommendation as lending a homely expressiveness.

swim. The past *swam* & p.p. *swum* are now almost invariable.

swine. Sing. & pl. the same; *swine* makes *swinish.*

swing. Past usually *swung.*

swivel has *-led, -ling,* US; *-lled, -lling,* &c. Brit.

swop. See SWAP.

sybarite. So spelled. Orig. an inhabitant of ancient Sybaris, a Greek colony in Southern Italy, noted for luxury; hence a voluptuary.

sybil. (See SIBYL.) This wrong spelling (the Greek is Sibulla) is especially common in the modern use as a feminine name.

syllabize &c. A verb & a noun are clearly sometimes needed for the notion of dividing words into syllables. Webster gives preference to *syllabify, syllabification;* ACD to *syllabicate, syllabication,* which COD also gives first. Fowler recommends acceptance of the verb *syllabize,* giving it the now nonexistent noun *syllabization.*

syllabus. Pl. *-buses,* or *-bi.*

syllepsis. (Pl. *-pses.*) *Syllepsis* & *zeugma* (Gram., Rhet.): 'taking together,' 'yoking.' Two figures distinguished by scholars, but confused in popular use, the second more familiar word being applied to both. Examples of syllepsis are: *Miss Bolo went home* in *a flood of tears & a sedan chair./He* lost *his hat & his temper./Washing clothes* with *happiness & Pears' soap.*

Examples of zeugma are: Kill *the boys & the luggage!/The pineapple* was *eaten & the apples neglected./With* weeping *eyes & hearts./See Pan with flocks, with fruits Pomona* crowned.

What is common to both figures is that a single word (that in roman in each example) is in relations that seem to be but are not the same with a pair of others. The difference is that syllepsis is grammatically correct, but requires the single word to be understood in a different sense with each of its pair (e.g. in the last *with* expresses first accompaniment, but secondly instrument), whereas in zeugma the single word actually fails to give sense with one of its pair, & from it the appropriate word has to be supplied—*destroy* or *plunder* the luggage, the apples *were* neglected, *bleeding* hearts, *Pan* surrounded.

syllogism. (Log.): 'combined reasoning.' Deduction, from two propositions containing three terms of which one appears in both, of a conclusion that is necessarily true if they are true. A syllogism of the simplest form is:

(*major premise*)
All men are mortal;
(*minor premise*)
All Germans are men;
(conclusion)
Hence all Germans are mortal.

The predicate of the conclusion (here *mortal*) is called the *major term;* the subject of the conclusion (here *Germans*) is called the *minor term;* the term common to both premises (here *men*) is called the *middle term.*

sylph. Elemental spirit of air, in Paracelsus's system. Hence *sylphlike*=slender, graceful.

sylvan. The usual spelling in US; see *silvan.*

symbol. *The Cross is the* symbol *of Christianity.* For synonyms see SIGN.

symbolic(al). The short form is more usual (there is no differentiation) and is recommended.

sympathetic. (1) *Macbeth is not made great by the mere loan of a poet's imagery, & he is not made* sympathetic, *however adequately his crime may be explained & palliated, by being the victim of a hallucination./ Let me first say that Elsie Lindtner is by no means* sympathetic *to the writer of this paper; if she were, the tragedy of the book would be more than one could bear.* It will be seen that in these passages the word does not mean capable of or prone to sympathy, but means capable of evoking sympathy. It is a GALLICISM, & if there is a possibility of confusion between the Gallic & the English senses the literary critic should deny himself the pleasure of using it. (2) *Sympathetic*=favorably disposed (to)—*I am not* sympathetic *to the idea*—is (US?) colloq.

sympathy. The exception sometimes taken to following *sympathy* with *for* instead of *with* is groundless; the OED, under the sense *compassion,* puts *for* before *with* as the normal construction (*sympathy for the unfortunate natives*—Burke). For the principle at issue, see DIFFERENT.

symposium. Originally a drinking party among the ancient Greeks; now a meeting for philosophical (&c.) discussion; a collection of articles by different authors on a single subject, published as a series in a periodical or in a single volume.

symptom. *It is already showing* symptoms *of decay.* For synonyms see SIGN.

synaeresis (Gram.): 'taking together.' The opposite of DIAERESIS; i.e. the making of two separate vowel sounds into one, as when *aerial* (adj.) is pronounced like *Ariel, naïve* like *nave,* or *cocaine* (originally three syllables) as *-cane.*

synchronize is not a word that we need regret the existence of, since there is useful work that it can do better than another; but it is a word that we may fairly desire to see as seldom as we may, one of the learned terms that make a passage in which they are not the best possible words stodgy & repellent; it may be compared with the lists in POPULARIZED TECHNICALITIES. The extracts below, for instance, would surely have been better without it: *The lock-out mania, therefore, has* synchronized [coincided?] *with an increased willingness for sacrifice on the part of the men./ The winter solstice, which north of the Equator* synchronizes with [determines] *the first day of the winter quarter, occurs at six minutes to eleven tonight.*

syncopation. (Gram., Mus.): 'cutting together.' In grammar, the use of SYNCOPE. In music the shifting of the regular metrical accent, e.g.: beginning a note on a normally unaccented part of the bar & sustaining it into the normally accented part, so as to produce the effect of shifting back or anticipating the accent. In modern popular dance music (*ragtime,* US 1900–; & *jazz*), characterized by continuous syncopation in the melody and a regular accent in the accompaniment.

syncope. (Pron. sin'kopĭ.) (Gram.): 'cutting together.' The shortening of a word by omission of a syllable or other part in the middle; cf. aphaeresis & APOCOPE. *Symbology* & *pacifist* & *idolatry* are examples.

synecdoche. (Pron. -dokĭ.) (Rhet.): 'inclusive extended acceptation.' The mention of a part when the whole is to be understood, as in *A fleet of fifty* sail (i.e. ships), or vice versa as in *England* (i.e. the English tennis team) *won.*

synonymity, synonymy. There is work for both words, the first meaning synonymousness, & the second the subject & supply of synonyms.

synonymous. Constr. *with* (rarely *to*). *'Since' is loosely* synonymous with *'meaning.' Synonymous* should not be used as if it were synonymous with *similar.* WRONG: *Much as Russia berated Fascism, she now is using* synonymous *tactics over her own people.*

SYNONYMS, in the narrowest sense, are separate words whose meaning, both denotation & connotation, is so fully identical that one can always be substituted for the other without change in the effect of the sentence in which it is done. Whether any such perfect synonyms exist is doubtful; *gorse* & *furze* may perhaps be a pair; but if it is a fact that one is much more often used than the other, or prevails in a different geographical or social region, then exchange between them does alter the effect on competent hearers, & the synonymy is not perfect. At any rate, perfect synonyms are extremely rare.

Synonyms in the widest sense are words either of which in one or other of its acceptations can sometimes be substituted for the other without affecting the meaning of a sentence. Thus it does not matter (to take the nearest possible example) whether I say a word has 'two senses' or 'two meanings,' & *sense* & *meaning* are therefore loose synonyms; but if 'He is a man of sense' is rewritten as 'He is a man of meaning,' it becomes plain that *sense* & *meaning* are far from perfect synonyms; see FIELD, & SIGN, for sets of this kind.

Synonyms, or words like in sense but unlike in look or sound, have as their converse *homonyms* & *homophones,* or words like in look or sound but unlike in sense. The *pole* of a tent or coach or punt, & the *pole* of the earth or the sky or a magnet, are in spite of their identical spelling separate words & *homonyms*. *Gauge* & *gage*, not spelled alike, but so sounded, are *homophones*.

Misapprehension of the degree in which words are synonymous is responsible for much bad writing of the less educated kind. From the notion that CONSERVATIVE is a synonym of *moderate*, as it is when compared with *radical* in politics, come the absurdities, illustrated under the word, of its use with *estimate* &c.; so with REGARD (& *consider*), OPTIMISTIC (& *hopeful*), SUBSTITUTION (& *replacement*), DILEMMA (& *difficulty*), ERE (& *before*), SAVE (& *except*), EXTENUATE (& *excuse*), FEASIBLE (& *possible*), ILK (& *same*), PERCENTAGE (& *part*), PROPORTION (& *portion*), as well as numberless others. To appreciate the differences between partial synonyms is therefore of the utmost importance. There are unluckily two obstacles to setting them out in this book. One is that nearly all words are partial synonyms, & the treatment of them all from this point of view alone would fill not one but many volumes; the other is that synonym books in which differences are analyzed, engrossing as they may have been to the active party, the analyst, offer to the passive party, the reader, nothing but boredom. Everyone must, for the most part, be his own analyst; & no one who does not expend, whether expressly & systematically or as a half-conscious accompaniment of his reading & writing, a good deal of care upon points of synonymy is likely to write well.

A writer's concern with synonyms is twofold. He requires first the power of calling up the various names under which the idea he has to express can go; everyone has this in some degree; everyone can develop his gift by exercise; but copiousness in this direction varies, & to those who are deficient in it ready-made lists of synonyms are a blessed refuge, even if the ease they bring has a doubtful effect on their style. Such lists, to be of much use, must be voluminous, & those who need them should try Roget's *Thesaurus* or some other work devoted to that side of synonymy. Secondly, he requires the power of choosing rightly out of the group at his command, which depends on his realizing the differences between its items. As has been implied already, such differences cannot be expounded for a language in anything less than a vast dictionary devoted to them alone; no attempt at it has been made in this book except in cases where experience shows warnings to be necessary.

synopsis. Pl. *-pses.*

syntax. (Grammar): 'combined order.' The part of grammar concerned not with the etymology, formation, & inflection of words, but with the arrangement of them in sentences.

synthesis. Pl. *-theses.* The scientific sound of the word often tempts the pretentious to use it instead of more appropriate words such as *combination, alliance,* or *union.* WRONG: *A flickering gleam on the subject may be found in a pamphlet which propounds the idea of a* synthesis *between the tariff & the opposition to Home Rule.*

synthetic, in the sense of 'made by artificial synthesis' (*synthetic dyes, rubber,* &c.), is of recent use, as is the extended derog. sense 'not genuine, artificial' (*a synthetic humor*).

synthetize, not *synthesize,* is the right formation. *Synthesize* is established, however, at least in US.

Syrian, Syriac. There is the same difference in application as between ARAB(IAN) & ARABIC.

syrup, syrupy. In US usually *sirup, sirupy.*

systematize, systemize. The longer form is the regular; the second should be dropped as a NEEDLESS VARIANT.

systemic, as compared with the regular *systematic,* is excused by its usefulness in distinguishing a sense required in physiology &c., 'of the system or body as a whole'; other wrong formations, *systemist, systemize,* &c., have no such excuse.

T

tableau. Pl. *-eaux,* sometimes (US) *-eaus. Tableau vivant* ('living picture'), pl. *-x -ts.*

table d'hôte. Pron. täbl' dōt'. ('Host's table.') Now usually a meal at a restaurant at a fixed price.

table tennis. In US known by the trade name *Ping-pong.*

tabloid. Orig. a trade mark for drugs, medicines, &c., held by the court of appeal in England in 1884 to be a 'fancy word' & restricted to the preparations of the original firm. In 1903, the term was released to the public as applying to 'a compressed form or dose of anything.' Now (US) usually applied to *tabloid newspapers,* in which news is presented in a condensed form and there is a preponderance of photographs.

taboo. Accent last syllable; though this accent is English only, it is established, & to correct it is pedantry; to spell *tabu* (except in ethnological dissertations) is no better. Past & p.p. *tabooed.*

tabulate makes *-lable.*

tacit. Silent; wordless; implied but not expressed. *A tacit acknowledgment.*

tack. Confusion between the nautical word used figuratively & *tact* is not unknown in speech, though it seldom gets into print (e.g. WRONG: *I think we have been on the wrong* tact).

tactics. In naval & military use, usually construed as sing.; transf. & fig., usually pl.: *These are strange tactics to be used by a member of the Senate.* (*A tactic,* sometimes heard, is wrong.) See STRATEGY for the Military distinction.

tactile, tactual. The pair are used almost indiscriminately. Careful writers confine *tactile* to the meaning capable of feeling or being felt by touch, & apply it to organs & qualities (*the tactile corpuscles; the tactile values of a painting*), while *tactual* should mean of or by touch & be more generally applied—*tactual tests, sensation, anesthesia, union.*

tail, v.,=follow closely and spy upon (*an undercover man* tailed *him to the Bronx*) is US (police and detective-story) slang.

talent, genius. Dr. Henry Bradley, in the OED, sums up the familiar contrast thus: 'The difference between genius & talent has been formulated very variously by different writers, but there is general agreement in regarding the former as the higher of the two, as "creative" & "original," & as achieving its results by instinctive perception & spontaneous activity, rather than by processes which admit of being distinctly analysed.'

talisman. Pl. *-mans.*

tall is to *short* as *high* is to *low.* In the sense extravagant, excessive, *tall* is slang (or colloq.), e.g. *tall talk, a tall order,* but *tall tale* is the accepted name of the (US) frontier stories of Paul Bunyan, Mike Fink, and other fictitious heroes whose amazing deeds were the subject of constant elaboration.

tame makes *-mable.*

-t & -ed. Some typical words are *bereaved* & *bereft, burned* & *burnt, dreamed* & *dreamt, kneeled* & *knelt, leaned* & *leant, leaped* & *leapt, learned* & *learnt, spilled* & *spilt, spoiled* & *spoilt, tossed* & *tost.*

In the last of these the point is purely one of spelling, & the sound is the same either way; but *tost,* esp. in p.p. compounds such as *storm-tost,* is current, by the side of *tossed.*

Of the rest the spelling may affect the sound in some, & does affect it in others. Thus, *burned* may be sounded with *d,* but perhaps most even of those who spell it so sound it as with *t,* whereas *leaped* & *leapt* are pronounced by everyone with different vowels—lēpt, & lĕpt. In US the *-ed* ending is much more general, esp. in writing; in Brit., the *-t.*

tantalize. To subject to torment like that given to Tantalus; i.e. to torment by the sight or promise of a desired thing that is withheld. WRONG: *To the motor industry Free Trade has become as* tantalizing *as a red rag to a bull;* see SLIPSHOD EXTENSION. He who is tantalized is usually irritated, but he who is irritated is comparatively seldom tantalized; & to apply *tantalize* to a wrong kind of irritation is to betray ignorance.

Taoism. Pron. tow´ĭzm.

tar=sailor. See SOBRIQUETS.

targeted. So spelled.

Tartar, Tatar. The second spelling may well be left to the ethnologists; see PRIDE OF KNOWLEDGE.

tassel makes US *-led;* Brit. *-lled.*

tasty has been displaced, except in uneducated or facetious use, in its primary sense by *savory* & in its secondary by *tasteful. Tastily* & *tastiness* are also now colloq. only.

tattler. Now so spelled; formerly, & esp. in the name of the 18th-c. periodical, *Tatler.*

tattoo makes *tattooed.*

TAUTOLOGY (lit. 'saying the same thing,' i.e. as one has already said) is a term used in various senses. To repeat the words or the substance of a preceding sentence or passage may be impressive & a stroke of rhetoric, or wearisome & a sign of incompetence, mainly according as it is done deliberately or unconsciously. In either case it may be called *tautology* (though the word is in fact seldom used except in reproach), but it is with neither of these kinds that we are here concerned. Another sense is the allowing of a word or phrase to recur without point while its previous occurrence is still unforgotten; this kind of tautology will be found fully discussed in the articles REPETITION, & ELEGANT VARIATION. Yet another form of tautology is that dealt with in PLEONASM 2, in which synonyms, either capable of serving the purpose by itself, are conjoined, as in *save & except*. Again, the word is sometimes applied to identical propositions such as 'I don't like my tea too hot'; for such statements see the *truism* section of COMMONPLACE.

What remains to be illustrated here is the way in which writers who are careless of form & desirous of emphasis often fail to notice that they are wasting words by expressing twice over in a sentence some part of it that is indeed essential but needs only one expression. It is true that words are cheap, &, if the cost of them as such to the writer were the end of the matter, it would not be worth considering; the intelligent reader, however, is wont to reason, perhaps unjustly, that if his author writes loosely he probably thinks loosely also, & is therefore not worth attention. A few examples follow, & under BOTH 2 & EQUALLY AS 2 will be found collections of the same kind of tautology: *The motion on constitutional reforms aims at placing women on* the same equality *with men in the exercise of the franchise* (as no other equality has been in question, *same & equality* are tautological; *in the same position as,* or *on an equality with*)./*The wool profits were* again *made the subject of* another *attack last night* (omit either *again* or *another*)./*May I be permitted to state that the activities of the club are not* limited only *to aeronautics?* (*limited & only* are tautological; *limited to,* or *directed only to*)./*It is sheer pretense to suppose that speed* & speed alone *is the* only *thing which counts* (omit either *& speed alone,* or *only*).

taxi. Pl. *taxis* better than *-ies.* The verb makes *taxiing, taxied.*

technic is used rather than *technique* when the meaning is *Technicology,* i.e. as having to do with the systematic knowledge of the industrial or applied sciences, or arts, or the terminology used in science & arts. *Technic* is older than *technique* in English but the latter can now be used in all contexts & the former is unusual when the reference is to artistic qualities. Pron. tĕk′nĭk, tĕk nēk′.

teens (*in one's teens* &c.). No apostrophe. *A teen-age girl* (not *-aged*).

teetotal makes *teetotaler* (US; Brit. *-ller*), *teetotalism.*

tele-. (1) Combining Gr. prefix meaning (*a*)*far,* (*telegram, television*); (2) *tele-* (before a vowel), *teleo-,* combining Gr. prefix meaning *end* (*teleology,* doctrine of final causes).

television makes *televise* (NOT *-ize*). *The parade was* televised (but *It was* telecast *over all the major networks*).

temerarious. See LITERARY WORDS. *Temerity*=rashness, excessive boldness, foolhardiness.

temperament, temperature. Pron. four syllables.

tempest. *Tempest in a teapot* (US)=*storm in a tea-cup* (Brit.).

templar. So spelled.

temptress. Established; see FEMININE DESIGNATIONS.

tend (=attend). *Tend the fire, tend the needs of the patients,* are current idiomatic usage. *Tend to business, tend to the baby* (=attend to) are colloq.

tendentious, -cious. The first is better. A new word, not in some of the shorter dictionaries. The first quotation in OED is 1900, the definition, 'having a purposed tendency; composed or written with such a tendency or aim.' Webster's 'marked by an intruded reformatory intent' is the sense in which it is usually used (*Even his poetry has a tendentious undertone*).

tender v., except in its legal use, is a FORMAL WORD for *offer, present,* or *give* (*tender my regrets, tender my services*).

tenet. Pron. tĕ′nĭt.

tenor. So spelled (not *-our*) US & Brit.

TENSES &c. Present, *I go;* past, *I went;* future, *I shall go;* present perfect, *I have gone,* past perfect, *I had gone,* future perfect, *I shall have gone.* Certain points requiring care will be found under SEQUENCE OF TENSES, SUBJUNCTIVES, PERFECT INFINITIVE, AS 4, HAD, LEST, SHALL, WILL.

tenterhooks. Sharp hooked nails by which cloth is fastened to a tenter (drying or stretching frame). Fig., *to be on tenterhooks,* in a state of suspense or nervous strain. (Brit. usually hyphened.) NOT *tenderhooks.*

tercentenary. The 300th anniversary. Pron. preferably tersĕn′tĕnĕrĭ (US & Brit.), but -tĕn′- is perhaps commoner.

term. For *major, minor, middle, term* in logic, see SYLLOGISM.

terminate makes *-nable,* & *-tor.* It is often a FORMAL WORD for *end.*

Terpsichore. Muse of dancing. Pron. terpsĭ′korĭ; & see MUSES.

terra cotta. *Made of terra cotta; a terra-cotta vase.* (Brit. one word.)

terrain. The justification of the word is that it expresses a complex notion briefly. When it is used as a substitute for *ground, tract, region,* or *district* —good ordinary words—it lacks the justification that an out-of-the-way word requires, & becomes pretentious. It means a piece of ground with all the peculiarities that fit or unfit it for military or other purposes; & to speak of 'the peculiarities of the terrain,' 'the nature of the terrain,' &c., instead of simply 'the terrain,' is, though the readers' assumed ignorance may excuse it, a PLEONASM.

tertium quid. 'A third something.' Originally a mixture of two things, having properties not so well ascertained as those of its elements. In this sense an alloy, or a chord ('not a fourth sound, but a star'), or Anglo-Catholicism, might be called *tertium quid.* Now often in the changed sense (the notion of unknown qualities being lost) of another alternative, a middle course, or third member of a set; so temperance as between drunkenness & teetotalism, suicide as an escape from the choice between poverty & dishonor, or the third person playing propriety for a pair of lovers, is in popular language a *tertium quid.*

terza rima. (Pl. *-ze -me.*) (Poet.): 'Third rhyme.' Dante's meter in the *Divina Commedia.* In English usually iambic pentameter arranged in tercets.

tessera. Pl. *-rae* (ē).

test. *Success is the* test *of character.* For synonyms see SIGN.

testatrix. Pl. *-trices* (-trīsēz).

te(t)chy, touchy. In the sense irritable, oversensitive, the OED suggests that *touchy* is perhaps an alteration of *techy; tetchy* is the usual modern spelling of those who do not prefer *touchy.* As the etymology of *te(t)chy* is unknown, & the much commoner *touchy* gives the same meaning without being a puzzle, any attempt to keep *te(t)chy* alive seems due to a liking for curiosities.

tête-à-tête. 'Head to head.' n. Private interview or conversation; adj., confidential. Pron. tāt à tāt. But see FRENCH WORDS.

tetralogy. In modern general use, any set of four connected plays, books, &c.

tetrameter. In modern verse, consisting of four feet.

textbook. US one word; Brit. hyphen.

textile. The pronunciation -tĭl is more usual in US, -tīl in Brit.

thalamus. Pl. *-mi.*

Thalia. Muse of comedy & pastoral poetry. See MUSES. One of the three Graces. Pron. thalī'*a.*

than. This article is divided into ten sections: 1. *Than* & *preferable.* 2. *Than* & inversion. 3. Verb after *rather than.* 4. *Hardly* & *scarcely than.* 5. *Than* after *the more.* 6. *Than* as conj. & prep. 7. Double comparison. 8. *Than* after non-comparatives. 9. *Than* & ellipsis. 10. Flounderings.

1. *Than* & *prefer(able).* RIGHT: *He preferred to drown* rather than *forsake the ship; rather* is necessary after *prefer, preferable,* before *than;* see PREFER(ABLE) 3.

2. *Than* & inversion. *Than* often tempts writers into unjustified inversion: WRONG: *No tariff-armed nation has got better entry for its potatoes* than has *Ireland./The visit will be much more direct in its effect upon the war* than could be *any indiscriminate bombing of open towns.* The normal order is *than Ireland has, than any indiscriminate bombing of open towns could.* Such inversions are deprecated; see INVERSION, esp. the section on inversion after relatives & comparatives.

3. Infinitive, or gerund &c., after *rather than. They were all in favor of 'dying in the last ditch'* rather than sign *their own death warrant.* The justification of *sign* instead of *signing* is discussed in -ING 5.

4. *Hardly than, scarcely than.* WRONG: *But* hardly *had I landed* than *the Mikado's death recalled me to Japan.* Read *no sooner* for *hardly,* or *when* for *than;* & see under HARDLY 2, SCARCELY 1.

5. *Than* after *the more, the less,* &c. The right forms are: *I am no better* than *if I had not taken them; I am* none the better *for taking them;* NOT *I am* none the better than *if I had taken them.* WRONG: *If we simply take the attitude of accepting her theory of naval policy, we make it* so much the less probable *that she will change her law* than *if we enter into violent contention.* Omit *the,* and see THE for the wrong-

ness of this construction.

6. *Than* used as conj. & prep. *Than* is properly a conjunction, NOT a preposition: *You treat her worse* than I (*treat her*); *You treat her worse* than I (*do*); *You treat her better* than (*you treat*) me; *You treat her better* than (*you do*) me. In the first two examples *than* is a strong conjunction connecting the two clauses of parallel construction (*You treat . . . than I treat*); in the second two, a weak conjunction connecting the two pronouns (*treat her . . . than me*). In *We both treat her miserably, but you treat her worse* than me (i.e. *than I do*), *than* is made to serve as a preposition. Doubts whether a word is a preposition or a conjunction or both are not unknown; usage, also, changes in such matters with time. It is obvious, however, that recognition of *than* as a preposition makes some sentences ambiguous that could otherwise have only one meaning & is to that extent undesirable. The OED statement on the preposition use is that, with the special exception of *than whom*, which is preferred to *than who* unless both are avoided, 'it is now considered incorrect.' That incorrectness occurs in the following examples (WRONG): *That international accord will finish by reaching the great mass of the proletariat; no one wishes it more* than us (read *than we do.*)/*The butcher of the last few months has been a good deal more obliging* than him *of the war period* (read *than he*). On the other hand, in the following sentences the *he*'s had better have been *him*, since the ellipsis required is in each piece awkward; here *than* is more properly a weak conjunction connecting *artist* and *him, friend* and *him*. AWKWARD: *If ever O'Connor gives us a second volume, we beg him to engage no other artist* than he *who illustrated the first./The Entente had no better friend* than he *on the other side of the Atlantic.*

7. Double standard of comparison; *more* & *more than*. *Than* should never be used after *more & more*. WRONG: *My eyes are* more & more *averse to light* than *ever./The order has gradually found* more & more *room for educational & learned work* than *was possible in the early centuries.* Both sentences would be right if *& more* were omitted; but the introduction of it implies the tacit introduction of other *thans* which conflict with those that are expressed. *More & more* means more yesterday than the day before, & more today than yesterday; to combine that shifting date with the unshifting dates *ever* & *in early centuries* is impossible.

8. *Than* after non-comparatives. *Else, other,* & their compounds are the only words outside true comparatives whose right to be followed by *than* is unquestioned; & 'true comparatives' is to be taken as excluding such Latin words as *superior* & *inferior, senior* & *junior,* all of which, as well as *prefer*(*able*), require not *than,* but *to.* The use of *than,* on the analogy of *other than,* after *different, diverse, opposite,* &c., is 'now mostly avoided' (OED). Two examples follow of irregularities that should not appear in print. WRONG: *What, then, remains if this measure of agreement still continues* than *to dispose of the Bill by fair discus-*

sion in reasonable time?/(Read *what . . . but* or *what else . . . than.*)/*There is obviously a vastly increased number of people who can & do follow reasoned arguments in books & newspapers* than *there was before educational methods were so efficient.* (For *increased* read *greater.*)

9. *Than* with ellipsis or brachylogy. Some kinds of ellipsis are so customary in *than* constructions that to write out the whole sense would be much more noticeable than the ellipsis. But hasty writers are encouraged by this to think that any slovenliness will pass muster. WRONG: *Many of them take tea & coffee to excess, & I am convinced myself the evil consequences of excess of these beverages is much greater* than^ *alcohol* (are *much greater* than those of *alcohol*)./*The proceedings were more humiliating to ourselves* than^*I can recollect in the course of my political experience* (than anything I)./*The interpretations of the words are more uniformly admirable* than could have been produced by *any other person* (than any other person could have made them).

10. Flounderings. There is often a difficulty in getting the things to be compared into sufficient grammatical conformity to stand on either side of a *than;* but writers who take so little trouble about it as the authors of the following sentences must not be surprised if their readers are indignant. WRONG: *In countries where a Referendum is a recognized part of the constitutional machinery, the House of Representatives* is much more ready to pass, *provisionally, constitutional reforms, & submit them to the electorate,* than are Bills *passed by the Houses of Parliament in a country like England.*/*'The Awkward Age,' which was just published, was being received with a little more intelligence & sympathetic comprehension* than had been the habit of greeting *his productions.*

Thanksgiving. In formal speech or writing, *Thanksgiving Day.*

thank you, thanks, &c. *I thank you* is now reserved for formal occasions or tongues; *thank you* is the ordinary phrase, but tends more & more to be lengthened with or without occasion into *thank you very much; thanks* is a shade less ceremonious than *thank you,* & *many* & *best* & *a thousand thanks* are frequent elaborations of it; *much thanks* is archaic, but not obs.; *thanks much* is a hybrid form, confusing the noun with the verb, & an affectation.

that, adj. & adv. 1. *That*= such a, so great a, to such an extent. The adj. use (*He has* that *confidence in his theory that he would act on it tomorrow*) was formerly normal English, & survives colloquially, but in literary use *such a, so great a,* &c., are substituted. The adv. use (*when I was* that *high; he was* that *angry*) is still more unliterary; & in spoken English it now passes only where, as in the first example, actual demonstration with the hand is possible; where it is impossible, as in the second example, *that* is held uneducated or slang.

2. *That* with a noun & a participle or other equivalent of a defining relative clause. The type meant is shown in *that*

part affected, that land lying fallow, that theory now in question, & the contention is that it is a bad type. In the OED there is a solitary example, & that justifiable for special reasons; but in modern use it is growing very common. The three specimens are NOT RECOMMENDED: *It was essential that both these phases of his art should be adequately represented in* that *branch of the National Gallery devoted to native talent.*/That *part relating to the freedom of the seas was given fairly fully in the 'Times.'/ Aphorisms & maxims are treated with* that *respect usually reserved for religious dogma.*

The use of *that* (demonstrative adj.) with the sole function of pointing forward to a defining relative clause is established English, & 'that part which concerns us' is as common as 'the part that concerns us'; but when for the relative clause is substituted a participle or phrase, it is an innovation to keep the *that;* it may safely be said that most good writers take the trouble to clear away the now needless *that,* & write *the* instead. In the first sentence above, the full form should have been *that branch which is devoted* (or *the branch that is devoted*), & the short form *the branch devoted;* & similarly for the rest.

It should be observed that sentences occur at first sight similar to those condemned, but with the difference that another purpose is served by *that* instead of, or as well as, that of heralding the participle &c. One such is (RIGHT): *On* that *peninsulated rock called La Spilla;* here *that* is justified as meaning 'the well-known.' Compare also (RIGHT): *The world needs peace. You will always find us at your side to preserve* that *peace bought by so much blood.* Here the justification of *that* is its referring back to the *peace* of the previous sentence.

The misuse here objected to is still commoner with THOSE.

that, conj. 1. Kinds of *that* clauses. 2. Omission of *that.* 3. *that* with *doubt(ful).* 4. Interim *that.* 5. *That* after *(in)so far.* 6. Nonparallel *that* clauses.

1. In adj. or relative clauses that begin with *that,* it is a relative pronoun, not a conj.; see the next article. *That* conj. attaches a substantival (noun) clause to the verb, noun, &c., to which it is object (*I hear* that he is dead), subject (That pain exists *is certain*), in apposition (*The fact* that pain exists), &c.; or else an adv. clause to the word &c. modified (*The heat is such* that it will boil water). The only point needing to be insisted on is that in either case, whether the *that* clause is substantival or adverbial, the sentence out of which it is made by prefixing *that* must be of the statement form, not a question, command, or exclamation. WRONG: *I should like to point out* that, *had the brave defender known he could hold out for another two months,* would he not have *informed General Butler of the fact?* Sentences of this other kind can be subordinated or turned into clauses but not by prefixing *that.* Read *I should like to ask* &c. & leave out the *that,* & the sentence is idiomatic. The mistake is not made by good writers, but yet occurs often enough to need mention. One way of avoiding it is so to arrange that there is unsubordi-

nated quotation of the question &c., & the other is, before subordinating, to convert the question &c. into a statement giving the same meaning. The remedy for each of the incorrect examples follows in parentheses. WRONG: *Your correspondent suggests* that *if we lend money* let us send *it to Canada for railways there* (read *suggests: If . . .* or *we should send*)./*Crises, international or national, arise so rapidly in these days* that who can say *what a few years may bring forth?* (read *arise rapidly in these days; who . . .* or *that none can*)./*One can only comment* that *if such a refuge was open to the Romans,* how much more available is it *to our own people* (read *comment: If . . .* or *Romans, it is much more available*).

2. Omission of *that* in substantival clauses. *I know* that *my Redeemer liveth; I know‸I can trust you.* These are equally good English; if *that* were shifted from the first to the second, both would still be grammatically correct, but each less idiomatic than as it is. That is, the use or omission of the *that* of a substantival clause depends partly on whether the tone is elevated or colloquial. But a glance at the following examples of obviously wrong omission will show that there is not free choice after all verbs or in all constructions. WRONG: *I assert‸the feeling in Canada today is such against annexation that . . ./In reply to Mr. Baker, may I point out‸in the circular entitled 'A Word to Women' the opposition to the Bill is expressly proclaimed?/I am abashed to see‸in my notice of Mr. Birt's book I have credited the elder W. M. Thackeray with 'sixteen' children./The enormous rents which would be asked for new houses would naturally render owners of existing properties restless & envious, with the result‸they would continually strive to raise their own rents./Mr. Balfour blurted out that his own view was‸the House of Lords was not strong enough.* It at once occurs to the reader that *assert,* & *point out,* are words that stand on their dignity & will not dispense with the attendance of *that.* The same idea is not suggested about *see,* since a moment's thought assures us that *I see,* & *I see that, Vesuvius is active again* are equally good. The reason why *that* is required in the third example is that by omitting it the chance is lost of making plain the arrangement of the sentence & showing that *in . . . Thackeray* belongs not to *see,* but *to have credited.* The lesson of the last two examples is that omission is unadvisable when the substantival clause is in apposition to a noun, as here to *result,* & *view.*

It may be useful to give tentative lists, to which everyone can make additions for his own use, of verbs that (1) prefer *that* expressed, (2) prefer *that* omitted, & (3) vary according to the tone of the context. (1) *That* is usual with *agree, assert, assume, aver, calculate, conceive, hold, learn, maintain, reckon, state, suggest;* (2) *that* is unusual with *believe, presume, suppose, think;* (3) *that* is used or omitted with *be told, confess, consider, declare, grant, hear, know, perceive, propose, say, see, understand.* The verbs with which the question may arise are many more than these few, which may however be enough to assist observation.

3. *That* & *whether* with *doubt(ful)*. UNIDIOMATIC: *It gave him cause for wonder that no serviceable 'pool' had been revealed in England;* that *any existed, however,* seemed doubtful. The choice allowed by idioms is between *Whether any existed seemed doubtful,* & *That any existed seemed unlikely,* according to the meaning required. See DOUBT(FUL).

4. Interim *that.* It often happens to a writer to embark upon a substantival *that* clause, to find that it is carrying him further than he reckoned, & to feel that the reader & he will be lost in a chartless sea unless they can get back to port & make a fresh start. His way of effecting this is to repeat his initial *that.* This relieves his own feeling of being lost; whether it helps the inattentive reader is doubtful; but it is not doubtful that it exasperates the attentive reader, who from the moment he saw *that* has been on the watch for the verb that it tells him to expect, & realizes suddenly, when another *that* appears, that his chart is incorrect. These interim *thats* are definite grammatical blunders, which can often be mended by leaving out the offending *that* with or without other superfluous words. The first example shows the most venial form of the mistake, the resumptive *that* being inserted at the point from which progress to the expected verb is not to be again interrupted by subordinate clauses; the others are worse. WRONG: *He must have astonished the 'First Gentleman in Europe' when he wrote to him* that *if he did not adopt the new principles, as laid down in his 'Grammar'* that *neither he nor his subjects could possibly hope to be saved.* (Omit second *that.*)/*Is there any man of sane judgment who does not know in his heart* that, *if the Unionist Party were free from the Protectionist entanglement, &* that *if it would reject the Budget, its position & prospects of the present moment would be vastly improved?* (Omit *that if it.*)/*It has been shown* that *if that inheritance be widening, as it is,* & that *if the means of increasing it exist, as they do, then growth of numbers must add to the power.* (Omit second *that if.*)

5. *That* & *as* after (*in*) *so far.* For the rather elusive distinction & its importance, see FAR 4.

6. Nonparallel *that* clauses in combination. Parallel *that* clauses can be strung together *ad libitum,* & may be rhetorically effective. It is otherwise with interdependent or dissimilar *that* clauses; for the principle see REPETITION. The unpleasantness of the construction deprecated is sufficiently shown in: *It is thoroughly in accordance with this recognition* that *the people have rights superior to those of any individual* that *the President is seeking legislation* that *will perpetuate Government title to the oil lands.*

that, rel. pron. 1. *That* & *which.* 2. *That*-ism. 3. Elliptical *that,* rel. adv. 4. *That* clause not close up. 5. One *that* in two cases. 6. Double government.

1. *That* & *which.* The two kinds of relative clause, to one of which *that* & to the other of which *which* is appropriate, are

the defining & the non-defining (in US often called the *restrictive* & *nonrestrictive*). If writers would agree to regard *that* as the defining relative pronoun, & *which* as the non-defining, there would be much gain both in lucidity & in ease. Some follow this principle now; but it would be idle to pretend that it is the practice either of most or of the best writers.

A *defining* (=*restrictive*) relative clause is one that identifies the person or thing meant by limiting the denotation of the antecedent: *Each made a list of books* that *had influenced him;* not *books generally,* but *books* as defined by the *that* clause. Contrast with that a *non-defining* clause: *I always buy his books,* which *have influenced me greatly;* the clause does not limit *his books,* which needs no limitation; it gives a reason (=*for they have*), or adds a new fact (=*& they have*). There is no great difficulty, though often more than in this chosen pair, about deciding whether a relative clause is defining or not; & the practice of using *that* if it is, & *which* if it is not, would also be easy but for certain peculiarities of *that.* One is that it has no possessive of its own, but must use *whose* (*The only place* whose *supply of baths is adequate*). The other, and most important, is its insistence on being the first word of its clause; it cannot, like *whom* & *which,* endure that a preposition governing it should, by coming before it, part it from the antecedent or the main clause; such a preposition has to go, instead, at the end of the clause (*This is the one* that *I am partial* to). That is quite in harmony with the closer connection between a defining (or *that*) clause & the antecedent than between a non-defining (or *which*) clause & the antecedent; but it forces the writer to choose between ending his sentence or clause with a preposition, & giving up *that* for *which.* In the article PREPOSITION AT END it is explained that to shrink with horror from ending with a preposition is no more than foolish superstition (*the life-work that Acton collected innumerable materials for*); but there are often particular reasons for not choosing that alternative, & then the other must be taken, & the fact accepted that the preposition-governed case of *that* is borrowed from *which.* A third peculiarity of *that* is that in the defining clauses to which it is proper it may, if it is not the subject, be omitted & yet operative (*The man you saw* means the same as *The man* that *you saw*), while *which* in the non-defining clauses to which it is proper must be expressed (*This fact,* which *you admit condemns you,* cannot be changed without altering the sense to *This fact, you admit, condemns you*).

The reader is invited to compare the two versions of the following sentences & to say whether, even apart from the grammatical theory here maintained, the rewritings do not offer him a more natural & easy English than the others:

a. *Visualize the wonderful things* which *the airman sees & all the feelings* which *he has./ Visualize the wonderful things*$_\wedge$ *the airman sees and all the feelings*$_\wedge$*he has.* (Both *thats* understood.)

b. *It is necessary to root out*

the autocratic principles which *underlie militarism,* that *threatens the peace of the world.* (ELEGANT VARIATION; *which,* having been wrongly chosen the first time, is wrongly rejected the second time for variety's sake.) *It is necessary to root out the autocratic principles* that *underlie militarism,* which *threatens the peace of the world.*

c. *A hatred of the rule* that *is not only unable to give them protection,* but which *strikes at them blindly & without discrimination.* (What has caused the change from *that* to *which* here is the writer's realizing that *but that* is somehow undesirable; it is so, because of the repugnance of *that,* mentioned above, to being parted from its antecedent; but the way out is to let the previous *that* carry on for both clauses, a task it is quite equal to.) *A hatred of the rule* that *not only is unable to give them protection but*^ *strikes at them blindly & without discrimination.*

d. *After a search for several days he found a firm* which *had a large quantity of them &* which *they had no use for.* (Both clauses are defining, & *that* is required; but the relatives have not the same antecedent, & the *and* is therefore [see WHICH WITH AND OR BUT] wrong. But there is a legitimate choice between *that . . . for* & *for which,* & the latter gives an escape from one *that* clause depending on another.) *After a search for several days, he found a firm* that *had a large quantity of them* for which *they had no use.*

e. *The class* to which *I belong* & which *has made great sacrifices will not be sufferers under the new plan.* (Defining and non-defining wrongly coupled; omit *and,* & naturally prefer [*that*] *I belong to* to the equally legitimate *to which I belong* as better both in clearness & in sound.) *The class* that *I belong to,* which *has made great sacrifices, will not be sufferers under the new plan.*

To sum up: *That* is the natural defining relative pronoun. *There are grievances* that *flourish and reforms* that *call for attention.*

Which is the natural non-defining relative pronoun, & the clause it introduces is normally set off by a comma. *It seemed that the Derna,* which arrived safely, *was sent in the ordinary way.*

Which may be used instead of *that* as a defining relative pronoun if the clause it introduces is separated from its antecedent by a preposition or other word. See (d) above.

That can often be omitted idiomatically; *which,* as a non-defining pronoun, cannot. *Among the distinguished visitors*^*the Crawfords had at Rome was Longfellow.*

That & *which* should not be used interchangeably for ELEGANT VARIATION. WRONG: *The Queen and her party were welcomed with the pomp & circumstance* which *so often attends an event* that *is new in the experience of India.* Read *that so often attends an event new in the experience . . .*

2. *That*-ism. As has been explained, the tendency in modern writing is for *which* to supersede *that* even in the functions for which *that* is better fitted. On the other hand some writers seem deliberately, where most other people would use

which, to choose *that* under the impression that its archaic sound adds the grace of unusualness to their style. A few examples will show *that* in non-defining clauses to be certainly noticeable, & the reader will perhaps conclude that its noticeability is not a grace: *But her fate,* that *has lately been halting in its pursuits of her, overtakes her at last./At Lingard's shout for Jorgenson,* that *in the profound silence struck his ears ominously, he raised his eyes./His arguments on these points were heard by the great audience of businessmen in an almost unbroken silence,* that *gave place to an outburst of applause when he . . .* (*which* in all three).

3. Elliptical *that* as rel. adv. The familiar yet remarkable fact that a preposition governing *that* does not precede it but follows it at a distance has been mentioned in (1). The idiom now to be noticed may be traceable to that fact. In the following idiomatic examples *that* serves as a sort of relative adverb, equivalent to *which* with a preposition. RIGHT: *She found herself* in the same position that Rome found herself *after the destruction of the Carthaginian fleet* (=in which)./*He took him for his model for* the very reason that *he ought to have shunned his example* (=for which)./*Others, watching the fluctuating rates of exchange with* all the anxiety that *a mariner consults his barometer in a storm-menaced sea, are buying securities* (=with which).

This is a freedom that should no more be allowed to lapse than the right of putting a preposition last or of omitting an objective *that.* But idiom requires that *which* should not be so treated; it has been tried with obviously bad results in (WRONG): *It touched them* in a way‸which *no book in the world could touch them./The man who cleaned the slate* in the way‸which *Sir E. Satow has done both in Morocco & Japan* (*in* must be supplied in both sentences). And further, *that* itself cannot be so treated unless the preposition to be supplied in the clause has been actually expressed with the antecedent. WRONG: *One of the greatest dangers is the pace* that *the corners in the main streets are turned* (read *at which* for *that*).

4. *That* clause not close up. The clinging of the defining *that* to its antecedent has been noticed in (1). It is the gap between it & the antecedent that occasions a certain discomfort in reading the correct sentences below. Each *that* clause is, or at the least may be meant as, defining; but between each & the actual noun of the antecedent intervenes a clause or phrase that would suffice by itself for identification. In such circumstances a *that* clause, though correct, is often felt to be queer, & it is usually possible, though by no means necessary, to regard it as non-defining & change *that* to *which: The foolish* formulae *for which the Coalition was responsible,* & that *the Conservatives have taken over, are not good enough* (read *responsible, & which*)./*When Mr. Raleigh writes, as he does, as if America was a* country *of bounding megalomaniacs,* that *measured everything by size & wealth, he is talking nonsense* (read *which,* no comma).

5. One *that* in two cases. It is quite in order to let a relative

which or *that* carry on & serve a second clause as well, but only if three conditions are satisfied: the antecedent of the two must be the same; both must be defining or both non-defining; & the case of the relative must be the same. This last condition is violated in the example now to be given. If there is a change of case, *that* (or *which*) must be repeated; or, more often, the repetition should be saved by some change of structure. WRONG: *The art of war includes* a technique that it is *indispensable to acquire* & can only be *acquired by prolonged effort* (read *that must be acquired, but can*).

6. Double government. *A book that I heard of & bought* is a familiar & satisfactory form of speech; *that* is governed first by *of* & again by *bought;* but it is not good enough for those who consider that spoken *that* should become written *which,* & that a preposition should not end a clause; they change it to *A book of which I heard & bought,* forgetting that if they do not repeat 'which I' this commits them to 'A book of which I bought.' The first example below shows the right form for such needs, with *that;* the others illustrate the frequency of the mistake, which is naturally not made by those who recognize that in writing as well as in speech *that* is the true defining relative & the place for a preposition governing it is later in the clause. RIGHT: *'Command,' by William McFee, is one of those fine roomy books* that one lives in *with pleasure for a considerable time* & leaves *at the last page with regret.*/WRONG: *A great international conference* to which America is *to be invited,* or is *to be asked to convene at Washington* (that America is to be invited to)./*We must not be faced by a peace* of which we may disapprove & yet must *accept* (that we may disapprove of)./*An ammunition dump* on which he dropped *his remaining bombs* & left *blazing merrily* (that he dropped his remaining bombs on).

the. 1. *The Hague Conference* &c. 2. *By the hundred* &c. 3. *The good & (the) bad.* 4. *The* with two nouns. 5. Single adv. *the* with comparatives. 6. Double adv. *the* with comparatives.

1. The capital *T* of *The Hague* raises a question that, however trivial, is forever presenting itself with newspaper names: in 'the Conference at The Hague,' or 'the correspondent of *The Times,*' we know where to use a capital & where a small letter; but when one *the* is cut out by *using* (*The*) Hague attributively, is the remaining *the* that which belonged to *Hague,* or that which belonged to *Conference*? & is it consequently to be *The,* or *the*? *It is agreed that The* (or *the*) *Hague Conference is to be a meeting of experts.* Though compositors or writers often choose the wrong alternative & print *The,* a moment's thought shows that it is *Conference* that must have its *the,* while *Hague* can do without it. We say 'a *Times* correspondent' & 'the last Hague Conference,' stripping *Hague* & *Times* of their *The* without scruple; it follows that the indispensable *the* belongs to the other word. For a similar question with *Times's,* see POSSESSIVE PUZZLES.

2. *By the hundred* &c. WRONG: *The mild revelations of a gentle*

domestic existence which some royal personages have given us command readers by the hundreds of thousands. The idiomatic English is *by the hundred thousand; by hundreds of thousands* will also pass, but with the plural *the* is not used. So also with *dozen, score,* &c.

3. *The good & (the?) bad. Primitively splendid dresses, which appealed after the manner of barbaric magnificence to the most complex & elementary aesthetic instincts.* Is the omission of another *the most* between *and* & *elementary* tolerable? The purist will condemn it, & probably most of us will, for this particular case, endorse his condemnation. But he will add that neither must we say 'The French, German, & Russian figures are not yet to hand,' unless we are talking of their combined total; *the Germans* & *the Russians,* he will say, must have their separating *the;* & in these rigors sensible people will not follow him. What may fairly be expected of us is to realize that among expressions of several adjectives or nouns introduced by *the* some cannot have *the* repeated with each item (*the black & white penguins*), & some can logically claim the repetition (*the red & the yellow tomatoes*). A careful writer will have the distinction in mind, but he will not necessarily be a slave to logic; 'the red & yellow tomatoes' may be preferred for better reasons than ignorance or indolence. For other examples of needless rigidity, see ONLY, & NOT 1.

4. *The* with two nouns & singular verb. *It is* the single-handed courage & intrepidity *of these men which* appeal(s) *to the imagination,* & are (is) *even more marvelous than their adventures.* Two nouns of closely allied meaning are often felt to make no more than a single notion; *courage & intrepidity* is almost a hendiadys for *intrepid courage;* that feeling is here strengthened by the writer's choosing to use only one *the* instead of two; & to change *appeal* & *are* to *appeals* & *is* would be not only legitimate, but an idiomatic improvement.

5. Single adverbial *the* with comparatives. The type here to be discussed is seen in (WRONG) *They are* none the wiser (=*no wiser*) than *if they had not read it.* What is here maintained is that (a) good writers do not prefix *the* to comparatives when it conveys nothing at all; & (b) they do not allow themselves a *than* after a comparative that has *the* before it.

(a) The question of when *the* is appropriate & when it is out of place before a comparison, without the complication of the following *than,* is simpler. RIGHT: *I am* the more *interested in his exploits* because *he is my brother.* The function of this *the* is to acquaint the reader that by looking about he may find the cause of the excess stated by the comparative. If no such indication is to be found earlier or later in the passage, *the* has no justification, & merely sets readers searching for what they will not find. In the example given above, *the* anticipates *because* &c.; in (RIGHT) *Though he is my cousin I am not* the more *likely to agree with him, the* refers back to *though* &c.; in (RIGHT) *As the hour approached I grew* the more *nervous, the* means *by so much* & refers back to *as* &c.

In the examples that follow it will be found impossible to point to such a cause or measure of excess anticipated or recalled by *the*, & moreover it will probably be admitted at once that removal of *the* does not weaken the sense; but improves it. WRONG: *That was the principle asserted in the resolution, but what* the more *interests us is the reasons given for this advertised resistance* (omit *the*)./*It is especially inexpedient that the diseased should languish unattended because of inability to provide skilled assistance, & it is not* the less *inexpedient that the prisoner should stand unaided before justice because his means cannot secure legal representation.* (The *because* clause does not explain *the*, as one might guess, but belongs to *stand unaided.* Omit *the.*)/ *It is gratifying to receive such clear testimony to a widespread interest in an intelligent study of the Bible; & it is not* the less *gratifying that many recent books deal with the subject from a special point of view.* (The *that* clause looks like the explanation of *the*, but is in fact the subject of 'is not less gratifying.' Again omit *the.*) In these two last examples the use of *the* goes beyond mere ineptitude, & amounts to the serious offense of being misleading.

(b) *The* should never be used with a comparative if *than* follows, but where the *than* clause introduces a standard of comparison different from that implicit in *the*, the departure from idiom is much more glaring. In all the following extracts the *the* form should be got rid of by omission of *the*, with any consequential change; but they are arranged in three sets, the first tautological & unusual, the second *prima facie* illogical, & the third in which *the* is entirely meaningless.

TAUTOLOGICAL: *I do not believe that the productions would have pleased people any* the more than *at present by having money lavished upon scenery* (*any the more*=any more than if money had not been lavished; omit *the*)./*If we take the attitude of accepting her theory of naval policy, we make it so much* the less *probable that she will change her law* than *if we enter into violent contention* (*the less probable*=less probable than if we did not take the attitude of accepting).

ILLOGICAL: *Audiences are accustomed to foreign artists speaking in strange tongues, & Madame Rejane is not likely to be any* the less *heartily appreciated during her present stay* than *on the occasion of any of her former performances* (*any the less heartily*=any less heartily than if she did not speak in a strange tongue)./ *But does that make Sophocles more Greek than Aeschylus or Euripides? Each of the latter may be more akin to other poets; but he is none* the less *Greek* than *Sophocles* (*none the less Greek*=no less Greek than if he were not more akin to other poets; read *no less Greek*).

MEANINGLESS: *I am* the more *disposed to rely on Mr. Chamberlain's silence* than *on Mr. Anderson's attempt to resuscitate a quotation which less adventurous Tariff Reformers seemed disposed to let drop* (read *I am more disposed*).

6. Double adverbial *the* with comparatives. The most familiar example (RIGHT), 'the more,

the merrier,' is the short for 'by how much we are more, by so much we shall be merrier.' In this construction one *the* means *by how much* & the other *by so much.* WRONG: *Probably the less* that is *said by outsiders, the better.* (Omit *that is.*) It may perhaps safely be laid down that when in the measure (*by how much*) clause of a *the . . . the* comparison the question arises whether a relative pronoun should be inserted, the answer is *no.* WRONG: The *better education a girl can receive, & the* more *time* which *can be spent on her training, the better.* The first clause is right, and the *which can be* in the second must be omitted.

It should be kept in mind that this *the . . . the* idiom is suited chiefly to short, emphatic, pointed sentences of *The more, the merrier* type. A suitable example (in spite of its length) is: The less distinct *was the message he felt impelled to deliver,* the more beautiful *was the speech in which he proclaimed it.* Points of merit are: brevity; close correspondence between the two parts; occurrence of *the* in both parts; measure first & thing measured afterwards; no inversion in measure clause; no inversion in thing measured if it stands first, but inversion common if it has its normal later place. All these points are found in our example, except that it should read *the message was,* instead of *was the message.*

A specimen or two may be added with comments: The wider *was the League,* the greater *it would be.* A suitable case; but read *The wider the League was, the greater would it* (or *it would*) *be;* for the rights & wrongs of INVERSION, see the article so named./*The less distinct* was the message *which he felt impelled to deliver,* the more beautiful is often the speech *in which he proclaims it.* A particularly suitable case, in spite of its length, because of the detailed correspondence of the two parts; but read *the message was* instead of *was the message./The less* likely is the satisfaction *of France's claims* (*morally just, but practically impossible*), the more frantic grow *these appeals to force on the part of certain deputies.* An unsuitable case, because the parenthesis & the last phrase (*on* &c.) disturb the correspondence. If these two could be omitted, the sentence would be well enough, except that the inversion should be got rid of by either shifting *is to* after *claims* or omitting *it*—the latter for choice.

theater, -tre. US dictionaries all give *-er* first, but *-re* is still widely used and is invariable in many theater names; *-er* was the prevailing form in England from *c.*1550 to *c.*1720, but modern Brit. *theatre.*

their, as the possessive of *they,* is liable to the same kinds of misuse, for discussion of which see THEY. A mere specimen or two will here suffice. WRONG: *Dr. Hollander has brought within* 200 *pages a vast amount of evidence from 'the medical literature of the entire civilized world'; this is arranged in chapters according to* their *origin./ But* each *knew the situation of* their *own bosom, & could not but guess at that of the other.*

theirs. *It is theirs. Theirs is the sounder opinion. This atom of theirs.* See ABSOLUTE POSSESSIVES.

theism. 'Belief in a deity, as opp. to *atheism;* belief in one god, as opp. to *polytheism* or *pantheism;* belief in one God as creator & supreme ruler of the universe, without denial of revelation, as opp. to *deism*' (OED). See DEISM for the difference.

them. For misuses common to *them* & *they,* see THEY. The reflexive use of *them* (=themselves) is archaic, & as such usually to be avoided; but the following quotation is enough to show that with an archaic verb it is not well to avoid the archaic reflexive: *Together the two—employee & director—*hied themselves *to the superintendent's office.* Read: *hied them to.*

then. *The then-existing Constitution,* hyphen; *the then ruler,* no hyphen.

thenceforth means *from then forth* & does not need (but often has) a preceding *from.*

theoretic(al). The noun forms are *-ic,* & *-ics; -ical* is probably more often used in all adj. senses than *-ic.*

there. In the well-known special use of *there* before *be, exist,* & such verbs (*There have never been many cricket teams in India*), two things call for notice. First, the use is anticipatory, i.e. *there* accompanies & announces inversion of verb & subject, standing in the place usually occupied before the verb by the subject; consequently, when there is no inversion, this *there* is out of place. WRONG: *Bombay is without a doubt the headquarters of whatever cricket* there *exists in India today* (whatever cricket exists). An exception must however be made for the verb *be* itself; *whatever cricket there is* is English though 'whatever cricket there exists' is not. The reason is easy to see; *there* has become, where there is inversion, so regular an attendant on *is, are, was,* &c., in their very frequent use as parts of the substantive verb or verb of existence that even when there is no inversion the need is felt of inserting it as a sign of the particular sense in which *is* &c. is to be taken; but with other verbs, whose meaning is not obscured by the doubt whether they are here & now substantive or auxiliary or copulative, no such sign is wanted, & *there* is used only with inversion.

Secondly, since in the *there* idiom verb precedes subject, there is a danger of the verb's being hastily put into the wrong number (e.g. *There* was *present for the reading of the play only eleven men* (should be *were*); see also NUMBER 7.

thereafter, thereat, therein, thereof. All usually formal, legal, or archaic (*thereafter* least so). See remark under THEREFOR.

thereby. WRONG: *A special tribunal will be constituted to try the accused,* thereby *assuring him the guarantees essential to the right of defense.* For this use of *thereby* with an UNATTACHED PARTICIPLE (*assuring*'s noun is not *tribunal,* but an inferred *constitution*), see that article & THUS, which is more frequently resorted to in similar difficulties.

therefor, therefore. The two are now distinct in accent & meaning as well as in spelling. *Therefor* is accented on the second syllable, *therefore* on the first; & *therefor* is to be used only where *for that, for it, for them,* &c., could stand equally well. In grammatical terms, *therefore* is an adverbial conjunction, & *therefor* an adverbial or adjectival phrase (adv., *He was punished therefor,* & adj., *The penalty therefor is death*). The essential function of *therefore* is to make clear the relation of its sentence to what has gone before; that of *therefor* is the same as that of *thereafter, thereat, therein,* & *thereof,* to give a touch of formality or archaism to the sentence in which it is substituted for the *for it* &c. of natural speech.

therefore. Apart from the danger of meaning *therefor* & writing *therefore,* the only caution needed is that commas should be used or not used with discretion before & after the class of words to which *therefore* belongs. Like *then, accordingly, nevertheless, consequently,* & many others, it is an adverb often (itself, indeed, almost always) used as a conjunction; & it is a matter of taste whether such adverbial conjunctions shall or shall not be set off in commas from the rest of the sentence in which they stand. Light punctuators usually omit the commas (or comma, if *therefore* stands first), heavy punctuators usually give them, & both are within their rights. But it must be remembered that the putting of a comma before *therefore* inevitably has the effect of throwing a strong accent on the preceding word, & that some preceding words are equal to that burden & some are not. From the three following examples it will be at once apparent that *although* can bear the commas, & the *ands* cannot: RIGHT: *Although,* therefore, *the element of surprise could not come into play on this occasion, they were forced to withdraw.* AWKWARD: *It would be impossible for the State to pay such prices, and,* therefore, *we must content ourselves with . . ./Malaria was the cause of a very large proportion of the sickness, and,* therefore, *the disease deserves especial study by . . .*

Again, the word *it* is one that can seldom be emphasized & consequently abhors a commaed *therefore* such as follows it in: *It,* therefore, *comes rather as a shock to find in many papers this morning articles declaring . . ./It,* therefore, *behooves those who have made the passage of the Bill possible to attend once more.* But where emphasis can reasonably be laid on *it,* & *it* can mean 'it more than others' or the like, the commas become at least tolerable; so: *It is a concrete & definite idea, the embodiment of which in practicable shape is by far the most urgent constructive problem of international statesmanship; &* it, therefore, *calls for the most careful examination.*

Many words, however, are neither naturally emphatic like *although* nor naturally unemphatic like *and* & *it;* & after them care should be taken not to use the commas with *therefore* except when emphasis is intended. The personal pronouns are good examples; in the following, we ought to be able to conclude from the commas that 'we' are being deliberately contrasted with others who believe otherwise: *We,* therefore, *find great comfort in believing that loyalty depends not on . . . but on . . .* Probably that is the case, & the commas are justified; but if the light punctuation were generally accepted as the rule with these adverbial conjunctions, & commas used only when emphasis on the preceding word was desired, one of the numberless small points that make for lucidity would be gained.

A curious specimen may be added: *We* therefore *are brought again to the study of symptoms.* Here it is obvious that *We* is unemphatic; but the writer, though he has rightly abstained from commas, has been perverse enough to throw an accent on *We* by other means, viz. by putting *therefore* before instead of after *are;* see POSITION OF ADVERBS 4.

thesaurus. Pl. *-sauri.* Treasury (fig., esp. of words), comprehensive dictionary (e.g. *Thesaurus Linguæ Graecæ,* or a 'treasure house' like Roget's).

these. Although OED does not condemn *these kind of* (*sort of*), and it is often heard colloq., modern usage bans it. RIGHT: *This kind of bird; birds of this kind. Many birds migrate only after the first snow.* These kinds *will often be seen late in the winter.* See KIND.

thesis. Pl. *theses* (ēz).

they, them, their. 1. *One* &c. followed by *their* &c. WRONG: *And we trust that* everybody *interested will send a contribution, however small, to this object, thereby demonstrating* their *personal interest. Their* should be *his;* & the origin of the mistake is clearly reluctance to recognize that the right shortening of the cumbersome *he or she, his or her,* &c., is *he* or *him* or *his* though the reference may be to both sexes. The OED quotes examples from Fielding (*Everyone in the house were in* their *beds*), Goldsmith, Sydney Smith, Thackeray (*A person can't help* their *birth*), Bagehot (*Nobody in* their *senses*), & Bernard Shaw. It also says nothing more severe of the use than that it is 'Not favoured by grammarians.' That the grammarians are likely, nevertheless, to have their way on the point is suggested by the old-fashioned sound of the Fielding & Thackeray sentences quoted. Few good modern writers would flout the grammarians so conspicuously. The question is discussed in NUMBER 11; examples of the wrong *their,* in addition to those that follow, will be found under THEIR, & the article ONE 5, 6, 7, may be useful. WRONG: *The lecturer said that* everybody *loved* their *ideals./* Nobody *in* their *senses would give sixpence on the strength of a promissory note of that kind./ Elsie Lindtner belongs to the kind of* person *who suddenly discovers the beauty of the stars when* they themselves *are dull & have no one to talk with.* The last is amusing by the number of the emendations that hurry to the rescue: E. L. is one of the people who discover . . . ; . . . kind of people who discover . . . ; . . . when he himself is . . . ; . . . when she herself is . . . As to '. . . when she herself is . . .' without further change, it is needless to remark that *each, one, person,* &c., may be answered by *her* instead of *him* & *his* when the reference, though formally to both sexes, is especially, as here, to the female.

2. Confusions with nouns of multitude & personifications. What is meant appears from the quotations following, with *Government, is,* & *them,* in the first, & *journal, its, is,* & *their,* in the second: *The* Government *with the Clarke award before* them, is *yet unable to enforce it./A widely circulated* journal, *having discovered a mare's nest in* its *attempt to show that a woman's drawing room was to be open to the Government Inspector,* is *now trying to inflict a sort of revenge for* their *own mistake by . . .* Discussion, & other examples, will be found in PERSONIFICATION 2.

3. Unsatisfactory reference. For the many possibilities, see PRONOUNS. A few flagrant examples follow, the bracketed numbers referring to sections in PRONOUNS: *It must not repeat this history with* the Poles *or fall into a sudden skepticism about the* Minsk negotiations, *because* they *have succeeded in keeping the enemy from the capital* (3)./*If* adherents *to the Conference have to fight the* Bolshevists, *it is because, by attacking* their *decisions in advance, by waging war against States which* they *propose to set up, & by* their *unscrupulous propaganda,* they *have begun to fight the Conference* (4)./*That the error in date, & the deduction, are from Dr. Garnett's preface, I am well aware; but that does not make* them *either correct or accurate.* In this *error in date* is necessarily part of the reference of *them;* but, since a fact cannot make an error correct or accurate, it should have been 'the date' or 'the erroneous date.'

4. Case. Like *him* & HE (which see for comment), *them* & *they* occasionally go wrong, as in: *The whole foundation of our constitution depends upon* the King being *faithfully served by his advisers, &* they taking *complete responsibility for every act which he does* (read *upon the King's being . . . & their taking*)./*Several bodies of the tribesmen then undertook to help Maclean to escape to the sacred oasis, to which his captors had been careful to draw near in the event of* they themselves being *in danger* (read *in the event of their being in danger themselves*). See FUSED PARTICIPLES.

thimbleful. Pl. *-ls.*

thin makes *thinness.*

thine. *Thine eyes, thine arm* (but *thy garment; thy mansion*); *mine and thine; those cheeks of thine.* See ABSOLUTE POSSESSIVES.

thing. *Things musical, things canine, things Japanese,* & the like, are phrases sometimes serviceable & businesslike, as at the head of a newspaper column, but suggestive of affectation where the only reason for using them is that they are a slightly out-of-the-way form of expression.

think. 1. After *think, that* is usually omitted e.g. *I think*‸*you are right;* see THAT, CONJ. 2.

2. *Think to do* is at best colloq. *Did you* think to ask *him how his father is?* (*think of asking him* or *remember to ask him*).

3. *No thinking man.* One of the bluffing formulas, like *It stands to reason* (see REASON 2), that put the reader's back up & incline him to reject the view that is being forced on

him. In the following piece it will be noticed that the writer by implication rules out all who differ with him from rational humanity: *No thinking man can believe that, without fairer conditions of internal competition, without a broader basis of revenue . . . the State can continue to exist.*

thinkable (capable of being thought, i.e. cogitable; conceivable, imaginable) is a word of the same unfortunate ambiguity as its much more popular opposite UNTHINKABLE. *Protection is only* a thinkable expedient *on the assumption that competition in the home market is to be made unprofitable.*

third. The third estate=Commons; or=the French bourgeoisie before the Revolution. See ESTATE.

thirties. See EIGHTIES.

this. (1) *This three weeks, this five years,* &c., are as good English as *these* &c., the numeral & the plural noun being taken as the singular name of a period; but the modern grammatical conscience is sometimes needlessly uneasy about it.

thither. Now usually formal or literary except in *hither and thither.* See HITHER. An OED quotation shows how the word is still available, though rarely indeed, when real ambiguity would result from *there;* it is from a guidebook: *The road* thither *leaves the main road at right angles.*

those. 1. For *those kind of, those sort of* (worth avoiding in writing but forgivable in hasty conversation) see KIND, SORT.

2. *Those* (adj.)+noun+adjective. RIGHT: *Those named; the persons named;* WRONG: *those persons named. The winner will be selected from* those persons named; *persons* is the noun, & *named* the adj. This arrangement is now very common in writing of the inferior kind, but is little warranted by good literary usage. The word *adjective* in the formula above is to be taken as including participles active or passive, & adjectival phrases, as well as simple adjectives—whatever, in fact, is equivalent to a defining relative clause (WRONG: *those persons* following, *those persons* in the list below, *those persons* present—all equivalent to *the persons that* &c.). *Those named* is a proper substitute for (*the*) *persons named,* the pronoun (not adj.) *those* taking the place of the noun *persons* with or without *the;* & (*the*) *persons named* is itself a shortening of *the persons that are named.* But *those persons named* is a mixture of the long form (*the persons that are named*) & the short form (*those named*), in which mixture what was gained by using the pronoun *those* instead of *the persons* is thrown away by reinserting the noun & making *those* an adjective. It is true that there is another legitimate form in which *those* does appear as an adjective, viz. *those persons who are named;* but that is a form in which not lightness & brevity, but on the contrary formality & precision, are aimed at; it is therefore not one that should be abbreviated.

All this is offered not as a proof that *those persons named* is impossible grammar, but as a reasonable explanation of what is believed to be the fact, that good writers do not say it, but say either (*the*) *persons named* or *those named.* The following quotation is useful as containing samples both of the right & of the wrong usage: *It depends upon the extent to which* those in authority *understand their responsibility, & are able so to make their influence felt as to enlist the active support of* those boys with most influence *in the school. Those in authority* is right, whereas *those persons in authority* would have been wrong; & *those boys with most influence* is wrong, & should be either *the boys,* or *those with* &c. WRONG: *For he possessed just* those qualities needed—*courage, energy, driving power, & . . .* (read *just the*)./*The fitting of such a contrivance must give to* those people employing it *a considerable advantage* (read *to people, to the people,* or *to those employing*). The following use of *those* is quite another matter, & of no importance, but worth giving as a curiosity: *It is impossible for the Ambassador to issue invitations to* those other than Americans.

though. 1. *Though, although.* The definite differences between the two hardly need stating; they are: first, that *though* can be used as an adv., placed last (*He said he would come; he didn't, though*) & *although* cannot; & secondly that *though* is alone possible in the *as though* idiom. In the use common to both forms, i.e. as a complete conjunction, no definite line can be drawn between them, & either is always admissible; but it is safe to say, in the first place, that *though* is much commoner, & secondly that the conditions in which *although* is likely to occur are (a) in the more formal style of writing, (b) in a clause that precedes the main sentence, & (c) in stating an established fact rather than a mere hypothesis: *He wouldn't take an umbrella* though *it should rain cats & dogs;* Although *he attained the highest office, he was of mediocre ability.*

2. *As though.* WRONG: *It is not* as though *there* has *been cruelty & injustice. Had,* in place of *has,* is the only right English; see AS 4 for discussion & examples.

3. (*Al*)*though* with participle or adj. Like other conjunctions (*if, when, while,* &c.), (*al*)*though* is often followed by the significant word only of its clause, the subject & the auxiliary or copulative verb being readily supplied. RIGHT: *Though annoyed, I consented.* The convenience of this is obvious, but care is needed, as appears from the two quotations that follow. WRONG: *Though*^new *to mastership* herself, *a lady master is not new to the pack, for* she *follows Mrs. Garvey in the position.*/Though sympathizing *as I do with Poland,* I cannot resist *the impression that it would be doing Poland an ill service to . . .* The point shown by the first is that the omission must not be made when it leaves the participle or adjective apparently attached to a wrong noun; *new* in fact belongs to *she,* but seems to belong to *a lady master;* if *she is* had not been omitted after *though,* all would have been in order. In the *Poland* sentence, the correction really required is to omit *though,* 'sympathizing as I do' being self-sufficient; but, even if we suppose *as I*

do omitted, there is a wrong sound about *though sympathizing* itself that suggests a restriction; *though,* & other conjunctions, must not be constructed with a participle unless that participle would have been used in the unabridged clause; but that would not have been *though I am sympathizing,* but *though I sympathize;* contrast with this the perfectly satisfactory *Though living he is no longer conscious,* where the full form would be not *Though he lives,* but *Though he is living.*

4. Illogical use. The danger of using adversative conjunctions where two propositions are not strictly opposed, but in harmony, is explained & illustrated in BUT 3. In the following example, *though* would be right if the words 'is the only country in Europe that' were not there; as it stands, the sentence is nonsense: Though *it is only in recent times that* in England *the Jewish civil disabilities were repealed,* Turkey is the only country in Europe *that has throughout been free of any anti-Jewish propaganda.*

thral(l)dom. In US *-ll-*, Brit. *-l-*.

thrash, thresh. One word, with two pronunciations & spellings differentiated. To separate grain is almost always *thresh;* to flog is always *thrash;* in fig. & transf. use the spelling varies as the user thinks of one or the other of the two senses.

Threadneedle Street, *Old Lady of* (Bank of England), see SOBRIQUETS.

threefold. So spelled.

three quarter(s). The noun expressing a fraction has the *-s,* &, though usually hyphened, is better written as two separate words (*a mile and three quarters*). This noun is often used attributively with another noun, e.g. with *length* or *face* in portraiture; in those conditions a hyphen is required to show that the adj.+noun has become one word; but further, it is usual, when a plural noun is used attributively or compounded, to take its singular for the purpose, even if that singular does not otherwise exist; accordingly, *three-quarter length* & *three-quarter face* are the normal forms.

threnody, threnode. (Song of lamentation.) The first is now the standard form.

thrive. *Throve, thriven,* the usual past & p.p., but *thrived* permissible for either.

throat. For *a lump in one's throat;* see STOCK PATHOS.

throe. Now usually only in plural (=*pang(s), anguish,* lit. & fig.).

throstle. The second *-t-* is silent.

through=arrived at completion &c. (*as soon as he gets through, nearly through my work*) is US colloq.

Thule. Pron. thūlē. Orig. a land 'six days north of Britain'; among the ancients, the northernmost (is)land of the world. Transf., esp. *ultima Thule,* the uttermost or highest point; the acme, the limit.

Thunderer. For *the Thunderer=The Times,* see SOBRIQUETS.

Thursday. See FRIDAY.

thus. There is a particular use of *thus* that should be carefully avoided. In this use *thus* is placed before a present participle (*thus enabling* &c.), & its function, when it is not purely otiose, seems to be that of apologizing for the writer's not being quite sure what noun the participle belongs to, or whether there is any noun to which it can properly be attached (cf. UNATTACHED PARTICIPLES). The exact content of *thus* itself is often as difficult to ascertain as the allegiance of the participle. To each quotation is appended (1) a guess at the noun to which the participle belongs, & (2) a guess at the content of *thus*. The guesses are honestly aimed at making the best of a bad job, but readers may prefer other guesses of their own. WRONG: *Our object can only be successfully attained by the substantial contributions of wealthy sympathizers,* thus enabling *us to inaugurate an active policy* (contributions? by being substantial?)./*But now a fresh anxiety has arisen owing to the rising of the Seine,* thus making *the river navigation more difficult & slow* (rising? by occurring?)./*This circumstance is due to the sail innovation introduced at the eleventh hour,* thus necessitating *a remeasurement of some of Shamrock's sails* (innovation? by occurring?). It should be noticed that the resolution of the participle into a relative clause, & the omission of *thus* gets rid of the difficulty every time (*which would enable; which makes; which will necessitate*).

thusly (colloq., facet.) is unnecessary & no longer (if it ever was) amusing.

tidbit. US (& former Brit.) spelling. Modern Brit. TITBIT.

tiers état. (Fr.) The THIRD ESTATE.

tike. Better spelled TYKE.

tilde. (Pron. tĭl′dĕ). The mark put over *n* (ñ) in Spanish when it is to be followed by a *y* sound, as in señor (sênyor′).

till, until. The first is the usual form. The statement that '*till* is inferior in formal prose or verse' is untrue (as seen from quotations in OED) and smacks of SUPERIORITY. For what difference of usage exists, see UNTIL. '*Till* with an apostrophe is wrong; '*til* useless, since *till* is available & means the same thing.

timbal(e). The kettledrum is *-bal;* the pastry &c., *-bale.*

timbre. Tone, tonal quality, resonance. Pron. tămbr′ or as Fr.

time. Under this, as the most general term, may be collected some synonyms. Of the five following words each is given a single definition with a view merely to suggesting the natural relation between them. Though each is often used in senses here assigned not to it but to another (or not mentioned at all), the words *date, epoch, era, period, cycle,* form a series when they are strictly interpreted, & to keep that series in mind is helpful in choosing the right word.

A *date* is the identifiable or intelligibly stated point of time at which something occurs.

An *epoch* is the date of an occurrence that starts things going under new conditions.

An *era* is the time during which the conditions started at an epoch continue.

A *period* is an era regarded as destined to run its course & be succeeded by another.

A *cycle* is a succession of periods itself succeeded by a similar succession.

A *time* & an *age* are words often exchangeable with all or most of the others, & less precise in meaning. Cf. also the words *term, span, spell, season, duration, juncture, moment, occasion.*

timid, timorous. In many contexts, the words are interchangeable. *Timid* is the usual word applied to people (*a timid soul*); *timorous* is more usual in the sense indicating or proceeding from fear (*timorous doubts; a timorous policy*). But *a timid* or *timorous hare.*

timidity, temerity are often confused. The first is fearfulness, the second rashness.

tin. Brit. *tin of soup*=US *can of soup.* (But Brit. *the canning industry.*)

tinge makes *-geable,* but *tinging.*

tinker. *Not worth a tinker's* damn, NOT *dam.*

tint, shade, hue. All are available as substitutes for the dominant word *color.* Different *hues* are, so far as meaning goes, simply different colors, so called because for good or bad reasons the everyday word is held to be unworthy of the context. Different *tints* & *shades* are properly speaking not different colors but varieties of any particular color, *tints* produced by its modification with various amounts of white, & *shades* by various admixtures of black. These distinctions, however little present to the mind, have a growing influence in determining the choice of a synonym for color.

tintinnabulum. Pl. *-la.*

-TION & OTHER -ION ENDINGS. Turgid flabby English of the kind common in inferior leading articles is full of abstract nouns; the commonest ending of abstract nouns is *-tion;* & to count the *-ion* words in what one has written, or, better, to cultivate an ear that without special orders challenges them as they come, is one of the simplest & most effective means of making oneself less unreadable. It is as an unfailing sign of a nouny abstract style that a cluster of *-ion* words is chiefly to be dreaded; but some nouny writers are so far from being awake to that aspect of it that they fall into a still more obvious danger, & so stud their sentences with *-ions* that the mere sound becomes an offense. These points are so simple that quotations need not be multiplied: Speculation *on the subject of the* constitution *of the British* representation *at the Washington* inauguration *will, presumably, be satisfied.*

tipsy (=drunk), see GENTEELISMS.

tiptoe, v., makes *tiptoeing.*

tire, tyre, nn. Of a wheel, US (& COD) *tire;* but Brit. often *tyre.*

tiro, ty-. Beginner, novice. US (and Brit. through the 18th c.) *tyro;* modern Brit. usually *tiro.*

tissue. The OED & US dictionaries give precedence to tĭ'shu; COD, to tĭsū.

titbit, tid-. The older (and usual US) spelling is *tid-,* modern Brit. *tit-.*

titled. *The first chapter of the book is* entitled *'We Rush at Africa.'* This is traditional &

correct usage. The recent (US?) vogue use of *titled* in this sense (*A strong piece* titled *'On Sincerity in Literature'*) is to be discouraged. RIGHT: *A well-titled book; a scion of a titled family;* but NOT *A novel* titled *Dragon Watch.* See VOGUE WORDS.

TITLES. Whereas we used, except on formal occasions, to talk & write of *Lord Salisbury, Lord Derby, Lord Palmerston,* & to be very sparing of the prefixes *Marquis, Earl,* & *Viscount,* the newspapers are now full of *Marquis Curzon, Earl Beatty, Viscount Rothermere,* & similarly Marchioness this & Countess that have replaced the *Lady* that used to be good enough for ordinary wear. We have taken a leaf in this from the Japanese book; it was when Japan took to European titles that such combinations as *Marquis Ito* first became familiar to us, & the adoption of the fashion is more remarkable than pleasing. See also LORD.

tmesis. (Pron. tmē′sis) (Gram.): 'cutting.' Separation of the parts of a compound word by another word inserted between them, as when 'toward us' is written *to usward,* or 'whatsoever things' *what things soever.* (Cf. the modern Brit. facet. *absobloodylutely.*)

to. 1. *To* wrongly substituted for some other preposition. WRONG: *After three years' experience of the official machine I am of opinion that the causes are to be found in the rottenness of the present system,* to *the absence of any system at all so far as Cabinet control is concerned,* & to *the system of bestowing honors on the recommendations of Ministers.* The *tos* result from indecision between *are to be found* & some loosely equivalent phrase such as *may be traced,* perhaps assisted by the writer's glancing back to recover his construction & having his eye caught by *to.* This sort of mistake occurs much more often with OF, under which it will be found fully illustrated.

2. Unidiomatic *to* & infinitive. WRONG: *The impossibility* to assert *himself in any manner galled his very soul./The two factors are the obvious necessity* to put *an end once & for all to the misrule over alien races, & the . . .* *To assert* & *to put* should be *of asserting* & *of putting.* Discussion will be found under GERUND; but it may be added here that it is not difficult to account for this very common lapse, sequences apparently similar being familiar enough. There is, for instance, nothing against saying *It was an impossibility to assert himself,* or *It is an obvious necessity to put an end;* the difference is that *to assert* &c. & *to put* &c. are not there, as in the examples, adjectival appendages of *impossibility* & *necessity,* but the real subjects of the sentences, which might have run *To assert himself was an impossibility,* & *To put an end to so-&-so is a necessity.*

toady makes *toadied, toadying.* Originally 'toad-eater,' i.e. one employed by a charlatan to eat (poisonous) toads; hence (v.) to fawn servilely upon a person.

tobacco. Pl. *-os.*

today, tomorrow, tonight. The lingering of the hyphen, which is still sometimes used after the *to* of these words, is a very singular piece of conservatism. It helps no one to pronounce, it distinguishes between no words that without it might be confused, &, as the *to* retains no vestige of its original meaning, a reminder that the words are compounds is useless.

toffee. The successive forms seem to have been *taffy, toffy, toffee;* it may be guessed that the last is due to the influence of *coffee,* but it is now established in Brit.; US usually *taffy.*

together. *All together* must be carefully distinguished from ALTOGETHER, often written instead of it.

toilet, -ette. The word in all senses should be completely anglicized in spelling & sound (NOT *-ette,* nor twahlĕt′). The sense bathroom, water closet, is chiefly US (originally a GENTEELISM).

toilless. So written, but pronounced with two separate *ls.*

token. Sign, symbol: *By what* token *could it manifest its presence?* For synonyms see SIGN. *By the same token, more by token,* are phrases that probably those who know most about their meaning are least likely to use. The one thing clear is that, when they were part of everyday English, they did not mean what they are usually made to by those who now adorn their writings with them. See WARDOUR STREET.

tolerant. Constr.: *Tolerant* of *little mannerisms; tolerant* of (*or* to) *the faults of others. Tolerant* toward *the persons of heretics, we are intolerant* of *the heresies themselves.* In Medicine, capable of enduring without injury; hence transf., *trees tolerant of shade* (chiefly US).

toll, n. The quotation from Donne (and the title of the Hemingway novel) is 'for whom the bell tolls,' not 'bells toll'; see MISQUOTATION.

tomato. Pl. *-oes.* Most US dictionaries give -ā- first; Brit. -ah- (which is nearer the original Spanish & Mexican, from which the word came).

tomorrow. So spelled.

ton (weight). *Ton,* the weight; *tun,* the cask, vat, & wine measure.

tonight. So spelled.

tonsil makes *tonsillitis; tonsillectomy.*

tonsorial. A word used almost only in PEDANTIC HUMOR.

too. 1. With passive participles, *too* is subject to the same limitations, though the point has been less noticed, as VERY. The line, however, between the adjectival & the verbal p.p. is often hard to draw. In the following quotations the addition of *with* &c. & *in* &c. to the participles turns the scale, & *too much* should have been written instead of *too: Belfast is* too *occupied* with *its own affairs, too confident of itself, to be readily stirred to any movement which would endanger its prosperity./But he was* too *engrossed* in *Northern Europe to realize his failure.*

2. Illogical uses. These are very common, so common as to deserve a place among the STURDY INDEFENSIBLES & to be almost idiomatic. They result from confusing two logical ways of making a statement, one with & the other without *too,* & are better avoided. WRONG: *Praise which perhaps was scarcely meant to be taken* too *literally* (a, which may easily be taken too literally; b, which was not

meant to be taken literally)./ *It is yet far* too early *to generalize* too widely *as to origins & influences* (a, If we generalize too early we may generalize too widely; b, It is too early to generalize widely).

top-. Writing of compounds. *Topcoat, -knot, -mast, -most, -notch, -sail, -side, -soil,* all best single words, no hyphen. *Top-dressing, top-heavy, top-secret* (adj.), all hyphened. *Top hat, top sergeant,* two words each.

topiary. Of a garden, one in which the shrubs &c. are trimmed into ornamental shapes. Pron. tō-.

torment makes *tormentor, -tress* (see FEMININE DESIGNATIONS).

tornado, torpedo. Pl. *-oes.*

torpor. So spelled.

torso. Pl. *-os.*

tortoise. Pron. tor′tŭs.

tortuous, full of twists or turns; transf. devious, circuitous; *torturous,* full of, involving, or causing torture; fig. (of style &c.) involving perversion or dislocation (of words). *Tortious,* law, involving a tort, wrongful.

toss makes *tossed,* poet. *tost* (e.g. *storm-tost*).

total. The adj. makes *-ally, -alize(r), -ality;* the verb, US *-aled, -aling,* Brit. *-lled, -lling.* Since World War II *total* has become a VOGUE WORD: *total war, total disarmament, total defense.*

totalitarian, of a polity that allows no rival parties or loyalties and is controlled by a strong centralized government dominated by a single political party or group.

tother, now colloq., was formerly in good literary use, & was then more often written *tother* than *t'other;* there is therefore no need for the apostrophe.

toto caelo. Literally, 'by the whole sky,' i.e. by the greatest possible distance. Properly used only with *differ, different,* & words of similar meaning (*it differs* toto caelo *from the normal construction*); but the writer of the following extract has guessed that it is a high-class variant of *totally.* WRONG: . . . *had the effect of habitually repealing its own canon in part, during the lifetime of parties . . . , & of repealing it,* toto caelo, *after the death of either of them.* See FOREIGN DANGER.

touchy. The modern word. See TETCHY.

toupee, toupet. The first is the form common in England in the 18th c. and still standard in US, written without an accent & pronounced tōōpā (or formally tōōpē); the second is the French spelling, now used in England & pronounced tōō′pā.

tour de force. A feat of strength or skill; now sometimes used of one merely adroit or ingenious: [*His book*] *holds the interest but the reader eventually realizes that it is only a* tour de force.

tourniquet. Pron. tōōr′nĭkĕt.

tousle. So spelled.

toward, towards, towardly. The adjs. *toward* (including the predicative use as in *a storm is toward,* i.e. coming) & *towardly* are pronounced tō′ard(lĭ). The prepositions are best pronounced tōrd (z), but in recent use the influence of spelling is forcing tōōward′(z) on the half educated. The adjs.

in all senses are obsolescent, or at any rate archaic. Of the prepositions the *-s* form is the prevailing one in Brit., *toward* in US.

town. *Town clerk, council, crier, hall,* & *house* should all be written as separate words without hyphens; *townward, township, townsman, townspeople,* single words.

trace, n. In the sense *vestige, indication* (*no trace of inhabitation*), for synonyms see SIGN.

trace, v., makes *-ceable.*

trachea. In US pron. trā′kêa (though trakē′*a* is etym. preferable & first in COD).

trade. *Trade mark* is two words in Brit. & was formerly so written in US; now *trade-mark* and *trademark* vie with each other, but the latter has been adopted by the Government & might well become general; the hyphen, esp. in a noun, is undesirable. *Trade union* is better as two words; *tradesman,* one word; *trade wind,* two words.

tradition(al)ism, -ist. The longer forms are usual.

traduce makes *-cible.* The only current sense is to speak evil of, calumniate, malign.

traffic, v., makes *-icked, -icker, -icking.*

tragedienne. Pron. tr*a* jē′dĭ-ĕn′.

tragic(al). It may almost be said that the longer form is, in serious use, dead. It survives, however, in playful use, often with a memory of the 'very tragicall mirth' of Pyramus & Thisbe in *Midsummer Night's Dream.* For *tragic* (dramatic) *irony,* see IRONY 2.

tragicomedy, tragicomic, &c. So spelled.

TRAILERS. Under this name a few specimens are collected of the sort of sentence that tires the reader out by again & again disappointing his hope of coming to an end. It is noticeable that writers who produce trailers produce little else, & that where one fine example occurs there are sure to be more in the neighborhood. The explanation probably is that these gentlemen have on the one hand a copious pen, & on the other a dislike (most natural, their readers must agree) to reading over what it may have set down. Whatever its cause, the trailer style is perhaps of all styles the most exasperating. Anyone who was conscious of this weakness might do much to cure himself by taking a pledge to use no relative pronouns for a year; but perhaps most of its victims are unconscious. *It is true that part of the traffic here is heavy,* but *at least the surface might be conditioned by modern methods,* even *if the form of paving cannot well be altered,* though *I think it ought to be—*e.g. *if Sydney Smith's suggestion as to the wood pavement problem perplexing an old vestry—'Gentlemen, put your heads together, & the thing's done' —is impracticable, there are now improved means open to a modern City Council,* both *in surface dressing, in hard woods,* & even *in macadam,* by the use *of slag—locally called dross—*from *the iron furnaces in Yorkshire,* which *makes the hardest & smoothest surface./* *But* so far *as I could see, nobody carried away burning candles to rekindle with holy fire the lamp in front of the ikon at home,* which *should burn* *throughout the year* except *for the short time it is extinguished* in order *to receive anew the light that is relit every year* throughout *the Christian world* by *Christ's victory over death.*

traipse. Colloq. To trail in an untidy way (esp. of women with skirts trailing, according to OED). So spelled in US. But see TRAPES.

trait. The final *t* is sounded in US, but still usually silent in Brit. In the sense distinguishing feature or quality (. . . *no national* trait *about them but their language*), for synonyms, see SIGN.

traitor makes *traitorous* and *traitress* (fem.).

tranquil makes, US, *-ilize;* Brit. *-illize;* both, *tranquillity, tranquilly.*

trans-. Prefix meaning *across* (or *crossing*), *through, beyond: Transcontinental, transoceanic, transatlantic, transalpine* (no hyphen, no capitalization); but *trans-Canadian, trans-Indian, trans-Mississippi, trans-Appalachian.*

transcendence, -cy. No differentiation. See -CE, -CY.

transcendent(al). These words, with their many specialized applications in philosophy, are for the most part beyond the scope of this book; but there are popular uses in which the right form should be chosen. (1) The word that means surpassing, of supreme excellence or greatness, &c., is *transcendent,* & the following is WRONG: *The matter is of* transcendental *importance, especially in the present disastrous state of the world.* See LONG VARIANTS for similar pairs. (2) The word applied to God in contrast with IMMANENT is *transcendent.* (3) The word that means visionary, idealistic, outside of experience, &c., is *transcendental.* (4) The word applied to Emerson & his 'religio-philosophical teaching' is *transcendental.*

transcendentalism. New England transcendentalism, as interpreted by Emerson, Thoreau, Margaret Fuller, Alcott, Theodore Parker, Brownson, &c., 'in its larger outlines . . . had as its base a monism holding to the unity of the world & God, and the immanence of God in the world . . . The soul of each individual is identical with the soul of the world, & latently contains all that the world contains. Man may fulfil his divine potentialities either through a rapt mystical state . . . or through coming into contact with the truth, beauty, & goodness embodied in nature, & originating in the Over-Soul. Through belief in the divine authority of the soul's intentions . . . there developed the doctrine of self-reliance & individualism, the disregard of authority, traditionalism, & logical demonstration, & the absolute optimism of the movement.' (From Hart, *Oxford Companion to American Literature.*)

transfer. *Transferred, -erring, -errer,* but *transferable* & *transference, transferee* & *transferor.* Of *transferrer* & *transferor,* the first is the general agent-noun, a person or mechanism that passes something on, & the second a legal term for the person who conveys his property to another, the *transferee.*

transfuse makes *-sible.*

transgress makes *transgressor.*

tranship, transship, trans-ship. The second is usual US, the third Brit., the first etymologically unjustifiable. But the OED accepts *tranship,* saying only 'less commonly trans-ship.' Generations of clerks have saved themselves trouble & nearly made away with the *s* & the hyphen; of 28 OED quotations, including those for *tran(s)-shipment,* 9 only show *s-s* or *ss;* 9 & the right against 19 & the wrong.

transient, transitory. In many contexts the words are interchangeable; both are defined as brief, fleeting, momentary. Webster adds of the first 'that which is actually short in duration or stay'; of the second, 'that which by its nature or essence is bound to pass or go.' A *transient* or *transitory view; the transient hours we call our own; this vain & transitory world.* The sense *transient guest, transient residents* (or 'transients,' n.) is chiefly US.

TRANSITIVE VERB. One taking a direct object. In 'Lay the book on the table,' *lay* is transitive, the object being *the book;* in 'Lie down for a minute,' *lie* is intransitive, *down* being an adverb showing where to lie. (In schoolbook rules, a transitive verb is one completed by a word, phrase, or clause telling what.)

translucence, -cy. No important differentiation. See -CE, -CY.

translucent. See TRANSPARENT.

transmit makes *-itted, -itter, -itting,* & *-issible* or *-ittable. Transmit* should not be used as a FORMAL WORD for *send.*

transparence, -ency. The second is the usual form. The first is marked 'rare' in the OED: & indeed, in its only two *-ence* quotations that are as late as 1800 euphony plainly accounts for the avoidance of *-cy: Motive may be detected through the transparence of tendency./ Adamantine solidity, transparence, & brilliancy.*

transparent, & the synonyms *diaphanous, pellucid, translucent. Transparent* is the general word for describing what is penetrable by sight (lit. or fig.) or by light, & it can be substituted for any of the others unless there is some point of precision or of rhetoric to be gained. All three synonyms have the rhetorical value of being less common than *transparent,* & therefore appear more often in poetical writing. As regards precision, the following definitions of the words' narrower senses are offered, & to each are appended some specially appropiate nouns, & the adjective or participle that seems most directly opposed.

That is *diaphanous* which does not preclude sight of what is behind it; *garments, vapor, membrane;* opp. *shrouding.*

That is *transparent* which does not even obscure sight of what is behind it; *glass, candor, pretense;* opp. *obscuring.*

That is *pellucid* which does not distort images seen through it; *water, literary style;* opp. *turbid.*

That is *translucent* which does not bar the passage of light; *alabaster, tortoise shell;* opp. *opaque.*

transpire. The notorious misuse of this word consists in making it mean *happen* or *turn out* or *go on* (COD says 'vulg.'; 'a sense disapproved by most authorities but used by authors of good standing'); & the legitimate meaning that has been misinterpreted into this is to emerge from secrecy into knowledge, to leak out, to become known by degrees. It is needless to do more than give a single example of the right use, followed by several of the wrong. RIGHT: *The conditions of the contract were not allowed to* transpire./WRONG: *That strike has caused a not inconsiderable increase in the cost of production, while nothing similar has* transpired *within the past few years to produce any such effect./In view of the fact that only two years have* transpired *since the date of publication, we should appreciate . . ./Both men opened in a subdued mood in what* transpired *to be the last game of this grand fight.* The last of these adds to the wrong meaning of *transpire* an unidiomatic construction after it in the infinitive *to be.* That construction will not do even when *transpire* has its true sense; that sense is complete in itself, & *transpired to be* is as little English as *came to light to be.* Here is the right sense followed by the wrong construction: *They must have been aware of the possibility that the facts might be as they ultimately* transpired to be.

transposal. Use *transposition* (see -AL NOUNS).

transship(ment). So spelled but see TRANSHIP.

trapes, traipse. The first seems to be at present the orthodox Brit. spelling; but the word in this form has so puzzling a look that it would surely be better to use TRAIPSE, which is usual in US & allowed by the OED as an alternative, is quoted from Swift & Pope, & can be pronounced only one way.

trapezium. Pl. *-ia, -ms.*

travail. Pron. trăʹvāl.

travel. US usually *-led, -ler;* Brit. *-lled, -ller,* &c.

travelogue, -log, an irregular and recent form (not in OED). The dictionaries give *-logue* first but *-log* is just as reasonable. Cf. *ship's log.*

travesty. A grotesque imitation. See BURLESQUE.

trayful. Pl. *-fuls.*

treat of (formerly *on* or *upon*)=deal with, handle (a subject) usually in a speech or writing (*The book* treats of *economic & social problems*); now usually formal.

treble. See TRIPLE.

trecento, -tist. Pron. trāchĕnʹtō, -tĭst. This & *quattrocento, -ist, cinquecento, -ist,* are words constantly used by writers on Italian art. Though their true meaning is 300, 400, 500, they are used as abbreviations for the centuries 1300–1399 (1301–1400 is to us the 14th c.), 1400–1499 (our 15th c.), & 1500–1599 (our 16th). There is therefore a double puzzle, Italian 300 for Italian 1300, & Italian 13th c. for English 14th c. The words in *-ist* mean painters &c. of the century.

trefoil. Pron. trē-. (COD admits trĕ- also.)

trek, v., makes *trekked, trekking.* To travel (orig. by ox or wagon); to migrate; hence loosely, to make one's way arduously.

trellis makes *-ised.*

tremolo. Pl. *-os.*

tremor. So spelled. Pron. trĕmẽr, not trē-.

trend. The essential idea of *trend* is direction. It is a word that, whether as noun or as verb, should be used by no one who is not sure of both its meaning & its idiomatic habits. WRONG: *There has unquestionably been a* trend *of policy* to strengthen *our naval position by making relations closer with . . ./His chapter on . . ., although it has little to do with the rest of his volume,* & trends *very closely* upon *the forbidden theme of history, is interesting.* 'There is a trend of policy to do' is not English, though 'The trend of our policy is to do' would be. *Trends very closely upon* is perhaps a confusion with *trenches* &c.; *trend* does not mean encroach.

trepan. Pron. trĕpăn′. Both verbs, that meaning entrap, & the surgical, make *trepanned, -nning.*

trial. *Trial and error* properly means finding the desired solution by experimenting with various means and eliminating errors or causes of failure; colloq. (or loosely), trying this & that till something works. See POPULARIZED TECHNICALITIES.

tribunal. Pron. preferably trībū′nal.

tribute. A SLIPSHOD EXTENSION of the less excusable kind—since the meaning of *tribute* is surely no mystery—is that which sets *a tribute to* to do the work of *a proof* (or *illustration* &c.) *of;* WRONG: *The debate on the whole was* a tribute to the good taste & good form *of the House of Commons./All these & many other prominent English works have been fairly & critically analyzed, & it is* a tribute to the modesty *of the American editors that the European works received first place.*

tricentenary. *Tercentenary* is the prevailing form.

triceps. Pl. *-cepses* (-sĕpsēz).

tricolor, tricolore, tricolour. The first is a Latin adj. (trī′kolor); the second is the French adj. used in describing the French flag (*le drapeau tricolore*); the third is a badly formed English noun (see COLOR, & HYBRID derivatives) used by itself as a name (*the tricolour*) for the French flag, & usually pronounced trī′kŭler. It would be better to use *tricolor* (trī′kolor, US usually trī′-) in this sense also, & drop the other two forms.

trillion. In US & Fr., 1000 millions; in Brit. & Ger., a million millions.

trilogy. (Lit.): 'three pieces.' In ancient Athens, there were dramatic competitions at which each dramatist presented three plays, originally giving successive parts of the same legend; the extant *Agamemnon, Choephoroe,* & *Eumenides* of Aeschylus formed a trilogy, &, with the addition of the lost *Proteus,* a tetralogy. Later trilogies were connected not necessarily by a common subject, but by being works of the same poet presented on the same occasion. In modern use the word is applied to a work such as Shakespeare's *Henry VI,* comprising three separate plays, or to a novel &c. with two sequels.

trio. Pl. -os.

triolet. (Pron. trī- or trē-.) (Poet.): 'three-piece.' An eight-line poem in which the first line occurs thrice (1, 4, 7) & the second twice (2, 8), & the other lines rhyme with these two. An example (Robert Bridges) is:

All women born are so perverse
No man need boast their love
possessing.
If nought seem better, nothing's
worse:
All women born are so perverse.
From Adam's wife, that proved
a curse
Though God had made her for
a blessing,
All women born are so perverse
No man need boast their love
possessing.

triple, treble. If the musical sense of *treble* is put aside, there are perhaps no senses in which one is possible & the other impossible. In US *triple* is perhaps more common in all senses (except music); in Brit. *treble* is the more usual verb & noun, & *triple* the more usual adj.

tripod. Pron. preferably trī'pŏd.

triptych. Pron. *-k.*

Tristan in *Tristan und Isolde; Tristram* in most English versions.

triumphal, -phant. The meanings are quite distinct, but to use the first for the second is usually a worse mistake than the converse, because the idea it ought to convey is narrower & more definite. *Triumphal* means only of or in the celebration of a victory, & belongs to the original 'triumph' or victorious general's procession; *triumphant* belongs to *triumph* in any of its senses, especially those of brilliant success or exultation. In the following quotations each word is used where the other was required. The 'progress' of the first was not almost, but quite *triumphant;* & the 'career' of the second, if it lasted 66 years & was troubled, may have been *triumphant*, but hardly *triumphal.* WRONG: *He had almost a* triumphant *progress through the streets, with women clinging about his car, manifesting in every possible way their delight at his presence./The story he told us of the sixty-six previous years of his troubled,* triumphal *career.* See also MALAPROPS, & PAIRS & SNARES.

triumvir. Pl. *-rs* or less usually *-ri.*

trivia, n. pl.,=trifles, unimportant matters, a BACK FORMATION from *trivial;* no sing.

-TRIX. As any Latin agent-noun in *-tor* could form a feminine in *-trix*, some of these when taken into English continue to do so, especially such as are, like *testator* & *prosecutor*, in legal use. It is a serious inconvenience that the Latin plural is *-ices* (-ī'sēz), as the pronunciation and accent resulting make many of the words hardly recognizable.

This sort of confusion would be best cured by giving them all the ordinary English plural—*testa'trixes* &c. instead of *testatri'ces* or *testa'trices.* For some of them the further anglicizing of *-trix* into *-tress* would also be possible. For the other escape of using the masculine form & dropping the feminine, see FEMININE DESIGNATIONS.

The chief words concerned are: *administratrix, cicatrix, executrix, matrix, prosecutrix, testatrix.*

troche (the medicinal lozenge). OED allows the pronunciations trōsh, trōch, & trōk; of trōkĕ it says 'in vulgar & commercial use.' Nevertheless, it is now so pronounced, US & Brit.

trochee. (Poet.): 'running.' The foot –⌣, as in *blun'der.* Pron. trō'kē.

troop, troupe. Both mean a

band, company, but the latter is used only of actors. *Swear like a trooper;* but *he's a real trouper* (i.e. veteran [traveling] actor who would play his part under any conditions).

trouble makes *trouble-maker, trouble shooter* (US? colloq.).

troublous. 'Now only literary or archaic' says the OED; & one of its quotations shows well the bad effect of diversifying commonplace contexts with words of the sort; the ordinary *troublesome* was the word wanted: *Mr. Walpole took on himself the management of the Home Office, little knowing what a* troublous *business he had brought upon his shoulders.* For *these troublous times,* see HACKNEYED PHRASES.

trounce makes *-ceable.* To thrash, castigate (lit. & fig.).

trousseau. Pl. *-eaux* or *-eaus.*

trout. Pl. usually the same.

trow, when still in ordinary use, was pronounced trō.

truck. There are two nouns, one originally meaning *barter,* which on the one hand deteriorated into (worthless) dealings and on the other is the source of our *truck farming, truck gardening* (market garden produce). The second noun originally meant *wooden wheel,* from which eventually came the *motor truck* and the British *freight truck.*

There are also two verbs, one from noun (1), now chiefly colloq. (*Private communities have no business to* truck *with the State*), the other from noun (2), to convey by truck & also (US colloq.) to have charge of a truck (*I've been* trucking *for the company for a dozen years*).

TRUE & FALSE ETYMOLOGY. English being the one of all languages that has gathered its material from the most various sources, the study of its etymology is naturally of exceptional interest. It is a study, however, worth undertaking for that interest, & as an end in itself, rather than as a means to the acquiring either of a sound style or even of a correct vocabulary. What concerns a writer is much less a word's history than its present meaning & idiomatic habits. The etymologist is aware, & the person who has paid no attention to the subject is probably unaware, that a *fuse* is so called not because it fuses anything, but because it is spindle-shaped; that a *belfry* is not named from its bell; that a child's *cot* & a *sheepcot(e)* come from different languages; that *Welsh rabbit* is amusing & right, & *Welsh rarebit* stupid & wrong; that *isle* & *island* have nothing in common; & that *pygmy* is a more significant spelling than *pigmy.* But to know when it is & when it is not well to call an island *an isle* is worth more than to know all these etymological facts (see SEMANTICS). *Still,* etymology has its uses, even for those whose sole concern with it is as an aid to writing & a preventive of blunders. It may save us from treating *protagonist* as the opposite of *antagonist,* or from supposing a *watershed* to be a *river basin,* or from materializing the *comity of nations* into either a *committee* or a *company* of them, or from thinking that *to demean oneself* is to lower oneself or do a mean thing. But it must be added that the etymology providing such stray scraps of useful knowledge is much more that which deals with the French & Latin elements in our language than that which deals with its native or Teutonic substratum. Those who start with a knowledge of Latin & French have in this way a very real if not very calculable advantage over writers who are without it; but to advise the latter to acquire Latin & French at a late stage with a view to ridding themselves of the handicap, still more to incite them to a course of pure English etymology, would be foolish indeed.

After this much of warning, which amounts to a confession that etymological knowledge is of less importance to writers than might be supposed, a selection of words is offered exemplifying the small surprises that reward or disappoint the etymologist. They are arranged alphabetically, but are a very low percentage of what might have been collected. With each word the barest indication only is given of the point, which to many readers will be already known, & by others may be easily verified in any good dictionary. The object of the list is not to give etymologies, but to provide anyone who is curious about the value of such knowledge with the means of testing it. The words in small capitals are the few that happen to have been treated in their places in any way that at all bears upon the present subject. (E=English, L=Latin.)

arbo(u)r, not L *arbor* tree
barberry, not E *berry*
bastard, not E *base*
blindfold, not E *fold*
bliss, not E *bless*
bound (homeward &c.), not E *bind*
BOXING-DAY, not pugilistic
buttonhole, not *hole* but *hold*
card (comb wool &c.), not from *card* (paper)
cockroach, not *cock* or *roach*
COCOA, *coconut*, unconnected
cookie (bun &c.), not E *cook*
core, not L *cor* heart
crayfish, not E *fish*
curtail, not E *tail*
cutlet, not E *cut*
egg on, not *egg* but *edge*
fingering (wool), not E *finger*
FORBEARS=fore-beërs
GINGERLY, not E *ginger*
GLOSS, one word colored by another
GREYHOUND, not E *grey*
incentive, not L *incendo* to fire
lutestring, not *lute* or *string*
pen, pencil, unconnected
recover, not E *cover*
river, not L *rivus* river
SORRY, sorrow, unconnected
TUBEROSE, not *tube* or *rose*
vile, villain, unconnected.

truffle. Best pron. trŭ′fl.

truism. The word's two meanings (an indisputable truth, e.g. *man cannot live without food;* a statement that says nothing not already implied) have been compared both with each other & with some synonyms under COMMONPLACE. *It is not permissible to be* too sanguine *of the outcome of the Conference,* & *A leading personage at the Conference declares that there is no cause for* undue alarm, are examples of the sort of truism that writers should not allow themselves; mend them by changing *too* into *very* & *undue* into *much,* & see TOO 2. As to the use of the word itself, the temptation to say that a thing is a truism when no more is meant than that it is true, because it has a smarter sound, should be resisted. WRONG: *It probably owes much to the dialect in which it is played; but* *that is a truism of almost every Irish or Scotch play.*

trunkful. Pl. *-ls.*

trust. (1) The OED's definition of the commercial sense is here given, for comparison with CARTEL: 'A body of producers or traders in some class of business, organized to reduce or defeat competition, lessen expenses, & control production & distribution for their common advantage; spec., such a combination of commercial or industrial companies, with a central governing body of trustees which holds a majority or the whole of the stock of each of the combining firms, thus having a controlling vote in the conduct & operation of each.' (2) *A trust company* is a company or corporation (usually a bank) organized to execute the functions of a trustee.

trusty, adj.=*trustworthy,* is chiefly archaic (or facet.): *my trusty steed* &c.; *trusty* n.,=a convict allowed special privileges for good behavior, is US.

try. (1) The idiom *try & do* something is described as colloq. for *try to do.* Its use is almost confined to exhortations & promises: *Do try & stop coughing; I will try & have it ready for you.* And it is hardly applicable to past time; *He tried & made the best of it* is not English in the sense required, though *He did try & make the best of it* is conceivable. It is, therefore, colloquial, if that means specially appropriate to actual speech; but not if colloquial means below the proper standard of literary dignity. Though *try to do* can always be substituted for *try & do,* the latter has a shade of meaning that justifies its existence. In exhortations it implies encouragement—the effort will succeed; in promises it implies assurance—the effort shall succeed. It is an idiom that should be not discountenanced, but used when it comes natural. See PEDANTRY. (2) *Try,* n. (*let's have a* try *at it; at first* try), is chiefly colloq., though not so labeled in most US dictionaries.

trysail. Pron. (naut.) trī'sl'.

tryst. OED gives trĭst only; most recent dictionaries give trīst also, & trīst is more usual in US.

Tsar. OED & Webster give Tsar, as nearer the Russian; COD & some other US dictionaries prefer *Czar.*

tsetse. So spelled; pron. tsĕ'-tsĭ.

T square, so spelled; *tee shirt* better so spelled (from golf).

-t-, -tt-. Words ending in *-t* are very numerous (cf. *-s*), & there seems to be some hesitation about making them conform to the rules that prevail for most consonants: forms like *rivetter, blanketty, docketted,* are often seen, though good usage is against them. Monosyllables ending in *-t* double it before suffixes beginning with vowels if the sound preceding it is a single vowel, but not if it is a diphthong or a doubled vowel or a vowel & *r: pettish, potted, cutter,* but *flouting, sooty, skirting.* Words of more than one syllable follow the rule for monosyllables if their last syllable is accented (*coquettish,* but *repeater*); but *combatant, wainscoting, balloted.*

tuber is the darling of the lower class of ELEGANT VARIATONists—the class that indulges in the practice not as a troublesome duty but for pleasure. A potato is a tuber, but the fact should be left in the decent obscurity of agricultural textbooks. *There was no difficulty in getting* potatoes *one day—the next, so to speak, you could search Paris without discovering a single* tuber./*Sir Walter Raleigh popularized them, & in all probability Sir Francis Drake was the first to bring the* tuber *from the New World.*

tuber, bulb, corm. A dahlia *tuber*, a tulip *bulb*, a gladiolus *corm.*

tuberculosis. Pref. pron. tūbûrkūlō′sĭs, but as three preceding unstressed syllables are too difficult for most people, now usually tūbûr′kūlō′sĭs.

tuberose. Pref. pron. tū′berōs (not tūbrōz); not from *tube* or *rose*, but from (*Polianthes*) *tuberosa*=tuberous, or grown from tubers.

tubful. Pl. *-ls.*

Tuesday. See FRIDAY.

tug. For *tug at one's heartstrings*, see STOCK PATHOS.

tumefy. So spelled, NOT *tumi-*. (Cf. Lat. *tumere*, to swell.)

tumidity, -ness. The first is more usual.

tumultuary, tumultuous. The distinction between the two is not very definite, & sentences may easily be made in which either might be used & give the same sense. But *-tuous* is now the much commoner word, which should be chosen unless there is good reason to prefer the other; & what is emphasized by *-tuous* is rather the violence & impetus & force, while *-tuary* emphasizes the irregularity & unorganized nature, of the thing described: *tumultuous applause, seas, attack, joy, crowd; tumultuary forces* (hastily levied), *thoughts* (thronging confusedly), *risings* (sporadic).

tumulus. Pl. *-li.*

tun. The vat for wine & the liquid measure. See TON.

tunnel makes US *-led, -ling;* Brit. *-lled* &c.

tu quoque. (Rhet.): 'thou also.' The meeting of a charge or argument not by disproof &c. but by retorting it upon its user. E.g. Why don't you go yourself? to a civilian urging one to enlist.

turbidity, turbidness. OED prefers *-ness* in both lit. & fig. uses (muddy; confused); but *-ity* is seen as often, esp. figuratively.

tureen. The right pronunciation is terēn′, in accordance with the derivation (*terra*, earth) & the older English spelling (*terrene* &c.); but tū- (US) and tū- (Brit.) are often heard.

turf. Pl. *-fs* (archaic, *-ves*).

turgid. Swollen. Fig., of language, bombastic, pompous. *Turgid & loquacious rhetoric; verbose & turgid style. Turgidity* is more usual than *turgidness.*

Turk makes US *Turko-*, Brit. *Turco-*, in compounds, as *Turkophil, -phobe, -mania.* But *Turkoman* now preferred to *Turcoman*, US & Brit.

turn, v. In the *age* idiom two constructions are recognized: *I have turned* 20, & *I am turned* 20; the second is apparently of more recent origin than the first, but is now more usual. *Turn of the century*, see HACKNEYED PHRASES.

turnover. The *turnover* in business & the pastry, no hyphen.

turquoise. Pron. -koiz, or -kwois (Brit. & US); -kwahz is an affectation.

turret makes *-eted.*

twelfth. So spelled & pronounced.

twenties, thirties, &c. See EIGHTIES.

twilit. The formation implies a verb *to twilight* made from the noun; & that verb, though unknown to most of us, is recorded to have been used; it also implies that *to twilight* has p.p. *twilit* rather than *twilighted,* which is not impossible. But, though *twilit* cannot be absolutely ruled out, it is better to use *twilight* attributively where, as usually, that does the work as well, & elsewhere to do without. In the two following quotations, *twilight* would have served at least as well: *He found himself free of a fanciful world where things happened as he preferred—a* twilit *world in which substance melted into shadow./The years of the war were a clear & brilliantly lit passage between two periods of* twilit *entanglement.*

-TY & -NESS. The number of legitimate words in *-ness* is limited only by that of the adjs. that exist in English; but, though any adj. may be formed into a noun on occasion by the addition of *-ness,* the nouns of that pattern actually current are much fewer, there being hundreds, usually preferred to the *-ness* forms, that are made from Latin adjs. with *-ty, -ety,* or *-ity* as their ending. Thus from *one* & *loyal* & *various* we can make for special purposes *oneness, loyalness,* & *variousness;* but ordinarily we prefer *unity, loyalty,* & *variety.* Of the *-ty* words that exist, a very large majority are for all purposes commoner & better than the corresponding *-ness* words, usage & not anti-latinism being the right arbiter. Scores of words could be named, such as *ability, honesty, notoriety, prosperity, stupidity,* for which it is hard to imagine any good reason for substituting *ableness, notoriousness,* &c. On the other hand words in *-ness* that are better than existent forms in *-ty* are rare; perhaps *acuteness* & *conspicuousness* have the advantage of *acuity* & *conspicuity;* & if *perspicuousness* could be established in place of *perspicuity* it might help to obviate the common confusion with *perspicacity;* but in general a *-ty* word that exists is to be preferred to its rival in *-ness,* unless total or partial differentiation has been established, or is designed for the occasion. Total differentiation has taken place between *ingenuity* & *ingenuousness, casualty* & *casualness, sensibility* & *sensibleness, enormity* & *enormousness;* the use of either form instead of the other necessarily changes or destroys the meaning. Partial differentiation results from the more frequent use made of the *-ty* words; both terminations have, to start with, the abstract sense of the quality for which the adj. stands; but while most of the *-ness* words, being little used, remain abstract & still denote quality only, many of the *-ty* words acquire by much use various concrete meanings in addition; e.g. *humanity, curiosity, variety,* beside the senses 'being human, curious, various,' acquire those of 'all human beings,' 'a curious object,' & 'a subspecies.' Or again they are so habitually applied in a limited way that the full sense of the adj. is no longer naturally suggested by them; *preciosity* is limited to literary or artistic style, *maturity* suggests the moment of reaching rather than the state of matureness, *purity* & *frailty* take a sexual tinge that *pureness* & *frailness* are without, *poverty* is more nearly confined to lack of money than *poorness.* It is when lucidity requires the excluding of some such meaning or implication attached only to the *-ty* form that a *-ness* word may reasonably be substituted.

Some of the articles under which special remarks will be found are BARBARISM &c., ENORMOUS, OBLIQUENESS, OPACITY, POVERTY, PRECIOSITY, SENSIBILITY. For similar distinctions between other nearly equivalent terminations, see -CE, -CY, -IC(AL), -ION & -NESS, -ION & -MENT, -ISM & -ITY.

A few specimens may be added & classified that have not been cited above, but are notable in some way. (A) Some words in *-ty* for which there is no companion in *-ness: celerity, cupidity, debility, fidelity, integrity, utility.* (B) Some more in which the *-ty* word has a marked concrete or limited sense not shared by the other: *capacity, commodity, fatality, festivity, monstrosity, nicety, novelty, subtlety.* (C) Some of the few in *-ness* that are as much used as those in *-ty,* or more, though the *-ty* words exist: *clearness* (clarity), *crudeness, falseness, graciousness, inevitableness, jocoseness, literalness, morbidness, moroseness, passiveness, ponderousness, positiveness, punctiliousness, spaciousness, sublimeness, tenseness, unctuousness.* (D) Some *-ness* words that have no corresponding form in *-ty: crispness, facetiousness, firmness, largeness, massiveness, naturalness, obsequiousness, pensiveness, proneness, robustness, rudeness, seriousness, tardiness, tediousness, vastness, vileness.*

tycoon=great prince. The official so named was the military ruler of Japan in the times (before 1867) when the Mikado's temporal power was usurped; & the title *tycoon* was substituted in diplomatic dealings for that of *shogun* (army leader), used at home, in order to represent him to foreigners as the real sovereign. The recent use of *tycoon* (business leader of wealth and power) is US colloq.

tyke, tike. The OED (& US) prefer *tyke* (COD allows either). Orig. a dog, cur; a low fellow; used of a child (*a cute little tyke*), US colloq.

tympanist. A drum player, pron. tĭm′.

TYPE, PROTOTYPE, ANTITYPE, ANTETYPE. *Prototype* & *antitype* both owe their existence to *type,* & have no meaning except with reference to it, but *type* has many meanings besides. That in which alone it has anything to do with *prototype* & *antitype* is symbol or emblem or pattern or model considered with regard to the person or object or fact or event in the sphere of reality that answers to its specifications; this answering reality, or thing symbolized &c., is called the *antitype, anti* (against) conveying the notion of match or answer or correspondence. *Type* & *antitype,* then, are a complementary pair, or correlatives & opposites. It is very different with *type* & *prototype;* far from being opposed to a *type,* a *pro-*

totype is a *type*, & serves as a synonym for it, though with limitations; it is preferred to *type*, first when stress is to be laid on the priority in time of a particular type over its *antitype*, such priority not being essential to the notion of *type* & *antitype;* secondly when *type*, which has other senses than that to which *antitype* is opposed, might be ambiguous; & thirdly when typification itself is of no great consequence, & the sense wanted is no more than 'the earliest form' of something. For those who feel a temptation to use the word *prototype* without being sure that they know the difference between the three words, it is well to remember that *antitype* is much more likely to be safe than *prototype*, but that real safety lies in abstaining from so tricky a set of words altogether.

The word *antetype* may be set aside as one that should hardly ever be used, first because its similarity in sound & opposition in sense to the established *antitype* is inconvenient, secondly as being liable to confusion with *prototype* also from their closeness in meaning, & thirdly because *forerunner* & *anticipation* are ready to take its place when it really does not mean *prototype*. Even with that ruled out, the relations between the other three are such as to make mistakes likely, but not pardonable.

There is much confusion & other misuse of these words. WRONG: *Foremost among them is the aged Wu Ting Fang, an Oriental* prototype *of the vicar of Bray* (should be *antitype*, or better *parallel*)./*The fees of the most successful barristers in France do not amount to more than a fraction of those earned by their* prototypes *in England* (should be *fellows* or *confreres* or *likes*)./*The type of mind which prompted that policy finds its modern* prototype *in Unionist Ulster* (should be *antitype* or *manifestation*). See also PROTOTYPE.

typo=typographical error (US), typogographer (Brit.). See CURTAILED WORDS.

typographic(al). Both forms are in use, with seemingly no difference.

tyrannic(al). *Tyrannic* is now not at home outside verse.

tyrannize. *This attempt to coerce &* tyrannize *us will produce results which the Government will have good reason to regret./They were 'the strong, rugged, God-fearing people' who were to be* tyrannized *& oppressed* by *a wicked Government.* Most readers of good modern writing will have the familiar slight shock incident to meeting a solecism & want to insert 'over.' But the OED's comment on the transitive use is merely 'now rare,' & it produces abundant examples from older writers; still, the present idiom is *to tyrannize over*, not to tyrannize, *one's subjects*.

tyrant. The original Greek sense of the word is so far alive still that readers must be prepared for it. Neither cruel nor despotic conduct was essential to the Greek notion of a tyrant, who was merely one who, or whose ancestors, had seized a sovereignty that was not his or theirs by hereditary right. Despotic or tyrannical use of the usurped position was natural & common, but incidental only.

tyre. Of a wheel &c., US *tire*.

tyro. Beginner, novice, so spelled in US (& in Brit. until late 18 c.); modern Brit. *tiro.*

Tzar, tzetze. Variants of TSAR, TSETSE.

Tzigane, -ny. Hungarian gypsy. The first spelling is better; pron. tsēgahn′. OED would prefer *tsigan* (if the word was not already established), pronounced tsĭgān′.

U

u. N.B. In this article the symbol *u* stands for the sound yōō or yŏŏ. The pronunciation of long *u* (as ū, or ōō) is a point that is discussed at length for the special case in which *l* precedes the *u;* ilyōōmĭnāt or ilōōmĭnāt? The traditional dictionaries give the first; the 'progressive' give the second. This book suggests that an affected yōō is worse than an untraditional but natural ōō, but advises that the orthodox pronunciation is yōō.

Most of us now, whatever the dictionaries say, never think of saying glū or blū, but content ourselves with glōō & blōō, however refined we like to be where the trials of articulation are less severe. The same question presents itself, but the answers are less doubtful, when the preceding letter is not *l.* (1) When it is the other liquid, *r,* attempts at ū are difficult; few people make them, & ōō (or ŏŏ) being generally accepted should be made universal; so rōōl (rule), krōōd (crude), intrōō′zhn (intrusion), kwer′ōōlus & gar′ōōlus (querulous, garrulous), grōō (grew), frōōt (fruit). (2) When no letter precedes, ū is invariable (unit, ubiquity, &c.) except in foreign words such as *uhlan, Ural, umlaut.* (3) After the sounds ch, j, sh, zh, attempts at ū are as ill advised as after *r;* so chōō, jōōn, jōōt, jōōs, shōōt, shōōr, for *chew, June, jute, juice, chute, sure.* (4) After *s* & *z* there is a tendency to convert the orthodox ū to ōō or ŏŏ, e.g. in *superior, Susan, supreme, suzerain, suicide, suet, suit, presume, Zulu;* this class is comparable to the *lu* words, but the decline of *u* is far less marked. (5) Outside the positions stated, ū rarely changes to ōō; dōōs (deuce), stōō′ard (steward), lōō′ard (leeward), are often heard, but these & others are generally regarded as carelessnesses. See PRONUNCIATION.

uglify sounds like a recent arrival, but it dates back, in good usage, to the 17th c.

ukase. Pron. ūkās′.

ulna. Pl. *-nae.*

ultima, 'last.' *Ultima Thule,* farthest-away region; fig. the highest point or degree attainable; see THULE.

ultimatum. Pl. *-tums, -ta.* Considering that *-tums* is about 200 years old (Swift is quoted in OED), it is strange that anglicization is still delayed, & that *-ta* is so often used; *-tums* is here recommended.

ultimo, ult. In the month preceding the present. If used, no reason not to abbreviate.

ultra-, prefix meaning *beyond;* joined to other words, in US, usually without hyphen (Webster gives *ultra-ambitious* but *ultraexclusive*); Brit., new and nonce combinations usually hyphened.

ultramontane. 'Beyond the Alps.' In modern use applied, chiefly by opponents, to the party of Italian predominance whose principle is the absolute supremacy of the Pope, & the denial of independence to national Churches.

ululate. Most recent dictionaries give ūlū-, &, unless there are reasons against it, the imitative effect got by repeating the same sound should not be sacrificed; ūlūl- suggests howling much more vividly than ŭlūl-.

-um. For general remarks on the plural of Latin nouns adopted in English, see LATIN PLURALS. Those in *-um* are numerous & demand special treatment. The Latin plural being *-a*, & the English *-ums*, three selections follow of nouns (1) that now always use *-ums*, either as having completed their naturalization (as it is to be hoped that the rest may do in time), or for special reasons (those followed by * are not Latin nouns but might be given the wrong plurals by mistake); (2) that show no signs at present of conversion, but always use *-a;* (3) that vacillate, sometimes with a differentiation of meaning, sometimes in harmony with the style of writing, & sometimes unaccountably. In deciding between the two forms for words in the third list, it should be borne in mind that, while anglicization is to be desired, violent attempts to hurry the process actually retard it by provoking ridicule.

1. Plural in *-ums* only: *albums; asylums; delphiniums; Elysiums; factotums**; *forums; lyceums; nostrums; pendulums; petroleums; premiums; quantums**; *quorums**; *vellums**.

2. Plurals in *-a* only or usually: *agenda; bacteria* (& many scientific terms); *corrigenda; desiderata; errata; scholia* (& other such learned words); *strata.*

3. Words with either plural; some notes are inserted as suggestions only: *aquarium* (usu. *-ms*); *compendium; curriculum* (usu. *-a*); *emporium; encomium* (usu. *-ms*); *interregnum* (usu. *-ms*); *medium* (*-ms* in spiritualism); *memorandum* (usu. *-a*); *millennium* (usu. *-ms*); *rostrum* (usu. *-a*); *spectrum* (usu. *-a*); *trapezium* (usu. *-a*); *ultimatum* (*-ms* better).

umbrage in its orig. literal sense, 'shadow,' is now archaic or poetic. Its transf. fig. use, 'offense,' 'annoyance,' is current chiefly in the phrases *to take* or *give umbrage.*

umlaut. Pron. o͞om′lowt. Loosely, the two dots used in Ger. words to indicate a vowel that has been changed because of assimilation of a vowel in the following syllable; e.g. *röntgen* may be so written with an umlaut or may be written *roentgen.*

un-, prefix. 1. Danger of ellipsis after *un-*. *Untouched* means *not touched,* but with the difference that it is one word & not two, a difference that in some circumstances is important. In *I was not touched & you were* the word *touched* is understood to be repeated, & not to carry the *not* with it; but *I was untouched & you were* cannot be substituted with the same effect; if it means anything it means that both were untouched, the *un-* having to be understood as well as the *touched.* Needless as such a statement may sound in a simple case like that above, where there is nothing to distract attention from the wording, blunders essentially similar are frequent. A couple of examples follow & the state of mind that produces them is illustrated in the articles NEGATIVE & AFFIRMATIVE CLAUSES 5, 6, & 7. WRONG: *Dr. Rashdall's scholarship is* unquestioned; *most of his writings & opinions on ecclesiastical matters* are. What is meant is that most of them are questioned, not unquestioned./*When I sat in the square of Oudenarde, opposite the old Hôtel de Ville, which happily has come through the war* untouched *by vandal hands, methought, if it* had been, *who in Belgium could have built the like of it?* That is, had been touched, not untouched; correct *untouched* into *without being touched.*

2. *Un-, in-.* When positive adjectives, including participles, are to be converted into negative, it is usually done by prefixing one of these. Which of the two it should be is a question that most people can answer without difficulty for most words, & the laying down of exhaustive rules would be both tedious & useless; some of the tendencies have been shown in the article IN- & UN-. One or two quotations are here given to prove that the wrong decision is sometimes made. WRONG: *The Government let loose their 'Black & Tans' to deal out summary &* indiscriminating *punishment./ Olrig, of whose* incompleted *labors we spoke lately in these columns./ It was inevitable that many men of* instable *nervous organization should be included.*/Read *undiscriminating, uncompleted,* & *unstable.* All three lapses result from the commonest cause of error, the existence of a familiar allied word beginning rightly with the prefix that, in the word used, is wrong—here *indiscriminate, incomplete,* & *instability.* One other point is perhaps worth stressing. It is a general truth that, while it is legitimate to prefix *un-*, but not *in-*, to any adjective of whatever form, those negative adjectives in *in-* that exist are normally preferred to the corresponding *un-* forms; but when an *in-* (or *il-* or *im-* or *ir-*) adjective has developed a sense that is something more than the negation of the positive adjective, an *un-* form is often used to discharge that function without risk of ambiguity; *immoral* having come to mean offending against morality or wicked, *unmoral* is called in to mean not moral or outside the sphere of morality; others are *ir* & *un -religious; in* & *un -human; in* & *un -artistic; in* & *un -artificial; im* & *un -material.*

unable is now usually restricted to the sense *not able* (to do &c. something at a given time): *I am* unable *to accept your offer now, much as I should like to. Incapable* suggests lack of ability, inefficiency: *He is* incapable *of telling the truth in any circumstances.* There are many contexts in which either word is possible, but the difference in connotation is worth remembering.

unaccountable. Now usually inexplicable, mysterious. UNIDIOMATIC: *Occurrences that are for the time being, & to the* *spiritualist,* unaccountable *by natural causes;* the writer means 'not to be accounted for.'

unanimous. Of one mind or opinion; an absolute that should not be compared; e.g. (WRONG) *A* more unanimous *endorsement cannot be imagined.*

unapt, inapt, inept. *Inept* has developed a special sense: out of place, absurd, silly; *an inept remark.* We have also the normal negative of *apt, unapt: I am a soldier and* unapt *to weep;* & this, not the hybrid *inapt,* is recommended when *inept* is not meant; in US *inapt* is sometimes used for backward, without aptitude or capacity; *he is hopelessly* inapt; but better, *inept.*

unartistic, in-. The second is the usual word; but since it has acquired a sort of positive sense, 'outraging the canons of art' &c., the other has been introduced for contexts in which such condemnation is not desired; *the unartistic* are those who are not concerned with art.

unashamedly. Five syllables if used.

UNATTACHED PARTICIPLES & ADJECTIVES (or wrongly attached). A firm sent in its bill with the following letter: *Dear Sir, We beg to enclose herewith statement of your account for goods supplied, &* being desirous *of clearing our books to end May* will you *kindly favor us with check in settlement per return, & much oblige.* The reply ran: *Sirs, You have been misinformed. I have no wish to clear your books.* It may be hoped that the desire on which they based their demand was ultimately (though not *per return*) satisfied, but they had certainly imputed it to the wrong person by attaching *being desirous* not to the noun it belonged to (*we*), but to another (*you*). The duty of so arranging one's sentences that they will stand grammatical analysis is now generally recognized & it is not a sufficient defense for looseness of this kind to produce parallels, as can very easily be done, even from great writers of past generations; on this see ILLOGICALITIES. On the other hand it is to be remembered that there is a continual change going on by which certain participles or adjectives acquire the character of prepositions or adverbs, no longer needing the prop of a noun to cling to; we can say *Considering the circumstances* you *were justified,* or *Roughly speaking* they *are identical,* & need not correct into *I acquit you* & *I should call them identical* in order to regularize the participles. The difficulty is to know when this development is complete. May I write *Referring to your letter,* you *do not state . . . ,* or must it be *I find you do not state . . .* ? i.e. is *referring* still undeveloped? In all such cases, it is best to put off recognition.

The conscious or unconscious assumption that a participle or adjective has acquired the powers of preposition or adverb when it has in fact not done so perhaps accounts for most of the unattached & wrongly attached; but there are many for which no such excuse is possible. Before proceeding to them, let us make a few sentences containing undoubtedly converted participles, sentences in which the seeming participle is not felt to need a noun. RIGHT: Talking *of test matches,* who *won the last?;* Coming *to details,* the spoiled ballots *were* 17; Granting *his honesty,* he *may be mistaken;* Failing *you,* there *is no chance left;* Twelve *were saved, not* counting *the dog;* Allowing *for exceptions,* the rule *may stand.* It is only fanatical purists who will condemn such sentences; & a clear acknowledgment of their legitimacy should strengthen rather than weaken the necessary protest against the slovenly uses now to be illustrated. After each extract will be given first the noun, whether present or not, to which the participle or adjective ought to be attached, & secondly the noun, if any, to which careless grammar has in fact attached it. WRONG: *Experiments have shown that, while* affording *protection against shrapnel,* the direct bullet *at moderate range would carry fragments of the* plate *into the body* (plate; bullet)./ Based *on your figures of membership,* you *suggest that the Middle Classes Union has failed* (suggestion; you)./I *would also suggest that, while* admitting *the modernity,* the proofs *offered by him as to the recent date of the loss of aspiration are not very convincing* (I; proofs).

unauspicious. Use *in-*.

unavowedly. Five syllables if used.

unaware is an adj. & is now used as an adv. (=*unawares*) only poetically. RIGHT: *He was* unaware *of the approaching storm; he came upon them* unawares.

unbeknown(st). Both forms are now out of use except in dialect or uneducated speech or in imitations of these. The *-st* form is more exclusively adverbial; cf. *unawares* as the adv. of *unaware.*

unbias(s)ed. The spelling varies; *unbiased* is recommended.

uncial. (Palaeog.): 'inch.' The style of writing, consisting of large letters, some of them rounded from the angular capital forms, but not run together, found in early Greek & Latin MSS. The later & smaller writing in MSS., in which the letters are further rounded, slanted, & run together, is called *cursive.* The terms *majuscule* & *minuscule* are sometimes used as synonyms of *uncial* & *cursive,* but strictly *majuscule* includes both capital & uncial writing, whereas *minuscule* & *cursive,* applied to MSS., are coextensive.

Uncle Sam. See SOBRIQUETS.

unconcernedly, unconstrainedly. Five syllables if used.

unconscionable. Since *conscionable* (=just; according to good conscience) is now archaic, the negative becomes increasingly rare in speech and is often self-conscious in writing when used by those to whom it is unfamiliar.

uncontrollable. Better than *in-*.

undependable. So spelled.

under, prep. The opp. of *over* (*below,* opp. of *above*). See BELOW for distinctions; & UNDERNEATH. For justification of *under the circumstances* (as opposed to *in*) see CIRCUMSTANCE. A boat is *under way,* NOT *weigh.*

underneath (prep.), compared with BELOW & *under,* is not, like BENEATH, a word that tends to become archaic. On the contrary, it is still in full colloq. as well as literary use. Its range is much narrower than that of *under*, being almost confined to the physical relation of material things (cf. 'underneath the bed' with 'under the stimulus of competition'), but within that range it is often preferred as expressing more emphatically the notion of being covered over, & carrying a step further the difference pointed out between BELOW and *under*.

undigested, undisciplined, undiscriminating. All better than the *in-* forms.

undisposed=not disposed of (*undisposed-of lands*); indisposed=rendered unfit; made averse (*to, toward*); now, usually in the p.p., slightly ill (often a GENTEELISM).

undistinguishable. *In-* is better.

undistributed middle. (Log.) A fallacy. The undistributed middle is the logical name for a middle term that is not made universal; in the syllogism *All men are mortal/All Germans are men/Therefore all Germans are mortal* the middle term is made universal by the word *all*, or 'distributed.' Such distribution is necessary to the validity of the conclusion, & *the fallacy of the undistributed middle* consists in allowing a middle term that is not universalized to pass as universally true. An example is: *Colds are wet-feet products./My trouble is a cold./Therefore my trouble is a wet-feet product*—which would be sound if *colds* meant *all colds*, but not if it merely means *some colds*.

undue, unduly. *There is no need for* undue alarm. Well, no; that seems likely. See TRUISMS; in the making of truisms *undue* is at present the favorite ingredient.

uneconomic(al). It is *uneconomic* to buy more cows when the market in butter has fallen. It is *uneconomical* to buy a cow when you don't need it, just because it has a fine coat. For the distinction see ECONOMIC(AL).

unedited. Better than the *in-* form, which is now restricted to the literary use 'unpublished.'

unequal. Constr. *to* (+noun or gerund); *unequal* to *the task*, to undertaking *so large a task*.

UNEQUAL YOKEFELLOWS. The phrase is here used in a comprehensive sense enabling a number of faults, most of them treated at length in other articles, to be exhibited side by side as varieties of one species. They are all such as not to obstruct seriously the understanding of the passage in which they occur but to inflict a passing discomfort on fastidious readers. To a writer who is not fastidious it is an irksome task to keep in mind the readers who are, & he inclines to treat symmetry as troublesome or even obtrusive formalism. To shape one's sentences aright as one puts them down, instinctively avoiding lopsidedness & checking all details of the framework, is not the final crown of an accomplished writer, but part of the rudiments. If one has neglected to acquire that habit in early days, one has no right to grumble at the choice that later confronts one between slovenliness & revision.

Conspicuous among the slights commonly inflicted upon the minor symmetries are those illustrated below.

The nine employees whose record of service ranged between

61 down to 50 *years* (61 and 50); see BETWEEN.

The enemy despairs both *of victory on land* or *of such success as will give him a compromise peace* (of victory . . . and such success); see BOTH.

Diderot presented a bouquet which was neither *well* or *ill received* (well nor ill); see NEITHER 6.

Neither *John* nor *Richard* were *English* (was English); see NEITHER 4.

Scarcely *was the drain finished* than *several sickened with diphtheria* (before several sickened); see SCARCELY.

The opportunities which each are *capable of turning to account* (is capable); see EACH.

The Government has never & does not now *close the door to overtures* (has never closed); see ELLIPSIS.

If the appeal be made & results *in* . . . (appeal is made *or* be made & result in); see SUBJUNCTIVES (arrivals).

Even were this tract *of country level plain & the* roads lent *themselves to the manœuvre* . . . (even if this track were); see INVERSION.

Does he *dislike its methods,* & will only mention . . .? (will he); see PARALLEL SENTENCE DANGERS.

One or two other types may be added without cross-reference: Either *he did not know* or‸was *lying* (read *He either*); *The old one was* as good‸*if not better than this* (read *as good as this if not better*); *One of the worst* kings *that* has *ever reigned* (read *have*); *It is* all & more than *I expected* (read *all I expected, & more*); *He was* young, rich,‸handsome, & enjoyed *life* (read *& handsome*).

unequaled. US usually so spelled; Brit. *-lled.*

unescapable, unessential. Better than *in-*.

Unesco. United Nations Educational, Scientific & Cultural Organization. (So spelled in its bulletins but in *NY Times,* UNESCO.)

unexceptionable, -al. *An* unexceptionable *authority; an* unexceptional *rule.* See EXCEPTIONABLE.

unfrequented, NOT *in-*.

unhuman. *Means so* unhuman, *so divine; curious and* unhuman *objects.* But *An* inhuman *tyrant;* inhuman *cruelty.*

UNIDIOMATIC -LY. As the lapses from idiom here to be illustrated probably owe their origin to the modern wider extension of grammatical knowledge, it may be prudent to start by conciliating the sticklers for grammar & admitting that an *-ly* is sometimes missing where it is wanted. So (WRONG): *If the Government is going to nationalize the coal, we believe it would do* wise *to leave its hands free to* . . . (more wisely)./*Surely no peace-loving man or woman will deny that it would be advisable to prevent strikes & lock-outs* consistent *with the principles of liberty as set forth by John Stuart Mill.*

But if grammar is inexorable against *consistent, wise,* &c., it would in the following sentences allow *contrary* & *irrespective* without a frown, while idiom for its part would welcome them: UNIDIOMATIC: *The provision is quite inadequate & very grudgingly granted, & often,* contrarily *to the spirit of the Act, totally denied./Loyal obedience is due to the 'powers that be,' as such,* irrespectively *of their historical origin.* *Contrary* & *irrespective* are among the adjectives that have, with others mentioned in UNATTACHED &c. & in QUASI-ADVERBS, developed adverbial force; to ignore that development is bad literary judgment, but, among the mistakes made with *-ly*, one of the least.

A degree worse is the use of an *-ly* adverb where idiom requires not an adverb at all, but a predicative adjective. (See LARGE-(LY) for the phrases *bulk* & *loom large.*) UNIDIOMATIC: *But over the rival claims controversy waxed* vigorously./*In neither direction can we fix our hopes very* highly./*This country was brought much more* closely *to disaster at sea than ever the Allies were on land.* Substitute *vigorous, high,* & *much closer.*

Yet a little worse is the officious bringing up to date of such time-honored phrases as *mighty kind* & *sure enough.* WRONG: *Still, it is* mightily kind *of the 'Morning Post' to be so anxious to shield the Labour party from the wrath to come./We begin to remember the story of the detective who died murmuring to himself 'More clues!' & toward the end of the book,* surely enough, *more clues there are.*

But much more to be deprecated than all the particular departures from idiom already mentioned is the growing notion that every monosyllabic adjective, if an adverb is to be made of it, must have an *-ly* clapped on to it to proclaim the fact. Of very many that is not true; see MOST, RIGHT, & STRAIGHT. Two such words may here be taken for special treatment, *much(ly)* as the least, & *hard(ly)* as the most, important of all. Probably most of us would guess that *muchly* was a modern facetious formation, perhaps meant to burlesque the ultra-grammatical & at any rate always used jocosely. We should be wrong; it is 300 years old, its earliest use was serious. Nevertheless, as it seems to have lain dormant for over 200 years, our guess is not so far out, & its revival in the 19th c. illustrates the belief that adverbs must end in *-ly.* *Muchly* does not often make its way into print, & has been worth attention only in contrast with *hardly.* That, as will appear, is substituted in print for the idiomatic *hard* neither seldom nor with any burlesque intention, but seemingly in ignorance. Ignorance that *hard* can be an adverb seems incredible when one thinks of *It froze hard, Hit him hard, Work hard, Try hard,* & so forth; the ignorance must be of idiom rather than of grammar. Neglect of idiom is, in this case, aggravated by the danger that *hardly,* written as meaning *hard,* may be read as meaning *scarcely;* for some proofs that that danger is real, see the article HARDLY. The examples that here follow are free from such ambiguity, but in each of them idiom demands expulsion of the *-ly.* WRONG: *Another sign of how* hardly *the great families are pressed in these times./The invasion of Henley by the fashionable world bears very* hardly *on those who go only for the sport./But what about the agriculturist, who is so* hardly *hit by our present system?/If there is a man* more hardly hit *by ex-*

isting conditions than the average holder of a season ticket he is hard to find (harder hit).

Other such adverbs are *wide, late, high,* each spoiled in the appended extracts by an unidiomatic *-ly.* WRONG: *And then he'd know that betting & insurance were* widely *apart./Several drawings in the new volume are dated as* lately *as August & September./He played* highly, *but he has lost his stake. Middling, soft,* & *sharp,* are specimens of the many others that might be named.

unilateral, multilateral, &c. Often used as FORMAL WORDS for *one-sided, many-sided,* &c. But right in *unilateral treaty* &c.

uninformed in print often turns up as *uniformed (the uniformed public).*

uninterested. The usual sense now is apathetic, indifferent; DISINTERESTED=unbaised, impartial. Uninterested *in the play or in any of its characters.* A disinterested *third party to be chosen by both sides.*

unique. *Unique* is applicable only to what is in some respect the sole existing specimen, the precise like of which may be sought in vain. That gives a clean line of division between it & the many adjs. for which the illiterate tend to substitute it—*remarkable, exceptional, rare, marvelous,* & the like. In the qualities represented by those epithets there are degrees; but *uniqueness* is a matter of yes or no only; no unique thing is *more* or *less unique* than another unique thing, as it may be *rare* or *less rare.* The adverbs that *unique* can tolerate are e.g. *quite, almost, nearly, really, surely, perhaps, absolutely,* or *in some respects;* & it is nonsense to call anything *more, most, very, somewhat, rather,* or *comparatively unique.* Such nonsense, however, is often written. WRONG: *This is a* rather unique *distinction./I have just come across the production of a boy aged seven, which is, in my experience,* somewhat unique./A very unique *child, thought I.*

But, secondly, there is another set of synonyms—*sole, single, peculiar to,* &c.—from which *unique* is divided not by a clear difference of meaning, but by an idiomatic limitation of the contexts to which it is suited. It will be admitted that we improve the two following sentences if we change *unique* in the first into *sole,* & in the second into *peculiar: In the always delicate & difficult domain of diplomatic relations the Foreign Minister must be the* unique *medium of communication with foreign Powers./He relates Christianity to other religions, & notes what is* unique *to the former & what is common to all of them.* The emendations are easy to make or accept; to explain the need of them is more difficult; but the reason why *unique* is unsuitable is perhaps that it belongs to the class of epithets discussed in POSITIVE WORDS.

United Kingdom. (United Kingdom of Great Britain and Northern Ireland.) Abbr. U.K.

United Nations. Abbr. U.N. (periods often omitted).

United States. Abbr. U.S. (periods; their omission in this book is for economy of space & not recommended). In usual contexts *these United States* is not only archaic (or pompous) but also apt to lead to a wrong verb or pronoun. *These United States* must be plural; *the United States* is usually singular.

unity. The unities, or dramatic unities, are the unity of time, the unity of place, & the unity of action. The first has been observed if all that happens in a play can be conceived as sufficiently continuous to fill only something like the same time (stretched by generous reckoning to a day) as the performance. The second is observed when changes of scene, if any, are slight enough to spare an audience the sensation of being transported from one place to another. The third is observed when nothing is introduced that has no bearing upon the central action of the play. The last only is universally recognized as among the essentials of good modern drama.

unlearned, -nt. In US, *-ed.* But see LEARN.

unless & until. See PLEONASM 2 for other such duplications; one of the conjunctions is always superfluous, as in the still commoner IF & WHEN, the discussion in which article may serve for this pair also; but a few quotations will allow the reader to judge whether 'unless &' might not in each be left out with advantage: Unless & until *it is made possible for a builder or householder to obtain an economic rent,* so long *will building be at a standstill./Speaking for himself he said that* unless & until *the Second Chamber was reformed . . . he treated every measure that proceeded from the House of Commons as at present constituted as coming from a tainted source./Sir Albert Stanley assured some alarmed manufacturers that a certain embargo which he had temporarily removed should be speedily reimposed & not removed again* unless & until *they had been consulted.*

unlike, in its less simple uses, i.e. when we get beyond 'unlike things,' 'the two cases are unlike,' & 'this is unlike that,' to 'unlike you, I feel the cold,' & further developments, is subject to the complications set out in LIKE, though occasions for it are much fewer. In addition to what is there said, two special warnings may be given. WRONG: *I counted eighty-nine rows of men standing,* & unlike *in London, only occasionally could women be distinguished. Unlike* is there treated as though it had developed the adverbial power described in the article UNATTACHED &c., as acquired by *owing* (*to*) but not by *due* (*to*); it has not, & something adverbial (*in contrast with London ways*?) must be substituted./*M. Berger, however, does not appear to have*—unlike his Russian masters—*the gift of presenting female characters.* As with many negatives, the placing of *unlike* is important; standing where it does, it must be changed to *like; unlike* would be right if the phrase were shifted to before 'does not appear.'

unmaterial, if chosen instead of the ordinary *im-,* confines the meaning to 'not consisting of matter' (e.g. *the scholar who lives an inward* unmaterial *life*), & excludes the other common meaning of *immaterial,* viz. 'that does not matter,' 'not important or essential.'

unmentionables. See WORN-OUT HUMOR.

unmoral. See UN-, & AMORAL.

unnavigable. Better so, NOT

in-. See IN- AND UN-.

unparalleled. NOT *-lled.*

unpractical. Better so, NOT *in-*.

unreligious, chosen instead of the usual *ir-*, excludes the latter's implications of sin &c., & means outside the sphere of religion.

unsanitary, in-. *In-* is the established form; but it would not be used, as *un-* might, of a place &c. that neither had nor needed provisions for sanitation: *a primitive &* unsanitary *but entirely healthy life* or *village; insanitary* implies danger.

unsolvable differs from *insoluble* in having its reference limited to the sense of the English verb *solve,* & not covering, as *insoluble* does, various senses (*dissolve* as well as *solve*) of the Latin verb *solvere;* it is therefore sometimes useful in avoiding ambiguity.

unstable. Better than *in-*.

unthinkable is now a sort of expletive. When we say *damn,* it relieves us because it is a strong word & yet means nothing; we do not intend the person or thing or event that we damn to be burned in hell fire; far from it; but the faint aroma of brimstone that hangs forever about the word is savory in wrathful nostrils. So it is with *unthinkable,* 'that cannot be thought.' That a thing at once exists & does not exist, & 'the things which God hath prepared for them that love him,' are unthinkable, i.e. the constitution of the human mind bars us from conceiving or apprehending them; but we do not mean all that with our VOGUE WORD *unthinkable* at present. Anything is now *unthinkable,* from what reason declares impossible or what imagination is helpless to conceive, down to what seems against the odds (as that a rival college should win the boat race), or what is slightly distasteful to the speaker (as that the political party we dislike should ever be elected). The word is so attractive because the uncompromising intensity of its proper sense in metaphysics & philosophy lingers around it, like the brimstone of *damn,* even when it is transferred to ordinary regions; & this recommends it to all who like to combine the most forcible sound with the haziest meaning. The haziness is easily accounted for; the *un-* & *-able* meaning 'that cannot be -ed' are regarded as affixed to (1) *think* in the philosophic sense 'frame a conception of,' (2) *think* in the everyday sense 'believe' or 'be of opinion,' (3) *think* of in the sense 'consider advisable' or 'contemplate doing,' (4) *think likely.* To attach to so protean a verb notion the affixes that make it mean 'that cannot be which-you-please-of-four-different-things-ed' does result & could not but result in haziness. A few quotations, beginning with the philosophic use, but chiefly of the bad trivial kinds, are added, not because anyone cannot find such things for himself, but because their variety may have a chance of disgusting those who do not reckon shiftiness a virtue in the words they use. RIGHT: *'Ultimate' scientific ideas may be* unthinkable *without prejudice to the 'thinkableness' of 'proximate' scientific ideas.*/POSSIBLE: *It is* unthinkable *that we should continue a policy under which a given locality may be allowed to commit a crime against a friendly nation.* In this, with a *that* clause as the unthinkable thing, the defense is possible that *think* has its ordinary meaning, the one numbered (2) above, & that *unthinkable* cannot be deprived of its right to embody this; the answer is that the defense is, for the particular construction, sound, but that abstention would nevertheless be better./NOT JUSTIFIED: *A tariff, having regard to its effects upon the textile industries of the country, is* unthinkable. (Impracticable?)/ *With all respect to the advocates of a third amendment, such a course appears to us to be simply* unthinkable. (A course that has advocates unthinkable!)/*It is* unthinkable *that hundreds upon hundreds of people should be getting their freedom on the ground of adultery, while thousands of innocent sufferers under desertion, drink, cruelty, & insanity, are left outside any relief.* He is plainly stating what he takes to be the existing position; how can that be unthinkable? read *flagrant injustice.*

until. 1. *Until* has very little of the archaic effect as compared with *till* that distinguishes *unto* from *to,* & substitution of it for *till* would seldom be noticeable, except in any such stereotyped phrase as *true till death.* Nevertheless, *till* is now the usual form, & *until* gives a certain leisurely or deliberate or pompous air; but when the clause or phrase precedes the main sentence, *until* is perhaps actually the commoner (*until his accession he had been unpopular*).

2. Neither *until* nor *till* is idiomatic in sentences of a certain type, which require *when* or *before.* WRONG: *He was seated at one end of a bench, & had not been there long* until *a sparrow alighted at the other end.* The reason is that *till* & *until,* strictly defined, mean (if there is no negative) 'throughout the interval between the starting point (i.e. here, his sitting down) & the goal' (here, the sparrow's arrival); 'at any point' in that interval is meaningless. The OED calls the misuse 'dial, & U.S.'

3. For *unless & until,* see UNLESS.

untoward. Pron. ŭntō′ard.

up. 1. The phrase *up to date* is three words unhyphened, except when it is used as an attributive adj.; then, it is hyphened: *An* up-to-date *bungalow;* but *You are not* up to date, *Bring the ledger* up to date.

2. *Up against* (faced or confronted with), & *up to* (incumbent upon), are good examples of the rapidity with which in modern English new slang phrases make their way into literary respectability.

3. *Up* as an intensive is accepted idiom (*burn up the trash, clean up the room, eat up your food*). It is unnecessary but often used with other verbs (*settle up the account, finish up your work,* &c.).

upgrade, v. *When student nurses show initiative, unusual responsiveness, or any other signs of leadership ability, they are immediately* upgraded. This comparatively new verb (US?) is useful in civil service, business, & personnel management, &c. What advantage it has over *advance* in other contexts it is hard to see.

upon, on. For a list of other such pairs, see TILL. The difference is much the same as between UNTIL & *till;* but euphony plays a considerable part in the choice, *upon* being usually rejected when its position would cause it to be pronounced as two unaccented syllables instead of with a clear -ŏ-; compare *upon my word* with *on no account*, & *that depends on who it was* with *depend upon it;* at the end of a sentence, consequently, *upon* is often preferred: *There is very little to go upon.*

upper. For upper case (capital letters), see LOWER 1.

us. 1. Case. WRONG: *They are as competent* as us *as regards manufacture./The Germans are involved* like ourselves *in a blind struggle of forces, & no more* than us *to be blamed or praised./Let us be content—*we Liberals, *at any rate—to go on in the possession of our old principles.* In the first two, after *as* & *than,* there can be no objection to letting grammar have its rights with the correct *we;* in the last, if it is obtrusively formal to keep the required case in mind for the duration of a dash & repeat it on the other side, *Let us Liberals at any rate be content* would not have been unbearably ordinary.

2. *Our,* or *his* &c., after *of us.* RIGHT: *Types, it must be admitted, under which each* of us *can classify a good many* of his *acquaintances.* That is the logical arrangement, which, as the quotation shows, is free from any taint of over-precision; but much more commonly *our acquaintances* is substituted owing to the attraction *of us.*

-us. The plural of nouns in *-us* are troublesome. (1) Most are from Latin second-declension words, whose Latin plural is *-i* (pron. ī); but when *-i* should be used, & when the English plural *-uses* is better, has to be decided for each separately; see LATIN PLURALS, -I, & the individual words. (2) Many are from Latin fourth-declension words, whose Latin plural is *-us* (pron. ūs); but the English plural *-uses* is almost always preferred, as *prospectuses; hiatus* (*ūs*) is occasionally seen as a plural but *hiatuses* is better; words of this class, which must never have plural in *-i,* are *afflatus, apparatus, conspectus, impetus, nexus, plexus, status.* (3) Some are from Latin third-declension neuters, whose plurals are of various forms in *-a;* so *corpus, genus, opus,* make *corpora, genera, opera,* which are almost always preferred in English to *-uses.* (4) *Callus, octopus, polypus,* & *virus,* nouns variously abnormal in Latin, can all have plural *-uses.* (5) Some English nouns in *-us* are in Latin not nouns but verbs &c.; so *ignoramus, mandamus, mittimus, omnibus;* for these the only possible plural is the English *-uses.*

use, n. The forms *What is the use of complaining?* & *There is no use in complaining* are current & uncriticized. The forms *It is no use complaining* (or *to complain*) & *Complaining* (or *To complain*) *is no use* are still more current, but much criticized, & the critics would have us correct them by inserting *of* (*is* of *no use*). General adoption of their *of* is at this time of day past praying for; we should all take refuge instead in *useless,* which would do well enough if we could remember to say it. Most of us would like to be allowed our *It is no use,* if it is but on the footing of a STURDY INDEFENSIBLE; we should welcome the rites of the church, but if they are withheld, we mean, like Touchstone, to live in bawdry. In so full-dress a sentence as the following, however, the writer might have been wise to defer to strict etiquette: *If the Government yields to these counsels, its voluntary recruiting campaign will be*^*no more use than its threat of conscription.*

user. The words meaning (1) person who uses, & (2) right or act of using, as a legal term, are not one, but two of distinct formation.

usual. For *as per usual,* see WORN-OUT HUMOR.

utilitarian. One who believes in the doctrine that the useful is good (e.g. the greatest happiness to the greatest number). See HEDONIST.

utilize, utilization. FORMAL WORDS if *use* will do the job.

utmost, uttermost. In most contexts *utmost* is better, *uttermost* being now obsolescent or literary.

V

V. *V-shaped, V-E Day, V-J Day* so written. (But *D day, D day*+6, &c.)

vaccinate makes *-nable,* & *-tor.*

vacillate. So spelled.

vacuity, -uousness. The first is the usual word; the second may reasonably be chosen when a noun is wanted for *vacuous* as applied to the face, eyes, expression, &c.

vacuum. Pl. now usually *-ms; -ua* esp. in philosophic & scientific writing.

vagary. Caprice; whimsical or extravagant notion. Pron. vagār'ĭ.

vainness. So spelled. Sometimes preferred to *vanity* when the notion of conceit is to be excluded (e.g. *The vainness of the attempt*).

valance (pron. vă-) is the preferred spelling of the drapery; *valence* (pron. vā-), less often *valency,* in chemistry.

valet. Pron. both n. & v. văl'ĭt (vălā', formerly preferred in US, is now listed only as a var. in most dictionaries); the verb makes *-eted, eting.*

valiant. Brave, courageous, heroic. See FORMAL WORDS.

valise. Except in military use as the official term for a soldier's kitbag, the word is now archaic in England, but survives in US.

Valkyrie. The prevailing spelling in modern English; pl. *-s.* Pron. văl'kĭrĭ, vălkĭr'ĭ, vălkī'rĭ. (OED prefers the first, US dictionaries the second; the third is often heard & listed as a var.) The opera is *Die Walküre.*

valo(u)r. US usually *-or,* Brit. *-our,* but both *valorous.*

value, n. (1) WRONG: *What* value *will our Second Chamber be to us if it is not to exercise such control?* Read *Of what value.* An interesting specimen of ANALOGY. *What good will it be?* is unexceptionable; *What use will it be?* is not, but a plea has been put in for it in USE, n.; *What value will it be?* is ruled out, because no instinct tells us, as about *Of what use,* that *Of what value* is a piece of pedantry. *Is no good* is both grammatical & idiomatic; *is no use* is idiomatic but not grammatical; & *is no value* is neither. (2) *Value* has become a VOGUE WORD in pedagogy. *The* values *a child receives from co-operative play, owning a pet, crossing* *the street alone; transfer* values, *social* values, &c.

vamoose. US slang. If used, so spelled and pron. -mōōs′. That *vamose* is closer to the Spanish (*vamos,* let us go) is not important.

Van Dyck, Vandyke, vandyke. The painter's name, originally *Van Dyck,* was anglicized into (Sir Anthony) *Vandyke;* the derived noun & verb is *vandyke;* the painter or a picture of his may properly be called either *Van Dyck* or preferably *Vandyke.*

vanity. The Catechism phrase is *The pomps & vanity of this wicked world* (NOT *vanities*); see MISQUOTATION.

vantage is now obs. except in *point of vantage, coign of vantage, vantage point,* &c. (and in tennis=*advantage*).

vapid. Pron. vă-. Of its nouns, *vapidness* is usually better than *vapidity,* except when the sense is a vapid remark; then *-ity* prevails, & still more the plural *-ities.*

vapo(u)r & its belongings. US *-or, -orish, -orless, -ory;* Brit. *-our, -ourish, -ourless, -oury;* both *vaporific, vaporize* (*-zation, -zer*), *vaporous* (*-osity*).

variability, -bleness. Both are in constant use, without any clear difference of sense or application.

variance. Constr.: *At variance* among *ourselves,* with *the authorities* (or *each other*), *some variance* between *their systems.*

variant, n., as compared with *variation* & *variety,* is the least ambiguous name for a thing that varies or differs from others of its kind; for it is concrete only, while the others are much more often abstract; *variation* is seldom concrete except in the musical sense, & *variety* seldom except as the classifying name for a plant, animal, mineral, &c., that diverges from the characteristics of its species. It is worth while to help on the differentiation by preferring *variant* in all suitable contexts.

variation. For fear of using the same word twice, see ELEGANT VARIATION.

variorum, n., pl. *-ums.* (*The Variorum Shakespeare*='*cum notis variorum*' &c., i.e. with the notes of several editors–not, as sometimes thought, with variant readings.)

various as a pronoun. WRONG: *The flowers were forwarded to* various *of the local hospitals.* Analogy has lately been playing tricks with the word & persuading many people that they can turn it at will, as *several, few, many, divers, certain, some,* & other words are turned, from adj. into pronoun. Most dictionaries have no hint of such a use (COD says 'vulg., abs. or quasi pron. . . . *among the letters are* various *anent motor-driving* . . .') but the following quotations will show that it cannot safely be passed by without a warning. To write *various of them* &c. is no better than to write *different of them,* or *numerous* or *innumerable of them.* WRONG: *Mr. William Watson is only the latest of many poets–* various *of them Poets Laureate –who have* . . . (some of them)./*A like series of conflagrations in* various *of our towns & villages* (several of our towns &c.). *In* various *of the territories under the control of the Colonial Powers the minimum has been exceeded.* Omission of *of the,* without the trouble of finding a substitute for *various,* suffices.

varlet. Now, outside the historical novel, PEDANTIC HUMOR.

varmint, besides its reputed use as a rustic variant of *vermin* in the sense of rascal &c., is an established SOBRIQUET for the fox that is being hunted.

varsity. Colloq. shortening of *university,* but only in expressions such as *The varsity crew, varsity eleven,* &c.

vase. For most Americans the natural pronunciation is vās. This is not a 'US illiteracy'; it was the earlier pronunciation in England. Swift made it rhyme with *face,* Byron with *place.* For an American to say vāz or vahz is right if natural; vawz stigmatizes the speaker, US or Brit., as ignorant or affected.

vastly. In contexts of measure or comparison, where it means 'by much,' 'by a great deal,' as *is vastly improved, a vastly larger audience, vastly* is still in regular use. Where the notion of measure is wanting, & it means no more than *much* or *to a great degree,* as in *I should* vastly *like to know, is* vastly *popular,* it is an affectation; see WARDOUR STREET.

vaudeville. Pron. vô′devĭl or vōd′vĭl.

-VE(D), -VES, &c., from words in *-f* & *-fe.* Corresponding to the change of sound that takes place in the plural &c. of words ending in *-th,* like *truth,* there is one both of sound & of spelling in many words ending in *-f* or *-fe,* which become *-ves, -ved, -vish,* &c. As the change is far from regular, & sometimes in doubt, the chief words are given in their dictionary places. When alternatives are given, the first, if either, is better.

beef, pl. *beeves* oxen, *beefs* kinds of beef; *beefy.*
belief, v. *believe.*
calf, pl. *calves;* v. *calve; -ed, plump-calved* (legs) &c.; *calfish; calves-foot* or *calfs-foot.*
elf, pl. *elves; elvish, elfish.*
grief, v. *grieve; grievous.*
half, pl. *halves;* v. *halve.*
hoof, pl. *hoofs, hooves;* v. *hoof; -ed, hoofed, hooved, hoofy.*
knife, pl. *knives;* v. *knife, knive; -ed, knived.*
leaf, pl. *leaves;* v. *leaf, leave; -ed, leaved, leafed; leafy, leavy.*
life, pl. *lives;* v. *live; -ed, -lived; liven, lifer.*
loaf, pl. *loaves;* v. *loaf, loave; -ed, loafed, loaved; loafy.*
mischief, mischievous.
oaf, pl. *oafs, oaves; oafish.*
proof, v. *prove.*
relief, v. *relieve; rilievo, relievo.*
safe, v. *save.*
scarf, pl. *scarfs, scarves; -ed, scarfed, scarved.*
scurf, scurfy, having scurf; *scurvy,* contemptible &c.
self, pl. *selves; selfish, selvedge.*
sheaf, pl. *sheaves;* v. *sheave, sheaf; -ed, sheaved; sheafage, sheafy.*
shelf, pl. *shelves;* v. *shelve; -ed, shelved; shelfy, shelvy.*
staff, pl. *staffs,* (arch. & mus.) *staves.*
strife, v. *strive.*
thief, pl. *thieves;* v. *thieve; thievery, thievish.*
turf, pl. *turfs, turves;* v. *turf; turfen* (adj.), *turfy.*
wharf, pl. *wharfs,* (US) *wharves; wharfage, wharfinger.*
wife, pl. *wives;* v. *wive; -ed, -wifed, -wived; -wifery.*

vehement, vehicle. Pron. vē′ĭ-, not vē′hĭ-, in both; but vêhĭk′ūlar.

veld(t). The modern form is *veld,* but the *-dt* still prevails in English use, & has the advantage of not disguising the sound, which is vĕlt.

velleity, volition. The first (pron. vĕlē′ĭtĭ) is chiefly used either in direct opposition to the second, or (when *volition* has its widest sense) as expressing a particular form of it that is sometimes described as 'mere volition.' *Volition* meaning in the wide sense will power or the exercise of it, & in a narrower but more usual sense such an exercise of it as shall if not baffled take effect, a choice or resolution or determination, *velleity* is an abstract & passive preference. The man in Browning—'And I think I rather . . . woe is me!—Yes, rather should see him than not see, If lifting a hand would seat him there Before me in the empty chair Tonight'—is expressing a *velleity,* but not in the ordinary sense a *volition.* And the OED quotes Bentham: 'In your Lordship will is volition, clothed & armed with power—in me, it is bare inert velleity.'

vellum. Fine-grained calfskin, lambskin, or kidskin used to write on or for bookbindings &c.; a type of paper made to look like parchment. Pl. *-ms;* adj. *vellumy.*

venal, venial. *Venal* (from *venum,* that which is sold or for sale), capable of being bought; hence subject to mercenary or corrupt influences. *Venal judges; a venal sale of office. Venial* (from *venia,* forgiveness, pardon), admitting forgiveness or remission; not heinous, but light; of sin, opp. to deadly or mortal: *venial frailties you may well forgive; provincialism in pronunciation . . . is venial in comparison with slovenly speech.*

vend makes *vendible. Vendor* & *vender* are both in frequent use, with a tendency to DIFFERENTIATION; *-or* is better when the contrast or relation between seller & buyer is prominent, & *-er* when purveyor or dealer is all that is meant.

venery. The existence of homonyms, one synonymous with hunting, the other with sexual indulgence, makes it necessary to provide against ambiguity in using either—the more that neither of them is now an everyday expression.

vengeance=retribution exacted (*revenge*=retaliation). See AVENGE.

venison. In US usually pron. vĕnĭzn; Brit. vĕn′zn.

ventilate makes *-lable, -tor.*

venturesome, venturous. The first is now the normal word. See ADVENTUROUS.

venue. Pron. vĕn′ū. Obs. except in legal senses.

Venus. Pl. *Venuses.* Poss. *Venus'* or (modern) *Venus's.*

veranda(h). Better no *h.*

verbal. *Verbal* meaning of or in words, *oral* meaning of or with the mouth, & words being as much used in writing as in speaking, it is obviously foolish to say 'in words' (*verbal*) when the sense wanted is 'in spoken words' (*oral*). All very true, but the OED gives as def. 4 'Conveyed by speech instead of writing,' with examples from 1591 to 1877, and to insist on the distinction is now both useless and pedantic.

verbal noun. In English usually the gerund or participle. *The* launching *of the ship was* *attended by a large crowd.* Launching *a ship is a serious business.* (Some grammarians include the inf.: To launch *a ship properly, you must have champagne.*)

verbum sap. (scil. *sapienti sat est*), 'a word is enough to the wise.' Ostensibly an apology for not explaining at greater length, or a hint that the less said the better, but more often in fact a way of soliciting attention to what has been said as weightier than it seems.

verdigris. The orthodox pronunciation is -ĭs, the popular -ēs; there seems no reason why the -ēs of the majority should not be accepted by the minority. Verdigrē, though often heard, is wrong; the origin is *vert de Grece* (green of Greece).

Vergil, see VIRGIL.

verily. Apart from its occasional appearance as a stylistic ornament, & its legitimate use in the dialogue of historical novels, *verily* is now perhaps confined to one single phrase—*I verily believe,* which has the special meaning, It is almost incredible, yet facts surprise me into the belief.

veritable, in its modern use, is probably to be classed as a journalistic GALLICISM, & its function is, when one contemplates an exaggeration, to say compendiously, but seldom truthfully, 'I assure you I am not exaggerating': e.g. *a* veritable *hail of slates* &c. It is a pity that the early 19th c. could not leave well alone; for the OED records that by about 1650 the word was dead, but the early 19th c. revived it. Would it had not! its appearance in a description has always the effect of taking down the reader's interest a peg or two, both as being a FORMAL WORD, & as the now familiar herald of a strained top note. The adv., which could equally well be spared, does the same service, or disservice, to adjs. as the adj. to nouns (*veritably portentous* &c.); it is also used with verbs as a supposed improvement on the various natural adverbs, as in: *If this is to be the last word, we shall find ourselves thrown back into a hopeless impasse, & there will* veritably *be no way of reforming our institutions* (actually? really? positively? absolutely? in very truth?).

vermilion (so spelled) makes *-oned.*

vermin. The plural form *-ns* is now hardly used; the word is a collective meaning either all the creatures entitled to the name, or any particular species or set of them, or some of them: it is treated usually as a plural (*these vermin; vermin infest everything*), but sometimes as singular & occasionally has *a* both in the collective sense (*a vermin that I hope to reduce the numbers of*) & as denoting an individual (*such a vermin as you*).

vermouth. So spelled; pron. US vẽr mōōth', Brit. vûr'mōōth.

vernacular. Language, idiom of one's native country; not of foreign origin or of learned formation. For *vernacular, idiom, slang,* &c., see JARGON. For the use of the word in apologies, see SUPERIORITY.

versatile. US pron. usually -ĭl, Brit. -īl. Adv. *versatilely.*

verse. Technically, one line; popularly, a stanza.

vers libre. (Pron. vĕr lēb'r.) (Lit.): 'free verse.' Versification in which different meters are mingled, or prosodical restrictions disregarded, or variable rhythm substituted for definite meter. The French phrase is still in general use; but there seems to be no good reason why 'free verse' should not be preferred. For the writers, we have to choose between 'free-verse writers' (since the handier 'freeverser' would probably be thought unduly familiar by the designated) & 'vers librist' (as queer a fish for English waters as *bellettrist,* but which seems to be accepted by both the writers & their critics).

verso (from *vertere,* to turn). The back of a leaf of a MS. or book (i.e. what you see when you turn it). Hence the left-hand page as opp. to *recto,* or right-hand page. Pl. *-os.*

vertebra. Pl. *-brae* (sometimes *-as*).

vertex. Pl. *-exes* or *-ices.*

vertigo. Pl. *-os.* The correct pronunciation in accordance with the Latin quantity is vertī′gō, but the OED gives ver′tĭgō precedence, & it is so pronounced in US & usually in Brit.

vertu. See VIRTU.

verve. Enthusiasm, vivacity, spirit, esp. in artistic & lit. work. (The earlier sense, aptitude, talent, is now obs.) See FRENCH WORDS.

very with passive participles. *I am* very *tired of hearing your complaints. I am* much *obliged to you for your kindness.* Everyone will agree that these sentences are idiomatic & no one would think of using *much* in the first or *very* in the second. But *a* very *celebrated poet* or *a* much *celebrated poet?* The legitimacy of using *very* with passive participles, or at least the line limiting its idiomatic use, is an old & not very easy puzzle. It will at once be admitted that *I was* much *tired* is improved by the substitution of *very* for *much,* whereas in *I was* very *inconvenienced, much* has undoubtedly to be substituted for *very. Very* & *much* are complementary, each being suited to places in which the other is unnatural or wrong.

A word that is in form a p.p., if it is to be qualified by *very* instead of *much* (or *very much*), must fall into one of the following classes: (1) It must have passed into a true adj. in common use, as *tired* has & *inconvenienced* has not. (RIGHT: *They were* very *discontented; They considered themselves* much *aggrieved.*)/(2) It must be used attributively, not predicatively. (RIGHT: *A* very *damaged reputation; Was the car* much *damaged?*)/(3) The noun to which it belongs must not be the name of the person or thing on which the verbal action is exercised but that of something else. (RIGHT: *His tone* was *very annoyed; He was* much *annoyed by the interruption.*)/(4) Its participial or verbal (as opp. to adjectival) character must be unbetrayed by e.g. a telltale preposition such as *by.* (RIGHT: *Opera engagements are also* very *limited and increasingly difficult to get; They are* much *limited* by *their failure to get backing.*)

All this amounts substantially to no more than that a participle (in *-ed*) that *is* a participle requires *much,* while a participle that is an adjective prefers *very;* but the bare rule is not very intelligible without some such expansion as has been given. In all of the following *very* should have been *much,* or *very much.* WRONG: *We should be* very *surprised if the agents ever received the alleged 'warning.'/The latter had been* very *annoyed on learning that . . ./We are not* very *concerned about these subtle distinctions./Both parties are very jealous, & very afraid of each other* (*afraid,* & other purely predicative adjs., rank with the p.p.)./*Your mind seems* very *exercised just now as to whether . . ./When the husband returned, he found her manner toward him* very *changed.*

In conclusion, the worst & the most venial misuses of *very* are represented by *I was* very *inconvenienced by it,* & *I shall be* very *pleased* (i.e. *glad, happy*) *to accept.*

-ves. See -VE(D).

vest. The older meanings, 'robe,' 'tunic,' or collectively clothes (=vesture), are still in poetic or archaic use; as a synonym for a man's waistcoat it is chiefly US (in Brit. 'a shop word').

veto. Pl. usually *-oes.*

via. 'By way of' or 'passing through,' pron. vīa or vēa. *Via media,* middle way, between the two extremes.

viable, viability. No relation to *via* above. Formed in French from *vie,* life, it means capable of living, & its special application is to newborn children (e.g. in contrast with stillborn); now also, of plant & animal life, capable of developing, e.g. *viable seeds;* and fig. in such phrases as *viable economy.* This last use should not, however, be transferred to ordinary contexts: *It bears the mark of faddism & hence would be impossible to sell in* viable *quantities.* See POPULARIZED TECHNICALITIES.

vicarious. Deputed, delegated, done for another (*vicarious sacrifice . . . or punishment by substitution; pebbles [swallowed by birds] perform the vicarious office of teeth; sin expiated by the vicarious virtues of other men*); in physiology, substitutive (*the vicarious action of the skin & lungs*). The sense 'experienced by one person through sympathetic participation in the feeling of another' (*vicarious education, a vicarious emotion*) is recent & probably of US origin (from psychiatry?) See POPULARIZED TECHNICALITIES. Best pron. vī-.

vice, prep. & prefix. (1) The preposition is pronounced vī′sĭ, & means in the place of (esp. in the sense succeeding to), being, like PACE, the ablative of a Latin noun followed by an English noun regarded as in the genitive (*appointed Secretary* vice *Mr. Jones deceased*). (2) The prefix is the same word treated as an adv. compounded with English nouns such as *chancellor, president, chairman, admiral,* but meaning rather deputy, & pronounced vīs.

vice. The tool, in US *vise.*

vicegerent, viceregent. The first (pron. vīs jĕr′ent) is a word of very wide application, including anyone who exercises authority committed or supposed to be committed to him by another, from the Pope as the Vicar of Christ on earth or the regent of a sovereign State to the clerk running an office during his employer's holiday. *Viceregent,* on the other hand, is 'One who acts in the place of a regent'; but from the quotations given in the OED it would appear that that is rather what it ought to mean than what it does. It is sometimes used in error for *vicegerent,* & sometimes used pleonastically for *regent* (which word includes the notion of *vice-*), so that it seems to have no right to exist, & may be classed among SUPERFLUOUS WORDS.

vice versa. Conversely, the relations being reversed. In US usually not ital.

vicinage is now, compared with *neighborhood,* a FORMAL WORD, &, compared with *vicinity,* a dying one.

vicious circle. In logic, *circle* & *vicious circle* mean the same —the basing of a conclusion on a premise that is itself based on this conclusion; for an example see ARGUING IN A CIRCLE. The phrase *vicious circle* is also applied outside logic to the reaction between two evils that aggravate each other: The wrecked sailor's thirst makes him drink salt water; the salt increases his thirst. WRONG: *There is a* vicious circle *in which starvation produces Bolshevism, & Bolshevism in its turn feeds on starvation.* What, then, produces starvation, & on what does starvation feed? The writer can no doubt retort with truth that nothing (i.e. no food) produces starvation, & that starvation feeds on nothing; but he will have proved his wit at the expense of his logic. Such blunders in stating the elements of a vicious circle are not uncommon.

victual. Pron. vĭ'tl. Now usually dial. or humorous.

vide. Pron. vī'dē; literally 'see' (imperative). It is properly used in referring readers to a passage in which they will find a proof or illustration of what has been stated, & should be followed by something in the nature of chapter & verse, or at least by the name of a book or author. But it is often used in extended senses with an incongruity of which the following is a comparatively mild specimen: (LOOSE) *Numbers count for nothing—*vide *the Coalition—it is the principles that tell.*

videlicet ('one may see') in its full form is now rare except in PEDANTIC HUMOR, the abbreviation *viz.* being used instead. In speech, use *namely.* See VIZ.

view forms part of three well-established idioms each equivalent to a preposition, & each liable to be confused in meaning or in form with the others. These are *in view of, with a view to,* & *with the view of. In view of* means taking into account, or not forgetting, or considering, & is followed by a noun expressing external circumstances that exist or must be expected: *In view of* these facts, *we have no alternative; In view of* his having promised *amendment; In view of* the Judgment *to come. With a view* to means calculating upon or contemplating as a desired result, & is followed by a verbal noun or a gerund or less idiomatically an infinitive: *With a view to* diminution *of waste,* or *to diminishing waste,* or (less well) *to diminish waste. With the view of* has the same meaning as *with a view to,* but is both less usual & less flexible, being naturally followed only by a gerund: *With the view of* proving *his sanity.* The forms of confusion are giving the first the meaning of the others or vice versa, & neglecting the correspondences *a* & *to, the* & *of,* in the second & third. RIGHT: *This may be interesting* in view of *the fact that the atmosphere has been reeking with pugilism for some time.* WRONG: *I will ask your readers to accept a few further criticisms on matters of detail,* in view of *ultimately* finding *a workable solution* (read *with a view to*)./*Dr. Deane was educated* with a view of becoming *a priest* (read *to* for *of*)./*They have been selected* with a view to illustrate *both the thought & action of the writer's life* (read *illustrating* for *illustrate*)./*The question of reducing the cost of bread production,* with the view both to preventing *the price of the loaf from rising* & of arresting *any increase in the subsidy.* (ELEGANT VARIATION again? read *of* for *to*).

viewpoint. *Point of view* is better. See POINT.

vignette. (Ornament of grape-leaves &c. in Arch.) Fig. thumbnail sketch. Pron. vēnyĕt′.

vigo(u)r, -gorous. US usually *vigor,* Brit. *-our;* both *vigorous.*

villain, villein. The retention of the second form for the word meaning *serf* is a useful piece of DIFFERENTIATION.

vindicate makes *-cable, -tor.*

vindictive has become so generally restricted to the notion of personal thirst for revenge or desire to hurt that the phrases in which it means punitive & not revengeful or cruel are apt to mislead; these are *vindictive damages* (designed to punish the offender & not, or not only, to indemnify the injured party), & *vindictive* (now more often *retributive*) *justice.*

vin ordinaire. Wine for ordinary table use (usually a cheap claret); *vin du pays,* wine of the locality.

viola. The flower is (best) vī′*ola,* the instrument vēō′*la.*

violate makes *-lable, -tor.*

violin. The victory of this over FIDDLE, to which it should have borne the same relation as, say, *savant* to *scientist,* or *belles lettres* to *literature,* or *robe de chambre* to *dressing gown*—the relation, that is, of refined journalese to ordinary plain language—may be deplored, but hardly now reversed. Already to talk of *fiddles* & *fiddlers* & *fiddling,* unless with contempt or condescension, is to be suspected of eccentricity.

violoncello. So spelled (NOT *-lin-*); pl. *-os.* For pronunciation, vēolonchĕ′lō is the approximation to the Italian; vīolonsĕ′lō, which the OED puts first, is the complete anglicization; & vīolonchĕ′lō is the usual compromise, which is here recommended.

virago. A turbulent woman, a termagant. Pron. vĭrā′gō. Pl. *-os.*

Virgil. Although we now know from inscriptions that the Latin spelling was *Vergilius, Virgil* & *Virgilian* gain or lose as much by being corrected into *Ver-* as MOHAMMED by the change to Muhammad. See PEDANTRY.

Virginia(n). The noun used attributively (*Virginia creeper, tobacco,* &c.) is established.

virile. US dictionaries & OED put vĭ′rĭl first. (Alternatives, vī′rĭl, vĭr′īl.) The proper sense is 'having the qualities of a male adult,' but the emphasis is on male, &, though *vigorous* can often be substituted for *virile* without affecting the required meaning, *virile* must not be substituted for *vigorous* where the notion *male* is out of place. WRONG: *Despite* her *great age,* Mrs. Jones *is fairly* virile, *& performs all her own household work.*

virtu. (Love of fine arts; productions of art, e.g. antiques, curios; *an article* or *object of virtu.*) So spelled (NOT *ver-*); pron. vertōō′.

virtual=that is so in essence or effect, though not formally or actually. *Although a minority party, it is the* virtual *leader of the country.* Hence *virtually,* for all practical purposes.

virtue. *To make a virtue of necessity* is one of the maltreated phrases illustrated in IRRELEVANT ALLUSION, being often applied to the simple doing of what one must, irrespective of the grace with which one does it.

virtuoso. Pl. *-si* (-sē).

virulent. Best. pron. -ū-.

virus. Pl. *-uses.* Pron. vī-.

visa. Spelling preferred by the US Dept. of State; but see VISÉ.

visage. Now a literary word for *face.* See COUNTENANCE.

vis-à-vis. Pron. vē′zà vē′. 'Face to face,' opposite to, in relation to. But see FOREIGN DANGER & FRENCH WORDS.

viscount. Pron. vī′kount. Noble ranking between an earl & a baron (esp. as courtesy title of earl's eldest son). For *Viscount Smith* & *Lord Smith,* see LORD & TITLES.

vise, the tool usually so spelled in US; Brit. *vice.*

visé, visa. Pron. vē′sā, vē′sa. The French form is widely used, in both US & Brit., though *visa* is the official US spelling. Verb, *viséd, viséing,* & *visaed, visaing.*

visibility, visibleness. The second has always been in more frequent use than most *-ness* words with partners in *-ty,* & the technical sense of *visibility,* with regard to conditions of light & atmosphere, has thrown more general work on the other.

vision, in the sense of statesmanlike foresight or political sagacity, is enjoying a noticeable vogue. Politicians who wish to be mysteriously impressive are much given to imputing *lack of vision* to their opponents & implying possession of it by themselves when they are at a loss for more definite matter; see VOGUE WORDS.

visit, v., makes *-tor.*

visor &c. *Visor* & *vizor* pron. vīz-; *vizard* & *visard* pron. vĭz-. The *-ard* forms differ in meaning by being restricted to the sense mask (lit. & fig.), whereas the *-or* forms have also, & chiefly, the sense movable helmet front.

vitamin. Pron. vī- (cf. *vitality, vital,* also from *vita*=life); Brit. also vĭ-.

vitiate means (1) impair the quality of, corrupt, & (2) make invalid or ineffectual, i.e. impair the legal effect of, as a contract. The adj. is *vitiable.*

vituperate. Pron. vītū′-.

viva. See VIVA VOCE.

viva, vivat, vive (pron. vē′vah, vī′vat, vēv) are the Italian, Latin, & French for 'long live —!' They can all be used as nouns also, with plural -s. The verbs have, like EXIT, plurals (*vivano, vivant, vivent*) for use with plural subjects—a fact forgotten in: *Cries of 'Vive les Anglais' attended us till we were inside the hotel.* The cries were undoubtedly *vivent* . . . , which is pronounced the same way.

vivace. Mus. 'In a lively manner.' Pron. vēvah′chā.

viva voce. 'With living voice,' i.e. orally. Pron. vīva vō′sĭ.

vividity. *Vividness* is better.

viz., sc(il)., i.e. Full form *videlicet, scilicet, id est.* The meanings are so close to one another that a less instead of the most appropriate is often chosen. *Viz.,* as is suggested by its usual spoken representative *namely,* introduces especially the items that compose what has been expressed as a whole (*For three good reasons,* viz. 1 . . . , 2 . . . , 3 . . .) or a more particular statement of what has been vaguely described (*My only means of earning,* viz. *my fiddle*). *Sc.* or *scil.* is in learned rather than popular use, is for instance commoner in notes on classical texts than elsewhere, & has as its most characteristic function the introducing of some word that has been not expressed, but left to be 'understood'; so *His performance failed to satisfy* (sc. *himself*)=not, as might be guessed, other people. What *i.e.* does is not so much to particularize like *viz.,* or supply omissions like *scil.,* as to interpret by paraphrasing a previous expression that may mislead or be obscure; *Now you are for it,* i.e. *punishment; Than that he should offend* (i.e. harm) *one of these little ones.* See also E.G.

vizard. See VISOR.

vizor. See VISOR.

V-J Day. So written. Either 14 Aug. or 2 Sept. 1945 (Japan's surrender or the formal surrender aboard the U.S.S. *Missouri*).

vocabulary. For distinctive senses (*A wide vocabulary. He has erased 'ought' & 'ought not' from his vocabulary. The Latin words in this vocabulary*) see GLOSSARY.

vocation. Orig. 'calling' (e.g. *vocation to the Church*); now also occupation, employment (as opp. to *avocation*).

VOGUE WORDS. Every now & then a word emerges from obscurity, or even from nothingness or a merely potential & not actual existence, into sudden popularity. It is often, but not necessarily, one that by no means explains itself to the average man, who has to find out its meaning as best he can. His wrestlings with it have usually some effect upon it. It does not mean quite what it ought to, but in compensation it means some things that it ought not to, before he has done with it. Ready acceptance of vogue words seems to some people the sign of an alert mind; to others it stands for the herd instinct & lack of individuality. The title of this article is perhaps enough to show that the second view is here taken; on the whole, the better the writer, or at any rate the sounder his style, the less will he be found to indulge in the vogue words. It is unnecessary here to discuss in detail the specimens that will be given; most of them are to be found in their dictionary places, & they will here be slightly classified only. The reason for collecting them under a common heading is that young writers may not even be aware, about some of them, that they are not part of the normal vocabulary but still replusive to the old & the well-read. Many, it should be added, are vogue words in particular senses only, & are unobjectionable, though liable to ambiguity, in the senses that belonged to them before they attained their vogue.

1. Old vogue words. *Individual* & *nice* may be instanced; the first now past its vogue but lingering in its vogue sense as a nuisance; the second established in a loose & general sense instead of its earlier & now infrequent precise one.

2. Words owing their vogue to the ease with which they can be substituted for any of several different & more precise words, saving the trouble of choosing the right: *area; asset; background; mentality; optimism; unthinkable.*

3. Words owing their vogue to the joy of showing that one has acquired them: *feasible; global; inferiority complex; idiosyncrasy; percentage; psychological moment.*

4. Words taken up merely as novel variants on their predecessors: *frock* for *dress; happening* for *event; intrigue* (v.) for *interest; melodic* for *melodious; titled* for *entitled.*

5. Words made or revived to suit a literary theory: *foreword; English,* v.

6. Words owing their vogue to some occasion: *acid test; atomic era; gesture*=beau geste.

7. Words of rhetorical appeal: *challenge; far-flung; vision.*

voice. Gram.: Active voice: *The car hit him.* Passive voice: *He was hit by the car.*

volatile. Pron. US usually -ĭl, Brit. -īl.

volcano. Pl. *-oes.*

Volkslied. German, *folksong.* Pron. fōˊkslēt. Pl. *-lieder* (lēdẽr).

volley. Pl. *-eys.*

voluminous. Pron. -lūˊ-.

vortex. Pl. *-texes, tices.*

votaress. So spelled.

vouch. Current chiefly in *vouch for,* i.e. confirm, answer for. See AVOUCH.

voyage. As distinct from *trip, journey,* &c., esp. a long journey by water.

vulgar(ly). For the use in apologies for slang, see SUPERIORITY.

VULGARIZATION. Many words depend for their legitimate effect upon rarity. When blundering hands are laid upon them & they are exhibited in unsuitable places, they are vulgarized. *Save* (prep.) & *ere* were in the days of our youth seldom seen in prose, & they then consorted well with any passage of definitely elevated style, lending to it & receiving from it the dignity that was proper to them. Things are now so different that the elevated style shuns them as tawdry ornament; it says what the man in the street says, *before* & *except,* & leaves *ere* & *save* to those who have not yet ceased to find them beautiful—which is naturally confusing, & an injury to the language. The fate of *awful* is of rather earlier date, but is still remembered, & *weird* has, almost in our own century, been robbed of all its weirdness. One would like to represent to the makers of fountain pens that the word *fount,* which some of them are desecrating, is sacrosanct; but they would probably be as indignant at the notion that their touch pollutes as the writer who should be told that he was injuring *faerie* & *evanish* & *mystic* & *optimistic* & *replica* by selecting them in honorable preference to *fairy* & *vanish* & *mysterious* & *hopeful* & *copy*. Vulgarization of words that should not be in common use robs some of their aroma, others of their substance, others again of their precision; but nobody likes to be told that the best service that he can do to a favorite word is to leave it alone, & perhaps the less said here on this matter the better.

Vulgate. Latin version of the Bible, prepared mainly by St. Jerome in the 4th c.; the authorized version of the R. C. Church. (The Vulgate was the first book printed, *c.* 1455.) Also (no capital), the vulgate text of any author, as distinct from a critical text. So *vulgate reading.*

W

WAC, Women's Army Corps (US), no periods necessary; sometimes *Wac;* formerly *WAAC,* Women's Army Auxiliary Corps. (Brit. *WAAC*).

WAF, Women in the Air Force (no periods); sometimes *Waf.* Brit. *WAAF,* Women's Auxiliary Air Force, now *WRAF,* Women's Royal Air Force.

wages, n. pl. of *wage,* pay given for labor, was formerly construed as a sing. (e.g. *The wages of sin* is *death*).

wag(g)on. US (and OED) *wagon;* Brit. *waggon* (but Fr. *wagon-lit,* sleeping car on a Continental railway).

wainscot (pron. wāns′kŭt) has *-oted, -oting.*

waistcoat. Pron. wĕs′kŭt.

wait. (1) The transitive use, as in *wait one's opportunity, wait the result, wait another's convenience* or *arrival,* is good English, but is described by the OED as 'now rare' & as being 'superseded' by *await* & *wait for;* the assignment of the intransitive uses to *wait* & of the transitive to *await* is a natural DIFFERENTIATION & may be expected to continue; see also AWAIT. (2) *To lie in wait (for)* is established usage. *To wait about* or (US) *wait around* is colloq.

waive. The broad distinction between *wave* & *waive,* viz. that to *wave* is, & to *waive* is not, proper to physical motion, is now generally observed; but confusion, & especially the assumption that the two forms are mere spelling variants, still occurs. The following example shows the form often taken by this confusion. WRONG: *The problem of feeding the peoples of the Central Empires is a very serious & anxious one, & we cannot* waive *it aside as though it were no concern of ours.* To *waive* is not a derivative, confined to certain senses, of to *wave,* but a derivative of *waif,* meaning to make waif or abandon; *to wave aside* or *away* is one method of *waiving;* but *to waive aside* or *away* is no better than *to abandon aside* or *to relinquish away.*

wake. Past *woke,* rarely *waked;* p.p., *waked,* rarely *woken. Wake* is the ordinary working verb, as opp. to *waken*

& *awake.* See AWAKE(N).

Walhalla. Var. of *Valhalla.*

Walkyrie. See VALKYRIE. The title of the opera is *Die Walküre.*

WALLED-UP OBJECT. *I shut & locked him in* is permissible English; *I scolded & sent him to bed* is not. In the first, *in* is common to *shut* & *locked; him* is therefore not walled up between *locked* & a word that is the private property of *locked.* In the second, *to bed* is peculiar to *sent,* & therefore *him,* enclosed between *sent* & *sent's* appurtenance *to bed,* is not available as object to *scolded;* it is necessary to say *I scolded him & sent him to bed,* though *I scolded & punished him* requires only one *him.* It is not in hasty colloq. use that such lapses are wicked, & the examples chosen were the simplest possible in order that the grammatical point might be unmistakable; but in print it is another matter. The quotations following show how common this slovenliness is, & no more need be said of them than that for nearly all the cure is to release the walled-up noun, place it as object to the unencumbered verb (which usually comes first), & fill its now empty place with a pronoun, *it, them,* &c.; this is done in parentheses after the first, & any change not according to this simple formula is shown for later ones. WRONG: *An earnest agitation for increasing*^*& rendering* that force *more efficient* (read *for increasing that force & rendering it . . .*)./*It is for its spirited reconstructions of various marches & battles that we counsel the reader* to buy^*& make* the book *his own.*/*He had to count, trim, press*^*& pack the furs into bales* (read *& press the furs, & pack them;* or, of course, the omission of *into bales* would put all right)./*There is no means of defense against submarines, & no means of fighting,* attacking^*or* driving them *from certain waters* (read *of fighting or attacking them, or of . . .*).

The great majority of such mistakes are of that form; one or two are added in which the principle infringed is the same, but some slight variation of detail occurs. WRONG: *We were not a little proud of the manner in which we* transported to & maintained *our Army* in *South Africa.* This is the old type, complicated by the well-meant but disastrous *to;* read *in which we transported our army to S.A. & maintained it there.*/*I trust you will kindly grant me a little space to express, in my own*^*& in the name of those elements whom I have the honor to represent, our indignation at . . .* The walled-up noun here (*name*) is governed not by a verb, but by a preposition; read *in my own name & in that of the elements . . .*/*The fourteen chapters explore the belief in immortality in primitive*^*& in the various civilizations of antiquity taken in order.* Like the preceding; read *in primitive civilization & in those of antiquity.*

wall-less. Write so.

wallop (slang) makes *-oped, -oping, -oper.*

wallpaper (or Brit.˙ *wall-paper*) so written.

Walpurgis Night. Eve of May Day, a witches' Sabbath. Pron. väl po͝or′gĭs.

waltz, valse. The first is the form that has established itself as the ordinary English, the other being confined to programs & the like.

wampum. Pron. wŏ-.

wanderlust. The impulse to wander or travel. In US the word is now pronounced as English; Brit. vän′derlo͝ost.

want. WRONG: *No man can say what* is wanted to be done *in regard to the military affairs of a nation.* For this ugly construction, see DOUBLE PASSIVE.

wanton makes *wantonness.*

war. (1) *Wars & rumors of wars* is the correct quotation (Matt. xxiv. 6); see MISQUOTATION. (2) *War between the States* is the name preferred by the Southern States for the (US) *Civil War.*

WARDOUR STREET ENGLISH. 'The name of a street in London mainly occupied by dealers in antique & imitation-antique furniture' (OED). (Today Wardour Street is associated with motion pictures.) As the antique dealer offers to those who live in modern houses the opportunity of picking up an antique or two that will be conspicuous for good or ill among their surroundings, so this article offers to those who write modern English a selection of oddments calculated to establish (in the eyes of some readers) their claim to be persons of taste & writers of beautiful English. And even as it is said of some dealers in the rare & exquisite that they have a secret joy when their treasures find no purchaser & are left on their hands, so the present collector, though he has himself no practical use for his articles of virtu, yet shows them without commendation for fear they should be carried off & unworthily housed.

albeit; ANENT; AUGHT; *belike;* ERE; ERST (*while*); *haply;* HOWBEIT; *maugre; more by* TOKEN; *oft;* PERCHANCE; SANS; SAVE, prep. or conj.; subjunctive as in *If it be; there*-compounds such as THEREFOR, *thereof, thereto;* THITHER; *to* WIT; *trow;* VARLET; WELL-NIGH; WHERE-compounds such as *wherein, whereof; whit; withal; wot.*

The words in small capitals are further commented upon in their dictionary places.

-ward(s). (Suffix.) Words ending with *-ward(s)* may most of them be used as advs., adjs., or nouns. The *-s* is usually present in the adv., & absent in the adj.; the noun, which is rather an absolute use of the adj., tends to follow it in being without *-s; moving eastwards; the eastward position; looking to the eastward.* This usage prevails esp. with the words made of a noun +*-ward(s)*, but is also generally true of the older words in which the first part is adverbial, such as *downward.* Some words, however, have peculiarities; see AFTERWARDS, FORWARD, ONWARD, TOWARD(S).

War of Independence. Usual in Brit. for the American Revolutionary War.

warp, n. The parallel (lengthwise) threads in the loom. See WOOF.

warrant, v., makes -tor.

warrantee, the person to whom a warranty is made.

washing. For *take in one another's washing,* see WORN-OUT HUMOR.

wassail. Pron. wŏ′sl.

wast, wert. *When thou* wast

true (past indic.); *if thou* wert *true* (past subj.). See BE 7.

wastage. There are contexts in which this word is for some reason better than *waste* (*Natural wastage in industry,* i.e. by death & superannuation—no implication of blame); in nearly all the places in which it nowadays appears in non-technical writing, it is not better; see LONG VARIANTS.

waste. (1) *Waste* makes *wastable.* (2) *Waste paper,* no hyphen. (3) *Wastebasket* is now usual for *wastepaper basket.*

wastrel. Pron. wăst'rel. The sense spendthrift (adj. & n.), now the most frequent one, is a recent development.

watchword. *The old Liberal* watchword *of Peace, Retrenchment, & Reform.* For synonyms, see SIGN.

water. The phrase *of the first water* comes from an earlier use meaning the transparency or luster of a diamond or pearl. (The quality of diamonds was formerly graded as of first, second, or third water.) Transf., usually derog.: *a swindler of the first water.*

watershed. The original meaning of the word, whether or not it is an anglicization of German *Wasserscheide* (lit. water-parting), was the line of high land dividing the waters that flow in one direction from those that flow in the other. Such classics as Lyell & Darwin & Geikie are all quoted for the correct sense & it is lamentable that the mistaken senses (drainage slope, river basin) should have found acceptance with those who could appreciate the risks of ambiguity; yet Huxley proposed that *water parting* should be introduced to do *watershed's* work, & *watershed* be allowed to mean what the ignorant thought it meant. The old sense should be restored & rigidly maintained. OED quotations from Lyell & Geikie follow to make the old use clear, & an extract from a newspaper shows the misuse. RIGHT: (Lyell) *The crests or* watersheds *of the Alps & Jura are about eighty miles apart.*/ (Geikie) *The* watershed *of a country or continent is thus a line which divides the flow of the brooks & rivers on two opposite slopes.*/ WRONG: *The Seine, between its source in the Côte d'Or & the capital, has many tributaries, & when there is bad weather in the* watershed *of each of these an excessive flow is bound to be the result.*

wave makes *-vable, wavy.*

waxen. *Wax dolls, wax candles,* but *a waxen image, the waxen faces of the children.*

way. (1) For *at the parting of the ways,* see HACKNEYED PHRASES. (2) *Under way* (NOT *weigh*) is the right phrase for in motion. (3) *See one's way* to. WRONG: *We hope that the Government will see their way* of *giving effect to this suggestion.* What has happened? The writer doubtless knows the idiomatic phrase as well as the rest of us, but finding himself saying 'will see their way to give effect to' has shied at the two *tos*; but he should have abandoned instead of mutilating his phrase; see OUT OF THE FRYING PAN, & CAST-IRON IDIOM.

ways. See -WISE.

we. 1. Case. Use of *us* for *we* has been illustrated under US 1; the converse is seen in (WRONG): *This man was en-*

titled to have four wives if he liked for chattels—which to we *Western people, with our ideas about women, is almost unintelligible./Whether the Committee's suggestions are dictated by patriotism or political expediency is not* for we *outside mortals to decide.* (Both should read *us.*)

2. National &c. uses: *We* may mean I & another or others, or the average man, or this newspaper, or this nation, or several other things. The writer occasionally forgets that he must not mix up his editorial with his national *we.* WRONG: *But still,* we *are distrusted by Germany, &* we *are loth, by explaining how our acts ought to be interpreted, to put her in a more invidious position.* The first *we* is certainly the nation, the second is probably the newspaper. See OUR 2 for similar confusions of different senses that are legitimate apart, but not together.

weaker sex, see SOBRIQUETS.

weal. In the sense welfare, well-being, now current only in *weal or woe, the public weal;* otherwise archaic.

weariless. *Tireless* or *untiring* is better.

weather. *Weather-beaten,* keep the hyphen. *Weather gauge,* so spelled (US); OED gives also *gage.*

weave. Ordinary p.p. *woven;* but *wove paper.*

web. In weaving, the fabric that comes from the loom is the web. See WOOF.

wed is a poetic or rhetorical synonym for *marry;* & the established past & p.p. is *wedded;* but it is noticeable that the need of brevity in newspaper headings is bringing into trivial use both the verb instead of *marry* (*PRINCE WEDS ACTRESS*), & the short instead of the long p.p. (*SUICIDE OF WED PAIR*): see INCONGRUOUS VOCABULARY.

wedge makes *wedgeable.*

Wednesday. See FRIDAY.

week makes *weekday,* (over the) *week end, workweek* (US; Brit. all hyphened); *a week-end vacation; he week-ended in the country* (the last, colloq.).

ween. See WARDOUR STREET.

weft. See WOOF.

weigh. Naut. *weigh anchor* (*anchors aweigh*), but the ship is *under way.*

weird. (Supernatural, uncanny, e.g. *the weird sisters* in *Macbeth.*) A word ruined by becoming a VOGUE WORD (strange, odd).

Welch. See WELSH.

well, adv. It is time for someone to come to the rescue of the phrase *as well as,* which is being cruelly treated. Grammatically, the point is that *as well as* is a conjunction & not a preposition; or, to put it in a less abstract way, its strict meaning is NOT *besides,* but *& not only;* or, to proceed by illustration, English requires NOT *You were there* as well as *me* (as it would if the phrase were a preposition & meant *besides*), but *You were there* as well as *I* (since the phrase is a conjunction & means *& not only*). The abuses occur, however, not in simple sentences like this with a common noun or pronoun following *as well as;* but in places where the part of a verb chosen reveals the grammar. WRONG: *The officer still has to put his hand in his pocket* as well as giving *his time.* (Read *give;* it depends on *has to;* or else substitute *besides.*)/As well as *closing the railway, it would make the river impracticable for traffic.* (Read *besides; as well as* should never precede; or else read *as well as close* & put this after *traffic.*)/*Germany* as well as *Austria* are *now ready to sign.* (*Are* should be *is:* Germany is ready to sign *as well as* (=*and not only*) Austria (i.e. is ready to sign).

well & well-. In combinations of a participle & *well* there is often a doubt whether the two parts should be hyphened or left separate. The danger of wrong hyphens is greater than that of wrong separation; e.g. to write *His courage is* well-known (where *well known* is the only tolerable form) is much worse than to write *His* well known *courage.* It may be here repeated that if a participle with *well* is attributive (*a well-aimed stroke*) the hyphen is desirable but not obligatory, but if the participle is predicative (*the stroke was well aimed*) the hyphen is wrong. Similarly in such phrases as *well off: They are not well off,* but *Well-off people cannot judge.*

well-nigh. See WARDOUR STREET: *Archaeology had strengthened its hold on art, & went* well-nigh *to strangling it.* The natural English would have been *& came near strangling it,* or *& nearly strangled it.* But if the writer was bent on displaying his antique, he should at least have said *& well-nigh strangled it;* the use of *well-nigh* is purely adverbial; i.e. it needs a following verb or adj. or noun to attach itself to; *well nigh worn to pieces,* & *well nigh dead,* says Shakespeare, & *well nigh half the angelic name,* says Milton. To say *come well-nigh to* is to put the antique in an incongruous frame.

Welsh, Welch. The modern spelling is *-sh,* both for the national adj. (except in the official names of regiments, for which *-ch* is used) and for the verb *to welsh* (to cheat by avoiding payment of [orig. racing] bets). Whether the verb is or is not etymologically connected with *Welsh* is a disputed question.

wen. For *the Wen* (=London), see SOBRIQUETS.

were. For the subjunctive uses in the singular, as *If I were you, Were he alive, It were futile,* some of which are more inconsistent than others with the writing of natural English, see SUBJUNCTIVES.

werewolf, werw-. The first is preferred; it is the more familiar, it suggests the usual pronunciation, & it dates back to Old English.

wert. Past subj., 2nd pers. (*wast,* past indic.). See BE 7.

westerly. *A westerly wind, took a westerly course, the most westerly batteries.*

westernmost. *The westernmost ridge of the Alleghenies.* See EASTERN.

westward(s). The adj. is always *-ward* (*a westward migration*); the adv. *-ward* or *-wards* (*lying five miles westward(s) from New York; -ward* is more usual in US). See -WARD(S).

wharf. Pl. US usually *wharves,* Brit. *wharfs.* (The *h* is best pronounced.)

wharfinger. Pron. -jer.

what is a word of peculiar interest, because the small problems that it poses for writers are such as on the one hand yield pretty readily to analysis, & on the other hand demand a slightly more expert analysis than they are likely to get from those who think they can write well enough without stopping to learn grammar. This article is divided into the following sections: 1. Wrong number attraction. 2. *What* sing. & pl. 3. One *what* in two cases. 4. *What* & *and, but, which.* 5. Miscellaneous.

1. Wrong number attraction. *What* (=that which, or a thing that) *is said* is *words.* This is idiomatic English; *what* is conceived as a sing. pron., since the first verb is sing. Therefore the second verb is sing. to agree with a sing. subject. *What is said* are *words* is not idiomatic English, the second verb being made plural due to the influence of a complement in the plural (*words*). The grammatical name for such influence is attraction; see NUMBER 1. In the quotations, the roman-type verb should have its number changed from plural to sing. WRONG: *What is of absorbing & permanent interest* are *the strange metamorphoses which this fear underwent./What is required* are *houses at rents that the people can pay./What is really at issue in the present conflict* are *not questions of territory, but the future of the democratic world.*

2. *What* sing. & *what* pl. In each of the quotations above, it is plain that *what* there is a sing. pronoun. But the word itself can equally well be plural. RIGHT: *I have few books, & what there* are *do not help me.* So arises another problem concerning the number of verbs after *what.* First comes a particular form of sentence in which plural *what* is better than singular, or in other words in which its verb should be plural. These are sentences in which *what,* if resolved, comes out as *the ——s that,* ——*s* standing for a plural noun actually present in the complement. After each quotation a correction is given if it is desirable, & the resolution that justifies the plural. WRONG: *We have been invited to abandon* what seems *to us to be the most valuable* parts *of our Constitution* (read *seem;* abandon the parts of our Constitution that seem)./*The City Council, for* what was *doubtless good & sufficient* reasons, *decided not to take any part* (read *were;* for reasons that were)./*The personal aspect is of little importance to English readers;* what are *important are* the criticisms *of the operation of protective duties in France* (the criticisms that; but *What is important is* would have been better, *what is* standing for *the thing that is,* in contrast with *aspect*)./*Confidence being inspired by the production of* what appears *to be* bricks *of solid gold* (read *appear;* production of bricks that appear).

But resolution of *what* often presents us not with a noun found in the complement, but with some other noun of wider meaning, or again with the still vaguer *that which.* A writer should make the resolution & act on it without allowing the number of the complement to force a plural verb on him if the most natural representative of *what* is *that which* or *the thing that.* In several of the following quotations the necessary courage has been lacking; corrections & resolutions are given as before.

What I now wish to point out are certain instances wherein philosophy has made serious error (read *is*;=the thing that)./*No other speaker has his peculiar power of bringing imagination to play on* what seems, *until he speaks, to be familiar platitudes* (read *seem*;=on sayings that *seem*)./What are *wanted are not small cottages, but the larger houses with modern conveniences that are now demanded by the working classes* (read *what is wanted is*;=the thing that *is wanted*—rather than *the buildings that* are)./*In order to reduce this material to utility & assimilate it,* what are *required are faith & confidence, & willingness to work* (read *what is required is;* but *the qualities that are required* justifies the plurals, though it does not make them idiomatic).

It will be observed that there is more room for difference of opinion on this set of examples than on either those in (1) or the previous set in (2), & probably many readers will refuse to accept the decisions given; but if it is realized that there are problems of number after *what*, & that solutions of them are possible, that is sufficient.

3. One *what* in two cases. For the general question whether in a language that like English has shed nearly all its case forms the grammatical notion of case still deserves respect, see CASES. It is here assumed that it does, to the extent that no word, even if it has not different forms such as *I* & *me* for the subjective & objective uses, ought to be so placed that it has, without being repeated, to be taken twice over first in one & then in the other case. The word *what* is peculiarly liable to such treatment. There are two chief ways of sparing grammatically minded readers this outrage on their susceptibilities; sometimes a second *what* should be inserted; sometimes it is better to convert a verb to the other voice, so that *what* becomes either object, or subject, to both. To correct Pater, from whom the last example comes, is perhaps impudence, but grammar is no respecter of persons. WRONG: *This is pure ignorance of* what *the House is &*^*its work consists of* (& what its)./*But it is not folly to give it* what *it had for centuries &*^*was only artificially taken from it by force rather more than a hundred years ago* (insert *what* where indicated or rephrase 'what belonged to it for')./*Mr. — tells us not to worry about Relativity or anything so brain-tangling, but to concentrate on* what *surrounds us, &*^*we can weigh & measure* (& can be weighed & measured)./*Impossible to separate later legend from original evidence as to* what *he was, &*^ *said, & how he said it* (& what he said).

4. *What* resumed by (*and, but*) *which*. In the following sentences a want of faith either in the lasting power of *what* (which has a good second wind & can do the two laps without turning a hair), or in the reader's possession of common sense, has led to a thrusting in of *which* as a sort of relay to take up the running. WRONG: *Palgrave, whose name is inseparably connected with* what is *probably the best, &* which *certainly has proved the most popular, of English anthologies* (what is probably the best, & has certainly proved)./*It is an instructive conspectus of views on* what *can hardly be de-*

scribed as a 'burning question,' but which *certainly interests many Irishmen* (omit *which*)./ *We are merely remembering* what *happened to our arboreal ancestors, &* which *has been stamped by cerebral changes into the heredity of the race* (omit *which*).

These sentences are not English; nothing can represent *what* —except indeed *what*. That is, it would be English, though hardly idiomatic English, to insert a second *what* in the place of the impossible *which* in each. If the reader will try the effect, he will find that the second *what*, though permissible, sometimes makes ambiguous what without it is plain. In the last example, for instance, 'what happened' & 'what has been stamped' might be different things, whereas 'what happened, & has been stamped' is clearly one & the same thing. The reason why *which* has been called 'impossible' is that *what* & *which* are of different grammatical values, *which* being a simple relative pronoun, while *what* (=*that which*, or *a thing that*) is a combination of antecedent & relative; but the second verb needs the antecedent-relative just as much as the first, if *but* or *and* is inserted; if neither *but* nor *and* is present, *which* will sometimes be possible, & so omission of *but* & *and* would be another cure for the last two examples.

Two specimens are added in which the remedy of simply omitting *which* or substituting for it a repeated *what* is not possible without further change. The difficulty is due to, & vanishes with, the superstition against PREPOSITION AT END. WRONG: *I can never be certain that I am receiving* what *I want* & for which *I am paying.* (Read *what I want & am paying for.*)/ *But now we have an ex-minister engaged daily in saying & doing* what *he frankly admits is illegal, &* for which *he could be severely punished.* Read *& what he could be severely punished for.* The repetition of *what* is required because the relative contained in the first *what* is subjective, & that in the second objective; see 3.

5. Miscellaneous. The beautiful conciseness belonging to *what* as antecedent-relative seems to lure the unwary into experiments in further concision. They must remember that both parts of it, the antecedent (*that* or *those*) & the relative (*which*), demand their share of attention. WRONG: What *I am concerned*^ *in the present article is to show that not only theory but practice support the unrestricted exercise of the prerogative.* Read *concerned to do.*/What *my friend paid less than $5 a day for last year he had to pay $10 a day*^ *at a minor establishment last Easter.* Read *$10 a day for./ Entering the church with feelings different from* what *he had ever entered a church*^*before, he could with difficulty restrain his emotions.* Read *entered a church with.*

The following shows a different *what*. WRONG: *When one reflects*^what *great importance it was to the success of the League that America should become a member of it.* Read *of what*, & see VALUE.

what ever, whatever. The various uses are complicated & cannot be all set out for readers who are not specialists in grammar, without elaborate explanations that would demand too much space. This article will avoid all technicalities except what are needed in dealing with two or three common mistakes.

1. The interrogative use. *What ever* is 'an uneducated or ultra-colloq.' means of emphasis for *what* (see EVER). WRONG: *What ever can it mean? What ever shall we do?* It should never appear in print except when familiar dialogue is being reproduced, & should then be in two separate words, differing in this from all other uses. Three examples follow in which both these rules are disregarded. In the second of them we have an indirect instead of a direct question, but the same rules hold. WRONG: *Which is pretty, but* whatever *can it mean?*/Whatever *you mean by 'patriotic' education I do not know, but Roberts's use of the term is plain enough./And, considering that* 180,000 *actually arrived in the country,* whatever *was the cost?*

2. The antecedent-relative use. *Whatever* in this use is an emphatic form of *what* as antecedent-relative (see WHAT 4, 5), and means *all that* or *any(thing* &c.) *that. We shall soon have stores of* whatever (=anything that) *you want.* The point ignored in the quotations below is that *whatever* contains in itself the relative (*that* or *which*), & that another relative cannot grammatically be inserted after it; *whatever that* is as absurd as *anything that that.* WRONG: *His cynical advice shows that* whatever *concession to Democracy* that *may seem to be involved in his words, may not be of permanent inconvenience.* (Omit *that.*)/*Keep close in touch with Him in* whatsoever *creed or form* that *brings you nearest to Him.* (Omit *that.*)/*They see in the shell, the gun—in* whatever *component, big or small,* upon which *their attention is concentrated—the essence of all that matters.* (Read: *in whatever component, big or small, their attention is concentrated upon.* Another example of trouble from the PREPOSITION-AT-END superstition.)

3. The concessive use. *Whatever one does, you are not satisfied; I am safe now, whatever happens; Whatever you do, don't lie.* These are concessive clauses, short for Though one does A or B or C, Though this or that or the other happens, Though you do anything else. They differ from the *whatever* clauses dealt with above in being adverbial, *whatever* meaning not *all* or *any that* (*that* beginning an adjectival clause), but *though all* or *any.* The difference is not a matter of hair-splitting; *Whatever he has done he repents* may mean (a) He is one of the irresolute people who always wish they had done something different, or (b) Though he may be a great offender, repentance should count for something; *whatever* antecedent-relative gives (a), & *whatever* concessive gives (b). In practice it should be noticed that proper punctuation distinguishes the two, the (a) meaning not having the two clauses parted by a comma, since *whatever* belongs to & is part of both, & the (b) meaning having them so parted, since *whatever* belongs wholly to one clause. In the following sentence, the reader is led by the wrong comma after *have* to mistake the *whatever* clause for a concessive & adverbial one. WRONG: *He has no reason to be displeased with this sequel to his effort,* and,

whatever responsibility he may have, *he will no doubt accept gladly*. The words concerned should run: *and whatever responsibility he may have he will no doubt* &c.

whatsoever. Intensive or formal form of *whatever*. *Whatso'er*, poetic or archaic.

wheaten. In US *wheaten* is archaic; *wheat cakes, wheat bread*, are the usual terms. See -EN ADJECTIVES.

whence, whither. The value of these subordinates of *where* for lucidity & conciseness seems so obvious that no one who appreciates those qualities can see such help being discarded without a pang of regret. But we who incline to weep over *whence* & *whither* must console ourselves by reflecting that in the less literal secondary senses the words are still with us for a time; 'Whither are we tending?' & 'Whence comes it that . . . ?' are as yet safe against *where . . . to* & *where . . . from;* & the poets may be trusted to provide our old friends with a dignified retirement in which they may even exercise all their ancient rights. But we shall do well to shun all attempts at restoration, & in particular to eschew the notion (see FORMAL WORDS) that the writer's duty is to translate the *where . . . from* or *where . . . to* of speech into *whence* & *whither* in print. On the other hand, let us not be ultra-modernists & assume that *whence* & *whither*, even in their primary senses, are dead & buried. That must have been the view of the journalist who wrote: *The Irregulars were compelled to withdraw their line from Clonmel*, to where *it is believed they transferred their headquarters when they had to flee from Limerick.* If *whither* was too antiquated, the alternative was 'to which place'; but occasions arise now & then to which *whence* & *whither* are, even for the practical purposes of plain speech, more appropriate than any equivalent.

whenever, the right form for the ordinary conjunction, should not be used instead of the colloq. *when ever* (*When ever will you be ready?*), for which see EVER.

where- compounds. (Whereas &c.) A small number of these are still in free general use, though chiefly in limited applications, with little or no taint of archaism. These are *whereabouts* (as purely local adv. & n.), *whereas* (in contrasts), *wherever, wherefore* (as noun pl. in *whys* & *wherefores*), *whereupon* (in narratives), & *wherewithal* (as noun). But the many others—*whereabout, whereat, whereby, wherefore* (adv. & conj.), *wherefrom, wherein, whereof, whereon, wherethrough, whereto, wherewith,* & a few more—have given way in both the interrogative & the relative uses either to the preposition with *what* & *which* & *that* (*whereof*=of what?, what . . . of?, of which, that . . . of), or to some synonym (*wherefore*=why). Resort to them generally suggests that the writer has a tendency either to FORMAL WORDS or to PEDANTIC HUMOR.

wherever, where ever. As WHENEVER.

wherewithal. The noun, as was mentioned in WHERE- COMPOUNDS, has survived in common use (*but I haven't got the wherewithal*), no doubt because the quaintness of it has struck the popular fancy. But the noun should remember that it is after all only a courtesy noun, not a noun in its own right. It means just 'with which,' but seems to have forgotten this in (WRONG): *They* [France's purchases] *have been merely the* wherewithal with which *to start business again.*

whether. (1) After *doubt(ful)*, *whether* is the idiomatic word, not *that*, except in negative sentences; see DOUBT(FUL). (2) *Whether or no(t). Whether he was there or was not there* easily yields by ellipsis *Whether he was there or not*, & that by transposition *Whether or not he was there. Whether or no he was there* is not so easily accounted for, since *no* is not ordinarily, like *not*, an adv. (see NO); & in fact the origin of the idiom is uncertain; but the fact remains that *whether or no* is idiomatic. Whichever form is used, such a doubling of the alternative as the following should be carefully avoided. WRONG: *But clearly,* whether or not *peers will* or will not *have to be made depends upon the number of the Die-Hards.* Omit either *or not* or *will not.* (3) *The question* as to *whether . . .* See AS 3. *Whether* seems to have an irresistible attraction to the ungrammatical or slovenly *as to.* WRONG: *The question* as to whether *any more suitable candidate can be suggested./ He was uncertain* as to whether *the commitments could be met./ Some doubt* as to whether *it will effect the situation.* (Omit *as to* in all.)

which. Relative pronouns are as troublesome to the inexpert but conscientious writer as they are useful to everyone, which is saying much. About *which*, in particular, problems are many, & some of them complicated. That the reader may not be frightened by an article of too portentous length, the two that require most space are deferred, & will be found in the separate articles WHICH, THAT, WHO, & WHICH WITH AND OR BUT. The points to be treated here can be disposed of with more certainty & at less length: 1. Relative instead of demonstrative. 2. One relative in two cases. 3. One rel. for main & subordinate verbs. 4. Break-away from relative. 5. Confused construction. 6. Late position. 7. *One of the best which.* 8. Commas. 9. *In which to.*

1. Relative instead of demonstrative. The WRONG type is: *He lost his temper,* which *proving fatal to him.* The essence of a relative is to do two things at once, to play the part of a noun in a sentence & to convert that sentence into, & attach it to another as, a subordinate clause. *He lost his temper; this proved fatal;* these can be made into one sentence (a) by changing the demonstrative *this* into the relative *which,* or (b) by changing the verb *proved* to the participle *proving;* one or the other, NOT both as in the false type above. WRONG: *Surely what applies to games should also apply to racing, the leaders* of which *being the very people from whom an example might well be looked for* (read *of this* or *of the latter;* or else *are* for *being*)./*Persons who would prefer to live in a land flowing with milk & honey if such could be obtained without undue exertion, but, failing* which, *are content to live in*

squalor, filth, & misery (read *failing that;* or else *failing which they* for *but failing which*)./*The World Scout principle—namely, of bringing into an Order of the young the boys of different races, by* which *means not only educating the children in scouting, but . . .* (read *by this means;* or else *we should not only educate* for *not only educating*).

2. One relative in two cases. See WHAT 3 for this question; in all the following extracts, a single *which* is once objective & once subjective. The cure is either to insert a second *which* in the second clause, or to convert one of the two verbs into the same voice as the other. WRONG: *Mr. Roche is practicing a definite system,* which *he is able to describe, &‸could be studied by others* (read *and others could study*)./*The queer piece,* which *a few find dull, but‸to most is irresistible in its appeal* (but which to most)./ *Shakespearian words & phrases* which *the author has heard, &‸ believes can be heard still, along this part of the Avon valley* (& which he believes).

3. One relative for main & subordinate verbs (or verb & preposition). (A) RIGHT BUT UNUSUAL: *This standard figure is called Bogey,* which *if you have beaten you are a good player.* In this the grammar is unexceptionable, *which* being the object of *have beaten,* & having no second job as a pronoun (though as relative it attaches to *Bogey* the clause that is also attached by *if* to *you are* &c.). In modern use, however, this arrangement is rare, being usually changed to 'if you have beaten which.' (B) QUESTIONABLE: *This standard figure is called Bogey,* which *if you have beaten‸you are apt to mention.* Here *which* is object first to *have beaten* & then to *mention;* English that is both easy & educated usually avoids this by making *which* object only to *mention,* & providing *have beaten* with another—*which, if you have beaten* it, *you are apt to mention.* Meeting the B form, we incline to ask whether the writer has used it because he knows no better, or because he knows better than we do & likes to show it. Grammatically, it must be regarded as an ellipsis, & to that extent irregular, but many ellipses are idiomatic. This particular kind is perhaps less called for as idiomatic than noticeable as irregular. (C) WRONG: *This standard figure is called Bogey,* which *if you have beaten is sometimes mentioned.* This is indefensible, the *which* having not only to serve twice (with *have beaten,* & with *is mentioned*), but to change its case in transit; see 2.

Illustrations follow of B & C; A, being both legitimate & unusual, & having been introduced only for purposes of comparison, need not be quoted for.

B, DOUBTFULLY ADVISABLE: *Mr. Masterman was a little troubled by the spirit of his past,* which, *if he had not evoked‸, no one would have remembered* (evoked it?)./*And it was doubtless from Weldon that he borrowed the phrase* which *his use of‸has made so famous* (of *it?* or *his use of which has made it?*). This is no more ungrammatical, though certainly more repulsive, than the other.

C, UNDOUBTEDLY WRONG: *The program is divided up into a*

series of walks, which, *if the industrious sightseer can undertake*$_\wedge$, *will supply him with a good everyday knowledge of Paris* (undertake them)./*In general the wife manages to establish a status* which *needs no legal proviso or trade-union rule to protect*$_\wedge$(*protect it;* or *which it needs;* or *to protect which needs no . . . rule*).

4. Break-away from relative. (A) WRONG: *It imposes a problem* which *we* either *solve* or *perish.* This is strictly ungrammatical. The break-away depends on the nature of *either . . . or* alternatives, in which whatever stands before *either* must be common to both the *either* & the *or* groups. *Either we solve this or we perish* can therefore become *We either solve this or perish*, but cannot become *This we either solve or perish*, because *this* is peculiar to the *either* group—else the full form would be *Either we solve this or we perish this.* With *this* as object the escape is easy—to put *this* after *solve;* with *which* as object that is not tolerable (*we either solve which or perish*), & strict grammar requires us to introduce into the *or* group something that can take *which* as object—*a problem which we either solve or perish by not solving, either solve or are destroyed by*, &c. Even those who ordinarily are prepared to treat *either* with proper respect (see EITHER 5, & UNEQUAL YOKEFELLOWS) may perhaps allow themselves the popular form; if not, *A problem which if we do not solve we perish* (see 3 A) is worth considering. (B) WRONG: *He shows himself extremely zealous against practices in some of* which *he had indulged &*$_\wedge$*was himself an example of their ill effects.* There are two possible correct versions of the second & third parts, (1) *some of which he had indulged in & himself exemplified the ill effect of*, or (2) *in some of which he had indulged, & of the ill effects of* (some of) *which he was himself an example.* (1) will be repudiated, perhaps more justifiably than usual, by those who condemn final prepositions; (2) fails to give the precise sense, whether the bracketed *some of* is inserted or not; to both these the break-away, which is not an uncommon construction, will be preferred by some.

5. Confused construction: *He may be expected to make a determined bid for the dual role* which is *his right & duty as Prime Minister* to occupy. In that sentence, is *which* subject to *is*, or object to *occupy?* It is in fact, of course, the latter, *occupy* having no other object, & not being able to do without one; but the writer has effectually put us off the track by dropping the *it* that should have parted *which* from *is*, *To occupy which is his right* becomes, when *which* is given its normal place, *which it is his right to occupy.* This mistake is very common, & will be found fully discussed under IT 1.

6. Late position. In the examples, which are arranged as a climax, the distance between *which* & its antecedent is shown by the roman type. Grammar has nothing to say on the subject, but common sense protests against abuse of this freedom. ILL-ADVISED: *She is wonderful in her brilliant* sketch of that querulous, foolish little old lady

which *she does so well./The whole art of clinching is explained in this little* book from the concentrated harvest of wisdom in which *we present some specimens to our readers./Nothing has more contributed to dispelling this illusion than the* camera, the remarkable & convincing evidence it has been possible to obtain with which *has enormously added to the knowledge of the habits of animals.*

7. *One of the best which* has, WRONG: *In which case one of the greatest & most serious strikes* which has occurred *in modern times will take place. Has* should be *have.* For this very common but inexcusably careless blunder see NUMBER 5.

8. Commas. In the present article the distinctions between *which* & other relatives—see WHICH, THAT, WHO—have been left alone, & it has been assumed that *which* can introduce either a defining clause or a non-defining one. A comma preceding *which* shows that the *which* clause is non-defining, & the absence of such a comma shows that it is defining. WRONG: *I always buy his books* which *have influenced me greatly.* There is no comma before *which,* & therefore the clause must be a defining one; i.e. it limits the books that I buy to those that have influenced me—that is what we are told. Or is it not so, & are we to understand rather that I buy all of his books, and they have all influenced me? Surely the latter is meant; but the loss of the comma forbids us to take it so. The difference between the two senses (or the sense & the nonsense) is not here of great importance, but is at least perfectly clear, & the importance of not misinterpreting will vary infinitely elsewhere. That right interpretation should depend on a mere comma is a pity, but, until *that* & *which* are differentiated, so it must be, & writers must see their commas safely through the press.

9. *In* &c. *which to.* STILTED: *England is, however, the last country* in which to *say so./I have no money* with which to *buy food.* The current English for the second is indisputably *I have no money to buy food with;* & there can hardly be a doubt that this has been formalized into the other by the influence of the PREPOSITION AT END superstition. No one need hesitate about going back to nature & saying *to buy food with.* And even for the first 'the last country to say so in' is here recommended, though the very light word *so* happens to make with the other very light word *in* an uncomfortably weak ending; much more is 'a good land to live in' superior to 'a good land in which to live.' A confessedly amateur guess at the genesis of these constructions is that there is no relative clause in the case at all, & that the form *to live in* originated in an adverbial infinitive attached to the adj. *good. He is a hard man to beat;* how hard? why, to beat; what Greek grammars call an epexegetic (or explanatory) infinitive. *It is a good land to in-habit* is precisely parallel, & *to live-in* is precisely the same as *to in-habit.* If this account should happen to be true, the unpleasant form 'in which to live' might be dismissed as a grammarians' mistaken pedantry.

which, that, who. 1. General.

2. *Which* for *that.* 3. *Which* after superlatives. 4. *Which* in *It is . . .* 5. *Which* as rel. adv. 6. Elegant variation. See also WHO 3 & 6, THAT, REL. PRON., & WHAT 4. Cf. also PERSONIFICATION.

1. Let it be stated broadly, before coming to particular dangers that: (A) of *which* & *that, which* is appropriate to non-defining & *that* to defining clauses: *The river,* which *here is tidal, is dangerous,* but *The river* that *flows through London is the Thames.* (B) Of *which* & *who, which* belongs to things, & *who* to persons; *The crews,* which *consisted of Lascars, mutinied,* but *Six Welshmen,* who *formed the crew, were drowned.* (C) Of *who* & *that, who* suits particular persons, & *that* generic persons: *You* who *are a walking dictionary,* but *He is a man* that *is never at a loss.* To substitute for the relative used in any of those six examples either of the others would be, if the principles maintained in this book are correct, a change for the worse; &, roughly speaking, the erroneous uses (if they are so) illustrated below are traceable to neglect or rejection of A, B, & C.

2. *Which* for *that.* The importance & convenience of using *that* as the regular token of the defining clause has been fully illustrated under THAT REL. PRON., & no more need be done here on that general point than to give an example or two of *whichs* that are misleading where *thats* would have been plain. AMBIGUOUS: *Serious works on Russia from Polish sources,* which *are not intended as merely propagandist pamphlets, are a valuable contribution toward a better understanding of that country.* If the clause is non-defining, as *which* suggests, none of these serious works are propagandist, & all are valuable. The real meaning is that some of them are free of propaganda, & are therefore valuable; but this real meaning requires *that* instead of *which.*/*The second statement* which, *taken as it stands in Mr. Wedgwood's letter, is misleading is that which implies that* . . . Impossible to tell, since there are no commas after *statement* & *misleading,* whether the clause is defining (=*the second misleading statement*) or non-defining (=*the second statement made—a misleading one*); probably it is defining, & should have *that* instead of *which.*

Much more often there is no danger of misinterpretation, but *that* is desirable because its regular association with defining clauses helps to establish a workmanlike distribution of the relatives to the work that has to be done. Examples need not be multiplied; *that* should be preferred to *which* in all such places as: *If the amending Bill is to serve the purpose* which *responsible men in all parties profess to desire.* Special circumstances that make *which* undesirable are set out in Nos. 3–5.

3. *Which* after superlative &c. When the antecedent of a defining clause includes a word of exclusive meaning, such as a superlative, an ordinal numeral, or 'the few,' the use of *which* instead of *that* (or *who* as second best) is bad enough to be almost a solecism even in the present undiscriminating practice. By rule B of the 1st section of this article, *who* is better than *which,* & by rule C

that is better than *who.* WRONG: *Lord Spencer came to be regarded as* one of the best *Viceroys* which *the country had ever had./The Bishop of Salisbury is* the third *bishop* which *his family has given to the world.*/One of the few *composers of the first rank* which *England has produced.* Read *that* for *which* in all.

4. *Which* after *It is . . .* The constructions are exemplified in simple forms by (RIGHT) *It was the war* that *caused it, It was yesterday* that *we came.* One thing can be confidently said about them, which is that they require *that* & not *which* —*that* the defining relative (*It was Jones* that *did it;* or, often tacit, as *It was Jones‸did it*), or *that* the conjunction (*It is with grief* that *I learn . . .*). WRONG: *It is to the State, & to the State alone,* to which *we must turn to acquire the transfer of freeholds compulsorily, expeditiously, & cheaply./It is in the relation between motive, action, & result in a given chain of historical causation,* in which *history consists./So once again East is West, & it is shown that it is not only the Japanese* which *have the imitative instinct strongly developed.* Read *that* for *to which, in which, which.*

5. *Which* as relative adverb. RIGHT: *In England the furthest north* that *I have heard the nightingale was near Concaster.* The curious & idiomatic use of *that* in this construction is explained in THAT REL. PRON. 3, where it is added that *which* is unsuitable for similar treatment. The clauses are defining, attached to such words, expressed or implied, as *way, extent, time, place.* WRONG (read *that* for *which* in each): *Parliament will be dissolved not later than Monday week—the earliest moment* which *it has ever been seriously considered possible for the dissolution to take place./Before we can find a Government expressing itself in the way* which *Americans express themselves./Before railway work was 'sped up' to the extent* which *it is at present, continuous work of this character was no great strain./The public will not be likely to misinterpret it in the way* in which *the party capital makers would desire.* In this last, singularly enough, the insertion of *in* makes matters worse; *which,* or better *that,* might have been a pronoun, object of *desire;* but with *in which* the clause needs to be completed with 'that they should' or some equivalent.

6. Elegant variation. A very well-known writer once stated his notion of the relation between *which* & *that:* When it struck him that there was too much *which* about, he resorted to *that* for a relief. So he said; it was doubtless only a flippant evasion, not a truthful account of his own practice. Of the unskilled writer's method it would be a true enough account; here is a specimen: *Governments find themselves almost compelled by previous & ill-informed pledges to do things* which *are unwise & to refrain from doing things* that *are necessary.* The two relative clauses are exactly parallel, & the change from *which* to *that* is ELEGANT VARIATION at its worst. When two relative clauses are not parallel, but one of them depends on the other, it is not such a simple matter; as is stated in REPETITION (dependent sequences), there is a reasonable objection to one

which clause, or one *that* clause, depending on another. Two examples will show the effect (a) of scorning consequences & risking repetition, & (b) of trying elegant variation; neither is satisfactory: (a) *Surely the 'reductio ad absurdum' of tariffs is found in a German treaty with Switzerland* which *contains a clause* which *deserves to remain famous* (read *containing a clause . . . that*). (b) *The task is to evolve an effective system* that *shall not imperil the self-governing principle*^which *is the cornerstone of the Empire.* The absence of a comma shows that the *which* is meant as a defining relative & should therefore be *that;* but, as a non-defining clause would here give a hardly distinguishable sense, the escape is to use one & keep *which,* merely inserting the necessary comma.

which with and or but. It is well known that *and which* & *but which* are kittle cattle, so well known that the more timid writers avoid the dangers associated with them by keeping clear of them altogether—a method that may be inglorious, but is effectual & usually not difficult. Others, less pusillanimous or more ignorant, put their trust in a rule of thumb & take the risks. That rule is: *and which* or *but which* should be used only if another *which* has preceded. It is not true; *and which* clauses may be legitimate without a preceding *which;* & its natural if illogical corollary—that *and which* is always legitimate if another *which* has preceded—induces a false security that begets many blunders. On the other hand, it probably saves many more bad *and whichs* than it produces. Anyone who asks no more of a rule of thumb than that it should save him the trouble of working out his problems separately, & take him right more often than it takes him wrong, should abandon the present article at this point.

Those for whom such a rule is not good enough may be encouraged to proceed by a few sentences in which it has not averted disaster. WRONG: *After a search for several days he found a firm* which *had a large quantity of them* & which *they had no use for./A period in* which *at times the most ungenerous ideas & the most ignoble aims have strutted across the stage,* & which *have promptly been exploited by unscrupulous journalists & politicians.* True, it is easy to see the flaw in these, viz. that the two *whichs* have not the same antecedent, & to say that common sense is to be expected of those who apply rules; but then rules of thumb are meant just for those who have not enough common sense to do without them, & ought to be made foolproof.

Here, on the other hand, are examples in which there is no preceding parallel *which,* & yet *and which* is blameless. RIGHT: *Mandates issued, which the member is bound blindly & implicitly to obey, to vote & to argue for, though contrary to the clearest conviction of his judgment & conscience—these are things*^*utterly unknown to the laws of this land,* and which *arise from a fundamental mistake of the whole order & tenor of our Constitution./Another natural prejudice,*^*of most extensive prevalence,* and which *had a great share in producing the errors fallen into by the an-*

cients in their physical inquiries, was this./In the case of calls‸within the London area, but which *require more than three pennies, the same procedure is followed.* (The carets indicate ellipses that make the *whichs* right.)

The first of these is from Burke, the second from Mill, & the last from the ordinary modern writing. Supporters of the rule of thumb will find it more difficult to appeal here to common sense, & will perhaps say instead that, no matter who wrote them, they are wrong; it will be maintained below that they are right. The rule of thumb fails, as such rules are apt to do, for want of essential qualifications or exceptions. The first qualification needed is that the *which* that has preceded must belong to the same antecedent as the one that is to be attached by *and* or *but;* our set of wrong examples would have been written otherwise if that had been part of the rule. The next amendment is both more important &, to the lovers of simple easy rules, more discouraging: the 'another *which*' that was to be the test must be changed to 'a clause or expression of the same grammatical value as the coming *which* clause.' Now what is of the same grammatical value as a *which* clause is either another *which* clause or its equivalent, & its equivalent may be an adjective or participle with its belongings (*utterly unknown to the laws of this land*), or an adjectival phrase (*of most extensive prevalence; within the London area*); for before these there might be inserted *which are, which was,* &c., without any effect on the meaning. But, secondly, what is of the same grammatical value as the *which* clause that is coming is an expression that agrees with it in being of the defining or of the non-defining kind; i.e. two defining expressions may be linked by *and* or *but,* & so may two non-defining, but a defining & a non-defining must not.

A defining expression is one that is inserted for the purpose of enabling the reader to identify the thing to which it is attached by answering about it such questions as *which* ––?, *what* ––?, *what sort of* ––?. If the Burke quotation had stopped short at *things* (*Mandates . . . are things.*), we should have said No doubt they are things, but what sort of things? we cannot tell what sort of things Burke has in mind till the expressions meaning 'unknown to law' & 'arising from mistake' identify them for us. Both expressions are therefore of the defining kind, & legitimately linked by *and;* whether *which* occurs in both, or only in one, is of no importance. In that example there can, owing to the vagueness of the antecedent *things,* be no sort of doubt that the expressions are defining. Often there is no such comfortable certainty; in the Mill sentence, for instance, 'another natural prejudice' is not a vague description like *things,* demanding definition before we know where we are with it; if the sentence had run simply *Another natural prejudice was this,* we should not have suspected a lacuna; it cannot be said with confidence whether the two expressions were defining, so that the summary might be *Another natural, widespread, & fatal prejudice was this,* or non-defining, so that it would be *Another natural prejudice—& it was a widespread & fatal one—was this.* It is clear, however, that whichever 'of most extensive prevalence' is, the *which* clause is also, & the *and which* is legitimate.

After these explanations a rule, as now amended, can be set down: *And which* or *but which* should not be used unless the coming *which* clause has been preceded by a clause or expression of the same grammatical value as itself. And a reasonable addition to this is the warning that, though the linking of a relative clause to a really parallel expression that is not a relative clause is logically & grammatically permissible, it has often an ungainly effect & is not unlikely to convict the writer of carelessness; if he had foreseen that a relative clause was to come (& not to foresee is carelessness), he could usually have paved the way for it by throwing his first expression into the same form.

WRONG: *A book the contributors to which come from many different countries* & who *are writing under conditions that necessarily impose some restrictions on them.* (No preceding parallel clause or equivalent; omit *who* & read *& are writing.*)/*He has attempted to give an account of certain events* of which, *without doubt, the enemy knew the true version,* & which version *is utterly at variance with the published report.* (Different antecedents here—*of which* refers to *events, & which* to *version;* inserting the second *version* did not mend matters: omit *and* & *version* & read *which is at variance.*)/*I have also much Russian literature on the subject,* but from which *out of respect to certain prejudices I forbear to quote.* (Defining and non-defining expressions linked; read *from this.*)/*I have noted the sagacious advice constantly given in your column* & which *may be summed up in the phrase 'Put your house in order.'* (Read *that has constantly been given . . . & may be summed up,* & see THAT REL. PRON.)/*He sent him what he spoke of as a 'severe rating'* but which *was in reality the mildest of remonstrances.* (Omit *but* & see WHAT 4.)/*The enormous wire nets, marked by long lines of floating barrels & buoys,* & which *reach to the bottom of the sea, were pointed out to me.* (Right but ungainly; read *which are marked . . . & reach.*)

whichever, which ever. See EVER.

while, whilst. (In US *while* is the usual form, *whilst* being regarded as 'chiefly Brit.' or poetic.) *While* (or *whilst*) is a conjunction of the kind called strong or subordinating, i.e. one that attaches a clause to a word or a sentence, not a weak or co-ordinating conjunction that joins two things of equal grammatical value; it is comparable, that is, with *if* & *although,* not with *and* & *or.* The distinction is of some importance to what follows. Nothing, perhaps, is more characteristic of the flabbier kind of journalese than certain uses of *while,* especially that which is described by the OED as 'colorless.' The stages of degradation may be thus exhibited:

1. Temporal strong conjunction=*during the time that:* While *she spoke, the tears were*

running down.

2. The same with inversion, a foolish variant of (1): *And* while *is being noticed just now the advance Germany & other nations are making in navigation, we see that . . .*

3. Non-temporal strong conjunction in contrasts=*whereas:* While *this is true of some, it is not true of all.*

4. Strong conjunction with correct ellipsis: While‸*walking in the road he was run over* (=while he was walking).

5. Strong conjunction with INCORRECT ellipsis of two kinds, (a) disregard of the full form, (b) wrongly attached participle &c., see UNATTACHED: *But* while being *in agreement with his main thesis, I am bound to confess my opinion that he* . . . (the full form is not *while I am being,* but *while I am,* which should be used without ellipsis)./While willing *to sympathize with those who would suffer by such an order,* they *can only console themselves with the thought how lucky they have been that the fortunes of war have not affected them sooner* (the full form would be not *while they are willing,* which could be got from what follows, but *while I am* or *we are willing,* which cannot, so that *willing* is wrongly attached; read *while we are willing*)./*An action was brought on account of injuries received in an accident* while being *driven in one of the company's cars* (were the injuries or the accident or the action being driven?).

6. Strong conjunction playing the part of weak, i.e. introducing what may be defended as a subordinate clause but is in sense a co-ordinate one, the 'colorless' use (=*and*) so common in bad writing that illustration is almost superfluous: *White outfought Ritchie in nearly every round, & the latter bled profusely,* while *both his eyes were nearly closed at the end.*

7. The same as (6), but with the defense prevented by the interrogative form of the *while* clause (=*and*): *We can only console ourselves with the thought that the German people are also 'slaves' on this showing;* while what are we *to think of a House of Lords which permitted this Slavery Act to become law?*

8. Use as FORMAL WORD or ELEGANT VARIATION for *and,* with complete abandonment of the strong conjunction character: *Archbishops, bishops, & earls were allowed eight dishes; lords, abbots, & deans six;* while *mere burgesses, or other 'substantious' men, whether spiritual or temporal, no more than three.*

whilom. For the adv. use (*the wistful eyes that* whilom *glanced down*), see WARDOUR STREET; for the adj.=*quondam, former* (a whilom *medical man*), see LATE.

whilst. See WHILE.

whimsy, -ey. US usually *-sey;* Brit. *-sy* (cf. *flimsy*).

whippoorwill. So spelled.

whir(r). US usually *whir;* Brit. *whirr.*

whisky, -ey. *Whisky* is now the dominant spelling, but in commercial use *-key* is often used of the US product, *-ky* of the imported. In Brit., *Scotch whisky,* but *Irish whiskey.*

whit. *He didn't care a whit,* current; but for variations (*The golf club, the bridge table,* in no whit less *than the factory, must relax their claims*) see WARDOUR STREET.

Whit. *Whitsunday* or *Whit Sunday* (seventh Sunday after Easter), NOT *Whitsun Day;* but *Whit-week, Whitsuntide.*

white-collar worker, job, &c. Though orig. (US) colloq., the term is so useful that it is now accepted by serious writers. It covers the salaried worker, from salesgirl to scientist, distinguished from the laborer & job worker (who wear work clothes or uniforms) on the one hand, and the self-employed (farmer, independent professional man, business owner, &c.) on the other. According to some economists, the white-collar worker derives part of his satisfaction from prestige & is therefore reluctant to join unions or unite with other workers to improve his status.

white(n), v. For the noun meaning prepared chalk, the old word, still in use, is *whiting;* but it is being ousted by *whitening,* perhaps partly because the verb is now *to whiten* instead of *to white,* & partly for distinction from the fish *whiting.*

Whitsun. See WHIT.

whither. Usually archaic. See WHENCE.

whiz(z). The single *z* is recommended, but *whizzed, whizzing.*

who & whom. 1. Case. 2. *Who(m) they supposed drown'd.* 3. *Who(m)* defining & non-defining. 4. *And* or *but whom.* 5. Person & number. 6. Personification. 7. *Who(m)* & participle.

1. Miscellaneous questions of case. *Who* being subjective & *whom* objective, & English speakers being very little conversant with case forms, mistakes are sure to occur. One is of importance as being extraordinarily common (whom *they supposed is drown'd*) & is taken by itself in (2); the others can be quickly disposed of here.

The interrogative *who* is often used in talk where grammar demands *whom,* as in *Who did you hear that from?* No further defense than 'colloquial' is needed for this, & in the sort of questions that occur in printed matter other than dialogue the liberty is seldom taken. The opposite mistake of a wrong *whom* is not uncommon in indirect questions. WRONG: *Speculation is still rife as to* whom *will captain the English side to Australia./The French-Canadian, who had learned* whom *the visitors were, tried to apologize.* The mistake is a bad one, but fortunately so elementary that it is nearly confined to patrons of the *as-to* style (see AS 3), & needs no discussion.

The relative *who* now & then slips in for *whom,* giving the educated reader a shock. WRONG: *There is the Lord Chancellor, for example,* who *in other days we knew as Galloper Smith./As Mr. Bevin reminds those* who *in other circumstances we should call his followers, the agreement provided for . . .* That is a mistake that should not occur in print; & at least as bad is the making of one *whom* serve two clauses of which the first requires it as the object, & the second as subject; this practice is untidy enough with words that, like *which* & *that,* have only one form for both cases (see THAT REL. PRON. 5,

WHICH 2), but is still worse with *who* & *whom.* The correct form should invariably be inserted in the second clause when a different case is wanted. WRONG: *He ran upstairs & kissed two children* whom *he only faintly recognized, & yet*^ *were certainly his own./But there has emerged to the finals a Spaniard* whom *few people would have supposed to have a good chance a fortnight ago but*^*is delighting the advocates of the older style by the beauty & rhythm of his strokes.* (Insert *who* as indicated.)

For the incorrect formula *whom failing,* see ABSOLUTE CONSTRUCTION; & for *than whom* see THAN 6.

2. *Young Ferdinand,* whom *they suppose is drown'd.*—*Tempest* III. iii. 92. It was said in (1) that the question between *who* & *whom* illustrated by this Shakespeare quotation is of importance. That is because the *whom* form, though probably no grammarian would have a word to say for it, is now so prevalent in the newspapers that there is real danger of its becoming one of those STURDY INDEFENSIBLES of which the fewer we have the better, & of good writers' taking to it under the hypnotism of repetition. What makes people write *whom* in such sentences? In the Shakespeare, the preceding words are 'while I visit' (Young Ferdinand) so that *Ferdinand* is objective; the relative, which should be *who* as subject to *is drown'd,* may have become *whom* by attraction to the case of *Ferdinand* or by confusion with another way of putting the thing—*whom they suppose* (to be) *drown'd.* A writer may have a general impression that with *who* & *whom* to choose between it is usually safer to play *whom* except where an immediately following verb decides at once for *who.* Any of these influences may be at work, but none of them can avail as a defense against the plain fact that the relative is the subject of its clause; nor can Shakespeare's authority protect the modern solecist; did not the Revisers, in an analogous case, correct the *whom* of a more familiar & sacred sentence (*But whom say ye that I am?*—Matt. xvi. 15) into conformity with modern usage? Of the extracts that follow, the earlier show easily intelligible *whoms,* because an active verb follows that could be supposed by a very careless person to be governing it, while in the later ones a passive verb or something equivalent puts that explanation out of court. WRONG: *Madame Vandervelde spoke for women,* whom, *she claimed, most* hated *war because they suffered most from it./The letter gives the name of a man* whom *the writer alleges* was *responsible for the child's death./A very modern Japanese, one* whom *it may be observed* spoke *English fluently./Among others* whom *it is hoped* will be *among the guests are . . .* That every *whom* in those quotations ought to be *who* is beyond question, & to prove it is waste of time since the offenders themselves would admit the offense; they commit it because they prefer gambling on probabilities to working out a certainty.

3. *Who*(*m*) defining & non-defining. As has been suggested in THAT, REL. PRON., the thing to aim at is the establishment of *that* as the universal defining

relative, with *which* & *who(m)* as the non-defining for things & persons respectively. That consummation will not be brought about just yet; but we contribute our little toward it every time we write *The greatest poet* that *ever lived*, or *The man* that *I found confronting me*, instead of using *who* & *whom*. Failing the use of *that* as the only defining relative, it is particularly important to see that *who* defining shall not, & *who* non-defining shall, have a comma before it. *Readers of the 'Westminster,'* who *are also readers at the great Bloomsburg institution, will be able to admire the new decorations for themselves.* Those wrong commas (see COMMAS) make the sentence imply that all readers of the 'Westminster' frequent the British Museum.

4. *And* or *but who(m)*. The use of these is naturally attended by the same dangers as that of *and which*. These have been fully discussed under WHICH WITH AND OR BUT, & nothing need here be added beyond a few specimens containing *who(m)*. WRONG: *A letter speaks of the sorrows of children* which *their parents are powerless to assuage*, & who *have little experience of the joys of childhood* (& of children who)./*The working classes, for long in enjoyment of all the blessings of 'Tariff Reform,'* & who *are therefore fully competent to appreciate their value, are moving with a startling rapidity toward Socialism* (read, *who for long have been in enjoyment . . . & are therefore* . . .)./*We should be glad of further assistance to pay the cost of putting up relatives of men* who *live in the provinces,* & to whom *we like to extend invitations to come & stay near them for a few days at a time* (the antecedent of *who* is *men*, but that of *whom* is *relatives*).

5. Person & number of *who(m)*. WRONG: *To me*, who has *also a copy of it, it seems a somewhat trivial fragment.* Read *have;* the relatives take the person of their antecedents; the Lord's Prayer & the Collects, with *which art, who shewest*, & scores of other examples, are overwhelming evidence that *who* is not a third-person word, but a word of whichever person is appropriate.

The relatives take also the number of their antecedents—a rule broken in (WRONG): *The death of Dr. Clifford removes one of the few Free Churchmen* whose *work had given* him *a national reputation.* The antecedent of *whose* is not *one*, but *Churchmen*, whereas the use of *him* instead of *them* shows that the writer assigned *whose* to *one;* read either *removes a Churchman whose work had given him*, or *removes one of the few Churchmen whose work has given them.*

6. Personification. *Who(m)* must be ventured on in personifications only with great caution. It will be admitted that in the following *who* is intolerable, & *which* the right word: *The joint operation for 'pinching out' the little kingdom of* Serbia, who *had the audacity to play in the Balkan Peninsula a part analogous to that* . . . Yet, if we had had *little Serbia* instead of *the little kingdom of Serbia, who* might have passed. Again, when we say that a ship has lost her rudder, we personify; yet, though *She had lost her rudder* is good English, *The*

ship, who *had lost her rudder* is not, nor even *The Arethusa, who* &c.; both these can do with *her,* but not with *who;* possibly *Arethusa, who* (& the naval writers drop the *the* with ships' names) is blameless; if so, it is because the name standing alone emphasizes personification, which must not be half-hearted or dubious if *who* is to follow. See PERSONIFICATION.

7. *Who(m)* & participle. WRONG: *I have been particularly struck by the unselfishness of the majority of sons & daughters, many* of whom *even* remaining *unmarried because they lacked the wherewithal to do more than help their parents.* The mistake has been treated under WHICH 1. Read *many of them remaining,* or *many of whom remain.*

whoever &c. 1. Forms. Subjective: *whoever, whosoever* (literary), *whoe'er* (poetic), *whose* (archaic). Objective: *whomever* (rare), *whoever* (colloq.), *whomsoever* (literary), *whomsoe'er* (poetic), *whomso* (archaic). Possessive: *whose ever, whoever's* (colloq.), *whosesoever* (literary).

2. *Who ever, whoever.* See EVER. *Whoever can it be?* is illiterate, & *Who ever can it be?* is colloq. only. In print, when an emphasizing *ever* is used, it should not come next to *who.* WRONG: *But* whoever *could have supposed that the business interests which are threatened would not have organized to resist?* (Read *who could ever* &c.)

3. Case. RIGHT: *For* whoever *was responsible for that deliberate lie there can be no forgiveness. Whoever,* not *whomever,* is correct in this sentence. *Whoever*=any person who. The case of *whoever* is that of the *who,* not that of the *any person,* that is, it is decided by the relative clause, not by the main clause. RIGHT: *He asked* whomever *he met,* but *He asked* whoever *came near him; For* whomever he met *he had a nod,* but *For* whoever met him *he had a nod.*

wholehearted, US so spelled (Brit. hyphened).

wholly. So spelled, but pron. as if it were *wholely.*

whom. See WHO.

whoop, whooping-cough, pron. hoop (but the US slang *whoopee,* whoopē).

whose. 1. General. The word is naturally liable to some of the same misuses as *who,* which need not be here discussed separately; see WHO & WHOM 3–6. Even the making of *whose* serve in two clauses requiring different cases (cf. WHO & WHOM 1) is not unexampled. WRONG: *The whole scheme may be likened to the good intentions of the dear old lady* whose concern *for the goldfish led her to put hot water into their bowl one winter's day, &* was *grievously surprised when they died* (and who was).

2. *Whose*=of which. RIGHT: *But what can one say of a book* whose *first two chapters run to* 190 *pages?* There are those who would have us correct this to *a book the first two chapters of which* . . . The tabooing of *whose* inanimate is on a level with that of the PREPOSITION AT END; both are great aids to flexibility; both are well established in older as well as in colloq. English; *My thought,* Whose *murder yet is but fantastical* (*Macbeth*), & *The fruit Of that forbidden tree* whose *mortal taste Brought death into the*

world (*Paradise Lost*), are merely the first instances that come to mind. The Milton happens to be a little out of the ordinary in that *whose* is not a mere possessive, but an objective genitive; but that even such a use is not obsolete is shown by the following from a newspaper. RIGHT: *Sir William Harcourt thrice refused an earldom,* whose *acceptance he feared might be a barrier to his son's political career.*

Let us, in the name of common sense, prohibit the prohibition of *whose* inanimate; good writing is surely difficult enough without the forbidding of things that have historical grammar, & present intelligibility, & obvious convenience, on their side, & lack only—starch.

wide. (1) For the distinction between *wide* & *broad*, which is of considerable idiomatic importance, see BROAD. (2) *Wide(ly)*. It should be remembered that there are many positions in which, though *widely* is grammatically possible, *wide* is the idiomatic form; see UNIDIOMATIC -LY for other such adjs.; *aim wide, wide apart, wide awake, open one's eyes wide, is widespread,* are all usually better than *widely apart* &c., & there are many more.

wide(-)awake. *He is wide awake; A very wide-awake person.*

widow. In printing, a short line or single word carried over from the foot of one page to the top of the next, not condoned in good book-making, but often unavoidable in dictionaries, dramas, books of verse, &c.

wife. *For all the world & his wife* see WORN-OUT HUMOR.

wild. (1) Hyphens &c. A *wild cat* is an untamed one of the domestic kind, *a wildcat* (US) or *wild-cat* (Brit.) one of the species so named; *wild oats,* NOT *wild-oats; wild flower* or *wildflower.* (2) *Wild(ly).* For *play, run, shoot, talk,* &c., *wild,* see UNIDIOMATIC -LY.

wilful. US usually *willful,* but the shorter (older) form is recommended.

will, n. Phrases like *the will to power,* in which a noun is tacked on to *will* by *to,* have come from Germany, and are unquestionably useful to psychologists, sociologists, and other technical writers. In literary writing, however, they are usually a clumsy substitute for the normal English expression: *It was now apparent that Jean had lost* the will to success. See POPULARIZED TECHNICALITIES.

will, v. There is a verb *to will,* conjugated regularly throughout—*will, willest, wills, willed, willedest, willing;* it means to intend so far as one has power that so-&-so shall come about, the so-&-so being expressed by a noun or a *that* clause or an infinitive with *to: You willed his death, that he should die, to kill him.* The much commoner auxiliary verb has none of these forms except *will,* & on the other hand has *wilt* & *would* & *would(e)st;* it has also none of these constructions, but is followed by an infinitive without *to: He will die, Would it be true?* The meaning of this auxiliary is curiously complicated by a partial exchange of functions with *shall,* the work of merely giving future & conditional forms to other verbs being divided between certain persons of *shall* & certain persons of *will,* while the parts of each not so employed retain something of the senses of ordering (*shall*) & intending (*will*) that originally belonged to the stems. It has been stated under *shall* that the distinction between *shall* & *will* in futurity &c. is fast disappearing in US. For those who wish to preserve it, the following comments & examples may be helpful.

1. Plain future or conditional statements & questions in the first person traditionally have *shall* & *should*. RIGHT: *If we add too much to these demands we* shall *be in grave danger of getting nothing./We are facing the consequences today, &* shall *have to face them for many years to come in the affairs of Europe./We have no proper place at the Coronation &* should *lay ourselves open to the gravest misunderstanding by departing, on this occasion, from the settled policy of our party.*

2. The verbs *like, prefer, care, be glad, be inclined* are very common in first person conditional statements (*I should like to know* &c.). In these *should,* not *would,* is the right form: *We* should like *to bring together two extracts dealing with the effects of the Budget on land./ But at any rate we* should *feel sorry to have missed anything that is told us of Edison in the biography.*

3. In clauses of indefinite future time & indefinite relative clauses, *will* is entirely unidiomatic; either *shall* is used, chiefly in formal contexts, or, much more often, futurity is allowed to be inferred from context & a present is used: WRONG: *The Gold Medal will go to a foreign astronomer when this evening the President presents* (NOT will present) *it to Professor Max Wolf.*

4. *Shall* & *will, should* & *would* are not material for ELEGANT VARIATION. WRONG: *The Greeks will now decide whether their country* shall *continue to be a Monarchy or* will *become a Republic./In a very few years we* shall *not remember, &* will *scarcely care to inquire, what companies were included.*

5. *That* clauses after *intend* or *intention, desire, demand, be anxious,* &c. have *shall* & *should* for all persons. Among the &c. are NOT included *hope, anticipate,* & the like. Roughly, *shall* & *should* are used when the word on which the *that* clause depends expresses an influence that affects the result, as a demand does, but a hope or a fear does not. *Mistresses expect* (i.e. demand) *that their maids* shall *wear uniforms;* but *we expect* (i.e. are of the opinion) *that tomorrow* will *be fine.* Read *shall* for *will* in the two sentences that follow: *The Queen has expressed a desire that on Sunday all flags* will *be flown at the masthead./It is intended that the exterior scenes in no fewer than four different pictures* will *be taken before they return.*

willful. Usually so spelled in US. But *wilful* is not a modern shortening; it has been in the language since the 14th c. & is the only accepted modern Brit. form.

willy-nilly. US so spelled (Brit. sometimes one word).

windward(s). Fig. (*To cast*) *an anchor to windward*=to take measures for security: *A policy based on the desire to keep an anchor to the windward.*

winebibber (Brit. hyphen), so spelled (NOT *-biber*).

winged. In literal contexts

pron. wingd (*a two-winged plane*); poet. & fig. wingéd: *winged words.*

winter. For *the winter of our discontent,* see IRRELEVANT ALLUSION.

wise, n. In the phrases *in no wise, in any wise,* &c., *wise* should be a separate noun unhyphened; if *in* does not precede, there is no objection to any of the three forms *no wise, no-wise, nowise.* In other phrases, *wise* n. is an ARCHAISM.

-wise, -ways. (1) The ending *-ways,* or occasionally *-way,* is often used indifferently with *-wise,* & is very seldom the only form without one in *-wise* by its side—perhaps only in *always.* (2) In a few established words, *-wise* is alone, esp. *clockwise, coastwise, likewise, otherwise, sunwise.* (3) In other established words both forms are used, as *broad-, end-, least-, length-, long-, no-, side-, slant-.* (4) In words made for the occasion from nouns, as in *Use it clubwise or pokerwise, Go crabwise or frogwise, Worn cloakwise, -wise* is now much the commoner.

wishful. Except in *wishful thinking,* borrowed from the psychiatrists, *wishful* has little current use.

wistaria. So spelled.

wit, n. See HUMOR; that the two are different names for the same thing is no doubt still a popular belief; but literary critics at least should not allow themselves to identify the two, as in: *It is to be doubted whether the author's gifts really do include that of* humor. *Two jests do not make a* wit.

wit, v. Archaic except in the infinitive, *to wit* (=namely; that is to say) and that is confined to legal contexts.

with. Writers who have become conscious of the ill effect of AS *to* & *in the* CASE *of,* casting about for a substitute that shall enable them still to pull something forward to the beginning of a sentence have hit upon *with,* which is sometimes found displacing *of* or some really appropriate preposition—a trick that should be avoided: With *pipes, as* with *tobacco, William Bragge was one of the most successful collectors./*[Collins, Blair, Parnell, &c.] *Collins has had his excellent editors, & we must suppose that the manuscript has finally disappeared;* but, with *the others, we suspect that the poems are extant.* Read *of pipes, of tobacco; the poems of the others . . . are.*

withal. See WARDOUR STREET.

without. 1. *Without*=outside. Both as adv. (*listening to the wind without; clean within & without*) & as prep. (*without the pale of civilization*) the word retains this meaning; but it is no longer for all styles, having now a literary or archaic sound that may be very incongruous.

2. *Without*=unless. *No high efficiency can be secured* without *we first secure the hearty co-operation of the* 30 *million or so workers.* The use is good old English, but bad modern English—one of the things that many people say, but few write; it should be left to conscious stylists who can rely on their revivals' not being taken for vulgarisms.

3. *Without . . . or without . . .* WRONG: *It can be done* without *any fear of his knowing it, or* without *other evil consequences.* See OR 4.

4. *Without hardly.* WRONG: *The introduction of the vast new refineries has been brought about silently, & effectively, &* without *the surrounding community* hardly *being aware of what was happening.* Again, like (2), common colloq., but unlike it, one that should never appear outside spoken or printed talk; the English for *without hardly* is *almost without.*

5. *Without him being.* The word is peculiarly apt to usher in a FUSED PARTICIPLE, e.g. *The formidable occasion had come & gone* without *anything* dreadful *happening.* The fused participle is no worse after *without* than elsewhere, but those who are prepared to eschew it altogether should take warning that *without* will sometimes try their virtue, so often does the temptation present itself. It is, for instance, a pure accident that the sentence quoted in (4) for a different point contains the fused participle *without the community being aware.* Escapes are usually not hard to find; here '& nothing dreadful had happened,' or 'without any dreadful results,' would do, but particular suggestions for a particular case are of little value; the great thing is general readiness to abandon & recast any of one's phrases that one finds faulty.

6. Negative confusion. Like all negative & virtually negative words, *without* often figures in such absurdities as (WRONG): *It is not* safe *for any young lady to walk along the road on a Sunday evening by herself* without *having unpleasant remarks spoken as she passes along.* (It is not possible)./*Rendering it possible for a government to accept some at any rate of the recommendations of the Committee* without *any loss of face, & least of all* without *loss of office* (most of all; see MUCH 2).

wive, v. Rare, & in most contexts it could be more so.

wizard. For *wizard of the North* (Scott), see SOBRIQUETS.

wizened, wizen, weazen. The first is now usual. Pron. wĭznd.

wolf. Pl. *-lves;* v. *wolfed, -fing.*

wolverene, -ine. OED treats *-ene* as the dominant form, but most of the quotations in OED spell *-ine,* which is the usual form in US for both animal and the *Wolverine State* (i.e. Michigan). (Pron. -ēn.)

woman. *Womankind,* NOT *womenkind,* for the whole sex or women in general; but *womenfolk(s),* dial. or colloq.

womanly. Having the qualities considered as characteristic of a woman (gentleness, compassion, modesty, virtuousness). See FEMALE, FEMININE.

wonder. For (WRONG) *I shouldn't wonder if it didn't rain* (i.e. I shouldn't wonder if it rained) see NOT 4, & STURDY INDEFENSIBLES.

wont, n., adj., v. Custom, accustomed, be accustomed (to). Best pron. wōnt.

wood. (1) *Wood anemone,* two words. (2) *Woodbine,* NOT *-bind,* is the established form, esp. with Shakespeare & Milton to maintain it. (3) *Tomorrow to fresh woods,* NOT *fields;* see MISQUOTATION.

wooden makes *woodenness.*

woof, warp, web, weft. The *warp* is a set of parallel threads stretched out; the threads woven across & between these are the *woof* or *weft;* & the fabric that results is the *web.*

wool makes, US, *woolen* & (best) *woolly;* Brit. *woollen, woolly.*

WORD PATRONAGE. Under SUPERIORITY, the tendency to take out one's words & look at them, to apologize for expressions that either need no apology or should be quietly refrained from, has been mentioned. To pat oneself on the back instead of apologizing for one's word is a contrary manifestation of the same weakness, viz. self-consciousness. It is rare, but perhaps deserves this little article all to itself: *That is a contingency which has been adumbrated* (to revive a word which has been rather neglected of late); *but this is one more case in which we must be content to wait & see.*

work, v. Past & p.p. also *wrought. Work,* n., makes US *workbench, workbook, workhouse, workman;* Brit. often hyphened. *Work load* usually two words.

workaday is now displaced, wholly in the noun use, & for the most part as an adj., by the normal *workday,* of which it is regarded as a slipshod pronunciation to be used only as a genial unbending; but *this workaday world* is still usual.

WORKING & STYLISH WORDS. Anyone who has not happened upon this article at a very early stage of his acquaintance with the book will not suppose that the word *stylish* is meant to be laudatory. Nor is it; but neither is this selection of stylish words to be taken for a blacklist of out-&-out undesirables. Many of them are stylish only when they are used in certain senses, being themselves in other senses working words; e.g. *category* is a working word in the philosopher's sense, though stylish as a mere synonym for *class; protagonist* a working word for the one person upon whom the interest centers, but aggressively stylish for an *advocate.* Others again, such as *bodeful* & *deem* & *dwell,* lose their unhappy stylish air when they are in surroundings of their own kind, where they are not conspicuous like an escaped canary among the sparrows.

What is to be deprecated is the notion that one can improve one's style by using stylish words. Those in the list below, like hundreds of others, have, either in certain senses or generally, plain homely natural companions. The writer who prefers to one of these the stylish word for no better reason than that he thinks it stylish, instead of improving his style makes it stuffy, or pretentious, or incongruous. Most of the words in the list below will be found with comments in their dictionary places:

STYLISH	WORKING
assist	help
beverage	drink
bodeful	ominous
category	class
collation	meal
commence	begin
comprise	include
cryptic	obscure
deem	think
description	kind, sort
envisage	face
feasible	possible
forenoon	morning
protagonist	champion
sufficient	enough

workless gives another illustration of how the newspaper headline is affecting the language. We have all known 'the unemployed' as long as we can remember. But *unemployed* fills up a good deal of headline; something shorter is wanted, & *workless* is invented for the need. But, secondly, *workless* by itself is shorter than *the workless;* so *workless* is turned from an adj. into an indeclinable plural noun—all to make possible such gems as: WORKLESS WANT TO SEE PREMIER./BILL TO AID WORKLESS.

WORN-OUT HUMOR. 'We are not amused'; so Queen Victoria baldly stated a fact that was disconcerting to someone; yet the thing was very likely amusing in its nature; it did not amuse the person whose amusement mattered, that was all. The writer's Queen Victoria is his public, & he would do well to keep a bust of the old Queen on his desk with the legend 'We are not amused' hanging from it. His public will not be amused if he serves it up the small facetiae that it remembers long ago to have taken delight in. Of the specimens of worn-out humor exhibited below nearly all have had point & liveliness in their time; but with every year that they remain current the proportion of readers who 'are not amused' to those who find them fresh & new inexorably rises.

Such grammatical oddities as *muchly;* such allusions as *the Chapter on Snakes in Iceland;* such parodies as *To — or not to —;* such quotations as *single blessedness,* or *suffer a sea change;* such oxymorons as *The gentle art of doing something ungentle;* such needless euphemisms as *unmentionables* or *a table's limbs;* such meioses as *Epithets the reverse of complimentary* or 'some' as a superlative; such playful archaisms as *hight* or *yclept;* such legalisms as (*the*) *said* —, & *the same;* such shiftings of application as *of the military persuasion,* or *to spell ruin* or *be too previous;* such metaphors as *sky pilot* & *priceless;* such happy thoughts as *taking in each other's washing*—with all these we, i.e. the average adult, not only are not amused; we feel a bitterness, possibly because they remind us of the lost youth in which we could be tickled with a straw, against the scribbler who has reckoned on our having tastes so primitive.

worsen. Still current & without the archaism of many -EN VERBS. *A general worsening of conditions.*

worship. In US dictionaries *-iped, -iping,* &c., but many US writers & publishers still prefer (the standard Brit.) *-ipped, -ipper.*

worsted, n. Pron. wŏŏs-.

worth, worth while. The adj. *worth* requires what is most easily described as an object; it is meaningless to say *This is worth,* but sense to say *This is worth a dollar,* or *This is worth saying* (i.e. the necessary expenditure of words), or *This is worth while* (i.e. the necessary expenditure of time); but one such object satisfies its requirements, so that *This is worth while saying,* with the separate objects *while* & *saying,* is ungrammatical. A less essential point, which must nevertheless be realized if all is to be clear, is the doubtful nature of the *It* that is often present in sentences containing *worth.* Though *This is worth while saying* is wrong, *It is* *worth while saying this* is right, but again *It* (viz. whatever has just been said) *is worth while saying* is wrong; the last *It* is the ordinary pronoun, & *this* or *that* might have stood instead of *it*, but the *It* of *It is worth while saying this* is what is called the anticipatory *it* (see IT 1, 2) & means not *this* or *that*, but *saying this*. In the following table, this source of confusion will be avoided, every *it* used being of the anticipatory kind.

RIGHT: A. This is worth saying.
B. To say this is worth while, *or* It is worth while to say this.
C. Saying this is worth while *or* It is worth while saying this (right but less idiomatic).
WRONG: a. This is worth while saying.
b. To say is worth while, *or* It is worth while to say.
c. Saying this is worth, *or* It is worth saying this.

Of the wrong forms, a is A spoiled by having *worth while* instead of *worth*, which means that *worth* has two objects; b is B spoiled by the verb *say*'s having no object, the cause being, as will appear when we come to examples, the mistaking of an anticipatory *it* for something else; c is C spoiled by *worth*'s having no object.

In the following examples the small letter indicates the wrong type to which it belongs, & the capital the right type to which it should be corrected. WRONG: *A spare captain, to take charge of any prize that might be* worth while *turning into a raider* (a. A. Omit *while*). *A problem which should be quite manageable—if we make up our minds that it is* worth while *tackling* (a. A. Omit *while*). *It is* worth *recalling Lord Salisbury's declaration in* 1885 *that, if she yielded to pressure, we should consider ourselves released from our obligations* (c. B. worth while to recall).

The next two are clear examples of C, & are given merely that the reader may try whether the conversion of them to B, by the change of *harking* & *remarking* to *to hark* & to *to remark* does not produce more idiomatic English: *It is not often* worth while harking *back to a single performance a fortnight old.* /*It is* worth while remarking *on Signor Nitti's very curious attitude toward the question of responsibility for the war.*

But of many sentences that are defensible as C it is open to doubt whether they are really C, or A gone wrong. These are sentences in which, while an anticipatory *It* is used, there are two possible views of what *It* stands for. *It is* worth while saying, *if one thinks so, that Mr. Kipling is a great writer, some of whose work will survive as long as anything contemporary with it.*/*It may be* worth while recalling *that the most interesting account of the novelist's visit to the little German capital is contained in his letter to George Henry Lewes. It is worth while to say . . . it may be worth while to recall,* are probably what the writers meant and certainly sound more idiomatic. The only further point that needs special discussion is the complication sometimes introduced by a relative clause. WRONG: *The Chinese Labor Corps & its organization was one of the side issues of the war which is* well worth while to hear *about.* Correct grammar would be (A) *which is well worth hearing about,* or (B) *which it is well worth while to hear about,* or (C) *which it is well worth while hearing about.*

Some mixed examples now follow, with reference to the table as before, & with a note where it seems called for. WRONG: *In your excellent account there is one omission, & it is* worth filling it *up* (c. A). Observe that the first *it* is *it* anticipatory (=filling it up), & the second is the ordinary pronoun(=the omission). Omit second *it./On that point it is* worth *quoting a passage from Mr. Carroll's election address* (c. B; worth while to quote)./*It is* worth quoting *the 'Echo de Paris,' which was one of the journals which cried loudest for large reparations* (c. B; worth while to quote).

worth-while. This attributive-adjective compound extracted from the phrase 'is worth while' (*a worth-while experiment* from *the experiment was worth while*) is at the best of doubtful value; &, having been seized upon as a VOGUE WORD, it is fast losing all precision of meaning: *That motherhood is a full-time job all* worth-while mothers *will readily admit./An attractive program of* worth-while topics *has been arranged for discussion. Worth-whileness,* more recently discovered, is worse: *There is no question of the* worth-whileness *of the project.*

worthy. The construction in which *worthy* was treated like *worth* & *like,* governing a noun (*in words worthy the occasion, a deed worthy remembrance,* without *of*), is now rare, & appropriate only in exalted contexts.

would. For (*we*) *would* or *should* see SHALL & WILL. A few specimens, in all of which *would* is wrong (in traditional usage) are here given to enable those who doubt their mastery of the idiom to test it: *If we were to go on borrowing money in this country* we would *keep the position of the unemployed better while borrowing, but* we would *have to pay for it./He might well have struck such a blow as* we would *have felt to the quick./*I would *feel safer in backing England had their batting not been so disappointing in the first Test.*

wove, p.p., instead of the usual *woven,* is chiefly in commercial terms, as *wove paper, hard-wove fabrics, wire-wove.*

wrack (rack), n.,=destruction, devastation, is obs. except in *wrack & ruin.* OED has quotations of the phrase with both spellings, but *wrack* is usually used. *Wreck & ruin* is wrong.

wrapt, wrapped, rapt. *Wrapt* as p.p. of *wrap* is archaic or poetic (*wrapt in conscious peace*); *wrapped* is the usual modern p.p. (*wrapped in slumber*). *Rapt*=absorbed, enraptured (*her rapt soul*). *Rapt meditation* but possibly *wrapped in meditation.* It might perhaps be well if the form *wrapt* could be abandoned, so that writers would have to make up their minds between *rapt* & *wrapped.*

wrath, wrathful, wroth. It is very desirable that differentiation should be clearly established. Many people ignore the existence of *wroth* & treat *wrath* as both noun & adj., pronouncing it always rawth. In modern usage *wrath* tends to be the noun only (=anger) & pronounced rawth (US also râth) & *wroth* the adj. (=angry) & pronounced rōth (US usually rŏth). This does not put *wrathful* out of use; it is the attributive adj., & *wroth* is the predicative: *A wrathful god,* but *God was wroth.*

write. *Write* with personal object. In *I shall write you the result,* there are two objects, (direct) *the result* & (indirect) *you.* In Brit. English an indirect object without *to* is used after *write* only if there is also a direct object (seldom observed in US), but the direct object may be used without an indirect; that is, *I shall write the result* & *I shall write you the result* are idiomatic, but *I shall write you soon,* or *about it,* is not; if a direct object is wanting, the person written to must be introduced by *to: I shall write to you about it.* In Brit. *We wrote you yesterday, Please write us at your convenience,* &c., are established in commercial use, but avoided elsewhere. The following from a novel would be condemned: *The Lady Henrietta . . . wrote*^*him regularly through his bankers, & once in a while he wrote*^*her.* (Insert two *tos.*)

wrong is one of the words whose adv. use should be remembered; *did his sum wrong* is better than with *wrongly,* but *a wrongly done sum.* See UNIDIOMATIC -LY.

wroth. See WRATH.

wry. In US *wrier, wriest* are more usual than (Brit.) *wryer, wryest;* but both *wryly, wryness, wryish.*

X

-x, as French plural. It is still usual, in various degrees, to write *-x* instead of the English *-s* in the plurals of words in *-eau* & *-eu* borrowed from the French, the pronunciation being *-z,* as in English plurals. It is to be hoped that some day all of these that are in familiar English use will be anglicized with *-s.* In US *adieus, beaus, plateaus,* are all permissible; why not also *chateaus, rondeaus,* &c.? Phrases such as *feux de joie* & *jeux d'esprit* would naturally keep their French *-x,* and so would any single words whose anglicization was so far from accomplished that the plural was still pronounced like the singular, without the sibilant; that is hardly true of any of the list above; we say not 'bō like Brummell,' but 'bōz like Brummell,' & 'all shatōz are not equally' interesting,' not 'all shatō . . .'

Xanthippe. Properly so spelled, but now usually *-tippe.*

xebec. Pron. zēbĕk.

-xion. About certain nouns there is a doubt whether they should be spelled with *-xion* or *-ction.* The forms *connexion, deflexion, inflexion,* & *reflexion* are called by the OED the 'etymological spellings,' and they are the usual Brit. forms; in US *-ction* is more usual in all.

Xmas. Not a modern commercial abbreviation, distasteful as it is to many people. *X* from early times was used as an abbreviation of *Christ* (*X* being the 1st letter of the Greek spelling); in English used as early as 1551 (OED).

X-ray. The adj. & v. so spelled (also sometimes *x-ray*). The noun better *X ray* or *x ray,* but *X-ray* is permissible for it too.

Y

-y. The adj. suffix is *-y,* not *-ey:* glass+y=*glassy.* If the noun ends in a mute *e,* the *e* is usually dropped: *stone, stony.* If the noun ends in *-y,* however, an *e* must be inserted: *clay, clayey.* Some words ending in mute *e* retain the *e,* to prevent confusion with another word; *hole, holey;* & the words ending in *ue* retain the *e, blue, bluey.* For full discussion see -EY & -Y in adjectives.

yacht. So spelled. So *yachtsman, yachtsmanship.*

Yahoo. In *Gulliver's Travels,* one of the brute tribe having the form & vices of men. Hence a degraded & vicious person.

Yahweh, also *Jahveh, Yahweh, Jahve, Yahwe,*=Jehovah.

y & i were in older English writing freely interchanged; that general liberty has long been abandoned, but there are still a few words in which usage varies or mistakes are common; they are, in the spelling here recommended: *cipher; gypsy; Libya(n); lichgate; pygmy; sibyl* & *Sibyl; silvan* (US *sylvan*) & *Silvanus; siphon; siren; stile* (in hedge) & *style* (manner); *stimy* (US *stymie*); *tire* (of wheel); *tiro.*

Yankee. Orig. a native of New England; by extension (to a Southerner), a Northerner; loosely (& esp. when the feeling is derog.), any inhabitant of the US. The derivation, much disputed, is probably from Jan (one source says Jan Kees, i.e. John Cheese, nickname applied by the Dutch of early N.Y. to the English of Conn.).

yankeefied. So spelled. See -FIED.

yardstick. Fig. a rule, criterion, by which something intangible is measured (with rigidity): *Success cannot be measured by the* yardstick *of the dollar.*

yclept. Archaic, 'called,' 'named'; see WORN-OUT HUMOR.

y^e^. The pronunciation of this is *the,* not *ye,* the *y* being not our letter, but a representation of the obs. single letter (þ, called thorn) now replaced by *th.*

ye, pronoun, is only nominative or vocative, never accusative (e.g. NOT *I tell* ye *of the works of God* but *O* ye *of little faith*).

year. Phrases such as *last year, next year,* may be either nouns or adverbs (*Next year may be warmer; We may have warmer weather next year*), but they should not be both at once. (WRONG): *Disquiet will be caused in Tariff Reform circles by the announcement that in the quinquennium ending & including* last year *Canada has borrowed the enormous sum of over six million dollars from this country.* The 'last year' that the quinquennium included was a noun; the 'last year' that the quinquennium ended was an adverb; indeed, far from the quinquennium's ending the year, the year ended the quinquennium. It is the same kind of mistake as making one word serve twice in two different cases, for which see, e.g., THAT REL. PRON. 5.

yearly. Adj. & adv. *His yearly dues; issued yearly.*

yelk, yolk. Spell *yolk*, pron. yōk.

yellow. The transf. & fig. sense 'sensational' (orig. US *yellow journalism, the yellow press*) is now standard usage; the sense 'cowardly' (*a yellow streak*) is still colloq.

yen. The monetary unit of Japan; 100 sen.

yen (from Chin. yen=opium, smoke), a longing, an urge (*a yen for far-off places*) is colloq. (US?).

yeoman. (Pron. yō-.) *Yeoman service* & *yeoman's service* are both in use. The meanings, good & faithful services, & a loyal servant, are now usually restricted to help in time of need.

yes. Pl. *yeses.*

yester-. Other combinations than *yesterday* are incongruous except in verse or in designedly poetic prose. It is true that *yester eve* is shorter than *yesterday evening*, but the saving of space is paid for by the proof that one has no literary sense.

yet. 1. Inversion. There is no reason for changing the normal order of words after *yet.* WRONG: *His works were burned by the hangman,* yet was the multitude *true to him.* The tendency of *yet* to inspire foolish inversions has been specially treated in INVERSION under the heading *Yet, Especially, Rather.*

2. Illogical pregnant use. When *yet* is used to point a contrast, the opposition between the fact it introduces & that which has gone before should be direct & clear. Examples of failure in this respect must necessarily be of some length; some simpler specimens of a rather similar kind will be found under BUT 3. In each of those that follow it will be noticed that the particular fact with which the *Yet* sentence is in contrast is by no means the essential content of the previous sentence, but has to be got out of it at the cost of some thought. WRONG: *We confess to being surprised at the line taken by the railwaymen with reference to Colonel Yorke's conclusion that the disaster occurred through the engine driver's having momentarily fallen asleep.* Yet *at a meeting railwaymen are very indignant at the suggestion, & denounce Colonel Yorke as an Army officer who does not understand the real working of railways.* Here the *Yet* fact is that the men are indignant. What is that in contrast with? Apparently with the correctness of Colonel Yorke's conclusion; but, though many other things not in contrast with their indignation can be got out of the sentence, the correctness of the conclusion is inferable only from the newspaper's surprise at the men's indignation at the conclusion. If *yet* were omitted, the second sentence would come in logically enough as an explanation of what the men's 'line' referred to had actually been./*I doubt if sufficient attention has been drawn to the injustice of throwing on the landlord in whose home they happen to be resident the cost of a large additional insurance benefit for*

those who are sick. Yet, *under Clause* 51, *a sick tenant would be able to live rent free for a year at the expense of his or her landlord.* This is a less glaring case. The essence of the *Yet* sentence is that a tenant has power to injure a landlord. What is that in contrast with? with the fact that justice would protect landlords; that is, not with the main clause preceding, which is a statement of why the writer is writing, but with a mere inference from a noun that occurs in it, viz. *injustice.* As in the first example, the logical work of the second sentence is to explain the nature of a noun contained in the first, viz. (again) *injustice,* but an explanation is presented in the guise of an opposition; the sentence would do its work properly if *yet* were omitted.

3. *Yet* to strengthen comparatives (*yet more painful*) is now usually replaced by *even* or *still.*

4. *We do not yet know* but *It is even yet not known.*

yodel, v., has US *-led, -ling;* Brit. *-lled* &c.

Yoga, the Hindu system of asceticism & meditation; *yogi,* one who practices it. (*Yogin,* a var. of *yogi.*)

yolk. Pron. yōk.

yon. Archaic. See WARDOUR STREET.

you. The indef. *you* is good usage both colloq. & in writing. You *can talk a mob into anything* (Ruskin); *The action is so confused that* you *often miss the significance of the lines;* & You *can fool some of the people some of the time* &c. See also ONE.

yours. (1) Your *and our efforts,* but *Our efforts and* yours. (2) *I have just received* yours *of the tenth,* vulg. (commercialese) for *your letter.* (3) *Trust* yours truly *to do the right thing,* see WORN-OUT HUMOR.

youth. Sing. & pl. Youth *must have its fling. The* youth *of our country will take* their *places when the time comes. Two handsome* youths.

Yucca. Pron. yŭkka.

Yugoslavia, Yugoslav. Brit. usually *Jugo-.*

Z

Zachariah, -as, Zech-. *Zachariah,* father of John the Baptist. *Zacharias,* in Douay Bible =Zachariah. *Zechariah,* prophet, in the Book of Zechariah.

zany. Orig. an attendant clown who mimicked his master; hence a buffoon, a crackbrain, simpleton.

Zarathustrian. See ZOROASTRIAN.

zed. Brit.=*z* (zeta). US usually spelled *Zee.*

Zeitgeist. 'Spirit of the times.' The general intelligence & feeling of a period, the drift of an era.

zenith. The point in the heavens directly overhead, opp. to *nadir.* Hence transf. summit, peak, culmination. *The zenith of his career.*

zephyr. West wind, personified (*Zephyr with Aurora playing*); a gentle breeze. Now chiefly poet.

zero. Pl. *-os. Zero hour* (orig. Brit., World War I), hour at which a planned movement is started; now transf., the time at which any ordeal is to begin, the moment of crisis. See VOGUE WORDS.

zeugma. (Pron. zūgma.) Pl. *-as* or *-ata.* A figure of speech in which a word is used to govern or modify two words, with only one of which it makes sense: *With weeping eyes and hearts* (i.e. grieving hearts). Intentional use of this figure has been so much overdone as to be now a peculiarly exasperating form of WORN-OUT HUMOR. To judge from the few specimens below, it is unfortunately still in favor. The first example is perhaps not the intentional kind meant to amuse: *Sir Charles Wilson, the newly elected member for Central Leeds,* took *the oath* & his seat./*Mr. Sydney played the Duke quite ably; & the* flood of *flowers and* enthusiasm *was terrific./Half-clad stokers toiled in an atmosphere consisting of one part air to ten parts mixed* perspiration, coal dust, & profanity.

zigzag, v., has *-gged, -gging.*

Zingaro. A gypsy. Accent first syllable. Fem. *-ara;* pl. *-ari.*

zither(n). In US *zither* is used for the modern instrument, but see CITHERN.

zodiac. A dictionary definition may be quoted as likely to be useful: A belt of the heavens outside which the sun & moon & major planets do not pass, divided crosswise into twelve equal areas called *signs of the zodiac,* each named after a zodiacal constellation formerly but not now contained in it. (*Signs of the zodiac: Aries* or Ram; *Taurus* or Bull, *Gemini* or Twins; *Cancer* or Crab; *Leo* or Lion; *Virgo* or Virgin; *Libra* or Balance or Scales; *Scorpio* or Scorpion; *Sagittarius* or Archer; *Capricornus* or Capricorn or Goat; *Aquarius* or Water-carrier; *Pisces* or Fishes.)

zodiacal. Pron. zōdī′-.

zoo. In general usage for zoological gardens. Pron. zōō, but *zō′ŏlogical* (not zōōo) & zō′ŏlogy. See also CURTAILED WORDS.

Zoroastrian, Zarathustrian. *Zoroastrian* is the usual form. For the substitution of *Zarathustra* &c., see DIDACTICISM, & VIRGIL.

-z-, -zz-. In *buz(z), fiz(z), quiz(z),* & *whiz(z), friz(z)* there is no need for a second *z,* & when it appears it is doubtless due to the influence of inflected forms like *buzzer, quizzed,* & *whizzing; buzz* & *fizz* are established, US & Brit., but *quiz* & *whiz* are recommended.